The Dragonriders of Pern

·· THE ··
DRAGONRIDERS
·· OF ··
PERN

DRAGONFLIGHT
DRAGONQUEST
THE WHITE DRAGON

Anne McCaffrey

DEL
REY

A DEL REY BOOK

THE RANDOM HOUSE PUBLISHING GROUP   NEW YORK

·· C O N T E N T S ··

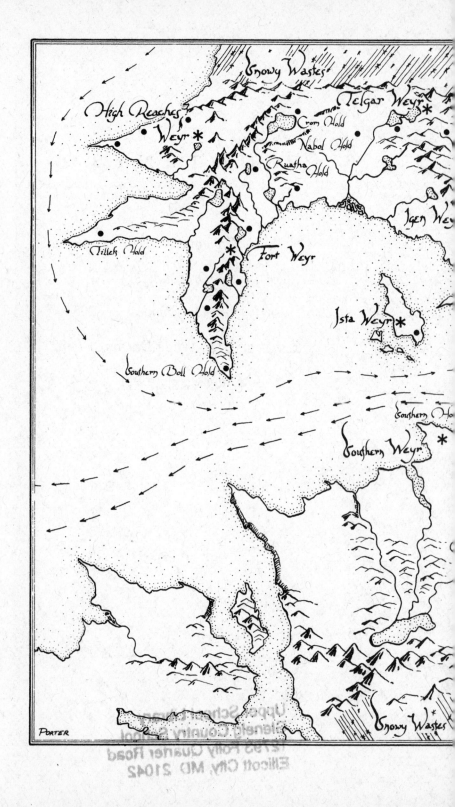

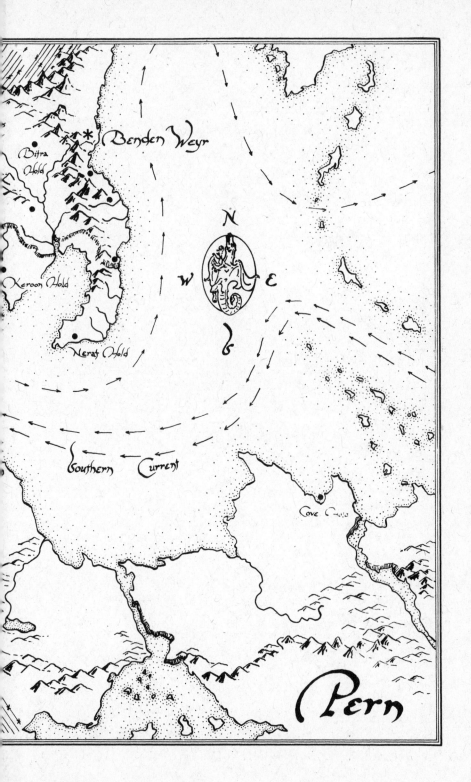

·· P R O L O G U E ··

Rukbat, in the Sagittarian Sector, was a golden G-type star. It had five planets, two asteroid belts and a stray planet that it had attracted and held in recent millennia. When men first settled on Rukbat's third world and called it Pern, they had taken little notice of the strange planet swinging around its adopted primary in a wildly erratic elliptical orbit. For two generations, the colonists gave the bright Red Star little thought—until the path of the wanderer brought it close to its stepsister at perihelion. When such aspects were harmonious and not distorted by conjunctions with other planets in the system, the indigenous life form of the wandering planet sought to bridge the space gap between its home and the more temperate and hospitable planet. At these times, silver Threads dropped through Pern's skies, destroying anything they touched. The initial losses the colonists suffered were staggering. As a result, during the subsequent struggle to survive and combat this menace, Pern's tenuous contact with the mother planet was broken.

To control the incursions of the dreadful Threads—for the Pernese had cannibalized their transport ships early on and abandoned such technological sophistication as was irrelevant to this pastoral planet—the more resourceful men embarked on a long-term plan. The first phase involved breeding a highly specialized variety of a life form indigenous to their new world. Men and women with high empathy ratings and some innate telepathic ability were trained to use and preserve these unusual animals. These dragons—named for the mythical Terran beast they resembled—had two valuable characteristics: they could get from one place to another instantaneously and, after chewing a phosphine-bearing rock, they would emit a flaming gas. Because the dragons could fly, they were able to char Thread in midair, and then escape from its ravages.

It took generations to develop to the fullest the potential of these dragons. The second phase of the proposed defense against the deadly incursions would take even longer. For Thread, a space-traveling mycorrhizoid spore, with mindless voracity devoured all organic matter and, once grounded, burrowed and proliferated with terrifying speed. So a symbiote of the same strain was developed to counter this parasite, and the resulting grub was introduced into the soil of the southern continent. The original plan was that the dragons would be visible protection, charring Thread while it was still skyborne and protecting the dwellings and the livestock of the colonists. The grub-symbiote would protect vegetation by devouring any Thread that managed to evade the dragons' fire.

The originators of the two-stage defense did not allow for change or for hard geological fact. The southern continent, overtly more attractive than the harsher nothern land, proved unstable and the entire colony was eventually forced to move north to seek refuge from the Threads in the natural caves on the continental shield rock of the north.

The original Fort, constructed in the eastern face of the Great West Mountain Range, soon grew too small to hold the colonists. Another settlement was started slightly to the north, alongside a great lake conveniently formed near a cave-filled cliff. But Ruatha Hold, as the settlement was called, became overcrowded within a few generations.

Since the Red Star rose in the east, the people of Pern decided to establish a holding in the eastern mountains, provided a suitable cavesite could be found. Only solid rock and metal, both of which were in distressingly short supply on Pern, were impervious to the burning score of Thread.

The winged, tailed, fire-breathing dragons had by then been bred to a size that required more spacious accommodations than the cliffside holds could provide. But ancient cave-pocked cones of extinct volcanoes, one high above the first Fort, the other in the Benden mountains, proved to be adequate and required only a few improvements to be made habitable. However, such projects took the last of the fuel for the great stonecutters, which had been programmed only for regular mining operations, not wholesale cliff excavations. Subsequent holds and weyrs had to be hand-hewn.

The dragons and their riders in their high places and the people in their cave holds went about their separate tasks, and each developed habits that became custom, which solidified into tradition as incontrovertible as law.

Then came an interval of two hundred Turns of the planet Pern around its primary—when the Red Star was at the other end of its erratic orbit, a frozen lonely captive. No Thread fell on Pern. The inhabitants erased the depredations of Thread and grew crops, planted orchards from precious seed brought with them, thought of reforestry for the slopes denuded by Thread. They even managed to forget that they had once been in grave danger of extinction. Then the Threads fell again when the wandering planet returned for another orbit around Pern, bringing fifty years of attack from the skies. The Pernese once again thanked their ancestors, now many generations removed, for providing the dragons who seared the dropping Thread midair with their fiery breath.

Dragonkind, too, had prospered during that interval and had settled in four other locations, following the master plan of interim defense.

The significance of the southern hemisphere—and of the grub—had been lost in the immediate struggle to establish new settlements. Recollections of Earth receded further from Pernese history with each successive generation until memory of their origins degenerated into legend or myth and passed into oblivion.

By the Third Pass of the Red Star, a complicated socio-political-economic structure had been developed to deal with this recurrent evil. The six Weyrs, as the old volcanic habitations of the dragonfolk were called, pledged themselves to protect Pern, each Weyr having a geographical section of the northern continent literally under its wing. The rest of the population agreed to tithe to support the Weyrs since these fighters, these dragonmen, did not have arable land in their volcanic homes. They could not afford to take time away from nurturing their dragons to learn other trades during peacetime, nor could they take time away from protecting the planet during Passes.

Settlements, called Holds, developed wherever natural caves were found—some, of course, more extensive or strategically placed than others. It took a strong man to hold frantic, terrified people in control during Thread attacks; it took wise administration to conserve victuals when nothing could be safely grown, and it took extraordinary measures to control population and keep it productive and healthy until such time as the menace passed.

Men with special skills in metalworking, weaving, animal husbandry, farming, fishing, mining formed Crafthalls in each large Hold and looked to one Mastercrafthall where the precepts of their craft were taught and craft skills were preserved and guarded from one generation to another. One Lord Holder could not deny the products of the Crafthall situated in his Hold to others, since the Crafts were deemed independent of a Hold affiliation. Each Craftmaster of a hall owed allegiance to the Master of that particular craft—an elected office based on proficiency in that craft and administrative ability. The Mastercraftsman was responsible for the output of his halls and the distribution, fair and unprejudiced, of all craft products on a planetary rather than parochial basis.

Certain rights and privileges accrued to different leaders of Holds and Masters of Crafts and, naturally, to the dragonriders whom all Pern looked to for protection during the Threadfall.

On occasion, the conjunction of Rukbat's five natural planets would prevent the Red Star from passing close enough to Pern to drop its fearful spores. To the Pernese these were Long Intervals. During one such Interval, the grateful people prospered and multiplied, spreading out across the land, carving more holds out of solid rock, just in case Thread returned. But they became so busy with their daily pursuits that they preferred to think that the Red Star had indeed passed beyond any danger to them.

No one realized that only a few dragons remained to take to the skies and that only one Weyr of dragonriders was left on Pern. Since the Red Star wasn't due to return for a long, long while, if ever, why worry? Within five generations, the descendants of the heroic dragonmen fell from disfavor; the legends of past braveries and the very reason for their existence fell into disrepute.

Then the Red Star, obeying natural forces, began to spin closer to Pern, winking with a baleful red eye on its ancient victim . . .

·· V O L U M E I ··

DRAGONFLIGHT

Dear God,
    Yes, there is a Virginia who helped me
create this planet and the marvels thereon.
And for whom I thank you.
                                    AMJ

·· CONTENTS ··

Weyr Search

Drummer, beat, and piper, blow,
Harper, strike, and soldier, go.
Free the flame and sear the grasses
Till the dawning Red Star passes.

Lessa woke, cold. Cold with more than the chill of the ever-
lastingly clammy stone walls. Cold with the prescience of a
danger stronger than the one ten full Turns ago that had then sent
her, whimpering with terror, to hide in the watch-wher's odorous lair.

Rigid with concentration, Lessa lay in the straw of the redolent
cheeseroom she shared as sleeping quarters with the other kitchen
drudges. There was an urgency in the ominous portent unlike any
other forewarning. She touched the awareness of the watch-wher,
slithering on its rounds in the courtyard. It circled at the choke limit
of its chain. It was restless, but oblivious to anything unusual in the
predawn darkness.

Lessa curled into a tight knot of bones, hugging herself to ease
the strain across her tense shoulders. Then, forcing herself to relax,
muscle by muscle, joint by joint, she tried to feel what subtle menace
it might be that could rouse her, yet not distress the sensitive watch-
wher.

The danger was definitely not within the walls of Ruath Hold.
Nor approaching the paved perimeter without the Hold where re-
lentless grass had forced new growth through the ancient mortar,
green witness to the deterioration of the once stone-clean Hold. The
danger was not advancing up the now little-used causeway from the
valley, nor lurking in the craftsmen's stony holdings at the foot of the
Hold's cliff. It did not scent the wind that blew from Tillek's cold
shores. But still it twanged sharply through her senses, vibrating every
nerve in Lessa's slender frame. Fully roused, she sought to identify it
before the prescient mood dissolved. She cast outward, toward the

Pass, farther than she had ever pressed. Whatever threatened was not in Ruatha . . . yet. Nor did it have a familiar flavor. It was not, then, Fax.

Lessa had been cautiously pleased that Fax had not shown himself at Ruath Hold in three full Turns. The apathy of the craftsmen, the decaying farmholds, even the green-etched stones of the Hold infuriated Fax, self-styled Lord of the High Reaches, to the point where he preferred to forget the reason he had subjugated the once proud and profitable Hold.

Relentlessly compelled to identify this oppressing menace, Lessa groped in the straw for her sandals. She rose, mechanically brushing straw from matted hair, which she then twisted quickly into a rude knot at her neck.

She picked her way among the sleeping drudges, huddled together for warmth, and glided up the worn steps to the kitchen proper. The cook and his assistant lay on the long table before the great hearth, wide backs to the warmth of the banked fire, discordantly snoring. Lessa slipped across the cavernous kitchen to the stable-yard door. She opened the door just enough to permit her slight body to pass. The cobbles of the yard were icy through the thin soles of her sandals, and she shivered as the predawn air penetrated her patched garment.

The watch-wher slithered across the yard to greet her, pleading, as it always did, for release. Comfortingly, she fondled the creases of the sharp-tipped ears as it matched her stride. Glancing fondly down at the awesome head, she promised it a good rub presently. It crouched, groaning, at the end of its chain as she continued to the grooved steps that led to the rampart over the Hold's massive gate. Atop the tower, Lessa stared toward the east where the stony breasts of the Pass rose in black relief against the gathering day.

Indecisively she swung to her left, for the sense of danger issued from that direction as well. She glanced upward, her eyes drawn to the red star that had recently begun to dominate the dawn sky. As she stared, the star radiated a final ruby pulsation before its magnificence was lost in the brightness of Pern's rising sun. Incoherent fragments of tales and ballads about the dawn appearance of the red star flashed through her mind, too quickly to make sense. Moreover, her instinct told her that, though danger might come from the northeast, too, there was a greater peril to contend with from due east. Straining her eyes as if vision would bridge the gap between peril and person, she stared intently eastward. The watch-wher's thin, whistled question reached her just as the prescience waned.

Lessa sighed. She had found no answer in the dawn, only discrepant portents. She must wait. The warning had come and she had accepted it. She was used to waiting. Perversity, endurance, and guile were her other weapons, loaded with the inexhaustible patience of vengeful dedication.

Dawnlight illumined the tumbled landscape, the unplowed fields in the valley below. Dawnlight fell on twisted orchards, where the sparse herds of milchbeasts hunted stray blades of spring grass. Grass in Ruatha, Lessa mused, grew where it should not, died where it should flourish. Lessa could hardly remember now how Ruatha Valley had once looked, sweetly happy, amply productive. Before Fax came. An odd brooding smile curved lips unused to such exercise. Fax realized no profit from his conquest of Ruatha . . . nor would he while she, Lessa, lived. And he had not the slightest suspicion of the source of this undoing.

Or had he, Lessa wondered, her mind still reverberating from the savage prescience of danger. West lay Fax's ancestral and only legitimate Hold. Northeast lay little but bare and stony mountains and the Weyr that protected Pern.

Lessa stretched, arching her back, inhaling the sweet, untainted wind of morning.

A cock crowed in the stable yard. Lessa whirled, her face alert, eyes darting around the outer Hold lest she be observed in such an uncharacteristic pose. She unbound her hair, letting the rank mass fall about her face concealingly. Her body drooped into the sloppy posture she affected. Quickly she thudded down the stairs, crossing to the watch-wher. It cried piteously, its great eyes blinking against the growing daylight. Oblivious to the stench of its rank breath, she hugged the scaly head to her, scratching its ears and eye ridges. The watch-wher was ecstatic with pleasure, its long body trembling, its clipped wings rustling. It alone knew who she was or cared. And it was the only creature in all Pern she had trusted since the dawn she had blindly sought refuge in its dark, stinking lair to escape the thirsty swords that had drunk so deeply of Ruathan blood.

Slowly she rose, cautioning it to remember to be as vicious to her as to all, should anyone be near. It promised to obey her, swaying back and forth to emphasize its reluctance.

The first rays of the sun glanced over the Hold's outer wall, and, crying out, the watch-wher darted into its dark nest. Lessa crept swiftly back to the kitchen and into the cheeseroom.

From the Weyr and from the Bowl,
Bronze and brown and blue and green,
Rise the dragonmen of Pern,
Aloft, on wing, seen, then unseen.

F'lar, on bronze Mnementh's great neck, appeared first in the skies above the chief Hold of Fax, so-called Lord of the High Reaches. Behind him, in proper wedge formation, the wingmen came into sight. F'lar checked the formation automatically; it was as precise as on the moment of their entry to *between.*

As Mnementh curved in an arc that would bring them to the perimeter of the Hold, consonant with the friendly nature of this visitation, F'lar surveyed with mounting aversion the disrepair of the ridge defenses. The firestone pits were empty, and the rock-cut gutters radiating from the pits were green-tinged with a mossy growth.

Was there even one Lord in Pern who maintained his Hold rocky in observance of the ancient Laws? F'lar's lips tightened to a thinner line. When this Search was over and the Impression made, there would have to be a solemn, punitive Council held at the Weyr. And by the golden shell of the queen, he, F'lar, meant to be its moderator. He would replace lethargy with industry. He would scour the green and dangerous scum from the heights of Pern, the grass blades from its stoneworks. No verdant skirt would be condoned in any farmhold. And the tithings that had been so miserly, so grudgingly presented, would, under pain of firestoning, flow with decent generosity into the Dragonweyr.

Mnementh rumbled approvingly as he vaned his pinions to land lightly on the grass-etched flagstones of Fax's Hold. The bronze dragon furled his great wings, and F'lar heard the warning claxon in the Hold's Great Tower. Mnementh dropped to his knees as F'lar indicated he wished to dismount. The bronze rider stood by Mnementh's huge wedge-shaped head, politely awaiting the arrival of the Hold Lord. F'lar idly gazed down the valley, hazy with warm spring sunlight. He ignored the furtive heads that peered at the dragonman from the parapet slits and the cliff windows.

F'lar did not turn as the rush of air past him announced the arrival of the rest of the wing. He knew, however, when F'nor, the brown rider who was coincidentally his half brother, took the customary position on his left, a dragon length to the rear. From the corner of his eye, F'lar glimpsed F'nor twisting to death with his boot heel the grass that crowded up between the stones.

An order, muffled to an intense whisper, issued from within the great Court, beyond the open gates. Almost immediately a group of men marched into sight, led by a heavy-set man of medium height.

Mnementh arched his neck, angling his head so that his chin rested on the ground. Mnementh's many-faceted eyes, on a level with F'lar's head, fastened with disconcerting interest on the approaching party. The dragons could never understand why they generated such abject fear in common folk. At only one point in his life span would a dragon attack a human, and that could be excused on the grounds of simple ignorance. F'lar could not explain to the dragon the politics behind the necessity of inspiring awe in the holders, Lord and craftsman alike. He could only observe that the fear and apprehension showing in the faces of the advancing squad which troubled Mnementh was oddly pleasing to him, F'lar.

"Welcome, bronze rider, to the Hold of Fax, Lord of the High Reaches. He is at your service," and the man made an adequately respectful salute.

The use of the third person pronoun could be construed by the meticulous to be a veiled insult. This fit in with the information F'lar had on Fax, so he ignored it. His information was also correct in describing Fax as a greedy man. It showed in the restless eyes that flicked at every detail of F'lar's clothing, at the slight frown when the intricately etched sword hilt was noticed.

F'lar noticed, in his own turn, the several rich rings that flashed on Fax's left hand. The overlord's right hand remained slightly cocked after the habit of the professional swordsman. His tunic, of rich fabric, was stained and none too fresh. The man's feet, in heavy wher-hide boots, were solidly planted, weight balanced forward on his toes. A man to be treated cautiously, F'lar decided, as one should the conqueror of five neighboring Holds. Such greedy audacity was in itself a revelation. Fax had married into a sixth : . . and had legally inherited, however unusual the circumstances, the seventh. He was a lecherous man by reputation. Within these seven Holds, F'lar anticipated a profitable Search. Let R'gul go southerly to pursue Search among the indolent if lovely women there. The Weyr needed a strong woman this time; Jora had been worse than useless with Nemorth. Adversity, uncertainty: those were the conditions that bred the qualities F'lar wanted in a Weyrwoman.

"We ride in Search," F'lar drawled softly, "and request the hospitality of your Hold, Lord Fax."

Fax's eyes widened imperceptibly at mention of a Search.

"I had heard Jora was dead," Fax replied, droping the third person abruptly as if F'lar had passed some sort of test by ignoring it. "So Nemorth has laid a queen, hmmm?" he continued, his eyes darting across the rank of the wing, noting the disciplined stance of the riders, the healthy color of the dragons.

F'lar did not dignify the obvious with an answer.

"And, my Lord—" Fax hesitated, expectantly inclining his head slightly toward the dragonman.

For a pulse beat, F'lar wondered if the man was deliberately provoking him with such subtle insults. The name of the bronze riders should be as well-known throughout Pern as the name of the dragon queen and her Weyrwoman. F'lar kept his face composed, his eyes on Fax's.

Leisurely, with the proper touch of arrogance, F'nor stepped forward, stopping slightly behind Mnementh's head, one hand negligently touching the jaw hinge of the huge beast.

"The bronze rider of Mnementh, Lord F'lar, will require quarters for himself. I, F'nor, brown rider, prefer to be lodged with the wingmen. We are, in number, twelve."

F'lar liked that touch of F'nor's, totting up the wing strength, as if Fax were incapable of counting. F'nor had phrased it so adroitly as to make it impossible for Fax to protest the return insult.

"Lord F'lar," Fax said through teeth fixed in a smile, "the High Reaches are honored with your Search."

"It will be to the credit of the High Reaches," F'lar replied smoothly, "if one of its own supplies the Weyr."

"To our everlasting credit," Fax replied as suavely. "In the old days many notable Weyrwomen came from my Holds."

"Your Holds?" asked F'lar, politely smiling as he emphasized the plural. "Ah, yes, you are now overlord of Ruatha, are you not? There have been many from that Hold."

A strange, tense look crossed Fax's face, quickly supplanted by a determinedly affable grin. Fax stepped aside, gesturing F'lar to enter the Hold.

Fax's troop leader barked a hasty order, and the men formed two lines, their metal-edged boots flicking sparks from the stones.

At unspoken orders, all the dragons rose with a great churning of air and dust. F'lar strode nonchalantly past the welcoming files. The men were rolling their eyes in alarm as the beasts glided above to the inner courts. Someone on the high Tower uttered a frightened yelp as Mnementh took his position on that vantage point. His great wings drove phosphoric-scented air across the inner court as he maneuvered his great frame onto the inadequate landing space.

Outwardly oblivious to the consternation, fear, and awe the dragons inspired, F'lar was secretly amused and rather pleased by the effect. Lords of the Holds needed this reminder that they still must deal with dragons, not just with riders, who were men, mortal and murderable. The ancient respect for dragonmen as well as dragonkind must be reinstilled in modern breasts.

"The Hold has just risen from table, Lord F'lar, if . . . " Fax suggested. His voice trailed off at F'lar's smiling refusal.

"Convey my duty to your lady, Lord Fax," F'lar rejoined, noticing with inward satisfaction the tightening of Fax's jaw muscles at the ceremonial request.

F'lar was enjoying himself thoroughly. He had not yet been born on the occasion of the last Search, the one that ill-fatedly provided the incompetent Jora. But he had studied the accounts of previous Searches in the Old Records that had included subtle ways to confound those Lords who preferred to keep their ladies sequestered when the dragonmen rode. For Fax to refuse F'lar the opportunity to pay his duty would have been tantamount to a major insult, discharged only in mortal combat.

"You would prefer to see your quarters first?" Fax countered.

F'lar flicked an imaginary speck from his soft wher-hide sleeve and shook his head.

"Duty first," he said with a rueful shrug.

"Of course," Fax all but snapped and strode smartly ahead, his heels pounding out the anger he could not express otherwise.

F'lar and F'nor followed at a slower pace through the double-doored entry with its great metal panels, into the Great Hall, carved into the cliffside. The U-shaped table was being cleared by nervous servitors, who rattled and dropped tableware as the two dragonmen entered. Fax had already reached the far end of the Hall and stood impatiently at the open slab door, the only access to the inner Hold, which, like all such Holds, burrowed deep into stone, the refuge of all in time of peril.

"They eat not badly," F'nor remarked casually to F'lar, appraising the remnants still on the table.

"Better than the Weyr, it would seem," F'lar replied dryly, covering his speech with his hand as he saw two drudges staggering under the weight on a tray that bore a half-eaten carcass.

"Young and tender," F'nor said in a bitter undertone, "from the look of it. While the stringy, barren beasts are delivered up to us."

"Naturally."

"A pleasantly favored Hall," F'lar said amiably as they reached Fax. Then, seeing Fax impatient to continue, F'lar deliberately turned back to the banner-hung Hall. He pointed out to F'nor the deeply set slit windows, heavy bronze shutters open to the bright noonday sky. "Facing east, too, as they ought. That new Hall at Telgar Hold actually faces south, I'm told. Tell me, Lord Fax, do you adhere to the old practices and mount a dawn guard?"

Fax frowned, trying to parse F'lar's meaning.

"There is always a guard at the Tower."

"An easterly guard?"

Fax's eyes jerked toward the windows, then back, sliding across F'lar's face to F'nor and back again to the windows.

"There are always guards," he answered sharply, "on all the approaches."

"Oh, just the approaches," and F'lar turned to F'nor and nodded wisely.

"Where else?" demanded Fax, concerned, glancing from one dragonman to the other.

"I must ask that of your harper. You do keep a trained harper in your Hold?"

"Of course. I have several trained harpers." Fax jerked his shoulders straighter.

F'lar affected not to understand.

"Lord Fax is the overlord of six other Holds," F'nor reminded his wingleader.

"Of course," F'lar assented, with exactly the same inflection Fax had used a moment before.

The mimicry did not go unnoticed by Fax, but as he was unable to construe deliberate insult out of an innocent affirmative, he stalked into the glow-lit corridors. The dragonmen followed.

"It is good to see one Holder keeping so many ancient customs," F'lar said to F'nor approvingly for Fax's benefit as they passed into the inner Hold. "There are many who have abandoned the safety of solid rock and enlarged their outer Holds to dangerous proportions. I can't condone the risk myself."

"Their risk, Lord F'lar. Another's gain," Fax snorted derisively, slowing to a normal strut.

"Gain? How so?"

"Any outer Hold is easily penetrated, bronze rider, with trained forces, experienced leadership, and well-considered strategy."

The man was not a braggart, F'lar decided. Nor, in these peaceful days, did he fail to mount Tower guards. However, he kept within his Hold, not out of obedience to ancient Laws, but through prudence. He kept harpers for ostentation rather than because tradition required it. But he allowed the pits to decay; he permitted grass to grow. He accorded dragonmen the barest civility on one hand and offered veiled insult on the other. A man to be watched.

The women's quarters in Fax's Hold had been moved from the traditional innermost corridors to those at the cliff-face. Sunlight poured down from the three double-shuttered, deep-casement windows in the outside wall. F'lar noted that the bronze hinges were well oiled. The sills were the regulation spear-length; Fax had not given in to the recent practice of diminishing the protective wall.

The chamber was richly hung with appropriately gentle scenes of women occupied in all manner of feminine tasks. Doors gave off the main chamber on both sides into smaller sleeping alcoves, and from these, at Fax's bidding, his women hesitantly emerged. Fax sternly gestured to a blue-gowned woman, her hair white-streaked, her face lined with disappointments and bitterness, her body swollen with pregnancy. She advanced awkwardly, stopping several feet from her lord. From her attitude, F'lar deduced that she came no closer to Fax than was absolutely necessary.

"The Lady of Crom, mother of my heirs," Fax said without pride or cordiality.

"My Lady—" F'lar hesitated, waiting for her name to be supplied.

She glanced warily at her lord.

"Gemma," Fax snapped curtly.

F'lar bowed deeply. "My Lady Gemma, the Weyr is on Search and requests the hospitality of the Hold."

"My Lord F'lar," the Lady Gemma replied in a low voice, "you are most welcome."

F'lar did not miss the slight slur on the adverb or the fact that Gemma had no trouble naming him. His smile was warmer than courtesy demanded, warm with gratitude and sympathy. Judging by the number of women in these quarters, Fax bedded well and frequently. There might be one or two Lady Gemma could bid farewell without regret.

Fax went through the introductions, mumbling names until he realized this strategy was not going to work. F'lar would politely beg the lady's name again. F'nor, his smile brightening as he took heed which ladies Fax preferred to keep anonymous, lounged indolently by the doorway. F'lar would compare notes with him later, although on cursory examination there was none here worthy of the Search. Fax preferred his women plump and small. There wasn't a saucy one in the lot. If there once had been, the spirit had been beaten out of them. Fax, no doubt, was stud, not lover. Some of the covey had not all winter long made much use of water, judging from the amount of sweet oil gone rancid in their hair. Of them all, if these were all, the Lady Gemma was the only willful one, and she was too old.

The amenities over, Fax ushered his unwelcome guests outside. F'nor was excused by his wingleader to join the other dragonmen. Fax peremptorily led the way to the quarters he had assigned the bronze rider.

The chamber was on a lower level than the women's suite and was certainly adequate to the dignity of its occupant. The many-colored hangings were crowded with bloody battles, individual swordplay, bright-hued dragons in flight, firestones burning on the ridges, and all that Pern's scarlet-stained history offered.

"A pleasant room," F'lar acknowledged, stripping off gloves and wher-hide tunic, throwing them carelessly to the table. "I shall see to my men and the beasts. The dragons have all been fed recently," he commented, pointing up Fax's omission in inquiring. "I request liberty to wander through the crafthold."

Fax sourly granted what was traditionally a dragonman's privilege.

"I shall not further disrupt your routine, Lord Fax, for you must have many demands on you, with seven Holds to supervise." F'lar inclined his body slightly to the overlord, turning away as a gesture of dismissal. He could imagine the infuriated expression on Fax's face and listened to the stamping retreat. He waited long enough to be sure Fax was out of the corridor and then briskly retraced his steps up to the Great Hall.

Bustling drudges paused in setting up additional trestle tables to eye the dragonman. He nodded pleasantly to them, looking to see if one of these females might possibly have the stuff of which Weyr-women are made. Overworked, underfed, scarred by lash and disease, they were just what they were—drudges, fit only for hard, menial labor.

F'nor and the men had settled themselves in a hastily vacated barrackroom. The dragons were perched comfortably on the rocky ridges above the Hold. They had so arranged themselves that every segment of the wide valley fell under their scrutiny. All had been fed before leaving the Weyr, and each rider kept his dragon in light but alert charge. There were to be no incidents on a Search.

As a group, the dragonmen rose at F'lar's entrance.

"No tricks, no troubles, but look around closely," he said laconically. "Return by sundown with the names of any likely prospects." He caught F'nor's grin, remembering how Fax had slurred over some names. "Descriptions are in order and craft affiliation."

The men nodded, their eyes glinting with understanding. They were flatteringly confident of a successful Search even as F'lar's doubts grew now that he had seen all of Fax's women. By all logic, the pick of the High Reaches should be in Fax's chief Hold, but they were not. Still, there were many large craftholds, not to mention the six other High Holds to visit. All the same . . .

In unspoken accord F'lar and F'nor left the barracks. The men would follow, unobtrusively, in pairs or singly, to reconnoiter the craft-hold and the nearer farmholds. The men were as overtly eager to be abroad as F'lar was privately. There had been a time when dragonmen were frequent and favored guests in all the great Holds throughout Pern, from southern Nerat to high Tillek. This pleasant custom, too, had died along with other observances, evidence of the low regard in which the Weyr was presently held. F'lar vowed to correct this.

He forced himself to trace in memory the insidious changes. The Records, which each Weyrwoman kept, were proof of the gradual but perceptible decline, traceable through the past two hundred full Turns. Knowing the facts did not alleviate the condition. And F'lar was of the scant handful in the Weyr itself who did credit Records and ballad alike. The situation might shortly reverse itself radically if the old tales were to be believed.

There was a reason, an explanation, a purpose, F'lar felt, for every one of the Weyr Laws from First Impression to the Firestones, from the grass-free heights to ridge-running gutters. For elements as minor as controlling the appetite of a dragon to limiting the inhabitants of the Weyr. Although why the other five Weyrs had been abandoned F'lar did not know. Idly he wondered if there were Records, dusty and crumbling, lodged in the disused Weyrs. He must contrive to check when next his wings flew patrol. Certainly there was no explanation in Benden Weyr.

"There is industry but no enthusiasm," F'nor was saying, drawing F'lar's attention back to their tour of the crafthold.

They had descended the guttered ramp from the Hold into the crafthold proper, the broad roadway lined with cottages up to the imposing stone crafthalls. Silently F'lar noted moss-clogged gutters on the roofs, the vines clasping the walls. It was painful for one of his calling to witness the flagrant disregard of simple safety precautions. Growing things were forbidden near the habitations of mankind.

"News travels fast," F'nor chuckled, nodding at a hurrying craftsman, in the smock of a baker, who gave them a mumbled good-day. "Not a female in sight."

His observation was accurate. Women should be abroad at this hour, bringing in supplies from the storehouses, washing in the river on such a bright warm day, or going out to the farmholds to help with planting. Not a gowned figure in sight.

"We used to be preferred mates," F'nor remarked caustically.

"We'll visit the Clothmen's Hall first. If my memory serves me . . . "

"As it always does . . . " F'nor interjected wryly. He took no advantage of their blood relationship, but he was more at ease with the bronze rider than most of the dragonmen, the other bronze riders included. F'lar was reserved in a close-knit society of easy equality. He flew a tightly disciplined wing, but men maneuvered to serve under him. His wing always excelled in the Games. None ever foundered in *between* to disappear forever, and no beast in his wing sickened, leaving a man in dragonless exile from the Weyr, a part of him numb forever.

"L'tol came this way and settled in one of the High Reaches," F'lar continued.

"L'tol?"

"Yes, a green rider from S'lel's wing. You remember."

An ill-timed swerve during the Spring Games had brought L'tol and his beast into the full blast of a phosphine emission from S'lel's bronze Tuenth. L'tol had been thrown from his beast's neck as the dragon tried to evade the blast. Another wingmate had swooped to catch the rider, but the green dragon, his left wing crisped, his body scorched, had died of shock and phosphine poisoning.

"L'tol would aid our Search," F'nor agreed as the two dragonmen walked up to the bronze doors of the Clothmen's Hall. They paused on the threshold, adjusting their eyes to the dimmer light within. Glows punctuated the wall recesses and hung in clusters above the larger looms where the finer tapestries and fabrics were woven by master craftsmen. The pervading mood was one of quiet, purposeful industry.

Before their eyes had adapted, however, a figure glided to them, muttering a polite if curt request for them to follow him.

They were led to the right of the entrance, to a small office, curtained from the main hall. Their guide turned to them, his face visible in the wallglows. There was that air about him that marked him indefinably as a dragonman. But his face was lined deeply, one side seamed with old burn marks. His eyes, sick with a hungry yearning, dominated his face. He blinked constantly.

"I am now Lytol," he said in harsh voice.

F'lar nodded acknowledgment.

"You would be F'lar," Lytol said, "and you F'nor. You both have the look of your sire."

F'lar nodded again.

Lytol swallowed convulsively, the muscles in his face twitching as the presence of dragonmen revived his awareness of exile. He essayed a smile.

"Dragons in the sky! The news spread faster than Threads."

"Nemorth has laid a female."

"And Jora dead?" Lytol asked concernedly, his face cleared of its nervous movement for a second. "Hath flew her?"

F'lar nodded.

Lytol grimaced bitterly. "R'gul again, huh?" He stared off in the middle distance, his eyelids quiet but the muscles along his jaw taking up the constant movement. "You have the High Reaches? All of them?" Lytol asked, turning back to the dragonman, a slight emphasis on "all."

F'lar gave an affirmative nod again.

"You've seen the women." Lytol's disgust showed through the words. It was a statement, not a question, for he hurried on. "Well, there are no better in all the High Reaches." His tone expressed utmost disdain. He eased himself down to the heavy table that half-filled one corner of the small room. His hands were clenched so tightly around the wide belt that secured the loose tunic to his body that the heavy leather was doubled.

"You would almost expect the opposite, wouldn't you?" Lytol continued. He was talking too much and too fast. It would have been insultingly rude in another, lesser man. It was the terrible loneliness of the man's exile from the Weyr that drove him to garrulity. Lytol skimmed the surfaces with hurried questions he himself answered, rather than dip once into matters too tender to be touched—such as his insatiable need for those of his kind. Yet he was giving the dragonmen exactly the information they needed. "But Fax likes his women comfortably fleshed and docile," Lytol rattled on. "Even the Lady Gemma has learned. It'd be different if he didn't need her family's support. Ah, it would be different indeed. So he keeps her pregnant, hoping to kill her in childbed one day. And he will. He will."

Lytol's laughter grated unpleasantly.

"When Fax came to power, any man with wit sent his daughters down from the High Reaches or drew a brand across their faces." He paused, his countenance dark and bitter memory, his eyes slits of hatred. "I was a fool and thought my position gave me immunity."

Lytol drew himself up, squaring his shoulders, turning full to the two dragonmen. His expression was vindictive, his voice low and tense.

"Kill that tyrant, dragonmen, for the sake and safety of Pern. Of the Weyr. Of the queen. He only bides his time. He spreads discontent among the other Lords. He—" Lytol's laughter had an hysterical edge to it now. "He fancies himself as good as dragonmen."

"There are no candidates then in this Hold?" F'lar said, his voice sharp enough to cut through the man's preoccupation with his curious theory.

Lytol stared at the bronze rider. "Did I not say it? The best either died under Fax or were sent away. What remains is nothing, nothing. Weak-minded, ignorant, foolish, vapid. You had that with Jora. She—" His jaw snapped shut over his next words. He shook his head, scrubbing his face to ease his anguish and despair.

"In the other Holds?"

Lytol shook his head, frowning darkly. "The same. Either dead or fled."

"What of Ruath Hold?"

Lytol stopped shaking his head and looked sharply at F'lar, his lips curling in a cunning smile. He laughted mirthlessly.

"You think to find a Torene or a Moreta hidden at Ruath Hold in these times? Well, bronze rider, all of Ruathan Blood are dead. Fax's blade was thirsty that day. He knew the truth of those harpers' tales, that Ruathan Lords gave full measure of hospitality to dragonmen and the Ruathan were a breed apart. There were, you know"—Lytol's voice dropped to a confiding whisper—"exiled Weyrmen like myself in that Line."

F'lar nodded gravely, unwilling to deprive the man of such a sop to his self-esteem.

"No, there is little, very little left in Ruatha Valley." Lytol chuckled softly. "Fax gets nothing from that Hold but trouble." This reflection restored Lytol to a semblance of normal behavior, and his face twisted into a better humor. "We of this Hold are now the best clothmen in all Pern. And our smithies turn out a better tempered weapon." His eyes sparkled with pride in his adopted community. "The conscripts from Ruatha tend to die of curious diseases or accidents. And the women Fax used to take . . . " His laugh was nasty. "It is rumored he was impotent for months after."

F'lar's active mind jumped to a curious conclusion. "There are none of the Blood left?"

"None!"

"Any families in the holdings with Weyr blood?"

Lytol frowned, glanced in surprise at F'lar. He rubbed the scarred side of his face thoughtfully.

"There were," he admitted slowly. "There were. But I doubt if any live on." He thought a moment longer, then shook his head emphatically. "There was such resistance at the invasion and no quarter given. At the Hold Fax beheaded ladies as well as babes. And he imprisoned or executed any known to have carried arms for Ruatha."

F'lar shrugged. The idea had been a probability only. With such severe reprisals, Fax undoubtedly had eliminated the resistance as well as the best craftsmen. That would account for the poor quality of Ruathan products and the emergence of the High Reaches' clothmen as the best in their trade.

"I wish I had better news for your, dragonman," Lytol murmured.

"No matter," F'lar reassured him, one hand poised to part the hanging in the doorway.

Lytol came up to him swiftly, his voice urgent.

"Heed what I say about Fax's ambitions. Force R'gul, or whoever is Weyrleader next, to keep watch on the High Reaches."

"Is Fax aware of your leanings?"

The haunted, hungry yearning crossed Lytol's face. He swallowed nervously, answering with no emotion in his voice.

"That would not signify if it suited the Lord of the High Reaches, but my guild protects me from persecution. I am safe enough in the craft. He is dependent on the proceeds of our industy." He snorted, mocking. "I am the best weaver of battle scenes. To be sure," he added, cocking one eyebrow waggishly, "dragons are no longer woven in the fabric as the comrades of heroes. You noticed, of course, the prevalence of growing greens?"

F'lar grimaced his distaste. "That is not all we have noted, either. But Fax keeps the other traditions. . . . "

Lytol waved this consideration aside. "He does that because it is basic military sense. His neighbors armed after he took Ruatha, for he did it by treachery, let me tell you. And let me warn you also"—Lytol jabbed a finger in the direction of the Hold—"he scoffs openly at tales of the Threads. He taunts the harpers for the stupid nonsense of the old ballads and has banned from their repertoire all dragonlore. The new generation will grow up totally ignorant of duty, tradition, and precaution."

F'lar was not surprised to hear that on top of Lytol's other disclosures, although it disturbed him more than anything else he had heard. Other men, too, denied the verbal transmissions of historic events, accounting them no more than the maunderings of harpers. Yet the Red Star pulsed in the sky, and the time was drawing near when they would hysterically re-avow the old allegiances in fear for their very lives.

"Have you been abroad in the early morning of late?" asked F'nor, grinning maliciously.

"I have," Lytol breathed out in a hushed, choked whisper. "I have. . . . " A groan was wrenched from his guts, and he whirled away from the dragonmen, his head bowed between hunched shoulders. "Go," he said, gritting his teeth. And, as they hesitated, he pleaded, "*Go!*"

F'lar walked quickly from the room, followed by F'nor. The bronze rider crossed the quiet dim Hall with long strides and exploded into the startling sunlight. His momentum took him into the center of the square. There he stopped so abruptly that F'nor, hard on his heels, nearly collided with him.

"We will spend exactly the same time within the other Halls," he announced in a tight voice, his face averted from F'nor's eyes. F'lar's throat was constricted. It was difficult suddenly for him to speak. He swallowed hard, several times.

"To be dragonless . . . " murmured F'nor pityingly. The encounter with Lytol had roiled his depths in a mournful way to which he was unaccustomed. That F'lar appeared equally shaken went far to dispel F'nor's private opinion that his half brother was incapable of emotion.

"There is no other way once First Impression has been made. You know that," F'lar roused himself to say curtly. He strode off to the Hall bearing the leather-men's device.

Honor those the dragons heed,
In thought and favor, word and deed.
Worlds are lost or worlds are saved
From those dangers dragon-braved.

Dragonman, avoid excess;
Greed will bring the Weyr distress;
To the ancient Laws adhere,
Prospers thus the Dragonweyr.

F'lar was amused . . . and unamused. This was their fourth
day in Fax's company, and only F'lar's firm control on self
and wing was keeping the situation from exploding into violence.

It had been a turn of chance, F'lar mused, as Mnementh held his
leisurely glide toward the Breast Pass into Ruatha, that he, F'lar, had
chosen the High Reaches. Fax's tactics would have been successful with
R'gul, who was very conscious of his honor, or S'lan or D'nol, who
were too young to have developed much patience or discretion. S'lel
would have retreated in confusion, a course nearly as disastrous for
the Weyr as combat.

He should have correlated the indications long ago. The decay
of the Weyr and its influence did not come solely from the Holding
Lords and their folk. It came also from within the Weyr, a result of
inferior queens and incompetent Weyrwomen. It came from R'gul's
inexplicable insistence on not "bothering" the Holders, on keeping
dragonmen within the Weyr. And yet within the Weyr there had been
too much emphasis on preparation for the Games until the internal
competition between wings had become the be-all and end-all of Weyr
activity.

The encroachment of grass had not come overnight, nor had the
Lords awakened one morning recently and decided in a flash not to
give all their traditional tithe to the Weyr. It had happened gradually
and had been allowed, by the Weyr, to continue, until the purpose
and reason of the Weyr and dragonkind had reached this low ebb,
where an upstart, collateral heir to an ancient Hold could be so contemptuous of dragonmen and the simple basic precautions that kept
Pern free of Threads.

F'lar doubted that Fax would have attempted such a program of
aggression against neighboring Holds if the Weyr had maintained its
old prominence. Each Hold must have its Lord to protect valley and
folk from the Threads. One Hold, one Lord—not one Lord claiming
seven Holds. That was against ancient tradition, and evil besides, for
how well can one man protect seven valleys at once? Man, except for

dragonman, can be in only one place at a time. And unless a man was dragon-mounted, it took hours to get from one Hold to another. No Weyrman of old would have permitted such flagrant disregard of ancient ways.

F'lar saw the gouts of flame along the barren heights of the Pass, and Mnementh obediently altered his glide for a better view. F'lar had sent half the wing ahead of the main cavalcade. It was good training for them to skim irregular terrain. He had issued small pieces of firestone with instructions to sear any growth as practice. It would do to remind Fax, as well as his troops, of the awesome ability of dragonkind, a phenomenon the common folk of Pern appeared to have all but forgotten.

The fiery phosphine emissions as the dragons belched forth gasses showed the pattern well flown. R'gul could argue against the necessity of firestone drills, he could cite such incidents as that which had exiled Lytol, but F'lar kept the tradition—and so did every man who flew with him, or they left the wing. None failed him.

F'lar knew that the men reveled as much as he did in the fierce joy of riding a flaming dragon; the fumes of phosphine were exhilarating in their own way, and the feeling of power that surged through the man who controlled the might and majesty of a dragon had no parallel in human experience. Dragonriders were forever men apart once First Impression had been made. And to ride a fighting dragon, blue, green, brown, or bronze, was worth the risks, the unending alertness, the isolation from the rest of mankind.

Mnementh dipped his wings obliquely to slide through the narrow cleft of the Pass that led from Crom to Ruatha. No sooner had they emerged from the cut than the difference between the two Holds was patent.

F'lar was stunned. Through the last four Holds he had been sure that the end of the Search lay within Ruatha.

There had been that little brunette whose father was a clothman in Nabol, but . . . And a tall, willowy girl with enormous eyes, the daughter of a minor Warder in Crom, yet . . . These were possibilities, and had F'lar been S'lel or K'net or D'nol, he might have taken the two in as potential mates, although not likely Weyrwomen.

But throughout he had reassured himself that the real choice would be found to the south. Now he gazed on the ruin that was Ruatha, his hopes dispersed. Below him, he saw Fax's banner dip in the sequence that requested his presence.

Mastering the crushing disappointment he felt, he directed Mnementh to descend. Fax, roughly controlling the terrified plunging of his earthbound mount, waved down into the abandoned-looking valley.

"Behold great Ruatha of which you had such hopes," he enjoined sarcastically.

F'lar smiled cooly back, wondering how Fax had divined that. Had F'lar been so transparent when he had suggested Searching the other Holds? Or was it a lucky guess on Fax's part?

"One sees at a glance why goods from the High Reaches are now preferred," F'lar made himself reply. Mnementh rumbled, and F'lar called him sharply to order. The bronze one had developed a distaste bordering on hatred for Fax. Such antipathy in a dragon was most unusual and of no small concern to F'lar. Not that he would have in the least regretted Fax's demise, but not at Mnementh's breath.

"Little good comes from Ruatha," Fax said in a voice that was close to a snarl. He jerked sharply at the bridle of his beast, and fresh blood colored the foam on its muzzle. The creature threw its head backward to ease the painful bar in its mouth, and Fax savagely smote it a blow between the ears. The blow, F'lar observed, was not intended for the poor, protesting beast but for the sight of unproductive Ruatha. "I am the overlord. My proclamation went unchallenged by any of the Blood. I am in my rights. Ruatha must pay its tribute to its legal overlord. . . . "

"And hunger the rest of the year," F'lar remarked dryly, gazing out over the wide valley. Few of its fields were plowed. Its pastures supported meager herds. Even its orchards looked stunted. Blossoms that had been so profuse on trees in Crom, the next valley over, were sparse, as if reluctant to flower in so dismal a place. Although the sun was well up, there seemed to be no activity in the farmholds or none near enough to be observed. The atmosphere was one of sullen despair.

"There has been resistance to my rule of Ruatha."

F'lar shot a look at Fax, for the man's voice was fierce, his face bleak, auguring further unpleasantness for Ruathan rebels. The vind- ictiveness that colored Fax's attitude toward Ruatha and its rebels was tinged with another strong emotion which F'lar had been unable to identify but which had been very apparent to him from the first time he had adroitly suggested this tour of the Holds. It could not be fear, for Fax was clearly fearless and obnoxiously self-assured. Revulsion? Dread? Uncertainty? F'lar could not label the nature of Fax's compound reluctance to visit Ruatha, but the man had not relished the prospect and now reacted violently to being within these disturbing boundaries.

"How foolish of the Ruathans," F'lar remarked amiably. Fax swung around on him, one hand poised above his sword hilt, eyes blazing. F'lar anticipated with a feeling close to pleasure that the usurper Fax might actually draw on a dragonman! He was almost dis- appointed when the man controlled himself, took a firm hold on the reins of his mount, and kicked it forward to a frantic run.

"I shall kill him yet," F'lar said to himself, and Mnementh spread his wings in concord.

F'nor dropped beside his bronze leader.

"Did I see him about to draw on you?" F'nor's eyes were bright, his smile acid.

"Until he remembered I was mounted on a dragon."

"Watch him, bronze rider. He means to kill you soon."

"If he can!"

"He's considered a vicious fighter," F'nor advised, his smile gone.

Mnementh flapped his wings again, and F'lar absently stroked the great, soft-skinned neck.

"I am at some disadvantage?" F'lar asked, stung by F'nor's words.

"To my knowledge, no," F'nor said quickly, startled. "I have not seen him in action, but I don't like what I have heard. He kills often, with and without cause."

"And because we dragonmen do not seek blood, we are not to be feared as fighters?" snapped F'lar. "Are you ashamed of being what you were bred?"

"I, no!" F'nor sucked in his breath at the tone of his leader's voice. "And others of our wing, no! But there is that in the attitude of Fax's men that . . . that makes me wish some excuse to fight."

"As you remarked, we will probably have that fight. There is something here in Ruatha that unnerves our noble overlord."

Mnementh and now Canth, F'nor's brown, extended their wings, flapping to catch their riders' attention.

F'lar stared as the dragon slewed his head back toward his rider, the great eyes gleaming like sunstruck opals.

"There is a subtle strength in this valley," F'lar murmured, gathering the import of the dragon's agitated message.

"A strength, indeed; even my brown feels it," F'nor replied, his face lighting.

"Careful, brown rider," F'lar cautioned. "Careful. Send the entire wing aloft. Search this valley. I should have realized. I should have suspected. It was all there to be evaluated. What fools have dragonmen become!"

The Hold is barred,
The Hall is bare,
   And men vanish.
The soil is barren,
The rock is bald.
   All hope banish.

Lessa was shoveling ashes from the hearth when the agitated messenger staggered into the Great Hall. She made herself as inconspicuous as possible so the Warder would not dismiss her. She had contrived to be sent to the Great Hall that morning, knowing that the Warder intended to brutalize the head clothman for the shoddy quality of the goods readied for shipment to Fax.

"Fax is coming! With dragonmen!" the man gasped out as he plunged into the dim Great Hall.

The Warder, who had been about to lash the head clothman, turned, stunned, from his victim. The courier, a farmholder from the edge of Ruatha, stumbled up to the Warder, so excited with his message that he grabbed the Warder's arm.

"How dare you leave your Hold?" The Warder aimed his lash at the astonished Holder. The force of the first blow knocked the man from his feet. Yelping, he scrambled out of reach of a second lashing. "Dragonmen indeed! Fax? Ha! He shuns Ruatha. There!" The Warder punctuated each denial with another blow, kicking the helpless wretch for good measure, before he turned breathless to glare at the clothman and the two underwarders. "How did he get in here with such a threadbare lie?" The Warder stalked to the Great Hall door. It was flung open just as he reached for the iron handle. The ashen-faced guard officer rushed in, nearly knocking the Warder down.

"Dragonmen! Dragons! All over Ruatha!" the man gibbered, arms flailing wildly. He, too, pulled at the Warder's arm, dragging the stupefied official toward the outer courtyard, to bear out the truth of his statement.

Lessa scooped up the last pile of ashes. Picking up her equipment, she slipped out of the Great Hall. There was a very pleased smile on her face under the screen of matted hair.

A dragonman at Ruatha! An opportunity: she must somehow contrive to get Fax so humiliated or so infuriated that he would renounce his claim to the Hold, in the presence of a dragonman. Then she could claim her birthright.

But she would have to be extraordinarily wary. Dragonriders were men apart. Anger did not cloud their intelligence. Greed did not sully their judgment. Fear did not dull their reactions. Let the dense-witted believe human sacrifice, unnatural lusts, insane revels. She was not so gullible. And those stories went against her grain. Dragonmen were still human, and there was Weyr blood in *her* veins. It was the same color blood as that of anyone else; enough of hers had been spilled to prove that.

She halted for a moment, catching a sudden shallow breath. Was this the danger she had sensed four days ago at dawn? The final encounter in her struggle to regain the Hold? No, Lessa cautioned herself, there was more to that portent than revenge.

The ash bucket banged against her shins as she shuffled down the low-ceilinged corridor to the stable door. Fax would find a cold welcome. She had laid no new fire on the hearth. Her laugh echoed back unpleasantly from the damp walls. She rested her bucket and propped her broom and shovel as she wrestled with the heavy bronze door that gave into the new stables.

They had been built outside the cliff of Ruatha by Fax's first Warder, a subtler man than all eight of his successors. He had achieved more than all the others, and Lessa had honestly regretted the necessity of his death. But he would have made her revenge impossible. He would have found her out before she had learned how to camouflage herself and her little interferences. What had his name been? She could not recall. Well, she regretted his death.

The second man had been properly greedy, and it had been easy to set up a pattern of misunderstanding between Warder and craftsmen. That one had been determined to squeeze all profit from Ruathan goods so that some of it would drop into his pocket before Fax suspected a shortage. The craftsmen who had begun to accept the skillful diplomacy of the first Warder bitterly resented the second's grasping, high-handed ways. They resented the passing of the Old Line and, even more so, the way of its passing. They were unforgiving of the insult to Ruatha, its now secondary position in the High Reaches, and they resented the individual indignities that Holders, craftsmen and farmers alike, suffered under the second Warder. It took little manipulation to arrange for matters at Ruatha to go from bad to worse.

The second was replaced and his successor fared no better. He was caught diverting goods—the best of the goods, at that. Fax had had him executed. His bony head still rolled around in the main firepit above the great Tower.

The present incumbent had not been able to maintain the Holding in even the sorry condition in which he had assumed its management. Seemingly simple matters developed rapidly into disasters. Like the production of cloth. Contrary to his boasts to Fax, the quality had not improved, and the quantity had fallen off.

Now Fax was here. And with dragonmen! Why dragonmen? The import of the question froze Lessa, and the heavy door closing behind her barked her heels painfully. Dragonmen used to be frequent visitors at Ruatha—that she knew and even vaguely remembered. Those memories were like a harper's tale, told of someone else, not something within her own experience. She had limited her fierce attention to Ruatha only. She could not even recall the name of queen, or Weyrwoman from the instructions of her childhood, nor could she recall hearing mention of any queen or Weyrwoman by anyone in the Hold these past ten Turns.

Perhaps the dragonmen were finally going to call the Lords of the Holds to task for the disgraceful show of greenery about the Holds. Well, Lessa was to blame for much of that in Ruatha, but she defied even a dragonman to confront her with her guilt. If all Ruatha fell to the Threads, it would be better than remaining dependent to Fax! The heresy shocked Lessa even as she thought it.

Wishing she could as easily unburden her conscience of such blasphemy, she ditched the ashes on the stable midden. There was a sudden change in air pressure around her. Then a fleeting shadow caused her to glance up.

From behind the cliff above glided a dragon, its enormous wings spread to their fullest as he caught the morning updraft. Turning effortlessly, he descended. A second, a third, a full wing of dragons followed in soundless flight and patterned descent, graceful and awesome. The claxon rang belatedly from the Tower, and from within the kitchen there issued the screams and shrieks of the terrified drudges.

Lessa took cover. She ducked into the kitchen where she was instantly seized by the assistant cook and thrust with a buffet and a kick toward the sinks. There she was put to scrubbing the grease-encrusted serving utensils with cleansing sand.

The yelping canines were already lashed to the spitrun, turning a scrawny herdbeast that had been set to roast. The cook was ladling seasonings on the carcass, swearing at having to offer so poor a meal to so many guests, some of them of high rank. Winter-dried fruits from the last scanty harvest had been set to soak, and two of the oldest drudges were scraping roots to be boiled.

An apprentice cook was kneading bread and another carefully spicing a sauce. Looking fixedly at him, Lessa diverted his hand from one spice box to a less appropriate one as he gave a final shake to the concoction. She innocently added too much wood to the wall oven to insure the ruin of the breads. She controlled the canines deftly, slowing one and speeding the other so that the meat would be underdone on one side, burned on the other. That the feast should result in fast, with the food presented found inedible, was her whole intention.

Above, in the Hold, she had no doubt that certain other measures, undertaken at different times for this exact contingency, were being discovered.

Her fingers bloodied from a beating, one of the Warder's women came shrieking into the kitchen, hopeful of refuge there.

"Insects have eaten the best blankets to shreds! And a canine who had littered on the best linens snarled at me as she gave suck. And the rushes are noxious, and the best chambers full of debris driven in by the winter wind. Somebody left the shutters ajar. Just a tiny bit, but it was enough," the woman wailed, clutching her hand to her breast and rocking back and forth.

Lessa bent with great industry to shine the plates.

Watch-wher, watch-wher,
In your lair,
Watch well, watch-wher!
Who goes there?

"The watch-wher is hiding something," F'lar told F'nor as they consulted in the hastily cleaned great chamber. The room delighted to hold the wintry chill, although a generous fire now burned on the hearth.

"It was but gibbering when Canth spoke to it," F'nor remarked. He was leaning against the mantel, turning slightly from side to side to gather some warmth. He watched his wingleader's impatient pacing.

"Mnementh is calming it down," F'lar replied. "He may be able to sort out the nightmare. The creature may be more senile than sane, but . . . "

"I doubt it," F'nor concurred helpfully. He glanced with apprehension up at the web-hung ceiling. He was certain he'd found most of the crawlers, but he didn't fancy their sting. Not on top of the discomforts already experienced in this forsaken Hold. If the night stayed mild, he intended curling up with Canth on the heights. "That would be a more reasonable suggestion than Fax or his Warder have made."

"Hmmm," F'lar muttered, frowning at the brown rider.

"Well, it's unbelievable that Ruatha could have fallen to such disrepair in ten short Turns. Every dragon caught the feeling of power, and it's obvious the watch-wher has been tampered with. That takes a good deal of control."

"From someone of the Blood," F'lar reminded him.

F'nor shot his wingleader a quick look, wondering if he could possibly be serious in the light of all information to the contrary.

"I grant you there is power here, F'lar," F'nor conceded. "But it could as easily be a hidden male bastard of the old Blood. And we need a female. But Fax made it plain, in his inimitable fashion, that he left none of the old Blood alive in the Hold the day he took it. Ladies, children, all. No, no." The brown rider shook his head, as if he could dispel the lack of faith in his wingleader's curious insistence that the Search would end in Ruath with Ruathan blood.

"That watch-wher is hiding something, and only someone of the Blood of its Hold can arrange that, brown rider," F'lar said emphatically. He gestured around the room and toward the window. "Ruatha has been overcome. But she resists . . . subtly. I say it points to the old Blood *and* power. Not power alone."

The obstinate expression in F'lar's eyes, the set of his jaw, suggested that F'nor seek another topic.

"I'll see what may be seen around fallen Ruatha," he mumbled and left the chamber.

F'lar was heartily bored with the lady Fax had so courteously assigned him. She giggled incessantly and sneezed constantly. She waved about, but did not apply to her nose, a scarf or handkerchief long overdue for a thorough washing. A sour odor, compounded of sweat, sweet oil, and rancid food smells, exuded from her. She was also pregnant by Fax. Not obviously so, but she had confided her condition to F'lar, either oblivious to the insult to the dragonman or directed by her Lord to let drop the information. F'lar deliberately ignored the matter and, except when her company was obligatory on this Search journey, had ignored her, too.

Lady Tela was nervously jabbering away at him about the terrible condition of the rooms to which Lady Gemma and the other ladies of the Lord's procession had been assigned.

"The shutters, both sets, were ajar all winter long, and you should have seen the trash on the floors. We finally got two of the drudges to sweep it all into the fireplace. And then that smoked something fearful till a man was sent up." Lady Tela giggled. "He found the access blocked by a chimney stone fallen aslant. The rest of the chimney, for a wonder, was in good repair."

She waved her handkerchief. F'lar held his breath as the gesture wafted an unappealing odor in his direction.

He glanced up the Hall toward the inner Hold door and saw the Lady Gemma descending, her steps slow and awkward. Some subtle difference about her gait attracted him, and he stared at her, trying to identify it.

"Oh, yes, poor Lady Gemma," Lady Tela babbled, sighing

deeply. "We are so concerned. Why my Lord Fax insisted on her coming I do not know. She is not near her time, and yet . . . " The lighthead's concern sounded sincere.

F'lar's incipient hatred for Fax and his brutality matured abruptly. He left his partner chattering to thin air and courteously extended his arm to the Lady Gemma to support her down the steps and to the table. Only the brief tightening of her fingers on his forearm betrayed her gratitude. Her face was very white and drawn, the lines deeply etched around mouth and eyes, showing the effort she was expending.

"Some attempt has been made, I see, to restore order to the Hall," she remarked in a conversational tone.

"Some," F'lar admitted dryly, glancing around the grandly proportioned Hall, its rafters festooned with the webs of many Turns. The inhabitants of those gossamer nests dropped from time to time, with ripe splats, to the floor, onto the table, and into the serving platters. Nothing replaced the old banners of the Ruathan Blood, removed from the stark brown stone walls. Fresh rushes did obscure the greasy flagstones. The trestle tables appeared recently sanded and scraped, and the platters gleamed dully in the refreshed glows. Those unfortunately, were a mistake, for brightness was much too unflattering to a scene that would have been more reassuring in dimmer light.

"This was such a graceful Hall," the Lady Gemma murmured for F'lar's ears alone.

"You were a friend?" he asked politely.

"Yes, in my youth." Her voice dropped expressively on the last word, evoking for F'lar a happier girlhood. "It was a noble line!"

"Think you *one* might have escaped the sword?"

The Lady Gemma flashed him a startled look, then quickly composed her features, lest the exchange be noted. She gave a barely perceptible shake of her head and then shifted her awkward weight to take her place at the table. Graciously she inclined her head toward F'lar, both dismissing and thanking him.

He returned to his own partner and placed her at the table on his left. As the only persons of rank who would dine that night at Ruatha Hold, Lady Gemma was seated on his right; Fax would be beyond her. The dragonmen and Fax's upper soldiery would sit at the lower tables. No guildmen had been invited to Ruatha.

Fax arrived just then with his current lady and two underleaders, the Warder bowing them effusively into the Hall. The man, F'lar noticed, kept a good distance from his overlord—as well a Warder might whose responsibility was in this sorry condition. F'lar flicked a crawler away. Out of the corner of his eye he saw the Lady Gemma wince and shudder.

Fax stamped up to the raised table, his face black with suppressed rage. He pulled back his chair roughly, slamming it into the Lady

Gemma's before he seated himself. He pulled the chair to the table with a force that threatened to rock the none too stable trestle-top from its supporting legs. Scowling, he inspected his goblet and plate, fingering the surface, ready to throw them aside if they displeased him.

"A roast, my Lord Fax, and fresh bread, Lord Fax, and such fruits and roots as are left."

"Left? Left? You said there was nothing harvested here."

The Warder's eyes bulged and he gulped, stammering, "Nothing to be sent on. Nothing *good* enough to be sent on. Nothing. Had I but known of your arrival, I could have sent to Crom . . . "

"Sent to Crom?" roared Fax, slamming the plate he was inspecting onto the table so forcefully that the rim bent under his hands. The Warder winced again as if he himself had been maimed.

"For decent foodstuffs, my Lord," he quavered.

"The day one of my Holds cannot support itself *or* the visit of its rightful overlord, I shall renounce it."

The Lady Gemma gasped. Simultaneously the dragons roared. F'lar felt the unmistakable surge of power. His eyes instinctively sought F'nor at the lower table. The brown rider, all the dragonmen, had experienced that inexplicable shaft of exultation.

"What's wrong, dragonman?" snapped Fax.

F'lar, affecting unconcern, stretched his legs under the table and assumed an indolent posture in the heavy chair.

"Wrong?"

"The dragons!"

"Oh, nothing. They often roar . . . at the sunset, at a flock of passing wherries, at mealtimes," and F'lar smiled amiably at the Lord of the High Reaches. Beside him his tablemate gave a little squeak.

"Mealtimes? Have they not been fed?"

"Oh, yes. Five days ago."

"Oh. Five . . . days ago? And are they hungry . . . now?" Her voice trailed into a whisper of fear, her eyes grew round.

"In a few days," F'lar assured her. Under cover of his detached amusement, F'lar scanned the Hall. That surge had come from nearby. Either in the Hall or just without it. It must have been from within. It came so soon upon Fax's speech that his words must have triggered it. F'lar saw that F'nor and the other dragonmen were surreptitiously searching every face in the Hall. Fax's soldiers could be disqualified, and the Warder's men. And the power had an indefinably feminine touch to it.

One of Fax's women? F'lar found that hard to credit. Mnementh had been close to all of them, and none had shown a vestige of power, much less—with the exception of Lady Gemma—any intelligence.

One of the Hall women? So far he had seen only the sorry drudges and the aging females the Warder had as housekeepers. The Warder's personal woman? He must discover if that man had one. One of the Hold guards' women? F'lar suppressed an intense desire to rise and search.

"You mount a guard?" he asked Fax casually.

"Double at Ruath Hold!" he was told in a tight, hard voice, ground out from somewhere deep in Fax's chest.

"Here?" F'lar all but laughed out loud, gesturing around the sadly appointed chamber.

"Here!" Fax changed the subject with a roar. "Food!"

Five drudges, two of them women in such grimy brown-gray rags that F'lar hoped they had had nothing to do with the preparation of the meal, staggered in under the emplattered herdbeast. No one with so much as a trace of power would sink to such depths, unless . . .

The aroma that reached him as the platter was placed on the serving table distracted him. It reeked of singed bone and charred meat. Even the pitcher of *klah* being passed smelled bad. The Warder frantically sharpened his tools as if a keen edge could somehow slice acceptable portions from this unlikely carcass.

The Lady Gemma caught her breath again, and F'lar saw her hands curl tightly around the armrests. He saw the convulsive movement of her throat as she swallowed. He, too, did not look forward to this repast.

The drudges reappeared with wooden trays of bread. Burnt crusts had been scraped and cut, in some places, from the loaves before serving. As other trays were borne in, F'lar tried to catch sight of the faces of the servitors. Matted hair obscured the face of the one who presented Lady Gemma with a dish of legumes swimming in greasy liquid. Revolted, F'lar poked through the legumes to find properly cooked portions to offer Lady Gemma. She waved them aside, her face ill concealing her discomfort.

As F'lar was about to turn and serve Lady Tela, he saw Lady Gemma's hand clutch convulsively at the chair arms. He realized then that she was not merely nauseated by the unappetizing food. She was seized with the onslaught of labor contractions.

F'lar glanced in Fax's direction. The overlord was scowling blackly at the attempts of the Warder to find edible portions of meat to serve.

F'lar touched Lady Gemma's arms with light fingers. She turned her face just enough so that she could see F'lar out of the corner of her eye. She managed a socially correct half-smile.

"I dare not leave just now, Lord F'lar. He is always dangerous at Ruatha. And it may only be false pangs . . . at my age."

F'lar was dubious as he saw another shudder pass through her frame. The woman would have been a fine Weyrwoman, he thought ruefully, if she were younger.

The Warder, his hands shaking, presented Fax the sliced meats, slivers of overdone flesh, portions of almost edible meats, but not much of either.

One furious wave of Fax's broad fist and the Warder had the plate, meats and juice, square in the face. Despite himself, F'lar sighed, for those undoubtedly constituted the only edible portions of the entire beast.

"You call this food? *You call this food?*" Fax bellowed. His voice boomed back from the bare vault of the ceiling, shaking crawlers from their webs as the sound shattered the fragile strands. *"Slop! Slop!"*

F'lar rapidly brushed crawlers from the Lady Gemma, who was helpless in the throes of a very strong contraction.

"It's all we had on such short notice," the Warder squealed, bloody juices streaking down his cheeks. Fax threw the goblet at him, and the wine went streaming down the man's chest. The steaming dish of roots followed, and the man yelped as the hot liquid splashed over him.

"My Lord, my Lord, had I but known!"

"Obviously, Ruatha can*not* support the visit of its Lord. You must renounce it," F'lar heard himself saying.

His shock at such words issuing from his mouth was as great as that of everyone else in the Hall. Silence fell, broken by the splat of crawlers and the drip of root liquid from the Warder's shoulders to the rushes. The grating of Fax's boot heel was clearly audible as he swung slowly around to face the bronze rider.

As F'lar conquered his own amazement and rapidly tried to predict what to do next to mend matters, he saw F'nor rise slowly to his feet, hand on dagger hilt.

"I did not hear you correctly?" Fax asked, his face blank of all expression, his eyes snapping.

Unable to comprehend how he could have uttered such an arrant challenge, F'lar managed to assume a languid pose.

"You did mention, my Lord," he drawled, "that if any of your Holds could not support itself and the visit of its rightful overlord, you would renounce it."

Fax stared back at F'lar, his face a study of swiftly suppressed emotions, the glint of triumph dominant. F'lar, his face stiff with the forced expression of indifference, was casting swiftly about in his mind. In the name of the Egg, had he lost all sense of discretion?

Pretending utter unconcern, he stabbed some vegetables onto his knife and began to munch on them. As he did so, he noticed F'nor glancing slowly around the Hall, scrutinizing everyone. Abruptly F'lar realized what had happened. Somehow, in making that statement, he, a dragonman, had responded to a covert use of the power. F'lar, the bronze rider, was being put into a position where he would *have* to fight Fax. Why? For what end? To get Fax to renounce the Hold? Incredible! But there could be only one possible reason for such a turn of events. An exultation as sharp as pain swelled within F'lar. It was all he could do to maintain his pose of bored indifference, all he could do to turn his attention to thwarting Fax, should he press for a duel. A duel would serve no purpose. He, F'lar, had no time to waste on it.

A groan escaped Lady Gemma and broke the eye-locked stance of the two antagonists. Irritated, Fax looked down at her, fist clenched and half-raised to strike her for her temerity at interrupting her lord and master. The contraction that rippled across the swollen belly was as obvious as the woman's pain. F'lar dared not look toward her, but he wondered if she had deliberately groaned aloud to break the tension.

Incredibly, Fax began to laugh. He threw back his head, showing big, stained teeth, and roared.

"Aye, renounce it, in favor of her issue, if it is male . . . and lives!" he crowed, laughing raucously.

"Heard and witnessed!" F'lar snapped, jumping to his feet and pointing to his riders. They were on their feet in an instant. "Heard and witnessed!" they averred in the traditional manner.

With that movement, everyone began to babble at once in nervous relief. The other women, each reacting in her way to the imminence of birth, called orders to the servants and advice to each other. They converged toward the Lady Gemma, hovering undecidedly out of Fax's reach like silly wherries disturbed from their roosts. It was obvious they were torn between their fear of their Lord and their desire to reach the laboring woman.

He gathered their intentions as well as their reluctance and, still stridently laughing, knocked back his chair. He stepped over it, strode down to the meat stand and stood hacking off pieces with his knife, stuffing them, juice dripping, into his mouth without ceasing to guffaw.

As F'lar bent toward the Lady Gemma to assist her out of her chair, she grabbed his arm urgently. Their eyes met, hers clouded with pain. She pulled him closer.

"He means to kill you, bronze rider. He loves to kill," she whispered.

"Dragonmen are not easily killed, brave lady. I am grateful to you."

"I do not want you killed," she said softly, biting at her lip. "We have so few bronze riders."

F'lar stared at her, startled. Did she, Fax's lady, actually believe in the Old Laws? He beckoned to two of the Warder's men to carry her up into the Hold. He caught Lady Tela by the arm as she fluttered past him in their wake.

"What do you need?"

"Oh, oh," she exclaimed, her face twisted with panic; she was distractedly wringing her hands. "Water, hot, clean. Cloths. And a birthing-woman."

F'lar looked about for one of the Hold women, his glance sliding over the first disreputable figure who had started to mop up the spilled food. He signaled instead for the Warder and peremptorily ordered him to send for the birthing-woman. The Warder kicked at the drudge on the floor.

"You . . . you! Whatever your name is, go get her from the craft-hold. You must know who she is."

With a nimbleness at odds with her appearance of extreme age and decrepitude, the drudge evaded the parting kick the Warder aimed in her direction. She scurried across the Hall and out the kitchen door.

Fax sliced and speared meat, occasionally bursting out with a louder bark of laughter as his thoughts amused him. F'lar sauntered down to the carcass and, without waiting for invitation from his host, began to carve neat slices also, beckoning his men over. Fax's soldiers, however, waited till their Lord had eaten his fill.

Lord of the Hold, your charge is sure
In thick walls, metal doors, and no verdure.

Lessa sped from the Hall to find the crafthold birthing-woman, her mind seething with frustration. So close! So close! How could she come so close and yet fail? Fax should have challenged the dragonman. And the dragonman was strong and young, his face that of a fighter, stern and controlled. He should not have temporized. Was all honor dead in Pern, smothered by green grass?

And why, oh, why, had the Lady Gemma chosen that precious moment to go into labor? If her groan hadn't distracted Fax, the fight would have begun, and not even Fax, for all his vaunted prowess as a vicious fighter, would have prevailed against a dragonman who had Lessa's support. The Hold must be secured to its rightful Blood again. Fax would not leave Ruatha alive!

Above her, on the High Tower, the great bronze dragon gave forth a weird croon, his many-faceted eyes sparkling in the gathering darkness.

Unconsciously she silenced him as she would have done the

watch-wher. Ah, that watch-wher. He had not come out of his den at her passing. She knew the dragons had been at him. She could hear him gibbering in his panic. They'd drive him to his death.

The slant of the road toward the crafthold lent impetus to her flying feet, and she had to brace herself to a sliding stop at the birthing-woman's stone threshold. She banged on the closed door and heard the frightened exclamation of surprise within.

"A birth. A birth at the Hold," Lessa cried in time to her thumping.

"A birth?" came the muffled cry, and the latches were thrown up on the door. "At the Hold?"

"Fax's lady and, as you love life, hurry, for if it is male, it will be Ruatha's own Lord."

That ought to fetch her, thought Lessa, and in that instant the door was flung open by the man of the house. Lessa could see the birthing-woman gathering up her things in haste, piling them into her shawl. Lessa hurried the woman out, up the steep road to the Hold, under the Tower gate, grabbing the woman as she tried to run at the sight of a dragon peering down at her. Lessa drew her into the Court and pushed her, resisting, into the Hall.

The woman clutched at the inner door, balking at the sight of the gathering there. Lord Fax, his feet up on the trestle table, was paring his fingernails with his knife blade, still chuckling. The dragonmen in their wher-hide tunics, were eating quietly at one table while the soldiers were having their turn at the meat.

The bronze rider noticed their entrance and pointed urgently toward the inner Hold. The birthing-woman seemed frozen to the spot. Lessa tugged futilely at her arm, urging her to cross the Hall. To her surprise, the bronze rider strode to them.

"Go quickly, woman, Lady Gemma is before her time," he said, frowning with concern, gesturing imperatively toward the Hold entrance. He caught her by the shoulder and led her, all unwilling, toward the steps, Lessa tugging away at her other arm.

When they reached the stairs, he relinquished his grip, nodding to Lessa to escort her the rest of the way. Just as they reached the massive inner door, Lessa noticed how sharply the dragonman was looking at them. At her hand on the birthing-woman's arm. Warily, she glanced at her hand and saw it, as if it belonged to a stranger— the long fingers, shapely despite dirt and broken nails, a small hand, delicately boned, gracefully placed despite the urgency of the grip. She blurred it.

The Lady Gemma was indeed in hard labor, and all was not well. When Lessa tried to retire from the room, the birthing-woman shot her such a terrified glance that Lessa reluctantly remained. It was obvious that Fax's other ladies were of no use. They were huddled at one side of the high bed, wringing their hands and talking in shrill, excited tones. It remained to Lessa and the birthing-woman to remove Gemma's clothing, to ease her and hold her hands against the contractions.

There was little left of beauty in the gravid woman's face. She was perspiring heavily, her skin tinged with gray. Her breath was sharp and rasping, and she bit her lips against outcry.

"This is not going well," the birthing-woman muttered under her breath. "You there, stop your sniveling," she ordered, swinging around to point at one of the gaggle. She lost her indecision as the requirements of her calling gave her temporary authority over those of rank. "Bring me hot water. Hand those cloths over. Find something warm for the babe. If it is born alive, it must be kept from drafts and chill."

Reassured by her tyranny, the women stopped their whimpering and did her bidding.

If it survives, the words echoed in Lessa's mind. *Survives to be Lord of Ruatha. One of Fax's Get?* That had not been her intention, although . . .

The Lady Gemma grabbed blindly for Lessa's hands, and despite herself, Lessa responded with such comfort as a strong grip would afford the woman.

"She bleeds too much," the birthing-woman muttered. "More cloths."

The women resumed their wailing, uttering little shrieks of fear and protestation.

"She should not have been made to journey so far."

"They will both die."

"Oh, it *is* too much blood."

Too much blood, thought Lessa. *I have no quarrel with her. And the child comes too early. It will die.* She looked down at the contorted face, the bloodied lower lip. *If she does not cry out now, why did she then?* Fury swept through Lessa. This woman had, for some obscure reason, deliberately diverted Fax and F'lar at the crucial moment. She all but crushed Gemma's hands in hers.

Pain from such an unexpected quarter roused Gemma from her brief respite between the shuddering contractions that seized her at shorter and shorter intervals. Blinking sweat from her eyes, she focused desperately on Lessa's face.

"What have I done to you?" she gasped.

"Done? I had Ruatha almost within my grasp again when you uttered your false cry," Lessa said, her head bent so that not even the birthing-woman at the foot of the bed could hear them. She was so angry that she had lost all discretion, but it would not matter, for this woman was close to death.

The Lady Gemma's eyes widened. "But . . . the dragonman . . . Fax cannot kill the dragonman. There are so few bronze riders. They are all needed. And the old tales . . . the star . . . star . . . " She could not continue, for a massive contraction shook her. The heavy rings on her fingers bit into Lessa's hands as she clung to the girl.

"What do you mean?" Lessa demanded in a hoarse whisper.

But the woman's agony was so intense that she could scarcely breathe. Her eyes seemed to start from her head. Lessa, hardened though she had become to all emotion save that of revenge, was shocked to the deeper feminine instinct of easing a woman's pain in her extremity. Even so, the Lady Gemma's words rang through her mind. The woman had not, then, protected Fax, but the dragonman. The star? Did she mean the Red Star? Which old tales?

The birthing-woman had both hands on Gemma's belly, pressing downward, chanting advice to a woman too far gone in pain to hear. The twisting body gave a convulsive heave, lifting from the bed. As Lessa tried to support her, Lady Gemma opened her eyes wide, her expression one of incredulous relief. She collapsed into Lessa's arms and lay still.

"She's dead!" shrieked one of the women. She flew, screaming, from the chamber. Her voice reverberated down the rock halls. "Dead . . . ead . . . ead . . . ddddd," echoed back to the dazed women, who stood motionless in shock.

Lessa laid the woman down on the bed, staring amazed at the oddly triumphant smile on Gemma's face. She retreated into the shadows, far more shaken than anyone else. She who had never hesitated to do anything that would thwart Fax or beggar Ruatha further was trembling with remorse. She had forgotten in her single-mindedness that there might be others motivated by a hatred of Fax. The Lady Gemma was one, and one who had suffered far more subjective brutalities and indignities than Lessa had. Yet Lessa had hated Gemma, had poured out that hatred on a woman who had deserved her respect and support rather than her condemnation.

Lessa shook her head to dispel the aura of tragedy and self-revulsion that threatened to overwhelm her. She had no time for regret or contrition. Not now. Not when, by affecting Fax's death, she could avenge not only her own wrongs but Gemma's!

That was it. And she had the lever. The child . . . yes, the child. She'd say it lived. That it was male. The dragonman would have to fight. He had heard and witnessed Fax's oath.

A smile, not unlike the one on the dead woman's face, crossed Lessa's as she hurried down the corridors to the Hall.

She was about to dash into the Hall itself when she realized she had permitted her anticipation of triumph to destroy her self-discipline.

Lessa halted at the portal, deliberately took a deep breath. She dropped her shoulders and stepped down, once more the colorless drudge.

The harbinger of death was sobbing in a heap at Fax's feet.

Lessa gritted her teeth against redoubled hatred for the overlord. He was glad the Lady Gemma had died, birthing his seed. Even now he was ordering the hysterical woman to go tell his latest favorite to attend him, doubtless to install her as his first lady.

"The child lives," Lessa cried, her voice distorted with anger and hatred. "It is male."

Fax was on his feet, kicking aside the weeping woman, scowling viciously at Lessa. "What are you saying, woman?"

"The child lives. It is male," she repeated, descending. The incredulity and rage that suffused Fax's face was wonderful to see. The Warder's men stifled their inadvertent cheers.

"Ruatha has a new Lord." The dragons roared.

So intent was she on achieving her purpose that she failed to notice the reactions of others in the hall, failed to hear the roaring of the dragons without.

Fax erupted into action. He leaped across the intervening space, bellowing denials of the news. Before Lessa could dodge, his fist crashed down across her face. She was swept off her feet, off the steps, and fell heavily to the stone floor, where she lay motionless, a bundle of dirty rags.

"Hold, Fax!" F'lar's voice cut across the silence as the Lord of the High Reaches lifted his leg to kick the unconscious body.

Fax whirled, his hand automatically closing on his knife hilt.

"It was heard and witnessed, Fax," F'lar cautioned him, one hand outstretched in warning, "by dragonmen. Stand by your sword and witnessed oath!"

"Witnessed? By dragonmen?" cried Fax with a derisive laugh. "Dragonwomen, you mean," he sneered, his eyes blazing with contempt, one sweeping gesture of scorn dismissing them all.

He was momentarily taken aback by the speed with which the bronze rider's knife appeared in his hand.

"Dragonwomen?" F'lar queried, his lips curling back over his teeth, his voice dangerously soft. Glowlight flickered off his circling blade as he advanced on Fax.

"Women! Parasites on Pern. The Weyr power is over! Over for good," roared Fax, leaping forward to land in a combat crouch.

The two antagonists were dimly aware of the scurry behind them, of tables pulled roughly aside to give the duelists space. F'lar could spare no glance at the crumpled form of the drudge, yet he was sure, through and beyond instinct sure, that she was the source of the power. He had felt it as she entered the room. The dragons' roaring confirmed it. If that fall had killed her . . . He advanced on Fax, leaping away to avoid the slashing blade as Fax unwound from the crouch with a powerful lunge.

F'lar evaded the attack easily, noticing his opponent's reach, deciding he had a slight advantage there. He told himself sternly that wasn't much advantage. Fax had had much more actual hand-to-hand killing experience than had he whose duels had always ended at first blood on the practice floor. F'lar made due note to avoid closing with the burly Lord. The man was heavy-chested, dangerous from sheer mass. F'lar must use agility as a weapon, not brute strength.

Fax feinted, testing F'lar for weakness or indiscretion. The two crouched, facing each other across six feet of space, knife hands weaving, their free hands, spread-fingered, ready to grab.

Again Fax pressed the attack. F'lar allowed him to close, just close enough to dodge away with a backhanded swipe. He felt fabric tear under the tip of his knife and heard Fax's snarl. The overlord was faster on his feet than his bulk suggested, and F'lar had to dodge a second time, feeling the scoring of Fax's knife across his heavy wherhide jerkin.

Grimly the two circled, looking for an opening in each other's defense. Fax plowed in, trying to turn his weight and mass to advantage against the lighter, faster man by cornering him between raised platform and wall.

F'lar countered, ducking low under Fax's flailing arm, slashing obliquely across Fax's side. The overlord caught at him, yanking savagely, and F'lar was trapped against the other man's side, straining desperately with his left hand to keep the knife arm up. F'lar brought up his knee, timing a sudden collapse with that blow. He ducked away as Fax gasped and buckled from the pain in his groin. F'lar danced away, sudden fire in his left shoulder witness that he had not escaped unscathed.

Fax's face was red with bloody anger, and he wheezed from pain and shock. But F'lar had no time to follow up the momentary advantage, for the infuriated Lord straightened up and charged. F'lar was forced to sidestep quickly before Fax could close with him. F'lar put the meat table between them, circling warily, flexing his shoulder to assess the extent of his injury. The slash felt as if it had been scored by a brand. Motion was painful, but the arm could be used.

Suddenly Fax seized up a handful of fatty scraps from the meat tray and hurled them at F'lar. The dragonman ducked, and Fax closed the distance around the table with a rush. Instinct prompted F'lar to leap sideways as Fax's flashing blade came within inches of his abdomen. His own knife sliced down the outside of Fax's arm. Instantly the two pivoted to face each other again, but Fax's left arm hung limply at his side.

F'lar darted in, pressing his luck as the Lord of the High Reaches staggered. But F'lar misjudged the man's condition and suffered a terrific kick in the side as he tried to dodge under the feinting knife. Doubled with pain, F'lar rolled frantically away from his charging adversary. Fax was lurching forward, trying to fall on him, to pin the lighter dragonman down for a final thrust. F'lar somehow got to his feet, attempting to straighten up to meet Fax's stumbling charge. His very position saved him. Fax overreached his mark and staggered off balance. F'lar brought his right hand over with as much strength as he could muster, and his knife blade plunged through Fax's unprotected back until he felt the point stick in the chest plate.

The defeated Lord fell flat to the flagstones, the force of his descent dislodging the dagger from his chest bone so that an inch of the bloody blade reemerged from the point of entry.

A thin wailing penetrated the haze of pain and relief. F'lar looked up and saw, through sweat-blurred eyes, women crowding in the Hold doorway. One held a closely swathed object in her arms. F'lar could not immediately grasp the significance of that tableau, but he knew it was very important to clear his thoughts.

He stared down at the dead man. There was no pleasure in killing the man, he realized, only relief that he himself was still alive. He wiped his forehead on his sleeve and forced himself erect, his side throbbing with the pain of that last kick and his left shoulder burning. He half-stumbled to the drudge, still sprawled where she had fallen.

He gently turned her over, noting the terrible bruise spreading across her cheek under the dirty skin. He heard F'nor take command of the tumult in the Hall.

The dragonman laid a hand, trembling in spite of an effort to control himself, on the woman's breast to feel for a heartbeat. . . . It was there, slow but strong.

A deep sigh escaped him, for either blow or fall could have proved fatal. Fatal, perhaps, for Pern as well.

Relief was colored with disgust. There was no telling under the filth how old this creature might be. He raised her to his arms, her light body no burden even to his battle-weary strength. Knowing F'nor would handle any trouble efficiently, F'lar carried the drudge to his own chamber.

He put the body on the high bed, then stirred up the fire and added more glows to the bedside bracket. His gorge rose at the thought of touching the filthy mat of hair, but nonetheless and gently, he pushed it back from the face, turning the head this way and that. The features were small, regular. One arm, clear of rags, was reasonably clean above the elbow but marred by bruises and old scars. The skin was firm and unwrinkled. The hands, when he took them in his, were dirt-encrusted but all the same, well-shaped and delicately boned.

F'lar began to smile. Yes, she had blurred that hand so skillfully that he had actually doubted what he had first seen. And yes, beneath grime and grease, she was young. Young enough for the Weyr. And no born drab. She was not young enough, happily, to be Fax's seed. One of the previous Lords' by-blows? No, there was no taint of common blood here. It was pure, no matter whose line, and he rather thought she was indeed Ruathan. One who had by some unknown agency escaped the massacre ten Turns ago and bided her time for revenge. Why else force Fax to renounce the Hold?

Delighted and fascinated by this unexpected luck, F'lar reached out to tear the dress from the unconscious body and found himself constrained not to. The girl had roused. Her great, hungry eyes fastened on his, not fearful or expectant; wary.

A subtle change occurred in her face. F'lar watched, his smile deepening, as she shifted her regular features into an illusion of disagreeable ugliness.

"Trying to confuse a dragonman, girl?" he chuckled. He made no further move to touch her but settled against the great carved post of the bed. He crossed his arms on his chest and then shifted suddenly to ease his sore arm.

"Your name, girl, and rank."

She drew herself upright slowly, her features no longer blurred. Deliberately she slid back against the headboard so they faced each other across the length of the high bed.

"Fax?"

"Dead. Your name!"

A look of exulting triumph flooded her face. She slipped from the bed, standing unexpectedly tall. "Then I reclaim my own. I am of the Ruathan Blood. I claim Ruath," she announced in a ringing voice.

F'lar stared at her a moment, delighted with her proud bearing. Then he threw back his head and laughed.

"This? This crumbling heap?" He could not help but mock the disparity of her manner and her dress. "Oh, no. Besides, fair lady, we dragonmen heard and witnessed Fax's oath renouncing the Hold in favor of his heir. Shall I challenge the babe, too, for you? And choke him with his swaddling clothes?"

Her eyes flashed, her lips parted in a terrible smile.

"There is no heir. Gemma died, the babe unborn. I lied."

"Lied?" F'lar demanded, angry.

"Yes," she taunted him with a toss of her chin. "I lied. There was no babe born. I merely wanted to be sure you challenged Fax."

He grabbed her wrist, stung that he had twice fallen to her prodding.

"You provoked a dragonman to fight? To kill? *When he is on Search?*"

"Search? What should I care for a Search? I have Ruatha as my

Hold again. For ten Turns I have worked and waited, schemed and suffered for that. What could your Search mean to me?"

F'lar wanted to strike that look of haughty contempt from her face. He twisted her arm savagely, bringing her to his feet before he released his pressure. She laughed at him and had scuttled to one side and was on her feet and out the door before he could realize what she was about and give chase.

Swearing to himself, he raced down the rocky corridors, knowing she would have to make for the Hall to get out of the Hold. However, when he reached the Hall, there was no sign of her fleeing figure among those still loitering there.

"Has that creature come this way?" he called to F'nor, who was, by chance, standing by the door to the Court.

"No. Is she the source of power, after all?"

"Yes, she is," F'lar answered, galled all the more by her escape. Where had she gone to? "And of the Ruathan Blood, at that!"

"Oh-ho! Does she depose the babe, then?" F'nor asked, gesturing toward the birthing-woman who occupied a seat close to the now blazing hearth.

F'lar paused, about to return to search the Hold's myriad passages. He stared, momentarily confused, at his brown rider.

"Babe? What babe?"

"The male child Lady Gemma bore," F'nor replied, surprised by F'lar's uncomprehending look.

"It lives?"

"Yes. A strong babe, the woman says, for all that he was premature and taken forcibly from the dead dame's belly."

F'lar threw back his head with a shout of laughter. For all her scheming, she had been outdone by Truth.

At that moment he heard the unmistakable elation in Mnementh's roar, followed by the curious warble of the other dragons.

"Mnementh has caught her," F'lar cried, grinning with jubilation. He strode down the steps, past the body of the former Lord of the High Reaches and out into the main court.

He saw the bronze dragon was gone from his Tower perch and called him. An agitation drew his eyes upward. He saw Mnementh spiraling down into the Court, his front paws clasping something. Mnementh informed F'lar that he had seen her climbing from one of the high windows and had simply plucked her from the ledge, knowing the dragonman sought her. The bronze dragon settled awkwardly onto his hind legs, his wings working to keep him balanced. Carefully he set the girl on her feet and carefully he formed a cage around her with his huge talons. She stood motionless within that circle, her face turned toward the wedge-shaped head that swayed above her.

The watch-wher, shrieking terror, anger, and hatred, was lunging violently at the end of its chain, trying to come to Lessa's aid. It grabbed at F'lar as he strode to the two.

"You've courage enough to fly with, girl," he admitted, resting one hand casually on Mnementh's upper claw. Mnementh was enormously pleased with himself and swiveled his head down for his eye ridges to be scratched.

"You did not lie, you know," F'lar said, unable to resist taunting the girl.

Slowly she turned toward him, her face impassive. She was not afraid of dragons, F'lar realized with approval.

"The babe lives. And it is male."

She could not control her dismay, and her shoulders sagged briefly before she pulled herself erect again.

"Ruatha is mine," she insisted in a tense, low voice.

"Aye, and it would have been had you approached me directly when the wing arrived here."

Her eyes widened. "What do you mean?"

"A dragonman may champion anyone whose grievance is just. By the time we reached Ruath Hold, my lady, I was quite ready to challenge Fax given any reasonable cause, despite the Search." This was not the whole truth, but F'lar must teach this girl the folly of trying to control dragonmen. "Had you paid any attention to your harper's songs, you'd know your rights. And"—F'lar's voice held a vindictive edge that surprised him—"the Lady Gemma might not now lie dead. She, brave soul, suffered far more at that tyrant's hand than you."

Something in her manner told him that she regretted Lady Gemma's death, that it had affected her deeply.

"What good is Ruatha to you now?" he demanded, a broad sweep of his arm taking in the ruined Court yard and the Hold, the entire unproductive valley of Ruatha. "You have indeed accomplished your ends, a profitless conquest and its conqueror's death."

F'lar snorted. "As well, too. Those Holds will all revert to their legitimate Blood, and time they did. One Hold and One Lord. Anything else is against tradition. Of course, you might have to fight others who disbelieve that precept: who have become infected with Fax's greedy madness. Can you hold Ruatha against attack . . . now . . . in her condition?"

"Ruatha is mine!"

"Ruatha?" F'lar's laugh was derisive. "When you could be Weyrwoman?"

"Weyrwoman?" she breathed, staring at him in shocked amazement.

"Yes, little fool. I said I rode in Search . . . it's about time you attended to more than Ruatha. And the object of my Search is . . . you!"

She stared at the finger he pointed at her, as if it were dangerous.

"By the First Egg, girl, you've power in you to spare when you can turn a dragonman, all unwitting, to do your bidding. Ah, but never again, for I am now on guard against you."

Mnementh crooned approvingly, the sound a soft rumble in his throat. He arched his neck so that one eye was turned directly on the girl, gleaming in the darkness of the Court.

F'lar noticed with detached pride that she neither flinched nor blanched at the proximity of an eye greater than her own head.

"He likes to have his eye ridges scratched," F'lar remarked in a friendly tone, changing tactics.

"I know," she said softly and reached out a hand to do that service.

"Nemorth has laid a golden egg," F'lar continued persuasively. "She is close to death. This time we must have a strong Weyrwoman."

"The Red Star?" the girl gasped, turning frightened eyes to F'lar. That alone surprised him, for she had never once evinced any fear.

"You've seen it? You understand what it means?" He saw her swallow nervously.

"There is danger . . . " she began in a bare whisper, glancing apprehensively eastward.

F'lar did not question by what miracle she appreciated the imminence of danger. He had every intention of taking her to the Weyr by sheer force if necessary. But something within him wanted very much for her to accept the challenge voluntarily. A rebellious Weyrwoman would be even more dangerous than a stupid one. This girl had too much power and was too used to guile and strategy. It would be a calamity to antagonize her with injudicious handling.

"There is danger for all Pern. Not just Ruatha," he said, allowing a note of entreaty to creep into his voice. "And *you* are needed. Not by Ruatha." A wave of his hand dismissed that consideration as a negligible one compared to the total picture. "We are doomed without a strong Weyrwoman. Without you."

"Gemma said all the bronze riders were needed," she murmured in a dazed whisper.

What did she mean by that statement? F'lar frowned. Had she heard a word he had said? He pressed his argument, certain only that he had already struck one responsive chord.

"You've won here. Let the babe"—he saw her startled rejection of that idea and ruthlessly qualified it—"Gemma's babe—be reared at Ruatha. You have command of all the Holds as Weyrwoman, not ruined Ruatha alone. You'ave accomplished Fax's death. Leave off vengeance."

She stared at F'lar with wondering eyes, absorbing his words.

"I never thought beyond Fax's death," she admitted slowly. "I never thought what should happen then."

Her confusion was almost childlike and struck F'lar forcibly. He had had no time or desire to consider her prodigious accomplishment. Now he realized some measure of her indomitable character. She could not have been above ten Turns of age herself when Fax had murdered her family. Yet somehow, so young, she had set herself a goal and managed to survive both brutality and detection long enough to secure the usurper's death. What a Weyrwoman she would be! In the tradition of those of Ruathan Blood. The light of the paler moon made her look young and vulnerable and almost pretty.

"You can be Weyrwoman," he repeated with gentle insistence.

"Weyrwoman," she breathed, incredulous, and gazed around the inner Court bathed in soft moonlight. He thought she wavered.

"Or perhaps you enjoy rags?" he said, making his voice harsh, mocking. "And matted hair, dirty feet, and cracked hands? Sleeping in straw, eating rinds? You are young . . . that is, I assume you are young." His voice was frankly skeptical. She glared at him coolly, her lips firmly pressed together. "Is this the be-all and end-all of your ambition? What are you that this little corner of the great world is *all* you want?" He paused, then with utter contempt added, "The Blood of Ruatha has thinned, I see. You're afraid!"

"I am Lessa, daughter of the Lord of Ruath," she countered, stung to responding by the Blood insult. She drew herself erect, her eyes flashing, her chin high. "I am afraid of nothing!"

F'lar contented himself with a slight smile.

Mnementh, however, threw up his head and stretched out his sinuous neck to its whole length. His full-throated peal rang out down the valley. The bronze communicated his awareness to F'lar that Lessa had accepted the challenge. The other dragons answered back, their warbles shriller than Mnementh's male bellow. The watch-wher which had cowered at the end of its chain lifted its voice in a thin, unnerving screech until the Hold emptied of its startled occupants.

"F'nor," the bronze rider called, waving his wingleader to him. "Leave half the flight to guard the Hold. Some nearby Lord might think to emulate Fax's example. Send one rider to the High Reaches with the glad news. You go directly to the clothmen's Hall and speak to L'to . . . Lytol." F'lar grinned. "I think he would make an exemplary Warder and Lord Surrogate for this Hold in the name of the Weyr and the baby Lord."

The brown rider's face expressed enthusiasm for his mission as he began to comprehend his leader's intentions. With Fax dead and Ruatha under the protection of dragonmen, particularly that same one who had dispatched Fax, the Hold would be safe and flourish under wise management.

"She caused Ruatha's deterioration?" he asked his leader.

"And nearly ours with her machinations," F'lar replied, but having found the admirable object of his Search, he could now be magnanimous. "Suppress your exultation, brother," he advised quickly as he took note of F'nor's expression. "The new queen must also be Impressed."

"I'll settle arrangements here. Lytol is an excellent choice," F'nor said, although he knew that F'lar needed no one's approval.

"Who is this Lytol?" demanded Lessa pointedly. She had twisted the mass of filthy hair back from her face. In the moonlight the dirt was less noticeable. F'lar caught F'nor looking at her with an all too easily read expression. He signaled F'nor with a peremptory gesture to carry out his orders without delay.

"Lytol is a dragonless man," F'lar told the girl, "no friend to Fax. He will ward the Hold well, and it will prosper." He added persuasively with a quelling stare full on her, "Won't it?"

She regarded him somberly, without answering, until he chuckled softly at her discomfiture.

"We'll return to the Weyr," he announced, proffering a hand to guide her to Mnementh's side.

The bronze one had extended his head toward the watch-wher, who now lay panting on the ground, its chain limp in the dust.

"Oh," Lessa sighed, and dropped beside the grotesque beast. It raised its head slowly, crying piteously.

"Mnementh says it is very old and soon will sleep itself to death."

Lessa cradled the repulsive head in her arms, stroking the eye ridges, scratching behind its ears.

"Come, Lessa of Pern," F'lar said, impatient to be up and away.

She rose slowly but obediently. "It saved me. It knew me."

"It knows it did well," F'lar assured her brusquely, wondering at such an uncharacteristic show of sentiment in her.

He took her hand again, to help her to her feet and lead her back to Mnementh.

In one split second he was knocked off his feet, sprawling across the stones and trying to roll to his feet again, to face his adversary. The force of the initial blow, however, had dazed him, and he lay sprawled on his back, startled to see the watch-wher, its scaly body launched—straight at him.

Simultaneously he heard Lessa's startled exclamation and Mnementh's roar. The bronze's great head was swinging around to knock the watch-wher aside, away from the dragonman. But just as the watch-wher's body was fully extended in its leap, Lessa cried out.

"Don't kill! Don't kill!"

The watch-wher, its snarl turning into an anguished cry of alarm, executed an incredible maneuver in mid-air, turning aside from its trajection. As it fell to the stone yard at his feet, F'lar heard the dull crack as the force of its landing broke its back.

Before he could get to his feet, Lessa was cradling the hideous head in her arms, her face stricken.

Mnementh lowered his head to tap the dying watch-wher's body gently. He informed F'lar that the beast had guessed Lessa was leaving Ruatha, something one of her Blood should not do. In its senile confusion it could only assume Lessa was in danger. When it heard Lessa's frantic command, it had corrected its error at the expense of its life.

"It was truly only defending me," Lessa added, her voice breaking. She cleared her throat. "It was the only one I could trust. My only friend."

F'lar awkwardly patted the girl's shoulder, appalled that anyone could be reduced to claiming friendship with a watch-wher. He winced because the fall had reopened the knife wound in his shoulder and he hurt.

"In truth a loyal friend," he said, standing patiently until the light in the watch-wher's green-gold eyes dimmed and died out.

All the dragons gave voice to the eerie, hair-raising, barely audible, high keening note that signified the passing of one of their kind.

"He was only a watch-wher," Lessa murmured, stunned by the tribute, her eyes wide.

"The dragons confer honor where *they* will," F'lar remarked dryly, disclaiming the responsibility.

Lessa looked down for one more long moment at the repulsive head. She laid it down to the stones, caressed the clipped wings. Then, with quick fingers, she undid the heavy buckle that fastened the metal collar around the neck. She threw the collar violently away.

She rose in a fluid movement and walked resolutely to Mnementh without a single backward glance. She stepped calmly to Mnementh's raised leg and seated herself, as F'lar directed her, on the great neck.

F'lar glanced around the Court at the remainder of his wing which had reformed there. The Hold folk had retreated into the safety of the great Hall. When his wingmen were all astride, he vaulted to Mnementh's neck, behind the girl.

"Hold tightly to my arms," he ordered her as he took hold of the smallest neck ridge and gave the command to fly.

Her fingers closed spasmodically around his forearm as the great bronze dragon took off, the enormous wings working to achieve height from the vertical takeoff. Mnementh preferred to fall into flight from a cliff or tower. Dragons tended to indolence. F'lar glanced behind him, saw the other dragonmen form the flight line, spread out to cover the gaps of those still on guard at Ruatha Hold.

When they had reached a sufficient altitude, he told Mnementh to transfer, going *between* to the Weyr.

Only a gasp indicated the girl's astonishment as they hung *between*. Accustomed as he was to the sting of the profound cold, to the awesome utter lack of light and sound, F'lar still found the sensations unnerving. Yet the uncommon transfer spanned no more time than it took to cough thrice.

Mnementh rumbled approval of this candidate's calm reaction as they flicked out of the eerie *between*. She had not been afraid or screamed in panic as other women had. F'lar did feel her heart pounding against his arm that pressed against her ribs, but that was all.

And then they were above the Weyr, Mnementh setting his wings to glide in the bright daylight, half a world away from nighttime Ruatha.

Lessa's hands tightened on his arms, this time in surprise as they circled above the great stony trough of the Weyr. F'lar peered at Lessa's face, pleased with the delight mirrored there; she showed no trace of fear that they hung a thousand lengths above the high Benden mountain range. Then, as the seven dragons roared their incoming cry, an incredulous smile lit her face.

The other wingmen dropped into a wide spiral, down, down, while Mnementh elected to descend in lazy circles. The dragonmen peeled off smartly and dropped, each to his own tier in the caves of the Weyr. Mnementh finally completed his leisurely approach to their quarters, whistling shrilly to himself as he braked his forward speed with a twist of his wings, dropping lightly at last to the ledge. He crouched as F'lar swung the girl to the rough rock, scored from thousands of clawed landings.

"This leads only to our quarters," he told her as they entered the corridor, vaulted and wide for the easy passage of great bronze dragons.

As they reached the huge natural cavern that had been his since Mnementh achieved maturity, F'lar looked about him with eyes fresh from his first prolonged absence from the Weyr. The huge chamber was unquestionably larger than most of the halls he had visited in Fax's procession. Those halls were intended as gathering places for men, not the habitations of dragons. But suddenly he saw his own quarters were nearly as shabby as all Ruatha. Benden was, of a certainty, one of the oldest dragonweyrs, as Ruatha was one of the oldest Holds, but that excused nothing. How many dragons had bedded in that hollow to make solid rock conform to dragon proportions! How many feet had worn the path past the dragon's Weyr into the sleeping chamber, to the bathing room beyond where the natural warm spring provided ever-fresh water! But the wall hangings were faded and unraveling, and there were great stains on lintel and floor that could easily be sanded away.

He noticed the wary expression on Lessa's face as he paused in the sleeping room.

"I must feed Mnementh immediately. So you may bathe first," he said, rummaging in a chest and finding clean clothes for her, discards of former occupants of his quarters, but far more presentable than her present covering. He carefully laid back in the chest the white wool robe that was traditional Impression garb. She would wear that later. He tossed several garments at her feet and a bag of sweetsand, gesturing to the hanging that obscured the way to the bath.

He left her then, the clothes in a heap at her feet, for she made no effort to catch anything.

Mnementh informed him that F'nor was feeding Canth and that he, Mnementh, was hungry, too. *She* didn't trust F'lar, but she wasn't afraid of himself.

"Why should she be afraid of you?" F'lar asked. "You're cousin to the watch-wher who was her only friend."

Mnementh informed F'lar that he, a fully matured bronze dragon, was no relation to any scrawny, crawling, chained, and wing-clipped watch-wher.

"Then why did you accord him a dragon tribute?" F'lar asked.

Mnementh told him haughtily that it was fitting and proper to mourn the passing of a loyal and self-sacrificing personality. Not even a blue dragon could deny the fact that that Ruathan watch-wher had not divulged information he had been enjoined to keep, though the beast had been sorely pressed to do so by himself, Mnementh. Also, in managing, by some physical feat, to turn aside its attack on F'lar, at the cost of its own life, it had elevated itself to dragonlike bravery. Of course, the dragons had uttered a tribute at its passing.

F'lar, pleased at having been able to tease the bronze one, chuckled to himself. With great dignity Mnementh curved down to the feeding ground.

F'lar dropped off as Mnementh hovered near F'nor. The impact with the ground reminded him he had better get the girl to dress his shoulder for him. He watched as the bronze one swooped down on the nearest fat buck in the milling herd.

"The Hatching is due at any hour," F'nor greeted his brother, grinning up at him as he squatted on his haunches. His eyes were bright with excitement.

F'lar nodded thoughtfully. "There will be plenty to choose from for the males," he allowed, knowing F'nor was tauntingly withholding choicer news.

They both watched as F'nor's Canth singled out a doe. The brown dragon neatly grabbed the struggling beast in one claw and rose up, settling on an unoccupied ledge to feast.

Mnementh dispatched his first carcass and glided in again over the herd, to the pens beyond. He singled out a heavy ground bird and lifted with it in his claws. F'lar observed his ascent, experiencing as always the thrill of pride in the effortless sweep of the great pinions, the play of the sun on the bronze hide, the flash of silvery claws, unsheathed for landing. He never tired of watching Mnementh in flight or admiring the unconscious grace and strength.

"Lytol was overwhelmed by the summons," F'nor remarked, "and sends you all honor and respect. He will do well at Ruatha."

"The reason he was chosen," grunted F'lar, nonetheless gratified by Lytol's reaction. Surrogate Lordship was no substitute for loss of one's dragon, but it was an honorable responsibility.

"There was much rejoicing in the High Reaches," F'nor continued, grinning widely, "and honest grief at the passing of Lady Gemma. It will be interesting to see which of the contenders takes title."

"At Ruatha?" F'lar queried, frowning down at his half brother.

"No. At the High Reaches and the other Holds Fax conquered. Lytol will bring his own people to secure Ruatha and to give any soldiery pause before they might attempt that Hold. He knew of many in the High Reaches who would prefer to make a change of Hold, even though Fax no longer dominates the High Reaches. He intended to make all haste to Ruatha so that our men will soon rejoin us."

F'lar nodded approval, turning to salute two more of his wing, blue riders, who dropped with their beasts to the feeding ground. Mnementh went back for another fowl.

"He eats light," F'nor commented. "Canth's still gorging."

"Browns are slow to get full growth," F'lar drawled, watching with satisfaction as F'nor's eyes flashed angrily. That would teach him to withhold news.

"R'gul and S'lel are back," the brown rider finally announced.

The two blues had the herd in a frenzy, stampeding and screaming in fright.

"The others are recalled," F'nor continued. "Nemorth is all but rigid in death." Then he could no longer contain himself. "S'lel brought in two. R'gul has five. Strong-willed, they say, and pretty."

F'lar said nothing. He had expected those two would bring in multiple candidates. Let them bring hundreds if they chose. He, F'lar, the bronze rider, had in his one choice the winner.

Exasperated that his news elicited so little response, F'nor rose.

"We should have backtrailed for that one in Crom and the pretty . . ."

"Pretty?" F'lar retorted, cocking one eyebrow high in disdain. "Pretty? Jora was pretty," he spat out cynically.

"K'net and T'bor bring contenders from the west," F'nor added urgently, concerned.

The wind-torn roar of homecoming dragons crackled through the air. Both men jerked their heads skyward and saw the double spirals of two returning wings, twenty strong.

Mnementh tossed his head high, crooning. F'lar called him in, pleased the bronze one made no quarrel at recall, although he had eaten very lightly. F'lar, saluting his brother amiably, stepped onto Mnementh's spread foot and was lifted back to his own ledge.

Mnementh hiccuped absently as the two walked the short passage to the vaulted inner chamber. He lumbered over to his hollowed bed and settled himself into the curved stone. When Mnementh had stretched and comfortably laid down his wedge-head, F'lar approached him. Mnementh regarded his friend with the near eye, its many facets glinting and shifting, the inner lids gradually closing as F'lar scratched the eye-ridge soothingly.

Those unfamiliar with it might find such a regard unnerving. But since that moment, twenty Turns before, when the great Mnementh had broken through his shell and stumbled across the Hatching Ground to stand, weaving on weak legs, before the boy F'lar, the dragonman had treasured these quiet moments as the happiest of a long day. No greater tribute could man be paid than the trust and companionship of the winged beasts of Pern. For the loyalty that dragonkind gave their chosen one of mankind was unswerving and complete from the instant of Impression.

Mnementh's inner content was such that the great eye quickly closed. The dragon slept, only the tip of his tail erect, a sure sign that he would be instantly on the alert if the need arose.

By the Golden Egg of Faranth
By the Weyrwoman, wise and true,
Breed a flight of bronze and brown wings,
Breed a flight of green and blue.
Breed riders, strong and daring,
Dragon-loving, born as hatched
Flight of hundreds soaring skyward,
Man and dragon fully matched.

Lessa waited until the sound of the dragonman's footsteps proved he had really gone away. She rushed quickly through the big cavern, heard the scrape of claw and the whoosh of the mighty wings. She raced down the short passageway, right to the edge of the yawning entrance. There was the bronze dragon circling down to the wider end of the mile-long barren oval that was Benden Weyr. She had heard of the Weyrs, as any Pernese had, but to be in one was quite a different matter.

She peered up, around, down that sheer rock face. There was no way off but by dragon wing. The nearest cave mouths were an unhandy distance above her, to one side, below her on the other. She was neatly secluded here.

Weyrwoman, he had told her. His woman? In his weyr? Was that what he had meant? No, that was not the impression she got from the dragon. It occurred to her suddenly that it was odd she had understood the dragon. Were common folk able to? Or was it the dragonman Blood in her Line? At all events, Mnementh had implied something greater, some special rank. They must mean her, then, to be Weyrwoman to the unhatched dragon queen. Only how did she, or they, go about it? She remembered vaguely that when dragonmen went on Search, they looked for certain women. Ah, certain women. She was one, then, of several contenders. Yet the bronze rider had offered her the position as if she and she alone qualified. He had his own generous portion of conceit, that one, Lessa decided. Arrogant he was, though not the bully Fax had been.

She could see the bronze dragon swoop down to the running herdbeasts, saw the strike, saw the dragon wheel up to settle on a far ledge to feed. Instinctively she drew back from the opening, back into the dark and relative safety of the corridor.

The feeding dragon evoked scores of horrid tales. Tales at which she had scoffed, but now . . . Was it true, then, that dragons did eat human flesh? Did . . . Lessa halted that trend of thought. Dragonkind was no less cruel than mankind. The dragon, at least, acted from bestial need rather than bestial greed.

Assured that the dragonman would be occupied awhile, she crossed the larger cave into the sleeping room. She scooped up the clothing and the bag of cleansing sand and proceeded to the bathing room. It was small but ample for its purpose. A wide ledge formed a partial lip to the uneven circle of the bathing pool. There was a bench and some shelves for drying cloths. In the glowlight she could see that the near section of the pool had been sanded high so a bather could stand comfortably. Then there was a gradual dip approaching the deeper water that slapped the very rock wall on the farther side.

To be clean! To be completely clean and to be able to stay that way. With a distaste at touching them no less acute than the dragonman's, she stripped off the remains of the rags, kicking them to one side, not knowing where to dispose of them. She shook out a generous handful of the sweetsand and, bending to the pool, wet it.

Quickly she made a soft mud with the sweet soap, and she

scoured hands and bruised face. Wetting more sand, she attacked her arms and legs, then her body and feet. She scrubbed hard until she drew blood from half-healed cuts. Then she stepped, or rather jumped, into the pool, gasping as the warm water made the sweetsand foam in her scratches. She ducked under the surface, shaking her head to be sure her hair was thoroughly wetted. Then briskly she rubbed in more sweetsand, rinsing and scrubbing until she felt her hair might possibly be clean. Years, it had been. Great strands floated away in tangles like immense crawlers with attenuated legs, toward the far edge of the pool and then were drawn out of sight. The water, she was glad to note, constantly circulated, the cloudy and dirty replaced with clear. She turned her attention again to her body, scrubbing at ingrained dirt until her skin smarted. It was a ritual cleansing of more than surface soil. She felt a pleasure akin to ecstasy for the luxury of cleanliness.

Finally satisfied her body was as clean as one long soaking could make her, she sanded her hair yet a third time. She left the pool almost reluctantly, wringing out her hair and tucking it up on her head as she dried herself. She shook out the clothing and held one garment against her experimentally. The fabric, a soft green, felt smooth under her water-shrunken fingers, although the nap caught on her roughened hands. She pulled it over her head. It was loose, but the darker-green overtunic had a sash that she pulled in tight at the waist. The unusual sensation of softness against her bare skin made her wriggle with voluptuous pleasure. The skirt, no longer a ragged hem of tatters, swirled heavily around her ankles, making her smile in sheer feminine delight. She took up a fresh drying cloth and began to work on her hair.

A muted sound came to her ears, and she stopped, hands poised, head bent to one side. Straining, she listened. Yes, there were sounds without. The dragonman and his beast must have returned. She grimaced to herself with annoyance at this untimely interruption and rubbed harder at her hair. She ran fingers through the half-dry tangles, the motions arrested as she encountered snarls. She tried patting her hair into place, pushing it defiantly behind her ears. Vexed, she rummaged on the shelves until she found, as she had hoped to, a coarse-toothed metal comb. With this she attacked her unruly hair and, by the dint of much yanking and groaning as she pulled ruthlessly through years of tangles, she was able to groom the mass.

Now dry, her hair suddenly had a life of its own, crackling about her hands and clinging to face and comb and dress. It was difficult to get the silky stuff under control. And her hair was longer than she had thought, for, clean and unmatted, it fell to her waist—when it did not cling to her hands.

She paused, listening, and heard no sound at all. Apprehensively, she stepped to the curtain and glanced warily into the sleeping room. It was empty. She listened and caught the perceptible thoughts of the sleepy dragon. Well, she would rather meet the man in the presence of a sleepy dragon than in a sleeping room. She started across the floor and, out of the corner of her eye, caught sight of a strange woman as she passed a polished piece of metal hanging on the wall.

Amazed, she stopped short, staring, incredulous, at the face the metal reflected. Only when she put her hands to her prominent cheekbones in a gesture of involuntary surprise and the reflection imitated the gesture did she realize she looked at herself.

Why, that girl in the reflector was prettier than the Lady Tela, than the clothman's daughter! But so thin. Her hands of their own volition dropped to her neck, to the protruding collarbones, to her breasts, which did not entirely reflect the gauntness of the rest of her. The dress was too large for her frame, she noted with an unexpected emergence of conceit born in that instant of delighted appraisal. And her hair . . . it stood out around her head like an aureole. It wouldn't lie contained. She smoothed it down with impatient fingers, automatically bringing locks forward to hang around her face. As she irritably pushed them back, dismissing a need for disguise, the hair drifted up again.

A slight sound, the scrape of a boot against stone, caught her back from her bemusement. She waited, momentarily expecting him to appear. She was suddenly timid. With her face bare to the world, her hair behind her ears, her body outlined by a clinging fabric, she was stripped of her accustomed anonymity and was therefore, in her estimation, vulnerable.

Sternly she controlled the desire to run away, the irrational shock of fearfulness. Observing herself in the looking metal, she drew her shoulders back, tilted her head high, chin up; the movement caused her hair to crackle and cling and shift about her head. She was Lessa of Ruatha, of a fine old Blood. She no longer needed to resort to artifice to preserve herself, so she must stand proudly bare-faced before the world . . . and that dragonman.

Resolutely she crossed the room, pushing aside the hanging on the doorway to the great cavern.

He was there, beside the head of the dragon, scratching its eye ridges, a curiously tender expression on his face. It was a tableau completely at variance with all she had heard of dragonmen.

She had, of course, heard of the strange affinity between rider and dragon, but this was the first time she realized that love was part of that bond. Or that this reserved, cold man was capable of such deep emotion. He had been brusque enough with her over the old watchwher. No wonder it had thought he had meant her harm. The dragons had been more tolerant, she remembered with an involuntary sniff.

He turned slowly, as if loath to leave the bronze beast. He caught sight of her and pivoted completely around, his eyes intense as he took note of her altered appearance. With quick, light steps he closed the distance between them and ushered her back into the sleeping room, one strong hand holding her by the elbow.

"Mnementh has fed lightly and will need quiet to rest," he said in a low voice, as if this were the most important consideration. He pulled the heavy hanging into place across the opening.

Then he held her away from him, turning her this way and that, scrutinizing her closely, a curious and slightly surprised expression fleeting across his face.

"You wash up . . . pretty, yes, almost pretty," he allowed with such amused condescension in his voice that she pulled roughly away from him, piqued. His low laugh mocked her. "How could one guess, after all, what was under the grime of . . . ten full Turns, I would say? Yes, you are certainly pretty enough to placate F'nor."

Thoroughly antagonized by his attitude, she asked in icy tones, "And F'nor must be placated at all costs?"

He stood grinning at her till she had to clench her fists at her sides to keep from beating that grin off his face.

At length he said, "No matter, we must eat, and I shall require your services." At her startled exclamation, he turned, grinning maliciously now as his movement revealed the caked blood on his left sleeve. "The least you can do is bathe wounds honorably received in fighting your battle."

He pushed aside a portion of the drapery that curtained the inner wall. "Food for two!" he roared down a black gap in the sheer stone.

She heard a subterranean echo far below as his voice resounded down what must be a long shaft.

"Nemorth is nearly rigid," he was saying as he took supplies from another drapery-hidden shelf, "and the Hatching will soon begin, anyhow."

A coldness settled in Lessa's stomach at the mention of a Hatching. The mildest tales she had heard about that part of dragonlore were chilling, the worst dismayingly macabre. Numbly she took the things he handed her.

"What? Frightened?" the dragonman taunted, pausing as he stripped off his torn and bloodied shirt.

With a shake of her head, Lessa turned her attention to the wide-shouldered, well-muscled back he presented her, the paler skin of his body decorated with random bloody streaks. Fresh blood welled from the point of his shoulder, for the removal of his shirt had broken the tender scabs.

"I will need water," she said and saw she had a flat pan among the items he had given her. She went swiftly to the pool for water, wondering how she had come to agree to venture so far from Ruatha. Ruined though it was, it had been hers and was familiar to her, from

Tower to deep cellar. At the moment the idea had been proposed and insidiously prosecuted by the dragonman, she had felt capable of anything, having achieved, at last, Fax's death. Now it was all she could do to keep the water from slopping out of the pan that shook unaccountably in her hands.

She forced herself to deal only with the wound. It was a nasty gash, deep where the point had entered and torn downward in a gradually shallower slice. His skin felt smooth under her fingers as she cleansed the wound. In spite of herself, she noticed the masculine odor of him, compounded not unpleasantly of sweat, leather, and an unusual muskiness that must be from close association with dragons.

Although it must have hurt him when she cleansed away clotted blood, he gave no indication of discomfort, apparently oblivious to the operation. It annoyed her still more that she could not succumb to the temptation of treating him roughly in return for his disregard of her feelings.

She ground her teeth in frustration as she smeared on the healing salve generously. Making a small pad of bandage, she secured the dressing deftly in place with other strips of torn cloth. She stood back when she had finished her ministrations. He flexed his arm experimentally in the constricting bandage, and the motion set the muscles rippling along his side and back.

When he faced her, his eyes were dark and thoughtful.

"Gently done, my lady. My thanks." His smile was ironic.

She backed away as he rose, but he only went to the chest to take out a clean, white shirt.

A muted rumble sounded, growing quickly louder.

Dragons roaring? Lessa wondered, trying to conquer the ridiculous fear that rose within her. Had the Hatching started? There was no watch-wher's lair to secrete herself in here.

As if he understood her confusion, the dragonman laughed good-humoredly and, his eyes on hers, drew aside the wall covering just as some noisy mechanism inside the shaft propelled a tray of food into sight.

Ashamed of her unbased fright and furious that he had witnessed it, Lessa sat rebelliously down on the fur-covered wall seat, heartily wishing him a variety of serious and painful injuries that she could dress with inconsiderate hands. She would not waste future opportunities.

He placed the tray on the low table in front of her, throwing down a heap of furs for his own seat. There were meat, bread, a pitcher of *klah*, a tempting yellow cheese, and even a few pieces of winter fruit. He made no move to eat, nor did she, though the thought of a piece of fruit that was ripe instead of rotten set her mouth to watering. He glanced up at her and frowned.

"Even in the Weyr, the lady breaks bread first," he said and inclined his head politely to her.

Lessa flushed, unused to any courtesy and certainly unused to being first to eat. She broke off a chunk of bread. It was like nothing she remembered having tasted before. For one thing, it was fresh-baked. The flour had been finely sifted, without trace of sand or hull. She took the slice of cheese he proffered her, and it, too, had an uncommonly delicious sharpness. Much emboldened by this indication of her changed status, Lessa reached for the plumpest piece of fruit.

"Now," the dragonman began, his hand touching hers to get her attention.

Guiltily she dropped the fruit, thinking she had erred. She stared at him, wondering at her fault. He retrieved the fruit and placed it back in her hand as he continued to speak. Wide-eyed, she nibbled, disarmed, and gave him her full attention.

"Listen to me. You must not show a moment's fear at whatever happens on the Hatching Ground. And you must not let her overeat." A wry expression crossed his face. "One of our main functions is to keep a dragon from excessive eating."

Lessa lost interest in the taste of the fruit. She placed it carefully back in the bowl and tried to sort out what he had not said but what his tone of voice implied. She looked at the dragonman's face, seeing him as a person, not a symbol, for the first time.

His coldness was caution, she decided, not lack of emotion. His sternness must be assumed to offset his youth, for he couldn't be that much her senior in Turns. There was a blackness about him that was not malevolent; it was a brooding sort of patience. Heavy black hair waved back from a high forehead to brush his shirt collar. Heavy black brows were too often pulled together in a glower or arched haughtily as he looked down a high-bridged nose at his victim; his eyes (an amber, light enough to seem golden) were all too expressive of cynical emotions or cold hauteur. His lips were thin but well-shaped and in repose almost gentle. Why must he always pull his mouth to one side in disapproval or in one of those sardonic smiles? Handsome he must be considered, she supposed candidly, for there was a certain compelling air about him that was magnetic. And at this moment he was completely unaffected.

He meant what he was saying. He did not want her to be afraid. There was no reason for her, *Lessa, to* fear.

He very much wanted her to succeed. In keeping whom from overeating what? Herd animals? A newly hatched dragon certainly wasn't capable of eating a full beast. That seemed a simple enough task to Lessa. The watch-wher had obeyed her and no one else, at Ruath Hold. She had understood the great bronze dragon and had even managed to hush him up as she raced under his Tower perch for the birthing-woman. Main function? *Our* main function?

The dragonman was looking at her expectantly.

"Our main function?" she repeated, an unspoken request for more information inherent in her inflection.

"More of that later. First things first," he said, impatiently waving off other questions.

"But what happens?" she insisted.

"As I was told, so I tell you. No more, no less. Remember those two points. Turn out fear and do not let her overeat."

"But . . . "

"You, however, need to eat. Here." He speared a piece of meat on his knife and thrust it at her, frowning until she managed to choke it down. He was about to force more on her, but she grabbed up her half-eaten fruit and bit down into the firm sweet sphere instead. She had already eaten more at this one meal than she was accustomed to having all day at the Hold.

"We shall soon eat better at the Weyr," he remarked, regarding the tray with a jaundiced eye.

Lessa was surprised, for in her opinion this was a feast.

"More than you're used to? Yes, I forgot you left Ruatha with bare bones indeed."

She stiffened.

"You did well at Ruatha. I mean no criticism," he added, smiling at her reaction. "But look at you," and he gestured at her body, that curious expression crossing his face, half-amused, half contemplative. "No, I should not have guessed you'd clean up pretty," he remarked. "Nor with such hair." This time his expression was frankly admiring.

Involuntarily she put one hand to her head, the hair crackling over her fingers. But what reply she might have made him, indignant as she was, died a-borning. An unearthly keening filled the chamber.

The sounds set up a vibration that ran down the bones behind her ear to her spine. She clapped both hands to her ears. The noise rang through her skull, despite her defending hands. As abruptly as it started, it ceased.

Before she knew what he was about, the dragonman had grabbed her by the wrist and pulled her over to the chest.

"Take those off," he ordered, indicating dress and tunic. While she stared at him stupidly, he held up a loose white robe, sleeveless and beltless, a matter of two lengths of fine cloth fastened at shoulder and side seams. "Take it off, or do I assist you?" he asked with no patience at all.

The wild sound was repeated, and its unnerving tone made her fingers fly faster. She had no sooner loosened the garments she wore, letting them slide to her feet, than he had thrown the other over her head. She managed to get her arms in the proper places before he grabbed her wrist again and was speeding with her out of the room, her hair whipping out behind her, alive with static.

As they reached the outer chamber, the bronze dragon was standing in the center of the cavern, his head turned to watch the sleeping room door. He seemed impatient to Lessa; his great eyes, which fascinated her so, sparkled iridescently. His manner breathed an inner excitement of great proportions, and from his throat a high-pitched croon issued, several octaves below the unnerving cry that had roused them all.

Rushed and impatient as they both were, the dragon and dragonman paused. Suddenly Lessa realized they were conferring about her. The great dragon's head was suddenly directly in front of her, his nose blotting out everything else. She felt the warm exhalation of his breath, slightly phosphorus-laden. She heard him inform the dragonman that he approved more and more of this woman from Ruatha.

With a yank that rocked her head on her neck, the dragonman pulled her along the passage. The dragon padded beside them at such speed that Lessa fully expected they would all catapult off the ledge. Somehow, at the crucial stride, she was perched on the bronze neck, the dragonman holding her firmly about the waist. In the same fluid movement they were gliding across the great bowl of the Weyr to the higher wall opposite. The air was full of wings and dragon tails, rent with a chorus of sounds, echoing and reechoing across the stony valley.

Mnementh set what Lessa was certain would be a collision course with other dragons, straight for a huge round blackness in the cliff-face, high up. Magically, the beasts filed in, the greater wingspread of Mnementh just clearing the sides of the entrance.

The passageway reverberated with the thunder of wings. The air compressed around her thickly. Then they broke out into a gigantic cavern.

Why, the entire mountain must be hollow, thought Lessa, incredulous. Around the enormous cavern dragons perched in serried ranks, blues, greens, browns, and only two great bronze beasts like Mnementh, on ledges meant to accommodate hundreds. Lessa gripped the bronze neck scales before her, instinctively aware of the imminence of a great event.

Mnementh wheeled downward, disregarding the ledge of the bronze ones. Then all Lessa could see was what lay on the sandy floor of the great cavern: dragon eggs. A clutch of ten monstrous, mottled eggs, the shells moving spasmodically as the fledglings within tapped their way out. To one side, on a raised portion of the floor, was a golden egg, larger by half again the size of the mottled ones. Just beyond the golden egg lay the motionless ocher hulk of the old queen.

Just as she realized Mnementh was hovering over the floor in the vicinity of that egg, Lessa felt the dragonman's hands on her, lifting her from Mnementh's neck.

Apprehensively she grabbed at him. His hands tightened and inexorably swung her down. His eyes, fierce with amber fire locked with hers.

"Remember, Lessa!"

Mnementh added an encouraging note, one great compound eye turned on her. Then he rose from the floor. Lessa half-raised one hand in entreaty, bereft of all support, even that of the sure inner compulsion that had sustained her in her struggle for revenge on Fax. She saw the bronze dragon settle on the first ledge, at some distance from the other two bronze beasts. The dragonman dismounted, and Mnementh curved his sinuous neck until his head was beside his rider. The man reached up and absently, it seemed to Lessa, caressed his mount.

Loud screams and wailings diverted Lessa, and she saw more dragons descend to hover just above the cavern floor, each rider depositing a young woman until there were twelve girls, including Lessa. She remained a little apart from them as they clung to one another. She regarded them curiously, contemptuous of their tears, although her heart was probably beating no less rapidly than theirs. It did not occur to her that tears were any help. The girls were not injured in any way that she could see, so why such weeping? Her contempt of their bleating made her aware of her own temerity, and she took a deep breath against the coldness within her. Let *them* be afraid. She was Lessa of Ruatha and did not need to be afraid.

Just then, the golden egg moved convulsively. Gasping as one, the girls edged away from it, back against the rocky wall. One, a lovely blonde, her heavy plait of golden hair swinging just above the ground, started to step off the raised floor and stopped, shrieking, backing fearfully toward the scant comfort of her peers.

Lessa wheeled to see what cause there might be for the look of horror on the girl's face. She stepped back involuntarily herself.

In the main section of the sandy arena, several of the handful of eggs had already cracked wide open. The fledglings, crowing weakly, were moving toward—and Lessa gulped—the young boys standing stolidly in a semicircle. Some of them were no older than she had been when Fax's army had swooped down on Ruath Hold.

The shrieking of the women subsided to muffled gasps and sobs as one fledgling reached out with claw and beak to grab a boy.

Lessa forced herself to watch as the young dragon mauled the boy, throwing him roughly aside as if unsatisfied in some way. The boy did not move, and Lessa could see blood seeping onto the sand from dragon-inflicted wounds.

A second fledgling lurched against another boy and halted, flapping its damp wings impotently, raising its scrawny neck and croaking a parody of the encouraging croon Mnementh often gave. The boy uncertainly lifted a hand and began to scratch the eye ridge. Incredulous, Lessa watched as the fledgling, its crooning increasingly more mellow, ducked its head, pushing at the boy. The child's face broke into an unbelieving smile of elation.

Tearing her eyes from this astounding sight, Lessa saw that another fledgling was beginning the same performance with another boy. Two more dragons had emerged in the interim. One had knocked a boy down and was walking over him, oblivious of the fact that its claws were raking great gashes. The fledgling who followed its hatch-mate stopped by the wounded child, ducking its head to the boy's face, crooning anxiously. As Lessa watched, the boy managed to struggle to his feet, tears of pain streaming down his cheeks. She could hear him pleading with the dragon not to worry, that he was only scratched a little.

It was over very soon. The young dragons paired off with boys. Green riders dropped down to carry off the unacceptable. Blue riders settled to the floor with their beasts and led the couples out of the cavern, the young dragons squealing, crooning, flapping wet wings as they staggered off, encouraged by their newly acquired Weyrmates.

Lessa turned resolutely back to the rocking golden egg, knowing what to expect and trying to divine what the successful boys had or had not done that caused the baby dragons to single them out.

A crack appeared in the golden shell and was greeted by the terrified screams of the girls. Some had fallen into little heaps of white fabric, others embraced tightly in their mutual fear. The crack widened and the wedge head broke through, followed quickly by the neck, gleaming gold. Lessa wondered with unexpected detachment how long it would take the beast to mature, considering its by no means small size at birth. For the head was larger than that of the male dragons, and they had been large enough to overwhelm sturdy boys of ten full Turns.

Lessa was aware of a loud hum within the Hall. Glancing up at the audience, she realized it emanated from the watching bronze dragons, for this was the birth of their mate, their queen. The hum increased in volume as the shell shattered into fragments and the golden, glistening body of the new female emerged. It staggered out, dipping its sharp beak into the soft sand, momentarily trapped. Flapping its wet wings, it righted itself, ludicrous in its weak awkwardness. With sudden and unexpected swiftness, it dashed toward the terror-stricken girls. Before Lessa could blink, it shook the first girl with such violence that her head snapped audibly and she fell limply to the sand. Disregarding her, the dragon leaped toward the second girl but misjudged the distance and fell, grabbing out with one claw for support and raking the girl's body from shoulder to thigh. Screaming, the mortally injured girl distracted the dragon and released the others from their horrified trance. They scattered in panicky confusion, racing, running, tripping, stumbling, falling across the sand toward the exit the boys had used.

As the golden beast, crying piteously, lurched down from the raised arena toward the scattered women, Lessa moved. Why hadn't that silly clunk-headed girl stepped aside, Lessa thought, grabbing for the wedge-head, at birth not much larger than her own torso. The dragon was so clumsy and weak she was her own worst enemy.

Lessa swung the head around so that the many-faceted eyes were forced to look at her . . . and found herself lost in that rainbow regard.

A feeling of joy suffused Lessa; a feeling of warmth, tenderness, unalloyed affection, and instant respect and admiration flooded mind and heart and soul. Never again would Lessa lack an advocate, a defender, an intimate, aware instantly of the temper of her mind and heart, of her desires. How wonderful was Lessa, the thought intruded into Lessa's reflections, how pretty, how kind, how thoughtful, how brave and clever!

Mechanically Lessa reached out to scratch the exact spot on the soft eye ridge.

The dragon blinked at her wistfully, extremely sad that she had distressed Lessa. Lessa reassuringly patted the slightly damp, soft neck that curved trustingly toward her. The dragon reeled to one side and one wing fouled on the hind claw. It hurt. Carefully Lessa lifted the erring foot, freed the wing, folding it back across the dorsal ridge with a pat.

The dragon began to croon in her throat, her eyes following Lessa's every move. She nudged at Lessa, and Lessa obediently attended the other eye ridge.

The dragon let it be known that she was hungry.

"We'll get you something to eat directly," Lessa assured her briskly and blinked back at the dragon in amazement. How could she be so callous? It was a fact that this little menace had just seriously injured, if not killed, two women.

She couldn't believe her sympathies could swing so alarmingly toward the beast. Yet it was the most natural thing in the world for her to wish to protect this fledgling.

The dragon arched her neck to look Lessa squarely in the eyes. Ramoth repeated wistfully how exceedingly hungry she was, so long confined in that shell without nourishment.

Lessa wondered how she knew the golden dragon's name, and Ramoth replied: Why shouldn't she know her own name since it was hers and no one else's? And then Lessa was long in the wonder of those magnificently expressive eyes.

Oblivious to the descending bronze dragons, oblivious to the presence of their riders, Lessa stood caressing the head of the most wonderful creature of all Pern, fully prescient of troubles and glories, but most immediately aware that Lessa of Pern was Weyrwoman to Ramoth the Golden for now and forever.

Dragonflight

Seas boil and mountains move,
Sands heat, dragons prove
Red Star passes.
Stones pile and fires burn,
Green withers, arm Pern.
Guard all passes.
Star Stone watch, scan sky.
Ready the Weyrs, all riders fly;
Red Star passes.

"If a queen isn't meant to fly, why does she have wings?" asked Lessa. She was genuinely trying to maintain a tone of sweet reason.

She had had to learn that, although it was her nature to seethe, she must seethe discreetly. Unlike the average Pernese, dragonriders were apt to perceive strong emotional auras.

R'gul's heavy eyebrows drew together in a startled frown. He snapped his jaws together with exasperation. Lessa knew his answer before he uttered it.

"Queens don't fly," he said flatly.

"Except to mate," S'lel amended. He had been dozing, a state he achieved effortlessly and frequently, although he was younger than the vigorous R'gul.

They are going to quarrel again, Lessa thought with an inward groan. She could stand about half an hour of that, and then her stomach would begin to churn. Their notion of instructing the new Weyrwoman in "Duties to Dragon, Weyr, and Pern" too often deteriorated into extended arguments over minor details in the lessons she had to memorize and recite word-perfect. Sometimes, as now, she entertained the fragile hope that she might wind them up so tightly in their own inconsistencies that they would inadvertently reveal a truth or two.

"A queen flies only to mate," R'gul allowed the correction.

"Surely," Lessa said with persistent patience, "if she can fly to mate, she can fly at other times."

"Queens don't fly," R'gul's expression was stubborn.

"Jora never did fly a dragon at all," S'lel mumbled, blinking rapidly in his bemusement with the past. His expression was vaguely troubled. "Jora never left these apartments."

"She took Nemorth to the feeding grounds," R'gul snapped irritably.

Bile rose in Lessa's throat. She swallowed. She would simply have to force them to leave. Would they realize that Ramoth woke all too conveniently at times? Maybe she'd better rouse R'gul's Hath. Inwardly she permitted herself a smug smile as her secret ability to hear and talk to any dragon in the Weyr, green, blue, brown, or bronze, momentarily soothed her.

"When Jora could get Nemorth to stir at all," S'lel muttered, picking at his underlip worriedly.

R'gul glared at S'lel to silence him and, succeeding, tapped pointedly on Lessa's slate.

Stifling her sigh, she picked up the stylus. She had already written this ballad out nine times, letter-perfect. Ten was apparently R'gul's magic number. For she had written every single one of the traditional Teaching Ballads, the Disaster Sagas, and the Laws, letter-perfect, ten times each. True, she had not understood half of them, but she knew them by heart.

"*Seas boil, and mountains move,*" she wrote.

Possibly. If there is a major inner upheaval of the land. One of Fax's guards at Ruath Hold had once regaled the Watch with a tale from his great-grandsire's days. A whole coastal village in East Fort had slid into the sea. There had been monumental tides that year and, beyond Ista, a mountain had allegedly emerged at the same time, its top afire. It had subsided years later. That might be to what the line referred. Might be.

"*Sands heat . . .*" True, in summer it was said that Igen Plain could be unendurable. No shade, no trees, no caves, just bleak sand desert. Even dragonmen eschewed that region in deep summer. Come to think of it, the sands of the Hatching Ground were always warm underfoot. Did those sands ever get hot enough to burn? And what warmed them, anyway? The same unseen internal fires that heated the water in the bathing pools throughout Benden Weyr?

"*Dragons prove . . .*" Ambiguous for half a dozen interpretations, and R'gul won't even suggest one as official. Does it mean that dragons prove the Red Star passes? How? Coming out with a special keen, similar to the one they utter when one of their own kind passes to die *between*? Or did the dragons prove themselves in some other way *as* the Red Star passes? Besides, of course, their traditional function of burning the Threads out of the skies? Oh, all the things these ballads don't say, and no one ever explains. Yet there must originally have been a reason.

"Stone pile and fires burn/Green withers, arm Pern."

More enigma. Is someone piling the stones on the fires? Do they mean firestone? Or do the stones pile themselves as in an avalanche? The balladeer might at least have suggested the season involved—or did he, with *"green withers"*? Yet vegetation purportedly attracted Threads, which was the reason, traditionally, that greenery was not permitted around human habitations. But stones couldn't stop a Thread from burrowing underground and multiplying. Only the phosphine emissions of a firestone-eating dragon stopped a Thread. And nowadays, Lessa smiled thinly, no one, not even dragonmen—with the notable exceptions of F'lar and his wingmen—bothered to drill with firestone, much less uproot grass near houses. Lately hilltops, scoured barren for centuries, were allowed to burgeon with green in the spring.

"Guard all passes."

She dug the phrase out with the stylus, thinking to herself: So no dragonrider can leave the Weyr undetected.

R'gul's current course of inaction as Weyrleader was based on the idea that if no one, Lord or holder, saw a dragonrider, no one could be offended. Even traditional patrols were flown now over uninhabited areas, to allow the current agitation about the "parasitical" Weyr to die down. Fax, whose open dissension had sparked that movement, had not taken the cause to his grave. Larad, the young Lord of Telgar, was said to be the new leader.

R'gul as Weyrleader. That rankled Lessa deeply. He was so patently inadequate. But his Hath had taken Nemorth on her last flight. Traditionally (and that word was beginning to nauseate Lessa for the sins of omission ascribable to its name) the Weyrleader was the rider of the queen's mate. Oh, R'gul looked the part—a big, husky man, physically vigorous and domineering, his heavy face suggesting a sternly disciplined personality. Only, to Lessa's thinking, the discipline was misdirected.

Now F'lar . . . he had disciplined himself and his wingriders in what Lessa considered the proper direction. For he, unlike the Weyrleader, not only sincerely believed in the Laws and Traditions he followed, he understood them. Time and again she had managed to make sense of a puzzling lesson from a phrase or two F'lar tossed in her direction. But, traditionally, only the Weyrleader instructed the Weyrwoman.

Why, in the name of the Egg, hadn't Mnementh, F'lar's bronze giant, flown Nemorth? Hath was a noble beast, in full prime, but he could not compare with Mnementh in size, wingspread, or strength.

There would have been more than ten eggs in that last clutch of Nemorth's if Mnementh had flown her.

Jora, the late and unlamented Weyrwoman, had been obese, stupid, and incompetent. On this everyone agreed. Supposedly the dragon reflected its rider as much as the rider the dragon. Lessa's thoughts turned critical. Undoubtedly Mnementh had been as repelled by the dragon, as a man like F'lar would be by the rider—unrider, Lessa corrected herself, sardonically glancing at the drowsing S'lel.

But if F'lar had gone to the trouble of that desperate duel with Fax to save Lessa's life back in Ruath Hold to bring her to the Weyr as a candidate at the Impression, why had he not taken over the Weyr when she proved successful, and ousted R'gul? What was he waiting for? He had been vehement and persuasive enough in making Lessa relinquish Ruatha and come to Benden Weyr. Why, now, did he adopt such an aloof pose of detachment as the Weyr tumbled further and further into disfavor?

"To save Pern," F'lar's words had been. From what if not R'gul? F'lar had better start salvation procedures. Or was he biding his time until R'gul blundered fatally? R'gul won't blunder, Lessa thought sourly, because he won't *do* anything. Most particularly he wouldn't explain what she wanted to know.

"Star Stone watch, scan sky." From her ledge, Lessa could see the gigantic rectangle of the Star Stone outlined against the sky. A watchrider always stood by it. One day she'd get up there. It gave a magnificent view of the Benden Range and the high plateau that came right up to the foot of the Weyr. Last Turn there had been quite a ceremony at Star Stone, when the rising sun seemed to settle briefly on Finger Rock, marking the winter solstice. However, that only explained the significance of the Finger Rock, not the Star Stone. Add one more unexplained mystery.

"Ready the Weyrs," Lessa wrote morosely. Plural. Not Weyr but Weyrs. R'gul couldn't deny there were five empty Weyrs around Pern, deserted for who knows how many Turns. She'd had to learn the names, the order of their establishment, too. Fort was the first and mightiest, then Benden, High Reaches, Hot Igen, Ocean Ista and Plainland Telgar. Yet no explanation as to why five had been abandoned. Nor why great Benden, capable of housing five hundred beasts in its myriad weyr-caverns, maintained a scant two hundred. Of course, R'gul had fobbed their new Weyrwoman off with the convenient excuse that Jora had been an incompetent and neurotic Weyrwoman, allowing her dragon queen to gorge unrestrained. (No one told Lessa why this was so undesirable, nor why, contradictorily, they were so pleased when Ramoth stuffed herself.) Of course, Ramoth was growing, growing so rapidly that the changes were apparent overnight.

Lessa smiled, a tender smile that not even the presence of R'gul and S'lel could embarrass. She glanced up from her writing to the passageway that led from the Council Room up to the great cavern that was Ramoth's weyr. She could sense that Ramoth was still deeply asleep. She longed for the dragon to wake, longed for the reassuring regard of those rainbow eyes, for the comforting companionship that made life in the Weyr endurable. Sometimes Lessa felt she was two people: gay and fulfilled when she was attending Ramoth, gray and frustrated when the dragon slept. Abruptly Lessa cut off this depressing reflection and bent diligently to her lesson. It did pass time.

"Red Star passes."

That benighted, begreened Red Star, and Lessa jammed her stylus into the soft wax with the symbol for a completed score.

There had been that unforgettable dawn, over two full Turns ago, when she had been roused by an ominous presentiment from the damp straw of the cheeseroom at Ruatha. And the Red Star had gleamed at her.

Yet here she was. And that bright, active future F'lar had so glowingly painted had not materialized. Instead of using her subtle power to manipulate events and people for Pern's good, she was forced into a round of inconclusive, uninstructive, tedious days, bored to active nausea by R'gul and S'lel, restricted to the Weyrwoman's apartments (however much of an improvement that was over her square foot of the cheeseroom floor) and the feeding grounds and the bathing lake. The only time she used her ability was to terminate these sessions with her so-called tutors. Grinding her teeth, Lessa thought that if it weren't for Ramoth, she would just leave. Oust Gemma's son and take Hold at Ruatha as she ought to have done once Fax was dead.

She caught her lip under her teeth, smiling in selfderision. If it weren't for Ramoth, she wouldn't have stayed here a moment past Impression anyway. But, from the second in which her eyes had met those of the young queen on the Hatching Ground, nothing but Ramoth mattered. Lessa was Ramoth's and Ramoth was hers, mind and heart, irrevocably attuned. Only death could dissolve that incredible bond.

Occasionally a dragonless man remained living, such as Lytol, Ruatha's Warder, but he was half shadow and that indistinct self lived in torment. When his rider died, a dragon winked into *between*, that frozen nothingness through which a dragon somehow moved himself and his rider, instantly, from one geographical position on Pern to another. To enter *between* held danger to the uniniated, Lessa knew, the danger of being trapped *between* for longer than it took a man to cough three times.

Yet Lessa's one dragonflight on Mnementh's neck had filled her with an insatiable compulsion to repeat the experience. Naïvely she had thought she would be taught, as the young riders and dragonets were. But she, supposedly the most important inhabitant of the Weyr next to Ramoth, remained earthbound while the youngsters winked in and out of *between* above the Weyr in endless practice. She chafed at the intolerable restriction.

Female or not, Ramoth must have the same innate ability to pass *between* as the males did. This theory was supported—unequivocally in Lessa's mind—by "The Ballad of Moreta's Ride." Were not ballads constructed to inform? To teach those who could not read and write? So that the young Pernese, whether he be dragonman, Lord, or holder, might learn his duty toward Pern and rehearse Pern's bright history? These two arrant idiots might deny the existence of that Ballad, but how had Lessa learned it if it did not exist? No doubt, Lessa thought acidly, for the same reason queens had wings!

When R'gul consented—and she would wear him down till he did—to allow her to take up her "traditional" responsibility as Keeper of the Records, she would find that Ballad. One day it was going to have to be R'gul's much delayed "right time."

Right time! she fumed. *Right time! I have too much of the wrong time on my hands. When will this particular right time of theirs occur? When the moons turn green? What are they waiting for? And what might the superior F'lar be waiting for? The passing of the Red Star he alone believes in?* She paused, for even the most casual reference to that phenomenon evoked a cold, mocking sense of menace within her.

She shook her head to dispel it. Her movement was injudicious. It caught R'gul's attention. He looked up from the Records he was laboriously reading. As he drew her slate across the stone Council table, the clatter roused S'lel. He jerked his head up, uncertain of his surroundings.

"Humph? Eh? Yes?" he mumbled, blinking to focus sleep-blurred eyes.

It was too much. Lessa quickly made contact with S'lel's Tuenth, himself just rousing from a nap. Tuenth was quite agreeable.

"Tuenth is restless, must go," S'lel promptly muttered. He hastened up the passageway, his relief at leaving no less than Lessa's at seeing him go. She was startled to hear him greet someone in the corridor and hoped the new arrival would provide an excuse to rid herself of R'gul.

It was Manora who entered. Lessa greeted the headwoman of the Lower Caverns with thinly disguised relief. R'gul, always nervous in Manora's presence, immediately departed.

Manora, a stately woman of middle years, exuded an aura of quiet strength and purpose, having come to a difficult compromise with life which she maintained with serene dignity. Her patience tacitly chided Lessa for her fretfulness and petty grievances. Of all the women she had met in the Weyr, (when she was permitted by the dragonmen to meet any) Lessa admired and respected Manora most. Some instinct in Lessa made her bitterly aware that she would never be on easy or intimate terms with any of the women in the Weyr. Her carefully formal relationship with Manora, however, was both satisfying and satisfactory.

Manora had brought the tally slates of the Supply Caves. It was her responsibility as headwoman to keep the Weyrwoman informed of the domestic management of the Weyr. (One duty R'gul insisted she perform.)

"Bitra, Benden, and Lemos have sent in their tithes, but that won't be enough to see us through the deep cold this Turn."

"We had only those three last Turn and seemed to eat well enough."

Manora smiled amiably, but it was obvious she did not consider the Weyr generously supplied.

"True, but that was because we had stores of preserved and dried foods from more bountiful Turns to sustain us. That reserve is now gone. Except for those barrels and barrels of fish from Tillek . . ." Her voice trailed off expressively.

Lessa shuddered. Dried fish, salted fish, fish, had been served all too frequently of late.

"Our supplies of grain and flour in the Dry Caves are very low, for Benden, Bitra, and Lemos are not grain producers."

"Our biggest needs are grains and meat?"

"We could use more fruits and root vegetables for variety," Manora said thoughtfully. "Particularly if we have the long cold season the weather-wise predict. Now we did go to Igen Plain for the spring and fall nuts, berries . . ."

"We? to Igen Plain?" Lessa interrupted her, stunned.

"Yes," Manora answered, surprised at Lessa's reaction. "We always pick there. And we beat out the water grains from the low swamplands."

"How do you get there?" asked Lessa sharply. There could be only one answer.

"Why, the old ones fly us. They don't mind, and it gives the beasts something to do that isn't tiring. You knew that, didn't you?"

"That the women in the Lower Caverns fly with dragonriders?" Lessa pursed her lips angrily. "No. I wasn't told." Nor did it help Lessa's mood to see the pity and regret in Manora's eyes.

"As Weyrwoman," she said gently, "your obligations restrict you where . . ."

"If I should ask to be flown to . . . Ruatha, for instance," Lessa cut in, ruthlessly pursuing a subject she sensed Manora wanted to drop, "would it be refused me?"

Manora regarded Lessa closely, her eyes dark with concern. Lessa waited. Deliberately she had put Manora into a position where the woman must either lie outright, which would be distasteful to a person of her integrity, or prevaricate, which could prove more instructive.

"An absence for any reason these days might be disastrous. Absolutely disastrous," Manora said firmly and, unaccountably, flushed. "Not with the queen growing so quickly. You *must* be here." Her unexpectedly urgent entreaty, delivered with a mounting anxiety, impressed Lessa far more than all R'gul's pompous exhortations about constant attendance on Ramoth.

"You must be here," Manora repeated, her fear naked.

"Queens do not fly," Lessa reminded her acidly. She suspected Manora was about to echo S'lel's reply to that statement, but the older woman suddenly shifted to a safer subject.

"We cannot, even with half-rations," Manora blurted out breathlessly, with a nervous shuffling of her slates, "last the full Cold."

"Hasn't there ever been such a shortage before . . . in all Tradition?" Lessa demanded with caustic sweetness.

Manora raised questioning eyes to Lessa, who flushed, ashamed of herself for venting her frustrations with the dragonmen on the headwoman. She was doubly contrite when Manora gravely accepted her mute apology. In that moment Lessa's determination to end R'gul's domination over herself and the Weyr crystallized.

"No," Manora went on calmly, "traditionally," and she accorded Lessa a wry smile, "the Weyr is supplied from the first fruits of the soil and hunt. True, in recent Turns we have been chronically shorted, but it didn't signify. We had no young dragons to feed. They do eat, as you know." The glances of the two women locked in a timeless feminine amusement over the vagaries of the young under their care. Then Manora shrugged. "The riders used to hunt their beasts in the High Reaches or on the Keroon plateau. Now, however . . ."

She made a helpless grimace to indicate that R'gul's restrictions deprived them of that victual relief.

"Time was," she went on, her voice soft with nostalgia, "we would pass the coldest part of the Turn in one of the southern Holds. Or, if we wished and could, return to our birthplaces. Families used to take pride in daughters with dragonfolk sons." Her face settled into sad lines. "The world turns and times change."

"Yes," Lessa heard herself say in a grating voice, "the world does turn, and times . . . times will change."

Manora looked at Lessa, startled.

"Even R'gul will see we have no alternative," Manora continued hastily, trying to stick to her problem.

"To what? Letting the mature dragons hunt?"

"Oh, no. He's so adamant about that. No. We'll have to barter at Fort or Telgar."

Righteous indignation flared up in Lessa.

"The day the Weyr has to buy what should be given . . ." and she halted in midsentence, stunned as much by such a necessity as by the ominous echo of other words. "The day one of my Holds cannot support itself *or* the visit of its rightful overlord . . ." Fax's words rang in her head. Did those words again foreshadow disaster? For whom? For what?

"I know, I know," Manora was saying worriedly, unaware of Lessa's shock. "It does against the grain. But if R'gul will not permit judicious hunting, there is no other choice. He will not like the pinch of hunger in his belly."

Lessa was struggling to control her inner terror. She took a deep breath.

"He'd probably then cut his throat to isolate his stomach," she snapped, her acid comment restoring her wits. She ignored Manora's startled look of dismay and went on. "It is traditional for you as head-woman of the Lower Cavern to bring such matters to the attention of the Weyrwoman, correct?"

Manora nodded, unsettled by Lessa's rapid switches of mood.

"I, then, as Weyrwoman, presumably bring this to the attention of the Weyrleader who, presumably,"—she made no attempt to moderate her derision—"acts upon it?"

Manora nodded, her eyes perplexed.

"Well," Lessa said in a pleasant, light voice, "you have dutifully discharged your traditional obligation. It is up to me now to discharge mine. Right?"

Manora regarded Lessa warily. Lessa smiled at her reassuringly.

"You may leave it in my hands, then."

Manora rose slowly. Without taking her eyes from Lessa, she began to gather up her records.

"It is said that Fort and Telgar had unusually good harvests," she suggested, her light tone not quite masking her anxiety. "Keroon, too, in spite of that coastal flooding."

"Is that so?" Lessa murmured politely.

"Yes," Manora continued helpfully, "and the herds at Keroon and Tillek had good increase."

"I'm happy for them."

Manora shot her a measuring look, not at all assured by Lessa's sudden affability. She finished gathering up her Records, then set them down again in a careful pile.

"Have you noticed how K'net and his wingriders chafe at R'gul's restrictions?" she asked, watching Lessa closely.

"K'net?"

"Yes. And old C'gan. Oh, his leg is still stiff, and Tagath may be more gray with age than blue, but he was of Lidith's hatching. Her last clutch had fine beasts in it," she remarked. "C'gan remembers other days . . ."

"Before the world turned and times changed?"

Lessa's sweet voice did not mislead Manora now.

"It is not just as Weyrwoman that you are attractive to the dragonmen, Lessa of Pern," Manora said sharply, her face stern. "There are several of the brown riders, for instance . . ."

"F'nor?" Lessa asked pointedly.

Manora drew herself up proudly. "He is a man grown, Weyrwoman, and we of the Lower Caverns have learned to disregard the ties of blood and affection. It is as a brown rider, not the son I bore, that I recommend him. Yes, I'd recommend F'nor, as I would also recommend T'sum and L'rad."

"Do you suggest them because they are of F'lar's wing and bred in the true traditions? Less apt to be swayed by my blandishments . . ."

"I suggest them because they believe in the tradition that the Weyr must be supplied from the Holds."

"All right." Lessa grinned at Manora, seeing the woman could not be baited about F'nor. "I shall take your recommendations to heart, for I do not intend . . ." She broke off her sentence. "Thank you for apprising me of our supply problems. We need fresh meat most of all?" she asked, rising to her feet.

"Grains, too, and some of the southern root vegetables would be very welcome," Manora replied formally.

"Very well," Lessa agreed.

Manora left, her expression thoughtful.

Lessa reflected for long moments on that interview, sitting like a slim statuette in the capacious stony chair, her legs curled up under her on the padding.

Foremost was the disturbing knowledge that Manora was deeply afraid of the mere prospect of Lessa absent from the Weyr, from Ramoth's side, for any reason, for any length of time. Her instinctive fear reaction was a far more effective argument than any of R'gul's sententious mouthings. However, Manora had given no hint of the reason for that necessity. Very well, Lessa would not try to fly one of the other dragons, with or without the rider, as she had been beginning to think she could.

As for this matter of short supplies; on that Lessa would act. Especially since R'gul would not. And, since R'gul could not protest what he did not know, she would contrive, with the help of K'net or F'nor or however many she needed, to keep the Weyr decently supplied. Eating regularly had become a pleasant habit she did not wish to curtail. She did not intend being greedy, but a little judicious pilfering of a bountiful harvest would go unnoticed by the Hold Lords.

K'net, though, was young; he might be rash and indiscreet. Perhaps F'nor would be the wiser choice. But was he as free to maneuver as K'net, who was, after all, a bronze rider? Maybe C'gan. The absence of a retired blue rider, time heavy on his hands, might not be noticed at all.

Lessa smiled to herself, but her smile faded quickly.

"The day the Weyr has to barter for what should be given . . ." She thrust back the premonitory shudder, concentrated on the ignominy of that situation. It certainly emphasized the measure of her self-delusion.

Why had she thought being at the Weyr would be so different from Ruath Hold? Had her early childhood training instilled such a questionless reverence for the Weyr that life must alter its pattern because Lessa of Ruatha had been Impressed by Ramoth? How could she have been such a romantic little fool?

Look around you, Lessa of Pern, look around the Weyr with unveiled eyes. Old and hallowed is the Weyr? Yes, but shabby and worn—and disregarded. Yes, you were elated to sit in the Weyrwoman's great chair at the Council Table, but the padding is thin and the fabric dusty. Humbled to think your hands rest where Moreta's and Torene's had rested? Well, the stone is ingrained with dirt and needs a good scrubbing. And your rump may rest where theirs did—but that's not where you have your brains.

The shabby Weyr reflected the deterioration of its purpose in the scheme of life on Pern. Those handsome dragonriders, too, so brave in their wher-hide accouterments, proud on the necks of their great beasts—they did not submit kindly to close examination without a few disappointing revelations. They were only men, with manlike lusts and ambitions, full of very human faults and frustrations, unwilling to disrupt their easy existence for the harsh exigencies that would reestablish the Weyr. They had settled too deeply in their isolation from the rest of their race; they did not realize they were little thought of. There was no real leader at their head . . .

F'lar! What was he waiting for? For Lessa to see through R'gul's ineffectiveness? No, Lessa decided slowly, for Ramoth to grow up. For Mnementh to fly her when he can . . . traditionalist that F'lar is, and Lessa thought this excuse to be specious . . . when the mating dragon's rider became, traditionally, the Weyrleader. That rider!

Well, F'lar might just find events not turning out as *he* planned.

My eyes were dazzled by Ramoth's, but I can see around the rainbow now, Lessa thought, steeling herself against the tenderness that always accompanied any thought of the golden beast. Yes, I can see into the black and gray shadows now, where my apprenticeship at Ruatha should stand me in good stead. True, there's more to control than one small Hold and far more perceptive minds to influence. Perceptive but dense in their own way. A greater hazard if I lose. But how can I? Lessa's smile broadened. She rubbed her palms against her thighs in anticipation of the challenge. They can do nothing with Ramoth without me, and they must have Ramoth. No one can coerce Lessa of Ruatha, and they're as stuck with me as they were with Jora. Only, I'm no Jora!

Elated, Lessa jumped from the chair. She felt alive again. And more powerful in herself than she felt when Ramoth was awake.

Time, time, time. R'gul's time. Well, Lessa had done with marking his time. She'd been a silly fool. Now she'd be the Weyrwoman F'lar had beguiled her to think she could be.

F'lar . . . her thoughts returned to him constantly. She'd have to watch out for him. Particularly when she started "arranging" things to suit herself. But she had an advantage he couldn't know—that she could speak to all the dragons, not just Ramoth. Even to his precious Mnementh.

Lessa threw back her hand and laughed, the sound echoing hollowly in the large, empty Council Room. She laughed again, delighted with an exercise she had had rare occasion to use. Her mirth roused Ramoth. The exultation of her decision was replaced by that of knowing the golden dragon was waking.

Ramoth stirred again and stretched restlessly as hunger pierced slumber. Lessa ran up the passage on light feet, eager as a child for the first sight of the glorious eyes and the sweetness that characterized the dragon's personality.

Ramoth's huge golden wedge-shaped head swiveled around as the sleepy dragon instinctively sought her Weyrmate. Lessa quickly touched her blunt chin, and the searching head was still, comforted. The several protecting lids parted over the many-faceted eyes, and Ramoth and Lessa renewed the pledge of their mutual devotion.

Ramoth had had those dreams again, she told Lessa, shuddering slightly. It was so cold *there!* Lessa caressed the soft down above her eye-ridge, soothing the dragon. Linked firmly to Ramoth as she had become, she was acutely aware of the dismay those curious sequences produced.

Ramoth complained of an itch by the left dorsal ridge.

"The skin is flaking again," Lessa told her, quickly spreading sweet oil on the affected area. "You're growing so fast," she added with mock and tender dismay.

Ramoth repeated that she itched abominably.

"Either eat less so you'll sleep less or stop outgrowing your hide overnight."

She chanted dutifully as she rubbed in the oil, "The dragonet must be oiled daily as the rapid growth in early development can overstretch fragile skin tissues, rendering them tender and sensitive."

They itch, Ramoth corrected petulantly, squirming.

"Hush. I'm only repeating what I was taught."

Ramoth issued a dragon-sized snort that blew Lessa's robe tightly around her legs.

"Hush. Daily bathing is compulsory, and thorough oiling must accompany these ablutions. Patchy skin becomes imperfect hide in the adult dragon. Imperfect hide results in skin ruptures that may prove fatal to a flying beast."

Don't stop rubbing, Ramoth entreated.

"Flying beast indeed!"

Ramoth informed Lessa she was so hungry. Couldn't she bathe and oil later?

"The moment that cavern you call a belly is full, you're so sleepy you can barely crawl. You've gotten too big to be carried."

Ramoth's tart rejoinder was interrupted by a low chuckle. Lessa whirled, hastily controlling the annoyance she felt at seeing F'lar lounging indolently against the archway to the ledge-corridor.

He had obviously been flying a patrol, for he still wore the heavy wher-hide gear. The stiff tunic clung to the flat chest, outlined the long, muscular legs. His bony but handsome face was still reddened by the ultra-cold of *between*. His curiously amber eyes glinted with amusement and, Lessa added, conceit.

"She grows sleek," he commented, approaching Ramoth's couch with a courteous bow to the young queen.

Lessa heard Mnementh give a greeting to Ramoth from his perch on the ledge.

Ramoth rolled her eyes coquettishly at the wingleader. His smile of almost possessive pride in her doubled Lessa's irritation.

"The escort arrives in good time to bid the queen good day."

"Good day, Ramoth," F'lar said obediently. He straightened, slapping his heavy gloves against his thigh.

"We interrupted your patrol pattern?" asked Lessa, sweetly apologetic.

"No matter. A routine flight," F'lar replied, undaunted. He sauntered to one side of Lessa for an unimpeded view of the queen. "She's bigger than most of the browns. There have been high seas and flooding at Telgar. And the tidal swamps at Igen are dragondeep." His grin flashed as if this minor disaster pleased him.

As F'lar said nothing without purpose, Lessa filed that statement away for future reference. However irritating F'lar might be, she preferred his company to that of the other bronze riders.

Ramoth interrupted Lessa's reflections with a tart reminder: If she had to bathe before eating, could they get on with it before she expired from hunger?

Lessa heard Mnementh's amused rumble without the cavern.

"Mnementh says we'd better humor her," F'lar remarked indulgently.

Lessa suppressed the desire to retort that she could perfectly well hear what Mnementh said. One day it was going to be most salutary to witness F'lar's stunned reaction to the knowledge that she could hear and speak to every dragon in the Weyr.

"I neglect her shockingly," Lessa said, as if contritely.

She saw F'lar about to answer her. He paused, his amber eyes narrowing briefly. Smiling affably, he gestured for her to lead the way.

An inner perversity prompted Lessa to bait F'lar whenever possible. One day she would pierce that pose and flay him to the quick. It would take doing. He was sharp-witted.

The three joined Mnementh on the Ledge. He hovered protectingly over Ramoth as she glided awkwardly down to the far end of the long oval Weyr Bowl. Mist, rising from the warmed water of the small lake, parted in the sweep of Ramoth's ungainly wings. Her growth had been so rapid that she had had no time to coordinate muscle and bulk. As F'lar set Lessa on Mnementh's neck for the short drop, she looked anxiously after the gawky, blundering queen.

Queens don't fly because they can't, Lessa told herself with bitter candor, contrasting Ramoth's grotesque descent with Mnementh's effortless drift.

"Mnementh says to assure you she'll be more graceful when she gets her full growth," F'lar's amused voice said in her ear.

"But the young males are growing just as fast, and they're not a bit . . ." She broke off. She wouldn't admit anything to that F'lar.

"They don't grow as large, and they constantly practice . . ."

"Flying! . . ." Lessa leaped on the word, and then, catching a glimpse of the bronze rider's face, said no more. He was just as quick with a casual taunt.

Ramoth had immersed herself and was irritably waiting to be sanded. The left dorsal ridge itched abominably. Lessa dutifully attacked the affected area with a sandy hand.

No, her life at the Weyr was no different from that at Ruatha. She was still scrubbing. And there was more of Ramoth to scrub each day, she thought as she finally sent the golden beast into the deeper water to rinse. Ramoth wallowed, submerging to the tip of her nose. Her eyes, covered by the thin inner lid, glowed just below the surface—watery jewels. Ramoth languidly turned over, and the water lapped around Lessa's ankles.

All occupations were suspended when Ramoth was abroad. Lessa noticed the women clustered at the entrance to the Lower Caverns, their eyes wide with fascination. Dragons perched on their ledges or idly circled overhead. Even the weyrlings, boy and dragonet, wandered forth curiously from the fledgling barracks of the training fields.

A dragon trumpeted unexpectedly on the hiehgts by the Star Stone. He and his rider spiraled down.

"Tithings, F'lar, a train in the pass," the blue rider announced, grinning broadly until he became disappointed by the calm way his unexpected good news was received by the bronze rider.

"F'nor will see to it," F'lar told him indifferently. The blue dragon obediently lifted his rider to the wing-second's ledge.

"Who could it be?" Lessa asked F'lar. "The loyal three are in."

F'lar waited until he saw F'nor on brown Canth wheel up and over the protecting lip of the Weyr, followed by several green riders of the wing.

"We'll know soon enough," he remarked. He turned his head thoughtfully eastward, an unpleasant smile touching the corner of his mouth briefly. Lessa, too, glanced eastward where, to the knowing eye, the faint spark of the Red Star could be seen, even though the sun was full up.

"The loyal ones will be protected," F'lar muttered under his breath, "when the Red Star passes."

How and why they two were in accord in their unpopular belief in the significance of the Red Star Lessa did not know. She only knew that she, too, recognized it as Menace. It had actually been the foremost consideration in all F'lar's arguments that she leave Ruatha and come to the Weyr. Why *he* had not succumbed to the pernicious indifference that had emasculated the other dragonmen she did not know. She had never asked him—not out of spite, but because it was so obvious that his belief was beyond question. He *knew*. And she *knew*.

And occasionally that knowledge must stir in the dragons. At dawn, as one, they stirred restlessly in their sleep—if they slept—or lashed their tails and spread their wings in protest if they were awake. Manora, too, seemed to believe. F'nor must. And perhaps some of F'lar's surety had infected his wingriders. He certainly demanded implicit obedience to tradition in his riders and received it, to the point of open devotion.

Ramoth emerged from the lake and half-flapped, half-floundered her way to the feeding grounds. Mnementh arranged himself at the edge and permitted Lessa to seat herself on his foreleg. The ground away from the Bowl rim was cold underfoot.

Ramoth ate, complaining bitterly over the stringy bucks that made her meal and resenting it when Lessa restricted her to six.

"Others have to eat, too, you know."

Ramoth informed Lessa that she was queen and had priority.

"You'll itch tomorrow."

Mnementh said she could have his share. He had eaten well of a fat buck in Keroon two days ago. Lessa regarded Mnementh with considerable interest. Was that why all the dragons in F'lar's wing looked so smug? She must pay more attention as to who frequented the feeding grounds and how often.

Ramoth had settled into her weyr again and was already drowsing when F'lar brought the train-captain into the quarters.

"Weyrwoman," F'lar said, "this messenger is from Lytol with duty to you."

The man, reluctantly tearing his eyes from the glowing golden queen, bowed to Lessa.

"Tilarek, Weyrwoman, from Lytol, Warder of Ruath Hold," he said respectfully, but his eyes, as he looked at Lessa, were so admiring as to be just short of impudence. He withdrew a message from his belt and hesitated, torn between the knowledge that women did not read and his instructions to give it to the Weyrwoman. Just as he caught F'lar's amused reassurance, Lessa extended her hand imperiously.

"The queen sleeps," F'lar remarked, indicating the passageway to the Council Room.

Adroit of F'lar, Lessa thought, to be sure the messenger had a long look at Ramoth. Tilarek would spread the word on his return journey, properly elaborated with each retelling, of the queen's unusual size and fine health. Let Tilarek also broadcast his opinion of the new Weyrwoman.

Lessa waited until she saw F'lar offer the courier wine before she opened the skin. As she deciphered Lytol's inscription, Lessa realized how glad she was to receive news of Ruatha. But why did Lytol's first words have to be:

The babe grows strong and is healthy . . .

She cared little for that infant's prosperity. Ah . . .

Ruatha is green-free, from hill crown to crafthold verge. The harvest has been very good, and the beasts multiply from the new studs. Herewith is the due and proper tithe of Ruath Hold. May it prosper the Weyr which protects us.

Lessa snorted under her breath. Ruatha knew its duty, true, but not even the other three tithing holds had sent proper greetings. Lytol's message contained ominously:

A word to the wise. With Fax's death, Telgar has come to the fore in the growing sedition. Meron, so-called Lord of Nabol, is strong and seeks, I feel, to be first: Telgar is too cautious for him. The dissension strengthens and is more widespread than when I last spoke with Bronze Rider F'lar. The Weyr must be doubly on its guard. If Ruatha may serve, send word.

Lessa scowled at the last sentence. It only emphasized the fact that too few Holds served in any way.

". . . laughed at we were, good F'lar," Tilarek was saying, moistening his throat with a generous gulp of Weyr-made wine, "for doing as men ought.

"Funny thing, that, for the nearer we got to Benden Range the less laughing we heard. Sometimes it's hard to make sense of some things, being as how you don't do 'em much. Like if I were not to keep my sword arm strong and used to the weight of a blade," and he made vigorous slashes and thrusts with his right arm, "I'd be put to it to defend myself come a long-drawn fight. Some folk, too, believe what the loudest talker says. And some folk because it frightens them not to. However," he went on briskly, "I'm soldier-bred and it goes hard to take the gibes of mere crafters and holders. But we'd orders to keep our swords sheathed, and we did. Just as well," he said with a wry grimace, "to talk soft. The Lords have kept full guard since . . . since the Search . . ."

Lessa wondered what he had been about to say, but he went on soberly.

"There are those that'll be sorry when the Threads fall again on all that green around their doors."

F'lar refilled the man's cup, asking casually about the harvests seen on the road here.

"Fine, fat and heavy," the courier assured him. "They do say this Turn has been the best in memory of living man. Why, the vines in Crom had bunches this big!" He made a wide circle with his two huge hands, and his listeners made proper response. "And I've never seen the Telgar grain so full and heavy. Never."

"Pern prospers," F'lar remarked dryly.

"Begging your pardon"—Tilarek picked up a wizened piece of fruit from the tray—"I've scooped better than this dropped on the road behind a harvest wagon." He ate the fruit in two bites, wiping his hands on the tunic. Then, realizing what he had said, he added in hasty apology, "Ruatha Hold sent you its best. First fruits as man ought. No ground pickings from us. You may be sure."

"It is reassuring to know we have Ruatha's loyalty as well as its full measure," F'lar assured him. "Roads were clear?"

"Aye, and there's a funny thing this time of year. Cold, then suddenly warm like the weather couldn't remember the season. No snow and little rain. But winds! Like you'd never believe. They do say as how the coasts have been hit hard with high water." He rolled his eyes expressively and then, hunching his shoulders, confidentially added, "They do say Ista's smoking mountain that does appear and then . . . phffst . . . disappears . . . has appeared again."

F'lar looked properly skeptical, although Lessa did not miss the gleam of excitement in his eyes. The man sounded like one of R'gul's ambiguous verses.

"You must stay a few days for a good rest," F'lar invited Tilarek genially, guiding him out past sleeping Ramoth.

"Aye and grateful. Man gets to the Weyr maybe once or twice in his life," Tilarek was saying absently, craning his neck to keep Ramoth in sight as F'lar led him out. "Never knew queens grew so big."

"Ramoth is already much larger and stronger than Nemorth," F'lar assured him as he turned the messenger over to the weyrling waiting to escort him to quarters.

"Read this," Lessa said, impatiently shoving the skin at the bronze rider as soon as they were again in the Council Room.

"I expected little else," F'lar remarked, unconcerned, perching on the edge of the great stone table.

"And . . . ?" Lessa demanded fiercely.

"Time will tell," F'lar replied serenely, examining a fruit for spots.

"Tilarek implied that not all the holders echo their Lords' seditious sentiments," Lessa commented, trying to reassure herself.

F'lar snorted. "Tilarek says 'as will please his listeners,'" he said in a passable imitation of the man's speech.

"You'd better know, too," F'nor said from the doorway, "he doesn't speak for all his men. There was a good deal of grumbling in the escort." F'nor accorded Lessa a courteous if absentminded salute. "It was felt that Ruatha has been too long poor to give such a share to the Weyr its first profitable Turn. And I'll say that Lytol was more generous than he ought to be. We'll eat well . . . for a while."

F'lar tossed the messageskin to the brown rider.

"As if we didn't know that," F'nor grunted after he had quickly scanned the contents.

"If you know that, what will you do about it?" Lessa spoke up. "The Weyr is in such disrepute that the day is coming when it can't feed its own."

She used the phrase deliberately, noticing with satisfaction that it stung the memories of both dragonmen. The look they turned on her was almost savage. Then F'lar chuckled so that F'nor relaxed with a sour laugh.

"Well?" she demanded.

"R'gul and S'lel will undoubtedly get hungry," F'nor said, shrugging.

"And you two?"

F'lar shrugged, too, and, rising, bowed formally to Lessa. "As Ramoth is deep asleep, Weyrwoman, your permission to withdraw."

"Get out!" Lessa shouted at them.

They had turned, grinning at each other, when R'gul came storming into the chamber, S'lel, D'nol, T'bor, and K'net close on his heels.

"What is this I hear? That Ruatha alone of the High reaches sends tithes?"

"True, all too true," F'lar conceded calmly, tossing the messageskin at R'gul.

The Weyrleader scanned it, mumbling the words under his breath, frowning at its content. He passed it distastefully to S'lel, who held it for all to read.

"We fed the Weyr last year on the tithings of three Holds," R'gul announced disdainfully.

"*Last* year," Lessa put in, "but only because there were reserves in the supply caves. Manora has just reported that those reserves are exhausted. . ."

"Ruatha has been very generous," F'lar put in quickly. "It should make the difference."

Lessa hesitated a moment, thinking she hadn't heard him right.

"Not that generous." She rushed on, ignoring the remanding glare F'lar shot her way.

"The dragonets require more this year, anyway. So there's only one solution. The Weyr must barter with Telgar and Fort to survive the Cold."

Her words touched off instant rebellion.

"Barter? Never!"

"The Weyr reduced to bartering? Raid!"

"R'gul, we'll raid first. Barter never!"

That had stung all the bronze riders to the quick. Even S'lel reacted with indignation. K'net was all but dancing, his eyes sparkling with anticipation of action.

Only F'lar remained aloof, his arms folded across his chest, glaring at her coldly.

"Raid?" R'gul's voice rose authoritatively above the noise. "There can be no raid!"

Out of conditioned reflex to his commanding tone, they quieted momentarily.

"No raids?" T'bor and D'nol demanded in chorus.

"Why not?" D'nol went on, the veins in his neck standing out.

He was not the one, groaned Lessa to herself, trying to spot S'lan, only to remember that he was out on the training field. Occasionally he and D'nol acted together against R'gul in Council, but D'nol was not strong enough to stand alone.

Lessa glanced hopefully toward F'lar. Why didn't he speak up now?

"I'm sick of stringy old flesh, of bad bread, of wood-tasting roots," D'nol was shouting, thoroughly incensed. "Pern prospered this Turn. Let some spill over into the Weyr as it ought!"

T'bor, standing belligerently beside him, growled agreement, his eyes fixing on first one, then another of the silent bronze riders. Lessa caught at the hope that T'bor might act as substitute for S'lan.

"One move from the Weyr at this moment," R'gul interrupted, his arm raised warningly, "and all the Lords will move—against us." His arm dropped dramatically.

He stood, squarely facing the two rebels, feet slightly apart, head high, eyes flashing. He towered a head and a half above the stocky, short D'nol and the slender T'bor. The contrast was unfortunate: the tableau was of the stern patriarch reprimanding errant children.

"The roads are clear," R'gul went on portentously, "with neither rain nor snow to stay an advancing army. The Lords have kept full guards under arms since Fax was killed." R'gul's head turned just slightly in F'lar's direction. "Surely you all remember the scant hospitality we got on Search?" Now R'gul pinned each bronze rider in turn with a significant stare. "You know the temper of the Holds, you saw their strength." He jerked his chin up. "Are you fools to antagonize them?"

"A good firestoning . . ." D'nol blurted out angrily and stopped. His rash words shocked himself as much as anyone else in the room.

Even Lessa gasped at the idea of deliberately using firestone against man.

"Something has to be done . . ." D'nol blundered on desperately, turning first to F'lar, then, less hopefully, to T'bor.

If R'gul wins, it will be the end, Lessa thought, coldly furious, and reacted, turning her thoughts toward T'bor. At Ruatha it had been easiest to sway angry men. If she could just . . . A dragon trumpeted outside.

An excruciatingly sharp pain lanced from her instep up her leg. Stunned, she staggered backward, unexpectedly falling into F'lar. He caught her arm with fingers like iron bands.

"You dare control . . ." he whispered savagely in her ear and, with false solicitude, all but slammed her down into her chair. His hand grasped her arm with vise-fingered coercion.

Swallowing convulsively against the double assault, she sat rigidly. When she could take in what had happened, she realized the moment of crisis had passed.

"*Nothing* can be done at this time," R'gul was saying forcefully.

"At this time . . ." The words ricocheted in Lessa's ringing ears.

"The Weyr has young dragons to train. Young men to bring up in the proper Traditions."

Empty Traditions, Lessa thought numbly, her mind seething with bitterness. And they will empty the very Weyr itself.

She glared with impotent fury at F'lar. His hand tightened warningly on her arm until his fingers pressed tendon to bone and she gasped again with pain. Through the tears that sprang to her eyes, she saw defeat and shame written on K'net's young face. Hope flared up, renewed.

With an effort she forced herself to relax. Slowly, as if F'lar had really frightened her. Slowly enough for him to believe in her capitulation.

As soon as she could, she would get K'net aside. He was ripe for the idea she had just conceived. He was young, malleable, attracted to her anyway. He would serve her purpose admirably.

"Dragonman, avoid excess," R'gul was intoning. "Greed will cause the Weyr distress."

Lessa stared at the man, honestly appalled that he could clothe the Weyr's moral defeat with hypocritical homily.

Honor those the dragons heed
In thought and favor, word and deed.
Worlds are lost or worlds are saved
From the dangers dragon-braved.

"What's the matter? Noble F'lar going against tradition?" Lessa demanded of F'nor as the brown rider appeared with a courteous explanation of the wingleader's absence.

Lessa no longer bothered to leash her tongue in F'nor's presence. The brown rider knew it was not directed at himself, so he rarely took offense. Some of his half brother's reserve had rubbed off on him.

His expression today, however, was not tolerant; it was sternly disapproving.

"He's tracing K'net," F'nor said bluntly, his dark eyes troubled. He pushed his heavy hair back from his forehead, another habit picked up from F'lar, which added fuel to Lessa's grievance with the absent weyrman.

"Oh, is he? He'd do well to imitate him instead," she snapped.

F'nor's eyes flashed angrily.

Good, thought Lessa. I'm getting to him, too.

"What you do not realize, Weyrwoman, is that K'net takes your instructions too liberally. A judicious pilfering would raise no protest, but K'net is too young to be circumspect."

"My instructions?" Lessa repeated innocently. Surely F'nor and F'lar hadn't a shred of evidence to go on. Not that she cared. "He's just too fed up with the whole cowardly mess!"

F'nor clamped his teeth down tightly against an angry rebuttal. He shifted his stance, clamped his hands around the wide rider's belt until his knuckles whitened. He returned Lessa's gaze coldly.

In that pause Lessa regretted antagonizing F'nor. He had tried to be friendly, pleasant, and had often amused her with anecdotes as she became more and more embittered. As the world turned colder, rations had gotten slimmer at the Weyr in spite of the systematic additions of K'net. Despair drifted through the Weyr on the icy winds.

Since D'nol's abortive rebellion, all spirit had drained out of the dragonmen. Even the beasts reflected it. Diet alone would not account for the dullness of their hide and their deadened attunement. Apathy could—and did. Lessa wondered that R'gul did not rue the result of his spineless decision.

"Ramoth is not awake," she told F'nor calmly, "so you do not need to dance attendance on *me*."

F'nor said nothing, and his continued silence began to discomfit Lessa. She rose, rubbing her palms on her thighs as if she could erase her last hasty words. She paced back and forth, glancing from her sleeping chamber into Ramoth's, where the golden queen, now larger than any of the bronze dragons, lay in deep slumber.

If only she would wake, Lessa thought. When she's awake, everything's all right. As right as it can be, that is. But she's like a rock.

"So . . ." she began, trying to keep her nervousness out of her voice, "F'lar is at last doing something, even if it is cutting off our one source of supply."

"Lytol sent in a message this morning," F'nor said curtly. His anger had subsided, but not his disapproval.

Lessa turned to face him, expectantly.

"Telgar and Fort have conferred with Keroon," F'nor went on heavily. "They've decided the Weyr is behind their losses. Why," and his anger flared hot again, "if you picked K'net, didn't you keep a close check on him? He's too green. C'gan, T'sum, I would have . . ."

"You? You don't sneeze without F'lar's consent," she retorted.

F'nor laughed outright at her.

"F'lar did give you more credit than you deserve," he replied, contemptuous of his own turn. "Haven't you realized why he must wait?"

"No," Lessa shouted at him. "I haven't! Is this something I must divine, by instinct, like the dragons? By the shell of the first Egg, F'nor, no one *explains* anything to me!

"But it is nice to know that he has a reason for waiting. I just hope it's valid. That it is not too late already. Because I think it is."

It was too late when he stopped me from reinforcing T'bor, she thought, but refrained from saying. Instead, she added, "It was too late when R'gul was too cowardly to feel the shame of . . ."

F'nor swung on her, his face white with anger. "It took more courage than you'll ever have to watch that moment slide by."

"Why?"

F'nor took a half step forward, so menacingly that Lessa steeled herself for a blow. He mastered the impulse, shaking his head violently to control himself.

"It is not R'gul's fault," he said finally, his face old and drawn, his eyes troubled and hurt. "It has been hard, hard to watch and to know you *had* to wait."

"*Why?*" Lessa all but shrieked.

F'nor would no longer be goaded. He continued in a quiet voice.

"*I* thought you ought to know, but it goes against F'lar's grain to apologize for one of his own."

Lessa bit back the sarcastic remark that rose to her lips, lest she interrupt this long-awaited enlightenment.

"R'gul is Weyrleader only by default. He'd be well enough, I suppose, if there hadn't been such a long Interval. The Records warn of the dangers . . ."

"Records? Dangers? What do you mean by Interval?"

"An Interval occurs when the Red Star does not pass close enough to excite the Threads. The Records indicate it takes about two hundred Turns before the Red Star swings back again. F'lar figures nearly twice that time has elapsed since the last Threads fell."

Lessa glanced apprehensively eastwad. F'nor nodded solemnly.

"Yes, and it'd be rather easy to forget fear and caution in four hundred Turns. R'gul's a good fighter and a good wingleader, but he has to see and touch and smell danger before he admits it exists. Oh, he learned the Laws and all the Traditions, but he never understood them in his bones. Not the way F'lar does or the way I have come to," he added defiantly, seeing the skeptical expression on Lessa's face. His eyes narrowed, and he pointed an accusing finger at her. "Nor the way you do, only you don't know why."

She backed away, not from him but from the menace she *knew* existed, even if she didn't know why she believed.

"The moment F'lar Impressed Mnementh, F'lon began training him to take over. Then F'lon got himself killed in that ridiculous brawl." An expression comprised of anger, regret, and irritation passed over F'nor's face. Belatedly Lessa realized the man was speaking of his father. "F'lar was too young to take over, and before anyone could intervene, R'gul got Hath to fly Nemorth and *we* had to wait. But R'gul couldn't control Jora's grief over F'lon, and she deteriorated rapidly. And he misinterpreted F'lon's plan for carrying us over the last of the Interval to mean isolation. Consequently"—F'nor shrugged expressively—"the Weyr lost prestige faster all the time."

"Time, time, time," Lessa railed. "It's always the wrong time. When is *now* the time?"

"Listen to me." F'nor's stern words interrupted her tirade as effectively as if he had grabbed and shaken her. She had not suspected F'nor of such forcefulness. She looked at him with increased respect.

"Ramoth is full-grown, ready for her first mating flight. When she flies, all the bronzes rise to catch her. The strongest does not always get the queen. Sometimes it is the one everyone in the Weyr wants to have win her." He enunciated his words slowly and clearly. "That was how R'gul got Hath to fly Nemorth. The older riders wanter R'gul. They couldn't stomach a nineteen-year-old over them as Weyrleader, son though he was to F'lon. So Hath got Nemorth. And they got R'gul. They got what they wanted. And look what they've got!" His scornful gesture took in the threadbare weyr.

"It is too late, it is too late," Lessa moaned, understanding a great deal, too well, too late.

"It may be, thanks to your prodding K'net into uncontrolled raiding," F'nor assured her cynically. "You didn't need him, you know. Our wing was handling it quietly. But when so much kept coming in, we cut our operations down. It's a case of too much too soon, since the Hold Lords are getting imprudent enough to retaliate. Think, Lessa of Pern," and F'nor leaned toward her, his smile bitter, "What R'gul's reaction will be. You didn't stop to think of that, did you? Think, now, what he will do when the well-armed Lords of the Hold appear, to demand satisfaction?"

Lessa closed her eyes, appalled at the scene she could picture all too clearly. She caught at her chair arm, limply sat down, undone by the knowledge she had miscalculated. Overconfident because she had been able to bring haughty Fax to his death, she was about to bring the Weyr to its ruin through that same arrogance.

There was suddenly noise enough for half the Weyr to be storming up the passageway from the ledge. She could hear the dragons calling excitedly to each other, the first outburst she had heard from them in two months.

Startled, she jumped up. Had F'lar failed to intercept K'net? Had K'net, by some horrible chance, been caught by the Lords? Together she and F'nor rushed out into the queen's weyr.

It was not F'lar and K'net and an angry Lord—or several—in tow who entered. It was R'gul, his cautious face distorted, his eyes wide with excitement. From the outside ledge Lessa could hear Hath generating the same intense agitation. R'gul shot a quick glance at Ramoth, who slumbered on obliviously. His eyes as he approached Lessa were coldly calculating. D'nol came rushing into the weyr at a dead run, hastily buckling on his tunic. Close on his heels came S'lan, S'lel, T'bor. They all converged in a loose semicircle around Lessa.

R'gul stepped forward, arm outstretched as if to embrace her. Before Lessa could step back, for there was something in R'gul's expression that revolted her, F'nor moved adroitly to her side, and R'gul, angry, lowered his arm.

"Hath is blooding his kill?" the brown rider asked ominously.

"Binth and Orth, too," T'bor blurted out, his eyes bright with the curious fever that seemed to be affecting all the bronze riders.

Ramoth stirred restlessly, and everyone paused to watch her intently.

"Blood their kill?" Lessa exclaimed, perplexed but knowing that this was strangely significant.

"Call in K'net and F'lar," F'nor ordered with more authority than a brown rider should use in the presence of bronzes.

R'gul's laugh was unpleasant.

"No one knows where they went."

D'nol started to protest, but R'gul cut him off with a savage gesture.

"You wouldn't dare, R'gul," F'nor said with cold menace.

Well, Lessa would dare. Her frantic appeal to Mnementh and Piyanth produced a faint reply. Then there was absolute blankness where Mnementh had been.

"She will wake," R'gul was saying, his eyes piercing Lessa's. "She will wake and rise ill-tempered. You must allow her only to blood her kill. I warn you she will resist. If you do not restrain her, she will gorge and cannot fly."

"She rises to mate," F'nor snapped, his voice edged with cold and desperate fury.

"She rises to mate with whichever bronze can catch her," R'gul continued, his voice exultant.

And he means for F'lar not to be here, Lessa realized.

"The longer the flight, the better the clutch. And she cannot fly well or high if she is stuffed with heavy meat. She must not gorge. She must be permitted only to blood her kill. Do you understand?"

"Yes, R'gul," Lessa said, "I understand. For once I do understand you, all too well. F'lar and K'net are not here." Her voice grew shrill. "But Ramoth will never be flown by Hath if I have to take her *between*."

She saw naked fear and shock wipe R'gul's face clear of triumph, and she watched as he got himself under control. A malevolent sneer replaced surprise at her threat. Did he think her defiance was empty?

"Good afternoon," said F'lar pleasantly from the entrance. K'net grinned broadly at his side. "Mnementh informs me that the bronzes blood their kill. How kind of you to call us in for the spectacle."

Relief temporarily swept her recent antagonism for F'lar out of Lessa's mind. The sight of him, calm, arrogant, mocking, buoyed her.

R'gul's eyes darted around the semicircle of bronze riders, trying to pick out who had called in these two. And Lessa knew R'gul hated as well as feared F'lar. She could sense, too, that F'lar had changed. There was nothing passive or indifferent or detached about him now. Instead, there was tense anticipation. F'lar was done with waiting!

Ramoth roused, suddenly and completely awake. Her mind was in such a state that Lessa candidly realized F'lar and K'net had arrived none too soon. So intense were Ramoth's hunger pangs that Lessa hastened to her head to soothe her. But Ramoth was in no mood for placation.

With unexpected agility she rose, making for the ledge. Lessa ran after her, followed by the dragonmen. Ramoth hissed in agitation at the bronzes who hovered near the ledge. They scattered quickly out of her way. Their riders made for the broad stairs that led from the queen's weyr to the Bowl.

In a daze Lessa felt F'nor place her on Canth's neck and urge his dragon quickly after the others to the feeding grounds. Lessa watched, amazed, as Ramoth glided effortlessly and gracefully in over the alarmed, stampeding herd. She struck quickly, seizing her kill by the neck and furling her wings suddenly, dropping down on it, too ravenous to carry it aloft.

"Control her!" F'nor gasped, depositing Lessa unceremoniously to the ground.

Ramoth screamed defiance of her Weyrwoman's order. She sloughed her head around, rustling her wings angrily, her eyes blazing opalescent pools of fire. She extended her neck skyward to its full reach, shrilling her insubordination. The harsh echoes reverberated against the walls of the Weyr. All around, the dragons, blue, green, brown, and bronze, extended their wings in mighty sweeps, their answering calls brass thunder in the air.

Now indeed must Lessa call on the strength of will she had developed through hungry, vengeful years. Ramoth's wedge-shaped head whipped back and forth; her eyes glowed with incandescent rebellion. This was no amiable, trusting dragon child. This was a violent demon.

Across the bloody field Lessa matched wills with the transformed Ramoth. With no hint of weakness, no vestige of fear or thought of defeat. Lessa forced Ramoth to obey. Screeching protest, the golden dragon dropped her head to her kill, her tongue lashing at the inert body, her great jaws opening. Her head wavered over the steaming entrails her claws had ripped out. With a final snarl of reproach, Ramoth fastened her teeth on the thick throat of the buck and sucked the carcass dry of blood.

"Hold her," F'nor murmured. Lessa had forgotten him.

Ramoth rose, screaming, and with incredible speed landed on a second squealing buck. She made a second attempt to eat from the soft belly of her kill. Again Lessa exerted her authority and won. Shrilling defiance, Ramoth reluctantly blooded again.

She did not resist Lessa's orders the third time. The dragon had begun to realize now that irresistible instinct was upon her. She had not known anything but fury until she got the taste of hot blood. Now she knew what she needed: to fly fast, far, and long, away from the Weyr, away from these puny, wingless ones, far in advance of those rutting bronzes.

Dragon instinct was limited to here-and-now, with no ability to control or anticipate. Mankind existed in partnership with them to supply wisdom and order, Lessa found herself chanting silently.

Without hesitation, Ramoth struck for the fourth time, hissing with greed as she sucked at the beast's throat.

A tense silence had fallen over the Weyr Bowl, broken only by the sound of Ramoth's feeding and the high keening of the wind.

Ramoth's skin began to glow. She seemed to enlarge, not with gorging but with luminescence. She raised her bloody head, her tongue forking out to lick her muzzle. She straightened, and simultaneously a hum arose from the bronzes ringing the feeding ground in silent anticipation.

With a sudden golden movement Ramoth arched her great back. She sprang into the sky, wings wide. With unbelievable speed she was airborne. After her, in the blink of an eye, seven bronze shapes followed, their mighty wings churning buffets of sand-laden air into the faces of the watching weyrfolk.

Her heart in her mouth at the prodigious flight, Lessa felt her soul lifting with Ramoth.

"Stay with her," F'nor whispered urgently. "Stay with her. She must not escape your control now."

He stepped away from Lessa, back among the folk of the Weyr, who, as one, turned their eyes skyward to the disappearing shining motes of the dragons.

Lessa, her mind curiously suspended, retained only enough physical consciousness to realize that she was in fact earthbound.

All other sense and feeling were aloft with Ramoth. And she, Ramoth-Lessa, was alive with limitless power, her wings beating effortlessly to the thin heights, elation surging through her frame, elation and—desire.

She sensed rather than saw the great bronze males pursuing her. She was contemptuous of their ineffectual efforts. For she was wingfree and unconquerable.

She snaked her head under one wing and mocked their puny efforts with shrill taunts. High above them she soared. Suddenly, folding her wings, she plummeted down, delighting to see them veer off in wingcrowding haste to avoid collision.

She soared quickly above them again as they labored to make up their lost speed and altitude.

So Ramoth flirted leisurely with her lovers, splendid in her new-found freedom, daring the bronze ones to outfly her.

One dropped, spent. She crowed her superiority. Soon a second abandoned the chase as she played with them, diving and darting in intricate patterns. Sometimes she was oblivious of their existence, so lost was she in the thrill of flight.

When, at last, a little bored, she condescended to glance at her followers, she was vaguely amused to see only three great beasts still pursuing. She recognized Mnementh, Orth, and Hath. All in their prime; worthy, perhaps, of her.

She glided down, tantalizing them, amused at their now labored flights. Hath she couldn't bear. Orth? Now Orth was a fine young beast. She dropped her wings to slide between him and Mnementh.

As she swung past Mnementh, he suddenly closed his wings and dropped beside her. Startled, she tried to hover and found her wings fouled with his, his neck winding tightly about hers.

Entwined, they fell. Mnementh, calling on hidden reserves of strength, spread his wings to check their downward fall. Outmaneuvered and startled by the terrific speed of their descent, Ramoth, too, extended her great wings. And then . . .

Lessa reeled, her hands wildly grabbing out for any support. She seemed to be exploding back into her body, every nerve throbbing.

"Don't faint, you fool. Stay with her." F'lar's voice grated in her ear. His arms roughly sustained her.

She tried to focus her eyes. She caught a startled glimpse of the walls of her own weyr. She clutched at F'lar, touching bare skin, shaking her head, confused.

"Bring her back."

"How?" she cried, panting, unable to comprehend what could possibly entice Ramoth from such glory.

The pain of stinging blows on her face made her angrily aware of F'lar's disturbing proximity. His eyes were wild, his mouth distorted.

"Think with her. She cannot go *between*. Stay with her."

Trembling at the thought of losing Ramoth *between*, Lessa sought the dragon, still locked wing to wing with Mnementh.

The mating passion of the two dragons at that moment spiraled wide to include Lessa. A tidal wave rising relentlessly from the sea of her soul flooded Lessa. With a longing cry she clung to F'lar. She felt his body rock-firm against hers, his hard arms lifting her up, his mouth fastening mercilessly on hers as she drowned deep in another unexpected flood of desire.

"Now! *We* bring them safely home," he murmured.

Dragonman, dragonman,
Between thee and thine,
Share me that glimpse of love
Greater than mine.

F'lar came suddenly awake. He listened attentively, heard and was reassured by Mnementh's gratified rumble. The bronze was perched on the ledge outside the queen's weyr. All was peacefully in order in the Bowl below.

Peaceful but different. F'lar, through Mnementh's eyes and senses, perceived this instantly. There was an overnight change in the Weyr. F'lar permitted himself a satisfied grin at the previous day's tumultuous events. Something might have gone wrong.

Something nearly did, Mnementh reminded him.

Who had called K'net and himself back? F'lar mused again. Mnementh only repeated that he had been called back. Why wouldn't he identify the informer?

A nagging worry intruded on F'lar's waking ruminations.

"Did F'nor remember to . . ." he began aloud.

F'nor never forgets your orders, Mnementh reassured him testily. *Canth told me that the sighting at dawn today puts the Red Star at the top of the Eye Rock. The sun is still off, too.*

F'lar ran impatient fingers through his hair. "At the top of the Eye Rock. Closer, and closer the Red Star came," just as the Old Records predicted. And that dawn when the Star gleamed scarlet at the watcher *through* the Eye Rock heralded a dangerous passing and . . . the Threads.

There was certainly no other explanation for that careful arrangement of gigantic stones and special rocks on Benden Peak. Nor for its counterpart on the eastern walls of each of the five abandoned Weyrs.

First, the Finger Rock on which the rising sun balanced briefly at dawn at the winter solstice. Then, two dragon lengths behind it, the rectangular, enormous Star Stone, chest-high to a tall man, its polished surface incised by two arrows, one pointing due east toward the Finger Rock, the other slightly north of due east, aimed directly at the Eye Rock, so ingeniously and immovably set into the Star Stone.

One dawn, in the not too distant future, he would look through the Eye Rock and meet the baleful blink of the Red Star. And then . . .

Sounds of vigorous splashing interrupted F'lar's reflections. He grinned again as he realized it was the girl bathing. She certainly cleaned up pretty, and undressed . . . He stretched with leisurely recollection, reviewing what his reception from that quarter might be. She ought to have no complaints at all. What a flight! He chuckled softly.

Mnementh commented from the safety of his ledge that F'lar had better watch his step with Lessa.

Lessa, is it? thought F'lar back to his dragon.

Mnementh enigmatically repeated his caution. F'lar chuckled his self-confidence.

Suddenly Mnementh was alert to an alarm.

Watchers were sending out a rider to identify the unusually persistent dust clouds on the plateau below Benden Lake, Mnementh informed his wingleader crisply.

F'lar rose hastily, gathered up his scattered clothes, and dressed. He was buckling the wide rider's belt when the curtain to the bathing room was flipped aside. Lessa confronted him, fully clothed.

He was always surprised to see how slight she was, an incongruous physical vessel for such strength of mind. Her newly washed hair framed her narrow face with a dark cloud. There was no hint in her composed eyes of the dragon-roused passion they had experienced together yesterday. There was no friendliness about her at all. No warmth. Was this what Mnementh meant? What was the matter with the girl?

Mnementh gave an additional alarming report, and F'lar set his jaw. He would have to postpone the understanding they must reach intellectually until after this emergency. To himself he damned R'gul's green handling of her. The man had all but ruined the Weyrwoman, as he had all but destroyed the Weyr.

Well, F'lar, bronze Mnementh's rider, was now Weyrleader, and changes were long overdue.

Long overdue, Mnementh confirmed dryly. *The Lords of the Holds gather in force on the lake plateau.*

"There's trouble," F'lar announced to Lessa by way of greeting. His announcement did not appear to alarm her.

"The Lords of the Hold come to protest?" she asked coolly.

He admired her composure even as he decried her part in this development.

"You'd have done better to let me handle the raiding. K'net's still boy enough to be carried away with the joy of it all."

Her slight smile was secretive. F'lar wondered fleetingly if that wasn't what she had intended in the first place. Had Ramoth not risen yesterday, it would be a different story altogether today. Had she thought of that?

Mnementh forewarned him that R'gul was at the ledge. R'gul was all chest and indignant eye, the dragon commented, which meant he was feeling his authority.

"He has none," F'lar snapped out loud, thoroughly awake and pleased with events, despite their precipitation.

"R'gul?"

She was quick-witted all right, F'lar admitted.

"Come, girl." He gestured her toward the queen's weyr. The scene he was about to play with R'gul ought to redeem that shameful day in the Council Room two months back. He knew it had rankled in her as in him.

They had no sooner entered the queen's weyr than R'gul, followed by an excited K'net, stormed in from the opposite side.

"The watch informs me," R'gul began, "that there is a large body of armed men, with banners of many Holds, approaching the Tunnel. K'net here"—R'gul was furious with the youngster—"confesses he has been raiding systematically—against all reason and most certainly against my distinct orders. Of course, we'll deal with him later," he informed the errant rider ominously, "that is, if there is a Weyr left after the Lords are through with us."

He turned back to F'lar, his frown deepening as he realized F'lar was grinning at him.

"Don't stand there," R'gul growled. "There's nothing to grin about. We've got to think how to placate them."

"No, R'gul," F'lar contradicted the older man, still grinning, "the days of placating the Lords are over."

"What? Are you out of your mind?"

"No. But *you* are out of order," F'lar said, his grin gone, his face stern.

R'gul's eyes widened as he stared at F'lar as if he had never seen him before.

"You've forgotten a very important fact," F'lar went on ruthlessly. "Policy changes when the leader of the Weyr is replaced. *I*, F'lar, Mnementh rider, am Weyrleader now."

On that ringing phrase, S'lel, D'nol, T'bor, and S'lan came striding into the room. They stopped, shock-still, staring at the motionless tableau.

F'lar waited, giving them a chance to absorb the fact that the dissension in the room meant that authority had indeed passed to him.

"Mnementh," he said aloud, "call in all wingseconds and brown riders. We've some arrangements to make before our . . . guests arrive. As the queen is asleep, dragonmen, into the Council Room, please. After you, Weyrwoman."

He stepped aside to permit Lessa to pass, noticing the slight flush on her cheeks. She was not completely in command of her emotions, after all.

No sooner had they taken places at the Council Table than the brown riders began to stream in. F'lar took careful note of the subtle difference in their attitudes. They walked taller, he decided. And— yes, the air of defeat and frustration was replaced by tense excitement.

All else being equal, today's events ought to revive the pride and purpose of the Weyr.

F'nor and T'sum, his own seconds, strode in. There was no doubt of their high, proud good humor. Their eyes flashed around daring anyone to defy their promotion as T'sum stood by the archway and F'nor marched smartly around to his position behind F'lar's chair. F'nor paused to make a deeply respectful bow to the girl. F'lar saw her flush and drop her eyes.

"Who's at our gate, F'nor?" the new Weyrleader asked affably.

"The Lords of Telgar, Nabol, Fort, and Keroon, to name the principal banners," F'nor answered in a similar vein.

R'gul rose from his chair; the half-formed protest died on his lips as he caught the expression in the faces of the bronze riders. S'lel, beside him, started to mumble, picking at his lower lip.

"Estimated strength?"

"In excess of a thousand. In good order and well-armed," F'nor reported indifferently.

F'lar shot his second a remonstrating look. Confidence was one thing, indifference preferable to defeat, but there was no wisdom in denying the situation was very tight.

"Against the Weyr?" S'lel gasped.

"Are we dragonmen or cowards?" D'nol snapped, jumping up, his fist pounding the table. "This is the final insult."

"Indeed it is," F'lar concurred heartily.

"It has to be put down. We'll swallow no more," D'nol continued vehemently, encouraged by F'lar's attitude. "A few flaming . . ."

"That's enough," F'lar said in a hard voice. "We are dragonmen! Remember that, and remember also—never forget it—this fellowship is sworn to *protect*." He enunciated that word distinctly, pinning each man with a fierce stare. "Is that point clear?" He glared questioningly at D'nol. There were to be no private heroics today.

"We do not need firestone," he continued, certain that D'nol had taken his meaning, "to disperse these foolish Lords." He leaned back and went on more calmly, "I noticed on Search, as I'm sure you all did, that the common holder has not lost one jot of his . . . let us say . . . respect for dragonkind."

T'bor grinned, and someone chuckled reminiscently.

"Oh, they follow their Lords quickly enough, incited with indignation and lots of new wine. But it's quite another matter to face a dragon, hot, tired, and cold sober. Not to mention on foot without a wall or Hold in sight." He could sense their concurrence. "The mounted men, too, will be too much occupied with their beasts to do any serious fighting," he added with a chuckle, echoed by most of the men in the room.

"However consoling these reflections are, there are more powerful factors in our favor. I doubt the good Lords of the Hold have bothered to review them. I suspect"—he glanced around sardonically at his riders—"they have probably forgotten them . . . as they have conveniently forgotten so much dragonlore . . . and tradition.

"It is now time to reeducate them." His voice was steel. An affirming mutter answered him. Good, he had them.

"For instance, they are here at our gates. They've traveled long and hard to reach this remote Weyr. Undoubtedly some units have been marching for weeks. F'nor," he said in a calculated aside, "remind me to discuss patrol schedules later today. Ask yourselves this, dragonmen, if the Lords of the Holds are here, who is holding the Holds for the Lords? Who keeps guard on the Inner Hold, over all the Lords hold dear?"

He heard Lessa chuckling wickedly. She was quicker than any of the bronze riders. He had chosen well that day in Ruatha, even if it had meant killing while on Search.

"Our Weyrwoman perceives my plan. T'sum, implement it." He snapped that order out crisply. T'sum, grinning broadly, departed.

"I don't understand," S'lel complained, blinking in confusion.

"Oh, let me explain," Lessa put in quickly, her words couched in the sweet, reasonable tone F'lar was learning to identify as Lessa at her worst. He couldn't blame her for wanting to get some of her own back from S'lel, but this taste of hers for vengeance could become pernicious.

"Someone ought to explain something," S'lel said querulously. "I don't like what's going on. Holders at the Tunnel Road. Dragons permitted firestone. I don't understand."

"It's so simple," Lessa assured him sweetly, not waiting for F'lar's permission. "I'm embarrassed to have to explain."

"Weyrwoman!" F'lar called her sharply to order.

She didn't look at him, but she did stop needling S'lel.

"The Lords have left their Holds unprotected," she said. "They appear not to have considered that dragons can move *between* in seconds. T'sum, if I am not mistaken, has gone to assemble sufficient hostages from the unguarded Holds to insure that the Lords respect the sanctity of the Weyr." F'lar nodded confirmation. Lessa's eyes flashed angrily as she continued. "It is not the fault of the Lords that they have lost respect for the Weyr. The Weyr has . . ."

"The Weyr," F'lar cut in sharply. Yes, he would have to watch this slim girl very carefully and very respectfully. ". . . the Weyr is about to insist on its traditional rights and prerogatives. Before I outline exactly how, Weyrwoman, would you greet our newest guests? A few words might be in order to reinforce the object lesson we will impress on all Pernese today."

The girl's eyes sparkled with anticipation. She grinned with such intense pleasure that F'lar wondered if he was wise to let her instruct the defenseless hostages.

"I rely on your discretion," he said emphatically, "and intelligence to handle the assignment adroitly." He caught her glance, held it until she briefly inclined her head in acknowledgement of his admonition. As she left, he sent a word ahead to Mnementh to keep an eye on her.

Mnementh informed him that that would be wasted effort. Hadn't Lessa shown more wit than anyone else in the Weyr? She was circumspect by instinct.

Circumspect enough to have precipitated today's invasion, F'lar reminded his dragon.

"But . . . the . . . Lords," R'gul was sputtering.

"Oh, freeze up," K'net suggested. "If we hadn't listened to you for so long, we wouldn't be in this position at all. Shove *between* if you don't like it, but F'lar is Weyrleader now. And I say about time!"

"K'net! R'gul!" F'lar called them to order, shouting over the cheers K'net's impudent words produced. "These are my orders," he went on when he had their complete attention. "I expect them to be followed exactly." He glanced at each man to be sure there was no further question of his authority. Then he outlined his intentions concisely and quickly, watching with satisfaction as uncertainty was replaced with admiring respect.

Assured that every bronze and brown rider understood the plan perfectly, he asked Mnementh for the latest report.

The advancing army was streaming out across the lake plateau, the foremost units on the Tunnel road, the one ground entrance to the Weyr. Mnementh added that the Holders' women were profiting from their stay in the Weyr.

"In what way?" F'lar demanded immediately.

Mnementh rumbled with the dragon equivalent of laughter. Two of the young greens were feeding, that was all. But for some reason such a normal occupation appeared to upset the women.

The woman was diabolically clever, F'lar thought privately, careful not to let Mnementh sense his concern. That bronze clown was as besotted with the rider as he was with the queen. What kind of fascination did the Weyrwoman have for a bronze dragon?

"Our guests are at the lake plateau," he told the dragonmen. "You have your positions. Order your wings out." Without a backward look, he marched out, conquering an intense urge to hurry to the ledge. He absolutely did not want those hostages scared witless.

Down the valley by the lake, the women were lightly attended by four of the smallest greens—big enough for the uninitiated—and the women were probably too scared at having been seized to notice that all four riders were barely out of adolescence. He spotted the slight

figure of the Weyrwoman, seated to one side of the main group. A
sound of muffled weeping drifted up to his ears. He looked beyond
them, to the feeding grounds, and saw a green dragon single out a
buck and run it down. Another green was perched on a ledge above,
eating with typical messy, dragon greed. F'lar shrugged and mounted
Mnementh, clearing the ledge for the hovering dragons who waited
to pick up their own riders.

As Mnementh circled above the confusion of wings and gleaming
bodies, F'lar nodded approvingly. A high, fast mating flight coupled
with the promise of action improved everyone's morale.

Mnementh snorted.

F'lar paid him no attention, watching R'gul as he assembled his
wing. The man had taken a psychological defeat. He would bear watching and careful handling. Once the Threads started to fall and R'gul's
faith was restored, he'd come around.

Mnementh asked him if they should pick up the Weyrwoman.

"She doesn't belong in this," F'lar said sharply, wondering why
under the double moons the bronze had made such a suggestion. Mnementh replied that he thought Lessa would like to be there.

D'nol's wing and T'bor's rose in good formation. Those two were
making good leaders. K'net took up a double wing to the Bowl lip and
winked out neatly, bound to reappear behind the approaching army.
C'gan, the old blue rider, had the youngsters organized.

F'lar told Mnementh to have Canth tell F'nor to proceed. With a
final look to be sure the stones to the Lower Caverns were in place,
F'lar gave Mnementh the signal to go *between*.

From the Weyr and from the Bowl,
Bronze and brown and blue and green,
Rise the dragonmen of Pern,
Aloft, on wing; seen, then unseen.

Larad, Lord of Telgar, eyed the monolithic heights of Benden
Weyr. The striated stone looked like frozen waterfalls at sunset. And about as hospitable. A long moribund awe squirmed at the
back of his mind for the blasphemy he and the army he led were about
to commit. He stifled that thought firmly.

The Weyr had outlived its usefulness. That was obvious. There
was no longer any need for the Holders to give up the profits of their

sweat and labor to the lazy weyrfolk. The Holders had been patient. They had supported the Weyr in good part out of gratitude for past services. But the dragonmen had overstepped the borders of grateful generosity.

First, this archaic Search foolishness. So a queenegg was laid. Why did the dragonmen need to steal away the prettiest women among the Holders when they had women of their own in the Weyr proper? No need to appropriate Larad's sister, Kylora, eagerly awaiting a far different alliance with Brant of Igen one evening and gone on that ridiculous Search the next. Never heard from since, either.

And killing Fax! Albeit the man had been dangerously ambitious, he was of the Blood. And the Weyr had not been asked to meddle in the affairs of the High Reaches.

But this steady pilfering. That was beyond enough. Oh, a holder might excuse a few bucks now and again. But when a dragon appeared out of nowhere (a talent that disturbed Larad deeply) and snatched the best stud bucks from a herd carefully protected and nurtured, that tore it!

The Weyr must be made to understand its subordinate position in Pern. It would have to make other provisions to victual its people, for no further tithes would come from anyone. Benden, Bitra, and Lemos would come around soon. They ought to be pleased to end this superstitious domination by the Weyr.

Nevertheless, the closer they came to the gigantic mountain, the more doubts Larad experienced as to just how in the world the Lords would penetrate that massif. He signaled Meron, so-called Lord of Nabol (he didn't really trust this sharp-faced ex-Warder with no Blood at all) to draw his riding beast closer.

Meron whipped his mount abreast of Larad.

"There is no other way into the Weyr proper but the Tunnel?"

Meron shook his head. "Even the locals are agreed."

This did not dismay Meron, but he caught Larad's doubtful expression.

"I have sent a party on ahead, to the southern lip of the Peak," and he indicated the area. "There might be a low, scalable cliff there where the brow dips."

"You sent a party without consulting us? I was named leader . . ."

"True," Meron agreed, with an amiable show of teeth. "A mere notion of mine."

"A distinct possibility, I agree, but you'd have done better . . ." Larad glanced up at the Peak.

"They have seen us, have no doubt of that, Larad," Meron assured him, contemptuously regarding the silent Weyr. "That will be sufficient. Deliver our ultimatum and they will surrender before such a force as ours. They've proved themselves cowards over and over. I gave insult twice to the bronze rider they call F'lar, and he ignored it. What *man* would?"

A sudden rustling roar and a blast of the coldest air in the world interrupted their conference. As he mastered his plunging beast, Larad caught a confused panorama of dragons, all colors, sizes, and everywhere. The air was filled with the panic-stricken shrieks of plunging beasts, the cries of startled, terrified men.

Larad managed, with great effort, to drag his beast around to face the dragonmen.

By the Void that spawned us, he thought, struggling to control his own fear, I'd forgotten dragons are so big.

Foremost in that frightening array was a triangular formation of four great bronze beasts, their wings overlapping in a tremendous criss-cross pattern as they hovered just above the ground. A dragon's length above and beyond them, there ranged a second line, longer, wider, of brown beasts. Curving beyond them and higher up were blue and green and more brown beasts, all with their huge wings fanning cold air in great drafts on the terrified mob that had been an army moments before.

Where did that piercing cold come from, Larad wondered. He yanked down on his beast's mouth as it began to plunge again.

The dragonmen just sat there on their beasts' necks, watching, waiting.

"Get them off their beasts and the things away so we can talk," Meron shouted to Larad as his mount cavorted and screamed in terror.

Larad signaled foot soldiers forward, but it took four men per mount to quiet them enough so the Lords could dismount.

Miscalculation number two, Larad thought with grim humor. We forgot the effect of dragons on the beasts of Pern. Man included. Settling his sword, pulling his gloves up onto his wrists, he jerked his head at the other Lords, and they all moved forward.

As he saw the Lords dismount, F'lar told Mnementh to pass the word to land the first three ranks. Like a great wave, the dragons obediently settled to the ground, furling their wings with an enormous rustling sigh.

Mnementh told F'lar that the dragons were excited and pleased. This was much more fun than Games.

F'lar told Mnementh sternly that this was not fun at all.

"Larad of Telgar," the foremost man introduced himself, his voice crisp, his manner soldierly and confident for one relatively young.

"Meron of Nabol."

F'lar immediately recognized the swarthy face with the sharp features and restless eyes. A mean and provocative fighter.

Mnementh relayed F'lar an unusual message from the Weyr. F'lar nodded imperceptibly and continued to acknowledge introductions.

"I have been appointed spokesman," Larad of Telgar began. "The Holder Lords unanimously agree that the Weyr has outlived its function. Consequently demands from the Weyr are out of order. There are to be no more Searches among our Holds. No more raiding on the herds and barns of any Hold by any dragonfolk."

F'lar gave him courteous attention. Larad was well-spoken and succinct. F'lar nodded. He looked at each of the Lords before him carefully, getting their measure. Their stern faces expressed their conviction and righteous indignation.

"As Weyrleader, I, F'lar, Mnementh's rider, answer you. Your complaint is heard. Now listen to what the Weyrleader commands." His casual pose was gone. Mnementh rumbled a menacing counterpoint to his rider's voice as it rang harshly metallic across the plateau, the words carried clearly back so that even the mob heard him.

"You will turn and go back to your Holds. You will then go into your barns and among your herds. You will make a just and equable tithe. This will be on its way to the Weyr within three days of your return."

"The Weyrleader is ordering the Lords to tithe?" Meron of Nabol's derisive laugh rang out.

F'lar signaled, and two more wings of dragonmen appeared to hover over the Nabolese contingent.

"The Weyrleader gives orders to the Lords to tithe," F'lar affirmed. "And until such time as the Lords do send their tithings, we regret that the ladies of Nabol, Telgar, Fort, Igen, Keroon must make their homes with us. Also, the ladies of Hold Balan, Hold Gar, Hold. . ."

He paused, for the Lords were muttering angrily and excitedly among themselves as they heard this list of hostages. F'lar gave Mnementh a quick message to relay.

"Your bluff won't work," Meron sneered, stepping forward, his hand on his sword hilt. Raiding among the herds could be credited; it had happened. But the Holds were sacrosanct! They'd not dare—

F'lar asked Mnementh to pass the signal, and T'sum's wing appeared. Each rider held a Lady on the neck of his dragon. T'sum held his group aloft but close enough so the Lords could identify each scared or hysterical woman.

Meron's face contorted with shock and new hatred.

Larad stepped forward, tearing his eyes from his own Lady. She was a new wife to him and much beloved. It was small consolation that she neither wept nor fainted, being a quiet and brave little person.

"You have the advantage of us," Larad admitted bleakly. "We

will retire and send the tithe." He was about to wheel when Meron pushed forward, his face wild.

"We tamely submit to their demands? Who is a dragonman to order us?"

"Shut up," Larad ordered, grabbing the Nabolese's arm.

F'lar raised his arm in an imperious signal. A wing of blues appeared, carrying Meron's would-be mountaineers, some bearing evidence of their struggle with the southern face of Benden Peak.

"Dragonmen do order. And nothing escapes their notice." F'lar's voice rang out coldly.

"You will retire to your Holds. You will send proper tithing because we shall know if you do not. You will then proceed, under pain of firestone, to clear your habitations of green, croft and Hold alike. Good Telgar, look to that southern outer Hold of yours. The exposure is acutely vulnerable. Clear all firepits on ridge defenses. You've let them become fouled. The mines are to be reopened and firestone stockpiled."

"Tithes, yes, but the rest . . ." Larad interrupted.

F'lar's arm shot skyward.

"Look up, Lord. Look well. The Red Star pulses by day as well as night. The mountains beyond Ista steam and spout flaming rock. The seas rage in high tides and flood the coast. Have you all forgotten the Sagas and Ballads? As you've forgotten the abilities of dragons? Can you dismiss these portents that always presage the coming of Threads?"

Meron would never believe until he saw the silver Threads streaking across the skies. But Larad and many of the others, F'lar knew, now did.

"And the queen," he continued, "has risen to mate in her second year. Risen to mate and flown high and far."

The heads of all before him jerked upward. Their eyes were wide. Meron, too, looked startled. F'lar heard R'gul gasp behind him, yet he dared not look, himself, lest it be a trick.

Suddenly, on the periphery of his vision, he caught the glint of gold in the sky.

·Mnementh, he snapped, and Mnementh merely rumbled happily. The queen wheeled into view just then, a brave and glowing sight, F'lar grudgingly admitted.

Dressed in flowing white, Lessa was distinctly visible on the curved golden neck. Ramoth hovered, her wing-span greater than even Mnementh's as she vaned idly. From the way she arched her neck, it was obvious that Ramoth was in good and playful spirits, but F'lar was furious.

The spectacle of the queen aloft had quite an effect on all beholders. F'lar was aware of its impact on himself and saw it reflected in the faces of the incredulous Holders, knew it from the way the dragons hummed, heard it from Mnementh.

"And, of course, our greatest Weyrwomen—Moreta, Torene, to name only a few—have all come from Ruath Hold, as does Lessa of Pern."

"Ruatha . . ." Meron grated out the name, clenched his jaw sullenly, his face bleak.

"Threads are coming?" asked Larad.

F'lar nodded slowly. "Your harper can reinstruct you on the signs. Good Lords, the tithe is required. Your women will be returned. The Holds are to be put in order. The Weyr prepares Pern, as the Weyr is pledged to protect Pern. Your cooperation is expected—" he paused significantly—"and will be enforced."

With that, he vaulted to Mnementh's neck, keeping the queen always in sight. He saw her golden wings beat as the dragon turned and soared upward.

It was infuriating of Lessa to take this moment, when all his energy and attention ought to go to settling the Holders' grievance for a show of rebellion. Why did she have to flaunt her independence so, in full sight of the entire Weyr and all the Lords? He longed to chase immediately after her and could not. Not until he had seen the army in actual retreat, not until he had signaled for the final show of Weyr strength for the Holders' elucidation.

Gritting his teeth, he signaled Mnementh aloft. The wings rose behind him with spectacular trumpetings and dartings so that there appeared to be thousands of dragons in the air instead of the scant two hundred Benden Weyr boasted.

Assured that that part of his strategy was proceeding in order, he bade Mnementh fly after the Weyrwoman, who was now dipping and gliding high above the Weyr.

When he got his hands on that girl, he would tell her a thing or two. . . .

Mnementh informed him caustically that telling her a thing or two might be a very good idea. Much better than flying so vengefully after a pair who were only trying their wings out. Mnementh reminded his irate rider that, after all, the golden dragon had flown far and wide yesterday, having blooded four, but had not eaten since. She'd be neither capable of nor interested in any protracted flying until she had eaten fully. However, if F'lar insisted on this ill-considered and completely unnecessary pursuit, he might just antagonize Ramoth into jumping *between* to escape him.

The very thought of that untutored pair going *between* cooled F'lar instantly. Controlling himself, he realized that Mnementh's judgment was more reliable than his at the moment. He'd let anger and anxiety influence his decisions, but . . .

Mnementh circled in to land at the Star Stone, the tip of Benden Peak being a fine vantage point from which F'lar could observe both the decamping army and the queen.

Mnementh's great eyes gave the appearance of whirling as the dragon adjusted his vision to its farthest reach.

He reported to F'lar that Piyanth's rider felt the dragons' supervision of the retreat was causing hysteria among the men and beasts. Injuries were occurring in the resultant stampedes.

F'lar immediately ordered K'net to assume surveillance altitude until the army camped for the night. He was to keep close watch on the Nabolese contingent at all times, however.

Even as F'lar had Mnementh relay these orders, he realized his mind had dismissed the matter. All his attention was really on that high-flying pair.

You had better teach her to fly between, Mnementh remarked, one great eye shining directly over F'lar's shoulder. *She's quick enough to figure it out for herself, and then where are we?*

F'lar let the sharp retort die on his lips as he watched, breathless. Ramoth suddenly folded her wings, a golden streak diving through the sky. Effortlessly she pulled out at the critical point and soared upward again.

Mnementh deliberately called to mind their first wildly aerobatic flight. A tender smile crossed F'lar's face, and suddenly he knew how much Lessa must have longed to fly, how bitter it must have been for her to watch the dragonets practice when she was forbidden to try.

Well, he was no R'gul, torn by indecision and doubt.

And she is no Jora, Mnementh reminded him pungently. *I'm calling them in*, the dragon added. *Ramoth has turned a dull orange.*

F'lar watched as the flyers obediently began a downward glide, the queen's wings arching and curving as she slowed her tremendous forward speed. Unfed or not, she could fly!

He mounted Mnementh, waving them on, down toward the feeding grounds. He caught a fleeting glimpse of Lessa, her face vivid with elation and rebellion.

Ramoth landed, and Lessa dropped to the ground, gesturing the dragon on to eat.

The girl turned then, watching Mnementh glide in and hover to let F'lar dismount. She straightened her shoulders, her chin lifted belligerently as her slender body gathered itself to face his censure. Her behavior was like that of any weyrling, anticipating punishment and determined to endure it, soundless. She was not the least bit repentant!

Admiration for this indomitable personality replaced the last trace of F'lar's anger. He smiled as he closed the distance between them.

Startled by his completely unexpected behavior, she took a half-step backward.

"Queens can, too, fly," she blurted out, daring him.

His grin broadening to suffuse his face, he put his hands on her shoulders and gave her an affectionate shake.

"Of course they can fly," he assured her, his voice full of pride and respect. "That's why they have wings!"

PART III

Dust Fall

The Finger points
At an Eye blood-red.
Alert the Weyrs
To sear the Thread.

"You still doubt, R'gul?" F'lar asked, appearing slightly amused by the older bronze rider's perversity.

R'gul, his handsome features stubbornly set, made no reply to the Weyrleader's taunt. He ground his teeth together as if he could grind away F'lar's authority over him.

"There have been no Threads in Pern's skies for over four hundred Turns. There are no more!"

"There is always that possibility," F'lar conceded amiably. There was not, however, the slightest trace of tolerance in his amber eyes. Nor the slightest hint of compromise in his manner.

He was more like F'lon, his sire, R'gul decided, than a son had any right to be. Always so sure of himself, always slightly contemptuous of what others did and thought. Arrogant, that's what F'lar was. Impertinent, too, and underhanded in the matter of that young Weyrwoman. Why, R'gul had trained her up to be one of the finest Weyrwomen in many Turns. Before he'd finished her instruction, she'd known all the Teaching Ballads and Sagas letter-perfect. And then the silly child had turned to F'lar. Didn't have sense enough to appreciate the merits of an older, more experienced man. Undoubtedly she felt a first obligation to F'lar for discovering her on Search.

"You do, however," F'lar was saying, "admit that when the sun hits the Finger Rock at the moment of dawn, winter solstice has been reached?"

"Any fool knows that's what the Finger Rock is for," R'gul grunted.

"Then why don't you, you old fool, admit that the Eye Rock was placed on Star Stone to bracket the Red Star when it's about to make a Pass?" burst out K'net.

R'gul flushed, half-starting out of his chair, ready to take the young sprout to task for such insolence.

"K'net!" F'lar's voice cracked authoritatively. "Do you really like flying the Igen patrol so much you want another few weeks at it?"

K'net hurriedly seated himself, flushing at the reprimand and the threat.

"There is, you know, R'gul, incontrovertible evidence to support my conclusions," F'lar went on with deceptive mildness. 'The Finger points/At an Eye blood-red. . .'"

"Don't quote me verses I taught you as a weyrling," R'gul exclaimed heatedly.

"Then have faith in what you taught," F'lar snapped back, his amber eyes flashing dangerously.

R'gul, stunned by the unexpected forcefulness, sank back into his chair.

"You cannot deny, R'gul," F'lar continued quietly, "that no less than half an hour ago the sun balanced on the Finger's tip at dawn and the Red Star was squarely framed by the Eye Rock."

The other dragonriders, bronze as well as brown, murmured and nodded their agreement to that phenomenon. There was also an undercurrent of resentment for R'gul's continual contest of F'lar's policies as the new Weyrleader. Even old S'lel, once R'gul's avowed supporter, was following the majority.

"There have been no Threads in four hundred Turns. There are no Threads," R'gul muttered.

"Then, my fellow dragonman," F'lar said cheerfully, "all you have taught is falsehood. The dragons are, as the Lords of the Holds wish to believe, parasites on the economy of Pern, anachronisms. And so are we.

"Therefore, far be it from me to hold you here against the dictates of your conscience. You have my permission to leave the Weyr and take up residence where you will."

Someone laughed.

R'gul was too stunned by F'lar's ultimatum to take offense at the ridicule. Leave the Weyr? Was the man mad? Where would he go? The Weyr had been his life. He had been bred up to it for generations. All his male ancestors had been dragonriders. Not all bronze, true, but a decent percentage. His own dam's sire had been a Weyrleader just as he, R'gul, had been until F'lar's Mnementh had flown the new queen.

But dragonmen never left the Weyr. Well, they did if they were negligent enough to lose their dragons, like that Lytol fellow at Ruath Hold. And how could he leave the Weyr *with* a dragon?

What did F'lar want of him? Was it not enough that he was Weyr-leader now in R'gul's stead? Wasn't F'lar's pride sufficiently swollen by having bluffed the Lords of Pern into disbanding their army when they were all set to coerce the Weyr and dragonmen? Must F'lar dominate *every* dragonman, body and will, too? He stared a long moment, incredulous.

"I do not believe we are parasites," F'lar said, breaking the silence with a soft, persuasive voice. "Nor anachronistic. There have been long Intervals before. The Red Star does not always pass close enough to drop Threads on Pern. Which is why our ingenious ancestors thought to position the Eye Rock and the Finger Rock as they did . . . to confirm *when* a Pass will be made. And another thing"—his face turned grave— "there have been other times when dragonkind has all but died out . . . and Pern with it because of skeptics like you." F'lar smiled and relaxed indolently in his chair. "I prefer not to be recorded as a skeptic. How shall we record you, R'gul?"

The Council Room was tense. R'gul was aware of someone breathing harshly and realized it was himself. He looked at the adamant face of the young Weyrleader and knew that the threat was not empty. He would either concede to F'lar's authority completely, though concession rankled deeply, or leave the Weyr.

And where could he go, unless to one of the other Weyrs, deserted for hundreds of Turns? And—R'gul's thoughts were savage—wasn't that indication enough of the cessation of Threads? Five empty Weyrs? No, by the Egg of Faranth, he would practice some of F'lar's own brand of deceit and bide his time. When all Pern turned on the arrogant fool, he, R'gul, would be there to salvage something from the ruins.

"A dragonman stays in his Weyr," R'gul said with what dignity he could muster.

"And accepts the policies of the current Weyrleader?" The tone of F'lar's voice made it less of a question and more of an order.

So as not to perjure himself, R'gul gave a curt nod of his head. F'lar continued to stare at him and R'gul wondered if the man could read his thoughts as his dragon might. He managed to return the gaze calmly. His turn would come. He'd wait.

Apparently accepting the capitulation, F'lar stood up and crisply delegated patrol assignments for the day.

"T'bor, you're weather-watch. Keep an eye on those tithing trains as you do. Have you the morning's report?"

"Weather is fair at dawning . . . all across Telgar and Keroon . . . if all too cold," T'bor said with a wry grin. "Tithing trains have good hard roads, though, so they ought to be here soon." His eyes twinkled with anticipation of the feasting that would follow the supplies' arrival—a mood shared by all, to judge by the expressions around the table.

F'lar nodded. "S'lan and D'nol, you are to continue an adroit Search for likely boys. They should be striplings, if possible, but do not pass over anyone suspected of talent. It's all well and good to present, for Impression, boys reared up in the Weyr traditions." F'lar gave a one-sided smile. "But there are not enough in the Lower Caverns. We, too, have been behind in begetting. Anyway, dragons reach full growth faster than their riders. We must have more young *men* to Impress when Ramoth hatches. Take the southern holds, Ista, Nerat, Fort, and South Boll where maturity comes earlier. You can use the guise of inspecting Holds for greenery to talk to the boys. And take along firestone and run a few flaming passes on those heights that haven't been scoured in—oh—dragon's years. A flaming beast impresses the young and arouses envy."

F'lar deliberately looked at R'gul to see the ex-Weyrleader's reaction to the order. R'gul had been dead set against going outside the Weyr for more candidates. In the first place, R'gul had argued that there were eighteen youngsters in the Lower Caverns, some quite young, to be sure, but R'gul would not admit that Ramoth would lay more than the dozen Nemorth had always dropped. In the second place, R'gul persisted in wanting to avoid any action that might antagonize the Lords.

R'gul made no overt protest, and F'lar went on.

"K'net, back to the mines. I want the dispositions of each firestone-dump checked and quantities available. R'gul, continue drilling recognition points with the weyrlings. They must be positive about their references. If they're used as messengers and suppliers, they may be sent out quickly and with no time to ask questions.

"F'nor, T'sum"—F'lar turned to his own brown riders—"you're clean-up squad today." He allowed himself a grin at their dismay. "Try Ista Weyr. Clear the Hatching Cavern and enough Weyrs for a double wing. And, F'nor, don't leave a single Record behind. They're worth preserving.

"That will be all, dragonmen. Good flying." And with that, F'lar rose and strode from the Council Room up to the queen's weyr.

Ramoth still slept, her hide gleaming with health, its color deepening to a shade of gold closer to bronze, indicating her pregnancy. As he passed her, the tip of her long tail twitched slightly.

All the dragons were restless these days, F'lar reflected. Yet when he asked Mnementh, the bronze dragon could give no reason. He woke, he went back to sleep. That was all. F'lar couldn't ask a leading question for that would defeat his purpose. He had to remain discontented with the vague fact that the restlessness was some kind of instinctive reaction.

Lessa was not in the sleeping room, nor was she still bathing. F'lar snorted. That girl was going to scrub her hide off with this constant bathing. She'd had to live grimy to protect herself in Ruath Hold, but bathing twice a day? He was beginning to wonder if this might be a subtle Lessa-variety insult to him personally. F'lar sighed. That girl. Would she never turn to him of her own accord? Would he ever touch that elusive inner core of Lessa? She had more warmth for his half brother, F'nor, and for K'net, the youngest of the bronze riders than she had for F'lar who shared her bed.

He pulled the curtain back into place, irritated. Where had she gone to today when, for the first time in weeks, he had been able to get all the wings out of the Weyr just so he could teach her to fly *between*?

Ramoth would soon be too egg-heavy for such activity. He had promised the Weyrwoman, and he meant to keep that promise. She had taken to wearing the wherhide riding gear as a flagrant reminder of his unfulfilled pledge. From certain remarks she had dropped, he knew she would not wait much longer for his aid. That she should try it on her own didn't suit him at all.

He crossed the queen's weyr again and peered down the passage that led to the Records Room. She was often to be found there, poring over the musty skins. And that was one more matter that needed urgent consideration. Those Records were deteriorating past legibility. Curiously enough, earlier ones were still in good condition and readable. Another technique forgotten.

That girl! He brushed his thick forelock of hair back from his brow in a gesture habitual to him when he was annoyed or worried. The passage was dark, which meant she could not be below in the Records Room.

"Mnementh," he called silently to his bronze dragon, sunning on the ledge outside the queen's weyr. "What is that girl doing?"

Lessa, the dragon replied, stressing the Weyrwoman's name with pointed courtesy, *is talking to Manora. She's dressed for riding,* he added after a slight pause.

F'lar thanked the bronze sarcastically and strode down the passage to the entrance. As he turned the last bend, he all but ran Lessa down.

You hadn't asked me where *she was,* Mnementh plaintively answered F'lar's blistering reprimand.

Lessa rocked back on her heels from the force of their encounter. She glared up at him, her lips thin with displeasure, her eyes flashing.

"Why didn't I have the opportunity of seeing the Red Star through the Eye Rock?" she demanded in a hard, angry voice.

F'lar pulled at his hair. Lessa at her most difficult would complete the list of this morning's trials.

"Too many to accommodate as it was on the Peak," he muttered, determined not to let her irritate him today. "And you already believe."

"I'd've liked to see it," she snapped and pushed past him toward the weyr. "If only in my capacity as Weyrwoman and Recorder."

He caught her arm and felt her body tense. He set his teeth, wishing, as he had a hundred times since Ramoth rose in her first mating flight, that Lessa had not been virgin, too. He had not thought to control his dragon-incited emotions, and Lessa's first sexual experience had been violent. It had surprised him to be first, considering that her adolescent years had been spent drudging for lascivious warders and soldiertypes. Evidently no one had bothered to penetrate the curtain of rags and the coat of filth she had carefully maintained as a disguise. He had been a considerate and gentle bedmate ever since, but, unless Ramoth and Mnementh were involved, he might as well call it rape.

Yet he knew someday, somehow, he would coax her into responding wholeheartedly to his lovemaking. He had a certain pride in his skill, and he was in a position to persevere.

Now he took a deep breath and released her arm slowly.

"How fortunate you're wearing riding gear. As soon as the wings have cleared out and Ramoth wakes, I shall teach you to fly *between*."

The gleam of excitement in her eyes was evident even in the dimly lit passageway. He heard her inhale sharply.

"Can't put it off too much longer or Ramoth'll be in no shape to fly at all," he continued amiably.

"You mean it?" Her voice was low and breathless, its usual acid edge missing. "You will teach us today?" He wished he could see her face clearly.

Once or twice he had caught an unguarded expression on her face, loving and tender. He would give much to have that look turned on him. However, he admitted wryly to himself, he ought to be glad that melting regard was directed only at Ramoth and not at another human.

"Yes, my dear Weyrwoman, I mean it. I will teach you to fly *between* today. If only," and he bowed to her with a flourish, "to keep you from trying it yourself."

Her low chuckle informed him his taunt was well-aimed.

"Right now, however," he said, indicating for her to lead the way back to the weyr, "I could do with some food. We were up before the kitchen."

They had entered the well-lighted weyr, so he did not miss the trenchant look she shot him over her shoulder. She would not so easily forgive being left out of the group at the Star Stone this morning, certainly not with the bribe of flying *between*.

How different this inner room was now that Lessa was Weyrwoman, F'lar mused as Lessa called down the service shaft for food. During Jora's incompetent tenure as Weyrwoman, the sleeping quarters had been crowded with junk, unwashed apparel, uncleared dishes. The state of the Weyr and the reduced number of dragons were as much Jora's fault as R'gul's, for she had indirectly encouraged sloth, negligence, and gluttony.

If he, F'lar, had been just a few years older when F'lon, his father, had died . . . Jora had been disgusting, but when dragons rose in mating flight, the condition of your partner counted for nothing.

Lessa took a tray of bread and cheese, and mugs of the stimulating *klah* from the platform. She served him deftly.

"You'd not eaten, either?" he asked.

She shook her head vigorously, the braid into which she had plaited her thick, fine dark hair bobbing across her shoulders. The hairdressing was too severe for her narrow face, but it did not, if that was her intention, disguise her femininity or the curious beauty of her delicate features. Again F'lar wondered that such a slight body contained so much shrewd intelligence and resourceful . . . cunning— yes, that was the word, cunning. F'lar did not make the mistake, as others had, of underestimating her abilities.

"Manora called me to witness the birth of Kylara's child."

F'lar maintained an expression of polite interest. He knew perfectly well that Lessa suspected the child was his, and it could have been, he admitted privately, but he doubted it. Kylara had been one of the ten candidates from the same Search three years ago which had discovered Lessa. Like others who survived Impression, Kylara had found certain aspects of Weyr life exactly suited to her temperament. She had gone from one rider's weyr to another's. She had even seduced F'lar—not at all against his will, to be sure. Now that he was Weyrleader, he found it wiser to ignore her efforts to continue the relationship. T'bor had taken her in hand and had had his hands full until he retired her to the Lower Caverns, well advanced in pregnancy.

Aside from having the amorous tendencies of a green dragon, Kylara was quick and ambitious. She would make a strong Weyrwoman, so F'lar had charged Manora and Lessa with the job of planting the notion in Kylara's mind. In the capacity of Weyrwoman . . . of another Weyr . . . her intense drives would be used to Pern's advantage. She had not learned the severe lessons of restraint and patience that Lessa had, and she didn't have Lessa's devious mind. Fortunately she was in considerable awe of Lessa, and F'lar suspected that Lessa was subtly influencing this attitude. In Kylara's case, F'lar preferred not to object to Lessa's meddling.

"A fine son," Lessa was saying.

F'lar sipped his *klah*. She was not going to get him to admit any responsibility.

After a long pause Lessa added, "She has named him T'kil."

F'lar suppressed a grin at Lessa's failure to get a rise from him. "Discreet of her."

"Oh?"

"Yes," F'lar replied blandly. "T'lar might be confusing if she took the second half of her name as is customary. 'T'kil,' however, still indicates sire as well as dam."

"While I was waiting for Council to end," Lessa said after clearing her throat, "Manora and I checked the supply caverns. The tithing trains, which the Holds have been so gracious as to send us"—her voice was sharp—"are due within the week. There will shortly be bread fit to eat," she added, wrinkling her nose at the crumbling gray pastry she was attempting to spread with cheese.

"A nice change," F'lar agreed.

She paused.

"The Red Star performed its scheduled antic?"

He nodded.

"And R'gul's doubts have been wiped away in the enlightening red glow?"

"Not at all." F'lar grinned back at her, ignoring her sarcasm. "Not at all, but he will not be so vocal in his criticism."

She swallowed quickly so she could speak. "You'd do well to cut out his criticism," she said ruthlessly, gesturing with her knife as if plunging it into a man's heart. "He is never going to accept your authority with good grace."

"We need every bronze rider . . . there are only seven, you know," he reminded her pointedly. "R'gul's a good wingleader. He'll settle down when the Threads fall. He needs proof to lay his doubts aside."

"And the Red Star in the Eye Rock is not proof?" Lessa's expressive eyes were wide.

F'lar was privately of Lessa's opinion—that it might be wiser to remove R'gul's stubborn contentiousness. But he could not sacrifice a wingleader, needing every dragon and rider as badly as he did.

"I don't trust him," she added darkly. She sipped at her hot drink, her gray eyes dark over the rim of her mug. As if, F'lar mused, she didn't trust him, either.

And she didn't, past a certain point. She had made that plain, and, in honesty, he couldn't blame her. She did recognize that every action F'lar took was toward one end . . . the safety and preservation of dragonkind and weyrfolk and consequently the safety and preservation of Pern. To effect that end, he needed her full cooperation. When Weyr business or dragonlore were discussed, she suspended the antipathy he knew she felt for him. In conferences she supported him wholeheartedly and persuasively, but always he suspected the double edge to her comments and saw a speculative, suspicious look in her eyes. He needed not only her tolerance but her empathy.

"Tell me," she said after a long silence, "did the sun touch the Finger Rock before the Red Star was bracketed in the Eye Rock or after?"

"Matter of fact, I'm not sure, as I did not see it myself . . . the concurrence lasts only a few moments . . . but the two are supposed to be simultaneous."

She frowned at him sourly. "Whom did you waste it on? R'gul?" She was provoked, her angry eyes looked everywhere but at him.

"I am Weyrleader," he informed her curtly. She was unreasonable.

She awarded him one long, hard look before she bent to finish her meal. She ate very little, quickly and neatly. Compared to Jora, she didn't eat enough in the course of an entire day to nourish a sick child. But then, there was no point in ever comparing Lessa to Jora.

He finished his own breakfast, absently piling the mugs together on the empty tray. She rose silently and removed the dishes.

"As soon as the Weyr is free, we'll go," he told her.

"So you said." She nodded toward the sleeping queen, visible through the open arch. "We still must wait upon Ramoth."

"Isn't she rousing? Her tail's been twitching for an hour."

"She always does that about this time of day."

F'lar leaned across the table, his brows drawn together thoughtfully as he watched the golden-forked tip of the queen's tail jerk spasmodically from side to side.

"Mnementh, too. And always at dawn and early morning. As if somehow they associate that time of day with trouble . . ."

"Or the Red Star's rising?" Lessa interjected.

Some subtle difference in her tone caused F'lar to glance quickly at her. It wasn't anger now over having missed the morning's phenomenon. Her eyes were fixed on nothing; her face, smooth at first, was soon wrinkled with a vaguely anxious frown as tiny lines formed between her arching, well-defined brows.

"Dawn . . . that's when all warnings come," she murmured.

"What kind of warnings?" he asked with quiet encouragement.

"There was that morning . . . a few days before . . . before you and Fax descended on Ruath Hold. Something woke me . . . a feeling, like a very heavy pressure . . . the sensation of some terrible danger threatening." She was silent. "The Red Star was just rising." The fingers of her left hand opened and closed. She gave a convulsive shudder. Her eyes refocused on him.

"You and Fax did come out of the northeast from Crom," she said sharply, ignoring the fact, F'lar noticed, that the Red Star also rises north of true east.

"Indeed we did," he grinned at her, remembering that morning vividly. "Although," he added, gesturing around the great cavern to emphasize, "I prefer to believe I served you well that day . . . you remember it with displeasure?"

The look she gave him was coldly inscrutable.

"Danger comes in many guises."

"I agree," he replied amiably, determined not to rise to her bait. "Had any other rude awakenings?" he inquired conversationally.

The absolute stillness in the room brought his attention back to her. Her face had drained of all color.

"The day Fax invaded Ruath Hold." Her voice was a barely articulated whisper. Her eyes were wide and staring. Her hands clenched the edge of the table. She said nothing for such a long interval that F'lar became concerned. This was an unexpectedly violent reaction to a casual question.

"Tell me," he suggested softly.

She spoke in unemotional, impersonal tones, as if she were reciting a Traditional Ballad or something that had happened to an entirely different person.

"I was a child. Just eleven. I woke at dawn . . ." Her voice trailed off. Her eyes remained focused on nothing, staring at a scene that had happened long ago.

F'lar was stirred by an irresistible desire to comfort her. It struck him forcibly, even as he was stirred by this unusual compassion, that he had never thought that Lessa, of all people, would be troubled by so old a terror.

Mnementh sharply informed his rider that Lessa was obviously bothered a good deal. Enough so that her mental anguish was rousing Ramoth from sleep. In less accusing tones Mnementh informed F'lar that R'gul had finally taken off with his weyrling pupils. His dragon, Hath, however, was in a fine state of disorientation due to R'gul's state of mind. Must F'lar unsettle everyone in the Weyr . . .

"Oh, be quiet," F'lar retorted under his breath.

"Why?" Lessa demanded in her normal voice.

"I didn't mean you, my dear Weyrwoman," he assured her, smiling pleasantly, as if the entranced interlude had never occurred. "Mnementh is full of advice these days."

"Like rider, like dragon," she replied tartly.

Ramoth yawned mightily. Lessa was instantly on her feet, running to her dragon's side, her slight figure dwarfed by the six-foot dragon head.

A tender, adoring expression flooded her face as she gazed into Ramoth's gleaming opalescent eyes. F'lar clenched his teeth, envious, by the Egg, of a rider's affection for her dragon.

In his mind he heard Mnementh's dragon equivalent of laughter.

"She's hungry," Lessa informed F'lar, an echo of her love for Ramoth lingering in the soft line of her mouth, in the kindness in her gray eyes.

"She's always hungry," he observed and followed them out of the weyr.

Mnementh hovered courteously just beyond the ledge until Lessa and Ramoth had taken off. They glided down the Weyr Bowl, over the misty bathing lake, toward the feeding ground at the opposite end of the long oval that comprised the floor of Benden Weyr. The striated, precipitous walls were pierced with the black mouths of single weyr entrances, deserted at this time of day by the few dragons who might otherwise doze on their ledges in the wintry sun.

As F'lar vaulted to Mnementh's smooth bronze neck, he hoped that Ramoth's clutch would be spectacular, erasing the ignominy of the paltry dozen Nemorth had laid in each of her last few clutches.

He had no serious doubts of the improvement after Ramoth's remarkable mating flight with his Mnementh. The bronze dragon smugly echoed his rider's certainty, and both looked on the queen possessively as she curved her wings to land. She was twice Nemorth's size, for one thing; her wings were half-a-wing again longer than Mnementh's, who was the biggest of the seven male bronzes. F'lar looked to Ramoth to repopulate the five empty Weyrs, even as he looked to himself and Lessa to rejuvenate the pride and faith of dragonriders and of Pern itself. He only hoped time enough remained to him to do what was necessary. The Red Star had been bracketed by the Eye Rock. The Threads would soon be falling. Somewhere, in one of the other Weyrs' Records, must be the information he needed to ascertain *when*, exactly, Threads would fall.

Mnementh landed. F'lar jumped down from the curving neck to stand beside Lessa. The three watched as Ramoth, a buck grasped in each of her forefeet, rose to a feeding ledge.

"Will her appetite never taper off?" Lessa asked with affectionate dismay.

As a dragonet, Ramoth had been eating to grow. Her full stature attained, she was, of course, now eating for her young, and she applied herself conscientiously.

F'lar chuckled and squatted, hunter fashion. He picked up shale-flakes, skating them across the flat dry ground, counting the dust puffs boyishly.

"The time will come when she won't eat everything in sight," he assured Lessa. "But she's young . . ."

". . . and needs her strength," Lessa interrupted, her voice a fair imitation of R'gul's pedantic tones.

F'lar looked up at her, squinting against the wintry sun that slanted down at them.

"She's a finely grown beast, especially compared to Nemorth." He gave a contemptuous snort. "In fact, there *is* no comparison. However, look here," he ordered peremptorily.

He tapped the smoothed sand in front of him, and she saw that his apparently idle gestures had been to a purpose. With a sliver of stone, he drew a design in quick strokes.

"In order to fly a dragon *between*, he has to know where to go. And so do you." He grinned at the astonished and infuriated look of comprehension on her face. "Ah, but there are certain consequences to an ill-considered jump. Badly visualized reference points often result in staying *between*." His voice dropped ominously. Her face cleared of its resentment. "So there are certain reference or recognition points arbitrarily taught all weyrlings. That,"—he pointed first to his facsimile and then to the actual Star Stone with its Finger and Eye Rock companions, on Benden Peak—"is the first recognition point a weyrling learns. When I take you aloft, you will reach an altitude just above the Star Stone, near enough for you to be able to see the hole in the Eye Rock clearly. Fix that picture sharply in your mind's eye, relay it to Ramoth. That will always get you home."

"Understood. But how do I learn recognition points of places I've never seen?"

He grinned up at her. "You're drilled in them. First by your instructor," and he pointed the sliver at his chest, "and then by going there, having directed your dragon to get the visualization from her instructor," and he indicated Mnementh. The bronze dragon lowered his wedge-shaped head until one eye was focused on his rider and his mate's rider. He made a pleased noise deep in his chest.

Lessa laughed up at the gleaming eye and, with unexpected affection, patted the soft nose.

F'lar cleared his throat in surprise. He had been aware that Mnementh showed an unusual affection for the Weyrwoman, but he had had no idea Lessa was fond of the bronze. Perversely, he was irritated.

"However," he said, and his voice sounded unnatural to himself, "we take the young riders constantly to and from the main reference points all across Pern, to all the Holds so that they have eyewitness impressions on which to rely. As a rider becomes adept in picking out landmarks, he gets additional references from other riders. Therefore, to go *between*, there is actually only one requirement: a clear picture of where you want to go. *And* a dragon!" He grinned at her. "Also, you should always plan to arrive above your reference point in clear air."

Lessa frowned.

"It is better to arrive in open air"—F'lar waved a hand above his head—"rather than underground," and he slapped his open hand onto the dirt. A puff of dust rose warningly.

"But the wings took off within the Bowl itself the day the Lords of the Hold arrived," Lessa reminded him.

F'lar chuckled at her uptake. "True, but only the most seasoned riders. Once we came across a dragon and a rider entombed together in solid rock. They . . . were . . . very young." His eyes were bleak.

"I take the point," she assured him gravely. "That's her fifth," she added, pointing toward Ramoth, who was carrying her latest kill up to the bloody ledge.

"She'll work them off today, I assure you," F'lar remarked. He rose, brushing off his knees with sharp slaps of his riding gloves. "Test her temper."

Lessa did so with a silent, *Had enough?* She grimaced at Ramoth's indignant rejection of the thought.

The queen went swooping down for a huge fowl, rising in a flurry of gray, brown and white feathers.

"She's not as hungry as she's making you think, the deceitful creature," F'lar chuckled and saw that Lessa had reached the same conclusion. Her eyes were snapping with vexation.

"When you've finished the bird, Ramoth, do let us learn how to fly *between*," Lessa said aloud for F'lar's benefit, "before our good Weyrleader changes his mind."

Ramoth looked up from her gorging, turned her head toward the two riders at the edge of the feeding ground. Her eyes gleamed. She bent her head again to her kill, but Lessa could sense the dragon would obey.

It was cold aloft. Lessa was glad of the fur lining in her riding gear, and the warmth of the great golden neck which she bestrode. She decided not to think of the absolute cold of *between* which she had experienced only once. She glanced below on her right where bronze Mnementh hovered, and she caught his amused thought.

F'lar tells me to tell Ramoth to tell you to fix the alignment of the Star Stone firmly in your mind as a homing. Then, Mnementh went on amiably, *we shall fly down to the lake. You will return from* between *to this exact point. Do you understand?*

Lessa found herself grinning foolishly with anticipation and nodded vigorously. How much time was saved because she could speak directly to the dragons! Ramoth made a disgruntled noise deep in her throat. Lessa patted her reassuringly.

"Have you got the picture in your mind, dear one?" she asked, and Ramoth again rumbled, less annoyed, because she was catching Lessa's excitement.

Mnementh stroked the cold air with his wings, greenish-brown in the sunlight, and curved down gracefully toward the lake on the plateau below Benden Weyr. His flight line took him very low over the rim of the Weyr. From Lessa's angle, it looked like a collision course. Ramoth followed closely in his wake. Lessa caught her breath at the sight of the jagged boulders just below Ramoth's wing tips.

It was exhilarating, Lessa crowed to herself, doubly stimulated by the elation that flowed back to her from Ramoth.

Mnementh halted above the farthest shore of the lake, and there, too, Ramoth came to hover.

Mnementh flashed the thought to Lessa that she was to place the picture of where she wished to go firmly in her mind and direct Ramoth to get there.

Lessa complied. The next instant the awesome, bone-penetrating cold of black *between* enveloped them. Before either she or Ramoth was aware of more than that biting touch of cold and impregnable darkness, they were above the Star Stone.

Lessa let out a cry of pure triumph.

It is extremely simple. Ramoth seemed disappointed.

Mnementh reappeared beside and slightly below them.

You are to return by the same route to the Lake, he ordered, and before the thought had finished, Ramoth took off.

Mnementh was beside them above the lake, fuming with his own and F'lar's anger. *You did not visualize before transferring. Don't think a first successful trip makes you perfect. You have no conception of the dangers inherent in* between. *Never fail to picture your arrival point again.*

Lessa glanced down at F'lar. Even two wingspans apart, she could see the vivid anger on his face, almost feel the fury flashing from his eyes. And laced through the wrath, a terrible sinking fearfulness for her safety that was a more effective reprimand than his wrath. Lessa's safety, she wondered bitterly, or Ramoth's?

You are to follow us, Mnementh was saying in a calmer tone, *rehearsing in your mind the two reference points you have already learned. We shall jump to and from them this morning, gradually learning other points around Benden.*

They did. Flying as far away as Benden Hold itself, nestled against the foothills above Benden Valley, the Weyr Peak a far point against the noonday sky, Lessa did not neglect to visualize a clearly detailed impression each time.

This was as marvelously exciting as she had hoped it would be, Lessa confided to Ramoth. Ramoth replied: yes, it was certainly preferable to the timeconsuming methods others had to use, but she didn't think it was exciting at all to jump *between* from Benden Weyr to Benden Hold and back to Benden Weyr again. It was dull.

They had met with Mnementh above the Star Stone again. The bronze dragon sent Lessa the message that this was a very satisfactory initial session. They would practice some distant jumping tomorrow.

Tomorrow, thought Lessa glumly, some emergency will occur or our hard-working Weyrleader will decide today's session constitutes keeping his promise and that will be that.

There was one jump she could make *between*, from anywhere on Pern, and not miss her mark.

She visualized Ruatha for Ramoth as seen from the heights above the Hold . . . to satisfy that requirement. To be scrupulously clear, Lessa projected the pattern of the firepits. Before Fax invaded and she had had to manipulate its decline, Ruatha had been such a lovely, prosperous valley. She told Ramoth to jump *between*.

The cold was intense and seemed to last for many heartbeats. Just as Lessa began to fear that she had somehow lost them *between*, they exploded into the air above the Hold. Elation filled her. That for F'lar and his excessive caution! With Ramoth she could jump anywhere! For there was the distinctive pattern of Ruatha's fire-guttered heights. It was just before dawn, the Breast Pass between Crom and Ruatha, black cones against the lightening gray sky. Fleetingly she noticed the absence of the Red Star that now blazed in the dawn sky. And fleetingly she noticed a difference in the air. Chill, yes, but not wintry . . . the air held that moist coolness of early spring.

Startled, she glanced downward, wondering if she could have, for all her assurance, erred in some fashion. But no, this was Ruath Hold. The Tower, the inner Court, the aspect of the broad avenue leading down to the crafthold were just as they should be. Wisps of smoke from distant chimneys indicated people were making ready for the day.

Ramoth caught the tenor of her insecurity and began to press for an explanation.

This is Ruatha, Lessa replied stoutly. *It can be no other. Circle the heights. See, there are the firepit lines I gave you. . .*

Lessa gasped, the coldness in her stomach freezing her muscles.

Below her in the slowly lifting predawn gloom, she saw the figures of many men toiling over the breast of the cliff from the hills beyond Ruatha, men moving with quiet stealth like criminals.

She ordered Ramoth to keep as still as possible in the air so as not to direct their attention upward. The dragon was curious but obedient.

Who would be attacking Ruatha? It seemed incredible. Lytol was, after all, a former dragonman and had savagely repelled one attack already. Could there possibly be a thought of aggression among the Holds now that F'lar was Weyrleader? And what Hold Lord would be foolish enough to mount a territorial war in the winter?

No, not winter. The air was definitely springlike.

The men crept on, over the firepits to the edge of the heights. Suddenly Lessa realized they were lowering rope ladders over the face of the cliff, down toward the open shutters of the Inner Hold.

Wildly she clutched at Ramoth's neck, certain of what she saw.

This was the invader Fax, now dead nearly three Turns—Fax and his men as they began their attack on Ruatha nearly thirteen Turns ago.

Yes, there was the Tower guard, his face a white blot turned toward the Cliff itself, watching. He had been paid his bribe to stand silent this morning.

But the watch-wher, trained to give alarm for any intrusion— why was it not trumpeting its warning? Why was it silent?

Because, Ramoth informed her rider with calm logic, *it senses your presence as well as mine, so how could the Hold be in danger?*

No, No! Lessa moaned. *What can I do now? How can I wake them? Where is the girl I was? I was asleep, and then I woke. I remember. I dashed from my room. I was so scared. I went down the steps and nearly fell. I knew I had to get to the watch-wher's kennel. . . . I knew. . . .*

Lessa clutched at Ramoth's neck for support as past acts and mysteries became devastatingly clear.

She herself had warned herself, just as it was her presence on the queen dragon that had kept the watch-wher from giving alarm. For as she watched, stunned and speechless, she saw the small, gray-robed figure that could only be herself as a youngster, burst from the Hold Hall door, race uncertainly down the cold stone steps into the Court, and disappear into the watch-wher's stinking den. Faintly she heard it crying in piteous confusion.

Just as Lessa-the-girl reached that doubtful sanctuary, Fax's invaders swooped into the open window embrasures and began the slaughter of her sleeping family.

"Back—back to the Star Stone!" Lessa cried. In her wide and staring eyes she held the image of the guiding rocks like a rudder for her sanity as well as Ramoth's direction.

The intense cold acted as a restorative. And then they were above the quiet, peaceful wintry Weyr as if they had never paradoxically visited Ruatha.

F'lar and Mnementh were nowhere to be seen.

Ramoth, however, was unshaken by the experience. She had only gone where she had been told to go and had not quite understood that going where she had been told to go had shocked Lessa. She suggested to her rider that Mnementh had probably followed them to Ruatha so if Lessa would give her the *proper* references, she'd take her there. Ramoth's sensible attitude was comforting.

Lessa carefully drew for Ramoth not the child's memory of a long-vanished, idyllic Ruatha but her more recent recollection of the Hold, gray, sullen, at dawning, with a Red Star pulsing on the horizon.

And there they were again, hovering over the Valley, the Hold below them on the right. The grasses grew untended on the heights, clogging firepit and brickwork; the scene showed all the deterioration she had encouraged in her effort to thwart Fax of any profit from conquering Ruath Hold.

But, as she watched, vaguely disturbed, she saw a figure emerge from the kitchen, saw the watch-wher creep from its lair and follow the raggedly dressed figure as far across the Court as the chain permitted. She saw the figure ascend the Tower, gaze first eastward, then northeastward. This was still not Ruatha of today and now! Lessa's mind reeled, disoriented. This time she had come back to visit herself of three Turns ago, to see the filthy drudge plotting revenge on Fax.

She felt the absolute cold of *between* as Ramoth snatched them back, emerging once more above the Star Stone. Lessa was shuddering, her eyes frantically taking in the reassuring sight of the Weyr Bowl, hoping she had not somehow shifted backward in time yet again. Mnementh suddenly erupted into the air a few lengths below and beyond Ramoth. Lessa greeted him with a cry of intense relief.

Back to your weyr! There was no disguising the white fury in Mnementh's tone. Lessa was too unnerved to respond in any way other than instant compliance. Ramoth glided swiftly to their ledge, quickly clearing the perch for Mnementh to land.

The rage on F'lar's face as he leaped from Mnementh and advanced on Lessa brought her wits back abruptly. She made no move to evade him as he grabbed her shoulders and shook her violently.

"How dare you risk yourself and Ramoth? Why must you defy me at every opportunity? Do you realize what would happen to all Pern if we lost Ramoth? Where did you go?" He was spitting with anger, punctuating each question that tumbled from his lips by giving her a head-wrenching shake.

"Ruatha," she managed to say, trying to keep herself erect. She reached out to catch at his arms, but he shook her again.

"Ruatha? We were there. You weren't. Where did you go?"

"Ruatha!" Lessa cried louder, clutching at him distractedly because he kept jerking her off balance. She couldn't organize her thoughts with him jolting her around.

She was at Ruatha, Mnementh said firmly.

We were there twice, Ramoth added.

As the dragons' calmer words penetrated F'lar's fury, he stopped shaking Lessa. She hung limply in his grasp, her hands weakly plucking at his arms, her eyes closed, her face gray. He picked her up and strode rapidly into the queen's Weyr, the dragons following. He placed her upon the couch, wrapping her tightly in the fur cover. He called down the service shaft for the duty cook to send up hot *klah*.

"All right, what happened?" he demanded.

She didn't look at him, but he got a glimpse of her haunted eyes. She blinked constantly as if she longed to erase what she had just seen.

Finally she got herself somewhat under control and said in a low, tired voice, "I did go to Ruatha. Only . . . I went *back* to Ruatha."

"Back to Ruatha?" F'lar repeated the words stupidly; the significance momentarily eluded him.

It certainly does, Mnementh agreed and flashed to F'lar's mind the two scenes he had picked out of Ramoth's memory.

Staggered by the import of the visualization, F'lar found himself slowly sinking to the edge of the bed.

"You went *between* times?"

She nodded slowly. The terror was beginning to leave her eyes.

"*Between* times," F'lar murmured. "I wonder . . ."

His mind raced through the possiblities. It might well tip the scales of survival in the Weyr's favor. He couldn't think exactly how to use this extraordinary ability, but there *must* be an advantage in it for dragonfolk.

The service shaft rumbled. He took the pitcher from the platform and poured two mugs.

Lessa's hands were shaking so much that she couldn't get hers to her lips. He steadied it for her, wondering if going *between* times would regularly cause this kind of shock. If so, it wouldn't be any advantage at all. If she'd had enough of a scare this day, she might not be so contemptuous of his orders the next time; which would be to his benefit.

Outside in the weyr, Mnementh snorted his opinion on that. F'lar ignored him.

Lessa was trembling violently now. He put an arm around her, pressing the fur against her slender body. He held the mug to her lips, forcing her to drink. He could feel the tremors ease off. She took long, slow, deep breaths between swallows, equally determined to get herself under control. The moment he felt her stiffen under his arm, he released her. He wondered if Lessa had ever had someone to turn to. Certainly not after Fax invaded her family Hold. She had been only eleven, a child. Had hate and revenge been the only emotions the growing girl had practiced?

She lowered the mug, cradling it in her hands carefully as if it had assumed some undefinable importance to her.

"Now. Tell me," he ordered evenly.

She took a long deep breath and began to speak, her hands tightening around the mug. Her inner turmoil had not lessened; it was merely under control now.

"Ramoth and I were bored with the weyrling exercises," she admitted candidly.

Grimly F'lar recognized that, while the adventure might have taught her to be more circumspect, it had not scared her into obedience. He doubted that anything would.

"I gave her the picture of Ruatha so we could go *between* there." She did not look at him, but her profile was outlined against the dark fur of the rug. "The Ruatha I knew so well—I accidentally sent myself backward in time to the day Fax invaded."

Her shock was now comprehensible to him.

"And . . ." he prompted her, his voice carefully neutral.

"And I saw myself—" Her voice broke off. With an effort she continued. "I had visualized for Ramoth the designs of the firepits and the angle of the Hold if one looked down from the pits into the Inner Court. That was where we emerged. It was just dawn"—she lifted her chin with a nervous jerk—"and there was no Red Star in the sky." She gave him a quick, defensive look as if she expected him to contest this detail. "And I saw men creeping over the firepits, lowering rope ladders to the top windows of the Hold. I saw the Tower guard watching. Just watching." She clenched her teeth at such treachery, and her eyes gleamed malevolently. "And I saw myself run from the Hall into the watch-wher's lair. And do you know why"—her voice lowered to a bitter whisper—"the watch-wher did not alarm the Hold?"

"Why?"

"Because there was a dragon in the sky, and *I*, Lessa of Ruatha, was on her." She flung the mug from her as if she wished she could reject the knowledge, too. "Because *I* was there, the watch-wher did not alarm the Hold, thinking the intrusion legitimate, with one of the Blood on a dragon in the sky. So I"—her body grew rigid, her hands clasped so tightly that the knuckles were white—"*I* was the cause of my family's massacre. Not Fax! If I had not acted the captious fool today, I would not have been there with Ramoth and the watch-wher would—"

Her voice had risen to an hysterical pitch of recrimination. He slapped her sharply across the cheeks, grabbing her, robe and all, to shake her.

The stunned look in her eyes and the tragedy in her face alarmed him. His indignation over her willfulness disappeared. Her unruly independence of mind and spirit attracted him as much as her curious dark beauty. Infuriating as her fractious ways might be, they were too vital a part of her integrity to be exorcised. Her indomitable will had taken a grievous shock today, and her self-confidence had better be restored quickly.

"On the contrary, Lessa," he said sternly, "Fax would still have murdered your family. He had planned it very carefully, even to scheduling his attack on the morning when the Tower guard was one who could be bribed. Remember, too, it was dawn and the watch-wher, being a nocturnal beast, blind by daylight, is relieved of responsibility at dawn and knows it. Your presence, damnable as it may appear to you, was not the deciding factor by any means. It did, and I draw your attention to this very important fact, cause you to save youself, by warning Lessa-the-child. Don't you see that?"

"I could have called out," she murmured, but the frantic look had left her eyes and there was a faint hint of normal color in her lips.

"If you wish to flail around in guilt, go right ahead," he said with deliberate callousness.

Ramoth interjected a thought that, since the two of them had been there that previous time as Fax's men had prepared to invade, it had already happened, so how could it be changed? The act was inevitable both that day and today. For how else could Lessa have lived to come to the Weyr and impress Ramoth at the hatching?

Mnementh relayed Ramoth's message scrupulously, even to imitating Ramoth's egocentric nuances. F'lar looked sharply at Lessa to see the effect of Ramoth's astringent observation.

"Just like Ramoth to have the final word," she said with a hint of her former droll humor.

F'lar felt the muscles along his neck and shoulders begin to relax. She'd be all right, he decided, but it might be wiser to make her talk it all out now, to put the whole experience into proper perspective.

"You said you were there twice?" He leaned back on the couch, watching her closely. "When was the second time?"

"Can't you guess?" she asked sarcastically.

"No," he lied.

"When else but the dawn I was awakened, feeling the Red Star was a menace to me? . . . Three days before you and Fax came out of the northeast."

"It would seem," he remarked dryly, "that you were your own premonition both times."

She nodded.

"Have you had any more of these presentiments . . . or should I say reinforced warnings?"

She shuddered but answered him with more of her old spirit.

"No, but if I should, *you* go. I don't want to."

F'lar grinned maliciously.

"I would, however," she added, "like to know why and how it could happen."

"I've never run across a mention of it anywhere," he told her candidly. "Of course, if you have done it—and you undeniably have," he assured her hastily at her indignant protest, "it obviously can be done. You say you thought of Ruatha, but you thought of it as it was on that particular day. Certainly a day to be remembered. You thought of spring, before dawn, no Red Star—yes, I remember your mentioning that—so one would have to remember references peculiar to a significant day to return *between* times to the past."

She nodded slowly, thoughtfully.

"You used the same method the second time, to get to the Ruatha of three Turns ago. Again, of course, it was spring."

He rubbed his palms together, then brought his hands down on his knees with an emphatic slap and rose to his feet.

"I'll be back," he said and strode from the room, ignoring her half-articulated cry of warning.

Ramoth was curling up in the Weyr as he passed her. He noticed that her color remained good in spite of the drain on her energies by the morning's exercises. She glanced at him, her many-faceted eye already covered by the inner, protective lid.

Mnementh awaited his rider on the ledge, and the moment F'lar leaped to his neck, took off. He circled upward, hovering above the Star Stone.

You wish to try Lessa's trick, Mnementh said, unperturbed by the prospective experiment.

F'lar stroked the great curved neck affectionately. *You understand how it worked for Ramoth and Lessa?*

As well as anyone can, Mnementh replied with the approximation of a shrug. *When did you have in mind?*

Before that moment F'lar had had no idea. Now, unerringly, his thoughts drew him backward to the summer day R'gul's bronze Hath had flown to mate the grotesque Nemorth, and R'gul had become Weyrleader in place of his dead father, F'lon.

Only the cold of *between* gave them any indication that they had transferred; they were still hovering above the Star Stone. F'lar wondered if they had missed some essential part of the transfer. Then he realized that the sun was in another quarter of the sky and the air was warm and sweet with summer. The Weyr below was empty; there were no dragons sunning themselves on the ledges, no women busy at tasks in the Bowl. Noises impinged on his senses: raucous laughter, yells, shrieks, and a soft crooning noise that dominated the bedlam.

Then, from the direction of the weyrling barracks in the Lower Caverns, two figures emerged—a stripling and a young bronze dragon. The boy's arm lay limply along the beast's neck. The impression that reached the hovering observers was one of utter dejection. The two halted by the lake, the boy peering into the unruffled blue waters, then glancing upward toward the queen's weyr.

F'lar knew the boy for himself, and compassion for that younger self filled him. If only he could reassure that boy, so torn by grief, so filled with resentment, that he would one day become Weyrleader. . . .

Abruptly, startled by his own thoughts, he ordered Mnementh to transfer back. The utter cold of *between* was like a slap in his face, replaced almost instantly as they broke out of *between* into the cold of normal winter.

Slowly, Mnementh flew back down to the queen's weyr, as sobered as F'lar by what they had seen.

> Rise high in glory,   Count three months and more,
> Bronze and gold.   And five heated weeks,
> Dive entwined,   A day of glory and
> Enhance the Hold.   In a month, who seeks?
>
> A strand of silver
> In the sky . . .
> With heat, all quickens
> And all times fly.

"I don't know why you insisted that F'nor unearth these ridiculous things from Ista Weyr," Lessa exclaimed in a tone of exasperation. "They consist of nothing but trivial notes on how many measures of grain were used to bake daily bread."

F'lar glanced up at her from the Records he was studying. He sighed, leaned back in his chair in a bone-popping stretch.

"And I used to think," Lessa said with a rueful expression on her vivid, narrow face, "that those venerable Records would hold the total sum of all dragonlore and human wisdom. Or so I was led to believe," she added pointedly.

F'lar chuckled. "They do, but you have to disinter it."

Lessa wrinkled her nose. "Phew. They smell as if we had . . . and the only decent thing to do would be to rebury them."

"Which is another item I'm hoping to find . . . the old preservative technique that kept the skins from hardening and smelling."

"It's stupid, anyhow, to use skins for recording. There ought to be something better. We have become, dear Weyrleader, entirely too hidebound."

While F'lar roared with appreciation of her pun, she regarded him impatiently. Suddenly she jumped up, fired by another of her mercurial moods.

"Well, you won't find it. You won't find the facts you're looking for. Because I know what you're really after, and it isn't recorded!"

"Explain yourself."

"It's time we stopped hiding a rather brutal truth from ourselves."

"Which is?"

"Our mutual feeling that the Red Star is a menace and that the Threads *will* come! We decided that out of pure conceit and then went back *between* times to particularly crucial points in our lives and strengthened that notion, in our earlier selves. And for you, it was when you decided you were destined"—her voice made the word mocking—"to become Weyrleader one day."

"Could it be," she went on scornfully, "that our ultraconservative R'gul has the right of it? That there have been no Threads for four hundred Turns because there are no more? And that the reason we have so few dragons is because the dragons sense they are no longer essential to Pern? That we *are* anachronisms as well as parasites?"

F'lar did not know how long he sat looking up at her bitter face or how long it took him to find answers to her probing questions.

"Anything is possible, Weyrwoman," he heard his voice replying calmly. "Including the unlikely fact that an eleven-year-old child, scared stiff, could plot revenge on her family's murderer and—against all odds—succeed."

She took an involuntary step forward, struck by his unexpected rebuttal. She listened intently.

"I prefer to believe," he went on inexorably, "that there is more to life than raising dragons and playing spring games. That is not enough for me. And I have made others look further, beyond self-interest and comfort. I have given them a purpose, a discipline. Everyone, dragonfolk and Holder alike, profits.

"I am not looking in these Records for reassurance. I'm looking for solid facts."

"I can prove, Weyrwoman, that there have been Threads. I can prove that there have been Intervals during which the Weyrs have declined. I can prove that if you sight the Red Star directly bracketed by the Eye Rock at the moment of winter solstice, the Red Star will pass close enough to Pern to throw off Threads. Since I can prove those facts, I believe Pern is in danger. *I* believe . . . not the youngster of fifteen Turns ago. F'lar, the bronze rider, the Weyrleader, believes it!"

He saw her eyes reflecting shadowy doubts, but he sensed his arguments were beginning to reassure her.

"You felt constrained to believe in me once before," he went on in a milder voice, "when I suggested that you could be Weyrwoman. You believed me and . . ." He made a gesture around the weyr as substantiation.

She gave him a weak, humorless smile.

"That was because I had never planned what to do with my life once I did have Fax lying dead at my feet. Of course, being Ramoth's Weyrmate is wonderful, but"—she frowned slightly—"it isn't enough anymore, either. That's why I wanted so to learn to fly and . . ."

". . . that's how this argument started in the first place," F'lar finished for her with a sardonic smile.

He leaned across the table urgently.

"Believe with me, Lessa, until you have cause not to. I respect your doubts. There's nothing wrong in doubting. It sometimes leads to greater faith. But believe with me until spring. If the Threads have not fallen by then . . ." He shrugged fatalistically.

She looked at him for a long moment and then inclined her head slowly in agreement.

He tried to suppress the relief he felt at her decision. Lessa, as Fax had discovered, was a ruthless adversary and a canny advocate. Besides these, she was Weyrwoman: essential to his plans.

"Now, let's get back to the contemplation of trivia. They do tell me, you know, time, place, and duration of Thread incursions," he grinned up at her reassuringly. "And those facts I must have to make up my timetable."

"Timetable? But you said you didn't know the time."

"Not the day to the second when the Threads may spin down. For one thing, while the weather holds so unusually cold for this time of year, the Threads simply turn brittle and blow away like dust. They're harmless. However, when the air is warm, they are viable and . . . deadly." He made fists of both hands, placing one above and to one side of the other. "The Red Star is my right hand, my left is Pern. The Red Star turns very fast and in the opposite direction from us. It also wobbles erratically."

"How do you know that?"

"Diagram on the walls of the Fort Weyr Hatching Ground. That was the very first Weyr, you know."

Lessa smiled sourly. "I know."

"So, when the Star makes a pass, the Threads spin off, down toward us, in attacks that last six hours and occur approximately fourteen hours apart."

"Attacks last six hours?"

He nodded gravely.

"When the Red Star is closest to us. Right now it is just beginning its Pass."

She frowned.

He rummaged among the skin sheets on the table, and an object dropped to the stone floor with a metallic clatter.

Curious, Lessa bent to pick it up, turning the thin sheet over in her hands.

"What's this?" She ran an exploratory finger lightly across the irregular design on one side.

"I don't know. F'nor brought it back from Fort Weyr. It was nailed to one of the chests in which the Records had been stored. He brought it along, thinking it might be important. Said there was a plate like it just under the Red Star diagram on the wall of the Hatching Ground."

"This first part is plain enough: 'Mother's father's father, who departed for all time *between*, said this was the key to the mystery, and it came to him while doodling: he said that he said: ARRHENIUS? EUREKA! MYCORRHIZA. . . .' Of course, that part doesn't make any sense at all," Lessa snorted. "It isn't even Pernese—just babbling, those last three words."

"I've studied it, Lessa," F'lar replied, glancing at it again and tipping it toward him to reaffirm his conclusions. "The only way to depart for all time *between* is to die, right? People just don't fly away on their own, obviously. So it is a death vision, dutifully recorded by a grandchild, who couldn't spell very well either. 'Doodling' as the present tense of dying!" He smiled indulgently. "And as for the rest of it, after the nonsense—like most death visions, it 'explains' what everyone has always known. Read on."

"'Flamethrowing fire-lizards to wipe out the spores. Q.E.D.'?"

"No help there, either. Obviously just a primitive rejoicing that he is a dragonman, who didn't even know the right word for Threads." F'lar's shrug was expressive.

Lessa wet one fingertip to see if the patterns were inked on. The metal was shiny enough for a good mirror if she could get rid of the designs. However, the patterns remained smooth and precise.

"Primitive or no, they had a more permanent way of recording their visions that is superior to even the well-preserved skins," she murmured.

"Well-preserved babblings," F'lar said, turning back to the skins he was checking for understandable data.

"A badly scored ballad?" Lessa wondered and then dismissed the whole thing. "The design isn't even pretty."

F'lar pulled forward a chart that showed overlapping horizontal bands imposed on the projection of Pern's continental mass.

"Here," he said, "this represents waves of attack, and this one"— he pulled forward the second map with vertical bandings—"shows time zones. So you can see that with a fourteen-hour break only certain parts of Pern are affected in each attack. One reason for spacing of the Weyrs."

"Six full Weyrs," she murmured, "close to three thousand dragons."

"I'm aware of the statistics," he replied in a voice devoid of expression. "It meant no one Weyr was overburdened during the height of the attacks, not that three thousand beasts must be available. However, with these timetables, we can manage until Ramoth's first clutches have matured."

She turned a cynical look on him. "You've a lot of faith in one queen's capacity."

He waved that remark aside impatiently. "I've more faith, no matter what your opinion is, in the startling repetitions of events in these Records."

"Ha!"

"I don't mean how many measures for daily bread, Lessa," he

retorted, his voice rising. "I mean such things as the time such and such a wing was sent out on patrol, how long the patrol lasted, how many riders were hurt. The brooding capacities of queens, during the fifty years a Pass lasts and the Intervals between such Passes. Yes, it tells that. By all I've studied here," and he pounded emphatically on the nearest stack of dusty, smelly skins, "Nemorth should have been mating twice a Turn for the last ten. Had she even kept to her paltry twelve a clutch, we'd have two hundred and forty more beasts. . . . Don't interrupt. But we had Jora as Weyrwoman and R'gul as Weyrleader, and we had fallen into planet-wide disfavor during a four hundred Turn Interval. Well, Ramoth will brood over no measly dozen, and she'll lay a queen egg, mark my words. She will rise often to mate and lay generously. By the time the Red Star is passing closest to us and the attacks become frequent, we'll be ready."

She stared at him, her eyes wide with incredulity. "Out of Ramoth?"

"Out of Ramoth and out of the queens she'll lay. Remember, there are Records of Faranth laying sixty eggs at a time, including several queen eggs."

Lessa could only shake her head slowly in wonder.

"'A strand of silver/In the sky. . . . With heat, all quickens/And all times fly,'" F'lar quoted to her.

"She's got weeks more to go before laying, and then the eggs must hatch . . ."

"Been on the Hatching Ground recently? Wear your boots. You'll be burned through sandals."

She dismissed that with a guttural noise. He sat back, outwardly amused by her disbelief.

"And then you have to make Impression and wait till the riders—"she went on.

"Why do you think I've insisted on older boys? The dragons are mature long before their riders."

"Then the system is faulty."

He narrowed his eyes slightly, shaking the stylus at her.

"Dragon tradition started out as a guide . . . but there comes a time when man becomes too traditional, too—what was it you said?— too hidebound? Yes, it's traditional to use the weyrbred, because it's been convenient. And because this sensitivity to dragons strengthens where both sire and dam are weyrbred. That doesn't mean weyrbred is best. You, for example . . ."

"There's Weyrblood in the Ruathan line," she said proudly.

"Granted. Take young Naton; he's craftbred from Nabol, yet F'nor tells me he can make Canth understand him."

"Oh, that's not hard to do," she interjected.

"What do you mean?" F'lar jumped on her statement.

They were both interrupted by a high-pitched, penetrating whine. F'lar listened intently for a moment and then shrugged, grinning.

"Some green's getting herself chased again."

"And that's another item these so-called all-knowing Records of yours never mention. Why is it that only the gold dragon can reproduce?"

F'lar did not suppress a lascivious chuckle.

"Well, for one thing, firestone inhibits reproduction. If they never chewed stone, a green could lay, but at best they produce small beasts, and we need big ones. And, for another thing"—his chuckle rolled out as he went on deliberately, grinning mischievously—"if the greens could reproduce, considering their amorousness and the numbers we have of them, we'd be up to our ears in dragons in next to no time."

The first whine was joined by another, and then a low hum throbbed as if carried by the stones of the Weyr itself.

F'lar, his face changing rapidly from surprise to triumphant astonishment, dashed up the passage.

"What's the matter?" Lessa demanded, picking up her skirts to run after him. "What does that mean?"

The hum, resonating everywhere, was deafening in the echo-chamber of the queen's weyr. Lessa registered the fact that Ramoth was gone. She heard F'lar's boots pounding down the passage to the ledge, a sharp *ta-ta-tat* over the kettledrum booming hum. The whine was so high-pitched now that it was inaudible, but still nerve-racking. Disturbed, frightened, Lessa followed F'lar out.

By the time she reached the ledge, the Bowl was a-whir with dragons on the wing, making for the high entrance to the Hatching Ground. Weyrfolk, riders, women, children, all screaming with excitement, were pouring across the Bowl to the lower entrance to the Ground.

She caught sight of F'lar, charging across to the entrance, and she shrieked at him to wait. He couldn't have heard her across the bedlam.

Fuming because she had the long stairs to descend, then must double back as the stairs faced the feeding grounds at the opposite end of the Bowl from the Hatching Ground, Lessa realized that she, the Weyrwoman, would be the last one there.

Why had Ramoth decided to be secretive about laying? Wasn't she close enough to her own weyrmate to want her with her?

A dragon knows what to do, Ramoth calmly informed Lessa.

You could have told me, Lessa wailed, feeling much abused.

Why, at the time F'lar had been going on largely about huge clutches and three thousand beasts, that infuriating dragon-child had been doing it!

It didn't improve Lessa's temper to have to recall another remark of F'lar's—on the state of the Hatching Grounds. The moment she stepped into the mountain-high cavern, she felt the heat through the soles of her sandals. Everyone was crowded in a loose circle around the far end of the cavern. And everyone was swaying from foot to foot. As Lessa was short to begin with, this only decreased the likelihood of her ever seeing what Ramoth had done.

"Let me through!" she demanded imperiously, pounding on the wide backs of two tall riders.

An aisle was reluctantly opened for her, and she went through, looking neither to her right or left at the excited weyrfolk. She was furious, confused, hurt, and knew she looked ridiculous because the hot sand made her walk with a curious mincing quickstep.

She halted, stunned and wide-eyed at the mass of eggs, and forgot such trivial things as hot feet.

Ramoth was curled around the clutch, looking enormously pleased with herself. She, too, kept shifting, closing and opening a protective wing over her eggs, so that it was difficult to count them.

No one will steal them, silly, so stop fluttering, Lessa advised as she tried to make a tally.

Obediently Ramoth folded her wings. To relieve her maternal anxiety, however, she snaked her head out across the circle of mottled, glowing eggs, looking all around the cavern, flicking her forked tongue in and out.

An immense sigh, like a gust of wind, swept through the cavern. For there, now that Ramoth's wings were furled, gleamed an egg of glowing gold among the mottled ones. A queen egg!

"A queen egg!" The cry went up simultaneously from half a hundred throats. The Hatching Ground rang with cheers, yells, screams, and howls of exultation.

Someone seized Lessa and swung her around in an excess of feeling. A kiss landed in the vicinity of her mouth. No sooner did she recover her footing than she was hugged by someone else—she thought it was Manora—and then pounded and buffeted around in congratulation until she was reeling in a kind of dance between avoiding the celebrants and easing the growing discomfort of her feet.

She broke from the milling revelers and ran across the Ground to Ramoth. Lessa came to a sudden stop before the eggs. They seemed to be pulsing. The shells looked flaccid. She could have sworn they were hard the day she Impressed Ramoth. She wanted to touch one, just to make sure, but dared not.

You may, Ramoth assured her condescendingly. She touched Lessa's shoulder gently with her tongue.

The egg was soft to touch and Lessa drew her hand back quickly, afraid of doing injury.

The heat will harden it, Ramoth said.

"Ramoth, I'm so proud of you," Lessa sighed, looking adoringly up at the great eyes that shone in rainbows of pride. "You are the most marvelous queen ever. I do believe you will redragon all the Weyrs. I do believe you will."

Ramoth inclined her head regally, then began to sway it from side to side over the eggs, protectingly. She began to hiss suddenly, raising from her crouch, beating the air with her wings, before settling back into the sands to lay yet another egg.

The weyrfolk, uncomfortable on the hot sands, were beginning to leave the Hatching Ground now that they had paid tribute to the arrival of the golden egg. A queen took several days to complete her clutch so there was no point to waiting. Seven eggs already lay beside the important golden one, and if there were seven already, this augured well for the eventual total. Wagers were being made and taken even as Ramoth produced her ninth mottled egg.

"Just as I predicted, a queen egg, by the mother of us all," F'lar's voice said in Lessa's ear. "And I'll wager there'll be ten bronzes at least."

She looked up at him, completely in harmony with the Weyrleader at this moment. She was conscious now of Mnementh, crouching proudly on a ledge, gazing fondly at his mate. Impulsively Lessa laid her hand on F'lar's arm.

"F'lar, I do believe you."

"Only now?" F'lar teased her, but his smile was wide and his eyes proud.

Weyrman, watch; Weyrman, learn
Something new in every Turn.
Oldest may be coldest, too.
Sense the right; find the true!

If F'lar's orders over the next months caused no end of discussion and muttering among the weyrfolk, they seemed to Lessa to be only the logical outcomes of their discussion after Ramoth had finished laying her gratifying total of forty-one eggs.

F'lar discarded tradition right and left, treading on more than R'gul's conservative toes.

Out of perverse distaste for outworn doctrines against which she

herself had chafed during R'gul's leadership, and out of respect for
F'lar's intelligence, Lessa backed him completely. She might not have
respected her earlier promise to him that she would believe with him
until spring if she had not seen his predictions come true, one after
another. These were based, however, not on the premonitions she no
longer trusted after her experience *between* times, but on recorded facts.

As soon as the eggshells hardened and Ramoth had rolled her
special queen egg to one side of the mottled clutch for attentive brooding, F'lar brought the prospective riders into the Hatching Ground.
Traditionally the candidates saw the eggs for the first time on the day
of Impression. To this precedent F'lar added others: very few of the
sixty-odd were weyrbred, and most of them were in their late teens.
The candidates were to get used to the eggs, touch them, caress them,
be comfortable with the notion that out of these eggs young dragons
would hatch, eager and waiting to be Impressed. F'lar felt that such a
practice might cut down on casualties during Impression when the
boys were simply too scared to move out of the way of the awkward
dragonets.

F'lar also had Lessa persuade Ramoth to let Kylara near her precious golden egg. Kylara readily enough weaned her son and spent
hours, with Lessa acting as her tutor, beside the golden egg. Despite
Kylara's loose attachment to T'bor, she showed an open preference for
F'lar's company. Therefore, Lessa took great pains to foster F'lar's plan
for Kylara since it meant her removal, with the new-hatched queen,
to Fort Weyr.

F'lar's use of the Hold-born as riders served an additional purpose. Shortly before the actual Hatching and Impression, Lytol, the
Warder appointed at Ruath Hold, sent another message.

"The man positively delights in sending bad news," Lessa remarked as F'lar passed the message skin to her.

"He's gloomy," F'nor agreed. He had brought the message. "I
feel sorry for that youngster cooped up with such a pessimist."

Lessa frowned at the brown rider. She still found distasteful any
mention of Gemma's son, now Lord of her ancestral Hold. Yet . . . as
she had inadvertently caused his mother's death and she could not be
Weyrwoman and Lady Holder at the same time, it was fitting that
Gemma's Jaxom be Lord at Ruatha.

"I, however," F'lar said, "am grateful for his warnings. I suspected Meron would cause trouble again."

"He has shifty eyes, like Fax's," Lessa remarked.

"Shifty-eyed or not, he's dangerous," F'lar answered. "And I
cannot have him spreading rumors that we are deliberately choosing
men of the Blood to weaken Family Lines."

"There are more craftsmen's sons than Holders' boys, in any
case," F'nor snorted.

"I don't like him questioning that the Threads have not appeared," Lessa said gloomily.

F'lar shrugged. "They'll appear in due time. Be thankful the weather has continued cold. When the weather warms up and still no Threads appear, then I will worry." He grinned at Lessa in an intimate reminder of her promise.

F'nor cleared his throat hastily and looked away.

"However," the Weyrleader went on briskly, "I can do something about the other accusation."

So, when it was apparent that the eggs were about to hatch, he broke another long-standing tradition and sent riders to fetch the fathers of the young candidates from craft and Hold.

The great Hatching Cavern gave the appearance of being almost full as Holder and Weyrfolk watched from the tiers above the heated Ground. This time, Lessa observed, there was no aura of fear. The youthful candidates were tense, yes, but not frightened out of their wits by the rocking, shattering eggs. When the ill-coordinated dragonets awkwardly stumbled—it seemed to Lessa that they deliberately looked around at the eager faces as though pre-Impressed—the youths either stepped to one side or eagerly advanced as a crooning dragonet made his choice. The Impressions were made quickly and with no accidents. All too soon, Lessa thought, the triumphant procession of stumbling dragons and proud new riders moved erratically out of the Hatching Ground to the barracks.

The young queen burst from her shell and moved unerringly for Kylara, standing confidently on the hot sands. The watching beasts hummed their approval.

"It was over too soon," Lessa said in a disappointed voice that evening to F'lar.

He laughed indulgently, allowing himself a rare evening of relaxation now that another step had gone as planned. The Holder folk had been ridden home, stunned, dazed, and themselves impressed by the Weyr and the Weyrleader.

"That's because you were watching this time," he remarked, brushing a lock of her hair back. It obscured his view of her profile. He chuckled again. "You'll notice Naton . . ."

"N'ton," she corrected him.

"All right, N'ton—Impressed a bronze."

"Just as you predicted," she said with some asperity.

"And Kylara is Weyrwoman for Pridith."

Lessa did not comment on that, and she did her best to ignore his laughter.

"I wonder which bronze will fly her," he murmured softly.

"It had better be T'bor's Orth," Lessa said, bridling.

He answered her the only way a wise man could.

ᴎ

Crack dust, blackdust,
Turn in freezing air.
Waste dust, spacedust,
From Red Star bare.

Lessa woke abruptly, her head aching, her eyes blurred, her mouth dry. She had the immediate memory of a terrible nightmare that, just as quickly, escaped recall. She brushed her hair out of her face and was surprised to find that she had been sweating heavily.

"F'lar?" she called in an uncertain voice. He had evidently risen early. "F'lar," she called again, louder.

He's coming, Mnementh informed her. Lessa sensed that the dragon was just landing on the ledge. She touched Ramoth and found that the queen, too, had been bothered by formless, frightening dreams. The dragon roused briefly and then fell back into deeper sleep.

Disturbed by her vague fears, Lessa rose and dressed, forgoing a bath for the first time since she had arrived at the Weyr.

She called down the shaft for breakfast, then plaited her hair with deft fingers as she waited.

The tray appeared on the shaft platform just as F'lar entered. He kept looking back over his shoulder at Ramoth.

"What's gotten into her?"

"Echoing my nightmare. I woke in a cold sweat."

"You were sleeping quietly enough when I left to assign patrols. You know, at the rate those dragonets are growing, they're already capable of limited flight. All they do is eat and sleep, and that's . . ."

". . . what makes a dragon grow," Lessa finished for him and sipped thoughtfully at her steaming hot *klah.* "You are going to be extra-careful about their drill procedures, aren't you?"

"You mean to prevent an inadvertent flight *between* times? I certainly am," he assured her. "I don't want bored dragonriders irresponsibly popping in and out." He gave her a long, stern look.

"Well, it wasn't my fault no one taught me to fly early enough," she replied in the sweet tone she used when she was being especially malicious. "If I'd been drilled from the day of Impression to the day of my first flight, I'd never have discovered that trick."

"True enough," he said solemnly.

"You know, F'lar, if I discovered it, someone else must have, and someone else may. If they haven't already."

F'lar drank, making a face as the *klah* scalded his tongue. "I don't know how to find out discreetly. We would be foolish to think we were

the first. It is, after all, an inherent ability in dragons, or you would
never have been able to do it."

She frowned, took a quick breath, and then let it go, shrugging.

"Go on," he encouraged her.

"Well, isn't it possible that our conviction about the imminence
of the Threads could stem from one of us coming back when the
Threads are actually falling? I mean . . ."

"My dear girl, we have both analyzed every stray thought and
action— even your dream this morning upset you, although it was no
doubt due to all the wine you drank last night—until we wouldn't
know an honest presentiment if it walked up and slapped us in the
face."

"I can't dismiss the thought that this *between* times ability is of
crucial value," she said emphatically.

"That, my dear Weyrwoman, *is* an honest presentiment."

"But why?"

"Not why," he corrected her cryptically. *"When."* An idea stirred
vaguely in the back of his mind. He tried to nudge it out where he
could mull it over. Mnementh announced that F'nor was entering the
weyr.

"What's the matter with you?" F'lar demanded of his half brother,
for F'nor was choking and sputtering, his face red with the paroxysm.

"Dust . . ." he coughed, slapping at his sleeves and chest with
his riding gloves. "Plenty of dust, but no Threads," he said, describing
a wide arc with one arm as he fluttered his fingers suggestively. He
brushed his tight wher-hide pants, scowling as a fine black dust drifted
off.

F'lar felt every muscle in his body tense as he watched the dust
float to the floor.

"Where did you get so dusty?" he demanded.

F'nor regarded him with mild surprise. "Weather patrol in Tillek.
Entire north has been plagued with dust storms lately. But what I came
in for . . ." He broke off, alarmed by F'lar's taut immobility. "What's
the matter with dust?" he asked in a baffled voice.

F'lar pivoted on his heel and raced for the stairs to the Record
Room. Lessa was right behind him, F'nor belatedly trailing after.

"Tillek, you said?" F'lar barked at his wingsecond. He was clearing the table of stacks for the four charts he then laid out. "How long
have these storms been going on? Why didn't you report them?"

"Report dust storms? You wanted to know about warm air
masses."

"How long have these storms been going on?" F'lar's voice
crackled.

"Close to a week."

"How close?"

"Six days ago the first storm was noticed in upper Tillek. They have been reported in Bitra, Upper Telgar, Crom, and the High Reaches," F'nor reported tersely.

He glanced hopefully at Lessa but saw she, too, was staring at the four unusual charts. He tried to see why the horizontal and vertical strips had been superimposed on Pern's land mass, but the reason was beyond him.

F'lar was making hurried notations, pushing first one map and then another away from him.

"Too involved to think straight, to see clearly, to understand," the Weyrleader snarled to himself, throwing down the stylus angrily.

"You did say only warm air masses," F'nor heard himself saying humbly, aware that he had somehow failed his Weyrleader.

F'lar shook his head impatiently.

"Not your fault, F'nor. Mine. I should have asked. I knew it was good luck that the weather held so cold." He put both hands on F'nor's shoulders, looking directly into his eyes. "The Threads have been falling," he announced gravely. "Falling into cold air, freezing into bits to drift on the wind"—F'lar imitated F'nor's finger-fluttering—"as specks of black dust."

"'Crack dust, blackdust,'" Lessa quoted. "In 'The Ballad of Moreta's Ride,' the chorus is all about black dust."

"I don't need to be reminded of Moreta right now," F'lar growled, bending to the maps. "She could talk to any dragon in the Weyrs."

"But I can do that!" Lessa protested.

Slowly, as if he didn't quite credit his ears, F'lar turned back to Lessa. "What did you just say?"

"I said I can talk to any dragon in the Weyr."

Still staring at her, blinking in utter astonishment, F'lar sank down to the table top.

"How long," he managed to say, "have you had *this* particular skill?"

Something in his tone, in his manner, caused Lessa to flush and stammer like an erring weyrling.

"I . . . I always could. Beginning with the watch-wher at Ruatha." She gestured indecisively in Ruatha's westerly direction. "And I talked to Mnementh at Ruatha. And . . . when I got here, I could . . ." Her voice faltered at the accusing look in F'lar's cold, hard eyes. Accusing and, worse, contemptuous.

"I thought you had agreed to help me, to believe in me."

"I'm truly sorry, F'lar. It never occurred to me it was of any use to anyone, but . . ."

F'lar exploded onto both feet, his eyes blazing with aggravation.

"The one thing I could not figure out was how to direct the wings and keep in contact with the Weyr during an attack, how I was going to get reinforcements and firestone in time. And you . . . you have been sitting there, spitefully hiding the . . ."

"I am NOT spiteful," she screamed at him. "I said I was sorry. I am. But you've a nasty, smug habit of keeping your own counsel. How was I to know you didn't have the same trick? You're F'lar, the Weyrleader, you can do *anything*. Only you're just as bad as R'gul because you never *tell* me half the things I ought to know . . ."

F'lar reached out and shook her until her angry voice was stopped.

"Enough. We can't waste time arguing like children." Then his eyes widened, his jaw dropped. "Waste time? That's it."

"Go *between* times?" Lessa gasped.

"*Between* times!"

F'nor was totally confused. "What are you two talking about?"

"The Threads started falling at dawn in Nerat," F'lar said, his eyes bright, his manner decisive.

F'nor could feel his guts congealing with apprehension. At dawn in Nerat? Why, the rainforests would be demolished. He could feel a surge of adrenalin charging through his body at the thought of danger.

"So we're going *back* there, *between* times, and be there when the Threads started falling, two hours ago. F'nor, the dragons can go not only where we direct them but *when*."

"Where? When?" F'nor repeated, bewildered. "That could be dangerous."

"Yes, but today it will save Nerat. Now, Lessa," and F'lar gave her another shake, compounded of pride and affection, "order out all the dragons, young, old, any that can fly. Tell them to load themselves down with firestone sacks. I don't know if you can talk across time . . ."

"My dream this morning . . ."

"Perhaps. But right now rouse the Weyr." He pivoted to F'nor. "If Threads are falling . . . were falling . . . at Nerat at dawn, they'll be falling on Keroon and Ista right now, because they are in that time pattern. Take two wings to Keroon. Arouse the plains. Get them to start the firepits blazing. Take some weyrlings with you and send them on to Igen and Ista. Those Holds are not in as immediate danger as Keroon. I'll reinforce you as soon as I can. And . . . keep Canth in touch with Lessa."

F'lar clapped his brother on the shoulder and sent him off. The brown rider was too used to taking orders to argue.

"Mnementh says R'gul is duty officer and R'gul wants to know . . ." Lessa began.

"C'mon, girl," F'lar said, his eyes brilliant with excitement. He grabbed up his maps and propelled her up the stairs.

They arrived in the weyr just as R'gul entered with T'sum. R'gul was muttering about this unusual summons.

"Hath told me to report," he complained. "Fine thing when your own dragon . . ."

"R'gul, T'sum, mount your wings. Arm them with all the firestone they can carry, and assemble above Star Stone. I'll join you in a few minutes. We go to Nerat at dawn."

"Nerat? I'm watch officer, not patrol . . ."

"This is no patrol," F'lar cut him off.

"But, sir," T'sum interrupted, his eyes wide, "Nerat's dawn was two hours ago, the same as ours."

"And that is *when* we are going to, brown riders. The dragons, we have discovered, can go *between* places temporally as well as geographically. At dawn Threads fell at Nerat. We're going back, *between* time, to sear them from the sky."

F'lar paid no attention to R'gul's stammered demand for explanation. T'sum, however, grabbed up firestone sacks and raced back to the ledge and his waiting Munth.

"Go on, you old fool," Lessa told R'gul irascibly. "The Threads are here. You were wrong. Now be a dragonman! Or go *between* and stay there!"

Ramoth, awakened by the alarms, poked at R'gul with her man-sized head, and the ex-Weyrleader came out of his momentary shock. Without a word he followed T'sum down the passageway.

F'lar had thrown on his heavy wher-hide tunic and shoved on his riding boots.

"Lessa, be sure to send messages to all the Holds. Now, this attack will stop about four hours from now. So the farthest west it can reach will be Ista. But I want every Hold and craft warned."

She nodded, her eyes intent on his face lest she miss a word.

"Fortunately, the Star is just beginning its Pass, so we won't have to worry about another attack for a few days. I'll figure out the next one when I get back.

"Now, get Manora to organize her women. We'll need pails of ointment. The dragons are going to be laced, and that hurts. Most important, if something goes wrong, you'll have to wait till a bronze is at least a year old to fly Ramoth . . ."

"No one's flying Ramoth but Mnementh," she cried, her eyes sparkling fiercely.

F'lar crushed her against him, his mouth bruising hers as if all her sweetness and strength must come with him. He released her so abruptly that she staggered back against Ramoth's lowered head. She clung for a moment to her dragon, as much for support as for reassurance.

That is, if Mnementh can catch me, Ramoth amended smugly.

Wheel and turn
Or bleed and burn.
Fly between,
Blue and green.
Soar, dive down,
Bronze and brown
Dragonmen must fly
When Threads are in the sky.

As F'lar raced down the passageway to the ledge, firesacks bumping against his thighs, he was suddenly grateful for the tedious sweeping patrols over every Hold and hollow of Pern. He could see Nerat clearly in his mind's eye. He could see the many-petaled vineflowers which were the distinguished feature of the rainforest at this time of the year. Their ivory blossoms would be glowing in the first beams of sunlight like dragon eyes among the tall, wide-leaved plants.

Mnementh, his eyes flashing with excitement, hovered skittishly over the ledge. F'lar vaulted to the bronze neck.

The Weyr was seething with wings of all colors, noisy with shouts and countercommands. The atmosphere was electric, but F'lar could sense no panic in that ordered confusion. Dragon and human bodies oozed out of openings around the Bowl walls. Women scurried across the floor from one Lower Cavern to another. The children playing by the lake were sent to gather wood for a fire. The weyrlings, supervised by old C'gan, were forming outside their barracks. F'lar looked up to the Peak and approved the tight formation of the wings assembled there in close flying order. Another wing formed up as he watched. He recognized brown Canth, F'nor on his neck, just as the entire wing vanished.

He ordered Mnementh aloft. The wind was cold and carried a hint of moisture. A late snow? This was the time for it, if ever.

R'gul's wing and T'bor's fanned out on his left, T'sum and D'nol on his right. He noted each dragon was well-laden with sacks. Then he gave Mnementh the visualization of the early spring rainforest in Nerat, just before dawn, the vineflowers gleaming, the sea breaking against the rocks of the High Shoal. . . .

He felt the searing cold of *between*. And he felt a stab of doubt. Was he injudicious, sending them all possibly to their deaths *between* times in this effort to outtime the Threads at Nerat?

Then they were all there, in the crepuscular light that promises day. The lush, fruity smells of the rainforest drifted up to them. Warm, too, and that was frightening. He looked up and slightly to the north. Pulsing with menace, the Red Star shone down.

The men had realized what had happened, their voices raised in astonishment. Mnementh told F'lar that the dragons were mildly surprised at their riders' fuss.

"Listen to me, dragonriders," F'lar called, his voice harsh and distorted in an effort to be heard by all. He waited till the men had moved as close as possible. He told Mnementh to pass the information on to each dragon. Then he explained what they had done and why. No one spoke, but there were many nervous looks exchanged across bright wings.

Crisply he ordered the dragonriders to fan out in a staggered formation, keeping a distance of five wings' spread up or down.

The sun came up.

Slanting across the sea, like an ever-thickening mist, Threads were falling, silent, beautiful, treacherous. Silvery gray were those space-traversing spores, spinning from hard frozen ovals into coarse filaments as they penetrated the warm atmospheric envelope of Pern. Less than mindless, they had been ejected from their barren planet toward Pern, a hideous rain that sought organic matter to nourish it into growth. One Thread, sinking into fertile soil, would burrow deep, propagating thousands in the warm earth, rendering it into a black-dusted wasteland. The southern continent of Pern had already been sucked dry. The true parasites of Pern were Threads.

A stifled roar from the throats of eighty men and dragons broke the dawn air above Nerat's green heights—as if the Threads might hear this challenge, F'lar mused.

As one, dragons swiveled their wedge-shaped heads to their riders for firestone. Great jaws macerated the hunks. The fragments were swallowed and more firestone was demanded. Inside the beasts, acids churned and the poisonous phosphines were readied. When the dragons belched forth the gas, it would ignite in the air into ravening flame to sear the Threads from the sky. And burn them from the soil.

Dragon instinct took over the moment the Threads began to fall above Nerat's shores.

As much admiration as F'lar had always held for his bronze companion, it achieved newer heights in the next hours. Beating the air in great strokes, Mnementh soared with flaming breath to meet the downrushing menace. The fumes, swept back by the wind, choked F'lar until he thought to crouch low on the lea side of the bronze neck. The dragon squealed as a Thread flicked the tip of one wing. Instantly F'lar and he ducked into *between*, cold, calm, black. The frozen Thread cracked off. In the flicker of an eye, they were back to face the reality of Threads.

Around him F'lar saw dragons winking in and out of *between*, flaming as they returned, diving, soaring. As the attack continued and they drifted across Nerat, F'lar began to recognize the pattern in the dragons' instinctive evasion-attack movements. And in the Threads. For, contrary to what he had gathered from his study of the Records, the Threads fell in patches. Not as rain will, in steady unbroken sheets, but like flurries of snow, here, above, there, whipped to one side suddenly. Never fluidly, despite the continuity their name implied.

You could see a patch above you. Flaming, your dragon would rise. You'd have the intense joy of seeing the clump shrivel from bottom to top. Sometimes, a patch would fall between riders. One dragon would signal he would follow and, spouting flame, would dive and sear.

Gradually the dragonriders worked their way over the rainforests, so densely, so invitingly green. F'lar refused to dwell on what just one live Thread burrow would do to that lush land. He would send back a low-flying patrol to quarter every foot. One Thread, just one Thread, could put out the ivory eyes of every luminous vineflower.

A dragon screamed somewhere to his left. Before he could identify the beast, it had ducked *between*. F'lar heard other cries of pain, from men as well as dragons. He shut his ears and concentrated, as dragons did, on the here-and-now. Would Mnementh remember those piercing cries later? F'lar wished he could forget them now.

He, F'lar, the bronze rider, felt suddenly superfluous. It was the dragons who were fighting this engagement. You encouraged your beast, comforted him when the Threads burned, but you depended on his instinct and speed.

Hot fire dripped across F'lar's cheek, burrowing like acid into his shoulder . . . a cry of surprised agony burst from F'lar's lips. Mnementh took them to merciful *between*. The dragonman battled with frantic hands at the Threads, felt them crumble in the intense cold of *between* and break off. Revolted, he slapped at injuries still afire. Back in Nerat's humid air, the sting seemed to ease. Mnementh crooned comfortingly and then dove at a patch, breathing fire.

Shocked at self-consideration, F'lar hurriedly examined his mount's shoulder for telltale score marks.

I duck very quickly, Mnementh told him and veered away from a dangerously close clump of Threads. A brown dragon followed them down and burned them to ash.

It might have been moments, it might have been a hundred hours later when F'lar looked down in surprise at the sunlit sea. Threads now dropped harmlessly into the salty waters. Nerat was to the east of him on his right, the rocky tip curling westward.

F'lar felt weariness in every muscle. In the excitement of frenzied battle, he had forgotten the bloody scores on cheek and shoulder. Now, as he and Mnementh glided slowly, the injuries ached and stung.

He flew Mnementh high and when they had achieved sufficient altitude, they hovered. He could see no Threads falling landward. Below him, the dragons ranged, high and low, searching for any sign of a burrow, alert for any suddenly toppling trees or disturbed vegetation.

"Back to the Weyr," he ordered Mnementh with a heavy sigh. He heard the bronze relay the command even as he himself was taken *between*. He was so tired he did not even visualize where—much less, when—relying on Mnementh's instinct to bring him safely home through time and space.

Honor those the dragons heed,
In thought and favor, word and deed.
Worlds are lost or worlds are saved
From those dangers dragon-braved.

Craning her neck toward the Star Stone at Benden Peak, Lessa watched from the ledge until she saw the four wings disappear from view.

Sighing deeply to quiet her inner fears, Lessa raced down the stairs to the floor of Benden Weyr. She noticed that someone was building a fire by the lake and that Manora was already ordering her women around, her voice clear but calm.

Old C'gan had the weyrlings lined up. She caught the envious eyes of the newest dragonriders at the barracks windows. They'd have time enough to fly a flaming dragon. From what F'lar had intimated, they'd have Turns.

She shuddered as she stepped up to the weyrlings but managed to smile at them. She gave them their orders and sent them off to warn the Holds, checking quickly with each dragon to be sure the rider had given clear references. The Holds would shortly be stirred up to a froth.

Canth told her that there were Threads at Keroon, falling on the Keroon side of Nerat Bay. He told her that F'nor did not think two wings were enough to protect the meadowlands.

Lessa stopped in her tracks, trying to think how many wings were already out.

K'net's wing is still here, Ramoth informed her. *On the Peak.*

Lessa glanced up and saw bronze Piyanth spread his wings in

answer. She told him to get *between* to Keroon, close to Nerat Bay. Obediently the entire wing rose and then disappeared.

She turned with a sigh to say something to Manora when a rush of wind and a vile stench almost overpowered her. The air above the Weyr was full of dragons. She was about to demand of Piyanth why he hadn't gone to Keroon when she realized there were far more beasts a-wing than K'net's twenty.

But you just left, she cried as she recognized the unmistakable bulk of bronze Mnementh.

That was two hours ago for us, Mnementh said with such weariness in his tone that Lessa closed her eyes in sympathy.

Some dragons were gliding in fast. From their awkwardness it was evident that they were hurt.

As one, the women grabbed salve pots and clean rags and beckoned the injured down. The numbing ointment was smeared on score marks where wings resembled black and red lace.

No matter how badly injured he might be, every rider tended his beast first.

Lessa kept one eye on Mnementh, sure that F'lar would not keep the huge bronze hovering like that if he'd been hurt. She was helping T'sum with Munth's cruelly pierced right wing when she realized the sky above the Star Stone was empty.

She forced herself to finish with Munth before she went to find the bronze and his rider. When she did locate them, she also saw Kylara smearing salve on F'lar's cheek and shoulder. She was advancing purposefully across the sands toward the pair when Canth's urgent plea reached her. She saw Mnementh's head swing upward as he, too, caught the brown's thought.

"F'lar, Canth says they need help," Lessa cried. She didn't notice then that Kylara slipped away into the busy crowd.

F'lar wasn't badly hurt. She reassured herself about that. Kylara had treated the wicked burns that seemed to be shallow. Someone had found him another fur to replace the tatters of the Thread-bared one. He frowned—winced because the frown creased his burned cheek. He gulped hurriedly at his *klah*.

Mnementh, what's the tally of able-bodied? Oh, never mind, just get 'em aloft with a full load of firestone.

"You're all right?" Lessa asked, a detaining hand on his arm. He couldn't just go off like this, could he?

He smiled tiredly down at her, pressed his empty mug into her hands, giving them a quick squeeze. Then he vaulted to Mnementh's neck. Someone handed him a heavy load of sacks.

Blue, green, brown, and bronze dragons lifted from the Weyr Bowl in quick order. A trifle more than sixty dragons hovered briefly above the Weyr where eighty had lingered so few minutes before.

So few dragons. So few riders. How long could they take such toll?

Canth said F'nor needed more firestone.

She looked about anxiously. None of the weyrlings were back yet from their messenger rounds. A dragon was crooning plaintively, and she wheeled, but it was only young Pridith, stumbling across the Weyr to the feeding grounds, butting playfully at Kylara as they walked. The only other dragons were injured or—her eye fell on C'gan, emerging from the weyrling barracks.

"C'gan, can you and Tagath get more firestone to F'nor at Keroon?"

"Of course," the old blue rider assured her, his chest lifting with pride, his eyes flashing. She hadn't thought to send him anywhere, yet he had lived his life in training for this emergency. He shouldn't be deprived of a chance at it.

She smiled her approval at his eagerness as they piled heavy sacks on Tagath's neck. The old blue dragon snorted and danced as if he were young and strong again. She gave them the references Canth had visualized to her.

She watched as the two blinked out above the Star Stone.

It isn't fair. They have all the fun, said Ramoth peevishly. Lessa saw her sunning herself on the Weyr ledge, preening her enormous wings.

"You chew firestone and you're reduced to a silly green," Lessa told her Weyrmate sharply. She was inwardly amused by the queen's disgruntled complaint.

Lessa passed among the inured then. B'fol's dainty green beauty moaned and tossed her head, unable to bend one wing that had been threaded to bare cartilage. She'd be out for weeks, but she had the worst injury among the dragons. Lessa looked quickly away from the misery in B'fol's worried eyes.

As she did the rounds, she realized that more men were injured than beasts. Two in R'gul's wing had sustained serious head damages. One man might lose an eye completely. Manora had dosed him unconscious with numb-weed. Another man's arm had been burned clear to the bone. Minor though most of the wounds were, the tally dismayed Lessa. How many more would be disabled at Keroon?

Out of one hundred and seventy-two dragons, fifteen already were out of action, some only for a day or two, however.

A thought struck Lessa. If N'ton had actually ridden Canth, maybe he could ride out on the next dragonade on an injured man's beast, since there were more injured riders than dragons. F'lar broke traditions as he chose. Here was another one to set aside—if the dragon was agreeable.

Presuming N'ton was not the only new rider able to transfer to another beast, what good would such flexibility do in the long run?

F'lar had definitely said the incursions would not be so frequent at first, when the Red Star was just beginning its fifty-Turn-long circling pass of Pern. How frequent was frequent? He would know, but he wasn't here.

Well, he *had* been right this morning about the appearance of Threads at Nerat, so his exhaustive study of those old Records had proved worthwhile.

No, that wasn't quite accurate. He had forgotten to have the men alert for signs of black dust as well as warming weather. As he had put the matter right by going *between* times, she would graciously allow him that minor error. But he did have an infuriating habit of guessing correctly. Lessa corrected herself again. He didn't guess. He studied. He planned. He thought and then he used common good sense. Like figuring out where and when Threads would strike according to entries in those smelly Records. Lessa began to feel better about their future.

Now, if he would just make the riders learn to trust their dragons' sure instinct in battle, they would keep casualties down, too.

A shriek pierced air and ear as a blue dragon emerged above the Star Stone.

Ramoth! Lessa screamed in an instinctive reaction, hardly knowing why. The queen was a-wing before the echo of her command had died. For the careening blue was obviously in grave trouble. He was trying to brake his forward speed, yet one wing would not function. His rider had slipped forward over the great shoulder, precariously clinging to his dragon's neck with one hand.

Lessa, her hands clapped over her mouth, watched fearfully. There wasn't a sound in the Bowl but the flapping of Ramoth's immense wings. The queen rose swiftly to position herself against the desperate blue, lending him wing support on the crippled side.

The watchers gasped as the rider slipped, lost his hold, and fell— landing on Ramoth's wide shoulders.

The blue dropped like a stone. Ramoth came to a gentle stop near him, crouching low to allow the weyrfolk to remove her passenger.

It was C'gan.

Lessa felt her stomach heave as she saw the ruin the Threads had made of the old harper's face. She dropped beside him, pillowing his head in her lap. The weyrfolk gathered in a respectful, silent circle.

Manora, her face, as always, serene, had tears in her eyes. She knelt and placed her hand on the old rider's heart. Concern flickered in her eyes as she looked up at Lessa. Slowly she shook her head. Then, setting her lips in a thin line, she began to apply the numbing salve.

"Too toothless old to flame and too slow to get *between*," C'gan mumbled, rolling his head from side to side. "Too old. But 'Dragonmen must fly/ when Threads are in the sky. . . .'" His voice trailed off into a sigh. His eyes closed.

Lessa and Manora looked at each other in anguish. A terrible, ear-shattering note cut the silence. Tagath sprang aloft in a tremendous leap. C'gan's eyes rolled slowly open, sightless. Lessa, breath suspended, watched the blue dragon, trying to deny the inevitable as Tagath disappeared in mid-air.

A low moan sprang up around the Weyr, like the torn, lonely cry of a keening wind. The dragons uttered tribute.

"Is he . . . gone?" Lessa asked, although she knew.

Manora nodded slowly, tears streaming down her cheeks as she reached over to close C'gan's dead eyes.

Lessa rose slowly to her feet, motioning to some of the women to remove the old rider's body. Absently she rubbed her bloody hands dry on her skirts, trying to concentrate on what might be needed next.

Yet her mind turned back to what had just happened. A dragonrider had died. His dragon, too. The Threads had claimed one pair already. How many more would die this cruel Turn? How long could the Weyr survive? Even after Ramoth's forty matured, and the ones she soon would conceive, and her queendaughters, too?

Lessa walked apart to quiet her uncertainties and ease her grief. She saw Ramoth wheel and glide aloft, to land on the Peak. One day soon would Lessa see those golden wings laced red and black from Thread marks? Would Ramoth . . . disappear?

No, Ramoth would not. Not while Lessa lived.

F'lar had told her long ago that she must learn to look beyond the narrow confines of Hold Ruatha and mere revenge. He was, as usual, right. As Weyrwoman under his tutelage, she had further learned that living *was* more than raising dragons and Spring Games. Living was struggling to do something impossible—to succeed, or die, knowing you had tried!

Lessa realized that she had, at last, fully accepted her role: as Weyrwoman and as mate, to help F'lar shape men and events for many Turns to come—to secure Pern against the Threads.

Lessa threw back her shoulders and lifted her chin high.

Old C'gan had had the right of it.

Dragonmen must fly
When Threads are in the sky!

Worlds are lost or worlds are saved
By those dangers dragon-braved.

As F'lar had predicted, the attack ended by high noon, and weary dragons and riders were welcomed by Ramoth's high-pitched trumpeting from the Peak.

Once Lessa assured herself that F'lar had taken no additional injury, that F'nor's were superficial and that Manora was keeping Kylara busy in the kitchens, she applied herself to organizing the care of the injured and the comfort of the worried.

As dusk fell, an uneasy peace settled on the Weyr—the quiet of minds and bodies too tired or too hurtful to talk. Lessa's own words mocked her as she made out the list of wounded men and beasts. Twenty-eight men or dragons were out of the air for the next Thread battle. C'gan was the only fatality, but there had been four more seriously injured dragons at Keroon and seven badly scored men, out of action entirely for months to come.

Lessa crossed the Bowl to her Weyr, reluctant but resigned to giving F'lar this unsettling news.

She expected to find him in the sleeping room, but it was vacant. Ramoth was asleep already as Lessa passed her on the way to the Council Room—also empty. Puzzled and a little alarmed, Lessa half-ran down the steps to the Records Room, to find F'lar, haggard of face, poring over musty skins.

"What are you doing here?" she demanded angrily. "You ought to be asleep."

"So should you," he drawled, amused.

"I was helping Manora settle the wounded . . ."

"Each to his own craft." But he did lean back from the table, rubbing his neck and rotating the uninjured shoulder to ease stiffened muscles.

"I couldn't sleep," he admitted, "so I thought I'd see what answers I might turn up in the Records."

"More answers? To what?" Lessa cried, exasperated with him. As if the Records ever answered anything. Obviously the tremendous responsibilities of Pern's defense against the Threads were beginning to tell on the Weyrleader. After all, there had been the stress of the first battle, not to mention the drain of the traveling *between* time itself to get to Nerat to forestall the Threads.

F'lar grinned and beckoned Lessa to sit beside him on the wall bench.

"I need the answer to the very pressing question of how one understrength Weyr can do the fighting of six."

Lessa fought the panic that rose, a cold flood, from her guts.

"Oh, your time schedules will take care of that," she replied gallantly. "You'll be able to conserve the dragon-power until the new forty can join the ranks."

F'lar raised a mocking eyebrow.

"Let us be honest between ourselves, Lessa."

"But there have been Long Intervals before," she argued, "and since Pern survived them, Pern can again."

"Before there were always six Weyrs. And twenty or so Turns before the Red Star was due to begin its Pass, the queens would start to produce enormous clutches. All the queens, not just one faithful golden Ramoth. Oh, how I curse Jora!" He slammed to his feet and started pacing, irritably brushing the lock of black hair that fell across his eyes.

Lessa was torn with the desire to comfort him and the sinking, choking fear in her belly that made it difficult to think at all.

"You were not so doubtful . . ."

He whirled back to her. "Not until I had actually had an encounter with the Threads and reckoned up the numbers of injuries. That sets the odds against us. Even supposing we can mount other riders to uninjured dragons, we will be hard put to keep a continuously effective force in the air and still maintain a ground guard." He caught her puzzled frown. "There's Nerat to be gone over on foot tomorrow. I'd be a fool indeed if I thought we'd caught and seared every Thread in mid-air."

"Get the Holders to do that. They can't just immure themselves safely in their Inner Holds and let us do all. If they hadn't been so miserly and stupid . . ."

He cut off her complaint with an abrupt gesture. "They'll do their part all right," he assured her. "I'm sending for a full Council tomorrow, all Hold Lords and all Craftmasters. But there's more to it than just marking where Threads fall. How do you destroy a burrow that's gone deep under the surface? A dragon's breath is fine for the air and surface work but no good three feet down."

"Oh, I hadn't thought of that aspect. But the firepits . . ."

". . . are only on the heights and around human habitations, not on the meadowlands of Keroon or on Nerat's so green rainforests."

This consideration was daunting indeed. She gave a rueful little laugh.

"Shortsighted of me to suppose our dragons are all poor Pern needs to dispatch the Threads. Yet . . ." She shrugged expressively.

"There are other methods," F'lar said, "or there were. There must have been. I have run across frequent mention that the Holds were organizing ground groups and that they were armed with fire. What kind is never mentioned because it was so wellknown." He threw up his hands in disgust and sagged back down on the bench. "Not even five hundred dragons could have seared all the Threads that fell today. Yet *they* managed to keep Pern Thread-free."

"Pern, yes, but wasn't the Southern Continent lost? Or did they just have their hands too full with Pern itself?"

"No one's bothered with the Southern Continent in a hundred thousand Turns," F'lar snorted.

"It's on the maps," Lessa reminded him.

He scowled disgustedly at the Records, piled in uncommunicative stacks on the long table.

"The answer must be there. Somewhere."

There was an edge of desperation in his voice, the hint that he held himself to blame for not having discovered those elusive facts.

"Half those things couldn't be read by the man who wrote them," Lessa said tartly. "Besides that, it's been your *own* ideas that have helped us most so far. You compiled the time maps, and look how valuable they have been already."

"I'm getting too hidebound again, huh?" he asked, a half smile tugging at one corner of his mouth.

"Undoubtedly," she assured him with more confidence than she felt. "We both know the Records are guilty of the most ridiculous omissions."

"Well said, Lessa. So let us forget these misguiding and antiquated precepts and think up our own guides. First, we need more dragons. Second, we need them now. Third, we need something as effective as a flaming dragon to destroy Threads which have burrowed."

"Fourth, we need sleep, or we won't be able to think of anything," she added with a touch of her usual asperity.

F'lar laughed outright, hugging her.

"You've got your mind on one thing, haven't you?" he teased, his hands caressing her eagerly.

She pushed ineffectually at him, trying to escape. For a wounded, tired man, he was remarkably amorous. One with that Kylara. Imagine that woman's presumption, dressing his wounds.

"My responsibility as Weyrwoman includes care of you, the Weyrleader."

"But you spend hours with blue dragonriders and leave me to Kylara's tender ministrations."

"You didn't look as if you objected."

F'lar threw back his head and roared. "Should I open Fort Weyr and send Kylara on?" he taunted her.

"I'd as soon Kylara were Turns as well as miles away from here," Lessa snapped, thoroughly irritated.

F'lar's jaw dropped, his eyes widened. He leaped to his feet with an astonished cry.

"You've said it!"

"Said what?"

"Turns away! That's it. We'll send Kylara back, *between* times, with her queen and the new dragonets." F'lar excitedly paced the room while Lessa tried to follow his reasoning. "No, I'd better send at least one of the older bronzes. F'nor, too . . . I'd rather have F'nor in charge. . . . Discreetly, of course—"

"Send Kylara back . . . where to? When to?" Lessa interrupted him.

"Good point." F'lar dragged out the ubiquitous charts. "Very good point. Where can we send them around here without causing anomalies by being present at one of the other Weyrs? The High Reaches are remote. No, we've found remains of fires there, you know, still warm, and no inkling as to who built them or why. And if we had already sent them back, they'd've been ready for today, and they weren't. So they can't have been in two places already. . . ." He shook his head, dazed by the paradoxes.

Lessa's eyes were drawn to the blank outline of the neglected Southern Continent.

"Send them there," she suggested sweetly, pointing.

"There's nothing there."

"They bring in what they need. There must be water, for Threads can't devour that, we fly in whatever else is needed, fodder for the herdbeasts, grain. . . ."

F'lar drew his brows together in concentration, his eyes sparkling with thought, the depression and defeat of a few moments ago forgotten.

"Threads wouldn't be there ten Turns ago. And haven't been there for close to four hundred. Ten Turns would give Pridith time to mature and have several clutches. Maybe more queens."

Then he frowned and shook his head dubiously. "No, there's no Weyr there. No Hatching Ground, no . . . ."

"How do we know that?" Lessa caught him up sharply, too delighted with many aspects of this project to give it up easily. "The Records don't mention the Southern Continent, true, but they omit a great deal. How do we know it isn't green again in the four hundred Turns since the Threads last spun? We do know that Threads can't last long unless there is something organic on which to feed and that once they've devoured all, they dry up and blow away."

F'lar looked at her admiringly. "Now, why hasn't someone wondered about that before?"

"Too hidebound." Lessa wagged her finger at him. "Besides, there's been no need to bother with it."

"Necessity—or is it jealousy?—hatches many a tough shell." There was a smile of pure malice on his face, and Lessa whirled away as he reached for her.

"The good of the Weyr," she retorted.

"Furthermore, I'll send you along with F'nor tomorrow to look, Only fair, since it is your idea."

Lessa stood still. "You're not going?"

"I feel confident I can leave this project in your very capable, interested hands." He laughed and caught her against his uninjured side, smiling down at her, his eyes glowing. "I must play ruthless Weyrleader and keep the Hold Lords from slamming shut their Inner Doors. And I'm hoping"—he raised his head, frowning slightly—"one of the Craftmasters may know the solution to the third problem—getting rid of Thread burrows."

"But . . ."

"The trip will give Ramoth something to stop her fuming." He pressed the girl's slender body more closely to him, his full attention at last on her odd, delicate face. "Lessa, you are my fourth problem." He bent to kiss her.

At the sound of hurried steps in the passageway, F'lar scowled irritably, releasing her.

"At this hour?" he muttered, ready to reprove the intruder scathingly. "Who goes there?"

"F'lar?" It was F'nor's voice, anxious, hoarse.

The look on F'lar's face told Lessa that not even his half brother would be spared a reprimand, and it pleased her irrationally. But the moment F'nor burst into the room, both Weyrleader and Weyrwoman were stunned silent. There was something subtly wrong with the brown rider. And as the man blurted out his incoherent message, the difference suddenly registered in Lessa's mind. He was tanned! He wore no bandages and hadn't the slightest trace of the Thread-mark along his cheek that she had tended this evening!

"F'lar, it's not working out! You can't be alive in two times at once!" F'nor was exclaiming distractedly. He staggered against the wall, grabbing the sheer rock to hold himself upright. There were deep circles under his eyes, visible despite the tan. "I don't know how much longer we can last like this. We're all affected. Some days not as badly as others."

"I don't understand."

"Your dragons are all right," F'nor assured the Weyrleader with a bitter laugh. "It doesn't bother them. They keep all their wits about them. But their riders . . . all the weyrfolk . . . we're shadows, half alive, like dragonless men, part of us gone forever. Except Kylara." His face contorted with intense dislike. "All she wants to do is go back and watch herself. The woman's egomania will destroy us all, I'm afraid."

His eyes suddenly lost focus, and he swayed wildly. His eyes widened, and his mouth fell open. "I can't stay. I'm here already. Too close. Makes it twice as bad. But I had to warn you. I promise, F'lar, we'll stay as long as we can, but it won't be much longer . . . so it won't be long enough, but we tried. We tried!"

Before F'lar could move, the brown rider whirled and ran, half-crouched, from the room.

"But he hasn't gone yet!" Lessa gasped. "He hasn't even gone yet!"

·· P A R T I V ··

The Cold Between

F'lar stared after his half brother, his brows contracting with the keen anxiety he felt.

"What can have happened?" Lessa demanded of the Weyrleader. "We haven't even told F'nor. We ourselves just finished considering the idea." Her hand flew to her own cheek. "And the Thread-mark—I dressed it myself tonight—it's gone. Gone. So he's been gone a long while." She sank down to the bench.

"However, he has come back. So he did go," F'lar remarked slowly in a reflective tone of voice. "yet we now know the venture is not entirely successful even before it begins. And knowing this, we have sent him back ten Turns for whatever good it is doing." F'lar paused thoughtfully. "Consequently we have no alternative but to continue with the experiment."

"But what could be going wrong?"

"I think I know and there is no remedy." He sat down beside her, his eyes intent on hers. "Lessa, you were very upset when you got back from going *between* to Ruatha that first time. But I think now it was more than just the shock of seeing Fax's men invading your own Hold or in thinking your return might have been responsible for that disaster. I think it has to do with being in two times at once." He hesitated again, trying to understand this immense new concept even as he voiced it.

Lessa regarded him with such awe that he found himself laughing with embarrassment.

"It's unnerving under any conditions," he went on, "to think of returning and seeing a younger self."

156

"That must be what he meant about Kylara," Lessa gasped, "about her wanting to go back and watch herself . . . as a child. Oh, that wretched girl!" Lessa was filled with anger for Kylara's self-absorption. "Wretched, selfish creature. She'll ruin everything."

"Not yet," F'lar reminded her. "Look, although F'nor warned us that the situation in his time is getting desperate, he didn't tell us how much he was able to accomplish. But you noticed that his scar had healed to invisibility—consequently some Turns must have elapsed. Even if Pridith lays only one good-sized clutch, even if just the forty of Ramoth's are mature enough to fight in three days' time, we have accomplished something. Therefore, Weyrwoman," and he noticed how she straightened up at the sound of her title, "we must disregard F'nor's return. When you fly to the Southern Continent tomorrow, make no allusion to it. Do you understand?"

Lessa nodded gravely and then gave a little sigh. "I don't know if I'm happy or disappointed to realize, even before we get there tomorrow, that the Southern Continent obviously will support a Weyr," she said with dismay. "It was kind of exciting to wonder."

"Either way," F'lar told her with a sardonic smile, "we have found only part of the answers to problems one and two."

"Well, you'd better answer number four right now!" Lessa suggested. "Decisively!"

ᐁ

Weaver, Miner, Harper, Smith,
Tanner, Farmer, Herdsman, Lord,
Gather, wingsped, listen well
To the Weyrman's urgent word.

They both managed to guard against any reference to his premature return when they spoke to F'nor the next morning. F'lar asked brown Canth to send his rider to the queen's weyr as soon as he awoke and was pleased to see F'nor almost immediately. If the brown rider noticed the curiously intent stare Lessa gave his bandaged face, he gave no sign of it. As a matter of fact, the moment F'lar outlined the bold venture of scouting the Southern Continent with the possibility of starting a Weyr ten Turns back in time, F'nor forgot all about his wounds.

"I'll go willingly only if you send T'bor along with Kylara. I'm not waiting till N'ton and his bronze are big enough to take her on.

T'bor and she are as—" F'nor broke off with a grimace in Lessa's direction. "Well, they're as near a pair as can be. I don't object to being . . . importuned, but there are limits to what a man is willing to do out of loyalty to dragonkind."

F'lar barely managed to restrain the amusement he felt over F'nor's reluctance. Kylara tried her wiles on every rider, and, because F'nor had not been amenable, she was determined to succeed with him.

"I hope two bronzes are enough. Pridith may have a mind of her own, come matingtime."

"You can't turn a brown into a bronze!" F'nor exclaimed with such dismay that F'lar could no longer restrain himself.

"Oh, stop it!" And that touched off Lessa's laughter. "You're as bad a pair," F'nor snapped, getting to his feet. "If we're going south, Weyrwoman, we'd better get started. Particularly if we're going to give this laughing maniac a chance to compose himself before the solemn Lords descend. I'll get provisions from Manora. Well, Lessa? *Are* you coming with me?"

Muffling her laughter, Lessa grabbed up her furred flying cloak and followed him. At least the adventure was starting off well.

Carrying the pitcher of *klah* and his cup, F'lar adjourned to the Council Room, debating whether to tell the Lords and Craftmasters of this southern venture or not. The dragons' ability to fly *between* times as well as places was not yet well-known. The Lords might not realize it had been used the previous day to forestall the Threads. If F'lar could be sure that project was going to be successful—well, it would add an optimistic note to the meeting.

Let the charts, with the waves and times of the Thread attacks clearly visible, reassure the Lords.

The visitors were not long in assembling. Nor were they all successful in hiding their apprehension and the shock they had received now that Threads had again spun down from the Red Star to menace all life on Pern. This was going to be a difficult session, F'lar decided grimly. He had a fleeting wish, which he quickly suppressed, that he had gone with F'nor and Lessa to the Southern Continent. Instead, he bent with apparent industry to the charts before him.

Soon there were but two more to come, Meron of Nabol (whom he would have liked not to include, for the man was a troublemaker) and Lytol of Ruatha. F'lar had sent for Lytol last because he did not wish Lessa to encounter the man. She was still overly—and, to his mind, foolishly—sensitive at having had to resign her claim to Ruatha Hold for the Lady Gemma's posthumous son. Lytol, as Warder of Ruatha, had a place in this conference. The man was also an ex-dragonman, and his return to the Weyr was painful enough without Lessa's compounding it with her resentment. Lytol was, with the exception of young Larad of Telgar, the Weyr's most valuable ally.

S'lel came in with Meron a step behind him. The Holder was furious at this summons; it showed in his walk, in his eyes, in his haughty bearing. But he was also as inquisitive as he was devious. He nodded only to Larad among the Lords and took the seat left vacant for him by Larad's side. Meron's manner made it obvious that that place was too close to F'lar by half a room.

The Weyrleader acknowledged S'lel's salute and indicated the bronze rider should be seated. F'lar had given thought to the seating arrangements in the Council Room, carefully interspersing brown and bronze dragonriders with Holders and Craftsmen. There was now barely room to move in the generously proportioned cavern, but there was also no room in which to draw daggers if tempers got hot.

A hush fell on the gathering, and F'lar looked up to see that the stocky, glowering ex-dragonman from Ruatha had stopped on the threshold of the Council. He slowly brought his hand up in a respectful salute to the Weyrleader. As F'lar returned the salute, he noticed that the tic in Lytol's left cheek jumped almost continuously.

Lyton's eyes, dark with pain and inner unquiet, ranged the room. He nodded to the members of his former wing, to Larad and Zurg, head of his own weavers' craft. Stiff-legged, he walked to the remaining seat, murmuring a greeting to T'sum on his left.

F'lar rose.

"I appreciate your coming, good Lords and Craftmasters. The Threads spin once again. The first attack has been met and seared from the sky. Lord Vincet," and the worried Holder of Nerat looked up in alarm, "we have dispatched a patrol to the rainforest to do a low-flight sweep to make certain there are no burrows."

Vincet swallowed nervously, his face paling at the thought of what Threads could do to his fertile, lush holdings.

"We shall need your best junglemen to help—"

"Help? But you said . . . the Threads were seared in the sky?"

"There is no point in taking the slightest chance," F'lar replied, implying that the patrol was only a precaution instead of the necessity he knew it would be.

Vincet gulped, glancing anxiously around the room for sympathy, and found none. Everyone would soon be in his position.

"There is a patrol due at Keroon and at Igen." F'lar looked first at Lord Corman, then at Lord Banger, who gravely nodded. "Let me say by way of reassurance that there will be no further attacks for three days and four hours." F'lar tapped the appropriate chart. "The Threads will begin approximately here on Telgar, drift westward through the southenmost portion of Crom, which is mountainous, and on, through Ruatha and the southern end of Nabol."

"How can you be so certain of that?"

F'lar recognized the contemptuous voice of Meron of Nabol.

"The Threads do not fall like a child's jackstraws, Lord Meron," F'lar replied. "They fall in a definitely predictable pattern; the attacks last exactly six hours. The intervals between attacks will gradually shorten over the next few Turns as the Red Star draws closer. Then, for about forty full Turns, as the Red Star swings past and around us, the attacks occur every fourteen hours, marching across our world in a timeable fashion."

"So *you* say," Meron sneered, and there was a low mumble of support.

"So the Teaching Ballads say," Larad put in firmly.

Meron glared at Telgar's Lord and went on, "I recall another of your predictions about how the Threads were supposed to begin falling right after Solstice."

"Which they did," F'lar interrupted him. "As black dust in the Northern Holds. For the reprieve we've had, we can thank our lucky stars that we have had an unusually hard and long Cold Turn."

"Dust?" demanded Nessel of Crom. "That dust was Threads?" The man was one of Fax's blood connections and under Meron's influence: an older man who had learned lessons from his conquering relative's bloody ways and had not the wit to improve on or alter the original. "My Hold is still blowing with them. They're dangerous?"

F'lar shook his head emphatically. "How long has the black dust been blowing in your Hold? Weeks? Done any harm yet?"

Nessel frowned.

"I'm interested in your charts, Weyrleader," Larad of Telgar said smoothly. "Will they give us an accurate idea of how often we may expect Threads to fall in our own Holds?"

"Yes. You may also anticipate that the dragonmen will arrive shortly before the invasion is due," F'lar went on. "However, additional measures of your own are necessary, and it is for this that I called the Council."

"Wait a minute," Corman of Keroon growled. "I want a copy of those fancy charts of yours for my own. I want to know what those bands and wavy lines really mean. I want . . . "

"Naturally you'll have a timetable of your own. I mean to impose on Masterharper Robinton"—F'lar nodded respectfully toward that Craftmaster—"to oversee the copying and make sure everyone understands the timing involved."

Robinton, a tall, gaunt man with a lined, saturnine face, bowed deeply. A slight smile curved his wide lips at the now hopeful glances favored him by the Hold Lords. His craft, like that of the dragonmen, had been much mocked, and this new respect amused him. He was a man with a keen eye for the ridiculous, and an active imagination.

The circumstances in which doubting Pern found itself were too ironic not to appeal to his innate sense of justice. He now contented himself with a deep bow and a mild phrase.

"Truly all shall pay heed to the master." His voice was deep, his words enunciated with no provincial slurring.

F'lar, about to speak, looked sharply at Robinton as he caught the double barb of that single line. Larad, too, looked around at the Masterharper, clearing his throat hastily.

"We shall have our charts," Larad said, forestalling Meron, who had opened his mouth to speak. "We shall have the dragonmen when the Threads spin. What are these additional measures? And why are they necessary?"

All eyes were on F'lar again.

"We have one Weyr where six once flew."

"But word is that Ramoth has hatched over forty more," someone in the back of the room declared. "And why did you Search out still more of our young men?"

"Forty-one as yet unmatured dragons," F'lar said. Privately, he hoped that this southern venture would still work out. There was real fear in that man's voice. "They grow well and quickly. Just at present, while the Threads do not strike with great frequency as the Red Star begins its Pass, our Weyr is sufficient . . . if we have your cooperation on the ground. Tradition is that"—he nodded tactfully toward Robinton, the dispenser of Traditional usage—"you Holders are responsible for only your dwellings, which, of course, are adequately protected by firepits and raw stone. However, it is spring and our heights have been allowed to grow wild with vegetation. Arable land is blossoming with crops. This presents vast acreage vulnerable to the Threads which one Weyr, at this time, is not able to patrol without severely draining the vitality of our dragons and riders."

At this candid admission, a frightened and angry mutter spread rapidly throughout the room.

"Ramoth rises to mate again soon," F'lar continued in a matter-of-fact way. "Of course, in other times, the queens started producing heavy clutches many Turns before the critical solstice as well as more queens. Unfortunately, Jora was ill and old, and Nemorth intractable. The matter—" He was interrupted.

"You dragonmen with your high and mighty airs will bring destruction on us all!"

"You have yourselves to blame," Robinton's voice stabbed across the ensuing shouts. "Admit it, one and all. You've paid less honor to the Weyr than you would your watch-wher's kennel—and that not much! But now the thieves are on the heights, and you are screaming because the poor reptile is nigh to death from neglect. Beat him, will you? When you exiled him to his kennel because he tried to warn you?

Tried to get you to prepare against the invaders? It's on *your* conscience, not the Weyrleader's or the dragonriders', who have honestly done their duty these hundreds of Turns in keeping dragonkind alive . . . against your protests. How many of you"—his tone was scathing— "have been generous in thought and favor toward dragonkind? Even since I became master of my craft, how often have my harpers told me of being beaten for singing the old songs as is their duty? You earn only the right, good Lords and Craftsmen, to squirm inside your stony Holds and writhe as your crops die a-borning."

He rose.

"'No Threads will fall. It's a harper's winter tale,'" he whined, in faultless imitation of Nessel. "'These dragonmen leech us of heir and harvest,'" and his voice took on the constricted, insinuating tenor that could only be Meron's. "And now the truth is as bitter as a brave man's fears and as difficult as mockweed to swallow. For all the honor you've done them, the dragonmen should leave you to be spun on the Threads' distaff."

"Bitra, Lemos, and I," spoke up Raid, the wiry Lord of Benden, his blunt chin lifted belligerently, "have always done our duty to the Weyr."

Robinton swung around to him, his eyes flashing as he gave that speaker a long, slow look.

"Aye, and you have. Of all the Great Holds, you three have been loyal. But you others," and his voice rose indignantly, "as spokesman for my craft, I know, to the last full stop in the score, your opinion of dragonkind. I heard the first whisper of your attempt to ride out against the Weyr." He laughed harshly and pointed a long finger at Vincet. "Where would you be today, good Lord Vincet, if the Weyr had *not* sent you packing back, hoping your ladies would be returned you? All of you," and his accusing finger marked each of the Lords of that abortive effort, "actually rode against the Weyr because . . . 'there . . . were . . . no . . . more . . . Threads!'"

He planted his fists on either hip and glared at the assembly. F'lar wanted to cheer. It was easy to see why the man was Masterharper, and he thanked circumstance that such a man was the Weyr's partisan.

"And now, at this critical moment, you have the incredible presumption to protest against any measure the Weyr suggests?" Robinton's supple voice oozed derision and amazement. "Attend what the Weyrleader says and spare him your petty carpings!" He snapped those words out as a father might enjoin an erring child. "You were," and he switched to the mildest of polite conversational tones as he addressed F'lar, "I believe, asking our cooperation, good F'lar? In what capacities?"

F'lar hastily cleared his throat.

"I shall require that the Holds police their own fields and woods, during the attacks if possible, definitely once the Threads have passed. All burrows which might land must be found, marked, and destroyed. The sooner they are located, the easier it is to be rid of them."

"There's no time to dig firepits through all the lands . . . we'll lose half our growing space," Nessel exclaimed.

"There were other ways, used in olden times, which I believe our Mastersmith might know." F'lar gestured politely toward Fandarel, the archetype of his profession if ever such existed.

The Smith Craftmaster was by several inches the tallest man in the Council Room, his massive shoulders and heavily muscled arms pressed against his nearest neighbors, although he had made an effort not to crowd against anyone. He rose, a giant tree-stump of a man, hooking thumbs like beast-horns in the thick belt that spanned his waistless midsection. His voice, by no means sweet after Turns of bellowing above roaring hearths and hammers, was, by comparison to Robinton's superb delivery, a diluted, unsupported light baritone.

"There were machines, that much is true," he allowed in deliberate, thoughtful tones. "My father, it was he, told me of them as a curiosity of the Craft. There may be sketches in the Hall. There may not. Such things do not keep on skins for long." He cast an oblique look under beetled brows at the Tanner Craftmaster.

"It is our own hides we must worry about preserving," F'lar remarked to forestall any intercraft disputes.

Fandarel grumbled in his throat in such a way that F'lar was not certain whether the sound was the man's laughter or a guttural agreement.

"I shall consider the matter. So shall all my fellow craftsmen," Fandarel assured the Weyrleader. "To sear Threads from the ground without damaging the soil may not be so easy. There are, it is true, fluids which burn and sear. We use an acid to etch design on daggers and ornamental metals. We of the Craft call it agenothree. There is also the black heavy-water that lies on the surface of pools in Igen and Boll. It burns hot and long. And if, as you say, the Cold Turn made the Threads break into dust, perhaps ice from the coldest northlands might freeze and break grounded Threads. However, the problem is to bring such to the Threads where they fall since they will not oblige us by falling where we want them. . . " He screwed up his face in a grimace.

F'lar stared at him, surprised. Did the man realize how humorous he was? No, he was speaking with sincere concern. Now the Mastersmith scratched his head, his tough fingers making audible grating sounds along his course hair and heat-toughened scalp.

"A nice problem. A nice problem," he mused, undaunted. "I shall give it every attention." He sat down, the heavy bench creaking under his weight.

The Masterfarmer raised his hand tentatively.

"When I became Craftmaster, I recall coming across a reference to the sandworms of Igen. They were once cultivated as a protective—"

"Never heard Igen produced anything useful except head and sand," quipped someone.

"We need every suggestion," F'lar said sharply, trying to identify that heckler. "Please find that reference, Craftmaster. Lord Banger of Igen, find me some of those sandworms!"

Banger, equally surprised that his arid Hold had a hidden asset, nodded vigorously.

"Until we have more efficient ways of killing Threads, all Holders must be organized on the ground during attacks, to spot and mark burrows, to set firestone to burn in them. I do not wish any man to be scored, but we know how quickly Threads burrow deep, and no burrow can be left to multiply. You stand to lose more," and he gestured emphatically at the Holder Lords, "than any others. Guard not just yourselves, for a burrow on one man's border may grow across to his neighbor's. Mobilize every man, woman, and child, farm and crafthold. Do it now."

The Council Room was fraught with tension and stunned reflection until Zurg, the Masterweaver, rose to speak.

"My craft, too, has something to offer . . . which is only fair since we deal with thread every day of our lives . . . in regard to the ancient methods." Zurg's voice was light and dry, and his eyes, in their creases of spare, lined flesh, were busy, darting from one face in his audience to another. "In Ruath Hold I once saw upon the wall . . . where the tapestry now resides, who knows?" He slyly glanced at Meron of Nabol and then at Bargen of the High Reaches who had succeeded to Fax's title there. "The work was as old as dragonkind and showed, among other things, a man on foot, carrying upon his back a curious contraption. He held within his hand a rounded, sword-long object from which tongues of flame . . . magnificently woven in the orange-red dyes now lost to us . . . spouted toward the ground. Above, of course, were dragons in close formation, bronzes predominating . . . again we've lost that true dragon-bronze shade. Consequently I remember the work as much for what we now lack as for its subject matter."

"A flamethrower?" the Smith rumbled. "A flamethrower," he repeated with a falling inflection. "A flamethrower," he murmured thoughtfully, his heavy brows drawn into a titanic scowl. "A thrower of what sort of flame? It requires thought." He lowered his head and didn't speak, so engrossed in the required thought that he lost interest in the rest of the discussion.

"Yes, good Zurg, there have been many tricks of every trade lost in recent Turns," F'lar commented sardonically. "If we wish to continue living, such knowledge must be revived . . . fast. I would particularly like to recover the tapestry of which Master Zurg speaks."

F'lar looked significantly at those Lords who had quarreled over Fax's seven Holds after his death.

"It may save all of you much loss. I suggest that it appear at Ruatha. Or at Zurg's or Fandarel's crafthall. Whichever is most convenient."

There was some shuffling of feet, but no one admitted ownership.

"It might then be returned to Fax's son, who is now Ruatha's Lord," F'lar added, wryly amused at such magnanimous justice.

Lytol snorted softly and glowered around the room. F'lar supposed Lytol to be amused and experienced a fleeting regret for the orphaned Jaxom, reared by such a cheerless if honest guardian.

"If I may, Lord Weyrleader," Robinton broke in, "we might all benefit, as your maps prove to us, from research in our own Records." He smiled suddenly, an unexpectedly embarrassed smile. "I own I find myself in some disgrace for we Harpers have let slip unpopular ballads and skimped on some of the longer Teaching Ballads and Sagas . . . for lack of listeners and, occasionally, in the interest of preserving our skins."

F'lar stifled a laugh with a cough. Robinton was a genius.

"I must see that Ruathan tapestry," Fandarel suddenly boomed out.

"I'm sure it will be in your hands very soon," F'lar assured him with more confidence than he dared feel. "My Lords, there is much to be done. Now that you understand what we all face, I leave it in your hands as leaders in your separate Holds and crafts how best to organize your own people. Craftsmen, turn your best minds to our special problems: review all Records that might turn up something to our purpose. Lords Telgar, Crom, Ruatha, and Nabol, I shall be with you in three days. Nerat, Keroon, and Igen, I am at your disposal to help destroy any burrow on your lands. While we have the Masterminer here, tell him your needs. How stands your craft?"

"Happy to be so busy at our trade, Weyrleader," piped up the Masterminer.

Just then F'lar caught sight of F'nor, hovering about in the shadows of the hallway, trying to catch his eye. The brown rider wore an exultant grin, and it was obvious he was bursting with news.

F'lar wondered how they could have returned so swiftly from the Southern Continent, and then he realized that F'nor—again—was tanned. He gave a jerk of his head, indicating that F'nor take himself off to the sleeping quarters and wait.

"Lords and Craftmasters, a dragonet will be at the disposal of each of you for messages and transportation. Now, good morning."

He strode out of the Council Room, up the passageway into the queen's weyr, and parted the still swinging curtains into the sleeping room just as F'nor was pouring himself a cup of wine.

"Success!" F'nor cried as the Weyrleader entered. "Though how you knew to send just thirty-two candidates I'll never understand. I thought you were insulting our noble Pridith. But thirty-two eggs she laid in four days. It was all I could do to keep from riding out when the first appeared."

F'lar responded with hearty congratulations, relieved that there would be at least that much benefit from this apparently ill-fated venture. Now all he had to figure out was how much longer F'nor had stayed south until his frantic visit the night before. For there were no worry lines or strain in F'nor's grinning, well-tanned face.

"No queen egg?" asked F'lar hopefully. With thirty-two in the one experiment, perhaps they could send a second queen back and try again.

F'nor's face lengthened. "No, and I was sure there would be. But there are fourteen bronzes. Pridith outmatched Ramoth there," he added proudly.

"Indeed she did. How goes the Weyr otherwise?"

F'nor frowned, shaking his head against an inner bewilderment. "Kylara's . . . well, she's a problem. Stirs up trouble constantly. T'bor leads a sad time with her, and he's so touchy everyone keeps a distance from him." F'nor brightened a little. "Young N'ton is shaping up into a fine wingleader, and his bronze may outfly T'bor's Orth when Pridith flies to mate the next time. Not that I'd wish Kylara on N'ton . . . or anyone."

"No trouble then with supplies?"

F'nor laughed outright. "If you hadn't made it so plain we must not communicate with you here, we could supply you with fruits and fresh greens that are superior to anything in the north. We eat the way dragonmen should! F'lar, we must consider a supply Weyr down there. Then we shall never have to worry about tithing trains and . . . "

"In good time. Get back now. You know you must keep these visits short."

F'nor grimaced. "Oh, it's not so bad. I'm not here in this time, anyway."

"True," F'lar agreed, "but don't mistake the time and come while you're still here."

"Hmmm? Oh, yes, that's right. I forget time is creeping for us and speeding for you. Well, I shan't be back again till Pridith lays the second clutch."

With a cheerful good-bye, F'nor strode out of the weyr. F'lar watched him thoughtfully as he slowly retraced his steps to the Council Room. Thirty-two new dragons, fourteen of them bronzes, was no small gain and seemed worth the hazard. Or would the hazard wax greater?

Someone cleared his throat deliberately. F'lar looked up to see Robinton standing in the archway that led to the Council Room.

"Before I can copy and instruct others about those maps, Weyrleader, I must myself understand them completely. I took the liberty of remaining behind."

"You make a good champion, Masterharper."

"You have a noble cause, Weyrleader," and then Robinton's eyes glinted maliciously. "I've been begging the Egg for an opportunity to speak out to so noble an audience."

"A cup of wine first?"

"Benden grapes are the envy of Pern."

"If one has the palate for such a delicate bouquet."

"It is carefully cultivated by the knowledgeable."

F'lar wondered when the man would stop playing with words. He had more on his mind than studying the time-charts.

"I have in mind a ballad which, for lack of explanation, I had set aside when I became the Master of my crafthall," he said judiciously after an appreciative savoring of his wine. "It is an uneasy song, both the tune and the words. One develops, as a harper must, a certain sensitivity for what will be received and what will be rejected . . . forcefully," and he winced in retrospect. "I found that this ballad unsettled singer as well as audience and retired it from use. Now, like that tapestry, it bears rediscovery."

After his death C'gan's instrument had been hung on the Council Room wall till a new Weyrsinger could be chosen. The guitar was very old, its wood thin. Old C'gan had kept it well-tuned and covered. The Masterharper handled it now with reverence, lightly stroking the strings to hear the tone, raising his eyebrows at the fine voice of the instrument.

He plucked a chord, a dissonance. F'lar wondered if the instrument was out of tune or if the harper had, by some chance, struck the wrong string. But Robinton repeated the odd discord, then modulating into a weird minor that was somehow more disturbing than the first notes.

"I told you it was an uneasy song. And I wonder if you know the answers to the questions it asks. For I've turned the puzzle over in my mind many times of late."

Then abruptly he shifted from the spoken to the sung tone.

Gone away, gone ahead,
Echoes away, die unansweréd.
Empty, open, dusty, dead,
Why have all the Weyrfolk fled?

Where have dragons gone together?
Leaving Weyrs to wind and weather?
Setting herdbeasts free of tether?
Gone, our safeguards, gone, but whither?

Have they flown to some new Weyr
Where cruel Threads some others fear?
Are they worlds away from here?
Why, oh, why, the empty Weyr?

The last plaintive chord reverberated.

"Of course, you realize that the song was first recorded in the craft annals some four hundred Turns ago," Robinton said lightly, cradling the guitar in both arms. "The Red Star had just passed beyond attack-proximity. The people had ample reason to be stunned and worried over the sudden loss of the populations of five Weyrs. Oh, I imagine at the time they had any one of a number of explanations, but none . . . not one explanation . . . is recorded." Robinton paused significantly.

"I have found none recorded, either," F'lar replied. "As a matter of fact, I had all the Records brought here from the other Weyrs . . . in order to compile accurate attack timetables. And those other Weyr Records simply end—" F'lar made a chopping gesture with one hand. "In Benden's Records there is no mention of sickness, death, fire, disaster—not one word of explanation for the sudden lapse of the usual intecourse between the Weyrs. Benden's Records continue blithely, but only for Benden. There is one entry that pertains to the mass disappearance . . . .the initiation of a Pern-wide patrol routing, not just Benden's immediate responsibility. And that is all."

"Strange," Robinton mused. "Once the danger from the Red Star was past, the dragons and riders may have gone *between* to ease the drain on the Holds. But I simply cannot believe that. Our craft Records do mention that harvests were bad and that there had been several natural catastrophes . . . other than the Threads. Men may be gallant and your breed the most gallant of all, but mass suicide? I simply do not accept that explanation . . . not for dragonmen."

"My thanks," F'lar said with mild irony.

"Don't mention it," Robinton replied with a gracious nod.

F'lar chuckled appreciatively. "I see we have been too weyrbound as well as too hidebound."

Robinton drained his cup and looked at it mournfully until F'lar refilled it.

"Well, your isolation served some purpose, you know, and you handled that uprising of the Lords magnificently. I nearly choked to death laughing," Robinton remarked, grinning broadly. "Stealing their women in the flash of a dragon's breath!" He chuckled again, then suddenly sobered, looking F'lar straight in the eye. "Accustomed as I am to hearing what a man does *not* say aloud, I suspect there is much you glossed over in that Council meeting. You may be sure of my discretion . . . and . . . you may be sure of my wholehearted support and that of my not ineffectual craft. To be blunt, how may my harpers aid you?" and he strummed a vigorous marching air. "Stir men's pulses with ballads of past glories and success?" The tune, under his flashing fingers, changed abruptly to a stern but determined rhythm. "Strengthen their mental and physical sinews for hardship?"

"If all your harpers could stir men as you yourself do, I should have no worries that five hundred or so additional dragons would not immediately end."

"Oh, then despite your brave words and marked charts, the situation is"—a dissonant twang on the gitar accented his final words—"more desperate than you carefully did not say."

"It may be."

"The flamethrowers old Zurg remembered and Fandarel must reconstruct—will they tip the scales?"

F'lar regarded this clever man thoughtfully and made a quick decision.

"Even Igen's sandworms will help, but as the world turns and the Red Star nears, the interval between daily attacks shortens and we have only seventy-two new dragons to add to those we had yesterday. One is now dead and several will not fly for several weeks."

"Seventy-two?" Robinton caught him up sharply. "Ramoth hatched but forty, and they are still too young to eat firestone."

F'lar outlined F'nor and Lessa's expedition, taking place at that moment. He went on to F'nor's reappearance and warning, as well as the fact that the experiment had been successful in part with the hatching of thirty-two new dragons from Pridith's first clutch. Robinton caught him up.

"How can F'nor already have returned when you haven't heard from Lessa and him that there is a breeding place on the Southern Continent?"

"Dragons can go *between* times as well as places. They go as easily to a *when* as to a *where*."

Robinton's eyes widened as he digested this astonishing news.

"That is how we forestalled the attack on Nerat yesterday morning. We jumped back two hours *between* time to meet the Threads as they fell."

"You can actually jump backward? How far back?"

"I don't know. Lessa, when I was teaching her to fly Ramoth, inadvertently returned to Ruath Hold, to the dawn thirteen Turns ago when Fax's men invaded from the heights. When she returned to the present, I attempted a *between* times jump of some ten Turns. To the dragons it is a simple matter to go *between* times or spaces, but there appears to be a terrific drain on the rider. Yesterday, by the time we returned from Nerat and had to go on to Keroon, I felt as though I had been pounded flat and left to dry for a summer on Igen Plain." F'lar shook his head. "We have obviously succeeded in sending Kylara, Pridith, and the others ten Turns *between*, because F'nor has already reported to me that he has been there several Turns. The drain on humans, however, is becoming more and more marked. But even seventy-two more mature dragons will be a help."

"Send a rider ahead in time to see if it is sufficient," Robinton suggested helpfully. "Save you a few days' worrying."

"I don't know how to get to a *when* that has not yet happened. You must give your dragon reference points, you know. How can you refer him to times that have not yet occurred?"

"You've got an imagination. Project it."

"And perhaps lose a dragon when I have none to spare? No, I must continue . . . because obviously I have, judging by F'nor's returns . . . as I decided to start. Which reminds me, I must give orders to start packing. Then I shall go over the time-charts with you."

It wasn't until after the noon meal, which Robinton took with the Weyrleader, that the Masterharper was confident that he understood the charts and left to begin their copying.

Across a waste of lonely tossing sea,
Where no dragonwings had lately spread,
Flew a gold and a sturdy brown in spring,
Searching if a land be dead.

As Ramoth and Canth bore Lessa and F'nor up to the Star Stone, they saw the first of the Hold Lords and Craftmasters arriving for the Council.

In order to get back to the Southern Continent of ten Turns ago,

Lessa and F'nor had decided it was easiest to transfer first *between* times to the Weyr of ten Turns back which F'nor remembered. Then they would go *between* places to a seapoint just off the coast of the neglected Southern Continent which was as close to it as the Records gave any references.

F'nor put Canth in mind of a particular day he remembered ten Turns back, and Ramoth picked up the references from the brown's mind. The awesome cold of *between* times took Lessa's breath away, and it was with intense relief that she caught a glimpse of the normal weyr activity before the dragons took them *between* places to hover over the turgid sea.

Beyond them, smudged purple on this overcast and gloomy day, lurked the Southern Continent. Lessa felt a new anxiety replace the uncertainty of the temporal displacement. Ramoth beat forward with great sweeps of her wings, making for the distant coast. Canth gallantly tried to maintain a matching speed.

He's only a brown, Lessa scolded her golden queen.

If he is flying with me, Ramoth replied coolly, *he must stretch his wings a little.*

Lessa grinned, thinking very privately that Ramoth was still piqued that she had not been able to fight with her weyrmates. All the males would have a hard time with her for a while.

They saw the flock of wherries first and realized that there would have to be some vegetation on the Continent. Wherries needed greens to live, although they could subsist on little else besides occasional grubs if necessary.

Lessa had Canth relay questions to his rider. *If the Southern Continent was rendered barren by the Threads, how did new growth start? Where did the wherries come from?*

Ever notice the seed pods split open and the flakes carried away by the winds? Ever notice that wherries fly south after the autumn solstice?

Yes, but . . .

Yes, but!

But the land was Thread-bared!

In less than four hundred Turns even the scorched hilltops of our Continent begin to sprout in the springtime, F'nor replied by way of Canth, *so it is easy to assume the Southern Continent could revive, too.*

Even at the pace Ramoth set, it took time to reach the jagged shoreline with its forbidding cliffs, start stone in the sullen light. Lessa groaned inwardly but urged Ramoth higher to see over the masking highlands. All seemed gray and desolate from that altitude.

Suddenly the sun broke through the cloud cover and the gray dissolved into dense greens and browns, living colors, the live greens of lush tropical growth, the browns of vigorous trees and vines. Lessa's cry of triumph was echoed by F'nor's hurrah and the brass voices of the dragons. Wherries, startled by the unusual sound, rose in squeaking alarm from their perches.

Beyond the headland, the land sloped away to jungle and grassy plateau, similar to mid-Boll. Though they searched all morning, they found no hospitable cliffs wherein to found a new Weyr. Was that a contributing factor in the southern venture's failure, Lessa wondered.

Discouraged, they landed on a high plateau by a small lake. The weather was warm but not oppressive, and while F'nor and Lessa ate their noonday meal, the two dragons wallowed in the water, refreshing themselves.

Lessa felt uneasy and had little appetite for the meat and bread. She noticed that F'nor was restless, too, shooting surreptitious glances around the lake and the jungle verge.

"What under the sun are we expecting? Wherries don't charge, and wild whers would come nowhere near a dragon. We're ten Turns before the Red Star, so there can't be any Threads."

F'nor shrugged, grimacing sheepishly as he tossed his unfinished bread back into the food pouch.

"Place feels so empty, I guess," he tendered, glancing around. He spotted ripe fruit hanging from a moonflower vine. "Now that looks familiar and good enough to eat, without tasting like dust in the mouth."

He climbed nimbly and snagged the orange-red fruit.

"Smells right, feels ripe, looks ripe," he announced and deftly sliced the fruit open. Grinning, he handed Lessa the first slice, carving another for himself. He lifted it challengingly. "Let us eat and die together!"

She couldn't help but laugh and saluted him back. They bit into the succulent flesh simultaneously. Sweet juices dribbled from the corners of her mouth, and Lessa hurriedly licked her lips to capture the least drop of the delicious liquid.

"Die happy—I will," F'nor cried, cutting more fruit.

Both were subtly reassured by the experiment and were able to discuss their discomposure.

"I think," F'nor suggested, "it is the lack of cliff and cavern and the still, still quality of the place, the knowing that there are no other men or beasts about but us."

Lessa nodded her head in agreement. "Ramoth, Canth, would having no Weyr upset you?"

We didn't always live in caves, Ramoth replied, somewhat haughtily as she rolled over in the lake. Sizable waves rushed up the shore almost to where Lessa and F'nor were seated on a fallen tree trunk. *The sun here is warm and pleasant, the water cooling. I would enjoy it here, but I am not to come.*

"She is out of sorts," Lessa whispered to F'nor. "Let Pridith have it, dear one," she called soothingly to the golden queen. "You've the Weyr and all!"

Ramoth ducked under the water, blowing up a froth in disgruntled reply.

Canth admitted that he had no reservations at all about living Weyrless. The dry earth would be warmer than stone to sleep on, once a suitably comfortable hollow had been achieved. No, he couldn't object to the lack of the cave as long as there was enough to eat.

"We'll have to bring herdbeasts in," F'nor mused. "Enough to start a good-sized herd. Of course, the wherries here are huge. Come to think of it, I believe this plateau has no exits. We wouldn't need to pasture it off. I'd better check. Otherwise, this plateau with the lake and enough clear space for Holds seems ideal. Walk out and pick breakfast from the tree."

"It might be wise to choose those who were not Hold-reared," Lessa added. "They would not feel so uneasy away from protecting heights and stone-security." She gave a short laugh. "I'm more a creature of habit than I suspected. All these open spaces, untenanted and quiet, seem . . . indecent." She gave a delicate shudder, scanning the broad and open plain beyond the lake.

"Fruitful and lovely," F'nor amended, leaping up to secure more of the orange-red succulents. "This tastes uncommonly good to me. Can't remember anything this sweet and juicy from Nerat, and yet it's the same variety."

"Undeniably superior to what the Weyr gets. I suspect Nerat serves home first, Weyr last."

They both stuffed themselves greedily.

Further investigation proved that the plateau was isolated, and ample to pasture a huge herd of foodbeasts for the dragons. It ended in a sheer drop of several dragonlengths into denser jungle on one side, the sea-side escarpment on the other. The timber stands would provide raw material from which dwellings could be made for the Weyrfolk. Ramoth and Canth stoutly agreed dragonkind would be comfortable enough under the heavy foliage of the dense jungle. As this part of the continent was similar, weatherwise, to Upper Nerat, there would be neither intense heat nor cold to give distress.

However, if Lessa was glad enough to leave, F'nor seemed reluctant to start back.

"We can go *between* time and place on the way back," Lessa insisted finally, "and be in the Weyr by late afternoon. The Lords will surely be gone by then."

F'nor concurred, and Lessa steeled herself for the trip *between*. She wondered why the *when between* bothered her more than the *where*, for it had no effect on the dragons at all. Ramoth, sensing Lessa's depression, crooned encouragingly. The long, long black suspension of the utter cold of *between* where and when ended suddenly in sunlight above the Weyr.

Somewhat startled, Lessa saw bundles and sacks spread out before the Lower Caverns as dragonriders supervised the loading of their beasts.

"What has been happening?" F'nor exclaimed.

"Oh, F'lar's been anticipating success," she assured him glibly.

Mnementh, who was watching the bustle from the ledge of the queen's weyr, sent a greeting to the travelers and the information that F'lar wished them to join him in the weyr as soon as they returned.

They found F'lar, as usual, bent over some of the oldest and least legible Record skins that he had had brought to the Council Room.

"And?" he asked, grinning a broad welcome at them.

"Green, lush, and livable," Lessa declaired, watching him intently. He knew something else, too. Well, she hoped he'd watch his words. F'nor was no fool, and this foreknowledge was dangerous.

"That is what I had so hoped to hear you say," F'lar went on smoothly. "Come, tell me in detail what you observed and discovered. It'll be good to fill in the blank spaces on the chart."

Lessa let F'nor give most of the account, to which F'lar listened with sincere attention, making notes.

"On the chance that it would be practical, I started packing supplies and alerting the riders to go with you," he told F'nor when the account was finished. "Remember, we've only three days in this time in which to start you back ten Turns ago. *We* have no moments to spare. And we must have many more mature dragons ready to fight at Telgar in three days' time. So, though ten Turns will have passed for you, three days only will elapse here. Lessa, your thought that the farm-bred might do better is well-taken. We're lucky that our recent Search for rider candidates for the dragons Pridith will have come mainly from the crafts and farms. No problem there. And most of the thirty-two are in their early teens."

"Thirty-two?" F'nor exclaimed. "We should have fifty. The dragonets must have some choice, even if we get the candidates used to the dragonets before they're hatched."

F'lar shrugged negligently. "Send back for more. *You'll* have time, remember," and F'lar chuckled as though he had started to add something and decided against it.

F'nor had no time to debate with the Weyrleader, for F'lar immediately launched on other rapid instructions.

F'nor was to take his own wingriders to help train the weyrlings. They would also take the forty young dragons of Ramoth's first clutch: Kylara with her queen Pridith, T'bor and his bronze Piyanth. N'ton's young bronze might also be ready to fly and mate by the time Pridith was, so that gave the young queen two bronzes at least.

"Suppose we'd found the continent barren?" F'nor asked, still puzzled by F'lar's assurance. "What then?"

"Oh, we'd've sent them back to, say, the High Reaches," F'lar replied far too glibly, but quickly went on. "I should send on other bronzes, but I'll need everyone else here to ride burrow-search on Keroon and Nerat. They've already unearthed several at Nerat. Vincet, I'm told, is close to heart attack from fright."

Lessa made a short comment on that Hold Lord.

"What of the meeting this morning?" F'nor asked, remembering.

"Never mind that now. You've got to start shifting *between* by evening, F'nor."

Lessa gave the Weyrleader a long hard look and decided she would have to find out what had happened in detail very soon.

"Sketch me some references, will you, Lessa?" F'lar asked.

There was a definite plea in his eyes as he drew clean hide and a stylus to her. He wanted no questions from her now that would alarm F'nor. She sighed and picked up the drawing tool.

She sketched quickly, with one or two details added by F'nor until she had rendered a reasonable map of the plateau they had chosen. Then, abruptly, she had trouble focusing her eyes. She felt light-headed.

"Lessa?" F'lar bent to her.

"Everything's . . . moving . . . circling . . . " and she collapsed backward into his arms.

As F'lar raised her slight body into his arms, he exchanged an alarmed look with his half brother.

"How do you feel?" the Weyrleader called after his brother.

"Tired but no more than that," F'nor assured him as he shouted down the service shaft to the kitchens for Manora to come and for hot *klah*. He needed that, and no doubt of it.

F'lar laid the Weyrwoman on the sleeping couch, covering her gently.

"I don't like this," he muttered, rapidly recalling what F'nor had said of Kylara's decline, which F'nor could not know was yet to come in his future. Why should it start so swiftly with Lessa?

"Time-jumping makes one feel slightly—" F'nor paused, groping for the exact wording. "Not entirely . . . whole. You fought *between* times at Nerat yesterday. . . . "

"I fought," F'lar reminded him, "but neither you nor Lessa battled anything today. There may be some inner . . . mental . . . stress simply to going *between* times. Look, F'nor, I'd rather only you came back once you reach the southern Weyr. I'll make it an order and get Ramoth to inhibit the dragons. That way no rider can take it into his head to come back even if he wants to. There is some factor that may be more serious than we can guess. Let's take no unnecessary risks."

"Agreed."

"One other detail, F'nor. Be very careful which times you pick to come back to see me. I wouldn't jump *between* too close to any time you were actually here. I can't imagine what would happen if you walked into your own self in the passageway, and I can't lose you."

With a rare demonstration of affection, F'lar gripped his half brother's shoulder tightly.

"Remember, F'nor. I was here all morning and you did not arrive back from the first trip till midafternoon. And remember, too, *we* have only three days. You have ten Turns."

F'nor left, passing Manora in the hall.

The woman could find nothing obviously the matter with Lessa, and they finally decided it might be simple fatigue; yesterday's strain when Lessa had to relay messages between dragons and fighters followed by the disjointing *between* times trip today.

When F'lar went to wish the southern venturers a good trip, Lessa was in a normal sleep, her face pale, but her breathing easy.

F'lar had Mnementh relay to Ramoth the prohibition he wished the queen to instill in all dragonkind assigned to the venture. Ramoth obliged, but added in an aside to bronze Mnementh, which he passed on to F'lar, that everyone else had adventures while she, the Weyr queen, was forced to stay behind.

No sooner had the laden dragons, one by one, winked out of the sky above the Star Stone than the young weyrling assigned to Nerat Hold as messenger came gliding down, his face white with fear.

"Weyrleader, many more burrows have been found, and they cannot be burned out with fire alone. Lord Vincet wants you."

F'lar could well imagine that Vincet did.

"Get yourself some dinner, boy, before you start back. I'll go shortly."

As he passed through to the sleeping quarters, he heard Ramoth rumbling in her throat. She had settled herself down to rest.

Lessa still slept, one hand curled under her cheek, her dark hair trailing over the edge of the bed. She looked fragile, childlike, and very precious to him. F'lar smiled to himself. So she was jealous of Kylara's attentions yesterday. He was pleased and flattered. Never would Lessa learn from him that Kylara, for all her bold beauty and sensuous nature, did not have one tenth the attraction for him that the unpredictable, dark, and delicate Lessa held. Even her stubborn intractableness, her keen and malicious humor, added zest to their relationship. With a tenderness he would never show her awake, F'lar bent and kissed her lips. She stirred and smiled, sighing lightly in her sleep.

Reluctantly returning to what must be done, F'lar left her so. As he paused by the queen, Ramoth raised her great, wedge-shaped head; her many-faceted eyes gleamed with bright luminescence as she regarded the Weyrleader.

"Mnementh, please ask Ramoth to get in touch with the dragonet at Fandarel's crafthall. I'd like the Mastersmith to come with me to Nerat. I want to see what his agenothree does to Threads."

Ramoth nodded her head as the bronze dragon relayed the message to her.

She has done so, and the green dragon comes as soon as he can. Mnementh reported to his rider. *It is easier to do, this talking about, when Lessa is awake,* he grumbled.

F'lar agreed heartily. It had been quite an advantage yesterday in the battle and would be more and more of an asset.

Maybe it would be better if she tried to speak, across time, to F'nor . . . but no, F'nor had come back.

F'lar strode into the Council Room, still hopeful that somewhere within the illegible portions of the old Records was the one clue he so desperately needed. There must be a way out of this impasse. If not the southern venture, then something else. Something!

Fandarel showed himself a man of iron will as well as sinew; he looked calmly at the exposed tangle of perceptibly growing Threads that writhed and intertwined obscenely.

"Hundreds and thousands in this one burrow," Lord Vincet of Nerat was exclaiming in a frantic tone of voice. He waved his hands distractedly around the plantation of young trees in which the burrow had been discovered. "These stalks are already withering even as you hesitate. Do something! How many more young trees will die in this one field alone? How many more burrows escaped dragon's breath yesterday? Where is a dragon to sear them? Why are you just standing there?"

F'lar and Fandarel paid no attention to the man's raving, both fascinated as well as revolted by their first sight of the burrowing stage of their ancient foe. Despite Vincet's panicky accusations, it was the only burrow on this particular slope. F'lar did not like to contemplate how many more might have slipped through the dragons' efforts and had reached Nerat's warm and fertile soil. If they had only had time enough to set out watchmen to track the fall of stray clumps. They could, at least, remedy that error in Telgar, Crom, and Ruatha in three days. But it was not enough. Not enough.

Fandarel motioned forward the two craftsmen who had accompanied him. They were burdened with an odd contraption: a large cylinder of metal to which was attached a wand with a wide nozzle. At the other end of the cylinder was another short pipe-length and then a short cylinder with an inner plunger. One craftsman worked the plunger vigorously, while the second, barely keeping his hands steady, pointed the nozzle end toward the Thread burrow. At a nod from this pumper, the man released a small knob on the nozzle, extending it carefully away from him and over the burrow. A thin spray danced from the nozzle and drifted down into the burrow. No sooner had the spray motes contacted the Thread tangles than steam hissed out of the burrow. Before long, all that remained of the pallid writhing tendrils was a smoking mass of blackened strands. Long after Fandarel had waved the craftsmen back, he stared at the grave. Finally he grunted and found himself a long stick with which he poked and prodded the remains. Not one Thread wriggled.

"Humph," he grunted with evident satisfaction. "However, we can scarcely go around digging up every burrow. I need another."

With Lord Vincet a hand-wringing moaner in their wake, they were escorted by the junglemen to another undisturbed burrow on the sea-side of the rainforest. The Threads had entered the earth by the side of a huge tree that was already drooping.

With his prodding stick Fandarel made a tiny hole at the top of the burrow and then waved his craftsmen forward. The pumper made vigorous motions at his end, while the nozzle-holder adjusted his pipe before inserting it in the hole. Fandarel gave the sign to start and counted slowly before he waved a cutoff. Smoke oozed out of the tiny hole.

After a suitable lapse of time, Fandarel ordered the junglemen to dig, reminding them to be careful not to come in contact with the agenothree liquid. When the burrow was uncovered, the acid had done its work, leaving nothing but a thoroughly charred mass of tangles.

Fandarel grimaced but this time scratched his head in dissatisfaction.

"Takes too much time, either way. Best to get them still at the surface," the Mastersmith grumbled.

"Best to get them in the air," Lord Vincet chattered. "And what will that stuff do to my young orchards? What will it do?"

Fandarel swung around, apparently noticing the distressed Holder for the first time.

"Little man, agenothree in diluted form is what you use to fertilize your plants in the spring. True, this field has been burned out for a few years, but it is *not* Thread-full. It *would* be better if we could get the spray up high in the air. Then it would float down and dissipate harmlessly—fertilizing very evenly, too." He paused, scratched his head gratingly. "Young dragons could carry a team aloft. . . . Hmmm. A possibility, but the apparatus is bulky yet." He turned his back on the surprised Hold Lord then and asked F'lar if the tapestry had been returned. "I cannot yet discover how to make a tube throw flame. I got this mechanism from what we make for the orchard farmers."

"I'm still waiting for word on the tapestry," F'lar replied, "but this spray of yours is effective. The Thread burrow is dead."

"The sandworms are effective too, but not really efficient," Fandarel grunted in dissatisfaction. He beckoned abruptly to his assistants and stalked off into the increasing twilight to the dragons.

Robinton awaited their return at the Weyr, his outward calm barely masking his inner excitement. He inquired politely, however, of Fandarel's efforts. The Mastersmith grunted and shrugged.

"I have all my craft at work."

"The Mastersmith is entirely too modest," F'lar put in. "He has already put together an ingenious device that sprays agenothree into Thread burrows and sears them into a black pulp."

"Not efficient. *I* like the idea of flamethrowers," the smith said, his eyes gleaming in his expressionless face. "A thrower of flame," he repeated, his eyes unfocusing. He shook his heavy head with a bone-popping crack. "I go," and with a curt nod to the harper and the Weyrleader, he left.

"I like that man's dedication to an idea," Robinton observed. Despite his amusement with the man's eccentric behavior, there was a strong undercurrent of respect for the smith. "I must set my apprentices a task for an appropriate Sage on the Mastersmith. I understand," he said, turning to F'lar, "that the southern venture has been inaugurated."

F'lar nodded unhappily.

"Your doubts increase?"

"This *between* times travel takes its own toll," he admitted, glancing anxiously toward the sleeping room.

"The Weyrwoman is ill?"

"Sleeping, but today's journey affected her. We need another, less dangerous answer!" and F'lar slammed one fist into the other palm.

"I came with no real answer," Robinton said then, briskly, "but with what I believe to be another part of the puzzle. I have found an entry. Four hundred Turns ago the then Masterharper was called to Fort Weyr not long after the Red Star retreated away from Pern in the evening sky."

"An entry? What is it?"

"Mind you, the Thread attacks had just lifted and the Masterharper was called one late evening to Fort Weyr. An unusual summons. However," and Robinton emphasized the distinction by pointing a long, callous-tipped finger at F'lar, "no further mention is ever made of that visit. There ought to have been, for all such summonses have a purpose. All such meetings are recorded, yet no explanation of this one is given. The record is taken up several weeks later by the Masterharper as though he had not left his crafthall at all. Some ten months afterward, the Question Song was added to compulsory Teaching Ballads."

"You believe the two are connected with the abandonment of the five Weyrs?"

"I do, but I could not say why. I only feel that the events, the visit, the disappearances, the Question Song, are connected."

F'lar poured them both cups of wine.

"I have checked back, too, seeking some indications." He shrugged. "All must have been normal right up to the point they disappeared. There are Records of tithing trains received, supplies stored, the list of injured dragons and men returning to active patrols. And then the Records cease at full Cold, leaving only Benden Weyr occupied."

"And why that one Weyr of the six to choose from?" Robinton demanded. "Island Ista would be a better choice if only one Weyr was to be left. Benden so far north is not a likely place to pass four hundred Turns."

"Benden is high and isolated. A disease that struck the others and was prevented from reaching Benden?"

"And no explanation of it? They can't all—dragons, riders, weyrfolk—have dropped dead on the same instant and left no carcasses rotting in the sun."

"Then let us ask ourselves, why was the harper called? Was he told to construct a Teaching Ballad covering this disappearance?"

"Well," Robinton snorted, "it certainly wasn't meant to reassure us, not with that tune—if one cares to call it a tune at all, and I don't— nor does it answer any questions! It poses them."

"For us to answer?" suggested F'lar softly.

"Aye." Robinton's eyes shone. "For us to answer, indeed, for it is a difficult song to forget. Which means it was meant to be remembered. Those questions are important, F'lar!"

"Which questions are important?" demanded Lessa, who had entered quietly.

Both men were on their feet. F'lar, with unusual attentiveness, held a chair for Lessa and poured her wine.

"I'm not going to break apart," she said tartly, almost annoyed at the excess of courtesy. Then she smiled up at F'lar to take the sting out of her words. "I slept and I feel much better. What were you two getting so intense about?"

F'lar quickly outlined what he and the Masterharper had been discussing. When he mentioned the Question Song, Lessa shuddered.

"That's one I can't forget, either. Which, I've always been told," and she grimaced, remembering the hateful lessons with R'gul, "means it's important. But why? It only asked questions." Then she blinked, her eyes went wide with amazement.

"'Gone away, gone . . . *ahead!*'" she cried, on her feet. "That's it! All five Weyrs went . . . *ahead*. But to when?"

F'lar turned to her, speechless.

"They came ahead to our time! Five Weyrs full of dragons," she repeated in an awed voice.

"No, that's impossible," F'lar contradicted.

"Why?" Robinton demanded excitedly. "Doesn't that solve the problem we're facing? The need for fighting dragons? Doesn't it explain why they left so suddenly with no explanation except that Question Song?"

F'lar brushed back the heavy lock of hair that overhung his eyes.

"It would explain their actions in leaving," he admitted, "because they couldn't leave any clues saying where they went, or it would cancel the whole thing. Just as I couldn't tell F'nor I knew the southern venture would have problems. But how do they get here—if here is *when* they came? They aren't here now. How would they have known they were needed—or *when* they were needed? And this is the real problem—how can you conceivably give a dragon references to a *when* that has not yet occurred?"

"Someone here must go back to give them the proper references," Lessa replied in a very quiet voice.

"You're mad, Lessa," F'lar shouted at her, alarm written on his face. "You know what happened to you today. How can you consider going back to a *when* you can't remotely imagine? To a *when* four hundred Turns ago? Going back ten Turns left you fainting and half-ill."

"Wouldn't it be worth it?" she asked him, her eyes grave. "Isn't Pern worth it?"

F'lar grabbed her by the shoulders, shaking her, his eyes wild with fear.

"Not even Pern is worth losing you, or Ramoth. Lessa, Lessa, don't you dare disobey me in this." His voice dropped to an intense, icy whisper, shaking with anger.

"Ah, there may be a way of effecting that solution, momentarily beyond us, Weyrwoman," Robinton put in adroitly. "Who knows what tomorrow holds? It certainly is not something one does without considering every angle."

Lessa did not shrug off F'lar's viselike grip on her shoulders as she gazed at Robinton.

"Wine?" the Masterharper suggested, pouring a mug for her. His diversionary action broke the tableau of Lessa and F'lar.

"Ramoth is not afraid to try," Lessa said, her mouth set in a determined line.

F'lar glared at the golden dragon who was regarding the humans, her neck curled around almost to the shoulder of her great wing.

"Ramoth is young," F'lar snapped and then caught Mnementh's wry thought even as Lessa did.

She threw her head back, her peal of laughter echoing in the vaulting chamber.

"I'm badly in need of a good joke myself," Robinton remarked pointedly.

"Mnementh told F'lar that he was neither young nor afraid to try, either. It was just a long step," Lessa explained, wiping tears from her eyes.

F'lar glanced dourly at the passageway, at the end of which Mnementh lounged on his customary ledge.

A laden dragon comes, the bronze warned those in the Weyr. *It is Lytol behind young B'rant on brown Fanth.*

"Now he brings his own bad news?" Lessa asked sourly.

"It is hard enough for Lytol to ride another's dragon or come here at all, Lessa of Ruatha. Do not increase his torment one jot with your childishness," F'lar said sternly.

Lessa dropped her eyes, furious with F'lar for speaking so to her in front of Robinton.

Lytol stumped into the queen's weyr, carrying one end of a large rolled rug. Young B'rant, struggling to uphold the other end, was sweating with the effort. Lytol bowed respectfully toward Ramoth and gestured the young brown rider to help him unroll their burden. As the immense tapestry uncoiled, F'lar could understand why Masterweaver Zurg had remembered it. The colors, ancient though they undoubtedly were, remained vibrant and undimmed. The subject matter was even more interesting.

"Mnementh, send for Fandarel. Here's the model he needs for his flamethrower," F'lar said.

"That tapestry is Ruatha's," Lessa cried indignantly. "I remember it from my childhood. It hung in the Great Hall and was the most cherished of my Blood Line's possessions. Where has it been?" Her eyes were flashing.

"Lady, it is being returned to where it belongs," Lytol said stolidly, avoiding her gaze. "A masterweaver's work, this," he went on, touching the heavy fabric with reverent fingers. "Such colors, such patterning. It took a man's life to set up the loom, a craft's whole effort to complete, or I am no judge of true craftsmanship."

F'lar walked along the edge of the immense arras, wishing it could be hung to afford the proper perspective of the heroic scene. A flying formation of three wings of dragons dominated the upper portion of half the hanging. They were breathing flame as they dove upon gray, falling clumps of Threads in the brilliant sky. A sky just that perfect autumnal blue, F'lar decided, that cannot occur in warmer weather. Upon the lower slopes of the hills, foliage was depicted as turning yellow from chilly nights. The slatey rocks suggested Ruathan country. Was that why the tapestry had hung in Ruatha Hall? Below, men had left the protecting Hold, cut into the cliff itself. The men were burdened with the curious cylinders of which Zurg had spoken. The tubes in their hands belched brilliant tongues of flame in long streams, aimed at the writhing Threads that attempted to burrow in the ground.

Lessa gave a startled exclamation, walking right onto the tapestry, staring down at the woven outline of the Hold, its massive door ajar, the details of its bronze ornamentation painstakingly rendered in fine yarns.

"I believe that's the design on the Ruatha Hold door," F'lar remarked.

"It is . . . and it isn't," Lessa replied in a puzzled voice.

Lytol glowered at her and then at the woven door. "True. It isn't and yet it is, and I went through that door a scant hour ago." He scowled down at the door before his toes.

"Well, here are the designs Fandarel wants to study," F'lar said with relief, as he peered at the flamethrowers.

Whether or not the smith could produce a working model from this woven one in time to help them three days hence F'lar couldn't guess. But if Fandarel could not, no man could.

The Mastersmith was, for him, jubilant over the presence of the tapestry. He lay upon the rug, his nose tickled by the nap as he studied the details. He grumbled, moaned, and muttered as he sat cross-legged to sketch and peer.

"Has been done. Can be done. Must be done," he was heard to rumble.

Lessa called for *klah*, bread, and meat when she learned from young B'rant that neither he nor Lytol had eaten yet. She served all the men, her manner gay and teasing. F'lar was relieved for Lytol's sake. Lessa even pressed food and *klah* on Fandarel, a tiny figure beside the mammoth man, insisting that he come away from the tapestry and eat and drink before he could return to his mumbling and drawing.

Fandarel finally decided that he had enough sketches and disappeared, to be flown back to his crafthold.

"No point in asking him when he'll be back. He's too deep in thought to hear," F'lar remarked, amused.

"If you don't mind, I shall excuse myself as well," Lessa said, smiling graciously to the four remaining around the table. "Good Warder Lytol, young B'rant should soon be excused, too. He's half asleep."

"I most certainly am not, Weyrlady," B'rant assured her hastily, widening his eyes with stimulated alertness.

Lessa merely laughed as she retreated into the sleeping chamber. F'lar stared thoughtfully after her.

"I mistrust the Weyrwoman when she uses that particularly docile tone of voice," he said slowly.

"Well, we must all depart," Robinton suggested, rising.

"Ramoth is young but not that foolish," F'lar murmured after the others had left.

Ramoth slept, oblivious of his scrutiny. He reached for the consolation Mnementh could give him, without response. The big bronze was dozing on his ledge.

Black, blacker, blackest,
And cold beyond frozen things.
Where is between *when there is naught*
To Life but fragile dragon wings?

"I just want to see that tapestry back on the wall at Ruatha," Lessa insisted to F'lar the next day. "I want it where it belongs."

They had gone to check on the injured and had had one argument already over F'lar's having sent N'ton along with the southern venture. Lessa had wanted him to try riding another's dragon. F'lar had preferred for him to learn to lead a wing of his own in the south, given the Turns to mature in. He had reminded Lessa, in the hope that it might prove inhibiting to any ideas she had about going four hundred Turns back, about F'nor's return trips, and he had borne down hard on the difficulties she had already experienced.

She had become very thoughtful, although she had said nothing.

Therefore, when Fandarel sent word that he would like to show F'lar a new mechanism, the Weyrleader felt reasonably safe in allowing Lessa the triumph of returning the purloined tapestry to Ruatha. She went to have the arras rolled and strapped to Ramoth's back.

He watched Ramoth rise with great sweeps of her wide wings, up to the Star Stone before going *between* to Ruatha. R'gul appeared on the ledge just then, reporting that a huge train of firestone was entering the Tunnel. Consequently, busy with such details, it was midmorning before he could get to see Fandarel's crude and not yet effective flamethrower . . . the fire did not "throw" from the nozzle of the tube with any force at all. It was late afternoon before he reached the Weyr again.

R'gul announced sourly that F'nor had been looking for him—twice, in fact.

"Twice?"

"Twice, as I said. He would not leave a message with me for you." R'gul was clearly insulted by F'nor's refusal.

By the evening meal, when there was still no sign of Lessa, F'lar sent to Ruatha to learn that she had indeed brought the tapestry. She had badgered and bothered the entire Hold until the thing was properly hung. For upward of several hours she had sat and looked at it, pacing its length occasionally.

She and Ramoth had then taken to the sky above the Great Tower and disappeared. Lytol had assumed, as had everyone at Ruatha, that she had returned to Benden Weyr.

"Mnementh," F'lar bellowed when the messenger had finished. "Mnementh, where are they?"

Mnementh's answer was a long time in coming.

I cannot hear them, he said finally, his mental voice soft and as full of worry as a dragon's could be.

F'lar gripped the table with both hands, staring at the queen's empty weyr. He knew, in the anguished privacy of his mind, where Lessa had tried to go.

Cold as death, death-bearing,
Stay and die, unguided.
Brave and braving, linger.
This way was twice decided.

B elow them was Ruatha's Great Tower. Lessa coaxed Ramoth slightly to the left, ignoring the dragon's acid comments, knowing that she was excited, too.

That's right, dear, this is exactly the angle at which the tapestry illustrates the Hold door. Only when that tapestry was designed, no one had carved the lintels or capped the door. And there was no Tower, no inner Court, no gate. She stroked the surprisingly soft skin of the curving neck, laughing to hide her own tense nervousness and apprehension at what she was about to attempt.

She told herself there were good reasons prompting her action in this matter. The ballad's opening phrase, "Gone away, gone ahead," was clearly a reference to *between* times. And the tapestry gave the required reference points for the jump *between* whens. Oh, how she thanked the Masterweaver who had woven that doorway. She must remember to tell him how well he had wrought. She hoped she'd be able to. Enough of that. Of course, she'd be able to. For hadn't the Weyrs disappeared? Knowing they had gone ahead, knowing how to go back to bring them ahead, it was she, obviously, who must go back and lead them. It was very simple, and only she and Ramoth could do it. Because they already had.

She laughed again, nervously, and took several deep, shuddering breaths.

"All right, my golden love," she murmured. "You have the reference. You know when I want to go. Take me *between*, Ramoth, *between* four hundred Turns."

The cold was intense, even more penetrating than she had imagined. Yet it was not a physical cold. It was the awareness of the absence of *everything*. No light. No sound. No touch. As they hovered, longer, and longer, in this nothingness, Lessa recognized full-blown panic of a kind that threatened to overwhelm her reason. She knew she sat on Ramoth's neck, yet she could not feel the great beast under her thighs, under her hands. She tried to cry out inadvertently and opened her mouth to . . . nothing . . . no sound in her own ears. She could not even feel the hands that she knew she had raised to her own cheeks.

I am here, she heard Ramoth say in her mind. *We are together*, and this reassurance was all that kept her from losing her grasp on sanity in that terrifying aeon of unpassing, timeless nothingness.

Someone had sense enough to call for Robinton. The Masterharper found F'lar sitting at the table, his face deathly pale, his eyes staring at the empty weyr. The craftmaster's entrance, his calm voice, reached F'lar in his shocked numbness. He sent the others out with a peremptory wave.

"She's gone. She tried to go back four hundred Turns," F'lar said in a tight, hard voice.

The Masterharper sank into the chair opposite the Weyrleader.

"She took the tapestry back to Ruatha," F'lar continued in that same choked voice. "I'd told her about F'nor's returns. I told her how dangerous this was. She didn't argue very much, and I know going *between* times had frightened her, if anything could frighten Lessa." He banged the table with in important fist. "I should have suspected her. When she thinks she's right, she doesn't stop to analyze, to consider. She just does it!"

"But she's not a foolish woman," Robinton reminded him slowly. "Not even she would jump *between* times without a reference point. Would she?"

"'Gone away, gone ahead'—that's the only clue we have!"

"Now wait a moment," Robinton cautioned him, then snapped

his fingers. "Last night, when she walked upon the tapestry, she was uncommonly interested in the Hall door. Remember, she discussed it with Lytol."

F'lar was on his feet and halfway down the passageway.

"Come on, man, we've got to get to Ruatha."

Lytol lit every glow in the Hold for F'lar and Robinton to examine the tapestry clearly.

"She spent the afternoon just looking at it," the Warder said, shaking his head. "You're sure she has tried this incredible jump?"

"She must have. Mnementh can't hear either her or Ramoth anywhere. Yet he says he can get an echo from Canth many Turns away and in the Southern Continent." F'lar stalked past the tapestry. "What is it about the door, Lytol? Think, man!"

"It is much as it is now, save that there are no carved lintels, there is no outer Court or Tower . . . "

"That's it. Oh, by the first Egg, it is so simple. Zurg said this tapestry is old. Lessa must have decided it was four hundred Turns, and she has used it as the reference point to go back *between* times."

"Why, then, she's there and safe," Robinton cried, sinking with relief in a chair.

"Oh, no, harper. It is not as easy as that," F'lar murmured, and Robinton caught his stricken look and the despair echoed in Lytol's face.

"What's the matter?"

"There is nothing *between*," F'lar said in a dead voice. "To go *between* places takes only as much time as for a man to cough three times. *Between* four hundred Turns. . . . " His voice trailed off.

> Who wills,
> Can.
> Who tries,
> Does.
> Who loves,
> Lives.

There were voices that first were roars in her aching ears and then hushed beyond the threshold of sound. She gasped as the whirling, nauseating sensation apparently spun her, and the bed which she felt beneath her, around and around. She clung to the sides of the bed as pain jabbed through her head, from somewhere directly in the middle of her skull. She screamed, as much in protest at the pain as from the terrifying, rolling, whirling, dropping lack of a solid ground.

Yet some frightening necessity kept her trying to gabble out the message she had come to give. Sometimes she felt Ramoth trying to reach her in that vast swooping darkness that enveloped her. She would try to cling to Ramoth's mind, hoping the golden queen could lead her out of this torturing nowhere. Exhausted, she would sink down, down, only to be torn from oblivion by the desperate need to communicate.

She was finally aware of a soft, smooth hand upon her arm, of a liquid, warm and savory, in her mouth. She rolled it around her tongue, and it trickled down her sore throat. A fit of coughing left her gasping and weak. Then she experimentally opened her eyes, and the images before her did not lurch and spin.

"Who . . . are . . . you?" she managed to croak.

"Oh, my dear Lessa . . . "

"Is that who I am?" she asked, confused.

"So your Ramoth tells us," she was assured. "I am Mardra of Fort Weyr."

"Oh, F'lar will be so angry with me," Lessa moaned as her memory came rushing back. "He will shake me and shake me. He always shakes me when I disobey him. But I was right. I was right. Mardra? . . . Oh, that . . . awful . . . nothingness," and she felt herself drifting off into sleep, unable to resist that overwhelming urge. Comfortingly, her bed no longer rocked beneath her.

The room, dimly lit by wallglows, was both like her own at Benden Weyr and subtly different. Lessa lay still, trying to isolate that difference. Ah, the weyrwalls were very smooth here. The room was larger, too, the ceiling higher and curving. The furnishings, now that her eyes were used to the dim light and she could distinguish details, were more finely crafted. She stirred restlessly.

"Ah, you're awake again, mystery lady," a man said. Light beyond the parted curtain flooded in from the outer weyr. Lessa sensed rather than saw the presence of others in the room beyond.

A woman passed under the man's arm, moving swiftly to the bedside.

"I remember you. You're Mardra," Lessa said with surprise.

"Indeed I am, and here is T'ton, Weyrleader at Fort."

T'ton was tossing more glows into the wallbasket, peering over his shoulder at Lessa to see if the light bothered her.

"Ramoth!" Lessa exclaimed, sitting upright, aware for the first time that it was not Ramoth's mind she touched in the outer weyr.

"Oh, that one," Mardra laughed with amused dismay. "She'll eat us out of the weyr, and even my Loranth has had to call the other queens to restrain her."

"She perches on the Star Stones as if she owned them and keens constantly," T'ton added, less charitably. He cocked an ear. "Ha. She's stopped."

"You can come, can't you?" Lessa blurted out.

"Come? Come where, my dear?" Mardra asked, confused. "You've been going on and on about our 'coming,' and Threads approaching, and the Red Star bracketed in the Eye Rock, and . . . my dear, don't you realize the Red Star has been past Pern these two months?"

"No, no, they've started. That's why I came back *between* times . . ."

"Back? *Between* times?" T'ton exclaimed, striding over to the bed, eyeing Lessa intently.

"Could I have some *klah*? I know I'm not making much sense, and I'm not really awake yet. But I'm not mad or still sick and this is rather complicated."

"Yes, it is," T'ton remarked with deceptive mildness. But he did call down the service shaft for *klah*. And he did drag a chair over to her bedside, settling himself to listen to her.

"Of course you're not mad," Mardra soothed her, glaring at her weyrmate. "Or she wouldn't ride a queen."

T'ton had to agree to that. Lessa waited for the *klah* to come; when it did, she sipped gratefully at its stimulating warmth.

Then she took a deep breath and began, telling them of the Long Interval between the dangerous passes of the Red Star: how the sole Weyr had fallen into disfavor and contempt, how Jora had deteriorated and lost control over her queen, Nemorth, so that, as the Red Star neared, there was no sudden increase in the size of clutches. How she had Impressed Ramoth to become Benden's Weyrwoman. How F'lar had outwitted the dissenting Hold Lords the day after Ramoth's first mating flight and taken firm command of Weyr and Pern, preparing for the Threads he knew were coming. She told her by now rapt audience of her own first attempts to fly Ramoth and how she had inadvertently gone back *between* time to the day Fax had invaded Ruath Hold.

"Invade . . . my family's Hold?" Mardra cried, aghast.

"Ruatha has given the Weyrs many famous Weyrwomen," Lessa said with a sly smile at which T'ton burst out laughing.

"She's Ruathan, no question," he assured Mardra.

She told them of the situation in which Dragonmen now found themselves, with an insufficient force to meet the Thread attacks. Of the Question Song and the great tapestry.

"A tapestry?" Mardra cried, her hand going to her cheek in alarm. "Describe it to me!"

And when Lessa did, she saw—at last—belief in both their faces.

"My father has just commissioned a tapestry with such a scene. He told me of it the other day because the last battle with the Threads was held over Ruatha." Incredulous, Mardra turned to T'ton, who no longer looked amused. "She must have done what she has said she'd done. How could she possibly know about the tapestry?"

"You might also ask your queen dragon, and mine," Lessa suggested.

"My dear, we do not doubt you now," Mardra said sincerely, "but it is a most incredible feat."

"I don't think," Lessa said, "that I would ever try it again, knowing what I do know."

"Yes, this shock makes a forward jump *between* times quite a problem if your F'lar must have an effective fighting force," T'ton remarked.

"You will come? You will?"

"There is a distinct possibility we will," T'ton said gravely, and his face broke into a lopsided grin. "You said we left the Weyrs . . . abandoned them, in fact, and left no explanation. We went somewhere . . . somewhen, that is, for we are still here now. . . . "

They were all silent, for the same alternative occurred to them simultaneously. The Weyrs had been left vacant, but Lessa had no way of proving that the five Weyrs reappeared in her time.

"There must be a way. There must be a way," Lessa cried distractedly. "And there's no time to waste. No time at all!"

T'ton gave a bark of laughter. "There's plenty of time at this end of history, my dear."

They made her rest then, more concerned than she was that she had been ill some weeks, deliriously screaming that she was falling and could not see, could not hear, could not touch. Ramoth, too, they told her, had suffered from the appalling nothingness of a protracted stay *between*, emerging above ancient Ruatha a pale yellow wraith of her former robust self.

The Lord of Ruatha Hold, Mardra's father, had been surprised out of his wits by the appearance of a staggering rider and a pallid queen on his stone verge. Naturally and luckily he had sent to his daughter at Fort Weyr for help. Lessa and Ramoth had been transported to the Weyr, and the Ruathan Lord kept silence on the matter.

When Lessa was strong enough, T'ton called a Council of Weyrleaders. Curiously, there was no opposition to going . . . provided they could solve the problem of time-shock and find reference points along the way. It did not take Lessa long to comprehend why the dragonriders were so eager to attempt the journey. Most of them had been born during the present Thread incursions. They had now had close to four months of unexciting routine patrols and were bored with monotony. Training Games were pallid substitutes for the real battles they had all fought. The Holds, which once could not do dragonmen favors enough, were beginning to be indifferent. The Weyrleaders could see these incidents increasing as Thread-generated fears receded. It was a morale decay as insidious as a wasting disease in Weyr and Hold. The alternative which Lessa's appeal offered was better than a slow decline in their own time.

Of Benden, only the Weyrleader himself was privy to these meetings. Because Benden was the only Weyr in Lessa's time, it must remain ignorant, and intact, until her time. Nor could any mention be made of Lessa's presence, for that, too, was unknown in her Turn.

She insisted that they call in the Masterharper because her Records said he had been called. But when he asked her to tell him the Question Song, she smiled and demurred.

"You'll write it, or your successor will, when the Weyrs are found to be abandoned," she told him. "But it must be your doing, not my repeating."

"A difficult assignment to know one must write a song that four hundred Turns later gives a valuable clue."

"Only be sure," she cautioned him, "that it is a Teaching tune. It must *not* be forgotten, for it poses questions that I have to answer."

As he started to chuckle, she realized she had already given him a pointer.

The discussions—how to go so far safely with no sustained sense deprivations—grew heated. There were more constructive notions, however impractical, on how to find reference points along the way. The five Weyrs had not been ahead in time, and Lessa, in her one gigantic backward leap, had not stopped for intermediate time marks.

"You did say that a *between* times jump of ten years caused no hardship?" T'ton asked of Lessa as all the Weyrleaders and the Masterharper met to discuss this impasse.

"None. It takes . . . oh, twice as long as a *between* places jump."

"It is the four hundred Turn leap that left you imbalanced. Hmmm. Maybe twenty or twenty-five Turn segments would be safe enough."

That suggestion found merit until Ista's cautious leader, D'ram, spoke up.

"I don't mean to be a Hold-hider, but there is one possibility we haven't mentioned. How do we know we made the jump *between* to Lessa's time? Going *between* is a chancy business. Men go missing often. And Lessa barely made it here alive."

"A good point, D'ram," T'ton concurred briskly, "but I feel there is more to prove that we do—did—will—go forward. The clues, for one thing—they were aimed at Lessa. The very emergency that left five Weyrs empty sent her back to appeal for our help—"

"Agreed, agreed," D'ram interrupted earnestly, "but what I mean is can you be sure we reached Lessa's time? It hadn't happened yet. Do we know it can?"

T'ton was not the only one who searched his mind for an answer to that. All of a sudden he slammed both hands, palms down, on the table.

"By the Egg, it's die slow, doing nothing, or die quick, trying. I've had a surfeit of the quiet life we dragonmen must lead after the Red Star passes till we go *between* in old age. I confess I'm almost sorry to see the Red Star dwindle farther from us in the evening sky. I say, grab the risk with both hands and shake it till it's gone. We're dragonmen, aren't we, bred to fight the Threads? Let's go hunting . . . four hundred Turns ahead!"

Lessa's drawn face relaxed. She had recognized the validity of D'ram's alternate possibility, and it had touched off bitter fear in her heart. To risk herself was her own responsibility, but to risk these hundreds of men and dragons, the weyrfolk who would accompany their men. . . ?

T'ton's ringing words for once and all dispensed with that consideration.

"And I believe," the Masterharper's exultant voice cut through the answering shouts of agreement, "I have your reference points." A smile of surprised wonder illuminated his face. "Twenty Turns or twenty hundred, you have a guide! And T'ton said it. As the Red Star dwindles in the evening sky . . . "

Later, as they plotted the orbit of the Red Star, they found how easy that solution actually was and chuckled that their ancient foe should be their guide.

Atop Fort Weyr, as on all the Weyrs, were great stones. They were so placed that at certain times of the year they marked the approach and retreat of the Red Star, as it orbited in its erratic two hundred Turn-long course around their sun. By consulting the Records which, among other morsels of information, included the Red Star's wanderings, it was not hard to plan jumps *between* of twenty-five Turns for each Weyr. It had been decided that the complement of each separate Weyr would jump *between* above its own base, for there would unquestionably be accidents if close to eighteen hundred laden beasts tried it at one point.

Each moment now was one too long away from her own time for Lessa. She had been a month away from F'lar and missed him more than she had thought possible. Also, she was worried that Ramoth would mate away from Mnementh. There were, to be sure, bronze dragons and bronze riders eager to do that service, but Lessa had no interest in them.

T'ton and Mardra occupied her with the many details in organizing the exodus, so that no clues, past the tapestry and the Question Song that would be composed at a later date, remained in the Weyrs.

It was with a relief close to tears that Lessa urged Ramoth upward in the night sky to take her place near T'ton and Mardra above the Fort Weyr Star Stone. At five other Weyrs great wings were ranged in formation, ready to depart their own times.

As each Weyrleader's dragon reported to Lessa that all were ready, reference points determined by the Red Star's travels in mind, it was this traveler from the future who gave the command to jump *between.*

ॐ

The blackest night must end in dawn,
The sun dispel the dreamer's fear:
When shall my soul's bleak, hopeless pain
Find solace in its darkening Weyr?

They had made eleven jumps *between,* the Weyrleaders' bronzes speaking to Lessa as they rested briefly between each jump. Of the eighteen hundred-odd travelers, only four failed to come ahead, and they had been older beasts. All five sections agreed to pause for a quick meal and hot *klah* before the final jump, which would be but twelve Turns.

"It is easier," T'ton commented as Mardra served the *klah,* "to go twenty-five Turns than twelve." He glanced up at the Red Dawn Star, their winking and faithful guide. "It does not alter its position as much. I count on you, Lessa, to give us additional references."

"I want to get us back to Ruatha before F'lar discovers I have gone." She shivered as she looked up at the Red Star and sipped hastily at the hot *klah.* "I've seen the Star just like that, once . . . no, twice . . . before at Ruatha." She stared at T'ton, her throat constricting as she remembered that morning: the time she had decided that the Red Star was a menace to her, three days after which Fax and F'lar had appeared at Ruatha Hold. Fax had died on F'lar's dagger, and she had gone to Benden Weyr. She felt suddenly dizzy, weak, strangely unsettled. She had not felt this was as they paused between other jumps.

"Are you all right, Lessa?" Mardra asked with concern. "You're so white. You're shaking." She put her arm around Lessa, glancing, concerned, at her Weyrmate.

"Twelve Turns ago I was at Ruatha," Lessa murmured, grasping Mardra's hand for support. "I was at Ruatha twice. Let's go on quickly. I'm too many in this morning. I must get back. I must get back to F'lar. He'll be so angry."

The note of hysteria in her voice alarmed both Mardra and T'ton. Hastily the latter gave orders for the fires to be extinguished, for the Weyrfolk to mount and prepare for the final jump ahead.

Her mind in chaos, Lessa transmitted the references to the other Weyrleaders' dragons: Ruatha in the evening light, the Great Tower, the inner Court, the land at springtime. . . .

A fleck of red in a cold night sky,
A drop of blood to guide them by,
Turn away, Turn away, Turn, be gone,
A Red Star becons the travelers on.

Between them, Lytol and Robinton forced F'lar to eat, deliberately plying him with wine. At the back of his mind F'lar knew he would have to keep going, but the effort was immense, the spirit gone from him. It was no comfort that they still had Pridith and Kylara to continue dragonkind, yet he delayed sending someone back for F'nor, unable to face the reality of that admission: that in sending for Pridith and Kylara, he had acknowledged the fact that Lessa and Ramoth would not return.

Lessa, Lessa, his mind cried endlessly, damning her one moment for her reckless, thoughtless daring, loving her the next for attempting such an incredible feat.

"I said, F'lar, you need sleep now more than wine." Robinton's voice penetrated his preoccupation.

F'lar looked at him, frowning in perplexity. He realized that he was trying to lift the wine jug that Robinton was holding firmly down.

"What did you say?"

"Come. I'll bear you company to Benden. Indeed, nothing could persuade me to leave your side. You have aged years, man, in the course of hours."

"And isn't it understandable?" F'lar shouted, rising to his feet, the impotent anger boiling out of him at the nearest target in the form of Robinton.

Robinton's eyes were full of compassion as he reached for F'lar's arm, gripping it tightly.

"Man, not even this Masterharper has words enough to express the sympathy and honor he has for you. But you must sleep; you have tomorrow to endure, and the tomorrow after that you have to fight. The dragonmen must have a leader. . . . " His voice trailed off. "Tomorrow you must send for F'nor . . . and Pridith."

F'lar pivoted on his heel and strode toward the fateful door of Ruatha's great hall.

Oh, Tongue, give sound to joy and sing
Of hope and promise on dragonwing.

Before them loomed Ruatha's Great Tower, the high walls of the Outer Court clearly visible in the fading light.

The claxon rang violent summons into the air, barely heard over the earsplitting thunder as hundreds of dragons appeared, ranging in full fighting array, wing upon wing, up and down the valley.

A shaft of light stained the flagstones of the Court as the Hold door opened.

Lessa ordered Ramoth down, close to the Tower, and dismounted, running eagerly forward to greet the men who piled out of the door. She made out the stocky figure of Lytol, a handbasket of glows held high above his head. She was so relieved to see him that she forgot her previous antagonism to the Warder.

"You misjudged the last jump by two days, Lessa," he cried as soon as he was near enough for her to hear him over the noise of settling dragons.

"Misjudged? How could I?" she breathed.

T'ton and Mardra came up beside her.

"No need to worry," Lytol reassured her, gripping her hands tightly in his, his eyes dancing. He was actually smiling at her. "You overshot the day. Go back *between*, return to Ruatha of two days ago. That's all." His grin widened at her confusion. "It is all right," he repeated, patting her hands. "Take this same hour, the Great Court, everything, but visualize F'lar, Robinton, and myself here on the flagstones. Place Mnementh on the Great Tower and a blue dragon on the verge. Now go."

Mnementh? Ramoth queried Lessa, eager to see her Weyrmate. She ducked her great head, and her huge eyes gleamed with scintillating fire.

"I don't understand," Lessa wailed. Mardra slipped a comforting arm around her shoulders.

"But I do, I do—trust me," Lytol pleaded, patting her shoulder awkwardly and glancing at T'ton for support. "It is as F'nor has said. You cannot be several places in time without experiencing great distress, and when you stopped twelve Turns back, it threw Lessa all to pieces."

"You know that?" T'ton cried.

"Of course. Just go back two days. You see, I *know* you have. I shall, of course, be surprised then, but now, tonight, I know you reappeared two days earlier. Oh, go. Don't argue. F'lar was half out of his mind with worry for you."

"He'll shake me," Lessa cried, like a little girl.

"Lessa!" T'ton took her by the hand and led her back to Ramoth, who crouched so her rider could mount.

T'ton took complete charge and had his Fidranth pass the order to return to the references Lytol had given, adding by way of Ramoth a description of the humans and Mnementh.

The cold of *between* restored Lessa to herself, although her error had badly jarred her confidence. But then there was Ruatha again. The dragons happily arranged themselves in tremendous display. And there, silhouetted against the light from the Hall, stood Lytol, Robinton's tall figure, and . . . F'lar.

Mnementh's voice gave a brassy welcome, and Ramoth could not land Lessa quickly enough to go and twine necks with her mate.

Lessa stood where Ramoth had left her, unable to move. She was aware that Mardra and T'ton were beside her. She was conscious only of F'lar, racing across the Court toward her. Yet she could not move.

He grabbed her in his arms, holding her so tightly to him that she could not doubt the joy of his welcome.

"Lessa, Lessa," his voice raggedly chanted in her ear. He pressed her face against his, crushing her to breathlessness, all his careful detachment abandoned. He kissed her, hugged her, held her, and then kissed her with rough urgency again. Then he suddenly set her on her feet and gripped her shoulders. "Lessa, if you ever . . . " he said, punctuating each word with a flexing of his fingers, then stopped, aware of a grinning circle of strangers surrounding them.

"I told you he'd shake me," Lessa was saying, dashing tears from her face. "But, F'lar, I brought them all . . . all but Benden Weyr. And that is why the five Weyrs were abandoned. I brought them."

F'lar looked around him, looked beyond the leaders to the masses of dragons settling in the Valley, on the heights, everywhere he turned. There were dragons, blue, green, bronze, brown, and a whole wingful of golden queen dragons alone.

"You brought the Weyrs?" he echoed, stunned.

"Yes, this is Mardra and T'ton of Fort Weyr, D'ram and . . . "

He stopped her with a little shake, pulling her to his side so he could see and greet the newcomers.

"I am more grateful than you can know," he said and could not go on with all the many words he wanted to add.

T'ton stepped forward, holding out his hand, which F'lar seized and held firmly.

"We bring eighteen hundred dragons, seventeen queens, and all that is necessary to implement our Weyrs."

"And they brought flamethrowers, too," Lessa put in excitedly.

"But—to come . . . to attempt it . . . " F'lar murmured in admiring wonder.

T'ton and D'ram and the others laughed.

"Your Lessa showed the way . . . "

" . . . with the Red Star to guide us . . . " she said.

"We are dragonmen," T'ton continued solemnly, "as you are yourself, F'lar of Benden. We were told there are Threads here to fight, and that's work for dragonmen to do . . . in any time!"

Drummer, beat, and piper, blow,
Harper, strike, and soldier, go.
Free the flame and sear the grasses
Till the dawning Red Star passes.

Even as the five Weyrs had been settling around Ruatha Valley, F'nor had been compelled to bring forward in time his southern weyrfolk. They had all reached the end of endurance in double-time life, gratefully creeping back to quarters they had vacated two days and ten Turns ago.

R'gul, totally unaware of Lessa's backward plunge, greeted F'lar and his Weyrwoman, on their return to the Weyr, with the news of F'nor's appearance with seventy-two new dragons and the further word that he doubted any of the riders would be fit to fight.

"I've never seen such exhausted men in my life," R'gul rattled on, "can't imagine what could have gotten into them, with sun and plenty of food and all, and no responsibilities."

F'lar and Lessa exchanged glances.

"Well, the southern Weyr ought to be maintained, R'gul. Think it over."

"I'm a fighting dragonman, not a womanizer," the old dragon-rider grunted. "It'd take more than a trip *between* times to reduce me like those others."

"Oh, they'll be themselves again in next to no time," Lessa said and, to R'gul's intense disapproval, she giggled.

"They'll have to be if we're to keep the skies Thread-free," R'gul snapped testily.

"No problem about that now," F'lar assured him easily.

"No problem? With only a hundred and forty-four dragons?"

"Two hundred and sixteen," Lessa corrected him firmly.

Ignoring her, R'gul asked, "Has that Mastersmith found a flame-thrower that'll work?"

"Indeed he has," F'lar assured R'gul, grinning broadly.

The five Weyrs had also brought forward their equipment. Fandarel all but snatched examples from their backs and, undoubtedly, every hearth and smithy through the continent would be ready to duplicate the design by morning. T'ton had told F'lar that, in his time, each Hold had ample flamethrowers for every man on the ground. In the course of the Long Interval, however, the throwers must have been either smelted down or lost as incomprehensible devices. D'ram, particularly, was very much interested in Fandarel's agenothree sprayer, considering it better than thrown-flame, since it would also act as a fertilizer.

"Well," R'gul admitted gloomily, "a flamethrower or two will be some help day after tomorrow."

"We have found something else that will help a lot more," Lessa remarked and then hastily excused herself, dashing into the sleeping quarters.

The sounds that drifted past the curtain were either laughter or sobs, and R'gul frowned on both. That girl was just too young to be Weyrwoman at such a time. No stability.

"Has she realized how critical our situation is? Even with F'nor's additions? That is, if they can fly?" R'gul demanded testily. "You oughtn't to let her leave the Weyr at all."

F'lar ignored that and began pouring himself a cup of wine.

"You once pointed out to me that the five empty Weyrs of Pern supported your theory that there would be no more Threads."

R'gul cleared his throat, thinking that apologies—even if they might be due from the Weyrleader—were scarcely effective against the Threads.

"Now there was merit in that theory," F'lar went on, filling a cup for R'gul. "Not, however, as you interpreted it. The five Weyrs were empty because they . . . they came here."

R'gul, his cup halfway to his lips, stared at F'lar. This man also was too young to bear his responsibilities. But . . . he seemed actually to believe what he was saying.

"Believe it or not, R'gul—and in a bare day's time you will—the five Weyrs are empty no longer. They're here, in the Weyrs, in this time. And they shall join us, eighteen hundred strong, the day after tomorrow at Telgar, with flamethrowers and with plenty of battle experience."

R'gul regarded the poor man stolidly for a long moment. Carefully he put his cup down and, turning on his heel, left the weyr. He refused to be an object of ridicule. He'd better plan to take over the leadership tomorrow if they were to fight Threads the day after.

The next morning, when he saw the clutch of great bronze dragons bearing the Weyrleaders and their wingleaders to the conference, R'gul got quietly drunk.

Lessa exchanged good mornings with her friends and then, smiling sweetly, left the weyr, saying she must feed Ramoth. F'lar stared after her thoughtfully, then went to greet Robinton and Fandarel, who had been asked to attend the meeting, too. Neither Craftmaster said much, but neither missed a word spoken. Fandarel's great head kept swiveling from speaker to speaker, his deep-set eyes blinking occasionally. Robinton sat with a bemused smile on his face, utterly delighted by ancestral visitors.

F'lar was quickly talked out of resigning his titular position as Weyrleader of Benden on the grounds that he was too inexperienced.

"You did well enough at Nerat and Keroon. Well indeed," T'ton said.

"You call twenty-eight men or dragons out of action good leadership?"

"For a first battle, with every dragonman green as a hatchling? No, man, you were on time at Nerat, however you got there," and T'ton grinned maliciously at F'lar, "which is what a dragonman must do. No, that was well flown, I say. Well flown." The other four Weyrleaders muttered complete agreement with that compliment. "Your Weyr is understrength, though, so we'll lend you enough odd-wing riders till you've gotten the Weyr up to full strength again. Oh, the queens love these times!" And his grin broadened to indicate that bronze riders did, too.

F'lar returned that smile, thinking that Ramoth was about ready for another mating flight, and this time, Lessa . . . oh, that girl was being too deceptively docile. He'd better watch her closely.

"Now," T'ton was saying "we left with Fandarel's crafthold all the flamethrowers we brought up so that the groundmen will be armed tomorrow."

"Aye, and my thanks," Fandarel grunted. "We'll turn out new ones in record time and return yours soon."

"Don't forget to adapt that agenothree for air spraying, too," D'ram put in.

"It is agreed," and T'ton glanced quickly around at the other riders, "that all the Weyrs will meet, full strength, three hours after dawn above Telgar, to follow the Thread's attack across to Crom. By the way, F'lar, those charts of yours that Robinton showed me are superb. We never had them"

"How did you know when the attacks would come?"

T'ton shrugged. "They were coming so regularly even when I was a weyrling, you kind of knew when one was due. But this way is much, much better."

"More efficient," Fandarel added approvingly.

"After tomorrow, when all the Weyrs show up at Telgar, we can request what supplies we need to stock the empty Weyrs," T'ton grinned. "Like old times, squeezing extra tithes from the Holders." He rubbed his hands in anticipation. "Like old times."

"There's the southern Weyr," F'nor suggested. "We've been gone from there six Turns in this time, and the herdbeasts were left. They'll have multiplied, and there'll be all that fruit and grain."

"It would please me to see that southern venture continued," F'lar remarked, nodding encouragingly at F'nor.

"Yes, and continue Kylara down there, please, too," F'nor added urgently, his eyes sparkling with irritation.

They discussed sending for some immediate supplies to help out the newly occupied Weyrs, and then adjourned the meeting.

"It is a trifle unsettling," T'ton said as he shared wine with Robinton, "to find that the Weyr you left the day before in good order has become a dusty hulk." He chuckled. "The women of the Lower Caverns were a bit upset."

"We cleaned up those kitchens," F'nor replied indignantly. A good night's rest in a fresh time had removed much of his fatigue.

T'ton cleared his throat. "According to Mardra, no man can *clean* anything."

"Do you think you'll be up to riding tomorrow, F'nor?" F'lar asked solicitously. He was keenly aware of the stress showing in his half brother's face, despite his improvement overnight. Yes those strenuous Turns had been necessary, nor had they become futile even in hindsight with the arrival of eighteen hundred dragons from past time. When F'lar had ordered F'nor ten Turns backward to breed the desperately needed replacements, they had not yet brought to mind the Question Song or known of the tapestry.

"I wouldn't miss that fight if I were dragonless," F'nor declared stoutly.

"Which reminds me," F'lar remarked, "we'll need Lessa at Telgar tomorrow. She can speak to any dragon, you know," he explained, almost apologetically, to T'ton and D'ram.

"Oh, we know," T'ton assured him. "And Mardra doesn't mind." Seeing F'lar's blank expression, he added, "As senior Weyrwoman, Mardra, of course, leads the queens' wing."

F'lar's face grew blanker. "Queens' wing?"

"Certainly," and T'ton and D'ram exchanged questioning glances at F'lar's surprise. "You don't keep your queens from fighting, do you?"

"Our *queens*? T'ton, we at Benden have had only *one* queen dragon—at a time—for so many generations that there are those who denounce the legends of queens in battle as black heresy!"

T'ton looked rueful. "I had not truly realized till this instant how small your numbers were." But his enthusiams overtook him. "Just the same, queens are very useful with flamethrowers. They get clumps other riders might miss. They fly in low, under the main wings. That's one reason D'ram's so interested in the agenothree spray. Doesn't singe the hair off the Holders' heads, so to speak, and is far better over tilled fields."

"Do you mean to say that you allow your queens to fly—against Threads?" F'lar ignored the fact that F'nor was grinning, and T'ton, too.

"Allow?" D'ram bellowed. "You can't stop them. Don't you know your Ballads?"

" 'Moreta's Ride?' "

"Exactly."

F'nor laughed aloud at the expression on F'lar's face as he irritably pulled the hanging forelock from his eyes. Then, sheepishly, he began to grin.

"Thanks. That gives me an idea."

He saw his fellow Weyrleaders to their dragons, waved cheerfully to Robinton and Fandarel, more lighthearted than he would have thought he'd be the morning before the second battle. Then he asked Mnementh where Lessa might be.

Bathing, the bronze dragon replied.

F'lar glanced at the empty queen's weyr.

Oh, Ramoth is on the Peak, as usual. Mnementh sounded aggrieved.

F'lar heard the sound of splashing in the bathing room suddenly cease, so he called down for hot *klah*. He was going to enjoy this.

"Oh, did the meeting go well?" Lessa asked sweetly as she emerged from the bathing room, drying-cloth wrapped tightly around her slender figure.

"Extremely. You realize, of course, Lessa, that you'll be needed at Telgar?"

She looked at him intently for a moment before she smiled again.

"I *am* the only Weyrwoman who can speak to any dragon," she replied archly.

"True," F'lar admitted blithely. "And no longer the only queen's rider in Benden. . . . "

"I hate you!" Lessa snapped, unable to evade F'lar as he pinned her cloth-swathed body to his.

"Even when I tell you that Fandarel has a flamethrower for you so you can join the queens' wing?"

She stopped squirming in his arms and stared at him, disconcerted that he had outguessed her.

"And that Kylara will be installed as Weyrwoman in the south . . . in this time? As Weyrleader, I need my peace and quiet between battles. . . . "

The cloth fell from her body to the floor as she responded to his kiss as ardently as if dragon-roused.

From the Weyr and from the Bowl,
Bronze and brown and blue and green,
Rise the dragonmen of Pern,
Aloft, on wing; seen, then unseen.

Ranged above the Peak of Benden Weyr, a scant three hours after dawn, two hundred and sixteen dragons held their formations as F'lar on bronze Mnementh inspected their ranks.

Below in the Bowl were gathered all the weyrfolk and some of those injured in the first battle. All the weyrfolk, that is, except Lessa and Ramoth. They had gone on to Fort Weyr where the queens' wing was assembling. F'lar could not quite suppress a twinge of concern that she and Ramoth would be fighting, too. A holdover, he knew, from the days when Pern had had only one queen. If Lessa could jump four hundred Turns *between* and lead five Weyrs back, she could take care of herself and her dragon against Threads.

He checked to be sure that every man was well loaded with firestone sacks, that each dragon was in good color, especially those in from the southern Weyr. Of course, the dragons were fit, but the faces of the men still showed evidences of the temporal strains they had endured. He was procrastinating, and the Threads would be dropping in the skies of Telgar.

He gave the order to go *between*. They reappeared above, and to the south of Telgar Hold itself, and were not the first arrivals. To the west, to the north, and, yes, to the east now, wings arrived until the horizon was patterned with the great V's of several thousand dragon wings. Faintly he heard the claxon bell on Telgar Hold Tower as the unexpected dragon strength was acclaimed from the ground.

"Where is she?" F'lar demanded of Mnementh. "We'll need her presently to relay orders . . ."

She's coming, Mnementh interrupted him.

Right above Telgar Hold another wing appeared. Even at this distance, F'lar could see the difference: the golden dragons shone in the bright morning sunlight.

A hum of approval drifted down the dragon ranks, and despite his fleeting worry, F'lar grinned with proud indulgence at the glittering sight.

Just then the eastern wings soared straight upward in the sky as the dragons became instinctively aware of the presence of their ancient foe.

Mnementh raised his head, echoing back the brass thunder of the war cry. He turned his head, even as hundreds of other beasts turned to receive firestone from their riders. Hundreds of great jaws masticated the stone, swallowed it, their digestive acids transforming dry stone into flame-producing gases, igniting on contact with oxygen.

Threads! F'lar could see them clearly now against the spring sky. His pulses began to quicken, not with apprehension, but with a savage joy. His heart pounded unevenly. Mnementh demanded more stone and began to speed up the strokes of his wings in the air, gathering himself to leap upward when commanded.

The leading Weyr already belched gouts of orange-red flame into the pale blue sky. Dragons winked in and out, flamed and dove.

The great golden queens sped at cliff-skimming height to cover what might have been missed.

Then F'lar gave the command to gain altitude to meet the Threads halfway in their abortive descent. As Mnementh surged upward, F'lar shook his fist defiantly at the winking Red Eye of the Star.

"One day," he shouted, "we will not sit tamely here, awaiting your fall. We will fall on you, where you spin, and sear you on your own ground."

By the Egg, he told himself, if we can travel four hundred Turns backward and across seas and lands in the blink of an eye, what is travel from one world to another but a different kind of step?

F'lar grinned to himself. He'd better not mention that audacious notion in Lessa's presence.

Clumps ahead, Mnementh warned him.

As the bronze dragon charged, flaming, F'lar tightened his knees on the massive neck. Mother of us all, he was glad that now, of all times conceivable, he, F'lar, rider of bronze Mnementh, was a dragonman of Pern!

··VOLUME II··
DRAGONQUEST

To
Anne Dorothy McElroy McCaffrey
my mother

·· C O N T E N T S ··

·· CHAPTER I ··

Morning at Mastercrafthall, Fort Hold
Several Afternoons Later at Benden Weyr

Midmorning (Telgar Time) at
Mastersmithcrafthall, Telgar Hold

How to begin? mused Robinton, the Masterharper of Pern. He frowned thoughtfully down at the smoothed, moist sand in the shallow trays of his workdesk. His long face settled into deep-grooved lines and creases, and his eyes, usually snapping blue with inner amusement, were gray-shadowed with unusual gravity.

He fancied the sand begged to be violated with words and notes while he, Pern's repository and glib dispenser of any ballad, saga or ditty, was inarticulate. Yet he had to construct a ballad for the upcoming wedding of Lord Asgenar of Lemos Hold to the half-sister of Lord Larad of Telgar Hold. Because of recent reports of unrest from his network of drummers and Harper journeymen, Robinton had decided to remind the guests on this auspicious occasion—for every Lord Holder and Craftmaster would be invited—of the debt they owed the dragonmen of Pern. As the subject of his ballad, he had decided to tell of the fantastic ride, *between* time itself, of Lessa, Weyrwoman of Benden Weyr on her great gold queen, Ramoth. The Lords and Craftsmen of Pern had been glad enough then for the arrival of dragonriders from the five ancient Weyrs from four hundred Turns in the past.

Yet how to reduce those fascinating, frantic days, those braveries, to a rhyme? Even the most stirring chords could not recapture the beat of the blood, the catch of breath, the chill of fear and the hopeless surge of hope of that first morning after Thread had fallen over Nerat Hold; when F'lar had rallied all the frightened Lords and Craftmasters at Benden Weyr and enlisted their enthusiastic aid.

It had not been just a sudden resurgence of forgotten loyalties that had prompted the Lords, but the all too real sense of disaster as they envisioned their prosperous acres blackened with the Thread they had dismissed as myth, of the thought of burrows of the lightning propagating parasites, of themselves walled up in the cliff-Holds behind thick metal doors and shutters. They'd been ready to promise F'lar their souls that day if he could protect them from Thread. And it was Lessa who had bought them that protection, almost with her life.

Robinton looked up from the sandtrays, his expression suddenly bleak.

"The sand of memory dries quickly," he said softly, looking out across the settled valley toward the precipice that housed Fort Hold. There was one watchman on the fire ridges. There ought to be six, but it was planting time; Lord Holder Groghe of Fort Hold had everyone who could walk upright in the fields, even the gangs of children who were supposed to weed spring grass from stone interstices and pull moss from the walls. Last spring, Lord Groghe would not have neglected that duty no matter how many dragonlengths of land he wanted to put under seed.

Lord Groghe was undoubtedly out in the fields right now, prowling from one tract of land to another on one of those long-legged running beasts which the Masterherdsman Sograny was developing. Groghe of Fort Hold was indefatigable, his slightly protuberant blue eyes never missing an unpruned tree or a badly harrowed row. He was a burly man, with grizzled hair which he wore tied in a neat band. His complexion was florid, with a temper to match. But, if he pushed his holders, he pushed himself as well, demanding nothing of his people, his children nor his fosterlings that he was not able to do himself. If he was conservative in his thinking, it was because he knew his own limitations and felt secure in that knowledge.

Robinton pulled at his lower lip, wondering if Lord Groghe was an exception in his disregard for this traditional Hold duty of removing all greenery near habitations. Or was this Lord Groghe's answer to Fort Weyr's growing agitation over the immense forest lands of Fort Hold which the dragonriders ought to protect? The Weyrleader of Fort Weyr, T'ron, and his Weyrwoman, Mardra, had become less scrupulous about checking to see that no Thread burrows had escaped their wing riders to fall on the lush forests. Yet Lord Groghe had been scrupulous in the matter of ground crews and flamethrowing equipment when Thread fell over his forests. He had a stable of runners spread out through the Hold in an efficient network so that if dragonriders were competent in flight, there was adequate ground coverage for any Thread that might elude the flaming breath of the airborne beasts.

But Robinton had heard ugly rumors of late, and not just from Fort Hold. Since he eventually heard every derogatory whisper and accusation uttered in Pern, he had learned to separate fact from spite, calumny from crime. Not basically an alarmist, because he'd found much sifted itself out in the course of time, Robinton was beginning to feel the stirrings of alarm in his soul.

The Masterharper slumped in his chair, staring out on the bright day, the fresh new green of the fields, the yellow blossoms on the fruit trees, the neat stone Holds that lined the road up to the main Hold, the cluster of artisans' cotholds below the wide ramp up to the Great Outer Court of Fort Hold.

And if his suspicions were valid, what could he do? Write a scolding song? A satire? Robinton snorted. Lord Groghe was too literal a man to interpret satire and too righteous to take a scold. Furthermore, and Robinton pushed himself upright on his elbows, if Lord Groghe was neglectful, it was in protest at Weyr neglect of far greater magnitude. Robinton shuddered to think of Thread burrowing in the great stands of softwoods to the south.

He ought to sing his remonstrances to Mardra and T'ron as Weyrleaders—but that, too, would be vain effort. Mardra had soured lately. She ought to have sense enough to retire gracefully to a chair and let men seek her favors if T'ron no longer attracted her. To hear the Hold girls talk, T'ron was lusty enough. In fact, T'ron had better restrain himself. Lord Groghe didn't take kindly to too many of his chattels bearing dragonseed.

Another impasse, thought Robinton with a wry smile. Hold customs differed so from Weyr morals. Maybe a word to F'lar of Benden Weyr? Useless, again. In the first place there was really nothing the bronze rider could do. Weyrs were autonomous and not only could T'ron take umbrage for any advice F'lar might see fit to offer, but Robinton was sure that F'lar might tend to take the Lord Holders' side.

This was not the first time in recent months that Robinton regretted that F'lar of Benden Weyr had been so eager to relinquish his leadership after Lessa had gone back *between* to bring the five lost Weyrs forward in time. For a brief few months then, seven Turns ago, Pern had been united under F'lar and Lessa against the ancient menace of Thread. Every Holder, Craftmaster, landsman, crafter, all had been of one mind. That unity had dissipated as the Oldtime Weyrleaders had reasserted their traditional domination over the Holds bound to their Weyr for protection, and a grateful Pern had ceded them those rights. But in four hundred Turns the interpretation of that old hegemony had altered, with neither party sure of the translation.

Perhaps now was the time to remind Lord Holders of those perilous days seven Turns ago when all their hopes hung on fragile dragon wings and the dedication of a scant two hundred men.

Well, the Harper has a duty, too, by the Egg, Robinton thought, needlessly smoothing the wet sand. And the obligation to broadcast it.

In twelve days, Larad, Lord of Telgar, was giving his half-sister, Famira, to Asgenar, Lord of Lemos Hold. The Masterharper had been enjoined to appear with appropriate new songs to enliven the festivities. F'lar and Lessa were invited as Lemos Hold was weyrbound to Benden Weyr. There'd be other notables among Weyr, Lord and Craft to signalize so auspicious an occasion.

"And among my jolly songs, I'll have stronger meat."

Chuckling to himself at the prospect, Robinton picked up his stylus.

"I must have a tender but intricate theme for Lessa. She's legend already." Unconsciously the Harper smiled as he pictured the dainty, child-sized Weyrwoman, with her white skin, her cloud of dark hair, the flash of her gray eyes, heard the acerbity of her clever tongue. No man of Pern failed of respect for her, or braved her displeasure, with the exception of F'lar.

Now a well-stated martial theme would do for Benden's Weyrleader, with his keen amber eyes, his unconscious superiority, the intense energy of his lean fighter's frame. Could he, Robinton, rouse F'lar from his detachment? Or was he perhaps unnecessarily worried about these minor irritations between Lord Holder and Weyrleader? But without the dragonriders of Pern, the land would be sucked dry of any sustenance by Thread, even if every man, woman and child of the planet were armed with flame throwers. One burrow, well established, could race across plain and forest as fast as a dragon could fly it, consuming everything that grew or lived, save solid rock, water or metal. Robinton shook his head, annoyed with his own fancies. As if dragonmen would ever desert Pern and their ancient obligation.

Now—a solid beat on the biggest drum for Fandarel, the Mastersmith, with his endless curiosity, the great hands with their delicate skill, the ranging mind in its eternal quest for efficiency. Somehow one expected such an immense man to be as slow of wit as he was deliberate of physical movement.

A sad note, well sustained, for Lytol who had once ridden a Benden dragon and lost his Larth in an accident in the Spring Games— had it been fourteen or fifteen Turns ago? Lytol had left the Weyr— to be among dragonfolk only exacerbated his tremendous loss—and taken to the craft of weaving. He'd been Crafthall Master in the High Reaches Hold when F'lar had discovered Lessa on Search. F'lar had appointed Lytol to be Lord Warder of Ruatha Hold when Lessa had abdicated her claim to the Hold to young Jaxom.

And how did a man signify the dragons of Pern? No theme was grand enough for those huge, winged beasts, as gentle as they were great, Impressed at Hatching by the men who rode them, flaming against Thread, who tended them, loved them, who were linked, mind to mind, in an unbreakable bond that transcended speech! (What was that really like? Robinton wondered, remembering that his youthful ambition had been to be a dragonman.) The dragons of Pern who could transfer themselves in some mysterious fashion *between* one place and another in the blink of an eye. *Between* even one Time and another!

The Harper's sigh came from his soul but his hand moved to the sand and pressed out the first note, wrote the first word, wondering if he would find some answer himself in the song.

He had barely filled the completed score with clay to preserve the text, when he heard the first throb of the drum. He strode quickly to the small outer court of the Crafthall, bending his head to catch the summons; it was his sequence all right, in urgent tempo. He concentrated so closely on the drumroll that he did not realize that every other sound common to the Harper's Hall had ceased.

"Thread?" His throat dried instantly. Robinton didn't need to consult the timetable to realize that the Threads were falling on the shores of Tillek Hold prematurely.

Across the valley on Fort Hold's ramparts, the single watchman made his monotonous round, oblivious to disaster.

There was a soft spring warmth to the afternoon air as F'nor and his big, brown Canth emerged from their weyr in Benden Weyr. F'nor yawned slightly and stretched until he heard his spine crack. He'd been on the western coast all the previous day, Searching for likely lads—and girls, since there was a golden egg hardening on the Benden Weyr Hatching Grounds—for the next Impression. Benden Weyr certainly produced more dragons, and more queens, than the five Old-timers' Weyrs, F'nor thought.

"Hungry?" he asked courteously of his dragon, glancing down the Weyr Bowl to the Feeding Grounds. No dragons were dining and the herdbeasts stood in their fenced pasture, legs spraddled, heads level with their bony knees as they drowsed in the sunlight.

Sleepy, said Canth, although he had slept as long and deeply as his rider. The brown dragon proceeded to settle himself on the sun-warmed ledge, sighing as he sank down.

"Slothful wretch," F'nor said, grinning affectionately at his beast.

The sun was full on the other side of the enormous mountain cup that formed the dragonman's habitation on the eastern coast of Pern. The cliffside was patterned with the black mouths of the individual dragon weyrs, starred where sun flashed off mica in the rocks. The waters of the Weyr's spring-fed lake glistened around the two green dragons bathing as their riders lounged on the grass verge. Beyond, in front of the weyrling barracks, young riders formed a semicircle around the Weyrlingmaster.

F'nor's grin broadened. He stretched his lean body indolently, remembering his own weary hours in such a semicircle, twenty odd Turns ago. The rote lessons which he had echoed as a weyrling had far more significance to this present group of dragonriders. In his Turn, the Silver Thread of those teaching songs had not dropped from the Red Star for over four hundred Turns, to sear the flesh of man and beast and devour anything living which grew on Pern. Of all the dragonmen in Pern's lone Weyr, only F'nor's half-brother, F'lar, bronze Mnementh's rider, had believed that there might be truth in those old legends. Now Thread was an inescapable fact, falling to Pern from the skies with diurnal regularity. Once more, its destruction was a way of life for dragonriders. The lessons these lads learned would save their skins, their lives and, more important, their dragons.

The weyrlings are promising, Canth remarked as he locked his wings to his back and curled his tail against his hind legs. He settled his great head to his forelegs, the many-faceted eye nearest F'nor gleaming softly on his rider.

Responding to the tacit plea, F'nor scratched the eye ridge until Canth began to hum softly with pleasure.

"Lazybones!"

When I work, I work, Canth replied. *Without my help, how would you know which holdbred lad would make a good dragonrider? And do I not find girls who make good queen riders, too?*

F'nor laughed indulgently, but it was true that Canth's ability to spot likely candidates for fighting dragons and breeding queens was much vaunted by Benden Weyr dragonmen.

Then F'nor frowned, remembering the odd hostility of the small holders and crafters he'd encountered in Southern Boll's Holds and Crafts. Yes, the people had been hostile until—until he'd identified himself as a Benden Weyr dragonrider. He'd have thought it'd be the other way round. Southern Boll was weyrbound to Fort Weyr. Traditionally—and F'nor grinned wryly since the Fort Weyrleader, T'ron, was so adamant in upholding all that was traditional, customary . . . and static—traditionally, the Weyr which protected a territory had first claim on any possible riders. But the five Oldtime Weyrs rarely sought beyond their own Lower Caverns for candidates. Of course, thought F'nor, the Oldtime queens didn't produce large clutches like the modern queens, nor many golden queen eggs. Come to think on it, only three queens had been Hatched in the Oldtime Weyrs in the seven Turns since Lessa brought them forward.

Well, let the Oldtimers stick to their ways if that made them feel superior. But F'nor agreed with F'lar. It was only common sense to give your dragonets as wide a choice as possible. Though the women in the Lower Caverns of Benden Weyr were certainly agreeable, there simply weren't enough weyrborn lads to match up the quantity of dragons hatched.

Now, if one of the other Weyrs, maybe G'narish of Igen Weyr or R'mart of Telgar Weyr, would throw open their junior queens' mating flights, the Oldtimers might notice an improvement in size of clutch and the dragons that hatched. A man was a fool to breed only to his own Bloodlines all the time.

The afternoon breeze shifted and brought with it the pungent fumes of numbweed a-boil. F'nor groaned. He'd forgotten that the women were making numbweed for salve that was the universal remedy for the burn of Thread and other painful afflictions. That had been one main reason for going on Search yesterday. The odor of numbweed was pervasive. Yesterday's breakfast had tasted medicinal instead of cereal. Since the preparation of numbweed salve was a tedious as well as smelly process, most dragonmen made themselves scarce during its manufacture. F'nor glanced across the Weyr Bowl to the queen's weyr. Ramoth, of course, was in the Hatching Ground, hovering over her latest clutch of eggs, but bronze Mnementh was absent from his accustomed perch on the ledge. F'lar and he were off somewhere, no doubt escaping the smell of numbweed as well as Lessa's uncertain temper. She conscientiously took part in even the most onerous duties of Weyrwoman, but that didn't mean she had to like them.

Numbweed stink notwithstanding, F'nor was hungry. He hadn't eaten since late afternoon yesterday, and, since there was a good six hours' time difference between Southern Boll on the western coast and Benden Weyr in the east, he'd missed the dinner hour at Benden Weyr completely.

With a parting scratch, F'nor told Canth that he'd get some food, and started down the stone ramp from his ledge. One of the privileges of being Wing-second was choice of quarters. Since Ramoth as senior queen would permit only two junior queens in Benden Weyr, there were two unoccupied Weyrwoman quarters. F'nor had appropriated one and did not need to disturb Canth when he wished to descend to a lower level.

As he approached the entrance of the Lower Caverns, the aroma of boiling numbweed made his eyes smart. He'd grab some *klah*, bread and fruit and go listen to the Weyrlingmaster. They were upwind. As Wing-second, F'nor liked to take every opportunity to measure up the new riders, particularly those who were not weyrbred. Life in a Weyr required certain adjustments for the craft and holdbred. The freedom and privileges sometimes went to a boy's head, particularly after he was able to take his dragon *between*—anywhere on Pern—in the space it takes to count to three. Again, F'nor agreed with F'lar's preference in presenting older lads at Impression though the Oldtimers deplored that practice at Benden Weyr, too. But, by the Shell, a lad in his late teens recognized the responsibility of his position (even if he were holdbred) as a dragonrider. He was more emotionally mature and, while there was no lessening of the impact of Impression with his dragon, he could absorb and understand the implications of a lifelong link, of an in-the-soul contact, the total empathy between himself and his dragon. An older boy didn't get carried away. He knew enough to compensate until his dragonet's instinctive sensibility unfolded. A baby dragon had precious little sense and, if some silly weyrling let his beast eat too much, the whole Weyr suffered through its torment. Even an older beast lived for the here and now, with little thought for the future and not all that much recollection—except on the instinctive level—for the past. That was just as well, F'nor thought. For dragons bore the brunt of Thread-score. Perhaps if their memories were more acute or associative, they'd refuse to fight.

F'nor took a deep breath and, blinking furiously against the fumes, entered the huge kitchen Cavern. It was seething with activity. Half the female population of the Weyr must be involved in this operation. F'nor thought, for great cauldrons monopolized all the large hearths set in the outside wall of the Cavern. Women were seated at the broad tables, washing and cutting the roots from which the salve was extracted. Some were ladling the boiling product into great earthenware pots. Those who stirred the concoction with long-handled paddles wore masks over nose and mouth and bent frequently to blot eyes watering from the acrid fumes. Older children were fetching and carrying, fuelrock from the store caves for the fires, pots to the cooling caves. Everyone was busy.

Fortunately the nighthearth, nearest the entrance, was operating for normal use, the huge *klah* pot and stew kettle swinging from their hooks, keeping warm over the coals. Just as F'nor had filled his cup, he heard his name called. Glancing around, he saw his blood mother, Manora, beckon to him. Her usually serene face wore a look of puzzled concern.

Obediently F'nor crossed to the hearth where she, Lessa, and another young woman who looked familiar though F'nor couldn't place her, were examining a small kettle.

"My duty to you, Lessa, Manora—" and he paused, groping for the third name.

"You ought to remember Brekke, F'nor," Lessa said, raising her eyebrows at his lapse.

"How can you expect anyone to see in a place dense with fumes?" F'nor demanded, making much of blotting his eyes on his sleeve. "I haven't seen much of you, Brekke, since the day Canth and I brought you from your crafthold to Impress young Wirenth."

"F'nor, you're as bad as F'lar," Lessa exclaimed, somewhat testily. "You never forget a dragon's name, but his rider's?"

"How fares Wirenth, Brekke?" F'nor asked, ignoring Lessa's interruption.

The girl looked startled but managed a hesitant smile, then pointedly looked towards Manora, trying to turn attention from herself. She was a shade too thin for F'nor's tastes, not much taller than Lessa whose diminutive size in no way lessened the authority and respect she commanded. There was, however, a sweetness about Brekke's solemn face, unexpectedly framed with dark curly hair, that F'nor did find appealing. And he liked her self-effacing modesty. He was wondering how she got along with Kylara, the tempestuous and irresponsible senior Weyrwoman at Southern Weyr, when Lessa tapped the empty pot before her.

"Look at this, F'nor. The lining has cracked and the entire kettle of numbweed salve is discolored."

F'nor whistled appreciatively.

"Would you know what it is the Smith uses to coat the metal?" Manora asked. "I wouldn't dare use tainted salve, and yet I hate to discard so much if there's no reason."

F'nor tipped the pot to the light. The dull tan lining was seamed by fine cracks along one side.

"See what it does to the salve?" and Lessa thrust a small bowl at him.

The anesthetic ointment, normally a creamy, pale yellow, had turned a reddish tan. Rather a threatening color, F'nor thought. He smelled it, dipped his finger in and felt the skin immediately deaden.

"It works," he said with a shrug.

"Yes, but what would happen to an open Thread score with that foreign substance cooked into the salve?" asked Manora.

"Good point. What does F'lar say?"

"Oh, him." Lessa screwed her fine delicate features into a grimace. "He's off to Lemos Hold to see how that woodcraftsman of Lord Asgenar's is doing with the wood pulp leaves."

F'nor grinned. "Never around when you want him, huh, Lessa?"

She opened her mouth for a stinging reply, her gray eyes snapping, and then realized that F'nor was teasing.

"You're as bad as he is," she said, grinning up at the tall Wingsecond who resembled her Weyrmate so closely. Yet the two men, though the stamp of their mutual sire was apparent in the thick shocks of black hair, the strong features, the lean rangy bodies (F'nor had a squarer, broader frame with not enough flesh on his bones so that he appeared unfinished), the two men were different in temperament and personality. F'nor was less introspective and more easygoing than his half brother, F'lar, the elder by three Turns. The Weyrwoman sometimes found herself treating F'nor as if he were an extension of his half brother and, perhaps for this reason, could joke and tease with him. She was not on easy terms with many people.

F'nor returned her smile and gave her a mocking little bow for the compliment.

"Well, I've no objections to running your errand to the Master-smithhall. I'm supposed to be Searching and I can Search in Telgar Hold as well as anywhere else. R'mart's nowhere near as sticky as some of the other Oldtime Weyrleaders." He took the pot off the hook, peering into it once more, then glanced around the busy room, shaking his head. "I'll take your pot to Fandarel but it looks to me as though you've already got enought numbweed to coat every dragon in all six—excuse me—seven Weyrs." He grinned at Brekke for the girl seemed curiously ill at ease. Lessa could be snaptempered when she was preoccupied and Ramoth was fussing over her latest clutch like a novice—which would tend to make Lessa more irritable. Strange for a junior Weyr-woman from Southern Weyr to be involved in any brewing at Benden.

"A Weyr can't have too much numbweed," Manora said briskly.

"That isn't the only pot that's showing cracks, either," Lessa cut in, testily. "And if we've got to gather more numbweed to make up what we've lost . . ."

"There's the second crop at the Southern Weyr," Brekke suggested, then looked flustered for speaking up.

But the look Lessa turned on Brekke was grateful. "I've no intention of shorting you, Brekke, when Southern Weyr does the nursing of every fool who can't dodge Thread."

"I'll take the pot. I'll take the pot," F'nor cried with humorous assurance. "But first, I've got to have more in me than a cup of *klah*."

Lessa blinked at him, her glance going to the entrance and the late afternoon sun slanting in on the floor.

"It's only just past noon in Telgar Hold," he said, patiently. "Yesterday I was all day Searching at Southern Boll so I'm hours behind myself." He stifled a yawn.

"I'd forgotten. Any luck?"

"Canth didn't twitch an ear. Now let me eat and get away from the stink. Don't know how you stand it."

Lessa snorted. "Because I can't stand the groans when you riders don't have numbweed."

F'nor grinned down at his Weyrwoman, aware that Brekke's eyes were wide in amazement at their good-natured banter. He was sincerely fond of Lessa as a person, not just as Weyrwoman of Benden's senior queen. He heartily approved of F'lar's permanent attachment of Lessa, not that there seemed much chance that Ramoth would ever permit any dragon but Mnementh to fly her. As Lessa was a superb Weyrwoman for Benden Weyr, so F'lar was the logical bronze rider. They were well matched as Weyrwoman and Weyrleader, and Benden

Weyr—and Pern—profited. So did the three Holds bound to Benden for protection. Then F'nor remembered the hostility of the people at Southern Boll yesterday until they learned that he was a Benden rider. He started to mention this to Lessa when Manora broke his train of thought.

"I am very disturbed by this discoloration, F'nor," she said, "Here. Show Mastersmith Fandarel these," and she put two small pots into the larger vessel. "He can see exactly the change that occurs. Brekke, would you be kind enough to serve F'nor?"

"No need," F'nor said hastily and backed away, pot swinging from his hand. He used to be annoyed that Manora, who was only his mother, could never rid herself of the notion that he was incapable of doing for himself. She was certainly quick enough to make her fosterlings fend for themselves, as his foster mother had made him.

"Don't drop the pot when you go *between*, F'nor," was her parting admonition.

F'nor chuckled to himself. Once a mother, always a mother, he guessed, for Lessa was as broody about Felessan, the only child she'd borne. Just as well the Weyrs practiced fostering. Felessan—as likely a lad to Impress a bronze dragon as F'nor had seen in all his Turns at Searching—got along far better with his placid foster mother than he would have with Lessa had she had the rearing of him.

As he ladled out a bowl of stew, F'nor wondered at the perversity of women. Girls were constantly pleading to come to Benden Weyr. They'd not be expected to bear child after child till they were worn-out and old. Women in the Weyrs remained active and appealing. Manora had seen twice the Turns that, for instance, Lord Sifer of Bitra's latest wife had, yet Manora looked younger. Well, a rider preferred to seek his own loves, not have them foisted on him. There were enough spare women in the Lower Caverns right now.

The *klah* might as well be medicine. He couldn't drink it. He quickly ate the stew, trying not to taste his food. Perhaps he could pick something up at Smithcrafthall at Telgar Hold.

"Canth! Manora's got an errand for us," he warned the brown dragon as he strode form the Lower Cavern. He wondered how the women stood the smell.

Canth did, too, for the fumes had kept him from napping on the warm ledge. He was just as glad of an excuse to get away from Benden Weyr.

F'nor broke out into the early morning sunshine above Telgar Hold, then directed brown Canth up the long valley to the sprawling complex of buildings on the left of the Falls.

Sun flashed off the water wheels which were turned endlessly by the powerful waters of the three-pronged Falls and operated the forges of the Smithy. Judging by the thin black smoke from the stone buildings, the smelting and refining smithies were going at full capacity.

As Canth swooped lower, F'nor could see the distant clouds of dust that meant another ore train coming from the last portage of Telgar's major river. Fandarel's notion of putting wheels on the barges had halved the time it took to get raw ore downriver and across land from the deep mines of Crom and Telgar to the crafthalls throughout Pern.

Canth gave a bugle cry of greeting which was instantly answered by the two dragons, green and brown, perched on a small ledge above the main Crafthall.

Beth and Seventh from Fort Weyr, Canth told his rider, but the names were not familiar to F'nor.

Time was when a man knew every dragon and rider in Pern.

"Are you joining them?" he asked the big brown.

They are together, Canth replied so pragmatically that F'nor chuckled to himself.

The green Beth, then, had agreed to brown Seventh's advances. Looking at her brilliant color, F'nor thought their riders shouldn't have brought that pair away from their home Weyr at this phase. As F'nor watched, the brown dragon extended his wing and covered the green possessively.

F'nor stroked Canth's downy neck at the first ridge but the dragon didn't seem to need any consolation. He'd no lack of partners after all, thought F'nor with little conceit. Greens would prefer a brown who was as big as most bronzes on Pern.

Canth landed and F'nor jumped off quickly. The dust made by his dragon's wings set up twin whirls, through which F'nor had to walk. In the open sheds which F'nor passed on his way to the Crafthall, men were busy at a number of tasks, most of them familiar to the brown rider. But at one shed he stopped, trying to fathom why the sweating men were winding a coil of metal through a plate, until he realized that the material was extruded as a fine wire. He was about to ask questions when he saw the sullen, closed expressions of the crafters. He nodded pleasantly and continued on his way, uneasy at the indifference—no, the distaste—exhibited at his presence. He was beginning to wish that he hadn't agreed to do Manora's errand.

But Smithcraftmaster Fandarel was the obvious authority on metal and could tell why the big kettle had suddenly discolored the vital anesthesic salve. F'nor swung the kettle to make sure the two sample pots were within, and grinned at the self-conscious gesture; for an instance he had a resurgence of his boyhood apprehension of losing something entrusted to him.

The entrance to the main Smithcrafthall was imposing: four land-beasts could be driven abreast through that massive portal and not scrape their sides. Did Pern breed Smithcraftmasters in proportion to that door? F'nor wondered as its maw swallowed him, for the immense metal wings stood wide. What had been the original Smithy was now converted to the artificers' use. At lathes and benches, men were polishing, engraving, adding the final touches to otherwise completed work. Sunlight streamed in from the windows set high in the building's wall, the eastern shutters were burnished with the morning sun which reflected also from the samples of weaponry and metalwork in the open shelves in the center of the big Hall.

At first, F'nor thought it was his entrance which had halted all activity, but then he made out two dragonriders who were menacing Terry. Surprised as he was to feel the tension in the Hall, F'nor was more disturbed that Terry was its brunt, for the man was Fandarel's second and his major innovator. Without a thought, F'nor strode across the floor, his bootheels striking sparks from the flagstone.

"And a good day to you, Terry, and you, sirs," F'nor said, saluting the two riders with airy amiability. "F'nor, Canth's rider, of Benden."

"B'naj, Seventh's rider of Fort," said the taller, grayer of the two riders. He obviously resented the interruption and kept slapping an elaborately jeweled belt knife into the palm of his hand.

"T'reb, Beth's rider, also of Fort. And if Canth's a bronze, warn him off Beth."

"Canth's no poacher," F'nor replied, grinning outwardly but marking T'reb for a rider whose green's *amours* affected his own temper.

"One never knows just what is taught at Benden Weyr," T'reb said with thinly veiled contempt.

"Manners, among other things, when addressing Wing-seconds," F'nor replied, still pleasant. But T'reb gave him a sharp look, aware of a subtle difference in his manner. "Good Master Terry, may I have a word with Fandarel?"

"He's in his study . . ."

"And you told us he was not about," T'reb interrupted, grabbing Terry by the front of his heavy wher-hide apron.

F'nor reacted instantly. His brown hand snapped about T'reb's wrist, his fingers digging into the tendons so painfully that the green rider's hand was temporarily numbed.

Released, Terry stood back, his eyes blazing, his jaw set.

"Fort Weyr manners leave much to be desired," F'nor said, his teeth showing in a smile as hard as the grip with which he held T'reb. But now the other Fort Weyr rider intervened.

"T'reb! F'nor!" B'naj thrust the two apart. "His green's proddy, F'nor. He can't help it."

"Then he should stay weyrbound."

"Benden doesn't advise Fort," T'reb cried, trying to step past his Weyrmate, his hand on his belt knife.

F'nor stepped back, forcing himself to cool down. The whole episode was ridiculous. Dragonriders did not quarrel in public. No one should use a Craftmaster's second in such a fashion. Outside, dragons bellowed.

Ignoring T'reb, F'nor said to B'naj, "You'd better get out of here. She's too close to mating."

But the truculent T'reb would not be silenced.

"Don't tell me how to manage my dragon, you . . ."

The insult was lost in a second volley from the dragons to which Canth now added his warble.

"Don't be a fool, T'reb," B'naj said. "Come! Now!"

"I wouldn't be here if you hadn't wanted that knife. Get it and come."

The knife B'naj had been handling lay on the floor by Terry's foot. The Craftsman retrieved it in such a way that F'nor suddenly realized why there had been such tension in the Hall. The dragonriders had been about to confiscate the knife, an action his entrance had forestalled. He'd heard too much lately of such extortions.

"You'd better go," he told the dragonriders, stepping in front of Terry.

"We came for the knife. We'll leave with it," T'reb shouted and, feinting with unexpected speed, ducked past F'nor, grabbing the knife from Terry's hand, slicing the smith's thumb as he drew the blade.

Again F'nor caught T'reb's hand and twisted it, forcing him to drop the knife.

T'reb gave a gurgling cry of rage and, before F'nor could duck or B'naj could intervene, the infuriated green rider had plunged his own belt knife into F'nor's shoulder, viciously slicing downward until the point hit the shoulder bone.

F'nor staggered back, aware of nauseating pain, aware of Canth's scream of protest, the green's wild bawl and the brown's trumpeting.

"Get him out of here," F'nor gasped to B'naj, as Terry reached out to steady him.

"Get out!" the Smith repeated in a harsh voice. He signaled urgently to the other craftsmen who now moved decisively toward the dragonmen. But B'naj yanked T'reb savagely out of the Hall.

F'nor resisted as Terry tried to conduct him to the nearest bench. It was bad enough that dragonrider should attack dragonrider, but F'nor was even more shocked that a rider should ignore his beast for the sake of a coveted bauble.

There was real urgency in the green's shrill ululation now. F'nor willed T'reb and B'naj on their beasts and away. A shadow fell across the great portal of the Smithhall. It was Canth, crooning anxiously. The green's voice was suddenly still.

"Are they gone?" he asked the dragon.

Well gone, Canth replied, craning his neck to catch sight of his rider. *You hurt.*

"I'm all right. I'm all right," F'nor lied, relaxing into Terry's urgent grip. In a blackening daze, he felt himself lifted, then the hard surface of bench under his back before the dizzying shock and pain overwhelmed him. His last conscious thought was that Manora would be annoyed that he had not seen Fandarel first.

Evening (Fort Weyr Time).

Meeting of the Weyrleaders at Fort Weyr

When Mnementh burst out of *between* above Fort Weyr, he entered so high above the Weyr mountain that it was a barely discernible black point in the darkening land below. F'lar's exclamation of surprise was cut off by the thin cold air that burned his lungs.

You must be calm and cool, Mnementh said, doubling his rider's astonishment. *You must command at this meeting.* And the bronze dragon began a long spiral glide down to the Weyr.

F'lar knew that no admonitions could change Mnementh's mind when he used that firm tone. He wondered at the great beast's unexpected initiative. But the bronze dragon was right.

F'lar could accomplish little if he stormed in on T'ron and the other Weyrleaders, bent on extracting justice for his wounded Wingsecond. Or if F'lar was still seething from the subtle insult implicit in the timing of this meeting. As Weyrleader of the offending rider, T'ron had delayed answering F'lar's courteously phrased request for a meeting of all Weyrleaders to discuss the untoward incident at the Craftmasterhall. When T'ron's reply finally arrived, it set the meeting for the first watch, Fort Weyr time; or high night, Benden time, a most inconsiderate hour for F'lar and certainly inconvenient for the other easterly Weyrs, Igen, Ista and even Telgar. D'ram of Ista Weyr and R'mart of Telgar, and probably G'narish of Igen would have something sharp to say to T'ron about such timing, though their lag was not as great as Benden Weyr's.

So T'ron wanted F'lar off balance and irritated. Therefore, F'lar would appear all amiability. He'd apologize to D'ram, R'mart and

G'narish for inconveniencing them, while making certain that they knew T'ron was responsible.

The main issue, to F'lar's now calm mind, was not the attack on F'nor. The real issue was the abrogation of two of the strongest Weyr restrictions; restrictions that ought to be so ingrained in any dragon-rider that their fracture was impossible.

It was an absolute that a dragonrider did not take a green dragon or a queen from her Weyr when she was due to rise for mating. It made no difference whatsoever that a green dragon was sterile because she chewed firestone. Her lust could affect even the most insensitive commoners with sexual cravings. A mating female dragon broadcast her emotions on a wide band. Some green-brown pairings were as loud as bronze-gold. Herdbeasts within range stampeded wildly and fowls, wherries and whers went into witless hysterics. Humans were susceptible, too, and innocent Hold youngsters often responded with embarrassing consequences. That particular aspect of dragon matings didn't bother weyrfolk who had long since disregarded sexual inhi-bitions. No, you did not take a dragon out of her Weyr in that state.

It was irrelevant to F'lar's thinking that the second violation stemmed from the first. From the moment riders could take their drag-ons *between*, they were abjured to avoid situations that might lead to a duel, particularly since dueling was an accepted custom among Craft and Hold. Any differences between riders were settled in unarmed bouts, closely refereed within the Weyr. Dragons suicided when their riders died. And occasionally a beast panicked if his rider was badly hurt or remained unconscious for long. A berserk dragon was almost impossible to manage and a dragon's death severely upset his entire Weyr. So armed dueling, which might injure or kill a dragon, was the most absolute proscription.

Today, a Fort Weyr rider had deliberately—judging from the tes-timony F'lar had from Terry and the other smithcrafters present—abrogated these two basic restrictions. F'lar experienced no satisfaction that the offending rider came from Fort Weyr even if T'ron, the major critic of Benden Weyr's relaxed attitudes toward some traditions, was in a very embarrassing position. F'lar might argue that his innovations breached no fundamental Weyr percepts, but the five Oldtime Weyrs categorically dismissed every suggestion originating from Benden Weyr. And T'ron bleated the most about the deplorable manners of modern Holders and Crafters, so different—so less subservient, F'lar amended—to the acquiescence of Holders and Crafters in their distant past Turn.

It would be interesting, F'lar mused, to see how T'ron the Tra-ditionalist explained away the actions of his riders, now guilty of far worse offenses against Weyr traditions than anything F'lar had suggested.

Common sense had dictated F'lar's policy—eight Turns ago—of throwing open Impressions to likely lads from Holds and Crafts; there hadn't been enough boys of the right age in Benden Weyr to match the number of dragon eggs. If the Oldtimers would throw open the mating flights of their junior queens to bronzes from other Weyrs, they'd soon have clutches as large as the ones at Benden, and undoubtedly queen eggs, too. However, F'lar could appreciate how the Oldtimers felt. The bronze dragons at Benden and Southern Weyr were larger than most Oldtimer bronzes. Consequently, they'd fly the queens. But, by the Shell, F'lar hadn't suggested that the senior queens be flown openly. He did not intend to challenge the Oldtimer Weyr-leaders with modern bronzes. He did feel that they'd profit by new blood among their beasts. Wasn't an improvement in dragonkind anywhere of benefit to all the Weyrs?

And it was practical diplomacy to invite Holders and Crafters to Impressions. There wasn't a man alive in Pern who hadn't secretly cherished the notion that he might be able to Impress a dragon. That he could be linked for life to the love and sustaining admiration of these gentle great beasts. That he could transverse Pern in a twinkling, astride a dragon. That he would never suffer the loneliness that was the condition of most men—a dragonrider always had his dragon. So, whether the commoners had a relative on the Hatching Ground hoping to attach a dragonet or not, the spectators enjoyed the vicarious thrill of being present, at witnessing this "mysterious rite." He'd observed that they were also subtly reassured that such dazzling fortune was available to some lucky souls not bred in the Weyrs. And those bound to a Weyr should, F'lar felt, get to know the riders since those riders were responsible for their lives and livelihoods.

To have assigned messenger dragons to every major Hold and Craft had been a very practical measure, too, when Benden had been Pern's only dragonweyr. The northern continent was broad. It took days to get messages from one coast to the other. The Harpercraft's system of drums was a poor second when a dragon could transport himself, his rider and an ungarbled message instantly anywhere on the planet.

F'lar, too, was exceedingly aware of the dangers of isolation. In the days before the first Thread had again fallen on Pern—could it be only seven Turns ago?—Benden Weyr had been vitiated by its isolation, and the entire planet all but lost. Where F'lar earnestly felt that dragonmen should make themselves accessible and friendly, the Old-timers were obsessed by a need for privacy. Which only fertilized the ground for such incidents as had just occurred. T'reb on a disturbed green had swooped down on the Smithmastercrafthall and demanded—not requested—that a craftsman give up an artifact, which had been made by commission for a powerful Lord Holder.

With thoughts that were more disillusioned than vengeful, F'lar realized that Mnementh was gliding fast toward Fort Weyr's jagged rim. The Star Stones and the watchrider were silhouetted against the dying sunset. Beyond them were the forms of three other bronzes, one a good half-tail larger than the others. That would be Orth, so T'bor was already arrived from Southern Weyr. But only three bronzes? Who was yet to come to the meeting?

Salth from High Reaches and Branth with R'mart of Telgar Weyr are absent, Mnementh informed his rider.

High Reaches and Telgar Weyrs missing? Well, T'kul of High Reaches was likely late on purpose. Odd though; that caustic Oldtimer ought to enjoy tonight. He'd have a chance to snipe at both F'lar and T'bor and he'd thoroughly enjoy T'ron's discomfiture. F'lar had never felt any friendliness for or from the dour, dark-complected High Reaches Weyrleader. He wondered if that was why Mnementh never used T'kul's name. Dragons ignored human names when they didn't like the bearer. But for a dragon not to name a Weyrleader was most unusual.

F'lar hoped that R'mart of Telgar would come. Of the Oldtimers, R'mart and G'narish of Igen were the youngest, the least set in their ways. Though they tended to side with their contemporaries in most affairs against the two modern Weyrleaders, F'lar and T'bor, F'lar had noticed lately that those two were sympathetic to some of his suggestions. Could he work on that to his advantage today—tonight? He wished that Lessa could have come with him for she was able to use deft mental pressures against dissenters and could often get the other dragons to answer her. She had to be careful, for dragonriders were apt to suspect they were being manipulated.

Mnementh was now within the Bowl of Fort Weyr itself and veering toward the ledge of the senior queen's weyr. T'ron's Fidranth was not there, guarding his queen Weyrmate as Mnementh would have been. Or perhaps Mardra, the senior Weyrwoman, was gone. She was as quick to find exception and slights as T'ron, though once she hadn't been so touchy. In those first days after the Weyrs had come up, she and Lessa had been exceedingly close. But Mardra's friendship had gradually turned into an active hatred. Mardra was a handsome woman, with a full, strong figure, and while she was nowhere near as promiscuous with her favors as Kylara of Southern Weyr, she was much sought after by bronze riders. By nature she was intensely possessive and not, F'lar realized, particularly intelligent. Lessa, dainty, oddly beautiful, already a Weyr legend for that spectacular ride *between* time, had unconsciously attracted attention from Mardra. Mardra evidently didn't consider the fact that Lessa made no attempt to entice any favorite from Mardra, did not, indeed, dally with any man (for which F'lar was immensely pleased). Add to that the ridiculous matter of their mutual Ruathan origin—Mardra conceived a hatred for Lessa. She seemed to feel that Lessa, the only survivor of that Bloodline, had had no right to renounce her claim on Ruatha Hold to young Lord Jaxom. Not that a Weyrwoman could take Hold or would want to. The bases for Mardra's hatred of Lessa were spurious. Lessa had no control over her beauty and had had no real choice about taking Hold at Ruatha.

So it was as well the Weyrwomen had not been included in this meeting. Put Mardra in the same room with Lessa and there'd be problems. Add Kylara of the Southern Weyr who was apt to make trouble for the pure joy of getting attention by disrupting others, and nothing would be accomplished. Nadira of Igen Weyr liked Lessa but in a passive way. Bedella of Telgar Weyr was stupid and Fanna of Ista, taciturn. Merika of the High Reaches was as much as a sour sort as her Weyrleader T'kul.

This was a matter for men to settle.

F'lar thanked Mnementh as he slid down the warm shoulder to the ledge, stumbling as his bootheels caught on the ridges of claw scars on the edge. T'ron might have put out a basket of glows, F'lar thought irritably, and then caught himself. Another trick to put everyone in as unreceptive a mood as possible.

Loranth, senior queen dragon of Fort Weyr, solemnly regarded F'lar as he entered the main room of the Weyr. He gave her a cordial greeting, suppressing his relief that there was no sign of Mardra. If Loranth was solemn, Mardra would have been downright unpleasant. Undoubtedly the Fort Weyrwoman was sulking beyond the curtain between weyr and sleeping room. Maybe this awkward time had been her idea. It was after western dinner hours and too late for more than wine for those from later time zones. She thus avoided the necessity of playing hostess.

Lessa would never resort to such mean-spirited strategies. F'lar knew how often the impulsive Lessa had bitten back quick answers when Mardra had patronized her. In fact, Lessa's forbearance with the haughty Fort Weyrwoman was miraculous, considering Lessa's temper. F'lar supposed that his Weyrmate felt responsible for uprooting the Oldtimers. But the final decision to go forward in time had been theirs.

Well, if Lessa could endure Mardra's condescension out of gratitude, F'lar could try to put up with T'ron. The man did know how to fight Thread effectively and F'lar had learned a great deal from him at first. So, in a determinedly pleasant frame of mind, F'lar walked down the short passage to the Fort Weyr Council Room.

T'ron, seated in the big stone chair at the head of the Table, acknowledged F'lar's entry with a stiff nod. The light of the glows on the wall cast unflattering shadows on the Oldtimer's heavy, lined face.

It struck F'lar forcibly that the man had *never* known anything but fighting Thread. He must have been born when the Red Star began that last fifty-Turn long Pass around Pern, and he'd fought Thread until the Star had finished its circuit. Then followed Lessa forward. A man could get mighty tired of fighting Thread in just seven short Turns. F'lar halted that line of thought.

D'ram of Ista Weyr and G'narish of Igen also contented themselves with nods. T'bor, however, gave F'lar a hearty greeting, his eyes glinting with emotion.

"Good evening, gentlemen," F'lar said to all. "I apologize for taking you from your own affairs or rest with this request for an emergency meeting of all Weyrleaders, but it could not wait until the regular Solstice Gathering."

"I'll conduct the meetings at Fort Weyr, Benden," T'ron said in a cold harsh voice. "I'll wait for T'kul and R'mart before I have any discussion of your—your complaint."

"Agreed."

T'ron stared at F'lar as if that hadn't been the answer he'd anticipated and he'd gathered himself for an argument that hadn't materialized. F'lar nodded to T'bor as he took the seat beside him.

"I'll say this now, Benden," T'ron continued. "The next time you elect to drag us all out of our Weyrs suddenly, you apply to me first. Fort's the oldest Weyr on Pern. Don't just irresponsibly send messengers out to everyone."

"I don't see that F'lar acted irresponsibly," G'narish said, evidently surprised by T'ron's attitude. G'narish was a stocky young man, some Turns F'lar's junior and the youngest of the Weyrleaders to come forward in time. "Any Weyrleader can call a joint meeting if circumstances warrant it. And these do!" G'narish emphasized this with a curt nod, adding when he saw the Fort Weyrleader scowling at him, "Well, they do."

"Your rider was the aggressor, T'ron," D'ram said in a stern voice. He was a rangy man, getting stringy with age, but his astonishing shock of red hair was only lightly grizzled at the temples. "F'lar's within his rights."

"You had the choice of time and place, T'ron," F'lar pointed out, all deference.

T'ron's scowl deepened.

"Wish Telgar'd get here," he said in a low, irritated tone.

"Have some wine, F'lar?" T'bor suggested, an almost malicious smile playing on his lips for T'ron ought to have offered immediately. "Of course, it's not Benden Hold wine, but not bad. Not bad."

F'lar gave T'bor a long warning look as he took the proffered cup. But the Southern Weyrleader was watching to see how T'ron reacted.

Benden Hold did not tithe of its famous wines as generously to the other Weyrs as it did to the one which protected its lands.

"When are we going to taste some of those Southern Weyr wines you've been bragging about, T'bor?" G'narish asked, instinctively trying to ease the growing tensions.

"Of course, we're entering our fall season now," T'bor said, making it seem that Fort was to blame for the chill outside—and inside—the Weyr. "However, we expect to start pressing soon. We'll distribute what we can spare to you northerners."

"What do you mean? What you can spare?" T'ron asked, staring hard at T'bor.

"Well, Southern plays nurse to every wounded dragonrider. We need sufficient on hand to drown their sorrows adequately. Southern Weyr supports itself, you must remember."

F'lar stepped on T'bor's booted foot as he turned to D'ram and inquired of the Istan Weyrleader how the last Laying had gone.

"Very well, thanks," D'ram replied pleasantly, but F'lar knew the older man did not like the mood that was developing. "Fanna's Mirath laid twenty-five and I'll warrant we've half a dozen bronzes in the clutch."

"Ista's bronzes are the fastest on Pern," F'lar said gravely. When he heard T'bor stirring restlessly beside him, he reached swiftly to Mnementh with a silent *"Ask Orth to please tell T'bor to speak with great thought for the consequences. D'ram and G'narish must not be antagonized."* Out loud he said, "A weyr can never have too many good bronzes. If only to keep the queens happy." He leaned back, watching T'bor out of the corner of his eye to catch his reaction when the dragons completed the message relay. T'bor gave a sudden slight jerk, then shrugged, his glance shifting from D'ram to T'ron and back to F'lar. He looked more rebellious than cooperative. F'lar turned back to D'ram. "If you need some likely prospects for any green dragons, there's a boy . . ."

"D'ram follows tradition, Benden," T'ron cut in. "Weyrbred is best for dragonkind. Particularly for greens."

"Oh?" T'bor glared with malicious intent at T'ron.

D'ram cleared his throat hastily and said in a too loud voice, "As it happens, we've a good group of likely boys in our Lower Caverns. The last Impression at G'narish's Weyr left him with a few he has offered to place at Ista Weyr. So I thank you kindly, F'lar. Generous indeed when you've eggs hardening at Benden too. And a queen, I hear?"

D'ram exhibited no trace of envy for another queen egg at Benden Weyr. And Fanna's Mirath hadn't produced a single golden egg since she'd come time *between*.

"We all know Benden's generosity," T'ron said in a sneering tone, his eyes flicking around the room, everywhere but at F'lar. "He extends help everywhere. And interferes when it isn't needed."

"I don't call what happened at the Smithhall interference," D'ram said, his face assuming grave lines.

"I thought we were going to wait for T'kul and R'mart," G'narish said, glancing anxiously up the passageway.

So, F'lar mused, D'ram and G'narish are upset by today's events.

"T'kul's better known for the meetings he misses than the ones he attends," T'bor remarked.

"R'mart always comes," G'narish said.

"Well, they're neither of them here. And I'm not waiting on their pleasure any longer," T'ron announced, rising.

"Then you'd better call in B'naj and T'reb," D'ram suggested with a heavy sigh.

"They're in no condition to attend a meeting." T'ron seemed surprised at D'ram's request. "Their dragons only returned from flight at sunset."

D'ram stared at T'ron. "Then why did you call the meeting for tonight?"

"At F'lar's insistence."

T'bor rose to protest before F'lar could stop him, but D'ram waved him to be seated and sternly reminded T'ron that the Fort Weyrleader had set the time, not F'lar of Benden.

"Look, we're here now," T'bor said, banging his fist on the table irritably. "Let's get on with it. It's full night in southern Weyr. I'd like . . ."

"I conduct the Fort Weyr meetings, Southern," T'ron said in a loud, firm voice, although the effort of keeping his temper told in the flush of his face and the brightness of his eyes.

"Then conduct it," T'bor replied. "Tell us why a green rider took his dragon out of your Weyr when she was close to heat."

"T'reb was not aware she was that close . . ."

"Nonsense," T'bor cut in, glaring at T'ron. "You keep telling us how much of a traditionalist you are, and how well trained your riders are. Then don't tell me a rider as old as T'reb can't estimate his beast's condition."

F'lar began to think he didn't need an ally like T'bor.

"A green changes color rather noticeably," G'narish said, with some reluctance, F'lar noted. "Usually a full day before she wants to fly."

"Not in the spring," T'ron pointed out quickly. "Not when she's off her feed from Threadscore. It can happen very quickly. Which it did." T'ron spoke loudly, as if the volume of his explanation would bear more weight than its logic.

"That is possible," D'ram admitted slowly, nodding his head up and down before he turned to see what F'lar thought.

"I accept that possibility," F'lar replied, keeing his voice even. He saw T'bor open his mouth to protest and kicked the man under the table. "However, according to the testimony of Craftmaster Terry, my rider urged T'reb repeatedly to take his dragon away. T'reb persisted in his attempt to—to acquire the belt knife."

"And you accept the word of a commoner against a rider?" T'ron leaped on F'lar's statement with a great show of surprised indignation and incredulity.

"What would a Craftmaster," and F'lar emphasized the title, "gain by bringing false witness?"

"Those smithcrafters are the most notorious misers of Pern," T'ron replied as if this were a personal insult. "The worst of all the crafts when it comes to parting with an honest tithe."

"A jeweled belt knife is not a tithe item."

"What differrence does that make, Benden?" T'ron demanded.

F'lar stared back at the Fort Weyrleader. So T'ron was trying to set the blame on Terry! Then he knew that his rider had been at fault. Why couldn't he just admit it and discipline the rider? F'lar only wanted to see that there'd be no repetitions of such an incident.

"The difference is that that knife had been crafted for Lord Larad of Telgar as a gift to Lord Asgenar of Lemos Hold for his wedding six days from now. The blade was not Terry's to give or withhold. It already belonged to a Lord Holder. Therefore, the rider was . . ."

"Naturally you'd take the part of your rider, Benden," T'ron cut in with a slight, unpleasant smile on his face. "But for a rider, a Weyrleader, to take the part of a Lord Holder against dragonfolk—" and T'ron turned to D'ram and G'narish with a helpless shrug of dismay.

"If R'mart were here, you'be—" T'bor began.

D'ram gestured at him to be quiet. "We're not discussing possession but what seems to be a grave breach of Weyr discipline," he said in a voice that overwhelmed T'bor's protest. "However, F'lar, you do admit that a green, off her feed from Threadscore, can suddenly go into heat without warning?"

F'lar could feel T'bor urging him to deny that possibility. He knew that he had made a mistake in pointing out that the knife had been commissioned for a Lord Holder. Or in taking the part of a Holder not bound to Benden Weyr. If only R'mart had been here to speak in Lord Larad's behalf. As it was, F'lar had prejudiced his case. The incident had disturbed D'ram so much that the man was deliberately closing his eyes to fact and seeking any extenuating circumstance he could. If F'lar forced him to see the event clearly, would he prove anything to a man unwilling to believe that dragonriders could be guilty of error? Would he get D'ram to admit that Craft and Hold had privileges, too?

He took a slow deep breath to control the frustrated anger he felt. "I have to concede that it is possible a green can go into heat without warning under those conditions." Beside him, T'bor cursed under his breath. "But for exactly that reason, T'reb ought to have known to keep his green in the Weyr."

"But T'reb's a Fort Weyr rider," T'bor began heatedly, jumping to his feet. "And I've been told often enough that . . ."

"You're out of order, Southern," T'ron said in a loud voice, glaring at F'lar, not T'bor. "Can't *you* control your riders, F'lar?"

"That is quite enough, T'ron," D'ram cried, on his feet.

As the two Oldtimers locked glances, F'lar murmured urgently to T'bor. "Can't you see he's trying to anger us? Don't lose control!"

"We're trying to settle the incident, T'ron," D'ram continued forcefully, "not complicate it with irrelevant personalities. Since you are involved in this business, perhaps I'd better conduct the meeting. With your permission, of course, Fort."

To F'lar's mind, that was a tacit admission that D'ram realized, however he might try to evade it, how serious the incident was. The Istan Weyrleader turned to F'lar, his brown eyes dark with concern. F'lar entertained a half hope that D'ram might have seen through T'ron's obstructiveness, but the Oldtimer's next words disabused him. "I do not agree with you, F'lar, that the Crafter acted in good part. No, let me finish. We came to the aid of your troubled time, expecting to be recompensed and supported in proper fashion, but the manner and the amount of tithing rendered the Weyrs from Hold and Craft has left much to be desired. Pern is much more productive than it was four hundred Turns ago and yet that wealth has not been reflected in the tithes. There is four times the population of our Time and much, much more cultivated land. A heavy responsibility for the Weyrs. And—" he cut himself off with a rueful laugh. "I'm digressing, too. Suffice it to say that once it was obvious a dragonrider found the knife to his liking, Terry should have gifted it him. As craftsmen used to, without any question or hesitation."

"Then" D'ram's face brightened slightly, "T'reb and B'naj would have left before the green went into full heat, your F'nor would not have become involved in a disgraceful public brawl. Yes, it is all too plain," and D'ram straightened his shoulders from the burden of decision, "that the first error of judgment was on the part of the craftsman." He looked at each man, as if none of them had control over what a craftsman might do. T'bor refused to meet his eyes and ground a bootheel noisily into the stone floor.

D'ram took another deep breath. Was he, F'lar wondered bitterly, having trouble digesting that verdict?

"We cannot, of course, permit a repetition of a green in mating heat outside her weyr. Or dragonriders in an armed duel . . ."

"There wasn't any duel!" The words seemed to explode from T'bor. "T'reb *attacked* F'nor without warning and sliced him up. F'nor never even drew his knife. That's no duel. That's an unwarranted attack . . ."

"A man whose green is in heat is unaccountable for his actions," T'ron said, loud enough to drown T'bor out.

"A green who never should have been out of her weyr in the first place no matter how you dance around the truth, T'ron," T'bor said, savage with frustration. "The first error in judgment was T'reb's. Not Terry's."

"Silence!" D'ram's bellow silenced him and Loranth answered irritably from her weyr.

"That does it," T'ron exclaimed, rising. "I'm not having my senior queen upset. You've had your meeting, Benden, and your—your grievance has been aired. This meeting is adjourned."

"Adjourned?" G'narish echoed him in surprise. "But—but nothing's been done." The Igen Weyrleader looked from D'ram to T'ron puzzled, worried. "And F'lar's rider was wounded. If the attack was . . ."

"How badly wounded is the man?" D'ram asked, turning quickly to F'lar.

"Now you ask!" cried T'bor.

"Fortunately," and F'lar held T'bor's angry eyes in a stern, warning glance before turning to D'ram to answer, "the wound is not serious. He will not lose the use of the arm."

G'narish sucked his breath in with a whistle. "I thought he'd only been scratched. I think we . . ."

"When a rider's dragon is lustful—" D'ram began, but broke off when he caught sight of the naked fury on T'bor's face, the set look on F'lar's. "A dragonrider can never forget his purpose, his responsibility, to his dragon or to his Weyr. This can't happen again. You'll speak to T'reb, of course, T'ron?"

T'ron's eyes widened slightly at D'ram's question.

"Speak to him? You may be sure he'll hear from me about this. And B'naj, too."

"Good," said D'ram, with the air of a man who has solved a difficult problem equitably. He nodded toward the others. "It would be wise if we Weyrleaders caution all our riders against the possibility of a repetition. Put them all on their guard. Agreed?" He continued nodding, as if to spare the others the effort. "It is hard enough to work with some of these arrogant Holders and Crafters without giving them any occasion to fault us." D'ram sighed deeply and scratched his head. "I never have understood how commoners can forget how much they owe dragonriders!"

"In four hundred Turns, a man can learn many new things," F'lar replied. "Coming, T'bor?" and his tone was just short of command. "My greetings to your Weyrwomen, riders. Good night."

He strode from the Council Room, T'bor pounding right behind him, swearing savagely until they got to the outer passageway to the Weyr ledge.

"That old fool was in the wrong, F'lar, and you know it!"

"Obviously."

"Then why didn't you . . . ."

"Rub his nose in it?" F'lar finished, halting in mid-stride and turning to T'bor in the dark of the passageway.

"Dragonriders don't fight. Particularly Weyrleaders."

T'bor let out a violent exclamation of utter disgust.

"How could you let a chance like that go by? When I think of the times he's criticized you—us—" T'bor broke off. "Never understand how commoners can forget all they owe dragonriders?" and T'bor mimicked D'ram's pompous intonation, "If they really want to know . . ."

F'lar gripped T'bor by the shoulder, appreciating the younger man's sentiments all too deeply.

"How can you tell a man what he doesn't want to hear? We couldn't even get them to admit that T'reb was in the wrong. T'reb, not Terry, and not F'nor. But I don't think there'll be another lapse like today's and that's what I really worried about."

"What?" T'bor stared at F'lar in puzzled confusion.

"That such an incident *could* occur worries me far more than who was in the wrong and for what reason."

"I can't follow that logic any more than I can follow T'ron's."

"It's simple. Dragonmen don't fight. Weyrleaders can't. T'ron was hoping I'd be mad enough to lose control. I think he was hoping I'd attack him."

"You can't be serious!" T'bor was plainly shaken.

"Remember, T'ron considers himself the senior Weyrleader on Pern and therefore infallible."

T'bor made a rude noise. Despite himself, F'lar grinned.

"True," he continued, "but I've never had a reason to challenge him. And don't forget, the Oldtimers taught us a great deal about Thread fighting we certainly didn't know."

"Why, our dragons can fight circles around the Oldtimers."

"That's not the point, T'bor. You and I, the modern Weyrs, have certain obvious advantages over the Oldtimers—size of dragons, number of queens—that I'm not interested in mentioning because it only makes for bad feeling. Nevertheless, we can't fight Thread without the Oldtimers. We need the Oldtimers more than they need us." F'lar gave T'bor a wry, bitter grin. "D'ram was partly right. A dragonman can never forget his purpose, his responsibility. When D'ram said 'to his dragon, to his Weyr', he's wrong. Our initial and ultimate responsibility is to Pern, to the people we were established to protect."

They had proceeded to the ledge and could see their dragons dropping off the height to meet them. Full dark had descended over Fort Weyr now, emphasizing the weariness that engulfed F'lar.

"If the Oldtimers have become introverted, we, Benden and Southern, cannot. We understand our turn, our people. And somehow we've got to make the Oldtimers understand them, too."

"Yes, but T'ron was in the wrong!"

"Would we have been more right to make him *say* it?"

T'bor bit back an angry response and F'lar hoped that the man's rebellion was dissipating. There was good heart and mind in the Southern Weyrleader. He was a fine dragonrider, a superb fighter, and his Wings followed him without hestiation. He was not as strong out of the skies, however, but with subtle guidance had built Southern Weyr into a productive, self-supporting establishment. He instinctively looked to F'lar and Benden Weyr for direction and companionship. Part of that, F'lar was sure, was because of the difficult and disturbing temperament of the Southern Weyrwoman, Kylara.

Sometimes F'lar regretted that T'bor proved to be the only bronze rider who could cope with that female. He wondered what subtle deep tie existed between the two riders, because T'bor's Orth consistently outflew every bronze to mate with Prideth, Kylara's queen, though it was common knowledge that Kylara took many men to her bed.

T'bor might be short-tempered and not the most diplomatic adherent, but he was loyal and F'lar was grateful to him. If he'd only held his temper tonight . . .

"Well, you usually know what you're doing, F'lar," the Southern Weyrleader admitted reluctantly, "but I don't understand the Oldtimers and lately I'm not sure I care."

Mnementh hovered by the ledge, one leg extended. Beyond him, the two men could hear Orth's wings beating the night air as he held his position.

"Tell F'nor to take it easy and get well. I know he's in good hands down at Southern," F'lar said as he scrambled up Mnementh's shoulder and urged him out of Orth's way.

"We'll have him well in next to no time. You need him," replied T'bor.

Yes, thought F'lar as Mnementh soared up out of the Fort Weyr Bowl, I need him. I could have used his wits beside me tonight. I could have used his thinking on T'ron's invidious attempts to switch blame.

Well, if it had been another rider, wounded under the same circumstances, he couldn't have brought F'nor anyhow. And T'bor with his short temper would still have been present, and played right into T'ron's hands. He couldn't honestly blame T'bor. He'd felt the same burning desire to *make* the Oldtimers see the facts in realistic perspective. But—you can't take a dragon to a place you've never seen. And T'bor's outbursts had not helped. Strange, T'bor hadn't been so touchy as a weyrling nor when he was a Benden Weyr Wing-second. Being weyrmate to Kylara had changed him but that woman was enough to unsettle; to unsettle D'ram.

F'lar entertained the wild mental image of the blonde sensual Kylara seducing the sturdy Oldtimer. Not that she'd even glanced at the Istan Weyrleader. And she certainly wouldn't have stayed with him. F'lar was glad that they'd eased her out of Benden Weyr. Hadn't she been found on the same Search as Lessa? Where'd she come from? Oh, yes, Telgar Hold. Come to think of it, she was the present Lord's full-blooded sister. Just as well Kylara was in Weyrlife. With her proclivity, she'd have had her throat sliced long ago in a Hold or a Crafthall.

Mnementh transferred them *between* and the cold of that awful nothingness made his bones ache. Then they emerged over the Benden Weyr Star Stones and answered the watchrider's query.

Lessa wasn't going to like his report of the meeting, F'lar thought. If only D'ram, usually an honest thinker, had seen past the obvious. He had a feeling that maybe G'narish had.

Yes, G'narish had been troubled. Maybe the next time the Weyrleaders met to confer, G'narish might side with the modern riders.

Only, F'lar hoped, there wouldn't be another occasion for this evening's grievance.

❧

Morning Over Lemos Hold

Ramoth, Benden's golden queen, was in the Hatching Ground when she got the green's frantic summons from Lemos Hold. *Threads at Lemos. Thread falls at Lemos!* Ramoth told every dragon and rider, her full-throated brassy bugle reverberating through the Bowl.

Men scrambled frantically from couch and bathing pool, upset tables and dropped tools before the first echo had rolled away. F'lar, idly watching the weyrlings drill, was dressed for fighting since the Weyr had expected to be at Lemos Hold late that day. Mnementh, his magnificent bronze, sunning himself on a ledge, swooped down at such a rate that he gouged a narrow trench in the sand of the floor with his left wingtip. F'lar was atop his neck and they were circling to the Eye Rock before Ramoth had had time to stamp out of the Hatching Cavern.

Thread at Lemos northeast, Mnementh reported, picking up the information from his mate Ramoth as she projected herself toward her weyr ledge for Lessa. Dragons were now streaming from every weyr opening, their riders struggling into fighting gear or securing bulging firesacks.

F'lar didn't waste time wondering why Thread was falling hours ahead of schedule or northeast instead of southwest. He checked to see if there were enough riders assembled and aloft to make up a full low altitude wing. He hesitated long enough to have Mnementh order every weyrling to proceed immediately to Lemos to help fly ground crews to the area and then told his dragon to take the wing *between*.

Thread was indeed falling, a great sheet plummeting down toward the delicate new leafing hardwoods that were Lord Asgenar's prime forestry project. Screaming, flaming, dragons broke out of *between*, skimming the spring forest to get quick bearings before they soared up to meet the attack.

Incredibly, F'lar believed they had actually managed to beat Thread to the forest. That green's rider would have his choice of anything in F'lar's power to give. The thought of Thread in those hardwood stands chilled the Weyrleader more thoroughly than an hour *between*.

A dragon screamed directly above F'lar. Even as he glanced upward to identify the wounded beast, both dragon and rider had gone *between* where the awful cold would shatter and break the entangling Threads before they could eat into membrane and flesh.

A casualty minutes into an attack? Even an attack that was so unpredictably early? F'lar winced.

Virianth, R'nor's brown, Mnementh informed his rider as he soared in search of a target. He craned his sinuous neck around in a wide sweep, eyeing the forest lest Thread had actually started burrowing. Then, with a warning to his rider, he folded his wings and dove toward an especially thick patch, braking his descent with neck-snapping speed. As Mnementh belched fire, F'lar watched, grinning with intense satisfaction as the Thread curled into black dust and floated harmlessly to the forests below.

Virianth caught his wingtip, Mnementh said as he beat upward again. *He'll return. We need him. This Thread falls wrong.*

"Wrong and early," F'lar said, gritting his teeth against the fierce wind of their ascent. If he hadn't been in the custom of sending a messenger on to the Hold where Thread was due . . .

Mnementh gave him just enough warning to secure his hold as the great bronze veered suddenly toward a dense clump. The stench of the fiery breath all but choked F'lar. He flung up an arm to protect his face from the hot charred flecks of Thread. Then Mnementh was turning his head for another block of firestone before swooping again at dizzying speed after more Thread.

There was no further time for speculation; only action and reaction. Dive. Flame. Firestone for Mnementh to chew. Call a weyrling for another sack. Catch it deftly mid-air. Fly above the fighting wings to check the pattern of flying dragons. Gouts of flame blossoming across the sky. Sun glinting off green, blue, brown, bronze backs as dragons veered, soared, dove, flaming after Thread. He'd spot a beast going *between*, tense until he reappeared or Mnementh reported their retreat. Part of his mind kept track of the casualties, another traced the wing line, correcting it when the riders started to overlap or flew too wide a pattern. He was aware, too, of the golden triangle of the queens' wing, far below, catching what Thread escaped from the upper levels.

By the time Thread had ceased to fall and the dragons began to spiral down to aid the Lemos Hold ground crews, F'lar almost resented Mnementh's summary.

Nine minor brushes, four just wingtips; two bad lacings, Sorenth and Relth, and two face-burned riders.

Wingtip injuries were just plain bad judgment. Riders cutting it too fine. They weren't riding competitions, they were fighting! F'lar ground his teeth . . .

Sorenth says they came out of between *into a patch that should not have been there. The Threads are not falling right,* the bronze said. *That is what happened to Relth and T'gor.*

That didn't assuage F'lar's frustration for he knew T'gor and R'mel as good riders.

How could Thread fall northeast in the morning when it wasn't supposed to drop until evening and in the southwest? he wondered, savage with frustrated worry.

Automatically, F'lar started to ask Mnementh to have Canth fly close in. But then he remembered that F'nor was wounded and half a planet away in Southern Weyr. F'lar swore long and imaginatively, wishing T'reb of Fort Weyr immured *between* with Weyrleader T'ron fast beside him. Why did F'nor have to be absent at a time like this? It still rankled F'lar deeply that Fort's Weyrleader had tried to shift the blame of the fight from his very guilty rider to Terry. Of all the specious, contrived, ridiculous contentions for T'ron to stand by!

Lamanth is flying well, the bronze dragon remarked, cutting into his rider's thoughts.

F'lar was so surprised at the unexpected diversion that he glanced down to see the young queen.

"We're lucky to have so many to fly today," F'lar said, amused despite his other concerns by the bronze's fatuous tone. Lamanth was the queen from Mnementh's second mating with Ramoth.

Ramoth flies well too, for one so soon from the Hatching Ground. Thirty-eight eggs and another queen, Mnementh added with no modesty.

"We're going to have to do something about that third queen."

Mnementh rumbled about that. Ramoth disliked sharing the bronze dragons of the Weyr with too many queens, in spite of the fact that she would mate only with Mnementh. Many queens were the mark of virility in a bronze and it was natural for Mnementh to want to flaunt his prowess. Benden Weyr had to maintain more than one golden queen to placate the rest of the bronzes and to improve the breed in general, but three?

After the meeting the other night at Fort Weyr, F'lar hesitated to suggest to any of the other Weyrleaders that he'd be glad of a home for the new queen: They'd probably contrive it to be bad management of Ramoth or coddling of Lessa. Still, Benden queens were bigger than

Oldtimer queens, just as modern bronzes were bigger, too. Maybe R'mart at Telgar Weyr wouldn't take offense. Or G'narish? F'lar couldn't think how many queens G'narish had at Igen Weyr. He grinned to himself, thinking of the expression of T'ron's face when he heard Benden was giving away a queen dragon.

"Benden's known for its generosity, but what's behind such a maneuver?" T'ron would say. "It's not traditional."

But it was. There were precedents. F'lar would far rather cope with T'ron's snide remarks than Ramoth's temper. He glanced down, sighting the gleaming triangle of the queens' wing, with Ramoth easily sweeping along, the younger beasts working hard to keep up with her.

Threads dropping out of pattern! F'lar gritted his teeth. Worse, out of a pattern which he'd so painstakingly researched from hundreds of disintegrating Record skins in his efforts seven Turns ago to prepare his ill-protected planet. Patterns, F'lar thought bitterly, which the Old-timers had enthusiastically acclaimed and *used*—though that was scarcely traditional. Just useful.

Now how could Thread, which had no mind, no intelligence at all, deviate from patterns it had followed to the split second for over seven Turns? How could it change time and place overnight? The last Fall in Benden's Weyr jurisdiction had been on time and over upper Benden Hold as expected.

Could he possibly have misread the timetables? F'lar thought back, but the carefully drawn maps were clear in his mind and, if he *had* made an error, Lessa would have caught it.

He'd check, double check, as soon as he returned to the Weyr. In the meantime, he'd better make sure they had cleared the Fall from Edge to Edge. He directed Mnementh to find Asgenar, Lord Holder of Lemos.

Mnementh obediently turned out of the leisurely glide and dropped swiftly. F'lar could thank good fortune that it was Lord As-genar of Lemos to whom he must explain, rather than Lord Sifer of Bitra Hold or Lord Raid of Benden Hold. The former would rant against the injustice and the latter would contrive to make a premature arrival of Thread a personal insult to him by dragonmen. Sometimes the Lords Raid and Sifer tried F'lar's patience. True, those three Holds, Benden, Bitra and Lemos, had conscientiously tithed to support Benden Weyr when it was the sole dragonweyr of Pern. But Lord Raid and Lord Sifer had an unpleasant habit of reminding Benden Weyr riders of their loyalty at every opportunity. Gratitude is an ill-fitting tunic that can chafe and smell if worn too long.

Lord Asgenar of Lemos Hold, on the other hand, was young and had been confirmed in his honors by the Lord Holders' Conclave only five Turns ago. His attitude toward the Weyr which protected his Hold-lands from Thread was refreshingly untainted by invidious reminders of past services.

Mnementh glided toward the expanse of the Great Lake which separated Lemos Hold from upper Telgar Hold. The Threads' advance edge had just missed the verdant softwoods that surrounded the northern shores. Mnementh circled down, causing F'lar to lean into the great neck, grasping the fighting straps firmly. Despite his weariness and worry, he felt the sharp surge of elation which always gripped him when he flew the huge bronze dragon; that curious merging of himself with the beast, against air and wind, so that he was not only F'lar, Weyrleader of Benden, but somehow Mnementh, immensely powerful, magnificently free.

On a rise overlooking the broad meadow that swept down to the Great Lake, F'lar spotted the green dragon. Lemos' Lord Holder, Asgenar, would be near her. F'lar smiled sardonically at the sight. Let the Oldtimers disapprove, let them mutter uneasily when F'lar put non-weyrfolk on dragonback, but if F'lar had not, Thread would have fallen unseen over those hardwoods.

Trees! Another bone of contention between Weyr and Hold, with F'lar staunchly upholding the Lord's position. Four hundred turns ago, such timber stands had not existed, were not permitted to grow. Too much living green to protect. Well, the Oldtimers were eager enough to own products of wood, overloading Fandarel's woodcraftsman, Bendarek, with their demands. On the other hand, they wouldn't permit the formation of a new Crafthall under Bendarek. Probably because, F'lar thought bitterly, Bendarek wanted to stay near the hardwoods of Lemos, and that would give Benden Weyr a Crafthall in its jurisdiction. By the Egg, the Oldtimers were almost more trouble than they were worth!

Mnementh landed with sweeping backstrokes that flattened the thick meadow grass. F'lar slid down the bronze's neck to join Lord Asgenar while Mnementh trumpeted approval to the green dragon and F'rad, his rider.

F'rad wants to warn you that Asgenar . . .

"Not much gets through Benden's wings," Asgenar was saying by way of greeting so that Mnementh didn't finish his thought. The young man was wiping soot and sweat from his face for he was one Lord who directed his ground crews personally instead of staying comfortably in his main Hold. "Even if Threads have begun to deviate. How do you account for all these recent variations?"

"Variations?" F'lar repeated the word, feeling stupid because he somehow realized that Asgenar was not referring just to this day's unusual occurrence.

"Yes! And here we thought your timetables were the last word. To be relied on forever, especially since they were checked and approved by the Oldtimers." Asgenar gave F'lar a sly look. "Oh, I'm not faulting you, F'lar. You've always been open in our dealings. I count myself lucky to be weyrbound to you. A man knows where he stands with Benden Weyr. My brother-in-law elect, Lord Larad, has had problems with T'kul of the High Reaches Weyr, you know. And since those premature falls at Tillek and Upper Crom, he's got a thorough watch system set up." Asgenar paused, suddenly aware of F'lar's tense silence. "I do not presume to criticize weyrfolk, F'lar," he said in a more formal tone, "but rumor can outfly a dragon and naturally I heard about the others. I can appreciate the Weyrs not wishing to alarm commoners but—well—a little forewarning would be only courteous."

"There was no way of predicting today's fall," F'lar said slowly, but his mind was turning so rapidly that he felt sick. Why had nothing been said to him? R'mart of Telgar Weyr hadn't been at the meeting about T'reb's transgressions. Could R'mart have been busy fighting Thread at that time? As for T'kul of the High Reaches Weyr imparting any information, particularly news that might show him in a bad light, that one wouldn't give coordinates to save a rider's life.

No, they'd have had good reason not to mention premature falls to F'lar that night. If T'kul had confided in anyone. But why hadn't R'mart let them know?

"But Benden Weyr's not caught sleeping. Once is all we'd need in those forests, huh, F'lar?" Asgenar was saying, his eyes scanning the spongewoods possessively.

"Yes. All we'd need. What's the report from the leading Edge of this Fall? Have you runners in yet?"

"Your queens' wing reported it safe two hours past." Asgenar grinned and rocked back and forth on his heels, his confidence not a bit jarred by today's unpredicted event. F'lar envied him.

Again the bronze rider thanked good fortune that he had Lord Asgenar to deal with this morning instead of punctilious Raid or suspicious Lord Sifer. He devoutly hoped that the young Lord Holder would not find his trust misplaced. But the question haunted him: how could Threads change so?

Both Weyrleader and Lord Holder froze as they watched a blue dragon hover attentively above a stand of trees to the northeast. When the beast flew on, Asgenar turned to F'lar with troubled eyes.

"Do you think these odd falls will mean that those forests must be razed?"

"You know my views on wood, Asgenar. It's too valuable a commodity, too versatile, to sacrifice needlessly."

"But it takes every dragon to protect . . ."

"Are you for or against?" F'lar asked with mild amusement. He gripped Asgenar's shoulder. "Instruct your foresters to keep constant watch. Their vigilance is essential."

"Then you don't know the pattern in the Thread shifts?"

F'lar shook his head slowly, unwilling to perjure himself to this man. "I'll leave the long-eyed F'rad with you."

A wide smile broke the thin troubled face of the Lord Holder.

"I couldn't ask, but it's a relief. I shan't abuse the privilege."

F'lar glanced at him sharply. "Why should you?"

Asgenar gave him a wry smile. "That's what the Oldtimers carp about, isn't it? And instant transportation to any place on Pern is a temptation."

F'lar laughed, remembering that Asgenar, Lord of Lemos, was to take Famira, the youngest sister of Larad, Lord of Telgar Hold, to wife. While the Telgar lands marched the boundaries of Lemos, the Holds were separated by deep forest and several ranges of steep rocky mountains.

Three dragons appeared and circled above them, wingriders reporting on the ground activities. Nine infestations had been sighted and controlled with minimum loss of property. Sweepriders had reported that the mid-Fall area was clear. F'lar dismissed them. A runner came loping up the meadow to his Lord Holder, carefully keeping several dragonlengths between himself and the two beasts. For all that every Pernese knew the dragons would harm no human, many would never lose their fearfulness. Dragons were confused by this distrust so that F'lar strolled casually to his bronze and scratched the left eye ridge affectionately until Mnementh allowed one lid to droop in pleasure over the gleaming opalescent eye.

The runner had come from afar, managing to gasp out his reassuring message before he collapsed on the ground, his chest heaving with the effort to fill his starved lungs. Asgenar stripped off his tunic and covered the man to prevent his chilling and made the runner drink from his own flask.

"The two infestations on the south slope are char!" Asgenar reported to the Weyrleader as he rejoined him. "That means the hardwood stands are safe." Asgenar's relief was so great that he took a swig on the bottle himself. Then hastily offered it to the dragonrider. When F'lar politely refused, he went on, "We may have another hard winter and my people will need that wood. Cromcoal costs!"

F'lar nodded. Free provision of fuelwood meant a tremendous saving to the average holder, though not every Lord saw it in this aspect. Lord Meron of Nabol Hold, for instance, refused to let his commoners chop fuelwood, forcing them to pay the high rates for Cromcoal, increasing his profit at their expense.

"That runner came from the south slope? He's fast."

"My forest men are the best in all Pern. Meron of Nabol has twice tried to lure that man from me."

"And?"

Lord Asgenar chuckled. "Who trusts Meron? My man had heard tales of how that Lord treats his people." He seemed about to add another thought but cleared his throat instead, glancing nervously away as if catching a glimpse of something in the woods.

"What all Pern needs is an efficient means of communication," remarked the dragonman, his eyes on the gasping runner.

"Efficient?" and Asgenar laughed aloud. "Is all Pern infected with Fandarel's disease?"

"Pern benefits by such an illness." F'lar must contact the Mastersmith the moment he got back to the Weyr. Pern needed the genius of the giant Fandarel now more than ever.

"Yes, but will we recover from the feverish urge for perfection?" Asgenar's smile faded as he added, in a deceptively casual fashion, "Have you heard whether a decision has been reached about Bendarek's guild?"

"None yet."

"*I* do not insist that a Craftmaster's Hall be sited in Lemos—" Asgenar began, urgent and serious.

F'lar held up his hand. "Nor I, though I have trouble convincing others of my sincerity. Lemos Hold has the biggest stands of wood, Bendarek needs to be near his best source of supply, and he comes of Lemos!"

"Every single objection raised has been ridiculous," Asgenar replied, his gray eyes sparkling with anger. "You know as well as I that a Craftmaster owes no allegiance to a Lord Holder. Bendarek's as unprejudiced as Fandarel as far as loyalty to anything but his craft is concerned. All the man thinks of is wood and pulp and those new leaves or sheets or what-you-ma-callums he's mucking about with."

"I know. I know, Asgenar. Larad of Telgar Hold and Corman of Keroon Hold side with you or so they've assured me."

"When the Lord Holders meet in Conclave at Telgar Hold, I'm going to speak out. Lord Raid and Sifer will back me, if only because we're weyrbound."

"It isn't the Lords or Weyrleaders who must make this decision." F'lar reminded the resolute young Lord. "It's the other Craftmasters. That's been my thought since Fandarel first proposed a new craft designation."

"Then what's holding matters up? All the Mastercraftsmen will be at the wedding at Telgar Hold. Let's settle it once and for all and let Bendarek alone." Asgenar threw his arms wide with frustration. "We need Bendarek settled, we need what he's been producing and he can't keep his mind on important work with all this shifting and shouting."

"Any proposal that smacks of change right now," (especially now, F'lar added to himself, thinking of this Threadfall,) "is going to alarm certain Weyrleaders and Lord Holders. Sometimes I think that only the Crafts constantly look for change, are interested and flexible enough to judge what is improvement or progressive. The Lord Holders and the—" F'lar broke off.

Fortunately another runner was approaching from the north, his legs pumping strongly. He came straight past the green dragon, right up to his Lord.

"Sir, the northern section is clear. Three burrows have been burned out. All is secure."

"Good man, Well run."

The man, flushed with praise and effort, saluted the Weyrleader and his Lord. Then, breathing deeply but without labor, he strode over to the prone messenger and began massaging his legs.

Asgenar smiled at F'lar. "There's no point in our rehearsing arguments. We are basically in agreement. If we could just make those others see!"

Mnementh rumbled that the wings were reporting an all-clear. He so pointedly extended his foreleg that Asgenar laughed.

"That does it," he said. "Any idea how soon before we have another Fall?"

F'lar shook his head. "F'rad is here. You ought to have seven days free. You'll hear from me as soon as we've definite news."

"You'll be at Telgar in six days, won't you?"

"Or Lessa will have my ears!"

"My regards to your lady."

Mnementh bore him upward in an elliptical course that allowed them to make one final check of the forest lands. Wisps of smoke curled to the north and farther to the east, but Mnementh seemed unconcerned. F'lar told him to go *between*. The utter cold of that dimension painfully irritated the Thread scores on his face. Then they were above Benden Weyr. Mnementh trumpeted his return and hung, all but motionless, until he heard the booming response of Ramoth. At that instant, Lessa appeared on the ledge of the weyr, her slight stature diminished still further by distance. As Mnementh glided in, she descended the long flight of stairs in much the same headlong fashion for which they criticized their weyrling son, Felessan.

Reprimands were not likely to break Lessa of that habit either, thought F'lar. Then he noticed what Lessa had in her hands and rounded angrily on Mnementh. "I'm barely touched and you babble on me like a weyrling!"

Mnementh was not the least bit abashed as he backwinged to land lightly by the Feeding Ground. *Thread hurts.*

"I don't want Lessa upset over nothing!"

I don't want Ramoth angry over anything!

F'lar slid from the bronze's neck, concealing the twinges he felt as the gritty wind from the Feeding Grounds aggravated the cold-seared lacerations. This was one of those times when the double bond between riders and dragons became a serious disadvantage. Particularly when Mnementh took the initiative, not generally a draconic characteristic.

Mnementh gave an awkward half-jump upward, clearing the way for Lessa. She hadn't changed from wher-hide riding clothes and looked younger than any Weyrwoman ought as she ran towards them, her plaited hair bouncing behind her. Although neither motherhood nor seven Turns of security had added flesh to her small-boned body, there was a subtle roundness to breast and hip, and that certain look in her great gray eyes that F'lar knew was for him alone.

"And you complain about the timing of other riders," she said, gasping, as she came to an abrupt stop at his side. Before he could protest the insignificance of his injuries, she was smearing numbweed on the burns. "I'll have to wash them once the feeling's gone. Can't you duck ash yet? Virianth will be all right but Sorenth and Relth took awful lacings. I do wish that glass craftsman of Fandarel's—Wansor's his name, isn't it?—would complete those eyeguards he's been blathering about. Manora thinks she can save P'ratan's good looks but we'll have to wait and see about his eye." She paused to take a deep breath. "Which is just as well because if he doesn't stop raiding Holds for new lovers, we won't be able to foster all the babies. Those holdbred girls are convinced it's evil to abort." She stopped short, set her lips in the thin line which F'lar had finally catalogued as Lessa veering away from a painful subject.

"Lessa! No, don't look away." He forced her head up so she had to meet his eyes. She who couldn't conceive must find it hard, too, to help terminate unwanted pregnancies. Would she never stop yearning for another child? How could she forget she had nearly died with Felessan? He'd been relieved that she had never quickened again. The thought of losing Lessa was not even to be thought. "Riding *between* so much makes it impossible for a Weyrwoman to carry to term."

"It doesn't seem to affect Kylara," Lessa said with bitter resentment. She had turned away, watching Mnementh rend a fat buck with such an intense expression in her eyes that F'lar had no difficulty guessing that she'd prefer Kylara thus rendered.

"That one!" F'lar said with a sharp laugh. "Dear heart, if you must model yourself after Kylara to bear children as Weyrwoman, I prefer you barren!"

"We've more important things to discuss than her," Lessa said, turning to him in a complete change of mood. "What did Lord Asgenar say about the Threadfall? I'd have joined you in the meadow, but Ramoth's got the notion she can't leave her clutch without someone spying on them. Oh, I sent messengers out to the other Weyrs to tell them what's happened here. They ought to know and be on their guard."

"It would've been courteous of them to have apprised us first," F'lar said so angrily that Lessa glanced up at him, startled. He told her then what the Lemos Lord Holder had said on the mountain meadow.

"And Asgenar assumed that we all knew? That it was simply a matter of changing the timetables?" Shock faced from her face and her eyes narrowed, flashing with indignation. "I would I had never gone back to get those Oldtimers. You'd have figured out a way for *us* to cope."

"You give me entirely too much credit, love." He hugged her for her loyalty. "However, the Oldtimers are here and we've got to deal with them."

"Indeed we will. We'll bring them up to date if . . ."

"Lessa," and F'lar gave her a little shake, his pessimism dispersed by the vehemence of her response and the transparency of her rapid calculations on how to bring about such changes. "You can't change a watch-wher into a dragon, my love . . ."

Who'd want to? demanded Mnementh from the Feeding Ground, his appetite sated.

The bronze dragon's tart observation elicited a giggle from Lessa. F'lar hugged her gratefully.

"Well, it's nothing we can't cope with," she said firmly, allowing him to tuck her under his shoulder as they walked back to the weyr. "And it's nothing I don't expect from that T'kul of the ever-so-superior High Reaches. But R'mart of Telgar Weyr?"

"How long have the messengers been gone?"

Lessa frowned up at the bright midmorning sky. "Only just. I wanted to get any last details from the sweepriders."

"I'm as hungry as Mnementh. Feed me, woman."

The bronze dragon had glided up to the ledge to settle in his accustomed spot just as a commotion started in the tunnel. He extended his wings to flight position, neck craned toward the one land entrance to the dragonweyr.

"It's the wine train from Benden, silly," Lessa told him, chuckling as Mnementh gave voice to a loud brassy grumble and began to arrange himself again, completely disinterested in wine trains. "Now don't tell Robinton the new wine's in, F'lar. It has to settle first, you know."

"And why would I be telling Robinton anything?" F'lar demanded, wondering how Lessa knew that he had only just started to think of the Masterharper himself.

"There has never been a crisis before us when you haven't sent for the Masterharper and the Mastersmith." She sighed deeply. "If we only had such cooperation from our own kind." Her body went rigid under his arm. "Here comes Fidranth and he says that T'ron's very agitated."

"*T'ron's* agitated?" F'lar's anger welled up instantly.

"That's what I said," Lessa replied, freeing herself and taking the steps two at a time. "I'll order you food." She halted abruptly, turning to say over her shoulder, "Keep your temper. I suspect T'kul never told anyone. He's never forgiven T'ron for talking him into coming forward, you know."

F'lar waited beside Mnementh as Fidranth circled smartly into the weyr. From the Hatching Cavern came Ramoth's crotchety challenge. Mnementh answered her soothingly that the intruder was only Fidranth and no threat. At least not to her clutch. Then the bronze rolled one scintillating eye toward his rider. The exchange, so like one between himself and Lessa, drained anger from F'lar. Which was as well, for T'ron's opening remarks were scarcely diplomatic.

"I found it! I found what you forgot to incorporate in those so-called infallible timetables of yours!"

"You've found what, T'ron?" F'lar asked, tightly controlling his temper. If T'ron had found anything that would be of help, he could not antagonize the man.

Mnementh had courteously stepped aside to permit Fidranth landing room, but with two huge bronze bodies there was so little space that T'ron slid in front of the Benden Weyrleader, waving a portion of a Record hide right under his nose.

"Here's proof your timetables didn't include every scrap of information from *our* Records!"

"You've never questioned them before, T'ron," F'lar reminded the exercised man, speaking evenly.

"Don't hedge with me, F'lar. You just sent a messenger with word that Thread was falling out of pattern."

"And I'd have appreciated knowing that Thread had fallen out of pattern over Tillek and High Crom in the past few days!"

The look of shock and horror on T'ron's face was too genuine to be faked.

"You'd do better to listen to what commoners say, T'ron, instead of immuring yourself in the Weyr," F'lar told him. "Asgenar knew of it yet neither T'kul nor R'mar thought to tell the other Weyrs, so we could prepare and keep watch. Just luck I had F'rad . . ."

"You've not been housing dragonmen in the Holds again?"

"I always send a messenger on ahead the day of a Fall. If I didn't follow the practice, Asgenar's forest lands would be gone by now."

F'lar regretted that heated reference. It would give T'ron the wedge he needed for another of his diatribes about overforestation. To divert him, F'lar reached for the piece of Record, but T'ron twitched it out of his grasp.

"You'll have to take my word for it . . ."

"Have I ever questioned your word, T'ron?" Those words, too, were out before F'lar could censor them. He could and did keep his face expressionless, hoping T'ron would not read in it an additional allusion to that meeting. "I can see that the Record's badly eroded, but if you've deciphered it and it bears on this morning's unpredicted shift, we'll all be in your debt."

"F'lar?" Lessa's voice rang down the corridor. "Where are your manners? The *klah's* cooling and it is predawn T'ron's time."

"I'd appreciate a cup," T'ron admitted, as obviously relieved as F'lar by the interruption.

"I apologize for rousing you . . ."

"I need none, not with this news."

Unaccountably F'lar was relieved to realize that T'ron had obviously not known of Threadfall. He had come charging in here, delighted at an opportunity to put F'lar and Benden in the wrong. He'd not have been so quick—witness his evasiveness and contradictions over the belt-knife fight—if he'd known.

When the two men entered the queen's weyr, Lessa was gowned, her hair loosely held by an intricate net, and seated gracefully at the table. Just as if she hadn't ridden hard all morning and been suited five minutes before.

So Lessa was all set to charm T'ron again, huh? Despite the unsettling events, F'lar was amused. Still, he wasn't certain that this ploy would lessen T'ron's antagonism. He didn't know what truth there was in a rumor that T'ron and Mardra were not on very good terms for a Weyrwoman and Weyrleader.

"Where's Ramoth?" T'ron asked, as he passed the queen's empty weyr.

"On the Hatching Ground, of course, slobbering over her latest clutch." Lessa replied with just the right amount of indifference.

But T'ron frowned, undoubtedly reminded that there was another queen egg on Benden's warm sands and that the Oldtimers' queens laid few gold eggs.

"I do apologize for starting your day so early," she went on, deftly serving him a neatly sectioned fruit and fixing *klah* to his taste. "But we need your advice and help."

T'ron grunted his thanks, carefully placing the Record hide side down on the table.

"Threadfall could come when it would if we didn't have all those blasted forests to care for," T'ron said, glaring at F'lar through the steam of the *klah* as he lifted his mug.

"What? And do without wood?" Lessa complained, rubbing her hands on the carved chair which Bendarek had made with his consummate artistry. "Those stone chairs may fit you and Mardra," she said in a sweet insinuating voice, "but I had a cold rear end all the time."

T'ron snorted with amusement, his eyes wandering over the dainty Weyrwoman in such a way that Lessa leaned forward abruptly and tapped the Record.

"I ought not to take your valuable time with chatter. Have you discovered something here which we missed?"

F'lar ground his teeth. He hadn't overlooked a single legible word in those moldy Records, so how could she imply negligence so casually?

He forgave her when T'ron responded by flipping over the hide. "The skin is badly preserved, of course," and he made it sound as if Benden's wardship were at fault, not the depredations of four hundred Turns of abandonment, "but when you sent that weyrling with this news, I happened to remember seeing a reference to a Pass where all previous Records were no help. One reason *we* never bothered with timetable nonsense."

F'lar was about to demand why none of the Oldtimers had seen fit to mention that minor fact, when he caught Lessa's stern look. He held his peace.

"See, this phrase here is partly missing, but if you put 'unpredictable shifts' here, it makes sense."

Lessa, her gray eyes wide with an expression of unfeigned awe (her dissembling nearly choked F'lar), looked up from the Record at T'ron.

"He's right, F'lar. That would make sense. See—" and she deftly slipped the Record from T'ron's reluctant fingers and passed it to F'lar. He took it from her.

"You're right, T'ron. Very right. This is one of the older skins which I had to abandon, unable to decipher them."

"Of course, it was much more readable when I first studied it four hundred Turns back, before it got so faded." T'ron's smug manner was hard to take, but he could be managed better so than when he was defensive and suspicious.

"But that doesn't tell us how the shift changes, or how long it lasted," F'lar said.

"There must be other clues, T'ron," Lessa suggested, bending seductively toward the Fort Weyrleader when he began to bristle at F'lar's words. "Why would Thread fall out of a pattern they've followed to the second for seven mortal Turns this Pass? You yourself told me that you followed a certain rhythm in your Time. Did it vary much then?"

T'ron frowned down at the blurred lines. "No," he admitted slowly, and then brought his fist down on the offending scrap. "Why have we lost so many techniques? Why have these Records failed us just when we need them most?"

Mnementh began to bugle from the ledge, with Fidranth adding his note.

Lessa "listened," head cocked.

"D'ram and G'narish," she said. "I don't think we need expect T'kul, but R'mart is not an arrogant man."

D'ram of Ista and G'narish of Igen Weyrs entered together. Both men were agitated, sparing no time for amenities.

"What's this about premature Threadfall?" D'ram demanded. "Where are T'kul and R'mart? You did send for them, didn't you? Were your wings badly torn up? How much Thread burrowed?"

"None. We arrived at first Fall. And my wings sustained few casualties, but I appreciate your concern, D'ram. We've sent for the others."

Though Mnementh had given no warning, someone was running down the corridor to the Weyr. Everyone turned, anticipating one of the missing Weyrleaders, but it was a weyrling messenger who came racing in.

"My duty, sirs," the boy gasped out, "but R'mart's badly hurt and there're so many wounded men and dragons at Telgar Weyr, it's an awful sight. And half the Holds of High Crom are said to be charred."

The Weyrleaders were all on their feet.

"I must send some help—" Lessa began, to be halted by the frown on T'ron's face and D'ram's odd expression. She gave a small impatient snort. "You heard the boy, wounded men and dragons, a Weyr demoralized. Help in time of disaster is *not* interference. That ancient law about Weyr autonomy can be carried to ridiculous lengths and this is one of them. Not to help Telgar Weyr, indeed!"

"She's right, you know," G'narish said, and F'lar knew the man was one step closer to gaining a modern perspective.

Lessa left the chamber, muttering something about personally flying to Telgar Weyr. The weyrling followed her, dismissed by F'lar's nod.

"T'ron found a reference to unpredictable shifts in this old Record Skin," F'lar said, seizing control. "D'ram, do you have any recollections from your studies of Istan Records four hundred Turns ago?"

"I wish I did," the Istan leader said slowly, then looked toward G'narish who was shaking his head. "Before I came here, I ordered immediate sweepwatches within my Weyr's bounds and I suggest we all do the same."

"What we need is a Pern-wide guard," F'lar began, carefully choosing his words.

But T'ron wasn't deceived and banged the table so hard that he set the crockery jumping. "Just waiting for the chance to lodge dragons in Holds and Crafthalls again, huh, F'lar? Dragonfolk stick together . . ."

"The way T'kul and R'mart are doing by not warning the rest of us?" asked D'ram in such an acid tone that T'ron subsided.

"Actually, why should dragonfolk weary themselves when there is so much more manpower available in the Holds now?" asked G'narish in a surprised way. He smiled slightly with nervousness when he saw the others staring at him. "I mean, the individual Holds could easily supply the watchers we'll need."

"And they've the means, too," F'lar agreed, ignoring T'ron's surprised exclamation. "It's not so very long ago that there were signal fires on every ridge and hill, across the plains, in case Fax began another of his acquisitive marches. In fact, I shouldn't be surprised if most of those beacon fireguards are still in place."

He was faintly amused by the expressions on the three faces. The Oldtimers never had recovered from the utter sacrilege of a Lord attempting to hold more than one territory. F'lar had no doubt this prompted such conservatives as T'kul and T'ron to impress on the commoners at every opportunity just how dependent they were on dragonfolk; and why they tried to limit and curtail contemporary freedoms and licenses. "Let the Holders light fires when Thread masses on the horizon—a few strategically placed riders could oversee great areas. Use the weyrlings; that'd keep them out of mischief and give 'em good practice. Once we know how the Thread falls now, we'll be able to judge the changes." F'lar forced himself to relax, smiling. "I don't think this is as serious a matter as it first appears. Particularly if shifts have occurred before. Of course, if we could find some reference to how long the shift lasted, if Thread went back to the original pattern, it'd help."

"It would have helped if T'kul had sent word as you did," D'ram muttered.

"Well, we all know how T'kul is," F'lar said tolerantly.

"He'd no right to withhold such vital information from us," T'ron said, again pounding the table. "Weyrs should stick together."

"The Lord Holders aren't going to like this," G'narish remarked, no doubt thinking of Lord Corman of Keroon, the most difficult one of the Holders bound to his Weyr.

"Oh," F'lar replied with more diffidence than he felt, "if we tell them we've expected such a shift at about this time in the Pass . . ."

"But—but the timetables they have? They're not fools," T'ron sputtered.

"*We're* the dragonfolk, T'ron. What they can't understand, they don't need to know—or worry about," F'lar replied firmly. "It's not their business to demand explanations of us, after all. And they'll get none."

"That's a change of tune, isn't it, F'lar?" asked D'ram.

"I never explained myself to them, if you'll think back, D'ram. I told them what had to be done and they did it."

"They were scared stupid seven Turns ago," G'narish remarked. "Scared enough to welcome us with wide-open arms and goods."

"If they want to protect all those forests and croplands, they'll do as we suggest or start charring their profits."

"Let Lord Oterel of Tillek or that idiot Lord Sangel of Boll start disputing my orders and I'll fire their forests myself," said T'ron, rising.

"Then we're agreed," said F'lar quickly, before the hypocrisy he was practicing overcame him with disgust. "We mount watches, aided by the Holders, and we keep track of the new shift. We'll soon know how to judge it."

"What of T'kul?" G'narish asked.

D'ram looked squarely at T'ron. "We'll explain the situation to him."

"He respects you two," F'lar agreed. "It might be wiser, though, not to suggest we knew about . . ."

"We can handle T'kul, without your advice, F'lar," D'ram cut him off abruptly, and F'lar knew that the momentary harmony between them was at an end. The Oldtimers were closing ranks against the crime of their contemporary, just as they had at that abortive meeting a few nights ago. He could console himself with the fact that they hadn't been able to escape all the implications of this incident.

Lessa came back into the weyr just then, her face flushed, her eyes exceedingly bright. Even D'ram bowed low to her in making his farewells.

"Don't leave, D'ram, T'ron. I've good word from Telgar Weyr," she cried, but catching F'lar's glance, did not try to keep them when they demurred.

"R'mart's all right?" G'narish asked, trying to smooth over the awkwardness.

Lessa recovered herself with a smile for the Igen leader.

"Oh that messenger—he's only a boy—he exaggerated. Ramoth bespoke Solth the senior queen at Telgar Weyr. R'mart is badly scored, yes. Bedella evidently overdosed him with numbweed powder. *She* hadn't the wit to send word to anyone. And the Wing-second assumed that we'd all been informed because he'd heard R'mart telling Bedella to send messengers, never dreaming she hadn't. When R'mart passed out, she forgot everything." Lessa's shrug indicated her low opinion of Bedella. "The Wing-second says he'd be grateful for your advice."

"H'ages is Wing-second at Telgar Weyr," G'narish said. "A sound enough rider but he's got no initiative. Say, you're Thread-bared your-self, F'lar."

"It's nothing."

"It's bleeding," Lessa contradicted. "And you haven't eaten a thing."

"I'll stop at Telgar Weyr, F'lar, and talk to H'ages," G'narish said.

"I'd like to come with you, G'narish, if you've no objections . . ."

"I've objections," Lessa put in, "G'narish's capable of ascertain-ing the extent of the Fall there and can relay the information to us. I'll see him to the ledge while *you* start *eating*." Lessa was so didactic that G'narish chuckled. She tucked her arm in his and started toward the corridor. "I've not made my duty to Gyarmath," she said, smiling sweetly up at G'narish, "and he's a favorite of mine, you know."

She was flirting so outrageously that F'lar wondered that Ramoth wasn't roaring protest. As if Gyarmath could ever catch Ramoth in flight! Then he heard Mnementh's rumble of humor and was reassured.

Eat, his bronze advised him. *Let Lessa flatter G'narish. Gyarmath doesn't mind. Nor Ramoth. Nor I.*

"What I do for my Weyr," said Lessa with an exaggerated sigh as she returned a few moments later.

F'lar gave her a cynical look. "G'narish is more of a modern mind than he knows."

"Then we'll have to make him conscious of it," Lessa said firmly.

"Just so long as it is 'we' who make him," F'lar replied with mock severity, catching her hand and pulling her to him.

She made a token resistance, as she always did, scowling feroc-iously at him and then relaxed against his shoulder all at once. "Signal fires and sweepriding are not enough, F'lar," she said thoughtfully. "Although I do believe we've worried too much about the change in Threadfall."

"That nonsense was to fool G'narish and the others, but I thought you'd . . ."

"But don't you see that you were right?"

F'lar gave her a long incredulous look.

"By the Egg, Weyrleader, you astonish me. Why can't there be deviations? Because you, F'lar compiled those Records and to spite the Oldtimers they must remain infallible? Great golden eggs, man, there were such things as Intervals when no Threads fell—as we both know. Why not a change of pace in Threadfall itself during a Pass?"

"But why? Give me one good reason why."

"Give me one good reason why not! The same thing that affects the Red Star so that it doesn't always pass close enough to cast Thread on us can pull it enough off course to change Fall! The Red Star is not the only one to rise and set with the seasons. There could be another heavenly body affecting not only us but the Red Star."

"Where?"

Lessa shrugged impatiently. "How do I know? I'm not long in the eye like F'rad. But we can try to find out. Or have seven full Turns of certainty and schedule dulled your wits?"

"Now, see here, Lessa . . ."

Suddenly she pressed herself close to him, full of contrition for her sharp tongue. He held her close, all too aware that she was right. And yet . . . There had been that long and lonely wait until he and Mnementh could come into their own. The terrible dichotomy of confidence in his own prophecy that Thread would fall and fear that nothing would rescue the Dragonriders from their lethargy. Then the crushing realization that those all too few dragonmen were all that could save an entire world from destruction; the three days of torture between the initial fall over the impending one at Nerat Hold and Telgar Hold with Lessa who-knew-where. Did he not have a right to relax his vigilance? Some freedom from the weight of responsibility?

"I've no right to say such things to you," Lessa was whispering in soft remorse.

"Why not? It's true enough."

"I ought never to diminish you, and all you've done, to placate a trio of narrow-minded, parochial, conservative . . ."

He stopped her words with a kiss, a teasing kiss that abruptly became passionate. Then he winced as her hands, curving sensuously around his neck, rubbed against the Thread-bared skin.

"Oh, I'm so sorry. Here, let me—" and Lessa's apology trailed off as she swiveled her body around to reach for the numbweed jar.

"I forgive you, dear heart, for all your daily machinations," F'lar assured her sententiously. "It's easier to flatter a man than fight him. I wish I had F'nor here right now!"

"I still haven't forgiven that old fool T'ron," Lessa said, her eyes narrowing, her lips pursed. "Oh, why didn't F'nor just let T'reb have the knife?"

"F'nor acted with integrity," F'lar said with stiff disapproval.

"He could've ducked quicker then. And you're no better." Her touch was gentle but the burns stung.

"Hmmm. What I have ducked is my responsibility to our Pern in bringing the Oldtimers forward. We've let ourselves get bogged down on small issues, like whose was the blame in that asinine fight at the Mastersmith's Hall. The real problem is to reconcile the old with the new. And we may just be able to make this new crisis work there to our advantage, Lessa."

She heard the ring in his voice and smiled back at him approvingly.

"When we cut through traditions before the Oldtimers came forward, we also discovered how hollow and restrictive some of them were; such as this business of minimal contact between Hold, Craft and Weyr. Oh, true, if we wish to bespeak another Weyr, we can go there in a few seconds on a dragon, but it takes Holder or Crafter days to get from one place to another. They had a taste of convenience seven Turns ago. I should never have acquiesced and let the Oldtimers talk me out of continuing a dragon in Hold and Craft. Those signal fires won't work, and neither will sweepriders. You're absolutely right about that, Lessa. Now if Fandarel can think up some alternative method of . . . What's the matter? Why are you smiling like that?"

"I knew it. I knew you'd want to see the Smith and the Harper so I sent for them, but they won't be here until you've eaten and rested." She tested the fresh numbweed to see if it had hardened.

"And of course you've eaten and rested, too?"

She got off his lap in one fluid movement, her eyes almost black. "*I'll* have sense enough to go to bed when I'm tired. *You'll* keep on talking with Fandarel and Robinton long after you've chewed your business to death. And you'll drink—as if you haven't learned yet that only a dragon could outdrink that Harper and that Smith—" She broke off again, her scowl turning into a thoughtful frown. "Come to think of it, we'd do well to invite Lytol, if he'd come. I'd like to know exactly what the Lord Holders' reactions are. But first, you eat!"

F'lar laughingly obeyed, wondering how he could suddenly feel so optimistic when it was now obvious that the problems of Pern were coming home to roost on his weyr ledge again.

·· C H A P T E R I V ··

❧

Midday at Southern Weyr

Kylara whirled in front of the mirror, turning her head to watch her slender image, observing the swing and fall of the heavy fabric of the deep red dress.

"I knew it. I told him that hem was uneven" she said, coming to a dead stop, facing her reflection, suddenly aware of her own engaging scowl. She practiced the expression, found one attitude that displeased her and carefully schooled herself against an inadvertent re-use.

"A frown is a mighty weapon, dear," her foster mother had told her again and again, "but do cultivate a pretty one. Think what would happen if your face *froze* that way."

Her posing diverted her until she twisted, trying to assess her profile, and again caught sight of the swirl of the guilty hem.

"Rannelly!" she called, impatient when the old woman did not answer instantly. "Rannelly!"

"Coming, poppet. Old bones don't move as fast. Been setting your gowns to air. There do be such sweetness from that blooming tree. Aye, the wonder of it, a fellis tree grown to such a size." Rannelly carried on a continuous monologue once summoned, as if the sound of her name turned on her mind. Kylara was certain that it did, for her old nurse voiced, like a dull echo, only what she heard and saw.

"Those tailors are no better than they should be, and sloppy about finishing details," Rannelly muttered on, when Kylara sharply interrupted her maundering with the problem. She exhaled on the note of a bass drone as she knelt and flipped up the offending skirt. "Aye and just see these stitches. Taken in haste they were, with too much thread on the needle . . ."

"That man promised me the gown in three days and was seaming it when I arrived. But I need it."

Rannelly's hands stopped; she stared up at her charge. "You weren't ever away from the Weyr without saying a word. . . ."

"I go where I please," Kylara said, staming her foot. "I'm no babe to be checking my movements with you. I'm the Weyrwoman here at Southern. I ride the queen. No one can do anything to me. Don't forget that."

"There's none as forgets my poppet's . . ."

"Not that this is a proper Weyr, at all . . ."

". . . And that's an insult to my nursling, it is, to be in . . ."

"Not that *they* care, but they'll see they can't treat a Telgar of the Blood with such lack of courtesy . . ."

". . . And who's been discourteous to my little . . ."

"Fix that hem, Rannelly, and don't be all week about it. I must look my best when I go home," Kylara said, turning her upper torso this way and that, studying the fall of her thick, wavy blonde hair. "Only good thing about this horrible, horrible place. The sun does keep my hair bright."

"Like a fall of sunbeams, my sweetling, and me brushing it to bring out the shine. Morning and night I brushes it. Never miss. Except when you're away. *He* was looking for you earlier . . ."

"Never mind *him*. Fix that hem."

"Oh, aye, that I can do for you. Slip it off. There now. Ooooh, my precious, my poppet. Whoever treated you so! Did *he* make such marks on . . ."

"Be quiet!" Kylara stepped quickly from the collapsed dress at her feet, all too aware of the livid bruises that stood out on her fair skin. One more reason to wear the new gown. She shrugged into the loose linen robe she had discarded earlier. While sleeveless, its folds almost covered the big bruise on her right arm. She could always blame that on a natural accident. Not that she cared a whistle what T'bor thought but it made for less recrimination. And he never knew what he did when he was well wined-up.

"No good will come of it." Rannelly was moaning as she gathered up the red gown and began to shuffle across to her cubby. "You're weyrfolk now. No good comes of weyrfolk mixing with Holders. Stick to your own. You're somebody here . . ."

"Shut up, you old fool. The whole point of being Weyrwoman is I can do what *I* please. I'm not my mother. I don't need your advice."

"Aye, and I know it," the old nurse said with such sharp bitterness that Kylara stared after her.

There, she'd frowned unattractively. She must remember not to screw her brows that way; it made wrinkles. Kylara ran her hands down her sides, testing the smooth curves sensuously, drawing one hand across her flat belly. Flat even after five brats. Well, there'd be no more. She had the way of it now. Just a few moments longer *between* at the proper time and . . .

She pirouetted, laughing, throwing her arms up to the ceiling in a tendon-snapping stretch and hissing as the bruised deltoid muscle pained her.

Meron need not . . . She smiled languorously. Meron did need to, because *she* needed it.

He is not a dragonrider, said Prideth, rousing from sleep. There was no censure in the golden dragon's tone; it was a statement of fact. Mainly the fact that Prideth was bored with excursions which landed her in Holds rather than Weyrs. When Kylara's fancy took them visiting other dragons, Prideth was more than agreeable. But a Hold, with only the terrified incoherencies of a watch-wher for company was another matter.

"No, he's *not* a dragonrider," Kylara agreed emphatically, a smile of remembered pleasure touching her full red lips. It gave her a soft, mysterious, alluring look, she thought, bending to the mirror. But the surface was mottled and the close inspection made her skin appear diseased.

I itch, Prideth said, and Kylara could hear the dragon moving. The ground under her feet echoed the effect.

Kylara laughed indulgently and, with a final swirl and a grimace at the imperfect mirror, she went out to ease Prideth. If only she could find a real man who could understand and adore her the way the dragon did. If, for instance, F'lar . . .

Mnementh is Ramoth's, Prideth told her rider as she entered the clearing which served as gold queen's Weyr in Southern. The dragon had rubbed the dirt off the bedrock just beneath the surface. The southern sun baked the slab so that it gave off comfortable heat right through the coolest night. All around, the great fellis trees drooped, the pink clustered blossoms scenting the air.

"Mnementh could be yours, silly one," she told her beast, scrubbing the itchy spot with the long-handled brush.

No. I do not contend with Ramoth.

"You would quick enough if you were in mating heat," Kylara replied, wishing she had the nerve to attempt such a coup. "It's not as if there was anything immoral about mating with your father or clutching your mother . . ."

Kylara thought of her own mother, a woman too early used and cast aside by Lord Telgar, for younger, more vital bedmates. Why, if she hadn't been found on Search, she might have had to marry that dolt what-ever-his-name-had-been. She'd never have been a Weyrwoman and had Prideth to love her. She scrubbed fiercely at the spot until Prideth, sighing in an excess of relief, blew three clusters of blooms off their twigs.

You are my mother, Prideth said, turning great opalescent eyes on her rider, her tone suffused with love, admiration, affection, awe and joy.

Despite her annoying reflections, Kylara smiled tenderly at her dragon. She couldn't stay angry with the beast, not when Prideth gazed at her that way. Not when Prideth loved her, Kylara, to the exclusion of all other considerations. Gratefully the Weyrwoman rubbed the sensitive ridge of Prideth's right eye socket until the protecting lids closed one by one in contentment. The girl leaned against the wedgeshaped head, at peace momentarily with herself, with the world, the balm of Prideth's love assuaging her discontent.

Then she heard T'bor's voice in the distance, ordering the weyrlings about, and she pushed away from Prideth. Why did it have to be T'bor? He was so ineffectual. He never came near making her feel the way Meron did, except of course when Orth was flying Prideth and then, then it was bearable. But Meron, without a dragon, was almost enough. Meron was just ruthless and ambitious enough so that together they could probably control all Pern . . .

"Good day, Kylara."

Kylara ignored the greeting. T'bor's forcedly cheerful tone told her that he was determined not to quarrel with her over whatever it was he had on his mind this time. She wondered what attraction he had ever held for her, though he was tall and not ill-favored; few dragonriders were. The thin lines of Thread scars more often gave them a rakish rather than repulsive appearance. T'bor was not scarred but a frown of apprehension and a nervous darting of his eyes marred the effect of his good looks.

"Good day, Prideth," he added.

I like him, Prideth told her rider. *And he is really devoted to you. You are not kind to him.*

"Kindness gets you nowhere," Kylara snapped back at her beast. She turned with indolent reluctance to the Weyrleader. "What's on your mind?"

T'bor flushed as he always did when he heard that note in Kylara's voice. She meant to unsettle him.

"I need to know how many weyrs are free. Telgar Weyr is asking."

"Ask Brekke. How should I know?"

T'bor's flush deepened and he set his jaw. "It is customary for the Weyrwoman to direct her own staff . . ."

"Custom be Thread-bared! She knows. I don't. And I don't see why Southern should be constantly host to every idiot rider who can't dodge Thread."

"You know perfectly well, Kylara, why Southern Weyr . . ."

"We haven't had a single casualty of any kind in seven Turns of Thread."

"We don't get the heavy, constant Threadfall that the northern continent does, and now I understand . . ."

"Well, I don't understand why their wounded must be a constant drain on our resources . . ."

"Kylara. Don't argue with every word I say."

Smiling, Kylara turned from him, pleased that she had pushed him so close to breaking his childish resolve.

"Find out from Brekke. *She* enjoys filling in for me." She glanced over her shoulder to see if he understood exactly what she meant. She was certain that Brekke shared his bed when Kylara was otherwise occupied. The more fool Brekke, who, as Kylara well knew, was pining after F'nor. She and T'bor must have interesting fantasies, each imagining the other the true object of their unrequited loves.

"Brekke is twice the woman and far more fit to be Weyrwoman than you!" T'bor said in a tight, controlled voice.

"You'll pay for that, you scum, you snivelling boy-lover," Kylara screamed at him, enraged by the unexpectedness of his retaliation. Then she burst out laughing at the thought of Brekke as the Weyrwoman, or Brekke as passionate and adept a lover as she knew herself to be. Brekke the Bony, with no more roundness at the breast than a boy. Why, even Lessa looked more feminine.

Thought of Lessa sobered Kylara abruptly. She tried again to convince herself that Lessa would be no threat, no obstacle in her plan. Lessa was too subservient to F'lar now, aching to be pregnant again, playing the dutiful Weyrwoman, too content to see what could happen under her nose. Lessa was a fool. She could have ruled all Pern if she had halftried. She'd had the chance and lost it. The stupidity of going back to bring up the Oldtimers when she could have had absolute dominion over the entire planet as Weyrwoman to Pern's only queen! Well, Kylara had no intention of remaining in the Southern Weyr, meekly tending the world's wounded weyrmen and cultivating acres and acres of food for everyone else but herself. Each egg hatched a different way, but a crack at the right time speeded things up.

And Kylara was all ready to crack a few eggs, *her* way. Noble Larad, Lord of Telgar Hold, might not have remembered to invite her, his only full-blood sister, to the wedding, but surely there was no reason why she should remain distant when her own half sister was marrying the Lord Holder of Lemos.

Brekke was changing the dressing on his arm when F'nor heard

T'bor calling her. She tensed at the sound of his voice, an expression of compassion and worry momentarily clouding her face.

"I'm in F'nor's weyr," she said, turning her head toward the open door and raising her light voice.

"Don't know why we insist on calling a hold made of wood a weyr," said F'nor, wondering at Brekke's reaction. She was such a serious child, too old for her years. Perhaps being junior Weyrwoman to Kylara had aged her prematurely. He had finally got her to accept his teasing. Or was she humoring him, F'nor wondered, during the painful process of having the deep knife wound tended.

She gave him a little smile. "A weyr is where a dragon is, no matter how it's constructed."

T'bor entered at that moment, ducking his head, though the door was plenty high enough to accommodate his inches.

"How's the arm, F'nor?"

"Improving under Brekke's expert care. There's a rumor," F'nor said, grinning slyly up at Brekke, "that men sent to Southern heal quicker."

"If that's why there are always so many coming back, I'll give her other duties." T'bor sounded so bitter that F'nor stared at him. "Brekke, how many more wounded can we accommodate?"

"Only four, but Varena at West can handle at least twenty."

From her expression, F'nor could tell she hoped there weren't that many wounded.

"R'mart asks to send ten, only one badly injured," T'bor said, but he was still resentful.

"He'd best stay here then."

F'nor started to say that he felt Brekke was spreading herself too thin as it was. It was obvious to him that, though she had few of the privileges, she had assumed all the responsibilities that Kylara ought to handle, while that one did much as she pleased. Including complaining that Brekke was shirking or stinting this or that. Brekke's queen, Wirenth, was still young enough to need a lot of care; Brekke fostered young Mirrim though she had had no children herself and none of the Southern riders seemed to share her bed. Yet Brekke also took it upon herself to nurse the most seriously wounded dragonriders. Not that F'nor wasn't grateful to her. She seemed to have an extra sense that told her when numbweed needed renewing, or when fever was high and made you fretful. Her hands were miracles of gentleness, cool, but she could be ruthless, too, in disciplining her patients to health.

"I appreciate your help, Brekke," T'bor said. "I really do."

"I wonder if other arrangements ought to be made," F'nor suggested tentatively.

"What do you mean?"

Oh-ho, thought F'nor, the man's touchy. "For hundreds of Turns, dragonriders managed to get well in their own Weyrs. Why should the Southern ones be burdened with wounded useless men, constantly dumped on them to recuperate?"

"Benden sends very few," Brekke said quietly.

"I don't mean just Benden. Half the men here right now are from Fort Weyr. They could as well bask on the beaches of Southern Boll . . ."

"T'ron's no leader—" T'bor said in a disparaging tone.

"So Mardra would like us to believe," Brekke interrupted with such uncharacteristic asperity that T'bor stared at her in surprise.

"You don't miss much, do you, little lady?" said F'nor with a whoop of laughter. "That's what Lessa said and I agree."

Brekke flushed.

"What do you mean, Brekke?" asked T'bor.

"Just that five of the men most seriously wounded *were flying in Mardra's wing!*"

"Her wing?" F'nor glanced sharply at T'bor, wondering if this was news to him, too.

"Hadn't you heard?" Brekke asked, almost bitterly. "Ever since D'nek was Threaded, she's been flying . . ."

"A queen eating firestone? Is that why Loranth hasn't risen to mate?"

"I didn't say Loranth ate firestone," Brekke contradicted. "Mardra's got some sense left. A sterile queen's no better than a green. And Mardra'd not be senior *or* Weyrwoman. No, she uses a fire thrower."

"On an upper level?" F'nor was stunned. And T'ron had the nerve to prate how Fort Weyr kept tradition?

"That's why so many men are injured in her wing; the dragons fly close to protect their queen. A flame thrower throws 'down' but not out, or wide enough to catch airborne Thread at the speed dragons fly."

"That is without doubt . . . ouch!" F'nor winced at the pain of an injudicious movement of his arm. "That's the most ridiculous thing I've ever heard. Does F'lar know?"

T'bor shrugged. "If he did, what could he do?"

Brekke pushed F'nor back onto the stool to reset the bandage he had disarranged.

"What'll happen next?" he demanded of no one.

"You sound like an Oldtimer," T'bor remarked with a harsh laugh. "Bemoaning the loss of order, the permissiveness of—of times which are so chaotic . . ."

"Change is not chaos."

T'bor laughed sourly. "Depends on your point of view."

"What's your point of view, T'bor?"

The Weyrleader regarded the brown rider so long and hard, his face settling into such bitter lines, that he appeared Turns older than he was.

"I told you what happened at that farce of a Weyrleaders' meeting the other night, with T'ron insisting it was Terry's fault." T'bor jammed one fist into the palm of his other hand, his lips twitching with a bitter distaste at the memory. "The Weyr above all, even common sense. Stick to your own, the hindmost falls *between*. Well, I'll keep my own counsel. And I'll make my weyrfolk behave. All of them. Even Kylara if I have to . . ."

"Shells, what's Kylara up to now?"

T'bor gave F'nor a thoughtful stare. Then, with a shrug he said, "Kylara means to go to Telgar Hold four days hence. Southern Weyr hasn't been invited. I take no offense. Southern Weyr has no obligation to Telgar Hold and the wedding is Holder business. But she means to make trouble there, I'm sure. I know the signs. Also she's been seeing the Lord Holder of Nabol."

"Meron?" F'nor was unimpressed with him as a source of trouble. "Meron, Lord of Nabol, was outmaneuvered and completely discredited at that abortive battle at the Benden Weyr Pass, eight Turns ago. No Lord Holder would ally himself with Nabol again. Not even Lord Nessel of Crom who never was very bright. How he got confirmed as Lord of Crom by the Conclave, I'll never understand."

"It's not Meron we have to guard against. It's Kylara. Anything she touches gets—distorted."

F'nor knew what T'bor meant. "If she were going to, say, Lord Groghe's Fort Hold, I'd not be concerned. He thinks she should be strangled. But don't forget that she's full blood sister to Larad of Telgar Hold. Besides, Larad can manage her. And Lessa and F'lar will be there. She's not likely to tangle with Lessa. So what can she do? Change the pattern of Thread?"

F'nor heard Brekke's sharp intake of breath, saw T'bor's sudden twitch of surprise.

"She didn't change Thread patterns. No one knows why that happened," T'bor said gloomily.

"How *what* happened?" F'nor stood, pushing aside Brekke's hands.

"You heard that Thread is dropping out of pattern?"

"No, I didn't hear," and F'nor looked from T'bor to Brekke who managed to be very busy with her medicaments.

"There wasn't anything you could do about it, F'nor," she said calmly, "and as you were still feverish when the news came . . ."

T'bor snorted, his eyes glittering as if he enjoyed F'nor's discomposure. "Not that F'lar's precious Thread patterns ever included us here in the Southern continent. Who cares what happens in this part of the world?" With that, T'bor strode out of the Weyr. When F'nor would have followed, Brekke grabbed his arm.

"No, F'nor, don't press him. Please?"

He looked down at Brekke's worried face, saw the deep concern in her expressive eyes. Was that the way of it? Brekke fond of T'bor? A shame she had to waste affection on someone so totally committed to a clutching female like Kylara.

"Now, be kind enough to give me the news about that change in Thread pattern. My arm was wounded, not my head."

Without acknowledging his rebuke, she told him what had occurred at Benden Weyr when Thread had fallen hours too soon over Lemos Hold's wide forests. F'nor was disturbed to learn that R'mart of Telgar Weyr had been badly scored. He was not surprised that T'kul of High Reaches Weyr hadn't even bothered to inform his contemporaries of the unexpected falls over his weyrbound territories. But he had to agree that he would have worried had he known. He was worried now but it sounded as if F'lar was coping with his usual ingenuity. At least the Oldtimers had been roused. Took Thread to do it.

"I don't understand T'bor's remark about our not caring what happens in this part of the world . . ."

Brekke put her hand on his arm appealingly. "It's not easy to live with Kylara, particularly when it amounts to exile."

"Don't I just know it!" F'nor had had his run-ins with Kylara when she was still at Benden Weyr and, like many other riders, had been relieved when she'd been made Weyrwoman at Southern. The only problem with convalescing here in Southern, however, was her proximity. For F'nor's peace, her interest in Meron of Nabol couldn't have been more fortunate.

"You can see how much T'bor has made out of Southern Weyr in the Turns he's been Weyrleader here," Brekke went on.

F'nor nodded, honestly impressed. "Did he ever complete the exploration of the southern continent?" He couldn't recall any report on the matter coming in to Benden Weyr.

"I don't think so. The deserts to the west are terrible. One or two riders got curious but the winds turned them back. And eastward, there's just ocean. It probably extends right around to the desert. This is the bottom of the earthy, you know."

F'nor flexed his bandaged arm.

"Now you listen to me, Wing-second F'nor of Benden," Brekke said sharply, interpreting that gesture accurately. "You're in no condition to go charging back to duty or to go exploring. You haven't the stamina of a fledgling and you certainly can't go *between*. Intense cold is the worst thing for a half-healed wound. Why do you think you were flown here straight?"

"Why, Brekke, I didn't know you cared," F'nor said, rather pleased at her vehement reaction.

She gave him such a piercingly candid look that his smile faded. As if she regretted that all too intimate glance, she gave him a half-playful push toward the door.

"Get out. Take your poor lonely dragon and lie on the beach in the sun. Rest. Can't you hear Canth calling you?"

She slipped by him, out the door, and was across the clearing before he realized that *he* hadn't heard Canth.

"Brekke?"

She turned, hesitantly, at the edge of the woods.

"Can you hear other dragons?"

"Yes." She whirled and was gone.

"Of all the—" F'nor was astounded. "Why didn't you tell me?" he demanded of Canth as he strode into the sun-baked wallow behind the weyr and stood glaring at his brown dragon.

You never asked, Canth replied. *I like Brekke.*

"You're impossible," F'nor said, exasperated, and looked back in the direction Brekke had gone. "Brekke?" And he stared hard at Canth, somewhat disgusted by his obtuseness. Dragons as a rule did not name people. They tended to project a vision of the person referred to by pronoun, rarely by name. That Canth, who was of another Weyr, should speak of Brekke so familiarly was a double surprise. He must tell that to F'lar.

I want to get wet. Canth sounded so wistful that F'nor laughed aloud.

"You swim. I'll watch."

Gently Canth nudged F'nor on the good shoulder. *You are nearly well. Good. We'll soon be able to go back to the Weyr we belong to.*

"Don't tell me that you knew about the Thread pattern changing."

Of course, Canth replied.

"Why, you, wher-faced, wherry-necked . . ."

Sometimes a dragon knows what's best for his rider. You have to be well to fight Thread. I want to swim. And there was no arguing with Canth further, F'nor knew. Aware he'd been manipulated. F'nor also had no redress with Canth so he put the matter aside. Once he was well, his arm completely healed, however . . .

Although they had to fly straight toward the beaches, an irritatingly lengthy process for someone used to instantaneous transport from one place to another, F'nor elected to go a good distance west, along the coastline, until he found a secluded cover with a deep bay, suitable to dragon bathing.

A high dune of sand, probably pushed up from winter storms, protected the beach from the south. Far, far away, purple on the horizon, he could just make out the headland that marked Southern Weyr.

Canth landed him somewhat above the high-water mark in the cove, on the clean fine sand, and then, taking a flying leap, dove into the brilliantly blue water. F'nor watched, amused, as Canth cavorted—an unlikely fish—erupting out of the sea, reversing himself just above the surface and then diving deeply. When the dragon considered himself sufficiently watered, he floundered out, flapping his wings mightily until the breeze brought the shower up the beach to F'nor who protested.

Canth then irrigated himself so thoroughly with sand that F'nor was half-minded to send him back to rinse, but Canth protested, the sand felt so good and warm against his hide. F'nor relented and, when the dragon had finally made his wallow, couched himself on a convenient curl of tail. The sun soon lulled them into drowsy inertia.

F'nor, Canth's gentle summons penetrated the brown rider's delicious somnolence, *do not move.*

That was sufficient to dispel drowsy complacence, yet the dragon's tone was amused, not alarmed.

Open one eye carefully, Canth advised.

Resentful but obedient. F'nor opened one eye. It was all he could do to remain limp. Returning his gaze was a golden dragon, small enough to perch on his bare forearm. The tiny eyes, like winking green-fired jewels, regarded him with wary curiosity. Suddenly the miniature wings, no bigger than the span of F'nor's fingers, unfurled into gilt transparencies, aglitter in the sunlight.

"Don't go," F'nor said, instinctively using a mere mental whisper. Was he dreaming? He couldn't believe his eyes.

The wings hesitated a beat. The tiny dragon tilted its head.

Don't go, little one, Canth added with equal delicacy. *We are of the same blood.*

The minute beast registered an incredulity and indecision which were transmitted to man and dragon. The wings remained up but the tautness which preceded flight relaxed. Curiosity replaced indecision. Incredulity grew stronger. The little dragon paced the length of F'nor's arm to gaze steadfastly into his eyes until F'nor felt his eye muscles strain to keep from crossing.

Doubt and wonder reached F'nor, and then he understood the tiny one's problem.

"I'm not of your blood. The monster above us is," F'nor communicated softly. "You are of *his* blood."

Again the tiny head cocked. The eyes glistened actively as they whirled with surprise and increased doubt.

To Canth, F'nor remarked that perspective was impossible for the little dragon, one hundredth his size.

Move back then, Canth suggested. *Little sister, go with the man.*

The little dragon flew up on blurringly active wings, hovering as F'nor slowly rose. He walked several lengths from Canth's recumbent hulk, the little dragon following. When F'nor turned and slowly pointed back to the brown, the little beast circled, took one look and abruptly disappeared.

"Come back," F'nor cried. Maybe he *was* dreaming.

Canth rumbled with amusement. *How would you like to see a man as large to you as I am to her?*

"Canth, do you realize that *that was a fire-lizard?*"

Certainly.

"I actually had a fire-lizard on my arm! Do you realize how many times people have tried to catch one of those creatures?" F'nor stopped, savoring the experience. He was probably the first man to get that close to a fire-lizard. And the dainty little beauty had registered emotion, understood simple directions and then—gone *between.*

Yes, she went between, Canth confirmed, unmoved.

"Why, you big lump of sand, do you realize what that means? Those legends *are* true. You were bred from something as small as her!"

I don't remember, Canth replied, but something in his tone made F'nor realize that the big beast's draconic complacency was a little shaken.

F'nor grinned and stroked Canth's muzzle affectionately. "How could you, big one? When we—men—have lost so much knowledge and we can record what we know."

There are other ways of remembering important matters, Canth replied.

"Just imagine being able to breed tiny fire-lizards into a creature the size of you!" He was awed, knowing how long it had taken to breed faster landbeasts.

Canth rumbled restlessly. *I am useful. She is not.*

"I'd wager she'd improve rapidly with a little help." The prospect fascinated F'nor. "Would you mind?"

Why?

F'nor leaned against the great wedge-shaped head, looping his arm under the jaw, as far as he could reach, feeling extremely fond and proud of his dragon.

"No, that was a stupid question for me to ask you, Canth, wasn't it?"

Yes.

"I wonder how long it would take me to train her."

To do what?

"Nothing you can't do better, of course. No, now wait a minute. If, by chance, I could train her to take messages . . . You said she went *between*? I wonder if she could be taught to go *between*, alone, and come back. Ah, but will she come back here to us now?" At this juncture, F'nor's enthusiasm for the project was deflated by harsh reality.

She comes, Canth said very softly.

"Where?"

Above your head.

Very slowly, F'nor raised one arm, hand outstretched, palm down.

"Little beauty, come where we can admire you. We mean you no harm." F'nor saturated his mental tone with all the reassuring persuasiveness at his command.

A shimmer of gold flickered at the corner of his eye. Then the little lizard hovered at F'nor's eye level, just beyond his reach. He ignored Canth's amusement that the tiny one was susceptible to flattery.

She is hungry, the big dragon said.

Very slowly F'nor reached into his pouch and drew out a meatroll. He broke off a piece, bent slowly to lay it on the rock at his feet, then backed away.

"That is food for you, little one."

The lizard continued to hover, then darted down and, grabbing the meat in her tiny claws, disappeared again.

F'nor squatted down to wait.

In a second, the dragonette returned, ravenous hunger foremost in her delicate thoughts along with a wistful plea. As F'nor broke off another portion, he tried to dampen his elation. If hunger could be the leash . . . Patiently he fed her tiny bits, each time placing the food nearer to him until he got her to take the final morsel from his fingers. As she cocked her head at him, not quite sated, though she had eaten enough to satisfy a grown man, he ventured to stroke an eye ridge with a gentle fingertip.

The inner lids of the tiny opalescent eyes closed one by one as she abandoned herself to the caress.

She is a hatchling. You have Impressed her, Canth told him very softly.

"A hatchling?"

She is the little sister of my blood after all and so must come from an egg, Canth replied reasonably.

"There are others?"

Of course. Down on the beach.

F'nor, careful not to disturb the little lizard, turned his head over his shoulder. He had been so engrossed in the one at hand, he hadn't even heard above the surf sounds the pitiful squawks which were issuing from the litter of shining wings and bodies. There seemed to be hundreds of them on the beach, above the high-tide mark, about twenty dragon lengths from him.

Don't move, Canth cautioned him. *You'll lose her.*

"But if they're hatching . . . they can be Impressed . . . Canth, rouse the Weyr! Speak to Prideth. Speak to Wirenth. Tell them to come. Tell them to bring food. Tell them to hurry. Quickly or it'll be too late."

He stared hard at the purple blotch on the horizon that was the Weyr, as if he himself could somehow bridge the gap with his thoughts. But the frenzy on the beach was attracting attention from another source. Wild wherries, the carrion eaters of Pern, instinctively flocked to the shore, their wings making an ominous line of v's in the southern sky. The vanguard was already beating to a height, preparing to dive at the unprotected weak fledglings. Every nerve in F'nor's body yearned to go to their rescue, but Canth repeated his warning. F'nor would jeopardize his fragile rapport with the little queen if he moved. Or, F'nor realized, if he communicated his agitation to her. He closed his eyes. He couldn't watch.

The first shriek of pain vibrated through his body as well as the little lizard's. She darted into the folds of his arm sling, trembling against his ribs. Despite himself, F'nor opened his eyes. But the wherries had not stooped yet, though they circled lower and lower with rapacious speed. The fledglings were voraciously attacking each other. He shuddered and the little queen rattled her pinions, uttering a delicate fluting sound of distress.

"You're safe with me. Far safer with me. Nothing can harm you with me," F'nor told her repeatedly, and Canth crooned reassurance in harmony with that litany.

The strident shriek of the wherries as they plunged suddenly changed to their piercing wail of terror. F'nor glanced up, away from the carnage on the beach, to see a green dragon in the sky, belching flame, scattering the avian hunters. The green hovered, several lengths above the beach, her head extended downward. She was riderless.

Just then, F'nor saw three figures, charging, sliding, slipping down the high sand dune, heading as straight as possible toward the many-winged mass of cannibals. Although they looked as if they'd carom right into the middle, they somehow managed to stop.

Brekke said she has alerted as many as she could, Canth told him.

"Brekke? Why'd you call her? She's got enough to do."

She is the best one, Canth replied, ignoring F'nor's reprimand.

"Are they too late?" F'nor glanced anxiously at the sky and at the dune, willing more men to arrive.

Brekke was wading toward the struggling hatchlings now, her hands extended. The other two were following her example. Who had she brought? Why hadn't she got more riders? They'd know instantly how to approach the beasts.

Two more dragons appeared in the sky, circled and landed with dizzying speed right on the beach, their riders racing in to help. The skyborne green flamed off the insistent wherries, bugling to her fellows to help her.

Brekke has one. And the girl. So does the boy but the beast is hurt. Brekke says that many are dead.

Why, wondered F'nor suddenly, if he had only just seen the truth of the legend of fire-lizards, did he ache for their deaths? Surely the creatures had been hatching on lonely beaches for centuries, been eaten by wherries and their own peers, unseen and unmourned.

The strong survive, said Canth, undismayed.

They saved seven, two badly hurt. The young girl, Mirrim, Brekke's fosterling, attached three; two greens and a brown, seriously injured by gouges on his soft belly. Brekke had a bronze with no mark on him, the green's rider had a bronze, and the other two riders had blues, one with a wrenched wing which Brekke feared might never heal properly for flight.

"Seven out of over fifty," said Brekke sadly after they had disposed of the broken bodies with agenothree. A precaution which Brekke suggested as a frustration for the carrion eaters and to prevent other fire-lizards from avoiding the beach as dangerous to their kind. "I wonder how many would have survived if you hadn't called us."

"She was already far from the others when she discovered us," F'nor remarked. "Probably the first to hatch, or on top of the others."

Brekke'd had the wit to bring a full haunch of buck, though the Weyr might eat light that evening. So they had gorged the hatchlings into such a somnolent state that they could be carried, unresisting, back to the Weyr, or to Brekke's Infirmary.

"You're to fly home straight," Brekke told F'nor, in much the way a woman spoke to a rebellious weyrling.

"Yes, ma'am," F'nor replied, with mock humility, and then smiled because Brekke took him so seriously.

The little queen nestled in his arm sling as contentedly as if she'd found a weyr of her own. "A weyr is where a dragon is no matter how it's constructed," he murmured to himself as Canth winged steadily eastward.

When F'nor reached Southern, it was obvious the news had raced through the Weyr. There was such an aura of excitement that F'nor began to worry that it might frighten the tiny creatures *between*.

No dragon can fly when he is belly-bloated, Canth said. *Even a fire lizard.* And took himself off to his sun-warmed wallow, no longer interested.

"You don't suppose he's jealous, do you?" F'nor asked Brekke when he found in her Infirmary, splinting the little blue's wrenched wing.

"Wirenth was interested, too, until the lizards fell asleep," Brekke told him, a twinkle in her green eyes as she looked up at him briefly.

"And you know how touchy Wirenth is right now. Mercy, F'nor, what is there for a dragon to be jealous of? These are toys, dolls as far as the big ones are concerned. At best, children to be protected and taught like any fosterling."

F'nor glanced over at Mirrim, Brekke's foster child. The two green lizards perched asleep on her shoulders. The injured brown, swathed from neck to tail in bandage, was cradled in her lap. Mirrim was sitting with the erect stiffness of someone who dares not move a muscle. And she was smiling with an incredulous joy.

"Mirrim is very young for this," he said, shaking his head.

"On the contrary, she's as old as most weyrlings at their first Impression. And she's more mature in some ways than half a dozen grown women I know with several babes of their own."

"Oh-ho. The female of the species in staunch defense . . ."

"It's no teasing matter, F'nor," Brekke replied with a sharpness that put F'nor in mind of Lessa. "Mirrim will do very well. She takes every responsibility to heart." The glance Brekke shot her fosterling was anxious as well as tender.

"I still say she's young . . ."

"Is age a prerequisite for a loving heart? Does maturity always bring compassion? Why are some weyrbred boys left standing on the sand and others, never thought to have a chance, walk off with the bronzes? Mirrim Impressed three, and the rest of us, though we tried, with the creatures dying at our feet, only managed to attach one."

"And why am I never told what occurs in my own Weyr?" Kylara demanded in a loud voice. She stood on the threshold of the Infirmary, her face suffused with an angry flush, her eyes bright and hard.

"As soon as I finished this splinting, I was coming to tell you," Brekke replied calmly, but F'nor saw her shoulders stiffen.

Kylara advanced on the girl, with such overt menace that F'nor stepped around Brekke, wondering to himself as he did so whether Kylara was armed with more than a bad temper.

"Events moved rather fast, Kylara," he said, smiling pleasantly. "We were fortunate to save as many of the lizards as we did. Too bad you didn't hear Canth broadcast the news. You might have Impressed one yourself."

Kylara halted, the full skirts of her robe swirling around her feet. She glared at him, twitching the sleeve of her dress but not before he saw the black bruise on her arm. Unable to attack Brekke, she turned, spotting Mirrim. She swept up to the girl, staring down in such a way that the child looked appealingly toward Brekke. At this point, the tension in the room roused the lizards. The two greens hissed at Kylara but it was the crystal bugle of the bronze on G'sel's shoulder that diverted the Weyrwoman's attention.

"I'll have the bronze! Of course. The bronze'll do fine," she exclaimed. There was something so repellent about the glitter in her eyes and the nasty edge to her laugh that F'nor felt the hair rise on the back of his neck.

"A bronze dragon on my shoulder will be most effective, I think," Kylara went on, reaching for G'sel's bronze lizard.

G'sel put up a warning hand.

"I said they were Impressed, Kylara," F'nor warned her, quickly signaling the rider to refuse. G'sel was only a green rider and new to this Weyr at that; he was no match for Kylara, particularly not in this mood. "Touch him at your own risk."

"Impressed, you say?" Kylara hesitated, turning to sneer at F'nor. "Why, they're nothing but fire-lizards."

"And from what creature on Pern do you think dragons were bred?"

"Not that old nursery nonsense. How could you possibly make a fighting dragon from a fire-lizard?" She reached again for the little bronze. It spread its wings, flapping them agitatedly.

"If it bites you, don't blame G'sel," F'nor told her in a pleasant drawl though it cost him much to keep his temper. It was too bad you couldn't beat a Weyrwoman with impunity. Her dragon wouldn't permit it but a sound thrashing was what Kylara badly needed.

"You can't be certain they're that much like dragons," Kylara protested, glancing suspiciously around at the others. "No one's ever caught one and you just found them."

"We're not certain of anything about them," F'nor replied, beginning to enjoy himself. It was a pleasure to see Kylara frustrated by a lizard. "However, look at the similarities. My little queen . . ."

"You? Impressed a queen?" Kylara's face turned livid as F'nor casually drew aside a fold of his sling to expose the sleeping gold lizard.

"She went *between* when she was frightened. She communicated that fright, plus curiosity, and she evidently received our reassurances. At least she came back. Canth said she'd just hatched. I fed her and she's still with me. We managed to save only these seven because they got Impressed. The others turned cannibal. Now, how long these will be dependent on us for food and companionship is pure conjecture. But the dragons admit a blood relationship and they have ways of knowing beyond ours."

"Just how did you Impress them?" Kylara demanded, her intentions transparent. "No one's ever caught one before."

If it got her out of the Weyr and kept her on sand beaches and off Brekke's back, F'nor was quite agreeable to telling her.

"You Impress them by being there when they hatch, same as with dragons. After that, I assume the ones which survive stay wild. As to why no one ever caught any before, that's simple; the fire-lizards hear them coming and disappear *between*." And, my dear, may it be a warm night *between* before you catch one.

Kylara stared hard at Mirrim and so resentfully at G'sel that the young rider began to fidget and the little bronze rustled his wings nervously.

"Well, I want it clearly understood that this is a working Weyr. We've no time for pets who serve no purpose. I'll deal severely with anyone shirking their duties or—" She broke off.

"No shirking or tramping the beaches until you've had a chance to get one first, huh, Kylara?" asked F'nor, still grinning pleasantly.

"I've better things to do," She spat the words at him and then, skirts kicking out before her, swept out of the room.

"Maybe we ought to warn the lizards," F'nor said in a facetious way, trying to dispel the tension in the Infirmary.

"There's no protection against someone like Kylara," Brekke said, motioning the rider to take his bandaged blue. "One learns to live with her."

G'sel gave an odd gargle and rose, almost unsettling his lizard.

"How can you say that, Brekke, when she's so mean and nasty to you?" Mirrim cried, and subsided at a stern look from her foster mother.

"Make no judgments where you have no compassion," Brekke replied. "And I, too, will not tolerate any shirking of duties to care for these pretties. I don't know why we saved them!"

"Make no judgments where you have no compassion," F'nor retorted.

"*They* needed us," Mirrim said so emphatically that even she was surprised at her temerity, and immediately became absorbed in her brown.

"Yes, they did," F'nor agreed, aware of the little queen's golden body nestled trustingly against his ribs. She had twined her tail as far as it would reach around his waist. "And true weyrmen one and all, we responded to the cry for succor."

"Mirrim Impressed three and she's no weyrman," Brekke said in a dry, didactic correction. "And if they are Impressionable by non-riders, they might well be worth every effort to save."

"How's that?"

Brekke frowned a little at F'nor as if she didn't credit his obtuseness.

"Look at the facts, F'nor. I don't know of a commoner alive who hasn't entertained the notion of catching a fire-lizard, simply because they resemble small dragons—no, don't interrupt me. You know perfectly well that it's just in these last eight Turns that commoners were permitted on the Ground as candidates at Impression. Why, I remember my brothers plotting night after night in the hope of catching a fire-lizard, a personal dragon of their own. I don't think it ever occurred to anyone, really, that there might be some truth in that old myth that dragons—weyrdragons—were bred from lizards. It was just that fire-lizards were not proscribed to commoners, and dragons were. Out of our reach." Her eyes softened with affection as she stroked the tiny sleeping bronze in the crook of her arm. "Odd to realize that generations of commoners were on the right track and never knew it. These creatures have the same talent dragons have for capturing our feelings. I oughtn't to take on another responsibility but nothing would make me relinquish my bronze now he's made himself mine." Her lips curved in a very tender smile. Then, as if aware she was displaying too much of her inner feelings, she said very briskly, "It'd be a very good thing for people—for commoners—to have a small taste of dragon."

"Brekke, you can't mean you think that a fire-lizard's loving company would mellow someone like Vincet of Nerat or Meron of Nabol toward dragonriders?" Out of respect for her, F'nor did not laugh aloud. Brekke was a sackful of unexpected reactions.

She gave him such a stern look that he began to regret his words.

"If you'll pardon me, F'nor," G'sel spoke up, "I think Brekke's got a good thought there. I'm holdbred myself. You're weyrbred. You can't imagine how I used to feel about dragonriders. I honestly didn't know myself—until I Impressed Roth." His face lit with a startling joy at the memory. He paused, unabashed, to savor the moment anew. "It'd be worth a try. Even if the fire-lizards are dumb, it'd make a difference. *They* wouldn't understand how much more it is with a dragon. Look, F'nor, here's this perfectly charming creature, perched on my shoulder, adoring me. He was all ready to bite the Weyrwoman to stay with me. You heard how angry he was. You don't know how—spectacular—it'd make a commoner feel."

F'nor looked around, at Brekke, at Mirrim, who did not evade his eyes this time, at the other riders.

"Are you all holdbred? I hadn't realized. Somehow, once a man becomes a rider, you forget he ever had another affiliation."

"I was craftbred," Brekke said, "but G'sel's remarks are as valid for the Craft as the Hold."

"Perhaps we ought to get T'bor to issue an order that lizard-watching has now become a Weyr duty," F'nor suggested, grinning slyly at Brekke.

"That'll show Kylara," someone murmured very softly from Mirrim's direction.

·· CHAPTER V ··

❧

Midmorning at Ruatha Hold
Early Evening at Benden Weyr

Jaxom's pleasure in riding a dragon, in being summoned to
Benden Weyr, was severely diminished by his guardian's glowering disapproval. Jaxom had yet to learn that most of Lord Warder
Lytol's irritation was for a far larger concern than his ward's mischievous habit of getting lost in the unused and dangerous corridors of
Ruatha Hold. As it was, Jaxom was quite downcast. He didn't *mean*
to irritate Lytol, but he never seemed able to *please* him, no matter how
hard he tried. There was such an unconscionable number of things
that he, Jaxom, Lord of Ruatha Hold, must know, must do, must understand, that his head swam until he had to run away, to be by himself, to think. And the only empty places to think in in Ruatha, where
no one ever went or would bother you, were in the back portions of
the hollowed-out cliff that was Ruatha Hold. And while he could, just
possibly, get lost or trapped behind a rockfall (there hadn't been a
cave-in at Ruatha in the memory of living man or the Hold Records
as far back as they were still legible), Jaxom hadn't got into trouble or
danger. He knew his way around perfectly. Who could tell? His investigations might someday save Ruatha Hold from another invader
like Fax, his father. Here Jaxom's thoughts faltered. A father he had
never seen, a mother who died bearing him, had made him Lord of
Ruatha, though his mother had been of Crom Hold and Fax his father,
of the High Reaches. It was Lessa, who was now Weyrwoman at Benden, who had been the last of Ruathan Blood. These were contradictions he didn't understand and must.

He had changed his clothes now, from the dirty everyday ones
to his finest tunic and trousers, with a wher-hide overtunic and knee

boots. Not that even they could stop the horrible cold of *between*. Jaxom shuddered with delighted terror. It was like being suspended nowhere, until your throat closed and your bowels knotted and you were scared silly that you'd never again see the light of day, or even night's darkness, depending on local time of day where you were supposed to emerge. He was very jealous of Felessan, despite the fact that it was by no means sure his friend would be a dragonrider. But Felessan *lived* at Benden Weyr, and he had a mother and a father, and dragonriders all around him, and . . .

"Lord Jaxom!" Lytol's call from the Great Courtyard broke through the boy's reverie and he ran, suddenly afraid that they'd leave without him.

It was only a green, Jaxom thought with some disappointment. You'd think they'd send a brown at the very least, for Lytol, Warder of Ruatha Hold, one time dragonrider himself. Then Jaxom was overwhelmed by contrition. Lytol's dragon had been a brown and it was well known that half a man's soul left him when his dragon died and he remained among the living.

The green's rider grinned a welcome as Jaxom scrambled up the extended leg.

"Good morning, Jeralte," he said, slightly startled because he'd played in the Lower Caves with the young man only two Turns back. Now he was a full-fledged rider.

"J'ralt, please Lord Jaxom," Lytol corrected his ward.

"That's all right Jaxom," J'ralt said and looped the riding belt deftly around Jaxom's waist.

Jaxom wanted to sink; to be corrected by Lytol in front of Jer— J'ralt, and not to remember to use the honorific contraction! He didn't enjoy the thrill of rising, a-dragonback, over the great towers of Ruatha Hold, of watching the valley, spread out like a wall hanging under the dragon's sinuous green neck. But as they circled, Jaxom had to balance himself against the dragon's unexpectedly soft hide, and the warmth of that contact seemed to ease his inner misery. Then he saw the line of weeders in the fields and knew that they must be looking up at the dragon. Did those bullying Hold boys know that he, Jaxom, Lord of Ruatha, was a-dragonback? Jaxom was himself again.

To be a dragonman was surely the most wonderful thing in the world. Jaxom felt a sudden wave of overwhelming pity for Lytol who had had this joy and—lost it, and now must suffer agonies to ride another's beast. Jaxom looked at the rigid back in front of him, for he was sandwiched between the two men, and wished that he might comfort his Warder. Lytol was always fair, and if he expected Jaxom to be perfect, it was because Jaxom must be perfect to be the Lord of Ruatha Hold. Which was no little honor, even if it wasn't being a dragonrider.

Jaxom's reflections were brought to an abrupt stop as the dragon took them *between*.

You count to three slowly, Jaxom told his frantic mind as he lost all sense of sight and sound, of contact, even of the soft dragon hide beneath his hands. He tried to count and couldn't. His mind seemed to freeze, but just as he was about to shriek, they burst out into the late afternoon, over Benden Weyr. Never had the Bowl seemed so welcome, with its high walls softened and colored by the lambent sun. The black maws of the individual weyrs, set in the face of the inner wall, were voiceless mouths, greeting him all astonished.

As they circled down, Jaxom spotted bronze Mnementh, surely the hugest dragon ever hatched, lounging on the ledge to the queen's weyr. She'd be in the Hatching Ground, Jaxom knew, for the new clutch was still hardening on the warm sands. There'd be another Impression soon. And there was a golden queen egg in the new clutch. Jaxom had heard that another Ruathan girl had been one of those chosen on Search. Another Ruathan Weyrwoman, he was positive. His Hold had bred up more Weyrwomen . . . Mardra, of course, was nowhere near as important as Lessa or Moreta, but she had come from Ruatha. She'd some real funny notions about the Hold. She always annoyed Lytol. Jaxom knew that, because the twitch in his Warder's cheek would start jumping. It didn't when Lessa visited. Except that lately Lessa had stopped coming to Ruatha Hold.

The young Lord of Ruatha spotted Lessa now, as they circled again to bring the queen's weyr in flight line. She and F'lar were on the ledge. The green called, answered by Mnementh's bass roar. A muffled bellow reverberated through the Weyr. Ramoth, the queen, took notice of their arrival.

Jaxom felt much better, particularly when he also caught sight of a small figure, racing across the Bowl floor to the stairs up to the queen's weyr. Felessan. His friend. He hadn't seen him in months. Jaxom didn't want the flight to end but he couldn't wait to see Felessan.

Jaxom was nervously conscious of Lytol's critical eyes as he made his duty to the Weyrwoman and to Weyrleader. He'd rehearsed words and bows often enough. He ought to have it down heart-perfect, yet he heard himself stammering out the traditional words and felt the fool.

"You came, you came. I told Gandidan you'd come," cried Felessan, dashing up the steps, two at a time. He nearly knocked Jaxom down with his antics. Felessan was three Turns his junior but he was of the dragonfolk, and even if Lessa and F'lar had turned their son over to a foster mother, he ought to have more manners. Maybe what Mardra was always carping about was true. The new weyrmen had no manners.

In that instant, as if the younger boy sensed his friend's disapproval, he drew himself up and, still all smiles, bowed with commendable grace to Lytol.

"Good afternoon to you, Lord Warder Lytol. And thank you for bringing Lord Jaxom. May we be excused?"

Before any adult could answer, Felessan had Jaxom by the hand and was leading him down the steps.

"Stay out of trouble, Lord Jaxom," Lytol called after them.

"There's little trouble they can get into here," Lessa laughed.

"I had the entire Hold mustered this morning, only to find him in the bowels of the Hold itself, where a rockfall . . ."

Now why did Lytol have to tell Lessa? Jaxom groaned to himself, with a flash of his previous discontent.

"Did you find anything?" Felessan demanded as soon as they were out of earshot.

"Find anything?"

"Yes, in the bowels of the Hold." Felessan's eyes widened and his voice took on Lytol's inflections.

Jaxom kicked at a rock, pleased by the trajectory and the distance it flew. "Oh, empty rooms, full of dust and rubbish. An old tunnel that led nowhere but an old slide. Nothing great."

"C'mon, Jax."

Felessan's sly tone made Jaxom look at him closely.

"Where?"

"I'll show you."

The weyrboy led Jaxom into the Lower Cavern, the main chamber with a vaulting roof where the Weyr met for sociability and evening meals. There was a smell of warm bread and simmering meats. Dinner preparations were well along, tables set and women and girls bustling about, making pleasant chatter. As Felessan veered past a preparation table, he snatched up a handful of raw roots.

"Don't you dare spoil your dinner, you young wher-whelp," cried one of the women, swinging at the retreating pair with her ladle. "And a good day to you, Lord Jaxom," she added.

The attitude of the weyrfolk toward himself and Felessan never failed to puzzle Jaxom. Why, Felessan was just as important as a Lord Holder, but he wasn't always being watched, as if he might break apart or melt.

"You're so lucky," Jaxom sighed as he accepted his share of Felessan's loot.

"Why?" the younger boy asked, surprised.

"You're—you just are, that's all."

Felessan shrugged, chomping complacently on the sweet root. He led Jaxom out of the Main Cavern and into the inner one, which was actually not much smaller, though the ceiling was lower. A wide, banistered ledge circled the Cavern a half-dragonlength above the floor, giving access to the individual sleeping rooms that ringed the height. The main floor was devoted to other homey tasks. No one was at the looms now, of course, with dinner being prepared, nor was anyone bathing at the large pool to one side of the Cavern, but a group of boys Felessan's age were gathered by the miggsy circle. One boy made a loud, meant-to-be-over-heard remark which was fortunately lost in the obedient loud cackles of laughter from the others.

"C'mon, Jaxom. Before one of those baby boys wants to tag along," Felessan said.

"Where are we going?"

Felessan shushed him peremptorily, looking quickly over his shoulder to see if they were being observed. He walked very fast, making Jaxom lengthen his stride to keep up.

"Hey, I don't want to get in trouble here, too," he said when he realized they were heading still farther into the caves. It was one thing, according to Jaxom's lexicon, to be adventurous in one's own Hold, but quite another to invade the sanctity of another's, much less a Weyr! That was close to blasphemy, or so he'd been taught by his ex-dragonrider guardian. And while he could weather Lytol's wrath, he never, never wanted to anger Lessa . . . or—his mind whispered the name—*F'lar!*

"Trouble? We won't get caught. Everybody's too busy this near dinner. I'd've had to help if you hadn't come," and the boy grinned smugly. "C'mon!"

They had arrived at a fork in the passageway, one leading left, deeper into the Weyr, the other bending right. This one was ill-lit and Jaxom faltered. You didn't waste glows on unused corridors.

"What's the matter?" Felessan asked, frowning back at his reluctant guest. "You're not afraid, are you?"

"Afraid?" Jaxom quickly stepped to Felessan's side. "It's not a question of fear."

"C'mon then. And be quiet."

"Why?" Jaxom had already lowered his voice.

"You'll see. Only be quiet now, huh? And take this."

From a hidey-hole, Felessan handed Jaxom a half-shielded basket with one feebly gleaming glow. He had another for himself. Whatever objections Jaxom might have had were stilled by the challenge in the younger boy's eyes. He turned haughtily and led the way down the shadowy corridor. He was somewhat reassured by the footprints in the dust, all leading the same way. But this hall was not frequented by adults. All the footprints were smallish, not a bootheel among 'em. Where did it lead?

They passed locked, covered doorways, long unused and scary in the flickering light of the dim glows. Why couldn't Felessan have stolen some new ones while he was about it? These wouldn't last too long. Jaxom earnestly wanted to know how far they were going. He had no liking for a trip through back halls and dangerous corridors without full illumination to aid his vision and reduce his imagination. But he couldn't ask. What could there possibly be this far back in the Weyr? A huge rectangle of absolute black rose on his left and he swallowed against terror, as Felessan marched purposefully past it, his weak glow back-lighting the threatening maw into another innocently empty corridor junction.

"Hurry up," Felessan said, sharply.

"Why?" Jaxom was pleased with the steady, casual tone he managed.

"Because *she* always goes to the lake about this time of day and it's the only chance you'll ever get."

"Chance to what? Who's she?"

"Ramoth, thickwit," Felessan stopped so quickly that Jaxom bumped into him and the glow in his basket began to flicker.

"Ramoth?"

"Sure. Or are you afraid to sneak a look at her eggs?"

"At her eggs? Honest?" Breathless terror battled with insatiable curiosity and the knowledge that this would really put him one up on the Hold boys.

"Honest! Now, c'mon!"

The other corridors they passed held no unknown evils for Jaxom now, with such a promised end to this dark trek. And Felessan did seem to know where he was going. Their passage churned up the dust, further dimming the glows, but ahead was a sliver of light.

"There's where we're heading."

"Have you ever seen an Impression, Felessan?"

"Sure. A whole gang of us watched the last one and ooh, that was the most scary-velous time. It was just great. First the eggs wobbled back and forth, see, and then these great cracks appeared. Zig-zaggy ones down the eggs, longwise," Felessan excitedly illustrated the point with his glow basket. "Then, all of a sudden," and his voice dropped to a more dramatic pitch, "one enormous, dragon-sized split and the head—comes through. You know what color the first one was?"

"Don't you know that from the color of the shell?"

"No, except for the queen. They're biggest and they gleam kinda. You'll see."

Jaxom gulped but nothing could have kept him from continuing now. None of the Hold boys or even the other young lordlings had seen eggs, or an Impression. Maybe he could lie a little . . .

"Hey, keep off my heels," Felessan commanded.

The sliver of light ahead widened, touching the smooth wall opposite with a comforting rectangle. As they got closer and their glows augmented the outside light, Jaxom could make out the end of the corridor just beyond the fissure of the slot. The jumble of rock gave evidence of an ancient slide. But sure enough, they could really spy on the mottled eggs as they lay maturing on the mist-heated sands. Occasionally an egg rocked slightly as Jaxom watched, fascinated.

"Where's the queen egg?" he asked in a reverent undertone.

"You don't need to whisper. See? Ground's empty. Ramoth's gone to the lake."

"Where's the queen egg?" Jaxom repeated and was disgusted when his voice broke.

"It's kinda to that side, out of sight."

Jaxom craned his neck up and down, trying to get a glimpse of the golden egg.

"You really want to see it?"

"Sure. Talina's been taken on Search from my Hold and she'll be a Weyrwoman. Ruathan girls always become Weyrwomen."

Felessan gave him a long stare, then shrugged. He twisted sideways and inserted his body into the slit, easing his way past the rocks.

"C'mon," he urged his friend in a hoarse whisper.

Jaxom eyes the slit dubiously. He was heavier as well as taller than Felessan. He presented the side of his body to the slit and took a deep breath. His left leg and arm got through fine but his chest was caught against the rocks. Helpfully, Felessan grabbed his left arm and yanked. Jaxom manfully suppressed a yelp as knee and chest were scraped skin deep by rock.

"Eggshells, I'm sorry, Jaxom."

"I didn't tell you to *pull!*" Then he added as he saw Felessan's contrite expression, "I'm all right, I guess."

Felessan pulled his tunic up to dab at the young Lord's bloody bare chest. The rock had torn through fabric. Jaxom slapped his hand away. It smarted enough as it was. Then he saw the great golden egg, reposing by itself, a little apart from the motley group.

"It's—it's—so glisteny," he murmured, swallowing against awe and reverence, and a growing sense of sacrilege. Only the weyrbred had the right to see the Eggs.

Felessan was casting a judicious eye over the gold egg.

"And big, too. Bigger'n the last queen egg at Fort. Their stock is falling off noticeably," he remarked with critical detachment.

"Not to hear Mardra talk. She says it's obvious Benden stock is in trouble; the dragons are too large to maneuver properly."

"N'ton says Mardra's a pain in the ass, the way she treats T'ron."

Jaxom didn't like the trend of the conversation now. After all, Ruatha Hold was weyrbound to Fort Weyr and while he didn't much like Mardra, he ought not listen to such talk.

"Well, this one's not so big. Looks like a wherry egg. It's half the size of even the smallest one of the others," and he touched the smooth shell of an egg that lay almost against the rock wall, apart from the others.

"Hey, don't touch it!" Felessan protested, visibly started.

"Why not? Can't hurt it, can I? Hard as leather," and Jaxom rapped it gently with his knuckles and then spread his hand flat on the curve. "It's warm."

Felessan pulled him away from the egg.

"You don't touch eggs. Not ever. Not until it's your turn. And you're not weyrbred."

Jaxom looked disdainfully at him. "You're scared to." And he caressed the egg again to prove that he was not.

"I am *not* scared. But you *don't* touch eggs," and Felessan slapped at Jaxom's impious hand. "Not unless you're a candidate. And you're not. And neither am I, yet."

"No, I'm a Lord Holder," and Jaxom drew himself up proudly. He couldn't resist the urge to pat the small egg once more because, while it was all right to be a Lord Holder, he was more than a little jealous of Felessan, and fleetingly wished that he, too, could look forward to being a dragonrider one day. And that egg looked lonely, small and unwanted, so far from the others.

"Your being a Lord Holder wouldn't matter a grain of sand in Igen if Ramoth came back and caught us here," Felessan reminded him and jerked Jaxom firmly toward the slit.

A sudden rumble at the far end of the Hatching Ground startled them. One look at the shadow on the sand by the great entrance was enough. Felessan, being more agile and faster, got to the exit first and squeezed through. This time Jaxom did not object at all as Felessan frantically yanked him past the rock. They didn't even stop to see if it really was Ramoth, returning. They grabbed the glow baskets and ran.

When the light from the slit was lost in the curve of the corridor, Jaxom stopped running. His chest hurt from his exertions as well as from his rough passage through the fissure.

"C'mon," Felessan urged him, halting several paces further.

"I can't. My chest . . ."

"Is it bad?" Felessan held his glow up; blood traced smeared patterns on Jaxom's pale skin. "That looks bad. We'd better get you to Manora quick."

"I . . . got . . . to . . . catch . . . my . . . breath."

In rhythm with his labored exhalations, his glow sputtered and darkened completely.

"We'll have to walk slow then," Felessan said, his voice now shakier with anxiety than from running.

Jaxom got to his feet, determined not to show the panic he was beginning to feel; a cold pressure gripped his belly, his chest was hot and painful, while sweat was starting to creep down his forehead. The salty drops fell on his chest and he swore one of the wardguard's favorites.

"Let's walk fast," he said and, holding onto the now useless glow basket, suited action to words.

By common consent they kept to the outer edge of the corridor, where the now dimly seen footsteps gave them courage.

"It's not much further, is it?" Jaxom asked as the second glow flickered ominously.

"Ah—no. It better not be."

"What's the matter?"

"Ah—we've just run out of footprints."

They hadn't retraced their steps very far before they ran out of glow, too.

"Now what do we do, Jaxom?"

"Well, in Ruatha," Jaxom said, taking a deep breath, a precaution against his voice breaking on him, "when they miss me, they send out search parties."

"In that case, you'll be missed as soon as Lytol wants to go home, won't you? He never stays here long."

"Not if Lytol gets asked to dinner and he will, if dinner is as close as you said it was." Jaxom couldn't suppress his bitterness at this whole ill-advised exploration. "Haven't you any idea where we are?"

"No," Felessan had to admit, sounding suddenly out of his depth. "I always followed the footprints, just like I did now. There were footprints. You saw them."

Jaxom didn't care to agree for that would mean he was in part to blame for their predicament.

"Those other corridors we passed on the way to the hole, where do they go?" he finally asked.

"I don't know. There's an awful lot of the Weyr that's empty. I've—I've never gone any farther than the slit."

"What about the others? How far in have they gone?"

"Gandidan's always talking about how far he's gone but—but—I don't remember what he said."

"For the Egg's sake, don't blubber."

"I'm not blubbering. I'm just hungry!"

"Hungry? That's it. Can you smell dinner? Seemed to me we could smell it an awful long ways down the corridor."

They sniffed at the air in all directions. It was musty but not with stew. Sometimes, Jaxom remembered, you *could* smell fresher air and find your own way back. He put out a hand to touch the wall; the smooth, cold stone was somehow comforting. In *between*, you couldn't feel anything, though this corridor was just as dark. His chest hurt and throbbed, in a steady accompaniment to his blood.

With a sigh, he backed up against the smooth wall and, sliding down it, settled to the ground with a bump.

"Jaxom?"

"I'm all right. I'm just tired."

"Me, too," and with a sigh of relief, Felessan sat down, his shoulder touching Jaxom's. The contact reassured them both.

"I wonder what it was like," Jaxom mused at length.

"Wonder what what was like?" asked Felessan in some surprise.

"When the Weyrs and the Holds were full. When these corridors were lighted and used."

"They've never *been* used."

"Nonsense. No one wastes time carving out corridors that'll lead nowhere. And Lytol said there are over five hundred weyrs in Benden and only half-used . . ."

"We have four hundred and twelve fighting dragons at Benden now."

"Sure, but ten Turns ago there weren't two hundred, so why so many weyrs if they weren't all used once? And why are there miles and miles of halls and unused rooms in Ruatha Hold if they weren't used once . . ."

"So?"

"I mean, where did all the people go? And *how* did they carve out whole mountains in the first place?"

Clearly the matter had never troubled Felessan.

"And did you ever notice? Some of the walls are smooth as . . ."

Jaxom stopped, stunned by a dawning realization. Almost fearfully he turned and ran his hand down the wall behind him. It *was* smooth. He gulped and his chest hurt more than the throb of the scratches. "Felessan . . . ?"

"What—what's the matter?"

"This wall is smooth."

"So what?"

"But it's smooth. It's not rough!"

"Say what you mean." Felessan sounded almost angry.

"It's smooth. It's an old wall."

"So?"

"We're in the old part of Benden." Jaxom got to his feet, running a hand over the wall, walking a few paces.

"Hey!" Jaxom could hear Felessan scrambling to his feet. "Don't leave me, Jaxom! I can't see you."

Jaxom stretched his hand back, touched fabric, and jerked Felessan to his side.

"Now hang on. If this is an old corridor, sooner or later it'll run out. Into a dead end, *or* into the main section. It's got to."

"But how do you know you're going in the right direction?"

"I don't, but it's better than sitting on my rump getting hungrier." With one hand on the wall, the other clinging to Felessan's belt, Jaxom moved on.

They couldn't have walked more than twenty paces before Jaxom's fingers stumbled over the crack. An even crack, running perpendicular to the floor.

"Hey, warn a guy!" cried Felessan, who had bumped into him.

"I found something."

"What?"

"A crack up and down, evenly." Excitedly Jaxom stretched both arms out, trying to find the other side of what might even be a doorway.

At shoulder height, just beyond the second cut, he found a square plate and, in examining it, pressed. With a rumbling groan, the wall under his other hand began to slide back and light came up on the other side.

The boys had only a few seconds to stare at the brightly lit wonders on the other side of the threshold before the inert gas with which the room had been flooded rushed out to overcome them. But the light remained a beacon to guide the searchers.

"I had the entire Hold mustered this morning, only to find him in the bowels of the Hold itself where a rockfall had barred his way," Lytol said to Lessa as he watched the boys running toward the Lower Cavern.

"You've forgotten your own boyhood then," F'lar laughed, gesturing courteously for Lytol to proceed him to the weyr. "Or didn't you explore the back corridors as a weyrling?"

Lytol scowled and then gave a snort, but he didn't smile. "It was one thing for me. I wasn't heir to the Hold."

"But, Lytol, heir to the Hold or not," Lessa said, taking the man's arm, "Jaxom's a boy, like any other. No, now please, I am not criticizing. He's a fine lad, well grown. You may be proud of him."

"Carries himself like a Lord, too," F'lar ventured to say.

"I do my best."

"And your best is very well indeed," Lessa said enthusiastically. "Why, he's grown so since the last time I saw him!"

But the tic started in Lytol's cheek and Lessa fumed, wondering what Mardra had been complaining about in the boy lately. That woman had better stop interfering . . . Lessa caught herself, grimly reminded that she could be accused of interfering right now, having invited Jaxom here on a visit. When Mardra heard that Lytol had been to Benden Weyr . . .

"I'm glad *you* think so," Lytol replied, confirming Lessa's suspicions.

Harper Robinton rose to greet Lytol, and the Mastersmith Fandarel's face broke into the almost feral expression that passed as his smile. While F'lar seated them, Lessa poured wine.

"The new train is in, Robinton, but not settled enough to serve," she said, grinning down at him. It was a private joke that Robinton visited Benden more for the wine than for companionship or business. "You'll have to make do with last year's tithe."

"Benden wine is always acceptable to me," Robinton replied suavely, using the compliment as an excuse to take a sip.

"I appreciate your coming, gentlemen," F'lar began, taking charge of the meeting. "And I apologize for taking you from your business at such short notice, but I . . . ."

"Always glad to come to Benden," Robinton murmured, his eyes twinkling as he tipped his cup again.

"I have news for you so I was glad of this opportunity," Fandarel rumbled.

"And I," Lytol said in a dark voice, the tic moving agitatedly.

"My news is very serious and I need to know your reactions. There has been premature Threadfall . . ." F'lar began.

"Thread*falls*," Robinton corrected him with no vestige of his previous levity. "The drumroll brought me the news from Tillek and Crom Holds."

"I wish I'd as reliable messengers," F'lar said bitterly, gritting his teeth. "Didn't you question the Weyrs' silence, Robinton?" He had counted the Harper his friend.

"My craft is weyrbound to Fort, my dear F'lar," the Craftmaster replied, an odd smile on his lips, "although Weyrleader T'ron does not appear to follow custom in keeping the Master Harper advised of auspicious events. I had no immediate, or privy way to bespeak Benden Weyr."

F'lar took a deep breath; Robinton confirmed the fact that T'ron had not known. "T'kul saw fit not to inform the other Weyrleaders of the unscheduled Fall in Tillek Hold."

"That doesn't surprise me," the Harper murmured cynically.

"We learned only today that R'mar was so badly injured in the Fall at Crom Hold that he couldn't dispatch any messengers."

"You mean, that numbwitted Weyrwoman Bedella forgot to," Lessa interjected.

F'lar nodded and went on. "The first Benden knew of this was when Thread fell in Lemos northeast, midmorning, when the table indicated southwest and evening. Because I always send a rider on ahead to act as messenger for any last moment problems, we were able to reach Lemos before the leading Edge."

Robinton whistled with appreciation.

"You mean, the timetables are wrong?" Lytol exclaimed. All the color had drained from his swarthy face at the news. "I thought that rumor had to be false."

F'lar shook his head grimly; he'd been watching for Lytol's reaction to this news.

"They're not accurate any more; they don't apply to this shift," he said. "Lessa reminded me, as I do you, that there have been deviations in the Red Star's passage that cause long intervals. We must assume that something can cause a change in the rhythm of the Fall as well. As soon as we can gauge a pattern again, we'll correct the tables or make new ones."

Lytol stared at him uncomprehendingly. "But how long will it take you? With three Falls, you ought to have some idea now. I've acres of new plantings, forests. How can I protect them when I can't be sure where Thread will fall?" He controlled himself with an effort. "I apologize but this is—this is terrible news. I don't know how the other Lord Holders will receive it on top of everything else." He took a quick drink of wine.

"What do you mean, on top of everything else?" F'lar asked, startled.

"Why, the way the Weyrs are behaving. That disaster in Esvay valley in Nabol, those plantations of Lord Sangel's."

"Tell me about the Esvay Valley and Lord Sangel."

"You hadn't heard that either?" Robinton asked in real surprise. "Don't the Weyrs talk to one another?" And he glanced from F'lar to Lessa.

"The Weyrs are autonomous," F'lar replied. "We don't interfere . . ."

"You mean, the Oldtimers keep exchanges with us contemporary radicals to a bare minimum," Lessa finished, her eyes flashing indignantly. "Don't scowl at me, F'lar. You know it's true. Though I'm sure D'ram and T'ron were as shocked as we were that T'kul would keep premature Threadfall a secret. Now, what happened at Esvay Vale and in Lord Sangel's Southern Boll?"

It was Robinton who answered her in an expressionless voice. "Several weeks back, T'kul refused to help Meron of Nabol clear some furrows from wooded slopes above the Esvay valley. Said it was the job of the ground crews and Meron's men were lazy and inefficient. The whole valley had to be fired in order to stop the burrows' spreading. Lytol sent help; he knows. I went to see some of the families. They're holdless now and very bitter about dragonmen.

"A few weeks later, Weyrleader T'ron left Southern Boll Hold without clearing with Lord Sangel's groundchief. They had to burn down three adult plantations. When Lord Sangel protested to T'ron, he was told that the wings had reported the Fall under control.

"On another level but disturbing in the over-all picture, I've heard of any number of girls, snatched on the pretext of Search . . ."

"Girls beg to come to the Weyr," Lessa put in tartly.

"To Benden Weyr, probably," Robinton agreed. "But my harpers tell me of unwilling girls, forced from their babes and husbands, ending as drudges to Weyrladies. There is deep hatred building, Lady Lessa. There has always been resentment, envy, because weyrlife is different and the ease with which dragonriders can move across the continent while lesser folk struggle, the special privileges riders enjoy—" The Harper waved his hands. "The Oldtimers really believe in special privilege, and that exacerbates the dangers inherent in such outdated attitudes. As for matters in the Crafthalls, the belt knife incident at Fandarel's is a very minor item in the list of depredations. The crafts generously tithe of their products, but Weaver Zurg and Tanner Belesden are bitterly disillusioned now by the stiff rate of additional levies."

"Is that why they were so cool to me when I asked for gown material?" Lessa asked. "But Zurg himself helped me choose."

"I fancy that no one at Benden Weyr abuses privilege," Robinton replied. "No one at *Benden* Weyr. After all," and he grinned toothily, managing to resemble T'ron as he did so, "Benden is the backsliding Weyr which has forgotten true custom and usage, become lax in their dealings. Why, they permit Holds bound to Benden Weyr to retain dignity, possession and forest. They encourage the Crafts to proliferate, hatching bastard breeds of who-knows-what. But Benden Weyr," and Robinton was himself again, and angry, "is respected throughout Pern."

"As a dragonrider, I ought to take offense," F'lar said, so disturbed by this indictment that he spoke lightly.

"As Benden's Weyrleader, you ought to take charge," Robinton retorted, his voice ringing. "When Benden stood alone, seven Turns ago, you said that the Lord Holders and Craftsmen were too parochial in their views to deal effectively with the real problem. They at least learned something from their mistakes. The Oldtimers are not only incurably parochial, but worse—adamantly inflexible. They will not, they cannot adapt to our turn. Everything we accomplished in the four hundred Turns that separate our thinking is wrong and must be set aside, set back for *their* ways, their standards. Pern has grown—is growing and changing. They have not. And they are alienating the Lord Holders and Craftsmen so completely that I am sincerely concerned—no, I'm scared—about the reaction to this new crisis."

"They'll change their minds when Thread falls unexpectedly," Lessa said.

"Who will change? The Weyrleaders? The Holders? Don't count on it, Lady Lessa."

"I have to agree with Robinton," Lytol said in a tired voice. "There's been precious little cooperation from the Weyrs. They're overbearing, wrongheaded and demanding. I find that I, Lytol, ex-dragonrider, resent any more demands on me as Lytol, Lord Warder. And now it appears they are incapable even of doing their job. What, for instance, can be done right in the present crisis? Are they willing to do *any*thing?"

"There'll be cooperation from the Weyrs, I can guarantee it," F'lar told Lytol. He must rouse the man from his dejection. "The Oldtimers were shaken men this morning. Ruatha Hold's weyrbound to Fort and T'ron's setting up sweepriders. You're to man the watch fires on the heights and light them when Thread mass is sighted. You'll get prompt action the instant a watch fire is seen."

"I'm to rely on shaken men and fires on the heights?" Lytol demanded, eyes wide with disbelief.

"Fire is not efficient," Fandarel intoned. "Rain puts it out. Fog hides it."

"I'll gladly assign my drummers to you if you think they'd be of help," Robinton put in.

"F'lar," Lytol said urgently, "I know Benden Weyr sends messengers ahead to Holds under Threadfall. Won't the other Weyrleaders agree *now* to assign riders to the Holds? Just until we know about the shifts and learn to anticpate them? I don't like most of the Fort Weyr riders, but at least I'd feel secure knowing there was instant communication with the Weyr."

"As I was saying," Fandarel boomed in such a portentous voice that they all turned to him a little startled, "there has been a regrettable lack of efficient communication on this planet which I believe my craft can effectually end. That is the news I brought."

"What?" Lytol was on his feet.

"Why didn't you speak up sooner, you great lout?" demanded the Harper.

"How long would it take to equip all major Holds and Weyrs?" F'lar's question drowned the others.

Fandarel looked squarely at the Weyrleader before he answered what had been almost a plea.

"More time, unfortunately, than we apparently have as margin in this emergency. My halls have been overbusy turning out flame throwers. There's been no time to devote to my little toys."

"How long?"

"The instruments which send and receive distance writing are easy to assemble, but wire must be laid between them. That process is time-consuming."

"Man-consuming, too, I warrant," Lytol added and sat down, deflated.

"No more than watch fires," Fandarel told him placidly. "*If* each Lord and Weyr could be made to cooperate and work together. We did once before," and the Smith paused to look pointedly at F'lar, "when Benden called."

Lytol's face brightened and he grabbed F'lar urgently by the arm.

"The Lord Holders would listen to you, F'lar of Benden, because they trust you!"

"F'lar couldn't approach other Lords, not without antagonizing the Weyrleaders," Lessa objected, but she too was alert with hope.

"What the other Weyrleaders don't know—" Robinton suggested slyly, warming to the strategy. "Come, come, F'lar. This is not the time to stick at principles—at least ones which have proved untenable. Look beyond affiliations, man. You did before and we won. Consider Pern, all Pern, not one Weyr," and he pointed a long callused finger at F'lar; "one Hold," and he swiveled it to Lytol; "or one Craft," and he cocked it at Fandarel. "When we five combined our wits seven Turns ago, we got ourselves out of a very difficult position."

"And I set the stage for this one," Lessa said with a bitter laugh.

Before F'lar could speak, Robinton was waggling his finger at her. "Silly people waste time assigning or assuming guilt, Lessa. You went back and you brought the Oldtimers forward. *To save Pern.* Now we have a different problem. You're not silly. You and F'lar, and all of us, must find other solutions. Now we've that so conveniently scheduled wedding at Telgar Hold. There'll be a bevy of Lords and Craftmasters doing honor to Lemos and Telgar. We are all invited. Let us make very good use of that social occasion, my Lady Lessa, my lord F'lar, and bend them all to Benden's way of thinking. Let Benden Weyr be a model—and all the other Holds and Crafts will follow those weyr-bound to Benden . . ."

He leaned back suddenly, smiling with great anticipation.

F'lar said quietly, "Disaffection is apparently universal. We are going to need more than words and example to change minds."

"The Crafts will back you, Weyrleader, to the last Hall," Fandarel said. "You champion Bendarek. F'nor defended Terry, and against dragonmen because they were in the wrong. F'nor is all right, is he not?" The Smith turned questioningly to Lessa.

"He'll be back in a week or so."

"We need him now," Robinton said. "He'd be useful at Telgar Hold, the commoners account him a hero. What do you say, F'lar? We're yours to command again."

They all turned to him, Lessa slipping a hand to his knee, her eyes eager. This was what she wanted, all right; for him to assume the responsibility. It was what he knew he had to do, finishing the task he had relinquished, hopefully, to those he thought better qualified than he to protect Pern.

"About that distance-writer of yours, Fandarel, could you rig one to Telgar Hold in time for the marriage?" F'lar asked.

Robinton let out a whoop that reverberated through the chamber, causing Ramoth to grumble from the Hatching Ground. The Smith showed all his stained tusks and clenched his huge fists on the table as if choking any opposition a-borning. The tic in Lytol's cheek gave a spasmodic leap and stopped.

"Marvelous idea," Robinton cried. "Hope's a great encourager. Give the Lords a reliable means of keeping in touch and you've undone much of the Weyrs' isolation policies."

"Can you do it, Fandarel?" F'lar asked the Smith.

"To Telgar I could lay wire. Yes. It could be done."

"How is this distance writing done? I don't understand."

Fandarel inclined his head toward the Masterharper. "Thanks to Robinton, we have a code that permits us to send long and complicated messages. One must train a man to understand it, to send and receive it. If you could spare an hour of your time . . ."

"I can spare you as much time as you need, Fandarel," F'lar assured him.

"Let's go tomorrow. There's nothing could fall here tomorrow," Lessa urged, excited.

"Good. I shall arrange a demonstration. I shall put more people to work on the wire."

"I shall speak to Lord Sangel of Southern Boll and Lord Groghe of Fort Hold," Lytol said. "Discreetly, of course, but they know Ruatha is not favored by the Weyr." He got to his feet. "I have been a dragonrider, and a craftsman, and now I am a Holder. But Thread makes no distinction. It sears wherever, whatever it touches."

"Yes, we must remind everyone of that," Robinton said with an ominous grin.

"I shall, of course, agree to whatever T'ron orders me to do, now I have hopes of a surer deliverance." Lytol bowed to Lessa. "My duty to you, my lady. I'll collect Lord Jaxom and beg the favor of a return flight . . ."

"You've missed your lunch, stay for our dinner."

Lytol shook his head regretfully. "There'll be much to set in motion."

"In the interests of conserving dragon strength, I'll ride with Lytol and Jaxom," Robinton said, swallowing the rest of his wine after a rueful toast to such haste. "That will leave you two beasts to share the burden of Fandarel."

Fandarel stood up, a tolerantly smiling giant, his massive bulk dwarfing the Harper, who was by no measure a short man. "I sympathize with dragons, forced to endure the envy of frail, small creatures."

None of them left, however, because neither Jaxom nor Felessan could be located. One of Manora's women remembered seeing them pilfering vegetables and thought they'd gone to join the boys playing miggsy. On questioning, one of the children, Gandidan, admitted seeing them go toward the back corridors.

"Gandidan," Manora said sternly, "have you been teasing Felessan about the peekhole again?" The child hung his head and suddenly the others couldn't look at anyone. "Hmmm," and she turned to the anxious parents. "I've been missing used glows again, F'lar, so I imagine there've been some trips to look at the eggs."

"What?" Lessa exclaimed, as startled as the boys who had turned to guilty statues.

Before she could berate them, F'lar laughed aloud. "That's where they are, then."

"Where?"

The boys huddled together, terrified by the coldness in her voice, even if it was directed toward the Weyrleader.

"In the corridor behind the Hatching Ground. Oh, don't fuss, Lessa. That's all part of growing up in the Weyr, isn't it, Lytol? I did it when I was Felessan's age."

"You've been aware of these excursions, Manora?" Lessa demanded imperiously, ignoring F'lar.

"Certainly, Weyrwoman," Manora replied unintimidated. "And kept track to be sure they all returned. How long ago did they set out, Gandidan? Did they play with you for a time?"

"No wonder Ramoth's been so upset; I kept thinking she was only being broody. How could you allow such activities to continue?"

"Come now, Lessa," F'lar said soothingly. "It's a matter of adolescent pride," and F'lar dropped his voice to a whisper and widened his eyes dramatically, "not to shrink from the challenge of dark, dusty corridors; dim, flickering glows. Will the glows last long enough to get us to the peekhole and back? Or will we be lost forever in the blackness of the Weyr?"

The Harper was grinning, the boys stunned and openmouthed. Lytol was not amused, however.

"How long ago, Gandidan?" Manora repeated, tipping the boy's face up. When he seemed unable to speak, she glanced at the scared expressions of the others. "I think we'd better look. It's easy to take the wrong turning if you have inadequate glows. And they did."

There was no lack of searchers, and F'lar quickly split them up into sections to explore each corridor segment. Sounds echoed through halls undisturbed for hundreds of Turns. But it was not long before

F'lar and Lytol led their group to the guiding light. Once they saw the figures lying in the patch of light, F'lar sent for the others.

"What's the matter with them?" Lytol demanded, supporting his ward against him, and anxiously feeling for his pulse. "Blood?" He held up stained fingers, his face bleak, cheek a-twitch.

So, thought F'lar, Lytol's heart had unfrozen a little. Lessa was wrong to think Lytol too numb to care for the boy. Jaxom was a sensitive boy and children needed affection, but there are many ways of loving.

F'lar gestured for more glows. He turned back the dusty linen of the boy's shirt, baring the horizontal scratches.

"Doesn't look to me like more than scrapes. Probably stumbled against the wall in the dark. Who's got some numbweed on him? Don't look like that, Lytol. The pulse is strong."

"But he's not asleep. He doesn't wake." Lytol shook the limp figure, at first gently, then more insistently.

"There isn't a mark on Felessan," the Weyrleader said, turning his son in his arms.

Manora and Lessa came running then, kicking up dust in spite of F'lar's urgent caution. But Manora reassured them that the boys were all right and briskly delegated two men to carry them back to the Weyr proper. Then she turned to the curious crowd that had assembled in the corridor.

"The emergency is over. Everyone back. Dinner's ready, my lady, my lords. Pick up your feet, Silon. No need to stir up more dust." She glanced at the Weyrleader and the Mastersmith. As one, the two men approached the mysterious doorway, Lessa and Lytol joining them.

Her crisp instructions cleared the corridor quickly until there were only the five remaining.

"The light is *not* made by glows," announced the Mastersmith as he peered cautiously into the bright room. "And from the smoothness of the walls, this is part of the original Weyr." He scowled at F'lar. "Were you aware such rooms existed?" It was almost an accusation.

"There were rumors, of course," F'lar said, stepping inside, "but I don't think I ever got very far down any of the unused corridors when I was a weyrling. Did you, Lytol?"

The Lord Warder snorted irritably but now that he knew Jaxom was all right, he could not resist looking in.

"Perhaps you should give him leave to prowl in Ruatha if he can find treasure rooms like this one," Robinton suggested slyly. "And what under the sun could this represent? Lessa, you're our expert on wall hangings, what do you say?"

He pointed to a drawing, composed of weird interconnecting varicolored rods and balls which spread in several ladderlike columns from floor to ceiling.

"I wouldn't call it artistic, but the colors are pretty," she said, peering closely at the wall. She touched a portion with a finger. "Why, the color is baked on the wall. And look here! Someone didn't like it although I don't think their correction helps. It's more a scribble than a design. And it's not even in the same type of coloring."

Fandarel scrutinized the drawing, his nose an inch from the wall. "Odd. Very odd." Then he moved off to other wonders, his huge hands reverently caressing the metallic counters, the hanging shelves. His expression was so rapt that Less suppressed a giggle. "Simply amazing. I believe that this countertop was extruded in a single sheet." He clucked to himself. "If it has been done, it can be done. I must think about it."

F'lar was more interested in the scribble-design. There was something tantalizingly familiar about it.

"Lessa, I'd swear I've seen just such a nonsense before."

"But we've never been here. No one has."

"I've got it. It's like the pattern on that metal plate F'nor found at Fort Weyr. The one that mentioned fire-lizards. See, this word," his finger traced lines that would read "eureka" to older eyes, "is the same. I'd swear it. And it was obviously added after the rest of this picture."

"If you want to call it a picture," Lessa said dubiously. "But I do think you're right. Only why would they circle this part of the ladder— and that one over there—with a scribble?"

"There are so many, many puzzles in this room," Fandarel intoned. He'd opened a cabinet door, struggling briefly with the magnetic catch, then opened and closed it several times, smiling absently in delight for such efficiency. Only then did he notice the strange object on the deep shelf.

He exhaled in wonder as he took the ungainly affair down.

"Have a care. It may waddle away," Robinton said, grinning at the Smith's performance.

Though the device was as long as a man's arm, the Smith's great hands seemed to envelop it as his fingers explored its exterior. "And they could roll metal without seam. Hmmm. It's coated," and he glanced up at F'lar, "with the same substance used in the big kettles. Coated for protection? With what?" He looked at it, peered at the top. "Ah, glass. Fine glass. Something to look through?" He fiddled with the easily swiveled coated glass that was fitted under a small ledge at the base of the instrument. He placed his eye at the opening on the top of the tube. "Nothing to see but through." He straightened, his brows deeply furrowed. A rumbling sound issued from him as if the gears of his thinking were shifting audibly. "There is a very badly eroded diagram which Wansor showed me not long ago. A device," and his fingers rested lightly on the wheels placed alongside the barrel, "which magnifies objects hundreds of times their proper size. But it takes so long to make lenses, polish mirrors. Hmmm." He bent again and with extremely careful fingers played with the knobs at the side of the tube. He glanced quickly at the mirror, wiped it with one stained finger and looked at it once with his own eye, then again through the tube. "Fascinating. I can see every imperfection in the glass." He was completely unconscious of the fact that everyone else was watching him, fascinated by his behavior. He pulled a coarse short hair from his head and held it under the end of the barrel, above the mirror, right across a small aperture. Another careful adjustment and he gave a bellow of joy. "Look. Look. It is only my hair. But look at the size of it now. See dust like stones, see the scales, see the broken end."

Exuberantly, he pulled Lessa into position, all but holding her head down to the eyepiece. "If you can't see clearly, move this knob until you can."

Lessa complied, but with a startled exclamation, jumped back. Robinton stepped up before F'lar could.

"But that's fantastic," the Harper muttered, playing with the knobs and quickly taking a comparative look at the actual hair.

"May I?" asked F'lar so pointedly that Robinton grinned an apology for his monopoly.

Taking his place, F'lar in turn had to check the specimen to believe in what he saw through the instrument. The strand of hair became a coarse rope, motes of dust sparkling in the light along it, fine lines making visible segmentation points.

When he lifted his head, he turned toward Fandarel, speaking softly because he almost dared not utter this fragile hope aloud.

"If there are ways of making tiny things this large, are there ways of bringing distant objects near enough to observe closely?"

He heard Lessa's breath catch, was aware that Robinton was holding his, but F'lar begged the Smith with his eyes to give him the answer he wanted to hear.

"I believe there ought to be," Fandarel said after what seemed to be hours of reflection.

"F'lar?"

He looked down at Lessa's white face, her startled eyes black with awe and fear, her hands half-raised in frightened protest.

"You can't *go* to the Red Star!" Her voice was barely audible.

He captured her hands, cold and tense, and though he drew her to him reassuringly, he spoke more to the others.

"Our problem, gentlemen, has always been to get rid of Thread. Why not at its source? A dragon can go anywhere if he's got a picture of where he's going!"

When Jaxom woke, he was instantly aware that he was not in the Hold. He opened his eyes bravely, scared though he was, expecting darkness. Instead, above him was a curving roof of stone, its expanse sparkling from the full basket of glows in its center. He gave an inarticulate gasp of relief.

"Are you all right, lad? Does your chest hurt?" Manora was bending over him.

"You found us? Is Felessan all right?"

"Right as rain, and eating his dinner. Now, does your chest hurt?"

"My chest?" His heart seemed to stop when he remembered how he got that injury. But Manora was watching him. He felt cautiously. "No, thank-you-for-inquiring."

His stomach further embarrassed him with its grinding noises.

"I think you need some dinner, too."

"Then Lytol's not angry with me? Or the Weyrleader?" he dared to ask.

Manora gave him a fond smile, smoothing down his tousled hair.

"Not to worry, Lord Jaxom," she said kindly. "A stern word or two perhaps. Lord Lytol was beside himself with worry."

Jaxom had the most incredible vision of two Lytols side by side, cheeks a-twitch in unison.

"However, I wouldn't advise any more unauthorized expeditions anywhere." She gave a little laugh. "That is now the special pastime of the adults."

Jaxom was too busy worrying if she *knew* about the slit, if she knew the weyrboys had been peeking through. If she knew *he* had. He endured a little death, waiting to hear her say Felessan had confessed to their crime, then realized she had said they weren't to be more than scolded. You could always trust Manora. And if she knew and wasn't angry . . . But if she didn't know and he asked, she might be angry . . .

"You found those rooms, Lord Jaxom. I'd rest on my honors, now, were I you."

"Rooms?"

She smiled at him and held out her hand. "I thought you were hungry."

Her hand was cool and soft as she led him onto the balcony which circled the sleeping level. It must be late, Jaxom thought, as they passed the tightly drawn curtains of the sleeping rooms. The central fire was banked. A few women were grouped by one of the worktables, sewing. They glanced up as Manora and Jaxom passed, and smiled.

"You said 'rooms?'" Jaxom asked with polite insistence.

"Beyond the room you opened were two others and the ruins of a stairway leading up."

Jaxom whistled. "What was in the rooms?"

Manora laughed softly. "I never saw the Mastersmith so excited.

They found some odd-shaped instruments and bits and pieces of glass I can't make out at all."

"An Oldtimer room?" Jaxom was awed at the scope of his discovery. And he'd had only the shortest look.

"Oldtimers?" Manora's frown was so slight that Jaxom decided he'd imagined it. Manora never frowned. "Ancient timers, I'd say."

As they entered the Main Cavern, Jaxom realized that their passage interrupted the lively conversations of the dragonmen and women seated around the big dining area. Accustomed as he was to such scrutiny, Jaxom straightened his shoulders and walked with measured stride. He turned his head slowly, giving a grave nod and smile to the riders he knew and those of the women he recognized. He ignored a sprinkle of laughter, being used to that, too, but a Lord of the Hold must act with the dignity appropriate to his rank, even if he were not quite Turned twelve and in the presence of his superiors.

It was full dark, but around the great inner face of the Bowl, he could see the lambent circles of dragon eyes on the weyr ledges. He could hear the muted rush of air as several stirred and stretched their enormous pinions. He looked up toward the Star Rocks, black knobs against the lighter sky, and saw the giant silhouette of the watch dragon. Far down the Bowl, he could even hear the restless tramping of the penned herdbeasts. In the lake in the center, the stars were mirrored.

Quickening his step now, he urged Manora faster. Dignity could be forgotten in the darkness and he was desperately hungry.

Mnementh gave a welcoming rumble on the queen's weyr ledge, and Jaxom, greatly daring, glanced up at the near eye which closed one lid at him slightly in startling imitation of a human wink.

Do dragons have a sense of humor? he wondered. The watch-wher certainly didn't and he was the same breed.

The relationship is very distant.

"I beg your pardon?" Jaxom said, startled, glancing up at Manora.

"For what, young Lord?"

"Didn't you say something?"

"No."

Jaxom glanced back at the bulky shadow of the dragon, but Mnementh's head was turned. Then he could smell roasted meats and walked faster.

As they rounded the bend, Jaxom saw the golden body of the recumbent queen and was suddenly guilt-struck and fearful. But she was fast asleep, smiling with an innocent serenity remarkably like his foster mother's newest babe. He looked away lest his gaze rouse her, and saw the faces of all those adults at the table. It was almost too much for him. F'lar, Lessa, Lytol and Felessan he'd expected, but there was the Mastersmith and the Masterharper, too.

Only drill helped him respond courteously to the greetings of the celebrities. He wasn't aware when Manora and Lessa came to his assistance.

"Not a word until the child has had something to eat, Lytol," the Weyrwoman said firmly, her hands pressing him gently to the empty seat beside Felessan. The boy paused between spoonfuls to look up with a complex series of facial contractions supposed to convey a message that escaped Jaxom. "Jaxom missed lunch at the Hold and is several hours hungrier in consequence. He is well, Manora?"

"He took no more harm than Felessan."

"He looked a little glassy-eyed as you crossed the weyr." Lessa bent to peer at Jaxom who politely looked at her, chewing with sudden self-consciousness. "How do you feel?"

Jaxom emptied his mouth hurriedly, trying to swallow a half-chewed lump of vegetable. Felessan tendered a cup of water and Lessa deftly swatted him between the shoulder blades as he started to choke.

"I feel fine," he managed to say. "I feel fine, thank you." He waited, unable to resist looking at his plate and was relieved when the Weyrleader laughingly reminded Lessa that she was the one who said the boy should eat before anything else.

The Mastersmith tapped his stained, branchlike finger on the faded Record skin which draped the table, except where the boys were sitting. Fandarel had one arm wrapped possessively around something in his lap, but Jaxom couldn't see what it was.

"If I judge this accurately, there should be several levels of rooms in this section, both beyond the one the boys found and above."

Jaxom goggled at the map and caught Felessan's eye. He was excited, too, but he kept on eating. Jaxom spooned up another huge mouthful—it tasted so good—but he did wish that the skin were not upside down to him.

"I'd swear there were no upper weyr entrances on that side of the Bowl," F'lar muttered, shaking his head.

"There was access to the Bowl on the ground level," Fandarel said, his forefinger covering what he ought to be showing. "We found it, sealed up. Possibly because of that rockfall."

Jaxom looked anxiously at Felessan who became engrossed in his plate. When Felessan made those faces, had he meant he hadn't told them? Or he had? Jaxom wished he knew.

"That seam was barely discernible," the Masterharper said. "The sealing substance was more effective than any mortar I've ever seen; transparent, smooth and strong."

"One could not chip it," rumbled Fandarel, shaking his head.

"Why would they seal off an exit to the Bowl?" Lessa asked.

"Because they weren't using that section of the Weyr," F'lar suggested. "Certainly no one has used those corridors for the Egg knows how many Turns. There weren't even footprints in the dust of most of them we searched."

Waiting for the adult wrath that must surely descend on him now, Jaxom kept his eyes on his plate. He couldn't bear Lessa's recriminations. He dreaded the look in Lytol's eyes when he learned of his ward's blasphemous act. How could he have been so deaf to all Lytol's patient teachings?

"We found enough of interest in the dusty, moldy old Records that had been ignored as useless," F'lar's voice went on.

Jaxom hazarded a glance and saw the Weyrleader tousle Felessan's hair; watched as the man actually grinned at him, Jaxom. Jaxom was almost sick with relief. None of the adults knew what he and Felessan had done in the Hatching Grounds.

"These boys have already led us to exquisite treasures, eh, Fandarel?"

"Let us hope that they are not the only legacies left in forgotten rooms," the Mastersmith said in his deep rumble of a voice. Absently he stroked the smooth metal of the magnifying device cradled in the crook of his arm.

·· C H A P T E R   V I ··

🐉

Midmorning at Southern Weyr
Early Morning at Nabol Hold: Next Day

Hot, sandy and sticky with sweat and salt, triumph overrode all minor irritations as Kylara stared down at the clutch she had unearthed.

"They can have their seven," she muttered, staring in the general direction of northeast and the Weyr. "I've got an entire nest. And another gold."

Exultations welled out of her in a raucous laugh. Just wait until Meron of Nabol saw these beauties! There was no doubt in her mind that the Holder hated dragonmen because he envied them their beasts. He'd often carped that Impressions ought not to be monopolized by one inbred sodality. Well, let's see if mighty Meron could Impress a fire lizard. She wasn't sure which would please her more: if he could or if he couldn't. Either way'd work for her. But if he could Impress a fire-lizard, a bronze, say, and she had a queen on her wrist, and the two mated . . . It might not be as spectacular as with the larger beasts, but then, given Meron's natural endowment . . . Kylara smiled in sensuous anticipation.

"You'd better be worth this," she told the eggs.

She put the thirty-four hardened eggs into several thicknesses of the firestone bagging she'd brought along. She wrapped that bundle in wher-hides and then in her thick wool cloak. She'd been Weyrwoman long enough to realize that a suddenly cooled egg would never hatch. And these were mighty close to cracking shell.

So much the better.

Prideth had been tolerant of her rider's preoccupation with fire-lizard eggs. She had obediently landed in a hundred coves along the

302

western coast, waiting, not unhappily in the hot sun, while Kylara
quartered the burning sands, looking for any trace of fire-lizard bur-
yings. But Prideth grumbled anxiously when Kylara gave her the coordinates for Nabol Hold, not Southern Weyr.

It was just first light, Nabol time, when Kylara's arrival sent the
watch-wher screaming into its lair. The watchguard knew the Southern
Weyrwoman too well to protest her entry and some poor wit was dispatched to wake his Lord. Kylara blithely disregarded Meron's angry
frown when he appeared on the stairs of the Inner Hold.

"I've fire-lizard eggs for you, Lord Meron of Nabol," she cried,
gesturing to the lumpy bundle she'd had a man bring in. "I want tubs
of warm sand or we'll lose them."

"Tubs of warm sand?" Meron repeated with overt irritation.

So, he'd someone else in his bed, had he? Kylara thought, of half
a mind to take her treasure and disappear.

"Yes, you fool. I've a clutch of fire-lizard eggs about to hatch.
The chance of your lifetime. You there," and Kylara pointed imperiously at Meron's holdkeeper who'd come shuffling in, half-dressed.
"Pour boiling water over all the cleansing sand you've got and bring
it here instantly."

Kylara, born to a high degree in one Hold, knew exactly the tone
to take with lesser beings, and was, in fact, so much the female counterpart of her own irascible Lord that the woman scurried to her bidding without waiting for Meron's consent.

"Fire-lizard eggs? What on earth are you babbling about,
woman?"

"They're Impressionable. Catch their minds at their hatching,
just like dragons, feed 'em into stupidity and they're yours, for life."
Kylara was carefully laying the eggs down on the warm stones of the
grate fireplace. "And I've got them here just in time," she said in
triumph. "Assemble your men, quickly. We'll want to Impress as many
as possible."

"I'm trying," Meron said through gritted teeth as he watched her
performance with some skepticism and much malice, "to apprehend
exactly how this will benefit anyone."

"Use your wits, man," Kylara replied, oblivious to the Lord Holder's sour reaction to her imperiousness. "Fire-lizards are the ancestors
of dragons and *they have all their abilities.*"

It took only a moment longer for Meron to grasp the significance.
Even as he shouted orders for his men to be roused, he was beside
Kylara, helping her to lay the eggs out before the fire.

"They go *between*? They communicate with their owners?"

"Yes. Yes."

"That's a gold egg," Meron cried, reaching for it, his small eyes
glittering with cupidity.

She slapped his hand away, her eyes flashing. "Gold is for me. Bronze for you. I'm fairly sure that that second one—no, that one—is a bronze."

The hot sands were brought and shoveled onto the hearth stones. Meron's men came clattering down the steps from the Inner Hold, dressed for Threadfall. Peremptorily Kylara ordered them to put aside their paraphernalia and began to lecture them on how to Impress a fire lizard.

"No one can catch a fire-lizard," someone muttered, well back in the ranks.

"I have but I doubt *you* will, whoever you are," Kylara snapped.

There was something, she decided, in what the Oldtimers said: Holders were getting far too arrogant and aggressive. No one would have dared speak up in her father's Hold when he was giving instructions. No one in the Weyrs interrupted a Weyrwoman.

"You'll have to be quick," she said. "They hatch ravenous and eat anything in reach. They turn cannibal if you don't stop them."

"I want to hold mine till it hatches," Meron told Kylara in an undertone. He'd been stroking the three eggs whose mottled shells he fancied contained bronzes.

"Hands aren't warm enough," Kylara replied in a loud, flat voice. "We'll need red meat, plenty of it. Fresh-slaughtered is the best."

The platter which was subsequently brought in was contemptuously dismissed as inadequate. Two additional loads were prepared, still steamy from the body heat of the slaughtered animals. The smell of the bloody raw meat was another odor to mingle with the sweat of men, the overheated, crowded hall and the general tension.

"I'm thirsty, Meron. I require bread and fruit and some chilled wine," Kylara said.

She ate daintily when the food was brought, eyeing Lord Meron's sloppy table habits with veiled amusement. Someone passed bread and sourwine to the men, who had to eat standing about the room. Time passed slowly.

"I thought you said they were about to hatch," Meron said in an aggrieved voice. He was as restless as his men and beginning to have second thoughts about this ridiculous project of Kylara's.

Kylara awarded him a slightly contemptuous smile. "They are, I assure you. You Holders ought to learn patience. It's needed in dealing with dragonkind. You can't beat dragons, you know, or fire-lizards, as you do a landbeast. But it'll be worth it."

"You're sure?" Meron's eyes glittered with unconcealed irritation.

"Think of the effect on dragonmen when you arrive at Telgar Hold in a few days with a fire-lizard clinging to your arm."

The slight smile on Meron's face told Kylara that her suggestion appealed to him. Yes, Meron could be patient if it gave him any advantage over dragonmen.

"It will be at my beck and call?" Meron asked, his gaze avidly caressing his trio.

Kylara didn't hesitate to reassure him, though she wasn't at all sure a fire-lizard would be faithful, or intelligent. Still, Meron didn't require intelligence, just obedience. Or compliance. And if the fire-lizards did not live up to his expectation, she could always say the lack was in him.

"With such messengers, I'd have the advantage," Meron said so softly that she barely caught the words.

"More than mere advantage, Lord Meron," she said, her voice an insinuating purr. "Control."

"Yes, to have solid, dependable communications would mean I'd have control. I could tell that wherry-blooded High Reaches Weyrleader T'kul to . . ."

One of the eggs rocked on its long axis and Meron started from his chair. Hoarsely he ordered his men to come closer, swearing as they halted at the normal distance from him.

"Tell them again, Weyrwoman, tell them exactly how they are to capture these fire-lizards."

It never troubled Kylara that even after nine Turns in a Weyr and seven Turns as a Weyrwoman herself, she could not have given the criteria by which one candidate was accepted by a dragon and another, discernibly as worthy, was rejected by an entire Hatching. Nor why the queens invariably chose women raised outside the Weyr. (For instance, at the time that boy-thing Brekke had Impressed Wirenth, there had been three other girls, any of whom Kylara would have thought considerably more interesting to a dragonette queen. But Wirenth had made a skyline directly to the craftbred girl. The three rejected candidates had remained at Southern Weyr—any girl in her right mind would—and one of them, Varena, had been presented at the next queen Impression and taken. One simply couldn't judge.) Generally speaking, weyrbred lads were always acceptable at one Hatching or another, for a weyrboy could attend Hatchings until he was in his twentieth Turn. No one was ever required to leave his Weyr, but those few who did not become riders usually left, finding places in one of the crafts.

Now, of course, with Benden and Southern Weyrs producing more dragons' eggs than the weyrwomen bore babies, it was necessary to range Pern to find enough candidates to stand on the Hatching Grounds. Evidently a commoner simply couldn't realize that the dragons, usually the browns or bronzes, did the choosing, not their riders.

There seemed to be no accounting for draconic tastes. A well-favored commoner might find himself passed over for the skinny, the unattractive.

Kylara looked around the hall, at the variety of anxious expressions on the rough men assembled. It could be hoped that fire-lizards weren't as discriminating as dragons for there wasn't much to offer them in this motley group. Then Kylara remembered that that brat of Brekke's had Impressed three. In that case, anything on two legs in this room would stand a chance. It had been handed them, their one big opportunity to prove that dragonkind did not need special qualities for Impression, that common Pernese of Holds and Crafts need only be exposed to dragons to have the same chance as the elite of the Weyrs.

"You don't *capture* them," Kylara corrected Meron with a malicious smile. Let these Holders see that there is far more to being chosen by a dragon than physical presence at the moment of Hatching. "You lure them to you with thoughts of affection. A dragon cannot be possessed."

"We have fire-lizards here, not dragons."

"They are the same for our purposes," Kylara said sharply. "Now heed me or you'll lose the lot of them." She wondered why she'd bothered to sweat and toil and bring him a gift, an opportunity which he was obviously unable to accept or appreciate. And yet, if she had a gold and he a bronze, when they mated it *ought* to be worth her troubles. "Shut out any thought of fear or profit," she told the listening circle. "The first puts a dragon off, the second he can't understand. As soon as one will approach you, feed it. Keep feeding it. Get it on your hand, if possible, and move to a quiet corner and keep feeding it. Think how much you love it, want it to stay with you, how happy its presence makes you. Think of nothing else or the fire-lizard will go *between*. There's just the short time between its hatching and its first big meal in which to make Impression. You succeed or you don't. It's up to you."

"You heard what she said. Now do it. Do it right. The man who fails—" Meron's voice trailed off threateningly.

Kylara laughed, breaking the ominous silence that followed. She laughed at the black look on Meron's face, laughed until the Lord Holder, angered beyond caution, shook her arm roughly, pointing to the eggs which were now indulging in wild maneuvers as their occupants tried to break out.

"Stop that cackling, Weyrwoman. It'll prejudice the hatchlings."

"Laughter is better than threats, Lord Meron. Even you can't order the preference of dragonkind. And tell me, good Lord Meron, will you be subject to the same dire unspeakable punishment if *you* fail?"

Meron grabbed her arm in a painful grip, his eyes riveted on the cracks now showing in one of his chosen eggs. He snapped his fingers for meat. Blood oozed from the raw handful as he knelt by the eggs, his body bowed tautly in his effort to effect an Impression.

Trying to show no concern, Kylara rose languidly from her chair. She strolled to the table and picked over the meaty gobbets until she had a satisfactory heap on the trencher. She signaled the tense guardsmen to supply themselves as she moved sedately back to the hearth.

She could not suppress her own excitement and heard Prideth warbling from the heights above the Hold. Ever since Kylara had seen the tiny fledglings F'nor and Brekke had Impressed, she had craved one of these dainty creatures. She would never understand that her imperious nature had subconsciously fought against the emotional symbiosis of her dragon queen. Instinctively Kylara had known that only as a Weyrwoman, a queen's rider, could she achieve the unparalleled power, privilege and unchallenged freedom as a woman on Pern. Skilled at ignoring what she didn't wish to admit, Kylara never realized that Prideth was the only living creature who could dominate her and whose good opinion she had to have. In the fire-lizard, Kylara saw a miniature dragon which she could control—easily control—and physically dominate in a way she could not dominate Prideth.

And in presenting these fire-lizard eggs to a Holder, particularly the most despised Holder of all, Meron of Nabol, Kylara struck back at all the ignominies and imagined slights she had endured at the hands of both dragonmen and Pernese. The most recent insult—that the dish-faced fosterling of Brekke's had Impressed three, rejecting Kylara—would be completely avenged.

Well, Kylara would not be rejected here. She knew the way of it and, whatever else, she would be a winner.

The golden egg rocked violently, and a massive crack split it lengthwise. A tiny golden beak appeared.

"Feed her. Don't waste time," Meron whispered to her hoarsely.

"Don't tell me how to hatch eggs, you fool. Tend to your own."

The head had emerged, the body struggled to right itself, claws scrabbling against the wet shell. Kylara concentrated on thoughts of welcoming affection, of joy and admiration, ignoring the cries and exhortations around her.

The little queen, no bigger than her hand, staggered free of its casing and instantly looked around for something to eat. Kylara laid a glob of meat in its path and the beast swooped on it. Kylara placed a second a few inches from the first, leading the fire-lizard toward her. Squawking ferociously, the fire-lizard pounced, her steps less awkward, the wings spread and drying rapidly. Hunger, hunger, hunger was the pulse of the creature's thoughts and Kylara, reassured by receipt of this broadcast, intensified her thoughts of love and welcome.

She had the fire-lizard queen on her hand by the fifth lure. She rose carefully to her feet, popping food into the wide maw every time it opened, and moved away from the hearth and the chaos there.

For it was chaos, with the overanxious men making every mistake in the Record, despite her advice. Meron's three eggs cracked almost at once. Two hatchlings immediately set upon each other while Meron was awkwardly trying to imitate Kylara's actions. In his greed, he'd probably lose all three, she thought with malicious pleasure. Then she saw that there were other bronzes emerging. Well, all was not lost when her queen needed to mate.

Two men had managed to coax fire-lizards to their hands and had followed Kylara's example by removing themselves from the confused cannibalism on the hearth.

"How much do we feed them, Weyrwoman?" one asked her, his eyes shining with incredulous joy and astonishment.

"Let them eat themselves insensible. They'll sleep and they'll stay by you. As soon as they wake, feed them again. And if they complain about itchy skin, bathe and rub them with oil. A patchy skin breaks *between* and the awful cold can kill even a fire-lizard or dragon." How often she'd told that to weyrlings when she'd had to lecture them as Weyrwoman. Well, Brekke did that now, thank the First Egg.

"But what happens if they go *between*? How do we keep them?"

"You can't *keep* a dragon. He *stays* with you. You don't chain a dragon like a watch-wher, you know."

She became bored with her role as instructor and replenished her supply of meat. Then, disgustedly observing the waste of creatures dying on the hearth, she mounted the steps to the Inner Hold. She'd wait in Meron's chambers—there'd better be no one else there now—to see if he had, after all, managed to Impress a fire-lizard.

Prideth told her that she wasn't happy that she had transported the clutch to death on a cold, alien hearth.

"They lost more than this at Southern, silly one," Kylara told her dragon. "This time we've a pretty darling of our own."

Prideth grumbled on the fire ridge, but not about the lizard so Kylara paid her no heed.

·· CHAPTER VII ··

❧

Midmorning at Benden Weyr
Early Morning at Mastersmithcrafthall, Telgar Hold

F'lar received F'nor's message, five leaves of notes, just as he was about to set out to the Smithcrafthall to see Fandarel's distance-writing mechanism. Lessa was already aloft and waiting.

"F'nor said it was urgent. It's about the—" G'nag said.

"I'll read it as soon as I can," F'lar interrupted him. The man would talk your ear off. "My thanks and my apologies."

"But, F'lar . . ." The rest of the man's sentence was lost as Mnementh's claws rattled against the stone of the ledge and the bronze dragon began to beat his way up.

It didn't help F'lar's temper to realize that Mnementh was making a gentle ascent. Lessa had been so right when she had teased him about staying up drinking and talking with Robinton. The man was a sieve for wine. Around midnight Fandarel had left, taking his treasure of a contraption. Lessa had wagered that he'd never go to bed, and likely no one in his Hall would either. After extracting a promise from F'lar that he'd get some rest soon, too, she'd retired.

He had meant to, but Robinton knew so much about the different Holds, which minor Holders were important in swaying their Lords' mind—essential information if F'lar was going to effect a revolution.

Reverence for the older rider was part of weyrlife, and respect for the able Threadfighter. Seven Turns back, when F'lar had realized humbly how inadequate was Pern's one Weyr, Benden, and how ill-prepared for actual Threadfighting conditions, he had ascribed many virtues to the Oldtimers which were difficult—now—for him arbitrarily to sweep away. He—and all Benden's dragonriders—had learned the root of Threadfighting from the Oldtimers. Had learned the many tricks of dodging Thread, gauging the varieties of Fall, of conserving the strength of beast and rider, of turning the mind from the horrors of a full scoring or a phosphine emission too close. What F'lar didn't realize was how his Weyr and the Southerners had improved on the teaching; improved and surpassed, as they could on the larger, stronger, more intelligent contemporary dragons. F'lar had been able, in the name of gratitude and loyalty to his peers, to ignore, forget, rationalize the Oldtimers' shortcomings. He could do so no longer as the weight of their insecurity and insularity forced him to re-evaluate the results of their actions. In spite of this disillusionment, some part of F'lar, that inner soul of a man which requires a hero, a model against which to measure his own accomplishments, wanted to unite all the dragonmen; to sweep away the Oldtimers' intractable resistance to change, their tenacious hold on the outmoded.

Such a feat rivaled his other goal—and yet, the distance separating Pern and the Red Star was only a different sort of step *between*. And one man had to take if he was ever to free himself of the yoke of Thread.

The cool air—the sun was not full on the Bowl yet—reminded him of his face scores but it felt good against his aching forehead. As he bent forward to brace himself against Mnementh's neck, the leaves of the message pressed into his ribs. Well, he'd find out what Kylara was doing later.

He glanced below, squeezing his lids shut briefly as the dizzying speed affected his unfocusing eyes. Yes, N'ton was already directing a crew of men and dragons in the removal of the sealed entrance. With more light and fresher air flooding the abandoned corridors, exploration could go on effectively. They'd keep Ramoth out of the way so she'd not complain that men were coming too close to her maturing clutch.

She knows, Mnementh informed his rider.

"And?"

She is curious.

They were now poised above the Star Rocks, above and beyond the watchrider, who saluted them. F'lar frowned at the Finger Rock. Now, if a man had a proper lens, fitted into the Eye Rock, would he be able to see the Red Star? No, because at this time of year you did not see the Red Star at that angle. Well . . .

F'lar glanced down at the panorama, the immense cup of rock at the top of the mountain, the tail-like road starting at a mysterious point on the right face, leading down to the lake on the plateau below the Weyr. The water glittered like a gigantic dragon eye. He worried briefly about haring off on this project with Thread falling so erratically. He had set up sweep patrols and sent the diplomatic N'ton (again he regretted F'nor's absence) to explain the necessary new measures to those Holds for which Benden Weyr was responsible. Raid had sent a stiff reply in acknowledgment, Sifer a contentious rebuke, although that old fool would come round after a night's thought on the alternatives.

Ramoth dipped her wings suddenly and disappeared from sight. Mnementh followed. A cold instant later they were wheeling above Telgar's chain of brilliant stair lakes, startlingly blue in the early morning sun. Ramoth was gliding downward, framed briefly against the water, sunlight unnecessarily gilding her bright body.

She's almost twice the size of any other queen, F'lar thought with a surge of admiration for the magnificent dragon.

A good rider makes a good beast, Mnementh remarked voluntarily.

Ramoth coyly swooped into a high banking turn before matching her speed with her Weyrmate's. The two flew, wingtip to wingtip, up the lake valleys to the Smithcraft. Behind them the terrain dropped slowly seaward, the river which was fed by the lakes running through wide farm and pasturelands, converging with the Great Dunto River which finally emptied into the sea.

As they landed before the Crafthall, Terry came running out of one of the smaller buildings set back in a grove of stunted fellis trees. He urgently waved them his way. The Craft was getting an early start today, sounds of industry issued from every building. Their riders aground, the dragons said they were going to swim, and took off again. As F'lar joined Lessa, she was grinning, her gray eyes dancing.

"Swimming, indeed!" was her comment and she caught her arm around his waist.

"So I must suffer uncomforted?" But he put an arm around her shoulders and matched his long stride to hers as they crossed the distance to Terry.

"You are indeed well come," Terry said, bowing continuously and grinning from ear to ear.

"Fandarel's already developed a long-distance glass?" asked F'lar.

"Not quite yet," and the Craft-second's merry eyes danced in his tired face, "but not for want of trying all night."

Lessa laughed sympathetically but Terry quickly demured.

"I don't mind, really. It's fascinating what the fine-viewer can make visible. Wansor is jubilant and depressed by turns. He's been raving all night to the point of tears for his own inadequacy."

They were almost at the door of the small hall when Terry turned, his face solemn.

"I wanted to tell you how terribly I feel about F'nor. If I'd only given them that rackety knife in the first place, but it had been commissioned as a wedding gift for Lord Asgenar from Lord Larad and I simply . . ."

"You had every right to prevent its appropriation," F'lar replied, gripping the Craft-second's shoulder for emphasis.

"Still, if I had relinquished it . . ."

"If the skies fell, we'd not be bothered by Thread," Lessa said so tartly that Terry was obliged to desist from his apologies.

The Hall, though apparently two-storied to judge by the windows, was in fact a vast single room. There was a small forge at one of the two hearths that were centered in each end. The black stone walls, smoothed and apparently seamless, were covered with diagrams and numbers. A long table dominated the center of the room, its wide ends deep sand trays, the rest a conglomerate of Record skins, leaves of paper and a variety of bizarre equipment. The Smith was standing to one side of the door, spread-legged, fists jammed against the wide waist belt, chin jutting out, a deep frown scoring his brow. His bellicose mood was directed toward a sketch on the black stone before him.

"It *must* be a question of the visual angle, Wansor," he muttered in an aggrieved tone, as if the sketch were defying his will. "Wansor?"

"Wansor is as good as *between*, Craftmaster," Terry said gently, gesturing toward the sleeping body all but invisible under skins on the outsized couch in one corner.

F'lar had always wondered where Fandarel slept, since the main Hall had long ago been given over to working space. No ordinary craftcot would be spacious enough to house the Craftmaster. Now he remembered seeing couches like this in most of the major buildings. Undoubtedly Fandarel slept anywhere and anytime he could no longer stay awake. The Smith thrived on what could burn out another man.

The Smith glanced crossly at the sleeper, grunted with resignation and only then noticed Lessa and F'lar. He smiled down at the Weyrwoman with real pleasure.

"You come early, and I'd hoped to have some progress to report on a distance-viewer," he said, gesturing toward the sketch. Lessa and F'lar obediently inspected the series of lines and ovals, innocently white on the black wall. "It is regrettable that the construction of perfect equipment is dependent on the frailty of men's minds and bodies. I apologize . . ."

"Why? It is barely morning," F'lar replied with a droll expression. "I will give you until nightfall before I accuse you of inefficiency."

Terry tried to smother a laugh; what came out was a slightly hysterical giggle.

They were all somewhat startled to hear the booming gargle that was Fandarel's laugh. He nearly knocked F'lar down with a jovial slap on the shoulder blades as he whooped with mirth.

"You give me . . . until nightfall . . . before . . . inefficiency . . ." the Smith gasped between howls.

"The man's gone mad. We've put too much of a strain on him," F'lar told the others.

"Nonsense," Lessa replied, looking at the convulsed Smith with small sympathy. "He hasn't slept and if I know his single-mindedness, he hasn't eaten. Has he, Terry?"

Terry plainly had to search his mind for an answer.

"Rouse your cooks, then. Even *he*," and Lessa jerked her thumb at the exasperating Smith, "ought to stoke that hulk of his with food once a week."

Her insinuation that the Smith was a dragon was not lost on Terry who this time began to laugh uncontrollably.

"I'll rouse them myself. You're all next to useless, you men," she complained and started for the door.

Terry intercepted her, masterfully suppressing his laughter, and reached for a button in the base of a square box on the wall. In a loud voice he bespoke a meal for the Smith and four others.

"What's that?" F'lar asked, fascinated. It didn't look capable of sending a message all the way to Telgar.

"Oh, a loudspeaker. Very efficient," Terry said with a wry grin, "if you can't bellow like the Craftmaster. We have them in every hall. Saves a lot of running around."

"One day I will fix it so that we can channel the message to the one area we want to speak to." The Smith added, wiping his eyes, "Ah, but a man can sleep anytime. A laugh restores the soul."

"Is that the distance-writer you're going to demonstrate for us?" asked the Weyrleader, frankly skeptical.

"No, no, no," Fandarel reassured him, dismissing the accomplishment almost irritably and striding to a complex arrangement of wires and ceramic pots. "This is my distance-writer!"

It was difficult for Lessa and F'lar to see anything to be proud of in that mystifying jumble.

"The wallbox looks more efficient," F'lar said at length, bending to test the mixture in a pot with a finger.

The Smith struck his hand away.

"That would burn your skin as quick as pure agenothree," he exlaimed. "Based on that solution, too. Now, observe. These tubs contain blocks of metal, one each of zinc and copper, in a watered solution of sulfuric acid which makes the metal dissolve in such a way that a chemical reaction occurs. This gives us a form of activity I have called chemical reaction energy. The c.r. produced can be controlled at this point," and he ran a finger down the metal arm which was poised over an expanse of thin grayish material, attached at both ends to rollers. The Smith turned a knob. The pots began to bubble gently. He tapped the arm and a series of red marks of different lengths began to appear on the material which wound slowly forward. "See, this is a message. The Harper adapted and expanded his drum code, a different sequence and length of lines for every sound. A little practice and you can read them as easily as written words."

"I do not see the advantage of writing a message here," and F'lar pointed to the roll, "when you say . . ."

The Smith beamed expansively. "Ah, but as I write with this needle, another needle at the Masterminer's in Crom or at the Crafthall at Igen repeats the line simultaneously."

"That would be faster than dragon flight," Lesser whispered, awed. "What do these lines say? Where did they go?" She inadvertently touched the material with her finger, snatching it back for a quick examination. There was no mark on her finger but a blotch of red appeared on the paper.

The Smith chuckled raspingly.

"No harm in that stuff. It merely reacts to the acidity of your skin."

F'lar laughed. "Proof of your disposition, my dear!"

"Put *your* finger there and see what occurs," Lessa ordered with a flash of her eyes.

"It would be the same," the Smith remarked didactically. "The roll is made of a natural substance, litmus, found in Igen, Keroon and Tillek. We have always used it to check the acidity of the earth or solutions. As the chemical reaction energy is acid, naturally the litmus changes color when the needle touches its surface, thus making the message for us to read."

"Didn't you say something about having to lay wire? Explain."

The Smith lifted a coil of fine wire which was hooked into the contraption. It ran out the window to a stone post. Now F'lar and Lessa noticed that posts were laid in a line marching toward the distant mountains, and, one assumed, the Masterminer in Crom Hold.

"This connects the c.r. distance-writer here with the one at Crom. That other goes to Igen. I can send messages to either Crom or Igen, or both, by adjusting this dial."

"To which did you send that?" Lessa asked, pointing to the lines.

"Neither, my lady, for the c.r. was not being broadcast. I had the dial set to receive messages, not send. It is very efficient, you see."

At this point, two women, dressed in the heavy wher-hide garb of smithcrafters, entered the room, laden with trays of steaming food. One was evidently solely for the Smith's consumption, for the woman jerked her head at him as she placed the heavy platter on a rest evidently designed to receive it and not disturb work in the sand tray beneath. She bobbed to Lessa as she crossed in front of her, gesturing peremptorily to her companion to wait as she cleared space on the table. She did this by sweeping things out of her way with complete disregard for what might be disarranged or broken. She gave the bared surface a cursory swipe with a towel, signaled the other to put the tray down, then the two of them swept out before Lessa, stunned by such perfunctory service, could utter a sound.

"I see you've got your women trained, Fandarel," F'lar said mildly, catching and holding Lessa's indignant eyes. "No talking, no fluttering, no importunate demands for attention."

Terry chuckled as he freed one chair of its pile of abandoned clothing and gestured Lessa to sit. F'lar righted one overturned stool that would serve him while Terry hooked a foot round a second that had got kicked under the long table, seating himself with a fluid movement that proved he had long familiarity with such makeshift repasts.

Now that he had food before him, the Smith was eating with single-minded intensity.

"Then it is the wire-laying process that holds you up," F'lar said, accepting the *klah* Lessa poured for him and Terry. "How long did it take you to extend it from here to Crom Hold, for instance?"

"We did not stick to the work," Terry replied for his Craftmaster whose mouth was too full for speech. "The posts were set up first by apprentices from both halls and those Holders willing to take a few hours from their own tasks. It was difficult to find the proper wire, and it takes time to extrude perfect lengths."

"Did you speak to Lord Larad? Wouldn't he volunteer men?"

Terry made a face. "Lord Holder Larad is more interested in how many flame throwers we can make him, or how many crops he can plant for food."

Lessa had taken a sip of the *klah* and barely managed to swallow the acid stuff. The bread was lumpy and half-baked, the sausage within composed of huge, inedible chunks, yet both Terry and Fandarel ate with great appetite. Indifferent service was one matter; but decent food quite another.

"If this is the food he barters you for flame throwers, I'd refuse," she exclaimed. "Why, even the fruit is rotten."

"Lessa!"

"I wonder you can achieve as much as you do if you have to survive on this," she went on, ignoring F'lar's reprimand. "What's your wife's name?"

"Lessa," F'lar repeated, more urgently.

"No wife," the Smith mumbled, but the rest of his sentence came out more as breadcrumbs than words and he was reduced to shaking his head from side to side.

"Well, even a headwoman ought to be able to manage better than this."

Terry cleared his mouth enough to explain. "Our headwoman is a good enough cook but she's so much better at bringing up faded ink on the skins we've been studying that she's been doing that instead."

"Surely one of the other wives . . ."

Terry made a grimace. "We've been so pressed for help, with all these additional projects," and he waved at the distance-writer, "that anyone who can has turned crafter—" He broke off, seeing the consternation on Lessa's face.

"Well, I've women sitting around the Lower Cavern doing make-work. I'll have Kenalas and those two cronies of hers here to help as soon as a green can bring 'em. And," Lessa added emphatically, pointing a stern finger at the Smith, "they'll have strict orders to do nothing in the *craft*, no matter what!"

Terry looked frankly relieved and pushed aside the meat-roll he had been gobbling down, as if he had only now discovered how it revolted him.

"In the meantime," Lessa went on with an indignation that was ludicrous to F'lar. He knew who managed Benden Weyr's domestic affairs. "*I'm* making a decent brew of *klah*. How you could have choked down such bitter dregs as this is beyond my comprehension!" She swept out the door, pot in hand, her angry monologue drifting back to amused listeners.

"Well, she's right," F'lar said, laughing. "This is worse than the worst the Weyr ever got."

"To tell the truth, I never really noticed before," Terry replied, staring at his plate quizzically.

"That's obvious."

"It keeps me going," the Smith said placidly, swallowing a half-cup of *klah* to clear his mouth.

"Seriously, are you that short of men that you have to draft your women, too?"

"Not short of men, exactly, but of people who have the dexterity, the interest some of our projects require," Terry spoke up, in quick defense of his Craftmaster.

"I mean no criticism, Master Terry," F'lar said, hastily.

"We've done a good deal of reviewing of the old Records, too," Terry went on, a little defensively still. He flipped the pile of skins that had been spilled down the center of the table. "We've got answers to problems we didn't know existed and haven't encountered yet."

"And no answers to the troubles which beset us," Fandarel added, gesturing skyward with his thumb.

"We've had to take time to copy these Records," Terry continued solemnly, "because they are all but illegible now . . ."

"I contend that we lost more than was saved and useful. Some skins were worn out with handling and their message obliterated."

The two smiths seemed to be exchanging portions of a well-rehearsed complaint.

"Did it never occur to you to ask the Masterharper for help in transcribing your Records?" asked F'lar.

Fandarel and Terry exchanged startled glances.

"I can see it didn't. It's not the Weyrs alone who are autonomous. Don't you Craftmasters speak to each other?" F'lar's grin was echoed by the big Smith, recalling Robinton's words of the previous evening. "However, the Harperhall is usually overflowing with apprentices, set to copying whatever Robinton can find for them. They could as well take that burden from you."

"Aye, that would be a great help," Terry agreed, seeing that the Smith did not object.

"You sound doubtful—or hesitant? Are any Crafts secret?"

"Oh, no. Neither the Craftmaster nor I hold with cabalistic, inviolable sanctities, passed at deathbed from father to son . . ."

The Smith snorted with such powerful scorn that a skin on the top of the pile slithered to the floor. "No sons!"

"That's all very well when one can count on dying in bed and at a given time, but I—and the Craftmaster—would like to see all knowledge available to all who need it," Terry said.

F'lar gazed with increased respect at the stoop-shouldered Craftsecond. He'd known that Fandarel relied heavily on Terry's executive ability and tactfulness. The man could always be counted on to fill in the gaps in Fandarel's terse explanations or instructions, but it was obvious now that Terry had a mind of his own, whether it concurred with his Craftmaster's or not.

"Knowledge has less danger of being lost, then," Terry went on less passionately but just as fervently. "We knew so much more once. And all we have are tantalizing bits and fragments that do almost more harm than good because they only get in the way of independent development."

"We will contrive," Fandarel said, his ineffable optimism complementing Terry's volatility.

"Do you have men enough, and wire enough, to install one of those things at Telgar Hold in two days?" asked F'lar, feeling a change of subject might help.

"We could take men off flame throwers and hardware. And I can call in the apprentices from the Smithhalls at Igen, Telgar and Lemos," the Smith said and then glanced slyly at F'lar. "They'd come faster dragonback!"

"You'll have them," F'lar promised.

Terry's face lit up with relief. "You don't know what a difference it is to work with Benden Weyr. You *see* so clearly what needs to be done, without any hedging and hemming."

"You've had problems with R'mart?" asked F'lar with quick concern.

"It's not that, Weyrleader," Terry said, leaning forward earnestly. "You still care what happens, what's happening."

"I'm not sure I understand."

The Smith rumbled something but there seemed to be no interrupting Terry.

"I see it this way, and I've seen riders from every Weyr by now. The Oldtimers have been fighting Thread since their birth. That's all they've known. They're tired and not just from skipping forward in time four hundred Turns. They're heart-tired, bone-tired. They've had too much rising to alarms, seen too many friends and dragons die, Thread-scored. They rest on custom, because that's safest and takes the least energy. And they feel entitled to anything they want. Their minds may be numb with too much time *between*, though they think fast enough to talk you out of anything. As far as they're concerned, there's always been Thread. There's nothing else to look forward to. They don't remember, they can't really conceive of a time, *of four hundred* Turns without *Thread*. We can. Our fathers could and their fathers. We live at a different rhythm because Hold and Craft alike threw off that ancient fear and grew in other ways, in other paths, which we can't give up now. We exist only because the Oldtimers lived in their Time *and* in ours. And fought in both Times. We can see a way out, a life without Thread. They knew only one thing and they've taught us that. How to fight Thread. They simply can see that *we*, that anyone, could take it just one step further and destroy Thread forever."

F'lar returned Terry's earnest stare.

"I hadn't seen the Oldtimers in just that light," he said slowly.

"Terry's absolutely right, F'lar," said Lessa. She'd evidently paused on the threshold, but moved now briskly into the room, filling the Smith's empty mug from the pitcher of *klah* she'd brewed. "And it's a judgment we ought to consider in our dealings with them." She smiled warmly at Terry as she filled his cup. "You're as eloquent as the Harper. Are you sure you're a smith?"

"That is *klah*!" announced Fandarel, having drunk it all.

"Are you sure you're a Weyrwoman?" retorted F'lar, extending his cup with a sly smile. To Terry he said, "I wonder none of us realized it before, particularly in view of recent events. A man can't fight day after day, Turn after Turn—though the Weyrs were eager to come forward—" He looked questioningly at Lessa.

"Ah, but that was something new, exciting," she replied. "And it was new here, too, for the Oldtimers. What isn't new is that they have another forty-some Turns to fight Thread in our time. Some of them have had fifteen and twenty Turns of fighting Thread. We have barely seven."

The Smith put both hands on the table and pushed himself to his feet.

"Talk makes no miracles. To effect an end to Thread we must get the dragons to the source. Terry, pour a cup of that excellent *klah* for Wansor and let us attack the problem with good heart."

As F'lar rose with Lessa, F'nor's message rustled at his belt.

"Let me take a look at F'nor's message, Lessa, before we go."

He opened the closely written pages, his eye catching the repetition of "fire-lizard" before his mind grasped the sense of what he was reading.

"Impressing? A fire-lizard?" he exclaimed, holding the letter so that Lessa could verify it.

"No one's ever managed to catch a fire-lizard," Fandarel said.

"F'nor has," F'lar told him, "and Brekke, and Mirrim. Who's Mirrim?"

"Brekke's fosterling," the Weyrwoman replied absently, her eyes scanning the message as rapidly as possible. "One of L'trel's by some woman or other of his. No, Kylara wouldn't have liked that!"

F'lar shushed her, passing the sheets over to Fandarel who was curious now.

"Are fire-lizards related to dragons?" asked the Craft-second.

"Judging by what F'nor says, more than we realized." F'lar handed Terry the last page, looking up at Fandarel. "What do you think?"

The Smith began to realign his features into a frown but stopped, grinning broadly instead.

"Ask the Masterherder. *He* breeds animals. I breed machines."

He saluted Lessa with his mug and strode to the wall he had been comtemplating when they entered, immediately lost in thought.

"A good point," F'lar said with a laugh to his remaining audience.

"F'lar? Remember that flawed piece of metal, with that garble of words? The one with the scribble like last night's. It mentioned fire-lizards, too. That was one of the few words that made sense."

"So?"

"I wish we hadn't given that plate back to Fort Weyr. It was more important than we realized."

"There may be more at Fort Weyr that's important," F'lar said, gloomily. "It was the first Weyr. Who knows what we might find if we could search there!"

Lessa made a face, thinking of Mardra and T'ron.

"T'ron's not hard to manage," she mused.

"Lessa, no nonsense now."

"If fire-lizards are so much like dragons, could they be trained to go *between*, as dragons can, and be messengers?" asked Terry.

"How long would that take?" asked the Smith, less unaware of his surroundings than he looked. "How much time *have* we got this Turn?"

·· CHAPTER VIII ··

Midmorning at Southern Weyr

"No, Rannelly, I've not seen Kylara all morning," Brekke told the old woman patiently, for the fourth time that morning.

"And you've not taken a good look at your own poor queen, either, I'll warrant, fooling around with these—these nuisancy flitter-bys," Rannelly retorted, grumbling as she limped out of the Weyrhall.

Brekke had finally found time to see to Mirrim's wounded brown. He was so stuffed with juicy tidbits from the hand of his overzealous nurse that he barely opened one lid when Brekke inspected him. Numbweed worked as well on lizard as on dragon and human.

"He's doing just fine, dear," Brekke told the anxious girl, the greens fluttering on the child's shoulders in response to her exaggerated sigh of relief. "Now, don't overfeed them. They'll split their hides."

"Do you think they'll stay?"

"With such care as you lavish on them, sweeting, they're not likely to leave. But you have chores which I cannot in conscience permit you to shirk . . ."

"All because of Kylara . . ."

"Mirrim!"

Ashamed, the girl hung her head, but she deeply resented the fact that Kylara gave all the orders and did no work, leaving her tasks to fall to Brekke. It wasn't fair. Mirrim was very very glad that the little lizards had preferred her to that woman.

"What did old Rannelly mean about your queen? You take good care of Wirenth. She lacks for nothing," said Mirrim.

"Ssssh. I'll go see. I left her sleeping."

"Rannelly's as bad as Kylara. She thinks she's so wise and knows everything . . ."

Brekke was about to scold her fosterling when she heard F'nor calling her.

"The green riders are bringing back some of the meat hung in the salt caves," she said, issuing quick instructions instead. "None of that is to go to the lizards, Mirrim. Now, mind. The boys can trap wild wherries. Their meat is as good, if not better. We've no idea what effect too much redblood meat will have on lizards." With that caution to inhibit Mirrim's impulsive generosity, Brekke went out to meet F'nor.

"There's been no rider in from Benden?" he asked her, easing the arm sling across his shoulder.

"You'd've heard instantly," she assured him, deftly adjusting the cloth at his neck. "In fact," she added in mild rebuke, "there are no riders in the Weyr at all today."

F'nor chuckled. "And not much to show for their absence, either. There isn't a beach along the coastline that doesn't have a dragon couchant, with rider a-coil, feigning sleep."

Brekke put her hand to her mouth. It wouldn't do for Mirrim to hear her giggling like a weyrling.

"Oh, you laugh?"

"Aye, and they've made a note of both occasions that I did," she said with due solemnity, but her eyes danced. Then she noticed that the sling was missing its usual occupant. "Where's . . ."

"Grall is curled between Canth's eyes, so stuffed she'd likely not move if we went *between*. Which I've half a mind to do. If you hadn't told me I could trust G'nag, I'd swear he'd not delivered my letter to F'lar, or else he's lost it."

"You are not going *between* with that wound, F'nor. And if G'nag said he delivered the letter, he did. Perhaps something has come up."

"More important than Impressing fire-lizards?"

"There could be something. Threads are falling out of phase—" Brekke broke off, she oughtn't to have reminded F'nor of that, judging by the bleak expression on his face. "Maybe not, but they've got to get the Lord Holders to supply watchers and fires and it may be F'lar is occupied with that. It certainly isn't *your* fault you're not there to help. Those odious Fort riders have no self-control. Imagine taking a green out of her Weyr close to mating—" Brekke stopped again, snapping her mouth closed. "But Rannelly said 'my queen,' not 'her' queen."

The girl turned so white that F'nor thrust his good hand under her elbow to steady her.

"What's the matter? Kylara hasn't ducked Prideth out of here when she's due to mate? Where is Kylara, by the way?"

"I don't know. I must check Wirenth. Oh, no, she couldn't be!"

F'nor followed the girl's swift steps through the great hanging trees that arched over the Southern Weyr's sprawling compound.

"Wirenth's scarcely hatched," he called after her and then remembered that Wirenth was actually a long time out of her shell. It was just that he tended to think of Brekke as the most recent of the Southern Weyrwomen. Brekke looked so young, much too young . . .

She is the same age as Lessa was when Mnementh first flew Ramoth, Canth informed him.

"Is Wirenth ready to rise?" F'nor asked his brown, stopping dead in his tracks.

Soon. Soon. Bronzes will know.

F'nor ticked over in his mind the bronze complement of Southern. The tally didn't please him. Not that the bronzes were few in number, a discourtesy to a new queen, but that their riders had always contended for Kylara, whether Prideth's mating was at stake or not. No matter whose bronze flew Wirenth, the rider would have Brekke and the thought of anyone who had vyed for Kylara's bed favor making love to Brekke irritated the brown rider.

Canth's as big or bigger than any bronze here, he thought resentfully. He had never entertained such an invidious comparison before and ruthlessly put it out of his mind.

Now, if N'ton, a clean-cut lad and a top wingrider just happened to be in Southern? Or B'dor of Ista Weyr. F'nor had ridden with the Istan when his Weyr and Benden joined forces over Nerat and Keroon. Nicely conformed bronzes, both of them, and while F'nor favored N'ton more, if B'dor's beast flew Wirenth, she and Brekke would have the option of removing to Ista Weyr. They'd only three queens there, and Nadira was a far better Weyrwoman than Kylara, despite her coming from the Oldtime.

Pleased with this solution, though he hadn't a notion how to accomplish it, F'nor continued along the path to Wirenth's sun-baked clearing.

He paused at the edge, affected by the sight of Brekke, totally involved with her queen. The girl stood at Wirenth's head, her body gracefully inclined against the dragon, as she tenderly scratched the near eye ridge. Wirenth was somnolent, one lid turning back enough to prove she was aware of the attention, her wedge-shaped head resting on one foreleg, her hindquarters neatly tucked under and framed by her long, graceful tail. In the sun she gleamed with an orange-yellow of excellent health—a color which would very shortly turn a deeper-burnished gold. All too shortly, F'nor realized, for Wirenth had lost every trace of the fatty softness of adolescence; her hide was sleek and smooth, not a blemish to suggest imperfect care. She was an extremely well-proportioned dragon; not one bit too leggy, short-tailed or wherry-necked. Despite her size, for she was easily the length of Prideth, she had a more lithesome appearance. She was one of the best bred from Ramoth and Mnementh.

F'nor frowned slightly at Brekke, subtly changed in her dragon's presence. She seemed more feminine—and desirable. Sensing him, Brekke turned, and the languid look of adoration for her queen made her radiant face almost embarrassing to F'nor.

He hastily cleared his throat. "She'll rise soon, you realize," he said, more gruffly than he intended.

"Yes, I think she will, my beauty. I wonder how that will affect him," Brekke asked, her expression altering. She stepped to one side and pointed to the tiny bronze tucked between Wirenth's jaw and forearm.

"Can't tell, can we?" F'nor replied and, with another series of throat-clearings, covered his savagery at the thought of Brekke mating any of the bronze riders at Southern.

"You're not sickening with something, are you?" she asked with concern and was abruptly transformed back into the Brekke he knew best.

"No. Who's going to be the lucky rider?" he heard himself asking. It was a civil enough question. He was, after all, F'lar's Wing-second and had a right to be curious about such matters. "You can ask for an open flight, you know," he added defensively.

She turned pale and leaned back against Wirenth. As if for comfort.

As if for comfort, F'nor repeated the observation to himself, and remembered, with no relief, the way Brekke had looked at T'bor the day before. "It doesn't matter if the rider's already attached, you know, not in a first mating." He blurted it out, then realized like the greenest dolt that that was stupid. Brekke'd know exactly what Kylara's reaction would be if T'bor's Orth flew Wirenth. She'd know she would have no peace at all. He groaned at his ineptitude.

"Your arm is hurting?" she asked, solicitous.

"No. Not my arm," and he stepped forward, gripping her shoulder with his good hand. "Look, it'd be better if you called for an open flight. There are plenty of good bronzes. N'ton of Benden Weyr, B'dor of Ista Weyr. Both are fine men with good beasts. Then you could leave Southern . . ."

Brekke's eyes were closed and she seemed to go limp in his grasp.

"No! No!" The denial was so soft he barely heard it. "I belong here. Not—Benden."

"N'ton could transfer."

A shudder went through Brekke's body and her eyes flew open. She slipped away from his grip.

"No, N'ton—shouldn't come to Southern," she said in a flat voice.

"He's got no use for Kylara, you know," F'nor continued, determined to reassure her. "She doesn't succeed with every man, you know. And you're a very sweet person, you know."

With a shift of mood as sudden as any of Lessa's, Brekke smiled up at him.

"That's nice to know."

And somehow F'nor had to laugh with her, at his own blundering interference, at the notion of him, a brown rider, giving advice to someone like Brekke, who had more sense in her smallest finger than he.

Well, he was going to get a message to N'ton and B'dor anyhow. Ramoth would help him.

"Have you named your lizard?" he asked.

"Berd. Wirenth and I decided. She likes him," Brekke replied, smiling tenderly on the sleeping pair. "Although it's very confusing. Why do I have a bronze, you a queen and Mirrim *three?*"

F'nor shrugged and grinned at her. "Why not? Of course, once we tell them that's not how it's done, they may conform to time-honored couplings."

"What I meant was, if the fire-lizards—who seem to be miniature dragons—can be Impressed by anyone who approaches them at the crucial moment, then fighting dragons—not just queens who don't chew firestone anyhow—could be Impressed by women, too."

"Fighting Thread is hard work. Leave it to men."

"You think managing a Weyr isn't hard work?" Brekke kept her voice even but her eyes darkened angrily. "Or plowing fields and hollowing cliffs for Holds? And . . ."

F'nor whistled. "Why, Brekke, such revolutionary thoughts from a craftbred girl? Where women know there's only one place for them . . . Oh, you've got Mirrim in mind as a rider?"

"Yes, she'd be as good or better than some of the male weyrlings I know," and there was such asperity in Brekke's voice that F'nor wondered just which boys she found so lacking. "Her ability to Impress three fire-lizards indicates . . ."

"Hey—backwing a bit, girl. We've enough trouble with the Old-timers as it is without trying to get them to accept a girl riding a fighting dragon! C'mon, Brekke. I know your fondness for the child and she seems a good intelligent girl, but you must be realistic."

"I am," Brekke replied, so emphatically that F'nor looked at her in surprise. "Some riders should have been crafters or farmers—or—nothing, but they were acceptable to dragons on Hatching. Others are real riders, heart and soul and mind. Dragons are the beginning and end of their ambition. Mirrim . . ."

A dragon broke into the air above the Weyr, trumpeting.

"F'lar!" With such a wingspan, it could be no other.

F'nor broke into a run, motioning Brekke to follow him to the Weyr landing field.

"No. You go. Wirenth's waking. I'll wait."

F'nor was relieved that she preferred to stay. He didn't want her to come out with that drastic theory in front of F'lar, particularly when he wanted his half-brother to shift N'ton and B'dor here for her sake. Anything to spare Brekke the kind of scene Kylara would throw if T'bor's Orth flew Wirenth.

"Where is everyone?" was F'lar's curt greeting as his brother joined him. "Where's Kylara? Mnementh can't find Prideth. She's not to be haring off on her own."

"Everyone's out trying to trap fire-lizards."

"With Thread falling out of pattern? Of all the stupidities . . . This continent is by no means immune! Where in the image of all shells is T'bor? That'd be all we need—Threads ravaging the southern continent!"

The outburst was so uncharacteristic that F'nor stared at the Weyrleader. F'lar passed his hand over his eyes, rubbing his temples. The cold of *between* had started his headache again. The talk at the Crafthall had been unsettling. He gripped his half-brother's arm in apology.

"That was inexcusable of me, F'nor. I beg your pardon."

"Accepted, of course. That's Orth wheeling in right now." F'nor decided to wait before asking F'lar what was really bothering him. He could just imagine what Raid of Benden Hold or Sifer of Bitra Hold had had to say about new levies of manpower. Probably felt that the change of Threadfall was a personal insult, dreamed up by Benden Weyr to annoy the faithful Holds of Pern.

T'bor landed and strode toward the waiting men.

Perhaps Brekke was not so far off in her heretical doctrine, F'nor thought. T'bor had made Southern Weyr self-sufficient and productive, no small task. He'd obviously have made a good Holder.

"Orth said you were here, F'lar. What brings you to Southern? You heard our news about the fire-lizards?" T'bor called, brushing the sand from his clothes as he walked.

"Yes, I did," replied F'lar in so formal a tone that T'bor's welcoming smile faded. "And I thought you'd heard ours, that Thread is dropping out of pattern."

"There's a rider along every inch of coastline, F'lar, so don't accuse me of negligence," T'bor said, his smile returning. "Dragons don't need to be a-wing to spot Thread. Shells, man, you can hear it hissing across the water."

"I assume you were looking for fire-lizard eggs?" F'lar sounded testy and not completely reassured by T'bor's report. "Have you found any?"

T'bor shook his head. "There's evidence, far to the west, of another clutch, but there isn't a sign of shell or corpse. The wherries can make fast work of anything edible."

"Were I you, T'bor, I'd not release an entire Weyr to search for lizard eggs. There's no guarantee Thread will move in on this continent from the ocean."

"But it always has. What little we get."

"Thread fell ten hours before schedule across Lemos north when it should have fallen on Lemos south and Telgar southeast," F'lar told him in a hard voice. "I have since heard that Thread fell, unchecked," and he paused to let that sink in to T'bor's mind, "in Telgar Hold and Crom Hold, both times out of phase with the tables though we do not yet know the time differential. We can't rely on any previous performance."

"I'll mount guards immediately and send the wings to sweep as far south as we've penetrated," T'bor said briskly and, shrugging into his riding jacket, trotted back to Orth. They were aloft in one great leap.

"Orth looks well," F'lar said and then eyed his half-brother closely before he smiled, jabbing a fist affectionately at F'nor's good shoulder. "You do, too. How's the arm healing?"

"I'm at Southern," F'nor replied in oblique explanation. "Are Threadfalls really that erratic?"

"I don't know," F'lar said with an irritable shrug. "Tell me about these fire-lizards if you please. Are they worth the time of every able-bodied rider in this Weyr? Where's yours? I'd like to see it for myself before I go back to Benden." He glanced northeast, frowning.

"Shells, can't I leave Benden Weyr for a week without everything falling apart?" F'nor demanded so vehemently that F'lar stared at him in momentary surprise before he chuckled and seemed to relax. "That's better," F'nor said, echoing the grin. "Come. There are a couple of the lizards in the Weyrhall and I need some *klah*. I was not hunting clutches all morning myself, you know. Or would you prefer to sample some of Southern's wine?"

"Ha!" F'lar made the excalamation a challenge.

When they entered the Weyrhall, Mirrim was there alone, stirring the stew in the big kettles. The two greens were watching her from the long, wide mantel. She gave the appearance of having an odd deformity of chest until F'nor realized that she had rigged a sling around her shoulders in which the wounded brown was suspended, his little eyes pinpoints of light. At the sound of their boots on the paving, she swung round, her eyes wide with an apprehension which turned to surprise as she glanced from F'nor to F'lar. Her mouth made an "o" of astonishment as she recognized the Benden Weyrleader by his resemblance to F'nor.

"And you're the—the young lady who Impressed three?" F'lar asked, crossing the big room to her.

Mirrim bobbed a series of nervous curtsies, causing the brown to squawk in protest to such bouncing.

"May I see him?" F'lar asked and deftly stroked a tiny eye ridge. "He's a real beauty! Canth in miniature," and F'lar glanced slyly at his half-brother to see if the jibe registered. "Will he recover from his wounds—ah . . ."

"Mirrim is her name," F'nor prompted in a bland tone that implied his brother's memory was failing him.

"Oh, no, Weyrleader—he's healing nicely," the girl said with another bob.

"Full stomach, I see," F'lar commented approvingly. He glanced at the pair buddled together on the mantel and crooned soft encouragement. They began to preen, stretching fragile, translucent green wings, arching their backs and emitting an echoing hum in pleasure. "You'll have your hands full with this trio."

"I'll manage them, sir. I promise. And I won't forget my duties, either," she said breathlessly, her eyes still wide. With a gasp, she turned to give a splashing stir to the contents of the nearest pot, then whirled back again before the men could turn. "Brekke's not here. Would you like some *klah?* Or the stew? Or some . . ."

"We'll serve ourselves," F'nor assured her, picking up two mugs.

"Oh, I ought to do that, sir . . ."

"You ought to watch your kettles, Mirrim. We'll manage," F'lar told her kindly, mentally contrasting the state of domestic affairs at the Crafthall to the order and the cooking of good rich food at this hall.

He motioned the brown rider to take the table furthest from the kitchen hearth.

"Can you hear anything from the lizards?" he asked in a low voice.

"From hers, you mean? No, but I can easily see what they must be thinking from their reactions. Why?"

"Idle question. But she's not from a Search, is she?"

"No, of course not. She's Brekke's fosterling."

"Hmmm. Then she's not exactly proof, is she?"

"Proof of what, F'lar? I've suffered no head injury but I can't follow your thought."

F'lar gave his brother an absent smile and then exhaled wearily.

"We're going to have trouble with the Lord Holders; they're disillusioned and dissatisfied with the Oldtimer Weyrs and are going to balk at any more expeditious measures against Thread."

"Raid and Sifer give you a hard time?"

"I wish it were only that, F'nor. They'd come round." F'lar gave his half-brother a terse account of what he'd learned from Lytol, Robinton and Fandarel the day before.

"Brekke was right when she said something really important had come up," F'nor said afterward. "But . . ."

"Yes, that news's a hard roll to eat, all right, but our ever efficient Craftsmith's got what might be an answer, not only to the watch on Thread but to establishing decent communications with every Hold and Hall on Pern. Especially since we can't get the Oldtimers to assign riders outside the Weyrs. I saw a demonstration of the device today and we're going to rig one for the Lord Holders at Telgar's wedding . . ."

"And the Threads will wait for that?"

F'lar snorted. "They may be the lesser evil, frankly. The Threads prove to be more flexible in their ways than the Oldtimers and less trouble than the Lord Holders."

"One of the basic troubles between Lord Holders and Weyrmen are dragons, F'lar, and those fire-lizards might just ease matters."

"That's what I was thinking earlier, considering that young Mirrim had Impressed three. That's really astonishing, even if she is weyrbred."

"Brekke would like to see her Impress a fighting dragon," F'nor said in a casual way, watching his half-brother's face closely.

F'lar gave him a startled stare and then threw back his head and laughed.

"Can you . . . imagine . . . T'ron's reaction?" . . . he managed to say.

"Well enough to spare myself your version, but the fire-lizard may do the trick! *And*, have the added talent of keeping Hold in contact with Weyr *if* these creatures prove amenable to training."

"If—if! Just how similar to dragons are fire-lizards?"

F'nor shrugged. "As I told you, they are Impressionable—if rather undiscriminating," he pointed to Mirrim at the Hearth and then grinned maliciously, "although they detested Kylara on sight. They're slaves to their stomachs, though after Hatching that's very definitely draconic. They respond to affection and flattery. The dragons themselves admit the relationship, seem totally free of jealousy of the creatures. I can detect basic emotions in the thoughts of mine and they generally inspire affection in those who handle them."

"And they can go *between?*"

"Grall—my little queen—did. About chewing firestone I couldn't hazard a guess. We'll have to wait and see."

"And we don't have time," F'lar said, clenching his fists, his eyes restless with the current of his thoughts.

"*If* we could find a hardened clutch, all set to Hatch, in time for that wedding—*that*, combined with Fandarel's gadget—" F'nor let his sentence trail off.

F'lar got up in a single decisive movement. "I'd like to see your queen. You named her Grall?"

"You're solid dragonman, F'lar," F'nor chuckled, remembering what Brekke had said. "You had no trouble remembering the lizard's name but the girl's—? Never mind, F'lar. Grall's with Canth."

"Any chance you could call her—here?"

F'nor considered the intriguing possibility but shook his head. "She's asleep, full up the jawline."

She was and daintily curled in the hollow by Canth's left ear. Her belly was distended from the morning's meal and F'nor dabbed it with sweet oil. She condescended to lift two lids but her eye was so dull she did not take notice of the additional visitor, nor Mnementh peering down at her. He thought her a very interesting creature.

"Charming. Lessa'll want one, I'm sure," F'lar murmured, a delighted half-smile on his face as he jumped down from Canth's forearm on which he'd stood to observe her. "Hope she grows a little. Canth could yawn and inadvertently inhale her."

Never, and the brown's comment did not need to be passed to the bronze rider.

"If we'd only an estimate of how long it would take to train them, if they are trainable. But time's as inflexible as an Oldtimer." F'lar looked his half-brother squarely in the eye, no longer hiding the deep worry that gnawed at him.

"Not entirely, F'lar," the brown rider said, returning his gaze steadily. "As you said, the greater evil is the sickness in our own . . ."

A dragon's brassy scream, the klaxon of Thread attack, stopped F'nor midsentence. The brown rider had swung toward his dragon, instinctively reacting to the alert, when F'lar caught him by the arm.

"You can't fight thread with an unhealed wound, man. Where do they keep firestone here?"

Whatever criticism F'lar might have had of T'bor's permissiveness at Southern, he could not fault the instant response of the Weyr's fighting complement. Dragons swarmed in the skies before the alert had faded. Dragons swooped to weyrs while riders fetched fighting gear and firestone. The Weyr's women and children were at the supply shed, stuffing sacks. A message had been sent to the seahold where fishermen from Tillek and Ista had established a settlement. They acted as ground crew. By the time F'lar was equipped and aloft, T'bor was issuing the coordinates.

Thread was falling in the west, at the edge of the desert where the terrain was swampy, where sharp broad-edged grasses were interspersed with dwarfed spongewoods and low berry bushes. For Thread, the muddy swamp was superb burrowing ground, with sufficient organisms on which to feed as the burrow proliferated and spread.

The wings, fully manned and in good order, went *between* at T'bor's command. And, in a breath, the dragons hung again in sultry air and began to flame at the thick patches of Thread.

T'bor had signaled a low altitude entry, of which F'lar approved. But the wing movement was upward, seeking Thread at ever higher levels as they eliminated the immediate airborne danger. Weyrfolk and convalescents swelled the seahold group as ground crew but F'lar thought they'd need low ground support here. There were only three fighting queens, *and where was Kylara?*

F'lar directed Mnementh to fly a skim pattern just as the ground crews arrived, piling off the transport dragons, and flaming any patch of grass that seemed to move. They kept shouting to know where the leading Edge of the Fall was and F'lar directed Mnementh east by north. Mnementh complied, and abruptly turned due north, his head barely skimming the vegetation. He backwinged so abruptly that he nearly offset his rider. He hovered, peering so intently at the ground, that F'lar leaned over the great neck to see what attracted him. Dragons could adjust the focus of their eyes to either great distances or close inspection.

Something moved—away, the dragon said.

The gusts of his backwinging flattened grasses. Then F'lar saw the pin-sized, black-rimmed punctures of Thread on the leaves of the berry bushes. He stared hard, trying to discern the telltale evidence of burrows, the upheaval of soil, the consumption of the lush swamp greenery. The bush, the grass, the soil stood still.

"What moved?"

Something bright. It's gone.

Mnementh landed, his feet sinking into the oozing terrain. F'lar jumped off and peered closely at the bush. Had the holes been made by droplets of hot Thread during a previous Fall? No. The leaves would long since have dropped off. He examined every nearby hummock of grass. Not a sign of burrows. Yet Thread had fallen—and it had to be *this* Fall—had pierced leaves, grass and tree over a widespread area— and vanished without a trace. No, that was impossible! Gingerly, for viable Thread could eat through wher-hide gloves, F'lar dug around the berry bush. Mnementh helpfully scooped out a deep trench nearby. The displaced soil teamed with grub life, writhing in among the thick tough grass roots. The unexpectedly gray, gnarly taproots of the bush were thick with the black earth but not a sign of Thread.

Mystified, F'lar raised his eyes in answer to a summons from the hovering weyrlings.

They wish to know if this is the Edge of Threadfall, Mnementh reported to his rider.

"It must be further south," F'lar replied and waved the weyrlings in that direction. He stood looking down at the overturned earth, at the grubs burrowing frantically away from sunlight. He picked up a stout barkless branch and jabbed the earth of the trench Mnementh had made, prodding for the cavities that meant Thread infestations. "It has to be further south. I don't understand this." He ripped a handful of the leaves from a berry bush and sifted them through his gloves. "If this happened some time ago, rain would have washed the char from the punctures. The damaged leaves would have dropped."

He began to work his way south, and slightly east, trying to ascertain exactly where Thread had started. Foliage on every side gave evidence of its passage but he found no burrows.

When he located drowned Thread in the brackish water of a swamp pool, he had to consider that as the leading Edge. But he wasn't satisfied and bogged himself down in syrtis muds investigating, so that Mnementh had to pull him free.

So intent was he on the anomalies of this Fall, that he did not notice the passage of time. He was somewhat startled, then, to have T'bor appear overhead, announcing the end of Fall. And both men were alarmed when the ground-crew chief, a young fisherman from Ista named Toric, verified that the Fall had lasted a scant two hours since discovery.

"A short Fall, I know, but there's nothing above, and Toric here says the ground crews are mopping up the few patches that got through," T'bor said, rather pleased with the efficient performance of his Weyr.

Every instinct told F'lar that something was wrong. Could Thread have changed its habits that drastically? He had no precedent. It always fell in four-hour spans—yet clearly the sky was bare.

"I need your counsel, T'bor," he said and there was that edge of concern in his voice that brought the other to his side instantly.

F'lar scooped up a handful of the brackish water, showing him the filaments of drowned Thread.

"Ever notice this before?"

"Yes, indeed," T'bor replied in a hearty voice, obviously relieved. "Happens all the time here. Not many fish to eat Thread in these foot-sized pools."

"Then there's something in the swamp waters that does for them?"

"What do you mean?"

Wordlessly, F'lar tipped back the scarred foliage nearest him. He warily turned down the broad saw-edged swamp grasses. Catching T'bor's stunned eyes, he gestured back the way he had come, where ground crews moved without one belch of flame from their throwers.

"You mean, it's like that? How far back?"

"To Threadfall Edge, an hour's fast walk," F'lar replied grimly. "Or rather, that's where I assume Thread Edge is."

"I've seen bushes and grasses marked like that in these swampy deltas closer to the Weyr," T'bor admitted slowly, his face blanched under the tan, "but I thought it was char. We mark so few infestations—and there've been no burrows."

T'bor was shaken.

Orth says there have been no infestations, Mnementh reported quietly and Orth briefly turned glowing eyes toward the Benden Weyrleader.

"And Thread was always short-timed?" F'lar wanted to know.

Orth says this is the first, but then the alarm came late.

T'bor turned haunted eyes to F'lar.

"It wasn't a short Fall, then," he said, half-hoping to be contradicted.

Just then Canth veered in to land. F'lar suppressed a reprimand when he saw the flame thrower on his half-brother's back.

"That was the most unusual Fall I've ever attended," F'nor cried as he saluted the two bronze riders. "We can't have got it all airborne, but there's not a trace of burrow. And dead Thread in every water pocket. I suppose we should be grateful. But I don't understand it."

"I don't like it, F'lar," T'bor said, shaking his head. "I don't like it. Thread wasn't due here for another few weeks, and then, not in this area."

"Thread apparently is falling when and where it chooses."

"How can Thread choose?" T'bor demanded with the anger of a frightened man. "It's mindless!"

F'lar gazed up at tropical skies so brilliant that the fateful stare of the Red Star, low on the horizon, wasn't visible.

"If the Red Star deviates for four hundred Turn Intervals, why not a variation in the way it falls?"

"What do we do then?" asked T'bor, a note of desperation in his voice. "Thread that pierces and doesn't burrow! Thread falling days out of phase and then for only two hours!"

"Put out sweepriders, to begin with, and let me know where and when Thread falls here. As you said, Thread is mindless. Even in these new Shifts, we may find a predictable pattern." F'lar frowned up at the hot sun; he was sweating in the wher-hide fighting clothes more suited to upper levels and cold *between*.

"Fly a sweep with me, F'lar," T'bor suggested anxiously. "F'nor, are you up to it? If we missed even one burrow here . . ."

T'bor had Orth call in every rider, even the weyrlings, told them what to look for, what was feared.

The entire complement of Southern spread out, wingtip to wingtip, flying at minimum altitude, and scanned the swampy region right back to Fall Edge. Not one man or beast could report any unusual disturbance of greenery or ground. The land over which Thread had so recently fallen was now undeniably Threadfree.

The clearance made T'bor even more apprehensive, but another tour seemed pointless. The fighting wings went *between* to the Weyr then, leaving the convalescents to fly straight.

As T'bor and F'lar glided in over the Weyr compound, the roofs of the weyrholds and the bare black soil and rock of the dragonbeds flashed under them like a pattern through the leaves of the giant fellis and spongewood trees. In the main clearing by the Weyrhall, Prideth extended her neck and wings, bugling to her Weyrmates.

"Circle once again, Mnementh," F'lar said to his bronze. First he'd better get over the urge to beat Kylara, and give T'bor the chance to reprimand her privately. He regretted, once more, that he had ever suggested to Lessa that she pressure that female into being a Weyr-woman. It had seemed a logical solution at the time. And he was sincerely sorry for T'bor although the man did manage to keep her worst depredations under control. But the absence of a queen from a Weyr . . . Well, how could Kylara have known Thread would fall here ahead of schedule? Yet where was she that she couldn't hear that alarm? No dragon slept that deeply.

He circled as the rest of the dragons peeled off to their weyrs and realized that none had had to descend by the Infirmary.

"Fighting Thread with no casualties?"

I like that, Mnementh remarked.

Somehow that aspect of the day's encounter unsettled F'lar the most. Rather than delve into that, F'lar judged it time to land. He didn't relish the thought of confronting Kylara, but he hadn't had the chance to tell T'bor what had been happening north.

"I told you," Kylara was saying in sullen anger, "that I found a clutch and Impressed this queen. When I got back, there wasn't any-one left here who knew where you'd all gone. Prideth has to have coordinates, you know." She turned toward F'lar now, her eyes glittering. "My duty to you, F'lar of Benden," and her voice took on a caressing tone which made T'bor stiffen and clench his teeth. "How kind of you to fight with us when Benden Weyr has troubles of its own."

F'lar ignored the jibe and nodded a curt acknowledgement.

"See my fire-lizard. Isn't she magnificent?" She held up her right arm, exhibiting the drowsing golden lizard, the outlines of her latest meal pressing sharp designs against her belly hide.

"Wirenth was here and Brekke. They knew," T'bor told her.

"Her!" Kylara dismissed the weyrwoman with a negligent shrug of contempt. "She gave me some nonsensical coordinates, deep in the western swamp. Threads don't fall . . ."

"They did today," T'bor cried, his face suffused with anger.

"Do tell!"

Prideth began to rumble restlessly and Kylara, the hard defiant lines of her face softening, turned to reassure her.

"See, you've made her uneasy and she's so near mating again."

T'bor looked dangerously close to an outburst which, as Weyrleader, he could not risk. Kylara's tactic was so obvious that F'lar wondered how the man could fall for it. Would it improve matters to have T'bor supplanted by one of the other bronze riders here? F'lar considered, as he had before, throwing Prideth's next mating flight into open competition. And yet, he owed T'bor too much for coping with this—this female to insult him by such a measure. On the other hand, maybe one of the more vigorous Oldtime bronzes with a rider just sufficiently detached from Kylara's ploys, and interested enough in retaining a Leadership, might keep her firmly in line.

"T'bor, the map of this continent's in the Weyrhall, isn't it?" F'lar asked, diverting the man. "I'd like to set the coordinates of this Fall in my mind . . ."

"Don't you like my queen?" Kylara asked, stepping forward and raising the lizard right under F'lar's nose.

The little creature, unbalanced by the sudden movement, dug her razor-sharp claws into Kylara's arm, piercing the wher-hide as easily as Thread pierced leaf. With a yelp, Kylara shook her arm, dislodging the fire-lizard. In midfall the creature disappeared. Kylara's cry of pain changed to a shriek of anger.

"Look what you've done, you fool. You've lost her."

"Not I, Kylara," F'lar replied in a hard, cold voice. "Take good care you do not push others to their limit!"

"I've limits, too, F'lar of Benden," she screamed as the two men strode quickly toward the Weyrhall. "Don't push me. D'you hear? Don't push *me!*" She kept up her curses until Prideth, now highly agitated, drowned her out with piteous cries.

At first the two Weyrleaders went through the motions of studying the map and trying to figure out where Thread might have fallen elsewhere undetected on the Southern continent. Then Prideth's complaints died away and the clearing was vacant.

"It comes down to manpower again, T'bor," F'lar said. "There ought to be a thorough search of this continent. Oh, I'm aware," and he held up his hand to forestall a defensive rebuttal, "that you simply don't have the personnel to help, even with the influx of holderfolk from the mainland. But Thread can cross mountains," he tapped the southern chain, "and we don't know what's been happening in these uncharted areas. We've assumed that Threadfall occurred only in this coastline portion. Once established though, a single burrow could eat its way across any land mass and—" He made a slashing movement of both hands. "I'd give a lot to know how Thread could fall unnoticed in those swamps for two hours and leave no trace of a burrow!"

T'bor grunted agreement but F'lar sensed that his mind was not on this problem.

"You've had more than your share of grief with that woman, T'bor. Why not throw the next flight open?"

"No!" And Orth echoed that vehement refusal with a roar.

F'lar looked at T'bor in amazement.

"No, F'lar. I'll keep her in hand. I'll keep myself in hand, too. But as long as Orth can fly Prideth, Kylara's mine."

F'lar looked quickly away from the torment in the other's face.

"And you'd better know this, too," T'bor continued in a heavy low voice. "She found a full clutch. She took them to a Hold. Prideth told Orth."

"Which Hold?"

T'bor shook his head wearily. "Prideth doesn't like it so she doesn't name it. She doesn't like taking fire-lizards away from the weyrs either."

F'lar brushed his forelock back from his eyes in an irritated movement. This was the most unhealthy development. A dragon displeased with her rider? The one restraint they had all counted on was Kylara's bond with Prideth. The woman wouldn't be fool enough, wanton enough, perverted enough to strain that, too, in her egocentric selfishness.

Prideth will not hear me, Mnementh said suddenly. *She will not hear Orth. She is unhappy. That isn't good.*

Threads falling unexpectedly, fire-lizards in Holder hands, a dragon displeased with her rider and another anticipating his rider's questions! and F'lar had thought he'd had problems seven Turns ago!

"I can't sort this all out right now, T'bor. Please mount guards and let me know the instant you've any news of any kind. If you do uncover another clutch, I would very much appreciate some of the eggs. Let me know, too, if that little queen returns to Kylara. I grant the creature had reason, but if they frighten *between* so easily, they may be worthless except as pets."

F'lar mounted Mnementh and saluted the Southern Weyrleader, reassured by nothing in this visit. And he'd lost the advantage of surprising the Lord Holders with fire-lizards. In fact, Kylara's precipitous donation would undoubtedly cause more trouble. A Weyrwoman meddling in a Hold not bound to her own Weyr? He almost hoped that these creatures would be nothing more than pets and her action could be soft-talked. Still, there was the psychological effect of that miniature dragon, Impressionable by anyone. That would have been a valuable asset in improving Weyr-Hold relations.

As Mnementh climbed higher, to the cooler levels, F'lar worried most about that Threadfall. It had fallen. It had pierced leaf and grass, drowned in the water, and yet left no trace of itself in the rich earth. Igen's sandworms would devour Thread, almost as efficiently as agenothree. But the grub life that had swarmed in the rich black swamp mud bore little resemblance to the segmented, shelled worms.

Unable to leave Southern without a final check, F'lar gave Mnementh the order to transfer to the western swamp. The bronze obediently brought him right to the trench his claw had made. F'lar slid from his shoulder, opening the wher-hide tunic as the humid, sticky, sun-steamed swamp air pressed against him like a thick wet skin. There was a ringing, rasping chorus of tiny sound all around him, splashings and burblings, none of which he'd noted earlier in the day. In fact, the swamp had been remarkably silent, as if hushed by the menace of Thread.

When he turned back the hummock of grass by the roots of the berry bush, the earth was untenanted, the gray roots sleekly damp. Kicking up another section, he did find a small cluster of the larvae, but not in the earlier profusion. He held the muddy ball in his hand, watching the grubs squirm away from light and air. It was then that he saw that the foliage of that bush was no longer Thread-scored. The char had disappeared and a thin film was forming over the hole, as if the bush were mending itself.

Something writhed against the skin of his palm and he hastily dropped the ball of dirt, rubbing his hand against his leg.

He broke off a leaf, the sign of Thread healing in the green foliage.

Could the grubs possibly be the southern continent's equivalent of sandworms?

Abruptly he gave a running jump to Mnementh's shoulder, grabbing the riding straps.

"Mnementh, take me back to the beginning of this Fall. That'd make it six hours back. The sun would be at zenith."

Mnementh didn't grumble but his thoughts were plain: F'lar was tired, F'lar ought to go back to Benden and rest, talk to Lessa. Jumping *between* time was hard on a rider.

Cold *between* enveloped them, and F'lar hastily closed the tunic he'd opened, but not before the cold seemed to eat into his chest bone. He shivered, with more than physical chill, as they burst out over the steamy swamp again. It took more than a few minutes under that blazing sun to counteract the merciless cold. Mnementh glided briefly northward and then hovered, facing due south.

They didn't have long to wait. High above, the ominous grayness that presaged Threadfall darkened the sky. As often as he had watched it, F'lar never rid himself of fear. And it was harder still to watch that distant grayness begin to separate into sheets and patches of silvery Thread. To watch and to permit it to fall unchecked on the swamp below. To watch as it pierced leaf and green, hissing as it penetrated the mud. Even Mnementh stirred restlessly, his wings trembling as he fought every instinct to dive, flaming, at the ancient menace. Yet he, too, watched as the leading Edge advanced southward, across the swamp, a gray rain of destruction.

Without needing a command, Mnementh landed just short of the Edge. And F'lar, fighting an inward revulsion so strong that he was sure he'd vomit, turned back the nearest hummock, smoking with Thread penetration. Grubs, feverishly active, populated the concourse of the roots. As he held the hummock up, bloated grubs dropped to the ground and frantically burrowed into the earth. He dropped that clump, uprooted the nearest bush, baring the gray, twisted rootball. It also teemed with grub life that burrowed away from the sudden exposure to air and light. The leaves of the bush were still smoldering from Thread puncture.

Not quite certain why, F'lar knelt, pulled up another hummock and scooped up a clump of squirming grubs into the fingers of his riding glove. He twisted it tightly shut and secured it under his belt.

Then he mounted Mnementh and gave him the coordinates of the Masterherdsman's Crafthall in Keroon, where the foothills that rose eventually to the massive heights of Benden range gently merged with the wide plains of Keroon Hold.

Masterherdsman Sograny, a tall, bald, leathery man so spare of flesh that his bones seemed held in position by his laced vest, tight hide pants and heavy boots, showed no pleasure in an unexpected visit from Benden's Weyrleader.

F'lar had been met with punctilious courtesy, if some confusion, by crafters. Sograny, it seemed, was supervising the birth of a new mix of herdbeasts, the very swift plains type with the heavy-chested mountain one. A messenger led F'lar to the great barn. Considering the importance of the event, F'lar thought it odd that no one had left his tasks. He was led past neat cots of immaculately cleaned stone, well-tended gardens, past forcing sheds and equipment barns. F'lar thought of the absolute chaos that prevailed at the Smith's, but then remembered what marvels that man accomplished.

"You've a problem for the Masterherdsman, have you, Weyrleader?" Sograny asked, giving F'lar a curt nod, his eyes on the laboring beast in the box stall. "How does that happen?"

The man's attitude was so defensive that F'lar wondered what D'ram of Ista Weyr might have been doing to irritate him.

"Mastersmith Fandarel suggested that you would be able to advise me, Masterherdsman," F'lar replied, no trace of levity in his manner and no lack of courtesy in his address.

"The Smithcrafter?" Sograny looked at F'lar with narrowed, suspicious eyes. "Why?"

Now what could Fandarel have done to warrant the bad opinion of the Masterherdsman?

"Two anomalies have come to my attention, good Masterherdsman. The first, a clutch of fire-lizard eggs hatched in the vicinity of one of my riders and he was able to Impress the queen . . ."

Sograny's eyes widened with startled disbelief.

"No man can catch a fire-lizard!"

"Agreed, but he can Impress one. And certainly did. We believe that the fire-lizards are directly related to the dragons."

"That cannot be proved!" Sograny pulled himself straight up, his eyes darting toward his assistants who suddenly found tasks far from F'lar and the Masterherdsman.

"By inference, yes. Because the similar characteristics are obvious. Seven fire-lizards were Impressed on the sands of a beach at Southern. One by my Wing-second, F'nor, Canth's rider . . ."

"F'nor? The man who fought those two thieving weyrmen at the Smithcrafthall?"

F'lar swallowed his bile and nodded. That regrettable incident had hatched an unexpected brood of benefits.

"The fire-lizards exhibit undeniable draconic traits. Unfortunately, one of them is to stay close to their Impressor or I'd have proof positive."

Sograny only grunted, but he was suddenly receptive.

"I was hoping that you, as Masterherdsman, might know something about the fire-lizards. Igen certainly abounds with them . . ."

Sograny was cutting him off with an impatient wave of his hand.

"No time to waste on flitterbys. Useless creatures. No crafter of mine would . . ."

"There is every indication that they may be of tremendous use to us. After all, dragons were bred from fire-lizards."

"Impossible!" Sograny stared at him, thin lips firmly denying such an improbability.

"Well, they weren't bred up from watch-whers."

"Man can alter size but only so far. He can, of course, breed the largest to the largest and improve on the original stock," and Sograny gestured toward the long-legged cow. "But to breed a dragon from a fire-lizard? Absolutely impossible."

F'lar wasted no further time on that subject but took the glove from his belt and emptied the grubs into the other, gloved palm.

"These, sir. Have you seen such as these . . ."

Sograny's reaction was immediate. With a cry of fear, he grabbed F'lar's hand, tumbling the grubs to the stone of the barn. Yelling for agenothree, he stamped on the squirming grubs as if they were essence of evil.

"How could you—a dragonman—bring such filth into my dwellings?"

"Masterherdsman, control yourself!" F'lar snapped, grabbing the man and shaking him. "They devour Thread. Like sandworms. Like sandworms!"

Sograny was trembling beneath F'lar's hands, staring at him. He shook his skull-like head and the wildness died from his eyes.

"Only flame can devour Thread, dragonman!"

"I told you," F'lar said coldly, "that those grubs devoured Thread!"

Sograny glared at F'lar with considerable animus.

"They are an abomination. You waste my time with such nonsense."

"My deep apologies," F'lar said, with a curt bow. But his irony was wasted on the man. Sograny turned back to his laboring cow as though F'lar had never interrupted him.

F'lar strode off, pulling on his gloves, his forefinger coming into contact with the wet, slippery body of a grub.

"See the Masterherdsman, eh?" he muttered under his breath, waving aside the services of the guide as he left the breeding barn. A bellow from a herdbeast followed him out. "Yes, he breeds animals, but not ideas. Ideas might waste time, be useless."

As he and Mnementh circled upward, F'lar wondered how much trouble D'ram was having with that old fool.

· · C H A P T E R   I X · ·

Afternoon at Southern Weyr:
Same Day

It was a long flight, the straight way, from the western swamps to Southern Weyr's headland. At first, F'nor rebelled. A short hop *between* would not affect his healing arm, but Canth became unexpectedly stubborn. The big brown soared, caught the prevailing wind and, with great sweeps of his wings, sped through the cooler air, high above the monotonous terrain.

As Canth settled down into long-distance flying, the rhythm began to soothe F'nor. What ought to have been a tedious journey became the blessing of uninterrupted time for reflection. And F'nor had much to think about.

The brown rider had noticed the widespread Thread-scoring. He had turned back bush after bush, heavily pitted by Threadmark, to find no trace of burrow at all in the swamp mud around them. Not once had he used his flame thrower. And the ground crews told him they had so little to do they wondered the Weyr called them at all. Many were from the fishing settlement and they were beginning to resent being taken from their labors, for they were trying to complete stone holds against the winter storms. They all preferred Southern to their old homes, though they did not complain against Tillek's Lord Oterel, or Lord Warbret of Ista.

It had always amused F'nor that people he had scarcely met were willing to confide in him, but he had found that this was often an advantage, despite the hours he'd had to spend listening to maundering tales. One of the younger men, the ground-crew chief, Toric, informed him that he'd staked out a sandy cove near his hold. It was almost inaccessible from the landside, but he'd seen certain fire-lizard signs. He was determined to Impress one and positive that he could, for he'd been lucky with watch-whers. He'd tried to convince Fort Weyr that he should have a chance at Impressing a dragon, but he hadn't been given the courtesy of seeing T'ron. Toric was quite bitter about weyrmen and, knowing (as everyone seemed to, F'nor had discovered) about the belt-knife fight, Toric expected F'nor to be disaffected, too. He was surprised when F'nor brusquely cut off his carping recital.

It was this curious ambivalence of Holder feeling toward dragonmen that occupied F'nor's thought. Holders claimed that weyrfolk held themselves aloof, acted patronizing or condescending, or plain arrogant in their presence. Yet there wasn't a man or woman, Holder or Crafter, who hadn't at one time or another wished he or she had Impressed a dragon. And in many this turned to bitter envy. Weyrmen insisted they were superior to commoners even while they consistently exhibited the same appetites as other men for material possessions and nubile women. Yet they did indeed refute the Crafter contention that dragonriding was a skill no more exacting than any craft on Pern, for in no other craft did a man risk life as a matter of course. And far worse, the loss of half his life. Reflexively, F'nor's thought sheered sharply away from any hint of threat to the great brown he rode.

The little queen stirred inside the heavy arm sling where he had been carrying her.

Young Toric, now, would lose some of his bitterness if he did Impress a fire-lizard. He would feel that his claim was vindicated. And if fire-lizards did take to anyone, and could carry messages back and forth, what a boon that would be. A lizard for everyone? That would be quite a battle cry. F'nor chortled as he thought of the Oldtimers' reactions to that. Do them good, it would, and he chuckled at the vision of T'ron trying to lure a fire-lizard which ignored him to be Impressed by a lowly crafterchild. Something had better pierce the Oldtimers' blind parochiality. Yet even they, at a crucial moment in the sensitive awareness of adolescence, had appealed to dragonkind; they endured cold and possible death to fight an endless and mindless enemy. But there was more to living than that initial achievement and that eternal alert. Adolescence was only a step of life, not a career in itself. When one matured, one knew there was more to living.

Then F'nor remembered that he'd not had the chance to mention Brekke's problem to F'lar. And F'lar would probably have gone back to Benden Weyr by now. F'nor upbraided himself for what was downright interference. Comes from being a wing-second so long, he thought. You can't go around meddling in another's Weyr. T'bor had enough stress. But, by the First Egg, F'nor hated to think of the scenes Kylara would subject Brekke to, if Orth flew Wirenth.

He grew restless with traveling and wasn't even amused when Canth began to croon soothingly. But when the journey was accomplished, and they were circling down into the late afternoon sun over Southern, he felt no fatigue. A few riders were feeding their beasts in the pasture and he inquired if Canth wished to be fed.

Brekke wants to see you, Canth advised F'nor as he landed neatly in his weyr.

"Probably to scold me," F'nor said, slapping Canth's muzzle affectionately. He stood aside watching until the brown settled himself in the warmth of his dusty wallow.

Grall peeked out of the folds of the sling and F'nor transferred her to his shoulder. She squeaked a protest as he strode quickly toward Brekke's weyrhold and dug her claws into the shoulder pad for balance. She was thinking hungry thoughts.

Brekke was feeding her lizard, Berd, when F'nor entered. She smiled as she heard Grall's shrill demand, and pushed the bowl of meat toward F'nor.

"I was worried that you might fly *between*."

"Canth wouldn't let me."

"Canth has sense. How's the arm?"

"Took no hurt. There wasn't much to be done."

"So I hear." Brekke frowned. "Everything's askew. I have the oddest sensation . . ."

"Go on," F'nor urged when she broke off. "What kind of a sensation?" Was Wirenth about to rise? Brekke seemed to remain untouched by so many disturbances, a serene competent personality, tranquilly keeping the Weyr going, healing the wounded. For her to admit to uncertainty was disturbing.

As if she caught his thoughts, she shook her head, her lips set in a fierce line.

"No, it's not personal. It's just that everything is going awry—disorienting, changing . . ."

"Is that all? Didn't I hear you suggesting a minor change or two? Letting a girl Impress a fighting dragon? Handing out fire-lizards to placate the common mass?"

"That's change. I'm talking about a disorientation, a violent upheaval . . ."

"And your suggestions don't rank under that heading? Oh, my dear girl," and F'nor suddenly gave her a long, penetrating look. Something in her candid gaze disturbed him deeply.

"Kylara pestering you?"

Brekke's eyes slid from his and she shook her head.

"I told you, Brekke, you can request other bronzes. Someone from another Weyr, N'ton of Benden or B'dor of Ista . . . That would shut Kylara up."

Brekke shook her head violently, but kept her face averted.

"Don't keep foisting your friends on me!" Her voice was sharp. "I like Southern. I'm needed here."

"Needed? You're being shamelessly exploited and not just by Southerners!"

She stared at him, as surprised by the impulsive outburst as he was. For one moment he thought he understood why, but her eyes became guarded and F'nor wondered what Brekke could want to hide.

"The need is more apparent than the exploitation. I don't mind hard work," she said in a low voice and popped a piece of meat into the brown's wide-open mouth. "Don't rob me of what fragile contentment I can contrive."

"Contentment?"

"Sssh. You're agitating the lizards."

"They'll survive. They fight. The trouble with you, Brekke, is that you won't. You deserve so much more than you get. You don't know what a kind, generous, useful—oh, shells!" and F'nor broke off in confusion.

"Useful, worthwhile, wholesome, capable, dependable, the list is categoric, F'nor, I know the entire litany," Brekke said with a funny little catch in her voice. "Rest assured, my friend, I know what I am."

There was such a bitterness in her light words, and such a shadow in her usually candid green eyes that F'nor could not tolerate it. To erase that self-deprecation, to make amends for his own maladroitness, F'nor leaned across the table to kiss her on the lips.

He meant it as no more than a guerdon and was totally unprepared for the reaction in himself, in Brekke. Or for Canth's distant bugle.

His eyes never leaving Brekke's, F'nor rose slowly and circled the table. He slid beside her on the bench, pulling her against him with his good arm. Her head fell back on his shoulder and he bent to the incredible sweetness of her lips. Her body was soft and pliable, her arms went around him, pressing him to her with a total surrender to his virility that he had never before experienced. No matter how eager others had seemed, or gratified, there had never been such a total commitment to him. Such an innocence of . . .

Abruptly F'nor raised his head, looking deep into her eyes.

"You've never slept with T'bor." He stated it as a fact. "You've never slept with any man."

She hid her face in his shoulder, the pliancy of her body gone. He gently forced her head up.

"Why have you deliberately let it be assumed that you and T'bor . . ."

She was shaking her head slightly from side to side, her eyes concealing nothing, her face a mask of sorrow.

"To keep other men from you?" F'nor demanded, giving her a little shake. "Why? Whom are you keeping yourself for?"

He knew the answer before she spoke, knew it when she placed her finger on his lips to silence him. But he couldn't understand her sorrow. He'd been a fool but . . .

"I have loved you since the first day I saw you. You were so kind to us, yanked away from Craft and Hold, dazed because we'd been brought all the way here on Search for Wirenth. One of us would actually be a Weyrwoman. And you—you were all a dragonman should be, tall and handsome, so kind. I didn't know then—" and Brekke faltered. To F'nor's concern, tears filmed her eyes. "How *could* I know that only bronze dragons fly queens!"

F'nor held the weeping girl to his chest, his lips against her soft hair, her trembling hands folded in his. Yes, there was much about Brekke he could understand now.

"Dear girl," he said when her tears lessened, "is that why you refused N'ton?"

She nodded her head against his shoulder, unwilling to look at him.

"Then you're a silly clunch and deserve all the anguish you've put yourself through," he said, his teasing voice taking the sting from his words. He patted her shoulder and sighed exaggeratedly. "And craftbred as well. Have you taken in nothing you've been told about dragonfolk? Weyrwomen can't be bound by any commoner moralities. A Weyrwoman has to be subservient to her queen's needs, including mating with many riders if her queen is flown by different dragons. Most craft and holdbred girls envy such freedom . . ."

"Of that I'm all too aware," Brekke said and her body seemed to resent his touch.

"Does Wirenth object to me?"

"Oh, no," and Brekke looked startled. "I meant—oh, I don't know what I meant. I love Wirenth, but can't you understand? I'm *not* weyrbred. I don't have that kind of—of—wantonness in my nature. I'm—I'm inhibited. There! I said it. I am inhibited and I'm terrified that I'll inhibit Wirenth. I can't change all of me to conform to Weyr customs. I'm the way I am."

F'nor tried to soothe her. He wasn't sure now how to proceed, for this overwrought girl was a different creature entirely from the calm, serious, reliable Brekke he knew.

"No one wants or expects you to change completely. You wouldn't be our Brekke. But dragons don't criticize. Neither do their riders. Most queens tend to prefer one bronze above the others consistently . . ."

"You still don't understand." The accusation was a hopeless wail. "I never saw any man I wanted to—to have—" The word was an aspirated whisper. "Not that way. Not until I saw you. I don't want any other man to possess me. I'll freeze. I won't be able to draw Wirenth back. And I love her. I love her so and she'll be rising soon and I can't . . . I thought I'd be able to, but I know I'll . . ."

She tried to break away from him, but even with one arm the brown rider was stronger. Trapped, she began to cling to him with the strength of utter despair.

He rocked her gently against him, removing his arm from the sling so he could stroke her hair.

"You won't lose Wirenth. It's different when dragons mate, love. You're the dragon, too, caught up in emotions that have only one resolution." He held her tightly as she seemed to shrink with revulsion from him as well as the imminent event. He thought of the riders here at Southern, of T'bor, and he experienced a disgust of another sort. Those men, conditioned to respond to Kylara's exotic tastes, would brutalize this inexperienced child.

F'nor glanced round at the low couch and rose, Brekke in his arms. He started for the bed, halted, hearing voices beyond the clearing. Anyone might come.

Still holding her, he carried her out of the weyrhold, smothering her protest against his chest as she realized his intention. There was a place behind his weyrhold, beyond Canth's wallow, where the ferns grew sweet and thick, where they would be undisturbed.

He wanted to be gentle but, unaccountably, Brekke fought him. She pleaded with him, crying out wildly that they'd rouse the sleeping Wirenth. He wasn't gentle but he was thorough, and, in the end, Brekke astounded him with a surrender as passionate as if her dragon had been involved.

F'nor raised himself on his elbow, pushing the sweaty, fern-entangled hair from her closed eyes, pleased by the soft serenity of her expression; excessively pleased with himself. A man never really knew how a woman would respond in love. So much hinted at in play never materialized in practice.

But Brekke was as honest in love, as kind and generous, as wholesome as ever; in her innocent wholeheartedness more sensual than the most skilled partner he had ever enjoyed.

Her eyes opened, met his in a wondering stare for a long moment. With a moan, she turned her head, evading his scrutiny.

"Surely no regrets, Brekke?"

"Oh, F'nor, what will I do when Wirenth rises?"

F'nor began to curse then, steadily, hopelessly, as he cradled her now unresponsive body against him. He cursed the differences between Hold and Weyr, the throbbing wound in his arm that signalized the difference which existed even between dragonmen. He railed at the inescapable realization that what he loved most was insufficient to his need. He hated himself, aware that in his effort to help Brekke, he had compromised her values and was probably destroying her.

Instinctively his confused thoughts reached out to Canth, and he found himself trying to suppress that contact. Canth must never know his rider could fault him for not being a bronze.

I am as large as most bronzes, Canth said with unruffled equanimity. Almost as if he was surprised he had to mention the fact to his rider. *I am strong. Strong enough to outlast any bronze here.*

F'nor's exclamation roused Brekke.

"There's no reason Canth can't fly Wirenth. By the Shell, he could outfly any bronze here. And probably Orth, too, if he puts his mind to it."

"Canth fly Wirenth?"

"Why not?"

"But browns don't fly queens. Bronzes do."

F'nor hugged her fiercely, trying to impart his jubilation, his almost inarticulate joy and relief.

"The only reason browns haven't flown queens is that they're smaller. They don't have the stamina to last in a mating flight. But Canth's big. Canth's the biggest, strongest, fastest brown in Pern. Don't you see, Brekke?"

Her body uncurled. Hope was restoring color to her face, life to her green eyes.

"It's been done?"

F'nor shook his head impatiently. "It's time to discard custom that hampers. Why not this one?"

She permitted him to caress her but there was a shadow lingering in her eyes and a reluctance in her body.

"I want to, oh how I want to, F'nor, but I'm so scared. I'm scared to my bones."

He kissed her deeply, ruthlessly employing subtleties to arouse her. "Please, Brekke?"

"It can't be wrong to be happy, can it, F'nor?" she whispered, a shiver rippling along her body.

He kissed her again, using every trick learned from a hundred casual encounters to wed her to him, body, soul and mind, aware of Canth's enthusiastic endorsement.

Seething with fury, Kylara watched the men walk off and leave her, standing in the clearing. Her conflicting emotions made it impossible for her to retaliate suitably, but she'd make them both regret their words. She'd pay F'lar back for losing the lizard queen. She'd score T'bor for daring to reprimand her, the Weyrwoman of Southern, of the Telgar Bloodline, in the presence of F'lar. Oh, he'd regret that insult. They'd both regret it. She'd show them.

Her arm throbbed from the clawing and she cradled it against her, the pain acerbating her other complaints. Where was some numb-weed? Where was that Brekke? Where was everyone else at a time when the Weyr compound should be full of people? Was everyone avoiding her? Where was Brekke?

Feeding the lizard. I'm hungry, too, Prideth said so firmly that Kylara looked around in surprise at her queen.

"Your color isn't good," she said, her stream of mental vituperation deflected by the habit of concern for Prideth's well-being and the instinctive awareness that she must not alienate her dragon.

Well, she didn't want to have to look at Brekke's broad commoner face. She certainly didn't want to see a lizard. Not now. Horrible creatures, no gratitude. No real sensitivity or the thing would have *known* it was only being shown off. Prideth jumped them to the Feeding Ground and landed so smartly that Kylara gave a gasp of pain as her arm was jarred. Tears formed in her eyes. Prideth, too?

But Prideth gave a flying jump to the back of a fat, stupid herd-beast and began to feed with a savagery that fascinated Kylara out of her self-pity. The queen finished the beast with ravenous speed. She was upon a second buck and disemboweling it so voraciously that Kylara could not escape the fact that she had indeed been neglecting Prideth. She felt herself caught up in the hunger and vicariously dissipated her anger by imagining T'bor as the second buck, F'lar as the third, Lessa as the big wherry. By the time Prideth's hunger was sated, Kylara's mind was clear.

She took her queen back to the weyr and spent a long time sanding and brushing her hide until it lost all trace of dullness. Finally Prideth curled in a contented drowse on the sun-warmed rock and Kylara's guilt was absolved.

"Forgive me, Prideth. I didn't mean to neglect you. But they've slighted me so often. And a blow at me is a slam at your prestige, too. Soon they won't dare ignore us. And we won't stay immured in this dreary, underside Weyr. We'll have strong men and the most powerful bronzes begging us for favors. You'll be oiled and fed and scrubbed and scratched and pampered as you ought. You'll see. They'll regret their behavior."

Prideth's eyes were completely lidded now, and her breath came and went with a faint whistle. Kylara glanced at the bulging belly. She'd sleep a long time with that much to content her.

"I ought not to have let her gorge so," Kylara murmured, but there had been something so gratifying in the way Prideth tore into her meat; as if all indignities and affronts and discourtesy had leaked out of Kylara as blood from the slaughtered animals had seeped into the pasture grass.

Her arm began to hurt again. She'd removed the wher-hide tunic to groom Prideth, and sand and dust coated the new scabs. Suddenly Kylara felt filthy, disgustingly filthy with sand and dust and sweat. She was aware of fatigue, too. She'd bathe and eat, have Rannelly rub her well with sweet oil and cleansing sand. First, she'd get some numb-weed from little nurse-goody Brekke.

She came past the side window of Brekke's weyrhold and heard the murmur of a man's voice and the low delighted laughing response from Brekke. Kylara halted, astonished by the rippling quality of the girl's voice. She peered in, unobserved, because Brekke had eyes only for the dark head bent toward her.

F'nor! And Brekke?

The brown rider raised his hand slowly, stroked back a wayward strand of hair from Brekke's cheek with such loving tenderness that there was no doubt in Kylara's mind that they had only recently been lovers.

Kylara's half-forgotten anger burst into cold heat. Brekke and F'nor! When F'nor had repeatedly turned aside *her* favors? Brekke and F'nor indeed!

Because Kylara moved on, Canth did not tell his rider.

•• CHAPTER X ••

Early Morning in
Harpercrafthall at Fort Hold

Afternoon at Telgar Hold

Robinton, Masterharper of Pern, adjusted his tunic, the rich green pile of the fabric pleasing to the touch as well as the eye. He turned sideways, to check the fit of the tunic across his shoulders. Masterweaver Zurg had compensated for his tendency to slouch, so the hem did not hike up. The gilded belt and the knife were just the proper dress accouterments.

Robinton grimaced at his reflection. "Belt knives!" He smoothed his hair behind his ears, then stepped back to check the pants. Mastertanner Belesdan had surpassed himself. The fellis dye had turned the soft wher-hide into a deep green the same shade as the tunic. The boots were a shade darker. They fit snug to his calf and foot.

Green! Robinton grinned to himself. Neither Zurg nor Belesdan had been in favor of that shade, though it was easily obtainable. About time we shed another ridiculous superstition, Robinton thought.

He glanced out of his window, checking the sun's position. It was above the Fort range now. That meant midafternoon at Telgar Hold and the guests would be gathering. He'd been promised transport. T'ron of Fort Weyr had grudgingly acceded to that request, though it was a tradition of long standing that the Harper could request aid from any Weyr.

A dragon appeared in the northwest sky.

Robinton grabbed up his overcloak—the dress tunic would never keep out the full cold of *between*—his gloves and felted case that contained the best guitar. He'd hesitated about bringing it. Chad had a fine instrument at Telgar Hold, but fine wood and gut would not be chilled by those cold seconds of *between* as mere flesh would.

350

When he passed the window, he noticed a second dragon winging down, and was mildly surprised.

By the time he reached the small court of the Harpercrafthall, he
gave a snort of amusement. A third dragon had appeared from due
east.

Never around when you want 'em, though. Robinton sighed, for
it seemed the problems of the day had already begun, instead of waiting dutifully for him (as what trouble does?) at Telgar Hold, where
he'd expected it.

Green, blue—and ah-ha—bronze dragon wings in the early
morning sun.

"Sebell, Talmor, Brudegan, Tagetarl, into your fine rags. Hurry
or I'll skin you and use your lazy innards for strings," Robinton called
in a voice that projected into every room facing the Court.

Two heads popped out of an upper window of the apprentice
barracks, two more at the journeyman's Hold.

"Aye, sir." "Coming, sir." "In a moment!"

Yes, with four harpers of his own, and the three at Telgar Hold—
Sebell played the best bass line, not to mention Chad the Telgar Harper
improvising in the treble—they'd have a grand loud group. Robinton
tossed his overcloak to his shoulder, forgetting that the pile of the green
tunic might crush, and grinned sardonically at the wheeling dragons.
He half-expected them all to wink out again at the discovery of this
multiplicity.

He should pick the Telgar Weyr blue on the grounds that he
appeared first. However, the green dragon came from Fort Weyr, to
whom his Craft was weyrbound. Yet Benden Weyr did the honor of
sending a bronze. Perhaps I should take the first to land, though
they're all taking their time about it, he thought.

He stepped out of the Court quadrangle to the fields beyond,
since it was obvious that's where the beasts were landing.

The bronze landed last, which canceled that method of impartial
choice. The three riders met mid-field, some few dragonlengths from
the disputed passenger. Each man began arguing his claim at once.
When the bronze rider became the target of the other two, Robinton
felt obliged to intervene.

"He's weyrbound to Fort Weyr. We have the right," said the
green rider indignantly.

"He's guest of Telgar Hold. Lord Holder Larad himself
requested . . ."

The bronze rider (Robinton recognized him as N'ton, one of the
first non-weyrbred to Impress a dragon at Benden Weyr Turns ago)
appeared neither angry nor disconcerted.

"The good Masterharper will know the right of it," and N'ton
bowed graciously to Robinton.

The others gave him scarcely a glance but renewed their quarrel.

"Why, there's no problem at all," Robinton said in the firm, decisive tone he rarely employed and which was never contradicted.

The two wranglers fell silent and faced him, the one sullen, the other indignant.

"Still, it does the Craft honor that you vye to serve it," and Robinton accorded the two dissidents an ironic bow. "Fortunately, I have need of three beasts. I've four more harpers to transport to Telgar Hold to grace the happy occasion." He emphasized the adjective, noticing the glares that passed between blue and green riders. Young N'ton, though not weyrbred, had excellent manners.

"I was told to take *you*," the Fort Weyr man said in a sour voice.

"And took such joy of the assignment, it has made my morning merry," Robinton replied crisply. He saw the smug look on the blue rider's face. "And while I appreciate Weyrleader R'mart's thoughtfulness in spite of his recent—ah—problems at Telgar Hold, I shall ride the Benden Weyr dragon. For they do not grudge the Masterharper the prerogative."

His craftsmen came racing out of the Hall, riding cloaks askew on their shoulders, fitting their instruments in felt wrappings as they came. Robinton gave each a cursory glance as they came to a ragged line in front of him, breathless, flushed and, thank the Shell, happy. He nodded toward Sebell's pants, indicated that Talmor should adjust his twisted belt, approved Brudegan's immaculate appearance, and murmured that Tagetarl was to smooth his wild hair.

"We're ready, sirs," Robinton announced and, giving a curt bow of his head to the other riders, turned on his heel to follow N'ton.

"I've half a mind—" the green rider began.

"Obviously," Robinton cut, his voice as cold as *between* and as menacing as Thread. "Brudegan, Tagetarl, ride with him. Sebell, Talmor, on the green."

Robinton watched as Brudegan, with no expression on his face, gestured politely to the shorter, green rider to precede them. Of all men on Pern, harpers feared few. Any one deliberately antagonizing them for no cause found himself the butt of a satirical tune which would be played around the land.

There were no further protests. And Robinton was rather pleased to notice that N'ton gave no indication that there'd been any display of ill nature.

Robinton on N'ton's bronze arrived in the air, facing the cliff-palisade that was Telgar Hold. The swift river that had its source in the great striding eastern range of mountains had cut through the softer stone and made a deep incision that gradually widened until a series of high palisades flanked the green, wide Telgar valley. Telgar Hold was situated in one such soaring palisade, at the apex of a slightly triangular section of the cliffs. It faced south, with sides east and west and its hundred or so windows, on five distinct levels, must make pleasant and well-lit rooms. All had the heavy bronze shutters which marked Telgar Hold for a wealthy one.

Today the three cliff faces of Telgar Hold were brilliant with the pennants of every minor Hold which had ever aligned its Blood with theirs. The Great Court was festooned with hundreds of flowering branches and giant fellis blooms, so that the air was heavy with mingled fragrances and appetizing kitchen odors. Guests must have been arriving for hours, to judge by the mass of long-legged runners among the pastured herdbeasts. Every room in old Telgar Hold ought to be filled this night and Robinton was glad that his rank gave him a sure place. A little crowded perhaps because he'd brought four more harpers. They might be superfluous; every harper who could must have wangled his way in here today. Maybe it would be a happy occasion, after all.

I'll concentrate on positive, happy thoughts, Robinton mused to himself, coining Fandarel's phrase. "You'll be staying on, N'ton?"

The young man grinned back at the Harper, but there was a serious shadow in his eyes. "Lioth and I have a sweep to ride, Master Robinton," he said, leaning forward to slap his bronze affectionately on the neck. "But I did want to see Telgar Hold, so when Lord Asgenar asked me to oblige him by bringing you, I was glad of the chance."

"I, too," Robinton said in farewell, as he slid down the dragon's shoulder. "My thanks to you, Lioth, for a smooth journey."

The Harper has only to ask.

Startled, Robinton glanced up at N'ton, but the young man's head was turned toward a party of brightly garbed young women who were walking up from the pasture.

Robinton looked at Lioth, whose opalescent eye gleamed at him an instant. Then the dragon spread his great wings. Hastily Robinton backed away, still not positive he'd heard the dragon. Yet there was no other explanation. Well, this day was certainly unfolding surprises!

"Sir?" inquired Brudegan respectfully.

"Ah, yes, lads." He grinned at them. Talmor had never flown and the boy was a bit glassy in the eye. "Brudegan, you know the hall. Take them to the Harper's room so they'll know their way. And take my instrument, too. I'll not need it until the banquet. Then, lads, you're to mingle, play, talk, listen. You know the ditties I've been rehearsing. Use them. You've heard the drum messages. Utilize them. Brudegan, take Sebell with you, it's his first public performance. No, Sebell, you'd not be with us today if I'd no faith in your abilities. Talmor, watch that temper of yours. Tagetarl, wait until after the banquet to charm the girls. Remember, you'll be a full Harper too soon to jeopardize a good Holding. All of you, mind the distilled wines."

He left them so advised and went up the busy ramp into the Great Court, smiling and bowing to those he knew among the many Holders, Craftsmen and ladies passing to and fro.

Larad, Lord of Telgar Hold, resplendent in dark yellow, and the bridegroom Asgenar, Lord of Lemos, in a brilliant midnight blue, stood by the great metal doors to the Hold's Main Hall. The women of Telgar were in white with the exception of the Larad's half-sister, Famira, the bride. Her blond hair streamed to the hem of her traditional wedding dress of graduated shades of red.

Robinton stood for a moment to one side of the gate into the Court, slightly in the shadow of the right-hand tower, scanning the guests already making small groups around the decorated Courtyard. He spotted the Masterherdsman, Sograny, near the stable. The man oughtn't to look as if he smelled something distasteful. Probably not the vicinity, but his neighbors. Sograny disapproved of wasting time. Masterweaver Zurg and his nimble wife moved constantly from group to group. Robinton wondered if they were inspecting fabric and fit. Hard to tell, for Weaver Zurg and spouse nodded and beamed at everyone with good-natured impartiality.

Masterminer Nigot was deep in talk with Mastertanner Belesden and the Masterfarmer Andemon, while their women formed a close conversation knot to one side. Lord Corman of Keroon was apparently lecturing the nine young men ringing him: sons, foster and blood undoubtedly, since most of them bore the old man's nosy signature. They must be recently arrived for, at a signal from him, the boys all smartly turned on their heels and followed their parent, right up to the steps. Lord Raid of Benden was talking to his host and, seeing Corman approach, bowed and stepped away. Lord Sifer of Bitra gestured for Lord Raid to join him and a group of minor Holders conversing near the watchtower steps. Of the other Lord Holders, Groghe of Fort, Sangel of Boll, Meron of Nabol, Nessel of Crom, Robinton saw nothing. Dragons trumpeted on high and a half wing of them began to spiral down to the wide field where Robinton had landed. Bronzes, blues—ah, and five golden queens—came to rest briefly. Discharging their passengers, most of them leaped skyward again, toward the fire ridges above the Hold.

Robinton made his way hastily to his host then, before the newest arrivals swarmed up the ramp to the Great Court.

There was a hearty cheerfulness about Lord Larad's greeting that masked a deep inner anxiety. His eyes, blue and candid, restlessly scanned the Court. The Lord of Telgar was a handsome man though there was scant resemblance between him and his only full sibling, Kylara. Evidently if was Kylara who had inherited their sire's appetites. Just as well.

"Welcome, Master Harper, we all look forward to your entertaining songs," Lord Larad said, according the Harper a deep bow.

"We shall play in tune with the times and the occasion, Lord Larad," Robinton replied, grinning broadly at such bluntness. They both heard the ripple of music as the young harpers began to move among the guests.

The whoosh of great wings drew their eyes upward. The dragons flew across the sun, briefly shadowing the Court. All talk died for a moment, then renewed more loudly than before.

Robinton moved on, greeting Lord Larad's first lady and true love, for he had no others besides her. The young Lord of Telgar, at least, was constant.

"Lord Asgenar, my felicitations. Lady Famira, may I wish you all happiness, to have and to hold."

The girl blushed prettily, glancing shyly at Lord Asgenar. Her eyes were as blue as her half-brother's. She had her hand on Asgenar's arm, having known him a long time. Larad and Asgenar had been fosterlings at the Hold of Lord Corman of Keroon, though Larad had been elected earlier to his dignities than Asgenar. There'd be no problem with this wedding, although it remained for the Conclave of Lord Holders to ratify it, since the progeny of this marriage might one day Hold either Telgar or Lemos. A man cast his seed widely if he was a Lord Holder. He had many sons in the hope that one male of his Blood would train up strong enough to be acceptable to the Conclave, when the question of Succession arose. Not that that ancient custom was an scrupulously observed as it had been. The wise Lord extended fosterage to the Blooded children of other Lords, to gain support in Conclave as well as to insure his own progeny being well-fostered.

Robinton stepped quickly among the guests. To hear what he could, enter a conversation with an amusing story, climax another with a deft phrase. He helped himself to a handful of finger-sized meatrolls from the long tables set up near the kitchen entrance. He scooped up a mug of cider. They'd not sit to table until sunset. First the Lord Holders and the major Small Holders would have their Conclave. (He hoped that Chad had found a way for him to "attend" that meeting for he'd a notion that the discussion wouldn't be limited to the Bloodlines of Telgar and Lemos Holds.)

So he wandered, every perception tuned high, every nuance, shrug, laugh, gesture and frown weighed and measured. He observed the groupings, who shifted between the lines of region, craft and rank. When he realized he had seen nothing of the Mastersmith Fandarel or his Craft-second, Terry, or, indeed, any smithcrafters, he began to wonder. Had Fandarel's distance-writer been installed? He took a look down the side of the Hold and could see no posts as had been described to him. He chewed thoughtfully at a rough spot on his lower lip.

Voices and laughter seemed to have a strident edge. From his detached vantage point, he surveyed the Great Court, now so full it appeared as a moving carpet of solid bodies, here and there a tight knot of bent heads. As if—as if everyone were determined to enjoy themselves, frantically grasping pleasure . . .

Dragons trumpeted from the heights. Robinton grinned. They spoke in thirds, he noticed. Now, if a man could direct them—what an accompaniment to his Ballad.

"Good Masterharper, have you seen F'lar or Fandarel?" Lytol had come up to him, the young Lord Jaxom at his elbow.

"Not yet."

Lytol frowned, suggested pointedly that Jaxom look for the young Bloods of Telgar Hold and drew Robinton further from the nearest guests.

"How do you think the Lords will react to Lord Meron of Nabol?"

"React to Meron?" Robinton snorted derisively. "By ignoring him, of course. Not that his opinion would influence the Conclave . . ."

"I don't mean that. I mean his possession of a fire-lizard—" Lytol broke off as the Harper stared at him. "You didn't hear? The messenger went through Ruatha Hold yesterday, bound for Fort Hold and your Crafthall."

"He missed me or—was he free with his news?"

"To me, yes. I seem to attract confidences . . ."

"Fire-lizard? What about them? I used to spend hours trying to catch one. Never did. In fact I never heard of one being caught. How did Meron manage the trick?"

Lytol grimaced, the tic beginning in his cheek. "They can be Impressed. There always was that nursery tale that fire-lizards are the ancestors of dragons."

"And Meron of Nabol Impressed one?"

Lytol gave a mirthless laugh. "Unlikely, I grant you. The fire-lizards exhibit a woeful lack of taste. But you can rest assured that Meron of Nabol would not waste time on fire-lizards if they weren't of use to him."

Robinton considered this and then shrugged. "I don't think you need be concerned. But how did Nabol get one? How can they be Impressed? I thought that was strictly a draconic trait."

"How Lord Meron of Nabol acquired one is what bothers me the most," Lytol said, glowering. "That Southern Weyrwoman, Kylara, brought him a whole clutch of eggs. Of course, they lost most in the Hatching, but the few that survived are making quite a stir in Nabol Hold. The messenger had seen one, and he was all bright-eyed in the telling. 'A regular dragon in miniature,' he said, and he's all for trying his luck on the sandy beaches in Southern Boll and Fort from the gleam in his eye."

"'A regular dragon in miniature,' huh?" Robinton began to turn the significance of this around in his mind. He didn't like the angles he saw.

There wasn't a boy alive on Pern that hadn't at one time dreamed of suddenly becoming acceptable to dragonkind, of Impressing. Of having at his beck and call (little dreaming it was more the other way round) an immense creature, capable of going anywhere on Pern in a breath, of defeating all enemies with his flame-ridden breth (also fallacious as dragons never flamed anything but Thread and wouldn't knowlingly harm a human). Life at the mountaintop Weyrs assumed a glamor all out of proportion to reality, yet dragonmen were not stooped by the heavy labor of the fields, orchards and craft benches; they were straight and tall, dressed in beautifully tanned wher-hides, and seemed somehow superior. Very few boys could become Lord Holders, unless they were properly Blooded. But there was always that tantalizing possibility that a dragonrider might choose *you* to go to the Weyr for an Impression. So generations of boys had vainly tried to catch a fire-lizard, symbolic of that other yearning.

And a "regular miniature dragon" in the possession of a sly-faced underhanded malcontent like Meron of Nabol, who was sour about dragonmen anyway (with some justification in the matter of the Esvay valley against T'kul of the High Reaches Weyr), could be an embarrassment for F'lar at the least, and might disrupt their plans for the day at the worst.

"Well, if Kylara brought the fire-lizard eggs to Nabol Hold, F'lar will know," Robinton told the worried Lord Warder. "They keep pretty close tabs on that woman."

Lytol's glower deepened. "I hope so. Meron of Nabol will certainly let no chance pass to irritate or embarrass F'lar. Have you seen F'lar?"

They both glanced around, hopefully. Then Robinton caught sight of a familiar grizzled head, bobbing toward himself and the Warder.

"Speaking of Benden, here's old Lord Raid charging down on us. I've an idea what he wants and I will *not* sing that ancient lay about the Holders one more time. Excuse me, Lytol."

Robinton slipped into the milling guests, working as rapidly away from the Benden Lord Holder as possible. He happened to dislike Lord Raid's favorite ballad with a passion and, if Raid cornered him, he'd have no choice but to sing it. He felt no compunction about leaving Lytol exposed to Lord Raid's pompous manner. Lytol enjoyed an unusual status with the Lord Holders. They weren't certain how to treat a man who'd been a dragonrider, Weaverhallmaster, and was now

Lord Warder of a Ruatha prospering under his guidance. He could deal with Raid.

The Masterharper halted at a point where he could look up at the cliff, trying to spot Ramoth or Mnementh among the dragons lining the edge.

Fire-lizards? How was Meron going to use a fire-lizard? Unless it was *because* Kylara, a Weyrwoman, had given *him* one. Yes. That was guaranteed to sow dissension. Undoubtedly every Lord Holder here would want one, so as to be equal to Meron. There couldn't be enough eggs to go around. Meron would capitalize on forgotten yearnings, and chalk up one more irritation against dragonmen.

Robinton found that the meatrolls sat heavily in his stomach. Suddenly Brudegan detached himself from the crowd, bowing with a rueful grin to those he'd been serenading as if he were reluctantly answering his Master's summons.

"The undercurrent is something fierce," the journeyman said, pretending to tune his instrument. "Everyone's so determined to have a good time. Odd, too. It's not what they say, but how they say it that tips you off." The boy flushed as Robinton nodded approvingly. "For instance, they refer to 'that Weyrleader' meaning their own weyrbound leader. 'The Weyrleader' always means F'lar of Benden. 'The Weyrleader' had understood. 'The Weyrleader' had tried. 'She' means Lessa. 'Her' means their own Weyrwoman. Interesting?"

"Fascinating. What's the feeling about Threadfall?"

Brudegan bent his head to the gitar, twanged strings discordantly. He drew his hand across all eight in a dissonant chord that ran a chill down the Masterharper's spine. Then Brudegan turned away with a gay song.

Robinton wished that F'lar and Lessa would arrive. He did see D'ram of Ista Weyr talking earnestly to Igen's Weyrleader, G'narish. He liked that pair best of the Oldtimers, G'narish being young enough to change and D'ram essentially too honest to deny a truth when his nose was in it. Trouble was, he kept his nose inside Ista Weyr too much.

Neither man looked at ease, as much because there was an island of empty space around them—an obvious ostracization with the Court so crowded—as anything else. They greeted Robinton with grave relief.

"Such a happy occasion," he said and, when they reacted with surprise, he hurried on. "Have you heard from F'lar?"

"Should we? There's been more Thread?" G'narish asked, alarmed.

"Not that I know of."

"Have you seen T'ron or T'kul about? We just arrived."

"No, in fact, none of the western people seem to be here except Lord Warder Lytol of Ruatha."

D'ram clenched his teeth with an audible snap.

"R'mart of Telgar can't come," the Oldtimer said. "He took a bad scoring."

"I'd heard it was wicked at Crom Hold," Robinton murmured, sympathetically. "No way to predict it'd fall there at that time, either."

"I see Lord Nessel of Crom and his Holders are here in strength, though," D'ram said, his voice bitter.

"He could scarcely stay away without insulting Lord Larad. How bad were the Telgar Weyr's casualties? And if R'mart's out of action, who's leading?"

D'ram gave the Harper the distinct feeling that he'd asked an impertinent question, but G'narish answered easily.

"The wing-second, M'rek, took over but the Weyr is so badly understrength that D'ram and I talked it over and sent replacements. As it happens, we've enough weyrlings who've just started chewing stone so we're wing-full." G'narish glanced at the older dragonman as if he suddenly realized that he was discussing Weyr affairs with an outsider. He gave a shrug. "It makes more sense with Thread falling out of phase and the Crom Hold demoralized. We used to do it in the Oldtime when a Weyr was understrength. In fact, I flew with Benden one season as a weyrling."

"I'm certain that Crom and Telgar Holds will appreciate your cooperation, Weyrleaders," Robinton said. "Tell me, though, have you had any luck Impressing some fire-lizards? Igen and Ista ought to be good hunting grounds."

"Impressing? Fire-lizards?" D'ram snorted with as much incredulity as Robinton had expressed earlier.

"That'd be a trick," G'narish laughed. "Look, there's Ramoth and Mnementh now."

There was no mistaking the two beasts who were gliding to the fire heights. It was also unmistakable that the dragons already perched on the pinnacle moved aside to make room for them.

"Now, that's the first time—" G'narish muttered under his breath and stopped, because a sudden lull in the conversation had swept through the assembly, punctuated by audible hushings and scrapings as people turned to the Gate.

Robinton watched, with fond pride, as Lessa and F'lar mounted the steps to their hosts. They were both wearing the soft green of new leaves and the Harper wanted to applaud. However, he restrained himself and, signaling to the dragonmen, began to thread his way toward the new arrivals. Another dragon, closely followed by a bronze, swept in at dangerously low altitude. Gold wingtips showed above the outer wall of the Court and the wind from her backstrokes flung up dust, dirt and the skirts of the ladies nearest the Gate. There was a spate of screams and angry protests from those discommoded which settled into an ominous murmur.

Robinton, his height giving him an advantage, noticed Lord Larad hesitate in the act of bowing to Lessa. He saw Lord Asgenar and the ladies staring intently beyond. Irritated that he was missing something, Robinton pushed urgently on.

He broke through to the corner of the stairs, took the first four in two big strides and halted.

Resplendent in red, her golden hair unbound like a maiden's, Kylara approached the Hall entrance, her smile composed of pure malice, not pleasure. Her right hand rested on the arm of Lord Meron of Nabol Hold, whose red tunic was slightly too orange in cast to blend with hers. Such details Robinton remembered at another time. Now all he saw were the two fire-lizards, wings slightly extended for balance; a gold one on Kylara's left arm, a bronze on Meron's. "Regular miniature dragons," beautiful, evoking a feeling of envy and desire in the Harper. He swallowed hastily, firmly suppressing such unbecoming emotions.

The murmur grew as more people became aware of the newest arrivals.

"By the First Shell, they've got fire-lizards!" Lord Corman of Keroon Hold bellowed. He stepped out of the crowd into the aisle that had been opened to the Hall entrance, and stalked forward to have a good look.

The golden lizard screamed at his approach, and the little bronze hissed in warning. There was an irritatingly smug smirk on Meron's face.

"Did you know Meron had one?" D'ram demanded in a harsh whisper at the Harper's elbow.

Robinton raised a hand to still further questions.

"And here come Kylara of Southern and Lord Meron of Nabol Hold with living examples of this small token of our best wishes for the happy couple," F'lar's voice rang out.

Utter silence fell as he and Lessa presented felt-wrapped round bundles to Lord Asgenar and his bride, Lady Famira.

"They are just now hard," F'lar said in a loud voice that carried over the murmurings, "and must be kept in heated sands to crack, of course. They come to you through the generosity of one Toric, a seaholder at Southern Weyr, from a clutch he discovered only hours ago. Weyrleader T'bor brought them to me."

Robinton glanced back at Kylara. Her flushed face now matched Meron's tunic while *he* looked ready to kill. Lessa, smiling graciously, turned to Kylara.

"F'lar told me he'd seen your little pet . . . ."

"Pet nothing!" Kylara blazed with anger. "She ate Thread yesterday at High Reaches . . ."

What else she'd had to say was lost as her words, "ate Thread," "ate Thread," ricocheted back through the assembly. The raucous screams of the two lizards added cacophony and Kylara and Meron had all they could do to soothe their creatures. To Robinton it was plain that whatever effect Meron of Nabol had planned had been foiled. He was not the only Lord Holder to own "a regular miniature dragon."

Two minor Holders, from Nerat to judge by their devices, bore down on D'ram and G'narish.

"As you love your dragons, pretend you knew about the lizards," Robinton said in an urgent undertone to the two. D'ram started to protest but the anxious Holders closed in with a barrage of eager questions on how to acquire a fire lizard just like Meron's.

Recovering first, G'narish answered with more poise than Robinton thought he'd have. Pressing against the stone wall, the Harper inched his way up the stairs, to push in around the women clustered about Lord Asgenar, his lady Famira and F'lar.

"LORD HOLDERS, OF MAJOR AND MINOR DEGREE, PRESENT YOURSELVES FOR THE CONCLAVE," boomed out the Telgar Hold guard captain. A brass chorus of dragons echoed from the heights, satisfactorily stunning the guests into momentary silence.

The Captain repeated his summons and abjured the crowd to make room.

Lord Asgenar handed Famira his egg, murmuring something in her ear and pointing into the Hall. He stepped aside, gesturing for Lessa and Famira to pass inside. As well they did, for the Holders were now massing up the stairs. Robinton tried to signal F'lar but the dragonman was struggling toward Kylara, against the current. She was arguing heatedly with Meron who gave an angry shrug, left her and began shoving roughly into the Hall, past more polite Holders.

There was another exodus, Robinton noticed, of Craftmasters who congregated near the kitchen.

F'lar needs the Harper.

Robinton glanced around him, wondering who had spoken, amazed that so soft a voice had reached him over the gabbling. He was alerted by a dissonant twang of strings and, turning his head unerringly toward the sound, spotted Brudegan up on the sentry walk with Chad, from the look of him. Had the resident Harper of Telgar Hold found a way to overhear the Conclave?

As Robinton changed his direction for the tower steps, a dragonrider confronted him.

"F'lar wants you, Masterharper."

Robinton hesitated, looking back to the two harpers who were urgently signaling him to hurry.

Lessa listens.

"Did you speak?" Robinton demanded of the rider.

"Yes, sir. F'lar wants you to join him. It's important."

The Harper looked toward the dragons and Mnementh dipped his head up and down. Robinton shook his, trying to cope with another of this day's astonishing shocks. A piercing whistle reached him from above.

He pursed his lips and gave the "go-ahead" sequence, adding in its different tempo the tune for "report later."

Brudegan strummed an "understand" chord with which Chad apparently disagreed. Marks for the journeyman, Robinton thought, and whistled the strident trill for "comply." He wished the harpers had as flexible a code as the one he'd developed for the Smith—and where was he?

That was one man easily spotted in a crowd but, as Robinton followed the dragonrider, he didn't see a smithcrafter anywhere. Of course, the impact of the distance-writer would be anticlimactic to the introduction of the lizards. Robinton felt sorry for the Smith, quietly perfecting an ingenious means of communication only to have it overshadowed by Threadeating miniature dragons. Creatures who could be Impressed by non-weyrfolk. The average Pernese would be far more struck by a draconic substitute than by any mechanical miracle.

The dragonrider had led him to the watchtower to the right of the Gate. When Robinton looked back over his left shoulder, Brudegan and Chad were no longer visible on the sentry walk.

The lower floor of the tower was a single large room, the stone stairs which rose to the right side of the sentry walk were on the far wall. Sleeping furs were piled in one corner in readiness for such guests as might have to be lodged there that night. Two slit windows, facing each other on the long sides of the room, gave little light. G'narish, the Igen Weyrleader, was unshielding the glow basket in the ceiling as the Harper entered. Kylara was standing right under it, glaring furiously at T'bor.

"Yes, I went to Nabol. My queen lizard was there. And well I did, for Prideth saw Thread sign across the High Reaches Range!" She had everyone's attention now. Her eyes gleamed, her chin lifted and, Robinton noted, the shrewish rasp left her voice. Kylara was a fine-looking female, but there was a hard ruthlessness about her that repelled him.

"I flew instantly to T'kul." Her face twisted with anger. "He's no dragonman! He refused to believe me. Me! As if *any* Weyrwoman wouldn't know the sign when she sees it. I doubt he's even bothered with sweepriders. He kept harping on the fact that Thread had fallen six days ago at Tillek Hold and couldn't be falling this soon at High

Reaches. So I told him about Falls in the western swamp and north Lemos Hold, and he still wouldn't believe me."

"Did the Weyr turn out in time?" F'lar interrupted her coldly.

"Of course," and Kylara drew herself up, her posture tightening the dress against her full-bosomed body. "*I* had Prideth sound the alarm." Her smile was malicious. "T'kul had to act. A queen can't lie. And there isn't a male dragon alive that will disobey one!"

F'lar inhaled sharply, gritting his teeth. T'kul of the High Reaches was a taciturn, cynical, tired man. However justified Kylara's actions were, her methods lacked diplomacy. And she was contemporary weyrfolk. Oh, well, T'kul was a lost cause anyhow. F'lar glanced obliquely at D'ram and G'narish, to see what effect T'kul's behavior had on them. Surely now . . . They looked strained.

"You're a good Weyrwoman, Kylara, and *you* did well. Very well," F'lar said with such conviction that she began to preen and her smile was a smirk of self-satisfaction. Then she stared at him.

"Well, what are you going to do about T'kul? We can't permit him to endanger the world with that Oldtime attitude of his."

F'lar waited, half-hoping that D'ram might speak up. If just one of the Oldtimers . . .

"It seems that the dragonriders had better call a conclave, too," he said at length, aware of the tapping of Kylara's foot and the eyes on him. "T'ron of Fort Weyr must hear of this. And perhaps we'd all better go on to Telgar Weyr for R'mart's opinion."

"Opinion?" demanded Kylara, infuriated by this apparent evasion. "You ought to ride out of here now, confront T'kul with flagrant negligence and . . ."

"And what, Kylara?" F'lar asked when she broke off.

"And—well—there must be something you can do!"

For a situation that had never before arisen? F'lar looked at D'ram and G'narish.

"You've go to *do* something," she insisted, swinging toward the other men.

"The Weyrs are traditionally autonomous . . ."

"A fine excuse to hide behind, D'ram . . ."

"There can be no hiding now," D'ram went on, his voice rough, his expression bleak. "Something will have to be done. By *all* of us. When T'ron comes."

More temporizing? F'lar wondered. "Kylara," he said aloud, "you mentioned your lizard eating Thread." There was a lot more to be discussed in this matter than T'kul's incredible behavior. "And may I inquire how you knew your lizard had returned to Nabol?"

"Prideth told me. She Hatched there so she returned to Nabol Hold when you frightened her at Southern."

"You had her at High Reaches Weyr, though?"

"No. I told you. I saw Thread over the High Reach Range and went to T'kul. First! Once I'd roused the Weyr, I realized that there might have been Thread over Nabol so I went to check."

"And told Meron about the premature Threadfall?"

"Of course."

"Then?"

"I took the lizard back with me. I didn't want to lose her again." When F'lar ignored that jibe, she went on. "I picked up a flame thrower, so naturally I flew with Merika's wing. Scant thanks I got for my help from that Weyrwoman."

She was telling the truth, F'lar realized, for her emotions were very much in evidence.

"When my lizard saw Thread falling, she seemed to go mad. I couldn't control her. She flew right at a patch and—ate it."

"Did you give her firestone?" D'ram asked, his eyes keen with real interest.

"I didn't have any. Besides, I want her to mate," and Kylara's smile had a very odd twist to it as she stroked the lizard's back. "She'll burrow, too," she added, extolling her creature's abilities. "A ground crewman said he'd seen her enter one. Of course I didn't know that until later."

"Is the High Reaches Hold clear of Thread now?"

Kylara shrugged indifferently. "If they aren't, you'll hear."

"How long did Threadfall continue after you saw it? Were you able to determine the leading Edge when you flew over to Nabol?"

"It lasted about three hours. Under, I'd say. That is, from the time the wings *finally* got there." She gave a condescending smile. "As to the leading Edge, *I'd* say it must have been high up in the Range," and she dared them to dispute it, hurrying on when no one did. "It'd fall on bare rock and snow there. I did sweep the Nabol side but Prideth saw no sign."

"You did extremely well, Kylara, and we are exceedingly grateful to you," F'lar said, and the other Leaders endorsed his commendation so firmly that Kylara smiled expansively, turning from one man to another, her eyes glittering with self-appreciation.

"We've had five Falls now," F'lar went on gravely, glancing at the other Leaders, trying to see how far he could continue in his move to consolidate himself as their spokesman. T'kul's defection had shaken D'ram badly. What T'ron's reaction would be, F'lar didn't try to guess, but if the Fort Weyrleader found himself in a minority of one against the other four Leaders, would he decide to act against T'kul, even if it did mean siding with F'lar? "At Tillek Hold, eight days ago; Upper Crom Hold, five; high Lemos Hold north, three; Southern far west, two; and now High Reaches Hold. Undoubtedly Thread fell in the Western Sea but there is no question that Falls are more frequent and increasing in scope. No point on Pern is safe. No Weyr can afford to relax its vigil to a traditional six-day margin." He smiled grimly. "Tradition!"

D'ram looked about to argue, but F'lar caught and held his eyes until the man slowly nodded.

"That's easy to say, but what are you going to do about T'kul? Or T'ron?" Kylara had just realized no one was paying her any attention. "He's just as bad. He refuses to admit times have changed. Even when Mardra deliberately . . ."

There was a brisk knock on the door but it swung open instantly, to admit the giant frame of Fandarel.

"I was told you were here, F'lar, and we are ready."

F'lar scrubbed at his face, regretting the diversion.

"The Lord Holders are in Conclave," he began and the Smith grunted acknowledgment, "and there has been another unexpected development . . ."

Fandarel nodded toward the fire-lizard on Kylara's arm. "I was told about them. There are many ways to fight Thread, of course, but not all are efficient. The merits of such creatures remain to be seen."

"The merits—" Kylara began, ready to explode with outrage.

Robinton the Harper was beside her, whispering in her ear.

Grateful to Robinton, F'lar turned to attend the Smith, who had stepped to the door, obviously wanting the dragonmen to accompany him. F'lar was reluctant to see the distance-writer. It wouldn't receive the attention it deserved from the Lords or the people or the riders. The distance-writer made so much more sense in this emergency than unreliable lizards. And yet, if they did eat Thread . . .

He paused on the threshold, looking back toward Kylara and the Harper. Robinton looked directly at him.

Almost as if the Harper read his mind, F'lar saw him smile winningly down at Kylara (though F'lar knew the man detested her).

"F'lar, do you think it's wise for Kylara to go out into that mob? They'll scare the lizard," said the Harper.

"But I'm hungry—" Kylara protested. "And there's music —" as the nearby thrum of a gitar was plainly audible.

"That sounds like Tagetarl," Robinton said, with a bright grin. "I'll call him in and send you choice victuals from the kitchen. Far better than struggling with that noisome rabble out there, I assure you." He handed her to a chair with great courtesy, motioning behind his back to F'lar to leave.

As they stepped out into the bright sunlight, the crowd swirling noisily around them, F'lar saw the merry-faced young man, gitar in hand, who had answered the Harper's whistle. Undoubtedly Robinton would be free to join them in a few moments if he read matters rightly.

The young journeyman would definitely appeal to Kylara's—ah—nature.

Fandarel had set up his equipment in the far corner of the Court, where the outside wall abutted the cliff-Hold, a dragonlength from the stairs. Three men were perched atop the wall, carefully handing something down to the group working on the apparatus. As the Weyrleaders followed Fandarel's swath through the press of bodies (the fellis blossom fragrance had long since given way to other odors), F'lar was the object of many sidelong glances and broken conversations.

"You watch, you'll see," a young man in the colors of a minor Hold was saying in a carrying voice. "Those dragonmen won't let *us* near a clutch . . ."

"The Lord Holders, you mean," another said. "Fancy anything trusting that Nabolese. What? Oh. Great shells!"

Now, if everyone on Pern could possess a fire-lizard, wondered F'lar, would that really solve the problem?

More dragons in the sky. He glanced up and recognized T'ron's Fidranth and Mardra's queen, Loranth. He sighed. He wanted to see what Fandarel planned with his distance-writer before he had to tackle T'ron.

"Mnementh, what is happening at the Conclave?"

Talk. They await the other two Lord Holders.

F'lar tried to see if the Fort Weyrleaders had brought the missing Lords Groghe of Fort and Sangel of South Boll. Those two wouldn't take kindly to a Conclave adjudicating without them. But if Lord Groghe had heard about High Reaches Hold . . .

F'lar suppressed a shudder, trying to smile with sincere apologies as he edged past a group of small Holders who apparently couldn't see him. As if recognizing the smithcrafters as neutral, the Weyrwomen had gathered in a wary group to the right of the mass of equipment which Fandarel's people were setting up. They were pretending great interest, but even G'narish's pretty Weyrmate, Nadira, looked troubled and she was a sweet-tempered lady. Bedella, representing Telgar Weyr, looked completely confused but she wasn't bright.

Just then Mardra broke through the guests, demanding to know what was going on. Had T'kul and Merika arrived? Where were their Hosts? Modern Holds were certainly lacking in plain courtesy. She didn't expect traditional ceremonies any more but . . .

At that moment, F'lar heard the clang of steel against steel and saw Lord Groghe of Fort pounding the Hall door with his knife handle, his heavy featured face suffused with anger. The slighter, frosty Sangel, Lord of South Boll, was scowling darkly behind him. The door opened a slit, widened slightly to allow the two Lord Holders to enter. Judging by their expression, it would take time and more talk before these two were pacified.

"How much more needs to be done?" asked F'lar as he joined the Smith. He tried to remember how the distance-writer had looked in the Hall. This collection of tubes and wire seemed much too big.

"We need only attach this wire so," Fandarel replied, his huge fingers deftly fitting word to action, "and that one, here. Now. I place the arm in position over the roll and we shall send out a message to the Hall to be sure all is in order." Fandarel beamed down at his instrument as fondly as any queen over a golden egg.

F'lar felt someone rather too close behind him and looked irritably over his shoulder to see Robinton's intent face. The Harper gave him an abstracted smile and nodded for him to pay attention.

The Smith was delicately tapping out a code, the irregular lengths of red lines appearing on the gray paper as the needle moved.

"'Hook-up completed,'" Robinton murmured in F'lar's ear. "'Efficiently and on time.'" Robinton chuckled through that translation. "'Stand by.' That's the long and the short of it."

The Smith turned the switch to the receive position and looked expectantly at F'lar. At that moment, Mnementh gave a squall from the heights. He and all the dragons began to extend their wings. The mass movement blotted out the sun which was lowering over the Telgar Cliffs and sent shadows over the guests to still their chatter.

Groghe told the Lords that T'ron has found a distance-viewer at Fort. He has seen the Red Star through it. They are upset. Be warned, said Mnementh.

The doors of the Great Hall swung wide and the Lord Holders came striding out. One look at Lord Groghe's face confirmed Mnementh's report. The Lord Holders ranged themselves on the steps, in a solid front against the Dragonmen gathered in the corner. Lord Groghe had lifted his arm, pointed it accusingly at F'lar, when a disconcerting hiss split the pregnant silence.

"Look!" the Smith bellowed and all eyes followed his hand as the distance-writer began receiving a message.

"'Igen Hold reports Thread falling. Transmission broken off midsentence.'"

Robinton reported the sounds as they were printed, his voice growing hoarser and less confident with each word.

"What nonsense is this?" Lord Groghe demanded, his florid face brick-red as attention was diverted from his proposed announcement. "Thread fell in the High Reaches at noon yesterday. How could it fall at Igen Hold this evening? What the Shells is that contraption?"

"I don't understand," G'narish protested loudly, staring up at Lord Laudey of Igen Hold who stood in stunned horror on the steps. "I've sweepriders on constant patrol . . ."

The dragons bugled on the heights just as a green burst into the air over the court, causing the crowd to scream and duck, scurrying to the walls for safety.

Threads fall at Igen southwest, came the message loud and clear. To be echoed by the dragonriders in the court.

"Where are you going, F'lar?" bellowed Lord Groghe as the Benden Weyrleader followed G'narish's plunge to the Gate. The air was full of dragon wings now, the screams of frightened women counterpointing the curses of men.

"To fight Thread at Igen, of course," F'lar shouted back.

"Igen's my problem," G'narish cried, halting and wheeling toward F'lar, but there was gratitude, not rebuke in his surprised face.

"G'narish, wait! Where in Igen?" Lord Laudey was demanding. He pushed past the infuriated Lord Groghe to catch up with his Weyrleader.

"And Ista? Is the island in danger?" Lord Warbret wanted to know.

"We'll go and see," D'ram reassured him, taking his arm and urging him toward the Gate.

"Since when has Benden Weyr concerned itself with Igen and Ista?" T'ron planted himself squarely in F'lar's way. The menace in his voice carried to the steps of the Hall. His belligerent stance, obstructing the way to the Gate, halted them all. "And rushed to Nabol's aid?"

F'lar returned his scowl. "Thread falls, dragonman. Igen and Ista fly winglight, with riders helping at Telgar Weyr. Should we feast when others fight?"

"Let Ista and Igen fend for themselves!"

Ramoth screamed on high. The other queens answered her. What she challenged no one knew, but she suddenly winked out. F'lar had no attention to spare to wonder that she'd gone *between* without Lessa riding for he saw T'ron's hand on his belt knife.

"We can settle our difference of opinion later, T'ron. In private! Thread falls . . ."

The bronzes had begun to land outside the Gate, juggling to let as many land close as possible.

The green rider from Igen had directed his beast to perch on the Gate. He was repeatedly yelling his message to the static, tense group below.

T'ron would not stop. "Thread falls, huh, F'lar? Noble Benden to the rescue! And it's not *Benden's* concern." He let out a raucous shout of derisive contempt.

"Enough, man!" D'ram stepped up to pull T'ron aside. He gestured sharply at the silent spectators.

But T'ron ignored the warning and shook him off so violently that the heavy-set D'ram staggered.

"I've had enough of Benden! Benden's notions! Benden's superiority! Benden's altruism! *And* Benden's Weyrleader . . ."

With that last snarled insult, T'ron launched himself toward F'lar, his drawn knife raised for a slashing blow.

As the ragged gasp of fear swept through the ranks of spectators, F'lar held his ground until there was no chance T'ron could change his direction. Then he ducked under the blade, yanking his own out of its ornamental sheath.

It was a new knife, a gift from Lessa. It had cut neither meat nor bread and must now be christened with the blood of a man. For this duel was to the death and its outcome could well decide the fate of Pern.

F'lar had sunk to a semicrouch, flexing his fingers around the hilt, testing its balance. Too much depended on a single belt knife, a half-hand shorter than the blade in his opponent's fingers. T'ron had the reach of him and the added advantage of being in wher-hide riding gear whereas F'lar wore flimsy cloth. His eyes never left T'ron as he faced the older man. F'lar was aware of the hot sun on the back of his neck, the hard stones under his feet, of the deathly hush of the great Court, of the smells of bruised fellis blooms, spilled wines and fried food, of sweat—and fear.

T'ron moved forward, amazingly light on his feet for a man of his size and age. F'lar let him come, pivoted as T'ron angled off to his left, a circling movement designed to place him off balance—a transparent maneuver. F'lar felt a quick surge of relief; if this were the measure of T'ron's combat strategy . . .

With a bound the Oldtimer was on him, knife miraculously transferred to his left hand with a motion too quick to follow, his right arm coming over and down in a blow that struck F'lar's wrist as he threw himself backward to avoid, by the thickness of a hair, the hissing stroke of the foot-long blade. He backed, his arm half-numbed, aware of the shock that coursed through him like a drenching of icy water.

For a man blind with anger, T'ron was a shade too controlled for F'lar's liking. What possessed the man to pick a quarrel—here and now? For T'ron had pushed this fight, deliberatley baiting F'lar with that specious quibble. D'ram and G'narish had been relieved at his offer of help. So T'ron had *wanted* to fight. Why? Then suddenly, F'lar knew. T'ron had heard about T'kul's flagrant negligence and knew that the other Oldtimers could not ignore or obliquely condone it. Not with F'lar of Benden likely to insist that T'kul step aside as Weyrleader of High Reaches. If T'ron could kill F'lar, he could control the others. And F'lar's public death would leave the modern Lord Holders without a sympathetic Weyrleader. The domination of Weyrs over Hold and Craft would continue unchallenged, and unchanged.

T'ron moved in, pressing the attack. F'lar backed, watching the center of the Oldtimer's wherhide-cased chest. Not the eyes, not the knife hand. The chest! That was the spot that telegraphed the next move most accurately. The words of old C'gan, the weyrling instructor, seven Turns dead, seemed to echo in F'lar's mind. Only C'gan had never thought his training would prevent one Weyrleader from killing another, to save Pern in a duel before half the world.

F'lar shook his head sharply, rejecting the angry line his thoughts were taking. This wasn't the way to survive, not with the odds against him.

He saw T'ron's arm move suddenly, swayed back in automatic evasion, saw the opening, lunged . . .

The watchers gasped as the sound of torn fabric was clearly heard. The pain at his waist had been such a quick stab that F'lar had all but decided T'ron's swipe was only a scratch when a wave of nausea swept him.

"Good try. But you're just not fast enough, Oldtimer!" F'lar heard himself saying; felt his lips stretch into a smile he was far from feeling. He kept to the crouch, the belt pressing against his waist, but the torn fabric dangled, jerking as he breathed.

T'ron threw him a half-puzzled look, his eyes raking him, pausing at the hanging rag, flicking to the knife blade in his hand. It was clean, unstained. A second realization crossed T'ron's face, even as he lunged again; F'lar knew that T'ron was shaken by the apparent failure of an attack he had counted on to injure badly.

F'lar pulled to one side, almost contemptuously avoiding the flashing blade, and then charged in with a series of lightning feints of his own, to test the Oldtimer's reflexes and agility. There was no doubt T'ron needed to finish him off quickly—and F'lar hadn't much time either, he knew, as he ignored the hot agony in his midriff.

"Yes, Oldtimer," he said, forcing himself to breathe easily, keeping his words light, mocking. "Benden Weyr concerns itself with Ista and Igen. And the Holds of Nabol, and Crom, and Telgar, because Benden dragonmen have not forgotten that Thread burns anything and anyone it touches, Weyr and commoner alike. And if Benden Weyr has to stand alone against the fall of Thread, it will."

He flung himself at T'ron, stabbing at the horny leather tunic, praying the knife was sharp enough to pierce it. He spun aside barely in time, the effort causing him to gasp in pain. Yet he made himself dance outside T'ron's reach, made himself grin at the other's sweaty, exertion-reddened face.

"Not fast enough, are you, T'ron? To kill Benden. Or muster for a Fall."

T'ron's breathing was ragged, a hoarse rasping. He came on, his knife arm lower. F'lar backed, keeping to a wary crouch, wondering if it was sweat he felt trickling down his belly, or blood. If T'ron noticed . . .

"What's wrong, T'ron? All that rich food and easy living beginning to tell? Or is it age, T'ron? Age creeping up on you. You're four hundred and forty-five Turns old, you know. You can't move fast enough any more, with the times, or against me."

T'ron closed in, a guttural roar bursting from him. He sprang, with a semblance of his old vitality, aiming for the throat. F'lar's knife hand flashed up, struck the attacking wrist aside, slashed downward at the other's neck, where the wher-hide tunic had parted. A dragon screamed. T'ron's right fist caught him below the belt. Agony lashed through him. He doubled over the man's arm. Someone screamed a warning. With an unexpected reserve of energy, F'lar somehow managed to pull himself sharply up from that vulnerable position. His head rocked from the impact against T'ron's descending knife, but it was miraculously deflected. Both hands on the hilt of his decorative blade, F'lar rammed it through wher-hide until it grated against the man's ribs.

He staggered free, saw T'ron waver, his eyes bulging with shock, saw him step back, the jeweled hilt standing out beneath his ribs. T'ron's mouth worked soundlessly. He fell heavily to his knees, then sagged slowly sideways to the stones.

The tableau held for what seemed hours to F'lar, desperately sucking breath into his bruised body, forcing himself to keep to his feet for he could not, *could not* collapse.

"Benden's young, Fort. It's our Turn. Now!" he managed to say. "And there's Thread falling at Igen." He swung himself around, facing the staring mass of eyes and mouths. "There's Thread falling at Igen!"

He pivoted back, aware that he couldn't fight in a torn dress tunic. T'ron had on wher-hide. He let himself down heavily on one knee and began to tug at T'ron's belt, ignoring the blood that oozed out around the knife.

Someone screamed and beat at his hand. It was Mardra.

"You've killed him. Isn't that enough? Leave him alone!"

F'lar stared up at her, frowning.

"He's not dead, Fidranth hasn't gone *between*." It made him feel stronger somehow to know he hadn't killed the man. "Get wine, someone. Call the physician!"

He got the belt loose and was pulling at the right sleeve when other hands began to help.

"I need it to fight in," he muttered. A clean cloth was waved in his direction. He grabbed it and, holding his breath, jerked loose the knife. He looked at it a second and then cast it from him. It skittered across the stone, everyone jumping from its path. Someone handed him the tunic. He got up, struggling into it. T'ron was a heavier man;

the tunic was too big. He was belting it tightly to him when he became aware again of the hushed, awed audience. He looked at the blur of expectant faces.

"Well? Do you support Benden?" he cried.

There was a further moment of stunned silence. The crowd's multihead turned to the stairs where the Lord Holders stood.

"Those who don't had better hide deep in their Holds," cried Lord Larad of Telgar, stepping down on a level with Lord Groghe and Lord Sangel, his hand on his knife belt, his manner challenging.

"The Smiths support Benden Weyr!" Fandarel boomed out.

"The Harpers do!" Robinton's baritone was answered by Chad's tenor from the sentry walk.

"The Miners!"

"The Weavers!"

"The Tanners!"

The Lord Holders began to call out their names, loudly, as if by volume they could redeem themselves. A cheer rose from the guests to fall almost instantly to a hush as F'lar turned slowly to the other Weyrleaders.

"Ista!" D'ram's cry was a fierce, almost defiant hiss, overtaken by G'narish's exultant "Igen" and T'bor's enthusiastic "Southern!"

"What can we do?" cried Lord Asgenar, striding to F'lar. "Can Lemos runners and groundmen help Igen Hold now?"

F'lar lost his immobility, tightened the belt one further notch, hoping the stricture would dull the pain.

"It's your wedding day, man. Enjoy what you can of it. D'ram, we'll follow you. Ramoth's already called up the Benden wings. T'bor, bring up the Southern fighters. *Every* man and woman who can fit on the dragons!"

He was asking for more than complete mobilization of the fighters and T'bor hesitated.

"Lessa," for she had her arms around him now. He pushed them gently to one side. "Assist Mardra. Robinton, I need your help. Let it be known," and he raised his voice, harsh and steely enough to be heard throughout the listening Court. "Let it be known," and he stared down at Mardra, "that any of Fort Weyr who do not care to follow Benden's lead must go to Southern." He looked away before she could protest. "And that applies to any craftsman, Lord Holder or commoner, as well as dragonfolk. There isn't much Thread in Southern to worry you. And your indifference to a common menace will not endanger others."

Lessa was trying to undo his belt. He caught her hands tightly, ignoring her gasp as his grip hurt.

"Where was Thread seen?" he yelled up to the Igen rider still perched atop the Gate Wall.

"South!" The man's response was an anguished appeal. "Across the bay from Keroon Hold. Across the water."

"How *long* ago?"

"I'll take you there and then!"

The ripple of cheering grew as it spread back, as people were reminded that the Weyrs would go *between* time itself and catch Thread, erasing the interval of time lost in the duel.

Dragonriders were moving toward beasts who were impatiently keening outside the walls. Wher-hide tunics were being thrust at riders in dress clothes. Firestone sacks appeared and flame throwers were issued. Dragons ducked to accept riders, hopping awkwardly out of the way, to launch themselves skyward. The Igen green hovered aloft, joined by D'ram and his Weyrwoman Fanna, waiting for Mnementh.

"You can't come, love," F'lar told Lessa, confused that she was following him out to Mnementh. She could handle Mardra. She'd have to. He couldn't be everywhere at once.

"Not till you've had this numbweed." She glared up at him as fiercely as Mardra had and fumbled at his belt again. "You won't last if you don't. And Mnementh won't take you up until I do."

F'lar stared at her, saw Mnementh's great eye gleaming at him and knew she meant it.

"But—he wouldn't—" he stammered.

"Oh, wouldn't he?" flashed Lessa, but she had the belt loose, and he gasped as he felt the cold of the salve on the burning lips of the wound. "I can't keep you from going. You've got to, I know. But I can keep you from killing yourself with such heroics." He heard something rip, saw her tearing a sleeve from her new gown into bandage-length strips. "Well, I guess they're right when they say green is an unlucky color. You certainly don't get to wear it long."

She quickly pressed the material against him, his wound already numbing. Deftly overlapping the outsized tunic, she tightened the wide belt to hold the bandage securely in place.

"Now, go. It's shallow but long. Get the Threadfall under control and get back. I'll do my part here." She gave his hand a final grip and, picking up her skirts, half-ran up the ramp, as if she were too busy to watch him leave.

She's worried. She's proud. Let's go.

As Mnementh wheeled smartly upward, F'lar heard the sound of music, gitars accompanying a ragged chorus. How like the Harper to have the appropriate music for this occasion, he thought.

> *Drummer, beat, and piper, blow.*
> *Harper, strike, and soldier, go.*
> *Free the flame and sear the grasses*
> *Till the dawning Red Star passes.*

Odd, thought F'lar, four hours later, as he and Mnementh returned to Telgar with the wings from Igen, it was over Telgar, seven Turns ago, that the massed Weyrs flew against the second Fall of Thread.

He stifled keen regret at the recollection of that triumphant day when the six Weyrs had been solidly in accord. And yet, the duel at Telgar Hold today had been as inevitable as Lessa's flight backward in time to bring up the Oldtimers. There was a subtle symmetry, a balance of good and bad, a fateful compensation. (His side ached. He suppressed pain and fatigue. Mnementh would catch it and then he'd catch it from Lessa. Fine thing when a man's dragon acted nursy. But the effects of that half-kettle of numbweed Lessa'd slathered on him were wearing off.) He watched as the wings circled to land. All the riders had been bidden back to Telgar.

So many things were coming back to their starting point: from fire-lizards to dragons, a circle encompassing who knows how many thousands of Turns, to the inner circle of the Old Weyrs and Benden's resurgence.

He hoped T'ron would live; he'd enough on his conscience. Though it might be better if T'ron . . . He refused to consider that, in spite of the fact that he knew it would avoid another problem. And yet, if Thread could fall in Southern to be eaten by those grubs . . .

He wanted very much to see that distance-viewer T'ron had discovered. He groaned with a mental distress. Fandarel! How could he face him? That distance-writer *had* worked. It had relayed a very crucial message—faster than dragon wings! No fault of the Smith's that his finely extruded wire could be severed by hot Thread. Undoubtedly he would overcome that flaw in an efficient way—unless he'd thrown up his hands at the idea, what with being presented with a powerful, fully operative distance-viewer to compound the day's insults. Of all the problems undoubtedly awaiting him, he dreaded Fandarel's reproach the most.

Below, dragonriders streamed into the Court illumined by hundreds of glow baskets, to be met and absorbed into the throng of guests. The aroma of roasted meats and succulent vegetables drifted to him on the night air, reminding him that hunger depresses any man's spirits. He could hear laughter, shouts, music. Lord Asgenar's wedding day would never be forgotten!

That Asgenar! Allied to Larad, a fosterling of Corman's, he'd be of enormous assistance in executing what F'lar saw must be done among the Holder Lords.

Then he spotted the tiny figure in the gateway. Lessa! He told Mnementh to land.

About time, the bronze grumbled.

F'lar slapped his neck affectionately. The beast had known perfectly well why they'd been hovering. A man needed a few minutes to digest chaos and restore order to his thinking before he plunged into more confusions.

Mnementh agreed as he landed smoothly. He craned his neck around, his great eyes gleaming affectionately at his rider.

"Don't worry about me, Mnementh!" F'lar murmured in gratitude and love, stroking the soft muzzle. There was a faint odor of firestone and smoke though they'd done little flaming. "Are you hungry?"

Not yet. Telgar feeds enough tonight. Mnementh launched himself toward the fire ridge above the Hold, where the perching dragons made black, regular crags against the darkening sky, their jeweled eyes gleaming down on the festal activities.

F'lar laughed aloud at Mnementh's consideration. It was true that Lord Larad was stinting nothing, though his guest list had multiplied four-fold. Supplies had been flown in but Telgar Hold bore the brunt of it.

Lessa approached him with such slow steps that he wondered if something else had happened. He couldn't see her face in the shadow but as she slipped into step beside him, he realized that she'd been respecting his mood. Her hand reached up to caress his cheek, lingering on the healing Thread score. She wouldn't let him bend to kiss her.

"Come, love, I've fresh clothes and bandages for you."

"Mnementh's been telling on me?"

She nodded, still unusually subdued for Lessa.

"What's wrong?"

"Nothing," she assured him hastily, smiling. "Ramoth said you were thinking hard."

He squeezed her and the gesture pulled the muscles, making him wince.

"You're a trial to me," she said with mock exasperation and led him into the tower room.

"Kylara came back, didn't she?"

"Oh, yes," and there was an edge to Lessa's voice as she added, "she and Meron are as inseparable as their lizards."

She'd had a standing tub brought in, the water steaming invitingly. She insisted on bathing him while she reported what had happened while he'd fought Thread. He didn't argue, it was too pleasant to relax under her ministrations, though her gentle hands sometimes reminded him of other occasions and . . .

T'ron had been taken directly to Southern, swathed in heavy felt. Mardra had contested F'lar's authority to exile them but her protests fell on the deaf and determined front of Robinton, Larad, Fandarel, Lords Sangel and Groghe. They'd all accompanied Lessa and Kylara when Mardra was escorted back to Fort. Mardra had been certain she'd only to appeal to her weyrfolk to ensure her position as Weyrwoman. When she discovered that her arrogance and shrewishness had robbed her of all but a few adherents, she'd retired meekly to Southern with them.

"We nearly had a fight between Kylara and Mardra but Robinton intervened. Kylara was proclaiming herself Fort Weyrwoman."

F'lar groaned.

"Don't worry," Lessa assured him, briskly kneading the tight muscles across his shoulders. "She changed her mind directly she learned that T'kul and his riders were leaving the High Reaches Weyr. It's more logical for T'bor and the Southerners to take over that Weyr than Fort since most of the Fort riders are staying."

"That puts Kylara too near Nabol for my peace of mind."

"Yes, but that leaves the way clear for P'zar, Roth's rider, to take over as Fort Weyrleader. He's not strong but he's well-liked and it won't upset the Fort people as much. They're relieved to be free of both T'ron and Mardra but we oughtn't to press our luck too far."

"N'ton'd be a good Wing-second there."

"I thought of him so I asked P'zar if he'd object and he didn't."

F'lar shook his head at her tactics, then hissed, because she was loosening the old, dried numbweed.

"I'm not so sure but what I'd prefer the physician—" she began.

"No!"

"He'd be discreet but I'll warn you, all the dragons know."

He stared at her in surprise. "I thought it odd there were so many dragons shadowing me and Mnementh. I don't think we went *between* more than twice."

"The dragons appreciate you, bronze rider," Lessa said tartly, encircling him with clean, soft bandages.

"The Oldtimers, too?"

"Most of them. And more of their riders than I'd estimated. Only twenty riders and women followed Mardra, you know, from Fort. Of course," and she grimaced, "most of T'kul's people went. The fourteen who stayed are young riders, Impressed since the Weyr came forward. So there'll be enough at Southern . . . ."

"Southern is no longer our concern."

She was in the act of handing him the fresh tunic and hesitated, the fabric gathered up in her hands. He took it from her, pulling on the sleeves, ducking his head into the opening, giving her time to absorb his dictum.

She sat slowly down on the bench, her forehead creased with a slight, worried frown.

He took her hands and kissed them. When she still did not speak, he stroked the hair which had escaped the braids.

"We have to make the break clean, Lessa. They can do no harm there to any but themselves. Some may decide to come back."

"But they can perpetuate their grievances . . ."

"Lessa, how many queens went?"

"Loranth, the Weyr queen at High Reaches and the other two . . . Oh!"

"Yes. All old queens, well past their prime. I doubt Loranth will rise more than once. The clutches at High Reaches have produced only one queen since they came forward. And the young queen, Segrith, stayed, didn't she, with Pilgra?"

Lessa nodded and suddenly her face cleared. She eyed him with growing exasperation. "Anyone would think you've been planning this for Turns."

"Then anyone could call me a triple fool for underestimating T'ron, closing my mind to the facts in front of me and defying fortune. What's the mood among Holders and crafters?"

"Relief," she said, rolling her eyes. "I admit the laughter has a slightly hysterical tinge, but Lytol and Robinton were right. Pern will follow Benden . . ."

"Yes, until my first mistake!"

She grinned mischievously at him, waggling a finger under his nose. "Ah-ha, but you're not allowed to make mistakes, Benden. Not while . . ."

He caught her hand, pulling her into the crook of his arm, disregarding the stabbing pain at his waist for the triumph of her instant response, the surrender in her slender body. "Not while I have *you*." The words came out in a whisper, and because he couldn't express his gratitude to her, his pride in her, his joy of her any other way, he sought her lips, held them in a long, passionate kiss.

She gave a languorous sigh when he finally released her. He laughed down at her closed eyes, kissing them, too. She struggled to a sitting position and, with another reluctant sigh, rose determinedly to her feet.

"Yes, Pern will follow you, and your loyal advisers will keep you from making mistakes, but I do hope you've an answer for pop-eyed Old Lord Groghe!"

"Answer for Groghe?"

"Yes," and she gave him a stern look, "though I'm not surprised you've forgotten. He was going to demand that the dragonmen of Pern go directly to the Red Star and put an end to Thread forever."

F'lar got slowly to his feet.

"I've always said that you solve one problem and five more appear from *between*."

"Well, I think we've contrived to keep Groghe away from you

tonight, but we promised to have a joint meeting of Hold and Craft at Benden Weyr tomorrow morning."

"That's a blessing."

In the act of opening the door, he hesitated and groaned again.

"Isn't the numbweed helping?"

"Not me. It's Fandarel. Between fire lizards, Threads and T'ron, I can't face him."

"Oh, him!" Lessa pulled the door open, grinning up at her Weyr-mate. "He's already deep in plans to bury, coat or thicken those ungrateful wires. He's planning installations with every Lord Holder and Craft. Wansor's dancing like a sun-crazed wherry to get his hands on the distance-viewer, all the time wailing that he needn't've dismantled the first apparatus." She tucked her arm in his, lengthening her stride to match his. "The man who's really put out is Robinton."

"Robinton?"

"Yes. He'd composed the most marvelous ballad and teaching songs and how there's no reason to play them."

Whether Lessa had deliberately saved that until now, F'lar didn't know, but they crossed the courtyard, laughing, though it hurt his side.

Their passage would have been noted anyhow, but their smiling faces subtley reassured the diners seated at the makeshift tables about the yard. And suddenly F'lar felt there was indeed something to celebrate.

·· CHAPTER XI ··

Early Morning at Benden Weyr

"I wish you'd give me fair warning the next time you rearrange the social and political structure of this planet," F'nor told his half-brother when he strode into the queen's weyr at Benden the next morning. There wasn't, of course, a trace of resentment on his tanned, grinning face. "Who's where now?"

"T'bor is Weyrleader at the High Reaches with Kylara as Weyrwoman . . ."

"Kylara at High Reaches?" F'nor looked dubious but F'lar waved aside his half-born protest.

"Yes, there are disadvantages to that, of course. All but fourteen of the folk at High Reaches Weyr went with T'kul and Merika. Most of the Fort Weyr people wanted to stay . . ."

F'nor chuckled nastily. "Bet that was hard for Mardra to swallow." He looked expectantly at Lessa, knowing how often his Weyrwoman had mastered resentment and indigantion at Mardra's hands. Lessa returned his gaze with polite unconcern.

"So P'zar is acting Weyrleader until a queen rises . . ."

"Any chance of making that an open flight for any bronze?"

"That is my intention," F'lar replied. "However, I think the biggest of the modern bronzes had better be conspicuous by their absence."

"Then why have you assigned N'ton there as Wing-second?" demanded Lessa in surprise.

F'lar grinned at his Weyrmate. "Because by the time a Fort queen rises in flight, N'ton will be known and well-liked by the Fort Weyrfolk and they won't mind. He'll be considered a Fort rider, not a Benden replacement."

Lessa wrinkled her nose. "*He* doesn't have much choice at Fort Weyr."

"*He* is quite capable of taking care of himself," F'lar replied with a wicked grin.

"Well, you seem to have arranged everything to your satisfaction," F'nor remarked. "I, however, resent having been yanked out of Southern. I'd spotted a very promising clutch of fire-lizard eggs in a certain Southern cove. Note quite hard enough to move with impunity. If you had held off a few more days, I'd—" He broke off, sliding into the chair Lessa motioned him to. "Say, F'lar, what's the matter with you? You been time-*betweening* or something?"

"No, he's been knifed between his top and bottom," Lessa answered with a sour glance at her Weyrmate. "And it is with exceptional difficulty that I can keep him in a chair. He belongs in a bed."

F'lar waved her recriminations aside good-humoredly.

"If you're—" F'nor half-rose, his face concerned.

"If you're—" mocked F'lar, his look indicating a growing irritation with his disability and their protectiveness.

F'nor laughed, reseating himself. "And Brekke said I was a cantankerous patient. Ha! How bad is it? I heard various tales about that duel, well embroidered already, but not that you'd been clipped. Must it always be belt knives—for our Blood? And the other man armed with a wherry-skewer?"

"And dressed in wher-hide," Lessa added.

"Look, F'lar, Brekke has pronounced me fit to fly *between*," and F'nor flexed his arm, fully but carefully. "I can appreciate your wanting to keep quiet about your injury, so I'll do all your popping about."

F'lar chuckled at his half-brother's eagerness. "Back a-neck and ready to go, huh? Well, resume your responsibilities then. They've changed."

"Noticeably, O exalted one."

F'lar frowned at that and brushed his forelock back irritably.

"Not that much. Did you see T'kul when he arrived from High Reaches at Southern?"

"No, nor did I want to. I *heard* him." F'nor's right hand clenched. "The fighting wings had already gone to join you at Igen for the Threadfall. T'kul ordered everyone, including the wounded, out of Southern in an hour's time. What they couldn't pack and take, he confiscated. He made it clear that the southern continent was his to have and hold. That his sweepriders were challenging any dragon and would flame them down like Thread if they didn't get the proper response. Some of those Oldtimer dragons are stupid enough to do it, too." F'nor paused. "You know, I've been noticing lately . . ."

"Did the Fort Weyr people arrive?"

"Yes, and Brekke checked T'ron to be sure he'd survived the trip." F'nor scowled.

"He'll live?"

"Yes, but . . ."

"Good. Now, I rather suspected that T'kul would react in that fashion. To be sure we've all of Igen, Ista and Southern Boll as breeding ground for fire lizards, but I want you to get Manora to rig you something for those other lizard eggs you found and bring them back here. We need every one we can find. Where's your little queen? They go back to their first feeding place, you know . . ."

"Grall? She's with Canth, of course. She heard Ramoth grumbling on the Hatching Ground."

"Hmm, yes. Fortunately, those eggs'll hatch soon."

"Going to invite all Pern's notables as you did before the Old-timers got stuffy?"

"Yes," F'lar replied so emphatically that F'nor pretended alarm. "That courtesy did more good than harm. It'll be standard procedure at all the Weyrs now."

"And you've talked the Leaders into assigning riders to Hold and Hall?" F'nor's eyes gleamed when F'lar nodded.

"Can you slip through whatever patrol T'kul has mounted in Southern?" F'lar asked.

"No problem. There isn't a bronze there that Canth can't outfly. Which reminds me . . ."

"Good. I've two errands for you. Pick up those fire-lizard eggs and, do you remember the coordinates for the Threadfall in the western swamp?"

"Of course, but I wanted to ask you . . ."

"You saw the grub life in the soil there?"

"Yes . . ."

"Ask Manora for a tightly covered pot. I want you to bring me back as many of those grubs as you can. Not a pleasant job, I know, but I can't go myself and I don't want this—ah—project discussed."

"Grubs? A project?"

Mnementh bellowed a welcome.

"I'll explain later," F'lar said, gesturing toward the weyr entrance.

F'nor shrugged as he rose. "I'll fly the hazard, O inscrutable one!" Then he laughed as F'lar glared at him in angry reproach. "Sorry. Like the rest of Pern—the north, that is—I trust you." He gave them both a jaunty salute and left.

"The day F'nor doesn't tease you I'll start to worry," Lessa said, encircling his neck with her arms. She laid her cheek against his for an instant. "It's T'bor," she added, moving away just as the new High Reaches Weyrleader strode in.

The man looked as if he hadn't slept enough but he carried his shoulders back and his head high which made the Benden Weyrleader more aware of the worried and wary expression on his face.

"Kylara's—" F'lar began, remembering that she and Meron had been gabbling together all the last night.

"Not Kylara. It's that T'kul who thought himself such a great Weyrleader," T'bor said with utter disgust. "As soon as we brought our people up from Southern, I had the wings do a sweep check, really more to familiarize themselves with the coordinates than anything else. By the first Egg, I don't like seeing anyone run from dragonmen. Run. And hide!" T'bor sat down, automatically taking the cup of *klah* Lessa handed him. "There wasn't a watch fire or a watchman. But plenty of burn sign. I don't see how that much Thread could have got through. Not even if smokeless weyrlings were riding the sweep. So I dropped down to Tillek Hold and asked to see Lord Oterel." T'bor gave a low whistle. "That was some greeting I got, I want to tell you. I nearly had an arrow through my belly before I convinced the guard captain that I wasn't T'kul. That I was T'bor and there'd been a change of Leaders at the Weyr."

T'bor took a deep breath. "It took time to calm Lord Holder Oterel down to the point where I could tell him what had happened. And it seemed to me," and the Southerner looked nervously first at Lessa and then at F'lar, "that the only way to restore his confidence was to leave him a dragon. So—I left him a bronze and stationed two greens in those minor Holds along the Bay. I also left weyrlings at vantage heights along the Tillek Hold range. Then I asked Lord Oterel to accompany me to Lord Bargen's Hold at High Reaches. I'd a good idea I might not get past *his* guard at all. Now, we'd six eggs left over from that clutch Toric of the Seahold unearthed and so—I gave two each to the Lords and two to the Master-fisherman. It seemed the only thing to do. They'd heard Lord Meron had one—at Nabol Hold." T'bor straightened his shoulders as if to endure F'lar's opprobrium.

"You did the right thing, T'bor," F'lar told him heartily. "You did exactly the right thing. You couldn't have done better!"

"To assign riders to a Hold and a Craft?"

"There'll be riders in all Holds and Crafts before the morning's over," F'lar grinned at him.

"And D'ram and G'narish haven't objected?" T'bor glanced at Lessa, incredulous.

"Well," Lessa began, and was saved from answering by the arrival of the other Weyrleaders.

D'ram, G'narish and the Wing-second from Telgar Weyr entered first, with P'zar, the acting Weyrleader from Fort, very close behind them. The Telgar Weyr Wing-second introduced himself as M'rek, Zigeth's rider. He was a lanky, mournful-looking man, with sandy hair, about F'lar's age. As they settled themselves at the big table, F'lar tried to read D'ram's mood. He was the crucial one still, the oldest of the remaining Oldtimers and, if he'd cooled down from the stimulus of yesterday's tumultuous events and had changed his mind after sleeping, the proposal F'lar was about to suggest might die a-hatching. F'lar stretched his long legs under the table, trying to make himself comfortable.

"I asked you here early because we had little chance to talk last night. M'rek, how's R'mart?"

"He rests easily at Telgar Hold, thanks to the riders from Ista and Igen." M'rek nodded gravely to D'ram and K'dor.

"How many at Telgar Weyr wish to go south?"

"About ten, but they're old riders. Do more harm than good, feeding nonsense to the weyrlings. Speaking of nonsense, Bedella came back from Telgar Hold with some mighty confusing stories. About us going to the Red Star and fire-lizards and talking wires. I told her to keep quiet. Telgar Weyr's in no shape to listen to that kind of rumor."

D'ram snorted and F'lar looked at him quickly, but the Istan leader's head was turned toward M'rek. F'lar caught Lessa's eye and nodded imperceptibly.

"There *was* talk about an expedition to the Red Star," F'lar replied in a casual tone. Apprehension made the Telgar Weyr man's face more mournful than ever. "But there're more immediate undertakings." F'lar straightened cautiously. He couldn't get comfortable. "And the Lord Holders and other craftsmen will be here soon to discuss them. D'ram, tell me frankly, do you object to placing riders in Holds and Crafthalls while we can't pattern Thread—that is, until we can find another reliable form of quick communication?"

"No, F'lar, I've no objections," the Istan Weyrleader replied, slowly, not looking at anyone. "After yesterday—" He stopped and, turning his head, looked at F'lar with troubled eyes. "Yesterday, I think I finally realized just how big Pern is and how narrow a man can get, worrying so much about what he ought to have, forgetting what he's got. And what he's got to do. Times have changed. I can't say I like it. Pern had got so big—and we Oldtimers kept trying to make it small again because, I guess, we were a little scared at all that had happened. Remember it took us just four days to come forward four hundred Turns. That's too much time—too much to sink into a man's thinking." D'ram was nodding his head in unconscious emphasis. "I think we've clung to the old ways because everything we saw, from those great, huge hour-long sweeps of forests to hundreds and hundreds of new Holds and Crafthalls was familiar and yet—so different. T'ron was a good man, F'lar. I don't say I knew him well. None of us ever really got to know each other, you know, keeping to our Weyrs mostly and resting between Threadfalls. But all dragonmen are—are dragonmen. For a dragonman to go to *kill* another one—" D'ram shook his head slowly from side to side. "You could've killed *him*." D'ram looked F'lar straight in the eye. "You didn't. You fought Thread over Igen Hold. And don't think I didn't know T'ron's knife got you."

F'lar began to relax.

"Nearly made two of me, in fact."

D'ram gave another one of his snorts but the slight smile on his face as he leaned back in his chair indicated his approval of F'lar.

Mnementh remarked to his rider that everyone was arriving at once. A bigger ledge was needed. F'lar swore softly to himself. He'd counted on more time. He couldn't jeopardize the fragile new accord with D'ram by springing distasteful innovations on the man.

"I don't believe the Weyrs can remain autonomous these days," F'lar said, discarding all the ringing, smooth words he'd been rehearsing. "We nearly lost Pern seven Turns ago because dragonmen lost touch with the rest of the world; we've seen what happens when dragonman loses touch with dragonman. We need open mating flights, the exchange of bronzes and queens between Weyrs to strengthen Blood and improve the breed. We need to rotate the wings so riders get to know each other's Weyrs and territories. A man grows stale, careless, riding over ground he knows too well. We need public Impressions . . ."

They could all hear the rumble of greetings and the scuffling of heavy boots in the corridor.

"Ista Weyr followed Benden Weyr yesterday," D'ram interrupted him, his slow smile reaching his dark eyes. "But have a care which traditions you overset. Some cannot be discarded with impunity . . ."

They rose then as Lord Holders and Craftmasters strode into the weyr. Lord Asgenar, Mastersmith Fandarel and his wood Craftmaster, Bendarek, were first; Lord Oterel of Tillek Hold and Meron, Lord Holder of Nabol, his fire lizard squawking on his arm, arrived together, but Lord Oterel immediately sought Fandarel. A restless, eager atmosphere began to build, palpable with questions unanswered the previous evening. As soon as most were assembled, F'lar led the way into the Council Room. No sooner had the Weyrleaders ranged themselves behind him, facing the gathering of Lords and Craftsmen, than Larad, Lord of Telgar Hold, rose.

"Weyrleader, have you established where the next Thread is likely to fall?"

"Where you've evidently placed it, Lord Larad, on the western plains of Telgar Hold and Ruatha Hold." F'lar nodded toward Lord Warder Lytol of Ruatha. "Probably later today. It's early hours now in that part of the country and we don't intend to hold you here long . . ."

"And how long will we have riders assigned us?" asked Lord Corman of Keroon, staring pointedly at D'ram on F'lar's left.

"Until every Hold and Craft has an efficient communications system."

"I'll need men," Mastersmith Fandarel rumbled from his cramped position in the far corner. "Do you all really want those flame throwers you've been plaguing me for?"

"Not if the dragonmen *come* when we call." It was Lord Sangel of Boll Hold who answered, his face grim, his voice bitter.

"Is Telgar Weyr prepared to ride today?" Lord Larad went on, still holding the floor.

M'rek, the Telgar Weyr Wing-second, rose, glanced hesitantly at F'lar cleared his throat and then nodded.

"High Reaches Weyr will fly with Telgar riders!" T'bor said.

"And Ista!" D'ram added.

The unexpected unanimity sent a murmurous ripple through the meeting, as Lord Larad sat down.

"Will we have to burn the forests?" Lord Asgenar of Lemos rose to his feet. The quiet question was the plea of a proud man.

"Dragonriders burn Thread, not wood," F'lar replied calmly but there was a ring in his voice. "There are enough dragonriders," and he gestured to the Weyrleaders on either side of him, "to protect Pern's forests . . ."

"That's not what's needed most, Benden, and you know it," Lord Groghe of Fort shouted as he rose to his feet, his eyes bulging. "I say, go after Thread on the Red Star itself. Enough time's been wasted. You keep saying your dragons'll go anywhere, anywhen you tell 'em to."

"A dragon's got to know where he's going first, man," G'narish, the Igen Leader, protested, jumping up excitedly.

"Don't put me off, young man! You can *see* the Red Star, plain as my fist," and Lord Groghe thrust out his closed hand like a weapon, "in that distance-viewer! Go to the source. Go to the source!"

D'ram was on his feet beside G'narish now, adding his angry arguments to the confusion. A dragon roared so loudly that all were deafened for a moment.

"If that is the desire of the Lords and Craftsmen," F'lar said, "then we shall mount an expedition to fly on the morrow." He knew D'ram and G'narish had turned to stare at him, dumbfounded. He saw Lord Groghe bristle suspiciously, but he had the attention of the entire room. He spoke quickly, clearly. "You've seen the Red Star, Lord Groghe? Could you describe the land masses to me? Would you estimate that we had to clear as large an area as, say, the northern continent? D'ram, would you agree that it takes about thirty-six hours to fly straight across? More? Hmmm. Tip-to-tip sweeps would be most effective since

we couldn't count on ground-crew support. That would mean dragonweights of firestone. Masterminer, I'll need to know exactly what
supplies you have processed for use. Benden Weyr keeps about five
dragonweights on hand at all times, the other Weyrs about the same,
so we'd probably need all you've got. And every flame thrower on the
continent. Now, dragonmen, I admit we don't know if we can traverse
such a distance without harm to ourselves and the dragons. I assume
that since Thread survives on this planet, we can exist on that one.
However . . ."

"Enough!" Groghe of Fort Hold bellowed, his face flushed, his
eyes protruding form their sockets.

F'lar met Groghe's eyes steadily so that the choleric Lord Holder
would realize that he was not being mocked; that F'lar was in earnest.

"To be at all effective, Lord Groghe, such an undertaking would
leave Pern totally unprotected. I could not in conscience order such
an expedition now that I see how much is involved. I hope you will
agree that it is far more important, at this time, to secure what we
have." Better to risk Groghe's pride if necessary to defect that premature ambition. He couldn't afford to evade an issue that could become a convenient rallying cry for the disaffected. "I'd want to get a
good look at the Red Star before I took such a leap, Lord Groghe. And
the other Leaders would too. I can promise you that once we are able
to distinguish some jumping coordinates acceptable to the dragons,
we can send a volunteer group to explore. I've often wondered why
no one has gone before now. Or, if they have, what happened." He
had dropped his voice on those last words and there wasn't a sound
in the Chamber for a long moment.

The fire-lizard on Lord Meron's arm squawked nervously, causing
an instant, violent reaction from every man.

"Probably that Record deteriorated, too," F'lar said, raising his
voice to a level audible above the restless scraping and throat-clearing.
"Lord Groghe, Fort is the oldest of the Holds. Is there a chance that
your back corridors, too, hide treasures we can use?"

Groghe's reply was a curt nod of his head. He seated himself
abruptly, staring straight ahead. F'lar wondered if he had alienated
the man beyond reconciliation.

"I don't think I'd ever fully appreciated the enormity of such a
venture," Corman of Keroon Hold remarked in a thoughtful drawl.

"One jump ahead of us, again, Benden?" asked Larad of Telgar
Hold with a rueful grin.

"I shouldn't say that, Lord Larad," F'lar replied. "The destruction
of all Thread as its source has been a favorite preoccupation of dragonmen Turn after Turn. I know how much territory one Weyr can
cover, for instance; how much firestone is used by a Weyr in a Fall's
span. Naturally we," and he gestured to the other Leaders, "would

have information unavailable to you just as you could tell *us* how many guests you can feed at a banquet." That elicited a chuckle from many.

"Seven Turns ago, I called you together to prepare to defend Pern against its ancient scourge. Desperate measures were in order if we were to survive. We are in nowhere as difficult a condition as we were seven Turns ago but we have all been guilty of misunderstandings which have deflected us from the important concern. We have no time to waste in assigning guilt of awarding compensation. We are still at the mercy of Thread though we are better equipped to deal with it.

"Once before we found answers in old Records, in the helpful recollections of Masterweaver Zurg, Masterfarmer Andemon, Masterharper Robinton, and the efficiencies of Mastersmith Fandarel. You know what we've found in abandoned rooms at Benden and Fort Weyrs—objects made long Turns ago when we had not lost certain skills and techniques.

"Frankly," and F'lar grinned suddenly, "I'd rather rely on skills and techniques we, in our Turn, right now, can develop."

There was an unexpected ripple of assent to that.

"I speak of the skill of working together, the technique of crossing the arbitrary lines of land, craft and status, because we must learn more from each other than the simple fact that none of us can stand alone and survive!"

He couldn't go on because half the men were on their feet, suddenly cheering. D'ram was pulling at his sleeve, G'narish was arguing with the Telgar Weyr Second, whose expression was grievously undecided. F'lar got a glimpse of Groghe's face before someone stood in the way. Fort's Lord, too, was plainly anxious but that was better than overt antagonism. Robinton caught his eye and smiled broad encouragement. So F'lar had no choice but to let them unwind. They might as well infect each other with enthusiasm—probably with more effect than his best-chosen arguments. He looked around for Lessa and saw her slipping toward the hallway where she stopped, evidently warned of a late arrival.

It was F'nor who appeared in the entrance.

"I've fire-lizard eggs," he shouted. "Fire-lizard eggs," and he pushed into the room, an aisle opening for him straight to the Council Table.

There was silence as he carefully placed his cumbersome feltwrapped burden down and glanced triumphantly around the room.

"Stolen from under T'kul's nose. Thirty-two of them!"

"Well, Benden," Sangel of Southern Boll demanded in the taut hush, "who gets preference here?"

F'lar affected surprise. "Why, Lord Sangel, that is for you," and his gesture swept the room impartially, "to decide."

Clearly that had not been expected.

"We will, of course, teach you what we know of them, guide you in their training. They are more than pets or ornaments," and he nodded toward Meron who bristled, so suspicious of attention that his bronze hissed and restlessly fanned his wings. "Lord Asgenar, you've two lizard eggs already. I can trust you to be impartial. That is, if the Lords share my opinion."

As soon as they fell to arguing, F'lar left the Council Room. There was so much more to do this morning but he'd do it the better for a little break. And the eggs would occupy the Lords and Craftsmen. They wouldn't notice his absence.

•• CHAPTER XII ••

❦

Morning at Benden Weyr

Predawn at High Reaches Weyr

As soon as he could, F'nor left the Council Room in search of F'lar. He retrieved the pot of revolting grubs which he'd left in a shadowed recess of the weyr corridor.

He's in his quarters, Canth told his rider.

"What does Mnementh say of F'lar?"

There was a pause and F'nor found himself wondering if dragons spoke among themselves as men spoke to them.

Mnementh is not worried about him.

F'nor caught the faintest emphasis on the pronoun and was about to question Canth further when little Grall swooped, on whirring wings, to his shoulder. She wrapped her tail around his neck and rubbed against his cheek adoringly.

"Getting braver, little one?" F'nor added approving thoughts to the humor of his voice.

There was a suggestion of smug satisfaction about Grall as she flipped her wings tightly to her back and sunk her talons into the heavy padding Brekke had attached to the left tunic shoulder for that purpose. The lizards preferred a shoulder to a forearm perch.

F'lar emerged from the sleeping room, his face lighting with eagerness as he realized F'nor was alone and awaiting him.

"You've the grubs? Good. Come."

"Now, wait a minute," F'nor protested, catching F'lar by the shoulder as the Weyrleader began to move toward the outer ledge.

"Come! Before we're seen." They got down the stairs without being intercepted and F'lar directed F'nor toward the newly opened entrance by the Hatching Ground. "The lizards were parceled out fairly?" he asked, grinning as Grall tucked herself as close to F'nor's ear as she could when they passed the Ground entrance.

F'nor chuckled. "Groghe took over, as you probably guessed he would. The Lord Holders of Ista and Igen, Warbret and Laudey, magnanimously disqualified themselves on the grounds that their Holds were more likely to have eggs, but Lord Sangel of Boll took a pair. Lytol didn't!"

F'lar sighed, shaking his head regretfully.

"I didn't think he would but I'd hoped he'd try. Not a substitute for Larth, his dead brown, but—well . . ."

They were in the brightly lit, newly cleaned corridor now, which F'nor hadn't seen. Involuntarily he glanced to the right, grinning as he saw that any access to the old peephole on the Grounds had been blocked off.

"That's mean."

"Huh?" F'lar looked startled. "Oh, that. Yes. Lessa said it upset Ramoth too much. And Mnementh agreed." He gave his half brother a bemused grin, half for Lessa's quirk, half for the mutual nostalgic memory of their own terror-ridden exploration of that passage, and a clandestine glimpse of Nemorth's eggs. "There's a chamber back here that suits my purpose . . ."

"Which is?"

F'lar hesitated, giving F'nor a long, thoughtful look.

"Since when have you found me a reluctant conspirator?" asked F'nor.

"It's asking more than . . ."

"Ask first!"

They had reached the first room of the complex discovered by Jaxom and Felessan. But the bronze rider did not give F'nor time to examine the fascinating design on the wall or the finely made cabinets and tables. He hurried him past the second room to the biggest chamber where a series of graduated, rectangular open stone troughs were set around the floor. Other equipment had obviously been removed at some ancient time, leaving puzzling holes and grooves in the walls, but F'nor was startled to see that the tubs were planted with shrubs, grasses, common field and crop seedlings. A few small hardwood trees were evident in the largest troughs.

F'lar gestured for the grub pot which F'nor willingly handed over.

"Now, I'm going to put some of these grubs in all but this container," F'lar said, indicating the medium-sized one. Then he started to distribute the squirming grubs.

"Proving what?"

F'lar gave him a long deep look so reminiscent of the days when they had dared each other as weyrlings that F'nor couldn't help grinning.

"Proving what?" he insisted.

"Proving first, that these southern grubs will prosper in northern soil among northern plants . . ."

"And . . ."

"That they will eliminate Thread here as they did in the western swamp."

They both watched, in a sort of revolted fascination, as the wriggling gray mass of grubs broke apart and separately burrowed into the loose dark soil of the biggest tub.

"What?"

F'nor experienced a devastating disorientation. He saw F'lar as a weyrling, challenging him to explore and find the legendary peekhole to the Ground. He saw F'lar again, older, in the Records Room, surrounded by moldering skins, suggesting that they jump *between* time itself to stop Thread at Nerat. And he imagined himself suggesting to F'lar to support *him* when he let Canth fly Brekke's Wirenth . . .

"But we didn't see Thread do anything," he said, getting a grip on perspective and time.

"What else could have happened to Thread in those swamps? You know as surely as we're standing here that it was a four-hour Fall. And we fought only two. You saw the scoring. You saw the activity of the grubs. And I'll bet you had a hard time finding enough to fill that pot because they only rise to the surface when Thread falls. In fact, you can go back in time and see it happen."

F'nor grimaced, remembering that it had taken a long time to find enough grubs. It'd been a strain, too, with every nerve of man, dragon and lizard alert for a sign of T'kul's patrols. "I should have thought of that myself. But—Thread's not going to fall over Benden . . ."

"You'll be at Telgar and Ruatha Holds this afternoon when the Fall starts. This time, you'll *catch* some Thread."

If there had not been an ironical, humorous gleam in his half-brother's eyes, F'nor would have thought him delirious.

"Doubtless," F'nor said acidly, "you've figured out exactly how I'm to achieve this."

F'lar brushed the hair back from his forehead.

"Well, I am open to suggestion . . ."

"That's considerate, since it's my hand that's to be scored . . ."

"You've got Canth, and Grall to help . . ."

"If they're mad enough . . ."

"Mnementh explained it all to Canth . . ."

"That's helpful . . ."

"I wouldn't ask you to do it if I could myself!" And F'lar's patience snapped.

"I know!" F'nor replied with equal force, and then grinned because he knew he'd do it.

"All right." F'lar grinned in acknowledgment. "Fly low altitude near the queens. Watch for a good thick patch. Follow it down. Canth's skillful enough to let you get close with one of those long-handled hearthpans. And Grall can wipe out any Thread which burrows. I can't think of any other way to get some. Unless, of course, we were flying over one of the stone plateaus, but even then . . ."

"All right, let us assume I can catch some live, viable Thread," and the brown rider could not suppress the tremor that shook him, "and let us assume that the grubs do—dispose of them. What then?"

With a ghost of a smile on his lips, F'lar spread his arms wide. "Why then, son of my father, we breed us hungry grubs by the tankful and spread them over Pern."

F'nor jammed both fists into his belt. The man was feverish.

"No, I'm not feverish, F'nor," the bronze rider replied, settling himself on the edge of the nearest tank. "But if we *could* have this kind of protection," and he picked up the now empty pot, turning it back and forth in his hand as if it held the sum of his theory, "Thread could fall when and where it wanted to without creating the kind of havoc and revolution we're going through.

"Mind you, there's nothing remotely hinting at such events in any of the Harper Records. Yet I've been asking myself *why* it has taken us so long to spread out across this continent. In the thousands of Turns, given the rate of increase in population over the last four hundred, *why* aren't there more people? And why, F'nor, has no one tried to reach that Red Star before, if it is only just another kind of jump for a dragon?"

"Lessa told me about Lord Groghe's demand," F'nor said, to give himself time to absorb his brother's remarkable and logical questions.

"It isn't just that we could *see* the Star to find coordinates," F'lar went on urgently. "The Ancients had the equipment. They preserved it carefully, though not even Fandarel can guess how. They preserved it for us, perhaps? For a time when we'd know how to overcome the last obstacle?"

"Which is the last obstacle?" F'nor demanded, sarcastically, thinking of nine or ten offhand.

"There're enough, I know." And F'lar ticked them off on his fingers. "Protection of Pern while all the Weyrs are away—which might well mean the grubs on the land and a well-organized ground crew to take care of homes and people. Dragons big enough, intelligent enough to aid us. You've noticed yourself that our dragons are both bigger and smarter than those four hundred Turns older. If the dragons were bred for this purpose from creatures like Grall, they didn't grow to present size in the course of just a few Hatchings. Any more than the Masterherdsman could breed those long-staying long-legged runners he's *finally* developed; it's a project that I understand started about four hundred Turns ago. G'narish says they didn't have them in the Oldtime."

There was an undercurrent to F'lar's voice, F'nor suddenly realized. The man was not as certain of this outrageous notion as he sounded. And yet, wasn't the recognized goal of dragonmen the complete extermination of all Thread from the skies of Pern? Or was it? There wasn't a line of the Teaching Ballads and Sagas that even suggested more than that the dragonmen prepare and guard Pern when the Red Star passed. Nothing hinted at a time when there would *be* no Thread to fight.

"Isn't it just possible that we, now, are the culmination of thousands of Turns of careful planning and development?" F'lar was suggesting urgently. "Look, don't all the facts corroborate? The large population in support, the ingenuity of Fandarel, the discovery of those rooms and the devices, the grubs—everything . . ."

"Except one," F'nor said slowly, hating himself.

"Which?" All the warmth and fervor drained out of F'lar and that single word came in a cold, harsh voice.

"Son of my father," began F'nor, taking a deep breath, "if dragonmen clear the Star of Thread, what further purpose is there for them?"

F'lar, his face white and set with disappointment, drew himself to his feet.

"Well, I assume you've an answer to that, too," F'nor went on, unable to bear the disillusion in his half-brother's scornful regard. "Now where's that long-handled hearthpan I'm supposed to catch Thread in?"

When they had thoroughly discussed and rejected every other possible method of securing Thread, and how they were to keep this project a secret—only Lessa and Ramoth knew of it—they parted, both assuring the other that he'd eat and rest. Both certain that the other could not.

If F'nor appreciated the audacity of F'lar's project, he also counted up the flaws and the possible disasters. And then he realized that he still hadn't had a chance to broach the innovation he himself desired to make. Yet, for a brown dragon to fly a queen was far less revolutionary than F'lar wanting to terminate the Weyrs' duties. And, reinforced by one of F'lar's own theories, if the dragons were now big enough for their ultimate breeding purpose, then no harm was done the species if a brown, smaller than a bronze, was mated to a queen—just this once. Surely F'nor deserved that compensation. Comforted that it would be merely an exchange of favors, rather than the gross crime it might once have been considered, F'nor went to borrow the long-handled hearthpan from one of Manora's helpers.

Someone, probably Manora, had cleaned his weyr during his absence at Southern. F'nor was grateful for the fresh, supple skins on the bed, the clean, mended clothes in his chest, the waxed wood of table and chairs. Canth grumbled that someone had swept the sandy accumulation from his weyr-couch and he had nothing to scour his belly hide with now.

F'nor dutifully sympathized as he lay back on the silky furs of his bed. The scar on his arm itched a little and he rubbed it.

Oil is for itching skin, said Canth. *Imperfect hide cracks in* between.

"Be quiet, you. I've got skin not hide."

Grall appeared in his room, hovering over his chest, her wings wafting cool air across his face. She was curious, a curiosity with slight overtones of alarm.

He smiled, generating reassurance and affection. The gyrations of her lovely jewel-faceted eyes slowed and she made a graceful survey of his quarters, humming when she discovered the bathing room. He could hear her splashing about in the water. He closed his eyes. He would need to rest. He did not look forward to the afternoon's endeavor.

If the grubs did live to eat Thread, and if F'lar could maneuver the scared Lords and Craftsmen into accepting this solution, what then? They weren't fools, those men. They'd see that Pern would no longer be dependent on dragonriders. Of course, that's what they wanted. And what under the sun did out-of-work dragonriders do? The Lords Holders Groghe, Sangel, Nessel, Meron and Vincet would immediately dispense with tithes. F'nor wouldn't object to learning another trade, but F'lar had relinquished their tentative hold on the southern continent to the Oldtimers, so where would dragonmen farm? What commodity would they barter for the products of the Crafthalls?

F'lar couldn't be under the impression that he could mend that breach with T'kul, could he? Or maybe—well, they didn't know how large the southern continent was. Past the deserts to the west or the unexplored sea to the east, maybe there were other, hospitable lands. Did F'lar know more than he said? Grall chirruped piteously in his ear. She was clinging to the fur rug by his shoulder, her supple hide gleaming golden from her bath. He stroked her, wondering if she needed oil. She was growing, but not at the tremendous rate dragons did in the first few weeks after Hatching.

Well, his thoughts were disturbing her as well as himself. "Canth?"

The dragon was asleep. The fact was oddly consoling.

F'nor found a comfortable position and closed his eyes, determined to rest. Grall's soft stirrings ended and he felt her body resting against his neck, in the curve of his shoulder. He wondered how Brekke was doing at the High Reaches. And if her small bronze was as unsettled by weyrlife in a cliff as Grall. A memory of Brekke's face crossed his mind. Not as he had last seen her, anxious, worried, rapidly mobilizing her wits to cope with moving so precipitously after T'kul had swooped down on the unsuspecting settlement. But as loving had made her, soft, gentled. He'd have her soon to himself, all to himself, for he'd see that she didn't overextend herself, fighting everyone's battles except her own. She'd be asleep now, he realized, for it was still night at High Reaches . . .

Brekke was not asleep. She had awakened suddenly, as she was accustomed to doing in the morning, except that the dark stillness around her was not simply that of an inner room in the weyr cliff, but was full of the soft solitude of night. The fire-lizard, Berd, roused too, his brilliant eyes the only light in the room. He crooned apprehensively. Brekke stroked him, listening for Wirenth, but the queen was sound asleep in her stony couch.

Brekke tried to compose herself back into sleep, but even as she made her body relax, she realized it was a useless attempt. It might be late watch here at High Reaches, but it was dawn in Southern, and that's the rhythm her body was still tuned to. With a sigh, she rose, reassuring Berd who rustled around anxiously. But he joined her in the pool-bath, splashing with small vehemence in the warm water, utilizing the superfluous suds from her cleansing sands to bathe himself. He preened on the bench, uttering those soft voluptuous croons that amused her.

In a way, it was good to be up and about with no one to interrupt her for there was so much to be done to settle the weyrfolk in their new habitation. She'd have to plan around some of the most obvious problems. There was little fresh food. T'kul had gratuitously left behind the oldest, scrawniest bucks, the worst furnishings, had made off with most of the supplies of cloth, cured woods, leathers, all the wine, and managed to prevent the Southern folk from taking enough from their stores to make up the deficits. Oh, if she'd had even two hours, or any warning . . .

She sighed. Obviously Merika had been a worse Weyrwoman than Kylara, for High Reaches was in a bad state of disrepair. Those Holds which tithed to High Reaches Weyr would be in no mood to make up the differences now. Maybe a discreet word to F'nor would remedy the worst of the lacks . . . No, that would suggest incompetency. First, she'd inventory what they did have, discover the most pressing needs, see what they could manufacture themselves . . . Brekke stopped. She'd have to adjust her thinking to an entirely new way of life, a life dependent on the generosity of the Holds. In Southern, you had so much to work with. In her father's Crafthall, you always made what you could from things to hand—but there were always raw materials—or you grew it—or did without.

"One thing certain, Kylara will not do without!" Brekke muttered. She had dressed in riding gear which was warmer and less hampering if she was to delve into storage caves.

She didn't like the pinched-faced Meron Lord of Nabol Hold. To be indebted to him would be abhorrent. There must be an alternative.

Wirenth was twitching as Brekke passed her and the dragon's hide gleamed in the darkness. She was so deeply asleep that Brekke did not even stroke her muzzle in passing. The dragon had worked hard yesterday. Could it really have been only yesterday?

Berd chirped so smugly as he glided past the queen that Brekke smiled. He was a dear nuisance, as transparent as pool water—and she must check and see if Rannelly was right about the Weyr lake. The old woman had complained bitterly last evening that the water was fouled—deliberately; maliciously fouled by T'kul.

It was startling to come out into crisply cold air with the pinch of late frost in the early hour chill. Brekke glanced up at the watchrider by the Star stones and then hurried down the short flight of steps to the Lower Caverns. The fires had been banked but the water kettle was comfortingly hot. She made *klah*, found bread and fruit for herself and some meat for Berd. He was beginning to eat with less of the barbarous voracity, and no longer gorged himself into somnolence.

Taking a fresh basket of glows, Brekke went into the storage section to begin her investigations. Berd cheerfully accompanied her, perching where he could watch her industry.

By the time the Weyr began to stir, four hours later, Brekke was full of contempt for past domestic management and considerably relieved about the resources on hand. In fact, she suspected that the best fabrics and leathers, not to mention wines, had not gone south with the dissenters.

But the lake water was indisputably fouled by household garbage and would have to be dredged. It wouldn't be usable for several days at least. And there was nothing in which water could be transported in any quantity from the nearby mountain streams. It semed silly to send a dragon out for a couple of bucketsful, she reported to T'bor and Kylara.

"I'll get kegs from Nabol," Kylara announced, once she had recovered from ranting about T'kul's pettiness.

While it was obvious to Brekke that T'bor was not pleased to hear her solution, he had too much else to occupy his time to protest. At least, Brekke thought, Kylara was taking an interest in the Weyr and some of the responsibility.

So Kylara circled out of the Bowl, Prideth shining golden in the early morning sun. And T'bor took off with several wings for low-altitude sweeps, to get familiar with the terrain and set up appropriate watch fires and patrol check points. Brekke and Vanira, with the help of Pilgra, the only High Reaches Weyrwoman to stay behind, settled who would supervise which necessary duties. They set the weyrlings to dragging the lake, sent others for immediate supplies of fresh water.

Deeply occupied in counting sacks of flour, Brekke did not hear Wirenth's first cry. It was Berd who responded with a startled squawk, flying round Brekke's head to attract her attention.

As Brekke felt for Wirenth's mind, she was astonished at the incoherence, at the rough, wild emotions. Wondering what could have happened to a queen who'd been so peacefully asleep, Brekke raced through the corridors, to be met in the Lower Cavern by Pilgra, wide-eyed with excitement.

"Wirenth's ready to rise, Brekke. I've called back the riders! She's on her way to the Feeding Ground. You know what to do, don't you?"

Brekke stared at the girl, stunned. In a daze she let Pilgra pull her toward the Bowl. Wirenth was screaming, as she glided into the Feeding Ground. The terrified herdbeasts stampeded, keening their distress, adding to the frightening tension in the air.

"Go on, Brekke," Pilgra cried, pushing her. "Don't let her gorge. She won't fly well!"

"Help me!" Brekke pleaded.

Pilgra embraced her reassuringly, with an odd smile. "Don't be scared. It's wonderful."

"I—I can't . . ."

Pilgra gave Brekke a shake. "Of course you can. You must. I've got to scoot with Segrith. Vanira's already taken her queen away."

"Taken her away?"

"Of course. Don't be stupid. You can't have other queens around right now. Just be thankful Kylara's at Nabol Hold with Prideth. That one's too close to rising herself."

And Pilgra, with one last push at Brekke, ran toward her own queen.

Rannelly was at Brekke's elbow suddenly, batting at the excited fire-lizard who darted above their heads.

"Get away! Get away! You, girl, get to your queen or you're no Weyrwoman! Don't let her gorge!"

Suddenly the air was again full of dragon wings—the bronzes had returned. And the urgency of mating, the necessity of protecting Wirenth roused Brekke. She began to run toward the Feeding Ground, aware of the rising hum of the bronzes, the expectant sensuality of the browns and blues and greens who now perched on their ledges to watch the event. Weyrfolk crowded the Bowl.

"F'nor! F'nor! What shall I do?" Brekke moaned.

And then she was aware that Wirenth had come down on a buck, shrieking her defiance; an altered, unrecognizable Wirenth, voracious with more than a blood urge.

"She mustn't gorge!" someone shouted at Brekke. Someone gripped her arms to her sides, tightly. "Don't let her gorge, Brekke!"

But Brekke was with Wirenth now, was feeling the insatiable desire for raw, hot meat, for the taste of blood in her mouth, the warmth of it in her belly. Brekke was unaware of extraneous matters. Of anything but the fact that Wirenth was rising to mate and that she, Brekke, would be captive to those emotions, a victim of her dragon's lust, and that this was contrary to all she had been conditioned to believe and honor.

Wirenth had gutted the first buck by now and Brekke fought to keep her from eating the steaming entrails. Fought and won, controlling herself and her beast for the bond-love she had with the golden queen. When Wirenth rose from the blooded carcass, Brekke became momentarily aware of the heavy, hot, musty bodies crowding around her. Frantic, she glanced up at the circle of bronze riders, their faces intent on the scene on the Feeding Ground, intent and sensual, their expressions changing them from well-known features into strange parodies.

"Brekke! Control her!" Someone shouted hoarsely in her ear and her elbow was seized in a painful vise.

This was wrong! All wrong! Evil, she moaned, desperately crying with all her spirit for F'nor. He had said he'd come. He had promised that only Canth would fly Wirenth . . . *Canth! Canth!*

Wirenth was going for the throat of the buck, not to blood it, but to rend and eat the flesh.

Two disciplines warred with each other. Confused, distraught, torn as violently as the flesh of the dead buck, Brekke nevertheless forced Wirenth to obey her. And yet, which force would finally win? Weyr or Crafthall? Brekke clung to the hope that F'nor would come—the third alternate.

After the fourth buck, Wirenth seemed to glow. With an astonishing leap, she was suddenly aloft. Trumpeting roars reverberated painfully back and forth from the sides of the Weyr as the bronzes leaped after her, the wind from their wings sweeping dust and sand into the faces of the watching weyrfolk.

And Brekke was conscious of nothing but Wirenth. For she was suddenly Wirenth, contemptuous of the bronzes trying to catch her as she sped upward, eastward, high above the mountains, until the land below was hollow black and sand, the flash of blue lake in the sun blinding. Above the clouds, up where the air was thin but speed enhanced.

And then, out of the clouds below her, another dragon. A queen, as glowingly golden as herself. A queen? To lure her dragons from her?

Screaming in protest, Wirenth dove at the intruder, her talons extended, her body no longer exulting in flight but tensed for combat.

She dove and the intruder veered effortlessly, turning so swiftly to rake her talons down Wirenth's exposed flank that the young queen could not evade the strike. Injured, Wirenth fell, recovering valiantly and swooping into cloud cover. The bronzes had caught up and bugled their distress. They wanted to mate. They wanted to interfere. The other queen—it was Prideth—believing her rival vanquished, called enticingly to the bronzes.

Fury was added to the pain of Wirenth's humiliation. She exploded from the clouds, bellowing her challenge, her summons to the bronzes.

And her opponent was there! Beneath Wirenth. The young queen folded her wings and dove, her golden body dropping at a fearsome rate. And her dive was too unexpected, too fast. Prideth could not avoid the mid-air collision. Wirenth's claws sank into her back and Prideth writhed, her wings fouled by the talons which she could not disengage. Both queens fell like Thread, toward the mountains, escorted by the distraughtly bugling bronzes.

With the desperation born of frenzy, Prideth wrenched herself free, Wirenth's talons leaving gouges to the bone along her shoulders. But as she twisted free, beating for altitude, she slashed at Wirenth's unprotected head, across one gleaming eye.

Wirenth's tortured scream pierced the heavens just as other queens broke into the air around them; queens who instantly divided, one group flying for Prideth, the other for Wirenth.

Implacably they circled Wirenth, forcing her back, away from Prideth, their circles ever decreasing, a living net around the infuriated, pain-racked queen. Sensing only that she was being deprived of revenge on her foe, Wirenth saw the one escape route and folding her wings, dropped on the bottom of the net and darted toward the other group of queens.

Prideth's tail protruded, and on this Wirenth fastened her teeth, dragging the other from protective custody. No sooner were they clear than Wirenth bestrode the older queen's back, talons digging deeply into her wing muscles, her jaws sinking into the unprotected neck.

They fell, Wirenth making no attempt to stop their dangerous descent. She could see nothing from her damaged eye. She paid no attention to the screams of the other queens, the circling bronzes. Then something seized her body roughly from above, giving her a tremendous jerk.

Unable to see on the right, Wirenth was forced to relinquish her hold to contend with this new menace. But as she turned, she caught a glimpse of a great golden body directly below Prideth. Above her—Canth! Canth? Hissing at such treachery, she was unable to realize that he was actually trying to rescue her from sure death on the dangerously close mountain peaks. Ramoth, too, was attempting to stop their plunge, supporting Prideth with her body, her great wings straining with effort.

Suddenly teeth closed on Wirenth's neck, close to the major artery at the junction of the shoulder. Wirenth's mortal scream was cut off as she now struggled for breath itself. Wounded by foe, hampered by friends, Wirenth desperately transferred *between*, taking Prideth with her, jaws death-locked on her life's blood.

The bronze fire-lizard, Berd, found F'nor preparing to join the wings at the western meadows of Telgar Hold. The brown rider was so astonished at first to see the little bronze in Benden so far from his mistress that he didn't immediately grasp the frenzied creature's thoughts.

But Canth did.

Wirenth has risen!

All other considerations forgotten, F'nor ran with Canth to the ledge. Grall grabbed at her perch on his shoulder, wrapping her tail so tightly around F'nor's neck that he had to loosen it forcibly. Then Berd could not be brought to roost and precious moments were lost while Canth managed to calm the little bronze sufficiently to accept instruction. As Berd finally settled, Canth let out so mighty a bugle that Mnementh challenged from the ledge and Ramoth roared back from the Hatching Ground.

With no thought of the effect of their precipitous exit or Canth's exceptional behavior, F'nor urged his dragon upward. The small pulse of reason that remained untouched by emotion was trying to estimate how long it had taken the little bronze to reach him, how long Wirenth would blood before rising, which bronzes were at High Reaches. He was thankful that F'lar had not had time to throw mating flights open. There were some beasts against whom Canth stood no chance.

When they broke into the air again over High Reaches Weyr, F'nor's worst fears were realized. The Feeding Ground was a bloody sight and no queen fed there. Nor was there a bronze among the dragons who ringed the Weyr heights.

Without order, Canth wheeled sharply down at dizzying speed.

Berd knows where Wirenth is. He takes me.

The little bronze hopped down to Canth's neck, his little talons gripping the ridge tightly. F'nor slid from Canth's shoulder to the ground, staggering out of the way so the brown could spring back aloft.

Prideth also rises! The thought and the brown's scream of fear were simultaneous. From the heights the other dragons answered, extending their wings in alarm.

"Rouse Ramoth!" F'nor shouted, mind and voice, his body paralyzed with shock. "Rouse Ramoth! Bronze riders! Prideth also rises!"

Weyrfolk rushed from the Lower Cavern, riders appeared on their ledges around the Weyr face.

"Kylara! T'bor! Where's Pilgra? Kylara! Varena!" Shouting with a panic that threatened to choke him. F'nor raced for Brekke's weyr, shoving aside the people who crowded him, demanding explanations.

Prideth rising! How could that happen? Even the stupidest Weyrwoman knew you didn't keep a queen near her weyr during a mating flight—unless they were broody. How could Kylara . . . ?

"T'bor!"

F'nor raced up the short flight of steps, pounded down the corridor in strides that jolted his half-healed arm. But the pain cleared his head of panic. Just as he burst into the weyr cavern, Brekke's angry cry halted him. The bronze riders grouped around her were beginning to show the effects of the interrupted mating flight.

"What's she doing here? How dare she?" Brekke was shrieking in a voice shrill with lust as well as fury. "These are my dragons! How dare she! I'll kill her!" The litany broke into a piercing scream of agony as Brekke doubled up, right shoulder hunching as if to protect her head.

"My eye! My eye! My eye!" Brekke was covering her right eye, her body writhing in an uncontrollable, unconscious mimicry of the aerial battle to which she was tuned.

"Kill! I'll kill her! No! No! She cannot escape. Go away!" Suddenly Brekke's face turned crafty and her whole body writhed sensuously.

The bronze riders were changing now, no longer completely in the thrall of the strange mental rapport with their beasts. Fear, doubt, indecision, hopelessness registered on their faces. Some portion of the human awareness was returning, fighting with the dragon responsiveness and the interrupted mating flight. When T'bor reached for Brekke, human fear was reflected in his eyes.

But she was still totally committed to Wirenth, and the incredible triumph on her face registered Wirenth's success in evading capture, in dragging Prideth from the encircling queens.

"Prideth has risen, T'bor! The queens are fighting," F'nor shouted.

One rider began to scream and the sound broke the link of two others who stared, dazed, at Brekke's contorting body.

"Don't touch her!" F'nor cried, moving to fend off T'bor and another man. He moved as close to her as possible but her ranging eyes did not see him or anything in the weyr.

Then she seemed to spring, her left eye widening with an unholy joy, her lips bared as her teeth fastened on an imaginary target, her body arching with the empathic effort.

Suddenly she hissed, craning her head sideways, over her right shoulder, while her face reflecting incredulity, horror, hatred. As suddenly, her body was seized with a massive convulsion. She screamed again, this time a mortal shriek of unbelievable terror and anguish. One hand went to her throat, the other batted at some unseen attacker. Her body, poised on her toes, strained in an agonized stretch. With a cry that was more gasp than scream, she whirled. In her eyes was Brekke's soul again, tortured, terrified. Then her eyes closed, her body sagged in such an alarming collapse that F'nor barely caught her in time.

The stones of the weyr itself seemed to reverberate with the mourning dirge of the dragons.

"T'bor, send someone for Manora," F'nor cried in a hoarse voice as he bore Brekke to her couch. Her body was so light in his arms— as if all substance had been drained from it. He held her tightly to his chest with one arm, fumbling to find the pulse in her neck with the free hand. It beat—faintly.

What had happened? How could Kylara have allowed Prideth near Wirenth?

"They're both gone," T'bor was saying as he stumbled into the sleeping room and sagged down on the clothes chest, trembling violently.

"Where's Kylara? Where is she?"

"Don't know. I left this morning to fly patrols." T'bor scrubbed at his face, shock bleaching the ruddy color from his skin. "The lake was polluted . . ."

F'nor piled furs around Brekke's motionless body. He held his hand against her chest, feeling its barely perceptible rise and fall.

F'nor?

It was Canth, his call so faint, so piteous that the man closed his eyes against the pain in his dragon's tone.

He felt someone grip his shoulder. He opened his eyes to see the pity, the understanding in T'bor's. "There's nothing more you can do for her right now, F'nor."

"She'll want to die. Don't let her!" he said. "Don't let Brekke die!"

Canth was on the ledge, his eyes glowing dully. He was swaying with exhaustion. F'nor encircled the bow head with his arms, their mutual grief so intense they seemed afire with pain.

It was too late. Prideth had risen. Too close to Wirenth. Not even the queens could help. I tried, F'nor. I tried. She—she fell so fast. And she turned on me. Then went between. *I could not find her* between.

They stood together, immobile.

•

Lessa and Manora saw them as Ramoth circled into High Reaches Weyr. At Canth's bellow, Ramoth had come out of the Hatching Ground, loudly calling for her rider, demanding an explanation of such behavior.

But F'lar, believing he knew Canth's errand, had reassured her, until Ramoth had informed them that Wirenth was rising. And Ramoth knew instantly when Prideth rose, too, and had gone *between* to Nabol to stop the mortal combat if she could.

Once Wirenth had dragged Prideth *between*, Ramoth had returned to Benden Weyr for Lessa. The Benden dragons set up their keen so that the entire Weyr soon knew of the disaster. But Lessa waited only long enough for Manora to gather her medicines.

As she and the headwoman reached the ledge of Brekke's weyr and the motionless mourners, Lessa looked anxiously to Manora. There was something dangerous in such stillness.

"They will work this out together. They *are* together, more now than ever before," Manora said in a voice that was no more than a rough whisper. She passed them quietly, her head bent and her shoulders drooping as she hurried down the corridor to Brekke.

"Ramoth?" asked Lessa, looking down to where her queen had settled on the sands. It was not that she doubted Manora's wisdom, but to see F'nor so—so reduced—upset her. He was much like F'lar. . .

Ramoth gave a soft croon and folded her wings. On the ledges around the Bowl, the other dragons began to settle in uneasy vigil.

As Lessa entered the Cavern of the Weyr, she glanced away from the empty dragon couch and then halted midstep. The tragedy was only minutes past so the nine bronze riders were still in severe shock.

As well they might be, Lessa realized with deep sympathy. To be roused to performance intensity and then be, not only disappointed, but disastrously deprived of two queens at once! Whether a bronze won the queen or not, there was a subtle, deep attachment between a queen and the bronzes of her Weyr . . .

However, Lessa concluded briskly, someone in this benighted Weyr ought to have sense enough to be constructive. Lessa broke this train of thought off abruptly. Brekke had been the responsible member.

She turned, about to go in search of some stimulant for the dazed riders when she heard the uneven steps and stertorous breathing of someone in a hurry. Two green fire lizards darted into the weyr, hovering, chirping excitedly as a young girl came in at a half-run. She could barely manage the heavy tray she carried and she was weeping, her breath coming in ragged gasps.

"Oh!" she cried, seeing Lessa. She stifled her sobs, tried to bob a curtsey and blot her nose on her shoulder at one and the same time.

"Well, you're a child with wits about you," Lessa said briskly, but not without sympathy. She took one end of the tray and helped the girl deposit it on the table. "You brought strong spirits?" she asked, gesturing to the anonymous earthenware bottles.

"All I could find." And the consonant ended in a sob.

"Here," and Lessa held out a half-filled cup, nodding toward the nearest rider. But the child was motionless, staring at the curtain, her face twisted with grief, the tears flowing unnoticed down her cheeks. She was washing her hands together with such violent motions that the skin stretched white across her knuckles.

"You're Mirrim?"

The child nodded, her eyes not leaving the closed entrance. Above her the greens whirred, echoing her distress.

"Manora is with Brekke, Mirrim."

"But—but she'll die. She'll die. They say the rider dies, too, when the dragon is killed. They say . . ."

"*They* say entirely too much," Lessa began and then Manora stood in the doorway.

"She lives. Sleep is the kindest blessing now." She flipped the curtain shut and glanced at the men. "These could do with sleep. Have their dragons returned? Who's this?" Manora touched Mirrim's cheek, gently. "Mirrim? I'd heard you had green lizards."

"Mirrim had the sense to bring the tray," Lessa said, catching Manora's eye.

"Brekke—Brekke would expect—" and the girl could go no further.

"Brekke is a sensible person," Manora said briskly and folded Mirrim's fingers around a cup, giving her a shove toward a rider. "Help us now. These men need our help."

In a daze, Mirrim moved, rousing herself to help actively when the bronze rider could not seem to get his fingers to the cup.

"My lady," murmured Manora, "we need the Weyrleader. Ista and Telgar Weyrs would be fighting Thread by now and . . ."

"I'm here," F'lar said from the weyr entrance. "And I'll take a shot of that, too. Cold *between* is in my bones."

"We've more fools than we need right now," Lessa exclaimed, but her face brightened to see him there.

"Where's T'bor?"

Manora indicated Brekke's room.

"All right. Then where's Kylara?"

And the cold of *between* was in his voice.

By evening some order had been restored to the badly demoralized High Reaches Weyr. The bronze dragons had all returned, been fed, and the bronze riders weyred with their beasts, sufficiently drugged to sleep.

Kylara had been found. Or, rather, returned, by the green rider assigned to Nabol Hold.

"Someone's got to be quartered there," the man said, his face grim, "but not me or my green."

"Please report, S'goral." F'lar nodded his appreciation of the rider's feelings.

"*She* arrived at the Hold this morning, with some tale about the lake here being fouled and no kegs to hold any supply of water. I remember thinking that Prideth looked too gold to be out. She's been off cycle, you know. But she settled down all right on the ridge with my green so I went about teaching those Holders how to manage their fire-lizards." S'goral evidently did not have much use for his pupils. "*She* went in with the Nabolese Holder. Later I saw their lizards sunning on the ledge outside the Lord's sleeping room." He paused, glancing at his audience and looking grimmer still. "We were taking a breather when my green cried out. Sure enough, there were dragons, high up. *I* knew it was a mating flight. You can't mistake it. Then Prideth started to bugle. Next thing I knew, she was down among Nabol's prize breeding stock. I waited a bit, sure that *she'd* be aware of what was happening, but when there wasn't a sign of her, I went looking. Nabol's bodyguards were at the door. The Lord didn't want to be disturbed. Well, I disturbed him. I stopped him doing what he was doing. And that's what was doing it! Setting Prideth off. That and being so close to rising herself, and seeing a mating flight right over her, so to speak. You *don't* abuse your dragon that way." He shook his head then. "There wasn't anything me and my green could do there. So we took off for Fort Weyr, for their queens. But—" and he held out his hands, indicating his helplessness.

"You did as you should, S'goral," F'lar told him.

"There wasn't anything else I could do," the man insisted, as if he could not rid himself of some lingering feeling of guilt.

"We were lucky you were there at all," Lessa said. "We might never have known where Kylara was."

"What I want to know is what's going to happen to her—now?" A hard vindictiveness replaced the half-shame, half-guilt in the rider's face.

"Isn't loss of a dragon enough?" T'bor roused himself to ask.

"Brekke lost her dragon, too," S'goral retorted angrily, "and she was doing what she should!"

"Nothing can be decided in heat or hatred, S'goral," F'lar said, rising to his feet. "We've no precedents—" He broke off, turning to D'ram and G'narish. "Not in our time, at least."

"Nothing should be decided in heat or hatred," D'ram echoed, "but there were such incidents in our time." Unaccountably he flushed. "We'd better assign some bronzes here, F'lar. The High Reaches men and beasts may not be fit tomorrow. And with Thread falling every day, no Weyr can be allowed to relax its vigilance. For anything."

•• C H A P T E R X I I I ••

𝕎

Night at Fort Weyr: Six Days Later

Robinton was weary, with fatigue of the heart and mind that did not lift to the thrill the Masterharper usually experienced on dragonback. In fact, he almost wished he'd not had to come to Fort Weyr tonight. These past six days, with everyone reacting in varying ways to the tragedy at High Reaches, had been very difficult. (Must the High Reaches always push the knottiest problems on Pern?) In a way, Robinton wished that they could have put off this Red Star viewing until minds and eyes had cleared and were ready for this challenge. And yet, perhaps the best solution was to press this proposed expedition to the Red Star as far and as fast as possible—as an anodyne to the depression that had followed the death of the two queens. Robinton knew that F'lar wanted to prove to the Lord Holders that the dragonmen were in earnest in their desire to clear the air of Thread, but for once, the Masterharper found himself without a private opinion. He did not know if F'lar was wise in pushing the issue, particularly now. Particularly when the Benden Weyrleader wasn't recovered from T'ron's slash. When no one was sure how T'kul was managing in Southern Weyr or if the man intended to *stay* there. When all Pern was staggered by the battle and deaths of the two queens. The people had enough to rationalize, had enough to do with the vagaries of Threadfall complicating the seasonal mechanics of plowing and seeding. Leave the attack of the Red Star until another time.

Other dragons were arriving at Fort Weyr and the brown on which Robinton rode took his place in the circling pattern. They'd be landing on the Star Stones where Wansor, Fandarel's glassman, had set up the distance-viewer.

"Have you had a chance to look through this device?" Robinton asked the brown's rider.

"Me? Hardly, Masterharper. Everyone else wants to. It'll stay there until I've had my turn, I daresay."

"Has Wansor mounted it permanently at Fort Weyr?"

"It was discovered at Fort Weyr," the rider replied, a little defensively. "Fort's the oldest Weyr, you know. P'zar feels it should stay at Fort. And the Mastersmith, he agrees. His man Wansor keeps saying that there may be good reason. Something to do with elevation and angles and the altitude of Fort Weyr mountains. I didn't understand."

No more do I, Robinton thought. But he intended to. He was in agreement with Fandarel and Terry that there should be an interchange of knowledge between Crafts. Indisputably, Pern had lost many of the bemoaned techniques due to Craft jealousy. Lose a Craftmaster early, before he had transmitted all the Craft secrets, and a vital piece of information was lost forever. Not that Robinton, nor his predecessor, had ever espoused that ridiculous prerogative. There were five senior harpers who knew everything that Robinton did and three promising journeymen studying diligently to increase the safety factor.

It was one matter to keep dangerous secrets privy, quite another to guard Craft skills to extinction.

The brown dragon landed on the ridge height of Fort Weyr and Robinton slid down the soft shoulder. He thanked the beast. The brown rose a half-length from the landing and then seemed to drop off the side of the cliff, down into the Bowl, making room for someone else to land.

Glows had been set on the narrow crown of the height, leading toward the massive Star Stones, their black bulk silhouetted against the lighter night sky. Among those gathered there, Robinton could distinguish the Mastersmith's huge figure, Wansor's pear-shaped and Lessa's slender one.

On the largest and flattest rock of the Star Stones, Robinton saw the tripod arrangement on which the long barrel of the distance-viewer had been mounted. At first glance he was disappointed by its simplicity, a fat, round cylinder, with a smaller pipe attached to its side. Then it amused him. The Smith must be tortured with the yearning to dismantle the instrument and examine the principles of its simple efficiency.

"Robinton, how are you this evening?" Lessa asked, coming toward him, one hand outstretched.

He gripped it, her soft skin smooth under the calluses of his fingers.

"Pondering the elements of efficiency," he countered, keeping his voice light. But he couldn't keep from asking after Brekke and he felt Lessa's fingers tremble in his.

"She does as well as can be expected. F'nor insisted that we bring her to his weyr. The man's emotionally attached to her—far more than gratitude for any nursing. Between him, Manora and Mirrim, she is never alone."

"And—Kylara?"

Lessa pulled her hand from his. "She lives!"

Robinton said nothing and, after a moment, Lessa went on.

"We don't like losing Brekke as a Weyrwoman—" She paused and added, her voice a little harsher, "And since it is now obvious that a person can Impress more than once, and more than one dragonkind, Brekke will be presented as a candidate when the Bendon eggs Hatch. Which should be soon."

"I perceive," Robinton said, cautiously choosing his words, "that not everyone favors this departure from custom."

Although he couldn't see her face in the darkness, he felt her eyes on him.

"This time it's not the Oldtimers. I suppose they're so sure she can't re-Impress, they're indifferent."

"Who then?"

"F'nor and Manora oppose it violently."

"And Brekke?"

Lessa gave an impatient snort. "Brekke says nothing. She will not even open her eyes. She can't be sleeping all the time. The lizards and the dragons tell us she's awake. You see," and Lessa's exasperation showed through her tight control for she was more worried about Brekke than she'd admit even to herself, "Brekke can hear any dragon. Like me. She's the only other Weyrwoman who can. And all the dragons listen to her." Lessa moved restlessly and Robinton could see her slender white hands rubbing against her thighs in unconscious agitation.

"Surely that's an advantage if she's suicidal?"

"Brekke is not—not actively suicidal. She's craftbred, you know," Lessa said in a flat, disapproving tone of voice.

"No, I didn't know," Robinton murmured encouragingly after a pause. He was thinking that Lessa wouldn't ever contemplate suicide in a similar circumstance and wondered what Brekke's "breeding" had to do with a suicidal aptitude.

"That's her trouble. She can't actively seek death so she just lies there. I have this incredible urge," and Lessa bunched her fists, "to beat or pinch or slap her—anything to get some response from the girl. It's not the end of the world, after all. She *can* hear other dragons. She's not bereft of all contact with dragonkind, like Lytol."

"She must have time to recover from the shock . . ."

"I know, I know," Lessa said irritably, "but we don't *have* time. We can't get her to realize that it's better to *do* things . . ."

"Lessa . . ."

"Don't you 'Lessa' me too, Robinton." In the reflection of the glow lights, the Weyrwoman's eyes gleamed angrily. "F'nor's as draft as a weyrling, Manora's beside herself with worry for them both, Mirrim spends more of her time weeping which upsets the trio of lizards she's got and *that* sets off all the babes and the weyrlings. And, on top of everything else, F'lar . . ."

"F'lar?" Robinton had bent close to her so that no one else might hear her reply.

"He is feverish. He ought never to have some to High Reaches with that open wound. You know what cold *between* does to wounds!"

"I'd hoped he'd be here tonight."

Lessa's laugh was sour. "I dosed his *klah* when he wasn't looking."

Robinton chuckled. "And stuffed him with mosstea, I'll bet."

"Packed the wound with it, too."

"He's a strong man, Lessa. He'll be all right."

"He'd better be. If only F'nor—" and Lessa broke off. "I sound like a wherry, don't I?" She gave a sigh and smiled up at Robinton.

"Not a bit, my dear Lessa, I assure you. However, it's not as if Benden were inadequately represented," and he executed a little bow which, if she shrugged it off, at least made her laugh. "In fact," he went on, "I'm a trifle relieved that F'lar isn't here, railing at anything that keeps him from blotting out any Thread he happens to see in that contraption."

"True enough." And Robinton caught the edge to her voice. "I'm not sure . . ."

She didn't finish her sentence and turned so swiftly to mark the landing of another dragon that Robinton was certain she was at odds with F'lar's wishing to push a move against the Red Star.

Suddenly she stiffened, drawing in her breath sharply. "Meron! What does he think he's doing here?"

"Easy, Lessa. I don't like him around any better than you, but I'd rather keep him in sight, if you know what I mean."

"But he's got no influence on the other Lords . . ."

Robinton gave a harsh laugh. "My dear Weyrwoman, considering the influence he's been exerting in other areas, he doesn't need the Lords' support."

Robinton did wonder at the gall of the man, appearing in public anywhere a scant six days after he'd been involved in the deaths of two queen dragons.

The Lord Holder of Nabol strode insolently to the focal point of the gathering, his bronze fire-lizard perched on his forearm, its wings extended as it fought to maintain its balance. The little creature began to hiss as it became aware of the antagonism directed at Meron.

"And this—this innocuous tube is the incredible instrument that will show us the Red Star?" Meron of Nabol asked scathingly.

"Don't touch it, I beg of you." Wansor jumped forward, intercepting Nabol's hand.

"What did you say?" The lizard's hiss was no less sibilantly menacing than Meron's tone. The Lord's thin features, contorted with indignation, took on an added malevolence from the glow lights.

Fandarel stepped out of the darkness to his craftsman's side. "The instrument is positioned for the viewing. To move it would destroy the careful work of some hours."

"If it is positioned for viewing, then let us view!" Nabol said and, after staring belligerently around the circle, stepped past Wansor. "Well? What do you do with this thing?"

Wansor glanced questioningly at the big Smith, who made a slight movement of his head, excusing him. Wansor gratefully stepped back and let Fandarel preside. With two gnarled fingers, the Smith delicately held the small round protuberance at the top of the smaller cylinder.

"This is the eyepiece. Put your best seeing eye to it," he told Meron.

The lack of any courteous title was not lost on the Nabolese. Plainly he wanted to reprimand the Smith. Had Wansor spoken so, he would not have hesitated a second, Robinton thought.

Meron's lips slid into a sneer and, with a bit of a swagger, he took the final step to the distance-viewer. Bending forward slightly, he laid his eye to the proper place. And jerked his body back hastily, his face wearing a fleeting expression of shock and terror. He laughed uneasily and then took a second, longer look. Far too long a look to Robinton's mind.

"If there is any lack of definition in the image, Lord Meron—" Wansor began tentatively.

"Shut up!" Gesturing him away impatiently, Meron continued his deliberate monopoly of the instrument.

"That will be enough, Meron," Groghe, Lord of Fort said as the others began to stir restlessly. "You've had more than your fair turn this round. Move away. Let others see."

Meron stared insolently at Groghe for a moment and then looked back into the eyepiece.

"Very interesting. Very interesting," he said, his tone oily with amusement.

"That is quite enough, Meron," Lessa said, striding to the instrument. The man could not be allowed any privilege.

He regarded her as he might a body insect, coldly and mockingly.

"Enough of what—Weyrwoman?" And his tone made the title a vulgar epithet. In fact, his pose exuded such a lewd familiarity that Robinton found he was clenching his fists. He had an insane desire to wipe that look from Meron's face and change the arrangement of the features in the process.

The Mastersmith, however, reacted more quickly. His two great hands secured Meron's arms to his sides and, in a fluid movement, Fandarel picked the Nabolese Lord up, the man's feet dangling a full dragonfoot above the rock, and carried him as far away from the Star Stones as the ledge permitted. Fandarel then set Meron down so hard that the man gave a startled exclamation of pain and staggered before he gained his balance. The little lizard screeched around his head.

"My lady," the Mastersmith inclined his upper body toward Lessa and gestured with great courtesy for her to take her place.

Lessa had to stand on tiptoe to reach the eyepiece, silently wishing someone had taken into account that not all the viewers this evening were tall. The instant the image of the Red Star reached her brain, such trivial annoyance evaporated. There was the Red Star, seemingly no farther away than her arm could reach. It swam, a many-hued globe, like a child's miggsy, in a lush black background. Odd whitish-pink masses must be clouds. Startling to think that the Red Star could possess clouds—like Pern. Where the cover was pierced, she could see grayish masses, a lively gray with glints and sparkles. The ends of the slightly ovoid planet were completely white, but devoid of the cloud cover. Like the great icecaps of northern regions of Pern. Darker masses punctuated the grays. Land? Or seas?

Involuntarily Lessa moved her head, to glance up at the round mark of redness in the night sky that was this child's toy through the magic of the distance-viewer. Then, before anyone might think she'd relinquished the instrument, she looked back through the eyepiece. Incredible. Unsettling. If the gray was land—how could they possibly rid it of Thread? If the darker masses were land . . .

Disturbed, and suddenly all too willing that someone else be exposed to their ancient enemy at such close range, she stepped back.

Lord Groghe stepped forward importantly. "Sangel, if you please?"

How like the Fort Lord, Lessa thought, to play host when P'zar who was, after all, acting Weyrleader at Fort Weyr, did not act quickly enough to exert his rights. Lessa wished fervently that F'lar had been able to attend this viewing. Well, perhaps P'zar was merely being diplomatic with the Fort Lord Holder. Still, Lord Groghe would need to be kept . . .

She retreated—and knew it for a retreat—to Robinton. The Harper's presence was always reassuring. He was eager to have his turn but resigned to waiting. Groghe naturally would give the other Lord Holders precedence over a harper, even the Masterharper of Pern.

"I wish he'd go," Lessa said, glancing sideways at Meron. The Nabolese had made no attempt to re-enter the group from which he had been so precipitously expelled. The offensive stubbornness of the man in remaining where he clearly was not welcome provided a counterirritant to worry and her renewed fear of the Red Star.

Why must it appear so—so innocent? Why did it have to have clouds? It ought to be different. How it ought to differ, Lessa couldn't guess, but it ought to look—to look sinister. And it didn't. That made it more fearful than ever.

"I don't *see* anything," Sangel of Boll was complaining.

"A moment, sir." Wansor came forward and began adjusting a small knob. "Tell me when the view clarifies for you."

"What am I supposed to be seeing?" Sangel demanded irritably. "Nothing there but a bright—ah! Oh!" Sangel backed away from the eyepiece as if Thread had burned him. But he was again in position before Groghe could call another Lord to his place.

Lessa felt somewhat relieved, and a little smug, at Sangel's reaction. If the fearless Lords also got a taste of honest dread, perhaps . . .

"Why does it glow? Where does it get light? It's dark here," the Lord Holder of Boll babbled.

"It is the light of the sun, my Lord," Fandarel replied, his deep, matter-of-fact voice reducing that miracle to common knowledge.

"How can that be?" Sangel protested. "The sun's on the other side of us now. Any child knows that."

"Of course, but we are not obstructing the Star from that light. We are below it in the skies, if you will, so that the sun's light reaches it directly."

Sangel seemed likely to monopolize the viewer, too.

"That's enough, Sangel," Groghe said testily. "Let Oterel have a chance."

"But I've barely looked, and there was trouble adjusting the mechanism," Sangel complained. Between Oterel's glare and Groghe trying to shoulder him out of the way, Sangel reluctantly stepped aside.

"Let me adjust the focus for you, Lord Oterel," Wansor murmured politely.

"Yes, do. I'm not half blind like Sangel there," the Lord of Tillek said.

"Now, see here, Oterel . . ."

"Fascinating, isn't it, Lord Sangel?" said Lessa, wondering what reaction the man's blathering had concealed.

He harumphed irritably, but his eyes were restless and he frowned.

"Wouldn't call it fascinating, but then I had barely a moment's look."

"We've an entire night, Lord Sangel."

The man shivered, pulling his cloak around him though the night air was not more than mildly cool for spring.

"It's nothing more than a child's miggsy," exclaimed the Lord of Tillek. "Fuzzy. Or is it supposed to be?" He glanced away from the eyepiece at Lessa.

"No, my Lord," Wansor said. "It should be bright and clear, so you can see cloud formations."

"How would you know?" Sangel asked testily.

"Wansor set the instrument up for this evening's viewing," Fandarel pointed out.

"Clouds?" Tillek asked. "Yes, I see them. But what's the land? The dark stuff or the gray?"

"We don't know yet," Fandarel told him.

"Land masses don't look that way as high as dragons can fly a man," said P'zar the Fort Weyrleader, speaking for the first time.

"And objects seen at a far greater distance change even more," Wansor said in the dry tone of someone who does know what he's talking about. "For example, the very mountains of Fort which surround us change drastically if seen from Ruatha Heights or the plains of Crom."

"Then all that dark stuff is land?" Lord Oterel had difficulty not being impressed. And discouraged, Lessa thought. Tillek's Lord Holder must have been hoping to press the extermination of Thread on the Red Star.

"Of that we are not sure," replied Wansor with no lessening of the authority in his manner. Lessa approved more and more of Wansor. A man ought not be afraid to say he didn't know. Nor a woman.

The Lord of Tillek did not want to leave the instrument. Almost as if he hoped, Lessa thought, that if he looked long enough, he'd discover a good argument for mounting an expedition.

Tillek finally responded to Nessel of Crom's acid remarks and stepped aside.

"What do you think is the land, Sangel? Or did you really *see* anything?"

"Of course I did. Saw the clouds plain as I see you right now."

Oterel of Tillek snorted contemptuously. "Which doesn't say much, considering the darkness."

"I saw as much as you did, Oterel. Gray masses, and black masses and those clouds. A star having clouds! Doesn't make sense. Pern has clouds!"

Hastily Lessa changed her laugh at the man's indignation to a cough, but she caught the Harper's amused look and wondered what his reaction to the Red Star would be. Would he be for, or against this expedition? And which attitude did she want him to express?

"Yes, Pern has clouds," Oterel was saying, somewhat surprised at that observation. "And if Pern has clouds, and more water surface than land, then so does the Red Star . . ."

"You can't be sure of that," Sangel protested.

"And there'll be a way of distinguishing land from water, too," Oterel went on, ignoring the Boll Lord. "Let me have another look, there, Nessel," he said, pushing the Crom Lord out of the way.

"Now, wait a minute there, Tillek." And Nessel put a proprietary hand on the instrument. As Tillek jostled him, the tripod tottered and the distance-viewer, on its hastily rigged swivel, assumed a new direction.

"Now you've done it," Oterel cried. "I only wanted to see if you could distinguish the land from the water."

Wansor tried to get between the two Lords so that he could adjust his precious instrument.

"I didn't get my full turn," Nessel complained, trying to keep physical possession of the distance-viewer.

"You'll not see anything, Lord Nessel, if Wansor cannot have a chance to sight back on the Star," Fandarel said, politely gesturing the Crom Lord out of the way.

"You're a damned wherry fool, Nessel," Lord Groghe said, pulling him to one side and waving Wansor in.

"Tillek's the fool."

"I saw enough to know there's not as much dark as there is that gray," Oterel said, defensively. "Pern's more water than land. So's the Red Star."

"From one look you can tell so much, Oterel?" Meron's malicious drawl from the shadows distracted everyone.

Lessa moved pointedly aside as he strolled forward, stroking his bronze lizard possessively. It affronted Lessa that the little creature was humming with pleasure.

"It will take many observations, by many eyes," Fandarel said in his bass rumble, "before we will be able to say what the Red Star looks like with any certitude. One point of similarity is not enough. Not at all."

"Oh, indeed. Indeed." Wansor seconded his Craftmaster, his eyes glued to the piece as he slowly swung it across the night sky.

"What's taking you so long?" Nessel of Crom demanded irritably. "There's the Star. We can all see it with our naked eyes."

"And it is so easy to pick out the green pebble you drop on the sands of Igen at high noon?" asked Robinton.

"Ah. I've got it," Wansor cried. Nessel jumped forward, reaching for the tube. He jerked his hand back, remembering what an unwise movement could do. With both hands conspicuously behind him, he looked again at the Red Star.

Nessel, however, did not remain long at the distance-viewer. When Oterel stepped forward, the Masterharper moved quicker.

"My turn now, I believe, since all the Lord Holders have had one sighting."

"Only fair," Sangel said loudly, glaring at Oterel.

Lessa watched the Masterharper closely, saw the tightening of his broad shoulders as he, too, felt the impact of that first sight of their ancient enemy. He did not remain long, or perhaps she was deceived, but he straightened slowly from the eyepiece and looked thoughtfully toward the Red Star in the dark heavens above them.

"Well, Harper?" asked Meron superciliously. "You've a glib word for every occasion."

Robinton regarded the Nabolese for a longer moment than he had the Star.

"I think it wiser that we keep this distance between us."

"Ha! I thought as much." Meron was grinning with odious triumph.

"I wasn't aware you thought," Robinton remarked quietly.

"What do you mean, Meron?" Lessa asked in a dangerously edged voice, "you thought as much?"

"Why, it should be obvious," and the Lord of Nabol had not tempered his attitude toward her much since his first insult. "The Harper does as Benden Weyr decrees. And since Benden Weyr does not care to exterminate Thread at source . . ."

"And how do you know that?" Lessa demanded coldly.

"And, Lord Nabol, on what grounds do you base your allegation that the Harper of Pern does as Benden Weyr decrees? For I most urgently suggest that you either prove such an accusation instantly or retract it." Robinton's hand was on his belt knife.

The bronze lizard on Meron's arm began to hiss and extend his fragile wings in alarm. The Lord of Nabol contented himself with a knowing smirk as he made a show of soothing his lizard.

"Speak up, Meron," Oterel demanded.

"But it's so obvious. Surely you can all see that," Meron replied with malicious affability and a feigned surprise at the obtuseness of the others. "He has a hopeless passion for—the Benden Weyrwoman."

For a moment Lessa could only stare at the man in a stunned daze. It was true that she admired and respected Robinton. She was fond of him, she supposed. Always glad to see him and never bothering to disguise it but—Meron was mad. Trying to undermine the country's faith in dragonmen with absurd, vicious rumors. First Kylara and now . . . And yet Kylara's weakness, her promiscuity, the general attitude of the Hold and Craft toward the customs of the Weyrs made his accusation so plausible . . .

Robinton's hearty guffaw startled her. And wiped the smile from Nabol's face.

"Benden's Weyrwoman has not half the attraction for me that Benden's wine has!"

There was such intense relief in the faces around her that Lessa knew, in a sinking, sick way, that the Lord Holders had been halfway to believing Meron's invidious accusation. If Robinton had not responded just as he had, if she had started to protest the accusation . . . She grinned, too, managed to chuckle because the Masterharper's fondness for wine, for the Benden wines in particular, was such common knowledge, it was more plausible than Meron's slander. Ridicule was a better defense than truth.

"Furthermore," the Harper went on, "the Masterharper of Pern has no opinion, one way or another, about the Red Star—not even a verse. Because that—that—child's miggsy scares him juiceless and makes him yearn for some of that Benden wine, right now, in limitless quantity." Robinton had not the slightest trace of laughter in his voice now. "I'm too steeped in the history and lore of our beloved Pern, I've sung too many ballads about the evil of the Red Star to want to get any closer to it. Even that—" and he pointed to the distance-viewer, "brings it far too near me. But the men who have to fight Thread day after day, Turn after Turn, can look upon it with less fearfulness than the poor Harper. And, Meron, Lord Holder of Nabol, you can wager every field and cot and hall upon your lands that the dragonmen of every Weyr would like to be quit of any obligation to keep *your* hide Threadfree—even if it means wiping Thread from every squared length of that Star." The vehemence in the Harper's voice caused Meron to take a backward step, to clap a hand on the violently agitated fire lizard. "How can you, any of you," and the Harper's opprobrium fell equally now on the other four Lords, "doubt that the dragonriders wouldn't be as relieved as you to see the end of their centuries of dedication to your safety. They don't *have* to defend you from Thread. You, Groghe, Sangel, Nessel, Oterel, you all ought to realize that by now. You've had T'kul to deal with, and T'ron.

"You all know what Thread does to a man. And you know what happens when a dragon dies. Or must I remind you of that, too? Do you honestly believe that the dragonriders wish to prolong such conditions, such occurrences? What do they get out of it? Not much! Not much! Are the scores they suffer worth a few bags of grain, or a blade from the Smith's? Is a dragon's death truly recompensed by a length of goods or a scrawny herdbeast?

"And if there have been instruments for man with his puny eyes to view that bauble in the sky, why do we still have Thread? If it's just a question of finding coordinates and taking that jump? Could it be that it has been tried by dragonriders before? And they failed because those gray masses we see so clearly are not water, or land, but uncountable Threads, seething and writhing, until the topmost can, by some mysterious agency, win free to plague us? Could it be because, although there are clouds, they do not consist of water vapor as Pern's clouds, but something deadly, far more inimical to us than Thread? How do we know we will not find the bones of long-lost dragons and riders in the dark blots of the planet? There is so much we do *not* know that, yes, I think it wiser that we keep this distance between us. But I think the time for wisdom is now past and we must rely on the folly of the brave and hope that it will suffice them and us. For I do believe," and the Harper turned slowly toward Lessa, "though my heart is heavy and I am scared soulless, that the dragonmen of Pern will go to the Red Star."

"That is F'lar's intention," Lessa said in a strong, ringing voice, her head high, her shoulders straight. Unlike the Harper, she could not admit her fear, even to herself.

"Aye," rumbled Fandarel, nodding his great head slowly up and down, "for he has enjoined me and Wansor to make many observations on the Red Star so that an expedition can be sent as soon as possible."

"And how long must we wait until this expedition takes place?" Meron asked, as if the Harper's words had never been spoken.

"Come now, man, how can you expect any one to give a date— a time?" asked Groghe.

"Ah, but Benden Weyr is so adept at giving times and dates and patterns, is it not?" Meron replied so unctuously that Lessa wanted to scratch his face.

"And they saved your profit, Nabol," Oterel put in.

"Have you any idea, Weyrwoman?" Sangel asked Lessa in an anxious tone.

"I must complete the observations," Wansor put in, nervously dithering. "It would be folly—madness—until we have seen the entire Red Star, and plot in the distinctive features of the various color masses. See how often the clouds cover it. Oh, there is much preliminary investigation to be done. And then, some kind of protective . . ."

"I see," Meron broke in.

Would the man never cease smiling? And yet, Lessa thought, his irony might work in their favor.

"It could be a lifelong project," he went on.

"Not if I know F'lar," the Harper said dryly. "I've recently entertained the notion that Benden's Weyrleader takes these latest vagaries of our ancient scourge as a personal insult, since we had rather thought we'd got them neatly slotted in time and place."

There was such good-humored raillery in the Harper's tone that Oterel of Tillek gave a snort. Lord Groghe looked more thoughtful, probably not quite recovered from F'lar's rebuttal the other day.

"An insult to Benden?" asked Sangel, baffled. "But his timetables were accurate for Turns. Used them myself and never found them wrong until just recently."

Meron stamped his foot, his affected pose gone.

"You're all fools. Letting the Harper sweet-talk you into complacency. We'll never see the end of Thread. Not in his lifetime or ours. And we'll be paying tithes to shiftless Weyrs, deferring to dragonriders and their women as long as this planet circles the sun. And there's not one of you great Lords, not one, with the courage to force this issue. We don't need dragonriders. We don't need 'em. We've fire lizards which eat Thread . . ."

"Then shall I inform T'bor of the High Reaches Weyr that his wings need no longer patrol Nabol? I'm certain he would be relieved," Lessa asked in her lightest, sweetest voice.

The Nabolese Lord gave her a look of pure hatred. The fire-lizard gathered itself into a hissing launch position. A single clear note from Ramoth all but deafened those on the heights. The fire-lizard disappeared with a shriek. Strangling on his curses, Meron stamped down the lighted path to the landing, calling harshly for his dragon. The green appeared with such alacrity that Lessa was certain Ramoth had summoned him, even as she had warned the little lizard against attacking Lessa.

"You wouldn't order T'bor to stop patrolling Nabol, would you, Weyrwoman?" asked Nessel, Lord of Crom. "After all, my lands march with his . . ."

"Lord Nessel," Lessa began, intending to reassure him that she had no such authority in the first place and in the second . . . "Lord Nessel," she repeated instead, smiling at him, "you notice that the Lord of Nabol did *not* request it, after all. Though," and she sighed with dramatic dedication, "we have been sorely tempted to penalize him for his part in the death of the two dragon queens." She gave Nessel a wan, brave smile. "But there are hundreds of innocent people on his lands, and many more about him, who cannot be permitted to suffer because of his—his—how shall I phrase it—his irrational behavior."

"Which leads me to ask," Groghe said, hastily clearing his throat, "what is being done with that—that Kylara woman?"

"Nothing," Lessa said in a flat hard voice, trusting that would end the matter.

"Nothing?" Groghe was incensed. "She caused the deaths of two queens and you're doing nothing . . ."

"Are the Lord Holders doing anything about Meron?" she asked, glancing sternly at the four present. There was a long silence. "I must return to Benden Weyr. The dawn and another day's watch come all too soon there. We're keeping Wansor and Fandarel from the observations that will make it possible for us to go to that Star."

"Before they monopolize the thing, I'd like another look," Oterel of Tillek said loudly. "My eyes are keen . . ."

Lessa was tired as she called Ramoth to her. She wanted to go back to Benden Weyr, not so much to sleep as to reassure herself about F'lar. Mnementh was with him, true, and he'd have reported any change in his rider's condition . . .

And I'd've told you, Ramoth said, sounding a little hurt.

"Lessa," the Harper's low voice reached her, "are you in favor of that expedition?"

She looked up at him, his face lighted by the path glows. His expression was neutral and she wondered if he'd really meant what he'd said back at the Star Rocks. He dissembled so easily, and so often against his own inclination, that she sometimes wondered what his candid thoughts were.

"It scares me. It scares me because it seems so likely that someone must have tried. Sometime. It just doesn't seem logical . . ."

"Is there any record that anyone, besides yourself, ever jumped so far *between* times?"

"No." She had to admit it. "Not so far. But then, there hadn't been such need."

"And there's no need now to take this other kind of a jump?"

"Don't unsettle me more." Lessa was unsure of what she felt or thought, or what anyone felt or thought, should or shouldn't do. Then she saw the kind, worried expression of the Harper's eyes and impulsively gripped his arm. "How can we know? How can we be sure?"

"How were you sure that the Question Song could be answered—by you?"

"And you've a new Question Song for me?"

"Questions, yes." He gave her a smile as he covered her hand gently with his own. "Answer?" He shook his head and then stepped back as Ramoth alighted.

But his questions were as difficult to forget as the Question Song which had led her *between* time. When she returned to Benden, she found that F'lar's skin was hot to the touch; he slept restlessly. So much so that, although Lessa willed herself to sleep beside him on the wide couch, she couldn't succeed. Desperate for some surcease from her fears—for F'lar, of the intangible unknown ahead—she crept from their couch and into the weyr. Ramoth roused sleepily and arranged her front legs in a cradle. Lulled by the warm, musty comfort of her dragon, Lessa finally did sleep.

By the morning, F'lar was no better, querulous with his fever and worried about her report on the viewing.

"I can't imagine what you expected me to see," she said with some exasperation after she had patiently described for the fourth time what she had seen through the distance-viewer.

"I *expected*," and he paused significantly, "to find some—some characteristic for which the dragons could fly *between*." He plucked at the bed fur, then pulled the recalcitrant forelock back from his eyes. "We have *got* to keep that promise to the Lord Holders."

"Why? To prove Meron wrong?"

"No. To prove it is or is not possible to get rid of Thread permanently." He scowled at her as if she should have known the answer.

"I think someone else must have tried to discover that before," she said wearily. "And we still have Thread."

"That doesn't mean anything," he countered in such a savage tone that he began to cough, an exercise which painfully contracted the injured muscles across his waist.

Instantly Lessa was at his side, offering him distilled wine, sweetened and laced with fellis fruit juice.

"I want F'nor," he said petulantly.

Lessa looked down at him for the coughing spasm had left him limp.

"If we can pry him away from Brekke."

F'lar's lips set in a thin line.

"You mean, only you, F'lar, Benden Weyrleader, can flout tradition?" she asked.

"That isn't . . . ."

"If it's your pet project you're worrying about, I had N'ton secure Thread . . ."

"N'ton?" F'lar's eyes flew open in surprise.

"Yes. He's a good lad and, from what I heard at Fort Weyr last night, very deft in being exactly where he is needed, unobtrusively."

"And . . . ?"

"And? Well, when the next queen at Fort Weyr rises, he'll undoubtedly take the Leadership. Which is what you intended, isn't it?"

"I don't mean that. I mean, the Thread."

Lessa felt her guts turn over at the memory. "As you thought, the grubs rose to the surface the instant we put the Thread in. Very shortly there was no more Thread."

F'lar's eyes shown and he parted his lips in a triumphant smile.

"Why didn't you tell me sooner?"

At that, Lessa jammed both fists against her waist and awarded him one of her sternest looks.

"Because there have been a few other things to occupy my mind and time. This is not something we can discuss in open session, after all. Why, if even such loyal riders as . . ."

"What did N'ton say? Does he fully understand what I'm tyring to do?"

Lessa eyed her Weyrmate thoughtfully. "Yes, he does, which is why I chose him to substitute for F'nor."

That seemed to relieve F'lar, for he leaned back against the pillows with a deep sigh and closed his eyes. "He's a good choice. For more than Fort Weyrleadership. He'd carry on. That's what we need the most, Lessa. Men who think, who can carry on. That's what happened before." His eyes flew open, shadowed with a vague fear and a definite worry. "What time is it at Fort Weyr now?"

Lessa made a rapid calculation. "Dawn's about four hours away."

"Oh. I want N'ton here as soon as possible."

"Now wait a minute, F'lar, he's a Fort rider . . ."

F'lar grabbed for her hand, pulling her down to him. "Don't you see," he demanded, his voice hoarse, his urgency frightening, "he's got to know. Know everything I plan. Then, if something happens . . ."

Lessa stared at him, not comprehending. Then she was both furious with him for frightening her, irritated with his self-pity, and terrified that he might indeed be fatally ill.

"F'lar, get a grip on yourself, man," she said, half-angry, half-teasing; he felt so hot.

He flung himself back down on the bed, tossing his head from side to side.

"This is what happened before. I know it. I don't care what he says, get F'nor here."

Lioth is coming and a green from Telgar, Mnementh announced.

Lessa took consolation from the fact that Mnementh didn't seem the least bit distressed by F'lar's ravings.

F'lar gave a startled cry, glaring accusingly at Lessa.

"Don't look at me. I didn't send for N'ton. It isn't even dawn there yet."

The green is a messenger and the man he bears is very excited, Mnementh reported, and he sounded mildly curious.

Ramoth, who had taken herself to the Hatching Ground after Lessa awakened, rumbled a challenge to bronze Lioth.

N'ton came striding down the passageway, accompanied by Wansor, certainly the last person Lessa expected to see. The rotund little man's face was flushed with excitement, his eyes sparkling despite red rims and bloodshot whites.

"Oh, Weyrlady, this is the most exciting news imaginable. Really exciting!" Wansor babbled, shaking the large leaf under her nose. She had an impression of circles. Then Wansor saw F'lar. All the excitement drained out of his face as he realized that the Weyrleader was a very sick man. "Sir, I had no idea—I wouldn't have presumed . . ."

"Nonsense, man," F'lar said irritably. "What brings you? What have you there? Let me see. You've found a coordinate for the dragons?"

Wansor seemed so uncertain about proceeding that Lessa took charge, guiding the man to the bed.

"What's this leaf mean? Ah, this is Pern, and that is the Red Star, but what are these other circles you're marked?"

"I'm not certain I know, my lady, but I discovered them while scanning the heavens last night—or this morning. The Red Star is not the only globe above us. There is this one, too, which became visible toward morning, didn't it, N'ton?" The young bronze rider nodded solemnly but there was a gleam of amusement in his blue eyes for the glassman's manner of exposition. "And very faintly, but still visible as a sphere, is this third heavenly neighbor, to our northeast, low on the horizon. Then, directly south—it was N'ton's notion to look all around—we found this larger globe with the most unusual cluster of objects moving with visible speed about it. Why, the skies around Pern are crowded!" Wansor's dismay was so ludicrous that Lessa had to stifle her giggle.

F'lar took the leaf from the glassman and began to study it while Lessa pushed Wansor onto the stool by the sick man. F'lar tapped the circles thoughtfully as though this tactile contact made them more real.

"And there are four stars in the skies?"

"Indeed there are many more, Weyrleader," Wansor replied. "But only these," and his stained forefinger pointed to the three newly discovered neighbors, "appear so far as globes in the distance-viewer. The others are merely bright points of light as stars have always been. One must assume, then, that these three are also controlled by our sun, and pass around it, even as we do. For I do not see how they could escape the force that tethers us and the Red Star to the Sun—a force we know to be tremendous . . ."

F'lar looked up from the rude sketches, a terrible expression on his face.

"If these are so near, then does Thread really come from the Red Star?"

"Oh dear, oh dear," moaned Wansor softly and began caressing his fingertips with his thumbs in little fluttery gestures.

"Nonsense," said Lessa so confidently that the three men glanced at her in surprise. "Let's not make more complications than we already have. The ancients who knew enough to make that distance-viewer definitely stipulate the Red Star as the origin of Thread. If it were one of these others, they'd have said so. It is when the Red Star approaches Pern that we have Thread."

"In that drawing in the Council Room at Fort Weyr there is a diagram of globes on circular routes," N'ton said thoughtfully. "Only there are six circles and," his eyes widened suddenly; he glanced quickly down at the sheet in Wansor's hand, ". . . one of them, the next to the last, has clusters of smaller satellites."

"Well, then, except that we've seen it with our own eyes, what's all the worry?" demanded Lessa, grabbing up the *klah* pitcher and mugs to serve the newcomers. "We've only just discovered for ourselves what the ancients knew and inscribed on that wall."

"Only now," N'ton said softly, "we know what that design means."

Lessa shot him a long look and nearly flooded Wansor's cup.

"Indeed. The actual experience is the knowing, N'ton."

"I gather you have both spent the night at that distance-viewer?" asked F'lar. When they nodded, he asked, "What of the Red Star? Did you see anything that could guide us in?"

"As to that, sir," N'ton answered after a questioning glance at Wansor, "there is an odd-shaped protuberance which puts me in mind of the tip of Nerat, only pointed east instead of west—" His voice trailed off and he gave a diffident shrug of his shoulders.

F'lar sighed and leaned back again, all the eagerness gone from his face.

"Insufficient detail, huh?"

"Last night," N'ton added in hurried qualification.

"I doubt the following nights will alter the view."

"On the contrary, Weyrleader," said Wansor, his eyes wide, "the Red Star turns on its own axis much as Pern does."

"But it is still too far away to make out any details," Lessa said firmly.

F'lar shot her an annoyed look. "If I could only see for my- self . . ."

Wansor looked up brightly. "Well, now, you know, I had about figured out how to utilize the lenses from the magnifier. Of course, there'd be no such maneuverability as one can achieve with the ancient device, but the advantage is that I could set up those lenses on your own Star Stones. It's rather interesting, too, because if I put one lens in the Eye Rock and set the other on the Finger Rock, you will see— or, but then you won't see, will you?" And the little man seemed to deflate.

"Won't see what?"

"Well, those rocks are situated to catch the Red Star only at winter solstice, so of course the angles are wrong for any other time of year. But then, I could—no," Wansor's face was puckered with his intense frown. Only his eyes moved, restlessly, as the myriad thoughts he was undoubtedly sifting were reflected briefly. "I will think about it. But I am sure that I can devise a means of your seeing the Red Star, Weyrleader, without moving from Benden."

"You must be exhausted, Wansor," Lessa said, before F'lar could ask another question.

"Oh, not to mention," Wansor replied, blinking hard to focus on her.

"Enough to mention," Lessa said firmly and took the cup from his hand, half-lifting him from the stool. "I think, Master Wansor, that you had better sleep here at Benden a little while."

"Oh, could I? I'd the most fearful notion that I might fall off the dragon *between*. But that couldn't happen, could it? Oh, I can't stay. I have the Craft's dragon. Really, perhaps I'd just better . . ."

His voice trailed off as Lessa led him down the corridor. "He was up all last night too," N'ton said, grinning affectionately after Wansor.

"There is no way to go *between* to the Red Star?"

N'ton shook his head slowly. "Not that we could see tonight— last night. The same features of dark, reddish masses were turned toward us most of the time we watched. Just before we decided you should know about the other planets, I took a final look and that Neratlike promontory had disappeared, leaving only the dullish gray-red coloration."

"There must be some way to get to the Red Star."

"I'm sure you'll find it, sir, when you're feeling better."

F'lar grimaced, thinking that "unobtrusive" was an apt description of this young man. He had deftly expressed confidence in his superior, that only ill-health prevented immediate action, and that the ill-health was a passing thing.

"Since that's the way matters stand in that direction, let us proceed in another. Lessa said that you procured Thread for us. Did you see how those swampgrubs dealt with Thread?"

N'ton nodded slowly, his eyes glittering.

"If we hadn't had to cede the dissidents the continent, I'd've had a straight-flown Search discover the boundaries of the southern lands. We still don't know its extent. Exploration was stopped on the west by the deserts, and on the east by the sea. But it can't be just the swampy area that is infested with these grubs." F'lar shook his head. He sounded querulous to himself. He took a breath, forcing himself to speak more slowly and therefore less emotionally. "There's been Threadfall in the Southern Weyr for seven Turns and not a single burrow. The ground crews have never had to flame out anything. Now, even with the most careful, most experienced, sharpest-eyed riders, some Thread gets to the ground. T'bor insists there were never any burrows to be found anywhere after a Threadfall." F'lar grimaced. "His wings are efficient and Threadfall is light in the south, but I wished I'd known."

"And what would you have thought?" asked Lessa with her usual asperity as she rejoined them. "Nothing. Because until Thread started falling out of phase, and you had been at the swampfall, you'd never have correlated the information."

She was right, of course, but N'ton didn't have to look so torn between agreement with her and sympathy for him. Silently F'lar railed at this infuriating debility. He ought to be up and around, not forced to rely on the observations of others at a crucial time like this.

"Sir, in the Turns I've been a dragonrider," said N'ton, considering his words even as he spoke, "I've learned that nothing is done without purpose. I used to call my sire foolish to insist that one tanned leather in just one way, or stretched hide only a little at a time, well-soaked, but I've realized recently that there is an order, a reason, a rhyme for it." He paused, but F'lar urged him to go on. "I've been most interested in the methods of the Mastersmith. That man *thinks* constantly." The young man's eyes shown with such intense admiration that F'lar grinned. "I'm afraid I may be making a nuisance of myself but I learned so much from him. Enough to realize that there're gaps in the knowledge that's been transmitted down to us. Enough to understand that perhaps the southern continent was abandoned to let the grubs grow in strength there . . ."

"You mean, that if the ancients knew they couldn't get to the Red Star," Lessa exclaimed, "they developed the grubs to protect growing fields?"

"They developed the dragons from fire-lizards, didn't they? Why not grubs as ground crews?" And N'ton grinned at the whimsy of his thesis.

"That makes sense," Lessa said, looking hopefully at F'lar. "Certainly that explains why the dragons haven't jumped *between* to the Red Star. They didn't need to. Protection was being provided."

"Then why don't we have grubs here in the north?" asked F'lar contentiously.

"Ha! Someone didn't live long enough to transmit the news, or sow the grubs, or cultivate them, or something. Who can tell?" Lessa threw wide her arms. It was obvious to F'lar that she preferred this theory, subtle as she may have been in trying to block his desire to go to the Red Star.

He was willing to believe that the grubs were the answer, but the Red Star had to be visited. If only to reassure the Lord Holders that the dragonmen were trustworthy.

"We still don't *know* if the grubs exist beyond the swamps," F'lar reminded her.

"I don't mind sneaking in and finding out," N'ton said. "I know Southern very well, sir. Probably as well as anyone, even F'nor. I'd like permission to go south and check." When N'ton saw F'lar hesitate and Lessa frown, he went on hurriedly. "I can evade T'kul. That man's so obvious, he's pathetic."

"All right, all right. N'ton. Go. It's the truth I've no one else to send," and F'lar tried not to feel bitter that F'nor was involved with a woman; he was a dragonrider first, wasn't he? Then F'lar suppressed such uncharitable thoughts. Brekke had been a Weyrwoman; through no fault of hers (and F'lar still berated himself that he had not thought of keeping a closer check on Kylara's activities—he'd been warned), Brekke was deprived of her dragon. If she found some comfort in F'nor's presence, it was unforgivable to deprive her of his company. "Go, N'ton. Spot-check. And bring back samples of those grubs from every location. I *wish* Wansor had not dismantled that other contraption. We could look closely at the grubs. That Masterherder was a fool. The grubs might not be the same in every spot."

"Grubs are grubs," Lessa mumbled.

"Landbeasts raised in the mountains are different from landbeasts raised on the plains," N'ton said. "Fellis trees grown south are larger with better fruit than Nerat's best."

"You know too much," Lessa replied, grinning to take the sting from her words.

N'ton grinned. "I'm a bronze rider, Weyrwoman."

"You'd best be off. No, wait. Are you sure Fort is not going to need you and Lioth for Thread?" F'lar asked, wanting to be rid of this very healthy youngster who only emphasized his illness.

"Not for a while, sir. It's full night there still."

That underscored his youthfulness and F'lar waved him out, trying to suppress jealousy with gratitude. The moment he'd gone, F'lar let out a sudden exasperated oath that brought Lessa, all consideration, to his side.

"I'll get well, I'll get well," he fumed. He held her hand against his cheek, grateful, too, for the cool of her fingers as they curved to fit against his face.

"Of course you'll get well. You're never sick," she murmured softly, stroking his forehead with her free hand. Then her voice took on a teasing note. "You're just stupid. Otherwise you wouldn't have gone *between*, let cold into a wound, and developed fever."

F'lar, reassured as much by her caustic jibe as her cool and loving caresses, lay back and willed himself to sleep, to health.

·· C H A P T E R   X I V ··

𐤀

Early Morning at Ruatha Hold
Midday at Benden Weyr

When word came that the Hatching was likely to occur that bright spring day, Jaxom didn't know whether he was glad or not. Ever since the two queens had killed each other ten days before, Lytol had been sunk in such a deep gloom that Jaxom had tiptoed around the Hold. His guardian had always been a somber man, never given to joking or teasing, but this new silence unnerved the entire Hold. Even the new baby didn't cry.

It was bad, very bad, to lose one queen, Jaxom knew, but to lose two, in such a horrible way! It was almost as if *things* were pointing toward even direr events. Jaxom was scared, a deep voiceless feeling in his bones. He almost dreaded seeing Felessan. He had never shaken off his sense of blasphemy for invading the Hatching Ground, and wondered if this were his punishment. But he was a logical boy and the death of the two queens had not occurred at Ruatha, not over Fort Weyr to which Ruatha Hold was bound. He'd never met Kylara or Brekke. He did know F'nor and felt sorry for him if half what he'd heard was true—that F'nor had taken Brekke into his weyr and had abandoned his duties as a Wing-second to care for her. She was very sick. Funny, everyone was sorry for Brekke but no one mentioned Kylara, and she'd lost a queen, too.

Jaxom wondered about that but *knew* he couldn't ask. Just as he couldn't ask if he and Lytol were really going to the Hatching. Why else would the Weyrleader send them word? And wasn't Talina a Ruathan candidate for the queen egg? Ruatha ought to be represented at the Hatching. Benden Weyr always had open Impressions, even when the other Weyrs didn't. And he hadn't seen Felessan in ages. Not that anyone had done much more than Thread-watch since the wedding at Telgar.

Jaxom sighed. That had been some day. He shivered, remembered how sick, cold and—yes—how scared he'd been. (Lytol said a *man* wasn't afraid to admit to fear.) All the time he'd watched F'lar fighting T'ron, he'd been scared. He shuddered again, his spine rippling with reaction to that memory. Everything was going wrong on Pern. Dragon queens killing each other, Weyrleaders dueling in public, Thread falling here and there, with no rhyme or reason. Order had slipped away from life; the constants that made his routine were dissolving, and he was powerless to stop the inexorable slide. It wasn't fair. Everything had been going so well. Everyone had been saying how Ruatha Hold had improved. Now, this past six days, they'd lost that northeastern farmhold and, if things kept up, there wouldn't be much left of all Lytol's hard work. Maybe that's why he was acting so—so odd. But it wasn't fair. Lytol had worked so hard. And now, it looked as though Jaxom was going to miss the Hatching and see who Impressed that littlest egg. It wasn't at all fair.

"Lord Jaxom," gasped a breathless drudge from the doorway, "Lord Lytol said for you to change to your best. The Hatching's to start. Oh, sir, do you think Talina has a chance?"

"More than a chance," Jaxom said, rude with excitement. "She's Ruathan-bred after all. Now get out."

His fingers were clumsy with the fastenings of his trousers and the tunic which had been new for the Telgar wedding. *He* hadn't spilled on the fine fabric, but you could still see the greasy fingerprints on the right shoulder where an excited guest had pulled him away from his vantage point on the Telgar Hold steps during the fight.

He shrugged into the cloak, found the second glove under the bed and raced down into the Great Court where the blue dragon waited.

Sight of the blue, however, inevitably reminded Jaxom that Groghe's eldest son had been given one of the fire-lizard eggs. Lytol had deliberately refused the pair to which Ruatha Hold was entitled. That, too, was a rankling injustice. Jaxom should have had a fire-lizard egg, even if Lytol couldn't bear to Impress one. Jaxom was Lord of Ruatha and an egg had been his due. Lytol had no right to refuse him that perquisite.

"Be a good day for Ruatha if your Talina Impresses, won't it?" D'wer, the blue's rider, greeted him.

"Yes," Jaxom replied, and he sounded sullen even to himself.

"Cheer up, lad," D'wer said. "Things could be worse."

"How?"

D'wer chuckled and, while it offended Jaxom, he couldn't very well call a dragonman to task.

"Good morning, Trebith," Jaxom said to the blue, who turned his head, the large eye whirling with color.

They both heard Lytol's voice, dull-toned but clear as he gave instructions for the day's work to the stewards.

"For every field that gets scored, we plant two more as long as we can get seed in the ground. There's plenty of fallow land in the northeast. Move the Holders."

"But, Lord Lytol . . ."

"Don't give me the old wail about temporary dwellings. There'll be temporary eating if we aren't farsighted, and that's harder to endure than a draught or two."

Lytol gave Jaxom a cursory inspection and an absent good morning. The tic started in the Lord Holder's face the moment he climbed up Trebith's shoulder to take his seat against the neck ridges. He motioned curtly to his ward to get in front of him and then nodded to D'wer.

The blue dragonman gave a slight smile of response, as if he expected no more notice from Lytol, and suddenly they were aloft. Aloft, with Ruatha's fire height dwindling below. And *between* with Jaxom holding his breath against the frightening cold. Then above Benden's Star Stones, so close to other dragons also winging into the Weyr that Jaxom feared collision at any moment.

"How—how do they know where they are?" he asked D'wer.

The rider grinned at him. *"They* know. Dragons never collide." And a shadow of memory crossed D'wer's usually cheerful face.

Jaxom groaned. How stupid of him to make any reference to the queens' battle.

"Lad, everything reminds us of that," the blue rider said. "Even the dragons are off color. But," he continued more briskly, "the Impression will help."

Jaxom hoped so but, pessimistically, he was sure something would go wrong today, too. Then he clutched wildly at D'wer's riding tunic for it seemed as if they were flying straight into the rock face of the Weyr Bowl. Or worse, despite D'wer's reassurance, right into the green dragon also veering in that direction.

But suddenly they were inside the wide mouth of the upper entrance, a dark core that led into the immense Hatching Ground. The whirr of wings, a concentration of the musty scent of dragons, and then they were poised above the slightly steaming sands, in the great circle theatre with its tiers of perches for men and beasts.

Jaxom had a dizzying view of the eggs on the Hatching Ground, of the colored robes of those already assembled, and the array of dragon bodies, gleaming eyes and furled wings, the great, graceful, blue, green and brown hides. Where were the bronzes?

"They'll bring in the candidates, Lord Jaxom. Ah, there's the young scamp," D'wer said, and suddenly Jaxom's neck was jerked as Trebith backwinged to land neatly on a ledge. "Off you go."

"Jaxom! You did come!"

And Felessan was thumping him, his clothes so new they smelled of dye and were harsh against Jaxom's hands as he pounded his friend's back.

"Thanks so much for bringing him, D'wer. Good day to you, Lord Warder Lytol. The Weyrleader and the Weyrwoman said to give you their greetings and to ask you to stay to eat after Impression, if you would give them a moment of your time."

It all came out in such a rush that the blue rider grinned. Lytol bowed in such solemn acknowledgement that Jaxom felt a surge of irritation for his stuffy guardian.

Felessan was impervious to such nuances and pulled Jaxom eagerly away from the adults. Having achieved a certain physical distance, the boy chattered away in so loud a whisper that everyone two ledges up could hear him distinctly.

"I was sure you wouldn't be allowed to come. Everything's been so sour and horrible since the—you know—happened."

"Don't you *know* anything, Felessan?" Jaxom said in a rebuking hiss that startled his friend into wide-eyed silence.

"Huh? What'd I do wrong?" he demanded, this time in a more circumspect tone, glancing around him apprehensively. "Don't tell me something's gone wrong at Ruatha Hold?"

Jaxom pulled his friend as far from Lytol as they could go on that row of seats and then sat the younger boy down so hard that Felessan let out a yip of protest which he instantly muffled behind both hands. Jaxom glanced surreptitiously back at Lytol but the man was responding to the greetings of those in the level above. People were still arriving, both by dragonwing and by a climb up the flight of stairs from the hot sands. Felessan giggled suddenly, pointing toward a portly man and woman now crossing the Hatching Ground. They obviously wore thin-soled shoes for they kept picking their feet up and putting them down in a curious mincing motion, totally at variance with their physical appearance.

"Didn't think so many people would come what with all that's been happening," Felessan murmured excitedly, his eyes dancing. "Look at them!" and he pointed out three boys, all with the Nerat device on their chests. "They look as if they smelled something unpleasant. You don't think dragons smell, do you?"

"No, of course not. Only a little and its pleasant. They aren't candidates, are they?" Jaxom asked, disgusted.

"Nooo. Candidates wear white." Felessan made a grimace for Jaxom's ignorance. "They don't come in till later. Ooops! And later may be sooner. Didja see that egg rock?"

The motion had been observed, for the dragons began to hum. There were excited cries from late arrivals who now scurried for places. And Jaxom could scarcely see the rest of the eggs for the sudden flutter of dragon wings in the air. Just as suddenly, there were no more impediments to vision and all the eggs seemed to be rocking. Almost as if they finally found the hot sands underneath too much. Only one egg was motionless. The little one, still off by itself against the far wall.

"What's wrong with that one?" Jaxom asked, pointing.

"That smallest one?" Felessan swallowed, keeping his face averted.

"We didn't *do* anything to it."

"*I* didn't," Felessan said firmly, glaring at Jaxom. "You touched it."

"I may have touched it but that doesn't mean I hurt it," the young Lord Holder begged for reassurance.

"No, touching 'em doesn't hurt 'em. The candidates've been touching 'em for weeks and they're rocking."

"Why isn't that one then?"

Jaxom had difficulty making Felessan understand him for the humming had increased until it was a constant, exciting thrum reverberating back and forth across the Hatching Ground.

"I dunno," Felessan shrugged diffidently. "It may not even Hatch. That's what *they* say, at any rate."

"But I didn't *do* anything," Jaxom insisted, mostly for his own comfort.

"I told you that! Look, here come the candidates." Then Felessan leaned over, his lips right at Jaxom's ear, whispering something so unintelligible that he had to repeat it three times before Jaxom did hear him.

"Re-Impress Brekke?" Jaxom exclaimed, far louder than he meant to, glancing toward Lytol.

"Deafwit!" Felessan hissed at him, jerking him back in his seat. "You don't *know* what's been going on here. Let me tell you, it's been something!" Felessan's eyes were wide with suppressed knowledge.

"What? Tell me!"

Felessan glanced toward Lytol but the man seemed oblivious of them; his attention was on the young boys marching toward the rocking eggs, their faces white and purposeful, their bodies in the white tunics taut with excitement and anticipation.

"What do you mean about Brekke re-Impressing? Why? How?" Jaxom demanded, his mind assaulted by simultaneous conflicts: Lytol astride a dragon all his own, Brekke re-Impressing, Talina left out and crying because she was Ruathan-bred and should be dragonwoman.

"Just that. She Impressed a dragon once, she's young. They said she was a far better Weyrwoman than that Kylara." Felessan's tone echoed the universally bad opinion of the Southern ex-Weyrwoman. "That way Brekke'd get well. You see," and Felessan lowered his voice again, "F'nor loves her! And I heard—" he paused dramatically and looked around (as if anyone could overhear them), "I heard that F'nor was going to let Canth fly her queen."

Jaxom stared at his friend, shocked. "You're crazy! Brown dragons don't fly queens."

"Well, F'nor was going to try it."

"But—but . . ."

"Yes, it is!" Felessan agreed sagely. "You should've heard F'lar and F'nor." His eyes widened to double their normal size. "It was Lessa, my mother, who said what they ought to do. Make Brekke re-Impress. She was too good, Lessa said, to live half-dead."

Both boys glanced guiltily toward Lytol.

"Do they—do they think she can re-Impress?" asked Jaxom, staring at the stern profile of his guardian and wondering.

Felessan shrugged. "We'll know soon. Here they come."

And sure enough, out of the black maw of the upper tunnel, flew bronze dragons in such rapid succession that they seemed nose to tail.

"There's Talina!" Jaxom exclaimed, jumping to his feet. "There's Talina, Lytol," and he crossed to pull at his guardian's arm. Lytol wouldn't have noticed either Jaxom's importunities or Talina's entrance. The man had eyes only for the girl entering from the Ground level. Two figures, a man and a woman, stood by the wide opening, as if they could accompany her this far, no further.

"That's Brekke all right," Felessan said in a hushed tone as he slid beside Jaxom.

She stumbled slightly, halted, seeming impervious to the uncomfortably hot sands. She straightened her shoulders and slowly walked across to join the five girls who waited near the golden egg. She stopped by Talina, who turned and gestured for the newcomer to take a place in the loose semicircle about the queen egg.

The humming stopped. In the sudden, unquiet silence, the faint crack of a shell was clearly audible, followed by the pop and shatter of others.

The dragonets, glistening, awkward, ugly young things, began to flop from their casings, squawking, crooning, their wedge-shaped heads too big for the thin, sinuous necks. The young boys stood very still, their bodies tense with the mental efforts of attracting the dragonets to them.

The first was free of its encumbrance, staggering beyond the nearest boy who jumped adroitly out of its way. It fell, nose first at the feet of a tall black-haired lad. The boy knelt, helped the dragonet balance on his shaky feet, looked into the rainbow eyes. Jaxom saw Lytol close his, and saw the fact of Lytol's terrible loss engraved on the man's gray face, as much of a torture now as the day his Larth had died of phosphine burns.

"Look," Jaxom cried, "the queen egg. It's rocking. Oh, how I wish . . ."

Then he couldn't go on without compromising himself in his friend's good opinion. For much as he wanted Talina to Impress which would mean three living Ruathan-bred Weyrwoman, he knew that Felessan was betting on Brekke.

Felessan was so intensely involved in the scene below that he hadn't been aware of Jaxom's unfinished phrase.

The golden shell cracked suddenly, right down the center, and its inmate, with a raucous protest, fell to the sand on her back. Talina and two others moved forward quickly, trying to help the little creature right herself. The queen was no sooner on all four legs than the girls stepped back, almost as if they could not press their claim, by mutual consent leaving the first opportunity to Brekke.

She was oblivious. To Jaxom, it seemed she didn't care. She seemed limp, broken, pathetic, listing to one side. A dragon crooned softly and she shook her head as if only then aware of her surroundings.

The queen's head turned to Brekke, the glistening eyes enormous in the outsized skull. The queen lurched forward a step.

At that moment a small blur of bronze streaked across the Hatching Ground. With defiant screams, a fire-lizard hung just above the queen's head. So close, in fact, that the little queen reared back with a startled shriek and bit at the air, instinctively spreading her wings as protection for her vulnerable eyes.

Dragons protested from their ledges. Talina interposed her body between the queen and her small attacker.

"Berd! Don't!" Brekke moved forward, arm extended, to capture the irate bronze. The little queen cried out in protest, hiding her face in Talina's skirts. The two women faced one another, their bodies tense, wary.

Then Talina stretched her hand out to Brekke, smiling. Her pose lasted only a moment for the queen butted her legs peremptorily. Talina knelt, arms reassuringly about the dragonet. Brekke turned, no longer a statue immobilized by grief, and retraced her steps to the figures waiting at the entrance. All the time, the little bronze fire-lizard whirred around her head, emitting sounds that ranged from scolding to entreaty. The racket sounded so like the cook at Ruatha Hold at dinnertime that Jaxom grinned.

"She didn't want the queen," Felessan said, stunned. "She didn't try!"

"That fire-lizard wouldn't let her," Jaxom said, wondering why he was defending Brekke.

"It would be wrong, terribly wrong for her to succeed," Lytol said in a dead voice. He seemed to shrink in on himself, his shoulders sagging, his hands dangling limply between his knees.

Some of the newly Impressed boys were beginning to lead their beasts from the Ground. Jaxom turned back, afraid to miss anything. It was all happening much too quickly. It'd be over in a few minutes.

"Didja see, Jaxom?" Felessan was saying, pulling at his sleeve. "Didja see? Birto got a bronze and Pellomar only Impressed a green. Dragons don't like bullies and Pellomar's been the biggest bully in the Weyr. Good for you, Birto!" Felessan cheered his friend.

"The littlest egg hasn't cracked yet," Jaxom said, nudging Felessan and pointing. "Shouldn't it be hatching?"

Lytol frowned, roused by the anxiety in his ward's voice.

"They were saying it probably wouldn't hatch," Felessan reminded Jaxom, far more interested in seeing what dragons his friends had Impressed.

"But what if it doesn't hatch? Can't someone break it and help the poor dragon out? The way a birthing woman does when the baby won't come?"

Lytol whirled on Jaxom, his face suffused with anger.

"What would a boy your age know of birthing?"

"I know about mine," Jaxom replied stoutly, jerking his chin up. "I nearly died. Lessa told me so and she was there. Can a dragonet die?"

"Yes," Lytol admitted heavily because he never lied to the boy. "They can die and better so if the embryo is misformed."

Jaxom looked at his body quickly although he knew perfectly well he was as he should be; in fact, more developed than some of the other Hold boys.

"I've seen eggs that never hatched. Who needs to live— crippled?"

"Well, that egg's alive," Jaxom said. "Look at it rocking right now."

"You're right. It's moving. But it isn't cracking," Felessan said.

"Then why is everyone leaving?" Jaxom demanded suddenly, jumping to his feet. For there was no one anywhere near the wobbling small egg.

The Ground was busy with riders urging their beasts down to help the weyrlings, or to escort guests of the Weyr back to their Holds. Most of the bronzes, of course, had gone with the new queen. Vast as the Hatching Ground was, its volume shrank with so many huge beasts around. Yet not even the disappointed candidates spared any interest for that one small remaining egg.

"There's F'lar. He ought to be told, Lytol. Please!"

"He knows," Lytol said, for F'lar had beckoned several of the brown riders to him and they were looking toward the little egg.

"Go, Lytol. Make them help it!"

"Small eggs can occur in any queen's laying life," Lytol said. "This is not my concern. Nor yours."

He turned and began to make his way toward the steps, plainly certain that the boys would follow.

"But they're not doing anything," Jaxom muttered, rebelliously.

Felessan gave him a helpless shrug. "C'mon. We'll be eating soon at this rate. And there's all kinds of special things tonight." He trotted after Lytol.

Jaxom looked back at the egg, now wildly rocking. "It just isn't fair! They don't care what happens to you. They care about that Brekke, but not you. Come on, egg. Crack your shell! Show 'em. One good crack and I'll bet they'll do something!"

Jaxom had edged along the tier until he was just over the little egg. It was rocking in time with his urgings now, but there was no one within a dragonlength. There was something frenzied about the way it rocked, too, that made Jaxom think the dragonet was desperate for help.

Without thinking, Jaxom swung over the wall and let himself drop to the sands. He could now see the minute striations on the shell, he could hear the frantic tapping within, observe the fissures spreading. As he touched the shell, it seemed like rock to him, it was so hard. No longer leathery as it had been the day of their escapade.

"No one else'll help you. I will!" he cried and kicked the shell.

A crack appeared. Two more stout blows and the crack widened. A piteous cry inside was followed by the bright tip of the dragonet's nose, which battered at the tough shell.

"You want to get born. Just like me. All you need is a little help, same as me," Jaxom was crying, pounding at the crack with his fists. Thick pieces fell off, far heavier than the discarded shells of the other hatchlings.

"Jaxom, what are you doing?" someone yelled at him but it was too late.

The thick inner membrane was visible now and this was what had been impeding the dragonet's emergence. Jaxom ripped the slippery stuff open with his belt knife and, from the sac, fell a tiny white body, not much larger than Jaxom's torso. Instinctively Jaxom reached out, helping the backstranded creature to its feet.

Before F'lar or anyone could intervene, the white dragon had raised adoring eyes to the Lord of Ruatha Hold and Impression had been made.

Completely oblivious to the dilemma he had just originated, the incredulous Jaxom turned to the stunned observers.

"He says his name is Ruth!"

·· CHAPTER XV ··

Evening at Benden Weyr: Impression Banquet

It had been like coming up out of the very bowels of the deepest hold, thought Brekke. And Berd had shown her the way. She shuddered again at the horror of memory. If she slipped back down . . .

Instantly she felt F'nor's hand tighten on her arm, felt the touch of Canth's thoughts and heard the chitter of the two fire-lizards.

Berd had led her out of the Ground to F'nor and Manora. She'd been surprised at how tired and sad they both looked. She'd tried to talk but they'd hushed her. F'nor had carried her up to his weyr. She smiled now, opening her eyes, to see him bending over her. Brekke put her hand up to the dear, worried face of her lover; she could say that now, her lover, her Weyrmate, for he was that, too. Deep lines from the high-bridged nose pulled F'nor's mouth down at the corners. His eyes were darkly smudged and bloodshot, his hair, usually combed in crisp clean waves back from his high forehead, was stringy, oily.

"You need cozening, love," she said in a low voice which cracked and didn't seem to be hers at all.

With a groan that was close to a sob, F'nor embraced her. At first as if he were afraid of hurting her. Then, when he felt her arms tightening around him—for it was good to feel his strong back under her seeking hands—he almost crushed her until she cried out gladly for him to be careful.

He buried his lips in her hair, against her throat, in a surfeit of loving relief.

"We thought we'd lost you, too, Brekke," he said over and over while Canth crooned an exuberant descant.

"It was in my mind," Brekke admitted in a tremulous voice, burrowing against his chest, as if she must get even closer to him. "I was trapped in my mind and didn't own my body. I think that's what was wrong with me. Oh, F'nor," and all the grief that she'd not been able to express before came bursting out of her, "I even hated Canth!"

The tears poured down her cheeks and shuddering sobs shook a body already weakened by fasting. F'nor held her to him, patting her shoulders, stroking her until he began to fear that the convulsions would tear her apart. He beckoned urgently to Manora.

"She's got to cry, F'nor. It'll be an easing for her."

Manora's anxious expression, the way she folded and unfolded her hands, was strangely reassuring to F'nor. She, too, cared about Brekke, cared enough to let concern pierce that imperturbable serenity. He'd been so grateful to Manora for opposing a re-Impression, though he doubted his blood mother knew why he'd be against it. Or perhaps she did. Manora in her calm detachment missed few nuances or evasions.

Brekke's frail body was trembling violently now, torn apart by the paroxysm of her grief. The fire-lizards took to fluttering anxiously and Canth's croon held on a distressed note. Brekke's hands opened and closed pathetically on his shoulders but the tearing sobs did not permit her to speak.

"She can't stop, Manora. She can't."

"Slap her."

"Slap her?"

"Yes, slap her," and Manora suited actions to words, fetching Brekke several sharp blows before F'nor could shield her face. "Now into the bathing pool with her. The water's warm enough to relax those muscles."

"You didn't have to slap her," F'nor said, angrily.

"She did, she did," said Brekke in a ragged gasp, shuddering as they bundled her into the warm pool water. Then she felt the heat penetrate and relax muscles knotted by racking sobs. As soon as she felt Brekke's body easing, Manora dried her with warmed towels and gestured for F'nor to tuck her back under the furs.

"She needs feeding up now, F'nor. And so do you," she said, looking sternly at him. "And you are to kindly remember that you've duties to others tonight. It's Impression Day."

F'nor snorted at Manora's reminder and saw Brekke smiling wanly up at him.

"I don't think you've left me at all since . . ."

"Canth and I needed to be with you, Brekke," he cut in when she faltered. He smoothed her hair back from her forehead as if such an action were the most important occupation in the world. She caught his hand and he looked into her eyes.

"I felt you there, both of you, even when I wanted most to die." Then she felt anger in her guts. "But how could you force me onto the Hatching Ground, to face another queen?"

Canth grumbled a protest. She could see the dragon through the uncurtained archway, his head turned toward her, his eyes flashing a little. She was startled by the unhealthy green tinge to his color.

"We didn't want to. That was F'lar's idea. And Lessa's. They thought it might work and they were afraid we'd lose you."

The empty ache she tried not to remember threatened to become a hole down which she must go if only to end that tearing, burning pain of loss.

No, cried Canth.

Two warm lizard bodies pressed urgently against her neck and face, affection and worry so palpable in their thoughts it was like a physical touch.

"Brekke!" The terror, the yearning, the desperation in F'nor's cry were louder than the inner roaring and pushed it back, dispersed its threat.

"Never leave me! Never leave me alone. I can't stand being alone even for a second," Brekke cried.

I am here, said Canth, as F'nor's arms folded hard around her. The two lizards echoed the brown's words, the sound of their thoughts strengthening as their resolve grew. Brekke clung to the surprise of their maturity as a weapon against that other terrible pain.

"Why, Grall and Berd care," she said.

"Of course they care." F'nor seemed almost angry that she'd doubt it.

"No, I mean, they *say* they care."

F'nor looked into her eyes, his embrace less fiercely possessive. "Yes, they're learning because they love."

"Oh, F'nor, if I hadn't Impressed Berd that day, what would have happened to me?"

F'nor didn't answer. He held her against him in loving silence until Mirrim, her lizards flying in joyous circles around her, came briskly into the weyr, carrying a well-laden tray.

"Manora had to attend to the seasoning, Brekke," the girl said in a didactic tone. "You know how fussy she is. But you are to eat every bit of this broth, and you've a potion to drink for sleeping. A good night's rest and you'll be feeling more yourself."

Brekke stared at the young girl, watching in a sort of bemusement while Mirrim deftly pushed F'nor out of her way, settled pillows behind her patient, a napkin at her throat, and began to spoon the rich wherry broth to Brekke's unprotesting lips.

"You can stop staring at me, F'nor of Benden," Mirrim said, "and start eating the food I brought you before it gets cold. I carved you a portion of spiced wherry from the breast, so don't waste prime servings."

F'nor rose obediently, a smile on his face, recognizing the child's mannerisms as a blend of Manora and Brekke.

To her own surprise, Brekke found the broth delicious, warming her aching stomach and somehow satisfying a craving she hadn't recognized until now. Obediently she drank the sleeping potion, though the fellis juice did not entirely mask the bitter aftertaste.

"Now, F'nor, are you going to let poor Canth waste away to a watch-wher?" Mirrim asked as she began to settle Brekke for the night. "He's a sorry shade for a brown."

"He did eat—" F'nor began contritely.

"Ha!" Mirrim sounded like Lessa now.

I'll have to take that child in hand, Brekke thought idly, but an enervating lassitude had spread throughout her body and movement was impossible.

"You get that lazy lump of brown bones out of his couch and down to the Feeding Ground, F'nor. Hurry it up. They'll be out to feast soon and you know what a feeding dragon does to commoner appetites. C'mon now. You, Canth, get out of your weyr."

The last thing Brekke saw as F'nor obediently followed Mirrim out of the sleeping room was Canth's surprised look as she bore down on him, reached for his ear and began to tug.

They were leaving her, Brekke thought with sudden terror. Leaving her alone . . .

I am with you, was Canth's instant reassurance.

The two lizards, one on each side of her head, pressed lovingly against her.

And I, said Ramoth. *I, too*, said Mnementh and, mingled with those strong voices, were others, soft but present.

"There," said Mirrim with great satisfaction as she reentered the sleeping room. "They'll eat and come right back." She moved quietly around the room, turning the shields on the glow baskets so that the room was dark enough for sleeping. "F'nor says you don't like to be left alone so I'll wait until he comes back."

But I'm not alone, Brekke wanted to tell her. Instead, her eyes closed and she fell into a deep sleep.

As Lessa looked around the Bowl, at the tables of celebrants lingering long past the end of the banquet, she experienced a wistful yearning to be as uninhibited as they. The laughter of the hold and craftbred parents of the new riders, the weyrlings themselves fondling their hatchlings, even the weyrfolk, was untinged by bitterness or sorrow. Yet she was aware of a nagging sadness, which she couldn't shake, and had no reason to feel.

Brekke was herself, weak but no longer lost to reason; F'nor had actually left the girl long enough to eat with the guests; F'lar was recovering his strength and had come to realize that he must delegate some of his new responsibilities. And Lytol, the most distressing problem since Jaxom had Impressed that little white dragon—how *could* that have happened?—had managed to get roaring drunk, thanks to the tender offices of Robinton who had matched him drink for drink.

The two were singing some utterly reprehensible song that only a Harper could know. The Lord Warder of Ruatha Hold kept falling out of tune, though the man had a surprisingly pleasant tenor voice. Somehow, she'd have thought him a bass; he had a gloomy nature and bass voices are dark.

She toyed with the remains of the sweet cake on her platter. Manora's women had outdone themselves: the fowls had been stuffed with fermented fruits and breads, and the result was a remission of the "gamy" taste that wherry often had. River grains had been steamed to that each individual morsel was separate and tender. The fresh herbs must have come from Southern. Lessa made a mental note to speak to Manora about sneaking down there. It simply wouldn't do to have an incident with T'kul. Maybe N'ton had gathered them when he went on his "grubbing" expeditions. She'd always liked the young bronze rider. Now that she'd got to know him better . . .

She wondered what he and F'lar were doing. They'd left the table and gone to the Rooms. They were always there these days, she thought irritably. They must be cleaning the grubs' orifices. Could she, too, slip away? No, she'd better stay here. It wasn't courteous for both Weyrleaders to absent themselves on such an auspicious occasion. And people ought to be leaving soon.

What were they going to do about young Jaxom? She looked around, locating Jaxom easily by the white hide of his dragon in the group of weyrlings watering their beasts by the lakeside. The beast had charm, true, but had he a future? And why Jaxom? She was glad that Lytol could get drunk tonight, but that wouldn't make tomorrow easier for the ex-dragonrider to endure. Maybe they ought to keep that pair here, until the beast died. The consensus was that Ruth would not mature.

At the other end of the long "high" table were Larad, Lord of Telgar, Sifer of Bitra, Raid of Benden Hold, and Asgenar of Lemos with Lady Famira (she really did blush all the time). The Lemos Hold pair had brought their fire-lizards—fortunately a brown and a green—which had been the object of much overt interest by Lord Larad, who had a pair hardening on his hearth, and covert inspection by old Raid and Sifer of Bitra, who also had eggs from F'nor's last find. Neither older Lord Holder was entirely sure of the experiment with fire-lizards but they had watched the Lemos pair all evening. Sifer had finally unfrosted enough to ask how to care for one. Would this influence their minds in the matter of Jaxom and his Ruth?

By the Egg, they couldn't want to disrupt the territorial balance because Jaxom had Impressed a sport dragon that hadn't a chance in Threadfall of surviving! How could you make an honorific out of Jaxom? J'om, J'xom? Most weyrwomen chose names for their sons that could be contracted decently. Then Lessa was amused to be worrying over how to shorten a name, a trivial detail in this dilemma. No, Jaxom must remain at Ruatha Hold. She'd relinquished her Bloodright on Ruatha Hold to *him*, Gemma's son, because he *was* Gemma's son and had at least some minute quantity of Ruathan Blood. She certainly would contest the Hold going to any other Bloodline. Too bad Lytol had no sons. No, *Jaxom* must remain as Lord Holder at Ruatha. Just like men to make a piece of work over something so simple. The little beast would not survive. He was too small, his color—who ever heard of a white dragon?—indicated other abnormalities. Manora'd mentioned that white-skinned, pink-eyed child from Nerat Hold who hadn't been able to endure daylight. A nocturnal dragon?

Obviously, Ruth would never grow to full size; newhatched, he was more like a large fire-lizard.

Ramoth rumbled from the heights, disturbed by her rider's thoughts, and Lessa sent a hundred apologies to her.

"It's no reflection on you, my darling," Lessa told her. "Why, you've spawned more queens than any other three. And the largest of their broods is no better than the smallest of yours, love."

Ruth will prosper, Ramoth said.

Mnementh crooned from the ledge and Lessa stared up at them, their eyes glowing in the shadows over the glow-lit Bowl.

Did the dragons know something she didn't? They often seemed to these days, and yet, how could they? They never cared about tomorrow, or yesterday, living for the moment. Which was not a bad way to live, Lessa reflected, a trifle enviously. Her roving eyes fastened on the white blur of Ruth. Why had those two Impressed? Didn't she have troubles enough?

"Why should I mind? Why should I?" demanded Lytol suddenly in a loud, belligerent voice.

The Harper beamed up at him in an idiotish way. "Tha's what I say. Why should you?"

"I love the boy. I love him more than if he were flesh and blood of me, of me, Lytol of Ruatha Hold. Proved I love him, too. Proved I care for him. Ruatha's rich. Rich as when the Ruathan Bloodline ruled it. Undid all Fax's harm. And did it all, not for me. My life's spent. I've been everything. Been a dragonrider. Oh, Larth, my beautiful Larth. Been a weaver so I know the Crafts. Know the Holds now, too. Know everything. Know how to take care of a white runt. Why *shouldn't* the boy keep his dragon? By the First Shell, no one else wanted him. No one else wanted to Impress him. He's special, I tell you. Special!"

"Now, just a moment, Lord Lytol," Raid of Benden said, rising from his end of the table and stalking down to confront Lytol. "Boy's Impressed a dragon. That means he must stay in the Weyr."

"Ruth's not a proper dragon," Lytol said, neither speaking nor acting as drunk as he must be.

"Not a proper dragon?" Raid's expression showed his shock at such blasphemy.

"Never been a white dragon ever," Lytol said pontifically, drawing himself up to his full height. He wasn't much taller than the Lord Holder of Benden but he gave the impression of greater stature. "Never!" He appeared to feel that required a toast but found his cup empty. He managed to pour wine with creditable deftness for a man swaying on his feet. The Harper motioned wildly for his own glass to be filled but had trouble keeping it steady under the flow of wine.

"Never a whi' dragon," the Harper intoned and touched cups with Lytol.

"May not live," Lytol added, taking a long gulp.

"May not!"

"Therefore," and Lytol took a deep breath, "the boy must remain in his Hold. Ruatha Hold."

"Absolutely must!" Robinton held his cup high, more or less daring Raid to contradict him.

Raid favored him with a long inscrutable look.

"He must remain in the Weyr," he said finally, though he didn't sound as definite.

"No, he must come back to Ruatha Hold," said Lytol, steadying himself with a firm grip on the table edge. "When the dragon dies, the boy must be where obligations and responsibilities give him a hold on life. I know!"

To that Raid could give no answer, but he glowered in disapproval. Lessa held her breath and began to "lean" a little on the old Lord Holder.

"I know how to help the boy," Lytol went on, sinking slowly back into his chair. "I know what is best for him. I know what it is to lose a dragon. The difference in this case is that we *know* Ruth's days are numbered."

"Days are numbered," echoed the Harper and put his head down on the table suddenly. Lytol bent toward the man, curiously, almost paternally. He drew back, startled when the Harper began to snore gently.

"Hey, don't go to sleep. We haven't finished this bottle." When Robinton made no response, Lytol shrugged and drained his own cup.

Then he seemed to collapse slowly until his head was on the table, too, his snores filling the pause between Robinton's.

Raid regarded the pair with sour disgust. Then he turned on his heel and walked back to his end of the head table.

"I don't know but what there isn't truth in the wine," Larad of Telgar Hold commented as Raid reseated himself.

Lessa "leaned" quickly against Larad. He was nowhere near as insensitive as Raid. When he shook his head, she desisted and turned her attentions to Sifer. If she could get two of them to agree . . .

"Dragon and his rider both belong in the Weyr," Raid said. "You don't change what's natural for man and beast."

"Well now, take these fire-lizards," Sifer began, nodding toward the two across the table from him, in the arms of the Lord and Lady of Lemos Hold. "They're dragons of a sort, after all."

Raid snorted, "We saw today what happens when you go against natural courses. The girl—whatever her name is—lost her queen. Well, even the fire-lizard warned her off Impressing a new one. The creatures know more than we think they do. Look at all the years people've tried to catch 'em . . ."

"Catch 'em now, in nestsful," Sifer interrupted him. "Pretty things they are. Must say I look forward to mine hatching."

Somehow their quarreling reminded Lessa of old R'gul and S'lel, her first "teachers" in the Weyr, contradicting themselves endlessly as they purportedly taught her "all she'd need to know to become a Weyrwoman." It was F'lar who had done that.

"Boy has to stay here with that dragon."

"The boy in question is a Lord Holder, Raid," Larad of Telgar reminded him. "And the one thing we don't need is a contested Hold. It might be different if Lytol had male issue, or if he'd fostered long enough to have a promising candidate. No, Jaxom must remain Lord at Ruatha Hold," and the Telgar Lord scanned the Bowl in search of the boy. His eyes met Lessa's and he smiled in absent courtesy.

"I don't agree, I don't agree," Raid said, shaking his head emphatically. "It goes against all custom."

"Some customs need changing badly," said Larad, frowning.

"I wonder what the boy wants to do," interjected Asgenar in his bland way, catching Larad's eye.

The Telgar Lord threw back his head with a hearty laugh. "Don't complicate matters, brother. We've just decided his fate, will-he, won't-he?"

"The boy should be asked," Asengar said, no longer mild-spoken. His glance slid from Larad to the two older Lord Holders. "I saw his face when he came out of the Hatching Ground. He realized what he'd done. He was as white as the little dragon." Then Asgenar nodded in Lytol's direction. "Yes, Jaxom's all too aware of what he's done."

Raid harumphed irritably. "You don't *ask* youngsters anything. You tell 'em!"

Asgenar turned to his lady, touching her shoulder lightly, but there was no mistaking the warmth of his expression as he asked her to request young Jaxom's presence. Mindful of her sleepy green lizard, she rose and went on her errand.

"I've discovered recently that you find out a great deal by asking people," Asgenar said, looking after his wife with an odd smile on his face.

"People, yes, but not children!" Raid managed to get a lot of anger into that phrase.

Lessa "leaned" against him. He'd be more susceptible in this state of mind.

"Why doesn't he just pick the beast up?" the Benden Lord Holder demanded irritably as he watched the stately progress of the Lady of Lemos Hold, the young Lord of Ruatha and the newly hatched white dragon, Ruth.

"I'd say he was establishing the proper relationship," Asgenar remarked. "It would be easier and faster to carry the little beast, but not wiser. Even a dragon that small has dignity."

Raid of Benden Hold grunted, whether in acknowledgment or disagreement Lessa couldn't tell. He began to fidget, rub the back of his head with one hand, so she stopped her "pushing."

The whir of dragon wings back-beating to land caught her attention. She turned and saw the gleam of a bronze hide in the darkness by the new entrance to the Rooms.

Lioth brings the Masterfarmer, Ramoth told her rider.

Lessa couldn't imagine why Andemon would be required, nor why N'ton would be bringing him. The Masterfarmerhall had its own beast now. She started to rise.

"D'you realize the trouble you've caused, young man?" Raid was asking in a stiff voice.

Lessa swung round, torn between two curiosities. It wasn't as if Jaxom were without champions in Asgenar and Larad. But she did wonder how the boy would answer Raid.

Jaxom stood straight, his chin up, his eyes bright. Ruth's head was pressed to his thigh as if the dragonet were aware that they stood on trial.

"Yes, my good Lord Raid, I am fully aware of the consequences of my actions and there may now be a grave problem facing the other Lord Holders." Without a hint of apology or contrition, Jaxom obliquely reminded Raid that, for all his lack of years, he was a Lord Holder, too.

Old Raid sat straighter, pulling his shoulders back, as if . . .

Lessa stepped past her chair.

"Don't . . ."

The whisper was so soft that at first Lessa thought she was mistaken. Then she saw the Harper looking at her, his eyes as keen as if he were cold sober. And he, the dissembler, probably was, for all that act he'd pulled earlier.

"Fully aware, are you?" Raid echoed, and suddenly launched himself to his feet. The old Lord Holder had lost inches as he gained Turns, his shoulders now rounding slightly, his belly no longer flat and his legs stringy in the tight hide of his trousers. He looked a caricature confronting the slim proud boy. "D'you know you've got to stay at Benden Weyr now you've Impressed a dragon? D'you realize that Ruatha's lordless?"

"With all due respect, sir, you and the other Lords present do not constitute a Conclave since you are not two-thirds of the resident Holders of Pern," replied Jaxom. "If necessary, I should be glad to come before a duly constituted Conclave and plead my case. It's obvious, I think, that Ruth is not a proper dragon. I am given to understand that his chances of maturing are slight. Therefore he is of no use to the Weyr which has no space for the useless. Even old dragons no longer able to chew firestone are retired to Southern Weyr—or were." His slight slip disconcerted Jaxom only until he saw Asgenar's approving grin. "It's wiser to consider Ruth more of an overgrown fire lizard than an undersized dragon." Jaxom smiled with loving apology down at Ruth, and caressed the upturned head. It was an action so adult, so beautiful that Lessa felt her throat tightening. "My first obligation is to my Blood, to the Hold which cared for me. Ruth and I would be an embarrassment here in Benden Weyr. We can help Ruatha Hold just as the other fire-lizards do."

"Well said, young Lord of Ruatha, well said," cried Asgenar of Lemos, and his applause started his lizard shrieking.

Larad of Telgar Hold nodded solemnly in accord.

"Humph. Shade too flip an answer for me," Raid grumbled. "All you youngsters act before you think these days."

"I'm certainly guilty of that, Lord Raid," Jaxom said candidly. "But I had to act fast today—to save the life of a dragon. We're taught to honor dragonkind, I more than most." Jaxom gestured toward Lytol. His hand remained poised and a look of profound sorrow came over his face.

Whether Jaxom's voice had roused him or the position of his head was too uncomfortable was debatable, but the Lord Warder of Ruatha Hold was no longer asleep. He rose, gripping the table, then pushing himself away from its support. With slow steps, as if he were forced to concentrate on each movement, Lytol walked the length of the table until he reached his ward. Lytol placed an arm lightly across Jaxom's shoulders. As though he drew strength from that contact, he straightened and turned to Raid of Benden Hold. His expression was proud and his manner more haughty than Lord Groghe at his worst.

"Lord Jaxom of Ruatha Hold is not to blame for today's events. As his guardian, I am responsible—if it *is* an offense to save a life. If I chose to stress reverence for dragonkind in his education, I had good reason!"

Lord Raid looked uneasily away from Lytol's direct gaze.

"*If*," and Lytol stressed the word as though he felt the possibility was remote, "the Lords decide to act in Conclave, I shall strongly urge that no man fault Lord Jaxom's conduct today. He acted in honor and at the promptings of his training. He best serves Pern, however, by returning to his Hold. At Ruatha, young Ruth will be cared for and honored—for as long as he is with us."

There was no doubt that Larad and Asgenar were of Lytol's mind. Old Sifer sat pulling at his lip, unwilling to look toward Raid.

"I still think dragonfolk belong in Weyrs!" Raid muttered, glum and resentful.

That problem apparently settled, Lessa turned to leave and nearly fell into F'nor's arms.

He steadied her. "A weyr is where a dragon is," he said in a low voice rippling with amusement. The strain of the past week still showed in his face but his eyes were clear and his lips no longer thin with tension. Brekke's resolution was evidently all in his favor.

"She's asleep," he said. "I told you she wouldn't Impress."

Lessa made an impatient gesture. "At least the experience snapped her out of that shock."

"Yes," and there was a wealth of relief in the man's soft affirmative.

"So, you'd better come with me to the Rooms. I want to find out why Masterfarmer Andemon has just flown in. And it's about time you got back to work!"

F'nor chuckled. "It is, if someone else has been doing *my* work. Did anyone bring F'lar his Threads?" There was a note in his voice that told Lessa he was concerned.

"N'ton did!"

"I thought he was riding Wing second to P'zar at Fort Weyr!"

"As you remarked the other morning, whenever you're not here to keep him under control, F'lar rearranges matters." She saw his stricken look and caught his arm, smiling up at him reassuringly; he wasn't up to teasing yet. "No one could take your place with F'lar— or me. Canth and Brekke needed you more for a while." She gave his hand a squeeze. "But that doesn't mean things haven't been happening and you'd better catch up. N'ton's been included in our affairs because F'lar had a sudden glimpse of his mortality when he was sick and decided to stop being secretive. Or it might be another four hundred Turns or so before we control Thread."

She gathered her skirt so she could move more rapidly over the sandy floor.

"Can I come, too?" asked the Harper.

"You? Sober enough to walk that far?"

Robinton chuckled, smoothing his rumpled hair back into place at his neck. "Lytol couldn't drink me drunk, my dear Lady Lessa. Only the Smith has the—ah—capacity."

There was no doubt that he was steady on his feet as the three walked toward the flow-marked entrance to the Rooms. The stars were brilliant in the soft black spring sky, and the glows on the lower levels threw bright circles of light on the sands. Above, on weyr ledges, dragons watched with gleaming opalescent eyes, occasionally humming with pleasure. High up, Lessa saw three dragon silhouettes by the Star Stones: Ramoth and Mnementh were perched to the right of the watchdragon, their wings overlapping. They were both smug tonight; she'd heard Ramoth's tenor often that evening. It was such a relief to have her in an agreeable mood for a while. Lessa rather hoped there'd be a long interval before the queen felt the urge to mate again.

When they entered the Rooms, the spare figure of the Masterfarmer was bending over the largest of the tubs, turning the leaves of the fellis sapling. F'lar watched him with a wary expression while N'ton was grinning, unable to observe the solemnity of the moment.

As soon as F'lar caught sight of F'nor, he smiled broadly and quickly crossed the room to clasp his half-brother's arm.

"Manora said Brekke had snapped out of shock. It's twice a relief, believe me. I'd have been happier still if she'd brought herself to re-Impress . . ."

"That would have served no purpose," F'nor said, so flatly contradictory that F'lar's grin faded a little.

He recovered and drew F'nor to the tubs.

"N'ton was able to get Thread and we infected three of the big tubs," F'lar told him, speaking in a low undertone as if he didn't wish to disturb the Masterfarmer's investigations. "The grubs devoured every filament. And where the Thread pierced the leaves of the fellis tree, the char marks are already healing. I'm hoping Master Andemon can tell us how or why."

Andemon straightened his body but his lantern jaw remained sunk to his chest as he frowned at the tub. He blinked rapidly and pursed his thin lips, his heavy, thick-knuckled hands twitching slightly in the folds of a dirt-stained tunic. He had come as he was when the Weyr messenger summoned him from the fields.

"I don't know how or why, Good Weyrleader. And if what you

have told me is the truth," he paused, finally raising his eyes to F'lar, "I am scared."

"Why, man?" And F'lar spoke on the end of a surprised laugh. "Don't you realize what this means? If the grubs can adapt to northern soil and climate, and perform as well—all of us here," his gesture took in the Harper and his Wingsecond as well as Lessa, "have seen them, Pern does not need to fear Thread ever again."

Andemon took a deep breath, throwing his shoulders back, but whether resisting the revolutionary concept or preparing to espouse it was not apparent. He looked toward the Harper as if he could trust this man's opinion above the others.

"You saw the Thread devoured by these grubs?"

The Harper nodded.

"And that was five days ago?"

The Harper confirmed this.

A shudder rippled the cloth of the Masterfarmer's tunic. He looked down at the tubs with the reluctance of fear. Stepping forward resolutely, he peered again at the young fellis tree. Inhaling and holding that deep breath, he poised one gnarled hand for a moment before plunging it into the dirt. His eyes were closed. He brought up a moist handful of earth and, opening his eyes, turned the glob over, exposing a cluster of wriggling grubs. His eyes widened and, with an exclamation of disgust, he flung the dirt from him as if he'd been burned. The grubs writhed impotently against the stone floor.

"What's the matter? There can't be Thread!"

"Those are parasites!" Andemon replied, glaring at F'lar, badly disillusioned and angry. "We've been trying to rid the southern parts of this peninsula of these larvae for centuries." He grimaced with distaste as he watched F'lar carefully pick up the grubs and deposit them back into the nearest tub. "They're as pernicious and indestructible as Igen sandworms and not half as useful. Why, let them get into a field and every plant begins to droop and die."

"There's not an unhealthy plant here," F'lar protested, gesturing at the burgeoning growths all around.

Andemon stared at him. F'lar moved, grabbing a handful of soil from each tub as he circled, showing the grubs as proof.

"It's impossible," Andemon insisted, the shadow of his earlier fear returning.

"Don't you recall, F'lar," Lessa said, "when we first brought the grubs here, the plants did seem to droop?"

"They recovered. All they needed was water!"

"They couldn't." Andemon forgot his revulsion enough to dig into another tub as if to prove to himself that F'lar was wrong. "There're no grubs in this one!" he said in triumph.

"That's never had any. I used it to check the others. And I must say, the plants don't look as green or healthy as the other tubs."

Andemon stared around. "Those grubs are pests. We've been trying to rid ourselves of them for hundreds of Turns."

"Then I suspect, good Master Andemon," F'lar said with a gentle, rueful smile, "that farmers have been working against Pern's best interests."

The Masterfarmer exploded into indignant denials of that charge. It took all Robinton's diplomacy to calm him down long enough for F'lar to explain.

"And you mean to tell me that those larvae, those grubs, were developed and spread on purpose?" Andemon demanded of the Harper who was the only one in the room he seemed inclined to trust now. "They were meant to spread, bred by the same ancestors who bred the dragons?"

"That's what we believe," Robinton said. "Oh, I can appreciate your incredulity. I had to sleep on the notion for several nights. However, if we check the Records, we find that, while there is no mention that *dragonmen* will attack the Red Star and clear it of Thread, there is the strong, recurring belief that Thread will one day not be the menace it is now. F'lar is reasonably . . ."

"Not reasonably, Robinton; completely sure," F'lar interrupted. "N'ton's been going back to Southern—jumping *between* time, as far back as seven Turns, to check on Threadfalls in the southern continent. Wherever he's probed, there're grubs in the soil which rise when Thread falls and devour it. That's why there have never been any burrows in Southern. The land itself is inimical to Thread."

In the silence, Andemon stared at the tips of his muddy boots.

"In the Farmercrafthall Records, they mention specifically that we are to watch for these grubs." He lifted troubled eyes to the others. "We always have. It was our plain duty. Plants wither wherever grub appears." He shrugged in helpless confusion. "We've always rooted them out, destroyed the larval sacks with—" and he sighed, "flame and angenothree. That's the only way to stop the infestations."

"Watch for the grubs, the Records say," Andemon repeated and then suddenly his shoulders began to shake, his whole torso became involved. Lessa caught F'lar's eyes, concerned for the man. But he was laughing, if only at the cruel irony. "Watch for the grubs, the Records say. They do not, they do not say *destroy* the grubs. They say most emphatically 'watch for the grubs.' So we watched. Aye, we have watched."

The Harper extended the wine bottle to Andemon.

"That's a help, Harper. My thanks," Andemon said, wiping his lips with the back of one hand after a long pull at the bottle.

"So someone forgot to mention why you were to watch the grubs,

Andemon," F'lar said, his eyes compassionate for the man's distress. "If only Sograny'd been as reasonable. Once, so many men must have known why you were to watch for the grubs, they didn't see a need for further implicit instructions. Then the Holds started to grow and people drifted apart. Records got lost or destroyed, men died before they'd passed on the vital knowledge they possessed." He looked around at the tubs. "Maybe they developed those grubs right here in Benden Weyr. Maybe that's the meaning of the diagram on the wall. There's so much that has been lost."

"Which will never be lost again if the Harpercraft has any influence," said Robinton. "If *all* men, Hold, Craft, Weyr have full access to every skin—" he held up his hand as Andemon started to protest, "well, we've better than skin to keep Records on. Bendarek now has a reliable, tough sheet of his wood pulp that holds ink, stacks neatly and is impervious to anything except fire. We can combine knowledge and disseminate it."

Andemon looked at the Harper, his eyes puzzled. "Master Robinton, there are some matters within a Craft that must remain secret or . . ."

"Or we lose a world to the Thread, is that it, Andemon? Man, if the truth about those grubs hadn't been treated like a Craft secret, we'd have been hundreds of Turns free of Thread by now."

Andemon gasped suddenly, staring at F'lar. "And dragonmen— we wouldn't need dragonmen?"

"Well, if men kept to their Holds during Threadfall, and grubs devoured what fell to the ground, no, you wouldn't need dragonmen," F'lar replied with complete composure.

"But dragonmen are su-supposed to fight Thread—" the Farmer was stuttering with dismay.

"Oh, we'll be fighting Thread for a while yet, I assure you. We're not in any immediate danger of unemployment. There's a lot to be done. For instance, how long before an entire continent can be seeded with grubs?"

Andemon opened and closed his mouth futilely. Robinton indicated the bottle in his hand, pantomimed a long swig. Dazedly the Farmer complied. "I don't know. I just don't know. Why, for Turn upon Turn, we've watched for those grubs—exterminating them, razing an entire field if it got infected. Spring's when the larval sacks break and we'd be . . ."

He sat down suddenly, shaking his head from side to side.

"Get a grip on yourself, man," F'lar said, but it was his attitude which caused Andemon the most distress.

"What—what will dragonmen do?"

"Get rid of Thread, of course. Get rid of Thread."

Had F'lar been a feather less confident, F'nor would have had trouble maintaining his composure. But his half-brother *must* have some plan in mind. And Lessa looked as serene as—as Manora could.

Fortunately Andemon was not only an intelligent man, he was tenacious. He had been confronted with a series of disclosures that both confused and disturbed basic precepts. He must reverse a long-standing Craft practice. He must rid himself of an inborn, carefully instilled prejudice, and he must accept the eventual abdication of an authority which he had good reason to respect and more reason to wish to perpetuate.

He was determined to resolve these matters before he left the Weyr. He questioned F'lar, F'nor, the Harper, N'ton and Manora when he learned she'd been involved in the project. Andemon examined all the tubs, particularly the one which had been left alone. He conquered his revulsion and even examined the grubs carefully, patiently uncoiling a large specimen as if it were a new species entirely. In a certain respect, it was.

Andemon was very thoughtful as he watched the unharmed larva burrow quickly back into the tub dirt from which he'd extracted it.

"One wishes fervently," he said, "to find a release from our long domination by Thread. It is just—just that the agency which frees us is . . ."

"Revolting?" the Harper suggested obligingly.

Andemon regarded Robinton a moment. "Aye, you're the man with words, Master Robinton. It is rather leveling to think that one will have to be grateful to such a—such a lowly creature. I'd rather be grateful to dragons." He gave F'lar a rather abashed grin.

"You're not a Lord Holder!" said Lessa, wryly, drawing a chuckle from everyone.

"And yet," Andemon went on, letting a handful of soil dribble from his fist, "we have taken the bounties of this rich earth too much for granted. We are from it, part of it, sustained by it. I suppose it is only mete that we are protected by it. If all goes well."

He brushed his hand off on the wher-hide trousers and with an air of decision turned to F'lar. "I'd like to run a few experiments of my own, Weyrleader. We've tubs and all at the Farmercrafthall . . ."

"By all means," F'lar grinned with relief. "We'll cooperate in every way. Grubs, Threads on request. But you've solved the one big problem I'd foreseen."

Andemon raised his eyebrows in polite query.

"Whether or not the grubs were adaptable to northern conditions."

"They are, Weyrleader, they are." The Farmer was grimly sardonic.

"I shouldn't think that would be the major problem, F'lar," F'nor said.

"Oh?" The quiet syllable was almost a challenge to the brown rider. F'nor hesitated, wondering if F'lar had lost confidence in him, despite what Lessa had said earlier.

"I've been watching Master Andemon, and I remember my own reaction to the grubs. It's one thing to say, to know, that these are the answer to Thread. Another—quite another to get the average man to accept it. And the average dragonrider."

Andemon nodded agreement and, judging by the expression on the Harper's face, F'nor knew he was not the only one who anticipated resistance.

But F'lar began to grin as he settled himself on the edge of the nearest tub.

"That's why I brought Andemon here and explained the project. We need help which only he can give us, once he himself is sure of matters. How long, Masterfarmer, does it take grubs to infest a field?"

Andemon dropped his chin to his chest in thought. He shook his head and admitted he couldn't estimate. Once a field showed signs of infestation, the area was seared to prevent spreading.

"So, we must find out how long first!"

"You'll have to wait for next spring," the Farmer reminded him.

"Why? We can import grubs from Southern."

"And put them where?" the Harper asked, sardonically.

F'lar chuckled. "Lemos Hold."

"Lemos!"

"Where else?" and F'lar looked smug. "The forests are the hardest areas to protect. Asgenar and Bendarek are determined to preserve them. Asgenar and Bendarek are both flexible enough to accept such an innovation and carry it through. You, Masterfarmer, have the hardest task. To convince your crafters to leave off killing . . ."

Andemon raised a hand. "I have my own observations to make first."

"By all means, Master Andemon," and F'lar's grin broadened. "I'm confident of the outcome. I remind you of your first journey to the Southern Weyr. You commented on the luxuriant growths, the unusual size of the trees and bushes common to both continents, the spectacular crops, the sweetness of the fruits. That is not due to the temperate weather. We have similar zones here in the north. It is due," and F'lar pointed his finger first at Andemon and then toward the tubs, "to the stimulation, the protection of the grubs."

Andemon was not totally convinced but F'lar did not press the point.

"Now, Master Andemon, the Harper will assist you all he can. You know your people better than we—you'll know whom you can tell. I urge you to discuss it with your trusted Masters. The more the better. We can't lose this opportunity for lack of disciples. We might be forced to wait until your Oldtimers die off." F'lar laughed wryly. "I guess the Weyrs are not the only ones to contend with Oldtimers; we've all got re-education to do."

"Yes, there will be problems." The magnitude of the undertaking had suddenly burst on the Masterfarmer.

"Many," F'lar assured him blithely. "But the end result is freedom from Thread."

"It could take Turns and Turns," Andemon said, catching F'lar's glance and, as if that consoled him somehow, straightened his shoulders. He was committed to the project.

"And well may take Turns. First," and F'lar grinned with pure mischief in his eyes, "we've got to stop you farmers from exterminating our saviors."

An expression of pure shock and indignation passed across Andemon's weather-lined face. It was swiftly replaced by a tentative smile as the man realized that F'lar was ribbing him. Evidently an unusual experience for the Masterfarmer.

"Think of all the rewriting I have to do," complained the Harper. "I'm dry just considering it." He looked mournfully at the now empty wine bottle.

"This certainly calls for a drink," Lessa remarked with a sidelong glance at Robinton. She took Andemon's arm to guide him out.

"I'm honored, my lady, but I've work to oversee, and the investigations I ought to conduct." He pulled away from her.

"Surely one drink?" Lessa pleaded, smiling in her most winning way.

The Masterfarmer ran his hand through his hair, clearly reluctant to refuse.

"One drink then."

"To seal the bargain of Pern's fate," said the Harper, dropping his voice to a sepulchral bass and looking solemnly portentous and amazingly like Lord Groghe of Fort.

As they all trooped out of the Rooms, Andemon looked down at Lessa.

"If it isn't presumptuous of me, the young woman, Brekke, who lost her queen—how is she?"

Lessa hesitated only a second. "F'nor here can answer you better than I. They're Weyrmates."

F'nor was forced to step in. "She's been ill. Losing one's dragon is a tremendous shock. She has made the adjustment. She won't suicide now."

The Masterfarmed halted, staring at F'nor. "That would be unthinkable."

Lessa caught F'nor's eye and he remembered he was talking to a commoner.

"Yes, of course, but the loss is unsettling."

"Certainly. Ah, does she have any position at all now?" The words came slowly from the Farmer, then he added in a rush, "she is from my Crafthall you see, and we . . ."

"She is well loved and respected by all Weyrs," Lessa broke in when Andemon faltered. "Brekke is one of those rare people who can hear any dragon. She will always enjoy a unique and high position with dragonfolk. She may, if she chooses, return to her home . . ."

"No!" The Masterfarmer was definite about that.

"Brekke is weyrfolk now," F'nor said on the heels of that denial.

Lessa was a little surprised at such vehemence from both men. She'd had the notion from Andemon's attitude that perhaps her Craft wanted her back.

"My apologies for being so brusque, my lady. It would be hard for her to live simply again." His voice turned hard and lost all hesitancy. "What of that adulterous transgressor?"

"She—lives," and there was an uncompromising echo of the Farmer's coldness in Lessa's voice.

"She lives?" The Masterfarmer stopped again, dropping Lessa's arm and staring at her with anger. "She lives? Her throat should be cut, her body . . ."

"She lives, Masterfarmer, with no more mind or wit than a babe. She exists in the prison of her guilt! Dragonfolk take no lives!"

The Farmer stared hard at Lessa for a moment longer, then nodded slowly. With great courtesy he offered Lessa his arm when she indicated they should continue.

F'nor did not follow for the events of the day were taking a revenge of fatigue on him.

He watched as Andemon and Lessa joined the others at the main table, saw the Lemos and Telgar Lords come over. Lytol and young Jaxom with his white Ruth were nowhere to be seen. F'nor hoped Lytol had taken Jaxom back to Ruatha. He was more grateful to his discovery of fire-lizards than at any other single time since Grall had first winked at him. He walked quickly toward the steep flight to his weyr, wanting to be with his own. Canth was in his weyr, all but one lid closed over his eyes. When F'nor entered, the final lids sagged shut. F'nor leaned his body against the dragon's neck, his hands seeking the pulsespots in the soft throat, warm and steadying. He could "hear" the soft loving thoughts of the two lizards curled by Brekke's head.

How long he stood there he couldn't gauge, his mind rehearsing the Impression, Brekke's release, Jaxom's performance, the dinner, everything that had jammed into one eventful afternoon.

There was much to be done, certainly, but he felt unable to move from the presence of Canth.

Most vividly he recalled Andemon's shock when the man realized that F'lar had proposed the end of dragonmen. Yet—F'lar hadn't. He certainly had some alternate in mind.

Those grubs—yes, they devoured Thread before it could burrow and proliferate. But they were repulsive to look at and commanded neither respect nor gratitude. They weren't obvious, or awesome, like dragons. People wouldn't *see* grubs devouring Thread. They wouldn't have the satisfaction of watching dragons flame, sear, char, destroy Thread mid-air, *before* the vicious stuff got to earth. Surely F'lar realized this, knew that men must have the visible proof of Thread's defeat. Would dragonmen become tokens? No! That would make dragonfolk more parasitic than Thread. Such an expedient would be repugnant, insupportable to a man of F'lar's integrity. But what had he in mind?

The grubs might be the ultimate answer but not—particularly after thousands of Turns of conditioning—not an answer acceptable to Pernese, Holder, Crafter, commoner *and* dragonman.

Evening at Benden Weyr
Later Evening at Fort Weyr

For the next few days, F'nor was too busy to worry. Brekke was recovering her strength and insisted that he return to his duties. She prevailed on Manora to permit her to come down to the Lower Caverns and be of some use. So Manora put her to tying off the woof ends of some finished wall hangings where Brekke could also be part of the busy Cavern activities. The fire-lizards rarely left her side. Grall twittered with conflicting wishes when F'nor went off on errands, so he would order her to stay with Brekke.

F'lar estimated correctly that Asgenar and Bendarek would accept any solution that might preserve the forests. But the incredulity and initial resistance he encountered showed him what a monumental task he had undertaken. Both Lord Holder and Craftmaster were frankly contemptuous of his claims until N'ton came in with a panful of live Thread—it could be heard hissing and steaming—and dumped it over a tub of verdant growths. Within a matter of moments, the tangle of Thread which they had seen poured over the fellis saplings had been completely consumed by grubs. Dazed, they even accepted F'lar's assertion that the pierced and smoking leaves would heal in a matter of days.

There were many things about grubs that the dragonmen did not know, as F'lar was careful to explain. How long it would take them to proliferate so that a given area could be considered "Threadproof"; the length of the grub life cycle, what density of grub life would be necessary to ensure the chain of protection.

But they did decide where to start in Lemos Hold: among the

precious softwoods so in demand for furniture, so vulnerable to Thread incursion.

Since the former residents of the Southern Weyr had not been farmcraft trained, they had been oblivious to the significance of the larval sacks in the southern woods. It was fall now in the southern hemisphere but F'nor, N'ton and another ride had agreed to jump *between* to the previous spring. Brekke helped, too, knowing as she did so many facets of the Southern management that she was able to tell them where they would not collide with others in the past. Though farmcraftbred, Brekke had been occupied with nursing during her tenure at Southern, and had deliberately stayed away from the farming aspects of the Weyr to sever connections with her past life.

Although F'lar did not press Masterfarmer Andemon, he proceeded with his plans as if he had Farmcraft cooperation. Several times, Andemon requested Thread and grubs which would be rushed to him, but he issued no progress reports.

Mastersmith Fandarel and Terry had been informed of the project and a special demonstration over the grubs and horror at being so close to live Thread, Terry had been as enthusiastic as anyone could wish. The performance of the grubs elicited only a deep grunt from the Mastersmith. He had limited his comments to a scornful criticism of the longhandled hearthpan in which the Thread was captured.

"Inefficient. Inefficient. You can only open it once to catch the things," and he had taken the pan, stalking off toward his waiting dragon-messenger.

Terry had been profuse in his assurance that the Mastersmith was undoubtedly impressed and would cooperate in every way. This was indeed a momentous day. His words were cut off by Fandarel's impatient bellow and he'd bowed his way out, still reassuring the somewhat disconcerted dragonriders.

"I'd've thought Fandarel would at least have found the grubs efficient," F'lar had remarked.

"He was struck dumb with amazement?" F'nor suggested.

"No," and Lessa grimaced, "he was infuriated by inefficiency!"

They'd laughed and gone on to the next job. That evening a messenger arrived from the Smithcrafthall with the purloined hearthpan and a truly remarkable contrivance. It was bulbous in shape, secured to a long handle from the end of which its lid could be opened, operated by a trigger inside the tubular handle. The lid was the truly ingenious part for it fanned open upward and outward so that Thread would be guided down into the vessel and could not escape if the lid was reopened.

The messenger also confided to F'lar that the Mastersmith was having difficulties with his distance-writer. All wire must be covered with a protective tubing or Thread cut right through the thinly extruded metal. The Smith had experimented with ceramic and metal casings but he could turn neither out in great or quick enough quantity. With Threadfall coming so frequently now, his halls were besieged with demands to fix flame throwers which clogged or burned out. Ground crews panicked when equipment failed them mid-Fall and it was impossible not to accede to every urgent request for repair. The Lord Holders, promised the distance-writers, as links between help and isolated Holds, began to press for solutions. And for the ultimate—to them—solution: the proposed expedition to the Red Star.

F'lar had begun to call a council of his intimate advisors and Wing-seconds daily so that no facet of the over-all plan could be lost. They also decided which Lords and Mastercraftsmen could accept the radical knowledge, but had moved cautiously.

Asgenar told them that Larad of Telgar Hold was far more conservative in his thinking than they'd supposed and that the limited demonstration in the Rooms would not be as powerful a persuader as a protected field under full attack by Thread. Unfortunately, Asgenar's young bride, Famira, on a visit to her home, inadvertently made a reference to the project. She'd had the good sense to send her lizard for her Lord who had bodily forced his blood relative to Benden Weyr for a full explanation and demonstration. Larad had been unconvinced and furious with what he called "a cruel deception and treacherous breach of faith" by dragonmen. When Asgenar then insisted Larad come to the softwood tract that was being protected and had live Thread poured over a sapling, uprooting the young tree to prove that it had been adequately protected, the Telgar Lord Holder's rage began to subside.

Telgar's broad valleys had been hard hit by the almost constant Threadfalls. Telgar's ground crews were disheartened by the prospect of ceaseless vigilance.

"Time is what we haven't got," Larad of Telgar had cried when he heard the grub protection would be a long-term project. "We lose fields of grain and root every other day. The men are already weary of fighting Thread interminably, they've little energy for anything. At best we've only the propsect of a lean winter, and I fear for the worst if these past months are any indication."

"Yes, it's hard to see help so close—and as far away as the life cycle of an insect no larger than the tip of your finger," said Robinton, an integral part of any such confrontation. He was stroking the little bronze fire-lizard which he had Impressed a few days earlier.

"Or the length of that distance-viewer," Larad said, his lips tight, his face lined with worry. "Has nothing been done about going to the Red Star?"

"Yes," F'lar replied, holding firmly to an attitude of patient reasonableness. "It's been viewed every clear night. Wansor has trained a wing of watchers and borrowed the most accurate draftsmen from Masterweaver Zurg and the Harper. They've made endless sketches of the masses on the planet. We know its faces now . . ."

"And . . ." Larad was adamant.

"We can see no feature distinct enough to guide the dragons."

The Lord of Telgar sighed with resignation.

"We do believe," and F'lar caught N'ton's eyes since the young bronze rider did as much of the investigating as Wansor, "that these frequent Falls will taper off in a few more months."

"Taper off? How can you tell that?" Hope conflicted with suspicion in the Telgar Lord's face.

"Wansor is of the opinion that the other planets in our sky have been affecting the Red Star's motion; slowing it, pulling it from several directions. We have near neighbors, you see; one is now slightly below the middle of our planet, two above and beyond the Red Star, a rare conjunction. Once the planets move away, Wansor believes the old routine of Threadfall will be established."

"In a few months? But that won't do us any good. And can you be sure?"

"No, we can't be sure—which is why we have not announced Wansor's theory. But we'll be certain in a few more weeks." F'lar held up his hand to interrupt Larad's protests. "You've surely noticed the brightest stars, which are our sister planets, move from west to east during the year. Look tonight, you'll see the blue one slightly above the green one, and very brilliant. And the Red Star below them. Now, remember the diagram in the Fort Weyr Council Room? We're positive that that is the diagram of skies around our sun. And you've watched your fosterlings play stringball. You've played it yourself. Substitute the planets for the balls, the sun for the swinger, and you get the general idea. Some balls swing more rapidly than others, depending on the speed of the swing, the length and tension of the cord. Basically, the principle of the stars around the sun is the same."

Robinton had been sketching on a leaf and passed the diagram over to Larad.

"I must see this in the skies for myself," the Telgar Lord replied, not giving an inch.

"It's a sight, I assure you," Asgenar said. "I've become fascinated with the study and *if*," he grinned, his thin face suddenly all creases and teeth, "Wansor ever has time to duplicate that distance-viewer, I want one on Lemos' fire height. We're at a good altitude to see the northern heavens. I'd like to see those showering stars we get every summer through a distance-viewer!"

Larad snorted at the notion.

"No, it's fascinating," Asgenar protested, his eyes dancing with enthusiasm. Then he added in a different tone, "Nor am I the only one beguiled by such studies. Every time I go to Fort I'm contending with Meron of Nabol for a chance to use the viewer."

"Nabol?"

Asgenar was a little surprised at the impact of his casual remark.

"Yes, Nabol's forever at the viewer. Apparently *he's* more determined than any dragonrider to find coordinates." No one else shared his amusement.

F'lar looked inquiringly at N'ton.

"Yes, he's there all right. If he weren't a Lord Holder—" and N'ton shrugged.

"Why? Does he say why?"

N'ton shrugged again. "He says he's looking for coordinates. But so are we. There aren't any features distinct enough. Just shapeless masses of gray and dark gray-greens. They don't change and while it's obvious they're stable, are they land? Or sea?" N'ton began to feel the accusatory tension in the room and shifted his feet. "So often the face is obscured by those heavy clouds. Discouraging."

"Is Meron discouraged?" asked F'lar pointedly.

"I'm not sure I like your attitude, Benden," Larad said, his expression hard. "You don't appear eager to discover any coordinates."

F'lar looked Larad full in the eyes. "I thought we'd explained the problem involved. We have to *know* where we're going before we can send the dragons." He pointed to the green lizard perched on Larad's shoulder. "You've been trying to train your fire-lizard. You can appreciate the difficulty." Larad stiffened defensively and his lizard hissed, its eyes rolling. F'lar was not put off. "The fact that no Records exist of any previous attempt to go there strongly indicates that the ancients—who built the distance-viewer, who knew enough to plot the neighbors in our sky—did not go. They must have had a reason, a valid reason. What would you have me do, Larad?" F'lar demanded, pacing in his agitation. "Ask for volunteers? You, you and you," F'lar whirled, jabbing a finger at an imaginary line of riders, "you go, jump *between* to the Red Star. Coordinates? Sorry, men, I have none. Tell your dragons to take a long look halfway there. If you don't come back, we'll keen to the Red Star for your deaths. But men, you'll die knowing you've solved our problem. Men can't go to the Red Star."

Larad flushed under F'lar's sarcasm.

"If the ancients didn't record any intimate knowledge of the Red Star," said Robinton quietly into the charged silence, "they did provide domestic solutions. The dragons, and the grubs."

"Neither proves to be effective protection right now, when we *need* it," Larad replied in a bitter, discouraged voice. "Pern needs something more conclusive than promises—and insects!" He abruptly left the Rooms.

Asgenar, a protest on his lips, started to follow but F'lar stopped him.

"He's in no mood to be reasonable, Asgenar," F'lar said, his face strained with anxiety. "If he won't be reassured by today's demonstrations, I don't know what more we can do or say."

"It's the loss of the summer crops which bothers him," Asgenar said. "Telgar Hold has been spreading out, you know. Larad's attracted many of the small Holders who've been dissatisfied in Nerat, Crom and Nabol and switched their allegiances. If the crops fail, he's going to have more hungry people—and more trouble—than he can handle in the winter."

"But what more can we do?" demanded F'lar, a desperate note in his voice. He tired so easily. The fever had left him little reserve strength, a state he found more frustrating than any other problem. Larad's obduracy had been an unexpected disappointment. They'd been so lucky with every other man approached.

"I know you can't send men on a blind jump to the Red Star," Asgenar said, distressed by F'lar's anxiety. "I've tried to tell my Rial where I want him to go. He gets frantic at times because he can't see it clearly enough. Just wait until Larad starts sending his lizard about. He'll understand. You see, what bothers him most is the realization that you *can't* plan an attack on the Red Star."

"Your initial mistake, my dear F'lar," and the Harper's voice was at its drollest, "was in providing salvation from the last imminent disaster in a scant three days by bringing up the Five Lost Weyrs. The Lord Holders really expect you to provide a second miracle in similar short order."

The remark was so preposterous that F'nor laughed out loud before he could stop himself. But the tension and anxiety dissolved and the worried men regained some needed perspective.

"Time is all we need," F'lar insisted.

"Time is what we don't have," Asgenar said wearily.

"Then let's use what time we have to the best possible advantage," F'lar said decisively, his moment of doubt and disillusion behind him. "Let's work on Telgar. F'nor, how many riders can T'bor spare us to hunt larval sacks *between* time at Southern? You and N'ton can work out coordinates with them."

"Won't that weaken Southern's protection?" asked Robinton.

"No, because N'ton keeps his eyes open. He noticed that a lot of sacks started in the fall get blown down or devoured during the winter months. So we've altered out methods. We check an area in spring to place the sacks that survive, go back to the fall and take some of those which didn't last. There were a few wherries who missed a meal but I don't think we disturbed the balance much."

F'lar began to pace, one hand absently scratching his ribs where the scar tissues itched.

"I need someone to keep an eye on Nabol, too."

Robinton let out a snort of amusement. "We do seem beholden to the oddest agencies. Grub life. Meron. Oh yes," and he chuckled at their irritation. "He may yet prove to be an asset. Let him strain his eyes and crick his neck nightly watching the Red Star. As long as he is occupied that way, we'll know we have time. The eyes of a vengeful man miss few details he can turn to advantage."

"Good point, Robinton. N'ton," and F'lar turned to the young bronze rider. "I want to know every remark that man makes, which aspects of the Red Star he views, what he could possibly see, what his reactions are. We've ignored that man too often to our regret. We might even be grateful to him."

"I'd rather be grateful to grubs," N'ton replied with some fervor. "Frankly, sir," he added, hesitant for the first time about any assignment since he'd been included in the council, "I'd rather hunt grubs or catch Thread."

F'lar eyed the young rider thoughtfuly for a moment, "Think of this assignment then, N'ton, as the ultimate Thread catch."

Brekke had insisted on taking over the care of the plants in the Rooms once she was stronger. She argued that she was farmcraftbred and capable of such duties. She preferred not to be present during the demonstrations. In fact she went out of her way to avoid seeing anyone but weyrfolk. She could abide their sympathy but the pity of outsiders was repugnant to her.

This did not affect her curiosity and she would get F'nor to tell her every detail of what she termed the best-known Craft secret on Pern. When F'nor narrated the Telgar Lord's bitter repudiation of what the Weyrs were trying to accomplish, she was visibly disturbed.

"Larad's wrong," she said in the slow deliberate way she'd adopted lately. "The grubs are the solution, the right one. But it's true that the best solution is not always easy to accept. And an expedition to the Red Star is *not* a solution, even if it's the one Pernese instinctively crave. It's obvious. Just as two thousand dragons over Telgar Hold was rather obvious seven Turns ago." She surprised F'nor with a little smile, the first since Wirenth's death. "I myself, like Robinton, would prefer to rely on grubs. They present fewer problems. But then I'm craftbred."

"You use that phrase a lot lately," F'nor remarked, turning her face toward him, searching her green eyes. They were serious, as always, and clear in the candid gaze was the shadow of a sorrow that would never lift.

She locked her fingers in his and smiled gently, a smile which did not disperse the sorrow. "I *was* craftbred," she corrected herself. "I'm weyrfolk now." Berd crooned approvingly and Grall added a trill of her own.

"We could lose a few Holds this Turn around," F'nor said bitterly.

"That would solve nothing," she said. "I'm relieved that F'lar is going to watch that Nabolese. He has a warped mind."

Suddenly she gasped, gripping F'nor's fingers so tight that her fingernails broke the skin.

"What's the matter?" He put both arms around her protectively.

"He *has* a warped mind," Brekke said, staring at him with frightened eyes. "And he also has a fire-lizard, a bronze, as old as Grall and Berd. Does anyone *know* if he's been training it? Training it to go *between?*"

"All the Lords have been shown how—" F'nor broke off as he realized the trend of her thought. Berd and Grall reacted to Brekke's fright with nervous squeals and fanning wings. "No, no Brekke. He can't," F'nor reassured her. "Asgenar has one a week or so younger and he was saying how difficult he found it to send his Rial about in his own Hold."

"But Meron's had his longer. It could be further along . . ."

"Nabol?" F'nor was skeptical. "That man has no conception of how to handle a fire-lizard."

"Then why is he so fascinated with the Red Star? What else could he have in mind but to send his bronze lizard there?"

"But he knows that dragonmen won't attempt to send dragons. How can he imagine that a fire-lizard could go?"

"He doesn't *trust* dragonmen," Brekke pointed out, obviously obsessed with the idea. "Why should he trust that statement? You've got to tell F'lar!"

He agreed to because it was the only way to reassure her. She was still so pathetically thin. Her eyelids looked transparent though there was soft flush of color in her lips and cheeks.

"Promise you'll tell F'lar."

"I'll tell him. I'll tell him, but not in the middle of the night."

With a wing of riders to direct *between* time for larval sacks the next day, his promise slipped F'nor's mind until late that evening. Rather than distress her with his forgetfulness, he asked Canth to bespeak N'ton's Lioth to pass the theory on to N'ton. If the Fort Weyr bronze rider saw anything that gave Brekke's premise substance, then they'd tell F'lar.

He had a chance to speak to N'ton the following day as they met in the isolated valley field which Larad of Telgar Hold had picked to be seeded by grubs. The field, F'nor noticed with some jaundice, was planted with a new hybrid vegetable, much in demand as a table luxury and grown successfully only in some upland areas of Telgar and the high Reaches Hold.

"Brekke may have something, F'nor," N'ton admitted. "The watchriders have mentioned that Nabol will stare for a long time into the distance-viewer and then suddenly stare into his fire-lizard's eyes until the creature becomes frantic and tries to rise. In fact, last night the poor thing went *between* screaming. Nabol stalked off in a bad mood, cursing all dragonkind."

"Did you check what he'd been looking at?"

N'ton shrugged. "Wasn't too clear last night. Lots of clouds. Only thing visible was that one gray tail—the place that resembles Nerat but points east instead of west. It was visible only briefly."

F'nor remembered that feature well. A mass of grayness formed like a thick dragon tail, pointing in the opposite direction from the planet's rotation.

"Sometimes," N'ton chuckled, "the clouds above the star are clearer than anything we can see below. The other night, for instance, there was a cloud drift that looked like a girl," N'ton made passes with his hands to describe a head, and a few to one side of the air-drawn circle, "braiding her hair. I could see her head, tilted to the left, the half-finished braid and then the stream of free hair. Fascinating."

F'nor did not dismiss that conversation entirely for he'd noticed the variety of recognizable patterns in the clouds around the Red Star and often had been more absorbed in that show than in what he was supposed to be watching for.

N'ton's report of the fire-lizard's behavior was very interesting. The little creatures were not as dependent on their handlers as dragons. They were quite apt to disappear *between* when bored or asked to do something they didn't feel like doing. They reappeared after an interlude, usually near dinnertime, evidently assuming people forgot quickly. Grall and Berd had apparently matured beyond such behavior. Certainly they had a nice sense of responsibility toward Brekke. One was always near her. F'nor was willing to wager that Grall and Berd were the most reliable pair of fire-lizards on Pern.

Nevertheless, Meron would be watched closely. It was just possible that he could dominate his fire-lizard. His mind, as Brekke said, was warped.

As F'nor entered the passageway to his weyr that evening, he heard a spirited conversation going on although he couldn't distinguish the words.

Lessa is worried, Canth told him, shaking his wings flat against his back as he followed his rider.

"When you've lived with a man for seven Turns, you *know* what's on his mind," Lessa was saying urgently as F'nor entered. She turned, an almost guilty expression on her face, replaced by relief when she recognized F'nor.

He looked past her to Brekke whose expression was suspiciously blank. She didn't summon even a welcoming smile for him.

"Know what's on whose mind, Lessa?" F'nor asked, unbelting his riding tunic. He tossed his gloves to the table and accepted the wine which Brekke poured him.

Lessa sank awkwardly into the chair beside her, her eyes darting everywhere but toward him.

"Lessa is afraid that F'lar may attempt to go to the Red Star himself," Brekke said, watching him.

F'nor considered that as he drank his wine. "F'lar's not a fool, my dear girls. A dragon has to know where he's going. And we don't know what to tell them. Mnementh's no fool either." But as F'nor passed his cup to Brekke to be refilled, he had a sudden flash of N'ton's hair-braiding cloud lady.

"He can't go," Lessa said, her voice harsh. "He's what holds Pern together. He's the only one who can consolidate the Lord Holders, the Craftmasters and the dragonriders. Even the Oldtimers trust him now. Him. No one else!"

Lessa was unusually upset, F'nor realized. Grall and Berd came gliding in to perch on the posts of Brekke's chair, chirping softly and preening their wings.

Lessa ignored their antics, leaning across the table, one hand on F'nor's to hold his attention. "I heard what the Harper said about miracles. Salvation in three days!" Her eyes were bitter.

"Going to the Red Star is salvation for no one, Lessa!"

"Yes, but we don't *know* that for certain. We've only assumed that *we* can't because the ancients didn't. And until we prove to the Lords what the actual conditions there are, they will not accept the alternative!"

"More trouble from Larad?" F'nor asked sympathetically, rubbing the back of his neck. His muscles felt unaccountably tight.

"Larad is bad enough," she said bitterly, "but I'd rather him than Raid and Sifer. They've somehow got hold of rumors and they're demanding instant action."

"Show 'em the grubs!"

Lessa abruptly released F'nor's hand, pursing her lips with exasperation. "If grubs didn't reassure Larad of Telgar, they'll have less effect on those old blow-hards! No, *they*," and in emphasizing the pronoun she underscored her contempt for the old Lord Holders, "are of the opinion that Meron of Nabol *has* found coordinates after nights of watching and is maliciously withholding them from the rest of Pern."

F'nor grinned and shook his head. "N'ton is watching Meron of

Nabol. The man has found nothing. He couldn't do anything without our knowledge. And he certainly isn't having any luck with his fire-lizard."

Lessa blinked, looking at him without comprehension.

"With his fire-lizard?"

"Brekke thinks Meron might attempt to send his fire-lizard to the Red Star."

As if a string in her back had been pulled, Lessa jerked up in her chair, her eyes huge and black as she stared first at him, then at Brekke.

"Yes, that would be like him. He wouldn't mind sacrificing his fire-lizard for that, would he? And it's as old as yours." Her hand flew to her mouth. "If he . . ."

F'nor laughed with an assurance he suddenly didn't honestly feel. Lessa had reacted far too positively to a notion he privately considered unlikely. Of course, she didn't have a fire-lizard and might not appreciate their limitations. "He may be trying," he felt obliged to say. "N'ton's been watching him. But he's not succeeding. I don't think Meron can. He doesn't have the temperament to handle fire-lizards. You simply can't order them about the way you do drudges."

Lessa clenched her fists in an excess of frustration.

"There's got to be something we can do. I tell you, F'nor, I *know* what F'lar has on his mind. I know he's trying to find some way to get to the Red Star if only to prove to the Lord Holders that there is no other alternative but the grubs!"

"He may be willing to risk his neck, my dear Lessa, but is Mnementh willing?"

Lessa flashed F'nor a look of pure dislike. "And put the notion in the poor beast's head that this is what F'lar wants? I could throttle Robinton. Him and his three-day salvation! F'lar can't stop thinking about that. But F'lar is not the one to go" and she broke off, biting her lip, her eyes sliding toward Brekke.

"I understand, Lessa," Brekke said very slowly, her eyes unwinking as she held Lessa's. "Yes, I understand you."

F'nor began to massage his right shoulder. He must have been *between* too much lately.

"Never mind," Lessa said suddenly, with unusual force. "I'm just overwrought with all this uncertainty. Forget what I said. I'm only imagining things. I'm as tired as—as we all are."

"You're right there, Lessa," F'nor agreed. "We're all seeing problems which don't exist. After all, no Lord Holder has come to Benden Weyr and thrown down any ultimatum. What could they do? F'lar certainly has been forthright, explained the project of grub protection so often I'll be ill if I have to listen to it once more. Certainly he's been open with the other Weyrleaders, the Craftmasters, being sure that everyone knows exactly what the over-all plan is. Nothing will go wrong this time. This is one Craft secret that won't get lost because someone can't read a Record skin!"

Lessa rose, her body taut. She licked her lips. "I think," she said in a low voice, "that's what scares me most. He's taking such precautions to be sure everyone knows. Just in case . . ."

She broke off and rushed out of the Weyr.

F'nor stared after her. That interpretation of F'lar's overtness began to assume frightening significance. Disturbed, he turned to Brekke, surprised to see tears in the girl's eyes. He took her in his arms.

"Look, I'll get some rest, we'll eat, and then I'll go to Fort Weyr. See Meron myself. Better still," and he hugged her reassuringly. "I'll bring Grall along. She's the oldest we've got. I'll see if *she'd* take the trip. If any of the fire-lizards would go, she'd be the one. There now! How's that for a good idea?"

She clung to him, kissing him so urgently that he forgot Lessa's disturbing idea, forgot he was hungry and tired, and responded with eager surprise to her ardent demands.

Grall hadn't wanted to leave Berd where the bronze fire-lizard was cuddled on the cushion by Brekke's head. But then, F'nor didn't much want to leave Brekke. She'd reminded him, after they'd loved each other deeply, that they had obligations. If Lessa had been worried enough about F'lar to confide in Brekke and F'nor, she was more deeply concerned than she'd admit. Brekke and F'nor must assume such responsibility as they could.

Brekke was a great one for assuming responsibility, F'nor thought with affectionate tolerance as he roused Canth. Well, it wouldn't take long to check on Meron. Or to see if Grall would consider going to the Red Star. That certainly was a better alternative than F'lar making the trip. *If* the little queen lizard would consider it.

Canth was in high good humor as they wheeled first above Benden Weyr, then burst out of *between* above Fort Weyr's Star Stones. There were glows along the crown of the Weyr rim and, beyond the Star Stones, the silhouettes of several dragons.

Canth and F'nor of Benden Weyr, the brown dragon announced in answer to the watchrider's query. *Lioth is here and the green dragon who must stay at Nabol,* Canth added as he backwinged to a light landing. Grall swooped above F'nor's head, waiting until Canth had taken off to join the other beasts before she took her shoulder perch.

N'ton stepped out of the shadows, his welcoming grin distorted by the path glows. He jerked his head back, toward the distance-viewer.

"He's here and his lizard's in a fine state. Glad you came. I was about to ask Lioth to bespeak Canth."

The bronze Nabol lizard began to screech with a distress which Grall echoed nervously. Her wings extended. F'nor stroked them down to her back, emitting the human version of a lizard croon which usually calmed her. She tightened her wings but started to hop from one foot to the other, her eyes whirling restlessly.

"Who's that?" demanded Meron of Nabol peremptorily. Meron's shadow detached itself from the larger one of the rock on which the distance-viewer was mounted.

"F'nor, Wing-second of Benden Weyr," the brown rider answered coldly.

"You've no business in Fort Weyr," Meron said, his tone rasping. "Get out of here!"

"Lord Meron," N'ton said, stepping in front of F'nor. "F'nor of Benden has as much right in Fort Weyr as you."

"How dare you speak to a Lord Holder in that fashion?"

"Can he have found something?" F'nor asked N'ton in a low voice.

N'ton shrugged and moved toward the Nabolese. The little lizard began to shriek. Grall extended her wings again. Her thoughts were a combination of dislike and annoyance, tinged with fear.

"Lord Nabol, you have had the use of the distance-viewer since full dark."

"I'll have the use of the distance-viewer as long as I choose, dragonman. Go away. Leave me!"

Far too accustomed to instant compliance with his orders, Nabol turned back to the viewer. F'nor's eyes were used to the darkness by now and he could see the Lord Holder bend to place his eye to the viewer. He also saw that the man held tight to his fire-lizard though the creature was twisting and writhing to escape. Its agitated screeching rose to a nerve-twitting pitch.

The little one is terrified, Canth told his rider.

"Grall terrified?" F'nor asked the brown dragon, startled. He could see that Grall was upset but he didn't read terror in her thoughts.

Not Grall. The little brother. He is terrified. The man is cruel.

F'nor had never heard such condemnation from his dragon.

Suddenly Canth let out an incredible bellow. It startled the riders, the other two dragons, and put Grall into flight. Before half the dragons of Fort Weyr roused to bugle a query, Canth's tactic had achieved the effect he'd wanted. Meron had lost his hold on the fire-lizard and it had sprung free and gone *between*.

With a cry of rage for such interference, Meron sprang toward the dragonriders, to find his way blocked by the menacing obstacle of Canth's head.

"Your assigned rider will take you back to your Hold, Lord

Meron," N'ton informed the Lord Holder. "Do not return to Fort Weyr."

"You've no right! You can't deny me access to that distance-viewer. You're not the Weyrleader. I'll call a Conclave. I'll tell them what you're doing. You'll be forced to act. You can't fool me! You can't deceive Nabol with your evasions and temporizing. Cowards! You're cowards, the pack of you! Always knew it. Anyone can get to the Red Star. Anyone! I'll call your bluff, you neutered perverts!"

The green dragon, her eyes redly malevolent, dipped her shoulder to Meron. Without a break in his ranting denunciation, the Lord of Nabol climbed the riding straps and took his place on her neck. She had not cleared the Star Stones before F'nor was at the distance-viewer, peering at the Red Star.

What could Meron have seen? Or was he merely bellowing baseless accusations to unsettle them?

As often as he had seen the Red Star with its boiling cover of reddish-gray clouds, F'nor still experienced a primitive stab of fear. Tonight the fear was like an extra-cold spine from his balls to his throat. The distance-viewer revealed the westward-pointing tail of the gray mass which resembled a featureless, backward Nerat. The jutting edge of the swirling clouds obscured it. Clouds that swirled to form a pattern—no lady braiding her hair tonight. Rather, a massive fist, thumb of darker gray curling slowly, menancingly over the clenched fingers as if the clouds themselves were grabbing the tip of the gray mass. The fist closed and lost its definition, resembling now a single facet of a dragon's complex eye, half-lidded for sleep.

"What could he have seen?" N'ton demanded urgently, tapping F'nor's shoulder to get his attention.

"Clouds," F'nor said, stepping back to let N'ton in. "Like a fist. Which turned into a dragon's eye. Clouds, that's all he could have seen, over backward Nerat!"

N'ton looked up from the eyepiece, sighing with relief.

"Cloud formations won't get us anywhere!"

F'nor held his hand up for Grall. She came down obediently and when she started to hop to his shoulder, he forestalled her, gently stroking her head, smoothing her wings flat. He held her level with his eyes and, without stopping the gentle caresses, began to project the image of that fist, lazily forming over Nerat. He outlined color, grayish-red, and whitish where the top of the imagined fingers might be sun-struck. He visualized the fingers closing above the Neratian peninsula. Then he projected the image of Grall taking the long step *between* to the Red Star, into that cloud fist.

Terror, horror, a whirling many-faceted impression of heat, violent wind, burning breathlessness, sent him staggering against N'ton as Grall, with a fearful shriek, launched herself from his hand and disappeared.

"What happened to her?" N'ton demanded, steadying the brown rider.

"I asked her," and F'nor had to take a deep breath because her reaction had been rather shattering, "to go to the Red Star."

"Well, that takes care of Brekke's idea!"

"But why did she overreact that way? Canth?"

She was afraid, Canth replied didactically, although he sounded as surprised as F'nor. *You gave vivid coordinates.*

"I gave vivid coordinates?"

Yes.

"What terrified Grall? You aren't reacting the way she did and you heard the coordinates."

She is young and silly. Canth paused, considering something. *She remembered something that scared her.* The brown dragon sounded puzzled by that memory.

"What does Canth say?" N'ton asked, unable to pick up the quick exchange.

"He doesn't know what frightened her. Something she remembers, he says."

"Remembers? She's only been hatched a few weeks."

"A moment, N'ton." F'nor put his hand on the bronze rider's shoulder to silence him for a thought had suddenly struck him. "Canth," he said taking a deep breath, "You said the coordinates I gave her were vivid. Vivid enough—for *you* to take me to that fist I saw in the clouds?"

Yes, I can see where you want me to go, Canth replied so confidently that F'nor was taken aback. But this wasn't a time to think things out.

He buckled his tunic slightly and jammed the gloves up under the wristbands.

"You going back now?" N'ton asked.

"Fun's over here for the night," F'nor replied with a nonchalance that astonished him. "Want to make sure Grall got back safely to Brekke. Otherwise I'll have to sneak in to Southern to the cove where she hatched."

"Have a care then," N'ton advised. "At least we've solved one problem tonight. Meron can't make that fire-lizard of his go to the Red Star ahead of us."

F'nor had mounted Canth. He tightened the fighting straps until they threatened to cut off circulation. He waved to N'ton and the watchrider, suppressing his rising level of excitement until Canth had taken him high above the Weyr. Then he stretched flat along Canth's neck and looped the hand straps double around his wrists. Wouldn't do to fall off during this jump *between*.

Canth beat steadily upward, directly toward the baleful Red Star, high in the dark heavens, almost as if the dragon proposed to fly there straight.

Clouds were formed by water vapors, F'nor knew. At least they were on Pern. But it took air to support clouds. Air of some kind. Air could contain various gases. Over the plains of Igen where the noxious vapors rose from the yellow mountains you could suffocate with the odor and the stuff in your lungs. Different gases issued from the young fire mountains that had risen in the shallow western seas to spout flame and boiling rock into the water. The miners told of other gases, trapped in tunnel hollows. But a dragon was fast. A second or two in the most deadly gas the Red Star possessed couldn't hurt. Canth would jump them *between* to safety.

They had only to get to that fist, close enough for Canth's long eyes to see to the surface, under the cloud cover. One look to settle the matter forever. One look that F'nor—not F'lar—would make.

He began to reconstruct that ethereal fist, its alien fingers closing over the westering tip of grayness on the Red Star's enigmatic surface. "Tell Ramoth. She'll broadcast what we see to everyone, dragon, rider, fire-lizard. We'll have to go slightly *between* time, too, to the moment on the Red Star when I saw that fist. Tell Brekke." And he suddenly realized that Brekke already knew, had known when she'd seduced him so unexpectedly. For that was why Lessa had confided in them, in Brekke. He couldn't be angry with Lessa. She'd had the courage to take just such a risk seven Turns ago, when she'd seen a way back through time to bring up the five missing Weyrs.

Fill your lungs, Canth advised him and F'nor felt the dragon sucking air down his throat.

He didn't have time to consider Lessa's tactics because the cold of *between* enveloped them. He felt nothing, not the soft hide of the dragon against his cheek, nor the straps scoring his flesh. Only the cold. Black *between* had never existed so long.

Then they burst out of *between* into a heat that was suffocating. They dropped through the closing tunnel of cloud fingers toward the gray mass which suddenly was as close to them as Nerat's tip on a high-level Thread pass.

Canth started to open his wings and screamed in agony as they were wrenched back. The snapping of his strong forelimbs went unheard in the incredible roar of the furnace-hot tornadic winds that seized them from the relative calm of the downdraft. There was air enveloping the Red Star—a burning hot air, whipped to flame-heat by brutal turbulences. The helpless dragon and rider were like a feather, dropped hundreds of lengths only to be slammed upward, end over end, with hideous force. As they tumbled, their minds paralyzed by the holocaust they had entered, F'nor had a nightmare glimpse of the

gray surfaces toward and away from which they were alternately
thrown and removed: the Neratian tip was a wet, slick gray that
writhed and bubbled and oozed. They they were thrown into the reddish clouds that were shot with nauseating grays and whites, here and
there torn by massive orange rivers of lightning. A thousand hot points
burned the unprotected skin of F'nor's face, pitted Canth's hide, penetrating each lid over the dragon's eyes. The overwhelming, multil-
eveled sound of the cyclonic atmosphere battered their minds ruthlessly to unconsciousness.

Then they were hurled into the awesome calm of a funnel of
burning, sand-filled heat and fell toward the surface—crippled and
impotent.

Painridden, F'nor had only one thought as his senses failed him.
The Weyr! The Weyr must be warned!

Grall returned to Brekke, crying piteously, burrowing into Brekke's
arms. She was trembling with fear but her thoughts made such chaotic
nonsense that Brekke was unable to isolate the cause of her terror.

She stroked and soothed the little queen, tempting her with morsels of meat to no effect. The little lizard refused to be quieted. Then
Berd caught Grall's anxiety and when Brekke scolded him, Grall's
excitement and anguish intensified.

Suddenly Mirrim's two greens came swooping into the weyr,
twittering and fluttering, also affected by the irrational behavior of the
little queen. Mirrim came running in then, escorted by her brown,
bugling and fanning his gossamer wings into a blur.

"Whatever is the matter? Are you all right, Brekke?"

"I'm perfectly all right," Brekke assured her, pushing away the
hand Mirrim extended to her forehead. "They're just excited, that's
all. It's the middle of the night. Go back to bed."

"Just excited?" Mirrim pursed her lips the way Lessa did when
she knew someone was evading her. "Where's Canth? Why ever did
they leave you alone?"

"Mirrim!" Brekke's tone brought the girl up sharp. She flushed,
looking down at her feet, hunching her shoulders in the self-effacing
way Brekke deplored. Brekke closed her eyes, fighting to be calm although the distress of the five fire-lizards was insidious. "Please get
me some strong *klah*."

Brekke rose and began to dress in riding clothes. The five lizards
started to keen now, flitting around the room, swooping in wild dives
as if they wanted to escape some unseen danger.

"Get me some *klah*," she repeated, because Mirrim stood watching her like a numbwit.

Her trio of fire-lizards had followed her out before Brekke realized
her error. They'd probably rouse the lower Caverns with their distress.

She called but Mirrim didn't hear her. Cold chills made her fingers awkward.

Canth wouldn't go if he felt it would endanger F'nor. Canth has sense, Brekke told herself trying to convince herself. He knows what he can and can't do. Canth is the biggest, fastest, strongest brown dragon on Pern. He's almost as large as Mnementh and nearly as smart.

Brekke heard Ramoth's brassy bugle of alarm just as she received the incredible message from Canth.

Going to the Red Star? On the coordinates of a cloud? She staggered against the table, her legs trembling. She managed to sit but her hands shook so, she couldn't pour the wine. Using both hands, she got the bottle to her lips and swallowed some that way. It helped.

She'd somehow not believed they'd see a way to go. Was that what had frightened Grall so?

Ramoth kept up her alarm and Brekke now heard the other dragons bellowing with worry.

She fumbled with the last closing of her tunic and forced herself to her feet, to walk to the ledge. The fire-lizards kept darting and diving around her, keening wildly; a steady, nerve-jangling double trill of pure terror.

She halted at the top of the stairs, stunned by the confusion in the crepuscular gloom of the Weyr Bowl. There were dragons on ledges, fanning their wings with agitation. Other beasts were circling around at dangerous speeds. Some had riders, most were flying free. Ramoth and Mnementh were on the Stones, their wings outstretched, their tongues flicking angrily, their eyes bright orange as they bugled to their weyrmates. Riders and weyrfolk were running back and forth, yelling, calling to their beasts, questioning each other for the source of this inexplicable demonstration.

Brekke futilely clapped her hands to her ears, searching the confusion for a sight of Lessa or F'lar. Suddenly they both appeared at the steps and came running up to her. F'lar reached Brekke first, for Lessa hung back, one hand steadying herself against the wall.

"Do you know what Canth and F'nor are doing?" the Weyrleader cried. "Every beast in the Weyr is shrieking at the top of voice and mind!" He covered his own ears, glaring furiously at her, expecting an answer.

Brekke looked toward Lessa, saw the fear and the guilt in the Weyrwoman's eyes.

"Canth and F'nor are on their way to the Red Star."

F'lar stiffened and his eyes turned as orange as Mnementh's. He stared at her with a compound of fear and loathing that sent Brekke reeling back. As if her movement released him, F'lar looked toward the bronze dragon roaring stentoriously on the heights.

His shoulders jerked back and his hands clenched into fists so tight the bones showed yellow through the skin.

At that instant, every noise ceased in the Weyr as every mind felt the impact of the warning the fire-lizards had been trying to inchoately to project.

Turbulence, savage, ruthless, destructive; a pressure inexorable and deadly. Churning masses of slick, sickly gray surfaces that heaved and dipped. Heat as massive as a tidal wave. Fear! Terror! An inarticulate longing!

A scream was torn from a single throat, a scream like a knife upon raw nerves!

"Don't leave me alone!" The cry came from cords lacerated by the extreme of anguish; a command, an entreaty that seemed echoed by the black mounts of the weyrs, by dragon minds and human hearts.

Ramoth sprang aloft. Mnementh was instantly beside her. Then every dragon in the Weyr was a-wing, the fire-lizards, too; the air groaned with the effort to support the migration.

Brekke could not see. Her eyes were filled with blood from vessels burst by the force of her cry. But she knew there was a speck in the sky, tumbling downward with a speed that increased with every length; a plunge as fatal as the one which Canth had tried to stop over the stony heights of the High Reaches range.

And there was no consciousness in that plummeting speck, no echo, however faint, to her despairing inquiry. The arrow of dragons ascended, great wings pumping. The arrow thickened, once, twice, three times as other dragons arrived, making a broad path in the sky, steadily striving for that falling mote.

It was as if the dragons became a ramp that received the unconscious body of their weyrmate, received and braked its fatal momentum with their own bodies, until the last segment of overlapping wings eased the broken-winged ball of the bloody brown dragon to the floor of the Weyr.

Half-blinded as she was, Brekke was the first person to reach Canth's bleeding body, F'nor still strapped to his burned neck. Her hands found F'nor's throat, her fingers the tendon where his pulse should beat. His flesh was cold and sticky to the touch and ice would be less hard.

"He isn't breathing," someone cried. "His lips are blue!"

"He's alive, he's alive," Brekke chanted. There, one faint shallow flutter against her seeking fingers. No, she didn't imagine it. Another.

"There wasn't any air on the Red Star. The blueness. He suffocated."

Some half-forgotten memory prompted Brekke to wrench F'nor's jaws apart. She covered his mouth with hers and exhaled deeply into his throat. She blew air into his lungs and sucked it out.

"That's right, Brekke," someone cried. "That may work. Slow and steady! Breathe for yourself or you'll pass out."

Someone grabbed her painfully around the waist. She clung to F'nor's limp body until she realized that they were both being lifted from the dragon's neck.

She heard someone talking urgently, encouragingly to Canth.

"Canth! Stay!"

The dragon's pain was like a cruel knot in Brekke's skull. She breathed in and out. Out and in. For F'nor, for herself, for Canth. She was conscious as never before of the simple mechanics of breathing; conscious of the muscles of her abdomen expanding and contracting around a column of air which she forced up and out, in and out.

"Brekke! Brekke!"

Hard hands pulled at her. She clutched the wher-hide tunic beneath her.

"Brekke! He's breathing for himself now. Brekke!"

They forced her away from him. She tried to resist but everything was a bloody blur. She staggered, her hand touching dragon hide.

Brekke. The pain-soaked tone was faint, as if from an incalculable distance, but it was Canth. *Brekke?*

"I am not alone!" And Brekke fainted, mind and body overtaxed by an effort which had saved two lives.

Spun out by ceaseless violence, the spores fell from the turbulent raw atmosphere of the thawing planet toward Pern, pushed and pulled by the gravitic forces of a triple conjunction of the system's other planets.

The spores dropped through the atmospheric envelope of Pern. Attenuated by the friction of entry, they fell in a rain of hot filaments on the surface of the planet.

. Dragons rose, destroying them with flaming breath. What Thread eluded the airborne beasts was efficiently seared into harmless motes by ground crews, or burrowed after by sandworm and fire lizard.

Except on the eastern slope of a nothern mountain plantation of hardwood trees. There men had carefully drawn back from the leading Edge of the Fall. They watched, one with intent horror, as the silver rain scorched leaf and fell hissing into the soil. When the leading Edge had passed over the crest of the mountain, the men approached the points of impact cautiously, the nozzles of the flames throwers they carried a half-turn away from the sprouting flame.

The still smoking hole of the nearest Thread entry was prodded with a metal rod. A brown fire-lizard darted from the shoulder of one man and, chirping to himself, waddled over to the hole. He poked an inquisitive half-inch of nose into the ground. Then he rose in a dizzying movement and resumed his perch on the specially padded shoulder of his handler and began to preen himself fastidiously.

His master grinned at the other men.

"No Thread, F'lar. No Thread, Corman!"

The Benden Weyrleader returned Asgenar's smile, hooking his thumbs in his broad riding belt.

"And this is the fourth Fall with no burrows and no protection, Lord Asgenar?"

The Lord of Lemos Hold nodded, his eyes sparkling. "No burrows on the entire slope." He turned in triumph to the one man who seemed dubious and said, "Can you doubt the evidence of your eyes, Lord Groghe?"

The ruddy-faced Lord of Fort Hold shook his head slowly.

"C'mon, man," said the white-haired man with the prominent, hooked nose. "What more proof do you need? You've seen the same thing on lower Keroon, you've seen it in Telgar Valley. Even that idiot Vincet of Nerat Hold has capitulated."

Groghe of Fort Hold shrugged, indicating a low opinion of Vincet, Lord Holder of Nerat.

"I just can't put any trust in a handful of squirming insects. Relying on the dragons makes sense."

"But you've seen grubs devour Thread!" F'lar persisted. His patience with the mean was wearing thin.

"It isn't right for a *man*," and Groghe drew himself up, "to be grateful to grubs!"

"I don't recall your being overgrateful to dragonkind either," Asgenar reminded him with pointed malice.

"I don't trust grubs!" Groghe repeated, jutting his chin out at a belligerent angle. The golden fire-lizard on his shoulder crooned softly and rubbed her down-soft head against his cheek. The man's expression softened slightly. Then he recalled himself and glared at F'lar. "Spent my whole life trusting dragonkind. I'm too old to change. But you're running the planet now. Do as you will. You will anyhow!"

He stalked away, toward the waiting brown dragon who was Fort Hold's resident messenger. Groghe's fire-lizard extended her golden wings, crooning as she balanced herself against his jolting strides.

Lord Corman of Keroon fingered his large nose and blew it out briskly. He had a disconcerting habit of unblocking his ears that way. "Old fool. He'll use grubs. He'll use them. Just can't get used to the idea that it's no good wanting to go to the Red Star and blasting Thread on its home ground. Groghe's a fighter. Doesn't sit well with him to barricade his Hold, as it were, and wait out the siege. He likes to charge into things, straighten them out *his* way."

"The Weyrs appreciate your help, Lord Corman," F'lar began.

Corman snorted, blew out his ears again before waving aside F'lar's gratitude. "Common sense. Protect the ground. Our ancestors were a lot smarter than we are."

"I don't know about that," Asgenar said, grinning.

"I do, young fellow," Corman retorted decisively. Then added hesitantly, "How's F'nor? And what's his name—Canth."

The days when F'lar evaded a direct answer were now past. He smiled reassuringly. "He's on his feet. Not much the worse for wear," although F'nor would never lose the scars on the cheek where particles had been forced into the bone. "Canth's wings are healing, though new membrane grows slowly. He looked like raw meat when they got back, you know. There wasn't a hand-span on his body, except where F'nor had lain, that hadn't been scoured bare. He has the entire Weyr hopping to when he itches and wants to be oiled. That's a lot of dragon to oil." F'lar chuckled as much to reassure Corman who looked uncomfortable hearing a list of Canth's injuries as in recollection of the sight of Canth dominating a Weyr's personnel.

"Then the beast will fly again."

"We believe so. And he'll fight Thread, too. With more reason than any of us."

Corman regarded F'lar levelly. "I can see it's going to take Turns and Turns to grub the continent thoroughly. This forest," and he gestured to the plantation of hardwood saplings, "my corner on Keroon plains, the one valley in Telgar, used all the grubs it's safe to take from Southern this Turn. I'll be dead, long since, before the job is finished. However, when the day comes that all land is protected, what do you dragonmen plan to do?"

F'lar looked steadily back at the Keroon Holder, then grinned at Asgenar who waited expectantly. The Weyrleader began to laugh softly.

"Craft secret," he said, watching Asgenar's face fold into disappointment. "Cheer up, man," he advised, giving the Lord of Lemos an affectionate clout on the shoulder. "Think about it. You ought to know by now what dragons do best."

Mnementh was settling carefully in the small clearing in response to his summons. F'lar closed his tunic, preparatory to flying.

"Dragons go places better than anything else on Pern, good Lord Holders. Faster, farther. We've all the southern continent to explore when this Pass is over and men have time to relax again. And there're other planets in our skies to visit."

Shock and horror were mirrored in the faces of the two Lord Holders. Both had had lizards when F'nor and Canth had taken their jump *between* the planets; they'd known intimately what had happened.

"They can't all be as inhospitable as the Red Star," F'lar said.

"Dragons belong on Pern!" Corman said and honked his big nose for emphasis.

"Indeed they do, Lord Corman. Be assured that there'll always be dragons in the Weyrs of Pern. It is, after all, their home." F'lar raised his arm in greeting and farewell and bronze Mnementh lifted him skyward.

··VOLUME III··
THE WHITE DRAGON

This book is irreverently dedicated
to my brothers
Hugh and Kevin
for sibling rivalries, and
the mature affections and loyalties that
develop from early brawling!

·· CONTENTS ··

•• C H A P T E R   I ••

At Ruatha Hold,
Present Pass, 12th Turn

"If he isn't clean enough now," Jaxom told N'ton as he gave Ruth's neck ridge a final swipe with the oiled cloth, "I don't know what clean is!" He wiped his sweaty forehead on his tunic sleeve. "What do you think, N'ton?" he asked politely, suddenly aware that he had spoken without due regard for his companion's rank as Weyrleader of Fort.

N'ton grinned and gestured toward the grassy bank of the lake. They squelched through the mud created by rinsing soapsand from the little dragon and, as one, turned for a full view of Ruth gleaming wetly in the morning sun.

"I've never seen him cleaner," N'ton remarked after due consideration, adding hastily, "not to imply that you haven't always kept him immaculate, Jaxom. However, if you don't ask him to move out of that mud, he won't stay clean long."

Jaxom passed on the request hastily. "And keep your tail up, Ruth, till you are on the grass."

From the corner of his eye, Jaxom noticed that Dorse and his cronies were creeping away, just in case N'ton had any further hard work for them. Jaxom had somehow managed to keep the smugness he felt under control all during Ruth's bath. Dorse and the others hadn't dared disobey the dragonrider when N'ton had blithely pressed them into service. To see them sweating over the "runt," the "oversized fire-lizard," unable to tease and taunt Jaxom as they'd planned to do this morning, had raised Jaxom's spirits considerably. He entertained no hopes that the situation would last long. But, if today the Benden Weyrleaders decided Ruth was strong enough to bear his weight in flight, then Jaxom would be free to fly away from the taunts he'd had to endure from his milk-brother and his cronies.

"You know," N'ton began, frowning slightly as he folded his arms across his damp-spattered tunic, "Ruth isn't really white."

Jaxom stared incredulously at his dragon. "He's not?"

"No. See how his hide has shadows of brown and gold, and ripples of blue or green on the near flank."

"You're right!" Jaxom blinked, surprised at discovering something totally new about his friend. "I guess those colors are much more noticeable because he's so clean and the sun's so bright today!" It was such a pleasure to be able to discuss his favorite topic with an understanding audience.

"He's . . . more . . . all dragon shades than the lack of any," N'ton continued. He slanted one hand against the angle of Ruth's heavily muscled shoulder, then cocked his head as he stared at the powerful hindquarters. "Beautifully proportioned, too. He may be small, Jaxom, but he's a fine-looking fellow!"

Jaxom sighed again, unconsciously straightening his shoulders and pushing out his chest with pride.

"Not too much flesh, not too little, eh, Jaxom?" N'ton shot an elbow to catch Jaxom on the top of his shoulder, a sly grin on his face for all the times Jaxom had had to call on the Weyrleader to help him cope with Ruth's indigestion. Jaxom had erroneously concluded that if he could stuff the proper amount of food down Ruth's gullet, the little dragon would grow to match the size of his clutch-mates. The results had not been good.

"Do you think he's strong enough to fly me?"

N'ton awarded Jaxom a thoughtful gaze. "Let's see, you Impressed him a Turn last spring, and we're into cool weather now. Most dragons achieve their full growth in their first Turn. I don't think Ruth's grown a half-hand in the last six months so we have to conclude that he has reached his full growth. Hey, now," N'ton reacted to Jaxom's sad sigh, "he's bigger than any runner beast by half a head, isn't he? They can be ridden for hours without tiring, right? And you're not exactly a heavyweight like Dorse there."

"Flying's a different sort of effort, isn't it?"

"True, but Ruth's wings are proportionally large enough to his body to support him in flight . . ."

"So he is a proper dragon, isn't he?"

N'ton stared at Jaxom. Then he put both hands on the boy's shoulders. "Yes, Jaxom, Ruth is a proper dragon, for all he's half the size of his fellows! And he'll prove it today when he flies you! So let's get you and him back to the Hold. You've got to get yourself fancied up to match his beauty!"

"C'mon, Ruth!"

I would rather sit here in the sun, Ruth replied, moving to Jaxom's left, his stride graceful as he kept pace with his friend and with the Fort Weyrleader.

"There's sun in our court, Ruth," Jaxom assured him, resting a light hand on Ruth's headknob, aware of the happy blue tone of Ruth's lightly whirling, jewel-faceted eyes.

As they walked on in silence, Jaxom raised his eyes to the imposing cliff face which was Ruatha Hold, the second oldest human habitation on Pern. It would be his to Hold when he came of age or when his guardian, Lord Lytol, former weaver-journeyman, former dragonrider, decided that he was wise enough—that is, if the other Lord Holders finally overcame their objections to his inadvertent Impression of the half-sized dragon, Ruth. Jaxom sighed, resigned to the fact that he would never be allowed to forget that moment.

Not that he wanted to, but Impressing Ruth had caused all kinds of problems for the Benden Weyrleaders, F'lar and Lessa, for the Lord Holders, and for himself since he was not allowed to be a real dragonrider and live in a Weyr. He had to remain Lord Holder of Ruatha or every younger Holdless son of every major Lord would fight to the death to fill that vacancy. The worst problem he had caused was to the man he desperately wanted most to please, his guardian, Lord Lytol. Had Jaxom only paused a moment to think before he jumped onto the hot sands of Benden's Hatching Ground to help break the tough shell for the little white dragon, he'd have realized what anguish he would bring to Lord Lytol by a constant reminder of what the man had lost at the death of his brown Larth. Never mind if Larth had died Turns before Jaxom's birth at Ruatha Hold, that tragedy was vividly, cruelly fresh in Lytol's mind, or so everyone told Jaxom repeatedly. If this was so, Jaxom often wondered, why then hadn't Lytol protested when the Weyrleaders and Lord Holders agreed that Jaxom must try to raise the little dragon at Ruatha?

Looking up to the fire-heights, Jaxom noticed that N'ton's bronze Lioth was nose to nose with Wilth, the elderly brown watch dragon. He wondered what the two dragons were talking about. His Ruth? The trial of the day? He noticed fire-lizards, tiny cousins to the big dragons, executing lazy spirals above the two dragons. Men were driving wherries and runner beasts from the main stables out to the pastures, north of the Hold. Smoke issued from the line of smaller cotholds that bordered the ramp into the Great Court and along the edge of the main road east. To the left of the ramp, new cots were being built since the inner recesses of Ruatha Hold were considered unsafe.

"How many fosterlings does Lytol have at Ruatha Hold, Jaxom?" N'ton suddenly asked.

"Fosterlings? None, sir." Jaxom frowned. Surely N'ton knew that.

"Why not? You've got to get to know the others of your rank."

"Oh, I accompany Lord Lytol quite often to the other Holds."

"I wasn't thinking of socializing as much as having companions here of your own age."

"There's my milk-brother, Dorse, and his friends from the cothold."

"Yes, that's true."

Something in the Weyrleader's tone made Jaxom glance at him but the man's expression told him nothing.

"See much of F'lessan these days? I remember that you two used to get into a lot of mischief at Benden Weyr."

Jaxom could not control the flush that rose to his hairline. Was it possible that N'ton had somehow found out that he and F'lessan had squeezed through a hole onto Benden's Hatching Ground for a close look at Ramoth's eggs? He didn't think F'lessan would have told that! Not to anyone! But Jaxom had often wondered if touching that little egg had somehow destined its occupant to be his!

"I don't see much of F'lessan these days. I don't have much time, taking care of Ruth and all."

"No, of course not," N'ton said. He seemed about to say more and then changed his mind.

As they walked on in silence, Jaxom wondered if he'd said something wrong. But he couldn't think about it for long. Just then N'ton's fire-lizard, brown Tris, whirled in for a landing on the padded shoulder of the Weyrleader, chirping excitedly.

"What's wrong?" asked Jaxom.

"He's too excited to make sense," N'ton replied with a laugh, and he stroked the little creature's neck, uttering a series of soothing noises until Tris, with a final chirp in Ruth's direction, folded his wings to his back.

He likes me, Ruth observed.

"All fire-lizards like you," Jaxom replied.

"Yes, I've noticed that too, and not just today when they were helping us wash him," N'ton said.

"Why do they?" Jaxom had always wanted to ask N'ton that, but he had never had the courage. He didn't like to take up the Weyrleader's valuable time with silly questions. But, today, it didn't seem like such a silly question.

N'ton turned his head to his fire-lizard and, in a moment, Tris gave a quick chirp and then busily cleaned his forepaw. N'ton chuckled. "He likes Ruth. That's all the answer I get from him. I'd hazard the notion that it's because Ruth is nearer their size. They can see him without having to back up several dragonlengths to do so."

"I suppose so." Jaxom still had reservations. "Whatever it is, fire-lizards come from all over to visit him. They tell him the most outrageous stories but that makes him happy, especially when I can't be right there with him."

They had reached the roadway and were heading for the ramp into the Great Court.

"Don't be long dressing, will you, Jaxom? Lessa and F'lar ought to arrive soon," N'ton said as he kept going straight on through the great gates toward the massive metal Hold door. "Finder'll be in his quarters at this hour?"

"He should be."

Then, as Jaxom and Ruth turned toward the kitchen and the old stables, the youth began to worry about the trial set for today. N'ton surely would not have raised his hopes about getting permission to fly Ruth if he wasn't pretty sure the Benden Weyrleaders would be agreeable.

To fly Ruth would be so marvelous. Besides it would prove once and for all that Ruth was a real dragon and not just an overgrown fire-lizard as Dorse so often teased him. And, too, he'd finally be able to get away from Dorse. Today was the first time in Turns he hadn't had to endure Dorse's teasing as he washed Ruth. Not that the boy was just jealous of Jaxom's having Ruth. Dorse had always taunted Jaxom, ever since he could remember. Before Ruth had come, Jaxom had managed to make himself scarce in the dark recesses of Ruatha's many levels. Dorse didn't like the dark, stuffy corridors and stayed away. But with Ruth's arrival, Jaxom no longer was able to disappear and avoid Dorse's attentions. He often wished that he didn't owe Dorse so much. But he was Lord of Ruatha and Dorse was his milk-brother so he owed him his life. For if Deelan hadn't given birth to Dorse two days before Jaxom's unexpected arrival, Jaxom would have died in his first hours. Therefore, Jaxom had been taught by Lytol and the Hold harper, he must share everything with his milk-brother. As far as Jaxom could see, Dorse benefitted far more than he did. The boy, a full hand taller than Jaxom and heavier set, certainly hadn't suffered for sharing his mother's milk. And Dorse made sure he got the best part of anything else Jaxom had.

Jaxom waved cheerily to the cooks, busy preparing a fine midday meal to celebrate, he fervently hoped, the occasion of his first flight on Ruth. He and the white dragon continued past the gates to the old stables which had been refitted as their quarters. Small though Ruth had been when he first arrived at Ruatha a Turn and a half ago, it had been obvious that he would quickly grow too large to enter the traditional apartment of the Lord Holder within the Hold proper.

So Lytol had decided that the old stables, with the vaulted ceiling, could be refurbished suitably for a sleeping quarters and a work room for Jaxom and a fine spacious Weyr for the little dragon. New doors had been specially designed by Mastersmith Fandarel and hung with such ingenuity that a slightly built lad and an awkward hatchling could manage them.

I will sit here in the sun, Ruth told Jaxom, poking his head past the entrance to their quarters. *My bed hasn't been swept.*

"Everyone's been so busy cleaning for Lessa's visit," Jaxom said, giggling as he remembered the terror in Deelan's face when Lytol had told her that the Weyrwoman was coming. In his milk-mother's eyes, Lessa was still only full-blooded Ruathan left alive after Fax's treacherous attack on the Hold over twenty Turns ago.

Jaxom stripped off his damp tunic as he entered his own room. The water in the jar by his sink was tepid and he grimaced. He really ought to be as clean as his dragon but he didn't think he'd have time to get to the Hold's hot baths before the Weyrleaders came. It wouldn't do for him to be absent when they arrived. He washed with soapsand and the tepid water.

They come, Ruth announced the words in Jaxom's mind just before old Wilth and Lioth heralded the visitors with appropriate trumpetings.

Jaxom rushed to the window and peered out, catching a glimpse of huge wings as the newcomers settled into the great courtyard. He didn't wait long enough to see the Benden dragons remove themselves to the fire-heights, accompanied by excited fairs of fire-lizards. Drying himself hurriedly, he wriggled out of his wet trousers. It didn't take him long to don his good new clothes and stamp into the boots made especially for this occasion and lined with downy wherry-hide for warmth in flight. Recent practice made it easy for him to rig the riding straps on the eager little dragon.

As Jaxom and Ruth emerged from their quarters, Jaxom was again assailed by apprehension. What if N'ton had been wrong? What if Lessa and F'lar decided to wait just a few more months to see if Ruth would grow? What if Ruth, being such a small dragon, didn't have enough strength to fly him? Supposing he hurt Ruth?

Ruth crooned encouragingly. *You couldn't hurt me. You are my friend.* And he butted Jaxom affectionately, whiffling against his face with warm sweet breath.

Jaxom inhaled deeply, hoping to settle his agitated belly. He then became aware of the gathering on the steps of the Hold. Why did there have to be so many people here today?

There are not many, Ruth told him, his tone surprised as he lifted his head to observe the gathering. *And many fire-lizards to see me, too. I know everyone here today. So do you.*

Jaxom realized that he did. Taking courage from his dragon's acceptance of such a large audience, he straightened his shoulders and strode forward.

F'lar and Lessa, as the chief dragonriders, were the most important guests. F'nor, brown Canth's rider and mate of the sad Brekke, was also present but he was a good friend to Jaxom. N'ton, of course, was there since he was Fort's Weyrleader and Ruatha was beholden to Fort Weyr. Master Robinton as Harper of Pern was here and, beside him, Jaxom was glad to see Menolly, the Haper girl who had often been his champion. Jaxom reluctantly admitted the right of Lord Sangel of South Boll and Lord Groghe of Fort to be present as representatives of the Holders.

At first Jaxom couldn't see Lord Lytol. Then Finder moved to say something to Menolly and Jaxom spotted his guardian. He hoped Lytol would *really* look at Ruth this once, if never again.

They had crossed the courtyard now and stood before the steps, Jaxom resting his right hand on Ruth's strong, gracefully curved neck, and squarely faced the judges.

Extending one hand in greeting towards Ruth, Lessa smiled at Jaxom as she stepped down to welcome him. "Ruth has filled out a great deal since last spring, Jaxom," she said, her manner reassuring as well as appreciative. "But you ought to eat more. Lytol, does Deelan never feed the child? He's nothing but bones."

Jaxom was shocked when he realized that he now was taller than Lessa, and she was cocking her head to look up at him. He'd always thought of Lessa as big. To be looking down on the Weyrwoman of Benden was somehow embarrassing.

"I'd say you've the advantage of F'lessan still, and he's getting longer every time I look," she added.

Jaxom began to stammer an apology.

"Nonsense, Jaxom, stand up to your inches," F'lar said, coming up beside his Weyrmate. His attention was centered on Ruth, and the white dragon raised his head slightly to be at eye level with the tall Weyrleader. "You've made more hands of height, Ruth, than I'd have given you at your Hatching! You've done well by your friend, Lord Jaxom." The Benden Weyrleader put a slight emphasis on the title as he turned his gaze from dragon to rider.

Jaxom winced, disliking the reminder of his equivocal position.

"However, I can't see that you'll ever reach the stature of our good Mastersmith, so I don't think you'll overburden Ruth in flight." F'lar glanced at the others on the steps. "Ruth's a full head higher in the shoulder than runner beasts. Sturdier, too."

"What's his wingspan now?" Lessa asked, her brows drawn in a thoughtful frown. "Jaxom, please ask him to extend?"

Lessa could easily have asked Ruth directly since she was able to speak to any dragon. Jaxom was considerably heartened to be accorded such a courtesy and he passed the request on to Ruth. Eyes whirling with excitement, the white dragon raised himself to his haunches and spread his wings, the muscles rippling through chest and shoulder with the clouded shades of all dragon colors.

"He's completely in proportion to himself," F'lar said, dipping under the wing to inspect the upper side of the broad, transparent membrane. "Oh, thank you, Ruth," he added as the white dragon obligingly tilted his wing. "I take it he's as eager to fly you as you are!"

"Yes, sir, because, sir, he *is* a dragon, and dragons all fly!"

The look F'lar shot him caused Jaxom to hold his breath, wondering if his quick answer had been too bold. When he heard Lessa laugh, he looked over at her. But she wasn't laughing at him, or at Ruth. Her eyes rested on her Weyrmate. F'lar's right eyebrow arched as he grinned back at her. Jaxom felt they weren't aware of him or Ruth at all.

"Yes, dragons do fly, don't they, Lessa?" the Weyrleader said softly, and Jaxom realized they were sharing some private joke.

Then F'lar raised his head to the fire-heights where golden Ramoth, bronze Mnementh, and the two browns, Canth and Wilth, maintained keen interest in the scene in the courtyard below.

"What does Ramoth say, Lessa?"

Lessa grimaced. "You know she's always said Ruth would do well."

F'lar glanced first at N'ton, who grinned, and then at F'nor, who shrugged acquiescence. "It's unanimous, Jaxom. Mnementh doesn't understand why we're all making such a fuss. Mount then, lad." F'lar stepped forward as if to give Jaxom a leg up to the neck of the white dragon.

Jaxom was torn between pleasure at having the Weyrleader of all Pern to assist him and indignation that F'lar thought him incapable of mounting unaided.

Ruth intervened by swinging his wings out of the way and bending his left knee. Jaxom stepped lightly on the proffered limb and swung to the proper position between the last two neck ridges. Those protuberances in a full dragon were sufficient to keep a man steady in ordinary flight, but Lytol had insisted that Jaxom use riding straps as a safety measure. As Jaxom secured the strap buckles to his belt's metal loops, he cast surreptitious glances at the crowd. But no one showed a trace of surprise or contempt for this precaution. When he was ready, that awful coldness of doubt rose once more in his belly. Supposing that Ruth couldn't . . .

He caught the confident grin on N'ton's face and saw Master Robinton and Menolly hold up their hands in salute. Then F'lar lifted his fist above his head in the traditional signal to rise.

Jaxom took a deep breath. "Let's fly, Ruth!"

He felt the bunching of muscle as Ruth assumed a semi-crouch, felt the tension through the back, the shift of musculature under his calves as the huge wings lifted for the all-important first downsweep. Ruth deepened his crouch slightly just as he kicked away from the ground with his powerful hind legs. Jaxom's head snapped on his neck. Instinctively he grabbed for the security of the straps, then hung on tightly as the little white dragon's powerful wing strokes lifted them upward, past the first rank of windows and the startled faces of the holders, up so quickly to the fire-heights that Jaxom saw the other tiers of windows in a blur. Then the great dragons extended their wings, bugling encouragement to Ruth. Fire-lizards swirled about them, adding their silvery voices. Jaxom just hoped they wouldn't startle Ruth or get in his way.

They are pleased to see us in the air together. Ramoth and Mnementh are very happy to see you on my back at last. I am very happy. Are you happier now?

The almost plaintive question caused a lump to lodge in Jaxom's throat. He opened his mouth to respond, only to have sound torn from his lips by the press of wind against his face.

"Of course, I'm happy. I'm always happy with you," he said joyfully. "I'm flying with you, just like I wanted to. This'll show everyone that you're a right dragon!"

You're shouting!

"I'm happy. Why shouldn't I shout?"

I'm the only one to hear you and I hear you very well indeed.

"You ought to. You're the one I'm happiest for."

They began a glide turn now and Jaxom leaned back away from the curve, holding his breath. Not that he hadn't flown on a dragon innumerable times before. But then he had been a passenger, usually crammed between two adult bodies. The intimacy of this flight was another sensation entirely, exhilarating, pleasantly scary and utterly marvelous.

Ramoth says you must grip more tightly with your legs as you do on runners.

"I didn't want to interfere with your breathing." Jaxom pressed his legs tightly into the warmth of the silken neck, heartened by the security the grip gave him.

That's better. You can't hurt my neck. You can't hurt me. You're my rider. Ramoth says we must land. Ruth sounded rebellious.

"Land? We just got airborne!"

Ramoth says I must not strain. Flying you is no strain. It is what I want to do. She says we may fly a little farther every day. I like that idea.

Ruth corrected his descending plane so that they approached the court from the southeast. People on the roadway stopped to stare and then to wave. Jaxom thought he heard cheers but the wind rushed past, making it difficult to be sure. Those in the court turned to follow his path. Every window on the second and first tier of the Hold had its observers.

"They'll all have to admit you're a proper flying dragon now, Ruth!"

The only thing Jaxom regretted was that this flight was so brief. A little longer every day, huh? Not Fall, fire or fog would keep him from flying every single day, longer and farther away from Ruatha.

Abruptly he was thrown forward, bruising his chest on a neck ridge as Ruth backwinged to settle neatly on the spot he had so recently vacated.

Sorry about that, Ruth said contritely. *I see that there are things I must learn now.*

Savoring the triumph of the airborne experience, Jaxom sat for a moment, rubbing his chest and reassuring Ruth. Then he was aware of F'lar, F'nor and N'ton coming towards him with expressions of approval. But why was the Harper looking so thoughtful? And why was Lord Sangel frowning?

The dragonriders say we can fly. They are the ones who matter, Ruth told him.

Jaxom could discern no expression at all on the face of Lord Lytol. That dulled Jaxom's pride in their achievement. How he had hoped that today of all days he might receive some flicker of approval, some kindly response from his guardian.

He never forgets Larth, Ruth said in his softest tone.

"See, Jaxom? I told you," N'ton cried as the three dragonriders ranged themselves by Ruth's shoulder. "Nothing to it."

"Very good first flight, Jaxom," F'lar said, running his eyes over Ruth for any signs of stress. "No bother to him at all."

"This fellow'll turn on a wing tip. Make sure you keep the straps on till you're used to each other," F'nor added, reaching up to grab Jaxom's forearm. It was the greeting gesture of equals, and Jaxom was enormously gratified.

"You've been mistaken then, Lord Sangel," Lessa's voice rang clearly to Jaxom. "There's never been any doubt that the white dragon could fly. We merely postponed the event until we were sure Ruth had reached his full growth."

F'nor winked at Jaxom and N'ton grimaced, while F'lar raised his eyes upward, indicating the need for patience. That intimacy made Jaxom realize that he, Jaxom of Ruatha, had indeed been admitted to a kinship with the three most powerful dragonriders of Pern.

"You're a dragonrider now, lad," N'ton said.

"Yes." F'lar frowned as he lengthened the word. "Yes, but you may not fly all over the world tomorrow, nor may you try going *between*. Not yet. You do realize that, I trust. Fine! You're to exercise Ruth in flight every day. Do you have a slate on those drills, N'ton?" F'lar passed N'ton's slate over to Jaxom. "Those wing muscles have got to be strengthened slowly, carefully, or you will place too great a strain on them. That's the danger. The time might come when you'd need speed or maneuverability and those unfit muscles wouldn't respond! You heard about that tragedy at High Reaches?" F'lar's expression was stern.

"Yes, sir. Finder told me." Jaxom didn't bother to mention that Dorse and his friends, once they'd heard of the incident, never let Jaxom forget the weyrling who had been dashed to death on the mountain slopes because he'd overflown his young dragon.

"You've a double responsibility at all times, Jaxom, to Ruth and to your Hold."

"Oh, yes sir; I know it, sir."

N'ton laughed and clapped Jaxom on the knee. "I'll wager you do, young Lord Jaxom, right up to the teeth!"

F'lar turned to the Fort Weyrleader, surprised at the tone of the rejoinder. Jaxom held his breath. Did Weyrleaders speak without thinking? Lord Lytol was always after Jaxom to think before he opened his mouth.

"I'll oversee Jaxom's initial training, F'lar, no need to worry about his sense of responsibility on that score. It's well ingrained," N'ton went on. "And, with your permission, I'll instruct him on flying *between* when I feel he's ready. I think," he gestured toward the two Lord Holders arguing with Lessa, "the less publicity for that phase of training, the better."

Jaxom could feel the slight tension in the air as N'ton and F'lar regarded each other. Suddenly Mnementh and then Ramoth bugled from the heights.

"They agree," N'ton said in a soft voice.

F'lar shook his head slightly and brushed away the lock of hair that fell into his eyes.

"It's obvious, F'lar, that Jaxom deserves to be a dragonrider," F'nor said in the same persuasive tone. "It's a question of Weyr responsibility in the final analysis. But it's not for those Lord Holders to decide. Besides Ruth *is* a Benden dragon."

"Responsibility is the overriding factor," F'lar said, frowning at the two riders. He glanced up at Jaxom, who wasn't certain exactly what they were talking about except that he knew he and Ruth were under discussion. "Oh, very well. He's to be trained to fly *between*. Otherwise, I suppose you'd try it on your own anyhow, wouldn't you, young Jaxom, being of Ruathan Blood?"

"Sir?" Jaxom didn't really quite believe his good fortune.

"No, F'lar, Jaxom wouldn't try such a thing on his own," N'ton replied in a curious tone. "That's the trouble. I think Lytol has done his job too well."

"Explain," F'lar said curtly.

F'nor held up his hand. "Here's Lytol himself," he said in quick warning.

"Lord Jaxom, if you would settle your friend in his quarters, and then join us all in the Hall?" The Lord Warder bowed politely to everyone. A muscle in his face started to twitch as he quickly turned and walked back to the steps.

He could have said something then . . . if he'd wanted to, Jaxom thought, staring sadly at his guardian's broad back.

N'ton gave him another clout on his knee and, when Jaxom looked at the Fort Weyrleader, he winked. "You're a good lad, Jaxom, and a good rider." Then he sauntered after the other dragonriders.

"You wouldn't by any chance be serving a Benden wine on this auspicious occasion, would you, Lytol?" the Masterharper's voice rang across the court.

"What else would anyone dare serve you, Robinton?" Lessa asked, laughing.

Jaxom watched them filing up the steps and through the Hall doors. With a concert of shrieks, the fire-lizards abandoned their aerial display and dove toward the entrance, narrowly missing the Harper's tall figure as they swarmed to get into the Hold.

The incident lifted Jaxom's spirits and he directed Ruth to their quarters. As his glance swept the windows, he saw people pulling back. He sincerely hoped that Dorse and all his pals had witnessed every moment, had noticed the handgrasp of F'nor and seen how he'd been talking to the three most important dragonriders on all Pern. Dorse would have to be more careful now that Jaxom was also going to be allowed to take his Ruth *between*. Dorse had never figured on that, had he? Nor, thought Jaxom, had he. Wasn't it just capital of N'ton to suggest it? And when Dorse heard, he'd just have to chew it raw and swallow!

Ruth answered his thoughts with a smug croon as the dragon paced into the old stable courtyard and dropped his left shoulder for Jaxom to dismount.

"We can fly now, and get away from here, Ruth. And we'll be able to go *between*, too, and go anywhere we want on Pern. You flew just beautifully, and I'm sorry I was such a poor rider, walloping you like that on your ridges. I'll learn. You'll see!"

Ruth's eyes wheeled affectionately in a brilliant blue as he followed Jaxom into the weyr. Then Jaxom kept telling Ruth how marvelous he was, turning on a wing tip and all, as he brushed away the worst of the ridge dust and hide fuzz that had accumulated on Ruth's bed overnight. Ruth settled himself, angling his head at Jaxom in a subtle bid for caresses. Jaxom obliged, somehow reluctant to join festivities at which the real guest of honor must be absent.

Warned by the shrieks of the fire-lizards, Robinton moved quickly to flatten himself against the righthand leaf of the great metal doors, then put his hands across his face as a shield. He'd been caught too often in frantic fire-lizard fairs not to take precautions. Generally speaking, however, the fire-lizards at the Harper Hall, thanks to Menolly's teachings, were well behaved. He smiled as he heard Lessa's exclamation of surprise and dismay. After he had felt the wind of their passing, he remained where he was and, sure enough, the fair swept back through the doorway. He heard Lord Groghe call his little queen, Merga, to order. Then his own Zair found him and, scolding as if Robinton had deliberately tried to hide from him, the little bronze fire-lizard settled on his padded left shoulder.

"There! There's a lad!" Robinton said, stroking the agitated bronze with his finger and receiving a headsweeping caress on his cheek in return. "I wouldn't leave you, you ought to know that. Were you flying with Jaxom, too?"

Zair stopped scolding and gave a happy cheep. Then he craned his neck to peer down the court. Curious, Robinton leaned forward to see what had attracted Zair and saw Ruth pacing toward the old stables. Robinton sighed. He almost wished Jaxom had not been allowed to fly Ruth. As he'd anticipated Lord Sangel was still vehemently against the youngster enjoying dragonrider prerogatives. Nor would Sangel be the only one of the older generation of Lord Holders who would dispute that liberty. Robinton felt that he'd done a fair job of influencing Groghe toward the boy, but then Groghe was smarter than Sangel. Besides, he owned a fire-lizard and that made him more charitably inclined toward Jaxom and Ruth. Robinton couldn't remember whether Sangel didn't want or had been unable to Impress a fire-lizard. He must ask Menolly. Her queen, Beauty, ought to be clutching soon. Useful that his journeywoman had a queen fire-lizard so that he could dispose of the eggs where he deemed it would do everyone the most good.

He watched a moment longer, rather touched by the sight. Between Jaxom and Ruth there was an aura of innocence and vulnerability, of dependence and protection of each for the other.

Jaxom had entered the world at a decided disadvantage, torn from his dead mother's body, with his father fatally wounded in a duel a half-hour later. Bearing in mind what N'ton and Finder had disclosed to him just before Jaxom's flight, Robinton was annoyed with himself for not keeping a close check on the boy. Lytol was not so stiff that he wouldn't take a hint, especially if it were for Jaxom's sake. But Robinton had so many claims on his time and his thinking, even with Menolly and Sebell in his confidence and as his devoted aides. Zair cheeped and brushed his head against the Harper's chin.

Robinton chuckled and stroked Zair. They weren't more than the length of a man's arm, these fire-lizards. They weren't as intelligent as dragons, but they were utterly satisfying as companions—and occasionally useful.

Now, he'd better join the others and see how he could insinuate his suggestion to Lytol. Young Jaxom would be a perfect addition to his scheme.

"Robinton!" F'lar called him from the doorway of the Hold's smaller reception room. "Hurry up here. Your reputation is at risk."

"My what? I'm coming . . ." The Harper's long legs brought him quickly into the room by the end of the sentence. From the smiles of those standing by the flasks of decanted wine, the Harper had no trouble guessing what was afoot.

"Ah! You think to catch me out!" he cried, dramatically gesturing at the wine. "Well, I'm sure I can manage to maintain my reputation here! Just as long as you've marked the flasks correctly, Lytol."

Lessa laughed and picked one up, exhibiting her choice to the assembled. She poured a glass of the deep red wine and held it out to Robinton. Aware that all eyes were on him, Robinton made his approach to the table, affecting a slow swaggering step. His eyes caught Menolly's and she gave him the barest wink, completely at her ease now in such prestigious company. Like the little white dragon, she was ready to fly on her own. She had certainly come a long Turn from the unsure, unappreciated girl of an isolated SeaHold. He really must get her out of the Harper Hall now and on her own.

Robinton made a proper show of wine-tasting, since this was obviously expected of him. He examined the color of the wine in the sunlight that streamed into the room, sniffed deeply of its aroma, then sipped ever so delicately and made a huge business of swishing the wine in his mouth.

"Hmmm, yes, well. There's no trouble in recognizing this vintage," he said, a shade haughtily.

"Well?" Lord Groghe demanded, his thick fingers twitching a bit on the broad belt in which he had hooked his thumbs. He rocked on his booted feet with impatience.

"One never hastens a wine!"

"Either you know or you don't," Sangel said with a skeptical sniff.

"Of course I know it. It's the Benden pressing of eleven Turns back, isn't it, Lytol?"

Robinton, aware of the silence in the room, was surprised by the look on Lytol's face. Surely the man couldn't still be upset about Jaxom flying the little dragon, could he? No, the muscle twitch had gone from his cheek.

"I'm right," Robinton said, drawling as he pointed an accusing finger at the Lord Warder. "And you know it, Lytol. To be precise, this is the later pressing as the wine is nicely fruity. Furthermore, this is from the first Benden shipment you managed to wheedle out of old Lord Raid, on the strength of Lessa's Ruathan Blood." He altered his voice to imitate Lytol's heavy baritone. " 'The Weyrwoman of Pern must have Benden wine when she visits her former Hold.' Am I not right, Lytol?"

"Oh, you're right on all counts," Lytol admitted with what sounded suspiciously like a chuckle. "About wines, Master Harper, you're infallible."

"What a relief!" F'lar said, clapping the Harper on the shoulder, "I could never have borne your loss of reputation, Robinton."

"It is proper wine to celebrate this occasion. I give you all Jaxom, young Lord of Ruatha Hold and proud rider of Ruth." Robinton knew he'd put a dragon among wherries with his words, but there was no point hiding from the fact that, though Jaxom was Lord-elect of Ruatha Hold, he was also and undeniably a dragonrider. Lord Sangel cleared his throat abruptly before taking the required sip. Lessa's scowl suggested she'd rather he made any other toast just then.

Then, after clearing his throat a second time, Sangel jumped in as Robinton had hoped he would. "Yes, about that, there must be some understanding as to how much of a dragonrider young Jaxom is to be. I was given to understand at his Hatching," Sangel waved his hand in the vague direction of the stables, "that the little creature was not likely to survive. Only reason I didn't protest at the time."

"We didn't deliberately mislead you, Lord Sangel," Lessa began in a testy voice.

"There will be no problem, Sangel," said F'lar diplomatically. "We've no shortage of large dragons in the Weyr. So he isn't needed to fight."

"We've no shortage of trained, Blooded men to take Hold here, either," Sangel said, shooting his jaw out belligerently. Trust old Sangel to come to the point, thought Robinton gratefully.

"Not with Ruathan Blood," Lessa said, her gray eyes flashing. "The whole point of my relinquishing my blood right to his Hold when I became Weyrwoman was to cede it to the one remaining male with any Ruathan Blood in his veins—Jaxom! As long as I live, I will not permit Ruatha, of all the Holds on Pern, to be the prize for continent-wide blood duels among younger sons. Jaxom remains as Lord Holder-elect of Ruatha; he will never be a fighting dragonrider."

"Just like to set matters straight," Sangel said, stepping aside to avoid the icy stare Lessa gave him. "But you've got to admit, Weyrwoman, that riding dragons, no matter in how limited a fashion, can be dangerous. Heard about that weyrling at High Reaches . . ."

"Jaxom's riding will be controlled at all times," F'lar promised. He threw a warning glance at N'ton. "He will never fly to fight the Thread. The danger would be too great."

"Jaxom is naturally a cautious lad," Lytol joined the debate, "and I've made him properly aware of his responsibilities."

Robinton saw N'ton's grimace.

"Too cautious, N'ton?" asked F'lar, who had also noticed the Fort Weyrleader's expression.

"Perhaps," N'ton replied tactfully, with an apologetic nod to Lytol. "Or perhaps, inhibited is a better description. No offense meant, Lytol, but I noticed today that the lad finds himself . . . isolated from others. Having his own dragon accounts for part of it, I'm sure. Since no lads his age have been allowed a chance to Impress fire-lizards, the hold boys have no appreciation of his problems."

"Dorse been nagging him again?" Lytol asked, pulling at his lower lip as regarded N'ton.

"Then you're not unaware of the situation?" N'ton appeared relieved.

"Certainly not. It's one reason I myself have pressed you, F'lar, to permit the boy to fly. He would then be able to visit the Holds which have boys his age and rank."

"But surely you've fosterlings?" Lessa cried, looking about the room as if she had somehow overlooked the presence of Holder younglings.

"I was about to arrange a half-Turn fostering for Jaxom when he Impressed." Lytol spread one hand to indicate an end to that plan.

"I can't support the notion of Jaxom leaving Ruatha for fostering," Lessa said with a frown. "Not when he's the last of the Bloodline . . ."

"Nor do I," Lytol said, "but it is necessary to reciprocate in fostering—"

"'Tis not," Lord Groghe said, clapping Lytol on the shoulder. "In fact, it's a blessing not to. I've a lad Jaxom's age to be fostered. Be a relief not to have to take another boy back. When I see what you've done to put Ruatha back on its feet and so prosperous, Lytol, the lad would learn from you how to Hold properly. That is, if there should be anything for him to Hold when he gets his majority."

"That's another matter I'd like to broach," Lord Sangel said, stepping up to F'lar with a glance at Groghe for support. "What are we Holders to do?"

"To do?" asked F'lar, momentarily perplexed.

"With the younger sons," Robinton said smoothly, "for whom there are no more holds to manage in South Boll, Fort, Ista, and Igen—to name the Lords with the largest families of hopeful sons."

"The Southern Continent, F'lar, when can we start opening the Southern Continent?" Groghe asked. "That Toric, who stayed behind in the Southern Hold, maybe he could use a strong, active, energetic, ambitious lad or two, or three?"

"The Oldtimers are in the Southern Continent," Lessa said

sternly. "They can do no one harm there, since the land is protected by grubs."

"I hadn't forgotten where the Oldtimers are, Weyrwoman," Groghe remarked, raising his eyebrows. "Best place for 'em, they don't bother us, they do what they want, without making honest folk suffer." There was a commendable lack of acrimony in Groghe's tone, Robinton noticed, considering how badly Fort Hold had suffered from T'ron's irresponsible conduct of Fort Weyr. "Point is, Southern's a fair size, grubbed, too, so it doesn't matter if the Oldtimers fly Thread or not, no real damage can be done."

"Have you ever remained outside your Hold during Threadfall?" F'lar asked Lord Groghe.

"Me? No! What d'you think I am, crazy? Not but what that gaggle of young men, fighting at the drop of a glove . . . Mind you, it's fists they fight with and I keep all weapons blunted, but their noise is enough to drive me *between* or outside. . . . Oh, I take your point, Weyrleader," Groghe added gloomily and his fingers did a rapid dance on his broad belt. "Yes, makes it difficult, doesn't it? We're not geared to live holdless, are we? Toric's not looking to increase his Holding at all? Something's got to be done about the youngbloods. Not just in my Hold, either, eh, Sangel?"

"If I may make a suggestion," Robinton broke in quickly when he saw F'lar hesitating. Considering the alacrity with which F'lar gestured him to proceed, he appeared grateful for the Harper's interruption. "Well, half a Turn ago, Lord Groghe's fifth son Benelek had an idea to improve a harvesting implement. The Fort Smithcraftmaster suggested that Fandarel ought to be interested. Indeed the good Mastersmith was. Young Benelek went to Telgar for special instruction and also talked one of the High Reaches' sons into joining him, that lad also having a mechanical bent. To shorten the tale, there are now eight Holder sons at the Smithcraft Hall, and three Crafthold boys who show an equal talent for the Smith's craft."

"What are you suggesting, Robinton?"

"Mischief needs idle hands. I'd like to see a special group of young people, recruited from all Crafts and Holds, exchanging ideas instead of insults."

Groghe grunted. "They want land to hold, not ideas. What about Southern?"

"That solution can surely be investigated," Robinton said, treating Groghe's insistence as offhandedly as he dared. "The Oldtimers won't live forever."

"In truth, Lord Groghe, we're by no means against expanding holds in the Southern," F'lar said. "It's just that . . ."

"The time must be chosen," Lessa finished when he faltered.

There was a curious gleam in her eyes that suggested to the Harper she had other reservations as well.

"We'll not have to wait until the end of this Pass, I hope," Sangel said peevishly.

"No, just until we are in no danger of dishonoring our word," F'lar said. "If you'll think back, the Weyrs have agreed to explore the Southern Continent . . ."

"The Weyrs agreed to get rid of Thread and the Red Star, too," Sangel said, irritated now.

"F'nor here and Canth still bear the scars of that Star," Lessa reminded him, indignant at having the Weyrs criticized.

"Meaning no offense, Weyrwoman, F'lar, F'nor," Sangel said, mumbling and not very subtly masking his annoyance.

"Another reason why it might be salutary to have young minds trained to discover new ways of doing things," Robinton said, smoothly diverting Lord Sangel.

Robinton was no end pleased at Sangel's attitude. He'd reminded F'lar and Lessa recently that the older Lord Holders persisted in believing that the dragonriders could, if they would put their minds to it, char Thread at its source on the Red Star and end forever the menace that kept people hold-fast. Mention, however, he deemed sufficient and quickly changed the subject.

"My archivist, Master Arnor, is going blind from trying to decipher eroding Record hides. He does well, but sometimes I think he doesn't at all understand what it is he is saving and thus unwittingly miscopies blurred words. Fandarel has commented on this problem, too. He's of the firm opinion that some of the mysteries from those old Records stem from miscopying. Now, if we had copyists who knew the discipline—"

"I'd like Jaxom to have some training that way," Lytol said.

"I was hoping you'd suggest him."

"Don't go back on your offer to take my son, Lytol," Groghe said.

"Well, if Jaxom's . . ."

"I see no reason why both solutions cannot be used," Robinton said. "We'd have boys his own age and rank fostering here where Jaxom must learn to Hold, but Jaxom would also learn skills with others of different rank and background."

"After the famine, a feast?" N'ton said in so low a voice that only Robinton and Menolly heard him. "And speaking of feasts, here's our honored guest!"

Jaxom stood, hesitating, on the threshold, remembering his manners sufficiently to swing a bow to the assembled.

"Ruth's settled, has he, Jaxom?" Lessa asked in a kind voice, gesturing the boy to come to her side.

"Yes, Lessa."

"Some other settlings been done, too, kinsman," she went on, smiling when she saw his apprehensive look.

"You know my son, Horon, don't you? Your age?" Groghe asked.

Jaxom nodded, startled.

"Well, he's going to foster here as company for you."

"And possibly some other lads," said Lessa. "Would you like that?"

Robinton noticed the incredulous widening of Jaxom's eyes as he glanced from Lessa to Groghe and back to Lytol where his glance remained until Lytol had nodded solemnly.

"And, when Ruth is flying well, how about coming to my Hall to see what I can teach you about Pern that Lytol doesn't know?" Robinton asked.

"Oh, sir," and Jaxom looked again to his guardian, "may I really do all this?" There was unadulterated relief and joy in Jaxom's voice.

·· C H A P T E R I I ··

Benden Weyr,
Present Pass, 13th Turn

Dusk was settling in Benden Weyr as Robinton climbed the stairs to the queen's weyr, something he had done so many times in the past thirteen Turns. He paused as much to catch his breath as to speak to the man just behind him.

"We've timed it well, Toric. I don't think anyone noticed our arrival. And they'll certainly not question N'ton," he said gesturing to the Fort Weyrleader dimly seen crossing the Bowl to the lighted kitchen caverns.

Toric wasn't looking at him. He was staring up at the ledge where bronze Mnementh was seated on his haunches, regarding the new arrivals, his jewel-faceted eyes gleaming in the dim light. Robinton's Zair reacted by digging his claws sharply into the Harper's ear and twining his tail more tightly about his neck.

"He won't hurt you, Zair," Robinton said, but he hoped the message would also satisfy the Southern Holder whose face and bearing were taut with surprise.

"He's almost twice as big as any of the Oldtimers' beasts," Toric said in a respectfully hushed voice. "And I thought N'ton's Lioth was big!"

"I believe that Mnementh's the largest bronze," Robinton said, continuing up the last few steps. He was concerned by that twinge in his chest. He'd have thought that all his recent and unexpected rest would have eased that condition. He must remember to speak to Master Oldive about it. "Good evening, Mnementh," he said as he reached the top step, inclining his body toward the great bronze. "It strikes me as disrespectful to barge by without acknowledging him," he said in an aside to Toric. "And this is my friend, Toric, whom Lessa and F'lar are expecting."

I know. I have told them you are come.

Robinton cleared his throat. He never expected an answer to his pleasantries but was always extremely flattered on those occasions when Mnementh responded. However, he did not share the dragon's comment with Toric. The man seemed unnerved enough as it was.

Toric moved quickly toward the short corridor, keeping Robinton between himself and bronze Mnementh.

"I'd better warn you," Robinton said, keeping amusement out of his voice, "that Ramoth's even larger!"

Toric's response was a grunt which dissolved into a gasp as the corridor opened up into the large rocky chamber which served as the home of Benden's queen. She was asleep on her stone couch, her wedge-shaped head pointing in their direction, gleaming golden in the glows that illuminated the weyr.

"Robinton, you are indeed safely back," Lessa cried, running toward him, a wide smile lighting her unusual face. "And so tanned!"

To the Harper's delighted surprise, she threw her arms about him in a brief and totally unexpected embrace.

"I should get storm-lost more often," he managed to say in a light tone, grinning as raffishly as he could with his heart pounding in his chest. Her body had been so vibrant, so light against him.

"Don't you dare!" She flashed him a look compounded of anger, relief and outrage, then her mobile face assumed a more dignified smile for the other guest. "Toric, you are very welcome here, and thank you for rescuing our good Masterharper."

"I did nothing," Toric said, surprised. "He'd a dollop of pure unadulterated good luck. He ought to have drowned in that gale."

"Menolly's not a Seaholder's daughter for naught," the Harper said, clearing his throat as he remembered those grim hours. "She kept us afloat. Though at one point, I wasn't at all sure I wanted to stay alive!"

"You're not a good seamen, then, Robinton?" F'lar asked with a laugh. He gripped the Southerner's arm in greeting and with his left hand gave the Harper an affectionate crack on the arm.

Robinton suddenly realized that his adventure had had disturbing repercussions in this Weyr. He was both gratified and chagrined. True, at the time of the gale, he'd been far too occupied with his rebellious stomach to think beyond surviving the next wave that crashed over their little boat. Menolly's skill had kept him from realizing the acute danger they were in. Afterward he would come to appreciate their position and wondered if Menolly had suppressed her own fear lest she lose honor in his eyes. She'd gone about her seamanship, managing to save most of the wind-torn sail, rigging a sea anchor, lashing him to the mast as he'd been made weak by nausea and retching.

"No, F'lar, I'm no seaman," Robinton said now, with a shudder. "I'll leave that to those born to the craft."

"And follow their advice," Toric warned, somewhat tartly. He turned to the Weyrleaders. "He's got no weather sense either. And, of course, Menolly didn't realize the strength of the Western Stream at this time of the year." He raised his shoulders to indicate his helplessness against such stupidity.

"Is that why you were dragged so far from Southern?" F'lar asked, gesturing at the newcomers to seat themselves at the round table set in the corner of the big room.

"So I'm informed," said Robinton, grimacing over the long lectures he'd received on current, tide, drift and wind. He knew more than he'd take care ever to need about those aspects of the seaman's craft.

Lessa laughed at his droll tone and poured wine.

"Do you realize," he asked, twirling the glass in his fingers, "that there wasn't a drop of wine on board?"

"Oh, no!" Lessa cried in comic dismay. F'lar's laughter joined hers. "What deprivation!"

Robinton then got down to the purpose of this visit. "It was, however, a felicitous accident. There is, my dear Weyrleaders, considerably more of the Southern Continent than we'd ever thought." He glanced at Toric, who produced the map he'd hastily copied from the larger one in his Hold. F'lar and Lessa obligingly held the corners to flatten the stiff hide. The Northern Continent was detailed as was the known portion of the Southern Continent. Robinton pointed to the thumb of the Southern peninsula which contained the Southern Weyr and Toric's Hold, then gestured to the right and left of that landmark where the coastline and a good part of the interior, marked off by two rivers, had been topographically detailed. "Toric has not been idle. You can see how much he has extended knowledge of the terrain beyond what F'nor was able to do during his journey south."

"I asked permission of T'ron to continue the exploration," the Southerner's expression mirrored contempt and dislike, "but he barely heard me out and said I could do as I liked just as long as the Weyr was properly supplied with game and fresh fruit."

"Supplied?" exclaimed F'lar. "They'd only to walk a few dragon lengths from the weyrs and pick what they needed."

"Sometimes they do. Mostly I find it easier to have my holders supply their demands. They don't bother us then."

"Bother you?" Lessa's voice was indignant.

"That's what I said, Weyrleader," Toric replied, a steely note in his voice; he turned back to the map. "My holders have been able to penetrate this far into the interior. Very difficult going. Tough jungle growth that dulls the keenest chopping blade in an hour. Never seen such vegetation! We know there are hills here and a mountain range farther back," he tapped the relevant area on the map, "but I'd not fancy carving my way there length by length. So we scouted along the shoreline, found these two rivers and proceeded up them as far as we could. The western river ends in a flat marshy lake, the southeastern one at a falls, six-seven dragon lengths high." Toric straightened, regarding the small portion of explored land with mild disgust. "I'd hazard the guess that even if the land went no farther south than that range, it's twice the size of South Boll or Tillek!"

"And the Oldtimers are not interested in examining what they have?" F'lar found that attitude unpalatable, Robinton realized.

"No, Weyrleader, they are not! And frankly, without some easier way to penetrate that vegetation," Toric tapped the hide. "I don't have the men, much less the energy, to bother. I've all the land I can hold right now and still be sure my people are safe from Thread." He paused. Although Robinton had a fair idea what he was hesitating about, the Harper wanted the Weyrleaders to know firsthand what this energetic Southerner thought. "Most of the time the dragonmen don't bother on that score, either."

"What?" Lessa exploded, but F'lar touched her shoulder.

"I'd wondered about that, Toric."

"How dare they?" Lessa continued, her gray eyes flashing. Ramoth stirred on her couch.

"They dare, all right," Toric said, looking nervously at the queen.

However, Robinton could see that Lessa's appalled reaction to the Oldtimers' delinquency gratified the man.

"But . . . but . . ." Lessa spluttered with indignation.

"Are you able to manage, Toric?" F'lar asked, calming his weyrmate with a firm hand.

"I've learned," he said. "We've plenty of flamethrowers, F'nor made sure they were left in my care. We maintain our holds grass-free and keep the beasts in the stone stables during Fall." He gave a diffident shrug, then grinned slightly as the indignant expression of the Weyrwoman. "They don't do us any harm, Lessa, even if they don't do us any good. Don't worry. We can handle them."

"That isn't the point," Lessa said angrily. "They are dragonmen, sworn to protect—"

"You sent them south because they weren't," Toric reminded her. "So they couldn't injure people here."

"That still doesn't give them any right to—"

"I told you, Lessa, they're not harming us. We manage fine without them!"

A sort of challenge in Toric's tone made Robinton hold his breath. Lessa had a quick temper.

"Is there anything you need from the North?" asked F'lar, in oblique apology.

"I was hoping you'd ask," the Southerner said, grinning. "I know you can't break your honor by interfering with the Oldtimers in the South. Not that I mind . . ." he added quickly as he saw Lessa about to protest again. "But we are running out of some things, like properly forged metal for my Craftsmith, and parts for the flamethrowers that he says only Fandarel can make."

"I'll see that you get them."

"And I'd like a young sister of mine, Sharra, to study with that healer the Harper was telling me about, a Master Oldive. We've some odd sorts of fevers and curious infections."

"Naturally she's welcome," Lessa said quickly. "And our Manora is adept in herb-brews."

"And . . ." Toric hesitated a moment, glancing at Robinton, who quickly reassured him with a smile and an encouraging gesture, "if there were some adventurous men and women who'd be willing to make do at my Hold, I think I could absorb them without the Oldtimers' knowing. Just a few, mind, because though we've all the space in the world, some people become unsettled when there aren't dragons in the sky during Threadfall!"

"Why, yes," F'lar said with a nonchalance that caused Robinton to stifle a laugh, "I believe there are a few hardy souls who would be interested in joining you."

"Good. If I've enough to Hold properly, then I can see my way clear to extending beyond the rivers next cool season." Toric's relief was visible.

"I thought you said it was impossible . . ." F'lar began.

"Not impossible. Just difficult," Toric replied, adding with a smile, "I've some men keen to continue despite the odds, and I'd like to know what's out there."

"So would we," Lessa said. "The Oldtimers won't last forever."

"That fact often consoles me," Toric replied. "One thing, though . . ." He paused, looking through narrowed eyes at the two Benden Weyrleaders.

So far, Toric's audacity had delighted Robinton. The Harper was very pleased at how he'd managed to prime the man into requesting the very thing that the North needed the most—a place to send the independent and capable men who had no chance of attaining holds in the North. The big Southerner's manner was quite a change for the Benden Weyrleaders: neither subservient and apologetic nor aggressive and demanding. Toric had become independent as a result of having no one, dragonmen, Craftmasters or Lord Holders, to fall back on. Because he had survived, he was self-confident and he knew what he wanted, and how to get it. Therefore he was addressing Lessa and F'lar as equals.

"One small matter," he continued, "which I'd like clarified?"

"Yes?" F'lar prompted him.

"What happens to Southern, to my holders, to me, when the last of those Oldtimers is gone?"

"I'd say that you will have more than earned the right to Hold," F'lar said slowly, with an unmistakable accent on the final word, "what you have managed to carve out of that jungle for yourself!"

"Good!" Toric gave a decisive nod of his head, his eyes never leaving F'lar's. Then, suddenly, his tanned face dissolved into a smile. "I'd forgotten what you Northerners can be like. Send me some more—"

"Will they hold what they have carved?" Robinton asked quickly.

"What they hold, they have," Toric replied in a grave manner. "But don't flood me with people. I've got to sneak them in when the Oldtimers aren't looking."

"How many can you sneak in . . . comfortably?" asked F'lar.

"Oh, six, eight, the first time. Then when we've got holds, the same again." He grinned. "The first ones build for themselves before the new ones come. But there's lots of room in the South."

"That's comforting because I've plans for the South myself," said F'lar. "That reminds me, Robinton, how far to the east did you and Menolly go?"

"I wish I could answer you. I know where we got to, when the storm finally blew out. The most beautiful place I've ever seen, a perfect semicircle of a white sanded beach, with this huge cone-shaped mountain far, far in the distance, right in the center of the cove . . ."

"But you came back along the shore, didn't you?" F'lar was impatient. "What was it like?"

"It was there," Robinton said uninformatively. "That's all I can say. . . ." He glared at Toric, who was chuckling at his discomfiture. "We had a choice of sailing very close to land which Menolly said was impossible as we didn't know the bottom, or with sufficient searoom to keep beyond the Western Current which would evidently have brought us right back to the cove. It is, as I've said, a very beautiful spot, but I was glad to leave it for a while. Consequently, while land was there, it was not close enough for any inspection by me."

"That's too bad." F'lar looked very unhappy.

"Yes and no," replied Robinton. "It took us nine days to sail back along that coast. That's a lot of land for Toric to explore."

"I'm willing, and I'll be ready if I get the supplies I need . . ."

"How do we get shipments to you, Toric?" F'lar asked. "Don't dare send them on dragonback, though that would be easiest and best from my point of view."

Robinton chuckled and gave a broad wink to the others. "As to that, if another ship should by chance be blown off course, south from Ista Hold . . . I had a word or two with Master Idarolan recently and he mentioned how bad the storms have been this Turn."

"Is that how you chanced to be South in the first place?" asked Lessa.

"How else?" Robinton said, assuming a very innocent expression. "Menolly was attempting to teach me to sail, a storm came up unexpectedly and blew us straight into Toric's harbor. Didn't it, Toric?"

"If you say so, Harper!"

·· CHAPTER III ··

❦

Morning at Ruatha Hold,
and Smithcrafthall at Telgar Hold,
Present Pass, 15.5.9

With a force that set all the cups and plates bouncing, Jaxom brought down both fists on the heavy wooden table.

"That is enough," he said into the stunned silence. He was on his feet, jerking his broad, bony shoulders back because his arms had been jarred by the blows. "That is quite enough!"

He didn't shout, he was oddly pleased to recall later, but his voice was deepened by this explosion of long suppressed anger and carried clearly to the edge of the Hall. The drudge who was bringing in another pitcher of hot klah paused in confusion.

"I am the Lord of this Hold," Jaxom went on, staring first at Dorse, his milk-brother. "I am Ruth's rider. He is unmistakably a dragon." Jaxom now bent his gaze on Brand, the head steward whose jaw had dropped in surprise. "He is, as usual," and Jaxom's glance flickered across Lytol's blankly puzzled face, "in the very good health he has enjoyed since his Hatching." Jaxom passed over the four fosterlings who were all too new at Ruatha Hold to have started jibing at him. "And yes," he said directly to Deelan, his milk-mother whose lower lip was quivering at her nursling's startling behavior, "this is the day when I go to the Smithcrafthall where, as you all well know, I shall be served with the food and courtesy adequate to my needs and station. Therefore," and his glance swept the faces around the table, "the subjects of this morning's conversation do not need to be aired again in my presence. Have I made myself clear?"

He didn't wait for an answer but strode purposefully from the Hall, elated at having finally said something and half-guilty because

513

he had lost control of his temper. He heard Lytol call his name but for once that summons did not exact obedience.

This time it would not be Jaxom, however young a Lord of Ruatha Hold he still was, who apologized for his behavior. The enormous backlog of similar incidents, manfully swallowed or overlooked for any number of logical reasons, swept aside every consideration except to put as much distance between himself and his invidious position, his too reasonable and conscientious guardian and the obnoxious group of people who mistook daily intimacy for license.

Ruth, picking up her rider's distress, came charging out of the old stable which made his weyr at Ruatha Hold. The white dragon's fragile-seeming wings were half-spread as he rushed to give whatever aid his mate needed.

With a breath that was half a sob, Jaxom vaulted to Ruth's back and urged him up out of the courtyard just as Lytol appeared at the massive Hold doors. Jaxom averted his face so that later he'd be able to say truthfully that he hadn't seen Lytol waving.

Ruth beat strongly upward, his lighter mass launched more readily than that of the regular-sized dragons.

"You're twice the dragon the others are. Twice! You're better at everything! Everything!" Jaxom's thought was so turbulent that Ruth trumpeted defiance.

The startled brown watchdragon queried them from the fire-heights and the entire Hold population of fire-lizards materialized around Ruth, dipping and swooping, chirping in echoed agitation.

Ruth cleared the fire-heights and then winked into *between*, unerringly going to the high mountain lake above the Hold which had become their special retreat.

The penetrating cold of *between*, brief passage though it was, reduced Jaxom's temper. He began shivering, since he wore only his sleeveless tunic, as Ruth glided down effortlessly to the water's edge.

"It's completely and utterly unfair!" he said, slamming his right fist into his thigh so hard that Ruth grunted with the impact.

What is troubling you today? the dragon asked as he landed daintily on the lake verge.

"Everything! Nothing!"

Which? Ruth reasonably wanted to know and turned his head to gaze at his rider.

Jaxom slid from the soft-skinned white back and encircled the dragon's neck with his arms, pulling the wedge-shaped head against him, for comforting.

Why do you let them *upset you?* Ruth asked, his eyes whirling with love and affection for his Weyrmate.

"A very good question," Jaxom replied after a full moment's consideration. "But they know exactly how." Then he laughed. "This is

where all that objectivity Robinton talks about ought to operate . . .
and doesn't."

The Masterharper is honored for his wisdom. Ruth sounded uncertain,
and his tone made Jaxom smile.

He was always being told that dragons had no ability to understand abstract concepts or complex relationships. Too often Ruth surprised him by remarks that cast doubt on the theory. Dragons, particularly Ruth in Jaxom's biased opinion, obviously perceived far more
than others credited to them. Even Weyrleaders like F'lar or Lessa and
even N'ton. Thinking about the Fort Weyrleader reminded Jaxom that
he now had a particular reason for going to the Mastersmithhall this
morning. N'ton, who would be there to hear Wansor, was the only
rider Jaxom felt would be likely to help him.

"Shells!" Jaxom kicked rebelliously at a stone, watching the ripples it caused when it skittered across the surface of the lake and finally
sank.

Robinton had often used the ripple effect to demonstrate how a
tiny action produced multiple reactions. Jaxom let out a snort, wondering how many ripples he'd caused this morning by storming out
of the Hall. And just why had this morning bothered him so much?
It had begun like other mornings, with Dorse's trite comments about
oversized fire-lizards, with Lytol's habitual query about Ruth's
health—as if the dragon were likely to deteriorate overnight—and with
Deelan snidely repeating that sickeningly old hoot about visitors starv-
ing at the Smithcrafthall. To be sure, Deelan's mothering had lately
begun to irritate Jaxom, especially when the dear soul invariably fondled him in front of her seething natural son, Dorse. All the time-
honored, worn-out nonsense that started a day, every day, at Ruatha
Hold. Why, today, should it jerk him to his feet in a fury and drive
him from the Hall he was Lord of, fleeing from people over whom, in
theory, he had all control and right?

And there was nothing wrong with Ruth. Nothing.

No. I am fine, Ruth said, then added in a plaintive tone, *except that
I didn't have time for my swim.*

Jaxom stroked the soft eye ridges, smiling indulgently. "Sorry to
spoil your morning, too."

You haven't. I'll swim in the lake. Quieter here, Ruth said and nuzzled
Jaxom. *It's better here for you, too.*

"I hope so." Anger was foreign to Jaxom and he resented the
violence of his inner feelings and those who had driven him to such
a point of fury. "Better swim. We've got to go on to the Smithcrafthall,
you know."

Ruth had no sooner spread his wings than a clutch of fire-lizards
appeared in the air above him, wildly chittering and loudly broad-
casting thoughts of smug satisfaction at their cleverness in finding him.

One winked out immediately and Jaxom felt another stab of resentment. Keeping track of him, huh? That'd be one more order from him when he got back to the Hold. Who did they think he was, an unbreeched child or an Oldtimer?

He sighed, repentant. Of course, they'd be worried about him when he'd stormed out of the Hold like that. Not that he was likely to go anywhere but to the lake. Not that he could possibly come to harm with Ruth, and not that he and Ruth could go anywhere on Pern where fire-lizards couldn't find them.

His resentment flared anew, this time against the silly fire-lizards. Why, of all dragons, did every fire-lizard have an insatiable curiosity about Ruth? Wherever they went on Pern, every fire-lizard in the neighborhood came popping in to gawk at the white dragon. This activity used to amuse Jaxom because the fire-lizards would give Ruth the most incredible images of things they remembered, and Ruth would pass the more interesting ones to him. But today, as with everything else, amusement had soured to irritation.

"Analyze," Lytol was fond of directing him. "Think objectively. You can't govern others until you can control yourself and see the broader, forward-looking view."

Jaxom took a couple of deep breaths, the kind Lytol recommended he take before speaking, to organize what he was going to say.

Ruth had winged over the deep-blue waters of the little lake now, fire-lizards outlining his graceful figure. He suddenly folded his wings and dove. Jaxom shuddered, wondering how Ruth could enjoy the biting cold waters fed by the snowcapped peaks of the High Ranges. In the muggy midsummer heat, Jaxom often found it refreshing, but now, with winter barely past? He shuddered again. Well, if dragons didn't feel the three-times-more-intense cold of *between*, a plunge in an icy lake would not be bothersome.

Ruth surfaced, waves lapping against the bank at Jaxom's feet. Jaxom idly stripped a branch of its thick needles and launched them one after another into the incoming ripples. Well, one wave of reaction to this morning's outburst was the dispatch of fire-lizards to find him.

Another, the look of stunned amazement on Dorse's face. That had been the first time Jaxom had ever rounded on his milk-brother, though, Shells, it was only the thought of Lytol's displeasure at his loss of control that had kept Jaxom's temper in check so long. Dorse loved nothing better than to taunt Jaxom about Ruth's lack of stature, masking his malicious jibes in mock-brotherly quarrels, knowing all too well that Jaxom could not retaliate without a rebuke from Lytol for conduct unbecoming his rank and station. Jaxom had long outgrown the need for Deelan's fussing but innate kindness and gratitude to her for the milk which had nourished him after his premature birth had long prevented Jaxom from asking Lytol to retire her.

So why, today, had all this suddenly come to a boil?

Ruth's head emerged from the waters again, the many-faceted eyes reflecting the bright morning sun in greens and brilliant clear blues. The fire-lizards attacked his back with rough tongues and talons, scrubbing off infinitesimal motes of dirt, splashing water over him with their wings, their own hides darkened by the wetting.

The green turned to batter her nose at one of the two blues and swatted the brown with her wing to make him work to her satisfaction. Despite himself, Jaxom laughed to see her scolding. She was Deelan's green and so much in manner like his milkmother that he was reminded of the weyr axiom that a drgon was no better than his rider.

In that way, Lytol had done Jaxom no disservice. Ruth was the best dragon in all Pern. If—and now Jaxom recognized the underlying cause of his rebellion—Ruth was ever *allowed* to be. Immediately all the frustrated anger of the morning returned, disrupting what little objectivity he had gained at the peaceful lakeside. Neither he, Jaxom, Lord of Ruatha, nor Ruth, the white runt of Ramoth's clutch, were allowed to be what they really were.

Jaxom was Lord Holder in name only, because Lytol administered the Hold, made all its decisions, spoke in Council for Ruatha. Jaxom had yet to be confirmed by the other Lord Holders as Lord of Ruatha. True, a matter of form only since there was no other male on Pern with Ruathan Blood. Besides, Lessa, the only living full-blooded Ruathan, had relinquished her blood right to Jaxom at the moment of his birth.

Jaxom knew he could never be a dragonrider because he had to be Lord Holder of Ruatha. Only he was not really a Lord Holder because he couldn't go up to Lytol and just say: "I'm old enough to take over now! Thanks and good-bye!" Lytol had worked too hard and long to make Ruatha prosper to take second place to the bumblings of an untried youth. Lytol only lived for Ruatha. He'd lost so much else: first his own dragon, then his small family to Fax's greed. All his life now centered about Ruathan fields and wheat, and runners, and how many wherry bucks . . .

No, in all fairness, he would simply have to wait until Lytol, who enjoyed vigorous health, died a natural death before he started Holding at Ruatha.

But, Jaxom continued his thoughts logically, if Lytol is active so that Ruatha Hold is not in dispute, why couldn't he and Ruth occupy their time learning to be proper dragon and rider. Every fighting dragon was needed now, what with Thread falling from the Red Star at unexpected intervals. Why should he have to trudge about the countryside, lugging a clumsy flamethrower when he could more effectively fight Thread if Ruth were only allowed to chew firestone? Just because

Ruth was half the size of the other dragons didn't mean he wasn't a proper dragon in all other respects.

Of course I am, Ruth said from the lake.

Jaxom grimaced. He'd been trying to think quietly.

I heard your feelings, not your thoughts, Ruth said calmly. *You are confused and unhappy.* He arched out of the water to shake his wings dry. He half-paddled, half-flew to the shore. *I am a dragon. You are my rider. No man can change that. Be what you are. I am.*

"But not really. They won't let us be what we are," Jaxom cried. "They're forcing me to be everything but a dragonrider."

You are a dragonrider. You are also, and Ruth said this slowly as if trying to understand it all himself, *a Lord Holder. You are a student with the Mastersmith and the Masterharper. You are a friend of Menolly, Mirrim, F'lessan and N'ton. Ramoth knows your name. So does Mnementh. And they know me. You have to be a lot of people. That is hard.*

Jaxom stared at Ruth, who gave his wings a final flick and then folded them fastidiously across his back.

I am clean. I feel well, the dragon said as if this announcement should resolve all of Jaxom's internal doubts.

"Ruth, whatever would I do without you?"

I don't know. N'ton comes to see you. He went to Ruatha. The little brown who followed looks to N'ton.

Jaxom sucked in his breath nervously. Trust Ruth to know which was whose fire-lizard. He had assumed the brown looked to someone at Ruatha Hold.

"Why didn't you tell me sooner?" Hurriedly Jaxom made to mount Ruth. He did most urgently want to see N'ton, and he wanted with equal intensity to keep in N'ton's good favor. The Fort Weyrleader didn't have that much free time to chat.

I wanted my swim, Ruth replied. *We will be in time.* Ruth rose from the ground when Jaxom had barely settled on his back. *We will not keep N'ton waiting.* Before Jaxom could remind Ruth that they weren't supposed to go *between* time, they had.

"Ruth, what if N'ton finds out we've been timing it," Jaxom said through chattering teeth as they broke out of *between* into the hot mid-morning sun of Telgar over the Mastersmithcrafthall.

He will not ask.

Jaxom wished that Ruth wouldn't sound so complacent. But then, the white dragon wouldn't have to take N'ton's tongue-lashing. Timing was bloody dangerous!

I always know when I'm going, Ruth replied, not at all perturbed. *That's something few other dragons can say.*

They were barely in a landing circle above the Smithcrafthall complex before N'ton's great bronze Lioth burst into the air above them.

"And how you know how to time it that close, I'll never know," Jaxom said.

Oh, Ruth said easily, *I heard* when *the brown returned to N'ton and just came to that* when.

Jaxom knew that dragons were not supposed to laugh but the feeling from Ruth was so close to laughter as to make no difference.

Lioth winged close enough to Jaxom and Ruth for the young Lord to see the bronze rider's expression—a pleased grin. Jaxom thought Ruth had said N'ton had been at Ruatha first. Then Jaxom noticed that N'ton raised his hand and was holding what could only be Jaxom's wherhide riding jacket.

As they circled downward, Jaxom saw that they were by no means the first arrivals. He counted five dragons, including F'lessan's bronze Golanth and Mirrim's green Path who warbled a greeting. Ruth landed lightly on the meadow before the Smithcrafthall with Lioth touching down the next moment. As N'ton slid down the bronze shoulder, his brown fire-lizard, Tris, appeared and settled impertinently on Ruth's upper crest, chirping smugly.

"Deelan said you'd gone off without this," N'ton said and tossed the jacket at Jaxom. "Well, I suppose you don't feel the cold the way my old bones do. Or are you practicing survival tactics?"

"Ah, N'ton, not you, too!"

"Me, too, what, young fella?"

"You know . . ."

"No, I don't know." N'ton gave Jaxom a closer look. "Or did Deelan's babbling this morning have real significance?"

"You didn't see Lytol?"

"No. I just asked the first person in the Hold where you were. Deelan was weeping because you'd gone off without your jacket." N'ton drolly pulled down his lower lip in a trembling imitation of Deelan. "Can't stand weeping women—at least women of that age— so I grabbed the jacket, promised on the shell of my dragon to force it about your frail body, sent Tris to see where Ruth was and here we are. Tell me, did something momentous happen this morning? Ruth looks fine."

Embarrassed, Jaxom looked away from the quizzical regard of the Fort Weyrleader and gave himself a bit more time by shrugging into his jacket.

"I told the entire Hold off this morning."

"I told Lytol it wouldn't be long now."

"What?"

"What tipped the scales? Deelan's blubbering?"

"Ruth is a dragon!"

"Of course he is," N'ton replied with such emphasis that Lioth turned his head to regard them. "Who says he's not?"

"They do. At Ruatha. Everywhere! They say he's nothing but an overgrown fire-lizard. And you know that's been said."

Lioth hissed. Tris took wing in surprise, but Ruth warbled complacently and the others settled.

"I know it's been said," N'ton replied, taking hold of Jaxom's shoulders. "But there isn't a dragonrider I know who hasn't corrected the speaker—somewhat forcefully on occasion."

"If *you* consider him a dragon, why can't he act like one?"

"He does!" N'ton gave Ruth a long look as if the creature had somehow changed in the last moment.

"I mean like other full fighting dragons."

"Oh." N'ton grimaced. "So that's it. Look, lad . . ."

"It's Lytol, isn't it? He's told you not to let me fight Thread on Ruth. That's why you'll never let me teach Ruth how to chew firestone."

"It's not that, Jaxom . . ."

"Then what is it? There isn't a place on Pern we can't get to, first time, right on. Ruth's small but he's faster, turns quicker midair, less mass to move—"

"It's not a question of ability, Jaxom," N'ton said, raising his voice slightly to make Jaxom hear what he had to say, "it's a matter of what is advisable."

"More evasions."

"No!" N'ton's firm negative cut through Jaxom's resentment. "Flying with a fighting wing during Threadfall is bloody dangerous, lad. I'm not impugning your courage, but bluntly, however keen you are, however quick and clever Ruth is, you'd be a liability to a fighting wing. You haven't the training, the discipline . . ."

"If it's only training—"

N'ton grabbed Jaxom by the shoulders to stop his contentiousness.

"It isn't." N'ton drew a deep breath. "I said it's not a question of Ruth's abilities or yours; it is solely a question of advisability. Pern can't afford to lose either you, young Lord of Ruatha, or Ruth, who is unique."

"But I'm not Lord of Ruatha either. Not yet! Lytol is. He makes all the decisions . . . I just listen, and nod my head like a sunstruck wherry." Jaxom faltered, aware he was implying criticism of Lytol. "I mean, I know Lytol has to manage until the Lord Holders confirm me . . . and I don't really want Lytol to leave Ruatha Hold. But if I could be a dragonrider, it wouldn't come to that. You see?"

As Jaxom caught the expression in N'ton's eyes, his shoulders slumped in defeat. "You see, but the answer's still no! It would just make different ripples, probably bigger ones, wouldn't it? So I've got to muck on as something in between everything. Not a real Lord

Holder, not a real dragonrider . . . not a real anything except a problem. A real problem to everybody!"

Not to me, Ruth said clearly and reassuringly touched his rider with his muzzle.

"You're not a problem, Jaxom, but I do see that you have one," N'ton said with quiet sympathy. "If it were up to me, I'd say it would do you a world of good to join a wing and teach Ruth to chew firestone. For the firsthand knowledge no other Lord Holder could contest."

For one hopeful moment, Jaxom thought N'ton was offering him the chance he so wanted.

"*If* it were my decision, Jaxom, which it isn't and can't be. But," and N'ton paused, his eyes searching Jaxom's face, "this is a matter that had better be discussed. You're old enough to be confirmed as Lord Holder *or* to do something else constructive. I'll speak to Lytol and F'lar on your behalf."

"Lytol will say that I am Lord Holder, and F'lar will say Ruth isn't big enough for a fighting wing—"

"And I won't say anything if you act like a sulky boy."

A bellow overhead interrupted them. Two more dragons were circling, indicating that they wanted to land. N'ton waved acknowledgment, and then he and Jaxom jogged out of the way toward the Smithcrafthall. Just short of the door, N'ton held him back.

"I won't forget, Jaxom, only . . ." and N'ton grinned, "for the sake of the First Shell, don't let anyone *catch* you giving Ruth firestone. And be bloody careful when you go!"

In a state of mild shock, Jaxom stared at N'ton as the Weyrleader hailed a friend inside the building. N'ton had understood. Jaxom's depression lifted instantly.

As he crossed the threshold of the Smithcrafthall, he hesitated, adjusting his sight to the interior after the bright spring sun. Intent on his own problems, he'd also forgotten how important a session this was to be. Masterharper Robinton was seated at the long work table, cleared for this occasion of its usual clutter, and F'lar, Benden's Weyrleader, was beside him. Jaxom recognized three other Weyrleaders and the new Masterherdsman Briaret. There were a good half a wing of bronze riders and Lord Holders, the leading smiths and more harpers than any other craft to judge by the color of tunics on men he didn't recognize immediately.

Someone was calling his name in an urgent hoarse whisper. Looking to his left, Jaxom saw that F'lessan and the other regular students had gathered humbly by the far window, the girls perched on stools.

"Half Pern's here," F'lessan remarked, pleased, as he made room against the back wall for Jaxom.

Jaxom nodded to the others who appeared far more interested in watching the new arrivals. "Didn't think there'd be so many people interested in Wansor's stars and maths," Jaxom said in a low voice to F'lessan.

"What? And miss the chance to ride dragonback?" F'lessan asked with good-natured candor. "I brought four in myself."

"A lot of people have assisted Wansor in collating the material," Benelek said in his usual didactic manner. "Naturally they want to hear what use has been made of their time and effort."

"They sure didn't come for the food," F'lessan said with a snicker.

Now why, wondered Jaxom, doesn't F'lessan's remark annoy me?

"Nonsense, F'lessan," Benelek replied, too literalminded to understand when someone was being faceticious. "Food's very good here. You eat enough of it."

"I'm like Fandarel," F'lessan said. "I make efficient use of anything edible. *Sush!* Here he is himself. Shells!" The young bronze rider grimaced with disgust. "Couldn't someone have made him change his clothes?"

"As if clothes mattered for a man with a mind like Wansor's." Benelek dropped his voice but he was nearly sputtering with contempt for F'lessan.

"Today of all days, Wansor should look tidy," Jaxom said. "That's what F'lessan meant."

Benelek grunted but did not pursue the subject. Then F'lessan nudged Jaxom in the ribs with a wink for Benelek's reaction.

Halfway inside the door, Wansor suddenly realized that the hall was filled. He stopped, peered around him, at first timidly. Then, when he recognized a face, he bobbed his head and smiled hesitantly. From all sides he met with encouraging grins and murmured greetings and gestures for him to continue to the front of the hall.

"Well, my, my . . . All for my stars? My stars, my, my!" His reaction sent a ripple of amusement through the hall. "This is most gratifying. I'd no idea . . . Most gratifying. And Robinton, you're *here* . . ."

"Where else?" The Masterharper's long face was suitably serious but Jaxom thought he saw the man's lips twitch in an effort not to smile. Robinton then half-guided, half-pushed Wansor toward the platform at the far end of the hall.

"Come on, Wansor," Fandarel said in his rolling tones.

"Oh yes, so sorry. Didn't mean to keep you waiting. Ah, and there's Lord Asgenar. How very good of you to come. I say, is N'ton here, too?" Wansor executed a full circle. Being nearsighted, he peered closely at faces, trying to spot N'ton. "He really should be—"

"Here I am, Wansor," N'ton raised his arm.

"Ah." The worried frown vanished from the round face of the Starsmith as Menolly had impudently, if accurately, labeled him. "My dear N'ton, you must come up front. You've done so much work, watching and looking at the most dreadful hours of the night. Come, you must—''

"Wansor!" Fandarel half-rose to project his commanding bellow. "You can't put everyone up front and they've all watched. That's why they're here. To see what their watching was all for. Not get up here and get on with it. You're wasting time. Sheer inefficiency."

Wansor muttered protestations and apologies as he bounced up the short distance to the platform. He did indeed look, Jaxom noticed, as if he'd been sleeping in those clothes. He probably hadn't changed since the last Threadfall to judge by the sharpness of the creases in the back of his tunic.

But there was nothing sloppy about the charts of star positions which Wansor now tacked up on the wall. Where did Wansor get that lurid red color for the Red Star—the color almost pulsed on the paper. Nothing dithering about his spoken presentation. Out of deference and respect for Wansor, Jaxom tried to pay close attention but he had heard it all before and his mind returned inexorably to N'ton's parting shot. "Don't let anyone catch you giving Ruth firestone!"

As if he would be that foolish. Here Jaxom hesitated. Although he knew in theory the whys and hows of teaching a dragon to chew firestone, he had also learned in his classes that between theory and practice anything could happen. Maybe he could enlist F'lessan's help?

He glanced at the friend of his boyhood, who had Impressed a bronze two Turns ago. Candidly, Jaxom did not consider F'lessan more than a boy and certainly not serious enough about his responsibilities as a bronze rider. He was grateful that F'lessan had never told anyone that Jaxom had actually touched Ruth's egg when the dragon was still in its shell on the Hatching Ground. Of course, that would have been a serious offense against the Weyr. F'lessan would scarcely regard teaching a dragon to chew firestone as anything at all remarkable.

Mirrim? Jaxom glanced toward the girl. The morning sun slanted through her browny hair, catching golden glints which he'd never noticed before. She was oblivious to anything but Wansor's words. She'd probably give Jaxom an argument and then set one of those fire-lizards of hers on him to be sure he didn't set himself ablaze.

Jaxom was privately convinced that T'ran, the other young bronze rider from Ista Weyr, thought Ruth was essentially an overgrown fire-lizard. He'd be even less help than F'lessan.

Benelek was out, too. He ignored dragons and fire-lizards as completely as they ignored him. But give Benelek a diagram or a machine, even the assorted parts of a machine found in the old holds and weyrs, and he'd spend days trying to figure out what it was supposed to be or do. Generally he could make a full machine work, even if he had to dismantle the whole thing to find out why it wasn't operating. Benelek and Fandarel understood each other perfectly.

Menolly? Menolly was just the person, if he did need someone, in spite of her predilection for putting anything she heard into a tune—a trick that was occasionally a real nuisance. But that talent made her an excellent Harper, in fact she was the first girl to be one in living memory. He stole a long look at her. Her lips were vibrating slightly and he wondered if she were already putting Wansor's stars to music.

"The stars mark time for us in every Turn and help us distinguish one Turn from another," Wansor was saying and Jaxom brought his attention guiltily back to the speakers. "The stars guided Lessa on her courageous trip back through time to bring the Oldtimers forward." Wansor cleared his throat at his somewhat unfortunate mention of the two dragonrider factions. "And the stars will be our constant guides in future Turns. Lands, seas, people and places may change but the stars are ordered in their courses and remain secure."

Jaxom remembered hearing some talk of trying to alter the course of the Red Star, deflecting it away from Pern. Had Wansor just proved that that couldn't be done?

Wansor went on to emphasize that once you understood the basic orbit and speed of any star, you could compute its position in the heavens as long as you also calculated the effect of its nearest neighbors at conjunction, at any given time.

"So, there is no doubt in our minds that we can now accurately predict Threadfall, according to the position of the Red Star when in conjunction with our other near neighbors in the skies."

Jaxom was amused that, whenever Wansor made a sweeping statement, he said *we* but when he announced a discovery, he said *I*.

"We believe that as soon as this blue star is released from the influence of the yellow star of our spring horizon and swings to the high east, Threadfall will resume the pattern which F'lar originally observed.

"With this equation," Wansor rapidly jotted the figures down on the board, and Jaxom again noticed that for a sloppy looking person, his notations were conversely precise, "we can compute further conjunctions which will affect Threadfall during this Pass. Indeed, we can now point to where the various stars have been at any time in the past and will be at any time in the future."

He was writing equations at a furious pace and explaining which stars were affected by which equations. He turned then, his round face settling into a very serious expression. "We can even predict, on the basis of this knowledge, the exact moment when the next Pass will begin. Of course, that's so many Turns in the future that none of us need worry about it. But I think it's comforting to know nonetheless."

Scattered chuckles caused Wansor to blink and then hesitantly grin, as if he belatedly realized that he'd said something humorous.

"And we must make sure that no one forgets in the long Interval this time," Mastersmith Fandarel said, his bass voice startling everyone after Wansor's light tenor. "That's what this union is all about, you know," Fandarel added, gesturing to the audience.

Several Turns before, when Ruth's life expectancy had been short, Jaxom had held a private if egocentric theory about the sessions at the Smithcrafthall. He had convinced himself that they had been initiated to give him an alternative interest in living in case Ruth died. Today's meeting let the substance out of that notion, and Jaxom snorted at his self-centered whimsy. The more people—in every Hold, in the Weyrs—who knew what was being done in each of the Crafthalls, by the individual Craftmasters and by their chief technicians, the less chance there was that the ambitious plans to preserve all Pern from the ravages of Thread would be lost again.

Jaxom, F'lessan, Benelek, Mirrim, Menolly, T'ran, Piemur, various other likely successors to Lord Holders and advanced junior craftsmen formed the nucleus of the regular school at the Smith and Harper crafthalls. Each student learned to appreciate the other crafts.

Communication is essential. That was one of Robinton's tenets. Wasn't he always saying, "Exchange information, learn to talk sensibly about any subject, learn to express your thoughts, accept new ones, examine them, analyze. Think objectively. Think toward the future."

Jaxom let his eyes drift about the room at the gathering, wondering how many of them could accept all of Wansor's explanations. True, with this lot he had the advantage that most of them had watched the stars form and reform their patterns, night after night, season after season until those stately patterns could be reduced to Wansor's clever diagrams and numbers. The trouble was that everyone was here in this room because he was willing to listen to new ideas and accept new thoughts. The ones who needed to be influenced were those who hadn't listened—such as the Oldtimers now exiled to the Southern Continent.

Jaxom surmised that some sort of a discreet watch was kept on happenings there. N'ton had once made an oblique reference to the Southern Hold. The students had a very detailed map of the land about the Hold and of some of the neighboring areas which indicated that the Southern Continent extended far deeper into the Southern seas than anyone had guessed even five Turns ago. During one of his talks with Lytol, Robinton had once let slip something that led Jaxom to believe the Masterharper had been in the Southern lands recently. It amused Jaxom to wonder how much the Oldtimers knew of what occurred on the mainland. There were some obvious changes which even those with the most closed minds would have to admit seeing. What of the ever-increasing spreads of forestland about which the Oldtimers had protested—expanses now protected by the burrowing grubs that farmers had once tried to exterminate, erroneously considering them a bane instead of a carefully contrived blessing and safeguard.

Jaxom's attention was reclaimed by the stamping of feet and the clapping of hands. He hastily added his own applause, wondering if he'd missed anything vital during his ruminations. He'd check with Menolly later. She remembered everything.

The ovation continued long enough to make Wansor blush with pleased embarrassment, until Fandarel rose and spread his tree-limb arms for silence. But Fandarel no more got his mouth open to speak when one of the Ista Hold watchers jumped to his feet to ask Wansor to clarify an anomaly concerning the fixed position of the trio of Stars known as the Day Sisters. Before Wansor could answer him, someone else informed the man that no anomaly existed and a spirited argument began.

"I wonder if we could use Wansor's equations to go ahead in time safely," F'lessan mused.

"You deadglow! You can't go to a time that hasn't happened!" Mirrim answered him tartly before the others could. "How would you know what's happening there? You'd end up in a cliff or a crowd, or surrounded by Thread! It's dangerous enough to go back in time when at least you can check on what happened or on who was there. Even then you could, and *you* would, muddle things. Forget it, F'lessan!"

"Going ahead could serve no logical purpose at this time," Benelek remarked in his sententious way.

"It'd be fun," F'lessan said, undeterred. "Like knowing what the Oldtimers are planning. F'lar's sure they're going to try something. They've been far too quiet down there."

"Close your jaw, F'lessan. That's Weyr business," Mirrim said sharply, glancing anxiously around her for fear some of the adults might have overheard his indiscreet remark.

"Communicate! Share your thoughts!" F'lessan spouted back some of Robinton's taglines.

"There's a difference between communication and gossip," Jaxom said.

F'lessan gave his boyhood friend a long measuring look. "You know, I used to think this school idea was a good one. Now I think it's turned the whole lot of us into do-nothing talkers. And thinkers!" He rolled his eyes upward in disgust. "We talk, we think everything to death. We never do anything. At least I have to do first and think later when we fight Thread!" He turned on his heel and then, brightening, announced, "Hey, there's food!" He began to weave through the crowd to the doors where heavily laden trays were being passed through to the central table.

Jaxom knew F'lessan's remarks had been general, but the young Lord keenly felt the jibe about fighting Thread.

"That F'lessan!" Menolly said at his ear. "He wants to keep glory in the bloodline. A bit of derring-do . . ." and her sea-blue eyes danced with laughter as she added, "for me to tune about!" Then she sighed. "And he's not the type at all. *He* doesn't think beyond himself. But he's got a good heart. C'mon! We'd better lend a hand with the food."

"Let us *do!*" Jaxom's quip was rewarded by Menolly's smile of appreciation.

There was merit in both viewpoints, Jaxom decided as he relieved an overburdened woman of a tray of steaming meatrolls, but he'd *think* about it later.

The Mastersmith's kitchen had prepared for the large gathering, and besides succulent meatrolls there were hot fish balls, bread slabbed with the firm cheeses of the High Range, two huge kettles of *klah*.

As he passed food around, Jaxom became conscious of something else that annoyed him. The other Lords Holder and Craftmasters were all cordial, inquiring courteously after Ruth and Lytol. They all seemed quite willing to exchange pleasantries with him but would not discuss Wansor's theories. Perhaps, Jaxom thought cynically, they hadn't understood what Wansor had said and were ashamed to show their ignorance before the younger man. Jaxom sighed. Would he ever be old enough to be considered on equal terms?

"Hey, Jaxom, dump that," F'lessan grabbed his sleeve. "Got something to show you."

Believing he had done his duty, Jaxom pushed his tray onto the table and followed his young friend out the door. F'lessan kept going, grinning like a dimwit, and then swung round to point at the roof of the Smithcrafthall.

The Hall was a large building with steep gables. The roof appeared to be in colorful motion, rippling with sound. A veritable fair of fire-lizards were perched on the gray slates, chirping and humming to one another in earnest conversation—a perfect parody of the intent discussions going on inside the building. Jaxom began to laugh.

"There can't be that many fire-lizards looking to those inside," he said to Menolly, who had just joined them. "Or have you acquired a couple more clutches?"

Brushing the laugh-tears from her eyes, she denied guilt. "I've only the ten and they go off on their own, sometimes for days. I don't think I could account for more than two besides Beauty, my queen. She sticks by me constantly. You know," she turned a serious face to him, "they're going to be a problem. Not mine, because I make mine behave, but this sort of thing." She gestured toward the covered roof. "They're such dreadful gossips. I'll wager most of the those don't look to the people within. They've been attracted by the dragons and by your Ruth in particular."

"A fair gathers like that wherever Ruth and I go," Jaxom said a bit sourly.

Menolly looked across the valley to where Ruth was lying on the sunny riverbank with three other dragons and the usual wing or two of ministering fire-lizards.

"Does Ruth mind?"

"No," Jaxom grinned tolerantly. "I think he rather enjoys it. They keep him company when I have to be elsewhere on Hold business. He says they have all sorts of fascinating and unlikely images in their minds. He likes looking . . . most times. Sometimes he gets annoyed— says they get carried away."

"How can they?" Menolly was bluntly dubious. "They don't have much imagination, not really. They only tell what they see."

"Or think they see, maybe?"

Menolly considered that. "What they see is usually pretty reliable. I know . . ." Then she stopped, looked dismayed.

"Never mind," Jaxom said. "I'd be as thick as a hold door if I didn't realize you Harpers keep busy down South." Jaxom then turned around to say something to F'lessan, who was nowhere to be seen.

"I'll tell you something, Jaxom," Menolly dropped her voice, "F'lessan was right. Something is going on down South. Some of my lot have been very agitated. I get an image of a single egg but it's not in an enclosed weyr. I thought maybe my Beauty had hidden another clutch. She sometimes does that. Then I got the impression that what she was seeing happened long ago. And Beauty's no older than Ruth, so how could she remember any more than five Turns back?"

"Fire-lizards with delusions of locating the First Shell?" Jaxom laughed heartily.

"I can't quite seriously laugh at their memories. They do know the oddest sorts of things. Remember F'nor's Grall not wanting to go to the Red Star? For that matter *all* the fire-lizards are terrified of the Red Star."

"Aren't we all?"

"They *knew*, Jaxom, knew before the rest of Pern had any knowledge."

Instinctively they both turned eastward, toward the malevolent Red Star.

"So?" Menolly asked cryptically.

"So? So what?"

"So fire-lizards have memories."

"Ah, leave off, Menolly. You can't ask me to believe that fire-lizards could remember things Man can't?"

"Got another explanation?" Menolly asked belligerently.

"No, but that doesn't mean there isn't one," and Jaxom grinned at her. His smile turned to alarm. "Say, what if some of those fellows up there are from the Southern Hold?"

"I'm not worried. The fire-lizards are outside, for one thing. For another, they can only visualize what they've understood." Menolly chuckled, a habit of hers which Jaxom found a pleasant change from the giggling of Holder girls. "Can you imagine what nonsense someone like T'kul would make of Wansor's equations? Seen through lizard eyes?"

Jaxom's personal recollections of the High Reaches Oldtimer Weyrleader were sparse, but he'd heard enough from Lytol and N'ton to realize that man's mind was closed to anything new. Though nearly six Turns of fending on his own down in the Southern Continent might have broadened his outlook.

"Look, it isn't me alone who's worried," Menolly went on. "Mirrim is, too. And if anyone today understands fire-lizards, it's Mirrim."

"You don't do badly yourself—for a mere Harper."

"Well, thank you, my Lord Holder." She gave him a facetious salute. "Look, will you find out what the fire-lizards are telling Ruth?"

"Don't they talk to Mirrim's green dragon?" Jaxom was reluctant to have more to do with fire-lizards at the moment than was absolutely necessary.

"Dragons don't remember things. You know that. But Ruth's different, I've noticed . . ."

"Very different . . ."

Menolly caught the sour note in his voice. "What's got your back up today? Or has Lord Groghe been to see Lytol?"

"Lord Groghe? What for?"

Menolly's eyes glinted with devilment and she beckoned him closer, as if anyone was near enough to hear what they'd been saying. "I think Lord Groghe fancies you for that beast-bosomed third daughter of his."

Jaxom groaned in horror.

"Don't worry, Jaxom. Robinton squashed the idea. He wouldn't do you a disservice there. Of course," Menolly glanced at him from the corners of her laughing eyes, "if you have anyone else in mind, now's the time to say so."

Jaxom was furious, not with Menolly but with her news, and it was hard to dissociate tidings and bearer.

"The one thing I don't want just now is a wife."

"Oh? Got yourself taken care of?"

"Menolly!"

"Don't look so shocked. We Harpers understand the frailties of human flesh. And you're tall, and nice-looking, Jaxom. Lytol's supposed to be giving you instruction in all the arts . . ."

"Menolly!"

"Jaxom!" She mimicked his tone perfectly. "Doesn't Lytol ever let you off to have some fun on your own? Or do you just *think* about it? Honestly, Jaxom," her tone became acerbic and her expression registered impatience with him, "between Robinton, though I love the man, and Lytol, F'lar, Lessa and Fandarel, I think they've turned you into a pale echo of themselves. Where is Jaxom?"

Before he could sort out a suitable answer for her impertinence, she gave him a piercing look through slightly narrowed eyes. "They do say the dragon is the man. Maybe that's why Ruth is so different!"

On that cryptic remark she rose and made her way back to the others.

Jaxom had half a mind to call Ruth and leave if all he was going to get were insults and slights.

"Like a sulky boy!" N'ton's words came back to him. Sighing, he settled back to the grass. No, he would not depart hastily from an awkward scene for the second time that morning. He would not act in an immature fashion. He would not give Menolly the satisfaction of knowing that her provocative comments bothered him at all.

He stared down the river where his dear companion played, and wondered? Why *is* Ruth different? Is the dragon the man? To be sure, if Ruth were different, he shared it. His birth had been as bizarre as Ruth's Hatching—he from a dead mother's body, Ruth from an eggshell too hard for the half-sized beak to break. Ruth was a dragon, but not weyrbred. He was Lord Holder, but not confirmed so.

Well then, to prove one would be to prove the other and hail the difference!

Don't let anyone catch you giving Ruth firestone! N'ton had said.

Wellaway, that would be his first goal!

•• C H A P T E R   I V ••

෴

Ruatha Hold, Fidello's Hold, and Various Points *Between*, 15.5.10–15.5.16

Over the next few days, Jaxom realized that it was one thing to form the resolution to teach Ruth to chew firestone, and quite another to find the time to do so. It was impossible to contrive a free hour. Jaxom entertained the unworthy thought that perhaps N'ton had tipped his plan to Lytol so that the Warder had consciously found activities to fill his days. As quickly, Jaxom discarded the notion. N'ton was not a treacherous or sly man. On sober examination, Jaxom had to admit that his days had always been full: with Ruth's care first, then lessons, Hold duties and, in past Turns, meetings at other Holders which Lytol felt he must attend—as a silent observer—to extend his knowledge of Hold management.

Jaxom simply hadn't realized the extent of his involvement until now, when he desperately wanted time to himself which did not have to be explained or arranged in advance.

The other problem which he hadn't seriously considered was that no matter where he and Ruth went, a fire-lizard was sure to appear. Menolly was correct in calling them gossips and he had no wish for them to oversee his unauthorized instruction. He experimented by popping Ruth up to a mountain ledge in the High Reaches which had been a practice ground when he was teaching Ruth to fly *between*. The area was deserted, barren, without so much as mountain weed peeping up from under the late hard snow. He'd given Ruth directions while they were airborne and, at that particular moment, unaccompanied by fire-lizards. He'd counted no more than twenty-two breaths before Deelan's green and the Hold steward's blue arrived over Ruth's head.

They squeaked in astonishment and then began to complain about the location.

Jaxom then tried two more equally unfrequented locations, one in the plains of Keroon and another on a deserted island off the coast of Tillek. He was followed to both places.

At first he seethed over such surveillance and envisioned himself tackling Lytol on the matter. Common sense urged that Lytol would scarcely have asked either the steward or Deelan to set their creatures on Jaxom. Misplaced zeal! If he tried to tell Deelan straight out, she'd weep and wail, wring her hands and run straight to Lytol. But Brand, the steward, was a different matter. He had come from Telgar Hold two Turns back when the old steward had proved unable to control the lustiness of the fosterlings. Jaxom paused. Now then, Brand *would* understand the problems of a young man.

So, when Jaxom returned to Ruatha Hold, he found Brand in his office, giving out discipline to some drudges for the depredations of tunnel-snakes in the storage rooms. To Jaxom's astonishment, the drudges were instantly dismissed with the injunction that if they didn't present him with two dead tunnel-snake carcasses apiece, they'd do without food for a few days.

Not that Brand had ever been lacking in courtesy to Jaxom, but such prompt attention surprised him, and he required a breath or two before he spoke. Brand waited with all the deference he would show to Lytol or a ranking visitor. With some embarrassment Jaxom remembered his outburst of a few mornings before and wondered. No, Brand wasn't the obsequious type. He had the steady eye, the steady hand, firm mouth and stance that Lytol had often told Jaxom to look for in the trustworthy man.

"Brand, I can't seem to go anywhere without fire-lizards from this Hold appearing. Deelan's green, and if you don't mind my saying so, your blue. Is all that really necessary anymore?"

Brand's surprise was honest.

"Occasionally," Jaxom hurried on, "a fellow likes to get off by himself, completely by himself. And, as *you* know, fire-lizards are the world's greatest gossips. They might get the wrong impression . . . if you know what I mean?"

Brand did but, if he was amused or surprised, he dissembled well.

"I do apologize, Lord Jaxom. An oversight, I assure you. You know how anxious Deelan used to be when you and Ruth first started flying *between* and the fire-lizards followed as a safeguard. I should have long ago altered that arrangement."

"Since when am I Lord Jaxom to you, Brand?"

The steward's lips actually twitched. "Since the other morning . . . Lord Jaxom."

"I didn't mean it like that, Brand."

Brand inclined his head slightly, forestalling further apology. "As Lord Lytol remarked, you are well old enough to be confirmed in your rank, Lord Jaxom, and we—" Brand grinned with uninhibited ease "—should act accordingly."

"Ah, well, yes. Thank you." Jaxom managed to leave Brand's office without further loss of poise and strode rapidly to the first bend of the corridor.

There he stopped, mulling over the implications of that interview. "Old enough to be confirmed in your rank . . ." And Lord Groghe thinking to marry him to his daughter. Surely the canny Fort Holder wouldn't do that if there was any doubt of Jaxom's being confirmed in rank. The prospect now alarmed and annoyed Jaxom whereas the day before it would have pleased him enormously. Once he officially became Lord of Ruatha, any chance he might have had of flying with the fighting wings would be gone. He didn't want to be Lord of Ruatha—at least not yet. And he certainly didn't want to be saddled with a female not of his own choosing.

He should have told Menolly that he had no trouble with any of the Holder girls . . . when he was of the mind. Not that he had followed some of the bawdier fosterlings' examples. He wasn't going to have the reputation of a lecher like Meron or that young fool of Lord Laudey's, whom Lytol had sent back to his home Hold with some cover excuse that no one really believed. It was all right for the Lord Holder to beget a few halfbloods, quite another to dilute Holder Blood with other lines. Nonetheless, he would have to find a pleasant girl to give him the alibi he needed, and then take the time for more important things.

Jaxom pushed himself off the wall, unconsciously straightening his shoulders. Brand's deference had been rather bracing. Now that he thought about it, he remembered other evidences of a change of attitude toward him, something his preoccupation with firestone had blinded him to until now. He suddenly realized that Deelan had not pestered him at the breakfast table to eat more than he wanted, that Dorse had been inexplicably absent the past few days. Nor had Lytol's morning remarks been prefaced with inquiries after Ruth's health but, rather, had concerned the day's upcoming business.

The night he had returned from the Mastersmithhall, Lytol and Finder had been eager to learn about Wansor's stars and that recital had taken up the whole evening. If the forsterlings and others had been unusually silent, Jaxom had only attributed that state of affairs to their interest in the discussion. Lytol, Finder and Brand had not had trouble finding their tongues.

The next morning there had been no time for more than a cup

of *klah* and a meatroll as Thread was due to fall across the spring-planted fields in the southwest and they had a long ride ahead.

I should have spoken out months ago, Jaxom thought as he entered his own quarters.

It had been established that Jaxom was not to be disturbed when he was caring for Ruth; a privacy that he was only now beginning to appreciate. Generally, Jaxom attended his dragon, oiling his skin and grooming him in the early morning or late evening. He hunted with Ruth every fourth day since the white dragon required more frequent meals than the larger ones. The Hold's fire-lizards usually accompanied Ruth, feasting with him. Most people fed their pets daily by hand, but the urge for hot, fresh-killed or self-caught food could never be trained out of the fire-lizards and it had been decided not to interfere with that instinct. Fire-lizards were quixotic creatures and although there was no doubt that they became genuinely attached at Hatching, they were subject to sudden fits and frights and would disappear, often for long periods of time. When they returned, they acted as if they'd never been gone, except for transmitting some rather outrageous images.

Ruth would be ready to hunt today, Jaxom knew. He heard his weyrmate's impatience to be off. Laughing, Jaxom shrugged on the heavy riding jacket and stamped into his boots as he politely inquired what sort of eating Ruth fancied.

Wherry, a juicy plain wherry, none of those stringy mountain ones. Ruth emphasized his distaste for the latter with a snort.

"You even sound hungry," Jaxom said, entering the dragon's weyr and approaching him.

Ruth laid his nose lightly on Jaxom's chest, his breath cool even through the heavy riding jacket. His eyes were wheeling with the red overtone of active appetite. He made his way to the huge metal doors that opened onto the stable courtyard and pushed them open with his forelegs.

Alerted by Ruth's hungry thoughts, the Hold's fire-lizards swirled about in eager anticipation. Jaxom mounted and directed Ruth aloft. The old brown watchdragon called good hunting from the fire-heights, and his rider waved.

From Hold tithings, the six Weyrs of Pern maintained their own herds and flocks on which the Weyr dragons fed. No Lord Holder ever objected to an occasional rider feeding his dragon off his land. As Jaxom was Lord Holder and technically had the right to anything within Ruatha's borders, Ruth's hunting was primarily a matter of courtesy. Lytol had not needed to instruct Jaxom to spread his beast's appetite so that no holder was overburdened.

On this particular morning Jaxom gave Ruth coordinates of a rich grass holding where Lytol had mentioned buck-wherries were being fattened for spring slaughtering. The holder was out on his runner when Jaxom and Ruth appeared, and he greeted the young Lord politely enough and replied to Jaxom's courteous inquiries for his health, the progress of the flock and the laying weight of the hens.

"A thing I'd like you to mention to Lord Lytol," the man began, and Jaxom detected resentment in his manner. "I've asked for a fire-lizard egg time and again. It's my due as a holder and I've the need. I can't hatch wherry eggs proper if vermin burrow under and crack shells. There are four or five from each clutch gone, lost to snakes and the like. Fire-lizard would keep 'em off. They do for your man down at Bald Lake Hold and others I've spoken to. Fire-lizards are mighty handy creatures, Lord Jaxom, and being a holder now these past twelve Turns, it's only my due. Bald Lake Palon, now he's got a fire-lizard and he's only held for ten Turns."

"I can't imagine why you've been slighted, Tegger. I'll see that something is done about it. We haven't a clutch at the moment but I'll do what I can when we have."

Tegger gave surly thanks and then suggested that Jaxom hunt the buck flock to be found browsing at the far end of the plain meadow. He wanted to take the nearer flock for slaughter and a hunting dragon ran a sevenday's weight off bucks.

Jaxom thanked the man and Ruth warbled his gratitude, startling Tegger's runner into bucking. Tegger grimly yanked the beast's head about, preventing a bolt.

Tegger was unlikely to Impress a fire-lizard, Jaxom thought as he leaped to Ruth's shoulder.

Ruth agreed. *That man had an egg once. The little one went* between *and never returned to its hatching place.*

"How did you remember that?"

The fire-lizards told me.

"When?"

When it happened. I have just remembered it. Ruth sounded very pleased with himself. *They tell me many things that are interesting when you're not with me.*

Jaxom only then became aware that the usual fire-lizard escorts weren't about, even though Ruth was hunting. He hadn't meant that Brand should curtail all fire-lizards excursions with them.

Ruth plaintively asked if they couldn't get on with the hunting since he was hungry. So they proceeded to the suggested area and Ruth let Jaxom down on a grassy rise with a good view of the hunt where he made himself comfortable. No sooner had Ruth become airborne than a flight of fire-lizards appeared, courteously landing to await the dragon's summons to join him after his kill.

Some dragons took their time selecting their meal, swooping on flock or herd to scatter it and isolate the fattest. Either Ruth made up his mind quickly or else he was influenced by Jaxom's knowledge that

Tegger would not appreciate overrun wherries. Whatever, the white dragon dispatched the first buck in one deft swoop, cracking the creature's long neck as he brought it down.

Ruth left the delighted fire-lizards picking the bones and killed a second time, eating as daintily as ever. The flock had barely settled at the far end of the meadow when he launched himself unexpectedly for the third.

I told you I was hungry, Ruth said so apologetically that Jaxom laughed and told him to stuff himself with all he wanted.

I am not stuffing myself, Ruth replied with a mild rebuke that Jaxom would think such a thing of him. *I am very hungry.*

Jaxom regarded the feasting fire-lizards thoughtfully. He wondered if any were from Ruatha. Ruth replied immediately that they had come from the surrounding area.

So, mused Jaxom, I've only solved the problem of keeping Ruathan fire-lizards from following. But what one fire-lizard knew, they all seemed to know so he would still have to keep his activities from their sight.

Jaxom knew a dragon needed time to chew and digest firestone for the best effect. Dragonriders would begin to feed their beasts stone several hours before Thread was due to fall. How fast could Ruth work up a full enough gullet of stone to produce the fire breath? He wondered. He'd have to go carefully. Since dragons differed in capacity and readiness, each rider had to find out for himself what his beast's peculiarities were. If only he could have trained Ruth in a Weyr and have the benefit of a weyrlingmaster's experience . . .

Well, firestone was no problem. The old watchdragon had to be supplied so there was a goodly pile on the fire-heights. And Ruth wouldn't need as much as a big dragon.

When still remained the problem. Jaxom had his morning free because Ruth was to hunt and it wasn't sound practice to take a full dragon *between*—all that rich warm food would sour a dragon belly in cold *between.* So Jaxom would have to take the time to fly Ruth straight to Ruatha Hold. This afternoon would be taken up with overseeing spring planting, and if Lytol were really going to arrange for him to be confirmed as Lord Holder, he couldn't get out of making an appearance.

Idly Jaxom wondered if the Lord Holders ever worried whether he might try to imitate his tyrannical father's taking ways or not. They would run on about Bloodlines, and blood telling, but weren't they the least bit nervous about his Fax blood telling? Or were they counting on the influence of his mother's blood. Everyone was right willing to discuss his Lady Mother Gemma with him, but did that ever fumble and fight to find another subject if he mentioned his unlamented father. Were they afraid to have him get ideas from his father's aggressive ways? Or was it merely courtesy not to talk about the dead unkindly? They certainly had no bar about discussing the living in destructive terms.

Jaxom toyed with the idea of conquest. How would *he* set about reducing Nabol or—since Fort Hold was too big a bite—Tillek? Or Crom, perhaps, though he liked Lord Nessel's oldest son, Kern, far too much to do him out of what was rightfully his. Shells, he was a fine one to talk of conquest, when he couldn't even control the destiny of himself and his dragon!

Ruth, waddling with a full, bulging belly, belched happily as he made his way to his rider. He settled himself in the sun-warmed sweet grasses and began to lick his talons. He was always neat.

"Can you fly when you're stuffed?" Jaxom asked when Ruth had finished tidying up.

Ruth turned his head, his eyes whirling in reproach. *I can always fly.* The dragon exhaled, his breath rather meaty and sweet. *You are worried again.*

"I want us to be proper dragon and rider, and fight Thread, me on your back, you flaming."

Then we will do it, Ruth said with unshakable faith. *I am a dragon, you are my rider. Why does this become a problem?*

"Well, wherever we go the fire-lizards come."

You told the thick man with the blue—Ruth's identification of Brand—*they were not to follow. They did not come here.*

"Others did, and you know how fire-lizards chatter." Then Jaxom recalled Menolly's comments. "What are that lot thinking of now?"

Their full bellies. The wherries were juicy and tender. Very good eating. They do not remember better in many Turns.

"Would they go away if you told them to?"

Ruth snorted, his eyes whirling a bit, more with amusement than irritation. *They would wonder why and come to see. I will tell them if you want me to. Maybe they would stay away long enough.*

"Just like them: they've more curiosity than sense. Well, as Robinton is always saying, there's a way to solve every problem. We'll just have to find a way."

On their return to Ruatha Hold, Ruth's digestion was working noisily. He wanted nothing more than to curl up on a sun-warmed rock and sleep, and since the brown watchdragon was away from his usual post, Ruth settled there. Jaxom waited in the Great Courtyard until he saw Ruth safely ensconced, and then he sought Lytol.

If Brand had commented on Jaxom's request to Lytol, the Lord Warder gave no sign, greeting Jaxom with his usual reserve and enjoining him to eat quickly as they had rather a long ride to make. Tordril and one of the other older fosterlings living under Lytol's supervision would accompany them. Masterfarmer Andemon had sent a new seed he had developed for a high-yield, fast-growing wheat. Southern fields, grub-infested and planted with this wheat seed, had produced phenomenally healthy, blight-resistant crops, that were able to survive long dry spells. Andemon wondered how the wheat would fare in a rainier, Northern climate.

Many of the older small holders were stubborn about trying something new. "As hidebound as Oldtimers," Lytol would mutter, but somehow or other he managed to prevail. For instance, Fidello, who owned the hold they were seeding, was only two Turns in the holding, the previous man having died of a fall while tracking wild wherries.

So, after a quick meal, the travelers set off on some of the specially bred runners that could pace a long summer's day without tiring. Though Jaxom used to find it tedious to take hours to cross country he could fly *between* on Ruth in a few breaths, he did enjoy an occasional runner ride. Today, with spring in the air and secure in the knowledge that he was still in Lytol's good graces, he enjoyed the trip.

Fidello's holding was in northeast Ruatha, on a plateau with the snow-capped mountains of Crom in the background. When they reached the plateau, the blue fire-lizard that rode on Tordril's arm shrilled a greeting and took off to make an aerial circle of introduction to a brown that was probably looking to Fidello and set to watch for the visitors. Immediately the two fire-lizards winked *between*. Tordril and Jaxom exchanged glances, knowing that a welcoming cup of klah and sweetbreads would be waiting at the holding. Their ride had given them an appetite.

Fidello himself rode out to escort them on the last part of the road. He was mounted on a sturdy workbeast whose summer coat gleamed with health through the rough and patchy winter fur. His hold, to which he welcomed them in an earnest but restrained manner, was small and well kept. His dependents, including those of the last holder, had assembled to serve the visitors.

"He's got a good cook," Tordril said in an aside to Jaxom as the three younger men made conspicuous inroads on the food laid out on the long Hall table. "And a deuced pretty sister," he added as the girl approached them bearing a steaming pitcher of klah.

She was pretty, Jaxom agreed, looking at her closely for the first time. Trust Tordril to spot the prettiest girl. Brand would have to keep his eye on this one when he ventured out of the Hold to the workers' cots below the bridge. This pretty girl, however, had a timid smile for Jaxom, not Tordril, and even though the prospective Lord of Ista tried to enage her in conversation, she gave him short answers, keeping her smiles for Jaxom. She left his side only when her brother joined them to say that perhaps they'd better seed the fields or it would be a long, dark ride back to the Hold.

"I wonder would you have got her so quick if I'd been Lord of

Ruatha?" Tordril asked Jaxom as they checked their saddle girths before mounting.

"Got her?" Jaxom stared blankly at Tordril. "We only chatted."

"Well, you could have her next time you . . . ah, have a chance to chat. Or does Lytol mind a few halfbloods around? Father says it keeps the full ones on their toes! Ought to be easy for you with Lytol weyrbred, and not as stuffy about such things."

Lytol and Fidello joined them at that point but Tordril's envious comment set Jaxom's thoughts on a very fruitful tack. What was her name? Corana? Well, Corana could be very useful. There was only the one fire-lizard about the Plateau Hold—and, if Ruth could just dissuade that creature from following them . . .

When they returned to the Hold late that night, Jaxom quietly climbed to the fire-heights and took a good sackful of firestone from the brown's supply while the old watchdragon and his rider were having a brief evening flight to stretch wings.

The next morning he casually asked Lytol if he thought they had brought enough seed for Fidello. Theirs did seem to be a very large field. Lytol regarded his ward from under half-closed lids for a moment and then agreed that perhaps another half-sack might be to the wise. Tordril's expression mirrored surprise, envy and, Jaxom felt, some respect for plausibility. Lytol duly ordered a half-sack of Andemon's seed from Brand's locked stores, and Jaxom sauntered off with it to don his riding gear.

Ruth, full of himself after a good feed, wanted to know if there was a nice lake near the hold. Jaxom thought that the river was wide enough for a respectable dragon's bath, but they weren't going there for water sports. They managed to take off without anyone seeing the second sack slung on Ruth—or the fighting straps. Although the fire-lizards engaged in their usual dizzy pattern around them while Ruth was becoming airborne, none emerged with them at the Plateau Hold.

Fidello himself took receipt of the additional seed with such profuse thanks that Jaxom was a bit abashed at his duplicity.

"Didn't like to mention it in front of the Lord Warder, Lord Jaxom, but that's a fair big field I've ready for this seed and I'd want to see a good return to justify Lord Lytol's opinion of me. Would you care for refreshment? My wife . . ."

Only his wife? "It would be welcome. The morning's nippy." He patted Ruth affectionately and dismounted, following Fidello into the hold. He was pleased to notice that the main Hall was as tidy as it had been for their expected visit. Corana was not in evidence, but Fidello's very pregnant wife was in no way misled by his casual return.

"Everyone else has gone to the river, to the place where it forms an island, to gather withies, Lord Jaxom," she said, glancing at him coquettishly, as she served him hot *klah*. "Oh your beautiful dragon, that's no more than a moment's trip for you, my Lord."

"Now why would Lord Jaxom want to see withies gathered?" Fidello asked, but received no direct answer.

The social amenities discharged, Jaxom directed Ruth aloft, circled while waving down at Fidello, and then took them *between* to the mountain well beyond the keenest eye of any hold. The brown fire-lizard followed.

Shells! Ruth, tell him to get lost."

Immediately the brown winked out.

"Good, now I can teach you to chew firestone."

I know.

"You think you know. I've been around dragonriders long enough to know that doing so is not quite as simple as that."

Ruth gave a sort of sniff as Jaxom dug a lump of firestone the size of his own generous fist out of the sack.

"Now *think* of your other stomach!"

Ruth lidded his eyes completely as he accepted the firestone. The noise as he chewed the lump startled him. His eyes came wide open, making Jaxom exclaim: "Should you make that much noise?"

It is rock.

He threw one lid over his eyes as he suddenly swallowed. *I am thinking of my other stomach,* he told Jaxom before he could be reminded. Later Jaxom swore that he could all but hear the chewed fragments rolling down the dragon's gullet. The two sat and regarded each other, waiting for the next step.

"You're supposed to belch."

I know. I know how to belch. But I can't.

Jaxom politely offered him another largish piece of firestone. This time the chewing did not resound so noticeably. Ruth swallowed, then seemed to settle more on his haunches.

OH!

On the heels of the mental exclamation, a rumble started that made Ruth look quickly at his white belly. His mouth opened. With a startled shout, Jaxom launched himself to one side just as a tiny trickle of flame appeared at the white dragon's muzzle. Ruth jerked backward, only saved from falling over by the set of his tail.

I think I need more firestone to make a respectable flame.

Jaxom offered several smallish lumps. Ruth made quick work of the chewing. And quicker work of the eruption of gas.

That was much more the thing, Ruth said with satisfaction.

"Wouldn't do much against Thread."

Ruth just opened his mouth for more firestone. What Jaxom had brought was all too quickly consumed. But with it, Ruth managed to sear a fair swath among the rock weeds.

"I don't think we've got the hang of it."

We also haven't burned any Thread midair.

"We aren't exactly ready to do that yet. But we have proved that you *can* chew firestone."

I never doubted it.

"I never did either, Ruth, but," Jaxom sighed heavily, "we're going to need a lot of firestone at hand, until you learn the way of sustaining a continuous eruption."

Ruth looked so disconsolate that Jaxom hastily reassured him, stroking his eye ridges and caressing his headbone.

"We should have been allowed to train you properly with the other weyrlings. It's just not fair. I've always said so. You can't help your difficulties today. But, by the First Shell, we'll eventually succeed together."

Ruth allowed himself to be reassured, then brightened. *We will work harder, that's all. But it would be easier with more firestone. Brown Wilth never uses much anymore. He's really too old to chew at all.*

"That's why he's a watchdragon."

Jaxom emptied the sack of any firestone rubble, tied it up by the neck thong and looped it around his belt. He hadn't needed the rope for fighting straps, after all. He was about to tell Ruth to transfer directly to Ruatha when he remembered that he had better consolidate his alibi for future use. He had no trouble finding the withie gatherers by the river island, and Corana eagerly came to meet him. She was very pretty, he realized, with a delicate flush to her skin and round greenish eyes. Her dark hair had escaped the braids about her face and now clung to her cheeks in damp waves.

"Has there been Thread?" she asked, her green eyes becoming round with alarm.

"No. Why?"

"I can smell firestone."

"Oh, these riding clothes. I always use them during Fall. Smell must cling to them. I just didn't notice." That was one hazard he hadn't considered and he'd have to do something about it. "I flew up with more seed for your brother . . ."

She thanked him sweetly for taking so much trouble for such a small hold as theirs. Then she became shy. Jaxom rather liked drawing her out and sent her into another spin by insisting on helping with the withie gathering.

"This Lord Holder wants to know how to do everything he requires of his holders," he said, to silence her protests.

Actually, he enjoyed himself. When they had amassed a huge bundle, he offered to fly it home on Ruth if she'd ride with him. Corana was honestly frightened but he assured her they'd only fly straight since she wasn't dressed for cold *between*. Jaxom got in a couple of

542 • THE DRAGONRIDERS OF PERN

kisses before Ruth circled to land his passengers at the hold. He decided that one way or another, Corana would no longer be just an excuse.

When he had deposited her and the withies, he directed Ruth *between* to their mountain lake. Though he was in no mood for a cold bath, Jaxom knew they'd better scrub off the firestone stink before going back to Ruatha. It took time to sandscrub the smell from Ruth's fair hide. Then Jaxom had to dry his impregnated shirt and pants, spreading them in full sun on the bushes. By that time the sun was well past zenith and he had spent far more time than dallying with Corana would cover. So he took a risk and returned to Ruatha *between* time to when the sun was still on the morning side of the sky. But one detail he forgot to take into his calculations nearly gave away their endeavor.

He was at dinner when his dragon let out a call for him, an urgent call. "Ruth!" he explained as he sprang from his chair at the table and raced across the Hall to the corridor to his quarters.

My stomach burns, Ruth began telling him in great distress.

"Shells, it's the stones," Jaxom replied as he ran down the deserted hallway. "Go outside, to the fire-heights. Where Wilth leaves his."

Ruth wasn't sure he could fly in his condition.

"Nonsense. You can always fly." Ruth had to disgorge his second stomach outside the weyr. Lytol might just follow to see what ailed the beast for him to interrupt Jaxom at dinner.

I can't move. I'm weighed down in the middle.

"You're just going to regurgitate the firestone ash. Dragons don't keep that in their stomachs: they can't pass it. The stuff has got to come back up."

I feel as if it will.

"Not in the weyr, Ruth. Please!"

Scarcely a second later, Ruth eyed him apologetically. In the middle of the weyr floor, a small pile of what looked like brownish gray wet sand exuded steam.

I feel much better now, Ruth said in a very small voice.

"Can you hear Lytol coming?" Jaxom asked Ruth, because his heart was pounding so from running that that was all he could hear. He dashed out the metal doors and into the kitchen yard to fetch a bucket and shovel. "If I can just get this outside before it smells up the place . . ." He worked as fast as he could and fortunately the mess just filled the one bucket. It wasn't as if Ruth had chewed enough firestone for a full four-hour Threadfall.

Jaxom pushed the bucket out and sprinkled sweet sand on the spot.

"No Lytol?" he asked, somewhat surprised.

No.

Jaxom exhaled heavily with relief, patted Ruth reassuringly. He wouldn't forget to have Ruth regurgitate in a safe spot next time.

When he resumed his place at the table, Jaxom offered no explanation and none was asked—one more example of the new respect from his familiars.

The next night he and Ruth filched as much firestone as the dragon could carry from the most logical place—the firestone mines in Crom. Half a dozen fire-lizards appeared during their raid, and Ruth merely sent each one on its way as soon as it appeared.

"Don't let them follow us."

They were only being courteous. They like me.

"There's such a thing as being too popular."

Ruth sighed.

"Is this too much firestone?" Jaxom asked, not wanting to overburden the beast.

Of course not. I'm very strong.

Jaxom directed Ruth *between* to the Keroon desert destination. There was the sea to bathe in afterward and plenty of sweetsand to scrub off firestone stench, and sun hot enough to dry his clothing in next to no time.

·· C H A P T E R V ··

❧

Morning in Harpercraft Hall, Fort Hold, Afternoon in Benden Weyr, Late Afternoon in Harpercraft Hall, 15.5.26

Another Threadfall passed before Jaxom could get off to the Plateau hold again. He seemed to have more success with Corana than in getting Ruth to sustain flame properly. The white dragon's throat was nearly burned from keeping in belches when fire-lizards would suddenly appear at the most inopportune times. Jaxom was certain that every single one in Keroon Hold had had a look-in. Even Ruth's patience was tried and they had to time it by a six-hour span so that their absence from Ruatha would not be considered exceptional. Timing it tired him, Jaxom realized, as he fell into bed that night, exhausted and frustrated.

To make matters worse he would have to go to the Masterharperhall the next day with Finder because the Ruathan Harper was scheduled to learn how to use Wansor's star equations. Every Harper was expected to master that so at least one other person besides the Holder could make an accurate check on Threadfall.

The Masterharperhall was part of the sprawling complex of dwellings inside and outside the Fort Hold cliffs. When Jaxom and Finder, on Ruth, burst into the air above the Harpercrafthall, they met chaos. Fire-lizards were swooping and diving, screaming in an ecstasy of agitation. The watchdragon on Fort Hold's fire-heights was up on his hind legs, front ones pawing the air, wings fanning at the stretch, bellowing in fury.

Angry! They are angry! was Ruth's startled comment. *Ruth! I am Ruth! Ruth!* he called in his inimitable tenor bugle.

"What's happened?" Finder demanded in Jaxom's ear.

"Ruth says they're angry."

"Angry? I've never seen a dragon that angry before!"

Filled with apprehension, Jaxom directed Ruth to the courtyard of the Harpercrafthall. So many people were dashing around, with fire-lizards zipping wildly about, that he had trouble finding a clear spot. No sooner had he landed than a wing of fire-lizards danced about him, projecting anxious, agitated thoughts that Ruth told Jaxom made no sense to him—and even less to Jaxom when he received them secondhand. He did perceive that these were Menolly's beasts, sent to find out where he was.

"There you are! You got my message?" Menolly came racing out of the Hall up to them, dragging on her flying gear as she ran. "We've got to go to Benden Weyr. They've stolen the queen egg."

She was scrambling up behind Finder on Ruth's back, apologizing for crowding him and urging Jaxom to get a move on. "Are three too many for Ruth?" Menolly asked with belated concern as the white dragon seemed to hesitate before launching himself.

Never.

"Who stole Ramoth's egg? How? When?" Finder asked.

"This half-hour past. They're calling in all the bronzes and the other queens. They're going to Southern in force and make them give the egg back."

"How do they know it was Southern?" asked Jaxom.

"Who else would need to steal a queen egg?"

Then all conversation was suspended as Ruth took them smartly *between*. They erupted into the air over Benden, and suddenly three bronzes were arrowing out of the sun right at them, flaming. Ruth let out a squeal and went *between*, emerging over the lake and chattering at his would-be attackers at the top of his voice.

I'm Ruth. I'm Ruth. I'm Ruth!

"That was close!" Finder said, gulping. His hands were pinching Jaxom's arms nerveless.

You just missed my wing tip. I'm Ruth! They apologized, the white dragon added in a calmer tone to his rider. But he turned his wing tip for a close look.

Menolly groaned. "I forgot to tell you we were to come in yelling who we were. You'd think Ruth at least would be passed without challenge."

As she spoke, more dragons appeared, trumpeting to the three bronzes guarding from the heights. The new arrivals circled tightly to land their riders by a crowd gathered around the entrance to the Hatching Ground. Jaxom, Finder and Menolly started across the Bowl to join them.

"Jaxom, have you ever seen so many dragons?" Menolly looked around at the crowded Weyr rim, at the dragons on weyr ledges, all with wings spread, ready for instant flight. "Oh, Jaxom, what if it comes to dragon fighting dragon?"

The terror in her voice echoed his own feelings perfectly.

"Those fool Oldtimers must be desperate," Finder said grimly.

"How could they get away with such bare-faced thievery?" Jaxom wanted to know. "Ramoth never leaves a clutch." Not since the time F'lessan and I disturbed her eggs, he added guiltily to himself.

"F'nor brought us the news," Menolly said. "He said she'd gone to feed. Half the Benden fire-lizards were in the Ground. They always are—"

"With an odd one or two visiting from the Southern Weyr, no doubt," Finder added.

Menolly nodded. "That's what F'nor said. So the Oldtimers would have known when she wasn't there. F'nor said she'd just killed when three bronzes appeared, passed the watchdragon. . . . I mean, why would the watchdragon question bronze dragons? They ducked in the upper tunnel to the Hatching Ground, Ramoth gave an almighty shriek and went *between*. The next thing three bronzes came flying out of the upper entrance, they had heard Ramoth scream. She came charging out of the Hatching Ground but they had gone *between* before she'd got a winglength off the ground."

"Didn't they send dragons after them?"

"Ramoth went after! With Mnementh but a breath behind her. Not that it did any good."

"Why not?"

"The bronzes went *between* time."

"And not even Ramoth would know *when*."

"Exactly. Mnementh checked the Southern Weyr and Hold and half the hot beaches."

"Not even the Oldtimers could be stupid enough to take a queen egg straight back to Southern."

"But surely the Oldtimers would not know," Finder added wearily, "that we know they took the egg."

By that time they had reached the outskirts of the crowd, where dragonriders from other Weyrs as well as Lords Holder and Craftmasters had gathered. Lessa stood on the ledge of her weyr, F'lar beside her along with Fandarel and Robinton, who both looked extremely grim and anxious. N'ton stopped halfway down the steps, talking earnestly and with angry gestures to two other bronze riders. Slightly to one side were the three other Benden weyrwomen, and several other women who must be queenriders from the other Weyrs. The atmosphere of outrage and frustration was oppressive. Dominating the entire scene was Ramoth, who paced up and down in front of the Hatching Ground, pausing now and again to peer in at the eggs remaining on the hot sands. Her tail started lashing and she let out angry buglings that obscured the discussions going on above her on the ledge.

"It's dangerous to take an egg *between*," someone in front of Jaxom and Menolly said.

"I suppose it could go a ways, so long as the egg was good and warm to start and took no hurt."

"We ought to just mount up and go down and sear those Old-timers out of the Weyr."

"And have dragon fight dragon? You're as bad as the Oldtimers."

"But we can't have dragons stealing our queen eggs! This is the worst insult Benden's ever taken from the Oldtimers. And I say, make them pay for it."

"The Southern Weyr is desperate," Menolly said in an undertone to Jaxom. "None of their queens has risen to mate. The bronzes are dying, and they don't even have any young greens."

Just then Ramoth gave a piteous cry, throwing her head up toward Lessa. Every dragon in the Weyr answered her call, deafening the humans. Jaxom could see Lessa leaning over the ledge, one hand outstretched toward the despairing queen. Then, because he was a good head above most of the crowd and looking that way, Jaxom saw something dark fluttering in the Hatching Ground. He heard a muffled cry of pain.

"Look! What's that? In the Hatching Ground!"

Only those around him heard his exclamation or noticed him pointing. All Jaxom could think of was that if the Southern bronzes were indeed dying, the Oldtimers might use this confusion to try and steal a bronze egg as well.

He took to his heels, followed by Menolly and Finder, but he was overcome by such a wave of weakness that he was forced to stop. Something seemed to be sapping his strength, but Jaxom had no idea what it could be.

"What's the matter, Jaxom?"

"Nothing." Jaxom pulled Menolly's hands from his arm and all but pushed her toward the Ground. "The eggs. The eggs!"

His injunction was drowned in Ramoth's bellow of surprise and exultation.

"The egg. The queen egg!"

By the time Jaxom had recovered from his inexplicable vertigo and reached the Hatching Ground, everyone was staring with relief at the sight of the queen egg, now safely positioned once again between Ramoth's forelegs.

A fire-lizard, reckless with curiosity, got a scant winglength into the Ground before Ramoth's bellow of fury sent it streaking away.

In relief, people began to chatter, as they moved back out of the Hatching Ground to where the sand was not so uncomfortable underfoot. Someone suggested that perhaps the egg had merely rolled away and Ramoth only thought it had been taken. But too many had seen the empty place, where the queen egg had too obviously been missing. And what about the three strange bronzes streaking out of the high entrance to the Ground. More acceptable was the notion that the Oldtimers had had second thoughts about the theft, that they, too, were reluctant to pit dragon against dragon.

Lessa had remained in the Ground, trying to persuade Ramoth to let her see if the egg had come to any harm. Soon she came hurrying out of the Ground to F'lar and Robinton.

"That's the same egg but it's older and harder, ready to Hatch anytime now. The girls must be brought."

For the third time that morning, Benden Weyr was in a state of high excitement—happier fortunately, but still generating as much chaos. Jaxom and Menolly managed to keep out of the way but remained close enough to hear what was going on.

"Whoever took that egg kept it at least ten days or more," they heard Lessa saying angrily. "That demands action."

"The egg is back safely," Robinton said, trying to calm her.

"Are we cowards to ignore such an insult?" she asked the other dragonmen, turning away from Robinton's calmer words.

"If to be brave," Robinton's voice laid scorn on the quality, "means to pit dragon against dragon, I'd rather be a coward."

Lessa's white-hot outrage noticeably cooled.

Dragon against dragon. The words echoed through the crowd. The thought turned sickeningly in Jaxom's mind and he could feel Menolly beside him shutting off the implications of such a contest.

"The egg was somewhen for long enough to be brought close to hatching hardness," Lessa went on, her face set with her anger. "It's probably been handled by their candidate. It could have been influenced enough so that the fledgling won't Impress here."

"No one has ever proved how much an egg is influenced by pre-Hatching contact," Robinton was saying in his most persuasive voice. "Or so you've had me understand any number of times. Short of dumping their candidate on top of the egg when it hatches, I can't think their conniving can do them any good or the egg any more harm."

The assembled dragonfolk were still very tense but the initial impetus to rise in wings and destroy the Southern Weyr had cooled considerably with the return of the egg, however mysterious that return was.

"Obviously, we can no longer be complacent," said F'lar, glancing up at the watchdragons, "or secure in the delusion of the inviolability of the Hatching Ground. Any Hatching Ground." Nervously he pushed the hair back from his forehead. "By the First Shell, they've a lot of gall, trying to steal one of Ramoth's eggs."

"The first way to secure this Weyr is to ban those dratted fire-lizards," Lessa said heatedly. "They're little tattlers, worse than useless . . ."

"Not all of them, Lessa," Brekke said, stepping up beside the Weyrwoman. "Some of them come on legitimate errands and give *us* a lot of assistance."

"Two were playing that game," Robinton said without humor.

Menolly dug Jaxom in the ribs, reminding him that the Harperhall's fire-lizards, hers included, did a lot of assisting.

"I don't care," Lessa told Brekke and glared around at the assembled, looking for fire-lizards. "I don't want to see them about here. Ramoth's not to be pestered by those plaguey things. Something's to be done to keep them where they belong."

"Mark 'em with their colors!" was Brekke's quick reply. "Mark 'em and teach them to speak their name and origin the way dragons do. They're quite capable of learning courtesy. At least the ones who come to Benden by order."

"Have them report to you, Brekke, or Mirrim," Robinton suggested.

"Just keep them away from Ramoth and me!" Lessa peered in at Ramoth and then whipped around. "And someone bring up that wherry that Ramoth didn't eat. She'll be the better for something in her belly right now. We'll discuss this violation of our Weyr later. In detail."

F'lar ordered several dragonmen to get the wherry and then courteously thanked the rest of the assembled for their prompt reply to his summons. He gestured to several of the Weyrleaders and Robinton to join him in the weyr above.

"There's not a fire-lizard in sight," Menolly said to Jaxom. "I told Beauty to stay away. She's answered me scared to her bones."

"So's Ruth," Jaxom said as they crossed the Bowl to him. "He's turned almost gray."

Ruth was more than scared, he was trembling with anxiety.

Something is wrong. Something is not right, he told his rider, his eyes whirling erratically with gray tones.

"Your wing was injured?"

No. Not my wing. Something is wrong in my head. I don't feel right. Ruth shifted from all four legs to his hindquarters, and then back again to all four, rustling his wings.

"Is it because all the fire-lizards have gone? Or the excitement about Ramoth's egg?"

Ruth said it was both and neither. The fire-lizards were all frightened; they remembered something which frightened them.

"Remembered? Huh!" Jaxom felt exasperated with fire-lizards

and their associative memories, and their ridiculous images which were making his sensible Ruth miserable.

"Jaxom?" Menolly had detoured to the Lower Caverns and shared with him the handful of meatrolls she'd cadged from the cooks. "Finder says Robinton wants me to go back to the Harpercrafthall and let them and Fort Hold know what's been happening. I'm also to start marking my fire-lizards. Look!" She pointed to the Weyr rim and the Star Stones. "The watch dragon is chewing firestone. Oh, Jaxom!"

"Dragon against dragon." He shuddered violently.

"Jaxom, it can't come to that," she said in a choked voice.

Neither of them could finish their meatrolls. Silently they mounted Ruth, who took them aloft.

As Robinton climbed the steps to the queen's weyr, he was thinking faster than he had ever done. Too much was going to depend on what happened now—the whole future course of the planet, if he read reactions correctly. He knew more than he ought about conditions in the Southern Weyr but his knowledge had done him no service today. He berated himself for being so naive, as unseeingly obtuse as any dragonrider for assuming that the Weyrs were inviolable and a Hatching Ground untouchable. He had had warnings from Piemur; but he simply hadn't correlated the information properly. Yet, in light of today's occurrence, he ought to have arrived at the logical conclusion that the desperate Southerners would make this prodigious attempt to revive their failing Weyr with the blood of a new and viable queen. Even if he had reached the proper conclusion, Robinton thought ruefully, how ever would he have been able to persuade Lessa and F'lar that that was what the Southerners planned today. The Weyrleaders would have been properly scornful of such a ridiculous notion.

No one was laughing today. No one at all.

Strange that so many people had assumed that the Oldtimers would meekly accept their exile and remain docilely on their continent. They had not been cramped in their accommodation, merely in their hope of a future. T'kul must have been the motivating force—T'ron had lost all his vigor and initiative after that duel with F'lar. Robinton was reasonably certain that the two Weyrwomen, Merika and Mardra, had had no part in the plan; they wouldn't wish to be deposed by a young queen and her rider. Had one of them returned the egg?

No, thought Robinton, it had to be someone with an intimate knowledge of the Benden Weyr Hatching Ground . . . or someone possessed of the blindest good luck and skill to go *between* into and out of the cavern.

Robinton relived briefly the compound terror he had experienced during the egg's absence. He winced thinking of Lessa's fury. She was still likely to arouse the Northern dragonriders. She was quite capable of sustaining the unthinking frenzy that had all but dominated the events of the morning. If she continued in her demand for vengeance against the guilty Southerners, it could be as much a disaster for Pern as the first Threadfall had been.

The egg had been returned. Robinton clung to the comforting fact that it was apparently unharmed despite its ageing in that elapsed subjective time. Lessa could choose to make its condition an issue. And, if the egg did not hatch an unimpaired queen, there was no doubt in Robinton's mind that Lessa would insist on retribution.

But the egg had been returned! He must drum in that fact, must emphasize that obviously not all Southerners had been party to this heinous action. Some Oldtimers still honored the old codes of conduct. No doubt one of them had been perceptive enough to guess what punitive action would be launched against the criminals and wished, as fervently as Robinton, to avoid such a confrontation.

"This is indeed a black moment," someone with a deep sad voice said. The Harper turned, grateful for the sane support of the Mastersmith. Fandarel's heavy features were etched with worry and, for the first time, Robinton noticed the puffiness of age blurring the man's features, yellowing his eyes. "Such perfidy must be punished—and yet it cannot be!"

The thought of dragon fighting dragon again seared Robinton's mind with terror. "Too much would be lost!" he said to Fandarel.

"*They* have already lost all they had, being sent into exile. I often wondered why they didn't rebel before."

"They have now. With a vengeance."

"To be met with more vengeance. My friend, we must keep our wits today as never before. I fear Lessa may be unreasonable and unthinking. Already she has let emotion dominate common sense." The Smith indicated the leather patch on Robinton's shoulder where his fire-lizard, Zair, customarily perched. "Where is your little friend now?"

"Brekke's weyr with Grall and Berd. I wanted him to return to the Harpercrafthall with Menolly, but he refused."

The Smith shook his great head again in sad slow sweeps as the two men entered the Council Chamber.

"I do not have a fire-lizard myself but I know only good of the little creatures. It never occurred to me that they constituted any threat for anyone."

"You will support me in this then, Fandarel?" asked Brekke, who had entered behind them with F'nor. "Lessa is not herself. I do really understand her anxiety but she cannot be allowed to damn all fire-lizards for the mischief of a few."

"Mischief?" F'nor was perturbed. "Don't let Lessa hear you call what happened mischief. Mischief? Stealing a queen egg?"

"The fire-lizard's part was only mischief . . . popping in to Ramoth's cave like how many others have been doing since the eggs were laid." Brekke spoke more sharply than she usually did, and the tightness about F'nor's eyes and mouth indicated to Robinton that this couple were not in accord. "Fire-lizards have no sense of wrong or right."

"They'll have to learn . . ." F'nor began with more heat than discretion.

"I fear that we, who have no dragons," said Robinton, quickly intervening—lest today's event fracture the bond between the two lovers—"have been making too much of our little friends, carting them about with us wherever we go, doting as parents of a late child, permitting too many liberties of conduct. *But* a more restrained attitude toward fire-lizards in our midst is a very minor consideration in today's affair."

F'nor had dampened his aggravation. He nodded now at the Harper. "Suppose that egg hadn't been returned, Robinton . . ." His shoulders jerked in a convulsive shake and he pushed at his forehead as if trying to eliminate all memory of that scene.

"If the egg hadn't been returned," Robinton said implacably, "dragon would have fought dragon!" He spaced out his words, putting as much force and distaste as he could in his tone.

F'nor quickly shook his head, denying that outcome. "No, it would not have come to that, Robinton. You were wise . . ."

"Wise?" Spat out by the infuriated Weyrwoman, the word cut like a knife. Lessa stood at the entrance to the Council Room, her slender frame taut with the emotions of the morning, her face livid with her anger. "Wise? To let them get away with such a crime? To let them plot even more base treacheries? Why did I ever think it necessary to bring them forward? When I remember that I pleaded with that excrescence T'ron to come and help us. Help us? He helps himself! To my queen's egg. If I could only undo my stupidity . . ."

"Your stupidity is in carrying on in this fashion," the Harper said coldly, knowing that what he had to say before the Weyrleaders and Craftmasters assembled in the Council Room might well alienate them all. "The egg has been returned—"

"Yes, and when I—"

"That was what you wanted half an hour, an hour ago, was it not?" Robinton demanded, raising his voice commandingly. "You wanted the egg returned. To achieve that end you were within your rights to send dragon against dragon, and no one to fault you. But the egg has been returned. To set dragon against dragon for revenge? Oh, no, Lessa. That you have no right to do. Not in revenge.

"And if you must have revenge to satisfy your queen and your angry self, just think: *They* failed! They don't have that egg. Their actions have put all the Weyrs on guard so they could never succeed a second time. They have lost their one chance, Lessa. Their one hope of reviving their dying bronzes has failed. They have been thwarted. And they face . . . nothing. No future, no hope.

"You can do nothing worse to them, Lessa. So with the return of that egg, you have no right in the eyes of the rest of Pern to do anything more."

"I have the right to revenge that insult to me, to my queen, and to my Weyr!"

"Insult?" Robinton gave a short bark of laughter. "My dear Lessa, that was no insult. That was a compliment of the highest order!"

His unexpected laughter as well as his startling interpretation stunned Lessa into silence.

"How many queen eggs have been laid this past Turn?" Robinton demanded of the other Weyrleaders. "And in Weyrs the Oldtimers would know more intimately than Benden. No, they wanted a queen of Ramoth's clutch! Nothing but the best that Pern could produce for the Oldtimers!" Adroitly Robinton left that argument. "Come, Lessa," he said with great sympathy and compassion, "we're all overwrought by this terrible event. None of us is thinking clearly . . ." He passed his hand across his face, no sham gesture for he was perspiring with effort to redirect the mood of so many. "Emotions are running far too high. And you've borne the brunt of it, Lessa." He took her by the arm and led the shocked but unresisting Weyrwoman to her chair, seating her with great concern and deference. "You must have been halfcrazed by Ramoth's distress. She is calmer now, isn't she?"

Lessa's jaw dropped in amazement and she continued to stare at Robinton with wide-open eyes. Then she nodded, closing her mouth and moistening her lips.

"So you'll be more yourself then, too." Robinton poured a cup of wine and passed it to her. Still bemused by his startling attitude, she even sipped it. "And able to realize that the worst catastrophe that could happen to this world would be for dragon to fight dragon."

Lessa set the cup down then, spilling wine on the stone table. "You . . . with your clever words . . ." and she pointed at Robinton, rising from the chair like an uncoiling spring. "You . . ."

"He was right, Lessa," F'lar said from the entrance where he'd been watching the scene. He walked into the room, toward the table where Lessa sat. "We only had cause to invade Southern to search for our egg. Once it was returned, we would be damned by all Pern to pursue vengeance." He spoke to her but his eyes had gone to each Weyrleader and Craftmaster to judge their reactions. "Once dragon fights dragon, for whatever reason," his gesture wiped away any possible consideration, "we, the dragonriders of Pern, lose the rest of Pern!"

He gave Lessa a long hard look which she returned with frozen implacability. Squarely he faced the room. "I wish with all my heart that there'd been some other solution that day at Telgar for T'ron and T'kul. Sending them to the Southern Continent seemed to be the answer. There they could do the rest of Pern scant harm . . ."

"No, just us—just Benden!" Lessa spoke with palpable bitterness. "It's T'ron and Mardra, trying to get back at you and me!"

"Mardra would not favor a queen to depose her," said Brekke, who did not turn aside when Lessa whirled on her.

"Brekke's right, Lessa," F'lar said, putting his hand on Lessa's shoulder with apparent casualness. "Mardra wouldn't like competition."

Robinton could see the pressure of the Weyrleader's fingers whitening his knuckles, although Lessa gave no sign.

"Neither would Merika, T'kul's Weyrwoman," said D'ram, the Istan Weyrleader, "and I knew her well enough to speak with surety now."

More than any of the others in this room, Robinton thought that the Oldtimer felt this turn of events most keenly. D'ram was an honest, loyal, fair-minded man. He had felt compelled to support F'lar against those of his own Time. By such backing, he had influenced R'mart and G'narish, the other Oldtime Weyrleaders, to side with the Benden Weyr at Telgar Hold. So many undercurrents and subtle pressures abounded in this chamber. Robinton thought. Whoever had conceived of kidnapping the queen egg might not have succeeded in that stratagem, but they had effectively shattered the solidarity of the dragonriders.

"I can't tell you how badly I feel about this, Lessa," D'ram continued, shaking his head. "When I heard, I couldn't believe. I just don't understand what good such an action would do them. T'kul's older than I. His Salth couldn't hope to fly a Benden queen. For that matter, none of the dragons in the South could fly a Benden queen!"

D'ram's puzzled comment did as much as Robinton's pointed remarks to ease the multiple strains in the Council Room. Unconsciously D'ram had supported Robinton's contention that an oblique compliment had been paid Benden Weyr.

"Why, for that matter, by the time the new queen was old enough to fly to mate," D'ram added as if he'd just realized it, "their bronzes would likely be dead. Eight Southern dragons have died this past Turn. We all know that. So they tried to steal an egg for nothing . . . for nothing." His face was lined with tragic regret.

"Not for nothing," Fandarel said, his voice heavy with sadness. "For just look at what has happened to us who have been friends and allies for how many Turns? You dragonriders," his great forefinger stabbed at them, "were a fingernail away from setting your beasts against the old ones at Southern." Fandarel shook his head slowly from side to side. "This has been a terrible, terrible day! I am sorry for all of you." His gaze rested longest on Lessa. "But I think I am sorrier for myself and Pern if your anger doesn't cool and your good sense return. I will leave you now."

With great dignity he bowed to each of the Weyrleaders and their women, to Brekke and last to Lessa, trying to catch her eyes. Failing, he gave a little sigh and left the room.

Fandarel had clearly stated what Robinton wanted to be sure Lessa heard and understood—that the dragonriders stood in grave peril of losing control over Hold and Craft if they permitted their outrage and indignation to control them. Enough had been said, in the heat of the moment, in front of those Holders summoned to the Weyr during the crisis. If no further action was to be taken now that the egg had been returned, no Holder or Craftmaster could fault Benden.

But how was anyone to get through to that stubborn Lessa, sitting there wallowing in fury and determined on a disastrous course of revenge? For the first time in his long Turn as Masterharper of Pern, Robinton was at a loss for words. Enough that he had lost Lessa's goodwill already! How could he make her see reason?

"Fandarel has reminded me that dragonriders can have no private quarrels without far-reaching effect," F'lar said. "I permitted insult to overcome sanity once. Today is the result."

D'ram's bowed head came up and he stared fiercely at F'lar, then shook his head vigorously. There were murmured disclaimers from other dragonriders, that F'lar had acted in all honor at Telgar.

"Nonsense, F'lar," Lessa said, roused from her immobility. "That wasn't a *personal* fight. You had to fight T'ron that day to keep Pern together."

"And today I cannot fight T'ron, or the other Southerners, or I won't keep Pern together!"

Lessa stared back at F'lar for another long moment and then her shoulders sagged as she reluctantly accepted that distinction.

"But . . . if that egg does not hatch, or if the little queen is in any way damaged . . ."

"If that should happen, we will certainly review the situation," F'lar promised her, raising his right hand to honor the condition.

Fervently Robinton hoped that the little hatchling would prove healthy and vigorous, not a whit the worse for its adventuring. By the Hatching, he ought to have some information that might appease Lessa and save F'lar's now pledged honor.

"I must return to Ramoth," Lessa announced. "*She* needs me." She strode from the room, past dragonriders who deferentially moved aside.

Robinton looked at the cup of wine he had poured for her and, taking it up, downed the contents in one gulp. His hand was trembling as he lowered the cup and met F'lar's gaze.

"We could all use a cup," F'lar said, gesturing the others to gather about while Brekke, rising quickly to her feet, began to serve them.

"We will wait until the Hatching," the Benden Weyrleader went on. "I don't think I have to suggest that you all take precautions against a similar occurrence."

"None of us have any clutches hardening right now, F'lar," said R'mart of Telgar Weyr. "And none of us have Benden queens!" He had a sly twinkle in his eye as he glanced toward the Harper. "So, if eight of their beasts died this past Turn, I make it that there are now two hundred and forty-eight dragonriders left, and only five bronzes. Who brought the egg back?"

"The egg is back: that's all that matters," F'lar said then half-emptied his cup at the first swallow. "Though I am deeply grateful to that rider."

"We could find out," N'ton said quietly.

F'lar shook his head. 'I'm not sure I want to know. I'm not sure we need to know—just as long as that egg hatches a live and kicking queen."

"Fandarel has his finger in the sore," Brekke said, moving gracefully to refill cups. "Just look what has happened to those of us who have been friends and allies for many Turns. I resent that more than anything else. And," she looked at everyone in turn, "I also resent the antagonism for all fire-lizards because some few, who were only being loyal to their friends, had a part in this hideous affair. I know I'm prejudiced," she smiled sadly, "but I have so much reason to be grateful to our little friends. I would like to see sense prevail as regards them, too."

"We'll have to go softly on that score, Brekke," F'lar said, "but I have taken your point. Much was said this morning in the heat and confusion that was not meant to stand!"

"I hope so. I sincerely hope so," said Brekke. "Berd keeps telling me that dragons have flamed fire-lizards!"

Robinton let out a startled exclamation. "I got that wild notion from Zair, too, before I sent him to stay in your weyr, Brekke. But no dragon flamed here . . ." He looked about at the other Weyrleaders, some of whom were agreeing with Brekke's remark, others expressing concern over such an unlikely occurrence.

"Not yet . . ." Brekke said, nodding significantly toward Ramoth's weyr.

"Then we must make sure that the queen is not further upset by any sight of fire-lizards," F'lar said, his glance sweeping around the room for agreement. "For the time being," he added, raising his hand to stop the half-formed protests. "It *is* the better part of wisdom

for them not to be seen or heard right now. I know they've been useful,
and some are proving to be very reliable messengers. I know many of
you have them. But direct them to Brekke if it is absolutely necessary
to send them here." He looked directly at Robinton.

"Fire-lizards do not go where they are not welcome," Brekke said.
Then she added with a wry smile to take the sting out of her comment:
"They're scared out of their hides right now anyway."

"So we do nothing until the egg has Hatched?" N'ton asked.

"Except to assemble the girls found on Search. Lessa will want
them here as soon as possible, to accustom Ramoth to their presence.
We'll all assemble again for the Hatching, Weyrleaders."

"A good Hatching," D'ram said with a fervor that was sincerely
seconded by everyone.

Robinton half-hoped that F'lar might hold him back as the others
dispersed. But F'lar was in conversation with D'ram, and Robinton
sadly decided that his absence would be appreciated. It grieved Robinton to be at odds with the Benden Weyrleaders and he felt weary
as he made his way back to the weyr entrance. Still, F'lar had supported
Robinton's plea for deliberation. As he reached the last turning of the
corridor, he saw Mnementh's bronze bulk on the ledge, and he hesitated, suddenly reluctant to approach Ramoth's mate.

"Don't fret so, Robinton," N'ton said, stepping to his side and
touching his arm. "You were so right and wise to speak out as you
did, and probably the only one who could stop Lessa's madness. F'lar
knows it." N'ton grinned. "But he does still have to contend with
Lessa."

"Master Robinton," F'nor's voice was low as if he didn't wish to
be overheard, "please join Brekke and me in my weyr. N'ton, too, if
you're not pressed to return to Fort Weyr."

"I can certainly spare any time you need today," the younger
bronze rider replied with cheerful compliance.

"Brekke will be right along." Then the Wingsecond led the way
across the Bowl, unnaturally silent except for the moans and mutters
that issued in muffled echoes from Ramoth in the Hatching Ground.
On his ledge, Mnementh swung his great head constantly so that every
portion of the rim was scrutinized.

No sooner had the men entered the weyr than they were assaulted by four hysterical fire-lizards that had to be petted and reassured that no dragon would flame them—a fear which seemed to be
common and persistent.

"What is this large darkness that I get from Zair's images?" Robinton asked when he had caressed his little bronze into a semblance
of order. Zair shivered frequently and, whenever the Harper's gentle
strokes lapsed, the bronze pushed imperiously at the negligent hand.

Meanwhile Berd and Grall were perched on F'nor's shoulders,

stroking his cheeks, their eyes bright yellow with anxiety and still whirling at a frantic rate. "When they're calmer, Brekke and I will try to sort the whole thing out. I get the impression that they are remembering something."

"Not something like the Red Star?" N'ton asked. At his unfortunate reference, Tris, who had been lying quietly on his forearm, began to bat his wings and the others squealed in fright. "I'm sorry. Calm down, Tris."

"No, not something like that," F'nor said. "Just something . . . something they remembered."

"We do know that they communicate instantly with one another and apparently broadcast anything seen that is strongly felt or experienced," Robinton said, picking his words as he vocalized his thoughts. "So this could be evidence of a mass reaction. But picked up from which fire-lizard or fire-lizards? However, Grall and Berd, and certainly that little creature of Meron's, could not have known through one of their own kind that the . . . you know what . . . was dangerous to them. So how did they know to the point of hysterics? How could it be something they remembered?"

"Runner beasts seem to know when to avoid treacherous ground . . ." N'ton offered.

"Instinct." Robinton pondered. "Could be instinct." Then he shook his head. "No, avoiding treacherous ground is not the same use of an instinctive fear: that's a generality. The . . . R-E-D-S-T-A-R," he spelled letter by letter, "is a specific. Ah, well!"

"Fire-lizards are basically gifted with the same skills as dragons. Dragons, however, have no memories to speak of."

"Which, let us fervently hope." F'nor said, raising his eyes toward the ceiling, "wipes out what happened today in record time."

"Lessa does not suffer that gift," Robinton said with a heavy sigh.

"She's not stupid either, Masterharper," N'ton said, adroitly reaffirming his respect for the man by the use of his title. "Nor is F'lar. Just worried. They'll both come round and appreciate your intervention today." Then N'ton cleared his throat and looked the Masterharper squarely in the eyes. "Do you know who took the egg?"

"I had *heard* that something was being planned. I knew, which would have been obvious to anyone counting Turns, that the Southern men and dragons are slowing with age, and desperate. I've had only the experience of Zair wanting to mate . . ." Robinton paused, remembering that astounding revival of desires he had thought himself well past, shrugged and met the understanding twinkle in N'ton's eyes. "So I can appreciate the pressures that randy brown and bronze dragons can exert on their riders. Even a willing green, young enough to be flown, would help . . ." He looked questioningly at the two dragonriders.

"Not after today," F'nor said emphatically. "If they'd approached one of the Weyrs . . . D'ram for instance," he glanced at N'ton for corroboration, "perhaps a green would have gone, if only to prevent something disastrous. But to attempt to solve their problems by kidnapping a queen egg?" F'nor frowned. "How much do you know, Robinton, about what goes on down in the Southern Weyr? I know I gave you all the maps I'd made when I was timing it in the South.

"Frankly, I know more about happenings in the Hold. I did get a message from Piemur recently that the dragonriders had been more private than is their custom. They don't mix much with holders, following the pattern of their own Time, but a certain amount of coming and going into the Weyr was permitted. That ceased abruptly and then no holders were allowed near the Weyr. Not for any reason. Nor was there much flying done. Piemur says the dragons would be seen midair and then they'd pop *between*. No circling, no cruising. Just going *between*."

"Timing it," F'nor said thoughtfully.

Zair squeaked piteously and Robinton soothed him. Again the fire-lizard inserted in his mind the image of dragons flaming fire-lizards: the black nothingness, and a glimpse of an egg.

"Did you both get that picture, too, from your friends?" he asked though their startled expression made the question unnecessary.

Robinton pressed Zair for a clearer image, a view of where the egg was, and received nothing but the impression of flame and fear.

"I wish they'd a bit more sense," Robinton said, forcing down his irritation. Tantalizing to be so close, thwarted by the limited scope of fire-lizard vision.

"They're still upset," F'nor said. "I'll try with Grall and Berd later on. I wonder if Menolly's getting the same reaction from hers. You might ask her when you've got back to the Harpercrafthall, Master Robinton. With ten, she might get that much more clarity."

Robinton agreed as he rose, but thought of one last thing. "N'ton, weren't you among the bronzes who went to Southern Weyr, to see if the egg had been taken there?"

"I was. The Weyr was deserted. Not even an old dragon left behind. Completely deserted."

"Yes, that would follow, wouldn't it?"

When Jaxom and Menolly, on Ruth, entered the air above Fort Hold, Ruth called his name to the watch dragon and was almost smothered by fire-lizards. They so impeded his progress that he dropped a few lengths before he could get them to give him wing room. The moment he landed, the fire-lizards swarmed over him and his riders, keening with anxiety.

Menolly called out reassurances as fire-lizards clung to her clothing, got tangled in her hair. Jaxom found two trying to sit on his head, several had tails wrapped around his neck and three were beating their wings frantically to remain at eye level with him.

"What's got into them?"

"They're terrified! Dragons breathing fire at them," Menolly cried. "But no one's doing that to you, you silly clunches. You only have to stay away from the Weyrs for a bit."

Other harpers, attracted by the commotion, came to their rescue, either taking the fire-lizards bodily from Jaxom and Menolly, or sternly recalling the ones that looked to them personally. When Jaxom started to shoo them away from Ruth, the dragon told him not to bother— he, Ruth, would calm them down himself shortly. They were frightened because they remembered being chased by dragon fire. Since the harpers were all now clamoring for news from Benden, Jaxom decided to let Ruth handle the fire-lizards.

The Harpers had received some pretty distorted images from the fire-lizards returning, terrified, to the Harpercrafthall: Benden full of immense bronze dragons, breathing fire, ready to fight; Ramoth acting like a blood-maddened watchwher, and curious images of the queen egg solitary in the sand. But what made the Harpers extremely apprehensive was the vision of dragons flaming at fire-lizards.

"Benden dragons did not flame any fire-lizards," Jaxom and Menolly both said.

"But all the fire-lizards must stay away from Benden unless they're sent to either Brekke or Mirrim," Menolly added firmly. "And we're to mark all those that look to harpers with harper colors."

Jaxom and Menolly were ushered into the Harperhall and given wine and hot soup. Neither of them got to eat it hot because no sooner were they served than some of the Hold people arrived, soliciting the news. Menolly recounted the major portion of the happening, being the trained Harper. Jaxom's respect for the girl increased greatly as he listened to her flowing voice evoke the emotions appropriate to each part of her narrative, without distorting what he knew to have happened. One of the senior Harpers, soothing the blue fire-lizard in the crook of his arm, kept nodding his head as if approving her use of Harper tricks.

When Menolly stopped speaking, a respectful murmur of thanks was heard throughout the room. Then the listeners became the speakers, dissecting the news, wondering who had returned the egg and how—and why, which was still the biggest question. How were the Weyrs going to protect themselves? Were the main Holds in any danger? Who knew to what lengths the Oldtimers might go if they'd steal a Benden egg. Now, there'd been some mysterious occurrences—insignificant in themselves but in total highly suspicious—which the Harpers felt ought to be reported to Benden Weyr. Those mysterious shortages at the iron mines, for instance. And what about those young girls who were carried off and no one could trace where? Could the Oldtimers be looking for more than dragon eggs?

Menolly eased her way out of the center of the audience and beckoned Jaxom to follow her. "I'm talked dry," she said with a heavy sigh and led him down the corridor to the huge copyroom where moldy Records were transcribed before their messages were lost forever. Her lizards suddenly appeared and she signaled them to land on one of the tables. "You lot are about to wear the very latest design for fire-lizards!" She rummaged in the cabinet under the table. "Help me find white and yellow, Jaxom. This can is dried up." She chucked it into a bin in the corner.

"And what is your design for fire-lizards?"

"Hmmmm. Here's white. Harper blue with journeyman light blue, separated by white and framed by Fort Hold lattice yellow. That ought to label them accurately, don't you think?"

Jaxom agreed and found himself required to hold fire-lizard necks still. This assignment was rendered all the more difficult because the fire-lizards seemed to want to look him straight in the eye.

"If they're trying to tell me something, I'm not getting the message," Jaxom told Menolly as he patiently endured the fifth soulful scrutiny.

"I suspect," Menolly said, speaking in disjointed phrases as she carefully applied her root colors, "what you've got—hold him still, Jaxom—is the only . . . dragon on Pern . . . that . . . they're not—hold him—scared silly of right now. Ruth doesn't . . . after all . . . chew firestone."

Jaxom sighed because he could see that Ruth's sudden popularity was going to ruin his private plans. Much as he was loath to do so, he was going to have to time it because if the fire-lizards didn't know *when* they went they couldn't follow him! That reminded him of his original errand to the Harpercrafthall.

"I started out this morning to get Wansor's equations from you. . . ."

"Hmmm, yes." Menolly grinned at him over a squirming blue fire-lizard. "That seems like Turns ago. Well, we'll just patch the white on Uncle, and I'll give 'em to you. I've also got some winter-summer season charts you might as well have, seeing as you've been so co-operative. Piemur hasn't written out many yet."

A blue fire-lizard came zipping into the paint room, chirping with relief when it saw Jaxom.

It is the thick man's blue, Ruth said from outside.

"I've only the blue fire-lizard and we just did him, didn't we?" Menolly asked in surprise, glancing about the room at the others.

"It's Brand's. I'd better get back to Ruatha Hold. I should've gone back hours ago."

"Well, don't be a fool and meet yourself coming," she said with a laugh. "You've been on legitimate business this time."

Managing a light laugh, Jaxom caught the roll of charts she threw in his direction. She couldn't know what he had in mind. He was entirely too sensitive to her random remarks. Sign of a guilty conscience.

"Then you'll alibi me to Lytol?"

"Anytime, Jaxom!"

Back at Ruatha Hold, he had the whole tale to tell again with an audience as rapt, astonished, angered and relieved as the harpers and the Fort Holders. He found himself unconsciously using Menolly's turns of phrase and he wondered how long before she'd make a Ballad of the event.

He finished by directing everyone owning a fire-lizard to band the creature with Ruatha colors: brown with red squares, banded by white and black. He got that task organized when he noticed that Lytol was still seated in his heavy chair, one hand playing with the corner of his lower lip, his eyes fixed on some indistinct point on the flagstones.

"Lytol?"

The Lord Warder recalled himself to the present with an effort and frowned at Jaxom. Then he sighed. "I've always feared that the conflict might come to dragon against dragon."

"It's not come to that, Lytol," Jaxom said quietly and as persuasively as he could.

The man looked intently into Jaxom's eyes. "It could, lad. It so easily could. And I, and you, owe so much to Benden. Should I go there now?"

"Finder remained."

Lytol nodded and Jaxom wondered if the Lord Warder felt he'd been slighted. "Better for Finder to travel on dragonback." He passed his hand over his eyes and shook his head.

"You're not well, Lytol. A cup of wine?"

"No, I'll be all right, lad." Lytol pushed himself vigorously to his feet. "I don't suppose in all the fuss that you remembered what you went to the Harpercrafthall for?"

Much relieved to hear Lytol sound like himself, Jaxom lightly announced that he had not only Wansor's equations but some charts to work with. From then until the evening meal, Jaxom wished he'd not been so thoughtful because Lytol had him instructing Brand and himself in accurately timing Threadfall.

Teaching someone else a method is a very good way to make it easier to do yourself, as Jaxom found later that night when he worked some private equations of his own, poring over the rough map he had of the Southern Continent. There was too much activity all over Pern for him to go to an alternate "when" with any safety. And since he was going to time it, he might just as well go back at least twelve Turns, before anyone had started using the Southern Continent at all. He knew just where firestone could be mined so there'd be no problem supplying Ruth. The night stars were halfway to morning before he felt he could find his way to the then he wanted to find.

Just before daybreak, he was awakened by the sound of Ruth's whimpering. He struggled from his furs and stumbled barefoot on the cold stones, blinking sleep from his eyes. Ruth's forelegs were churning and his wing elbows twitched with whatever dream disturbed him. Fire-lizards burrowed about him; most of them did not wear Ruathan colors. He shooed the creatures away and Ruth, sighing, dropped into a deeper, quiet sleep.

•• C H A P T E R   V I ••

Ruatha Hold and Southern Hold,
15.5.27–15.6.2

The hold day began by sending out fire-lizards with messages
to all the smaller holds and craftcottages, ordering that every
fire-lizard be appropriately marked and individually warned about approaching any Weyr. Some of the nearby holders had ridden in during
the morning for reassurances about the garbled accounts the fire-lizards had given. So Lytol, Jaxom and Brand were kept busy all day.
The next day, Thread was due to fall, and it fell at precisely the moment
Lytol had calculated. This gave him great pleasure and reassured the
more nervous holders.

Jaxom good-naturedly took his place with the flamethrower crew,
not that any Thread escaped the Fort Weyr dragons. It amused Jaxom
to think that at the next Threadfall, he too might be above ground on
a fire-breathing Ruth.

The third day after the egg was stolen, Ruth was famished and
wanted to hunt. But the fire-lizards came in such droves to accompany
him that he killed only once and ate the beast up, bones and hide.

I will not kill for them, Ruth told Jaxom so fiercely that he wondered
if Ruth might eventually flame the fire-lizards.

"What's the matter? I thought you liked them!" Jaxom met his
dragon on the grassy slope and caressed him soothingly.

*They remember me doing something I do not remember doing. I did not
do it.* Ruth's eyes whirled with red sparks.

"What do they remember you doing?"

I haven't done it. And there was a tinge of fearful uncertainty to
Ruth's mental tone. *I know I haven't done it. I couldn't do such a thing. I*

am a dragon. I am Ruth. I am of Benden! His last words sounded in a despairing tone.

"What do they remember you doing, Ruth? You've got to tell me."

Ruth ducked his head, as if he wished he could hide, but he turned back to Jaxom, his eyes wheeling piteously. *I wouldn't take Ramoth's egg. I know I didn't take Ramoth's egg. I was there by the lake all the time with you. I remember that. You remember that. They know where I was. But somehow they remember that I took Ramoth's egg too.*

Jaxom clung to Ruth's neck to keep from falling. Then he took several very deep breaths.

"Show me the images they've been giving you, Ruth!"

And Ruth did, the projections growing more clear and vivid as Ruth calmed in response to his rider's encouragement.

That's what they remember, he said finally with a deep sigh of relief.

Jaxom told himself to think logically so he said out loud, "Fire-lizards can only tell what they've seen. You say they remember. Do you know *when* they remember seeing you take Ramoth's egg?"

I could take you to that when.

"Are you sure?"

There are two queens—they've bothered me most because they remember best.

"They wouldn't just happen to remember it at night, when the stars are out, would they?"

Ruth shook his head. *Fire-lizards are not big enough to see enough stars. And that's when they got flamed. The bronzes who guard the egg chew firestone. They don't want any fire-lizards near.*

"That's smart of them."

None of the dragons like fire-lizards anymore. And if they knew what the fire-lizards remember about me, they won't like me, either.

"Then it's just as well that you're the only dragon who'll listen to fire-lizards, isn't it?" That observation wasn't much comfort to either Ruth or Jaxom. "But why, if the egg is already back in Benden Weyr, are the fire-lizards bothering you about it?"

Because they don't remember me going yet.

Jaxom felt he'd better sit down. This last statement would take a lot of thinking. No, he contradicted himself. F'lessan had been right. We think and talk things to death. He wondered briefly if Lessa and F'nor had been seized by this same sort of irrational compulsion at the moment of their decisions. He decided he'd better not think about that either.

"You're sure you know *when* we have to go?" he asked Ruth once more.

Two queens flitted up, crooning lovingly: one even bold enough to light on Jaxom's arm, her eyes wheeling with joy.

They know. I know.

"Well, I'm glad they're willing to take us. I sure wish they'd seen stars!"

Jaxom permitted himself one more deep breath and then he swung to Ruth's neck and told him to take them home.

Once he'd made his decision to act, it was amazing how easy it was to go ahead, just as long as he didn't think about it. He assembled his flying gear, the rope, a fur robe to cover the egg. He gobbled down some meatrolls, casually winked at Brand as he sauntered out of the Hall, overwhelmingly glad that he had a handy excuse in his suspected affair with Corana.

It took longer to persuade Ruth to roll in the black tidal mud of the Telgar River delta, but Jaxom managed to persuade his weyrmate that a white hide was remarkably visible against the black tropical night or in full daylight inside the Hatching Ground where he planned for them to stay in the shadows.

From the images given Ruth by the two queens, Jaxom felt he could safely assume that the Oldtimers had taken the egg back in time but lodged it in the most logical and fitting spot for an egg, in the warm sands of the old volcano that would eventually become Southern Weyr in the appropriate time. He had already memorized the positions of Southern night stars so he'd probably be able to tell *when* he was, within a Turn or two. He'd have to count heavily on Ruth's boast that he always knew *when* he was.

The fire-lizards arrived in full fair at the delta and enthusiastically helped him sully Ruth's white coat with the clinging black mud. Jaxom dabbed it on his hands and face, and the shiny parts of his accoutrements. The fur robe was already dark enough.

Somehow Jaxom wasn't quite sure that all this was happening to him, that he could be mixed up in such a wild venture. But he had to be. He was moving in inexorable steps toward a predestined event and nothing could stop him now. So he mounted Ruth calmly, trusting as he had never done before in his dragon's abilities. Jaxom took two deep breaths.

"You know *when*, Ruth. We'd better get there!"

It was without doubt the longest, coldest jump he had ever made. He had one advantage over Lessa, he expected it. But that didn't keep the jump from being frighteningly dark, or relieve a silence that was a noisy pressure in his ears, or keep the cold from striking his bones. He couldn't come straight back with the egg; he'd have to take several steps to warm it.

Then they were above a darkened moist warm world that smelled of lush greenery and slightly decaying fruit. For a moment Jaxom had the hideous feeling that this was all a sun-dream of the fire-lizards. But something in the eerie way that Ruth glided as noiselessly as possible, a part of the gentle night breeze, made it real and immediate. Then he saw the egg below, a luminescent spot slightly to the right of Ruth's searching head.

Jaxom let him glide a little farther to catch a glimpse of the Weyr's eastern edge, the point from which he wanted to enter at all possible speed, at early dawn. Then he told Ruth to change and there seemed to be no time spent *between*. All at once the rising sun was warm on their backs. Ruth arrowed in, winging low and fast, over the backs of the drowsy bronzes and their napping riders. A quick deft swoop, Ruth grabbing the egg in his sturdy forearms, a lunge up and, before the startled bronzes could rise to their feet, the little white dragon had enough free air to go *between* again.

Ruth was still only a winglength above the Weyr when they came out of *between*, a Turn in time ahead of Ruth's sunrise plunge.

Ruth had just enough strength left in his forearms and wings to let the egg down carefully into the warm sands. Jaxom dropped from the dragon's neck to check the egg for any cracks, but it looked all right. Certainly it was hard enough and still warm. With his gloved hands, he shoveled sun-hot sand over the egg and then, like Ruth, collapsed to catch his breath.

"We can't stay long. They might just try it day by day. They'd know we can't take the egg far at once."

Ruth nodded, his breath still coming in ragged gasps. Then he stopped, taut until Jaxom started with alarm. Two fire-lizards, a gold and a bronze, were watching them from the edge of the Weyr. In the brief glimpse Jaxom had of them before they winked out, he saw no colored bands about their necks.

"Do we know them?"

No.

"Where're those two queens?"

They showed me when. *That's all you wanted.*

Jaxom felt bereft of their fragile guidance and stupid because he hadn't insisted they stay.

There's firestone, Ruth said. *And flame scar. The bronzes did flame at the fire-lizards here! A long time ago. The scar is growing weed.*

"Dragon against dragon!" Apprehension nagged at Jaxom. He didn't feel safe here. He wouldn't feel safe until they actually had that egg back in Benden where it belonged.

"We've got to make another jump, Ruth. We don't dare wait here."

Resolutely he unlooped the rope from about his waist and started making a rough sling with the fur rug. There'd be less strain on Ruth if the egg were strapped between his forelegs. Jaxom had completed the corners when he heard a loud crunching.

"Ruth! You're not going to flame dragons!"

No, of course I'm not. But will they dare approach me if I am flaming?

Jaxom was unsettled enough not to protest. When Ruth had a gulletful, he called him over and got the sling around the egg. He looped the rope comfortably over Ruth's shoulders to take the weight. He started to check the knots again and then, some inner caution prompting him, he just mounted.

"We'll go five Turns more into Keroon, to our place there. Do you know when?"

Ruth thought a moment and then said he knew when.

In *between* Jaxom had time to worry if he was making the jumps too long to keep the egg warm. It hadn't actually Hatched before he'd left. Maybe he should have waited, to find out if the egg had hatched properly: then they'd've known how to judge the forward jumps. Maybe he'd even killed the little queen trying to save her. No, his mind reeled with *between* and paradoxes; the most important act, returning the queen egg, was in process. And dragon had not fought dragon—not yet.

The shimmering heat of Keroon desert warmed his failing spirit as well as his body. Ruth looked a ghastly shade under the caking black mud. Jaxom released the rope and lowered the egg to the sand. Ruth helped him cover it. It was midmorning, and not far from the hour when the egg must be back but at least six Turns in time-distance.

Ruth asked if he couldn't wash off the mud in the sea but Jaxom told him they'd have to wait until they'd got the egg safely back. No one had known who'd done it then: no one should know, and the safest way was not to have a white hide showing.

The fire-lizards?

That had worried Jaxom but he thought he had the answer. "They didn't know who brought the egg back that day. There weren't any in the Hatching Ground, so they don't know what they haven't seen." Jaxom decided not to think further on that subject.

He was very tired as he leaned back against Ruth's warm flank. They'd rest a little while and let the egg warm up well in the mid-morning sun before they'd make that last the trickiest jump. They had a position themselves to land just inside the Hatching Ground, where the arch of the entrance sloped abruptly down and obscured the view of anyone looking from the Bowl into the Ground. In fact, directly opposite the peephole and slit that F'lessan and Jaxom had used so many Turns ago. It was just luck that Ruth was small enough to risk going *between* inside the Ground but it'd been his own Hatching place so his feeling was innate. Thus far he'd lived up to his boast that he always knew when he was going. . . .

Even in the hot desert plains of Keroon there was some noise: infinitesimal rustlings of insect life, hot breezes riffling through dead grasses, snakes burrowing in the sand, the distant rush of water on the beach. The cessation of such sounds can be as remarkable as a thunderclap, and so it was the utter stillness and a minute change of air pressure that roused Jaxom and Ruth from somnolence to alarm.

Jaxom glanced up, expecting bronze dragons to appear and reclaim their prize. The sky above was clear and hot. Jaxom glanced around and saw the danger, the silver mist of descending Thread raining down across the desert. He slithered and scrambled to the egg. Ruth right beside him, both digging it free, pushing it into the sling, frantically trying to judge the leading edge of Fall, wondering and worrying that the skies weren't full of fighting dragons.

As fast as they worked to secure the precious burden to Ruth for flight, they were not quite quick enough. The leading edge of Threadfall fell hissing to the sand around them as Jaxom got to Ruth's neck and directed him upward. Ruth, giving a belch of flame, vaulted skyward, trying to sear a path far enough above the ground to go *between*.

A ribbon of fire sliced Jaxom's cheek, his right shoulder through the wherhide tunic, his forearm, his thigh. He felt, rather than heard, Ruth's bellow of pain, lost in the black of *between*.

Somehow Jaxom kept his mind on where and when they should be. They were finally in the Hatching Ground, Ramoth bellowing outside. Ruth could not quite suppress his cry as the hot sand rubbed the raw Threadscore on his hind foot. Jaxom bit his lips against his pain as he struggled with the rope. There was so little time and it seemed to take ages to release the sling. Ruth lowered the egg to the sand but it rolled down the slight incline from their shadowy corner of the Ground. They couldn't wait. Ruth sprang up toward the high ceiling and went *between*.

Dragon would not now fight dragon!

It was no surprise to Jaxom that Ruth came out of *between* above the little mountain lake. In what relative when, Jaxom was too concerned for his dragon to care at that moment. Ruth was whimpering with the pain in his foot and leg; all he wanted was to cool that Threadfire. Jaxom leaped from his neck to the shallows and splashed water on the sweaty gray hide, cursing himself that the nearest numbweed was at Ruatha Hold. He was so clever, he was, that he never thought one of them might get hurt.

The cool lake water was taking the sting from the Threadscores but Jaxom worried now about the mud causing an infection. Surely he could have used something less dangerous for camouflage than river mud. He didn't dare scour the wounds with sand: it would be too painful for Ruth and might just rub the cursed mud deeper into the wounds. For the first time in many days, Jaxom regretted the total absence of fire-lizards who could have helped him scrub his very dirty dragon. Once again he briefly wondered when, besides high noon of the day, they were.

It is the day after the evening we left, Ruth announced. *I always know when I am,* he added with justifiable pride in his ability. *Along the left dorsal, a terrible itch. You've left some mud.*

Jaxon could and did use sand on the rest of Ruth's hide and managed to ignore the way it smarted in his own scores. He was dead weary and aching by the time Ruth allowed that he was clean enough for a last plunge in the deeper part of the lake.

The ripples lapping around his soaked ankles brought Jaxom's memory back to that not so distant day of his rebellion.

"Well," he said with a self-deprecatory chuckle, "among other things, we did get to fight Thread." And what a dismal showing they'd made of it with proof patent on their hides.

We weren't exactly giving our complete attention to Thread, Ruth reminded him with a note of reproach. *I know how now. We'll be much better at it next time. I'm faster than any of the big dragons. I can turn on my tail and go* between *in a single length from the ground.*

Jaxom told Ruth fervently and gratefully that he was without doubt the best, fastest, cleverest beast in all Pern, North and South. Ruth's eyes whirled greenly with pleasure and he paddled to the shore, wings extended to dry.

You are cold and hungry and sore. My leg hurts. Let's go home.

Jaxom knew that was the wisest course; he had to get numbweed on Ruth's leg and on his own injuries. But scores they were and undeniably caused by Thread. How in the name of the First Shell was he ever going to explain all of this to Lytol?

Why explain anything? Ruth asked logically. *We only did what we had to do.*

"Think logically, huh?" Jaxom replied with a laugh, and patted Ruth's neck before he wearily pulled himself up. With understandable reluctance and apprehension, he told Ruth to take them home.

The watchdragon caroled a greeting and a mere half-dozen fire-lizards, all banded in Hold colors, swarmed up to escort Ruth down to his weyr courtyard.

One of the drudges came hurrying out of the kitchen entrance, eyes wide with excitement.

"Lord Jaxom, there's been a Hatching. The queen egg Hatched, it did. You were sent to come but no one could find you."

"I had other business. Fetch me some numbweed!"

"Numbweed?" The drudge's eyes widened further with concern.

"Numbweed! I'm sunburned."

Rather pleased with his resourcefulness considering he was shivering in wet clothes, Jaxom saw Ruth comfortably situated in his weyr, his injured leg propped up.

It hurt Jaxom to get the tunic over his shoulder because Thread had scored right down the muscle, caught him at the wrist and continued to cut a long furrow down his thigh.

A timid scratching on the door to the main Hold announced the incredibly speedy return of the drudge. Jaxom opened the door wide enough to get the jug of numbweed, and still keep his Threadscores from the curious eyes.

"Thanks, and I'll want something hot to eat, too. Soup, *klah*, whatever's on the fire."

Jaxom closed the door, scooped up a bathing sheet which he knotted about his middle as he made his way to Ruth. He slathered a fistful of the numbweed on his dragon's leg and grinned at the sigh of intense relief that Ruth gave as the salve took immediate effect.

Jaxom gratefully echoed the sentiments as he smeared his own wounds. Blessed, blessed numbweed. Never again would he begrudge his labor in gathering the plaguey, thorny greenery from which this incredible balm was stewed. He peered into his looking glass as he daubed his face cut. It'd leave a finger-long scar. No getting around that. Now if he could get around Lytol's wrath . . .

"Jaxom!"

Lytol strode into the room after the most perfunctory knock at the door. "You've missed the Hatching at Benden Weyr and—" At the sight of Jaxom, Lytol stopped so quickly in midstride that he rocked back on his heels. Clad only in a bathing sheet, the marks on Jaxom's shoulder and face were quite visible.

"The egg Hatched all right then? Good," Jaxom responded, picking up his tunic with a nonchalance he wasn't feeling. "I . . ." then he stopped, as much because his voice would be muffled in the fabric of his tunic as because he had been about to explain with his customary candor his bizarre night's work. He balked at the task. Ruth perhaps was right—they had only done what they had to. It was sort of his and Ruth's private affair. You might even say his actions reflected his unconscious wish to atone for violating Ramoth's Hatching Ground as a boy. He pulled the shirt over his head, wincing as it caught the numbweed on his cheek. "I heard at Benden," he said then, "that they were worried whether it would Hatch after all the coming and going *between*."

Lytol approached Jaxom slowly, his eyes on the young man's face, begging the question.

Jaxom settled his tunic, belted it, then smoothed the numbweed into the cut again. He didn't know what to say.

"Oh, Lytol, would you mind taking a look at Ruth's leg? See if I doctored it right?" Jaxom waited then, facing Lytol calmly. He noticed, with a sadness for the inevitability of this moment of reverse, that Lytol's eyes were dark with emotion. He owed the man so much, never more than at this moment. He wondered that he had ever considered Lytol cold or hard and unfeeling.

"There's a trick of ducking Thread," Lytol said quietly, "that you'd better teach Ruth, Lord Jaxom."

"If you'd be kind enough to tell me how, Lord Lytol . . ."

ᴗ

Morning at Ruatha Hold, 15.6.2

"I came to tell you that we have guests, Lord Jaxom; Master Robinton, N'ton and Menolly are above, just back from the Hatching. First, let's see to Ruth."

"Didn't you go to Benden for the Hatching?" Jaxom asked.

Lytol shook his head as he walked toward Ruth's weyr. The white dragon was settling in for a well-deserved nap. Lytol bowed courteously to him before peering closely at the thickly smeared scorings.

"You washed first in the lake, I presume?" Lytol's glance took in Jaxom's damp hair. "That water's pure enough, and the numbweed's been applied in good time. We'll check again in a few hours. But I think he's all right." Lytol's gaze went then to Jaxom's all-too-obvious scoring.

"I had no reason to excuse you to our guests." He sighed. "Be grateful it's N'ton above and not F'lar. I suppose Menolly knew what you were about?"

"I told no one what I intended, Lord Lytol," Jaxom said with some formality.

"At least you've learned discretion." The Lord Warder hesitated, his eyes sweeping the figure of his ward. "Ah, well, I'd best ask N'ton to take you for weyrling practice—safer that way and you'd be with others. Robinton will guess what you've been about, but he'd learn in due course no matter how we evaded. Come then, they'll not give you too hard a time for your clumsiness. Not that you don't deserve more than a ribbing, taking such a chance with yourself and Ruth. And right now, when order is all in pieces anyhow . . ."

"I apologize for distressing you, Lord Lytol . . ."

The man subjected his charge to another shrewd scrutiny.

"No distress, Lord Jaxom. Any apologies are on my head. I ought to have realized your need to prove Ruth's abilities. I *wish* that you were a few Turns older and that matters were in such order that I could let you take Hold—"

"I don't want to take Hold from you, Lord Lytol—"

"I don't think I'd be permitted to step down right now anyway, Jaxom. As you'll hear for yourself. Come, we've kept our guests waiting long enough as it is."

N'ton was facing the door of the smaller hall used at Ruatha when guests required privacy for their discussions. The bronze rider took one look at Jaxom's face and groaned. At his reaction, Master Robinton slewed round in his chair, his tired eyes registering surprise and, Jaxom hoped, a certain measure of approval.

"You're Threadscored, Jaxom," Menolly cried, and her expression was one of shocked dismay. "How could you take such a risk right now?" She, who had taunted him about thinking, not doing, was now furious with him.

"I should have known you'd try it, young Jaxom," N'ton said with a weary sigh, a rueful smile on his face. "You were bound to break out soon, but your timing is atrocious."

Jaxom would have liked to say that, in point of fact, his timing had been faultless, but N'ton went on: "Ruth wasn't hurt, was he?"

"A single score on thigh and foot," Lytol replied. "Well doctored."

"I do sympathize with your ambition, Jaxom," Robinton said, unusually solemn, "to fly Ruth with other dragons but I must counsel you to patience."

"I'd rather he learned how to fly properly now, Robinton. With my other weyrlings," N'ton interrupted unexpectedly, winning Jaxom's gratitude. "Particularly if he's mad enough, brave enough, to try it on his own without any guidance."

"I doubt we could get Benden to approve," Robinton said, shaking his head.

"*I* approve," Lytol said in a firm voice, his face set. "I am Lord Jaxom's guardian, not F'lar or Lessa. Let her manage her own concerns. Lord Jaxom is my charge. He can come to little harm with the Fort Weyrlings." Lytol stared fiercely at Jaxom. "And he will agree not to put his teaching to the test without consulting us. Will you abide by that, Lord Jaxom?"

Jaxom was relieved enough to know that the Benden Weyrleaders would not be queried so that he agreed to more stringent conditions than he might have. He nodded and was immediately beset by conflicting emotions—amusement because everyone had assumed the obvious and annoyance because, having achieved so much more that day, he was now reduced to apprentice level. Yet, his experience at Keroon had demonstrated too sharply how much he still had to learn about fighting Thread if he wished to keep whole his and his dragon's hides.

N'ton had been peering intently at Jaxom and his frown deepened so that, for one moment, Jaxom wondered if N'ton had somehow guessed what he and Ruth had actually been doing when they were Threadscored. If they ever found out, Jaxom would be twice bound with added restrictions.

"I think I'll require a further promise from you, Jaxom," the bronze rider said. "No more timing it. You've been doing far too much of that lately. I can tell from your eyes."

Startled, Lytol examined his ward's face more closely.

"I'm in no danger on Ruth, N'ton," Jaxom said, relieved at being accused of a lesser transgression. "He always knows *when* he is."

N'ton dismissed that talent impatiently. "Possibly, but the danger lies in the rider's mind—an inadvertent time clue that could set both in jeopardy. Coming too close to yourself in subjective time is dangerous. Besides it's draining for both dragon and rider. You don't need to time it, young Jaxom. You'll have enough for all you need to do."

N'ton's words caused Jaxom to recall the inexplicable weakness that had overcome him in the Hatching Ground. Was it possible that at that very moment—

"I don't think you can have realized, Jaxom," Robinton began, interrupting Jaxom's thoughts, "just how critical matters are in Pern right now. And you should know."

"If you mean about the egg-stealing, Master Robinton, and how close it came to dragon attacking dragon, I was in Benden Weyr that morning . . ."

"Were you?" Robinton was mildly surprised and shook his head as if he ought not to have forgotten. "Then you can guess at Lessa's temper today. If that egg hadn't hatched properly . . .

"But the egg *was* returned, Master Robinton." Jaxom was confused. *Why* should Lessa still be upset?

"Yes," the Harper replied, "apparently not everyone in Southern was blind to the consequences of the theft. But Lessa is not appeased."

"An insult was given Benden Weyr, and Ramoth and Lessa," N'ton said.

"Dragons can't fight dragons!" Jaxom was appalled. "That's why the egg was returned." If his risk and Ruth's injury had been futile . . .

"Our Lessa is a woman of strong emotions, Jaxom—revenge being one of those most highly developed in her. Remember how you came to be Lord here?" Robinton's expression indicated regret for reminding Jaxom of his origin. "I do not belittle the Benden Weyrwoman when I say that. Such perseverance in the face of incredible odds is laudable. But her tenacity over the insult could have a disastrous effect on all Pern. So far, reason has prevailed but currently that balance is shaky indeed."

Jaxom nodded, perceiving that he could never admit to his part, relieved that he had not blurted out his adventure to Lytol. No one must ever know that he, Jaxom, had returned the egg. Particularly Lessa. He sent a silent command to Ruth, who drowsily replied that he was too tired to talk to anyone about anything and couldn't he please sleep?

"Yes," Jaxom said in reply to Robinton, "I quite understand the need for discretion."

"There is another event," Robinton's mobile face drew into a sorrowful grimace as he sought the proper word, "an event which will shortly compound our problems." He glanced at N'ton. "D'ram."

"I think you're right, Robinton," the bronze rider said. "He's unlikely to remain Weyrleader if Fanna dies."

"If? I'm afraid we must say when. And, according to what Master Oldive told me, the sooner it happens, the kinder it will be."

"I didn't know that Fanna was ill," Jaxom said, and his thoughts leaped ahead to the sorrowful knowledge that Fanna's queen, Mirath, would suicide when her Weyrwoman died. A queen's death would upset every dragon—and Lessa and Ramoth!

Lytol's expression was bleak, as it always was whenever he was reminded of his own dragon's death. Jaxom swallowed the remainder of his pride and dismay about apprenticing as a weyrling; he would never risk injuring Ruth again.

"Fanna's been declining gradually," Robinton was saying, "a wasting sickness that nothing seems to halt. Master Oldive is at Ista with her now."

"Yes, his fire-lizard will summon me when he's ready to leave. I want to be available to D'ram," N'ton said.

"Fire-lizards, yes, hmmm," said Robinton. "Another sore subject at Benden Weyr." He glanced at his bronze, perched contentedly on his shoulder. "I felt naked without Zair at that Hatching. Upon my word!" He stared at his somnolent bronze, then over to N'ton's Tris, drowsy-eyed on the rider's arm. "They've calmed down!"

"Ruth's here," N'ton said, stroking Tris. "They feel safe with him."

"No, that isn't it," Menolly said, her eyes resting on Jaxom's face. "They were worried even with Ruth. But that wild restlessness is gone. No more visions of the egg!" She peered sideways at her little queen. "I suppose that makes sense. It's Hatched and healthy. Whatever was plaguing them hasn't happened. Or," she stared at Jaxom suddenly, "or has it?"

Jaxom affected surprise and confusion.

"They were worried about the egg hatching, Menolly?" Robinton asked. "Too bad we can't tell Lessa how concerned they've all been. It might help restore them to her good graces."

"I think it's high time something was done about fire-lizards," Menolly said severely.

"My dear girl . . ." Robinton was surprised.

"I don't mean ours, Master Robinton. They've proved to be extremely useful. Too many people take them for granted and make no effort to train them." She gave a peculiar laugh. "As Jaxom can vouch. They congregate wherever Ruth goes till he's driven *between* by their attentions. Isn't that right, Jaxom?" There was a strange quality about her gaze that puzzled him.

"I wouldn't say he objects . . . most of the time, Menolly," he replied coolly, casually stretching his long legs under the table. "But a fellow likes a little time to himself, you know."

Lytol gave a knowing snort which told Jaxom that Brand had had a word with the Warder about Corana.

"Why? To chew firestone?" N'ton asked, grinning.

"Was that what you were doing with your . . . time, Jaxom?" Menolly asked him, her eyes wide, affecting innocent inquiry.

"You might say so."

"Do the fire-lizards really present you with problems?" Robinton asked, "in their preference for Ruth's company?"

"Well, sir," Jaxom replied, "no matter where we go, every fire-lizard in the vicinity pops in to see Ruth. Generally it's no bother because they keep Ruth amused if I'm busy with Hold matters."

"They wouldn't by any chance have told Ruth why they've been troubled? Or did you know about those images?" Robinton leaned forward, eager to have Jaxom's answer.

"You mean fire-lizards being flamed? The dark nothingness and the egg? Oh yes, they've been driving Ruth frantic with that nonsense," said Jaxom. He scowled as if annoyed with his friend, and was careful not to look in Menolly's direction. "But that seems to have passed. Perhaps the disturbance was connected with the stolen egg. But it's hatched now and look, they're not the least bit as agitated as they've been, and they're letting Ruth sleep by himself again."

"Where were you when the egg was being Hatched?" Menolly pounced on Jaxom so swiftly with her question that Robinton and N'ton regarded her with surprise.

"Why," and Jaxom laughed as he touched his scored cheek, "trying to sear Thread!"

His ready answer threw Menolly into quiet confusion while Robinton, Lytol and N'ton all had another go at him for his foolhardiness. He endured the scolding in good part because it kept Menolly from plaguing him. She'd been suspicious after all. He wished that he could tell her the truth. Of all the people on Pern, she was the only one he could trust now that he knew how infinitely wiser it was to let everyone else believe a Southern dragonrider had returned the egg. He was discontented, though, because it would be a relief, a pleasure, to be able to tell *someone* what he'd done.

Food was served them and they kept the discussions to the problem of the fire-lizards—whether they were more nuisance than valuable—until Jaxom pointed out that everyone about the table was converted. What they needed was a way to pacify Lessa and Ramoth.

"Ramoth will forget her aggravation soon enough," N'ton said.

"Lessa won't, although I doubt there'll be that much reason for me to send Zair to Benden Weyr."

As N'ton and Lytol vigorously reassured the Harper, Jaxom realized there was a curious restraint about the man, an odd note in his voice when he mentioned Benden or the Weyrwoman. Robinton wasn't worried simply that Lessa had prohibited fire-lizards at Benden.

"There's another aspect of this affair that is nagging at the back of my overactive imagination," Robinton said. "The matter has brought Southern to everyone's attention."

"Why is that a problem?" Lytol asked.

Robinton took a sip of his wine, delaying his answer as he savored the taste. "Just this: these recent events have made everyone realize that that huge continent is occupied by a mere handful of people."

"So?"

"I know some restless Lord Holders whose halls are crowded, whose cots are jammed. And the Weyrs, instead of protecting the inviolability of the Southern Continent, were half-set to force their way in. What's to prevent the Lord Holders from taking the initiative and claiming whole portions of it?"

"There wouldn't be dragons enough to protect that much area, that's what," Lytol said. "The Oldtimers surely wouldn't."

"They don't really need dragonriders in the South," Robinton said slowly.

Lytol stared at him, aghast at such a statement.

"It's true," he said. "The land is thoroughly sowed by grubs. Traders have told me that they more or less ignore Falls; Holder Toric just makes certain everyone's safe and all stock is under cover."

"There will come a time when no dragonriders will be needed in the North either," N'ton said, slowly, compounding Lytol's shock.

"Dragonriders will always be needed on Pern while there is Thread!" Lytol emphasized his conviction by banging the table with his fist.

"At least in our lifetimes," Robinton said soothingly. "But I could have wished less interest in Southern. Think it over, Lytol."

"More of your thinking ahead, Robinton?" Lytol asked, a sour note in his voice and a jaundiced expression on his face.

"Looking ahead is far more constructive than looking behind," said Robinton. He held his clenched fist up. "I'd all the facts in my grasp and I couldn't see the water for the waves."

"You've been down to the Southern Continent often, Masterharper?"

Robinton gave Lytol a long considering look. "I have. Discreetly, I assure you. There are some things that must be seen to be believed."

"Such as?"

Robinton idly stroked Zair as he gazed out, over Lytol's head, at some distant view.

"Mind you, there are times when looking back can be helpful," he said and then turned back to the Lord Warder. "Are you aware that we originally, all of us, came from the Southern Continent?"

Lytol's first surprise at such a sudden turn of the conversation melded into a thoughtful frown. "Yes, that was implicit in the oldest Records."

"I've often wondered if there aren't older Records, moldering somewhere in the South."

Lytol snorted at the notion. "Moldering is right. There'd be nothing left after so many thousands of Turns."

"They had ways of tempering metal, those ancestors of ours, ways that made it impervious to rust and wear. Those plates found at Fort Weyr, the instruments, like the long-distance viewer that fascinates Wansor and Fandarel. I don't believe that time can have erased all traces of such clever people."

Jaxom glanced at Menolly, recalling hints that she'd let slip. Her eyes were sparkling with suppressed excitement. She knew something that the Harper wasn't saying. Jaxom looked then at the Fort Weyrleader and realized that N'ton knew all about this.

"The Southern Continent was ceded to the dissident Oldtimers," Lytol said heavily.

"And they have already broken their side of the agreement," N'ton said.

"Is that any reason for us to break ours?" Lytol asked, drawing his shoulders back and scowling at both Weyrleader and Harper.

"They occupy only a small tongue of land, jutting out into the Southern Sea," said Robinton in his smooth way. "They have been unaware of any activity elsewhere."

"You've already been exploring in the South?"

"Judiciously. Judiciously."

"And you'd not have your . . . judicious intrusions discovered?"

"No," answered Robinton slowly. "I shall make the knowledge public soon enough. I don't want every disgruntled apprentice and evicted smallholder running about indiscriminately, destroying what should be preserved because they haven't the wit to understand it."

"What have you discovered so far?"

"Old mine workings, shored up with lightweight but so durable a material that it is as unscratched today as when it was put in place in the shaft. Tools, powered by who can guess—bits and pieces that not even young Benelek can assemble."

There was a long silence which Lytol broke with a snort. "Harpers! Harpers are supposed to instruct the young."

"*And* first and foremost, to preserve our heritage!"

Ruatha Hold, Fort Weyr,
Fidello's Hold, 15.6.3–15.6.17

Jaxom was disappointed that all Lytol's coaxing could not draw more facts from the Harper about his explorations in the South. At the point where Jaxom's fatigue made it difficult for him to keep his eyes open, it occurred to him that Robinton had indeed succeeded in rousing Lytol to support his and N'ton's desire to keep interest in the South to a minimum.

Jaxom's last waking thought was one of admiration for the Harper's devious methods. No wonder he had not objected to Jaxom training with N'ton when he saw Lytol was in favor of it. The Harper needed the older man as the Lord Holder at Ruatha. Training Ruth to chew firestone kept the young Lord from wanting to take Hold in Lytol's place.

The next morning Jaxom was positive that he couldn't have moved during the night. He was bindingly stiff, his face and shoulder stung with the Threadscore and that reminded him of Ruth's injury. With no regard for his own discomfort, he whipped aside the furs and, grabbing the numbweed pot as he went, burst into Ruth's weyr.

The faintest rumble told him that the white dragon was still sound asleep. He also seemed not to have moved for his leg was propped in the same position. That made it easier for Jaxom to work and he smeared a new coating of numbweed along the line of the score. Only then did it occur to Jaxom that he and Ruth might have to wait until they'd healed before they could join the weyrlings at Fort Weyr.

Lytol did not share his thought. The reason Jaxom was going to Fort Weyr was to avoid scoring, to learn how to take care of his dragon and himself during Threadfall. If he got teased because he hadn't ducked fast enough, he deserved it. So, after breaking his fast, Jaxom flew Ruth to the Weyr.

Fortunately two of those in training were near his own age of eighteen Turns—not that being older would have bothered Jaxom as long as he could train Ruth properly. He did have to suppress the insidious urge to excuse Ruth's scoring with the real reason for the supposed clumsiness. He took refuge in knowing that he had achieved more than they'd ever guess—a small consolation.

His first problem in the weyrling class was to relieve Ruth of the embarrassment of the endless fire-lizards that settled on him. No sooner was one group dislodged and sent off than another appeared, to the disgust and exasperation of K'nebel, the Weyrlingmaster.

"Does this go on all day wherever you are?" the man asked Jaxom irritably.

"More or less. They just . . . come. Especially since . . . what happened at Benden Weyr."

K'nebel snorted his aggravation even as he nodded his understanding. "I don't like to put truth to these notions that dragons flamed fire-lizards, but you'll never get Ruth going if the fire-lizards don't leave him alone. And if they don't leave him alone, one of 'em will get flamed!"

So Jaxom had Ruth shoo the fire-lizards away as quickly as they arrived. It took time before Ruth remained unencumbered for any appreciable period. Then, either all the fire-lizards in the vicinity had looked in, or Ruth had been sufficiently firm and the rest of the morning's class was undisrupted.

Despite all the interruptions, K'nebel kept the weyrlings working until the noonday meal was called. Jaxom was invited to stay and, as a mark of his rank, was shown to the large table reserved for senior dragonriders.

The conversation was dominated by continued speculation about the return of the egg and which one of the queen riders had returned it. The discussions served to reinforce Jaxom's decision to remain silent. He cautioned Ruth, needlessly it appeared, since the white dragon was more interested in chewing firestone and dodging Thread than in past events.

The fire-lizards about him had lost all their previous agitation. Their primary concern now was eating, the secondary one was their hides. With the advent of the warmer weather, they had begun shedding and were plagued by itching. The images they projected to Ruth no longer had alarming content.

Since he was engaged at Fort Weyr in the mornings, Jaxom had to forego the classes at the Harper and Smith crafthalls. That meant he wouldn't have to endure Menolly's tendency to ask searching questions, and he was well pleased. He was also heartily amused when he realized that Lyton was leaving him several uncommitted hours in the afternoons. Obligingly he and Ruth took off for the Plateau Hold to see how the new wheat was prospering—of course.

Corana was about the hold these days since her brother's wife was near her time. When she showed a pretty concern for his healing score, he did not abuse her notion that he'd acquired it in a legitimate Fall, protecting the Hold from Thread. She rewarded him for that protection in a fashion that embarrassed him even as it relieved him. He'd as soon save his favors for honest endeavor. But he couldn't be annoyed with her when, in the languor that followed their pleasure, she made several references to fire-lizards and asked if he'd ever had a chance to find a clutch when he was fighting Thread.

"Every beach in the North is well staked," he told her and, noting her intense disappointment, added, "Of course, there are lots of empty beaches in the Southern Continent!"

"Could you fly in on your Ruth without those Oldtimers knowing?" Clearly Corana knew little of the most recent events, another relief to Jaxom, who was beginning to be bored by the Weyr's preoccupation with that topic.

Fly in on Ruth made the whole thing seem simple enough; especially as Ruth would not upset strange fire-lizards since he had apparently made friends with them all.

"I suppose I could." His hesitation was due to the complications of planning an absence long enough to allow him to go South. Corana misconstrued what he said, and again, he was too tenderhearted and too gratified to correct her.

As he and Ruth winged homeward from the Plateau, it occurred to Jaxom that the ripples from his initial outburst just a short while ago were still spreading. He had finally achieved proper training for Ruth and, if he hadn't taken Hold, at least he was finally enjoying more of the prerogatives of a Lord Holder. He grinned, savoring Corana's sweetness. Judging by her sister's warm welcome, he assumed the Plateau Hold would not object to a half-blooded addition. Success in that area would do him no harm in the eyes of Lord Holders. He considered bringing Corana to the Hold, but decided against it. That would be unfair to the other fosterlings and cause trouble for Brand and Lytol. It wasn't as if he didn't have Ruth and couldn't come and go at his leisure and speedily. Furthermore, if he brought Corana to his quarters, she'd demand more of his attention at Ruth's expense than he was willing to give.

The third afternoon he went to the Plateau Hold, Fidello's wife was in labor and Corana too distracted to do more than beg his pardon for the fuss and excitement. He asked if they wished the Hold's healer, but Fidello said that one of his dependents was skillful in such matters and had said that his wife would have no trouble with the birth. Jaxom made all the appropriate remarks, then left, feeling slightly put off by this unanticipated obstacle to his expectations.

Why are you laughing? Ruth asked as they winged back to the Hold.

"Because I'm a fool, Ruth. I'm a fool."

I don't think you are. She makes you feel good, not a fool.

"That's why I'm a fool now, silly dragon. I went up there expecting . . . expecting to feel good and she's too busy. And only a few sevendays ago I wouldn't have dreamed I'd be as lucky with her. That's why I'm a fool now, Ruth."

I will always love you, was Ruth's reply because he felt that was the response Jaxom needed.

Jaxom reassuringly caressed his dragon's neck ridge, but he couldn't suppress his self-deprecatory mirth. He discovered a second obstacle when he returned to the Hold. Lytol informed him that the remainder of Ramoth's clutch would probably Hatch the next day, and that Jaxom would have to put in an appearance at Benden. The Lord Warder peered intently at Jaxom's healed score and nodded.

"Do try to keep out of the Weyrleaders' sight. They'd know at a glance what that was," Lytol said. "No sense advertising your folly."

Jaxom privately thought the scar gave him a more mature appearance but he promised Lytol he'd stay well away from Lessa and F'lar.

Jaxom rather enjoyed Hatchings, more so when Lytol was not present. He felt guilty about that but he knew that, at each Hatching, painful memories of Lytol's beloved Larth tortured the man.

News of the imminent Hatching came to Fort Weyr while Jaxom was flying wing tip in weyrling Fall practice. He finished the maneuver, begged the Weyrlingmaster's pardon and took Ruth *between* to Ruatha so that he could change into proper clothing. Lytol along with Menolly's Rocky reached him at the same moment and requested that he collect Menolly, since Robinton was already at Ista Weyr with the Harperhall's dragon and rider.

Jaxom put a good face on the request since he could think of no excuse to refuse. Well, he'd hurry her out of the Hall and into the Weyr so quickly that she wouldn't have time to ask any questions.

When he and Ruth arrived at the Harpercrafthall, Ruth bellowing his name to the watchdragon on the fire-heights, Jaxom became furious. Why, there were enough Fort Weyr dragons on the meadow to take half the Hall. Why hadn't she asked one of them? He was determined that she wouldn't have a chance to nag at him and asked Ruth peremptorily to tell her fire-lizards that he was here and waiting in the meadow. He had barely formed the words in his mind when Menolly came dashing out of the archway toward him, Beauty, Rocky and Diver chittering in circles above her head. She began shrugging into her riding jacket, awkwardly juggling something from one hand to the other.

"Get down, Jaxom," she ordered imperiously. "I can't do it when your back's to me."

"Do what?"

"This!" She held up one hand to show him a small pot. "Get down."

"Why?"

"Don't be dense. You're wasting time. This is to cover that scar. You don't want Lessa and F'lar to see it, do you, and ask awkward questions? Come down! Or we'll be late. And you're not supposed to time it, are you?" She added the last comment as he still hesitated, not altogether reassured by her altruism.

"I've got my hair brushed over—"

"You'll forget and push it back," she said, gesturing him to do so now as she unscrewed the pot lid. "I got Oldive to make some without scent. There. Only takes a dab." She had applied it to his face and then brushed the residue on the skin of his wrist above his glove. "See? It blends in." She stared critically at him. "Yes, that does the trick. No one would ever know you've been scored." Then she chuckled. "What does Corana think of your scar?"

"Corana?"

"Don't glare at me. Get up on Ruth. We'll be late. Very clever of you, Jaxom, to cultivate Corana. You'd've made a good harper with your wits."

Jaxom mounted his dragon, furious with her but determined not to rise to her lure. It was just like her to find out such things, hoping to aggravate him. Well, she wasn't going to succeed.

"Thanks for thinking of the salve, Menolly," he said when he got his voice under control. "It certainly wouldn't do to annoy Lessa right now, and I do have to be at this Hatching."

"Indeed you do."

Her tone was loaded but he'd no time to figure out what she meant as Ruth took them up and, with no further direction, *between* to Benden Weyr. No, he wouldn't let her rouse him. But she was bloody clever, this Harper girl.

Ruth came out of *between* midsyllable. ". . . uth. I'm Ruth. I'm Ruth."

Which reminded Jaxom and he twisted his head about to look at Menolly's left shoulder.

"Don't worry. They're safely in Brekke's weyr."

"All of them?"

"Shells, no, Jaxom. Only Beauty and the three bronzes. She may be mating soon and the boys won't leave her alone for a moment." Menolly chuckled again.

"Are all that clutch spoken for?"

"What? Count the eggs before they're laid? Not at all!" Menolly sounded repressive. "Why? You don't want one, do you?"

"Not I."

Menolly burst out laughing at his telling rejoinder and he groaned. Well, let her have her laugh.

"What would I do with a fire-lizard?" he went on to settle her. "I promised Corana I'd see if I could get one for her. She's been very . . . kind to me, you know." He was rewarded by the sound of Menolly's gulp of surprise.

Then she smacked him across the shoulder blade with her closed fist and he winced, then ducked away from her.

"Leave off, Menolly! I've a score on that shoulder, too." He spoke with more irritation than he meant and then cursed himself for reminding her of what he avoided mentioning.

"I am sorry, Jaxom," she said with such contrition that Jaxom was mollified. "How much scoring did you get?"

"Face, shoulder and thigh."

She caught at his other shoulder. "Listen! They're thrumming wildly. And, look, there are candidates entering the Hatching Ground. Can we fly right in?"

Jaxom directed Ruth in through the upper entrance of the Hatching Ground. Bronzes were still bearing visitors to the Ground. As Ruth entered, Jaxom found his gaze going immediately to the spot by the arch where he and Ruth had transferred to return the egg. He felt a sudden surge of pride at his feat.

"I see Robinton, Jaxom. There on the fourth tier. Near the Istan colors. Would you sit with us, Jaxom?" There was an entreaty in her tone, and a slight emphasis that puzzled Jaxom. Who wouldn't want to sit with the Masterharper of Pern?

Ruth angled close to the tier, catching at the ledge with his claws and hovering long enough to permit Menolly and Jaxom to dismount.

As Jaxom settled his tunic before seating himself, he got a good long look at Master Robinton. He could understand Menolly's entreaty. The Harper seemed different. Oh, he had greeted Jaxom and Menolly brightly enough with a smile for his journeyman and a buffet on the shoulder for Jaxom but he had turned back to his own thoughts which, to judge by his expression, were sad. The Masterharper of Pern had a long face, generally mobile with quick expressions and reaction. Now, while the Harper apparently watched the progress of the young candidates as they moved across the warm sands of the Hatching Ground, his face was lined, his deep-set eyes shadowed with fatigue and worry, the skin of his cheeks and chin sagged. He looked old, tired, and bereft. Jaxom was appalled and looked quickly away, avoiding Menolly's gaze because his thoughts must have been all too apparent to the observant Harper girl.

Master Robinton old? Tired, worried, yes. But ageing? A cold emptiness assailed Jaxom's innards. Pern deprived of the humor and wisdom of the Master Harper? Even harder to contemplate was being without his vision and eager curiosity. Resentment replaced the sense of loss as Jaxom found himself, loyal to Robinton's precepts, trying to rationalize this wave of unpalatable reflection.

An urgent thrumming brought his attention back to the Hatching Ground. He'd been to enough Hatchings to realize that Ramoth's presence, when there was no queen egg, was unusual; her attitude was daunting. He wouldn't have wanted to brave her red whirling eyes, or the stabs of her head as she kept poking toward the oncoming candidates. Instead of fanning out so that they loosely circled the rocking eggs, the boys were in a tight group, as if that way they stood a better chance against her attentions.

"I don't envy them," Menolly said to Jaxom in an undertone.

"Will she let them Impress, sir?" Jaxom asked the Harper, momentarily forgetting his awareness of the man's mortality.

"You'd think she was inspecting each one to see if he smelled of the Southern Weyr, wouldn't you?" the Harper replied, his voice light with humor.

Jaxom glanced at him and wondered if there hadn't been some unflattering trick of lighting for the Harper grinned with mischief, very much his customary self.

"I'm not sure I'd care for such a scrutiny right now," he added, giving his left eyebrow a quirk upward.

Menolly coughed, her eyes dancing. Jaxom supposed they'd been South recently and wondered what they had learned.

Shells, he thought, in a sudden sweaty panic, the Southerners *knew* that none of them had returned the egg. Suppose Robinton had found that out?

An angry hiss from the Hatching Ground brought such a reaction from the audience that Jaxom quickly transferred his attention. One of the eggs had split, but Ramoth had moved so protectively over it that none of the candidates dared approach. Mnementh bellowed from his ledge outside and the bronzes within thrummed. Ramoth's head went up, her wings, shimmering gold and green, extended and she warbled a defiant answer. The other bronzes answered her in conciliating tones but Mnementh's bugle was clearly an order.

Ramoth is very upset, Ruth said to Jaxom. The white dragon had discreetly retired to a sunny spot by the Bowl lake. His absence did not keep him from knowing what was happening within the ground. *Mnementh tells her she is being silly. The eggs must Hatch; the Hatchlings must make Impression. Then she will not have to worry about them again. They will be safe with men.*

The croon of the bronzes deepened and Ramoth, still protesting an inevitable cycle of life, stepped slowly away from the eggs. Whereupon one of the older boys who had bravely led the first rank bowed formally to her and then stepped up to the split egg from which a young bronze was emerging, squealing as it tried to balance itself on wobbly legs.

"That boy has good presence of mind," Robinton said, nodding his approbation. He was intent on the scene below. "Just what Ramoth needed, that courtesy. Her eyes are slowing and she's retracting her wings. Good. Good!"

Following the example set, two more of the older candidates bowed to Ramoth and moved quickly toward eggs that had begun rocking violently with the efforts of the Hatchlings to pierce their shells. If subsequent obeisances were jerky or skimped, Ramoth had been mollified although she emitted curious little barks as each dragonet made its Impression.

"Look, he got the bronze! He deserved him!" Robinton said, applauding, as the newly linked pair moved toward the entrance of the Ground.

"Who's the lad?" Menolly asked.

"From Telgar Hold; he's got the build and coloring of the old Lord—and his wits."

"Young Kirnety from Fort Hold has another bronze," Menolly reported, delighted. "I told you he'd do it."

"I have been wrong before and will be again, my dear girl. Infallibility would be a bore," Master Robinton replied equably. "Are there any lads here from Ruatha, Jaxom?"

"Two, but I can't recognize them from this angle."

"It's a good-sized clutch," Robinton replied. "Plenty to choose from."

Jaxom was watching five boys who had circled one large egg covered with green splotches. He caught his breath as the dragonet's head emerged, turning to look at each of the boys as it shook shell fragments from its body. "And many boys disappointed," Jaxom said as the little brown dragon pushed past the five boys, out into the sands, crooning piteously, swinging its head from side to side. What if, Jaxom thought with a pang of cold in his guts, Ruth had not found me suitable? Almost all the candidates had left the Ground when he'd freed Ruth from the overhard shell.

The searching dragonet stumbled, its nose burying into the warm sand. It righted itself, sneezed and cried again. Ramoth called out in warning and the boys nearest her retreated hurriedly. One of them, a darkhaired, long-legged lad whose bony knees were scarred, almost stumbled over the little brown. He caught himself with a wild flailing of his arms, started to back away and then halted, staring at the brown dragon. Impression occurred!

I was there. You were there. We are now together, said Ruth, responding to Jaxom's emotion at that scene. Jaxom blinked away an excess
of moisture that collected in his eyes at that reaffirmation of their bond.

"It's all over so soon," Menolly said, her voice petulant with
regret. "I wish it wouldn't all happen in such a rush!"

"I'd say we'd had quite an afternoon," Robinton stated, gesturing
toward Ramoth. The queen was now glowering at the retreating pairs
and shifting from foreleg to foreleg.

"D'you suppose now that they're all safely Hatched and Impressed, her temper will improve?" Menolly asked.

"And Lessa's as well?" Robinton's lips twitched to suppress his
amusement. "No doubt once Ramoth can be persuaded to eat, both
will feel more charitable."

"I hope so." Menolly's reply was low and fervent, not meant,
Jaxom thought, to be heard by Robinton, for the Harper had turned
to the back of the tiers, evidently looking for someone.

Robinton had heard, however, and gave his journeyman a warm
grin. "Too bad we can't postpone this meeting until the happy res-
toration has occurred."

"Can't I come with you this once?"

"To protect me, Menolly?" The Harper gripped her by the shoulder, smiling affectionately. "No, it's not a general meeting and I cannot
offend by including you."

"He can come . . ." Menolly jerked her thumb at Jaxom, glaring
at him with resentment.

"I can what?"

"You hadn't learned from Lytol that a meeting's been called after
the Impression?" the Harper asked. "Ruatha must attend."

"They couldn't exclude you as Masterharper," said Menolly in a
tight voice.

"Why would they?" Jaxom asked, surprised by Menolly's uncharacteristic defensiveness.

"Because, you dim glow . . ."

"That's enough, Menolly. I appreciate your concern, but all things
come to pass in the fullness of time. My head is neither bloodied or
bowed. Once Ramoth has killed, I'll have no fear of being dragon bait,
either." Robinton patted her shoulder, reassuringly.

The queen was making her way out of the hatching Ground and,
as they watched, she took wing.

"There, you see. She's gone to feed," the Harper said. "I have
nothing to fear anymore."

Menolly gave him a long sardonic look. "I just wish I could be
with you, that's all."

"I know. Ah, Fandarel." The Harper raised his voice and waved to catch the eye of the big Mastersmith. "Come, Lord Jaxom, we've business in the Council Chamber."

This must be what Lytol had meant by his being required to attend the Hatching. But oughtn't Lytol to have been there if the meeting was as important as Menolly intimated? Jaxom was flattered by his guardian's confidence.

The two Masters, having met on their way down the tiers, attached other Craftmasters who nodded greetings with more solemnity than a Hatching generally occasioned. Menolly's hint that this was to be an unusual meeting was reinforced. Again Jaxom wondered that Lytol was not here. He had, Jaxom knew, agreed to support Robinton.

"Thought Ramoth was going to prevent Impression for a moment there," Fandarel said, nodding at Jaxom. "Hear you've deserted me for your favorite pastime, huh, lad?"

"Training only, Master Fandarel. All dragons must learn to chew firestone."

"Upon my soul," Masterminer Nicat exclaimed. "Never thought he'd live long enough to do that."

Jaxom caught the Masterharper's warning expression as he was about to reply with some heat, and rephrased his answer. "Ruth is very good at it, thank you."

"One forgets the passage of time, Master Nicat," Robinton said, smoothly, "and that growth and maturity come to those we remember first as very young. Ah, Andemon, how are you today?" The Harper beckoned to the Masterfarmer to join them as they made their way across the hot sands.

Nicat fell in beside Jaxom, chuckling. "Teaching the little white to chew firestone, huh? That wouldn't happen to be why some of our supplies appear short in the morning?"

"Master Nicat, I'm training at Fort Weyr and have all the firestone Ruth needs there."

"Training at Fort Weyr, are you?" Nicat's grin widened as his eyes flicked to Jaxom's cheek, stayed and moved on. "With dragonriders, huh, Lord Jaxom?" There was the barest stress of the title before Nicat looked ahead at the steps up to the queen's weyr and the ledge where Mnementh generally perched.

The bronze had gone off to watch his queen feed in the meadow below. Jaxom looked for the white hide of Ruth by the lake and felt his dragon's mental presence.

"Good Hatching, with a nice bit of suspense for starters, huh?" Nicat said conversationally.

"Did you have any lads on the Ground today?" Jaxom asked politely.

"Only one this time. Two lads had already gone to Telgar's last

Hatching so no complaints. No complaints. Although, if you've a clutch of fire-lizard eggs going a-begging, I wouldn't say no to a couple."

Nicat's gaze was guileless, and it certainly would be no hair off his hide if Jaxom chose to teach Ruth to chew firestone and had appropriated sacks from the mines.

"We've none presently, but you never can tell when a clutch'll be found."

"I only mention it in passing. They're pure death for those pesky, ruinous tunnel snakes, not to mention being very clever about discovering gas pockets *we* don't smell. And gas pockets are about all we're mining at present."

The Masterminer sounded depressed and worried. Jaxom wondered what was in the air these days to produce such a general atmosphere of anxiety and sorrow. He'd always liked Master Nicat and, during their lessons in the mines, had come to respect the short heavyset craftmaster whose face was still black-pored from working as an apprentice below the ground. As they climbed the stone steps to the queen's weyr, Jaxom wished again that he wasn't bound by that promise to N'ton not to time it. He had too many demands on ordinary daytime to risk a hop *between* to the Southern beaches although Ruth might be lucky enough to locate a clutch quickly. He would like to oblige Master Nicat; he'd also like to find an egg for Corana. It also wouldn't hurt to indulge the disgruntled Tegger, who might have learned how to keep a fire-lizard now. But there was no way, short of timing it, that Jaxom could complete a trip south right now.

Just as they reached the entrance, a bronze dragon appeared above the Star Stones, bugling. The watchdragon replied. Jaxom noticed that everyone had stopped stock still to hear the exchange. Shells and shards, but they were nervous here in Benden. He wondered who had arrived.

The Weyrleader from Ista, Ruth told him.

D'ram? It wasn't incumbent on other Weyrleaders to attend Hatchings, though generally, unless Threadfall was imminent in their own area, they did come—especially to Benden. Jaxom had already spotted N'ton, R'mart of Telgar Weyr, G'narish of Igen, T'bor of the High Reaches among those gathered. Then he remembered the Master Harper's talk about D'ram's Weyrwoman, Fanna. Was she worse?

When they reached the Council Chamber, Nicat parted from him. Jaxom took one look at Lessa, seated in the Weyrwoman's huge stone chair, her face intense in its frown, and he quickly moved to the far corner of the room. Her keen eyes wouldn't be able to spot the score on his cheek at that distance.

This was not to be a large meeting, the Harper had said. Jaxom watched the Mastercraftsmen file in, the other Weyrleaders, the major

Lord Holders, but there were no weyrwomen or wing-seconds except for Brekke and F'nor.

D'ram arrived in the company of F'lar and a younger man Jaxom didn't recognize though he wore wing-second colors. If Jaxom had been upset by the glimpse of the Masterharper's ageing, he was shocked by the change in D'ram's appearance. The man seemed to have shrunk in the past Turn to a husk, dried up and frail. The Istan Weyrleader's step was jerky and his shoulders rounded.

Lessa rose in one of her swift graceful gestures and went to meet the Istan, her hands outstretched, her expression unexpectedly compassionate. Jaxom had had the impression that she had been totally immersed in her brooding. Now, all her attention was centered on D'ram.

"We're all assembled as you asked, D'ram," Lessa said, pulling him to the chair beside her and pouring him a cup of wine.

D'ram thanked her for the wine and welcome, took a sip but, instead of seating himself, he turned to face the meeting. Jaxom could see that his face was marred by lines of fatigue as well as of age.

"Most of you already know my situation and Fanna's . . . illness," he said in a low hesitant voice. He cleared his throat, took a deep breath. "I wish to step down now as Istan Weyrleader. None of our queens is due to mate but I have no heart to continue longer. My Weyr has agreed. G'dened," and D'ram indicated the man who had accompanied him, "has led the past ten Falls on his Barnath. I should have stepped down sooner but . . ." he shook his head, smiling sadly, "we so hoped the illness would pass." He straightened his shoulders with an effort. "Caylith is oldest queen and Cosira a good Weyrwoman. Barnath has flown Caylith already and there's been a large strong clutch to prove them." Now he hesitated, glancing warily at Lessa. "It was the custom in the Oldtime, when a Weyr was leaderless, to throw open the first queen's flight in that Weyr to all young bronzes. In this fashion a new leader was fairly chosen. I would invoke that custom now." He said it almost belligerently and yet his manner toward Lessa was entreating.

"You must be very sure of G'dened's Barnath then," R'mart of Telgar Weyr said in a disgusted tone of voice that rose over the startled murmurs.

G'dened, grinning broadly, managed to avoid meeting anyone's glance.

"I want the best leadership for Ista," D'ram said, stiffly, resenting R'mart's implication of a token flight. "G'dened has proved his competence to my satisfaction. But he ought to prove it to everyone's."

"That's fairly put." F'lar rose to his feet, holding up his hands for silence. "I don't doubt G'dened has a good chance, R'mart, but D'ram's offer is exceedingly generous at this critical time. I'll inform all my bronze riders but I, for one, will permit only those whose drag-ons haven't yet had a chance to mate with a queen. I don't think it's fair to pile too many odds against Barnath, now is it?"

"Isn't Caylith a Benden queen?" Lord Corman of Keroon Hold asked.

"No, she's one of Mirath's laying. Pirith is the Benden Hatched queen."

"Caylith's an Oldtimer queen?"

"Caylith is an Istan queen," F'lar said firmly but quickly.

"And G'dened?"

"I was born in the old time," the man said in a quiet voice but the expression he turned to Lord Corman bore no trace of apology.

"He is also a son of D'ram," Lord Warbret of Ista Hold said, speaking directly to Lord Corman as if that qualification should ease the Holder's tacit objection.

"Good man. Good blood," Corman replied, not at all ruffled.

"His leadership is in question, not his bloodline," F'lar said. "The custom is a good one . . ."

Jaxom clearly heard someone remark that it was the only good Oldtime custom he'd ever heard about, and he hoped that the low whisper hadn't carried far.

"D'ram would be within his right to keep to the Weyr for lead-ership," F'lar continued, addressing the craftmasters and Lord Hold-ers. "I, for one, deeply appreciate his offer and the willingness of the Weyr to open the mating flight."

"I only want the best leadership for my Weyr," D'ram repeated. "This is the only way to be certain Ista gets it. The only way, the only right way."

Jaxom suppressed the urge to cheer and glanced about the room, willing the reactions to be favorable. All the Weyrleaders seemed to agree. As they should, since one of their riders might gain from it. Jaxom hoped that G'dened's Barnath would fly Caylith anyhow. That would prove there was good metal in the younger Oldtimers. No one would be able to say anything against Ista leadership once it was proved by competition!

"I have stated Ista's intention," D'ram said, raising his tired voice over the murmur of individual conversations. "It is the will of my Weyr. I must go back now. My duty to you, Lords, Masters, Weyrleaders, all."

He gave a quick sweeping nod to everyone, bowed more formally to Lessa, who rose, touched his arm in sympathy and let him pass.

To Jaxom's surprise and elation, everyone rose as D'ram left, but the Istan Weyrleader's head remained down. Jaxom wondered if he'd been aware of that spontaneous show of respect and felt a lump rise in his throat.

"I will take my leave as well, in case I'm needed," G'dened said, bowing formally to Benden's leaders and the others.

"G'dened?" Lessa incorporated a wealth of question in his name.

The man shook his head slowly. "I will inform all the Weyrs when Caylith is ready to fly." He quickly followed D'ram.

As the sound of his footsteps diminished down the corridor, voices began to rise. The Lord Holders weren't certain they approved of such an innovation. The Craftmasters were apparently divided, though Jaxom rather thought Robinton had known of D'ram's decision and was neutral. The Weyrleaders expressed complete satisfaction.

"Hope Fanna doesn't expire today," Jaxom heard a Craftmaster murmur to his neighbor. "A death at a Hatching is a bad sign."

"Besides spoiling the feast. I wonder just how strong G'dened's bronze is. Now if a Benden bronze rider got into Ista . . ."

Speaking of the feast reminded Jaxom that his stomach was roiling for lack of food. He'd been up early for his training as usual, and had had no more than time to change into good clothing at his Hold so he began to sidle to the exit. He could always coax a meatroll or a sweetbread from one of the Lower Cavern women to stay his hunger.

"Is this all the meeting there is?" Lord Begamon of Nerat Hold asked, his rasping voice falling into a momentary silence. He sounded peevish. "Haven't the Weyrs yet found out who took the egg? Even who returned it? That's what I thought we'd hear today."

"The egg was returned, Lord Begamon," F'lar said, extending his hand to Lessa.

"I know the egg was returned. I was right here when it happened. Was at its Hatching, too."

F'lar continued to lead Lessa down the length of the room.

"This is another Hatching, Lord Begamon," F'lar said. "A happy occasion for all of us. There will be wine below." And the two Weyrleaders had left the room.

"I don't understand." Begamon turned in confusion to the man beside him. "I thought we'd learn something today."

"You did," F'nor said, guiding Brekke past him. "That D'ram is stepping down as Weyrleader at Ista."

"That doesn't concern me," Begamon was growing more, rather than less, annoyed with the replies he was getting.

"That concerns you more than any puzzle over the egg," F'nor said as he and Brekke left the room.

"I think that's all the answer you're going to get," Robinton said to Begamon, a wry smile on his face.

"But . . . but aren't they doing anything about it? They're not just letting the Oldtimers insult them like that and not doing something?"

"Unlike Lord Holders," N'ton said, coming forward, "dragon-

riders are not free to indulge their passions or honors at the expense
of their primary duty, which is to protect all of Pern from Thread. *That*
is the important occupation of dragonriders, Lord Begamon."

"C'mon, Begamon," Lord Groghe of Fort Hold said as he took
the man by the arm. "It's Weyr business, not ours, you know. Can't
interfere. Shouldn't. They know what they're doing. And the egg was
returned. Too bad about D'ram's woman. Hate to see him go. Sensible
fellow. F'lar didn't say but it must be Benden wine."

Jaxom saw Lord Groghe searching the faces about him.

"Ah, Harper, it ought to be Benden wine here?"

The Harper agreed and left the Council room in the company of
the two Lords, Begamon still protesting the lack of information. Jaxom
followed them out as the room was clearing. When he got to the base
of the weyr steps, Menolly pounced on him.

"Well, what happened? Did they speak to him at all?"

"Did who speak to whom?"

"Did F'lar or Lessa address the Harper?"

"No reason why they would."

"Plenty of reason why they wouldn't. What happened?"

Jaxom sighed for patience with her as he rapidly reviewed what
had occurred.

"D'ram came here to ask—no, to tell them that he's stepping
down as Istan Weyrleader . . ." Menolly nodded encouragingly as if
this were no news to her. "And he said he was invoking an Oldtime
custom to throw the first queen's mating flight open to all bronzes."

Menolly's eyes widened and she made her mouth round with
surprise. "That must have rocked 'em back on their heels. Any
protests?"

"From the Lord Holders, yes." Jaxom grinned. "From the other
Weyrleaders, no. Except that R'mart made a snide remark about
G'dened being so strong there'd be no contest."

"I don't know G'dened, but he's a son of D'ram's."

"That doesn't always mean anything."

"True."

"D'ram kept saying that he wanted the best leadership for Ista
Weyr and this was the way to achieve it."

"Poor D'ram . . ."

"Poor Fanna, you mean."

"No, poor D'ram. Poor us. He was very strong as a leader. Did
Master Robinton speak at all?" she asked then, throwing off her reflections on D'ram for the more important consideration.

"He spoke to Begamon."

"Not to the Weyrleaders?"

"No reason to. Why?"

"They've been such close friends for so long . . . and they're so unfair about it. He had to speak up. Dragons can't fight dragons."

To which Jaxom stoutly agreed, his comment echoed by a rumble from his stomach so audible that Menolly glared at him. Jaxom was torn between embarrassment and amusement at such an internal betrayal. The laughter won and, even as he apologized to Menolly, he could see that the incident had triggered her sense of the ridiculous.

"Oh, come on. I won't get any sense out of you until you've eaten."

It was not the most memorable of Hatching feasts nor particularly merry. A restraint touched the dragonriders. Jaxom did not try to figure out how much was due to D'ram's resignation or how much to the theft of the egg. He preferred not to hear any more about that. He was uncomfortable in Menolly's company because he couldn't put aside his feeling that she knew he'd brought the egg back. The fact that she said nothing about her suspicions worried him more because he also felt that she was leaving him in suspense on purpose. He didn't particularly wish to share a table with F'lessan and Mirrim, who might notice the Threadscore. Benelek was not his choice of a companion at any time and he certainly wouldn't have been at ease taking the place at the main tables to which his rank entitled him. Menolly had been dragged away from him by Oharan, the Weyr's Harper, and he could hear them singing. Had there been new music he might have stayed by them, just to be part of some group. But the Lord Holders were asking for their favorite songs and so were the proud parents of boys who had Impressed.

Ruth was enjoying the emotional feast of the newly Hatched dragons but he did miss the ministrations of the fire-lizards.

They don't like being cooped up in Brekke's weyr, Ruth told his rider. *Why can't they come out? Ramoth's asleep with a very full belly. She wouldn't even know.*

"Don't be too sure of that," Jaxom said, glancing up at Mnementh, curled on the queen's ledge, his softly glowing eyes bright points on the other side of the darkening Weyr Bowl.

The outcome was that he and Ruth left the feast as soon after eating as courtesy permitted. While they were circling in to Ruatha Hold Jaxom began to worry about Lytol. His guardian would be extremely upset when Fanna died and her queen suicided. He wished he didn't have to bring the news of D'ram's resignation. He knew that Lytol respected the Oldtimer. He wondered what Lytol's reaction would be to the open mating flight.

Lytol merely grunted, gave a sharp nod of his head and asked Jaxom if any further development over the theft of the egg had been discussed. For Jaxom's recital of Lord Begamon's complaint, Lytol issued another sort of grunt, disgusted and contemptuous. Then he asked if there were any fire-lizard eggs available; two more small holders had been pressing him for eggs. Jaxom said he'd ask N'ton in the morning.

"Considering the bad odor of fire-lizards, I wonder anyone wants them," the Fort Weyrleader remarked the next day when Jaxom told him his errand. "Or maybe that's why there's so many requests. Everyone is convinced no one else will want 'em, so they get in there now. No, I don't have any. But I wanted to speak with you. Fort Weyr flies with the High Reaches Weyr tomorrow during the northernly Fall. If it were over Ruatha, I'd ask you to join the weyrling wing. As it is, I'd better not. Can you understand?"

Jaxom allowed that he could, but did N'ton mean that he would be able to fight Ruth the next time Thread was over Ruatha.

"I discussed it with Lytol." N'ton grinned, his eyes twinkling. "Lytol's reasoning is that you'd be so far above ground no Ruathan would realize his Lord Holder was risking his life and word wouldn't get back to Benden."

"I risk my life and limbs far more surely on the ground with that flamethrower crew."

"Quite likely, but we still don't want someone blurting the truth out to Lessa and F'lar. I've had a good report of you from K'nebel. Ruth is all you told me he could be—fast, clever and unusually quick in the air." N'ton grinned again. "Between you and me, K'nebel says the little beast changes direction on his tail. His chief concern is that some of the others might get the notion that their dragons can do the same thing, and we'd have riders coming adrift."

So the following morning, while the Weyr dealt with falling Thread, Jaxom hunted Ruth and then directed him to the lake for a good scrub and swim. While the fire-lizards were grooming Ruth's neck ridges, Jaxom did a careful brushing of the scar on his leg.

Suddenly the white dragon whimpered. Apologetic, Jaxom looked around and noticed that the fire-lizards had suspended their labors. All the animals had their heads cocked, as if listening to something beyond Jaxom's hearing.

"What's the matter, Ruth?"

The woman dies.

"Take me back to the Hold, Ruth. Hurry."

Jaxom gritted his teeth as his wet clothing froze against his body in the cold of *between*. Teeth chattering, Jaxom glanced toward the watchdragon on the fire-heights. Strangely enough, the beast was indolent in the sun when he ought to be responding to the death.

Now *she is not yet dying,* Ruth said.

It took Jaxom a moment to realize that Ruth had acted on his own initiative and timed it to just before the fire-lizards' alarm at the lake.

"We promised not to time it, Ruth." Jaxom could appreciate the circumstances but he didn't like the notion of going back on his word for any reason.

You promised. I did not. Lytol will need you in time.

Ruth landed Jaxom in the courtyard and the young Lord pelted up the stairs to the main Hall. He startled the drudge who was sweeping the dining hall with a demand to know Lytol's whereabouts. The drudge thought Lord Lytol was with Master Brand. Jaxom knew that Brand kept wine in his office but he ducked into the serving hall, grabbed up a wineskin by its thong, swept two cups into his other hand and strode to the steps of the inner hall, which he took two at a time. Catching the heavy inner door with the point of his shoulder, he worked the latch with his right elbow and continued without much loss of forward speed down the corridor to Brand's quarters.

Just as he threw open the door, Brand's little blue fire-lizard struck the very listening pose that had alerted Jaxom at the lake.

"What's the matter, Lord Jaxom?" Brand cried, rising to his feet. Lytol's face showed his disapproval of such a mannerless entrance and he was about to speak when Jaxom pointed to the fire-lizard.

The blue suddenly sat back on his haunches, opened his wings and began the shrill high ululation that was the keening of the fire-lizards. As all color drained from Lytol's face, the men heard the deeper, equally piercing cries of the watchdragon and Ruth, each giving voice to the passing of a queen dragon.

Jaxom splashed wine in a cup and held it to Lytol.

"It doesn't stop the pain, I know," he said in a rough tone, "but you can get drunk enough not to hear or remember."

•• C H A P T E R I X ••

Early Summer, Harpercraft and Ruatha Hold, 15.7.3

The first hint Robinton had was from Zair, who woke abruptly from a sound morning's sleep in the sun on the window ledge and flew to Robinton's shoulder, wrapping his tail firmly about the Harper's neck. Robinton, not having the heart to rebuke his friend, tried to ease the tension of the tail so that he didn't have the sensation of choking to death. Zair rubbed his cheek against the Harper's, crooning.

"Whatever is the matter with you?"

Just then the watchdragon on the fire-heights rose to his haunches and bugled. A dragon appeared in midair, answered the summons smartly before beginning a circle to land.

A knock on the door was followed so closely by its opening that the courtesy was hardly observed. Robinton was forming a reprimand as he slewed round in his chair and saw Menolly, with Beauty clinging tightly to her shoulder, Rocky, Diver and Poll doing an aerial dance about her.

"It's F'lar and Mnementh," she cried.

"So I had just perceived, my dear. Why the panic?"

"Panic? I'm not in a panic. I'm excited. This is the first time since the egg was taken that Benden has come to you."

"Then be a polite child and see if Silvina has any sweetbreads to eat with our *klah*. It is," he sighed wistfully, "a shade too early in the morning to offer wine."

"It's not too early in Benden's morning," Menolly said as she left the room.

Robinton sighed again, sadly, as he looked at the empty doorway.

She had grieved over the estrangement of the Harper Hall and Benden Weyr. So, in his own way, had he. He brought his thoughts sharply away from that. There'd been no hint of distress in Mnementh's acknowledgement of the watchdragon's challenge. What had brought F'lar to Benden? And, more important, did the Weyrleader come with Lessa's knowledge? And consent?

Mnementh had landed now. F'lar would be striding across the meadow. Robinton began to twitch with more impatience for that final walk than he had felt during the four sevendays of coolness between Weyr and Hall.

Robinton rose and paced to the window just as F'lar entered the inner courtyard of the Crafthall. He was walking with long strides, but F'lar always did, so there did not seem to be any haste in his errand. Then why was he coming to the Hall?

F'lar spoke to a journeyman, who was packing a runner for a trip. Fire-lizards congregated on the roof. Robinton saw F'lar raise his head and notice them. The Harper briefly considered whether he ought to ask Zair to leave while F'lar was present. No sense firing resentment of any consequence right now.

F'lar had entered the Hall. Through the open window, Robinton could hear the Weyrleader's voice and the pause for an answer. Silvina? More likely his journeyman, he thought, smiling to himself, lying in wait for the Weyrleader. Yes, he was right. He could hear Menolly's voice and F'lar's as they came up the stairs. The sounds of the voices were unmarked by emotion. Good girl! Easy does it.

"Ah, Robinton, Menolly informs me that her fire-lizards refer to Mnementh as 'the biggest one,'" F'lar said with a slight smile on his face as he entered the room.

"They're chary of awarding accolades, F'lar," Robinton replied, taking the tray from Menolly, who withdrew, closing the door. Not that her absence precluded her knowing what would happen, not with Beauty attuned to Zair.

"There's no trouble at Benden, is there?" Robinton asked the Weyrleader as he handed him a cup of klah.

"No, no trouble." Robinton waited. "But there is a puzzle that I thought you might be able to answer for us."

"If I can, I will," the Harper said, gesturing to F'lar to seat himself.

"We can't find D'ram."

"D'ram?" Robinton almost laughed in surprise. "Why can't you find D'ram?"

"He's alive. We know that much. We don't know where."

"Surely Ramoth could touch Tiroth?"

F'lar shook his head. "Perhaps I should have said *when*."

"When? D'ram's timed it somewhere? I mean, somewhen?"

"That's the only explanation. And we can't see how he could

possibly have gone *back* to his own Time. We don't believe that Tiroth has that much strength in him. Timing it, as you know, is very draining on both dragon and rider. But D'ram has gone."

"That's not unexpected surely," Robinton said slowly, his mind turning rapidly over the possiblities of *when*.

"No, not unexpected."

"He wouldn't have gone to the Southern Weyr?"

"No, because Ramoth would have no trouble locating him there. And G'dened went back quite a distance, before Threadfall, at Ista itself, thinking D'ram would stay where his memories are."

"Lord Warbret offered D'ram any one of those caves on the south side of Ista Island. He seemed agreeable." Then as F'lar's shrug negated that suggestion, the Harper added, "Yes, he was too agreeable."

F'lar rose, striding restlessly about, turning back to the Harper. "Have you any ideas where the man could have gone? You were with him a great deal. Can you remember anything?"

"He wasn't talking very much toward the end, just sat there holding Fanna's hand." Robinton found that he needed to swallow. As accustomed as he was to mortality, D'ram's devotion to his Weyrwoman and his silent grief at her death had the power to bring tears to the Harper's eyes. "I tendered offers of hospitality to him from Groghe and Sangel. In fact, I gather he could have gone anywhere on Pern and been welcome. Obviously he prefers the company of his memories. Might I ask if there is any reason to know where he is?"

"No reason other than our concern for him."

"Oldive said that he was completely in possession of his reason, F'lar, if that's your worry."

F'lar made a grimace and impatiently stroked back a forelock which invariably fell into his eyes when he was agitated. "Frankly, Robinton, it's Lessa. Ramoth can't find Tiroth. Lessa's certain he's gone far enough back in time to suicide without giving us distress. It's in D'ram's nature to do so."

"It is also his option," Robinton said gently.

"I know. I know. And no one would fault him but Lessa is very worried. D'ram may have stepped down, Robinton, but his knowledge, his opinions are valuable and valued. Right now more than ever. Bluntly we need him . . . need him available to us."

Robinton thought briefly about the possibility that D'ram had realized this and deliberately removed himself and Tiroth from easy access. But D'ram would serve Pern, and dragonfolk at any time.

"He perhaps needs time to recover from his grief, F'lar."

"He was worn out with tending Fanna. You know that. He could also be sick and who would be there to help? We're both worried."

"I hesitate to suggest this, but has Brekke tried with the fire-lizards? Hers as well as those at Ista Weyr."

A grin tugged at the worried line of F'lar's mouth. "Oh, yes. She insisted. No luck. The fire-lizards need a direction to go *between* time just like dragons."

"I didn't exactly mean sending them. I mean, asking them to *remember* a lone bronze dragon."

"Asking those creatures to *remember?*" F'lar laughed with incredulity.

"I'm serious, F'lar. They have good memories which can be triggered. For instance, how could the fire-lizards have known that the Red Star . . ." He was interrupted by a squeal of protest from Zair, who launched himself so quickly from Robinton's shoulder that he scratched the Harper's neck. "I will mention it in his presence!" Robinton said, ruefully patting the scratch. "My point is, F'lar, that the fire-lizards all knew that the Red Star was dangerous and could not be reached *before* F'nor and Canth tried to go there. If you can get a fire-lizard to make any sense when you mention the Red Star, they say they remember being afraid of it. They? Or their ancestors when our ancestors first attempted to go to it?"

F'lar gave the Masterharper a long searching stare.

"That isn't the first memory of theirs that has proved to be accurate," Robinton went on. "Master Andemon believes that it's entirely possible that these creatures can remember unusual events that one of their number has witnessed or felt. Instinct plays a part with all animals—why not in their memories, too?"

"I'm not sure I see how you intend to get this—this fire-lizard memory to work in helping to find D'ram, whenever he's got to."

"Simple. Ask them to remember seeing a lone dragon. That would be unusual enough to be noted . . . and remembered."

F'lar was not convinced it would work.

"Oh, I think so if we ask Ruth to ask them."

"Ruth?"

"When every fire-lizard was scared to death of the other dragons, they beleaguered Ruth. Jaxom's told me that they talk with his white wherever they are. With so many, there's bound to be one that might remember what we want to know."

"If I could relieve Lessa's fears, I'd even forget my antipathy to those nuisances."

"I trust you'll remember that statement." Robinton grinned to soften the remark.

"Will you come with me to Ruatha Hold?"

In that moment, Robinton remembered Jaxom's Threadscoring. Of course, it would be long healed. But he couldn't remember if N'ton had ever discussed Jaxom's training with Benden Weyr.

"Shouldn't we find out if Jaxom's at the Hold?"

"Why wouldn't he be?" F'lar asked, frowning.

"Because he's often about the Hold, learning the land, or at Fandarel's with the other young people."

"A point." F'lar looked away from the Harper, out the window, his eyes unfocused. "No, Mnementh says Ruth's at the Hold. See, I have my own message sender," F'lar added with a grin.

Robinton hoped that Ruth would think to tell Jaxom that Mnementh had bespoken him. He wished that he'd had time to send Zair with a message to Ruatha but he had no excuse and certainly no wish to jeopardize this gesture of F'lar's.

"More reliable than mine and farther reaching than Fandarel's little wire." Robinton donned the thick wherhide jacket and helmet he used when flying. "Speaking of Fandarel, he's got his lines as far as Crom's mines, you know." He gestured F'lar to precede him out of the room.

"Yes, I know. That's another reason to locate D'ram."

"It is?"

F'lar laughed at the Harper's bland question, a laugh that held no constraint so that Robinton sincerely hoped that this visit mended their relationship.

"Hasn't Nicat been at you, too, Robinton? To go south to those mines?"

"The ones Toric's been trading from?"

"I thought you'd know."

"Yes, I know that Nicat's worried about mining. The ores are getting very poor. Fandarel's a good sight more worried than Nicat. He needs the better quality metals."

"Once we allow the Crafts into the South, the Lord Holders will press for entry . . ." F'lar instinctively lowered his voice though the courtyard they were crossing was empty.

"The Southern Continent is large enough to take all of Northern Pern and rattle it. Why, we've only touched the fringes of it, F'lar. Great Shells and Shards!" Robinton slapped his forehead. "Talk about fire-lizards and associative memories. That's it! That's where D'ram has gone."

"Where?"

"At least I think that's where he might have gone."

"Speak, man. Where?"

"The problem is still when, I fancy. And Ruth is still our key."

They had only several dragonlengths to go before they reached Mnementh in the meadow. Zair fluttered above Robinton's head, chittering anxiously well away from the bronze dragon. He refused to alight on Robinton's shoulder, though the Harper gestured for him to land.

"I'm going to Ruatha to the white dragon, to Ruth. Join us there, then, you silly creature, if you won't ride on my shoulder."

"Mnementh doesn't mind Zair," F'lar said.

"It's still the other way round, I'm afraid," Robinton said.

A hint of anger danced in the bronze rider's eyes. "No dragon flamed a fire-lizard."

"Not here, Weyrleader, not here. But all of them remember seeing it happen. And fire-lizards can only tell what they or one of them have actually seen."

"Then let's get to Ruatha and see if one of them has seen D'ram."

So the fire-lizards were still tender subjects, thought Robinton sadly as he climbed up Mnementh's shoulder to sit behind F'lar. He wished that Zair had not been so wary of Mnementh.

Jaxom and Lytol stood on the Hold steps as Mnementh bugled his name to the watchdragon and circled to land in the huge courtyard. As the two visitors were being greeted, Robinton scanned Jaxom's face to see if the Threadscore was obvious. He couldn't see a trace of it and wondered if he was examining the right cheek. He could only hope that Ruth had healed as well. Of course, F'lar was so involved with this business of D'ram he wouldn't be looking for scoring on Ruth or Jaxom.

"Ruth said Mnementh inquired for him, F'lar," Jaxom said. "I trust nothing is wrong?"

"Ruth may be able to help us find D'ram."

"Find D'ram? He hasn't . . ." Jaxom paused, looking anxiously at Lytol, who was frowning and shaking his head.

"No, but he has timed it somewhen," Robinton said. "I thought perhaps if Ruth asked the fire-lizards, they might tell him."

Jaxom stared at the Harper, who wondered why the lad looked so stunned and, curiously, scared. Robinton did not miss the quick flick of Jaxom's eyes toward F'lar nor the convulsive swallowing.

"I remembered hearing you comment that fire-lizards often tell Ruth things," Robinton went on in a casual manner, giving Jaxom time to recover his composure. Whatever was bothering the boy?

"Where? Possibly. But when, Master Robinton?"

"I've a hunch I know where D'ram went. Would that help?"

"I'm not sure I understand," Lytol said, looking from one to the other. "What's this all about?" Lytol had been guiding the visitors into the Hold and toward the small private room. Wine and cups had been set on the table, together with cheese, bread and fruits.

"Well," Robinton said, eyeing the wineskin, "I'll explain . . ."

"And you'll be dry, I'm sure," Jaxom said, as he strode to the table to pour. "It's Benden wine, Master Robinton. Only the best for our distinguished visitors."

"The lad's growing up, Lytol," F'lar said, taking the cup and raising it approvingly toward Lytol.

"The lad has grown up," Lytol said in a half-growl. "Now, about those fire-lizards . . ."

Zair appeared midair, squealed and swooped to Robinton's shoulder, wrapping his tail tightly about the Harper's neck and chittering in a nervous tone as he reassured himself that Robinton had taken no harm riding the biggest one.

"Pardon me," Robinton said, and soothed Zair to silence. Then he explained to Lytol his theory that fire-lizards shared a vast pool of common knowledge which would explain their fear of—he cleared his throat and pointed east to spare them all his bronze's antics. Fire-lizards were able to communicate strong emotions as evidenced by Brekke's call to Canth that fateful night. They had had this fright about the queen's egg and all had been in a high state of turmoil until the egg had Hatched properly. They seemed to remember seeing it near a black nothingness, and they seemed to remember being flamed. Jaxom had told him on several occasions that the fire-lizards regaled Ruth with incredible things they said they'd remembered seeing. If this curious talent of theirs was not the sun-dreams of silly creatures—he had to placate an outraged Zair—then here was a case in which it could be proved, with Ruth's cooperation. D'ram had apparently gone off on his own, to a time when Ramoth could not reach the mind of his dragon. It was upsetting Ramoth and Lessa, who were worried that D'ram might be in physical distress. Despite his resignation as Weyrleader, Pern still had a need of and a place for D'ram and certainly did not wish to lose contact with him.

"Now," Robinton went on, "there have been occasions in recent Turns . . ." He cleared his throat, glanced toward F'lar for permission and received the nod. ". . . occasions when I have ventured South. On one such instance, Menolly and I were blown off course, far to the east where we came to rest in a beautiful cove, white-sanded, with red fruit trees abounding; the waters of the cove teemed with yellowtail and white fingerfish. The sun was warm and the waters of a stream just inland was sweet as wine." He looked into his cup wistfully. With a laugh, Jaxom refilled it. "I told D'ram of it, I've forgotten why now. I'm reasonably certain I described it well enough for a dragon of Tiroth's abilities to find his way there."

"D'ram would not wish to cause complications here," Lytol said slowly. "He'd have gone to a time when the Oldtimers were not in the South. A jump back of ten-twelve Turns wouldn't overtax Tiroth."

"A point, Robinton, that might complicate matters," F'lar said. "If these creatures can remember significant events that happened to their predecessors"—and F'lar was patently skeptical—"then none of the fire-lizards here could possibly have any recollections for our purpose. No ancestors from the area." He indicated Zair. "He's from that clutch Menolly brought up from below Half-Circle Sea Hold, isn't he?"

"Fire-lizards from all over converge on Ruth," Robinton said, looking to the young Lord for corroboration.

"F'lar has made a good point," Jaxom said.

"Not if you go to that cove, Jaxom. I'm sure the fatal fascination fire-lizards all have for Ruth will operate even there."

"You want me to go to the Southern Continent?"

Robinton noted the incredulity and sudden start of intense interest in Jaxom's eyes. So, the boy had discovered that flying a fire-breathing dragon was not enough to keep him content with his life.

"I don't *want* anyone to go South," F'lar replied, "since that . . . is a breach of our agreement, but I can't see any other way of locating D'ram."

"The cove is a long way from the Southern Weyr," Robinton said gently, "and we know the Oldtimers don't venture far from it."

"They ventured far enough from it a little while ago, didn't they?" Weyr asked with considerable heat in his voice and an angry shine in his amber eyes.

Wearily Robinton saw that the breach between Harper Hall and Benden Weyr was only thinly healed.

"Lord Lytol," the Benden Weyrleader continued, "I am remiss. May we have your permission to recruit Jaxom to this search?"

Lytol shook his head and gestured toward Jaxom. "It is entirely up to Lord Jaxom."

Robinton could see F'lar digesting the implications of that referral, and he gave Jaxom a long keen look. Then he smiled. "And your answer, Lord Jaxom?"

With commendable poise, Robinton thought, the young man inclined his head. "I'm flattered to be asked to assist, Weyrleader."

"You don't happen to have any maps of the Southern Continent in this Hold, do you?" asked F'lar.

"As a matter of fact, I do." Then Jaxom added a hasty explanation. "Fandarel gave us several sessions of chartmaking at his Hall."

The charts were, however, incomplete. F'lar recognized them as copies of F'nor's original explorations of the Southern Continent when the Benden Wingsecond had taken Ramoth's first clutch back ten Turns to mature before Thread would fall again—an undertaking marked by partial success.

"I have more comprehensive maps of the coastline," Robinton said casually and scribbled a note to Menolly which he attached to the clasp on Zair's collar. He sent the little bronze back to the Harper Hold with an entreaty not to forget his errand.

"And he'll bring the charts back directly?" F'lar asked, skeptical and somewhat contemptuous. "Brekke and F'nor keep trying to convince me of their usefulness, too."

"I suspect with something as important as the charts, Menolly will wheedle the watchdragon into bringing her." Robinton sighed, wishing he'd thought to insist she return the charts by fire-lizard. No opportunity should be wasted.

"How much timing it have you done, Jaxom?" F'lar asked suddenly.

A flush suffused Jaxom's face. With a start, Robinton saw the thin line of scar white against the reddened cheek. Luckily that side of Jaxom's face was turned away from the Weyrleader.

"Well, sir . . ."

"Come, lad, I don't know any young dragonrider who hasn't used the trick to be on time. What I want to establish is how accurate Ruth's time sense is. Some dragons don't have any at all."

"Ruth always knows when he is," Jaxom replied with quick pride. "I'd say he has the best time memory on Pern."

F'lar considered that for a long moment. "Have you ever tried any long jumps?"

Jaxom nodded slowly, his eyes flicking to Lytol whose face remained impassive.

"No wavering of the leap? No unduly long stay *between?*"

"No, sir. It's easy to be accurate anyhow if you jump at night."

"I'm not sure I follow that reasoning."

"Those star equations that Wansor worked out. I think you were at that session in the Smithcrafthall . . ." The young man's voice trailed off uncertainly until F'lar caught his drift and looked his surprise. "If you work out the position of the dominant stars in the skies, you can position yourself most accurately."

"If you jump at night," the Masterharper added, never having thought to put that use to Wansor's equations.

"Never occurred to me to do that," F'lar said.

"There is a precedent," Robinton remarked, grinning, "in your own Weyr, F'lar."

"Lessa used the stars from the tapestry to go back for the Old-timers, didn't she?" Jaxom had clearly forgotten that, and also, to judge by the sudden comic dismay on his face, forgotten that his reference to the Oldtimers was not adroit.

"We can't ignore them, can we?" the Weyrleader said with more tolerance than Robinton had anticipated. "Well, they exist and can't be ignored. To the present problem, Robinton. How long is it likely to take your fire-lizard?"

Just outside the Hold window a multivoiced squabbling arose, so obviously that of fire-lizards that they all hurried to the window.

"Menolly did it," Robinton said in an undertone to Jaxom. "They're here, F'lar."

"Who? Menolly with the watchdragon?"

"No, sir," Jaxom said, his voice triumphant, "Zair, and Menolly's queen and her three bronzes. They've all got charts strapped to their backs."

Zair flew in, chittering in a combination of anger, concern and confusion. Menolly's four followed. The little queen, Beauty, started scolding all of them as she circled about the room. Robinton easily lured Zair to his arm. But Beauty kept her bronzes in circulation, out of reach, while F'lar, grinning sardonically, and Lytol, expressionless, watched the attempts of Robinton and Jaxom to land the other four fire-lizards.

"Ruth, would you tell Beauty to behave and come to my arm?" Jaxom cried as his futile attempts to coax the little queen began to assume ludicrous proportions in front of someone he was trying to impress.

Beauty let out a startled squawk but immediately came to rest on the table. She scolded Jaxom furiously as he undid the chart. She kept up her monologue as the bronzes timidly landed, not quite furling their wings, to have their burdens removed. Once free of their encumbrances, the bronzes retreated out the window. Beauty gave everyone in the room one final raucous harangue and then, with a flick of her tail, disappeared from sight. Zair let out one sort of apologetic cheep and hid his face in Robinton's hair.

"Well," Robinton said as welcome silence settled on the room, "they did return promptly, didn't they?"

F'lar burst out laughing. "Return, yes. Delivery was another problem. I'd hate to have to argue for every message brought me."

"That was just because Menolly wasn't here," Jaxom said. "Beauty wasn't certain whom she could trust, you know. Meaning no offense, F'lar," he added hastily.

"Here's the one I need," Robinton said, unwinding it fully. He gestured for the others to unroll the segments they held. Shortly the maps were placed in sequence across the table, the curling ends weighted down with pieces of fruit and wine cups.

"It would appear," Lytol said mildly, "that you have been blown off course in every direction, Master Robinton."

"Oh, not me, sir," the Harper replied ingenuously. "SeaHolders have been very helpful here, here and here," and he pointed to the western portions where an intricate coastline was carefully delineated. "This is the work of Idarolan and the captains reporting to him." He paused, toying with the notion of mentioning just how much of Idarolan's explorations had been assisted by the various fire-lizards of the crews. "Toric and his holders, of course," he went on, deciding against gilding the matter now, "have a perfect right to discover their land. They've detailed this portion . . ." His hand swept across the peninsular thumb that was the southern Hold and Weyr and substantial portions of the territory on either side.

"Where're those mines located that Toric's trading from?"

"Here." Robinton's finger dropped to the foothilled shading, slightly to the west of the settlement and well inland.

F'lar considered the location, walking his fingers back across the well-stretched hide to the Weyr's location. "And where's this cove of yours?"

Robinton pointed to a spot which was as far distant from the Southern Weyr as Ruatha was from Benden. "In this area. There're quite a few small coves in the coastline. I couldn't say exactly which one it was, but in this general location."

F'lar mumbled about his recollection being all too general and how would a dragon take the specific direction he'd need to go *between*.

"Dead center in the cove is the cone of an old mountain, perfectly symmetrical." Robinton gestured appropriately. "Zair was with me and could give Ruth the proper image." Robinton turned his head slightly and gave Jaxom a private wink.

"Could Ruth take a direction from a fire-lizard?" F'lar asked Jaxom, frowning at the unreliability of the source.

"He has," Jaxom remarked, and Robinton caught the glint of amusement in the lad's eyes. He began to wonder where fire-lizards had already led the white dragon. Would Menolly know?

"What is this?" F'lar demanded suddenly. "A conspiracy to restore fire-lizards to good odor?"

"I thought we were forming a cooperative venture to locate D'ram," Robinton replied in mild rebuke.

F'lar snorted and bent to study the maps.

The cooperation, Robinton realized, would be all on Ruth's part. The outcome would finally depend on whether or not the Southern fire-lizards were attracted to the white dragon. Otherwise, Jaxom had agreed to try judicious time jumps backward in the cove . . . if, F'lar amended, Jaxom was able to find the proper one.

The subject of fire-lizard memory was discussed again; F'lar unwilling to concede that, unlike the dragons they otherwise resembled, the little creatures were capable of recall. Their tales might all be imaginary, the results of sun-dreams and insubstantial. To that Robinton replied that imagination relied on memory—without one, the other was impossible. The afternoon drew to a close, emphasized by the return of the fosterlings to the Hold after a day's field tour with Brand. F'lar noted that he'd been gone far longer than he had intended when he set out from Benden. He cautioned Jaxom to be careful timing it— advice which Robinton suspected F'lar had best take to heart himself— and to take no risks with himself or his dragon. If he didn't locate the cove, he was not to waste time and energy but return. If he did find D'ram, preferably he was to mark the time and place and return immediately to Benden with the coordinate for F'lar. F'lar did not want to intrude on D'ram's grief unnecessarily, and if Jaxom could avoid being seen, so much the better.

"I think you could trust Jaxom to handle the situation diplomatically," Robinton said, watching the young man through the side of his eyes. "He's already proved to be discreet." Now why would Jaxom react so to a simple compliment, Robinton wondered and smoothly made a fuss of rolling up the charts to divert attention from the discomposed young rider.

Robinton told Jaxom to get a good night's sleep, a good morning's breakfast, and to report to the Harpercrafthall immediately thereafter to acquire his guide. Then Robinton and F'lar left the Hold. As the Weyrleader and Mnementh brought the Harper back to his Hall, Robinton forebore to go beyond offering ordinary courtesies. The needs of Pern had brought the Benden Weyrleader back to the Hall. One step at a time!

As Robinton watched F'lar and bronze Mnementh climb above the fire-heights and wink out, Beauty appeared, scolding at Zair, who resumed his customary perch on the Harper's shoulder. Zair did not respond to her crackling, causing Robinton to grin. Menolly must be agitating for an account of the afternoon's doings. She wasn't presumptuous enough to nag at him, but that didn't keep Beauty from badgering his bronze. A good child, Menolly, and worth her weight in marks. He hoped she'd approve of a trip with young Jaxom. He hadn't mentioned her participating in front of Lytol since F'lar had long ago enjoined him to the strictest secrecy about his Southern trips. Zair would not have been enough for Jaxom to find the right cove, but with Menolly, who had been with him on that stormy trip, and her fire-lizards to act as reinforcement, they'd have no trouble at all. But the fewer people who knew about it the better.

The next day when the Harper informed Jaxom of this added insurance for success, Jaxom looked relieved and surprised.

"Mind you, young Jaxom, it's not to be discussed that Menolly and I have been exploring so far south. In point of fact, we hadn't planned that trip . . ."

Menolly chuckled. "I told you there'd be a storm."

"Thank you. I've heeded your weather wisdom since, as you well know." He grimaced as he recalled three days of storm-sickness and a desperate Menolly clinging to the tiller of their light craft.

He saddled them with no further advice, urged them to take a supply of food from the kitchens and said he hoped they'd have a favorable report.

"Of D'ram's whereabouts?" Menolly asked, her eyes dancing at him, "or the performance of the fire-lizards?"

"Both, of course, saucy girl. Away with you."

He had decided not to query Jaxom about his strong reactions to timing it and discretion. When he had told Menolly of his intention to send her and her fire-lizards to accompany Jaxom, she, too, had reacted in an unexpected fashion. He had casually asked her what was so amusing and she had merely shaken her head, convulsed in laughter. He couldn't imagine what the two of them had been up to together. Now, as he watched Ruth circle into the skies above the Hold, he reviewed their interactions. Good-natured chaffing, certainly—a dollop of contention for leadership but nothing beyond the exchanges of old friends. Not, he hastily told himself, that Menolly would not make an excellent Lady Holder for Jaxom if the two were sincerely attached. It was just that . . . the Harper chided himself for interfering and turned to dull matters of Craft management which he had been delaying far too long.

•• C H A P T E R X ••

🐚

From Harpercraft Hall
to the Southern Continent,
Evening at Benden Weyr, 15.7.4

As Ruth flew upward from the meadow, Jaxom experienced a tremendous sense of relief and excitement as well as the usual tension that gripped him when making a long jump *between*. Beauty and Diver were perched on Menolly's shoulders, tails twined about her neck. He had given shoulder room to Poll and Rocky since these four had accompanied the Harper and Menolly on that initial trip. Jaxom would have liked to ask what they'd been doing sailing in the Southern Continent. The boat made some sense since Menolly, being SeaHold-bred, was a good sailor. But there'd been a challenging gleam in Menolly's eyes that had kept him from asking. He was wondering, too, if she had told the Harper anything of her suspicions about his part in returning the egg.

They went *between* first to Nerat's tip, circling again while Menolly and her fire-lizards concentrated on imagining the cove far to the southeast. Jaxom had wanted to time it to the night before; he'd spent hours working out star positions in the Southern Hemisphere. Menolly and Robinton had overruled him unless Ruth couldn't get a vivid enough picture of the cove from the combination of Menolly and the fire-lizards.

Somewhat to Jaxom's disgruntlement, Ruth announced that he could clearly see where he was to go. *Menolly makes very sharp pictures,* he added.

Jaxom had no option but to ask him to change.

The quality of the air was Jaxom's first impression of the new location: softer, cleaner, less humid. Ruth was gliding toward the little cove, expressing pleasure in anticipation of a good swim. Their guiding mountain peak glistened in the sun, distant, serene and unusually symmetrical.

"I'd forgotten how lovely it was," Menolly said, breathing out a sigh in his ear.

The water had a clarity that made the sandy bottom of the cove quite visible, though Jaxom was sure that the water was by no means shallow. He noticed the brilliant reflection of yellowtails and the darting movements of whitefingers in the clear waters. Ahead of them was the perfect crescent of a white-sanded cove, trees of all sizes, some bearing yellow and red fruits, forming a shady border. As Ruth descended to the beach, Jaxom could see dense forest extending unbroken toward the low range of foothills that culminated in that magnificent mountain. Just beyond this cove, on both flanks, were other little bays, not perhaps as symmetrically shaped, but equally peaceful and untouched.

Ruth came to a back-winging halt on the sands, urging his passengers to disembark as he intended to have a proper bath.

"Go ahead, then," Jaxom said, patting Ruth's muzzle affectionately and laughing as the white dragon, too eager to dive, waddled ungracefully into the sea.

"These sands are as hot as at Hatching Grounds," Menolly explained, picking up her feet in fast order and heading toward the shaded area.

"They're not that hot," Jaxom said, following her.

"My feet are sensitive," she replied, casting herself down on the beach. She glanced up and down and then grimaced.

"No signs, huh?" Jaxom asked.

"Of D'ram?"

"No, fire-lizard."

She unslung the pack with their provisions.

"They're likely sleeping off their early-morning feed. You're still on your feet. See if there're some ripe redfruits in that tree there, would you, Jaxom? Meatroll makes dry eating."

Jaxom found sufficient ripe fruit to feed a Hold and brought as much as he could carry back to Menolly. He knew her fondness for them. Ruth was disporting himself in the water, diving and surfacing to tail length before crashing down with great splashings and wavemakings, the fire-lizards encouraging him with shrieks and buglings.

"Tide's full in," Menolly said as she bit into redfruit peel, tearing off a large hunk and squeezing the pulp for the juice. "Oh, this is heavenly! Why does everything Southern taste so good?"

"Forbidden, I guess. Does the tide make a difference to the fire-lizards' appearing?"

"Not that I know of. Ruth will make the difference, I think."

"So we have to wait until they notice Ruth?"

"That's the easiest way."

"Do we actually know there *are* fire-lizards in this part of the South?"

"Oh, yes, didn't I mention?" Menolly pretended to be contrite. "We saw a queen mating, and I nearly lost Rocky and Diver to her. Beauty was furious."

"Anything else that hasn't been mentioned that I should know?"

Menolly grinned at him. "I need to have the old memory jogged by association. You'll know what is needed when the time comes."

Jaxom decided that two could play that word game and grinned back at her, before choosing a redfruit to eat. It was so warm that he set aside his riding jacket and helmet. Ruth continued to enjoy a leisurely and lengthy bath as Menolly's fire-lizards performed alongside him, their combined show affording their indulgent audience considerable amusement.

It got hotter, the white sands reflecting the sun's rays and baking the cove even where they were in shade. The clear water and the fun the beasts were having was too much for Jaxom to watch any longer. He unlaced his boots, wriggled out of his trousers, whipped off his shirt and raced for the water. Menolly was soon splashing beside him before he was a dragonlength from the shore.

"We'd better not take too much sun," she told him. "I got a colossal burning the last time." She grimaced in recollection. "Peeled like a tunnel snake."

Ruth erupted beside them, blowing out water, all but swamping them with strokes from his wings, and then, solicitously extending a helping tail as the two choked and spluttered from the water they'd swallowed.

Menolly's body was trimmer than Corana's, Jaxom noticed as they waded out, happily exhausted by their swim with Ruth. She was longer in the leg and not nearly as rounded in the hip. A bit too flat in the breast, but she moved with a grace that fascinated Jaxom more than courtesy allowed. When he looked back, she had put on pants and overtunic, so that her slim bare arms were exposed to the sun as she dried her hair. He preferred long hair in a girl though, with all the dragonriding Menolly did, he could see why she'd keep it short enough to wear under a helmet.

They shared a yellow fruit which Jaxom had never eaten before. Its mild taste was well seasoned by the salt in his mouth.

Ruth emerged from the water, shaking water all over Jaxom and Menolly.

The sun is warm, he said when they complained of the shower. *Your clothes will dry quickly. They always do at Keroon.*

Jaxom shot a glance at Menolly but she evidently hadn't caught the significance of the remark. She was resettling herself, disgusted by the wet sand that now speckled her clothes and bare arms.

"It's not the wet that bothers," Jaxom told Ruth, as he brushed his face before lying down again, "it's the gritty sand."

Ruth worked himself into a good wallow of dry sand and the fire-lizards, giving little tired cheeps, nestled down against him.

Jaxom thought that one of them should stay awake to see if local fire-lizards responded to the lure of the white dragon, but the combination of exercise, food, sun and the limpid air of the cove were too much.

Ruth's soft call woke him. *Do not move. We have visitors.*

Jaxom was on his side, his head pillowed on his left hand. Opening his eyes slowly, he looked directly at Ruth's shade-dappled body. He counted three bronze fire-lizards, four greens, two golds and a blue. None of them wore neck paint or bands. As he watched, a brown came gliding in to land by one of the golds. The two exchanged nose touches and then cocked their heads at Ruth's head which was on the sand at their level. Ruth had the lids of one eye half-opened.

Beauty, who had been asleep on the other side of Ruth, minced carefully across the white dragon's shoulders and returned the courtesies of the strangers.

"Ask them if they remember seeing a bronze dragon?" Jaxom thought to Ruth.

I have. They're thinking about it. They like me. They've never seen anything like me before.

"Nor will again." But Jaxom was amused at the delight in his dragon's tone. Ruth did so like to be liked.

A long time ago there was a dragon, a bronze one, and a man who walked up and down the beach. They did not bother him. He didn't stay long, Ruth added, almost as an afterthought.

Now what did that mean? Jaxom wondered, apprehensive. Either we came and got him. Or he and Tiroth suicided.

"Ask them what else they remember about men," Jaxom said to Ruth. Maybe they saw F'lar with D'ram.

The new fire-lizards became so excited that Ruth's head came up out of the sand and his eyes flashed open and began to whirl with alarm. At his movement, Beauty lost her grip on his ridge and slid out of sight, reappearing with wings working furiously as she repositioned herself, squawking over her disarrangement.

They remember men. Why don't I remember such things?

"And dragons?" Jaxom suppressed a spurt of alarm, wondering how on earth the Oldtimers could know he and Menolly were here. Then his common sense asserted itself. They couldn't know.

He nearly jumped to his feet at the touch on his arm.

"Find out when, Jaxom," Menolly said in a soft whisper, "when was D'ram here?"

No dragons. But many many men, Ruth was saying and added that the fire-lizards were too excited now to remember anything about one man and a dragon. He didn't understand what they were remembering; each one seemed to have different memories. He was confused.

"Do they know we're here?"

They haven't seen you. They've only looked at me. But you aren't their men. Ruth's tone indicated he was as perplexed by this message as Jaxom.

"Can't you get them back to the subject of D'ram?"

No, Ruth said sadly and with some disappointment. *All they want to remember is men. Not my men, but their men.*

"Maybe if I stand up they will recognize me as a man." Slowly Jaxom got to his feet, gesturing cautiously to Menolly to rise as well. What the fire-lizards needed was the proper perspective.

You aren't the men they remember, Ruth said as the fire-lizards, startled by the two figures rising from the sands, took wing. They circled once, at a safe distance, and then disappeared.

"Call them back, Ruth. We've got to find out when D'ram is."

Ruth was silent for a moment, his eyes decreasing the speed of their whirl. Then he shook his head as he told his rider that they had gone away to remember their men.

"They couldn't mean Southerners," Menolly said, having received some images from her friends. "That mountain is in the background of their images." And she turned in that direction though she couldn't see the mountain for the trees. "And they wouldn't have meant Robinton and myself when we got storm-tossed here. Did they remember a boat, Ruth?" Menolly asked the white dragon, then looked at Jaxom for the answer.

No one told me to ask about a boat, Ruth said plaintively. *But they did say they saw a man and a dragon.*

"Would they react if . . . if Tiroth had gone *between*, Ruth?"

By himself? To the end? Yes, they didn't remember sadness. I remember sadness. I remember Mirath's going very well. The white dragon's tone was sad.

Jaxom hurried to comfort him.

"Did he?" Menolly asked anxiously, not hearing Ruth.

"Ruth doesn't think so. And besides, a dragon wouldn't let his rider harm himself. D'ram *can't* suicide with Tiroth alive. And Tiroth won't if D'ram is still alive."

"When?" Menolly sounded upset. "We still don't know when."

"No, we don't. But if D'ram was here, long enough for the fire-lizards to remember him, if he planned to stay here as he must have, he would have had to build some sort of shelter for himself. There are rains in this part of the world. And Thread . . ." Jaxom had started toward the verge of the forest to test his theory. He called, "Hey, Menolly, Thread's only been falling for the past fifteen Turns. That wouldn't be too long a jump for Tiroth. They came forward in time at twenty-five Turn intervals. I'll bet anything that's his *when*, before Thread. D'ram's had enough of Thread for several lifetimes." Jaxom scrambled across the sand back to his clothes and continued talking as he got dressed. That sense of rightness colored his speculation. "I'd say Dram's gone back about twenty or twenty-five Turns. I'll try then first. If we see any sign of D'ram or Tiroth, we'll come right back, I promise." He vaulted to Ruth's back, fastening his helmet as he urged the white dragon to wing.

"Jaxom, wait! Don't be so quick . . ."

Menolly's words were lost in the noise of Ruth's wings. Jaxom grinned to himself as he saw her jumping up and down in the sands in her frustration. He concentrated on the moment in time to when he wished to jump: predawn, with the Red Star far east, a pale, malevolent pink, not yet ready to swoop down on an unsuspecting Pern. But Menolly had a final say. He felt a tail wrapping about his neck just as he told Ruth to transfer *between* time.

It seemed a long moment, suspended in that cold nothingness that was *between*. He could feel that chill inching its way through skin and bones warmed by a kind sun. He steeled himself for the ordeal. Then they were out in the cool dawn, the pink gleam of the Red Star low on the horizon.

"Can you sense Tiroth, Ruth?" Jaxom could see nothing in the crepuscular light of this new day so many Turns before his birth.

He sleeps, so does the man. They are here.

Elation brimming inside him, Jaxom told Ruth to get back to Menolly but not too soon. Jaxom pictured the sun well over the forests and that was what he saw as Ruth burst back into *now* over the cove.

For a moment he couldn't see Menolly on the beach. Then Beauty and the other two bronzes—it was Rocky who had accompanied him— exploded beside them, Beauty blistering the air with her angry comments, while Diver and Poll chittered anxiously. Then Menolly appeared from the forest, planted both hands on her hip bones and just watched. He didn't need to see her face to know she was furious. She continued to glare balefully at him while Ruth settled to the sand, careful not to flick it over the girl.

"Well?"

Menolly was very pretty, Jaxom thought, with her eyes flashing like that, but she was daunting, too.

"D'ram was *then*. Twenty-five Turns back. I used the Red Star as a guide."

"I'm glad you used something constant. Do you realize that you've been gone from this time for hours?"

"You knew I was all right. You sent Rocky with me."

"That didn't help! You went so far Beauty couldn't touch him. We had no idea where you were!" She flung her arms wide with her exasperation. "You could've met up with those men the other fire-lizards saw. You could've miscalculated and never come back!"

"I'm sorry, Menolly, really I am." Jaxom was genuinely contrite, if only to spare himself the sharp edge of her tongue. "But I couldn't remember what time it was when we left, so I made sure we didn't double up on ourselves coming back."

She calmed down a trifle. "You didn't need to be that cautious. I was about to send Beauty for F'lar."

"You were worried!"

"Bloody right." She swooped and gathered up the pack, shrugging into her jacket and slapping her helmet on. "Incidentally I found the remains of a lean-to, near a stream back there," she said as she slung him the pack. Vaulting neatly to Ruth's back, she looked around for her fire-lizards that had disappeared. "Off again." She gave a call, and Jaxom instinctively ducked from the rush of wings about his head.

Menolly settled them down, Beauty and Poll on her shoulders, Rocky and Diver on Jaxom's, and they were ready.

When they emerged above Benden Weyr, Ruth caroled his name. Menolly's fire-lizards cheeped uncertainly.

"I wish I dared take you into the queen's weyr, but that wouldn't be smart. Off you go Brekke!"

As they disappeared, the watchdragon let out an outraged roar, wings extended, neck arching, eyes flashing with angry red. Startled, Menolly and Jaxom turned to see a fair of fire-lizards arrowing toward them.

"They followed us from the South, Jaxom. Oh, tell them to go back!"

The fair winked out abruptly.

They only wanted to see where we came from, Ruth said to Jaxom in an aggrieved tone.

"At Ruatha Hold, yes. Here, no!"

They won't come again, Ruth said sadly. *They got frightened.*

By that time the watchdragon's alarm had stirred up the Weyr. With sinking spirits, Jaxom and Menolly saw Mnementh raise himself on his ledge. They could hear Ramoth's bellow and before they had landed in the Bowl, half the dragons were bellowing, too. The unmistakable figures of Lessa and F'lar appeared on the ledge by Mnementh.

"We're in for it now," Jaxom said.

"Not as bearers of good tidings, we're not. Concentrate on that."

"I'm too bloody tired to concentrate on anything," Jaxom replied with more feeling than he'd intended. His skin itched, probably the sand. Or too much sun, but he was uncomfortable.

I am very hungry, Ruth said, looking wistfully toward the fenced killing ground of the Weyr.

Jaxom groaned. "I can't let you hunt here, Ruth." He gave his friend an encouraging pat and, noticing F'lar and Lessa waiting for them, he hitched up his trousers, settled his tunic and gestured to Menolly that they'd better go.

They'd taken no more than three steps, during which time Mnementh had turned his wedge-shaped head to F'lar, when the Weyrleader had spoken to Lessa and the two Benden leaders started down the steps, F'lar gesturing to Jaxom to move Ruth on to the killing ground.

Mnementh is a kind friend, Ruth said. *I may eat here. I am very very hungry*.

"Let Ruth go, Jaxom," F'lar was calling across the intervening distance. "He's gray!"

Ruth did indeed look gray, Jaxom realized, which was the shade he himself felt, now that the exhilaration of their quest was ebbing. Relieved, he signaled the white dragon to proceed to the ground.

As he and Menolly walked toward the Weyrleaders, he felt his knees weaken unaccountably and he lurched against Menolly. She had her hand under his arm instantly.

"What's the matter with him, Menolly? Is he ill?" F'lar strode to her assistance.

"He jumped back twenty-five Turns to find D'ram. He's exhausted!"

The next few moments were a blank to Jaxom. He re-established contact with the here and now when someone held a rank-smelling vial under his nose, the fumes of which cleared his head and made him back away from the stink. He realized that he was sitting on the steps to the queen's weyr, his body braced between F'lar and Menolly, with Manora and Lessa in front of him, everyone looking extremely anxious.

A high-pitched squeal told him that Ruth had killed and, curiously, he felt better immediately.

"Drink this slowly," Lessa ordered, curling his fingers about a warm cup. The soup was rich with meat juice, savory with herbs and just the right temperature for drinking. He took two long gulps and opened his mouth to speak when Lessa gestured him imperiously to keep drinking.

"Menolly's given us the salient points," the Weyrwoman said, pulling a disapproving grimace. "But you disappeared long enough to scare Menolly out of her harpered wits. How under the sun did you conclude he'd gone twenty-five Turns back? Don't answer that yet. Drink. You're transparent and I'd never hear the last of it from Lytol if you came to any harm over this numbwitted escapade." She glared at her weyrmate. "Yes, I've been worried over D'ram but not to the point where I would risk a fingertip of Ruth's hide to find him if he's trying that hard to be lost. Nor am I very pleased to find fire-lizards involved." She was tapping one foot now and her glare was divided equally between Menolly and Jaxom. "I still think they're pests. Barging in where they're not wanted. I suppose that unmarked fair that popped in followed you up from the South? I won't sanction that."

"Well, I can't keep them from following Ruth," Jaxom said, too weary to be prudent. "Don't think I haven't tried!"

"I'm sure you have, Jaxom," Lessa said in a milder tone.

A series of frightened wherry whistles was plainly heard from the killing ground. They saw Ruth swoop to dispatch a second fowl.

"He certainly is neat," Lessa remarked approvingly. "Doesn't run a flock to bone making a choice. Can you stand, Jaxom? I think you'd best plan on spending the night here. Send one of those dratted fire-lizards of yours to Ruatha Hold, Menolly, and tell Lytol. It'll take Ruth time to digest anyhow and I won't permit this lad to risk *between* tired out of his mind and on a tired and sated dragon."

Jaxom got to his feet.

"I'm all right now, thank you."

"Not when you're leaning at that angle," F'lar said with a snort as he slipped one arm around Jaxom. "Up to the weyr."

"I'll bring a proper meal," Manora promised and turned to go. "You can help me, Menolly. And send your message."

Menolly hesitated, obviously wanting to stay with Jaxom.

"I don't intend to eat him, girl," Lessa said, shooing Menolly off. "Much less scold him when he's reeling. I'll save that for later. Come up to the weyr when you've sent word to Ruatha."

Jaxom felt obliged to protest their assistance, but they were convinced he needed it and by the time they'd reached the top of the weyrsteps, he ruefully sagged against their support. Mnementh regarded him kindly as Lessa and F'lar guided him into the weyr.

This was not the first time Jaxom had been there, and, as they led him to the living corner, he wondered if he was always going to enter Ramoth's weyr consumed with guilt. Could Ramoth perceive his thoughts? Her jeweled eyes turned idly without a trace of agitation as he was solicitously settled in a chair, and a foot rest positioned. When Lessa was spreading a fur over him, muttering about watching for chills after exertion, she paused, staring at him. She put her hand under his chin and turned his head slightly, then traced the line of Threadscore with a light finger.

"Where did you acquire that, young Lord Jaxom?" she asked harshly, her eyes forcing him to look at her.

F'lar, alerted by the tone in her voice, returned to the table with the wine and cups he'd taken from the wall chest.

"Acquire what? Oh ho, the young man has trained his dragon to chew firestone but not to duck!"

"I thought it was decided that Jaxom was to remain in Holding at Ruatha."

"I thought you said you wouldn't scold him," F'lar replied as he winked at Jaxom.

"About timing it. But this . . ." she gestured angrily at Jaxom, "this is entirely different."

"Is it, Lessa?" F'lar asked in a tone that embarrassed Jaxom. They were momentarily unaware of him. "I seem to remember a girl wanting desperately to fly her queen."

"Flying was no danger. But Jaxom could be—"

"Jaxom has evidently learned a lesson. Haven't you? About ducking, that is."

"Yes, sir. N'ton's put me in with the weyrlings at Fort."

"Why wasn't I informed?" Lessa demanded.

"Jaxom's training is Lytol's responsibility and we've no complaints on that score. As far as Ruth is concerned, I'd say that he too falls under N'ton's jurisdiction. How long has this been going on, Jaxom?"

"Not that long, sir. I asked N'ton because . . . well . . ." Here Jaxom's conscience interfered with his glibness. Above all else, Lessa must not think he had any part in returning that blasted egg.

F'lar rescued him. "Because Ruth *is* a dragon, and dragons ought to fight Thread with firestone? Right?" He shrugged at Lessa. "What did you expect? He's Ruathan-blooded, like yourself. Just keep your hide and Ruth's intact."

"We haven't flown in a Threadfall yet," Jaxom admitted realizing as he spoke how much resentment showed in his voice.

F'lar gave him a friendly clout on the shoulder.

"He's a sound lad, Lessa, stop glowering. If he's singed himself once, he's less likely to risk doing so again. Was Ruth hurt?"

"Yes!" The anguish of that experience was plain in Jaxom's admission.

F'lar gave a laugh and waggled a finger at Lessa, who was still glaring at Jaxom. "There! That's the best deterrent in the world. Ruth wasn't badly hurt, was he? I can't say I've seen you that often recently . . ." F'lar turned toward the killing ground as if conjuring up the white dragon.

"No," Jaxom said quickly and F'lar grinned again at the relief in his reply. "It's well healed. You can barely see the scar. On his left thigh."

"I can't say that I like all this," Lessa said.

"We would have asked you, Weyrwoman," Jaxom began, not entirely truthful, "but there was so much trouble just then. . . ."

"Well . . ." she began.

"Well," echoed F'lar, "it really isn't up to you, Lessa, but you do understand, Jaxom, how awkward it would be for you to be seriously hurt right now. We can't afford to have a major Hold in contention."

"I appreciate that, sir."

"Nor, I'm afraid, is it wise to press your confirmation as Lord Holder—"

"I don't want Lytol to have to step down, sir. Not ever."

"Your loyalty does you credit but I really can understand and appreciate your ambiguous position. It's never easy to be patient, my friend, but patience can be rewarding."

Again Jaxom was embarrassed by the look that Lessa and F'lar exchanged.

"And," the Weyrleader continued more briskly, as if he realized Jaxom's discomfiture, "you've already proved your resourcefulness today, though, believe me, had I known you to be so thorough, I'd have been more explicit in my instructions." F'lar's expression was severe but Jaxom found himself grinning in relief. "Twenty-five Turns timing it . . ." The Weyrleader was both appalled and impressed.

Lessa gave a snort.

"It was your jumps, Lessa, that first gave me the notion," Jaxom said, and when he saw her startled expression, explained: "Remember, you came forward in twenty-five Turn jumps when you brought the Oldtimers forward. So I thought it likely that D'ram would go back that interval. It left him time enough before the Pass started so he wouldn't have to worry about Thread."

F'lar nodded approvingly, and Lessa appeared somewhat mollified.

Ramoth turned her head toward the entrance.

"Your meal is coming," Lessa said, smiling. "No more talk till you've eaten. Ruth's way ahead of you, just brought down his third wherry, Ramoth says."

"Don't worry about a bird or three or four," F'lar said, for Jaxom had winced at this report of Ruth's greed. "The Weyr can support the meal."

Menolly entered, breathing heavily from the climb and, to judge by the beads of perspiration on her brow, her haste. When Lessa exclaimed that she'd brought enough food to feed a fighting wing, Menolly replied that Manora said it was nearly dinnertime and they might as well all eat in the weyr.

If anyone had told Jaxom that morning that he'd enjoy a comfortable dinner with the Benden Weyrleaders, he'd have told them to open their glow baskets. Despite the reassurances of Mnementh and Ramoth that they conveyed to him, he wouldn't sit still and eat until he'd checked on Ruth. So Lessa permitted him to walk to the ledge and see the white dragon grooming himself by the lake. When Jaxom resumed his place at the table, he found himself shaking, and he applied himself to the roast meats to restore his energy.

"Tell me again what those fire-lizards said about men," F'lar asked when they were relaxing around the table.

"You can't always get fire-lizards to explain," Menolly said, glancing first at Jaxom to see if he wished to answer. "They got so excited when Ruth asked them if they remembered men that their images made no sense. Actually," Menolly paused, drawing her brows together in concentration, "the images were so varied that you didn't see much."

"Why would their images be varied?" Lessa asked, interested in spite of her present antagonism to fire-lizards.

"Generally a group will come up with one specific image . . ."

Jaxom inhaled wearily: she couldn't be foolish enough to mention the egg pictures.

"They echoed Canth's fall from the Red Star. My friends will often come back with rather good images, I think each reinforcing the other, of places they've been."

"Men!" F'lar said thoughtfully. "They could mean men elsewhere in the South. It is a vast continent."

"F'lar!" Lessa's voice was sharp and warning. "You are not exploring the Southern Continent. And, might I suggest that if there were men there, somewhere, they would certainly have ventured far enough north to be seen at some stage or another by F'nor when he was south, or by Toric's groups. There would have been signs of them other than the unreliable recollections of some fire-lizards."

"You're quite likely correct, Lessa," F'lar said, looking so disappointed that Jaxom realized for the first time that being Benden's Weyrleader and First Dragonrider of Pern might not be as enviable a position as he'd previously assumed.

So often lately he'd come to realize that things were not as they seemed. There were hidden facets to everything. You'd think you had what you wanted in your grasp and, when you looked closely, it wasn't what it had seemed to be from a distance. Like teaching your dragon to chew firestone—and getting caught at it, in one sense, as he had. Now he had to train earnestly with N'ton's weyrlings, which was fine as far as it went but it didn't go far enough to please Jaxom—flying high in a Fort Weyr wing so his holders wouldn't even know he was there!

"The problem is, Jaxom, that we," F'lar indicated Lessa, himself and the entire Weyr, "have other plans for the South—before the Lord Holders start parceling it out to their younger sons." He brushed his hair back from his face. "We learned a lesson from the Oldtimers, a valuable one. And I know what happens to a Weyr in a long Interval." F'lar grinned broadly at Jaxom. "We've been mighty busy protecting land by seeding the grubs. By the next Pass of the Red Star, all the Northern Continent," and the Weyrleader's gesture was wide, "will be seeded. And safe at least from Thread burrowing. If the Holds thought dragonriders were superfluous before, they certainly will have more cause then."

"People always feel better *seeing* dragons flame Thread," Jaxom said hastily, from a sense of loyalty although, from the expression on F'lar's face, the Weyrleader didn't seem to be in need of any reassurance.

"True, but I'd prefer it if the Weyrs no longer needed the bounty of the Holds. If we had land enough of our own . . ."

"*You* want the South!"

"Not all of it."

"Just the best part of it," said Lessa firmly.

·· C H A P T E R X I ··

Late Morning at Benden Weyr,
Early Morning at Harpercraft Hall,
Midday at Fidello's Hold, 15.7.5

Jaxom and Ruth spent the night in an empty weyr, but Ruth
felt sufficiently uneasy in a full-sized dragon bed that Jaxom
bundled his furs and curled up against his mount. Jaxom was conscious
of having to pull himself out of a soft, black enfolding pit from which
he was loath to move.

"I know you must be flattened with fatigue, Jaxom, but you've
got to wake up!" Menolly's voice penetrated the comfortable darkness.
"Besides, you'll get a pain in your neck sleeping like that."

Menolly was upside down, Jaxom thought as he opened his eyes.
Beauty was precariously perched, hind legs on the girl's shoulder, her
forepaws well down Menolly's breast, peering anxiously at him. He
felt Ruth stir.

"Jaxom, wake up! I've brought you all the *klah* you can drink."
Mirrim moved into his line of vision. "But F'lar's eager to go and he
wants Mnementh to talk to Ruth first."

Menolly winked solemnly at Jaxom, turning her shoulder to mask
her action from Mirrim. Jaxom groaned because he was never going
to keep straight in his mind who knew what was to be kept secret or
who could be told. He groaned again because his neck was indeed
stiff.

Ruth opened his inner lid just a crack, regarding his rider with
displeasure. *I am tired. I need to sleep.*

"You can't sleep any longer now. Mnementh needs to speak to
you."

Why didn't he speak to me last night?

"Because he probably wouldn't have remembered today."

Ruth's head came up and he turned one eye fully on Jaxom. *Mnementh would. He is the biggest dragon on all Pern.*

"Just because he let you gorge yourself on his killing ground, you like him. But he wants to speak to you so you'd better. Are you awake?"

If I am able to speak to you, I am not dreaming. I am awake.

"You are a bold fellow today," Jaxom said. In one massive heave, he pulled himself out of his impromptu bed. Dragging the furs about him, he half-fell toward the table where Menolly and Mirrim had politely withdrawn. The smell of klah was very welcome and he thanked the girls.

"What time is it?"

"Midmorning, Benden time," Menolly said, her face expressionless but her eyes dancing as she lightly stressed the last two words.

Jaxom grunted. They could all hear the creaks, groans and rumblings of Ruth as the dragon stretched himself in preparation for the day.

"When did you get Threadscored, Jaxom?" Mirrim asked with her usual forthrightness. She leaned over and traced the scar with a light touch, flattening her lips together in patent disapproval of the disfigurement.

"Teaching Ruth to chew firestone. At Fort Weyr," he added, after a malicious pause as he saw her gathering herself to scold him.

"Does Lessa know?" Mirrim asked, emphasizing the last word.

"Yes," Jaxom replied. Let Mirrim digest that truth. But Mirrim wouldn't let some matters alone.

"I don't think much of N'ton's Weyrlingmaster then," she said, sniffing disapproval, "letting you get scored that way."

"Not his fault," Jaxom mumbled through half-chewed bread.

"Wasn't Lytol furious? You shouldn't be risking yourself."

Jaxom shook his head vigorously. He did wish Menolly hadn't brought Mirrim with her.

"And I just don't see what good it's going to do you. You can't expect to fight Ruth."

Jaxom choked. "I am too going to fight Ruth, Mirrim."

"He already has," Menolly remarked, indicating the Threadscore. "Now shut your mouth and let the man eat."

"*Man?*" Mirrim's voice took a derisive swoop and she gave Jaxom a scathing glance.

Menolly made an exasperated sound. "If Path doesn't fly soon, Mirrim, you're not going to be on terms with anyone!"

Surprised, Jaxom looked at Mirrim, who was flushing deeply red.

"Oh ho, Path's ready to be flown! That'll sort out some of your high-headed notions." He couldn't resist crowing at her dismay. "Has Path shown a preference? Ha! Look at her blush! Never thought I'd see the day you'd lose the use of your tongue! And you'll be losing something more soon. I hope it's the wildest flight they've had at Benden since Mnementh first flew Ramoth!"

Mirrim exploded, her eyes narrowed with her anger, hands clenched into fists at her sides. "At least my Path will be flown! That's more than you'll ever do, with that white runt of yours!"

"*Mirrim!*" Menolly's sharp voice made the girl wince, but not soon enough to erase the angry retort that sank coldly into Jaxom's mind. He stared at Mirrim, trying to reject her taunt. "You take too much on yourself, Mirrim," Menolly was saying. "I think you'd better leave."

"You just bet I'll leave. And I don't care if you have to climb down from this weyr, Menolly. Indeed I don't." Mirrim ran from the room.

"Shells and Shards, but it'll be a relief when that green of hers rises to mate. And it might even be today the way Mirrim's reacting." Menolly spoke in a casual tone, almost chuckling at her friends's behavior.

Jaxom swallowed against the dryness in his mouth. Rigidly he controlled his intense emotional reaction for Ruth's sake. A surreptitious glance at the white dragon showed that his friend was still stretching and extending wings and legs. Jaxom only hoped that the dragon had been too sleepy to attend to what they had been saying. He leaned toward Menolly.

"Do you know anything about . . ." he jerked his head at Ruth, "that I don't know?"

"About Path?" Menolly deliberately misconstrued his direction. "Well, if you've never seen a rider reaction to a proddy dragon, Mirrim's given you a classic example."

Path is a well-grown dragon, Ruth said thoughtfully. Jaxom groaned, covering his face with one hand; he should have known that Ruth missed little.

Menolly tapped his hand imperiously, her eyes demanding an explanation.

"Would you like to fly Path?" Jaxom asked Ruth, his eyes meeting Menolly's.

Why should I fly her? I have already outflown her in every race we flew at Telgar. She isn't as fast as I am in the air.

Jaxom repeated to Menolly exactly what Ruth had said, trying to keep his voice as close to Ruth's puzzled tone as possible.

Menolly burst out laughing. "Oh, I wish Ruth had said that in Mirrim's hearing. That would bring her down a peg or two."

Mnementh wishes to speak to me, Ruth said in a very respectful manner, raising his head and turning toward Mnementh's ledge.

"Do you know something I don't? About Ruth?" Jaxom asked in a fierce whisper as he caught hold of Menolly's hand to bring her closer to him.

"You heard him, Jaxom." Menolly's eyes were bright with amusement. "He's simply not interested in dragons, not that way yet."

Jaxom gave her hand a hard squeeze.

"Just think logically, Jaxom," she said, leaning over to him. "Ruth's small, he's maturing more slowly than other dragons."

"You mean, he may never mature enough to mate, don't you?"

Menolly regarded him steadily and he searched her eyes for pity or evasion; and found neither. "Jaxom, aren't you enjoying Corana?"

"Yes, I am."

"You're upset. I don't think you need be. I have never heard a word to suggest you should worry. Only that Ruth *is* unusual."

I have told Mnementh what he wishes to know. They go now, Ruth said. *Do you think I could take a bath in the lake?*

"Didn't you get enough bathing yesterday in the cove?" Jaxom was relieved to find himself answering his dragon calmly.

That was yesterday, Ruth replied equably. *I have eaten since then and slept on a dusty surface. You need a bath, too, I think.*

"All right, all right," Jaxom replied. "Go along with you then. But don't let Lessa see you with any fire-lizards."

How will I get my back properly cleaned? Ruth asked in mild reproach. He stepped down from the bedstone.

"What's his problem?" Menolly wondered aloud, grinning at Jaxom's expression.

"Wants his back scrubbed."

"I'll send my friends to you, Ruth, once you're at the lake. Lessa won't notice."

Ruth paused in his progress to the weyr entrance, cocking his head, patiently considering. Then he arched his neck and moved forward confidently. *Yes, Mnementh has gone and Ramoth with him. They will not know that I will have a real bath with fire-lizards to scrub my ridges properly.*

Jaxom couldn't help but laugh at the smug satisfaction in Ruth's tone as he left the weyr.

"Sorry about inflicting Mirrim on you, Jaxom, but I couldn't get up to this level without Path. And her."

Jaxom took a long sip of *klah*. "I suppose, if Path's proddy, she has to be excused."

"Mirrim usually is, one way or another." Menolly's tone was acid.

"Huh?"

"Mirrim generally gets away with outrageous behavior—"

A sudden thought caused Jaxom to interrupt the harper girl abruptly. "You don't think Mirrim did sneak onto the Ground before that Hatching? I know she swears she didn't but I do know she wasn't supposed to Impress. . . ."

"Not any more than you were! Oh, for goodness sake, Jaxom,

can't I tease you? No, I don't think she tried to influence Path in the shell. She had her fire-lizards and was always content with them. Who wouldn't be with three? Also, you surely know how furious Lessa was after she Impressed Path? Well, no one came forward then to say they'd ever seen Mirrim sneaking onto the Ground and they would have! Mirrim can be managing, tactless, difficult and exasperating, but she's not devious. Weren't you at the Hatching? Oh, well, I was. Path came staggering over to the spot where Mirrim was sitting, crying her heart out and refusing every single candidate on the Ground until F'lar was forced to decide that Path wanted someone sitting among the spectators."

Menolly shrugged. "Someone who turned out to be Mirrim. Oddly enough, her fire-lizards never uttered a chirp of objection. No, I think the partnering was as much . . . well, destined to be as you and Ruth. Not at all like my acquisition of Poll. As if I needed another fire-lizard." She grimaced ruefully. "But his shell cracked just as I was passing him to that addle-handed child of Lord Groghe's. *He's* never faulted me, and the child got a green. A bronze would have been wasted on that brat!"

Jaxom pointed a forefinger at Menolly. "You are blathering! What is it you're hiding? What is it that you know about Ruth that I don't?"

Menolly looked Jaxom straight in the eye. "I don't *know* anything, Jaxom. But, by your own account to me a few minutes gone by, Ruth greeted the news of Path's imminent mating with all the enthusiasm of a weyrling asked to change glow baskets."

"That doesn't mean—"

"Doesn't mean anything. So don't get defensive. Ruth is maturing late. That's all you need to think about it . . . especially with Corana on hand."

"Menolly!"

"Don't explode! You'll undo all the good rest you had last night. You were faded!" She put her hand on his arm, giving it a squeeze. "I'm not prying about Corana. I'm commenting, although you might not appreciate the distinction."

"It does occur to me that Ruatha Hold is not Harper business," he said, gritting his teeth against the words he'd like to use.

"You, Jaxom, rider of white Ruth, are the Harper's business— not young Jaxom, Lord of Ruatha."

"You're making distinctions again."

"Yes, I am, Jaxom," and although her voice was serious, her eyes twinkled. "When Jaxom influences what happens to Pern, then he becomes Harper business."

Jaxom stared at her, still baffled by her silence on the matter of the egg's return. Then he caught the odd warning expression in her eyes; for some reason beyond his comprehension, she did not want him to confirm that adventure.

"You're several people at once, Jaxom," she went on, earnestly. "The Lord of a Hold which cannot be in contention, the rider of an unusual dragon and a young man who's not quite sure who or what he should be. You can, you know, *be* all and more, without being disloyal to anyone, or yourself."

Jaxom snorted. "Who's speaking? The Harper, or Menolly the Meddler?"

Menolly shrugged, gave a rueful twist of her mouth, neither smile nor denial. "Partly Harper, because I can't look at most things without thinking Harper, but Menolly mostly, right now, I think, because I don't want you to be upset. Particularly not after that feat you pulled off yesterday!" There was no doubt of the warmth of her smile.

Her fair of fire-lizards came swooping into the weyr. Jaxom suppressed his annoyance at the interruption because he'd have preferred to keep Menolly talking in this unsually expansive mood. But the fire-lizards were clearly excited and, before Menolly could calm them enough to find out, Ruth came into the weyr, his eyes whirling with myriad colors.

D'ram and Tiroth are here, and everyone is very excited, Ruth said, pushing his nose at Jaxom to be caressed. Jaxom obliged, and went on to rub eye ridges damp from Ruth's swimming. *Mnementh is very pleased with himself.* There was a note of grievance in that addition.

"Well, Mnementh couldn't have brought D'ram and Tiroth back without your help, Ruth," Jaxom replied staunchly. "Right, Menolly?"

I could not have found D'ram and Tiroth without the fire-lizards' help, Ruth remarked graciously. *And you thought of going back twenty-five Turns.*

Menolly sighed, unable to hear Ruth's last comment.

"Actually, we owe more to those Southern fire-lizards."

"That's just what Ruth said . . ."

"Dragons are honest people!" Menolly exhaled heavily and rose. "Come on, my friend. You and I had better return to our own halls. We've done what we were sent to do. Done it well. That's all the satisfaction we're likely to have." She shot him an amused look. "Isn't that so?" She gathered up her pack. "Which is the way some matters have to remain. Right?"

She slipped her arm through his, hauling him to his feet, grinning in a semi-conspiratorial fashion that oddly enough did dispel the resentment he was beginning to feel.

As they came out on the ledge, they could see the activity about the queen's weyr, as riders and women from the Lower Caverns came streaming across to greet D'ram and his bronze.

"I must admit, it's rather nice to leave Benden with everyone in a good frame of mind for a change," Menolly said as Ruth bore her and Jaxom upward.

Jaxom expected to deposit Menolly safely in the Harperhall and return home. No sooner had Ruth announced himself to the watch-dragon on the fire-heights than Zair and a harper-banded little queen attached themselves with precarious talon holds to Ruth's neck.

"That's Sebell's Kimi. He's back!" There was an exultant ring to Menolly's voice that Jaxom had never heard before.

The watchdragon says that the Harper wants to see us. So does Zair, Ruth told Jaxom. *He means me, too,* Ruth added with a note of pleasant surprise.

"Why shouldn't the Harper want to see you, Ruth? He's sure to give you the credit you're due," Jaxom said, still nursing a bit of re-sentment as he slapped the arched neck affectionately. Ruth had turned his head to choose a landing space in the courtyard.

Master Robinton and a man with a master's knot on his shoulder came striding down the Hall's steps. Master Robinton's arms were outstretched so he could encircle both Menolly and Jaxom with an enthusiasm that almost embarrassed Jaxom. Then, to his complete sur-prise, the other Harper grabbed Menolly from Robinton's grasp and began to swing her around and around, all the time kissing her soundly. Instead of protesting this treatment of their friend, the fire-lizards went into spectacular aerial maneuvers of twined necks and overlapped wings. Jaxom knew that fire-lizard queens rarely indulged in tactile contact with queens, but Beauty and the strange gold were as joyously indulging as Menolly and the man. Glancing to see what the Harper's reaction was to such excess, Jaxom was astonished to see Master Robinton grinning with smug pleasure, an expression quickly altered when he noticed Jaxom's regard.

"Come, Jaxom, Menolly and Sebell have several months' news to exchange and I want to hear *your* version of D'ram's discovery."

As Robinton guided Jaxom toward the Hall, Menolly cried out and pushed herself free of Sebell's arms, although Jaxom noticed that her fingers remained entwined in Sebell's as she took a hesitant step toward Robinton. "Master?"

"What?" Robinton affected dismay. "Cannot Sebell command a measure of your time after so long an absence?"

Jaxom was gratified to see Menolly caught by uncertainty and confusion. Sebell was grinning.

"Hear what *he* has to tell you first, girl," Robinton said, more kindly. "I'll make do admirably with Jaxom."

Glancing back at the pair as Robinton escorted him into the Hall, Jaxom saw their arms linked about each other's waists, heads inclined together. Their fire-lizards spiraled above, following them as they walked slowly toward the meadow beyond the Harper Hall.

"You brought D'ram and Tiroth back?" the Harper asked Jaxom.

"I found them. The Benden Weyrleaders returned them this morning, Benden time."

Robinton hesitated, his foot nearly missing the top step as he led Jaxom to his own quarters. "They were there, though, in that cove, all along? Just as I surmised."

"Twenty-five Turns back," and, with no further urging, Jaxom recounted the adventure from the beginning. His listener was more sympathetic and attentive than either Lessa or F'lar had been, so Jaxom began to enjoy his unaccustomed role.

"Men?" The Harper, who had been lounging in his chair, one booted foot propped on the table, abruptly came off the end of his spine. His heel rang on the stone floor. "They'd seen men?"

Jaxom was momentarily startled. Whereas the Weyrleaders had been alarmed and skeptical, the Master Harper acted almost as if he'd expected this news.

"I've always maintained that we came from the Southern Continent," the Harper said, more to himself than anyone else. Then he signaled Jaxom to continue.

Jaxom obeyed but was soon aware that only half the Harper's attention was on his narrative, though the man nodded and asked occasional questions. Jaxom told of his and Menolly's safe return to Benden Weyr, remembered to mention his gratitude to Mnementh for permitting Ruth to eat. He fell silent then, wondering how to ask a question of his own of the Harper, but Robinton was frowning at some private reflections.

"Tell me again what the fire-lizards said about these *men*," the Harper asked, leaning forward, elbows on the table, eyes fixed on Jaxom. On his shoulder, Zair echoed a querying note.

"They didn't *say* much, Master Robinton. That's the trouble! They got so excited, they made little sense at all. Menolly could probably tell you more because she had Beauty and the three bronzes with her. But—"

"What did Ruth say?"

Jaxom shrugged, unhappily aware that his half-answers were inadequate.

"He said the images were too confused, even if they were all about men, their men. And we, Menolly and I, weren't their sort of men."

Jaxom reached for the pitcher of *klah*, to slake the dryness of his mouth. He courteously filled a cup for the Harper who absently drained half of it while deep in thought.

"Men," Master Robinton said again, extending the last consonant and ending the sound with a click of his tongue. He got to his feet in such a fluid motion that Zair squawked, clawing for balance. "Men, and so long ago that the images the fire-lizards retain are vague. That is very interesting, very interesting indeed."

The Harper began to pace, stroking Zair, who chittered reprovingly.

Jaxom glanced out the window at Ruth, sunning himself in the courtyard, the local fire-lizards clustered about him. Jaxom listened idly to the chorus, wondering why they were stopped so often in the Ballad, for he couldn't detect discord in their harmonies. The breeze coming in the window was pleasant, soft with summer scents, and he was jerked back to his surroundings when Robinton's hand gripped his shoulder.

"You've done very well, lad, but you'd better get back to Ruatha now. You're half asleep. That time jump took more out of you than I think you realize."

As Master Robinton accompanied Jaxom to the courtyard, he had him rehearse the conversation with the fire-lizards just once more. This time the Harper nodded his head sharply at each point as if to insure accurate recall.

"That you found D'ram and Tiroth safe, Jaxom, is the least of this affair, I think. I knew I was right to involve you and Ruth. Don't be surprised if you hear more from me on this business, with Lytol's permission, of course."

With a final affectionate grip of his arm, Robinton stepped back to let Jaxom mount Ruth, the fire-lizards shrilling their disappointment at the end of their friend's visit. As Ruth obediently climbed higher, Jaxom waved a cheery farewell to the diminishing figure of the Master Harper. Then Jaxom looked down toward the river for Menolly and Sebell. He was annoyed with himself, at the same time, for wanting to know where they were—and further irritated, because, when he did spot them, the intimacy of their attitude proved that they enjoyed a relationship of which he had been totally unaware.

He did not go straight back to Ruatha Hold. Lytol would not be expecting him at any particular hour. As he also saw no fire-lizards abroad to betray his delinquency, he asked Ruth to take him to the Plateau Hold. In Ruth's cheerful compliance, he wondered if the white dragon knew his mind better than he did himself.

Now, it was close to midday in western Pern, and Jaxom wondered how he was going to attract Corana's attention without every dependent in the hold knowing of his visit. His need of her was great enough to make him irritable.

She comes, Ruth said, dipping his wing so that Jaxom could see the girl emerging from the hold, walking in the direction of the river, a basket balanced on one shoulder.

What could have been more fortuitous! He told Ruth to take them to the river edge where the women of her hold generally did their washing.

The stream is not very deep, Ruth said casually, *but there is a large rock in the sun where I can be comfortable and warm.* And before Jaxom could answer, he began to glide down to the river, past the rapid boiling waters flowing across treacherously strewn boulders, to the calm pool and the flat stone outcropping. Angling himself neatly so as not to foul his wings in the branches of the heavy shade trees that bordered the river, Ruth landed lightly on the biggest rock. *She comes,* he repeated, ducking his shoulder so that Jaxom could dismount.

Suddenly Jaxom was assailed by a conflict of desires and doubts. Mirrim's angry remarks resounded in his head. Ruth was indeed well beyond the usual age of mating and yet . . .

She comes and she is good for you. If she is good for you, it is good for me, Ruth said. *She makes you feel happy and relaxed and that is good. The sun here makes me warm and happy, too. Go.*

Startled by the strength of his weyrmate's tone, Jaxom stared up at Ruth's face. The eyes were whirling gently, with the blues and greens of a contentment at odds with the force of his voice.

Then Corana reached the last loop in the path to the river's edge and saw him. She dropped her basket, spilling the linen, and ran, embracing him so fiercely, kissing his face and neck with such uninhibited delight, that he was soon too involved to think.

Together they moved toward the soft moss that carpeted the ground beyond the stones, out of sight of the river bank, out of Ruth's actual vision. Corana was as willing and eager as he was to satisfy desires thwarted on his previous visit to the hold. As his hands touched her soft flesh and he felt her body press against his, he wondered briefly if she'd have been as willing a lover had he not been Ruatha's Lord. But he didn't care! He was her lover now! He gave himself to that pursuit with no further reservation. At the precise moment of his release, exquisite to the point of pain, he was aware of a gentle touch and knew, with a sense of relief that enhanced his own, that Ruth was joined to him then, as always.

◥

Ruatha Hold, Fidello's Hold, Threadfall, 15.7.6

Keeping a secret from one's dragon was not easy. About the only safe time for Jaxom to think of anything he didn't wish Ruth to perceive was very late at night when his friend was sound asleep, or in the morning if Jaxom happened to wake before Ruth. He had seldom needed to shield his thought from Ruth, which further complicated and inhibited the process. Then, too, the pace of Jaxom's life—the now-boring training with the weyrling wing, helping Lytol and Brand to gear up the Hold to full summer activity, not to mention excursions to the Plateau Hold—caused Jaxom to fall asleep as soon as he pulled his bed furs about his shoulders. Mornings, he was often dragged out of his bed by Tordril or another fosterling just in time to keep appointments.

Nevertheless, the problem of Ruth's maturity cropped up in Jaxom's mind at inconvenient times during his waking hours and had to be rigidly suppressed before a hint of his anxiety reached his dragon.

Twice at Fort Weyr, to intensify the problem, a proddy green had taken off on a flight, pursued by such browns and blues as felt able to rise to her. The first time, Jaxom was in the middle of drill sequence and only happened to notice the flight above and beyond the weyrlings' wing. His attention was abruptly diverted from them as a most unconcerned Ruth continued in the wing's maneuver. Jaxom had to grab at the fighting straps to remain in place.

The second time, Jaxom and Ruth were aground when the mating shrieks of a green blooding her kill startled the Weyr. The other weyrlings were immature enough to be disinterested but the Weyrlingmaster looked in Jaxom's direction for a long moment. All at once,

Jaxom realized that K'nebel was apparently wondering if Jaxom and Ruth were going to join those waiting for the green to launch herself.

Jaxom was assailed by such a gamut of emotions—anxiety, shame, expectation, reluctance, and pure terror—that Ruth reared, wings wide, in alarm.

What has upset you? Ruth demanded, settling to the ground and curving his neck about to regard his rider, his eyes whirling in quick response to Jaxom's emotions.

"I'm all right. I'm all right," Jaxom said hastily, stroking Ruth's head, desperately wanting to ask if Ruth felt at all like flying the green and hoping in a muted whisper deep inside him that Ruth did not!

With a challenging snarl, the green dragon was airborne, the blues and browns after her while she repeated her taunting challenge. Quicker, lighter than any of her prospective mates, her facility strengthened by her sexual readiness, she achieved a conspicuous distance before the first male had become airborne. Then they were all after her. On the killing ground, their riders closed into a knot about the green's rider. All too quickly, challenger and pursuers dwindled to specks in the sky. The riders half-ran, half-stumbled to the Lower Caverns and the chamber reserved there.

Jaxom had never witnessed a mating flight of dragons. He swallowed, trying to moisten his dry throat. He felt heart and blood thudding and a tension that he usually experienced only as he held Corana's slender body against him. He suddenly wondered which dragon had flown Mirrim's Path, which rider had—

The touch on his shoulder made him jump and cry out.

"Well, if Ruth isn't ready to fly, you certainly are, Jaxom," K'nebel said. The Weyrlingmaster glanced up at far-distant specks in the sky. "Even a green's mating can be unsettling." K'nebel's expression was understanding. He nodded at Ruth. "He wasn't interested? No, well, give him time! You'd better be off. Drill was all but over today, anyhow. I've just got to keep these younger ones occupied someplace else when that green gets caught."

Then Jaxom realized that the rest of the wing had dispersed. With a second encouraging clap on Jaxom's back, K'nebel walked off toward his bronze, agilely mounting and urging the beast up toward their weyr.

Jaxom thought of the skyborne beasts. Unwillingly he thought of their riders in the inner room, linked to their dragons in an emotional struggle that was resolved in a strengthening and fusing of the links between dragons and riders. Jaxom thought of Mirrim. And of Corana.

With a groan, he sprang on Ruth's neck, fleeing the emotional atmosphere of Fort Weyr, trying to flee from his sudden realization of what he had probably always known about riders but had only this very morning assimilated.

He had intended to go to the lake to immerse himself in the cold waters and let that icy shock cure his body and chill the torment in his mind. But Ruth took him instead to the Plateau Hold.

"Ruth! The lake. Take me to the lake!"

It is better for you to be here right now, was Ruth's astonishing reply. *The fire-lizard says the girl is in the upper field.* Once again Ruth seized the initiative, gliding toward the field where young grain waved, brilliantly green in the noonday sun, where Corana was diligently hoeing away the tenacious creeper vine that grew from the borders of the field and threatened to strangle the crop.

Ruth achieved a landing on the narrow margin between grain and wall. Corana, recovering from surprise at his unexpected arrival, waved a welcome. Instead of rushing toward him as she usually did, she smoothed back her hair and blotted the perspiration beading her face.

"Jaxom," she began as he strode toward her, the urgency in his loins increasing at the sight of her, "I wish you wouldn't—"

He silenced her half-teasing scold with a kiss, felt something hard clout him along his side. Pinning her against him with his right arm, he found the offending hoe with his left hand. Wrenching it from her grasp, he spun it away from them. Corana wriggled to get free, as unprepared for this mood in him as he was. He held her closer, trying to temper the pressures rising within him until she could respond. She smelled of the earth and her own sweat. Her hair, covering his face as he kissed her throat and breast, also smelled of sun and sweat, and the odors excited him further. Somewhere in the back of his mind was a green dragon, shrieking her defiance. Somewhere, too close to his need, was that vision of dragonriders in an inner room, waiting, with an excitement that matched his own, waiting until the green dragon had been captured by the fastest, the strongest or the smartest of her pursuers. But it was Corana he was holding in his arms, and Corana who was beginning to respond to his need. They were on the warm ground, the dampness of earth she had just hoed soft under his elbows and knees. The sun was warm on his buttocks as he tried to erase the memory of those riders half-stumbling toward the inner room, and the mocking taunt of a green dragon in flight. He did not resist or deny Ruth's familiar beloved touch as his orgasm released the turmoil of body and mind.

Jaxom could not bring himself to go to weyrling practice the next morning. Lytol and Brand were out early, riding to a distant holding with the fosterlings so no one questioned his presence. When he left the Hold in the afternoon, he firmly directed Ruth to the lake and scrubbed and scrubbed his dragon until Ruth meekly asked what was the matter.

"I love you, Ruth. You are mine. I love you," Jaxom said, wanting with all his heart to be able to add, with his former blithe confidence, that he would do anything in the world for his friend. "I love you!" he repeated through gritted teeth and dove from Ruth's back as deeply as he could into the ice-cold waters of the lake.

Perhaps I am hungry, Ruth said as Jaxom fought the pressure of water and airlessness in his lungs.

That could certainly provide a diversion, Jaxom thought as he erupted to the surface, gasping for breath. "There's a hold in South Ruatha where there're wherries fattening."

That would do very nicely.

Jaxom dried himself quickly, shrugged into his clothes and boots, absently coiling the damp bath sheet over his shoulders as he mounted Ruth and directed him up and *between* to the Southern Holding. He realized his foolishness the moment the deathly chill of *between* compounded the dampness about his neck. He'd surely contract a distressingly uncomfortable head cold from such stupidity.

Ruth hunted with his usual dispatch. Fire-lizards, local by their band colors, arrived, apparently invited by the white dragon to share the feast. Jaxom watched, freer to think while Ruth was totally involved with hunting and eating. Jaxom was not pleased with himself. He was thoroughly disgusted and revolted by the way he had used Corana. The fact that she seemed to have matched what he had to admit was a violent lust dismayed him. Their relationship, once innocent pleasure, had somehow been sullied. He wasn't at all certain that he cared to continue as her lover, an attitude that posed another unpleasant burden of guilt. One point in his favor, he had helped her finish the hoeing his importunity had interrupted. That way she'd not be in trouble with Fidello for shorting her task. The young grain was important. But he ought not to have taken Corana like that. Doing so was inexcusable.

She liked it very much. Ruth's thought touched him so unexpectedly that Jaxom jerked straight.

"How could you possibly know?"

When you are with Corana, her emotions are also very strong and just like yours. So I can feel her, too. Only at that time. Otherwise I do not hear her. Acceptance rather than regret colored Ruth's tone. Almost as if he were relieved that the contact was limited.

Ruth was padding up from the field as he spoke, having disposed of two fat wherries without leaving much for the fire-lizards to pick over. Jaxom regarded his friend, the whirl of the jeweled eyes slowing as the red of hunger paled into dark violet and then the blue of contentment.

"Do you like what you hear? Our lovemaking?" Jaxom asked, abruptly deciding to air his concern.

Yes. You enjoy it so much. It is good for you. I like it to be good for you.

Jaxom jumped to his feet, consumed by frustration and guilt. "But don't you want it for yourself? Why are you always worried about me? Why didn't you go fly that green?"

Why does that worry you? Why should I fly the green?

"Because you're a dragon."

I am a white dragon. Blues and browns, and occasionally a bronze, fly greens.

"You could have flown her. You could have flown her, Ruth!"

I did not wish to. You are upset again. I have upset you. Ruth extended his neck, his nose gently touching Jaxom's face in apology.

Jaxom threw his arms about Ruth's neck, burrowing his forehead against the smooth, spicy-smelling hide, concentrating on how very much he loved his Ruth, his most unusual Ruth, the only white dragon on all Pern.

Yes, I am the only white dragon there has ever been on Pern, Ruth said encouragingly, moving his body so that he could gather Jaxom closer within the circle of his foreleg. *I am the white dragon. You are my rider. We are together.*

"Yes," Jaxom said, wearily admitting defeat, "we *are* together."

A chill shook Jaxom and he sneezed. Shells, if he was heard sneezing about the Hold, he'd be subjected to some of those noxious medicines Deelan foisted on everyone. He closed his jacket, folded the now dry bathing sheet about his neck and chest and, mounting Ruth, suggested that they get back to the Hold as fast as possible.

He escaped the dosing only because he kept out of Deelan's way by staying in his own quarters. He announced that he was occupied in a task for Robinton and did not care to interrupt it for the evening meal. He hoped that his sneezing would abate by evening. Lytol would be sure to visit him, which reminded Jaxom that if he didn't have something to show for his afternoon's occupation Lytol might be difficult. Actually, Jaxom had wanted to set down his observations about that beautiful cove, with the cone of the huge mountain center so neatly in its curve. Using the soft carbon stick that Master Bendarek had developed to use on his paper leaves, Jaxom became absorbed in the project. Much easier to work with these tools, he thought, than with sandtable. Errors, since his memory of the cove did not appear to be that precise, could be rubbed out with a blob of softwood tree sap as long as he was careful not to abrade the leaf's surface too much.

He had achieved a respectable map of D'ram's cove when a knock on the door broke his concentration. He sniffed mightily before calling permission to enter. His voice didn't seem too affected by the congestion in his head.

Lytol entered, greeted Jaxom and approached the worktable, eyes courteously averted from the contents.

"Ruth did eat today?" he asked, "because N'ton sent to remind you that Thread falls north and you could fly with the wing. Ruth will have sufficient time to digest, won't he?"

"He'll be just fine," Jaxom replied, aware of both an excitement and a sense of inevitability at the prospect of fighting Thread from Ruth's back.

"Have you then completed your training with the weyrlings?"

So Lytol had noticed his morning's delinquency from the Weyr. Jaxom also heard the faint note of surprise in his guardian's voice.

"Well, you might say that I've learned about all I'd need to know since I'm not to fly regularly with a fighting wing. I've done this sketch of D'ram's cove. That's where we found him. Isn't it beautiful?" He offered the leaf to Lytol.

To Jaxom's satisfaction, Lytol's expression changed to one of surprised interest as he peered intently at the sketch and diagram.

"Your rendering of the mountain is accurate? It must surely be the largest volcano on Pern! You've got the perspective correct? How magnificent! And this area?" Lytol's hand washed across the space beyond the trees which Jaxom had carefully drawn in their variety and as accurately in position along the cove's edge as he could recall.

"Forest extends to low hills, but we stayed on the beach, of course—"

"Beautiful! One can appreciate why the Harper remembered the place so clearly."

With a noticeable reluctance, Lytol replaced the leaf on Jaxom's table.

"The drawing is a poor image of the real place," he said to his guardian, letting his voice end on an upward note. It wasn't the first time Jaxom regretted Lytol's aversion to riding on dragonback for any but the most vital excursions.

Lytol favored Jaxom with a brief smile, shaking his head. "It is good enough to guide a dragon, I'm sure. But do remember to tell me when you've the notion to return there."

With that Lytol bade him good evening, leaving Jaxom a trifle unsettled. Was Lytol giving him oblique permission to go back to the cove? Why? Critically, Jaxom examined the sketch, wondering if he really had drawn the trees correctly. It would be nice to go back there again. Say, after Threadfall, if flying didn't overtire Ruth. . .

I would like to swim off firestone stench in the cove waters, Ruth said sleepily.

By tilting his chair back, Jaxom could see the white bulk of Ruth on his couch, head facing Jaxom's door, though both sets of the dragon's eyelids were closed.

I would like that very much indeed.

"And maybe we could find out more about those men from the fire-lizards." Yes, thought Jaxom, relieved to have a definite objective, it would be very good. Neither F'lar nor Lessa had forbidden him to return to the cove. It was certainly far enough away from the Southern Hold to put him in no danger of compromising the Weyrleaders. Now if he could learn more about the men, he'd be doing Robinton a favor. He might even be able to find a clutch somewhere along that coastline. Maybe that's what Lytol had had in mind by giving him that oblique permission. Of course! Why hadn't Jaxom realized that before?

Threadfall was calculated to arrive the next morning at just past the ninth hour. Although Jaxom was not to ride out in his usual place with the flamethrower crews, he was nevertheless awakened early by a drudge who brought him a tray of *klah* and sweetbread as well as a package of meatrolls for his lunch.

Jaxom was conscious of a stuffiness in his head, a tightness in his throat and a general sense of unfitness. Under his breath he cursed himself for that moment's thoughtlessness that was going to make his first Threadfall mighty uncomfortable. What under the sun had possessed him to dive into a chill-watered lake, go *between* half-soaked, then cavort in lustful exercise on damp, just-turned earth? He sneezed several times as he dressed. That cleared his nose, but left his head aching. He put on his warmest underfur, heaviest tunic, pants and extra liners in his boots. He was sweltering when he and Ruth left their quarters. Holders were bustling about the courtyard, mounting runners, securing flamethrowers and equipment. The watchdragon and the hold fire-lizards were chewing firestone on the heights. Catching Lytol's eye where the Lord Warder stood on the top step of the Hold entrance, Jaxom gestured skyward, saw Lytol salute in reply before he continued giving orders for the day's emergency. Jaxom sneezed once more, an exhalation that rocked him back on his heels.

Are you all right? Ruth's eyes whirled faster in concern.

"For a damn fool who's caught a cold, yes, I'm all right. Let's get going. I'm boiling inside these furs."

Ruth complied and Jaxom was more comfortable with wind cooling the sweat from his face. He had Ruth fly direct to the Weyr for they had plenty of time. He would never be foolish enough to go *between* again in a sweat. Maybe he'd better change to lighter flying gear once at the Fort. He'd be warm enough once they were fighting Thread. However, the Weyr was situated higher in the mountains than Ruatha Hold and he did not feel overheated once they landed.

Following instructions well drilled into him, Jaxom took Ruth to collect their firestone sack. Then he directed Ruth to take stones from the supply laid about the Bowl for that purpose. Ruth began to chew firestone, preparing his second stomach for flame. With a good start, he'd have a steady flame that could be easily replenished in flight by additional stone from the sack he carried. While Ruth was chewing, Jaxom got himself a large mug of steaming *klah*, hoping that would revive him. He felt miserable, his nose clogging repeatedly.

Fortunately the noise of so many dragons chewing stone masked his fits of sneezing. If this wasn't to be his very first time to fight Ruth, Jaxom might have hesitated about continuing. Then he convinced himself that since the weyrlings would undoubtedly be flying in the wake of the other wings on the after-edge of Threadfall, he could probably keep from having to go *between* frequently, if at all, and so he would run little risk of aggravating the congestion. He didn't fancy sneezing just as Ruth had to duck *between* to avoid Thread.

N'ton and Lioth appeared on the Star Stones, Lioth bugling for silence as the Weyrleader raised his arm. Fort's four queens flanked the big bronze, larger than he but, in Jaxom's eyes, only enhancing his magnificence with their brilliance. Dragons on all weyr ledges listened to Lioth's silent orders and then the wings formed. Jaxom needlessly tested the fighting straps that held him securely to his ridge seat on Ruth's neck.

We are to ride with the queens' wing, Ruth told his rider.

"All of the weyrlings?" Jaxom asked, since he'd heard nothing from K'nebel about a change of position.

No, just us. Ruth sounded pleased but Jaxom wasn't at all sure of the honor.

His hesitation was noticed by the Weyrlingmaster, who gave him a curt signal to take his assigned position. So Jaxom directed Ruth upward to the Star Stones. As Ruth landed neatly on the left-hand side of Selianth, the youngest Fort queen, Jaxom wondered if he looked as silly as he felt, dwarfed by the golden dragon.

Lioth bugled again and the Weyrleaders took off from the Star Stones, dropping far enough for wing room before rising on strongly beating wings to the sky. Ruth needed no room at all for takeoff and hovered briefly before taking his position beside Selianth. Prilla, her rider, waved an encouraging fist and then Ruth told Jaxom that Lioth was giving him the command to go *between* to meet Threadfall.

When they emerged above the barren hills of northern Ruatha,

Jaxom found himself responding to an exhilaration he had never before experienced on Ruth. The wings of the fighting dragons spread above and all around his lower level position in the queens' wing. The sky appeared to be full of dragons, all facing east, the highest wing the first to contact the imminent Fall of Thread.

Jaxom snuffled back the mucus, irritated that his condition was dampening this personal triumph: Jaxom, Lord of Ruatha Hold, was actually going to fly his white dragon against Thread! Between his legs, he could feel Ruth's body rumbling with the stored gas and wondered if the feeling were in any way analogous to his own congested, heavy-headed state.

In a burst of speed, the uppermost wing moved forward and Jaxom had no further time for speculation as he, too, glimpsed the filming of the clear sky, that graying that heralded the advent of Thread.

Selinath wants me to stay above her at all times so her flamethrower won't singe me, Ruth said, his mental tone muffled as he retained fire-breath. He altered his position and now all the wings began to move.

The gray film visibly turned into the silver rain of Thread. Gouts of flame blossomed in the sky as the forward dragons seared their ancient mindless enemy into charred dust. Jaxom's excitement was tempered by the endless drills he had performed with the weyrlings, and by the cold logic of caution. He and Ruth would not return Thread-scored today!

The queens' wing nosed slightly earthward, to fly under the first wave of dragons, set to destroy whatever shred might have eluded the first flames. They flew through patches of fine dust, the residue of crisped Thread. Wheeling sharply, the queens' wing turned back and now Jaxom did spy a silver strand. Urging an all too willing Ruth upward, Jaxom heard his white dragon warn others off as the novice team encountered and demolished Thread in proper style.

Proudly, Jaxom wondered if anyone else noted the economy of Ruth's deadly flame: just enough, no more than was necessary. He stroked his friend's neck and felt Ruth's delight in the praise. Then they were off on another tangent as the queens' wing headed for a heavier concentration of Thread, eluding an easterly flying wing.

From that moment onward, throughout the Fall, Jaxom had no time for further thought. He became aware of the rhythm to the queens' wing pattern. Margatta on her golden Luduth seemed to have an uncanny instinct for those heavier patches that could escape even the closest flying wing. Each time the queens would be under the silver rain, destroying it. It became apparent to Jaxom that his position in the queens' wing was neither sinecure nor protective. The golden drag-ons could cover more territory in the air, but they were not as maneuverable. Ruth was. Ever maintaining his upper position, the little white dragon could flit from one side of the queens' V formation to the other, assisting wherever he was needed.

Abruptly, the Thread stopped falling. The upper reaches of the sky were clear of the graying mist. The highest wing began to circle down leisurely, to begin the final phase of the defense, the low-level sweep which assisted ground crews in locating any trace of viable Thread.

The exhilaration of combat drained from Jaxom and his physical discomfort began to manifest itself. His head felt twice its proper size, his eyes were unaccountably filled with grit and ached hotly. His chest felt tighter, his throat raw. The illness had a good hold on him now. He'd been a fool to fight Thread. To compound his miseries, he didn't even have any sense of personal achievement after four hours of bloody hard work. He was thoroughly depressed. He earnestly wished that he and Ruth could retire now but he had made such an issue of flying with the fighting wings that he must complete the exercise. Dutifully he continued on above the queens.

The big queen says we must go, Ruth said suddenly, *before the ground crews see us.*

Jaxom glanced down at Margatta and saw her signal of dismissal. He could not suppress the sense of injury that gesture gave him. He hadn't expected a round of cheers but he did think that he and Ruth had acquitted themselves well enough to rate some indication of approval. Had they done something wrong? He could not think with his head hot and aching. But he obeyed, directing Ruth to change flight to the Hold when he saw Selianth rise toward him. Prilla gave her right fist the pumping motion that signaled well done and thanks.

Her recognition reduced his grievance.

We fought well and no Thread passed us, Ruth said in a hopeful tone. *I was quite comfortable sustaining my flame.*

"You were marvelous, Ruth. You were such a clever dodger, we didn't have to go *between* once." Jaxom slapped with affectionate force the flight-extended neck. "D'you have more gas to exhale?"

He felt Ruth cough and just the merest trickle flicked beyond his head.

No more flame but I shall be very glad to be rid of the fire-ash. This is the most firestone I have ever chewed!

Ruth sounded so proud of himself that despite his general discomfort, Jaxom laughed, his own spirits buoyed up by Ruth's ingenuous satisfaction.

It was also obscurely comforting to find the Hold occupied by a few drudges only. The other Thread fighters were hours away from the rewards he could now enjoy. While Ruth drank long and deep at the courtyard well, Jaxom asked a drudge to bring him any warm food available and a mug of wine.

As Jaxom entered his own quarters to change out of his stinking fighting gear, he passed his worktable and, seeing the cove sketch, remembered his promise of the previous evening. He thought longingly of the hot sun in that cove. It'd bake the cold out of his bones and dry the wetness in his head and chest.

I would like to swim in the water, Ruth said.

"You're not too tired, are you?"

I am tired but I would like to swim in the cove and then lie in the sand. It would be good for you, too.

"It'd suit me down to the shell," Jaxom said as he stripped off the fighting clothes. He was pulling on fresh riding furs when the drudge, tapping nervously on the half-open door, arrived with the food.

Jaxom gestured toward the worktable and then asked the man to take the discarded clothing to be cleaned and well aired. He was sipping the hot wine, blowing out against the sting of it in his mouth, when he realized that it would be hours before Lytol returned to the Hold and so he couldn't inform his guardian of his intention. But he needn't wait. He could be there and back before Lytol had returned to the Hold. Then he groaned. The cove was halfway on the other side of the world, and the sun which he had wanted to bake the illness out of his body would be well down now on the cove's horizon.

It will remain warm enough long enough, Ruth said. *I really want to go there.*

"We'll go, we'll go!" Jaxom gulped down the last of the hot wine, and reached for the toasted bread and cheese. He didn't feel hungry. In fact the smell of the food made his stomach queasy. He rolled up one of his sleeping furs, to keep the sand off his skin, slung the small pack over his shoulder and started out of his quarters. He'd leave word with the drudge. No, that wasn't sufficient. Jaxom whirled back to his table, the pack banging against his ribs. He wrote a quick note to Lytol and left it propped up between mug and plate where it was clearly visible.

When are we going? Ruth asked, plaintive now with his impatience to be clean and to wallow in the warm sands.

"I'm coming. I'm coming!" Jaxom detoured through the kitchens, scooping up some meatrolls and cheese. He might be hungry later.

The head cook was basting a roast and the smell of it, too, made him feel nauseated.

"Batunon, I've left a message for Lord Lytol in my room. But, if you see him first, tell him I've gone to the cove to wash Ruth."

"Thread is gone from the sky?" Batunon asked, ladle poised above the roast.

"Gone to dust, all of it. I'm away to wash the stink from both our hides."

The yellow tinge in Ruth's whirling eyes was reproachful but Jaxom paid that no heed as he scrambled to the dragon's neck, loosely fastening the fighting straps which would need to be soaked and sunned as well. They were airborne in such haste that Jaxom was glad he had the straps about him. Ruth achieved only the barest minimum of wing room before he transferred them *between*.

·· CHAPTER XIII ··

A Cove in the Southern Continent, 15.7.7–15.8.7

Jaxom roused, felt something wet slip down from his forehead across his nose. He irritably brushed it aside.

You are feeling better? Ruth's voice held a volume of wistful hope that astonished his rider.

"Feel better?" Not quite awake, Jaxom attempted to lift himself up on one elbow but he couldn't move his head, which seemed to be wedged.

Brekke says to lie still.

"Lie still, Jaxom," Brekke ordered. He felt her hand on his chest preventing his movement.

He could hear water dripping somewhere nearby. Then another wet cloth, this one cool and aromatic with scent, was placed on his forehead. He could feel two large blocks, padded because they lay along his cheeks to his shoulder, on either side of his head, presumably to keep him from moving his head from side to side. He wondered what was wrong. Why was Brekke there?

You've been very sick, Ruth said, anxiety coloring his tone. *I was very worried. I called Brekke. She is a healer. She heard me. I couldn't leave you. She came with F'nor on Canth. Then F'nor went for the other one.*

"Have I been sick a long time?" Jaxom was dismayed to think he'd needed two nurses. He hoped that the "other one" wasn't Deelan.

"Several days," Brekke replied, but Ruth seemed to think a longer period of time. "You'll be all right now. The fever's finally broken."

"Lytol knows where I am?" Jaxom opened his eyes then, found them covered by the compress and reached to pull it away. But spots danced in front of his eyes, even shielded by the fabric of the compress, and he groaned and closed his lids.

"I told you to lie still. And don't open your eyes or try to remove the bandage," Brekke said, giving his hand a little slap. "Of course Lytol knows. F'nor took word to him immediately. I sent word when your fever had broken. Menolly's has too."

"Menolly? How could she catch my cold? She was with Sebell."

Someone else was in the room because Brekke couldn't speak and laugh at the same time. She began quietly explaining that he hadn't had a cold. He'd had an illness known as fire-head to Southerners; its initial symptoms were similar to those of a cold.

"But I'm going to be all right, aren't I?"

"Are your eyes bothering you?"

"I don't really want to open them again."

"Spots? As if you were staring at the sun?"

"That's it."

Brekke patted his arm. "That's normal, isn't it, Sharra? How long do they generally last?"

"As long as the headache. So keep your eyes covered, Jaxom." Sharra spoke slowly, almost slurring her words but her low voice had a rich lilt that made him wonder if she looked as good as her voice sounded. He doubted it. No one could. "Don't you dare look about. You've still got that headache, haven't you? Well, keep your eyes closed. We've got the place as dark as we can but you could do permanent damage to your eyes if you're not careful right now."

Jaxom felt Brekke adjust the compress. "Menolly got sick, too?"

"Yes, but Master Oldive sent word that she's responding to the medicine very well." Brekke hesitated. "Of course, she hadn't flown Thread or gone *between*, which aggravated the illness for you."

Jaxom groaned. "I've gone *between* with a cold before and got no worse for it."

"With a cold, yes, not with fire-head," Sharra said. "Here, Brekke. This is ready for him now."

He felt a reed placed at his lips. Brekke told him to suck through it as he should not lift his head to drink.

"What is this?" he mumbled around the straw.

"Fruit juice," Sharra said so promptly that Jaxom siped warily. "Just fruit juice, Jaxom. You need liquid in your body right now. The fever dried you out."

The juice was cool in his mouth and so mild in taste that he couldn't figure out from which fruit it came. But it was just what he wanted, not tart enough to irritate moisture-starved tissues in his mouth and throat, and not sweet enough to be nauseating to his empty stomach. He finished it and asked for more, but Brekke told him he'd had enough. He should try to sleep now.

"Ruth? Are you all right?"

Now that you are yourself again, I will eat. I will not go far. I don't need to.

"Ruth?" Alarmed by the thought that his dragon had neglected himself, Jaxom injudiciously tried to raise his head. The pain was incredible.

"Ruth is perfectly all right, Jaxom," Brekke said in a stern voice. Her hands had already pushed his shoulders flat to the bed. "Ruth's been covered with fire-lizards, and he's been bathed regularly morning and evening. He's never been more than two lengths from you. I've reassured him on every concern." Jaxom groaned, having completely forgotten that Brekke could speak to any dragon. "F'nor and Canth have hunted for him because he wouldn't leave you so he's by no means the skin and bones you are. He'll hunt now, none the worse for the waiting. You go to sleep."

He had no option and suspected as he drifted away from consciousness that there had been something besides fruit in that drink.

When he woke, feeling rested and restless, he remembered not to move his head. He began to cast back through distorted memories of being hot and cold. He distinctly remembered reaching the cove, staggering into the shade, collapsing at the base of a redfruit tree, struggling to reach the cluster of fruit, longing for the liquid to cool his parched mouth and throat. That must have been when Ruth realized he was ill.

Jaxom could vaguely recall fevered glimpses of Brekke and F'nor, could remember pleading with them to bring Ruth to him. He supposed they had erected some kind of temporary hold for shelter. Sharra had said something to that effect. He extended his left arm slowly, moved it up and down, without contacting more than the frame of the bed. He extended his right arm.

"Jaxom?" He heard Sharra's soft voice. "And Ruth too fast asleep himself to warn me. Are you thirsty?" She didn't sound contrite that she'd been asleep. She made a small sound of dismay as she touched the now dry compress. "Don't open your eyes."

She removed the bandage and he heard her dipping it in liquid, wringing it out and then he shivered at its touch on his skin. He reached up, holding the bandage against his forehead, lightly at first and then with more confident pressure.

"Hey, it doesn't hurt—"

"*Ssssh*. Brekke's asleep and she wakes so easily." Sharra's voice had been muted; now her fingers closed his lips.

"Why can't I move my head from side to side?" Jaxom tried not to sound as startled as he felt.

Sharra's low laugh reassured him. "We've got two blocks wedging your head so you can't move. Remember?" She guided his hands to them, then moved the restraints aside. "Turn your head, just a little now, from side to side. If your skin is no longer sensitive, you may be over the worst of the fire-head."

Gingerly he rotated his head, left and then right. He made a bolder motion. "It doesn't hurt. It actually doesn't hurt."

"Oh, no, you don't." Sharra grabbed his wrist as he reached for the compress. "I've a night light on. Wait till I shield it. The less light, the better."

He heard her fumbling with a glow-basket shield. "All right now?"

"I'm only permitting you to try," she stressed the last word as she covered his hand on the bandage with hers, "because it's a moonless hour of night and you couldn't do any harm. If you see even the tiniest patch of glare, cover your eyes instantly."

"It's that dangerous?"

"It can be."

Slowly she peeled the bandage back.

"I don't see anything!"

"Any glare or spots?"

"No? Nothing. Oh!" Something had been obscuring his vision for now he could see dim outlines.

"I had my hand in front of your nose, just in case," she said.

He could make out the dark blur of her body beside him. She must be on her knees. Slowly his sight improved as he blinked sandy incrustations from his lashes.

"My eyes are full of sand."

"Just a moment." Suddenly water was dribbled carefully into his eyes. He blinked furiously, complained loudly. "I told you to hush, you'll wake Brekke. She's worn out. Now, does that clear the sand?"

"Yes, it's much better. I didn't mean to be so much trouble."

"Oh? I thought you'd planned all this on purpose."

Jaxom caught one of her hands and brought it to his lips, holding it as fast as his weakened condition permitted because she gasped at the kiss and withdrew her hand.

"Thanks!"

"I'm putting your bandage back on," she said, the reproach in her voice unmistakable.

Jaxom chuckled, pleased to have disconcerted her. His only regret was the lack of light. He could see that she was slender. Her voice, despite her firmness, sounded young. Would her face be lovely enough to match that voice?

"Please drink all this juice," she said, and he felt the straw against his lips. "Another good sleep now and you're over the worst of it."

"You're a healer?" Jaxom was dismayed. Her voice had sounded so young. He'd assumed she was a fosterling of Brekke's.

"Certainly. You don't think they'd entrust the life of the Lord of Ruatha Hold to an apprentice? I've had a lot of experience getting people through fire-head."

The familiar floating sensation induced by fellis juice flooded him and he couldn't have answered her no matter how urgently he wanted to.

To his disappointment, when he awoke the next day, Brekke answered his call. It didn't seem courteous to inquire where Sharra was. Nor could he ask Ruth since Brekke could hear the exchange. But Sharra had evidently told Brekke of his middle-of-the-night awakening because her voice sounded lighter, almost gay as she greeted him. To celebrate his recovery, she permitted him a cup of weak *klah* and a bowl of moistened sweetbread.

Warning him to keep his eyes closed, she changed the bandage but the replacement was not as dense and when he opened his eyes, cautiously, he could distinguish light and dark areas about him.

Midday he was allowed to sit up and eat the light meal Brekke provided, but even that slight activity exhausted him. Nonetheless he complained petulantly to Brekke when she offered him more juice to drink.

"Fellis-laced? Am I expected to sleep my life away?"

"Oh, you'll be making up for this lost time, I assure you," she replied, a cryptic remark that puzzled him as he drifted off to sleep again.

The next day he chafed further at the restrictions imposed on him. He chafed but, when Sharra and Brekke assisted him to the bench so they could exchange rushbags on the bed, he was so weak after sitting up a few minutes that he was very grateful to be down again. He was all the more surprised then, that evening, to hear N'ton's voice in the other room.

"You look a lot better, Jaxom," N'ton said, walking quietly up to the bed. "Lytol will be immensely relieved. But if you ever," N'ton's harsh voice reflected his anxieties, "attempt to fight Thread again when you're ill, I'll . . . I'll . . . I'll throw you to Lessa's mercies."

"I didn't think I'd more than a stuffed head, N'ton," Jaxom replied, nervously poking at grassy bumps in his bedbag. "and it *was* my first Fall on Ruth . . ."

"I know, I know," N'ton said, his tone considerably less reproving. "You couldn't have known you were coming down with fire-head. You owe your life to Ruth, you know. F'nor says Ruth has more sense than most people. Half the dragons on Pern wouldn't have known what to do with their rider delirious; they would have been totally confused by the confusion in their riders' minds. No, you and Ruth are in very good odor at Benden. Very good! You just concentrate on getting your strength back. And when you're feeling stronger, D'ram said he'd be glad to bear you company and show you some of the interesting things he found while he was here."

"He didn't mind me and Ruth following him?"

"No," N'ton was genuinely surprised at Jaxom's question. "No, lad, I think he was surprised that he'd been missed and gratified that he's still needed as a dragonrider."

"N'ton!" Brekke's call was firm.

"I was told I couldn't stay long." Jaxom could hear N'ton's feet scraping on the ground as he rose. "I'll come again, I promise." Jaxom could hear Tris complaining and he visualized the little fire-lizard clutching N'ton's shoulder for balance.

"How's Menolly? Is she recovering? Tell Lytol that I'm very sorry to cause him worry!"

"He knows that, Jaxom. And Menolly's much better. I've seen her, too. She had a lighter touch of fire-head than you did. Sebell recognized the symptoms almost immediately and called in Oldive. Don't be in a rush to get up, though."

As glad as he'd been for N'ton's visit, Jaxom was relieved that it had been short. He felt limp and his head began to ache.

"Brekke?" Could he be having a relapse?

"She's with N'ton, Jaxom."

"Sharra! My head is aching." He couldn't help the waver in his voice.

Her cool hand touched his cheek. "No fever, Jaxom. You tire quickly, that's all. Sleep now."

The reasonable words, spoken in her gentle rich voice lulled him and, though he wanted to remain awake, his eyes closed. Her fingers massaged his forehead, descended to his neck, gently smoothing the tension, all the while her voice encouraged him to rest, to sleep. And he did.

The cool, moist sea breeze roused him at dawn, and he fumbled irritably to cover his exposed legs and back for he'd been sleeping on his stomach, tangled in the light blanket. Having rearranged himself with some difficulty, he couldn't drop back to sleep again though he had closed his eyes, expecting to do so. He opened them again, fretfully gazing beyong the raised curtains of the shelter. He exclaimed in surprise, tensing, just then aware that his eyes were no longer bandaged and his vision was unimpaired.

"Jaxom?"

Twisting around, he saw Sharra's tall figure swing from the hammock, noticed the length of dark hair streaming about her shoulders, obscuring her face.

"Sharra!"

"Your eyes, Jaxom?" she asked in a hushed worried tone and walked swiftly to his bed.

"My eyes are just fine, Sharra," he replied, catching her hand in his, keeping her where he could see her face clearly in the dim light. "Oh, no, you don't," he said with a low laugh as she tried to break his hold. "I've been waiting to see what you looked like." With his free hand, he pushed aside the hair that covered her face.

"And?" She drawled the word in proud defiance, unconsciously straightening her shoulders and tossing her hair back.

Sharra was not pretty. He'd expected that. Her features were too irregular, in particular her nose was too long for her face, and though her chin was well shaped it was a shade too firm for beauty. But her mouth had a lovely double curve, the left side twitching as she contained the humor which her deep-set eyes echoed. She arched her left eyebrow slowly, amused by his scrutiny.

"And?" she repeated.

"I know you may not agree but *I* think you're beautiful!" He resisted her second attempt to free her hand and rise. "You must be aware that you have a beautiful speaking voice."

"I have tried to cultivate *that*," she said.

"You've succeeded." He exerted pressure on her hand, pulling her still closer. It was immensely important to him to determine her age.

She laughed softly, wriggling her fingers in his tight grasp. "Let me go now, Jaxom, be a good boy!"

"I am not good and I am not a boy." He had spoken with a low intensity which drove the good-natured amusement from her expression. She returned his gaze steadily and then gave him a small smile.

"No, you're neither good nor a boy. You've been a very sick man and it's my job," she stressed the word just slightly as he let her withdraw her hand from his, "to make you well again."

"The sooner, the better." Jaxom lay back, smiling up at her. She'd be nearly his height when he stood, he thought. That they would be able to look eye to eye appealed to him.

She gave him one long, slightly puzzled look and then, with a cryptic shrug, turned away from him, gathering her hair and twining it neatly about her head as she left the room.

Although neither of them mentioned that dawn confidence, afterward Jaxom found it easier to accept the restraints of his convalescence in good grace. He ate what he was given without complaint, took the medicines, and obeyed instructions to rest.

One worry fretted him until he finally blurted it out to Brekke.

"When I was fevered, Brekke, did I . . . I mean . . ."

Brekke smiled and patted his hand reassuringly. "We never pay any attention to such ramblings. Generally, they're so incoherent they make no sense whatever."

Some note in her voice bothered him, though. ". . . so incoherent, they make no sense?" He had babbled his head off, then. Not that he minded about Brekke if he had said something about that dratted queen egg. But if Sharra had heard? She was from the Southern Hold. Would she be as quick to discount his ramblings about that double-blasted shard-shelled egg? He couldn't relax. What wretched luck to fall ill when you had a secret that must be kept! He worried over that until he fell asleep, and picked right up on the same train of thought the next morning, though he forced himself to be cheerful as he listened to Ruth bathing with the fire-lizards.

He comes, Ruth said suddenly, sounding startled. *And D'ram brings him.*

"D'ram brings whom?" Jaxom asked.

"Sharra," Brekke called from the other room, "our guests have arrived. Would you escort them from the beach?" She came quickly into Jaxom's room, smoothing the light blanket and peering intently at his face. "Is your face clean? How are your hands?"

"Who's coming that has you in a flurry? Ruth?"

He's pleased to see me, too. Ruth's sound of surprise was colored with delight.

Jaxom was forewarned by that remark, but he could only stare, stunned, as Lytol came striding into the room. His face was tense and pale under the flying helmet, and he hadn't bothered to unfasten his jacket on the walk up from the beach, so perspiration beads formed on his forehead and upper lip. He stood in the doorway, just looking at his ward.

Abruptly, he turned toward the outside wall, harshly clearing his throat, stripping off helmet and gloves, unbelting his jacket, grunting in surprise when Brekke appeared at his elbow to relieve him of the gear. As she passed Jaxom's bed on her way out of the room, she gave him such an intense look that he couldn't fathom what she was trying to convey.

She says that he is crying, Ruth told him. *And that you are not to be surprised or embarrass him.* Ruth paused. *She is also thinking that Lytol is healed, too? Lytol hasn't been ill.*

Jaxom didn't have time to sort out that oblique reference because his guardian had already recovered his composure and turned.

"Hot here after Ruatha," Jaxom said, struggling to break the silence.

"You want a bit of sun, boy," Lytol said at the same moment.

"I'm not allowed out of bed, yet."

"The mountain is just as you sketched it."

They spoke again simultaneously, answering each other's comments.

It was too much for Jaxom, who burst out laughing, waving Lytol to sit beside him on the bed. Still laughing, Jaxom grabbed Lytol's forearm, holding it firmly, trying in that grasp to apologize for all the concern he'd caused. Abruptly he was engulfed in Lytol's rough embrace, his back soundly thumped when the man released him. Tears sprang to Jaxom's eyes, too, at the unexpected demonstration. Lytol had always been scrupulous in caring for his ward but the older Jaxom had grown, the more he had wondered if Lytol really liked him at all.

"I thought I had lost you."

"I'm harder to lose than you'd think, sir."

Jaxom couldn't stop grinning foolishly because Lytol actually had a smile on his face: the first one Jaxom recalled.

"You're nothing but bones and white skin," Lytol said in his customary gruff manner.

"That'll pass. I'm allowed to eat all I want," Jaxom replied. "Care for something?"

"I didn't come to eat. I came to see you. And I'll tell you this, young Lord Jaxom, I think you'd better go back to the Mastersmith for more drafting lessons: you did not accurately place the trees along the cove shore in that sketch of yours. Though the mountain is very well done."

"I knew I had the trees wrong, sir, one of the things I planned to check out. Only when I got back here, it went clean out of my head."

"So I understand," and Lytol gave a rusty laugh.

"Give me the news of the Hold." Jaxom was suddenly eager for those minor details that had once bored him.

They chatted away in a companionable fashion that astonished Jaxom. He'd been ill at ease with Lytol, he realized now, ever since he had inadvertently Impressed Ruth. But that strain had evaporated. If this illness of his did no other good, it had brought him and Lytol closer than Jaxom in his boyhood could ever have imagined.

Brekke entered, smiling apologetically. "I'm sorry, Lord Lytol, but Jaxom tires easily."

Lytol obediently rose, glancing anxiously at Jaxom.

"Brekke, after Lytol has come all this distance, on dragonback, he *must* be allowed to . . ."

"No, lad, I can return." Lytol's smile startled Brekke. "I'd rather not take a risk with him." He gave Brekke a second surprise then as he embraced Jaxom with awkward affection before striding from the room.

Brekke stared at Jaxom, who shrugged to indicate she could put her own interpretation on his guardian's behavior. She quickly left to escort the visitors back to the beach.

He was very glad to see you, Ruth said. *He is smiling*.

Jaxom lay back, wriggling his shoulders into the rushes to get comfortable. He closed his eyes, chucking to himself. He had got Lytol to see his beautiful mountain.

Lytol wasn't the only one to come to see the mountain, and Jaxom. Lord Groghe arrived the next afternoon, grunting and puffing from the heat, shouting at his little queen not to get lost with all those strangers, and not to get completely soaked because he didn't want a wet shoulder on the way back.

"Heard you'd got ill of that fire-head stuff like the harper girl," Lord Groghe said, swinging into Jaxom's room with a vigor that produced instant fatigue in the convalescent.

More unnerving was Lord Groghe's scrutiny. Jaxom was certain the man counted his ribs, he had looked at them so long. "Can't you feed him up better than this, Brekke? Thought you were a top-flight healer. Boy's a rake! Can't have that. Must say you picked a beautiful place to fall ill in. Must have a look about me since I'm down here. Not that it took all that long to come. Hmmm. Yes, must have a look about." Groghe stuck his chin out as Jaxom, frowning again. "Did you? Before that sickness got hold of you?"

Jaxom realized that Lord Groghe's totally unexpected visit might have several objectives: one, to assure the Lord Holders that the Lord of Ruatha was in the land of the living, all rumor to the contrary. The second purpose made Jaxom a little uneasy when he could so clearly recall Lessa's remark about wanting "the best part of it."

When Brekke tactfully reminded the blustering and genial Lord Holder that he mustn't tire her patient, Jaxom nearly cheered.

"Don't worry, lad. I'll be back again, never fear." Lord Groghe waved cheerfully to him from the doorway. "Beautiful spot. Envy you."

"Does everyone in the North know where I am?" Jaxom asked when Brekke returned.

"D'ram brought him," she said, sighing heavily and frowning.

"D'ram ought to have known better," Sharra said, collapsing on the bench and plying a tree frond as a fan in exaggerated relief at the Lord's departure. "The man's enough to wear the healthy down, much less the convalescent."

"I would guess," Brekke continued, ignoring Sharra's remarks, "that the Lord Holders needed verification of Jaxom's recovery."

"He looked Jaxom over like a herdsman. Did you show him your teeth?"

"Don't let Lord Groghe's manner fool you, Sharra," Jaxom said. "He's got a mind as sharp as Master Robinton's. And if D'ram brought him, then F'lar and Lessa must have known he was coming. I don't think they'll like him returning—or scouting around here."

"If Lessa did permit Lord Groghe to come, she'll hear from me about it, you may be sure," Brekke replied, thinning her lips in disapproval. "He is not an easy visitor for a convalescent. You might as well know now, Jaxom, that you were ill of that fever for sixteen days . . ."

"What?" Jaxom sat upright in the bed, stunned. "But . . . but . . ."

"Fire-head is a dangerous disease for an adult," Sharra said. She glanced at Brekke, who nodded. "You nearly died."

"I did?" Appalled, Jaxom put his hand to his head.

Brekke nodded again. "So, if we seem to be restricting you to a very slow recovery, you will agree that we have cause."

"I nearly died?" Jaxom couldn't absorb that news.

"So we will go slowly to ensure your health. Now, I think it's time you had something to eat," Brekke said as she left the room.

"I nearly died?" Jaxom turned to Sharra.

"I'm afraid so." She sounded more amused by his reaction than concerned. "The important thing is that you didn't die." Involuntarily she glanced toward the beach and sighed, a quick exhalation of relief. She smiled, a brief one, but Jaxom noticed that her expressive eyes were dark with remembered sorrow.

"Who died of fire-head that saddens you, Sharra?"

"No one you know, Jaxom, and no one I knew very well. It's just . . . just that no healer likes to lose a patient."

He could tease no more from her on the subject and stopped trying to when he saw that she had felt that death so keenly.

The next morning, cursing with embarrassment at the unreliability of his legs, Jaxom was assisted to the beach by Brekke and Sharra. Ruth came charging up the sands, almost dangerous in his delight at seeing his friend. Brekke sternly ordered Ruth to stand still lest he knock Jaxom off his unsteady feet. Ruth's eyes rolled with concern and he crooned with apology as he extended his head very carefully toward Jaxom, almost afraid to muzzle him in greeting. Jaxom flung his arms about his dragon's neck, Ruth tightening his muscles to take the drag of his friend's body, almost thrumming with encouragement. Tears flowed down his cheeks which he quickly dried against his friend's soft hide. Dear Ruth. Marvelous Ruth. Unbidden came the thought to Jaxom's mind: "If I had died of fire-head . . ."

You did not, Ruth said. *You stayed. I told you to. And you are much stronger now. You will get stronger every day and we will swim and sun and it will be good.*

Ruth sounded so fierce that Jaxom had to soothe him with words and caresses until Brekke and Sharra insisted that he had better sit down before he fell. They had arranged a matting of woven streamer fronds against a landward-leaning trunk, well back from the shore, to avoid full exposure to the sun. To this couch they assisted him. Ruth stretched out so that his head rested by Jaxom's side, the jeweled eyes whirling with the lavenders of stress.

F'lar and Lessa arrived at midday, after Jaxom had had a short nap. He was surprised to find that Lessa, for all her abrasiveness on other occasions, made a soothing visitor, quiet and soft-voiced.

"We had to let Lord Groghe come in person, Jaxom, though I'm sure you didn't appreciate the visit. Rumor had you dead and Ruth, too." Lessa shrugged expressively. "Bad news needs no harper."

"Lord Groghe was more interested in where I was than how I was, wasn't he?" Jaxom asked pointedly.

F'lar nodded and grinned at him. "That is why we had D'ram bring him. The Fort Hold watchdragon is too old to take a placement from Lord Groghe's mind."

"He also had his fire-lizard with him," Jaxom said.

"Those pesky creatures," Lessa said, her eyes sparkling with annoyance.

"These same pesky creatures came in very handy saving Jaxom's life, Lessa," Brekke said firmly.

"All right, they have uses but, as far as I'm concerned, their bad habits still outweigh the good ones."

"Lord Groghe's little queen may be intelligent," Brekke went on, "but not clever enough to get him back here on his own."

"That isn't the real problem," F'lar grimaced. "He's now seen that mountain. And the scope of the land."

"So, we put in our claim here first," Lessa replied decisively. "I don't care how many sons Groghe wants to settle, the dragonriders of Pern have first choice. Jaxom can help—"

"Jaxom has some time to go before he can do very much of anything," Brekke said, breaking in so smoothly that Jaxom wondered if he'd misinterpreted the surprise on Lessa's face.

"Don't worry, I'll think of some way to stall Lord Groghe's ambitions," F'lar added.

"If one gets in, the others will follow," Brekke said thoughtfully, "and I can hardly blame them. This part of the Southern Continent is so much more beautiful than our original settlement."

"I have a yearning to get closer to that mountain," F'lar said, turning his head to the south. "Jaxom, I know you've not been very active yet, but how many of those fire-lizards about Ruth are Southerners?"

"They're not from the Southern Weyr, if that's what you're worried about," Sharra said.

"How can you tell?" Lessa asked.

Sharra shrugged. "They won't be handled. They go *between* if anyone gets close to them. It's Ruth that fascinates them. Not us."

"We are not *their* men," Jaxom said. "Now that I can get to Ruth, I'll see what I can find out about them from him."

"I wish you would," Lessa said. "And if there are any from the Southern Weyr . . ." She let her sentence trail off.

"I think we ought to let Jaxom rest," Brekke said.

F'lar chuckled, gesturing for Lessa to precede him. "Fine guests we are. Come to see the man and never let him talk."

"I've done nothing lately to talk about," and Jaxom shot a fierce look at Brekke and Sharra. "When you come back, I will."

"If anything interesting occurs, have Ruth bespeak Mnementh or Ramoth."

Brekke and Sharra left with the Weyrleaders, and Jaxom was grateful for the respite. He could hear Ruth talking to the two Benden dragons and he chuckled when Ruth told Ramoth firmly that there were no fire-lizards from the Southern Weyr among his new friends. Jaxom wondered why it hadn't occurred to him sooner to ask Ruth's acquaintances about their men. He sighed. He hadn't been thinking about much lately except his extraordinary brush with death, and that occupied his mind too morbidly. Much better for him to explore a living puzzle.

He had several. The most worrisome was still what he might have said in his delirium. Brekke's rejoinder had been no real assurance. He tried to force his thought back to that time but all he remembered was heat and cold, vivid but vague nightmares.

He thought about his guardian's visit. So Lytol did like him! Shells! He'd forgotten to ask Lytol about Corana. He ought to have sent her some kind of word. She must have heard of his illness. Not but what this didn't make it easier for him to complete the break in their relationship. Now that he'd seen Sharra, he couldn't have continued with Corana. He must remember to ask Lytol.

What *had* he said when he was fevered? How did a fever patient talk? In bits and snatches? Whole phrases? Maybe he needn't worry. Not about what he could have said in fever.

He didn't like Lord Groghe just appearing like that, to check up on him. And, if he hadn't taken ill, Lord Groghe would never have known about this part of Southern. At least, until the dragonriders wanted him to know. And that mountain! Too unusual a feature to forget. Any dragon would be able to find it. Or would they? Unless the rider had a very clear picture, the dragon did not always see vividly enough to jump *between*. And a secondhand vision? D'ram and Tiroth had done so from Master Robinton's description. But D'ram and Tiroth were experienced.

Jaxom wanted to be well. He wanted to get closer to that mountain. He wanted to be first. How long would it take him to recover?

•

He was allowed to swim a bit the next day, an exercise which Brekke said would tone his muscles, but which succeeded in proving he had none left. Exhausted, he was no sooner on his beachside couch than he fell deeply asleep.

Roused by Sharra's touch, he cried out and sat bolt upright, looking about him.

"What's the matter, Jaxom?"

"A dream! A nightmare!" He was sure something was wrong. Then he saw Ruth, stretched out, fast asleep, his muzzle only a handsbreadth from his feet, at least a dozen fire-lizards curled on and about him, twitching in their own dreams.

"Well, you're awake now. What's wrong?"

"That dream was so vivid . . . and yet it's all gone. I wanted so much to remember it."

Sharra placed a cool hand on his forehead. He pushed it away.

"I'm not fevered," he said, cranky.

"No, you're not. Any headache? Spots?"

Impatient and angry, he denied them, then sighed and smiled an apology at her. "Bad-tempered, aren't I?"

"Rarely." She grinned, then eased to the sand beside him.

"If I swim a little longer and further every day, how long will it take me to recover fully?"

"What makes you so anxious?"

Jaxom grinned, jerking his head back in the direction of the mountain. "I want to get there before Lord Groghe does."

"Oh, I think you'll manage that quite easily." Sharra's expression was mischievous. "You will get stronger every day now. We just don't want you to push yourself too quickly. Better a few more days now, than suffer a relapse and go through all this again."

"A relapse? How would I know if I was having one?"

"Easy. Spots and headaches. Do please do it our way, Jaxom."

The appeal in her blue eyes was genuine, and Jaxom liked to think it was for him, Jaxom, not for him, the patient. Not taking his eyes from hers, he nodded slowly in acquiescence and was rewarded by her slow smile.

F'nor and D'ram arrived late that afternoon, in fighting gear, with full firestone sacks draped across their dragons.

"Thread tomorrow," Sharra told Jaxom as she caught his look of inquiry.

"Thread?"

"It falls on all Pern, and has fallen here in this cove three times since you took ill. In fact, the day after you took ill!" She grinned at his openmouthed consternation. "It's been a rare treat to watch dragons in the sky. We'd only to keep the shelter area free. Grub takes care of the rest." She chuckled. "Tiroth complains that he's not fighting

full when he doesn't follow the Fall to its end. Just wait till you see
Ruth in action. Oh, yes, nothing could keep him out of the sky. Brekke
keeps her ear open for him and, of course, Tiroth and Canth are directing. He's so proud of himself, protecting you!"

Jaxom swallowed against a variety of emotions, chagrin being
foremost as he heard Sharra's casual explanation.

"You were aware of Thread, by the way. Once a dragonrider,
one evidently doesn't forget—even in fever. You kept moaning about
Thread coming and not being able to get off the ground." Fortunately
she was looking at the dragons as they glided to a landing on the beach
because Jaxom was certain that his expression gave him away. "Master
Oldive says that we humans have instincts, too, hidden deep in our
minds, to which we respond automatically. As you reacted to Threadfall, sick as you were. Ruth is such a dote. I made much of him after
each Fall, I assure you, and I made sure that the fire-lizards got all
firestone stink out of his hide."

She waved a greeting to F'nor and D'ram as they strolled up the
beach, loosening their fighting gear. Canth and Tiroth had already
shrugged off the firestone sacks on the beach and, wings extended
high, waddled with groans of pleasure into the soft warm water. Ruth
came slithering through the water to join them. A great fair of fire-
lizards chittered above the three dragons, overjoyed with such
company.

"You've more color, Jaxom, you look better!" F'nor said, grasping
Jaxom's arm in greeting.

D'ram nodded his head, agreeing with F'nor.

Aware of his indebtedness to both riders, Jaxom stammered out
his gratitude.

"Tell you something, Jaxom," F'nor said, squatting on his
haunches, "it's been a rare treat to watch your little fellow work in the
air. He's a superb chop-and-change artist. Caught three times as much
Thread as our big fellows could. You trained him well!"

"I don't suppose I'll be considered strong enough to fight Thread
tomorrow?"

"No, nor for some time to come," F'nor replied firmly. "Know
how you're feeling, Jaxom," he continued as he dropped beside him
on the mats. "Felt the same way when I was wounded and not allowed
to fly Thread. But now, your only responsibility to Hold and Weyr is
to get fit. Fit enough to take a good look about this country! I envy
you that chance, Jaxom. Indeed I do!" F'nor's grin was candidly envious. "Haven't had the time to fly far, even after Thread, down here.
Forest extends a long way on either side." F'nor gestured broadly with
one arm. "You'll see. Shall I bring you writing materials next trip down
so you can make a Record? You may not fly Thread yet awhile, Jaxom,
but you'll be working hard enough to make that a treat!"

"You're only saying that . . ." Jaxom broke off, surprised at the bitterness in his voice.

"Yes, because you need something to look forward to since you can't do what you want most," F'nor said. He reached out and gripped Jaxom's arm. "I understand, Jaxom. Ruth's been giving Canth a full report. Sorry. Awkward for you, but Ruth worries when you're upset, or didn't you know that?" He chuckled.

"I appreciate what you're trying to do. F'nor," Jaxom said.

Just then Brekke and Sharra emerged from the trees, Brekke walking quickly to her Weyrmate. She did not, as Jaxom half-expected, embrace the brown rider. But the way she regarded him, the gentle, almost hesitant way she rested her hand on his arm, spoke more tellingly of the love between the two than any more demonstrative welcome. A bit embarrassed, Jaxom turned his head and saw Sharra watching Brekke and F'nor, a peculiar expression on her face which she erased the moment she realized that Jaxom was looking at her.

"Drinks all round," she said in a brisk tone, handing a mug to D'ram as Brekke served F'nor.

It was a pleasant evening and they ate on the beach, Jaxom managing to suppress his frustration in the face of the morning's Threadfall. The three dragons made nests in the still warm sands above the high-tide lines, their eyes glistening like jewels in the dark beyond the firelight.

Brekke and Sharra sang one of Menolly's tunes while D'ram added a rough bass line. When Brekke noticed Jaxom's head lolling to one side, he didn't resist her ordering him back to the shelter. He drifted to sleep, face turned toward the fireglow, lulled by the singing voices.

Ruth's excitement roused him and he blinked without comprehension as the dragon's voice penetrated his sleep. *Thread!* Ruth was going to fight Thread today with D'ram's Tiroth and F'nor's Canth. Jaxom threw aside the blanket, struggled into his trousers, and strode quickly from the shelter to the beach. Brekke and Sharra were helping the two dragonriders load their beasts with the firestone sacks. With the four fire-lizards on the ground at his feet, Ruth was industriously chewing away at the pile of stone on the beach. Dawn was just breaking in the east, Jaxom peered through the dim light, straining to see the filmy discoloration that meant Thread. The three Dawn Sisters winked with unexpected brilliance high above him, paling to insignificance the other morning stars in the west. Jaxom frowned at their display. He hadn't realized how bright they were, how close they seemed. In Ruatha, they were duller, barely visible points on the southeastern horizon at dawn. He reminded himself to ask if F'nor could have the use of a long-distance viewer, and if Lytol would send down his star

equations and maps. Then Jaxom noticed the absence of the fairs of
Southern fire-lizards which haunted Ruth day and night.

"Jaxom!" Brekke noticed him. The two riders waved a greeting
and swung up on their beasts.

Jaxom checked Ruth to be sure he had enough stone in his gullet,
caressing his friend and applauding his willingness to fly Thread
though riderless.

*I remember all the drills we were taught at Fort Weyr. I have F'nor and
Canth, and D'ram and Tiroth to help. Brekke always watches me, too. I have
never listened to a woman before. But Brekke is good! She is also sad but Canth
says it is good for her to hear us. She knows that she is never alone.*

They were all facing east where the Red Star pulsed, round and
brightly orange-red. A film seemed to float across it and F'nor, raising
his hand, called Ruth to take wing. Canth and Tiroth leapt strongly
into the air, their wings beating in powerful strokes to assist their
rising. Ruth was well aloft before them and straining ahead. Beside
him four fire-lizards appeared, as dwarfed by him as he was by Canth
and Tiroth.

"Don't meet Thread alone, Ruth!" Jaxom cried.

"He won't," Brekke said, her eyes twinkling. "He is young
enough to want to be first. At that, he saves the older dragons a lot
of effort. But we must go in."

As one, the three paused for a last look at their defenders and
then moved quickly inside the shelter.

"You can't see much," Sharra told Jaxom, who had gone to stand
by the open doorway.

"I'd see if Thread got into this greenery."

"It won't. We've clever riders."

Jaxom felt the skin on his back begin to crawl and he gave a
massive shudder.

"Don't you dare catch a cold," Sharra said. She collected a shirt
from his room which she threw at him.

"I'm not cold. I'm just thinking of Thread and this forest."

Sharra made a disparaging sound. "I forget. You're Northern
Hold-bred! Thread can't do any more than tear or hole leaves which
heal in Southern forests. It's all grubbed. And, in case you're interested, that's the first thing F'nor and D'ram did—check to be sure the
land here is well-grubbed. It is!"

We have met Thread, Ruth told him, sounding elated. *I am flaming
well. I am to do V-sweeps while Canth and Tiroth pass east and west. We are
high. The fire-lizards flame well, too. Over there! Berd. You are closest! Meer,
get it to your offside. Talla! Help him. I come, I come. Down. I come. I flame!
I protect my friend!*

Brekke caught Jaxom's eyes, smiling at him. "He delivers a running comment so we all know how well he fights!" Her eyes lost their

focus on him and then she blinked. "Sometimes I see the Fall through three sets of dragon eyes. I don't know where I'm looking! It goes well!"

Later, Jaxom could not have said what he ate or drank. When Ruth's monologue resumed, Jaxom paid strict attention to what his dragon said, looking now and again at Brekke whose face reflected the intense concentration of listening to three dragons and four fire-lizards. Suddenly Ruth's commentary stopped and Jaxom gasped.

"It's all right. They don't pursue Thread through the Fall," Brekke said. "Just enough to insure our safety. Benden flies Thread tomorrow evening over Nerat. F'nor and Canth ought not overtire themselves today."

Jaxom rose so abruptly that his bench clattered to the floor. He mumbled an apology, righted it and then strode out the door in the direction of the beach. As he reached the sands, he kept peering westward and barely discerned the distant film of Thread. Another shudder gripped him and he had to smooth the hair down on the back of his neck. The cove before him, generally calm with leisurely waves, was roiled with the activity of fish diving, lifting their bodies above the surface and crashing awkwardly down again as if in the throes of pain.

"What's the matter with them?" he asked Sharra, who had joined him.

"The fish are having a good feed off Thread. They generally manage to clean up the cove in time for our dragons to bathe when they return. There! There they all are! Just popped back!"

It was a good Fall! Ruth was jubilant, then rebellious. *But we are not to follow it. Canth and Tiroth said that once across the big river there is nothing but stony waste and it is stupid to waste flame above what cannot be hurt by Thread. Ooooh!*

Sharra and Jaxom laughed as the little white dragon emitted a trail of flame, almost singeing his muzzle because he was at the wrong flight angle. He corrected instantly, continuing his downward glide on the correct plane.

Even as the big dragons landed, the waters had calmed. Ruth was full of boast that he'd not needed to replenish his fire once, that he now knew how much to take to last the Fall. Canth turned his head toward the little white in an attitude of amused tolerance.

Tiroth snorted and, relieved of his firesack, nodded once toward D'ram then waded into the water. Abruptly the air was full of fire-lizards, hovering eagerly above Tiroth. The old bronze threw his head skyward, snorted again and, with a loud sigh, rolled over in the water. The fire-lizards descended, dropping mouthsful of sand on him before attacking his hide with all four feet. Tiroth's eyes, lidded once against the water, gleamed just beneath the surface in an eerie submarine rainbow.

Canth bellowed and half the fair left Tiroth to minister to him as he splashed about. Ruth watched this pre-emption of his friends, blinked, gave himself a bit of a shake and meekly took to the water at some distance from the bronze and brown. Four fire-lizards, the banded ones, detached themselves from the big dragons and began to scrub the little white.

"Here, I'll help you, Jaxom," Sharra said.

Scrubbing a dragon's hide free of firestone stink is a tiring job under any circumstances and, although he only had to do one side of Ruth, Jaxom had to grit his teeth to finish.

"I told you not to overdo, Jaxom," Sharra said, her voice sharp as she straightened from scrubbing the fork of Ruth's tail and noticed Jaxom leaning against the dragon's rump. She gestured imperiously toward the beach. "Get out! I'll bring you some food. You're whiter than he is!"

"I'm never going to get myself fit if I don't try!"

"Stop muttering at me under your breath . . ."

"And don't tell me you're doing it for my own good . . ."

"No, for mine! I don't want to have to nurse you through a relapse!"

She glared at him so fiercely that he gathered himself erect and stalked out of the water. Though it wasn't far to his informal bed under the trees, his legs were leaden as he dragged them through the water. He lay down, heaving a sigh of relief, and closed his eyes.

When he opened them again someone was shaking him, and he discovered Brekke peering at him quizzically. "How do you feel now?"

"I was dreaming?"

"Hmmm. Bad ones again?"

"No, curious ones. Only nothing was in focus." Jaxom shook his head to clear the miasma of nightmare. He realized that it was midday. Ruth was asleep snoring, at his left. On the far right, he could see D'ram resting against Tiroth's front leg. There was no sign of F'nor or Canth.

"You're probably hungry," Brekke said, holding out the plate of food and the mug she'd brought.

"How long did I sleep?" Jaxom was disgusted with himself. He stretched his shoulders, feeling muscles stiff from the exercise of scrubbing a dragon.

"Several hours. Did you good,"

"I dream an awful lot lately. Aftereffect of the fire-head?"

Brekke blinked, then frowned thoughtfully. "Come to think of it, I've been dreaming rather more than usual myself. Too much sun perhaps."

At that point, Tiroth woke, bellowed, struggled to his feet, sprinkled his rider with sand. Brekke gasped and rose quickly, her eyes on the old bronze as he shook his body free of sand and extended his wings.

"Brekke, I must go!" D'ram shouted. "Did you hear?"

"Yes, I heard. Do go quicklly!" she called back, raising her hand in farewell.

Whatever had roused Tiroth excited the fire-lizards who began wheeling, diving, chittering raucously. Ruth raised his head, looked at them sleepily, then laid his head back on the sand, unmoved by the excitement. Brekke turned to regard the white dragon, with a curious frown.

"What's wrong, Brekke?"

"The bronzes at Ista Weyr are blooding their kills."

"Oh, Shards and Shells!" Jaxom's initial surprise melded into disappointed disgust with his weakness. He'd hoped to be allowed to attend that mating flight. He'd wanted to cheer G'dened and Barnath on.

"I'll know," Brekke said soothingly. "Canth will be there as well as Tiroth. They'll tell me all. Now, you eat!"

As Jaxom obeyed, still cursing his unfortuante condition, he noticed that Brekke was staring at Ruth again.

"What's the matter with Ruth?"

"Ruth? Nothing. Poor dear, he was so proud to fly Thread for you, and he's too tired to care about anything else right now."

She rose and as she left him Berd and Grall landed on her shoulders, murmuring softly as she disappeared into the shady forest.

Early Morning at Harpercraft Hall, Midmorning at Ista Weyr, Midafternoon at Jaxom's Cove, 15.8.28

In the dark of the early morning Robinton was awakened by Silvina.

"Master Robinton, word has come from Ista Weyr. The bronzes are blooding their kill. Caylith will fly soon. You're wanted there."

"Oh, yes, thank you, Silvina." He blinked against the light from the glow baskets she was unshielding. "You didn't by any chance bring me . . ." He saw the steaming mug by his bed. "Oh, good woman! My undying thanks!"

"That's what you always say," Silvina replied, chuckling as she left him to proceed with his wake-up routine.

He dressed quickly to avoid the predawn chill. Zair took his accustomed shoulder perch, squeaking softly as Robinton paced down the corridor.

With a glow torch to cast some light in the dark lower hall, Silvina awaited him at the massive iron doors. She whirled the release wheel and the great bar lifted from ceiling and floor. He gave the yank required to open the huge door and wondered at the sudden stitch in his side. Then Silvina passed him his gitar, stoutly encased against the bitter cold of *between*.

"I do hope Barnath flies Caylith," she said. "Look, here's Drenth now."

The Harper saw the brown dragon backwinging to land and he ran down the hall steps. Drenth was excited, his eyes gleaming orange and red in the night. Robinton greeted the dragon's rider, paused to sling his gitar across his back and then, reaching for D'fio's hand, climbed to the brown's back.

"How does the wagering stand?" he asked the rider.

"Ah, now Harper; Barnath is a fine beast. He'll fly Caylith. Although," a certain element of doubt tinged the man's voice, "the four bronzes N'ton is permitting to try are good strong young beasts, and mighty eager for the chance. It could be an upset. Put your mark where you will, it'll give you good value."

"I wish I could bet, but it's not the sort of thing I ought to do . . ."

"Now, if you were to pass me the marks, Master Robinton, I'd swear on the Shell of Drenth here that they were mine!"

"After the flight as well as before?" Robinton asked, amusement warring with his unprofessional desire to gamble.

"I'm a dragonrider, Master Robinton," D'fio said gruffly, "not one of those faithless Southerners."

"And I'm Master Harper of Pern," said Robinton. But he leaned into the man's back, pressing a two-mark piece into his hand. "Barnath, of course, and please let none be the wiser."

"As you wish, Master Robinton," D'fio sounded pleased.

They rose above the black shadow of the Fort Hold cliffs, the lighter darkness of night sky, moonless at this hour and season, just barely discernible. He felt the tension in D'fio's back, drew his own breath in sharply as they transferred *between*, and abruptly emerged with Drenth calling out his name to the Ista Weyr watchdragon.

Robinton shielded his eyes from the brilliance of the sun slanting off the water. As he glanced below, he saw the dramatic half-peak of Ista Weyr, the black stone like giant jagged fingers pointing to the bright blue skies. Ista was the smallest of the Weyrs, some of its complement of dragons making weyrs in the forest that surrounded the base. But the broad plateau beyond the cone was crowded with bronze beasts, their riders forming a cluster close to the golden queen who was crouched over her kill, sucking the blood from its body. At a farther and safe distance from this spectacle a large group of people looked on. Toward this area, Drenth glided.

Zair took wing from Robinton's shoulder, to join other fire-lizards in an aerial display of excitement. Robinton noticed that the little creatures kept a distance from the dragons. At least the fire-lizards were appearing at Weyrs again.

D'fio dismounted, too, and sent his brown for a swim in the warm waters of the bay below the Weyr plateau. Other dragons, uninvolved in this flight, were already taking advantage of the bathing at Ista Island.

Caylith vaulted from the ground toward the herd of beasts in the Weyr's corral. Cosira half-followed, keeping a firm control on her young queen so that she wouldn't gorge the meat and be too heavy for this all-important mating flight. Robinton counted twenty-six bronzes ringing the killing ground, gleaming in the harsh sunlight, their eyes wheeling red in rut agitation, their wings half-furled, their bodies at a crouch that would send them skyward the instant the queen ascended. They were all young, as F'lar had recommended, almost equal in size as they waited, never taking their glistening eyes from the object of their interest.

Caylith growled deep in her throat as she sucked the blood from the buck carcass. She raised her head to snarl contemptuously back at the bronze ring.

Suddenly the watchdragon roared a challenge and even Caylith turned to look. Arrowing in from the south, over the sea, came two bronzes.

Just as Robinton realized that the beasts must have flown in at sea level to get this close to the Weyr undetected, he also realized that these were older beasts, muzzles graying, necks thickened. Southerners. Two of the Oldtimers' bronzes. That had to be T'kul with Salth, and probably B'zon with Ranilth. Robinton began to run toward the killing ground, toward the queen's prospective mates, for that was the obvious goal of the two bronzes sweeping in from the south.

Their timing had been perfect, Robinton thought then saw two others making for the landing bronzes—the stocky figure of D'ram and F'lar's lean body. T'kul and B'zon jumped off their beasts. The dragons took one final leap to range themselves with the other bronzes who hissed and growled at the newcomers. Robinton prayed under his breath that none of the bronze riders would act first, think later. Most of them were so young they'd not recognize T'kul or B'zon. But D'ram and F'lar certainly had.

Robinton felt his heart pounding in his chest and a totally unfamiliar ache that caused him to grimace and slow his trot momentarily. B'zon was facing him, a set smile on his face. The Oldtimer touched T'kul's arm and the former High Reaches Weyrleader spared the Harper a quick glance. T'kul considered him no threat and turned back toward the two Weyrleaders.

D'ram reached T'kul first. "You fool, this is for young beasts. You'll kill Salth."

"What option have you left us?" B'zon demanded just as F'lar and Robinton skidded to either side of the two Southerners. There was a hysterical note in the man's voice. "Our queens are too old to rise: there are no greens to give the males relief. We *must* . . ."

Caylith bugled as she left the blood-sucked corpse of the buck and half-flew, half-ran to scatter the herd, one sweeping forepaw impaling another victim on its flank and dragging it back to her.

"D'ram, you declared this flight open, didn't you?" T'kul asked in a harsh voice, his features fine-drawn despite the tan of Southern suns. He looked from D'ram to F'lar.

"I did, but your bronzes are too old, T'kul." He gestured toward the eager young dragons. The difference between them and the two older ones was pathetically obvious.

"Salth's dying anyway. Let him go out flying. I made that choice, D'ram, when I brought him here." T'kul stared hard at F'lar, the bitterness and hatred so vivid that Robinton sucked in his breath. "*Why* did you take back the egg? How did you find it?" Desperation broke briefly through T'kul's cold pride and arrogance.

"Had you come to us, we would have helped you," F'lar said quietly.

"Or I," D'ram said, miserable before the plight of his one-time acquaintance.

Ignoring F'lar altogether, T'kul gave the Istan Weyrleader a long scornful glance then, straightening his shoulders, jerked his head at B'zon to move forward. F'lar was in his direct path to the other bronze riders. The Benden Weyrleader opened his mouth to speak, shook his head in regret and stepped to one side. The Southern riders moved the few paces forward just in time. Caylith, raising her bloody muzzle, seemed to pulse more golden than ever. Her eyes were whirling opalescence. With a fierce scream, she launched herself upward. Barnath was the first dragon off the ground after her, and, to Robinton's surprise, T'kul's Salth was not far behind the Istan bronze.

T'kul swung back to F'lar, the triumph on his face an insult. Then he strode to Cosira's side. The Weyrwoman was swaying with the effort of staying in mental contact with her queen. She didn't notice that it was G'dened and T'kul who were leading her back to her quarters to await the outcome of the flight.

"He'll kill Salth," D'ram was muttering, his face stricken.

That odd pressure against his chest kept Robinton from reassuring the worried man.

"And B'zon, too!" D'ram grabbed F'lar's arm. "Is there nothing we can do to stop it? Two dragons?"

"If they had come to us . . ." F'lar began, placing his hand consolingly on D'ram's. "But those Oldtimer riders always *took!* That was their error at the outset!" His face hardened.

"They're still taking," Robinton said, wanting to ease D'ram's distress. "They've taken what they wanted from the north all along. Here, there. What pleased them. Young girls, material, stone, iron, jewels. They looted with quiet system ever since they were exiled. I've had the reports. I've given them to F'lar."

"If only they had asked!" F'lar looked upward at the fast-dwindling specks of dragons in flight.

"What was that all about?" Lord Warbret of Ista Hold hurried up to them. "Those last two were old or I don't know dragons as well as I though I did."

"The mating flight was open," F'lar replied, but Warbret was looking at D'ram's anxious face.

"To old dragons? I thought you stipulated young ones that hadn't had a chance at a queen before! I don't see the point myself, in having another older Weyrleader. No offense intended, D'ram. Change upsets holders." He gazed at the sky. "How'll they keep up with the younger ones? That's a gruelling pace."

"They have the right to try," F'lar said. "While we await the outcome, some wine, D'ram?"

"Yes, yes, wine. Lord Warbret . . ." D'ram recovered his composure sufficiently to gesture the Lord Holder to accompany him toward the living cavern. He beckoned to the other guests to follow, but his step was heavy and slow.

"Don't worry, D'ram. That other dragon might have been quick off the mark," Lord Warbret said as he thumped D'ram's shoulder encouragingly, "but I've all the faith in the world in G'dened and Barnath. Fine young man! Splendid dragon. Besides he's mated Caylith before, hasn't he? That always tells, doesn't it?"

While Robinton breathed with relief that the Lord Holder was misinterpreting D'ram's concern, F'lar replied to the questions.

"Yes, Caylith had thirty-four eggs of her first clutch with Barnath. You don't want a young queen to overlay herself, but her hatchlings were healthy and strong. No queen egg, but that's often the case when a Weyr has enough queens. The bond of a previous mating can be a strong factor despite a queen's captiousness, but you never know."

Robinton noticed that the weyrfolk appeared to be somewhat tense as they served the visitors. He wondered how many had indeed identified the Southerners. He hoped no one blurted out their suspicions in front of the Lord Holder.

T'kul's Salth must have flown his queen dozens of times and won her. He'd be a canny old fellow, all right, but all his cleverness would be no good if he couldn't catch the queen in the first few minutes of flight. He simply wouldn't have the staying power of the younger dragons, and possibly not even the speed for the surge to catch her up. He flew against some fine beasts. Robinton knew how carefully N'ton had chosen the four bronze riders to present themselves from Fort. Each had been wing-seconds for Turns, men already proven in Falls as leaders with strong dragons. F'lar had also limited Benden's three contenders to men well able to lead a Weyr. Robinton could only assume that Telgar, Igen and High Reaches had honored D'ram's Weyr with good men. Ista was the smallest of the six Weyrs and needed a united folk.

He sipped at his wine, hoping his side would stop aching, wondering what had caused that unnerving pressure. Well, wine cured many ills. He waited until D'ram turned his head and then he refilled the man's cup, catching F'lar's approving gaze as he did.

Weyrfolk began to stop at the table now, greeting D'ram and Lord Warbret. Their obvious pleasure in seeing their former Weyrleader was a tonic for D'ram, and he responded with smiles and chatting. He looked tense but anyone would attribute that to understandable concern for the outcome of this flight.

Robinton had a puzzle to chew over: T'kul's bitter words about the egg. "Why did you take back the egg? How did you find it?" Didn't T'kul realize that someone from Southern had returned the egg? Then the Harper stiffened. No Southerner had returned that egg, for surely T'kul would have discovered the culprit by now.

Robinton began to hope fervently that neither of the two old dragons would die in their attempt to fly the young queen. Just like the Oldtimers to add a sour note to what ought to be a joyous occasion! Surely life in the Southern Weyr was not so unbearable that T'kul would cold-bloodedly allow his dragon to court death rather than continue there? Robinton knew the Weyr well; the setting in its own small valley was beautiful—a considerable improvement on T'kul's dour, barren High Reaches Weyr. There was a huge well-constructed hall in the center of a flagstone court where no Thread could find grass to burrow. Food for the picking, wild beasts in plenty to feed dragons, ideal weather, and their only obligation as dragonriders to the small Hold on the coast.

Then Robinton recalled the pulsing hatred for F'lar in T'kul's eyes. It was malice and spite that motivated the former High Reaches Weyrleader—and hatred for an exile not of his choosing.

The queens might be too old to rise, but that was only a recent occurrence, Robinton thought, and the bronzes could not be in that hard a case. They were ageing as well and the blood did not so easily quicken, so the old urgencies surely could be contained.

There was also the point that T'kul need not have gone South with Mardra, T'ron and the other obstinate and inflexible Oldtime weyrfolk. He could have accepted the leadership of Benden, acknowledged that Craft and Hold had earned rights for themselves in the four hundred Turns since the last Pass and conducted himself and his Weyr affairs accordingly.

Had any of the Southerners come forward, acting in honor, asking the assistance of the other Weyrs, he was certain such would have been forthcoming. He didn't doubt D'ram's sincerity, and he would have pressed for their requests himself, by the Shell he would have!

Looking at the worst possible conclusion to the day's events, what would happen to T'kul if Salth did overfly himself? The Harper sighed deeply, not liking to consider that possibility at all, but he'd better. The possibility meant that . . . Robinton glanced toward the Weyr-woman's quarters. T'kul had been wearing a belt knife. Everyone wore belt knives. Robinton felt his heart pounding. He knew it wasn't proper, but shouldn't he suggest to D'ram that someone be in the queen's weyr in case of trouble? Someone uninvolved in the mating flight. When a man's dragon died he could become insane, not know what he was doing. A vision of T'kul's hatred flashed vividly before the Harper's eyes. Robinton had many prerogatives but entering the chambers of a Weyrwoman whose dragon was mating was not one of them. Still . . .

Robinton blinked. F'lar was no longer seated at the table. The Harper glanced about the cavern, but caught no glimpse of the tall figure of the Benden Weyrleader. He rose, struggling to keep his progress casual, managed to nod pleasantly to D'ram and Warbret as he sauntered toward the entrance. The Istan Harper intersected his path.

"F'lar took two of our strongest riders with him, Master Robinton." The man nodded toward the Weyrwoman's quarters. "He's afraid of trouble."

Robinton nodded, blowing out with relief, then halted.

"How did he manage it? I saw no one using the steps."

Baldor grinned. "This Weyr is full of odd tunnels and entrances. It wouldn't do to compound the problem," he added, gesturing toward the guests in the cavern, "now would it?"

"Indeed not. Indeed not."

"We'll know what happens soon enough," Baldor said with a worried sigh. "Our fire-lizards'll tell us."

"True," and Zair on his shoulder cheeped at Baldor's brown.

Robinton was somewhat relieved by the precautions and made his way back to the table. He filled his cup again, and D'ram's. Not Benden wine, but it wasn't altogether unpalatable, if a trifle sweeter than he liked. Why was it that happy occasions seemed to fly past and one like today dragged interminably?

The watchdragon bugled, a fearful, unhappy sound. But not a keen! Not a death knell! Robinton felt the muscles in his chest relax. His relief was premature for there was a rustle of worried whispers sweeping through the living cavern. Several weyrfolk hurried out, looking up at the blue watchdragon, his wings extended. Zair crooned softly but Robinton sensed nothing definite from the creature. The little bronze merely repeated the dragon's muddled thoughts.

"One of the bronzes must have faltered," D'ram said, swallowing nervously, his face tinged gray under his tan. He looked hard at Robinton.

"One of those older ones, I'll wager," Warbret said, pleased at this justification of his opinion.

"You're likely right," Robinton said easily, "but the flight was declared open, so they had to be admitted."

"Aren't they taking a long time of it?" Warbret asked, frowning out at the sky just visible from their table.

"Oh, I don't think so," Robinton replied with what he hoped was a casual air, "though it sometimes seems that way. I expect that's because the outcome of this particular flight will have such consequences for the Weyr. Caylith is at least giving the bronzes a good run for her!"

"D'you think there'll be a queen egg this time?" Warbret asked eagerly.

"I would never make the error of counting eggs *this* soon, my Lord Warbret," the Harper said, trying to keep his countenance bland.

"Oh, yes, of course. I mean it would be quite an accomplishment for Barnath, wouldn't it? Having his queen lay a golden egg this flight?"

"It would indeed. That is, if . . . Barnath succeeds in flying her."

"Really, Master Harper, of course he will. Where's your sense of justice?"

"Where it generally is, but I doubt that Caylith is attuned to justice right now."

The words were no sooner out of his mouth than Zair, his eyes the bright yellow of distress, gave a frightened, gibbering squeak at the Harper. Mnementh erupted into the air just above the ground of the Bowl, bugling in alarm.

Robinton was on his feet and running, glancing about him for Baldor. The Istan Harper was equally alert to the danger. He and four large riders began pelting toward the Weyr.

"What's the matter?" Warbret demanded.

"Stay there," Robinton shouted.

The air was suddenly full of dragons, bugling and keening, barely avoiding midair collisions as they swept about, riderless, disturbed. Robinton pumped his long legs as fast as he could, regardless of the fierce pain in his side that he eased somewhat by digging the heel of his hand into his flesh. The weight on his chest seemed worse; it kept breath which he needed for running.

Zair began squealing over Robinton's head, projecting an image of a falling dragon and fighting men. Unfortunately the little bronze could not project the information Robinton most wanted—which dragon, which men! F'lar must be involved or Mnementh would not be here.

The huge bronze was landing on the queen's weyr ledge, preventing Baldor's men from entering the weyr. They flattened themselves against the wall, trying to avoid the frantic sweeps of his wide wings.

"Mnementh! Listen to me! Let us pass! We're going to aid F'lar. Listen to me!"

Robinton charged right up the steps, past Baldor and his men, and grabbed one wing tip. He was all but hauled off his feet as Mnementh pulled it back, bending his head to hiss at the Harper. The great eyes whirled violently yellow.

"Listen to me, Mnementh!" the Harper roared. "Let us pass!"

Zair flew at the bronze dragon, screaming at the top of his lungs.

I listen. Salth is no more. Help F'lar!

The great bronze dragon folded his wings, lifted his head, and Robinton thankfully waved Baldor and his men to go ahead. He needed a moment to catch his breath.

As Robinton turned to enter the passage, hand pressed against his side, Zair zipped in front of him, his cries full of encouragement now. The Harper wondered fleetingly if the tiny creature thought that he, and he alone, had turned aside the great bronze. Robinton could only be grateful that the bronze dragon *would* listen to him.

As Robinton entered the weyr, he could hear the sounds of fighting in the Weyrwoman's sleeping chamber. The curtain across the entrance was suddenly ripped from its pole as two struggling bodies staggered out into the larger room. F'lar and T'kul! Baldor and two of his helpers were close behind, trying to separate the men. In the room beyond them, locked in the mating flight contact with their beasts, were the rest of the bronze riders and the Weyrwoman, oblivious to the combat. Someone had collapsed on the floor. B'zon, probably, he thought as the scene registered in his mind in one split second.

What caught Robinton's horrified attention was the fact that F'lar had no knife in either hand. His left was closed about T'kul's right wrist, straining to keep the man's long knife—no short-bladed belt but a skinning tool—away from his collarbone. His fingers began digging into the tendons of T'kul's wrist, trying to force the fingers open, or to deaden the nerves. His right hand held T'kul's left arm down and out from their sides. T'kul writhed savagely; the maniacal gleam in his reddened eyes told Robinton that the man was beyond himself. As he must have intended, thought Robinton.

One of Baldor's men was trying to shove a knife in F'lar's hand but F'lar had to keep T'kul's left hand engaged.

"I'll kill you, F'lar," T'kul said through gritted teeth as he struggled to force his right hand down, closer and closer, the blade slanting toward the bronze rider's neck. "I'll kill you. As you killed my Salth. As you killed us! I'll kill you!" It sounded like a chant, the beats emphasized by the spurts of strength T'kul called up from the depths of his madness.

F'lar saved his breath, the strain of holding off that knife showing in the cords that stood out in his neck, in the drag on his face muscles, the tension in his legs and thighs.

"I'll kill you. I'll kill you as T'ron ought! I'll kill you, F'lar!"

T'kul's voice now came in ragged gasps as the point of the knife inched toward its goal.

Abruptly, F'lar kicked out with his left leg and, twining it about T'kul's left, yanked the foot out from under the crazed, overbalanced Oldtimer. With a yell, T'kul fell forward into F'lar, who neatly twisted him over and down, breaking T'kul's left-hand hold but keeping his own left hand firmly locked on T'kul's right wrist. The Oldtimer kicked out, caught F'lar viciously in the stomach. Although the bronze rider did not release the knife hand, he was doubled up, windless. A second kick from T'kul knocked his feet out from under him. F'lar fell heaving as T'kul wrenched his knife-hand free and scrambled to fall on the younger Weyrleader. But F'lar continued the roll with an agility that astonished the watchers, coming to his feet again even as T'kul stood up and launched an immediate attack. But that interval had been time enough for F'lar to grab the belt knife from Baldor.

The two antagonists faced each other. Robinton knew by the grim determination on F'lar's face that this time, with the man's beast already dead, the Benden Weyrleader would finish off his opponent. If he could.

Robinton disliked having doubts about F'lar's skill as a fighter, but T'kul was no ordinary antagonist, driven as he was by the griefmadness of Salth's death. The man, older by some twenty Turns, had the reach of F'lar, and a longer, more deadly blade in his hand. F'lar would have to elude that slashing blade long enough to wear T'kul past the point of the mad energy that possessed the Oldtimer.

An exultant shout burst from the Weyrwoman's room and her piercing shriek followed. That was just enough to divert T'kul. F'lar was ready for that tiny break in concentration. He dove at T'kul, knife arm down and, before the man could parry and guard himself at the lower angle, F'lar's thrust went up and through the ribs to the heart. T'kul, eyes protruding, fell dead at his feet.

F'lar sagged, dropping to one knee, gasping with his exertions.

Wearily he scrubbed at his forehead with the back of his left hand, every line of his body emphasizing the dejection he was experiencing.

"You could have done nothing else, F'lar," Robinton said softly, wishing he had the strength to move to F'lar's side.

From the Weyrwoman's chamber came the rejected suitors, dazed by their participation in the mating flight. They came out in a mass, and Robinton couldn't figure out who had remained with the Weyr-woman as her mate and was now the new Weyrleader of Ista.

His sudden inexplicable weakness confused the Harper. He couldn't catch his breath; he hadn't the energy to quiet Zair, who was chittering the wildest distress. The pain in his side had moved again to his chest, like a heavy rock sitting on him.

"Baldor!"

"Master Robinton!" The Istan Harper rushed to his side, his face expressing horror and consternation as he assisted Robinton to the nearest bench. "You're gray. Your lips. They're blue. What's wrong with you?"

"Gray is how I feel. My chest! Wine! I need wine!"

The room began pressing in on the Harper. He couldn't breathe. He was aware of shouts, sensed panic in the air and tried to bestir himself to take control of the situation. Hands pushed him down, then flat, making it totally impossible to breathe. He struggled to sit up.

"Let him. It will help his breathing."

Dimly Robinton identified the voice as Lessa's. How did she come to be here? Then he was propped against someone and could breathe more easily. If only he could rest, could sleep.

"Clear everyone from the weyr." Lessa was giving orders.

Harper, Harper, listen to us. Now listen to us. Harper, don't sleep. Stay with us. Harper, we need you. We love you. Listen to us.

The voices in his head were unfamiliar. He wished they would be silent so that he could think about the pain in his chest and the sleep he so desperately craved.

Harper, you cannot leave. You must stay. Harper, we love you.

The voices puzzled him. He didn't know them. It wasn't Lessa or F'lar speaking. The voices were deep, insistent, and he wasn't hearing them with his ears. The voices were in his mind where he couldn't ignore them. He wished they would leave him alone so that he could sleep. He was so very tired. T'kul had been too old to fly his dragon or win a fight. Yet he was older than T'kul, who now slept in death. If only the voices would let him sleep, too. He was so tired.

You cannot sleep yet, Harper. We are with you. Do not leave us. Harper, you must live! We love you.

Live? Of course, he would live. Silly voices. He was just tired. He wanted to sleep.

Harper, Harper, do not leave us. Harper, we love you. Do not go.

The voices were not loud, but they held on to him, in his mind. That was it. They were not letting his mind go.

Someone else, outside him, was holding something to his lips.

"Master Robinton, you must try to swallow the medicine. You must make the effort. It will ease the pain." That voice he recognized. Lessa. Distraught.

Of course, she would be, with F'lar having to kill a rider, and all the trouble with the theft of the egg, and Ramoth being so upset.

Harper, obey Lessa. You must obey Lessa, Harper. Open your mouth. You must try.

He could ignore Lessa, he could bat feebly at the cup at his lips and try to spit out the bitter-tasting pill which was melting on his tongue, but he could not ignore those insistent voices. He let them put wine in his mouth, and swallowed the pill with it. At least they had the kindness to give him wine, not water. Water would have been undignified for the Harper of Pern. He could never have swallowed water with the pain in his chest.

Something seemed to snap inside him. Ah, the pain in his chest. It was easing, as if the snap had been the loosening of the tight band that constricted his heart.

He sighed at the relief. One didn't fully appreciate the absence of pain, he thought.

"Take a sip of the wine, Master," He felt the cup at his lips again.

Wine, yes, that would complete his cure. Wine always did revive him. Only he still wanted to sleep. He was so very tired.

"And another!"

You may sleep later. You must listen to us and stay. Harper, listen! We love you. You must stay.

The Harper resented their insistence.

"How long does it take the man to get here?" That was Lessa's voice, sounding fiercer than he'd ever heard her. Why did she also sound as if she were weeping? Lessa weeping?

Lessa is weeping for you. You do not want her to weep. Stay with us, Harper. You cannot go. We will not let you go. Lessa should not weep.

No, that was right, Lessa should not weep. Robinton didn't really believe that she was. He forced his eyes to open and saw her bending over him. She was weeping! The tears were dropping from her cheeks to his hand which lay limp and upturned as if to receive the tears.

"You mustn't weep, Lessa. I will not have you weeping." Great Shells, he was losing his voice control. He cleared his throat. This would never do.

"Don't try to talk, Robinton," Lessa said, gulping back her sobs. "Just rest. You've got to rest. Oldive is coming. I told them to time it. Just rest. More wine?"

"Have I ever refused wine?" Why was his voice so faint?

"Never," and Lessa was laughing and crying at the same time.

"Who's been nagging me? They wouldn't let me go. Make them let me rest, Lessa. I'm so tired!"

"Oh, Master Robinton, please!"

Please what?

Harper, stay with us. Lessa will weep.

"Oh, Master Oldive. Over here!" That was Lessa again, leaving his side.

Robinton tried to reach for her.

"Don't exert yourself!" She was holding him down, but she was staying beside him. *Dear Lessa!* Even when he was angry with her, he loved her nonetheless. *Perhaps more, because she was angry so often and anger intensified her beauty.*

"Ah, Master Robinton." Oldive's soothing voice made him open his eyes. "The chest pain again? Just nod. I'd rather you didn't make the effort to speak."

"Ramoth says he has great pain and is very tired."

"Oh? Convenient having the dragon listen, too."

Master Oldive was putting cold instruments to his chest and on his arm. Robinton would have liked to protest.

"Yes, I know they're cold, my dear Harper, but necessary. Now listen to me, your heart has been overstrained. That was the pain in your chest. Lessa gave you a pill which has relieved that pain for the moment. But the immediate danger is past. I want you to try to sleep. You are going to need a lot of rest, my good friend. A lot of rest."

"Then tell them to be quiet and let me sleep."

"Who's to be quiet?" Oldive's voice was soothing, and Robinton was vaguely annoyed because he suspected Oldive didn't believe he'd heard them keeping him awake. "Here, take this pill and a sip of wine. I know you've never refused wine."

Robinton smiled weakly. *How well they knew him, Oldive and Lessa.*

"It's Ramoth and Mnementh talking to him, Oldive. They said he had nearly gone . . ." Lessa's voice broke on the last note.

Nearly gone, was I? Is that what it feels like to be so close to death? Like being very tired?

You will stay now, Harper. We can let you sleep. But we will be with you. We love you.

Dragons talking to me? Dragons keeping me from death? How kind they are for I did not want to die yet. There is so much to be done. Problems to be solved. There'd been a problem on my mind . . . about dragons, too . . .

"Who flew Caylith?"

Did he manage to say that out loud? He didn't even hear his own voice in his ears.

"Did you hear what he said, Oldive?"

"Something about Caylith."

"Wouldn't you know he'd worry about that at a time like this?" Lessa sounded more like herself, acerbic. "Barnath flew Caylith, Robinton. Now, will you sleep?"

Sleep, Master. We will listen.

The Harper drew a deep breath into his lungs and relaxed gratefully into sleep.

Evening at Jaxom's Cove and Late Evening at Ista Weyr, 15.8.28

Sharra was showing Brekke and Jaxom how to play a children's game in the sand with pebbles and sticks when Ruth, sleeping just beyond them with the fire-lizards, woke up. He reared to a sitting position, stretching his neck and keening the long piercing note that marked a dragon's passing.

"Oh no!" Brekke reacted just a shade faster than Jaxom. "Salth is gone!"

"Salth?" Jaxom wondered who that was.

"Salth!" Sharra's face drained of color. "Ask Ruth where!"

"Canth says he was trying to fly Caylith and burst his heart!" Brekke answered the question, her shoulders sagging in new grief and a poignantly remembered tragedy. "The fool! He must have known that the younger dragons would be faster, stronger than poor old Salth!"

"Serves T'kul right! And don't soar over me, Brekke." Sharra's eyes flashed as Brekke turned to reprimand her. "Remember, I've had to deal with T'kul and the rest of those Oldtimers. They are *not* like your Northern dragonfolk at all. They're . . . they're impossible! I could burn your ears with tales! If T'kul was fool enough to set his bronze to fly a young queen, with the competition there'd be for the Istan Weyrleadership, then he deserves to lose his beast! I'm sorry. Harsh words for you, Brekke, and Jaxom, but I know what those Southerns are like. You don't!"

"I knew there'd be real trouble sometime, exiling them like that," Brekke said slowly, "but . . ."

"From what I've heard, Brekke," Jaxom said from a compulsion to erase the desolate look from her face, "that was the only way to handle them. They weren't honoring their responsibilities to the people beholden to them. They were greedy, over and above proper tithing. Further," and he brought out his strongest point, "I heard Lytol criticizing those dragonriders!"

"I know, Jaxom. I know all that but they did come forward from their own time to save Pern . . ." Jaxom wondered if she realized she was wringing her hands till the knuckles showed white.

"To save Pern, yes, and then they demanded that we remember that every time we drew breath in their presence," Jaxom went on, recalling all too clearly the arrogant and contemptuous manner with which T'ron had treated Lytol.

"We ignore the Oldtimers," Sharra said, with a shrug. "We go about our business, keep our Hold green clear, pen up our animals during Fall. We just run a quick search with the flamethrowers to be sure the grubs have done their work."

"Don't they ride a Fall?" Brekke asked in surprise.

"Oh, now and again. If they feel like it, or if their dragons get too upset . . ." Sharra's contempt was trenchant. Then she noticed the dismay on the other two faces and added, "Oh, what's happened is not the *dragons'* fault, mind you. And I don't suppose that it's really the riders' either. I do think they should at least try to act what they are. To be sure, most of the Oldtimers stayed north. So just a few are giving dragonmen a poor reputation in Southern. Still . . . if they'd met us halfway . . . we would have helped."

"I should go, I think," Brekke said, rising and facing west. "T'kul is half a man now. I know how that feels . . ." Her voice petered out and her face drained of all color as she stared to the west, her eyes getting larger until a cry of horror burst from her lips. "Oh no!" Her hand went to her throat and she turned it palm outward as if warding off an attack.

"Brekke, what is it?" Sharra leaped to her feet, her arms about the woman.

Ruth whimpered and nudged against Jaxom for reassurance.

She is very afraid. She is speaking to Canth. He is unhappy. It is terrible. Another dragon is very weak. Canth is with him. It is Mnementh who talks now. T'kul fights F'lar!

"T'kul fights F'lar?" Jaxom reached out to Ruth's shoulder for balance.

The fire-lizards picked up the agitation, dipping and swooping, chittering in harsh cacophony that made Jaxom wave his arms at them to be silent.

"This is ghastly, Jaxom," Brekke cried. "I must go. They must see that T'kul is not responsible for what he's doing. Why don't they just overpower him? There must be someone with wits at Ista! What is D'ram doing? I'll get my flying things." She ran back to the shelter.

"Jaxom." Sharra turned to him, one hand raised, appealing for his reassurance. "T'kul hates F'lar. I've heard him blame F'lar for everything that happens in Southern. If T'kul's dragonless, he'd be insane. He'd kill F'lar!"

Jaxom drew the girl close to him, wondering which of them needed comfort more. T'kul trying to kill F'lar? He asked Ruth to listen hard.

I hear nothing. Canth is between. *I only hear trouble. Ramoth is coming . . .*

"Here?"

No, where they are! Ruth's eyes deepened to the purple of worry. *I do not like this.*

"What, Ruth?"

"Oh, please Jaxom, what's he saying? I'm scared."

"He is, too. And so am I."

Brekke came back through the woods, her flying gear in one hand, in the other her small pack of medicines, half-closed, and in danger of spilling its contents. She halted just before stepping onto the sands, blinked, frowning with impatience and dismay.

"I can't get there! Canth must stay with B'zon's Ranilth. We can't lose two bronzes today!" She looked this way and that as if the beach could sprout an answer to her dilemma. She bit her underlip and then exclaimed in frustration. "I've got to go!"

The second shock struck both Brekke and Jaxom at the same time as Ruth bugled in fear.

"Robinton!" Brekke reeled and would have fallen if Sharra and Jaxom had not jumped to her support. "Oh, no, not Robinton? How?"

The Master Harper.

"Not dead?" Sharra cried.

The Master Harper is very ill. They will not let him go. He will have to stay. As you did.

"I'll take you, Brekke. On Ruth. Just let me get my flying gear."

Both women reached out to restrain him.

"You can't fly yet, Jaxom. You can't go *between!*" The fear in Brekke's eyes was for him now.

"You really can't, Jaxom," Sharra said, shaking her head and pleading with her eyes. "The cold of *between* . . . you're just not well enough yet. Please!"

They are afraid for you now, Ruth said, sounding confused. *Very afraid. I do not know why it is wrong for you to ride me but it is!*

"He's right, Jaxom, it would be disastrous," Brekke said, her body slumping with defeat. Wearily she raised her hand to her head, and pulled off the now unnecessary helmet. "You mustn't attempt going *between* for at least another month or six sevendays. If you did, you'd risk headaches for the rest of your life and the possibility of blindness. . . ."

"How do you know that?" Jaxom demanded, struggling with fury at having been kept ignorant of such a restriction, with frustration at not being able to help either Brekke or the Harper.

"I know that," Sharra said, turning Jaxom to face her. "One of the dragonriders at Southern took fire-head. We didn't know the dangers of going *between*. He went blind first. Then mad with the pain in his head and . . . died. So did his dragon." Her voice caught, remembering that tragedy, and her eyes were misted with tears.

Jaxom could only stare at her, stunned.

"Why wasn't I told that before?"

"No reason to," Sharra said, her eyes never leaving his, pleading with him for understanding. "You're getting stronger daily. By the time you realized the restriction existed, it might not have been necessary to warn you anymore."

"Another four or six sevendays?" He ground the words out, conscious that he was working his fists and that his jaw muscles ached with the effort to control his temper.

Sharra nodded slowly, her face expressionless.

Jaxom took a deep breath, forcing emotion down. "That does make it awkward, doesn't it, because right now we need a dragonrider." He looked toward Brekke. Her head was turned slightly to the west. Jaxom could sense her longing to be where she was urgently needed, the restraint that kept her from claiming Canth's help when he was needed elsewhere. "We have a dragonrider!" he exclaimed, whooping. "Ruth, would you take Brekke to Ista without me?"

I would take Brekke anywhere. The little white dragon raised his head, his eyes wheeling quickly as he stepped forward, toward Brekke.

Brekke's face cleared miraculously of sorrow and helplessness. "Oh, Jaxom, would you really let me?"

He was well repaid by the overwhelming gratitude in that breathless question.

He took her arm, hurrying her to Ruth's side.

"You must go. If Master Robinton . . ." Jaxom choked on the rest of that sentence, panic at the thought closing his throat.

"Oh, thank you, Jaxom. Thank you, Ruth." Brekke fumbled with the strap of her helmet. She struggled with her jacket before she could get her arm into the sleeve, and buckled the riding belt in place. When she was ready Ruth dipped his shoulder for Brekke to mount, then turned his head to be sure she was safely seated.

"I'll send Ruth directly back, Jaxom. Oh, no, don't let him go! Don't let him sleep!" The last two sentences were directed to distant minds.

We will not let him go, Ruth said. He briefly nosed Jaxom on the shoulder and then sprang up, showering his friend and Sharra with dry sand. He was barely wing height above the waves before he winked out.

"Jaxom?" Sharra's voice was so unsteady that he turned to her in concern. "What can have happened? T'kul couldn't have been mad enough to attack the Harper, too?"

"The Harper may have tried to stop the fight, if I know him. Do *you* know Master Robinton?"

"I know more *of* him," she said, biting her underlip. She expelled her breath in a deep shudder, struggling to control her fears. "Through Piemur, and Menolly. I've seen him, of course, in our Hold and heard him sing. He's such a wonderful man. Oh, Jaxom! All those Southerners have run mad. *Mad!* They're sick, confused, lost!" She dropped her head against his shoulder, surrendering to her anxieties. Tenderly, he drew her against him.

He lives! Ruth's reassurance rang faint but true in his head.

"Ruth says he lives, Sharra."

"He must continue to live, Jaxom. He must! He must!" Her fists beat on his chest to emphasize her determination.

Jaxom caught her hands, holding them flat, and smiled into her wide, flashing eyes.

"He will. I'm sure he will, if it's in our power to think him so."

Jaxom was intensely aware, at this highly inappropriate moment, of Sharra's vibrant body pressing against his. He could feel her warmth through the thin fabric of her shirt, the long line of her thighs against his, the fragrance of her hair, scented with sun and a blossom she had tucked behind her ear. The startled look that crossed her face told him that she, too, was aware of the intimacy of their positions—aware and, for the first time since he had known her, confused.

He eased his grip on her hands, ready to release her completely if necessary. Sharra was not Corana, not a simple hold girl obedient to the Lord of her Hold. Sharra was not a bed partner for a passing indulgence of desire. Sharra was too important to him to risk destroying their relationship with an ill-timed demonstration. He was also aware that Sharra thought that his feelings for her stemmed from a natural gratitude for her nursing. He'd thought of that possibility in himself and decided that she was wrong. He liked too many things about her, from the sound of her beautiful voice, to the sure touch of her hands: hands he was aching to have caress him. He'd learned a good deal about her in the past few days, but he was aware of a hungry curiosity in himself to know much, much more. Her reaction to the Southerners had surprised him; she often surprised him. Part of her attraction, he supposed, was that he never knew what she'd say or how she'd say it.

Suddenly he broke their partial embrace and, circling her shoulders lightly with his arm, guided her to the mats where they'd been so blithely playing a child's game. He put both hands on her shoulders and gave her a gentle downward push.

"We may have a long wait, Sharra, before we know for certain the Harper's all right."

"I wish I knew *what* was wrong! If that T'kul has harmed our Harper . . ."

"What about his harming F'lar?"

"I don't know F'lar, although I'd naturally be very sorry if he were hurt by T'kul." She absently folded her legs as he sat down beside her, just close enough so that their shoulders nearly touched "And, in a sense, F'lar ought to fight T'kul. After all, *he* sent the Oldtimers into exile so *he* ought to finish it."

"And he'll finish it by killing T'kul?"

"Or being killed by him!"

"We'd be in a far worse state," Jaxom replied with more heat than he intended at her callous dismissal of F'lar's fate, "if the Benden Weyrleader gets killed! He *is* Pern!"

"Really?" Sharra was willing to be converted. "I've never seen him . . ."

There are many dragons here and many many people, Ruth told him, his tone still faint but clear. *Sebell is coming. Menolly cannot.*

"Is Ruth talking to you?" Sharra asked anxiously, leaning forward and grasping his arm. He covered her fingers with his, silencing her in that gesture. She bit her underlip and studied his face. He tried to reassure her with emphatic nods.

Her fire-lizards are here. The Harper sleeps. Master Oldive is with him, too. They *wait outside. We will not let him go. Should I return to you now?*

"Who are *they?*" Jaxom asked though he was fairly sure of the identity.

Lessa and F'lar. The man who attacked F'lar is dead.

"T'kul's dead, and F'lar is not hurt?"

No.

"Ask him what is wrong with the Harper," Sharra whispered.

Jaxom wanted to know, too, but there was a long pause before Ruth answered, and the little dragon sounded confused.

Mnementh said Robinton's chest hurt and he wanted to sleep. Wine helped him. Mnementh and Ramoth knew he should not sleep. He would go. May I come back now?

"Does Brekke need you?"

There are many dragons here.

"Come home, my friend!"

I come!

"His chest hurt?" Sharra repeated when Jaxom told her what Ruth had said. She frowned. "It could be the heart. The Harper is not a young man and he does a great deal!" She looked about her for her fire-lizards. "I could send Meer . . ."

"Ruth says there's an awful lot of people and dragons at Ista right now. I think we'd better wait."

"I know," and Sharra gave a long sigh. She picked up a handful of sand and let it run through her fingers. Then she gave Jaxom a sad smile. "I know how to wait, but that doesn't mean I like to!"

"We know he's alive, and F'lar . . ." Jaxom gave her a sly look.

"I didn't mean any disrespect to your Weyrleader, Jaxom, I want you to know that . . ."

Jaxom laughed, having managed to tease her. She let out an exclamation of annoyance and threw the handful of sand toward him, but he ducked and the sand went over his shoulder, some of it falling in the gentle waves that lapped up the shore.

Brushed out of existence by the next wave, no ripples lasted in this water. There was a fallacy in the Harper's analogy then, Jaxom thought, amused by this irrelevant thought.

Meer and Talla suddenly squawked, both heads turned toward the western arm of the cove. They raised their wings and crouched on their haunches, ready to spring into the air.

"What is it?"

As quickly as they had become alert, the two fire-lizards relaxed, Meer preening one wing as if she hadn't been startled the moment before.

"Is someone coming?" Sharra asked, turning to Jaxom with amazement.

Jaxom jumped to his feet, scanning the skies. "They wouldn't object to Ruth's return."

"It must be someone they know!" The possibility was as improbable to Sharra as it was to Jaxom. "And he's not flying in!"

They both heard the noises of something large moving through the forest on the point. A muffled curse indicated the visitor was human but the first head that penetrated the screen of thick foliage was undeniably animal. The body that followed the head belonged to the smallest runner beast Jaxom had ever seen.

The muffled curses resolved into intelligible words. "Stop snapping the branches back in my face, you ruddy, horn-nosed, flat-footed, slab-hided dragon-bait! Well, Sharra, so this is where you got to! I was told, but I was beginning to doubt it! Hear you've been ill, Jaxom? You don't look it now!"

"Piemur?" Although the appearance of the young harper was the unlikeliest of events, there was no mistaking the characteristic swagger in the short, compact figure that limped jauntily down the beach. "Piemur! What are you doing here?"

"Looking for you, of course. Have you any idea how many coves along this stretch of nowhere in the world answer the description Master Robinton gave me?"

"Well, the Weyr's all organized," F'lar told Lessa in a quiet voice as he joined her in the foreroom of the weyr which had been hastily vacated by its occupants so that the Master Harper of Pern could be accommodated. Master Oldive would not have him moved even as far as Ista Hold. The Healer and Brekke were with him now in the inner room as he slept, propped up in the bed, Zair perched above him, his glowing eyes never leaving the face of his friend.

Lessa held out her hand, needing her Weyrmate's touch. He pulled a stool beside hers, gave her a quick kiss and poured himself a cup of wine.

"D'ram has the Weyrfolk organized. He's sent the older bronzes to help Canth and F'nor bring Ranilth back. The poor old thing will live only a few more Turns . . . if B'zon does."

"Not another one today!"

F'lar shook his head. "No, he's just dead asleep. We've got the disappointed bronze riders drunk as winemakers' apprentices, and from every indication Cosira and G'dened are . . . so involved they haven't any notion of what else has been happening here in Ista."

"That's as well," Lessa replied, grinning from ear to ear.

F'lar stroked her cheek, grinning right back at her. "So when does Ramoth rise again, dear heart?"

"I'll remember to let you know!" As she saw F'lar glance in the direction of the inner room, she added, "He'll be all right!"

"Oldive wasn't hedging about his full recovery?"

"How could he? With every dragon on Pern listening in? Now that," she paused in thoughtful reflection, "was totally unexpected. I know the dragons will call him by name but . . . linking?"

"More incredible to me was Brekke arriving on Ruth, alone!"

"Why ever not?" Lessa asked, piqued. "She's been a rider! And she's had a special touch with dragons ever since she lost Wirenth!"

"I can't quite see you offering her Ramoth under similar circumstances. Now don't soar over me, Lessa. That was a fine gesture of Jaxom's. Brekke told me that he hadn't realized till that moment that he couldn't fly *between*. It must have been a bitter discovery for him and it's greatly to his credit that he could respond so generously."

"Yes, I see your point. It's a relief to have her here, too." Lessa glanced toward the curtain and sighed. "You know, I could almost get to like fire-lizards after today."

"What brought about this change of heart?" F'lar stared at her in surprise.

"I didn't say I had. I said I could almost—watching Brekke direct

Grall and Berd to bring her things, and that little bronze of Robinton's. The creatures can get vicious when their friends are hurt but he just crouched there, watching Robinton's face and crooning till I thought he'd shake his bones loose. Not that I didn't feel much the same myself. When I think . . ." Lessa broke off, her face blotchy with tears.

"Don't think of it, dear heart." F'lar squeezed her hand. "It didn't happen."

"When Mnementh called me, I don't think I've ever moved so fast. I fell off the ledge onto Ramoth's back. Bad enough trying to get here before T'kul tried to kill you, but to find Robinton . . . If only you'd killed T'ron at Telgar Hold . . ."

"Lessa!" He gripped her fingers so tightly she winced. "T'ron's Fidranth was very much alive at Telgar Hold. I couldn't cause *his* death no matter what insult T'ron had given me. T'kul I could kill with pleasure. Though I admit, he nearly had me. Our Harper's not the only one who's Turning old."

"So, thank goodness, are whoever's still left of the Oldtimers in Southern. And now, what are we to do with them?"

"I will go south and take charge of the Weyr," D'ram said. He'd entered, quiet with weariness, while they were talking. "I am, after all, an Oldtimer . . ." He gave a deep sigh. "They will accept from me what they would not endure from you, F'lar."

The Benden Weyrleader hesitated, appealing as this offer was. "I know you're willing, D'ram, but if it's going to overset you . . ."

D'ram raised his hand to cut off the rest of the sentence. "I'm fitter than I thought. Those quiet days in the cove worked a miracle. I will need help . . ."

"Any help we can give . . ."

"I'll take you at your word. I'll need some greens, preferably from R'mart at Telgar, or G'narish at Igen, for there are none to spare here at the moment. If they, too, are Oldtime, it will be easier for the Southerns. I'll need two younger bronzes, and enough blues and browns to make up two fighting wings."

"The Southern dragonriders haven't fought Thread in Turns," F'lar said with contempt.

"I know that. But it's time they did. That would give the dragons who remain purpose and strength. It would give their riders hope and occupation." D'ram's face was stern. "I learned things from B'zon today that grieve me. I have been so blind . . ."

"The fault is not yours, D'ram. Mine was the decision to send them south."

"I have honored that decision because it was the right one, F'lar. When . . . when Fanna died . . ." he got the words out in a rush, "I should have gone to the Southern Weyr. It would not have been disloyal to you if I had and it might have . . ."

"I doubt it," Lessa said, angry that D'ram was blaming himself. "Once T'kul plotted to steal a queen egg . . ." and she gestured her condemnation of the man.

"If he had come to you . . ."

Lessa's harsh expression did not alter. "I doubt that T'kul would have come," she said slowly. An expression of distaste crossed her mobile features and she made a sound of annoyance before she looked at D'ram again; this time her expression was rueful. "And I'd have probably sent him about his business. But you," she pointed her finger at D'ram, "wouldn't have. And I imagine that F'lar would also have been more tolerant." She grinned at her Weyrmate. "It wasn't in T'kul's nature to beg," she went on more briskly. "Nor in mine to forgive! I will never forgive the Southerns for stealing Ramoth's egg! When I think they brought *me* to the point where I was willing to set dragon against dragon! That I can never forgive!"

D'ram drew himself up. "Do you disagree, Weyrwoman, with my decision to go south?"

"Great Shells, no!" She was astonished, and then shook her head. "No, D'ram, I think you're wise and kind, more generous than I could ever be. Why, that idiot T'kul might have killed F'lar today! No, you must go. You're quite right about their accepting you. I don't think I ever realized what might be happening in the South. I didn't want to!" she added in candid acknowledgment of her own shortcomings.

"Then I may invite additional riders to join me?" D'ram looked first at her and then at F'lar.

"Ask anyone you want from Benden, except F'nor. It wouldn't be fair to ask Brekke to return to Southern."

D'ram nodded.

"I think the other Weyrleaders will help. This matter touches the honor of all dragonriders. And . . ." F'lar broke off, cleared his throat, "and we do not want the Lord Holders precipitously taking charge in the South on the grounds that we cannot maintain order in the Weyrs."

"They'd never . . ." D'ram began, frowning with indignation.

"They well might. For other very valid reasons—to their ways of thinking," F'lar replied. "I know," he paused to emphasize that surety, "that the Southerns under T'kul and T'ron would never permit the Lord Holders to extend their holdings one dragonlength. Toric's settlement has been steadily growing over the past Turns, a few people now and then, craftsmen, the dissatisfied, a few young holder sons without hope of land in the North. All very quietly, so as not to alarm the Oldtimers." F'lar rose, restlessly pacing. "This isn't common knowledge . . ."

"I knew that there were traders north and south," said D'ram.

"Yes, part of the problem. Traders talk, and word has passed back that there's a lot of land south. Granted some of this may be exaggeration but I've reason to believe that the Southern Continent is probably as large as this one—and one protected against Thread by thorough grubbing." He paused again, rubbing forefinger and thumb down the lines from nose to chin, scratching absently under his jaw. "This time, D'ram, the dragonriders will have first choice of land. In the next Interval, I do not intend that any dragonrider will be beholden to the generosity of Hold and Craft. We will have our own places, without prejudice. I, for one, will never beg wine or bread or meat from anyone!"

D'ram had listened, at first with surprise and then with a gleam of delight in his tired eyes. He straightened his shoulders and with a curt nod of his head, looked the Benden Weyrleader straight in the eye.

"You may rely on me, F'lar, to secure the South for that purpose. A grand purpose! By the First Shell, that's a superb notion. That lovely land, soon dragonrider land!"

F'lar gripped D'ram's arm, affirming the trust. Then his face broke into a sly smile. "If you hadn't volunteered to go South yourself, D'ram, I was going to suggest it to you! You're the only man to handle the situation. And I don't envy you!"

D'ram chuckled at the Benden Weyrleader's admission and returned the arm grip firmly. Then his expression cleared.

"I have grieved for my Weyrmate as is proper. But I still live. I liked being in that cove, but it wasn't enough. I was relieved when you came after me, and kept me busy, F'lar. It doesn't answer to give up the only life I've known. I couldn't. *Dragonmen must fly/When Threads are in the sky!*" He sighed once more, inclined his head respectfully to Lessa and then, turning smartly on his heel, strode from the weyr, his step firm, his stance proud.

"D'you think he can manage it, F'lar?"

"He's more likely to pull it off than anyone . . . except possibly F'nor. But I can't ask that of him. Or of Brekke!"

"I should think not!" She spoke sharply and, with a little cry as if regretting her asperity, she ran to embrace him. He put his arms about her, absently stroking her hair.

There are too many deep lines in his face, now, thought Lessa, lines that she hadn't noticed before. His eyes were sad, his lips thin with worry as he gazed after D'ram. But the muscles in his arm were as strong as ever, and his body lean and hard with the active life he led. He'd been fit enough to preserve his skin against a madman. There'd only been one time when weakness had frightened F'lar—just after that knife fight at Telgar, when his wound had been slow to heal and he'd been sick with fever from foolishly going *between*. He'd learned a lesson then and had started delegating some of the strain of leadership to F'nor and T'gellan in Benden, to N'ton and R'mart in

Pern, and to Lessa herself! Keenly sensible of her deep need of him, Lessa embraced F'lar fiercely.

He smiled down at her sudden demonstration, the tired lines smoothed away.

"I'm with you, dear heart, don't worry!" He kissed her soundly enough to leave her no room for doubt of his vitality.

The sound of boot heels thudding rapidly down the short corridor interrupted them and they moved apart. Sebell, face flushed from running, charged into the room, checking his pace when Lessa signaled him urgently to be quieter.

"He's all right?"

"He's asleep now, but see for yourself, Sebell," Lessa replied and gestured toward the curtained sleeping chamber.

Sebell rocked on his heels, wanting to reassure himself with a glimpse of his Master and anxious with fear he might disturb him.

"Go on, man." F'lar waved him forward. "Just be quiet."

Two fire-lizards winged into the room, squeaked when they saw Lessa and disappeared.

"I didn't know you had two queens."

"I don't," Sebell said, glancing over his shoulder to see where they'd gone. "The other one's Menolly's. She wasn't allowed to come!" His grimace told both Weyrleaders how Menolly had reacted to that restriction.

"Oh, tell them to come back. I don't eat fire-lizards!" Lessa said, curbing her irritation. She didn't know which annoyed her more, the fire-lizards themselves, or the way people cringed about her when the subject came up. "And that little bronze of Robinton's showed a commendable amount of common sense today. So tell Menolly's queen to come back. If the fire-lizard sees, she'll believe!"

Smiling with intense relief, Sebell held up his arm. Two queens popped in, eyes huge and whirling madly in their perturbation. One of them, Lessa didn't know whose, since they all looked alike to her, chirped as if in thanks. Then Sebell, careful not to disrupt their balance and set them squeaking, walked with exaggerated care toward the sick man's quarters.

"Sebell takes over the Harper Hall?" Lessa asked.

"Well able for it, too."

"If only the dear man had had the sense to delegate more to Sebell before this . . ."

"It's partly my fault, Lessa. Benden has asked much of the Harper Hall." F'lar poured himself a cup of wine, looking at Lessa to see if she wanted some as well, and poured another when she nodded. They made an unspoken toast. "Benden wine!"

"The wine that kept him alive!"

"Miss a cup of wine? Not Robinton!" She drank quickly to ease the pressure in her throat.

"And he'll drink many more skins limp," the quiet voice of Master Oldive said. He glided to the table, a curious figure with arms and legs apparently too long for his torso until his back was visible, with its hump. His handsome face was serene as he poured himself a cup of wine, regarding the rich crimson color a moment before he raised it, as Lessa had, and drank it down. "As you said, this helped keep him alive. It's seldom that a man's vice sustained life in his body!"

"Master Robinton will be all right?"

"Yes, with care and rest. He has rallied well. His pulse and heart are beating evenly again, if slowly. He cannot be fretted by any worries. I warned him repeatedly to reduce his activities. Not that I thought he'd listen! Sebell, Silvina and Menolly have done all they could to assist, but then Menolly took ill . . . There is so much to be done for his Hall and for Pern!" Oldive smiled, his long face lighting gently as he took Lessa's hand and put it in F'lar's. "You can do no more here, Weyrleaders. Sebell will wait to reassure Robinton when he rouses that all is well in his Hall. Brekke and I, and the good people of this Weyr, will nurse the Master Harper. You two need rest as well. Go back to your Weyr. This day has taken its toll of many. Go!" He gave them a shove toward the passage. "Go along now!" He spoke as to recalcitrant children, but Lessa was weary enough to obey and concerned enough to override the objections she saw rising in F'lar's eyes.

We do not leave the Harper alone, Ramoth said as F'lar helped Lessa mount her queen. *We are with him.*

All of us are with him, Mnementh said, his eyes slowly turning in quiet reassurance.

❦

At the Cove Hold, 15.8.28–15.9.7

When Jaxom and Sharra blurted out to Piemur the events at Ista Weyr, including the news of the Harper's illness, the young journeyman treated them to a colorful description of his Master's follies, shortcomings, stupid loyalties and altruistic hopes that quite stunned the listeners until they saw the tears leaking down Piemur's cheeks.

At that moment, Ruth returned, scaring Piemur's runner beast into the forest. Piemur had to coax the animal, cheerfully called Stupid, to come out again.

"He's really not stupid, you know," Piemur said, wiping sweat and tears from his face. "He knows that yon," Piemur jerked his thumb surreptitiously in Ruth's direction, "like his sort for eating." He tested the knot on the rope with which he had secured Stupid to a tree trunk.

I wouldn't eat him, Ruth replied. *He's small and not very plump.*

Laughing, Jaxom passed the message to Piemur, who grinned and bowed his gratitude to Ruth.

"I wish I could make Stupid understand that," Piemur said with a sigh, "but it's difficult for him to make distinctions between friendly dragons and hungry ones. As it is, his tendency to disappear into the nearest thicket when dragons come within his senses has saved my skin any number of times. You see, I'm not supposed to be doing exactly what I've been doing. Most of all, I'm not supposed to be caught doing it."

"Go on," Jaxom urged when Piemur stopped to assess the effect of his cryptic statement. "You wouldn't have told us this much if you didn't intend to say more. You did mention that you'd been looking for us?"

Piemur grinned. "Among other things." He stretched out on the sand, grunting and making a show of settling himself. He took the cup of fruit juice Sharra handed him, quaffed the contents and held it out to be refilled.

Jaxom regarded the young man patiently. He was used to Piemur's mannerisms from the days they had spent together in Master Fandarel's and the Harper Hall.

"Did you never wonder why I left the classes, Jaxom?"

"Menolly told me you'd been posted elsewhere."

"And everywhere," Piemur replied with a broad sweep of his arm, his fingers flicking southward in emphasis. "I'll wager that I've seen more of this planet than any living thing . . . including dragons!" He gave a decisive nod of his head to show the others they should be impressed. "I haven't quite . . ." he paused to stress the qualifier, "gone all around this Southern Continent, nor have I gone across it, but I intimately know everywhere I have been!" He pointed to the worn boots on his feet. "New they were, a scant four sevendays ago when I started east. Oh, the tales these boots could tell!" He squinted at Jaxom thoughtfully. "It's one thing, my Lord Jaxom, to soar serenely over land, seeing all from an exalted height. Quite another, I assure you, to stomp on it, through it, under it, around it. You *know* where you've been then!"

"Does F'lar know?"

"More or less," Piemur replied with a grin. "A little less than more, I'd wager. You see, about three Turns back, Toric started trading North with some fine samples of iron ore, copper and tin—all of which, as you might have heard Fandarel complain, Jaxom, are getting in short supply north. Robinton thought it prudent to investigate Toric's sources of supply. He was smart enough to send me over . . . You're sure he's going to be all right? You're not holding anything from me?" Piemur's anxiety cut through his brash manner.

"You know as much as we know, as much as Ruth knows." Jaxom paused to inquire of his dragon. "And Ruth says he sleeps. He also says the dragons won't let him go."

"The dragons won't let him go, huh? Don't that beat all!" Piemur shook his head from side to side. "Not that I'm surprised, mind you," he added with customary briskness. "The dragons know who're their friends. Now, as I was saying, Master Robinton decided it would be very smart of us to know more about the South, since he had a notion F'lar had an eye for this continent during the next Interval."

"How is it that you know so much about what F'lar and Robinton think?" Sharra asked.

Piemur chortled, wagging a finger at her. "That's for me to know and you to guess. But I'm right, aren't I, Jaxom?"

"I don't know what F'lar's plans might be but he's not the only one interested in the South, I'd wager."

"Truly spoken! But he's the only one that matters, don't you see?"

"No, frankly I don't see," Sharra said. "My brother's Lord Holder . . . Well he is," she added with some heat when Piemur started to contradict her. "Or would be, if his Hold had been acknowledged by the Northern Lord Holders. He risked settling south with F'nor when he timed it back. No one else was willing to try. He's put up with the Oldtimers, and made a fine, big, Threadfree Hold. No one can gainsay his right to hold what he has . . ."

"Nor do I!" Piemur assented quickly. "But . . . for all Toric's attracted a lot of new people from the North, he can only Hold so much! He can only protect and work so much. And there is so much more of the Southern Continent than anyone realizes. Except me! I'll bet I've already walked the breadth of Pern from Tillek Head to Nerat Tip on this continent and not gone its length." Piemur's tone changed abruptly from derision to awe. "There was this bay, you see, the opposite shore all but hid in the heat haze. Stupid and I had been struggling through really bad sand for two days. I'd only enough water to go back the way we'd come because I'd thought that the sand would have to give way to decent land soon. . . . I sent Farli out, first to the far shore, then down to the mouth of the bay, but all she brought back to me was more sand. So I knew I'd have to turn back. But," he turned to his listeners, "you see, there's probably as much land beyond that bay as I'd already transversed from Toric's Hold and I'd still not come full circle! Toric could not begin to hold the half of what I've seen. And that's only the western side. East now, it's taken me a full three sevendays to reach you from Toric's and we'd had to swim part of the way. Good swimmer, that Stupid of mine! As willing as a new day and never complains. When I think of how careful my father was to feed his runner stock on only the best fodder, and what Stupid makes do on with twice the work out of him . . ." Piemur broke off to shake his head at the inequity.

"So," he returned briskly to his narrative, "I've been exploring as I was told to, and heading in your general direction, as I was told to, only I expected to be here long before this! My word, but I'm tired, and no one knows how much further I've got to travel before I get where I'm going."

"I thought you were coming here."

"Yes, but I've to go on . . . eventually." He raised his left leg, the one which he'd been favoring, and squinched his face up in a grimace of pain. "Shards, but I can't go another step for a while! This leg's been walked half off, now, hasn't it, Sharra?"

Still elevating the leg, he swiveled in the sand toward the healer who was looking quite concerned. Deftly she unwound the shreds of what had probably been Piemur's cloak, and uncovered a long but recently healed scar.

"I can't walk any farther on that, now can I, Sharra?"

"No, I don't think you should, Piemur," Jaxom said, critically examining the healed wound. "Do you, Sharra?"

She looked from one to the other and then began to shake her head, her eyes dancing.

"No, positively not. It needs soaking in warm salt water, and plenty of sun, and you're a terrible rascal, Piemur. Just as well you're not a posted harper! You'd scandalize any sensible Holder!"

"Have you kept any Records of your traveling?" Jaxom asked, keenly interested and just a shade jealous of Piemur's freedom.

"Have *I* kept Records?" Piemur snorted derisively. "Most of what Stupid packs *is* Records! Why do you think I'm wearing rags? I haven't room to carry spare clothes." His voice lowered and he leaned urgently toward Jaxom. "You don't just possibly happen to have any of Bendarek's leaves down here, do you? There are a couple of—"

"Plenty of leaves. Drawing tools as well. C'mon!"

Jaxom was on his feet, Piemur not a second behind him with only a trace of a limp, following him to the shelter. Jaxom had not intended Piemur to see his bumbling attempts to map their immediate vicinity. But he'd forgot the young harper's keen eyes missed little, and Piemur had spotted the roll of neatly connected leaves and, without so much as a by-your-leave, laid it open. He soon was nodding his head and muttering under his breath.

"You haven't been wasting your time here, have you?" Piemur grinned, an oblique compliment to Jaxom's work. "You used Ruth as measure? Fair enough, I've taught my queen, Farli, to pace her flight. I count by the second, watch for her dip at the end of the run and record the distance by seconds. I figure it up later when I'm charting. N'ton double-checked the measure when he worked with me, so I know it's reasonably accurate, as long as I allow enough for a wind factor." He whistled as his gaze fell on the tall stack of fresh sheets. "I might need 'em, I might, to map what I've traveled over. If you'd give me a hand . . ."

"You do have to rest that leg, don't you?" Jaxom kept his face expressionless.

Piemur caught his eye in surprise and then they both burst out laughing until Sharra, joining them, wanted to share the joke.

The next few days passed most agreeably for the three, starting with Ruth's assurances about the Harper's continued improvement. The first morning, noticing that Stupid had cropped all the ground greens in the area, Piemur asked if there was any grassland nearby.

So Jaxom and Piemur flew Ruth to the river meadows that lay south and east of the cove, a good hour's flying inland. Ruth willingly helped harvest the tall waving grain grasses which Piemur pronounced fine fodder that might even put poor Stupid into condition. Ruth told Jaxom that he'd never seen such a hungry-looking runner.

"We're not fattening him up for you," Jaxom said, laughing.

He is Piemur's friend. Piemur is my friend. I do not eat the friends of friends.

Jaxom couldn't resist repeating this rationalization to Piemur, who howled with laughter and thumped Ruth with the same rough affection he used on Stupid.

They packed half a dozen heavy sheaves of grass on Ruth and were airborne when Piemur asked Jaxom if he'd been to the peak yet.

"Can't fly *between*." Jaxom didn't bother hiding his frustration from Piemur.

"Too bloody right you can't. Not with fire-head!"

Jaxom blinked at Piemur's unequivocal agreement.

"Don't worry! You'll get there soon enough." Piemur squinted at the symmetrical peak, shading his eyes with one hand. "May look near, but it's several, four-five maybe, days' travel. Rough country, I'd guess. You've . . ." he paused to give Jaxom an unexpected blow in the midriff which robbed him of breath, "got to get fit first! I heard you puffing, hacking down that grass. Huh!"

"Wouldn't it be easier to bring Stupid here and let him graze? There aren't any dragons about, except Ruth. And he's agreed not to eat Stupid!"

"Once he sees wild ones, he won't come back. He's too stupid to know he's much safer with me with a dragon to bring him food, instead of eating him as food."

Stupid was delighted with the contribution to his diet and whistled with pleasure as he munched away at the piled grass.

"Just how intelligent is Stupid?" Sharra asked, stroking the creature's rough dun-colored neck.

"Not as smart as Farli, but not really stupid. Limited is a fairer assessment of his scope. Within those limitations, he's pretty bright."

"For instance?" asked Jaxom. He'd never thought much of runner beasts.

"Well, for instance, I can send Farli ahead, telling her to fly so many hours in the direction I've pointed, land and pick up anything lying on the ground. Generally she brings back grasses or bush twigs, and sometimes stone and sand. I can send her to look for water. That's what fooled me about the Big Bay. She'd found water, all right, so Stupid and I humped after her. I didn't specify drinking water." Piemur shrugged and laughed. "But Stupid and I have to go on foot, and he's right smart about ground. Kept me from sinking in mud and those shifting sands time and again. He's clever about finding the easiest route over rough going. He's also good at finding water . . . drinking-type water. So I should have listened to him when he didn't want to cross the sands to the Big Bay. He knew there wasn't any real water over there, although Farli insisted there was. I trusted Farli that time. Generally speaking, the two make one good reliable guide between them. We're a team—Stupid, Farli and I.

"Which reminds me, I found a fire-lizard clutch, a queen's, five . . ." Farli chittered at him, "all right, maybe six or seven coves back. I kind of lost track there, but she'll remember where. . . . In case someone wants some. You know if green fire-lizards weren't as stupid as they are, we'd be up to our ears in little green ones. And they're downright useless."

Sharra grinned. "I remember the day I found my first clutch in the sands. *I* didn't know the difference between green and gold nests. Oh, how I watched that clutch . . . for days. Never told a soul. I was going to Impress all of them . . ."

"Four or five?" Piemur asked with a laugh.

"Six, in fact. Only I didn't realize that a sand snake had got the lot from beneath long before I found the nest."

"How is it, then, that sand snakes don't get a queen's eggs?" Jaxom asked.

"She's never far from her clutch," Sharra said. "She'd spot a snake tunnel right away and kill it." She gave a shudder. "I hate snakes worse than I hate Thread."

"Much the same thing, isn't it?" Piemur asked, "except for the direction of attack." He gestured with both hands, one coming down, the other coming up on an imaginary victim.

During the hot part of the day, Jaxom, Sharra and Piemur began to turn his Records, measurements and rough sketches into proper detailed maps. Piemur wanted to get the report back to Sebell, or Robinton or F'lar if so directed, as soon as possible.

In the cool of the next morning, with Stupid as pack animal and Ruth overhead, the three friends backtracked to Piemur's queen clutch. Twenty-one eggs were in the nest, all nicely hardened to within a day or two of Hatching. Their approach had sent the wild fire-lizard queen to cover so they were able to excavate the eggs, packing them carefully in the carrier they had strapped to Stupid's back. Jaxom asked Ruth to alert Canth that they had fire-lizard eggs.

Canth says that they are coming tomorrow anyway, Ruth replied. *The Harper ate well.*

Ruth gave them such snippets of information about Master Robinton periodically. It was as good as being in the same Hall with the invalid, without having to hear him complain, Piemur observed.

They returned to the shelter cover through the forest. The fruit trees near the clearing had been picked clean and if F'nor were coming, he'd surely appreciate some fresh fruit to take back to Benden Weyr.

"Should you be around when F'nor comes?" Jaxom asked the young harper.

"Why not? He knows what I've been doing. You know, Jaxom, when you see how beautiful this continent is, you wonder why our ancestors went north . . ."

"Maybe the South was too big an area to keep Threadfree until the grubs had been seeded," Sharra suggested.

"Good point!" Then Piemur snorted with derision. "Those old Records are worse than useless; they leave out the most important things. Like telling farmers to watch for the grubs in the North and not mentioning why! Like leaving the Southern Continent alone, and not why! Though if there were half as many earthshakes then as there are now, I can't fault them for common sense. When I was on the way to Big Bay, I bloody near got killed in a shake. Nearly lost Stupid from fright. If it hadn't been for Farli keeping her eye on him, I never would have caught up with the stupid idiot!"

"Earth-shakes happen in the North," Jaxom said, "in Crom and High Reaches and sometimes Igen and the Telgar Plain."

"Not the kind I've been through," Piemur said, shaking his head at the memory. "Not where the earth drops beneath your feet and two paces beyond you lifts above your head half a dragonlength."

"When did that happen? Three, four months ago?"

"That's when!"

"Earth only trembled at Southern, but that's scary enough!"

"Ever seen a volcano pop up out of the ocean and spew fiery rock and ash about?" asked Piemur.

"No, and I'm not sure you have, either, Piemur," Sharra said, eyeing him suspiciously.

"I have, and N'ton was with me, so I've a witness."

"Don't think I won't ask him."

"Where was it, Piemur?" Jaxom asked, fascinated.

"I'll show you on the map. N'ton's been keeping his eye on the place. Last time we met, he said the volcano had stopped smoking and it had built a regular island about itself as neat as . . . as neat as that mountain of yours!"

"I'd prefer to see it with my own eyes," Sharra said, still skeptical.

"I'll arrange it," the harper replied with good humor. "That's a likely tree!" he added and, leaping in the air, grabbed the lowest branch and swung himself neatly up. He began to sever the stems that held the redfruit, dropping them carefully into the waiting hands of Jaxom and Sharra.

It had taken them only two hours to walk to the fire-lizards' clutch along the beach. But it took them almost three times as long to hack a narrow path back to the shelter through the thick undergrowth. Jaxom began to appreciate the arduousness of Piemur's journey as he slashed valiantly away at the sticky-sapped bushes. His shoulders ached and he'd branch-spiked shins and skinned toes by the time they emerged near the shelter. Jaxom had lost all sense of direction. But Piemur had an uncanny sense and with Ruth and three fire-lizards, had kept them on a direct line to their goal.

Once there, only Jaxom's pride kept him from collapsing on his bed and sleeping off his exertions. Piemur was all for a swim to wash off the sweat and Sharra thought that broiled fish would make a good supper, so Jaxom struggled to keep going.

That might have been why, he thought later, he had such vivid dreams when he finally did crawl into bed to sleep. The mountain, smoking, and spewing out fire-ash and glowing rock, dominated the dream, which was full of streams of running people. To Jaxom that was very sensible but he was also part of those people rushing away and it seemed that he couldn't run fast enough. The red-orange glowing river that poured over the lip of the mountain threatened to engulf him and he couldn't make his legs move fast enough.

"Jaxom!" Piemur shook him awake. "You're dreaming! You'll wake Sharra." Piemur paused, and in the dim twilight of predawn, the sound of Sharr's moaning was clearly audible. "Maybe I should. She sounds like she's having a bad dream, too."

Piemur started to crawl out of his sleeping furs when they heard Sharra sigh deeply, and fall into a quieter sleep.

"I shouldn't have talked about that volcano. I relived that eruption. At least, I think that's what I was dreaming." Piemur sounded confused. "Probably too much fish and fruit! I made up for lost meals tonight." He sighed and made himself comfortable again.

"Thanks, Piemur!"

"For what?" Piemur asked in the middle of a yawn.

Jaxom turned over, found a good position and dropped easily back into a dreamless sleep.

Ruth's bugle woke all three the next morning.

"F'nor's coming," Jaxom said, having heard Ruth's message.

F'nor brings others, Ruth added.

Jaxom, Sharra and Piemur had reached the cove when four dragons erupted into the air, the other three dwarfed by brown Canth. Shrieking in surprise, the fire-lizards who had been draped about Ruth abruptly disappeared, leaving only Meer, Talla and Farli.

It is Piemur, Jaxom heard Ruth tell Canth. And then F'nor began to wave wildly, clasping two hands above his head in a signal of victory.

Canth deposited his rider on the sand. Roaring a command at

the other dragons, he waddled happily into the water where Ruth was quick to join him.

"Well met, Piemur," F'nor cried, unloosening his flying gear as he walked toward the others. "Began to wonder if you'd gotten lost!"

"Lost?" Piemur looked outraged. "That's the trouble with you dragonfliers. You've no respect for ground distances! You've got it too easy. Up, up and away! Wink out and you're where you want to be. No effort at all involved." He made a sound of disgust in his throat. "Not *I* know where *I've* been, every bloody finger's length of it!"

F'nor grinned at the young harper and pummeled his back with such vigor Jaxom was surprised to see Piemur unmoved. "You'll amuse your Master then, with the full and properly embroidered tale of your travels . . ."

"You're to bring me to Master Robinton?"

"Not yet. He's coming to you!" F'nor pointed to the ground.

"What?"

F'nor was searching in his belt pouch and brought out a folded leaf. "*This* is my reason for coming today! And don't let me forget the fire-lizard eggs, will you?"

"What's that?" Jaxom, Sharra and Piemur clustered close about the brown rider as he made a show of unfolding the sheet.

"This . . . is a hall for the Master Harper, to be built in this cove!"

"Here?" the three demanded in chorus.

"How'll he get here?" Jaxom asked. "He surely wouldn't be allowed to fly *between*." He couldn't help the edge of resentment in his voice. F'nor cocked an eyebrow at him.

"Master Idarolan has put his fastest, largest vessel at the Master Harper's disposal. Menolly and Brekke are accompanying him. On a sea voyage there is nothing that can disturb or worry the Harper."

"He gets seasick," remarked Jaxom.

"Only in small boats." F'nor looked at them with a very solemn expression. "So. We'll set to work at once. I've brought tools and extra help," and he gestured toward the three Weyrlings who had joined them. "We'll enlarge that shelter to a proper small hold," he said as he glanced down at the leaf. "I'll want every bit of that underbrush cleared off . . ."

"Then you'll fry the Harper in the sun which is unpleasant," Sharra pointed out.

"I beg your pardon . . ."

Sharra took the leaf from him, frowning critically at it. "Small hold? This is a bloody hall," she said, "and not the least bit suitable to this continent. Furthermore," and she dropped to the sand, picking up a long shell fragment with which she began another sketch. "First, I wouldn't build where the old shelter is—too close to the cove in rough seas and they have them here. There's a rise . . . with mature fruit trees screening it, over there . . ." She pointed to the east of the shelter.

"Mature trees? For Thread to eat?"

"Oh, you dragonriders! This is Southern, not the North. It's all been grubbed. Thread sears a leaf every sevenday or so, but the plant heals itself. Meanwhile, you're coming into the hot season and, believe me, you'll want as much green about you as possible to keep cool. You want to build off the ground, on pilings. There's plenty of reef rock for foundations. You want wide windows, not these tiny slits, to catch every breeze. All right, you can shutter them if you want to but I've lived south all my life, so I know how you should build here. You want windows, and corridors straight through the interior for breezeways . . ." As she spoke, she was delineating the revised hold with strokes that were strong enough to stay in the hot dry sand. "And you want an outdoor hearth for so many. Brekke and I did most of our baking here in stone pits," she pointed to the spot on the cove, "and you don't really need a bathing room with the cove a few steps from the door."

"You don't object to piped water, do you?"

"No, that would be handier than lugging it from the stream. Only put another tap in the cooking area as well as one in the house. Perhaps even a tank by the hearth so we can have heated water, too . . ."

"Anything else, Masterbuilder?" F'nor was more amused and admiring than sarcastic.

"I'll let you know when the thought occurs to me," she replied with dignity.

F'nor grinned at her and then frowned down at her drawing. "I'm not really certain how the Harper will like having so much greenery near him. You are, I know, used to being out during Threadfall . . ."

"So's Master Robinton," Piemur said. "Sharra's right about the heat and the building down here. We can always cut forest down, F'nor, but you can't build it back up so easily."

"A point. Now you three, B'refli, K'van and M'tok, loose your dragons. They can swim and sun with Ruth and Canth. They won't be needed until we've cut some wood. K'van, let me have your sack. You've got the axes, haven't you?" F'nor passed out the tools, ignoring Piemur's mutterings about slogging through days of forests only to end up cutting one down. "Sharra, take us to your preferred site. We'll clear some of those trees and use 'em for supports."

"They're stout enough," Sharra agreed and led the way.

Sharra was correct about the trees: F'nor marked off the proposed site of the hall and the trees to be cut. This was a lot easier said than done. The axes didn't seem to bite the wood, rather bounced off. F'nor was surprised, muttering about dull axes and brought out his sharpening stone. Having achieved a suitably sharp edge at the expense of a slit finger, he tried again with slightly more success.

"I don't understand it," he said, peering at the cuts in the trunk. "This wood shouldn't be that tough. It's a fruitwood, not a northern hardwood. Well, we've got to clear the site, boys!"

The only one who didn't have a fine set of blisters by midday was Piemur, who was used to hacking. More discouraging was the lack of progress—only six trees were down.

"Not for lack of trying, is it?" F'nor said, mopping the sweat from his forehead. "Well, let's see what Sharra's got for us to eat. Something smells good."

They had time for a swim before Sharra's meal was ready, the salt water stinging in their blisters which Sharra slathered with numbweed. When they'd eaten the broiled fish and baked roots, F'nor set them to sharpening their axes. They spent the rest of the afternoon lopping off branches before they asked the dragons to haul the timbers to one side. Sharra cleared underbrush and, with Ruth's help, brought black reef rock to mark out the piles of the foundation.

As soon as F'nor took his recruits back to the Weyr for the night, Jaxom and Piemur collapsed on the sand, rousing only long enough to eat the dinner Sharra served them.

"I'd sooner tramp around the Big Bay," Piemur muttered, wincing as he stretched his shoulders this way and that.

"It's for Master Robinton," Sharra said.

Jaxom regarded his blisters thoughtfully. "At the rate we're going it'd better take him months to get here!"

Sharra took pity on their aching muscles and rubbed salve that smelled aromatic and burned pleasantly into the soreness. Jaxom liked to think that she spent more time massaging his back than Piemur's. He'd been glad to see the young harper and was fascinated by the Records and the charts he was drawing from his travels, but he did wish that Piemur had taken a day or two longer before he'd reached the camp. There was no way he could consolidate his hold on her attentions with a third party about.

There was even less opportunity by the following morning. Sharra woke them to announce that F'nor had arrived, with more helpers.

Jaxom should have been more suspicious of her bland expression, and the calls and orders that he heard outside the shelter. But he was totally unprepared for the sight that met his eyes when he and Piemur, moving stiffly, emerged from the shelter.

The cove, the clearing, the sky—all were full of dragons and men. As soon as a dragon was unloaded, he took off to allow another to land. The waters of the cove were full of splashing, playing dragons. Ruth was standing on the eastern tip of the cove, head turned skyward, bugling welcome after welcome. A full fair of fire-lizards chattered at one another on the roof of the shelter.

"Sear and scorch it, will you look at that?" Piemur called at Jaxom's side. Then he chuckled and rubbed his hands. "One thing for sure, no chopping today!"

"Jaxom! Piemur!" The two swung round at F'nor's cheerful greeting and saw the brown rider striding toward them. Following close on his heels were the Mastersmith Fandarel, Masterwoodsman Bendarek, N'ton and, from his shoulder knots, a wingleader from Benden. Jaxom thought he was T'gellan.

"Did I give you the two drawings last night, Jaxom? I can't find them . . . Ah, here they are!" F'nor pointed to the sheets on the small table—Brekke's original drawing and the alterations suggested by Sharra. The brown rider retrieved the sheets and showed them to the Craftsmasters. "Now, here, Fandarel, Bendarek, this is our idea . . ."

Acting as one, the two men lifted the sheets from F'nor's hands and scrutinized first one then the other. Both shook their heads slowly from side to side in disapproval.

"Not very efficient, F'nor, but well meant," the huge Smith said.

"Weyrleader R'mart allowed me sufficient riders to bring in well-seasoned hardwoods for the frame," Bendarek told the Smith.

"I have piping for water and other conveniences, metals for a proper hearth and fitments, kitchen implements, windows . . ."

"Lord Asgenar insisted that I bring stonesmiths. Proper foundations and flooring must be well laid . . ."

"First we must correct this design, Master Bendarek . . ."

"I quite agree. This is a nice enough little cot but not at all suitable accomodation for the Masterharper of Pern."

The two Craftsmasters became so involved in amplifying the rough sketches that, oblivious to the other occupants of the room, they moved as one toward the table Jaxom had contrived for his charts. Piemur leaped forward and rescued his pouch of notes and sketches. The Masterwoodsman, ignoring any such interruptions to his thoughts, took a clean sheet, slipped a writing tool from a pocket and began, with neat lines, to draw what he had in mind. The Smith, taking a sheet of his own, began to delineate his ideas.

"Honest, Jaxom," F'nor said, his eyes crinkling with amusement, "all I did was ask F'lar and Lessa if I could draft a *few* more helpers. Lessa gave me a stern look; F'lar said I was to recruit as many free riders as I needed and, at dawn, the rim of the Weyr was packed solid with dragons and half of the Craftsmasters of Pern! Lessa must have bespoken Ramoth, who evidently told everyone in Pern . . ."

"You gave them the excuse they needed, F'nor," Piemur said, surveying the traffic on the once-quiet beach, the throngs of riders and craftsmen piling dragonloads on the already crowded perimeters.

"Yes, I know, but I hadn't expected such a response. And how could I tell 'em they couldn't come?"

"I think," said Sharra, who had joined them, "that this is quite a tribute to the Masterharper." Her eyes caught Jaxom's and he knew that she was aware of his ambivalent feelings about this invasion of their private, peaceful cove.

Then Jaxom saw F'nor watching him and managed a weak smile. "Yesterday's blisters will have a chance to heal, I guess. Right, Piemur?"

Piemur nodded, his jaw muscles working as he observed the activity on the beach. "I'd better find Stupid. All this confusion has probably scared him deep into the forest. Farli!" He held up his arm for his fire-lizard, who swooped down from the roof. "Find Stupid, Farli. Lead me to him!"

The fire-lizard looked over her left shoulder and chirped, and Piemur strode off in that direction without a backward glance.

"That young man's been alone too long," F'nor said.

"Yes!"

"You know how he feels?" F'nor asked, grinning at Jaxom's terse reply. He clapped him on the shoulder. "I wouldn't let it get to me, if I were you, Jaxom. With the amount of help we've got, the hold will be up in next to no time. You'll have your peace and quiet back."

"Idiots!" Sharra exclaimed suddenly.

Jaxom, avoiding F'nor's quizzical expression, looked at her. She'd been half-listening to the conversation between the two Masters.

"Now I have to have it out with *them!*" Her fists were clenched with exasperation as she strode purposefully up to the two Craftsmen. "Masters, I must point out something you have clearly overlooked. This is hot country. You're both used to cold winters and freezing rains. If you build this hold on those lines, people will stifle in the full heat of summer which is almost upon us. Now, where I live in Southern Hold, we build thick walls to keep the heat out and the cool in. We build off the ground so air circulates under the floor and keeps that cool. We build lots of windows—wide ones—and you've brought enough metal shutters, Master Fandarel, to outfit a dozen holds. Yes, I know, but Thread doesn't fall every day and the heat does. Now . . ."

F'nor made a clicking noise against his teeth. "She sounds like Brekke. And if she acts at all like my weyrmate when she's in that sort of mood, I'd rather be somewhere else. *You,*" F'nor poked Jaxom in the chest, "can show us where to hunt. Food was brought along but since you're in effect the resident Lord Holder, it's up to you to play host with some roasting meat . . ."

"I'll get my flying gear," Jaxom said with such a tone of relief that the three dragonriders laughed.

Jaxom quickly slipped long trousers over the short pants he'd been wearing for sunning and swimming, threw his jacket over his shoulder and joined the three riders by the doorway.

"I think we can mount on the left-hand arm of the cove, near Ruth," said F'nor.

Something whizzed by Jaxom's ear and instinctively ducking, he looked back as Meer came to a hover, clutching a piece of black reef rock in his front paws. Jaxom heard Sharra thanking her fire-lizard for his prompt return.

He hastily left before she could think of any errands for him. F'nor had hunting ropes for each of them which they checked and coiled over their shoulders. As they made their way past piles of assorted woods in various lengths and widths, past metal shutters and unlabeled bales, men hailed the riders and inquired how Jaxom was feeling.

Before they completed the short walk to the cove tip, Jaxom had identified men from every Weyr except Telgar—which was expecting Thread that day—and representatives of every craft in Pern, mostly journeyman rank and higher. Isolated as he'd been for so many sevendays, it hadn't occurred to Jaxom that his illness might have been a subject of widespread interest through Weyr, Craft, and Hold. He was embarrassed as well as gratified, but that did not ease his sense of being overwhelmed, or this violation, however well-intentioned, of the privacy and peace of his cove.

What had F'nor called him? Resident Lord Holder? He gave himself a shake just as Ruth, dripping wet, landed lightly beside him.

So many people. So many dragons! This is fun! Ruth's eyes were whirling with excitement and pleasure.

The white dragon, now dwarfed by two huge bronzes and a nearly as large brown dragon, was so delighted with all this excitement that Jaxom could not remain disgruntled.

Laughing, he thumped Ruth affectionately on the shoulder and sprang to his neck. The other riders were also mounted so, raising his arm, fist closed, he pumped it to indicate ascent. Still laughing, he braced himself as Ruth launched straight upward, leaving the heavier beasts sandbound while he was in free air. Politely Ruth circled while the others became airborne and then, heading southeast, he led the way.

He headed toward the farthest of the river meadows that he and Sharra had found. Wherries and runner beasts generally made their way there about midmorning, to wallow in the water and the cool mud. There would also be sufficient open space for the bigger dragons to maneuver and permit their riders good casts.

Sure enough, herd and flock were wandering about the river meadows, where the land sloped from the trees to the flood edges of the river in a series of banks where successive rainy seasons had made it impossible for trees to root. Grass abounded now, about to turn sere as the hotter weather burned it relentlessly to hay.

We are to hunt singly. F'nor asks that we get a large wherry. They will try for a buck apiece. That should be enough for today.

"If it isn't," Jaxom replied, "we can always go after one of the big fish."

In fact, Jaxom quite looked forward to the opportunity. He had never had occasion to use a spearheaded rope but . . . He spotted a wherry, a fine big one, fanning its tail spines as it stalked majestically after the wherry-fens. Jaxom tightened his legs on Ruth's neck, tested the weighted loop end of the rope in his hands. He pictured the wherry-male to Ruth, who turned his head obediently to point. Then Ruth dove, his wings back to give Jaxom room to throw, his tucked-up legs nearly touching the meadow grass. Jaxom leaned forward over Ruth's near side and threw the loop deftly about the wherry's big ugly head. The creature reared back, helpfully tightening the noose. As Jaxom dug his heels into Ruth, the dragon soared upward. With a deft yank, Jaxom neatly broke the wherry's neck.

It was a heavy bird, Jaxom realized as the dead weight pulled his arms almost from the sockets. Ruth took some of the strain as he caught the rope with his forepaw.

F'nor says good catch. He hopes he can do as well!

Jaxom guided Ruth to the edge of the meadow furthest from the other hunters. Then, letting the carcass down lightly, Ruth landed and Jaxom began to secure the snatch across Ruth's back. They were airborne again in time to see T'gellan valiantly pursuing the buck he'd missed on his frist throw. F'nor and N'ton had their beasts neatly dangling. F'nor pumped his arm in triumph as he and N'ton circled back to the ccve. As Ruth followed, Jaxom saw T'gellan succeed in his second throw; none too soon for they'd had to soar to miss the edge of the forest and nearly entangled the depending buck in the trees. A good quick hunt, though, which meant the quarry would forget quickly the small excitement. Undoubtedly they'd have to hunt again tomorrow. Jaxom couldn't see even that enormous work force finishing the Harper's new hold in a day! Maybe tomorrow they could go after the big fish.

They had not been gone long, although their return trip took slightly more time, burdened as they were. A massive clearing had been made in the center of the grove. Just as Jaxom wondered how on earth even that many men had been able to fell the necessary trees, he saw a dragon lift one out of the ground by the roots, and carry it to the beach of the next cove east where the tree was neatly stacked on others. As Ruth and he neared the site, Jaxom saw that pillars of black reef rock were in place and several crossbeams of the treated, seasoned hardwoods Masters Bendarek had brought were being secured in position. A wide avenue in a graceful curve had also been cleared and sand dumped from firestone sacks transported on drag-onback. Other workmen on the edges of the clearing were involved in a variety of tasks—sawing, planing, nailing, fitting—while another file of men carried black reef rock from piles on the cove edge.

On the eastern tip, Jaxom could see that pits had been dug for roasting, metal spits erected and fires started. Tables had been placed in the shade on which Jaxom could see the piled mounds of red, orange and green fruits.

Ruth hovered over the clearing, gently landing. Two men by the fire-pits leaped to Jaxom's assistance as he offloaded the wherry. Ruth immediately vaulted out of the way so that Jaxom could guide the other carcasses dangling from the hunting ropes of the bigger dragons.

F'nor, stripping off his flying gear, walked slowly up to Jaxom, squinting against the brilliant glare from the sands as he surveyed the activity in the once peaceful cove. He sighed deeply but began to nod his head as if unexpectedly satisfied by something.

"Yes, it'll work out all right," he said, more to himself than to Jaxom because he turned then, smiling, and gripped Jaxom by the shoulder. "Yes, they'll make the transition easily."

"Transition?"

F'nor clearly didn't mean the present building frenzy.

"Dragonfolk going back to the land, the hold. How much ex-ploring have you been able to do around here?"

"The coves, as far back as those river meadows, and some of the immediate interior the day before yesterday with Piemur."

As one, the two men turned toward the cone of the volcano that lay, cloud clad, in the distance.

"Yes, it does sort of draw your eye, doesn't it?" F'nor grinned. "You'll get there first, Jaxom. In fact, I'd prefer it if you and Piemur began some serious explorations with that as your goal. Yes, that pleases you, doesn't it? Better for you, too, and Piemur. Now, before I forget it again, where's that fire-lizard clutch you reported?"

"There's twenty-one eggs and I'd like to have five of them, if I may . . ."

"Of course!"

"To be taken to Ruatha!"

"By evening."

"You know, that's curious." Jaxom craned his body about, look-ing everywhere.

"What?"

"Usually there's a lot more fire-lizards around. I don't count more than a double handful. And they're all banded."

·· C H A P T E R   X V I I ··

❧

Fort Hold, Benden Weyr, at Cove Hold, and at Sea aboard the *Dawn Sister*, 15.10.1–15.10.2

When the three fire-lizards had made the first overtures of greeting, the three men, grinning at the enthusiasm shown by their friends, made themselves comfortable around the table in the small room at Fort Hold where Lord Groghe held his private meetings. Sebell had been there frequently, but never as spokesman for his Crafthall and never when Lord Groghe had summoned the Fort Weyrleader as well, in what was obviously a matter of some importance.

"Not sure how to begin," Lord Groghe said as he poured the wine. Sebell thought that was a very good way to begin, especially since the Lord Holder had honored them with Benden wine. "Might as well plunge. Problem's this . . . I backed F'lar when he fought T'ron," Groghe nodded at the current Fort Weyrleader, "because I knew he was right. Right to exile those misfits where they'd do no one any harm. While the Oldtimers were in the Southern Weyr, made sense to leave them alone, just as long as they left us alone—which they mostly did." Lord Groghe peered from under his heavy brows first at N'ton and then at Sebell.

Since both men were aware that there had been occasional depredations in Fort Hold which could only be attributed to the dissident Oldtimers, they nodded acknowledgment of that point. Lord Groghe cleared his throat, and folded his hands across his thick middle.

"Point is, they're mostly dead, or waiting to die. No trouble anymore. D'ram, being sort of F'lar's representative, is bringing in dragonfolk from other Weyrs, to make it a proper Weyr again, fighting Thread and all that! I approve!" He favored the Harpercraftmaster and

710

then the Weyrleader with long meaningful glances. "Hmmm. Well, that's all to the good, isn't it? Protecting the South against Thread! Thing of it is, with the Southern Weyr working again, as it were, that Southern land is safe. Now I know there's a hold established there. Young Toric. Wouldn't want to interfere with *his* Holding. No way! He's earned it. But a working Weyr can protect more than one small hold, now can't it?" He pinned his gimlet stare on N'ton, who contrived to maintain an attitude of courteous interest, forcing Lord Groghe to continue without any help.

"Well, hmmm. Trouble is, you bring up a fair of young 'uns to know how to hold proper and that's what they want to do. Hold! Terrible fights they get into. Terrible quarrels. Fostering 'em don't help much. Just got to foster others and *they* quarrel and fight. Scorch it! They all need holds of their own." Lord Groghe banged his fist on the table emphasizing this point. "I can't split my land more'n it is and I'm Holding every square length that isn't bare rock. Can't put out men who're beholden to me as their fathers and grandfathers and greats were? That's not proper Holding on my side. And I won't turm 'em out to please my kin. Not that it would.

"Thing of it is, while the Oldtimers were south, wouldn't have dreamed of suggesting it. But they aren't in command anymore. D'ram is and he's F'lar's man and he'll make it a proper Weyr so there could be more holdings, couldn't there?"

Lord Groghe glanced from Harper to Weyrleader, daring them to contradict him. "There's plenty of unheld land in the South, isn't there? No one really knows how much. But I heard Masterfisherman Idarolan say one of his ships cruised for days along a coastline. Hmmm yes, well." Then he started to chuckle, a mirth that increased into a wheeze that shook the large well-fleshed frame of the Lord Holder. He was reduced to speechlessness and impotently pointed his thick forefingers first at one and then the other, trying to indicate something by gesture which his laughter kept him from explaining by word.

Helplessly, N'ton and Sebell exchanged grins and shrugs, unable to perceive what amused Lord Groghe or what he wanted to convey to them. The monumental mirth subsided, leaving Lord Groghe weak to the point of wiping tears from his eyes.

"Well trained! That's what you pair are! Well trained!" he gasped, pounding his chest with his fist to stop his wheezing. He coughed long and then, as abruptly as the laughter had seized him, he turned solemn. "Can't fault either of you. Won't. Shouldn't give up Weyr secrets easily anyhow. Appreciate that. Do me one favor. Tell F'lar. Remind him that it's better to attack than defend. Not but what he doesn't already know that! I think," Lord Groghe stabbed at his chest with his thumb, "he'd better be prepared . . . soon. Trouble is, everyone in Pern knows that the Masterharper is going south to get well. Everyone wishes Master Robinton the best of luck. Yet everyone is beginning to wonder about that Southern Continent now it's not closed anymore."

"Southern is too big to be adequately protected against Thread which still falls there," N'ton said.

Lord Groghe nodded, mumbling that he was aware of that. "Point is, people know you can live without hold and survive Threadfall!" The Lord Holder's eyes narrowed as he glanced at Sebell. "That Menolly girl of yours did it! Hear tell Toric in Southern got little help from those Oldtimers during Falls."

"Tell me, Lord Groghe," Sebell asked in his quiet way, "have you ever been out in Fall?"

Lord Groghe shuddered a bit. "Once. Ohhh, well, yes, I take your point, Harper. I take your point. Still, one way to separate boys from men!" He gave a sharp nod of his head. "That's my notion. Separate boys from men!" He gazed up at N'ton, a sly look in his eyes though his expression continued bland. "Or don't the Weyrs want the boys separated?"

N'ton laughed, to the Lord's surprise. "It's time we separated more than the boys, Lord Groghe."

"Huh?"

"We will convey your message to F'lar today." The Fort Weyrleader raised his cup to the Lord Holder as a seal on that promise.

"Can't ask fairer than that! What news, Master Sebell, of Master Robinton?"

Sebell's eyes lit with amusement. "He's four days out of Ista Hold, resting comfortably."

"Ha!" Lord Groghe begged to disbelieve that.

"Well, I'm told he's comfortable," Sebell replied. "Whether he is of the same opinion or not."

"Going to that pretty place where young Jaxom's trapped, huh?"

"Trapped?" Sebell regarded Lord Groghe with mock horror. "He's not trapped, only restricted from flying *between* for a while longer."

"Been at that cove. Beautiful. Whereabouts is it exactly?"

"In the South," Sebell answered.

"Humph. All right, you won't tell? You won't tell! Don't blame you. Beautiful place. Now, off with the pair of you and tell F'lar what I've said. Don't think I'll be the last but it'd be a help to be the first. Help to him. Help to me! Dratted sons of mine drive me to drinking!" The Lord Holder rose and so did the two younger men. "Tell your Master I was asking for him when you see him next, Sebell."

"I will, sir!"

Lord Groghe's little queen, Merga, chirped brightly at Sebell's Kimi and N'ton's Tris as the three men walked to the Hall door. To

Sebell, it indicated that Lord Groghe was well pleased with the interview.

Neither man made any comment until they were well down the wide ramp that led from the courtyard of Fort Hold to the main paved roadway of the complex Hold.

Then N'ton heard Sebell's soft and satisifed chuckle. "It worked, N'ton, it worked."

"What worked?"

"The Lord Holder's asking the Weyrleaders' permission to go south!"

"Why shouldn't they?" N'ton seemed perplexed.

Sebell grinned broadly at his friend. "By the Shell, it worked with you, too! Do you have time to take me to Benden Weyr? Lord Groghe's right. He might be the first though I doubt it, knowing Lord Corman's ways, but he won't be the last."

"What worked with me, Sebell?"

Sebell's grin deepened and his brown eyes danced. "Now I'm well trained not to give away craft secrets, my friend."

N'ton made a noise of disgusted impatience and stopped in the middle of the dusty pavement. "Explain or you don't go."

"It should be so obvious, N'ton. Do think on it. While you take me to Benden. If you haven't figured out what I mean, I'll tell you there. I'll have to inform F'lar what's been done anyhow."

"Lord Groghe, too, eh?" F'lar regarded the two younger men thoughtfully.

He'd just returned from fighting Thread over Keroon and a surprising after-Fall interview with Lord Corman, punctuated with much honking of the Lord's large and perpetually runny nose.

"Threadfall over Keroon today?" Sebell asked and when F'lar grimaced sourly, the young Craftmaster grinned at N'ton. "Lord Groghe wasn't first!"

Giving vent to the irritation he felt, F'lar slapped his riding gauntlets down on the table.

"I apologize for barging in when you must wish to rest, Weyrleader," Sebell said, "but if Lord Groghe has thought of those empty lands to the south, others have, too. He suggested that you'd better be warned."

"Warned, huh?" F'lar brushed the forelock out of his eyes and grimly poured a cup of wine for himself. Recalling courtesy, he poured wine for N'ton and Sebell.

"Sir, the matter's not yet out of hand."

"Hordes of holdless men wanting to swarm south, and it's not out of hand?"

"They have to ask Benden's permission first!"

F'lar was in the act of swallowing wine and nearly choked in surprise.

"Ask Benden's permission? How does that come about?"

"Master Robinton's doing," N'ton said, grinning from ear to ear.

"Excuse me, I don't seem to be following you," F'lar said, sitting down. He dabbed the splattered wine from his lips. "What has Master Robinton, who is, I trust, safely at sea, to do with Groghe, Corman and who knows who else wanting Southern lands for their many sons?"

"Sir, you know that I've been sent about Pern—north and south—by the Masterharper? Lately I've had two important tasks to accomplish above and beyond my normal duties. First I was to take the temper of every small Hold as regarded duty to Hold and Weyr. Secondly I was to reinforce the belief that it is to Benden Weyr everyone on Pern must look!"

F'lar blinked, shook his head as if to clear his mind and then leaned forward to Sebell.

"Go on. This is very interesting."

"Benden Weyr only could appreciate the changes that had occurred to Hold and Craft during the Long Interval, because only Benden had changed *with* the Turns. You, as Benden Weyrleader, saved Pern from Thread when no one else felt Thread would ever fall again. You also protected your Time from the excesses of those Oldtimers, who could not accept the gradual changes of Hold and Craft. You upheld the rights of Hold and Craft against your own kind and exiled those who would not look to you for leadership."

"Hmmm. I haven't ever heard it put quite like that," F'lar said.

To N'ton's amustment, Benden's Weyrleader squirmed, partly embarrassed but most gratified by the summation.

"And so the South became closed off!"

"Not precisely closed off," F'lar said. "Toric's people always came and went." He grimaced at the present repercussions of that liberty.

"They came north, true, but traders or anyone else only went south with the permission of Benden Weyr."

"I don't remember saying that at Telgar Hold the day I fought T'ron!" F'lar struggled to recall clearly what had happened that day other than a wedding, a fight and a Threadfall.

"You didn't actually say so in so many words," Sebell replied, "but you asked for and received the support of three other Weyrleaders, and every Lord Holder and Craftmaster . . ."

"And Master Robinton construed that to mean Benden gives all orders regarding Southern?"

"More or less." Sebell made that admission cautiously.

"But not in so many words, eh, Sebell?" F'lar asked, appreciating afresh the devious mind of the Harper.

"Yes, sir. It seemed the course to take, sir, considering your own wish to secure some part of the Southern Continent for the dragonfolk during the next Interval."

"I'd no idea that Master Robinton had taken a chance remark of mine so much to heart."

"Master Robinton has always had the best interests of the Weyrs clearly in mind."

Grimly F'lar thought of the painful estrangement when the Harper had intervened on the day the egg had been stolen. But again, though it hadn't seemed so at the moment, the Harper had acted in the best interests of Pern. If Lessa had carried out her intention of setting the Northern dragons against the poor old beasts at Southern . . .

"We owe the Masterharper much."

"Without the Weyrs . . ." Sebell spread his hands wide to indicate that there was no other option.

"Not all the Holds would agree to that," F'lar said. "There is still that notion that the Weyrs do not destroy the Red Star because the end of Thread would mean the end of their dominance in Pern. Or has Master Robinton cleverly changed that notion, too?"

"Master Robinton didn't have to," Sebell said with a grin. "Not after F'nor and Canth tried to go to the Red Star. The notion is *Dragonmen must fly/When Threads are in the sky.*"

"Isn't it current knowledge now," F'lar tried to keep the contempt from his tone, "that the Southerners rarely stirred themselves to fly. Thread in the South?"

"That is, as you believe, now known. But, sir, I think you fail to appreciate that it is one thing to *think* about being holdless in the Fall, and quite another matter to endure it."

"You have?" F'lar asked.

"I have." Sebell's expression was solemn. "I would prefer above all else to be within a Hold." He shrugged his shoulders. "I know that it's a question of changing the habits of my early years, but I definitely prefer to be sheltered during Fall. And to me that will always imply protection by dragons!"

"So, in the final analysis, I've got the problem of Southern right back in my lap?"

"What's the problem with Southern now?" Lessa asked, entering the weyr just then. "I thought it was understood that *we* have first rights in Southern!"

"That," F'lar chuckled, "does not appear to be in contention. Not at all. Thanks to good Master Robinton."

"Then what is the problem?" She nodded at Sebell and N'ton by way of greeting, then looked sternly at her Weyrmate for his answer.

"Only which part of the Southern Continent we'll open to the holdless younger sons of the North before they become a problem in themselves. Corman spoke to me after Fall."

"I saw you two talking. Frankly, I've been wondering when the subject would come up now that we've had to interfere with the Old-timers again." Lessa loosened her riding belt, and sighed. "I wish I knew more. Has Jaxom done nothing with his time down at the cove?"

Sebell extracted a bulky packet from his tunic. "He has, among others. Perhaps this will ease your mind, Lessa." With an air of quiet triumph, Sebell unfolded the carefully joined leaves of a large chart, portions of which remained white. A clearly defined coastline was occasionally expanded inland with colored and shaded areas. In the margins were dates and the names of those who had surveyed the various sections. The thumb of land pointing at Nerat Tip was completely filled in and familiar to the Weyrleader as Southern Weyr and Hold. On either side of that landmark was an incredible sweep of continent, bounded on the west by the delineation of a great sandy waste on two sides of a huge bay. On the east, ever further from the thumb of Southern, a longer coastline stretched, dipping sharply south, punctuated at its most easterly point by the drawing of a high, symmetrical mountain and a small, starred cove.

"This is what we know of the Southern Continent," Sebelle said after a long interval while the dragonriders studied the map. "As you see, we still haven't managed to chart the entire coast, let alone the interior. This much has taken three full Turns of discreet survey to do."

"By whom?" Lessa inquired, now deeply interested.

"By many people, myself included, N'ton, Toric's holders, but most of it by a young harper named Piemur."

"So that's what happened to him when his voice changed," Lessa said in surprise.

"By the scale of this map," F'lar said slowly, "you could fit the North of Pern in the western half of the Bay."

Sebell laid his left thumb on the protuberance of Southern and planted the rest of his hand, fingers splayed on the western section of the map. "This area could easily occupy the Lord Holders." He heard Lessa's sharp intake of breath and smiled at her, spreading his right hand over the eastern portion. "But this, Piemur tells me, is the best part of the South!"

"Near that mountain?" Lessa asked.

"Near that mountain!"

Piemur, leading Stupid while Farli circled above him, reappeared from the forest just as full dark was falling on the cove. He swung a plaited string of ripe fruit to the ground in front of Sharra.

"There! That's to make up for cutting out this morning," he said, a tentative grin on his face as he squatted on his haunches. "Stupid wasn't the only one scared of that mob this morning." He made a show of wiping his forehead. "I haven't seen that many people in . . . since the last gather I attended a South Boll. *That* was two Turns ago! I was afraid they'd never leave! They'll be back tomorrow?"

Jaxom grinned at his plaintive question and nodded. "I wasn't much better than you, Piemur. I got away by having to hunt. Then I tracked down that clutch and spent the afternoon rigging fishnet." He gestured toward the next cove.

Piemur nodded. "Funny thing that, not wanting to be among people. Felt as if I couldn't breathe with so many using the same air supply. And that's downright foolish." He looked about him, at the black bulks of supplies lining the cove. "We're not stuffed in a Hold, with fans going!" He shook his head. "Me, Piemur, harper, a social fellow. And I turn and run from people . . . faster than Stupid did!" He gave a snort of laughter.

"If it'll make you two feel any better, I was a bit overwhelmed myself," Sharra said. "Thank you for the fruit, Piemur. That . . . that horde ate all we had. I think there's some roast wherry left, and a few rib bones from the buck."

"I could eat Stupid, only he'd be too tough." Piemur breathed a sigh of relief and eased himself down to the sand.

Sharra chuckled as she went to get him something to eat.

"I don't like to think of a lot of people here," Jaxom told Piemur.

"Know what you mean." The young harper grinned. "Jaxom, do you realize that I've been places no man has ever stepped before? I've seen places that scared me to leaking, and other spots that I had trouble leaving because they were so beautiful." He exhaled in resignation. "Oh, well, I got there first." Suddenly he sat up, pointing urgently into the sky. "There they are! If only I had a far-viewer!"

"Who are?" Jaxom slewed himself around to see where Piemur was pointing, expecting dragonriders.

"The so-called Dawn Sisters. You can only see them dusk and dawn down here and much higher in the sky. See, those three very bright points! Many's the time I've used them as guides!"

Jaxom could scarcely miss the three stars, gleaming in an almost constant light. He wondered that he hadn't noticed them before now.

"They'll fade soon," Piemur said, "unless one of the moons is out. Then you see them again just before dawn. Must ask Wansor about that when I see him. They don't act like proper stars. The Starsmith's not scheduled to come down and help build the Harper's hold, is he?"

"He's about the only one who isn't," Jaxom replied. "Cheer up, Piemur. The way they worked today, it won't take long to finish that hold. And what do you mean about the Dawn Sisters?"

"They just don't act like proper stars. Didn't you ever notice?"

"No. But we've been in most evenings and certainly every dawn."

Piemur pointed with several stabs of his right arm at the Dawn Sisters. "Most stars change position. They never do."

"Sure they do. In Ruatha they're almost invisible on the horizon . . ."

Piemur was shaking his head. "They're constant. That's what I mean. Every season I've been here, they're always in the same place."

"Can't be! It's impossible. Wansor says that stars have routes in the sky just like—"

"They stay still! They're always in the same position."

"And I tell you that's impossible."

"What's impossible? And don't snarl at each other," Sharra said, returning with a tray piled high with food and a wineskin slung over her shoulder. Giving Piemur the food, she filled cups all around.

Piemur guffawed as he reached for a buck rib. "Well, I'm going to send a message to Wansor. I say it's bloddy peculiar behavior for stars!"

A change in the breeze awakened the Master Harper. Zair chirped softly, curled on the pillows above Robinton's ear. A sunscreen had been rigged above the Harper's head but it was the airless heat that roused him.

For a change, no one was seated in watch over him. The respite of surveillance pleased him. He had been touched by the concern of everyone, though at times the attention bade fair to smother him. He'd curbed his impatience. He had no choice. Too weak and tired to resist the ministrations. Today must be another small indication of his general improvement: leaving him alone. He reveled in the solitude. Before him, the jib sheet flapped idly and he could hear the mainsail, behind him—aft, he corrected himself abruptly—rumbling windless as well. The gentle rolling swells seemed to be all that drove the ship forward. Waves, curls of foam on their crests, were mesmeric in their rhythm and he had to shake his head sharply to break their fascination. He raised his glance above the swell and saw nothing but water, as usual, on all sides. They would not see land for days more, he knew, though Master Idarolan said they were making good speed on their southeasterly course now that they had picked up the Great South Current.

The Master Fisherman was as pleased with this expedition as everyone else connected with it. Robinton snorted to himself with amusement. Everyone else apparently was profiting by his illness.

Now, now, Robinton chided himself, don't be sour. Why did you spend so much time training Sebell if not to take over when it became necessary? Only, Robinton thought, he hadn't ever expected that to happen. He wondered fleetingly if Menolly was faithfully reporting the daily messages from Sebell. She and Brekke could well be conspiring to keep any worrying problem from him.

Zair stroked his cheek with his soft head. Zair was the best humor-vane a man could have. The fire-lizard knew, with an instinct that outshone his own reliable sense of atmosphere, the emotional climate of those about Robinton.

He wished he could throw off this languor and use the journey time to good effect—catching up on Craft business, on those songs he had in mind to write, on any number of long-delayed projects that the press of immediate concerns had pushed further and further from completion. But Robinton had no ambition at all; he found himself content to lie on the deck of Master Idarolan's swift ship and do nothing. The *Dawn Sister*, that's what Idarolan called her. Pretty name. That reminded him. He must borrow the Fisherman's far-viewer this evening. There was something odd about those Dawn Sisters. They were visible, higher up than they ought to be, in the sky at dusk as well as dawn. Not that he'd been allowed to be awake at dawn to check. But they were mostly in the sky at sunset. He didn't think that stars should act that way. He must remember to write Wansor a note.

He felt Zair stir, heard him chirp a pleasant greeting before he heard the soft step behind him. Zair's mind imagined Menolly.

"Don't creep up on me," he said with more testiness than he intended.

"I thought you were asleep!"

"I was. What else do I do all day?" He smiled at her to take the petulance from his words.

Surprisingly, she grinned and offered him a cup of fruit juice, lightly laced with wine. They knew better now than to offer him plain juice.

"You sound better."

"Sound better? I'm as peevish as an old uncle! You must be heartily tired of my sulks by now!"

She dropped beside him, her hand on his forearm.

"I'm just so glad you're able to sulk," she said. Robinton was startled to see the glimmer of tears in her eyes.

"My dear girl," he began, covering her hand with his.

She laid her head on the low couch, her face turned from him. Zair chirped in concern, his eyes beginning to whirl faster. Beauty erupted into the air above Menolly's head, chittering in echoed distress. Robinton set down his cup and raised himself on one elbow, leaning solicitously over the girl.

"Menolly, I'm fine. I'll be up and about any day now, Brekke says." The Harper permitted himself to stroke her hair. "Don't cry. Not now!"

"Silly of me, I know. Because you are getting well, and we'll see to it that you never strain yourself again . . ." Menolly wiped her eyes impatiently with the back of her hand and sniffled.

It was an endearingly childlike action. Her face, now blotchy from crying, was suddenly so vulnerable that Robinton felt his heart give a startling thump. He smiled tenderly at her, stroked tendrils of her hair back from her face. Tilting her chin up, he kissed her cheek. He felt her hand tighten convulsively on his arm, felt her lean into his kiss with an appeal that set both fire-lizards humming.

Perhaps it was that response from their friends, or the fact that he was so startled that caused him to stiffen, but Menolly swiveled away from him.

"I'm sorry," she said, her head bent, her shoulders sagging.

"So, my dear Menolly, am I," the Harper said as gently as he could. In that instant, he regretted his age, her youth, how much he loved her—the fact that he never could—and the weakness that caused him to admit so much. She turned back to him, her eyes intense with her emotion.

He held up his hand, saw the quick pain in her eyes, as the merest shake of his fingers forestalled all she wanted to say. He sighed, closing his eyes against the pain in her loving eyes. Abruptly he was exhausted by an exchange of understanding that had taken so few moments. As few as at Impression, he thought, and as lasting. He supposed he had always known the dangerous ambivalence of his feelings for the young SeaHold-bred girl whose rare talent he had developed. Ironic that he should be weak enough to admit it, to himself and to her, at such an awkward moment. Obtuse of him not to have recognized the intensity and quality of Menolly's feelings for him. Yet, she'd seemed content enough with Sebell. Certainly they enjoyed a deep emotional and physical attachment. Robinton had done everything in his subtle power to insure that. Sebell was the son he had never had. Better that!

"Sebell . . ." he began, and stopped when he felt here fingers tentatively closing over his.

"I loved your first, Master."

"You've been a dear child to me," he said, willing himself to believe that. He squeezed her fingers in a brisk grip which he broke and, elbowing himself off the pillows, retrieved the cup he had set down and took a long drink.

He was able, then, to smile up at her, despite the lingering ache in his throat for what could never have been. She did manage a smile in return.

Zair flew up and beyond the sunscreen, though Robinton couldn't imagine why the approach of the Masterfisher would startle the creature.

"So, you wake. Rested, my good friend?" the Seamaster asked.

"Just the man I wanted to see. Master Idarolan, have you noticed those Dawn Sisters at dusk? Or has my eyesight deteriorated with the rest of me?"

"Oho, the eye is by no means dimmed, good Master Robinton. I've already sent word back to Master Wansor on that account. I confess that I have never sailed so far easterly in these Southern waters so I'd never observed the phenomenon before, but I do believe that there is something peculiar about the positioning of those three stars."

"If I'm allowed to stay up past dusk this evening," the Harper glared significantly at Menolly, "may I have the loan of your distance-viewer?"

"You certainly may, Master Robinton. I'd appreciate your observations. I know you've had a good deal more time to study Master Wansor's equations. Perhaps we can figure out between us this erratic behavior."

"I'd like nothing better. In the meantime, let us complete that game we started this morning. Menolly, have you the board handy?"

ᐁ

At the Cove Hold the Day of Master Robinton's Arrival, 15.10.14

With so many eager hands and skilled craftsmen, Cove Hold took only eleven days to complete, though the stonemen shook their heads a bit over rushing the drying of hardset. Another three days were spent on the interior. Lessa, Manora, Silvina and Sharra consulted long, and with much shifting of the furnishings finally achieved what they considered the effective use—not efficient, Sharra told Jaxom with a wicked grin, but effective—of the offerings which poured in from every hold, craft and cot.

Sharra's voice began to take on a tone that mixed suffering and pride. She'd spent the day unpacking, washing and arranging things. "What did you fall into?" she asked Piemur, noticing newly acquired scratches on his face and hands.

"Doing things his way," Jaxom replied, though he'd a few marks on his neck and forehead as well.

With so many to build the Hold, N'ton, F'nor, and F'lar, when he could arrange the time, had joined Piemur and Jaxom to increase their knowledge of the lands immediately adjacent to the Cove.

Piemur rather arrogantly told F'lar that dragons had to *be* to a place first to get there again *between*—or else get a sharp enough visualization from someone who had. But he, with his two feet and Stupid's four, had to be first so that mere dragonriders could then follow. The dragonriders ignored the somewhat disparaging remarks, but Piemur's attitude was beginning to get on Jaxom's nerves.

No matter the method of accomplishment, temporary camps at a good day's flight by dragon from Cove Hold were established in a wide arc fanning out from the new Hold. Each camp consisted of a small tile-roofed shelter and a stone bunker to secure emergency supplies and sleeping furs. By a tacit agreement, they had gone two days' flight on a direct bearing to the mountain and built a secondary camp.

The restriction on Jaxom flying *between* would shortly be removed. He had only to wait now, F'lar told him, until Master Oldive gave him a final examination. Since Master Oldive would soon be in Cove Hold to check Robinton's recovery, Jaxom wouldn't have long to wait.

"And, if I can go *between*, so can Menolly," Jaxom said.

"Why would you have to wait until Menolly can go *between*?" Sharra asked, with an edge to her voice that Jaxom hoped might be a twinge of jealousy.

"She and Master Robinton found this Cove first, you know." He wasn't glancing in the direction of the Cove when he spoke, but toward the omnipresent mountain.

"By sea," Piemur said with some disgust for such a mode of transport.

"I have to admit, Piemur," Sharra said after regarding him for a long moment, "that feet were used before wings and sail. I, for one, am thankful that there are other ways of getting from one place to another. And it's no disgrace to use them."

She then turned and walked off, leaving Piemur to stare after her in surprise.

The incident cleared the air and Jaxom was relieved to note that Piemur ceased his snide remarks about flying and riding.

Attesting to the accuracy of Piemur's charting was the fact that, once the Great South Current curved shoreward, Master Idarolan was able to identify his position by the contour of the now visible coast and to predict the arrival of the *Dawn Sister* at Cove Hold. She was twenty-two days out of Istan water before she rounded the west point of the Cove one bright morning, an event that was celebrated by a special, select welcoming committee.

Oldive and Brekke had forbidden a large reception and party. There was no point in undoing all the benefit of the long, restful voyage with the strain and fatigue of a feast. So Master Fandarel represented the hundreds of craftsmen and masters who had produced the beautiful Cove Hold. Lessa stood for all the Weyrs whose dragons had transported men and material, and Jaxom was the logical spokesman for the Lord Holders who had contributed the men and supplies.

These last moments, as the graceful three-masted ship headed up the Cove toward the stubby stone pier, seemed the hardest to endure. Jaxom strained his eyes as the ship glided closer and closer on the calm waters, and let out a jubilant whoop that made the fire-lizards squeak in surprise when he discerned the figure of the Harper standing in the prow, waving to those on shore. The fire-lizards executed aerial dances of great intricacy above the ship.

"Look, he's almost black with sun," Lessa cried, clutching Jaxom's arm in her excitement.

"Don't worry, he'll have had a good long rest," Fandarel said, grinning from ear to ear in anticipation of his friend's delight and pleasure in the new Hall. It was just out of sight from the pier.

The ship suddenly wheeled as Master Idarolan swung the tiller starboard, to slip his vessel deftly broadside to the dock. Seamen leapt to the pier, snubbing lines on the bollards. Jaxom jumped forward to lend a willing hand. The ship creaked as her timbers resisted the sudden halt. Bound bolsters were run over the side to prevent the ship rubbing against stone. Then a plank was dropped from an opening in the ship's rail to the pier.

"I've brought him safely to you, Benden, Mastersmith, Lord Holder," boomed the voice of the Master Seaman as he jumped to the cabin housing.

A spontaneous cheer burst from Jaxom's throat, echoed by a roar from Fandarel and a cry from Lessa. Jaxom and Fandarel stood on either side of the springy plank to grip Robinton's hands as he all but slid ashore.

Ramoth and Ruth bugled overhead, startling the fire-lizards into wilder extravagances of motion. Lessa embraced the Harper by standing on tiptoe and imperiously pulling his head down so she could kiss him soundly. Tears sparkled on her cheeks and, to Jaxom's surprise, he realized his own eyes were wet, too. He stood politely back while Fandarel gently thumped the Harper off balance, sticking out a hamlike hand to steady his friend. Then he turned to assist Brekke and Menolly down the bouncing plank. Everyone began talking at once. Brekke looked anxiously from Robinton to Jaxom, demanding if the latter had had any headaches or eye spots, then urging the Harper to get out of the fierce sun as if he hadn't been baking in it on board ship day after day.

Good-naturedly everyone seized bundles from those the seamen were passing from ship to shore—everyone except Robinton, who was only allowed to carry his gitar.

Brekke began to walk up the shore toward the old shelter when Fandarel, laughing hugely in anticipation, placed his big hand on her back and gently propelled her toward the sanded path that led to the new Cove Hold. When Brekke began to protest, Lessa hushed her and pointed decisively at the path, taking her arm and half-pulling her along.

"I'm sure the shelter was that way . . . "

"It was," replied Master Fandarel, striding along beside the Harper. "We found a better site, more suitable for our Harper!"

"More efficient, my friend?" Robinton asked, laughing as he clapped his hand on the Smith's bulging shoulder.

"Much more efficient. Much!" The Smith nearly choked with his laughter.

Brekke had reached the bend of the path and stared incredulously at the sight of the new Hold. "I don't believe it!" She glanced quickly from Lessa to the Smith to Jaxom. "What have you done? How have you done it? It just isn't possible!"

Robinton and Fandarel had reached the two women, the Smith beaming so broadly that every tooth in his head showed and his eyes were mere squints in the folds of his cheeks.

"I thought Brekke said the shelter was small," Robinton said, peering at the structure and smiling hesitantly. "Otherwise I'd have asked for . . ."

Lessa and Fandarel could bear the suspense no longer and, each taking one of the Harper's arms, urged him toward the wide porch steps.

"Just you wait until you see what's inside," Lessa said with a crow of satisfaction.

"Everyone on Pern helped, either sending craftsmen or material," Jaxom told Brekke, taking her limp arm and escorting her on. He beckoned Menolly to hurry and join them.

Menolly glanced about and saw only the peaceful cove, carefully raked sand, trees and flowering shrubs which bordered the beach looking as unscathed as the day she and Jaxom had arrived. Only the bulk of the Hold, with its peripheral path of sand and shells, gave evidence of any change. "I just don't believe it."

"I know, Menolly. They took pains to keep it lovely. And just wait till you see inside Cove Hold . . ."

"It's already been named?" That seemed to irritate her, but Jaxom could appreciate her reaction.

"Well, it is a hold in a cove, so 'Cove Hold.'"

"It's all so beautiful," Brekke said, turning her head this way and that to see everything. "Menolly, don't be annoyed. It's such a marvelous surprise. When I think what I thought we were coming to . . ." She laughed, a happy sound. "I must say, this *is* much more the suitable thing!"

They had reached the steps of black reef rock, filled with white hardset, making it sturdy and attractive at the same time. A creamy orange tile roof extended over the porch which ringed the Hold almost to the surrounding trees, their blooms adding spicy fragrance to the air. The metal shutters were folded back from the unusually wide windows so that they could see through the house and catch glimpses of the furnishings within. The Harper's voice was raised in delight and amazement as he moved about the main room. As Jaxom, Brekke and Menolly entered, Robinton had been peering into the room set aside as his study, and his expression was dazed as he realized that Silvina had sent down everything from his crowded workroom in the Harper Hall. Zair echoed his confusion, chittering high and excitedly from his perch on a crossbeam. Beauty and Berd flew to join him, and suddenly, Meer, Talla and Farli appeared. They all seemed to be comparing notes, Jaxom thought.

"That's Farli! I thought I'd heard that Piemur was here. But where is he?" The Harper sounded surprised and a trifle hurt.

"Sharra and he are tending the spits," Jaxom said.

"We didn't want too many people about, tiring you . . . " Lessa added in a soothing tone.

"Tiring me? Tiring me! I need a little tiring! PIEMUR!"

If his tanned and relaxed face had not been proof enough of his return to health, the bellow he let loose, as vigorous and deafening as ever, left no further doubts of his vitality.

Clearly audible was the distant startled reply: *"Master?"*

"REPORT, PIEMUR!"

"Thank goodness we put him on a ship to rest," Brekke said, smiling at the Weyrwoman. "Can you imagine the time we'd have had with him on land?"

"What you two cannot appreciate is how much my momentary disability has set back some very important—"

"Momentary disability?" Fandarel's eyes protruded in amazement. "My dear Robinton—"

"Master Robinton?" Menolly took a cup from the crowded cabinet, a beautiful glass goblet, its base stained harper blue, its cup incised with the Master's name and a harp. "Have you seen this?" She held it out to him, her eyes round with approval.

"My word, harper blue!" Robinton took and examined the beautiful thing.

"From my crafthall," Fandarel said, beaming. "Mermal thought to tint the entire glass blue but I argued that you would prefer to see the red of Benden wine in a clear cup."

Robinton's eyes gleamed with appreciation and gratitude as he examined the cup carefully. Then his long face fell into a sorrowful expression.

"But it's empty," he said in a plaintive, mournful tone.

At that moment a commotion started in the kitchen corner of the Hold. The curtain was flung roughly aside as Piemur, all but losing his balance in an effort not to careen into Brekke, lurched into the room.

"Master?" he gasped.

"Ah, yes, Piemur," the Harper drawled, eyeing his young journeyman as if he had momentarily forgotten why he had summoned the young man. The two regarded each other steadily, a puzzled frown on the Harper's face while Piemur's chest heaved as he panted, blinking sweat from his eyes. "Piemur, you've been here long enough to know where they store the wine? I've been given this lovely goblet and it's empty!"

Piemur blinked again and then shook his head slowly and said to the room at large, "There's nothing wrong with him anymore! And if that roast wherry burns . . . " He gave the Harper a thoroughly disgusted look, turned on his heel, whipped aside the curtain and could be heard noisily opening doors.

Jaxom caught Menolly's eye and she winked at him. Piemur's gruff manner and cracking voice had not disguised his emotion to those who knew him. He stamped back into the main hall, swinging a wineskin, with Benden wax on its stopper.

"Don't swing it, lad," the Harper cried, holding up a restraining hand at such sacrilegious treatment. "Wine must be handled with respect . . . " He took the skin from Piemur and peered at the seal. "Hmmm. One of the better vintages! Tsk, tsk, Piemur, have you learned nothing from me of how to treat wine?" He made a grimace as he expertly cracked the seal and sighed with relief as he saw the condition of the stopper's end. He passed it under his nose, sniffing delicately. "Ah! Yes! Beautiful! Took no harm from its travel! There's a good lad, Piemur, pour for us all, will you, please? I can see this Hold is admirably supplied with cups."

Jaxom and Menolly were already distributing them as Piemur, with the courtesy due good Benden vintages, poured. The Harper, holding his cup high, watched the ceremony with growing impatience.

"Your continued good health, my friend." Fandarel proposed the toast which was repeated firmly by everyone.

"I am truly overwhelmed by all this," the Harper said, giving strength to his claim by taking only a small sip of the excellent wine. He looked from one to another of his friends, nodding his head and then shaking it. "Truly overwhelmed!"

"You haven't seen everything yet, Robinton," Lessa said and took him by the hand. "Brekke, you come see, too. Piemur, Jaxom, bring the bundles."

"Not so fast, Lessa. I'll spill the wine!" The Harper watched his glass as Lessa pulled him behind her.

He was guided through the sliding panel into the small corridor that separated the main Hall from the sleeping quarters. Brekke followed, her face alight with keen interest and curiosity.

The Harper's sleeping room was the largest, occupying the corner opposite his workroom. Four more sleeping rooms had been furnished to accommodate two guests in each but, as Lessa pointed out, the porch itself could comfortably sleep half a Hold of guests. Not that Robinton was to be allowed that many. He expressed pleasure at the bathing room and was suitably impressed by the large kitchen, and dutifully peered at the auxiliary hearth outside. He sniffed as the aroma of roasting meat wafted on the sea breeze.

"Where's that being done, might I ask?"

"We've steaming and roasting pits on the beach," Jaxom said, "to use when there's a horde here."

The Harper laughed, agreed that horde was probably the proper term.

"Try your chair," Fandarel said, striding to the armed chair when they returned to the main room. He turned it about for the Harper to see. "Bendarek made it exactly to your measure. See if it suits. Bendarek will be anxious to hear."

The Harper took time to examine the beautifully carved, high-backed chair, covered with wherhide dyed a deep harper blue. He sat down, put his hands along the armrests, found they were precisely the length of his forearm, and that the seat of the chair admirably fit his long legs and torso.

"It *is* beautiful, tell Master Bendarek. And a perfect size. How considerate Bendarek is. How overwhelmed I am by this and every other single item in this Hold. It is . . . magnificent. That's the only word for it. I'm speechless. Rendered completely speechless. Never in my wildest flights of fancy did I expect such luxury in unexplored wilds, such beauty, such thoughtfulness, such comfort."

"If you're speechless, Robinton, spare us your eloquence," came a dry voice. All turned to see the Masterfisherman standing in the open main door.

Everyone laughed, and Master Idarolan was beckoned forward and given a cup of wine.

"There are more bundles for you, Master Robinton," the Seaman said, gesturing toward the porch.

"You and your crew are to eat with us, Master Idarolan," Lessa called out.

"I was hoping so. Don't noise it about, but occasionally I do get the craving for red meat, not white."

"Master Robinton! Look here!" Menolly's voice was high with surprise. She was looking inside one of the cabinets that lined the walls between windows. "I'd swear it's Dermently's hand! And every single Traditional song and ballad newly written on leaves and bound in blue wherhide! Just what you've been wanting to have Arnor do for you."

The Harper exclaimed with surprise and nothing would do but he had to open each folder and appreciate the craftsmanship and collection. Then he began to investigate all the cupboards and presses of Cove Hold until the midafternoon heat drove everyone to the beach to swim and cool off. Brekke fretted that the Harper should rest, quietly by himself, but Fandarel dismissed the notion, gesturing to Robinton, who was sporting in the water with the others.

"He is indulging in another type of rest right now. Leave him. Night's soon enough for sleeping!"

The evening breezes sprang up as the sun dipped closer to the western horizon. Rugs and woven mats as well as benches were brought out so that all the guests could be comfortable. When F'lar and F'nor arrived, they were enthusiastically welcomed by the Harper, who wanted to show them his beautiful Hold and was somewhat disappointed that they were already quite familiar with it.

"You forget how many people helped build it, Robinton," F'lar said. "It's probably the best known Hold on the entire world."

At that moment Sharra and the ship's cook—a thin man because that's the only sort, he told her, who could fit in the closet-sized excuse for a galley on the *Dawn Sister*—proclaimed that the feast was ready and were nearly run down by the hungry guests.

When no one could eat another morsel and even the Harper was reduced to small sips of wine, the guests settled into smaller groups: Jaxom, Piemur, Menolly and Sharra in one, the seamen in the largest, and the dragonriders and craftsmen in the third.

"I wonder what they're plotting for us to do now," Piemur said in a sour mutter after staring at the intense expressions of the third group.

Menolly laughed. "More of the same, I expect. Robinton's been going over those charts and reports of yours on shipboard until I thought he'd wear the ink out from looking." She pulled her knees up under her chin, a shy smile lighting her eyes. "Sebell's coming tomorrow with N'ton and Master Oldive." She went on quickly, before anyone could comment: "As I understand it, Sebell, N'ton and F'lar are overseeing Toric's people and that herd of holders' sons coming from the North. They'll chart the western part . . . the dividing line is that black rock river of yours, Piemur!"

Piemur groaned, writhing dramatically on the sand. "That place! May I never see it again!" He lifted one fist skyward to emphasize his determination. "Took me days to find a break in the cliffs on the other shore that we could climb out of. At that I had to ride Stupid off the cliffs into the water and swim him across. The fishes nearly made us their lunch."

"And the rest of us," Menolly continued. "with F'nor and the Harper, will explore this side."

"Inland, I hope?" Piemur asked sharply.

She nodded. "I understand," and she glanced over her shoulder at the Weyrleaders and Craftmasters, "that Idarolan may sail the coast . . ."

"More power to him. I've walked far enough!"

"Oh, hush, Piemur. No one forced you to . . ."

"Oh?"

"Enough, Piemur," Jaxom said, impatiently. "So we're to go inland?" Menolly nodded.

As one they looked over their shoulders toward the mountain, invisible though it was from their recumbent position.

Jaxom grinned at Menolly. "And Master Oldive'll be here tomorrow so I'll be able to go *between* again!"

"Lot of good that'll do you," Piemur said with a snort. "You still have to fly the route straight first."

"That doesn't put me out one little bit."

A fire-lizard squabble in the trees startled all of them and diverted Piemur from what Jaxom was certain was a renewal of his usual sour theme. Two gold streaks could be seen against the darker green of the foliage.

"Beauty and Farli to settle the matter!" Menolly cried, then looked around, curiously. "There're just our fire-lizards here now, Jaxom. Has all the activity frightened the Southern ones away?"

"I doubt it. They come and go. I suspect some of them are in the trees, fussing because they don't dare come near Ruth."

"Did you ever find out more about their men?"

Jaxom was chagrined to say that he hadn't even tried. "There's been too much else happening."

"I'd have thought you'd have given it one go." Menolly sounded irritated.

"What? And deprive you of the pleasure?" Jaxom affected surprised hurt. "I wouldn't dream of it . . ." He stopped abruptly, remembering those very peculiar dreams, as if he'd been seeing something out of hundreds of eyes. He also recalled what Brekke had said, the first day Ruth had flown Thread: "It was difficult to see the same scene through three pairs of eyes." Had he in fact been seeing, in his dreams, a scene from many fire-lizard eyes?

"What's wrong, Jaxom?"

"Maybe I did dream of it, after all," he said, with a hesitant laugh. "Look, Menolly, if you dream tonight, remember it, huh?"

"Dream?" Sharra asked, curious. "What kind of dreams?"

"Have you been having some?" Jaxom turned toward her. Sharra had assumed her usual intricate fold of leg, a posture which evidently fascinated and confounded Menolly.

"Certainly. Only . . . like you, I don't remember them, except that I couldn't seem to see clearly. As if my dream eye gets unfocused."

"That's a nice concept," Menolly said. "A dream eye unfocused."

Piemur groaned and flailed at the sand with his fists. "Here comes another song!"

"Oh, do be quiet!" Menolly regarded him with impatience. "All that lone traveling has changed you, Piemur, and I for one don't like the change."

"No one says you have to," Piemur snapped at her and, with a fluid motion, was on his feet and striding into the forest, angrily batting the underbrush out of his way.

"How long has he been so touchy?" Menolly asked Jaxom and Sharra.

"Since he arrived here," Jaxom said, shrugging to indicate that they hadn't been able to change him.

"Remember, he's been very worried about Master Robinton," Sharra said slowly.

"We've all been worried about Master Robinton," Menolly said, "but that's no reason to change one's temperament!"

There was an awkward silence. Sharra unfolded her legs and rose abruptly.

"I wonder if anyone remembered to feed Stupid this evening!" She walked off, not quite in the same direction as Piemur.

Menolly looked after her for a long moment. Her eyes were dark with concern as she turned back to Jaxom and then a wicked gleam changed them to their normal sea-blue.

"While they're out of earshot, Jaxom," she glanced about to be sure no one had come up behind her, "I'd better mention that it's been pretty well established now that no one at Southern Weyr returned Ramoth's egg."

"Oh? Really?"

"Oh! Really!"

She rose then, cup in hand, and strode across to the wineskin hanging from a tree branch.

Was she warning him? Not that it made any difference. His adventure had served a purpose at the time. Now that the Southern Weyr was being integrated into the others, there was less need than ever to admit his part in the affair.

Menolly wandered over to collect her gitar from the table and then seated herself at the bench, strumming softly to herself. A new song, about dream eyes, Jaxom wondered. Then he looked off in the direction Sharra had gone. Had he any legitimate reason for following her? He sighed. He liked Piemur, despite his acid tongue. He'd been glad to see the young Harper, grateful for his company and assistance. He just wished that Piemur had taken a day longer, even half a day longer, to reach the Cove. Since his arrival, Jaxom had had no time at all alone with Sharra. Was she avoiding him? Or was it just the circumstances of the building and getting Cove Hold ready for Master Robinton? He must figure out some way to separate Sharra from the others! Or else visit Corana!

CHAPTER XIX

Morning at the Cove Hold, Star-gazing
in Late Evening, Next Morning,
Discovery at the Mountain,
15.10.15–15.10.16

By the time Jaxom and Piemur had reluctantly struggled from their furs the next morning, Sharra told them that the Harper had risen at the first light of day, taken a bracing swim, made himself a breakfast and been long in his study, muttering over the charts and making copious notes. He now wished to have a few words with Jaxom and Piemur, if they didn't mind.

Master Robinton acknowledged their entry with a sympathetic grin for their deliberate and slow movements, the aftereffects of a very convivial evening. He then began asking for explanations of their latest additions to the main chart. When he had satisfied himself on that point, he asked how they had arrived at their conclusions. When they'd told him, he leaned back from the desk, fiddling with his drawing stick with such an unreadable expression on his face that Jaxom began to worry about what the Harper might be planning.

"Have either of you happened to notice the trio of stars we have been calling—erroneously, I might add—the Dawn Sisters?"

Jaxom and Piemur exchanged glances.

"Do you have a far-viewer with you, sir?" Jaxom asked.

The Harper nodded. "Master Idarolan has one aboard his ship. I construe that question to mean that you've noticed that they also appear at dusk?"

"And whenever there's enough moonlight . . . " Piemur added.

"And always in the same place!"

"I see you did profit by your classes," the Harper said, beaming at both of them. "Now, I've asked Master Fandarel if we could prevail

732

on Master Wansor to visit here for a few days. Why, might I ask, are you two grinning as if you'd eaten all the bubbly pies at a gather?''

Piemur's grin deepened at this reference to his apprentice pastime.

"I don't think anyone on Pern would refuse to come here, given the whisper of an invitation," he said.

"Does Master Wansor have his new far-viewer finished?" Jaxom asked.

"I certainly hope that he does . . . "

"Master Robinton . . . " Brekke stood in the doorway, a curious expression on her face.

"Brekke," the Harper held up a warning hand, "if you have come to tell me that I have to rest, or drink a potion of your making, I beg you, don't! I have far too much to do."

"All I have is a message which Kimi has just brought from Sebell," she said, handing him the small tube.

"Oh!"

"As to your resting, I've only to watch Zair to know when that's necessary!" Her glance, as she turned to leave the study, fell on Jaxom and Piemur. There was no doubt in Jaxom's mind that he and Piemur were under tacit orders not to overstrain the Harper's strength.

Master Robinton raised his eyebrows in surprise as he read the message. "Oh, dear. Toric was invaded by a shipload of holders' sons last evening. Sebell feels he should wait till they've settled into temporary quarters." He chuckled and, when he saw the expressions of Jaxom and Piemur, then added, "I infer that all did not progress as smoothly as the holder boys could wish!"

Piemur snorted, with the contempt born of his Turns' exploring and his knowledge of Toric and his Hold's accommodations.

"Once you can go *between*, Jaxom,"'Robinton continued, "our investigation can proceed more rapidly. I've in mind to set you and the girls out as teams."

"Harper and Holder?" Jaxom asked, seizing the opportunity he'd been waiting for.

"Harper and Holder? Oh, yes, of course. Piemur, you and Menolly have worked well together, I know. So Sharra can go with Jaxom. Now . . . " Oblivious to the sharp look Piemur gave Jaxom, the man went on. "One sees things from the air in a perspective not always possible at ground level. The reverse, of course, applies. So any exploration should involve both methods. Jaxom, Piemur knows what I'm looking for . . . "

"Sir?"

"Traces of the original habitation of this continent. I can't for the life of me imagine why our long-dead ancestors left this fruitful and beautiful continent for the colder, duller North, but I assume that they had good reasons. The oldest of our Records states: *When man came to Pern, he established a good Hold in the South.* We used to think," the Harper smiled apologetically for that error, "that Fort Hold was meant, since it is south in the Northern Continent. But that particular document goes on to state ambiguously: *but found it necessary to move north to shield.* That never made any sense, but so many of the old Records have deteriorated past deciphering, much less coherence.

"Well, then Toric discovered an iron mine, worked in the open fashion. And N'ton and I sighted unnatural formations set in a mountainside which, when we had finally reached the spot on foot, were clearly mine shafts.

"If the ancients had been long enough in the Southern Continent to discover ore and mine it, there must be other traces of their habitation somewhere here in the South."

"In hot weather and rainy forest, nothing survives very long," Jaxom said. "D'ram built a shelter here a scant twenty-five Turns back and not much remains of it. And what F'lessan and I stumbled on in Benden Weyr had been sealed up, protected from weather."

"Nothing," Piemur said emphatically, "could dent, scratch or mar the pit supports we found in that mine. And not even the best stoneman can carve through solid rock like cheese. Yet the ancients did."

"We have found some traces. There must be more."

Jaxom had never heard the Harper so adamant, but he couldn't suppress a sigh as he glanced at the size of the map before him.

"I know, Jaxom, the scope is daunting, but what a triumph when we find the place. Or places!" Master Robinton's eyes shone with anticipation. "Now," he went on briskly, "once Jaxom is pronounced fit enough to fly *between*, we will progress southward, using that symmetrical mountain as our guide. Any objections?" The man barely waited for an answer. "Piemur will start out on the ground with Stupid. Menolly can accompany him, if she wishes, or can wait for Jaxom to take her and Sharra on Ruth to the secondary camp. While the girls survey the immediate vicinity, which I understand has not been done, you, Jaxom, can fly ahead with Ruth to set up another camp to which you can fly *between* the next day. And so on.

"I think you must have been drilled at Fort Weyr," the Harper said, looking at Jaxom, "to be able to observe and distinguish ground formations from the air? However, I want to impress on you both that though this is a joint effort, Piemur is far more experienced, Jaxom, and you will please bear this in mind when problems occur. And send me your reports for this . . . " he tapped the chart, "every evening! Off with you both, now, and organize your equipment and supplies. And your partners!"

Though explaining the situation to Menolly and Sharra and organizing their supplies and equipment took very little time, the explorers did not leave Cove Hold that day.

Master Oldive arrived on Lioth with N'ton and was lavishly welcomed by the Harper, more sedately by Brekke and Sharra, and with some reservations by Jaxom. Robinton immediately insisted on showing the Healer the beautiful new hold before, as Robinton expressed it, Oldive had to see his old carcass.

"He's not fooling Master Oldive," Sharra said, her rich voice for Jaxom's ear alone as they watched the Harper striding vigorously about the holding, Master Oldive murmuring appropriate comments. "Not one fingertip is he fooling the Healer."

"That's a relief," Jaxom said. "Otherwise the Harper'll be coming with us."

"Not *between*, he won't."

"No, he'd ride Stupid."

Sharra laughed, but her amusement ended as they both watched the Healer firmly steer the Harper into his sleeping quarters and quietly close the door.

"No," Sharra said, shaking her head slowly, "Master Robinton wasn't fooling Master Oldive!"

Jaxom was very glad he didn't have to try to fool the Master Healer when it came his turn to be examined. The ordeal for him was brief— a few questions, Master Oldive's inspection of his eyes, tapping on his chest, listening to his heart and the pleased smile on the Healer's mobile face gave Jaxom the favorable verdict.

"Master Robinton will be all right, too, won't he, Master Oldive?" Jaxom couldn't resist asking.

When the Harper had emerged from his room, he had been too quiet, rather thoughtful, and the bounce had gone out of his step. Menolly had poured him a cup of wine which he had accepted with a wistful smile and a deep sigh.

"Of course, Master Robinton will be all right," Master Oldive said. "He's much improved. But," the Healer held up one long forefinger, "he must learn to pace himself, conserve his energy and ration his strength or he will bring on another attack. You young people can assist, with your strong legs and stouter hearts, without seeming to curtail his activities."

"Indeed we will. In fact, we do!"

"Good. Continue and he will soon be completely recovered. *If* he keeps in mind the lesson he learned from this seizure." Master Oldive glanced through the open window, mopping his forehead a little. "This beautiful place was a grand idea." He favored Jaxom with a sly smile. "The heat makes the Harper drowsy midday and forces him to rest. The prospects on all sides delight the eyes, and the scent of the air pleases the nose. How I envy you this spot, Lord Jaxom."

The beauties of Cove Hold had evidently worked their charm on the Masterharper as well, for he had recovered his good spirits even before the arrival of Master Fandarel and Master Wansor from Telgar. Robinton's delight was doubled when Fandarel and Wansor proudly exhibited the new distance-viewer that had occupied the Starsmith's time for the past half-Turn. The instrument, a tube as long as Fandarel's arm, and thick enough so that he needed two hands to surround it, was carefully encased in leather, with a curious eye-piece set, not on its end where Jaxom thought it ought to be, but on its side.

Master Robinton commented on that variation as well, and Wansor muttered something about reflective and refracting, ocular and objective and that this was the arrangement he thought best for the purposes of viewing distant objects. Whereas the instrument found in Benden Weyr made small things larger, the principles employed here were somewhat similar.

"That is neither here nor there but we are very pleased to use the new far-viewer in Cove Hold," Wansor went on, mopping his brow for he'd been so busy explaining his new device that he'd not bothered to remove his wherhide flying clothes.

Master Robinton winked at Menolly and Sharra and the two girls divested the lecturing Starsmith of his outer garments while he explained, almost oblivious to their assistance, that this was his first visit to the Southern Continent and yes, he had of course heard of the aberrant behavior of the three stars known as the Dawn Sisters. Until recently he had put the anomaly down to the inexperience of the observers. But, with Master Robinton himself noting their peculiarities, Wansor felt justified in bringing his precious instrument to the South to investigate the matter himself. Stars did not remain in fixed positions in the sky. All his equations, not to mention such experienced observers such as N'ton and Lord Larad, had verified this characteristic. Furthermore the Records handed down from the ancients, though they were in a shocking state, mentioned that stars undeniably followed a pattern of movement. Stars obeyed laws. Therefore when three stars had been observed to be in defiance of these natural laws, there had to be some explanation. He was hoping to find it this evening.

Not without a good deal of discussion, the site for this viewing was placed on the slight elevation of the stony eastern tip of Cove Hold, beyond the spot where the roasting and baking pits had been dug. Master Fandarel drafted Piemur and Jaxom to help him erect a frame on which he placed a swivel to mount the new viewer. Wansor, naturally, supervised this project until he was so in the Smith's way that the good man sat his Craftmaster on the edge of the promontory, near the trees, where he had a full view of all the activities but was no longer in his way. By the time the frame had been completed, Master

Wansor was fast asleep, his head cushioned on his hands, snoring in a soft rhythm.

Finger against his lips to indicate the little man was not to be disturbed, Fandarel led Jaxom and Piemur back to the main beach. They all took a refreshing swim before joining the others in the afternoon rest. Rather than miss a single moment of the dusky display of the Sisters, everyone ate on the promontory. Master Idarolan brought out his ship's viewer, and the Smith quickly constructed a second frame from the materials left over from making Wansor's.

Sunset, which had previously come upon them all too quickly, seemed delayed and delayed. Jaxom thought that if Wansor adjusted either the viewer or his bench, or his position on the bench, one more time, he would probably display some aberrant behavior of his own. Even the dragons who'd been playing in the water as if the sport had just been invented, were sprawled quietly on the beach, the fire-lizards sleeping about Ruth or perched on their friends' shoulders.

The sun finally went down, spreading its brilliant aftercolors across the western horizon. As the eastern sky darkened, Wansor put his eye to his instrument, let out a startled cry and nearly fell backward off his bench.

"It can't be. There is no possible logical explanation for such an arrangement." He righted himself and looked once again through the viewer, making delicate adjustments to the focus.

Master Idarolan had his eye pressed to his own viewer. "I see only the Dawn Sisters in their usual alignment. Just as they have always been."

"But they can't be. They are close together. Stars do not congregate so closely. They are always far distant."

"Here, let me have a look, man." The Smith was almost dancing in eagerness to have a glimpse through the instrument. Wansor reluctantly gave way to him, repeating the impossibility of what he had just seen.

"N'ton, your eyes are younger!" The Seaman passed his viewer to the bronze rider, who quickly accepted it.

"I see three round objects!" Fandarel announced in a booming voice. "Round metallic objects. Manmade objects. Those are not stars, Wansor," he said, looking at the distressed Starsmith, "those are things!"

Robinton, almost shoving the Smith's bulk to one side, bent his eye to the viewer, gasping.

"They are round. They do shine. As metal does. Not as stars do."

"One thing sure," Piemur said irreverently in the awed silence, "you have now found traces of our ancestors in the South, Master Robinton."

"Your observation is eminently correct," the Harper said in such

a curiously muffled tone Jaxom wasn't certain if the man was suppressing laughter or anger, "but not at all what I had in mind and you
know it!"

Everyone was given a chance to peer through Wansor's device,
since Master Idarolan's was not powerful enough. Everyone concurred
with Fandarel's verdict: the so-called Dawn Sisters were not stars.
Equally indisputable was that they were round, metallic objects that
apparently hung in a stationary position in the sky. Even the moons
had been observed to turn a different side to Pern in the course of their
regular cycles.

F'lar and Lessa as well as F'nor were asked to come with all urgency before the nightly appearance of the Dawn Sisters was over.
Lessa's irritation at such a summons evaporated when she saw the
phenomenon. F'lar and F'nor monopolized the instrument for the short
space of time that the peculiar objects remained visible in the slowly
darkening sky.

When Wansor was seen trying to work equations in the sand,
Jaxom and Piemur hurriedly brought out a table and some drawing
tools. The Starsmith wrote furiously for some minutes and then studied
the result he'd achieved as if this presented a more inscrutable puzzle.
Bewildered, he asked Fandarel and N'ton to check his figures for error.

"If there's no error, what is your conclusion, Master Wansor?"
F'lar asked him.

"Those . . . those things *are* stationary. They stay in the same
position over Pern all the time. As if they were following the planet."

"That would prove, would it not," Robinton said, unperturbed,
"that they are manmade."

"My conclusion precisely," but Wansor did not appear to be reassured. "They were made to stay where they are all the time."

"And we can't get from here to there," F'nor said in a regretful
murmur.

"Don't you dare, F'nor," Brekke said with such fervor that F'lar
and the Harper chuckled.

"They were made to stay there," Piemur began, "but they
couldn't have been made here, could they, Master Fandarel?"

"I doubt it. The Records give us hints of many marvelous things
made by men but no mention was ever made of stationary stars."

"But the Records say that men came to Pern . . . " Piemur looked
at the Harper for confirmation. "Perhaps they used those things to
travel from some other place, some other world, to get here. To Pern!"

"With all the worlds in the heavens to choose from," Brekke
began, breaking the thoughtful silence that followed Piemur's conclusion, "had they no better place to come to than Pern?"

"If you'd seen as much of it as I have lately," Piemur said, his spirit undaunted for any appreciable length of time, "you'd know that Pern's not all that bad a world . . . if you ignore the danger of Thread!"

"Some of us never can," F'lar replied in a wry tone.

Menolly gave Piemur a sharp jab in the ribs, but F'lar only laughed when Piemur suddenly realized the tactlessness of his remark.

"This is a most amazing development," Robinton said, his eyes sweeping the night sky as if more mysteries were to be revealed. "To see the very vehicles that brought our ancestors to this world."

"A good topic for some quiet reflections, eh, Master Robinton?" Oldive asked, with a sly grin on his face an an emphasis on the *quiet*.

The Harper made an impatient dismissal of that suggestion.

"Well, sir, you could hardly go there," the Healer said.

"I cannot," Master Robinton agreed. Then startling everyone, he suddenly thrust his right arm in the direction of the Three Sisters. "Zair, the round objects in the sky? Can you go there?"

Jaxom held his breath, felt the rigidity of Menolly's body beside him and knew she wasn't breathing either. He heard Brekke's sharp, quickly muffled cry. Everyone watched Zair.

The little bronze stretched his head toward Robinton's lips and made a soft quizzical noise in his throat.

"Zair? The Dawn Sisters?" Robinton repeated his words. "Would you go there?"

Now Zair cocked his head at his friend, clearly not understanding what was asked of him.

"Zair? The Red Star?"

The effect of that question was instantaneous. Zair vanished with a squawk of angry fear, and the fire-lizards nestling by Ruth woke and followed his lead.

"That does seem to answer both questions," F'lar said.

"What does Ruth say?" Menolly whispered in Jaxom's ear.

"About the Dawn Sisters? Or Zair?"

"Either."

"He's been asleep," Jaxom replied after consulting his dragon.

"He would be!"

"So? What did Beauty image before she winked out?"

"Nothing!"

Despite an evening of earnest debate and discussion, the humans solved nothing either. Robinton and Wansor would probably have kept the conversation up all night if Master Oldive hadn't slipped something into Robinton's wine. No one had actually seen him, but one moment Master Robinton was arguing forcefully with Wansor, the next he had wilted at the table. No sooner was his head down that he began to snore.

"He cannot neglect his health for talking's sake," Master Oldive remarked, signaling to the dragonriders to help him carry the Harper to his bed.

That effectively ended the evening. The dragonriders returned to their Weyrs, Oldive and Fandarel to their respective Halls. Wansor remained. A full wing of dragons would not have dragged him from Cove Hold.

It had been tactfully decided not to broadcast the true nature of the Dawn Sisters, at least until such time as Wansor and other interested starcrafters had had a chance to study the phenomenon and reach some conclusion that would not alarm people. There'd been enough shocks of late, F'lar commented. Some might construe those harmless objects to be a danger, much as the Red Star was.

"Danger?" Fandarel had exclaimed. "Were there any danger from those things, we should have known it many Turns past."

To that, F'lar agreed readily enough but, with everyone conditioned to believe that disaster fell from skyborne things, it was better to be discreet.

F'lar did agree to send anyone who could be spared from Benden to help search. It was, the Weyrleader felt, more important than ever to discover just what this land contained.

As Jaxom pushed his legs into his sleeping blanket, he tried not to be annoyed with the thought of another invasion in Cove Hold, just when he thought he and Sharra would be left alone for a while.

Had she been avoiding him? Or was it simply that circumstances had intervened? Such as Piemur's premature arrival in Cove Hold? The worry over Master Robinton, the need to explore which left them too tired to do more than crawl into their furs, the arrival of half of Pern to complete the Hold for the Harper, then his arrival, and now this! No, Sharra had not been avoiding him. She seemed . . . *there*. Her beautiful rich laugh, a tone below Menolly's, her face often hidden by the strands of dark hair which kept escaping thong and clip . . .

He wished, intensely, that Cove Hold would not be overrun again—a wish that did him little good since he had no control over what was going to happen here. He was Lord of Ruatha, not of the Cove. If the place belonged to anyone, it was Master Robinton's and Menolly's by virtue of their being storm-swept into it.

Jaxom sighed, his conscience nagging at him. Master Oldive had rated him fully recovered from the effects of fire-head. So he could go *between*. He and Ruth could return to Ruatha Hold. He ought to return to Ruatha Hold. But he didn't want to—and not just because of Sharra.

It wasn't as if he were needed in Ruatha. Lytol would manage the Hold as he'd always done. Ruth was not required to fight Thread either at Ruatha or at Fort Weyr. Benden had been lenient but F'lar had made it plain that the white dragon and the young Lord of Ruatha were not to be at risk.

There had been no prohibition, had there, Jaxom suddenly realized, to his exploring. In fact no one had suggested that he ought to return to Ruatha now.

Jaxom took some comfort in that thought, if he took none at all in the knowledge that tomorrow F'lar would be sending in riders—riders whose dragons could fly considerably faster and farther than his Ruth, riders who'd be able to reach the mountain before him. Riders who might just discover those traces which Robinton hoped existed somewhere in the interior of the Southern Continent. Riders who might also see in Sharra the beauty and gentle warmth of spirit that attracted Jaxom.

He tried, turning on the rushes yet again, to find a comfortable position, to find sleep. Maybe Robinton's plan for himself, Sharra, Menolly and Piemur would not undergo revision. As Piemur constantly reminded them all, dragons were great for flying over, but you still had to traverse the ground on foot to really know it. F'lar and Robinton might well want the dragonriders to spread out, cover as much territory as possible, and let the original explorers continue on to the mountain.

Jaxom then admitted to himself that he wanted to be first to the mountain! That serenely symmetrical cone had drawn him, sick and fevered, back to the Cove, had dominated his waking hours and intruded with nightmarish drama into his dreams. He wanted to be first to reach it, irrational as the notion might be.

Somewhere in the middle of these reflections, he did fall asleep. Again those overlapping scenes figured in his dreams: again the mountain erupted, one whole side shattering and spewing pulsingly red-orange flaming rocks and hot flows of molten lava down its side. Again Jaxom was both frightened refugee and dispassionate observer. Then the red wall began bearing down on him, so close to his heels that he could feel its hot breath on his feet . . .

He woke! The rising sun was slanting through the trees to caress his right foot which protruded from a rent in the light blanket. Rising sun!

Jaxom felt for Ruth. His dragon was still asleep in the clearing for the old shelter where a sandy wallow had been made to accommodate him.

Jaxom glanced across to Piemur, who slept in a neat ball, both hands resting under his right cheek. Slipping out of his bed, Jaxom noiselessly opened the door and, carrying his sandals, tiptoed out through the kitchen. Ruth stirred briefly, dislodging a fire-lizard or two from his back, as Jaxom passed him. Jaxom paused, struck by some puzzle. He stared at Ruth, then at the fire-lizards. None of those nestled against his friend were banded. He must ask Ruth when he woke if the Southern fire-lizards always slept with him. If they did, those dreams could be fire-lizard dreams—old memories triggered by the presence of men! That mountain! No, from this side a perfect cone appeared to the naked eye, unblemished by eruptive damage!

As soon as he reached the beach, Jaxom glanced up to see if he could sight the Dawn Sisters. But it was, unfortunately, already too late to catch their morning appearance.

The two viewers, Wansor's carefully covered with wherhide against morning dew and Idarolan's in its leather case, were still mounted on their frames. Grinning at the futility of his action, Jaxom nonetheless couldn't resist uncovering Wansor's viewer and peering skyward. He recovered the instrument carefully and stood looking southeast, toward the mountain.

In his dream the cone had blown out. And there were two sides to that mountain. Suddenly decisive, he removed the Seaman's viewer from its case. Though he might get more definition from Wansor's, he wouldn't presume to alter that careful focus. Besides, Idarolan's was strong enough for what he needed. Not that it could show the damage that Jaxom had half-hoped to see. Thoughtfully he lowered the instrument. He could go *between* now. Further, he was under Master Robinton's orders to explore the Southlands. More important, he wanted to be first to that mountain!

He laughed. This venture was scarcely as dangerous as the return of the egg. He and Ruth could go *between* and return before anyone in Cove Hold was aware of their intention. He took the viewer from its mounting. He'd need this with him. Once he and Ruth were airborne, he'd have to get a good long look at the mountain to find a point to which Ruth could move safely *between*.

He pivoted on his heel and lurched backward in surprise. Piemur, Sharra and Menolly were standing in a row, watching him.

"Do tell, Lord Jaxom, what you saw in the Seaman's viewer? A mountain, perhaps?" Piemur asked, showing all his teeth in that smug grin.

On Menolly's shoulder, Beauty chirped.

"Did he see enough?" Menolly asked Piemur, ignoring Jaxom.

"I'd say he had!"

"He wouldn't have planned to go without us, would he?" Sharra asked.

They regarded him with mocking expressions.

"Ruth can't carry four."

None of you are fat. I could manage, Ruth said.

Sharra laughed, covered her mouth to silence the sound and pointed an accusing finger at him.

"I'll bet anything Ruth just said he could!" she told the other two.

"I'll bet you're right." Menolly didn't take her eyes from Jaxom's face. "I think it really is best if you have some help on this venture." She drawled the last two words significantly.

"This venture?" Piemur echoed the words, alert as ever to nuances of speech.

Jaxom clenched his teeth, glaring at her. "You're sure you could carry four?" he asked Ruth.

The dragon emerged on the beach, his eyes glowing with excitement.

I have had to fly straight for many days now. That has made me very strong. None of you are heavy. The distance is not great. We are going to see the mountain?

"Ruth is obviously willing," Menolly said, "but if we don't make a move soon . . . " She gestured toward Cove Hold. "C'mon, Sharra, we'll get the flying gear."

"I'll have to rig flying straps for four."

"Then do it." Menolly and Sharra raced off down the sand.

Hunting ropes were handiest and Jaxom and Piemur had them in position when the girls returned with jackets and helmets. Jaxom hefted the Seaman's viewer and mentally promised that they'd be back so quickly that the man wouldn't have had time to notice its disappearance.

Ruth did have to strain to get himself off the beach, but once airborne, he assured Jaxom that he was flying easily. He veered southeast as Jaxom focused on the distant peak. Even at this altitude, he could discern no damage in the cone. He lowered the viewer fractionally until, clear and detailed, there was a distinctive ridge in the foreground of the mountain.

Jaxom asked Ruth if he visualized the objective. Ruth assured him he could. And took them *between* before Jaxom could have second thoughts on this venture. Abruptly, they were above the ridge, gasping. Breathless because of the incredible shock of cold *between* after months of baking in tropical suns, and because of the spectacular panorama before them.

As Piemur had once said, distance was deceptive. The mountain rose on the shoulders of a high plateau already thousands of dragonlengths above the sea. Far below them a broad sparkling inlet cut high cliffs: grassy on the mountain's side, densely forested on theirs. To the south, a towering range of mountains, snow-capped and misty in the distance, lay as a barrier east and west.

The mountain, still a good distance from them, dominated the scene.

"Look." Sharra suddenly pointed to their left, seaward. "More volcanoes. Some are smoking!"

Studding the open sea, a long chain of peak tops bent northeast, some with substantial islands at their feet, others mere cones poking from the water.

"A loan of the viewer, Jaxom?" Piemur took the instrument and peered. "Yes," he replied casually after a long look, "a couple of them are active. Far out though. No danger." Then he swung the viewer toward the barrier range, slowly shaking his head after a moment. "It could be the same barrier range I saw in the west." He sounded dubious. "Take months to get there! And cold!" He turned the viewer in a short arc. "Useful thing, this. That water goes deep inland. Idarolan could likely sail up if he has a mind to." He handed the viewer back to Jaxom and stared ahead at the mountain.

"That is the most beautiful sight," Sharra said on a long sigh.

"Must be the other side that blew out," Jaxom said, more to himself than to the others.

"The other side?" Sharra and Menolly spoke at once. And Jaxom could feel Piemur stiffening behind him.

"Did you dream, too, last night?" Jaxom asked.

"What on earth did you think had awakened us in time to hear you creeping out?" Menolly asked, a bit sharply.

"Well, let's go see the other," Piemur said as if he were merely suggesting a swim.

"Why not?" Sharra replied with the same carelessness.

I would like to see the place of my dreaming, Ruth said and, without any warning, he dropped from the ridge height.

Jaxom heard Menolly and Sharra exclaim in surprise and he was glad that he'd rigged flying straps for them. Ruth expressed apologies which Jaxom had no time to relay as the white dragon swooped into a current of warm air that bore them up and over the broad inlet. When his flying had leveled, Jaxom used the viewer and found a distinctive rock formation on the northern shoulder. He gave Ruth the visualization.

They were *between*: they were hovering above the rock formation and the mountain seemed to bend frighteningly toward them for the space of several breaths. Ruth recovered his flying speed and veered further north, beating strongly in a wide arc toward the eastern face of the mountain.

Momentarily they were all blinded by the full brilliance of the rising sun which had been occluded by the mountain's bulk. Ruth shifted to a southerly heading. Before them lay the most incredible sweep of land that Jaxom had ever seen—far broader, and deeper than Telgar's flatlands, or the desert of Igen. His eyes were drawn quickly from that spectacular vista to the mountain.

The view was suddenly all too familiar to Jaxom, the product of so many uneasy nights and unfocused dreams. The eastern lip of the mountain was gone! The gaping mouth seemed to snarl, its left-hand corner pulled down. Jaxom's eyes followed that line and he saw, crouching on the southeastern flank, three more volcano mouths, like malevolent offspring of the larger. The lava flowed down, south, toward the rolling plains.

Ruth continued to glide instinctively away from the mountain, toward the kinder valley.

As much as Jaxom had admired and feasted his eyes on the northern aspect of that volcano, now he turned from the malevolent teeth of the blown side, the side of his nightmares.

Jaxom all but anticipated Ruth's words: *This place I know. They say this is where their men were!*

Out of the sun, fairs of fire-lizards dove and veered out of Ruth's flightline. Beauty, Meer, Talla and Farli, who had ridden their friends' shoulders to this incredible place, took off to join the newcomers.

"Look, Jaxom! Look down!" Piemur yelled in his ear while tugging at his shoulder and pointing frantically to a spot below Ruth's left foreleg. The early sun threw the outlines in bold relief. Regular outlines, mounds, and then straight lines dissecting, forming curious squares where no such regular formations should be.

"That's what Master Robinton is looking for!" He grinned back over his shoulder at Piemur, who had turned to attract the girls' attention to the ground.

Then Jaxom gasped, pressuring Ruth with his legs to turn northeast. He felt Piemur clutch at his shoulders as the Harper, too, saw what he'd seen. Where the haze from the distant smoking volcanoes in the sea was joined by a gray haze from the skies—Thread!

"Thread!"

Thread! Before Jaxom could direct him, Ruth had taken them smartly *between*. In the next instant they were hovering above the Cove, its beaches accommodating the bulks of five dragons. Master Idarolan's fishermen were scurrying from shore to ship, placing slates on a frame rigged to protect the wooden decks from Threadfall!

Canth asks where have we been? I must chew firestone immediately. The fire-lizards are to help protect the ship. Everyone is annoyed with us. Why?

Jaxom asked Ruth to land them near the firestone pile on the beach and to start chewing.

"I've got to find Stupid!" Piemur dropped to the sand and was off in a run toward the forest.

"Give me Master Idarolan's viewer," Menolly said to Jaxom. "I got a look at his face and though I don't say it's his viewer he's angry about . . ."

"I'll brave the storm in Cove Hold," Sharra told Jaxom, grinning at him and gripping his arm in reassurance. "Don't look so depressed! I know I wouldn't have missed this morning's jaunt. Not even if I get scolded by Lessa."

We have been exploring south as we were told to do by the Harper! Ruth announced suddenly, lifting his head and staring in the direction of the other dragons. *We are back here in time to fight Thread. We have done nothing wrong.*

Jaxom flinched, surprised at the determination in Ruth's tone, particularly since Jaxom was certain the white dragon was answering Canth since the brown dragon was looking in their direction and his eyes were whirling. Jaxom saw Lioth next to Canth, Monarth and two other Benden browns whom he did not know on sight.

Yes, I will fly across your pattern, Ruth said, again responding to words Jaxom didn't hear. *As I have done before. I have enough stone to flame. Thread is nearly on the Cove.*

He craned his neck toward Jaxom, and his rider sprang to his neck, truly relieved that the imminence of Thread delayed a confrontation with either F'nor or N'ton. Not, Jaxom realized, that he was in the wrong with either rider.

We have done what the Harper told us to do, Ruth said as he launched himself into the sky. *No one told us not to fly to the mountain today. I am glad we did. I will not be bothered with dreams now that I have seen the place.* The Ruth added with some surprise: *Brekke does not think you are strong enough to fly Thread the first day you are allowed between. You are to tell me if you tire!*

Nothing would have induced Jaxom to admit fatigue after that, had they flown the entire four-hour Fall. As it was, they met Thread three coves east. Met and destroyed it, Ruth and Jaxom weaving over, under, through the other five who set the triangle pattern east and west. Jaxom hoped that Piemur had got Stupid to safety. After a moment, Ruth replied that Farli said the beast was on the porch of Cove Hold. She was ready to flame any Thread that attacked the Hold.

Jaxom noticed, as they wheeled above the Cove itself, that the tall masts of the *Dawn Sister* seemed to have sprouted fire and then realized that it must be the other fire-lizards protecting the ship. There seemed to be rather a lot of them flaming! Had the Southerners joined forces with the banded ones? Had they decided for some reason to help men?.

He hadn't time for more speculation in the dive, swoop and flame of Threadfall. He was very tired by the time the silver rain had dwindled to nothing and Canth bugled return. Ruth swept east and Jaxom saw F'nor give the signal: *Well done.* Then they glided back to the Cove.

Jaxom landed Ruth on the narrower portion of the western beach to allow the bigger dragons more space. He slid from Ruth's back, thumping the sweat-dampened neck, sneezing when the reek of firestone blew in his face. Ruth gave a little cough.

I am getting better and better at chewing. No flame left. He raised his head then, looking toward Canth, who had landed near them. *Why is*

F'nor annoyed? We have flown well. No Thread escaped us. Ruth craned his neck back at his rider, his eyes beginning to whirl faster, flicks of yellow appearing. *I do not understand.* He snorted once, the firestone fumes making Jaxom cough.

"Jaxom! I want a word with you!"

F'nor strode across the sand to him, unbelting his jacket and stripping off his helmet in sharp gray angry gestures.

"Yes?"

"Where were the lot of you this morning? Why did you leave with no word to anyone? What have you to say for yourself arriving so close to Thread? Did you forget Thread was due today?"

Jaxom regarded F'nor. The brown rider's face was suffused with anger and fatigue. The same cold rage that had erupted within Jaxom that day so long ago in his own Hold began to possess him. He straightened his shoulders and raised his head higher. His eyes were level with F'nor's, a fact he had not previously noted. He could not, he would not, permit himself to lose control of his temper as he had that morning in Ruatha.

"We were ready for Thread when it fell, brown rider," he responded calmly. "My duty as the rider of a dragon was to protect Cove Hold. I did. My pleasure and privilege was to fly with Benden." He gave a slight bow and had the satisfaction of seeing the anger in F'nor's face give way to surprise. "I'm sure the others have by now reported to Master Robinton what we discovered this morning. Into the water with you, Ruth. I'll be glad to answer all your questions, F'nor, when I've cleaned Ruth up." He gave F'nor, who was staring at him in honest amazement, a second bow and then stripped off hot and sweaty flying gear, leaving on only the shortened trousers that were more suitable to the heat.

F'nor was still staring at him when he ran and dove neatly into the water, coming up beside his wallowing white friend.

Ruth twisted, blowing water in a fountain above his head, his half-lidded eyes gleaming greenly just under the surface.

Canth says that F'nor is confused. What did you say that confuses a brown rider?

"What he didn't expect to hear from a white rider. I can't wash you when you're rolling over all the time."

You are angry. You will tear my hide scrubbing so hard.

"I am angry. Not at you."

Should we go to our lake? Ruth's question was tentative and he turned his head toward his rider in an anxious manner.

"What do we need with a freezing lake when we've an entire warm ocean? I'm just annoyed with F'nor. It isn't as if I were still sick, or a child that needed a guardian. I've fought Thread with you, and without you. If I'm old enough to do that, I don't need to account for any of my movements to any one for any reason."

I forgot that Thread would fall today!

Jaxom couldn't help but laugh at Ruth's humble admission.

"So did I. But don't you ever let on to anyone."

Fire-lizards descended now to assist, needing a bit of scrub themselves to judge by the reek their wet hides exuded. They scolded Ruth much more unkindly than Jaxom did if he wallowed too deeply in the waves when they wanted to rinse him. Among the fair were Meer, Talla and Farli. Jaxom bent to his task. He was tired but he decided that as long as he kept himself going, he'd be able to finish bathing Ruth. Then he'd have all afternoon to rest.

He didn't. He also didn't have to bathe Ruth all by himself because Sharra joined him.

"Would you like me to take the other side again?" she asked as she waded up to him.

"I'd appreciate it no end," he said with a grin and sigh.

She tossed him a handled brush. "Brekke brought these with her. Thought they'd help clean dragons, and things. Good stiff bristles. You'll like that, won't you, Ruth?"

She scooped handsful of sand from the cove floor, dribbling the wet stuff on Ruth's neck and then applying the brush with vigor. Ruth whistled through the water with pleasure.

"What happened to you while I was fighting Thread?" he asked her, pausing before attacking Ruth's rump.

"Menolly's still answering questions." Sharra regarded him over Ruth's recumbent body, her eyes dancing, her smile full of mischief. "She talked so fast he couldn't interrupt, and she was still talking when I left. I didn't realize anyong could outtalk the Master Harper. Anyway, he stopped fuming very early on. Did you get scorched by F'nor?"

"We exchanged . . . opinions."

"I'll just bet you did the way Brekke was carrying on. I told her that you'd got pretty fit while she was away. She acted as if you'd risen from your deathbed to ride Fall!" Sharra made a scornful sound.

Jaxom leaned over Ruth's back, grinning at her, thinking how pretty she was with the mischief in her eyes, and beads of water on her face where Ruth had splashed her. She glanced up at him, raising one eye in query.

"Did we really see what I thought we saw this morning, Sharra?"

"We surely did!" She pointed her brush at him, her expression severe. "And you're very lucky that we were along to vouch because I don't think anyone would have believed just you." She paused, the twinkle back in her eyes. "I'm not entirely sure they believe us anyhow."

"Who doesn't believe us?"

"Master Robinton, Master Wansor and Brekke. Weren't you listening to me?"

"No," he said, grinning, "I was looking at you."

"Jaxom!"

He laughed as the blush deepened the tan on her face and neck.

I have a severe itch where you are leaning against me, Jaxom.

"There now, you see?" Sharra said, slapping his hand with the bristles. "You're neglecting Ruth in a shocking fashion."

"How'd you know Ruth was speaking to me?"

"Your face always gives you away."

"Say, where's the *Dawn Sister* going?" Jaxom asked, noticing the ship, her sails billowing out in the breeze, standing out to sea.

"Fishing, of course. Threadfall always brings out schools. And our escapade this morning is going to bring people down here in droves. We'll need the fish to feed 'em."

Jaxom groaned, closing his eyes and shaking his head in dismay.

"That . . . " Sharra paused for emphasis, "is our punishment for the unauthorized jaunt this morning."

They were both dumped into the water as Ruth unexpectedly lunged out.

"Ruth!"

My friends are coming! The white dragon bugled happily as Jaxom saw, bleary-eyed from the ducking, a half-wing of dragons appearing in the sky.

There is Ramoth and Mnementh, Tiroth, Gyamath, Branth, Orth . . .

"All the Weyrleaders, Sharra!"

She was spitting and choking over the water she'd swallowed.

"Great!" She didn't sound happy. "My brush!" She began searching about her.

And Path, Golanth, Drenth and he's here on our watchdragon!

"There's Lytol! Stand still, Ruth. We've still got your tail to clean."

I must give a proper greeting to my friends, Ruth replied, pulling his tail out of Jaxom's grasp to sit up on his haunches and warble to the second group of dragonriders appearing over the Cove.

"He may not be clean," Sharra said with some acerbity as she began to wring her long hair dry, "but I am."

I am clean enough. My friends will want to swim, too.

"Don't count on another swim, Ruth. It's going to be a busy day!"

"Jaxom, did you get a chance to eat anything yet?" Sharra asked. When he shook his head, she grabbed his hand. "C'mon, quickly, the back way, before someone catches us."

He paused long enough on the shore to collect his flying gear, then they both ran up the old path to the kitchen entrance of Cove Hold. Sharra breathed an exaggerated sigh of relief to discover the place empty. Ordering him to sit, she poured a cup of *klah*, and served him slices of fruit and warm cereal from the pot on the back of the warming hearth.

They both heard the calls and exclamations from the new arrivals, Robinton's deep baritone dominating as he called greetings from the porch.

Jaxom half-rose from his bench, gulping down another mouthful, but Sharra pushed him back.

"They'll find you soon enough. Eat!"

"Ruth is on the beach," Lytol's voice was audible suddenly, "but I don't see Jaxom anywhere . . . "

"I know he's about . . . " Robinton began.

A bronze arrow whizzed into the kitchen, chittered and zipped away.

"He's through that door, Lytol, in the kitchen," Robinton said with a laugh.

"I could almost agree with Lessa," Jaxom said in a mutter of disgust. He scraped a huge spoonful out of his bowl, cramming it into his mouth. He had to rise, catching the overflow at the corners of his mouth as Lytol came striding in.

"Sorry, sir," Jaxom mumbled through his food. "Had no breakfast!"

Lytol stood, his eyes so intent that Jaxom grinned in nervous embarrassment. He wondered if Lytol could already know of his excursion that morning.

"You look a great deal better than when I last saw you, lad. Good day to you, Sharra." His greeting was absent-minded courtesy as he crossed the remaining distance to clasp Jaxom's arm strongly in his. A smile pulled at his lips before he stepped back. "You're tanned, you look fit. Now what is this trouble you created today?"

"Create it? Me? No, sir." Jaxom couldn't help grinning now. Lytol was delighted, not annoyed. "That mountain's been there a long time. I didn't create it. But I did want to see it, close up, first!"

"Jaxom!" The Harper's bellow was impossible to ignore.

"Sir?"

"Come here, Jaxom!"

In the hours that followed, Jaxom was grateful that Sharra had thought to feed him breakfast. He didn't get much time for more food. The moment he entered the main Hall, questions were thrown at him by the Weyrleaders and Craftmasters assembled. Piemur had been very busy during Fall because Master Robinton had already completed a sketch of the southeastern face of the mountain to show the incredulous visitors, and a rough, small-scale map of this section of Southern. From the almost rhythmic way Menolly described their jaunt, Jaxom decided she had already repeated the account many times.

What Jaxom remembered most of that session was feeling sorry that the Master Harper was unable to see the mountain first hand. But, if Jaxom had waited until Master Oldive permitted the Harper to fly *between* . . .

"I know you've just flown Fall, Jaxom, but if you'd just give Mnementh the visualization . . . " F'lar began.

N'ton burst out laughing, pointing to Jaxom. "The look on your face, lad. F'lar, he's got to lead us! Give him that!"

So Jaxom got back into slightly damp flying gear and roused Ruth from his sandy baking. Ruth was pleased enough with the honor of leading the bronzes of Pern, but Jaxom could barely contain behind a composed expression the thrill he was experiencing. Jaxom and the white dragon, leading the most important people on Pern.

He could have asked Ruth to jump directly to the southeastern side of the Two-Faced Mountain, his private designation. Somehow he wanted everyone to experience the full impact of those two sides—the benign and beautiful.

From the expressions on the riders' faces as they settled briefly on the ridge, he could see that he had achieved the desired effect. He allowed them time to sight the Barrier Range, glistening in the sun, ragged white teeth on the horizon. He gestured seaward where neither morning mists nor Thread now obscured the tail of volcanoes snaking northeasterly out into the sea, smoke just curling from the curve of the world in that direction.

At his request, Ruth soared across the inlet as he had done before, climbing high before he gave the coordinates of the next jump *between*. They came out above the broad expanse of the southeastern side of Two-Face, as dramatic an approach as anyone could have wished.

Mnementh suddenly surged into the fore and, as Ruth relayed to Jaxom, said that they should land. Politely, Ruth and Jaxom circled as the great bronze settled near the intersection of some of the regular lines, as far as possible from the three secondary cones. One by one the great bronze dragons of Pern settled in the grassy sward, their riders and passengers striding through the tall waving grasses to join F'lar, who had hunkered down to dig with his belt knife into the edge of one of those curious lines.

"Covered with Turns of blow dirt and old grasses," he said, giving up his attempt.

"Volcanoes often blow out quantities of ash," T'bor of the High Reaches said. He would know since quite a few old volcanoes were in Tillek which was beholden to the High Reaches Weyr. "If all those mountains blew at once, there'd be half a length of ash before you'd reach anything."

For a split second, Jaxom thought they were being threatened with ash. Sunlight was blotted out and a chittering, fluttering mass swooped down, almost touching Mnementh's head before the hundred fire-lizards lifted up again.

Amid shouts of consternation and surprise, Jaxom heard Ruth's announcement.

They are happy. Men have returned to them!

"Ask them about the three mountains, Ruth? Do they remember the mountains blowing up?"

There was no doubt they did. Suddenly there wasn't an unbanded fire-lizard in the sky.

They remember the mountains, Ruth said. *They remember fire in the air and fire crawling on the ground. They are afraid of the mountains. Men were afraid of the mountains.*

Menolly came running up to Jaxom, her face contorted with concern. "Did Ruth ask those fire-lizards about the mountains? Beauty and the others just had a fit. About those blasted mountains."

F'lar came striding up to them. "Menolly? What was all that fuss with the fire-lizards? I didn't see any banded ones. Were they all Southern ones?"

"Of course men were here. They're not telling us anything we didn't know. But for them to say they remembered?" F'lar was scornful. "I could accept your finding D'ram in the Cove with their aid . . . but that was only a matter of twenty-five Turns in the past. But . . . ." For want of appropriate expression of his skepticism, F'lar merely gestured at the dead volcanoes and the long-covered traces of a settlement.

"Two points, F'lar," Menolly said, boldly contradicting the Benden Weyrleader, "no fire-lizard in this time knew the Red Star, but they were, nonetheless, all afraid of it. They also . . . " Menolly paused, and Jaxom was certain she had been about to bring up the fire-lizard dreams about Ramoth's egg. He hastily interrupted.

"Fire-lizards must be able to remember, F'lar. Ever since I've been in the Cove, I've been troubled with dreams. At first I thought it was leftovers from fire-head fever. The other night I found out that Sharra and Piemur have had similar nightmares . . . about the mountain. This side of it, not the one facing the Cove."

"Ruth always sleeps with fire-lizards at night, F'lar," Menolly said, pressing their case. "He could be relaying those dreams to Jaxom! And our fire-lizards to us!"

F'lar nodded, as if granting them this possibility.

"And last night your dreams were more vivid than ever?"

"Yes, sir!"

F'lar began to chuckle, looking from Menolly to Jaxom. "So this morning you decided to see if there was any substance to the dreams?"

"Yes, sir!"

"All right, Jaxom." F'lar thumped him good-naturedly on the back. "I suppose I can't blame you. I'd have done the same thing given the opportunity. Now, what do you . . . and those precious fire-lizards of yours . . . suggest we do now?"

"I am no fire-lizard, F'lar, but I would dig," the Mastersmith said, striding up to them. His face was aglow with perspiration, his hands grass and dirt-stained. "We must dig beneath the grass and soil. We must find out how they managed to make lines straight as rules that last Turn after Turn. Why did they build in mounds, if that's what those things are. Dig, that's what we must do." He pivoted slowly, staring about him at the desultory digging efforts of some of the dragonriders. "Fascinating. Utterly fascinating!" The Smith beamed. "With your permission, I will ask Masterminer Nicat for some of his craftmasters. We will need skilled diggers. Also I promised Robinton that I would return immediately and tell him what I have seen with my own eyes."

"I'd like to go back, too, F'lar," Menolly said. "Master Robinton is in a swivet. Zair's been here twice. He must be impatient."

"I'll take them back, F'lar," Jaxom said. Suddenly he was as possessed by an irrational desire to leave as he had been eager to come that morning.

F'lar would not permit Ruth to carry weight again, not after the morning's excursion and Threadfall. He sent Master Fandarel and Menolly back to Cove Hold with F'lessan and Golanth, with instructions to the young bronze rider to take the Mastersmith wherever he wished to go. If he was surprised at Jaxom's wish to return, he gave no sign.

He and Ruth were away before the Smith and Menolly had mounted Golanth. They returned to a Cove delightfully empty of people. The warm, sultry air, after the cooler, clear atmosphere of the Plateau, was like an enveloping blanket, enervating Jaxom. He took advantage of his unremarked return and let Ruth take them to his clearing. It was cooler there and, when Ruth had settled himself, Jaxom gratefully curled up in the dragon's forearms. He was asleep in two breaths.

A touch on his shoulder roused him. His flying jacket had fallen from his shoulder and he felt chilly.

"I said I'd wake him, Mirrim," he heard Sharra say, her tone one of annoyance.

"Does it matter? Here, Jaxom, I've brought you some *klah*! Master Robinton wants to talk to you. You've slept all afternoon. We couldn't figure out where you'd got to."

Jaxom muttered under his breath, wishing with all his heart that Mirrim would go away. He resented her implication that he hadn't any right to sleep in the afternoon.

"Come on, Jaxom. I know you're awake."

"You're wrong. I'm half asleep." Jaxom indulged in a massive yawn before he opened his eyes. "Go away, Mirrim. Tell Master Robinton I'll be in directly."

"He wants you now!"

"He'll get me a lot sooner if you go tell him I'm coming. Now, get out of here!"

Mirrim gave him one more long hard look, brushed past Sharra and stomped up the stairs to the kitchen.

"You are my true friend, Sharra," Jaxom said. "Mirrim irritates me so! Menolly told me that once Path had flown, she'd improve. I haven't noticed any sign."

Sharra was peering at Ruth, who was still fast asleep, not even an eyelid twitching.

"I know what you're going to ask . . . " Jaxom said with a laugh, holding up a hand to forestall her words. "No, nary a dream."

"Nary a fire-lizard either." She smiled at him, shaking her head and retying her hair thong. "You were smart to come here and rest. There's none up at the Hall. Fire-lizards popping in and out, from Cove to the plateau, nearly hysterical! No one can make any sense out of what ours say or the Southern ones tell them. And it's not as if some of the Southern ones hadn't known we were here."

"And Master Robinton thinks Ruth can sort it all out?"

"He just might." She regarded the sleeping white dragon thoughtfully. "Poor darling, he's exhausted with all he's done today." Her rich voice was a tender croon and Jaxom could have wished her words included him. She saw him looking at her and flushed a little. "I'm so glad we got there first!"

"So'm I!"

"Jaxom!"

At Mirrim's shout, she moved back hastily.

"Scorch her!"

He grabbed Sharra's hand and ran with her toward the Hold, nor did he relinquish her hand when they entered the main Hall.

"Was I asleep an afternoon or a whole day?" Jaxom asked her in an undertone as he saw maps, charts, sketches and diagrams pinned on the walls and propped up on tables.

The Harper, his back to them, was bending over the long dining table. Piemur was occupied in sketching something; Menolly was looking at whatever absorbed the Harper, and Mirrim stood at one side, bored and irritated. Fire-lizards peered down from the crossbeams. Every now and then, one would flick out of the room and another would swoop in the window to take its place. An aroma of roasting fish filled the air as a sea breeze began to clear away the day's heat.

"Brekke's going to be furious with us," Jaxom said to Sharra.

"With us? Why? We're keeping him completely occupied at a sedentary task."

"Stop mumbling, Sharra. Jaxom, come over here and add your mark to what the others have told me," Robinton said, skewing his body about to frown at them.

"Sir, Piemur, Menolly and Sharra have done a lot more exploring than I have."

"Yes, but they don't have Ruth and his way with fire-lizards. Can he help us sort out their conflicting and confusing images?"

"I'm certainly willing to help, Master Robinton," Jaxom said, "but I think you might be asking more of Ruth and those fire-lizards than they can do."

Master Robinton straightened up. "If you'd explain?"

"Granted that the fire-lizards seem to share violent mutual experiences like . . ." Jaxom pointed in the direction of the Red Star, "and Canth's fall, and now, of course, the mountain. But these are all momentous events . . . not everyday routine."

"You did locate D'ram here in the Cove," Robinton said.

"And lucky at that. If I'd asked about men first, we'd never have got an answer," Jaxom replied with a grin.

"There was scarcely more detail to go on in your first venture."

"Sir?" Jaxom stared in stunned amazement because the Harper's drawl had been so deceptively mild, with just a slight emphasis on "first," yet the implication had been unmistakable; somehow the Harper knew Jaxom had rescued the egg. Jaxom shot an accusing glance at Menolly, whose expression was slightly perplexed as if the Harper's subtle reference surprised her, too.

"Come to think of it, I had much the same information from Zair," Master Robinton continued smoothly, "but not the wit to interpret it as cleverly as you did. My compliments, however belated," he inclined his head and went on as swiftly as if this were just some passing matter, "on the way you handled the feat. Now, if you and Ruth can turn your fine perceptions to today's problem, we can save ourselves endless hours of vain effort. As before, Jaxom, time is against us. This Plateau," Robinton tapped the sketches before him, "cannot remain a secret. It is the heritage of everyone on Pern—"

"But it's in the east, Master Robinton, which is to be dragonrider land," Mirrim said, her tone almost belligerent.

"Of course it is, my dear child," the Harper said soothingly. "Now if Ruth could charm the fire-lizards enough to focus their memories . . ."

"I'll certainly try, Master Robinton," Jaxom said when the Harper regarded him expectantly, "but you know how they are about . . ." and he pointed skyward. "They're nearly as incoherent about the eruption."

"As Sharra put it, the dream eye is unfocused," Menolly said, grinning at her friend.

"My point exactly," the Harper said, bringing the flat of his hand down hard on the table. "If Jaxom, through Ruth, can sharpen the focus, maybe those of us with fire-lizards can get distinct and helpful images from their minds, instead of this confusion of perspective."

"Why?" Jaxom asked. "We know the mountain erupted. We know the settlement had to be abandoned, that the survivors came north . . . "

"There's a lot we don't know, and we might find some answers, perhaps even some equipment left behind, just as the enlarging viewer was left in those deserted rooms at Benden Weyr. Look how that instrument has improved our understanding of our world and the heavens above us. Maybe even some models of those fascinating machines the old Records mention." He pulled the sketches over the map. "There are a lot of mounds, great and small, long and short. Some would have been for sleeping, storage, general living: some quite likely workhalls . . . "

"How do we even know that the ancients did things the way we do?" Mirrim demanded, "storage, and workhalls and such."

"Because, my dear child, neither human nature nor human needs have changed since the earliest Records we have."

"That doesn't mean they left anything in the mounds when they left the Plateau," Mirrim said, frankly dubious.

"The dreams have been consistent in some details," Robinton said with more patience for Mirrim's obstructionism than Jaxom would have accorded him. "The fiery mountain, the molten rock and lava raining down. People running . . . " He paused, looking expectantly at the others.

"People in a panic!" Sharra said. "They wouldn't have had time to take anything with them. Or very little!"

"They could have come back after the worst of the eruption was over," Menolly said. "Remember that time in western Tillek—"

"That's precisely what I had in mind," the Harper said, nodding approval.

"But, Master," Menolly went on, confused, "the ash spewed out of that volcano for weeks. The valley was eventually level with ash," she made a flat gesture with her hand, "and you could see nothing of what had been there for the debris."

"The prevailing wind on that plateau is southeast, and strong," Piemur said, and his gesture was one of sweeping clear. "Didn't you notice how strong it is?"

"That's precisely why something was left for us to see from the air," the Harper said. "I know it's just an off-chance, Jaxom, but my feeling is that the eruption caught the ancients completely unaware.

Why, I can't comprehend. Surely people who could hold the Dawn Sisters in the sky in a stationary position for who knows how many Turns ought to be wise enough to identify an active volcano. My surmise is that the eruption was spontaneous, totally unexpected. The people were caught going about their daily tasks in cot, hold, crafthall. If you can get Ruth to focus those disparate views, perhaps we could identify which of the mounds were important from the numbers of people coming from it, or them.

"I am not able to get to the Plateau to do my own exploring, but nothing prevents my brain from suggesting possibilities of what I'd do if I were there."

"We'll be your hands and legs," Jaxom offered.

"They'll be your eyes," Menolly added, gesturing to the fire-lizards on the crossbeams.

"I thought you'd see it my way," the Harper said, beaming fondly on them all.

"When would you like us to try?" Jaxom asked.

"Would tomorrow be too soon?" the Harper asked plaintively.

"All right by me. Piemur, Menolly, Sharra, I'll need you and your fire-lizards!"

"I can arrange to come, too," Mirrim said.

Jaxom caught Sharra's closed expression and realized that Mirrim's presence would be as unwelcome to her as to himself.

"I don't think that would work, Mirrim. Path would scare the Southern fire-lizards away!"

"Oh, don't be ridiculous, Jaxom," Mirrim replied, brushing aside that argument.

"He's right, Mirrim. Look out in the Cove right now. Not a single fire-lizard that isn't banded," Menolly said. "They all disappear the minute they see any other dragon but Ruth."

"It's ridiculous. I have three of the best-trained fire-lizards in Pern . . ."

"I must agree with Jaxom," the Harper said, smiling with sincere apology to the Benden dragongirl. "And, though I quite agree that yours are undoubtedly the best-trained fire-lizards in Pern, we don't have time for the Southern ones to get used to Path."

"Path needn't be in evidence—"

"Mirrim, the decision has been made," Robinton said firmly, with no trace of a smile now.

"Well, that's plain enough. Since I'm not needed here . . ." She stalked out of the hall.

Jaxom noticed the Harper's gaze following her, and he felt acutely embarrassed by her display of temperament. He could see that Menolly was also disturbed.

"Is her Path proddy today?" the Harper asked Menolly quietly.

"I don't think so, Master Robinton."

Zair chittered on the Harper's shoulder and his expression changed to chagrin. "Brekke's come back. I was supposed to rest."

He half-ran out of the hall, turning briefly at the door to put his finger to his lips as he quickly ducked into his room. Piemur, his expression bland, took a step sideways to fill the space so precipitously vacated. Fire-lizards zipped into the room. Jaxom spotted Berd and Grall.

"Master Robinton really should have rested," Menolly said, nervously twitching sketches across the table surface.

"He wasn't exerting himself," Piemur pointed out. "This sort of thing is bread and meat to him. He was going out of his skull with boredom and with Brekke fussing over him when you weren't. It isn't as if he was up on the Plateau, digging about . . ."

"I told you, Brekke," F'nor said, his voice carrying from the porch as he and his weyrmate mounted the last step, "you worried for no reason at all."

"Menolly, how long has Master Robinton been resting?" Brekke asked, coming right up to the table.

"Half a skinful," Piemur replied, grinning as he pointed to the wine on the back of the chair, "and he went without a protest."

Brekke gave the young harper a long and searching look. "I wouldn't trust you for a moment, Harper Piemur." Then she looked at Jaxom. "Have you been here all afternoon, too?"

"Me? No indeed. Ruth and I slept until Mirrim woke us."

"Where is Mirrim?" F'nor asked, glancing about.

"She's outside somewhere," replied Menolly in a voice so devoid of tone that Brekke glanced at her apprehensively.

"Has Mirrim been . . ." Brekke pressed her lips in a thin, disapproving line. "Drat that girl!" She looked up at Berd, and he immediately darted from the hall.

F'nor was bending over the maps now, shaking his head with pleased surprise.

"You lot work like twenty, don't you?" He grinned at all of them.

"Well, this part of the twenty has done quite enough work," Piemur said, stretching his arms until his joints cracked. "I want a swim, to wash the sweat from my brow, and the ink from my fingers. Anyone coming?"

Jaxom's acceptance was as enthusiastic as the two girls' and, with F'nor's jocular complaint about being deserted ringing in their ears, they all made for the beach. Jaxom managed to grab Menolly by the hand as Sharra and Piemur pelted around the bend.

"Menolly, how did Master Robinton know?"

She'd been laughing as they raced down the path, but now her eyes darkened.

"I didn't tell him, Jaxom. I didn't have to. I don't know when he figured it out. But the facts all point to you."

"How?"

She ticked off reasons on her fingers. "To start with, a dragon had to return the egg. Only way. Preferably a dragon who was totally familiar with Benden Hatching Ground. The dragon had to be ridden by someone who wanted earnestly to return that egg, and who could find it!" The last qualification seemed to be the most important. "More people will figure out it was you now."

"Why now?"

"No one in the Southern Weyr returned Ramoth's egg." Menolly smiled up at Jaxom, and put her hand to his cheek, giving him an affectionate slap. "I was so proud of you, Jaxom, when I realized what you and Ruth had managed to do! Prouder even because you didn't noise it about. And it was so critical just then for Benden to believe that a Southern rider had relented and restored Ramoth's egg . . . "

"Hey, Jaxom, Menolly, c'mon!" Piemur's roar distracted them.

"Race you?" Menolly said, turning and dashing for the beach.

They weren't to have much time for their swim. Master Idarolan's ship reappeared, the blue full-catch pennant flying from its foremast. Brekke called them to help gut enough fish for the evening's meal. She wasn't certain how many of those now at the Plateau would return to Cove Hold for dinner but cooked fish could be served in rolls the next day, she said, cheerfully ignoring the protests. She sent Mirrim off with supplies for Master Wansor and N'ton, who planned to make an evening of star-watching or, as Piemur said irreverently, the Dusk-Dawn and Midnight Sisters.

"And what do you bet Mirrim tries to stay there the night, too, to see if Path does keep away the Southern fire-lizards?" Piemur asked, a slightly malicious grin on his face.

"Mirrim does have well-trained fire-lizards," Menolly said.

"And they sound just like her when they scold everyone else's friends," Piemur added.

"Now that's not fair," Menolly said. "Mirrim's a good friend of mine . . . "

"And as her best friend you ought to explain to her that she can't manage everyone on Pern!"

As Menolly prepared to take umbrage, dragons began popping into the air over the Cove, and with their bugling no one could hear anything else.

The dragons were not the only ones in good moods. An atmosphere of intense excitement and expectation pervaded the evening.

Jaxom was grateful for his afternoon's nap, for he wouldn't have missed that evening. All seven Weyrleaders were there, D'ram with some private news for F'lar's ears about the affairs in the Southern

Weyr, and N'ton, who stayed only part of the evening since he was sky-watching with Wansor. There were also Mastercraftsmen Nicat, Fandarel, Idarolan, Robinton, and Lord Lytol.

To Jaxom's surprise, the three Oldtimer Weyrleaders, G'narish of Igen, R'mart of Telgar and D'ram now of Southern, were less interested in what might lie hidden in the settlement than N'ton, T'bor, G'dened and F'lar. The Oldtimers were far more eager to explore the broad lands and the distant range than dig to unearth their past.

"That *is* past," R'mart of Telgar said. "Past, dead, and very much buried. *We* have to live in the present, a trick, mind you, F'lar, that you taught us." He grinned to remove any sting from what he said. "Besides, wasn't it you, F'lar who suggested that it's useless to muddle our brains thinking how the ancients did things . . . that it's better to build for ourselves what is useful for our times and Turn?"

F'lar grinned, amused to have his words returned. "I suppose I'm hoping that we'll find undamaged records somewhere, filling in the holes in what came down to us. Maybe even another useful item like the enlarger viewer we discovered in Benden Weyr."

"Look where that got us!" R'mart exclaimed, whooping with laughter.

"Undamaged instruments would be invaluable," Fandarel said, very solemn.

"We might just find you some, Master Robinton," Nicat said thoughtfully, "because only one section of that settlement sustained much damage." He had everyone's attention. "Look," he drew out a sketch of the general site, "the flow of lava is to the south. Here, here, and here, the cones of the mountains broke, and the flow followed the slope of the land, away from much of the settlement. The prevailing wind also carried the ash away from the place. From the little digging I did today, I found only a thin layer of volcanic debris."

"Is there only this one settlement? When they had a whole world to occupy?" asked R'mart.

"We'll find the others tomorrow," the Harper assured them, "won't you, Jaxom?"

"Sir?" Jaxom rose, half-startled by his unexpected inclusion in the main discussion.

"No, to be serious, R'mart, you may be quite correct," F'lar said, leaning forward across the table. "And we really don't know if the eruption made the ancients leave the Plateau immediately afterward."

"We won't know anything until we've entered one of those mounds and discovered what they left behind, if anything," N'ton said.

"Go carefully, Weyrleader," Master Nicat told N'ton, but his glance took in everyone. "Better still, I'll send a craftmaster and a few steady journeymen to direct the excavations."

"Show the tricks of your craft, eh, Master Nicat," R'mart said. "We'd better learn a thing or two about mining, right, Masterminer?"

Jaxom stifled a chuckle at the expression of puzzlement and then indignation on the Masterminer's face.

"Dragonriders mining?"

"Why not?" F'lar asked. "Thread will Pass. There'll be another Interval on us all too soon. I promise you one thing, with the Southern lands open, never again will the Weyrs be beholden to anyone during an Interval."

"Ah, yes, a very sound idea, Weyrleader, very sound," Master Nicat prudently agreed, though he would plainly need time to assimilate such a revolutionary idea.

The dragons lounging on the shore crooned a welcome to someone.

N'ton suddenly rose. "I must join Wansor in our star-watch. That must be Path and Mirrim returning. My duty to you all."

"I'll light your way, N'ton," Jaxom said, grabbing a glow basket and unshielding it.

They were well out of hearing range of the others when N'ton turned to Jaxom. "This is more to your fancy, isn't it, Jaxom, than flying tamely in the queens' wing?"

"I didn't do it on purpose, N'ton," Jaxom said with a laugh. "I just wanted to see the mountain before anyone else did."

"No hunch this time?"

"Hunch?"

N'ton threw a companionable arm about his shoulders, chuckling. "No, I suppose it was inspired by the fire-lizards' images."

"The mountain?"

N'ton gave him a bit of a shake. "Good man!"

They saw the dark bulk of a dragon settling to the beach and then two gleaming circles as Lioth turned his head toward them.

"A white dragon has an advantage at night," N'ton said as he pointed to the visible hide of Ruth a little to one side of his bronze.

I'm glad you've come. I've an itch I cannot reach, said Ruth.

"He's in need of attention, N'ton."

"Leave the glows with me then, I'll pass them on to Mirrim so she can find her way to the point."

They separated as Jaxom moved aside to attend to Ruth. He heard N'ton greet Mirrim, their voices carrying on the quiet night air.

"Of course, Wansor's all right," Mirrim said, sounding peevish. "He's got his eyes glued to that tube of his. He never knew I came, never ate the food I brought, never knew I left. And further," she paused, taking a deep breath, "Path did not scare away the Southern fire-lizards."

"Why would she?"

"*I'm* not allowed to be on the Plateau when Jaxom and the others try to coax some sense out of the Southerners."

"Sense? Oh, yes, seeing if Ruth can focus the fire-lizards' images. Well, I shouldn't worry about it, Mirrim. There are so many other things you can do."

"At least my dragon is not an unsexed runt, good for nothing but consorting with fire-lizards!"

"Mirrim!"

Jaxom heard the coldness in N'ton's voice; it matched the sudden freezing in his own guts. Mirrim's petulant comment resounded over and over in his ears.

"You know what I mean, N'ton . . . "

Just like Mirrim, Jaxom thought, not to heed the warning in N'ton's voice.

"You ought to," she went on with the impetus of grievance. "Wasn't it you who told F'nor and Brekke that you doubted if Ruth would ever mate? Where are you going, N'ton? I thought you were going . . . "

"You don't think, Mirrim!"

"What's the matter, N'ton?" The sudden panic in her voice afforded Jaxom some consolation.

Don't stop, Ruth said. *The itch is still there.*

"Jaxom?" N'ton's call was not loud, meant to reassure, but the sound carried back.

"Jaxom?" Mirrim cried. "Oh, no!" Then Jaxom heard her running away, saw the glow basket jolting, heard her weeping. Just like the girl, speak first, think later and weep for days. She'd be repentant and hanging on about him, driving him *between* with her need to be forgiven her thoughtlessness.

"Jaxom!" N'ton was anxious.

"Yes, N'ton?" Jaxom dutifully continued to scratch Ruth's backbone, wondering why Mirrim's cruel remark did not rankle as it ought. Sexless runt! As he saw N'ton striding toward him, he was aware of a curious sense of relief, of relaxation deep inside him. The memory of those riders, waiting for the Fort green to mate, flashed through his mind. Yes, he'd been relieved then that Ruth had proved disinterested. He could somewhat regret that Ruth would be deprived of that experience; but he was relieved that he would never be called upon to endure it.

"You must have heard her." There was a tinge of hope in N'ton's voice that Jaxom hadn't.

"I heard. Sound carries near water."

"Blast the girl! Scorch the girl! We were going to explain . . . then you took the fire-head, and now this. The opportunity hasn't presented itself . . . " N'ton's explanations came out in a rush.

"I can live with it. Like Mirrim's Path, there are other things we can do."

N'ton's groan came from his guts. "Jaxom!" His fingers closed tightly on Jaxom's shoulder, trying in the contact to express his inarticulate regret.

"It's not your fault, N'ton."

"Does Ruth comprehend what was said?"

"Ruth comprehends that his back itches." Even as Jaxom said it, he found it curious that Ruth was not the least bit upset.

There, you have the exact spot. Harder now.

Jaxom could feel the slightly flaky dryness in the otherwise loose and soft hide.

"I think I guessed, N'ton," Jaxom went on, "that time at Fort Weyr, that something was wrong. I know K'nebel expected Ruth to rise for the green. I thought that Ruth, being born small, maybe would mature later than other dragons do."

"He's as mature as he'll ever be, Jaxom!"

Jaxom was rather touched by the genuine regret in the bronze rider's voice.

"So? He's my dragon and I'm his rider. We are together!"

"He's unique!" N'ton's verdict was fervent, and he stroked Ruth's hide with affectionate respect. "So, my young friend, are you!" He gripped Jaxom's shoulder again, letting the gesture stand for words unsaid. Lioth crooned in the darkness beyond them and Ruth, turning his head toward the bronze dragon, made a courteous response.

Lioth is a fine fellow. His rider is a kind man. They are good friends!

"We are ever your friends," N'ton said, giving Jaxom's shoulder a final, almost painful squeeze. "I must get to Wansor. You're sure you're all right?"

"Go along, N'ton. I'll just settle Ruth's itch!"

The Fort Weyrleader hesitated one more moment before he pivoted and walked quickly toward his bronze.

"I think I'd better oil that patch, Ruth," Jaxom said. "I've been neglecting you lately."

Ruth's head came around, his eyes gleamed more brilliantly blue in the darkness. *You never neglect me.*

"I have too, or you wouldn't be patchy!"

There has been much for you to do!

"There's a fresh pot of oil in the kitchen. Hold tight."

His eyes accustomed to the tropic darkness, Jaxom made his way to the Hold, found the pot in the kitchen press and trotted back. He was conscious of a weariness, in mind and body. Mirrim was the most awkward person! If he'd let her and Path come . . . Well, he'd have learned the verdict on Ruth sooner or later. *Why* wasn't Ruth upset? Maybe if he had been completely willing for his dragon to experience that part of his personality, Ruth would have matured. Jaxom railed at the fact that they had always been kept from being full dragon and rider: brought up as they were in the Hold, instead of the Weyr where the mating of dragons was an understood and accepted fact of the weyr life. It wasn't as if Ruth were immune to sexual experience. He was always present when Jaxom had sex.

I love with you and I love you. But my back itches fiercely.

That was clear enough, Jaxom thought as he hurried through the forest to his dragon.

Someone was with Ruth, scratching his back for him. If it was Mirrim . . . Jaxom strode forward angrily.

Sharra is with me, Ruth told him calmly.

"Sharra?" Swallowing an irrational surge of anger, he acknowledged her presence. "I've got the oil. Ruth's got a bad flaky patch. I've been neglecting him."

"You've never neglected Ruth," she said so emphatically that Jaxom had to smile in surprise.

"Did Mirrim . . . " He began, holding the oil pot out so she could dip her hand in.

"Yes, and no sympathy from any of us, let me assure you." Her anger translated itself to an overly hard rub on Ruth's back that made him complain. "Sorry, Ruth. They sent Mirrim back to Benden!"

Jaxom glanced up the beach to where Path had landed and, indeed, the green dragon was gone.

"And you were sent to me?" He found he didn't mind Sharra: her presence was, in fact, a boon.

"Not sent . . . " Sharra faltered. "I was . . . I was called!" She finished her sentence in a rush.

"Called?" Jaxom left off rubbing oil into Ruth's back and looked at her. Her face was a pale blur with dark spots for her eyes and mouth.

"Yes, called. Ruth called me. He said Mirrim . . . "

"*He* said?" Jaxom interrupted her as her words finally sank in. "You can hear Ruth?"

She needed to hear me when you were sick, Jaxom, Ruth said at the same moment Sharra was saying out loud, "I've been able to hear him ever since you were so ill."

"Ruth, why did you call Sharra?"

She is good for you. You need her. What Mirrim said, even what N'ton said but he was kinder, has made you close up. I do not like it when I cannot hear your mind. Sharra will open it for us.

"Will you do that for us, Sharra?"

This time Jaxom didn't hesitate. He took Sharra's hands, oily as they were, and drew her to him, inordinately pleased that she was so nearly his height and her mouth so close to his. All he had to do was tilt his head slightly.

"I would do anything for you, Jaxom, anything for you and Ruth!" Her lips moved delightfully against his until he made more speech impossible.

A warmth began in his belly, dispelling the cold closeness that distressed his dragon and himself—a warmth that had to do with Sharra's lithe body against his, the scent of her long heavy hair in his nostrils as he kissed her, the pressure of her arms on the skin of his back. And her hands, flat against his waist, were not the hands of a healer, but the hands of a lover.

They made love in the soft warm darkness, delighting in each other and fully responsive to the moment of ecstasy that came, totally aware that Ruth loved with them.

·· C H A P T E R X X ··

At the Mountain and at
Ruatha Hold, 15.10.18–15.10.20

Jaxom could not feel easy looking at the eastern face of the mountain. He arranged himself, Sharra and Ruth so that they did not have to see it. The other five made themselves comfortable in a loose semicircle about Ruth.

The seventeen banded fire-lizards—for at the last moment, Sebell and Brekke asked to be included in the group—settled on Ruth's back. The more trained fire-lizards, the better, reasoned Master Robinton, which, he went on to say, gave him the chance to include Zair.

Word of the ancients' settlement at the high Plateau had spread throughout Pern with a swiftness that had amazed even the Harper. Everyone clamored to see the place. F'lar sent the message that if Jaxom and Ruth were to prod the fire-lizards' memories, they'd better do so quickly, or not at all.

Once Ruth had settled, the Southern fire-lizards began arriving in fairs, led by their queens, dipping toward Ruth who crooned a greeting as Jaxom had suggested he do.

They are pleased to see me, Ruth told Jaxom. *And happy that men come to this place again.*

"Ask them about the first time they saw men."

Jaxom caught an instant image from Ruth of many dragons arriving over the shoulder of the mountain.

"That's not what I meant."

I know, Ruth acknowledged with regret. *I will ask again. Not the time with the dragons, but a long time ago, before the mountain blew up.*

The reaction of the fire-lizards was predictable and discouraging.

They flew up from their perches on and about Ruth and did wild sky-dances, chittering and bugling in dismay.

Disappointed, Jaxom turned to see Brekke's hand raised, a look of intense concentration on her face. He relaxed against Ruth, wondering what arrested her attention. Menolly also held up her hand. She was sitting near enough to Jaxom so that he saw her eyes were totally unfocused. On her shoulder, Beauty had assumed a rigid position, her eyes wheeling violently red. Above their circle, the fire-lizards chattered and continued their wild gyrations.

They are seeing the mountain on fire, said Ruth. *They see people running, the fire following them. They are afraid as they were afraid so long ago. This is the very dream we used to have.*

"Can you see the mounds? Before they were covered?" In his excitement, Jaxom forgot and spoke aloud.

I see only people running, this way and that. No, they are running toward . . . toward us? Ruth looked about him as if he half-expected to be overrun, so vivid were the fire-lizard images.

"Toward us, and then where?"

Down to the water? Ruth wasn't sure himself, and turned to look toward the distant, invisible sea.

They are afraid again. They don't like remembering the mountain.

"Any more than they like remembering the Red Star," Jaxom said imprudently. Every fire-lizard disappeared, including the banded ones.

"That did it, Jaxom," Piemur said in deep disgust. "You can't mention that bloody Red Star in front of fire-lizards. Flaming mountains, but not red stars."

"Undeniably," Sebell said in his deep quiet voice, "there are moments that are branded in the minds of our little friends. When they start remembering, everything else is excluded."

"It is association," Brekke said.

"What we need then," Piemur said, "is another spot that strikes less distressing memories in them. Memories . . . useful . . . to us . . ."

"Not so much that," Menolly considered her words carefully, "as interpretation. I saw something. I think I'm right . . . it wasn't the big mountain that erupted, it was . . ." She turned, and pointed to the smallest of the three. "That's the one that blew in our dreams!"

"No, it was the big one," Piemur contradicted, pointing higher.

"You're wrong, Piemur," Brekke said with quiet certainty. "It was the smallest one . . . everything is to the left in my images. The big mountain is too much higher than the one I'm sure I saw."

"Yes, yes," Menolly said, excited. "The angle is important. The fire-lizards couldn't see that high! Remember they're much, much smaller. And see, the angle. It's right!" She was on her feet, gesturing to illustrate her points. "People came from there, running this way, away from the smallest volcano! They came from those mounds. The largest ones!"

"That's the way I saw it," Brekke agreed. "Those mounds there!"

"So do we start with these?" F'lar asked, the next morning, sighing at the task of unearthing a small hill. Lessa stood beside him, surveying the silent mounds, with the Master Smith, Masterminer Nicat, F'nor and N'ton. Jaxom, Piemur, Sharra and Menolly remained discreetly to one side. "This large one?" he asked, but his eyes swept down the parallel ranks, squinting with resignation.

"We could be digging until the Pass is done," Lessa said, slapping her riding gloves against her thigh as she, too, did a slow thoughtful survey of the sprawl of anonymous earthen lumps.

"A vast area," Fandarel said, "vast! A larger settlement than the combined Holds at Fort and Telgar." He glanced up in the direction of the Dawn Sisters. "They *all* came from those?" He shook his head, staggered by the concept. "Where to start to best effect?"

"Is everyone on Pern coming here today?" Lessa asked as a bronze dragon burst into the air over their heads. "D'ram's Tiroth! With Toric?"

"I doubt we could exclude him if we wished, and it would be unwise to try," F'lar remarked in a droll tone.

"True," she replied and then smiled at her weyrmate. "I rather like him," she added, surprised at her own verdict.

"My brother makes himself likable," Sharra said quietly to Jaxom, a curious smile on her lips. "But to trust him?" She shook her head slowly, watching Jaxom's face. "He is a very ambitious man!"

"He's taking a good look, isn't he?" N'ton remarked, watching the circling dragon's lazy downward glide.

"It's worth looking at," F'nor replied, scanning the broad, mounded expanse.

"Is that Toric aloft?" Master Nicat asked, digging his boot toe into the large mound. "Glad he's here. He sent for me when he found those mine shafts in the Western Range."

"I'd forgot he's already had some experience with the ancients' handiwork," F'lar said.

"He's also got experienced men to help us without having to go back to the Lord Holders," N'ton said with a knowing grin.

"Whom I don't want too interested in these eastern lands," Lessa said firmly.

When D'ram and Toric had dismounted, Tiroth glided down the grassy plain to where the other dragons were lounging on an out-cropping of sun-warmed rock. As Toric and the bronze rider walked toward them, Jaxom regarded the Southerner with Sharra's remarks in his mind. Toric was a big man, as big as Master Fandarel in build and height. His hair was sun-streaked, his skin a deep brown and, while his smile was broad, there was a certain arrogant self-possession in the very way he strode that suggested he felt himself the equal of any awaiting him. Jaxom wondered just how that attitude would strike the Benden Weyrleaders.

"You certainly have discovered the Southern Continent, haven't you, Benden?" he said, gripping F'lar's arm in greeting and bowing as he smiled at Lessa. He nodded and murmured the name of the other leaders and masters present, glancing beyond them with a raking look at the younger people. When Toric's eyes came back to his face, just briefly, Jaxom knew he'd been identified. Resenting the way Toric's glance slid from him, as if he were negligible, he stiffened. Then he felt Sharra's hand lightly on his arm.

"He does that to irritate," she said in a very soft voice, with a ripple of her rich laughter in it. "Most of the time it's effective."

"It puts me in mind of the way my milk-brother used to tease me in front of Lytol, when he knew I couldn't retaliate," Jaxom said, surprising himself with such an unexpected comparison. He saw her approval in her dancing eyes.

"Trouble is," Toric was saying, his voice carrying to them, "that the ancients didn't leave much behind. Not if they could move it elsewhere and use it. Saving people they were!"

"Oh?" F'lar's exclamation invited Toric to explain.

The Southerner shrugged. "We've been through the mine shafts they left. They'd even pulled up the rails for their ore carts, and the brackets where they must have hung lights. One place had a largish shelter at the mouth," he gestured toward the smallest nearby mound, "about that size, carefully shut against the weather and totally bare inside. Again, you could see where things had been bolted to the floor. They'd prized the bolts out, too."

"If this thriftiness applies here," Fandarel said, "then if anything is likely to be found, it will be in those mounds." He pointed to a smaller cluster on the edge of the settlement nearest the lava flow. "They would have been too hot or too dangerous to approach for a long time."

"And if too hot to approach, what makes you think anything survived the heat?" Toric demanded.

"Because the mound has survived to this time," Fandarel replied as if he were only being logical.

Toric regarded him for a moment and then clouted the Smith on the shoulder. He was oblivious to the startled look awarded him by Fandarel, whom men tended to treat with distant respect.

"Point in your favor, Mastersmith," Toric said. "I'll dig gladly with you and hope you're right."

"I'd like to see what's in the smaller humps," Lessa said, wheeling and indicating one. "There are such a lot of them. Maybe they were used as small holds. Surely something would be left behind in the rush to leave."

"What would they have had in such big places?" F'lar asked, kicking at the grassy roundness of the large one nearest him.

"There're hands enough and . . . " Toric took three long strides to the pile of digging implements, "plenty of shovels and picks for everyone to take a dig at the mound of his choice." He picked up a long-handled shovel and tossed it to the Mastersmith, who caught it in a reflex action as he stared, bemused, at the big Southerner. Toric shouldered another shovel, selected two picks and with no more discussion strode toward the cluster of mounds that were the Smith's choice.

"Presuming Toric's theory is correct, is it worth digging here?" F'lar asked his Weyrmate.

"What we found in that long-forgotten room at Benden Weyr was obviously a discard of the ancients. And after all, mining equipment they could have used elsewhere. Besides, I want to *see* what's inside." Lessa said that with such determination that F'lar laughed.

"I guess I do, too. And I do wonder what they'd do in this size place! It's big enough to weyr a dragon or two!"

"We'll help you, Lessa," Sharra said, urging Jaxom to pick a tool.

"Menolly, shall we assist F'lar?" F'nor directed the Harper girl toward the tools.

N'ton shook his head as he hefted spade and pick. "Master Nicat, what's your preference?"

The Masterminer looked about him dubiously but his eyes kept returning to the mounds nearest the mountain toward which Toric and Fandarel moved purposefully. "I think our good Mastersmith might have the right of it. But we'll spread the effort. And try those." He pointed with sudden decision toward the sea side of the Plateau, where six smallish mounds made a loose circle.

It was not work to which any of them were accustomed despite the fact that Master Nicat had begun as an apprentice miner in the pits, and Master Fandarel still took long turns at the forges when he worked on something particularly intricate.

Jaxom, sweat pouring from his face and body, had the distinct feeling that he was under surveillance. But when he leaned on the pick for an occasional breather, or lifted colonies of grubs safely to one side, he could see no one looking in his direction. The sensation bothered him.

The big one watches you, Ruth said suddenly.

Jaxom shot a glance under his arm at the mound where Toric and Master Fandarel were working and, sure enough, Toric was looking in his direction. Beside him, Lessa groaned suddenly, jamming her shovel blade into the rough-rooted grass of the mound. She examined her hands, reddened and beginning to blister.

"It's a long time since these have worked so hard," she said.

"Use your flying gloves," Sharra suggested.

"A few moments in them and my hands would swim in sweat," Lessa replied, grimacing. She glanced at the other work parties and, chuckling to herself, sank gracefully to the mound. "Much as I dislike revealing this site to more people than necessary, I think we shall have to recruit strong hands and backs." She deftly captured a tangle of grubs and deposited them to one side, watching them tunnel back into the rich gray-black soil. She rubbed particles between her thumbs and forefinger. "Like ash. Gritty. Never thought I'd be dealing in ashes again. Did I ever tell you, Jaxom, that I was cleaning the fireplace in Ruatha Hold the day your mother arrived?"

"No," Jaxom said, surprised at this unexpected confidence. "But then, few people ever mention my parents to me."

Lessa's expression became severe. "Now I wonder why I called Fax to mind . . . " she said, glancing in Toric's direction and adding, more to herself than to Jaxom and Sharra, "except he was ambitious, too. But Fax made mistakes."

"Such as taking Ruatha Hold from its rightful Bloodline," Jaxom said, grunting as he swung the pick.

"That was his worst mistake," Lessa said with intense satisfaction. Then she noticed Sharra staring at her and smiled. "Which I rectified. Oh, Jaxom, leave off a moment. Your enthusiasm exhausts me." She mopped at the perspiration on her forehead. "Yes, I think some strong backs will have to be drafted. At least for my mound!" She patted it, almost affectionately. "There's no telling how deep the covering goes. Perhaps," the thought amused her, "the mounds aren't big at all, just so overloaded. We may end up with nothing larger than a wherhole for all our digging."

Jaxom, conscious of Toric's scrutiny, continued to dig, though his shoulders ached and his hands were hot and stiff with blisters.

Just then, Sharra's two fire-lizards popped into the air, chirruping at each other as if they didn't understand what their friend was doing. They dropped lightly to the spot where Sharra had just planted her shovel and, with tremendous energy, they began to dig, their strong forepaws lifting the dirt to either side, their hindquarters pushing it farther out of the way. They had tunneled almost an arm's length while Lessa, Sharra and Jaxom watched in amazement.

"Ruth? Would you lend us your aid?" Jaxom called.

The white dragon obediently rose from his sunny perch and glided over to his friend, his eyes beginning to whirl more quickly with curiosity.

"Would you mind digging holes for us, Ruth?"

Where? Here? Ruth indicated a spot to the left of the fire-lizards who had not stopped their efforts.

"I don't think it matters where, we just want to see what the grass covers!"

No sooner had the other dragonriders seen what Ruth was doing than they called on theirs. Even Ramoth felt inclined to lend her aid, with Lessa giving her every encouragement.

"I wouldn't have believed it," Sharra said to Jaxom. "Dragons digging?"

"Lessa wasn't too proud to dig, was she?"

"We're people, but they're dragons!"

Jaxom couldn't help laughing at her incredulity. "You've got a jaundiced view of dragons, living among the Oldtimers' lazy beasts." He caught her about the waist, pulling her toward him before he felt her stiffen. He looked in Toric's direction. "He's not watching, if that's what you're worried about."

"He might not have been," she pointed skyward, "but his fire-lizards are. I'd wondered where they were."

A trio of fire-lizards, a golden queen and two bronzes, were circling lazily above Jaxom and Sharra.

"So? I'll just speak to Master Robinton to mediate . . . "

"Toric has other plans for me . . . "

"Am I not included in your plans?" Jaxom asked, experiencing sudden shock.

"You know you are, which is why . . . we loved each other. I wanted you while I could." Sharra's eyes were troubled.

"Why should he interfere then? My rank is . . . " Jaxom took both her hands in his and retained them when she tried to pull away.

"He doesn't think much of the young Northern men, Jaxom. Not after coping with fairs of younger sons in the past three Turns who are really," Sharra sounded exasperated, "enough to try the patience of a harper. I know you're not like them, but Toric . . . "

"I'll prove myself to Toric, never fear." Jaxom brought her hands to his lips, holding her eyes with his, determined by the force of his will to banish the unhappiness in her eyes. "And I'll do it properly, through Lytol and Master Robinton. You will be my lady, won't you, Sharra?"

"You know I will, Jaxom. For as long as I can . . . "

"For as long as we live . . . " he corrected her, gripping her hands tight enough to make her wince.

"Jaxom! Sharra!" cried Lessa, who had been far too engrossed in Ramoth's industry to notice their quiet exchange.

Jaxom felt Sharra's hands struggle but, having decided to confront

Toric in all his arrogance, Jaxom was not about to defer before Lessa. He kept a tight hold on Sharra as they turned toward the Weyrwoman.

"Come and see. Ramoth has struck something solid. And it doesn't look like rock . . . "

Jaxom pulled Sharra up the slight incline to Lessa's side of the mound. Ramoth was sitting back on her haunches, peering over Lessa to look into the trench her forepaws had scored.

"Move your head slightly, Ramoth. You're in my light," Lessa said. "Here, take my shovel, Jaxom, and see what you think. Clear out a bit more dirt."

Jaxom jumped into a trench which reached to mid-thigh. "Feels solid enough," he said, pressing his weight down before he tapped with the shovel. "Sounds like stone?" But it didn't. The shovel thunked echoingly. Scraping clear a long swath, Jaxom stepped aside for all to see.

"F'lar, come here! We've reached something!"

"So have we!" came the Weyrleader's triumphant reply.

There was a mutual inspection from one dragon-dug trench to the other which exposed much the same material, except that in F'lar's case the rocklike substance had an amber panel set into the curve of the mound. Finally the Mastersmith raised his huge arms above his head and roared for silence.

"This is not efficient use of time and energy." A loud guffaw, almost contemptuous in agreement, came from Toric. "It is not funny," the Smith said at his most serious. "We will concentrate on Lessa's mound since it is smaller. Then we will work on Master Nicat's and then . . . " He pointed to his own choice as Toric interrupted.

"All in one day?" he asked, again with a tone of supercilious derision that irritated Jaxom.

"We will do as much as we can, certainly, so let us begin!"

Jaxom decided that the Smith chose to ignore Toric's attitude, an example for him to follow.

It also proved inefficient to have more than two dragons working on Lessa's small mound since it was scarcely longer than a dragon. So F'lar and N'ton urged their bronzes to help Master Nicat.

By midafternoon the curving sides of Lessa's mound had been unearthed to the original floor of the valley. Six panels, three on an arc of the curved roof, tantalized, but their surface, once undoubtedly transparent, was now badly scored and darkened. Attempts to see through to the interior were vain. Disappointing, but no openings were found on the long sides so one end was promptly dug out. The dragons, despite the gray-black dust that now dulled their hides, showed no sign of fatigue and considerable interest in this unlikely task. And shortly the access was unearthed.

A door made of an opaque form of the material used in the roof panels, slid across the opening on rails. The dirt-clogged tracks had to be cleared and dragonhide oil applied to the runners before the door could be forced wide enough to permit entry. Lessa, all set to enter first, was restrained by the Smith's hand.

"Wait! The air inside is sick with age! Smell! Let fresh air in first. The place has been shut who knows how many Turns!"

The Smith, Toric and N'ton, set their shoulders to the door and forced it fully open. The air that flooded out was fetid, and Lessa stepped back, sneezing and coughing. Dim rectangles of tan light fell on a dusty floor, touched cracked and water-stained walls. As Lessa and F'lar, followed by the others, made their way into the small building, dust swirled under their boots.

"What was it for?" Lessa asked in a hushed voice.

Toric, unnecessarily ducking his head, for the top of the doorway cleared even his height by another hand's breadth, pointed to a far corner, to the now-visible remnants of a wide, wooden frame.

"Someone could have slept on that!" He turned to the other corner, and then with a sudden movement that made Lessa gasp, he stooped and came up with an object which he then made a show of presenting to her. "A treasure from the past!"

"It's a spoon!" Lessa held it up for all to see, then ran her fingers over its shape. "But what's it made of? It's no metal I've ever seen. Certainly it's not wood. It's more like . . . like the panels, and the door, only transparent. But it's strong," and she tried to bend it.

The Smith asked to examine the spoon. "It does seem to be a similar material. Spoons and windows, huh? Hmmmm!"

Overcoming a sense of awe at being inside such an ancient place, everyone began to examine the interior. Shelves and cabinets had once hung on the walls, for marks of paint left outlines. The structure had once been partitioned into sections and there were distinct gouges in the tough material of the floor to indicate that large permanent objects had rested here and there. In one corner, Fandarel discovered circular outlets, leading down. When he checked the exterior, he had to assume that the piping went through the wall and underground. One, he maintained, was undoubtedly for water. But the other four puzzled him.

"Surely they can't all be empty!" Lessa said in a wistful tone, trying to hide a disappointment that everyone, Jaxom thought, was experiencing.

"One can assume," Fandarel said in a brisk voice when they had all left Lessa's building, "that many of these of the same shape were also living quarters for the ancients. They would, I feel, take all their personal things with them. I think we ought then to devote more effort to the larger or the much smaller places."

Then, without waiting to see if anyone concurred with his opinion, the Smith marched straight to the interrupted excavation of Nicat's mound. This building was square and once they had uncovered enough of the top to notice the same roof panels, they concentrated their efforts on the inner end. The tropical night was quickly descending when they finally unearthed the entrance, but they couldn't quite clear the door tracks to open it more than a crack. They were barely able to make out some sort of decorations on the walls. No one had thought to bring glow baskets with them and this second disappointment drained the last of their energy so that no one even suggested sending fire-lizards for glows.

Leaning against the half-open panel, Lessa gave a tired laugh and looked down at her muddied condition.

"Ramoth says she's tired and dirty and wants a bath."

"She's not the only one," F'lar promptly agreed. He made a vain effort to close the door, then laughed. "I don't suppose anything will happen overnight. Back to Cove Hold."

"You'll join us, Toric?" Lessa asked, cocking her head to look up at the big Southerner.

"I think not this evening, Lessa. I've a Hold to manage and cannot always please myself," he said. Jaxom saw the Southerner's eyes on him, the implication obvious to Jaxom. "All things being equal, I'll return tomorrow for a time to see if Fandarel's mound proves more profitable. Shall I bring more strong hands and spare your dragons?"

"Spare the dragons? They're enjoying themselves hugely," Lessa said. "I need the relief. What do you think, F'lar? Or should we draft some Benden riders?"

"I can appreciate that you'd like to keep this for yourself," Toric went on, smoothly, his eyes on F'lar.

"This Plateau will have to be available to everyone," F'lar said, ignoring Toric's implication. "And since dragons enjoy earth-moving . . . "

"I'd like to bring Benelek with me tomorrow, F'lar," said the Master Smith, rubbing his gray-mudded hands together and flicking off the dried pellets off his clothes. "And two other lads with good imaginations . . . "

"Imagination? Yes, you'll need a lot of that here to make sense out of what the ancients have left for you," Toric said, the faintest hint of scorn in his tone. "When you're ready, D'ram?"

For some reason Toric's manner toward the old Weyrleader was more respectful than to anyone else. At least to Jaxom's sensitive ears. He was inwardly seething over Toric's insinuation that he did not manage his own Hold but pleased himself. He seethed because it was a valid accusation. Yet why, Jaxom sought to console himself, would anyone have expected him to return tamely to Ruatha, which prospered under Lytol's expert management, when all the excitement in the world was happening here? He felt Sharra's fingers curl around his arm, and he reminded himself of his own analogy between Toric and Dorse.

"I'll have a job getting Ruth clean," he said with a rueful sigh as he undid Sharra's fingers from his arm and clasped them tightly, drawing her with him to Ruth.

As the dragons broke from *between* over the Cove, the Harper's tall figure was visible on the beach, his impatience to hear of their explorations echoed by the fire-lizards who did dizzy spirals about him. When he saw the state the group was in, and how impatient they were to swim clean, he simply divested himself of his clothes and swam from one to another, hearing their reports.

It was an altogether deflated group that sat about the fire that evening.

"There's no guarantee, is there," the Harper said, "that even if we had the energy to excavate all those hundred of mounds, we'd find anything of value left behind."

Lessa held up her spoon with a laugh. "No intrinsic value, but it does give me a tremendous thrill to hold something my hundred-times ancestress might have used!"

"Efficiently made, too," Fandarel said, politely taking the small object and examining it again. "The substance fascinates me." He bent toward the flames to scrutinize it. "If I could just . . . " and he reached for his belt knife.

"Oh, no you don't, Fandarel," Lessa said in alarm and retrieved her artifact. "There were other bits and pieces of the same stuff discarded in my building. Experiment on them."

"Is that all we are to have of the ancients, their bits and pieces?"

"I remind you, F'lar," Fandarel said, "their discards have already proved invaluable." The Smith then indicated the spot where Wansor's distance-viewer had been sited. "What men have once learned to do, can be relearned. It will take time and experimentation but . . . "

"We've only begun, my friends," said Nicat, whose enthusiasm had not been daunted. "And as our good Smith says, we can learn even from their discards. With your permission, Weyrleaders, I'd like to bring some experienced teams, and go about the excavations methodically. There may have been good reasons for the rank system. Each file might belong to a different craft or—"

"You don't believe, as Toric suggests, that they took everything with them?" F'lar asked.

"That's irrelevant," Nicat said, dismissing Toric's contentions. "The bed, for instance, was unneeded because they knew they could obtain wood wherever they went. The little spoon for another, because they could make more. There may be other pieces, useless to them, which might very well form the missing elements of the Records which did come down to us, in whatever mutilated fashion. Just think, my friends," Nicat held up one finger along his nose, closing an eye conspiratorially, "the sheer quantity they had to take from those buildings after the eruption. Oh, we'll find things, never fear!"

"Yes, they had to take great loads from those buildings after the eruption," Fandarel murmured, frowning as he lowered his chin to his chest in deep thought. "Where did they take their possessions? Certainly, not immediately to establish Fort Hold!"

"Yes, where did they go?" F'lar asked, puzzled.

"As far as we could tell from the fire-lizard images, they headed toward the sea," Jaxom said.

"And the sea wouldn't have been safe," Menolly said.

"The sea wouldn't," F'lar said, "but there's a lot of land between the Plateau and the sea." He stared at Jaxom a moment. "Can you get Ruth to find out from the fire-lizards where they did go?"

"Does that mean I can't excavate more thoroughly?" Nicat asked, sounding irritable.

"By all means, if you've the men to spare."

"I do," Nicat replied a bit grimly. "With three mines worked out."

"I thought you'd started to reopen the shafts Toric found in the Western Range?"

"We've been examining them, to be sure, but my Hall hasn't reached a miner's agreement with Toric yet."

"With Toric? Does he hold those lands? They're far to the southwest, well beyond Southern Hold," F'lar said, abruptly intent.

"It was an exploring party of Toric's which located the shafts," Nicat said, his eyes shifting from the Benden Weyrleader's to the Harper's and then to the Smith's.

"I told you my brother was ambitious," Sharra said softly to Jaxom.

"An exploring party?" F'lar seemed to relax again. "That doesn't make it a Holding then. At all events, mines come under your jurisdiction, Master Nicat. Benden supports your decision. I'll just have a word with Toric tomorrow."

"I think we should," Lessa said, holding her hand out to F'lar to assist her from the sands.

"I was hopeful you'd support my Hall," the Miner said with a bow of gratitude, his shrewd eyes glinting in the firelight.

"I'd say a talk was long overdue," the Harper remarked.

The dragonriders took their leave quickly, N'ton to deliver Master Nicat to Crom Hold from where they'd collect him the next morning. Robinton took Master Fandarel with him to Cove Hall. Piemur dragged Menolly off to check on Stupid, leaving Jaxom and Sharra to douse the fire and clear the beach.

"Your brother doesn't plan to hold the entire Southwest, does he?" Jaxom asked when the others had dispersed.

"Well, if not all, as much as he can," Sharra replied with a laugh. "I'm not being disloyal to him telling you this, Jaxom. You have your own Hold. You don't want Southern lands. Or do you?"

Jaxom considered that.

"You don't, do you?" Sharra sounded anxious and put her hand on his arm.

"No, I don't," he said. "No, much as I love this Cove, I don't want it. Today on the Plateau, I'd have given anything for a cool breeze from Ruatha's mountain, or a plunge in my lake. Ruth and I will take you there—it's such a beautiful place. Only a dragon can get to it easily." He picked up a flat pebble and skated it across the quiet swells that lapped the white sands of the beach. "No, I don't want a Southern Hold, Sharra. I was born in Ruatha, bred to Ruatha. Lessa obliquely reminded me of that this afternoon. She reminded me, too, of the price of my Holding and of all she's done to insure that I remain Lord of Ruatha. You do realize, don't you, that her son, F'lessan, is a Ruathan half-blood. That's more than I am."

"But he's a dragonrider!"

"Yes, and weyrbred, by Lessa's choice so that I would remain the uncontested Lord of Ruatha. I'd better start acting like one!" He rose and drew Sharra up.

"Jaxom?" and her tone was suspicious, "what are you going to do?"

He put both hands on her arms, looking her squarely in the eyes. "I've a Hold to manage, too, as your brother reminded me . . . "

"But you're needed here, with Ruth. He's the only one who can make sense out of fire-lizard images . . . "

"And with Ruth, I can handle both responsibilities. Manage my Hold and please myself. You'll see!" He drew her closer to kiss her, but suddenly she broke away from him, pointing over his shoulder, her face mirroring hurt and anger. "What's the matter? What have I done, Sharra?"

She pointed to the tree where two fire-lizards were intently watching.

"Those are Toric's. He's watching me. Us!"

"Great! Let him have no mistake about my intentions toward you!" He kissed her until he felt her taut body responding to his, till the angry set of her lips dissolved into willingness. "I'd give him more to see but I want to get back to Ruatha Hold this evening!" He rapidly drew on his riding gear and called to Ruth. "I'll be back in the morning, Sharra. Tell the others, will you?"

Do we have to leave? Ruth asked even as he bent his foreleg for Jaxom to mount.

"We'll be back in no time, Ruth!" Jaxom waved to Sharra, thinking how forlorn she looked standing there in the starlight.

Meer and Talla circled once with Ruth, whistling so cheerfully that he knew Sharra had accepted his precipitous departure.

His abrupt compulsion to return to Ruatha and set in train the formalities of his confirmation as Lord Holder was by no means entirely due to Toric's barbed comments. His own suppressed sense of responsibility had been heightened by Lessa's odd nostalgia at the mound. But it had also occurred to him, at the fireside, that a man of Lytol's vitality and experience might find the Plateau's mysteries a challenge sufficient to replace Ruatha. His return to his birthplace had the same inexorable quality of his decision to rescue the egg.

He asked Ruth to take them to Ruatha. The sharp bitter cold of *between* was instantly replaced by a damp moist cold as they entered Ruatha's skies, leaden and showing a fine light snow that must have been in progress for some time to have piled drifts in the southeast corners of the courts.

I used to like snow, Ruth said as if encouraging himself to accept the return.

Wilth trumped from the fire-heights in surprised welcome. Half the fire-lizards of the Hold exploded into the air about them, giving raucous greetings and spurts of chittering complaint about the snow.

"We won't stay long, my friend," Jaxom reassured Ruth, and shuddered with the damp cold even in his warm flying gear. How had he forgot the season here?

Ruth landed in the courtyard just as the Great Hall door opened. Lytol, Brand and Finder surged to the steps.

"Is anything wrong, Jaxom?" Lytol cried.

"Nothing, Lytol, nothing. Can fires be laid in my quarters? I forgot it was winter here. Ruth is going to feel the difference even through dragonhide!"

"Yes, yes," Brand said, jogging across the court toward the kitchen, yelling for drudges to bring coal fires, while Lytol and Finder hurriedly ushered Jaxom up the steps. Ruth obediently followed the steward.

"You'll take a chill changing climates like this," Lytol was saying. "Why didn't you check? What brings you back?"

"Isn't it about time I did return?" Jaxom asked, striding to the fireplace as he stripped off his flying gloves and let his hands take warmth from the blaze. Then he burst out laughing as the other men joined him there. "Yes, at this fireplace!"

"What? At this fireplace?" Lytol asked, pouring wine for his ward.

"This morning, in the hot sun of the Plateau, while we were digging up one of the mounds the ancients left to puzzle us, Lessa told me that she had been taking ashes out of this fireplace the day my unlamented sire, Fax, escorted my lady mother Gemma to this

Hold!" He raised his cup in a toast to the memory of the mother he had never known.

"Which obliquely reminded you that you are Lord of Ruatha now?" Lytol inquired, a slight lift to the corner of his mouth. His eyes, which before had seemed so expressionless to Jaxom, twinkled in the firelight.

"Yes, and showed me where a man of your talents could be better used now, Lord Lytol."

"Oh, tell me more," Lytol said, gesturing to the heavy carved chair which had been placed to get the most benefit of the fire.

"Don't let me take your chair," Jaxom said courteously, noticing that the cushions bore the recent imprint of buttocks and thighs.

"I suspect you're about to take more than that, Lord Jaxom."

"Not without due courtesy," Jaxom said, dragging a small footstool beside the chair for his own use. "And a challenge in its place." He was relieved at Lytol's placid reaction. "Am I, sir, ready to be Lord of Ruatha Hold now?"

"Are you trained, do you mean?"

"That, too, but I had in mind the circumstances which have made it wiser to leave Ruatha in your charge."

"Ay, yes."

Jaxom keenly watched Lytol to see if there was any constraint in his manner as he answered.

"The circumstances have indeed altered over the past two seasons," Lytol almost laughed, "thanks to you, in great part."

"To me? Oh, that wretched illness. So, there is now no real bar to my confirmation as Lord Holder?"

"I see none."

Jaxom heard the harper's soft intake of breath but he was watching Lytol closely.

"So," Lytol almost smiled, "may I know what has prompted you? Surely not just the realization that pressure is eased in the North? Or is it that pretty girl? Sharra, is that her name?"

Jaxom laughed. "She's a large part of my haste," lightly emphasizing the last word and then catching Finder's grin from the corner of his eye.

"A sister to Toric of the Southern Hold, isn't she?" Lytol pursued the subject, testing the suitability of the match.

"Yes, and tell me, Lytol, has there been any move to confirm Toric as a major Lord Holder?"

"No, nor any rumor that he's asked to be." Lytol scowled as he reflected on that circumstance.

"What's your opinion of Toric, Lord Lytol?"

"Why do you ask? Certainly the match is suitable, even if he hasn't rank to match yours."

"He doesn't need the rank. He has the ambition," Jaxom said with sufficient rancor to attract the undivided attention of both guardian and harper.

"Ever since D'ram became Southern Weyleader," Finder remarked in the silence that ensued, "I've heard it said that no holdless man is turned away."

"Does he promise them the right to hold what they can?" Jaxom asked, turning so quickly on Finder that the harper blinked in surprise.

"I'm not sure . . . "

"Two of Lord Groghe's sons have gone," Lytol said, pulling at his lower lip thoughtfully, "and my understanding from him is that they will hold. Of course, they retain their birthrank of Lords. Brand, what was Dorse promised?" he asked as the steward returned.

"Dorse? Has he gone south looking for a hold?" Jaxom gave a chuckle of relief and wonder.

"I saw no reason to refuse him the opportunity," Lytol replied calmly. "I didn't imagine you would object. Brand? What was promised him?"

"I think he was told he could have as much land as he wanted. I don't believe that the term *hold* came into the discussion. But then, the offer was made through one of the Southern traders, not directly from Toric."

"Still, if a man offered you land, you'd be grateful to him, and support him against those who had denied you land, wouldn't you?" Jaxom asked.

"Yes, gratitude would be reasonably expressed in loyalty," Lytol moved restlessly, considering another aspect of the situation. "However, it was clearly stated that the best land was too far from the protection of the Weyr. I gave Dorse one of our older flamethrowers, in good repair of course, with spare nozzles and hose," Lytol added.

"I'd give anything to watch Dorse in the open in Threadfall without a dragonrider in sight," Jaxom said.

"If Toric is as shrewd as he appears to be," Lytol said, "that may be the final consideration as to who may hold."

"Sir," Jaxom rose, finishing the rest of his wine, "I'll return tonight. Our blood's not yet thick enough for a snowstorm in Ruatha Hold. And there's a task set for Ruth and myself tomorrow. Would you be free to come South again? If Brand can hold matters in our absence?"

"At this time of year, I would welcome the sun," said Lytol.

Brand murmured that he could cope.

When Jaxom and Ruth returned to Cove Hold, grateful for the balmy warmth of the starlight night, Jaxom was more certain than ever that Lytol would not find the change hard to make. Even as Ruth circled to land, Jaxom felt himself relaxing in the warm air. He'd been very tense at Ruatha—tense not to rush Lytol and still achieve his own ends, and worried by the report of Toric's clever machinations.

He slid down Ruth's shoulder to the soft sand, at just the spot where he had so recently kissed Sharra. Thoughts of her were comforting. He waited until Ruth had curled into the still warm sand and then he made for the Hall, tiptoeing in, surprised to see even the Harper's room dark. It must be later than he thought in this part of the world.

He crept into his bed, heard Piemur mutter in his sleep. Farli, curled beside her friend, opened one lid to peer at him, before going back to sound sleep. Jaxom pulled the light blanket over him, thinking of the snows in Ruatha, and went gratefully to sleep.

He woke abruptly, thinking that someone had called his name. Piemur and Farli were motionless in the crepuscular light that briefly heralded the dawn. Jaxom lay taut, expecting a repetition of that call, and heard none. The Harper? He doubted that, for Menolly was attuned to wake at his call. He touched Ruth's sleepy mind and knew that the dragon was only just rousing.

Jaxom was stiff. Maybe that was what had awakened him for his shoulders were cramped, the long muscles in his arms and across his midriff ached from yesterday's digging. His back was uncomfortably warm from the sun on that Plateau. It was too early to be up. He tried to court sleep but the discomforts of his muscles and skin were sufficient to keep him wakeful. He rose quietly so as not to disturb Piemur or be heard by Sharra. A swim would ease his muscles and soothe his burn. He paused by Ruth and found the white dragon waking, eager to join him for Ruth felt certain that all the mud had not been washed from his hide the evening before.

The Dawn Sisters were clearly sparkling in a sun which was not yet visible over the far horizon. Could his ancestors have gone back to them for refuge after the eruption? And how?

Wading out to his waist in the quiet Cove, Jaxom dove and swam under water, mysteriously dark without the sun to lighten its depths. Then he shot himself to the surface. No, there must have been some other sanctuary between the settlement and the sea. The flight had been channeled in one direction.

He called Ruth, reminding the grumbling white dragon that the sun would be much warmer on the Plateau. He collected his flying gear and grabbed some cold meatrolls from the larder, listening for a long moment to see if he had roused anyone else. He'd rather test his theory now and surprise everyone with good news on waking. He hoped.

They were airborne just as the sun became visible on the horizon, touching the clear cloudless sky with yellow and gilding the benign face of the distant cone mountain.

Ruth took them *between* and then, at Jaxom's suggestion, circled wide and lazily above the Plateau. They'd made new mounds of their own, Jaxom noticed with amusement, from the debris which the dragons had clawed from the two ancient buildings. He lined Ruth up in the direction of the sea. That goal would have been a long day's march for terrified people. He decided against calling the fire-lizards at this point; they'd only overexcite themselves repeating memories of the eruption. He had to get them to a spot where their associative memories tapped a less frantic moment. Surely they would have something to recall of their men in whatever refuge the fleeing people had set out to reach.

Had there perhaps been stables for beasts and wherries built at some distance from the settlement? Considering the scale on which the ancients operated, such a stable would have been large enough to shelter hundreds from the burning rain of a volcano!

He asked Ruth to glide toward the sea, in the general direction of the panic-driven ancients. Once past the grassland, shrubs began to hold root in the ashen soil, giving way to larger trees and thicker vegetation. They'd be lucky if they could spot anything unusual in that thick green mass. He was just about to ask Ruth to turn back and fly another swath when he noticed a break in the jungle. They glided out over a long scar of grassland, several dragonlengths wide and several hundred long. Trees and bushes were sparse on either side, as if struggling to find soil for their roots. Ribbons of water glinted at the far end of the curious scar, like shallow interconnected pools.

Just then the sun rose above the rim of the Plateau, and turning his head to the left to escape that brilliance, Jaxom saw the three shadows lengthening across the top end of the grassy scar. Excitedly, he urged Ruth to the spot, circling until he was certain that these hills couldn't be hills and certainly were unlike the shape of the ancients' other buildings. For one thing, their placement was as unnatural as their shape. One was seven dragonlengths or more in advance of the other two, and there'd be ten or more dragonlengths between them.

He had Ruth fly past and noticed the curious conformation: a larger mass was discernible at one end, while the other tapered slightly downward, a difference visible despite grass, earth and the small bushes that covered these so-called hills.

As excited as he was, Ruth came to rest between the leading two. The hills were not as obviously unnatural on the ground but they would have appeared odd even to someone arriving on foot.

No sooner had he asked Ruth to land than fire-lizards erupted about them, chittering with wild excitement and unbelievable pleasure.

"What are they saying, Ruth? Let's try to keep them calm enough to make sense. Do they have any images about these hills?"

Too many. Ruth raised his head, crooning softly to the fire-lizards.

They were dipping and darting about so erratically that Jaxom gave up trying to see if any were banded. *They are happy. They are glad you are come back. It has been so long.*

"When was I first here?" Jaxom asked Ruth, having learned not to confuse the fire-lizards with generations. "Can they remember?"

When you came out of the sky in long gray things? Ruth sounded bewildered even as he relayed the answer.

Jaxom leaned against Ruth, scarcely crediting the reply. "Show me!"

Brilliant and conflicting images stunned him as he saw vistas, unfocused at first, then resolving into a clear picture as Ruth sorted out the myriad impressions into one single coherent view.

The cylinders were grayish, with stubby wings that were poor imitations of the graceful pinions of the dragons. The cylinders bore rings of smaller tubes at one end while the other was blunt-nosed. Suddenly an opening appeared about a third of the way from the tubed end of the first ship. Men and women walked down a ramp. A progression of images flashed across Jaxom's mind then, of people running about, embracing each other, jumping up and down. Then the images Ruth obtained from the chittering bugling fire-lizards dissolved into chaos—as if each separate fire-lizard had followed one person and each was trying to give Ruth *his* individual image rather than a group view of the landing and ensuing events.

There was no doubt in Jaxom's mind that here was where the ancients had taken refuge from the volcano's havoc, the ships that had brought them from the Dawn Sisters to Pern. And the ships were still here because for some reason they couldn't go back to the trio of stars.

The opening into the vessel had been a third of the way from the tube end? With ecstatic fire-lizards doing acrobatics about his head, Jaxom paced the grass covering the cylinder until he thought he'd reached the appropriate spot.

They say that you have found it, Ruth advised him, nudging Jaxom forward. His great eyes were spinning with yellow fire.

To support their verdict, scores of fire-lizards settled on the bush-covered place and began to tug at the vegetation.

"I should go back to the Hold and tell them," Jaxom muttered to himself.

They are asleep. Benden is asleep. We are the only ones awake in the world!

That was, Jaxom had to admit, rather likely.

I dug yesterday. I can dig today. We can dig until they wake, when they can come help us.

"You have claws. I don't. Let's get some of the tools from the Plateau."

They were accompanied in both directions by excited, happy fire-lizards. With a shovel, Jaxom marked out the approximate area he wanted them to unearth to reach the door to the vessel. Then it was only a question of supervising Ruth and the sometimes obstructive assistance of the fire-lizards. They stripped the tough grass from the earth, first, the fire-lizards depositing it in the bushes beyond the scar. Fortunately the covering was firmly packed dirt blown over the landing site in the course of thousands of Turns. Even so, rain and sun had hardened a thick covering. When his shoulders began to ache, Jaxom eased his pace. He munched on a breadroll, occasionally urging squabbling fire-lizards back to work.

Ruth's claws scrabbled on something. *It isn't rock!* Jaxom jumped to the spot, slamming his shovel through the loose dirt. The edge hit a hard, unyielding surface. Jaxom let out a wild yell that set all the fire-lizards gyrating in midair.

Brushing away the last of the covering dirt with his hands, he stared at what he had unearthed. With cautious fingers, he touched the curious surface. Not metal, not the stuff of the mounds, rather like—improbable as it seemed—clouded glass. But no glass could be that hard!

"Ruth, is Canth awake yet?"

No. Menolly and Piemur are. They wonder where we are.

Jaxom crowed in triumph. "I think we'll go tell them!"

They were waiting for him and Ruth when they arrived from *between* in Cove Hold—the Harper, Menolly and Piemur. Over their babble of questions about his disappearance to Ruatha the night before, Jaxom tried to explain what he'd found. The Harper had to silence the babble with a huge bellow that stunned every fire-lizard into *between*. Having obtained silence, the Harper took a deep breath.

"Who could think or hear in such noise? Now, Menolly, get us some food! Piemur, get drawing materials. Zair, come here, my beautiful rascal. You've to take a message to Benden. You are to bite Mnementh's nose if necessary to wake him. Yes, I know you're brave enough to fight the big one. Don't fight! Wake! High time those lazy louts at Benden were up anyway!" The Harper was in great spirits, his head high, his eyes sparkling, his gestures broad. "By Shard and Shell, Jaxom, you've started a dull day with a bright promise. I was laggard in bed because there was nothing to rise for but more disappointment!"

"They may be as empty . . . ."

"You said the fire-lizards imaged the landing? People emerging? Those cylinders could be as empty as grudging forgiveness but they'd still be worth seeing. The actual ships which brought our ancestors from the Dawn Sisters to Pern!" The Harper expelled his breath slowly, his eyes brilliant with excitement.

"You're not too stimulated, are you, Master Robinton?" Jaxom asked, looking about for Sharra. "Where is Sharra?" He saw Menolly and Piemur running on their errands. Surely Sharra wasn't still asleep. He glanced among the fire-lizards for Meer and Talla.

"A dragonrider came for Sharra last evening. There's some illness at Southern and she was urgently needed. I've been selfish, I suppose, keeping you all about me when the real need is over. In fact," the Harper said, "I'm surprised to find you here and not at Ruatha still." Robinton's eyebrows arched as an invitation to explain.

"I should have been back in my Hold some time ago, Master Robinton," Jaxom admitted in a contrite tone, then he shrugged at his reluctance to leave the Cove. "Furthermore, it was snowing when I got there. Lord Lytol and I had a long talk . . . "

"There'd be no opposition to you taking Hold now," the Harper said with a laugh, "and no more hedging and hawing about lands and you being a dragon's rider." The Harper's eyes twinkled as he mimicked Lord Sangel's pinched tones. Then his face altered and he put his hand on Jaxom's shoulder. "How did Lytol react?"

"He wasn't surprised," Jaxom said, allowing his relief and wonder to color his voice. "And I've been thinking, sir, that if Nicat continues to excavate the Plateau buildings, someone with Lytol's gift for organizing . . . "

"My own thinking exactly, Jaxom," the Harper said, giving Jaxom another clout on the shoulder in his enthusiasm. "The past is a fit occupation for two old men . . . "

"Sir," Jaxom cried in outraged tones, "you'll never be old. Nor will Lytol!"

"Kind of you to think so, young Jaxom, but I've had warning. Ah, here comes a dragon—Canth, if I don't mistake in the sun's glare!" Robinton shielded his eyes with his hand.

The glare might also account for the frown on F'nor's face as he strode up the beach toward them. Zair had given him the most confused images, which had excited Berd, Grall and every fire-lizard in Benden Weyr to the point where Lessa had told Ramoth to banish the whole lot. In proof of which, the air above the Cove was filled with fair upon fair of fire-lizards, making a tremendous clamor.

"Ruth, settle them down," Jaxom asked his dragon. "We'll not be able to see or hear for fire-lizards."

Ruth gave such a bellow he startled himself and drew an awed whirl of Canth's eyes. The ensuing silence was broken by a frightened lone chirp. And the sky emptied of fire-lizards as they rapidly found perches on the tree-ringed beach.

They obeyed me. Ruth sounded amazed, and smug.

The display of control put F'nor in a considerably better frame of mind.

"Now, tell me what you've been up to so early in the morning,

Jaxom?" F'nor asked, loosening his flying belt and helmet. "It's getting so Benden can't turn around without Ruatha's assistance."

Jaxom peered intently at F'nor in surprise, but the brown rider gave him such a look that Jaxom realized F'nor was being exceptionally cryptic. Could he be referring to that damned egg? Had Brekke mentioned something to him?

"Why not?" he said in answer. "Benden and Ruatha have the strongest ties, F'nor. Blood, as well as mutual interest."

F'nor's expression turned from daunting to amused. He clipped Jaxom hard enough on the shoulder to make him lose balance.

"Well said, Ruatha, well said! So, what did you discover today?"

With no little satisfaction, Jaxom recounted his morning's labor, and F'nor's eyes widened with excitement.

"The ships they landed in? Let's go!" He tightened his belt, fastened his helmet and gestured for Jaxom to speed up his dressing. "We've Thread tomorrow at Benden, but, if this is as you say . . . "

"I'm coming, too," the Harper announced.

Not even the boldest fire-lizard chirped in the silence that followed that remark.

"I'm coming, too," Master Robinton repeated in a firm reasonable tone to override the protest he saw in every face. "I've missed too much. The suspense is very bad for me!" He placed his hand dramatically on his chest. "My heart pounds harder and harder with every passing moment that I'm forced to wait until you decide to send me dribbles and drabbles of tantalizing details." He held up his hand as Menolly recovered her wits and opened her mouth to speak. "I will do no digging. I will merely watch! But, I assure you that the vexation, not to mention the loneliness and suspense while you are off making Records, will put a totally unnecessary and dangerous strain on my poor heart. What if I collapsed from the tension, with no one here?"

"Master Robinton, if Brekke knew . . . " Menolly's protest was very weak.

F'nor covered his eyes with one hand and shook his head at the Harper's base tactics. "Give the man a finger and he'll take a length." Then he looked up and shook his finger at Robinton. "If you move a muscle, pick up a pinch of dirt, I'll . . . I'll . . . "

"I'll sit on him," Menolly finished, giving her Master such a fierce glare that he pretended to ward off her glance.

"Get my flying gear, Menolly, there's a dear child." The Harper, with a cajoling expression, gave her a gentle push toward the Hold. "And my writing case from the worktable in my study. I really will behave myself, F'nor, and I'm certain I wouldn't come to harm in such a short journey *between*. Menolly," he raised his voice to a carrying roar, "don't forget the half-sack of wine on my chair! It was bad enough yesterday being unable to see the Plateau buildings!"

As soon as Menolly returned with his requirements, the wine sack bouncing on her back, there was no more discussion. F'nor mounted the Harper and Piemur on Canth, leaving Jaxom to settle Menolly behind him on Ruth. Fleetingly he wished that Sharra were still here. He wondered if Ruth could bespeak her all the way to Southern and then restrained the impulse. Day had not yet dawned that far west. The two dragons ascended with a dense escort of fire-lizards. Ruth gave Canth the direction and, even as Jaxom worried that the Harper's action was very rash, they had gone *between* and were gliding toward the three peculiar hills.

Jaxom grinned with delight at the response to his discovery. Menolly's arms gripped him more tightly and she cried out an intricate arpeggio in her excitement. He could see the Harper gesticulating wildly, and hoped he had a good grip on F'nor's belt. Canth, never taking his eyes from the hole in the hill, veered to land as close to it as possible. They settled the Harper in the nearest spot of shade and had Jaxom ask Ruth to get the local fire-lizards to image things for himself and Zair while he admired their labors.

To the chirping conversation of fire-lizards, the others began to dig, Ruth standing to one side since Canth could move far more earth than he and there was only room for one dragon. Jaxom was keenly aware of an internal excitement that had been utterly lacking at the Plateau.

They dug perpendicularly now, for Jaxom had unearthed the top of the vehicle. Canth's enthusiasm often showered the Harper with clods of dirt as they worked down to the door area, but they'd been digging only a short time before the seam of the doorway, a fine crack in the otherwise smooth surface, came to light. F'nor had Canth shift the angle of excavation slightly to the right and very shortly the entire upper edge of the opening was uncovered.

Much encouraged, fire-lizards joined Canth and the riders, and dirt flew everywhere. When the opening was all but clear, they had also uncovered the rounded, leading edge of one of the stubby wings as well, proving, as the Harper was quick to point out, that the fire-lizards did recall accurately what their ancestors had seen. Once you could get them to remember, of course.

When the whole doorway had been cleared, the workers stood aside for the Harper to approach and examine it.

"I think we really had better contact Lessa and F'lar now. And it would be unkind in the extreme to exclude Master Fandarel. He might even be able to tell us what they constructed this ship of."

"That's enough people to know of this," F'nor said before the Harper could include any other names. "I'll go for the Master Smith myself. It'll spare time and prevent gossip. Canth will tell Ramoth." He rubbed sweat from his face and neck and the worst of the mud stains from his hands before he shrugged into his flying gear. "Don't any of you do anything while I'm gone!" he added, glaring at each one in turn and most fiercely at the Harper.

"I wouldn't know what to do," the Harper said in a reproving tone. "We shall take refreshment," he said, reaching for the wineskin and gesturing the others to sit around him.

The diggers welcomed a respite and a chance to contemplate the marvel they were unearthing.

"If they flew in those things . . . "

"If, my dear Piemur. No doubt obtains. They did. The fire-lizards saw those vehicles land," Master Robinton said.

"I started to say that if they flew in those things, why didn't they fly them away from the Plateau after the explosion?"

"A very good point."

"Well?"

"Perhaps Fandarel can answer, for I certainly can't," Robinton said truthfully, regarding the door with some chagrin.

"Maybe they'd need to take off from a height, the way a lazy dragon does," Menolly said, casting a sly glance at Jaxom.

"How long does it take F'nor to go *between*?" the Harper asked with a wistful sigh, squinting up at the bright sky for any sign of returning dragons.

"Takes longer to take off and land."

The Benden Weyrleaders arrived first, Canth with F'nor and Fandarel only a few seconds behind them so that all three dragons landed together. The Smith was first off Canth, rushing to the new wonder to run reverent hands over the curious surface, murmuring under his breath. F'lar and Lessa came striding through the long grasses, picking their way past dragon-strewn dirt; neither took their eyes from the softly shining doorway.

"*Aha!*" the Smith cried in sudden triumph, startling everyone. He'd been examining the rim of the doorway minutely. "Perhaps this is meant to move!" He dropped to his knees to the exposed right-hand corner. "Yes, if one excavated the entire vessel, this would probably be man-height! I think I ought to press." He put action to words and a small panel slid open to one side of the main door. It displayed a depression occupied by several colored circles.

Everyone crowded about him as his big fingers wiggled preparatorily and then hovered first over the upper rank of green circles. The bottom ones were red.

"Red has always meant danger, a convention we undoubtedly learned from the ancients," he said. "Green we will therefore try first!" His thick forefinger hesitated a moment longer and then stabbed at the green button.

At first nothing happened. Jaxom felt a clenching, like a cold hand on his guts, the prelude to intense disappointment.

"No, look, it's opening!" Piemur's keen eyes caught the first barely perceptible widening of the crack.

"It's old," the Smith said reverently. "A very old mechanism," he added as they all heard the faint protest of movement.

Slowly the door moved inward and then, astonishingly, it moved sideways, into the hull of the ship. A *whoosh* of rank air sent them reeling and gasping backward. When they looked again, the door was fully retracted, sunlight streaming onto flooring, darker than the ship's hull but, when the Smith rapped it with his knuckles, apparently made of the same peculiar material.

"Wait!" Fandarel restrained the others from entering. "Give fresh air a chance to circulate. Did anyone think to bring glows?"

"There're some at the Cove," Jaxom said, reaching for his flying gear and jamming his helmet on his head as he raced to Ruth. He never did bother to belt up and the frigid moment of *between* was a shocking cooler after the exertions of digging. He got as many glow baskets as he could carry. On his return, he realized no one seemed to have moved in his brief absence. Awe of the unknown beyond that great entrance had restrained them. Awe and perhaps, Jaxom decided, a reluctance to repeat the disappointment of the Plateau.

"Well, we will never know anything standing out here like numbwits," Robinton said, taking a glow basket from Jaxom and unshielding it as he strode forward into the ship.

It was mete, Jaxom thought, as he passed out the other baskets, that the Master Harper should have the honor of entering first. Fandarel, F'lar, F'nor and Lessa walked abreast through the opening. Jaxom grinned at Piemur and Menolly as they fell in behind.

Another great door, with circular wheel for locking thick bars ceiling and floor, lay open and inviting. Master Fandarel was making inarticulate noises of praise and awe as he touched the walls and peered at what looked to be control levers and more colored circles. As they penetrated further, they came upon two more doors, an open one on the left and one closed on their right which would lead, Fandarel was certain, to the rear, tube-encircled end of the vehicle. How could tubes make a cumbersome, snub-winged thing like this fly? He simply had to bring Benelek here, if no one else was to see it.

They all turned to the left and entered a long narrow corridor, their boots making muffled noises on the nonmetallic floor.

"More of the substance they used for pit supports, I think," Fandarel said, kneeling and pressing his fingers against the floor. "Ha, what was in these?" he asked, fingering brackets which were empty now. "Fascinating. And no dust."

"No air or wind to carry it in here for who knows how long,"

F'lar remarked in a quiet tone. "As in those rooms we discovered in Benden Weyr."

They moved along a corridor of doors, some open, some closed. None locked, for Piemur and Jaxom were able to peer into the emptied cubicles. Holes in the flooring and on the inside walls proved that there had been fittings.

"All of you, come here!" came the excited voice of the Harper, who had prowled ahead.

"No, here!" F'nor called from further beyond the Harper. "Here's where they must have controlled the ship!"

"No, F'nor, this is important to us!"

And F'lar seconded the Harper's vibrant claim.

As everyone gathered about the two, their glow baskets adding to the illumination, it was clear what had arrested their attention. The walls were covered with maps. In great detail, the familiar contours of Northern Pern and the not-so-familiar Southern Continent, all of it in its immensity, had been drawn eradicably on the wall.

With a sound—half-moan, half-shout—Piemur touched the map, tracing with his forefinger the coast which he had so arduously tramped, but which was only a small portion of the total shoreline.

"Look, Master Idarolan can sail almost to the Eastern Barrier Range . . . and it's not the same range I saw in the west. And . . ."

"Now what would this map represent?" F'nor asked, interrupting Piemur's excited comments. He was standing to one side, his glow basket lighting another chart of Pern. The outlines were the same, but the bands of different colors covered the familiar contours in puzzling configurations. The seas were depicted with varying shades of blue.

"That would indicate the depth of the water," Menolly said, running her fingers along what she knew was the Nerat Deep, here colored a deep blue. "Look, here are arrows to indicate the Great South Current. And here's the Western Stream."

"If that is so," the Harper said slowly, "then this ought to indicate the height of the land? No. For here where there should be mountains in Crom, Fort, Benden and Telgar, the color is the same as this part of the Telgar Plains. Most puzzling. Whatever could this have meant to the ancients?" He glanced from Northern to Southern spheres. "And none of that shade except this little bit here on the underside of the world. Perplexing. I shall have to study this!" He felt along the edges of the map, but it was evidently drawn on the wall itself.

"Here's one for Master Wansor's eyes," Fandarel said, apparently so engrossed in the section he was studying that he hadn't attended Robinton's words.

Piemur and Jaxom turned their glows toward the Smith.

"A star map!" the young Harper cried.

"Not quite," the Smith said.

"Is it a map of our stars?" Jaxom asked.

The Smith's big finger touched the largest circle, a brilliant orange with licking flames jagging out from its circumference.

"This is our sun. This must be the Red Star." His finger described the orbit about the sun which had been designated for the wanderer. He now touched the third, very small, round world. "This is our Pern!" He grinned at the others, for the humble size of their world.

"What's this then?" Piemur asked, putting his finger on a dark-colored world on the other side of the sun, away from the other planets and their described lines of orbit.

"I don't know. It ought to be on this side of the sun, as the other planets are!"

"And what do these lines mean?" Jaxom asked, having traced the arrowed lines from the bottom of the chart to the Red Star and then off the edge of the chart on the far right.

"Fascinating," was all the Mastersmith would allow, rubbing his chin as he stared at the enigmatic drawings.

"I prefer this map," Lessa said, smiling with a great deal of satisfaction at the two continents.

"You do?" F'lar asked, turning from his examination of the star map. "Ah, yes, I take your point," he said as he watched her hand cover the western section. Then he laughed. "Yes, I quite agree, Lessa. Very instructive."

"How can that be?" Piemur asked with some scorn. "It's not accurate. Look," he pointed, "there's no sea volcanoes beyond the Plateau cliffs. And there's far too much shore in this section of the South. And no Great Bay. It doesn't go like that. I know. I've walked it."

"No, the map isn't accurate anymore," the Harper said before Lessa could level a criticism at Piemur. "Notice Tillek. There's a good deal more of the northern peninsula than there should be. And no mark for the volcano on the south shore." Then he added with a deep smile, "But I suspect the map was accurate, when it was drawn!"

"Of course," Lessa said in a cry of triumph. "All the Passes, each one stressing our poor world, caused upheaval and destruction . . . "

"See, this spur of land, where the Dragon Stones are now?" Menolly cried. "My great-grandsire remembers the land falling into the sea!"

"No matter that there have been minor changes," Fandarel said, dismissing these casually, "the maps are superb discoveries." He frowned again at the one with the anomalous shadings. "That shade of brown designates our first settlements in the North. See, Fort Hold, then Ruatha, Benden, Telgar," he looked at F'lar and Lessa, "and the Weyrs. They all are placed in this same coloration. Is that what it means, perhaps? Places where people could settle?"

"But they settled the Plateau first of all, and it's not that same brown," Piemur said, disgruntled.

"We must seek Master Wansor's opinion. And Master Nicat's."

"I'd like to see Benelek look over the controls by the doors and perhaps investigate the rear of the ship," F'nor said.

"My dear brown rider," the Smith said, "Benelek is very clever with mechanical things but these . . . " His broad gesture indicated that the highly advanced technology on the ship was well beyond his apprentice's skill.

"Perhaps one day, we will know enough to fathom all the ships' mysteries," F'lar said, smiling with intense pleasure as he tapped the maps. "But these . . . are current and exceedingly valuable to us, and Pern." He paused to grin at Master Robinton, who nodded his head in comprehension, and Lessa, who continued to smile, her eyes dancing with a mischief only the three seemed to share. "And, for the time being, no mention is to be made of them!" He was stern now, and held up his hand when Fandarel began to protest. "A short time only, Fandarel. I have very good reason. Wansor must certainly see these equations and drawings. And Benelek can puzzle what he may. As he talks only to inanimate objects, he's no risk to the necessary secrecy I feel we must impose on these ships. Menolly and Piemur are harper-bound, and you've already proved your discretion and abilities, Jaxom." F'lar's glance, direct and intense, caused Jaxom an inner pang because he was certain then that the Benden Weyrleader did know of his episode with the dratted egg. "There's going to be quite enough to confuse Hold, Craft, and Weyr on that Plateau without adding these riddles." His eyes went back to the broad expanse of the Southern Continent and, as he shook his head slowly, his smile and those of the Harper and Lessa increased. Suddenly a shocked expression crossed his face, and he looked up. "Toric! He said he'd be here today, to help excavate."

"Yes, and N'ton was to collect me," Fandarel said, "but not for an hour yet or more. I was dragged from my couch by F'nor . . . "

"And Southern is in Telgar's time area. Good! However, I want a copy of this map. Which of you three can we best spare today?" he asked.

"Jaxom!" the Harper said quickly. "He copies neatly and when the rider came for Sharra last evening, Jaxom had gone to Ruatha. Besides, it is wise to keep Ruth apart. The local fire-lizards will bear him company here and not chatter to Toric's trio."

The matter was quickly decided and Jaxom left with copying materials and all the glows. A screen of branches was contrived to hide the opening from any chance observer. Ruth was asked to entice the local fire-lizards to him and hopefully get them to nap. Because the morning's exertions had tired Ruth, he was quite willing to curl up in the sun and sleep. The others departed to Cove Hold and Jaxom began to copy this peculiarly significant map.

As he worked, he tried to figure out why it had so pleased the Weyrleaders and Master Robinton. To be sure, it was a gift to know the extent of Southern without having to walk it all.

Was that it? Of course. Toric didn't know how large the Southern Continent was! And now the Weyrleaders did. Jaxom regarded the Hold peninsula, estimating how much Toric and his holdless men had managed to explore. Never could Toric, even with his Hold swollen by younger sons from every Hold and cothold in Northern Pern, explore this vast continent. Why, even if he tried to Hold as far as the Western Range in the south, to the Great Bay in the West . . . Jaxom smiled, so pleased with his deduction that he nearly smeared the line he was drawing. Should he mark in the Great Bay as they now knew it, or copy the old map faithfully? Yes, it was this one that mattered. And when Toric finally saw it . . . Jaxom chuckled, imagining with intense pleasure the chagrin which Toric would feel at first sight.

•• **C H A P T E R   X X I** ••

🐦

Next Day at the Mountain, Cove Hold, and the Southern Hatching Ground, 15.10.21

"**I** know what was originally conceded to Toric," Robinton was saying to the Benden Weyrleaders as they sat drinking klah at Cove Hold.

"To Hold what he had acquired when the Oldtimers left the Southern Weyr," F'lar amended. "The pursuit would argue that, as the Oldtimers have not indeed all passed *between*, Toric may continue to extend his Holding."

"Or secure the loyalty of others in Holding?" Robinton remarked.

Lessa stared at him, absorbing his meaning. "Was that why he was amenable to settling so many holdless men?" She looked indignant for a moment and then laughed. "Toric is a man we shall have to watch these next Turns. I'd no idea he'd prove so ambitious."

"Farsighted, too," Robinton said in a dry tone. "He achieves as much by gratitude as by possession."

"Gratitude has a tendency to sour," F'lar said.

"He's not fool enough to rely on that alone," Lessa said with a rueful expression then looked about her, puzzled. "Did I see Sharra at all this morning?"

"No, a rider collected her last evening. There's illness at—oh!" The Harper's eyes widened to emphasize his surprised dismay. "Now there's no fool like an old one. It never occurred to me to doubt that message. Yes, he'd use Sharra, and his other sisters. He has several daughters as well to bind men to him. Jaxom will react to this situation, I think."

"I hope so," Lessa said with some asperity. "I rather approve of

795

Sharra as a match. If this is not a simple case of his being grateful for her nursing . . ." She clucked her tongue at the mention of gratitude.

Robinton laughed. "Brekke feels, and so does Menolly, that the attachment is sincere on both sides. I'm delighted you agree. I've been daily hoping he would ask me to officiate. Especially in view of today's reflections. By the way, only it isn't exactly by the way but to our point, Jaxom went back to Ruatha Hold last evening. He approached Lytol on the subject of his confirmation as Lord Holder."

"Did he?" F'lar was as pleased as his weyrmate. "Prompted by Sharra? Or by Toric's not-too-subtle jibing yesterday?"

"I missed far too much not being permitted to go the Plateau yesterday," the Harper said irritably. "What jibing?"

The bugling of Ramoth and Mnementh outside effectively prevented further discussion.

"N'ton's here, with Master Nicat and Wansor," F'lar said. He turned to Robinton and Lessa as he rose. "Shall we just let matters proceed naturally?"

"That's usually best," Robinton said.

Lessa smiled cryptically as she stroke toward the door.

N'ton had brought three journeymen miners as well as their Master. F'nor arrived immediately thereafter with Wansor, Benelek and two young apprentices apparently chosen for their generous size. Without waiting for Toric to appear with D'ram, they all went *between* to the Plateau, landing as close to Nicat's little mound as possible. Daylight provided the answer to its function—numerals and letters paraded as design across the far end, and rather fascinating animals, large and small and bearing no resemblance to anything walking Pern's surface, marched across the two long walls.

"A harper's room, for the very young learning first Teaching Songs and Ballads," the Harper said, not nearly as disappointed as the other since the building applied to his Craft.

"Well, then," Benelek added and, turning on his heel, pointed to the mound immediately on the left. "This is where the advanced students would be. If, of course," he sound dubious, "the ancients followed a logical sequence and progressed to the right in any circular formation." He executed a curt bow to the Weyrleaders and the three Craftmasters and, gesturing to one of the apprentices, marched decisively out, picked a shovel from the pile and proceeded to cut the grass from the inner end of the chosen mount.

Lessa, waiting until Benelek was out of hearing, gave way to laughter. "And if the ancients disappoint him, will he bother with any more mysteries?"

"It's time to unearth my large mound today," F'lar said, trying to imitate Benelek's decisiveness as he gestured the others to pick up tools and join him.

Bearing in mind that the entrances tended to be on the short ends, they abandoned F'lar's original trench on the roof. Ramoth and Mnementh obligingly shifted enormous mounds of the curious gray-black soil from the center of the end. The entrance was shortly revealed as a door, large enough to admit a green dragon, sliding on rails; a smaller opening pierced one corner. "Man size," F'lar said. It opened on hinges that were not of metal, a fact which delighted and puzzled Masters Nicat and Fandarel. Just as they opened the small door, Jaxom and Ruth arrived. No sooner had they landed on the mound's top, than three more dragons burst into the air.

"D'ram," Lessa said, "and two Benden browns that went south to help."

"Sorry to take so long, Master Robinton," Jaxom said, handing the Harper a neat roll as if it were of no moment. "Good morning, Lessa. What was in Nicat's building?"

The Harper tucked the roll carefully in his belt pouch, please with Jaxom's dissembling. "A children's hall. Go take a look."

"Could I have a word with you, Master Robinton. Unless . . ." Jaxom waved his hands toward the mound and the little door hanging so invitingly open.

"I can wait until the air is cleared out," Robinton said, having noticed the tense look in Jaxom's eyes and his air of polite entreaty. He moved with the young man to one side of the others. "Yes?"

"Sharra is being restrained at Southern by her brother," Jaxom said in a low voice that did not reveal his agitation.

"However did you find that out?" Robinton asked, glancing up at the circling bronze that bore the Southerner.

"She told Ruth. Toric has plans for her to marry one of his new holders. He considers the Northern lordlings useless!" There was a dangerous glint in Jaxom's eyes and a sternness to his features which, for the first time since Robinton had known the lad, gave him the look of his father, Fax, a resemblance which afforded Robinton some small pleasure.

"Some of the lordlings undoubtedly are," Robinton replied, amused. "What have you in mind, Jaxom?" he added, for there was no answering response to his drollery in the grim-faced young man. Somehow, the Harper had failed to appreciate the maturing that had occurred in Ruatha's Lord Holder during the past eventful two seasons.

"I intend to get her back," Jaxom said in a quiet firm tone, and gestured to Ruth. "Toric forgot to reckon with Ruth."

"You'd fly into Southern and just carry her off?" Robinton asked, trying to keep his expression straight, though Jaxom's romantic manner made it difficult.

"Why not?" Suddenly the glint of humor was restored to Jaxom's eyes. "I doubt if Toric expects me to take direct action. I'm one of those useless Northern lordlings!"

"Ah, but not before you receive some direct action yourself, I fancy," Robinton said with a quick undertone.

Toric and his group had dismounted in the clear space between two of the mound ranks. He had left his people to sort themselves out and, stripping off his flying gear, was striding toward Lessa and those clustered about the mound door. But, after giving her a greeting, he changed directions and there was no doubt his goal was Jaxom.

"Harper!" he said, coming to a halt with a courteous nod for Robinton before he looked at Jaxom.

To Robinton's pleasure, Ruatha's Lord did not so much as straighten his shoulders or turn to face Toric.

"Holder Toric," Jaxom said over his shoulder in a cool indifferent greeting. The title, which was certainly proper as Toric has never been invited to take full rank by the other Lord Holders of Pern, brought the Southerner up short. His eyes narrowed as he looked keenly at Jaxom.

"Lord Jaxom." Toric's drawl made an insult of that title, implying that it was not fully Jaxom's as yet.

Jaxom turned slowly toward him. "Sharra tells me," he said, noting as Robinton did the surprise twitch of Toric's eye muscles, and a quick darting glance at the fire-lizards about Ruth, "that you do not favor an alliance with Ruatha."

"No, lordling. I do not!" Toric flicked a glance at the Harper, a broad smile on his face. "She can do better than a table-sized Hold in the North." The last word held contemptuous emphasis.

"What did I hear. Toric?" Lessa asked, her voice light but with a hint of steel in her eyes as she squarely ranged herself beside Jaxom.

"Holder Toric has other plans for Sharra," Jaxom said, his tone more amused than aggrieved. "She can do better, it seems, than a table-sized Hold like Ruatha."

"I mean no offense to Ruatha," Toric said quickly when he caught the flicker of anger in Lessa's face, though the Weyrwoman continued to smile.

"That would be most unwise, considering my pride in my Bloodline and in the present Holder of that title," she said in the most casual tone.

"Surely, you might reconsider the matter, Toric," Robinton said, as affable as ever despite the palpable warning he conveyed that the Southerner was on very dangerous ground. "Such an alliance, so much desired by the two young people, would have considerable advantages for you, I think, aligning yourself with one of the most prestigious Holds on Pern."

"And be in favor with Benden," Lessa said, smiling so sweetly that Robinton almost chuckled at the man's predicament.

Toric stood there, absently rubbing the back of his neck, his smile slightly diminished.

"We should discuss the matter. At some length, I think." Lessa tucked her arm in Toric's and turned him about. "Master Robinton, will you join us? I think that little cot of mine would be an admirable spot in which to talk undisturbed."

"I thought we were here to dig up Pern's glorious past," Toric said, with a good-natured laugh. But he did not disengage his arm from Lessa's.

"There's surely no time like the present," Lessa continued at her sweetest, "to discuss the future. Your future."

F'lar had joined them, falling in step at Lessa's left, apparently aware through the link between Mnementh and Lessa of what had just occurred. The Harper shot a reassuring look over his shoulder to Jaxom but the young man was looking at his dragon.

"Yes, with so many ambitious holdless men pouring into Southern," F'lar said smoothly, "we've been remiss in making certain you'll have the lands you want, Toric. I don't fancy blood feuds in the South. Unnecessary, too, when there's space enough for this generation and several more."

Toric's answer was a full-bodied laugh and although he had adjusted his stride to match Lessa's, he still gave Robinton the impression of invulnerable self-assurance.

"And since there's so much space, why should I not be ambitious for my sister?"

"You've more than one, and we're not talking of Jaxom and Sharra just now," Lessa added with a hint of irritability as she dismissed the irrelevant. "F'lar and I had intended to arrange a more formal occasion to set your Holding," she went on, gesturing on the ancient, empty structure in which they now stood. "but there's Master Nicat wanting to formalize Minecrafthall affairs, and Lord Groghe is anxious that his two sons do not hold adjacent lands, and other questions have come up recently which require answers."

"Answers?" Toric asked politely as he leaned against one wall and crossed his arms on his chest.

Robinton began to wonder just how much of that pose of indolence was assumed. Was Toric's ambition going to overpower good sense?

"One answer required is how much land any one man should Hold in the South?" F'lar said, idly digging dirt from under his thumbnail with his knife point. He had lightly emphasized the *one*.

"And? Our original agreement was that I could Hold all the lands I had acquired by the time the Oldtimers had passed on."

"Which, in truth, they haven't," Robinton said.

Toric agreed to that. "I shan't insist on waiting," he admitted with a slight inclination of his head, "since the original circumstances have altered. And, since my Hold is thoroughly disorganized by the indigent and hopeful lordlings, and holdless men and boys, I am reliably informed that others have eschewed our help and landed wherever their ships be beached."

"All the more reason to be sure you are not deprived of one length of your just Hold," F'lar said. "I know that you have sent out exploring teams. How far have they actually penetrated?"

"With the help of D'ram's dragonriders," Toric said as Robinton noticed how keenly he watched F'lar's face to see if this unexpected assistance was known to Benden, "we have extended our knowledge of the terrain to the foot of the Western Range."

"That far?" The bronze rider appeared surprised and perhaps a trifle alarmed.

Robinton knew from that auspiciously discovered map that, while the area from the sea to the Western Range was immense, it was but a small segment of the total area of the vast Southern Continent.

"And, of course, Peimur reached the Great Desert Bay to the west," Toric was saying.

"My dear Toric, how can you possibly Hold all that?" F'lar seemed politely concerned.

"I've small cotholders with burgeoning families along most of the habitable shoreline, and at strategic points in the interior. The men you sent me these past few Turns proved most industrious." Toric's smile was more assured.

"I suspect they have pledged loyalty to you in return for your original generosity?" F'lar asked with a sigh.

"Naturally."

Lessa laughed. "I thought when we met at Benden that you were a shrewd and independent man."

"There's more land, my dear Weyrwoman, for any man who can hold it. Some small holds could turn out to be far more valuable than larger spreads, in the eyes of those who truly appreciate their worth."

"I'd say then," Lessa went on, pointedly ignoring Toric's allusion to Ruatha's size, "that you'll have more than enough to occupy you fully and to hold, from sea to Western Range to the Great Bay . . ."

Suddenly Toric straightened. Lessa had been looking at F'lar, obliquely seeking his approval for what she granted Toric, so it was only Robinton who caught the full alertness, the look of intense surprise and displeasure in the Southerner's eyes. He recovered himself quickly.

"To the Great Bay in the West, yes, that is my hope. I do have maps. In my Hold, but if I've your leave . . ."

He had taken one stride to the door when Ramoth's bugle halted him. And as Mnementh chimed in, F'lar moved swiftly to block his way.

"It's already too late, Toric."

As Jaxom watched the Benden Weyrleaders and the Harper walk toward the excavated house with Toric, he expelled with a deep breath the anger he had contained for Toric's belittling manner.

" 'Ruatha a table-sized Hold?' " Indeed! Ruatha, the second oldest and certainly one of the most prosperous Holds on Pern. If Lessa hadn't come then, he'd have shown—

Jaxom took another breath. Toric had the height and reach of him. He'd have been slaughtered by the Southerner if Lessa hadn't interfered and saved him from sheer folly. It had never occurred to Jaxom that Toric might not be honored by an alliance with Ruatha. He'd been stunned when Ruth had informed him of Sharra's contact— that she had been lured back to Southern—and told that Toric would not countenance a marriage for her in the North. Nor would Toric listen to Sharra's avowal of a true attachment to Jaxom. So he had set his queen on her two fire-lizards to keep her from sending messages to Jaxom. Toric hadn't known that Sharra could talk to Ruth, something she had done as soon as she'd awakened that morning. There was a hint of amusement in Ruth's tone for the secret exchange.

Jaxom waited until the four had entered the little dwelling before he moved to Ruth. "Fly into Southern and carry her off," the Harper had said in jest, but that was exactly what Jaxom intended.

"Ruth," he asked in his mind as he closed the distance between them, "are there any fire-lizards of Toric's about you?"

No! We are going to rescue Sharra? Where shall I tell her to meet us? We've only been to the Hatching Grounds in Southern. Shall I ask Ramoth?

"I'd prefer not to involve the Benden dragons in this. We'll go to the Hatching Ground. That egg is coming in useful to us after all," he added, appreciating the irony of the situation as he vaulted to Ruth's back. "Give her the picture, Ruth. Ask her if she can reach the place?"

She says yes.

"Let's get there then!"

Jaxom began laughing openly as Ruth took them *between*.

They came in low from the east, just as they had not quite a Turn before. Now, however, the ring of warm sand was unoccupied. Only briefly, for fire-lizards swooped down in cheerful greeting.

"Toric's?" Jaxom asked, wondering if he should dismount and search for Sharra.

She comes! Toric's queen is with her. Go away! You displease me, watching my friends!

Jaxom had no time to be astonished by his dragon's fierce attitude.

Sharra, trailing a blanket which she was endeavoring to wrap about her thinly clad body, came running across the Ground. She pelted toward him, her expression anxious, and she almost tripped on an edge of her blanket as she looked back over her shoulder.

She says two of Toric's men are after her. Ruth half-sprang, half-glided toward Sharra, while Jaxom leaned down, holding his hands out to catch her and swing her onto Ruth's neck. Two men, swords drawn, came tearing onto the Ground. But Ruth launched himself, leaving the two men swearing helplessly at them as the Ground dropped away. The watchdragon of the Southern Weyr called out to Ruth, who replied in a greeting as he beat upward on the warm air.

"I think your brother has miscalculated, Sharra."

"Take me away from here, Jaxom. Take me to Ruatha! I've never been so furious in all my life. I never want to see that brother of mine again. Of all the devious, misguided . . ."

"We have to see your brother again, for I'm not hiding from him. We'll have it out in the open today!"

"Jaxom!" There was real concern in Sharra's voice now. She clutched him tightly about the waist. "He'd kill you in a fight."

"Our affair will cause no duel, Sharra," Jaxom said with a laugh. "Bundle yourself well in that blanket. Ruth will take us *between* as quick as he can!"

"Jaxom, I hope you know what you're doing!"

Ruth took them back to the Plateau, caroling a greeting as he circled down.

"Oh, I'm frozen, but they took my flying gear away," Sharra cried. Her bare legs on Ruth's neck were blue with chill. Jaxom leaned over to rub warmth into them. "And there's Toric. With Lessa, F'lar and Robinton!"

"And the largest of the Benden dragons!"

"Jaxom!"

"Your brother does things his way, I do them in mine. In mine!"

"Jaxom!" There was surprise as well as respect in her voice and her arms tightened again about his waist.

Ruth landed and when they had dismounted, he walked to Jaxom's left as the two young lovers went to meet the others. Toric no longer wore his customary smile.

"Toric, you cannot contain Sharra anywhere on Pern where Ruth and I cannot find her!" Jaxom said after the barest of nods to the Benden Weyrleaders and the Harper. There was no hint of compromise in Toric's hard expression. Nor did he expect it. "Place and time are no barriers to Ruth. Sharra and I can go anywhere, anywhen on Pern."

A piteously crying queen fire-lizard attempted to land on Toric's shoulder, but the man brushed her away.

"Further, fire-lizards obey Ruth! Don't they, my friend?" Jaxom rested his hand on Ruth's headknob. "Tell every fire-lizard here on the Plateau to go away!"

Ruth did so, adding as the wide meadow was suddenly empty of the little creatures, that they didn't wish to leave.

Toric's eyes narrowed slightly at that show of ability. Then the fire-lizards were back. This time he permitted his little queen to land on his shoulder, but his eyes held Jaxom's.

"How did you know Southern? I was informed that you've never been there!" He made a half-turn as if to accuse Lessa and F'lar of complicity.

"Your informant erred," Jaxom said, wondering if it had been Dorse. "Today is not the first time I've retrieved something from the Southern Weyr which belongs to the North." He laid his arm possessively about Sharra's shoulders.

Toric's composure deserted him. "*You!*" He extended his arm, pointing at Jaxom; his face was a mixture of anger, indignant outrage, disappointment, frustration and, lastly, a grudging respect. "*You* took the egg back! You and that . . . but the fire-lizards' images were black!"

"I'd be stupid not to darken a white hide if I make a night pass, wouldn't I?" Jaxom asked with understandable scorn.

"I knew it wasn't one of T'ron's riders," Toric cried, his fists clenching and unclenching. "But for you to . . . Well now," and Toric's whole attitude changed radically. He began to smile again, a trifle sourly as he looked at the Benden Weyrleaders and then the Harper. Then he started to laugh, losing anger and frustration in that laughter. "If you knew, Lordling . . ." again he pointed fiercely at Jaxom, "the plans you ruined, the . . . How many people knew it was you?" Now he did turn accusingly on the dragonriders.

"Not many," Robinton said, wondering quickly if indeed Lessa and F'lar had ever guessed.

"I knew," Sharra said, "and so did Brekke. Jaxom worried about that egg the whole time he was fevered." Her gaze on his face was proud.

"Not that it matters now," Jaxom said. "What does matter is, do I now have your permission to marry Sharra and make her lady of Ruatha Hold?"

"I don't see how I can stop you." Toric's broad gesture of frustration took in the people and the dragons.

"Indeed you couldn't, for Jaxom's boast about Ruth's abilities is valid," F'lar said. "One must never underestimate a dragonrider, Toric." Then he grinned without softening the implicit warning. "Especially a Northern dragonrider."

"I shall bear that firmly in mind," Toric said, the intensity of his big voice indicating his chagrin. The affable grin reappeared on his face. "Especially in our present discussion. Before these impetuous youngsters interrupted us, we were discussing the extent of my Hold, were we not?"

He turned his back on Sharra and Jaxom, and gestured to the others to return to their temporary hall.

·· A F T E R W O R D ··

Spring had come again to Northern Pern and Ruatha Hold. Once the winter's damages had been repaired and the first crops set, there had been great business on the Hold itself, all aimed to have the old place look its best on the one spring morning when Wansor's equations said no Thread would fall anywhere but harmlessly far to the west at sea.

Ruatha's walls were scrubbed, its paving brightly sealed, and this day banners hung from every unshuttered window while flowers decked every corner of the courts and the Hall. Southern vines had been flown in the night before to garland the fire-heights. The broad meadows below the Hold proper were covered with tents and divided into fields for the runner beasts of the guests. Dragons began to arrive, greeted by the old brown watchdragon, Wilth, who would surely be hoarse from bugling welcome before the ceremonies began.

Fire-lizards were everywhere and had to be constantly called to order by dragon and friend. But the atmosphere was so relaxed, so jubilant, that pranks and antics, human or creature, were amicably tolerated.

To cater to so many guests, half Pern north and south it seemed, Fort Hold and Weyr, as well as Benden, had joined kitchen staffs with Ruatha. Toric had obligingly sent from Southern meadows dragonloads of fresh fruit, fish, wild bucks and wherries whose flesh was prized for its tender gamey taste, so distinct from Northern meats. Great roasting, baking and steaming pits had been in operation since the previous evening, the aromas commingling to set mouths watering.

There had been festivities the night before, dancing and singing until early morning, for traders had arrived well in advance, no one minding the multiple uses of this occasion. Now more people poured up the roads, flew down from the skies as the momentous hour for the ceremonious confirmation of the young Lord of Ruatha Hold drew close.

The Harper comes, Ruth told Jaxom and Sharra as the white dragon pushed open the doors of his weyr and stepped into his courtyard.

Jaxom and Sharra, in the main room of their ground-level apartment, heard his joyous bugle of welcome, just as if he hadn't said goodnight to the Harper in the early hours of that morning.

Lioth says for you to wait here. Harper and N'ton want to speak to you without other ears.

Jaxom turned to Sharra in surprise.

"Oh, it can't be anything untoward, Jaxom," she said, smiling. "Master Robinton would have told us last night. I still think that tunic is too tight across your chest."

"All the spring digging at Ship Meadow, my love," Jaxom said, inhaling so that the fabric of his brown tunic strained at the seams.

"If you split this new material, you'll have to wear it mended!" She smiled as she spoke her scold then kissed him.

Sharra's kisses were to be enjoyed whenever possible, so he held her tightly.

"Jaxom! I will not go mussed to your Confirmation."

Ramoth and Mnementh are here! Ruth rose on his haunches to bugle a sufficiently honorable greeting.

"You'd think he was the one being Confirmed as Lord Holder," Sharra said, her rich voice filled with laughter.

"It's been a joint effort," Jaxom said, grinning broadly. He hugged her swiftly just once more, relieved that the winter's uncertainty had given way to spring.

He'd never been busier: managing the Hold and delving into the ancient mysteries of the Plateau and the Ship Meadow whenever he could spare a few hours. Lytol, as Jaxom had hoped, had found himself tremendously involved in the excavations, spending more and more time with the Harper at Cove Hold. With his Confirmation now a certainty, Jaxom had been admitted to the inner councils of the Lord Holders, as much because of his association with Toric as his own rank. Jaxom doubted that Toric would tolerate much more of the conservatism that dominated the Lord Holders' attitudes to anything. Larad of Telgar Hold, Asgenar of Lemos, Begamon and Sigomel seemed more of Toric's mind, and Jaxom found himself willing to be ranked with them rather than side with Groghe, Sangel and some of the older men. Some of the old Lord Holders simply didn't understand the needs of today—nor the call of the vast Southern lands with their infinite variety and challenge.

Today's formalities were token and excuse for a gathering of Weyr, Craft and Hold, a festival of the end of the cold months of the Turn, a happy day when no Thread fell on any part of Pern.

Lioth landed in the small kitchen courtyard, Ruth backing into his quarters to give the great bronze dragon sufficient space. The Harper slid from his shoulder, waving a thick roll, and N'ton's crack-faced grin indicated they had news of great import.

"Lessa and F'lar must hear our news, too," N'ton said, as he and the Harper joined the young Holders. "They're just coming now." He signaled Lioth to the fire-heights.

The two men removed their flying jackets, Robinton never relinquishing hold on the roll as he did so. They watched with growing impatience as first golden Ramoth and then bronze Mnementh discharged their passengers and ascended to the fire-heights to join Lioth.

"Well, Harper, Mnementh says you're bursting with news," F'lar said, handing Jaxom his flying gear as Sharra assisted Lessa.

"Indeed I am, Benden," and the Harper exaggerated each syllable, brandishing his roll in emphasis.

"So, what have you here?" Lessa asked.

"Nothing but the key to that colored map in the ship!" the Harper said, grinning at their response. "Piemur figured it out, working with Nicat, because we had the feeling it had something to do with the lay of the land. It does! The rock underneath the land, to be precise." He was unrolling the map with Lessa and F'lar holding corners. "These dark-brown patches indicate very old rock, in places that have never known earthquake or volcanic action. Never changed from this map to our present ones. The Plateau, shaded here as yellow, obviously had to be abandoned because of the eruption. See, here and here on the south and in Tillek, we have the same coloration. My dear friends, the ancients came to the North, to Fort, Ruatha, Benden, Telgar, because that land was safer from natural disasters!"

"Thread being an unnatural disaster?" Lessa asked in a droll voice.

"I prefer to cope with my disasters one at a time," F'lar said. "Being attacked from the ground and the air would be a bit much!"

"Then Nicat and Piemur have also deduced where the ancients discovered metals, black water and black stone. The deposits are clearly marked both North and South! We've already worked many of the Northern mines."

"More in the South?" F'lar asked, deeply interested. "Show me!"

Robinton pointed to half a dozen small markings. "How rich the deposits are is not yet known but I'm sure Nicat will tell us soon enough. He and Piemur make a potent team."

"How many mines are in Toric's Hold?" F'lar asked.

N'ton chuckled. "No more than he's already discovered and produced. There're far more to be worked in dragonrider country," he said, tapping the southeast. "When this Pass is over, I think I'll turn miner!"

"When this Pass is over . . ." F'lar echoed the words, his eyes catching the Harper's, suddenly aware that neither of them were likely to see that moment.

"When this Pass is over," Jaxom said eagerly, his eyes scanning the map, "people can begin to concentrate on what we've found at the Plateau, too, and in those ships. We can rediscover the South! Maybe even solve the mystery of the ships—and how we can get dragons to cross that airless void to the Dawn Sisters . . ." Jaxom's gaze went to the southeast, to beacons now hidden from his sight.

"And how to wipe out forever the threat of Thread from the Red Star itself," Sharra said in a whisper.

F'lar gave a rueful laugh, brushing from his forehead the lock of hair, now gray-streaked, that fell across his eyes. "I once thought to reach the Red Star. Maybe you young people won't find it so daunting a task once we've caught up on what men used to know."

"Don't belittle your accomplishments, F'lar," Robinton said sternly. "You've kept Pern Threadfree and united . . . in spite of itself!"

"Why, if it hadn't been for you," Lessa said, looking about her, eyes flashing angrily for F'lar's self-denigration, "none of this would have happened!" Her gesture meant Ruatha bannered for a happy day and secure in the knowledge that no Thread would mar the occasion anywhere.

"LORD JAXOM!" Lytol's bellow rang clearly from an upper window of Ruatha Hold.

"Sir?"

"Benden? Fort? The other Weyrleaders and all the Lord Holders of Pern, North and South, have gatherd!"

Jaxom waved his hand in acknowledgment of the summons. F'lar rolled up the map and handed it back to Robinton with a bow.

"I'll examine it more closely later, Robinton."

Jaxom offered his arm to his Lady Sharra and would have gestured for the Master Harper and the dragonriders to precede them.

"By no means, it's your day, Lord Jaxom of Ruatha Hold," the Harper said, and he bowed low, his arm coming up with a flourish to indicate the honor of precedence.

Laughing, Jaxom and Sharra strode out into the court, N'ton and Robinton behind them. F'lar presented his arm to Lessa but she had turned her eyes about the small kitchen courtyard and it wasn't hard for the bronze rider to sense her thoughts.

"It's your day, too, Lessa," he said, taking her hand to his lips. "A day your determination and spirit made possible!" He turned her into his arms and made her look up at him. "Ruathan Blood Holds Ruatha lands today!"

"Which proves," she said, pretending to be haughty though her body was pliant against his, "that if you try hard enough, and work long enough, you can achieve anything you desire!"

"I hope you're right," F'lar said, unerringly turning his gaze toward the Red Star. "One day dragonriders will conquer that Star!"

"*BENDEN!*" The Harper's roar startled their private moment of triumph.

Grinning like errant children, Lessa and F'lar crossed the kitchen courtyard and raced up the steps to the Great Hall. The dragons on the fire-heights rose to their haunches, bugling their jubilation on this happy day while fire-lizards executed dizzy patterns in the Thread-free sky!

DRAGONDEX

The Weyrs in Order of Founding

Fort Weyr   Ista Weyr

Benden Weyr   Telgar Weyr

High Reaches Weyr   Southern Weyr

Igen Weyr

Pernese Oaths

By the Egg   By the shards of my dragon's egg

By the first Egg   Shells

By the Egg of Faranth   Through Fall, Fog, and Fire

Scorch it   Shards

Some Terms of Interest

agenothree: a common chemical on Pern, HNO_3. Agenothree fuels the flamethrowers used by groundcrews to burn Thread, and traditionally carried by riders of the queens' wings.

Belior: Pern's larger moon

between: an area of nothingness and and sensory deprivation between here and there

Dawn Sisters: a trio of stars visible from Pern; also called Day Sisters

Day Sisters: a trio of stars visible from Pern; also called Dawn Sisters

deadglow: a numbskull, stupid. Derived from "glow."

Dragon: the winged, fire-breathing creature that protects Pern from Thread. Dragons were originally developed by the early colonists of Pern, before they lost the ability to manipulate DNA. A dragon is hatched from an egg, and becomes empathically and telepathically bound to its rider for the duration of its life.

> **Green:** Female (20–24 meters). The smallest and most numerous of the dragons. Light, highly maneuverable and agile, the greens are the sprinters of dragonkind. They breathe short bursts of flame. Greens are rendered sterile through a sex-linked disability triggered by chronic use of firestone.
>
> **Blue:** Male (24–30 meters). The workhorse of the dragons. Medium-sized, the blues are as tough as the greens but not as maneuverable. They have more stamina under pressure and are capable of sustaining flame longer.
>
> **Brown:** Male (30–40 meters). Larger than greens and blues, some well-grown browns are as big as smaller bronzes and could actually mate with the queens if they so dared. The browns are the real wheel-horses of the dragons, reasonably agile and strong enough to go a whole Fall without faltering. They are more intelligent than blues or greens, with greater powers of concentration. Browns and their riders sometimes act as Weyrlingmasters, training the young dragons and riders.
>
> **Bronze:** Male (35–45 meters). The leaders of the dragons. All bronzes compete to mate with the gold queens; the rider whose dragon succeeds becomes Weyrleader. Bronzes are generally trained for leadership and assume Wingleader and Wingsecond positions along with browns. Bronzes and their riders often act as Weyrlingmasters, training the young dragons and riders.
>
> **Gold:** Queen, full female (40–45 meters). The bearer of the young, the queen is

traditionally mated by whichever bronze can catch her. Although browns can mate with queens—and sometimes do, in the case of junior queens—this is unusual and not encouraged. The queen is fertile and bears eggs which she oversees until they hatch. Clutch sizes range from ten to forty; generally, the larger clutches occur during a Pass. The senior queen, usually the dragon of the oldest queen rider, is the most prestigious dragon and is responsible for all the dragons in the Weyr and for the propagation of her species.

fellis: a flowering tree

fellis juice: a juice made from the fruit of the fellis tree; a soporific

firestone: a rock bearing phosphorous that, when eaten by a dragon, is digested to produce phosphine gas, which ignites on contact with air

glow: a light-source that can be carried in a hand-basket

harper: Harpers are the teachers and entertainers of Pern. They educate the young in hall, hold, Weyr, and cot; they guide the elders in the practice of their traditional duties. The Masterharper of Pern is responsible for the training of harpers, the appointment of trained harpers to Weyr, hold, hall, and cot, and the discipline of harpers. The Masterharper acts as judge, arbitrator, and mediator in disputes between Lords Holder and between Weyr and hold or hall, but any harper can be called in to mediate if necessary.

Headwoman: Selected by the Weyrwoman to run the Lower Caverns, the Headwoman supervises the general domestic machinery of the Weyr and the individual weyrs of the riders. Among her duties are the care of the young; the supervision of food collection, storage, and preparation; weyr maintenance; and nursing, under the aegis of the Weyr healer(s).

High Reaches: mountains on the northern continent of Pern (see map)

hold: A hold is where the "normal" folk of Pern live. Holds were initially caverns in rocky cliffs where Thread could gain no foothold; they began as places of refuge. They grew to become centers of government, and the Lord Holder became the man to whom everyone looked for guidance, both during and after the Pass of the Red Star.

Impression: the joining of minds of a dragon and his or her rider-to-be. At the moment of hatching, the dragon, not the rider, chooses his partner and telepathically communicates this choice to the chosen rider.

Interval: the period of time between Passes; generally two hundred Turns

klah: a hot, stimulating drink made from tree bark and tasting faintly of cinnamon

Long Interval: a period of time, generally twice the length of an Interval, during which no Thread falls and Dragonmen decrease in number. The last Long Interval is thought to herald the end of Threads.

looks to: is Impressed by

month: four sevendays

numbweed: a medicinal cream that, when smeared on a wound, kills all sensation; used as an anesthetic.

Oldtimer: a member of one of the five Weyrs that Lessa brought forward four hundred Turns in time. Used as a derogative term to refer to one who has moved to Southern Weyr.

Pass: a period of time during which the Red Star is close enough to drop Thread on Pern. A Pass generally lasts fifty Turns and occurs approximately every two hundred Turns. A Pass commences when the Red Star can be seen at dawn through the eye rock of the Star Stones.

Pern: third of the star Rukbat's five planets. It has two natural satellites.

Red Star: Pern's stepsister planet. The Red Star has an erratic orbit.

Rukbat: a yellow star in the Sagittarian Sector, Rukbat has five planets and two asteroid belts.

runnerbeast: also called "runner." An equine adapted to Pernese conditions from fetuses brought with the colonists. Quite a few distinct variations were bred: heavy-duty cart and plow animals; comfortable, placid riding beasts; lean racing types.

sevenday: the equivalent of a week on Pern

Star Stones: Stonehenge-type stones set on the rim of every Weyr. When the Red Star can be seen at Dawn through the eye rock, a Pass is imminent.

Thread: mycorrhizoid spores from the Red Star, which descend on Pern and burrow into it, devouring all organic material they encounter.

Timor: Pern's smaller moon

Tunnel-snakes: Tunnel-snakes are a minor danger and an annoyance on Pern. Of the myriad types of Tunnel-snakes, two are the most insidious: the type that lives in tunnels, and the type that makes tunnels by burrowing in the sand on beaches. The latter has a great appetite for fire-lizard eggs.

Turn: a Pernese year

watchdragon: the dragon whose rider has pulled watch duty on the Weyr roster. A watch is generally four hours long. Essentially Weyrs are military camps. Sentries are part of that ethos. During a Pass, they watch for any chance erratic Fall of Thread, for anyone entering or leaving the Weyr.

watch-wher: the ungainly, malodorous product of an attempt to breed larger, more useful animals from the genetic material of the fire-lizard, an indigenous Pernese life form. Watch-whers are nocturnal, exceedingly vicious when aroused, and highly protective of those they recognize as friends. A watch-wher is conditioned to know the people of its hold, hall, or cot, and to give warning of intruders of any sort; used as a watchdog, it is generally chained to the front entrance of the hold, hall, or cot. Watch-whers can communicate with dragons, but as they tend to be very trivial and rather stupid, dragons are not fond of touching their minds.

Weyr: a home of dragons and their riders

weyr: a dragon's den

Weyrleader: generally the rider of the bronze dragon who has mated with the senior queen dragon of the Weyr during her mating flight. The Weyrleader is in charge of the fighting wings of the Weyr, responsible for their conduct during Falls, and for the training and discipline of all riders. During an Interval, he is responsible for the continuance of all Thread-fighting tactics, for keeping alive the fighting abilities of dragons and riders. His rank symbol is a dragon.

weyrling: an inexperienced dragonrider under the tutelage of the Weyrlingmaster. His rank symbol is an inverted stripe.

Weyrlingmaster: usually an aging rider with good skills and the ability to discipline and inspire the young. Responsible for the training of young riders and their dragons.

Weyrsinger: the harper for the dragonriders, usually himself a dragonrider.

Weyrwoman: The rider of a dragon queen and coleader, with the Weyrleader, of the Weyr. She is responsible for the conduct of the queens' wing during Fall, under the Weyrleader's orders; for the care of dragons, riders, and all Weyrfolk; and for the peace and tranquility of the Weyr during a Pass and during Intervals. She appoints all subordinates, insures that all tithes are delivered or collected, and mediates all disputes except honor contests among riders. She is responsible for the training, fostering, and disposition of the Weyr's children and nonrider personnel, overseeing with the Weyrleader the training of weyrlings under the Weyrlingmaster. As any dragon will obey a queen, even against the wishes of his or her rider, the Weyrwomen are in fact the most powerful people on Pern. Weyrwomen have autonomy in their own Weyr, but will act in concert with other Weyrwomen when necessary for the good of the Weyrs. Her rank symbol is a dragon.

Each Weyr has from two to five queens, the larger numbers occurring during a Pass. In the event of the death or voluntary retirement of a Weyrwoman, the position will be assumed by the oldest of the other queenriders in the Weyr. Although candidates for Impression generally come from nearby holds and halls, the Search for a queen candidate may extend throughout the continent.

weyrwoman: a female dragonrider. Her rank symbol is a gold star.

wherries: a type of fowl roughly resembling the domestic turkey of Earth, but about the size of an ostrich

Wingleader: the dragonrider in command of a Weyr's fighting wing, subordinate to the Weyrleader. His rank symbol is double bars.

Wingsecond: the dragonrider second in command to the Wingleader. His rank symbol is a single bar.

withies: water plants resembling the reeds of Earth

The People of Pern

Abuna: Kitchen head of Harpercraft Hall, at Fort Hold

Alemi: Third of Seaholder's six sons, at Half-Circle Sea Hold

Andemon: Masterfarmer, Nerat Hold

Arnor: Craftmaster scrivenor, at Harpercraft Hall

Balder: Harper, at Ista Weyr

B'dor: at Ista Weyr

Bedella: Oldtimer Weyrwoman, at Telgar Weyr; dragon queen Solth

Belesdan: Mastertanner, Igen Hold

Bendarek: Craftmaster Woodsmith, at Lemos Hold

Benelek: Journeyman machinesmith, Smithhall

Benis: one of Lord Holder Groghe's 17 sons, at Fort Hold

B'fol: rider, at Benden Weyr; dragon green Gereth

B'iro: rider, at Benden Weyr; dragon bronze Cabenth

B'naj: rider, at Fort Weyr; dragon queen Beth

Brand: steward at Ruatha Hold; blue fire-lizard

B'rant: rider, at Benden Weyr; dragon brown Fanth

B'refli: rider, at Benden Weyr; dragon brown Joruth

Brekke: Weyrwoman, at Southern Weyr; dragon queen Wirenth; fire-lizard bronze Berd

Briala: student at Harper Hall

Briaret: Masterherder (replaces Sograny), Keroon Hold

Brudegen: Journeyman of chorus, at Harpercraft Hall, Fort Hold

Camo: a half-wit at Harpercraft Hall, Fort Hold

Celina: queenrider, at Benden Weyr; dragon queen Lamanth

C'gan: Weyrsinger, at Benden Weyr; dragon blue Tegath

Corana: sister of Fidello (holder at Plateau), at Ruatha Hold

Cosira: rider, at Ista Weyr; dragon queen Caylith

Deelan: milkmother to Jaxom, at Ruatha Hold

Dorse: milkbrother to Jaxom, at Ruatha Hold

D'nek: rider, at Fort Weyr; dragon bronze Zagenth

D'nol: rider, at Benden Weyr; dragon bronze Valenth

Domick: Craftmaster composer, at Harpercraft Hall, Fort Hold

D'ram: Oldtimer Weyrleader, at Ista Weyr; dragon bronze Tiroth

Dunca: cot-holder, girl's cottage, at Harpercraft Hall, Fort Hold

D'wer: rider, at Benden Weyr; dragon blue Trebeth

Elgion: the new harper, at Half-Circle Sea Hold

Fandarel: Mastersmith, at Smithcraft Hall, Telgar Hold

Fanna: Oldtimer Weyrwoman, at Ista Weyr; dragon queen Miranth

Fax: Lord of Seven Holds, father of Jaxom

Felena: second to the Headwoman Manora, at Benden Weyr

Fidello: holder, at Plateau in Ruatha Hold

Finder: Harper, at Ruatha Hold

F'lar: Weyrleader, at Benden Weyr; dragon bronze Mnementh

F'lessan: rider, at Benden Weyr, son of F'lar and Lessa; dragon bronze Golanth

F'lon: Weyrleader, at Benden Weyr, father of F'nor and F'lar.

F'nor: Wingsecond, at Benden Weyr; dragon bronze Canth, fire-lizard gold Grall

F'rad: rider, at Benden Weyr; dragon green Telorth

Gandidan: a child at Benden Weyr

Gemma, Lady: First Lady of Fax (Lord of the Seven Holds) and mother of Jaxom

G'dened: Weyrleader-to-be, at Ista Weyr, son of Oldtimer Weyrleader D'rami; dragon bronze Baranth

G'nag: at Southern Weyr; dragon blue Nelanth

G'narish: Oldtimer Weyrleader, at Igen Weyr; dragon bronze Gyamath

G'sel: rider, at Southern Weyr; bronze fire-lizard, dragon green Roth

Groghe: Lord Holder, at Fort Hold; fire-lizard queen Merga

H'ages: Wingsecond, at Telgar Weyr; dragon bronze Kerth

Horon: son of Lord Groghe; at Fort Hold

Idarolan: Masterfisher, at Tillek Hold

Jaxom: Lord Holder (underage) at Ruatha Hold; dragon white Ruth

Jerint: Craftmaster for instruments, at Harpercraft Hall, Fort Hold

Jora: Weyrwoman preceding Lessa, at Benden Weyr; dragon queen Nemorth

J'ralt: rider, at Benden Weyr; dragon queen Palanth

Kayla: drudge, at Harpercraft Hall, Fort Hold

K'der: rider, at Ista Weyr; dragon blue Warth

Kenelas: a woman of the lower caverns, at Benden Weyr

Kern: eldest son of Lord Nessel (the Lord Holder of Crom)

Kimety: a boy, at Telgar Hold; Impresses dragon bronze Fidirth

K'nebel: Weyrlingmaster, at Fort Weyr; dragon bronze Firth

K'net: rider, at Benden Weyr; dragon bronze Pianth

K'van: rider, at Benden Weyr; dragon bronze Heth

Kylara: a sister of Lord Holder Larad and a Weyrwoman at Southern Weyr who moved to High Reaches Weyr when Oldtimers were banished; dragon queen Prideth

Lessa: Weyrwoman, at Benden Weyr; dragon queen Ramoth

Lidith: Queen dragon before Nemorth, rider unknown

Ligand: Journeyman tanner, at Fort Hold

L'tol: rider, at Benden Weyr and, as Lytol, Warder of Ruatha Hold; dragon brown Larth (dies)

L'trel: father of Mirrim, at Southern Weyr; dragon blue Falgrenth

Lytol: Lord Warder for the underage Lord Holder Jaxom, at Ruatha Hold; dragon brown Larth (dies)

Manora: headwoman, at Benden Weyr

Mardra: Oldtimer Weyrwoman, at Fort Weyr, banished to Southern Weyr; dragon queen Loranth

Margatta: senior Weyrwoman, at Fort Weyr; dragon queen Ludeth

Mavi: Seaholder's (Yanis) Lady, at Half-Circle Sea Hold

Menolly: Journeyman, at Harpercraft Hold, Fort Hold, fire-lizards (10): gold Beauty, bronzes Rocky, Diver, Poll; browns Lazybones, Mimic, Brownie; greens Auntie One and Auntie Two; blue Uncle

Menolly: youngest child (daughter) of Seaholder (Yanis) at Half Circle Sea Hold

Merelan: mother of Robinton (Masterharper of Harpercraft Hold)

Merika: Oldtimer Weyrwoman, at High Reaches Weyr; exiled to Southern Weyr; dragon queen

Mirrim: greenrider, fosterling of Brekke, at Benden Weyr; dragon green Path; fire-lizards: green Reppa, green Lok, brown Tolly

Moreta: ancient Weyrwoman, at Benden Weyr; dragon queen Orlith

Morshall: Craftmaster for theory, at Harpercraft Hall, Fort Hold

M'rek: Wingsecond, at Telgar Weyr; dragon bronze Zigith

M'tok: rider, at Benden Weyr; a dragon bronze Litorth

Nadira: Weyrwoman, at Igen Weyr

Nanira: see Varena

Nicat: Masterminer, Crom Hold

N'ton: Wingleader, at Benden Weyr on dragon bronze Lioth; then Weyrleader at Fort Weyr (after T'ron), fire-lizard brown Tris

Oharan: Journeyman harper, at Benden Weyr

Oldive: Masterhealer, at Harpercraft Hall, Fort Hold

Old Uncle: great grandfather of Menolly, at Half-Circle Sea Hold

Palim: Journeyman baker, at Fort Hold

Petiron: the old Harper, at Half-Circle Sea Hold

Piemur: Apprentice/Journeyman, at Harpercraft Hold, Fort Hold; fire-lizard green Farli; runner-beast Stupid

Pilgra: Weyrwoman, at High Reaches Weyr; dragon queen Selgrith

P'llomar: rider, at Benden Weyr; dragon green Ladrarth

Pona: granddaughter to Lord Holder Sangel, at Southern Boll Hold

P'ratan: rider, at Benden Weyr; dragon green Poranth

Prilla: youngest Weyrwoman, at Fort Weyr; dragon queen Selianth

Rannelly: nurse and servant of Kylara

R'gul: Weyrleader before F'lar, at Benden Weyr; dragon bronze Hath

R'mart: Oldtimer Weyrleader, at Telgar Weyr; dragon bronze Branth

R'mel: rider, at Benden Weyr; dragon Sorenth

R'nor: rider, at Benden Weyr; dragon brown Virianth

Robinton: Masterharper, at Harpercraft Hall, Fort Hold; fire-lizard bronze Zair

Sanra: supervisor of children, at Benden Weyr

Sebell: Journeyman/Masterharper, Robinton's second, at Harpercraft Hall, Fort Hold; fire-lizard queen Kimi

Sella: Menolly's next-oldest sister, at Half-Circle Sea Hold

S'goral: rider, at Southern Weyr; dragon green Betunth

Sharra: Journeyman healer, at Southern Hold; fire-lizards bronze Meer and brown Talla

Shonagar: Craftmaster for voice, at Harpercraft Hall, Fort Hold

Silon: a child, at Benden Weyr

Silvina: headwoman, at Harpercraft Hall, Fort Hold

S'lan: rider, at Benden Weyr; dragon bronze Binth

S'lel: rider, at Benden Weyr; dragon bronze Tuenth

Sograny: Masterherder, at Keroon Hold

Soreel: wife of the First Holder, at Half-Circle Sea Hold

Tagetarl: Journeyman, at Harpercraft Hall, Fort Hold

Talina: Weyrwoman, at Benden Weyr, queenrider

Talmor: Journeyman teacher, at Harpercraft Hall, Fort Hold

T'bor: Weyrleader, at Southern Weyr, later moves to High Reaches when the Oldtimers are exiled; dragon bronze Orth

Tegger: holder, at Ruatha

Tela, Lady: one of Fax's ladies

Terry: Craftmaster smith, at Smithcraft Hall, Telgar Hold

T'gran: dragonrider, at Benden Weyr; dragon brown Branth

T'gellan: Wingleader, at Benden Weyr; dragon bronze Monarth

T'gor: rider, at Benden Weyr; dragon blue Relth

T'kul: Oldtimer, at High Reaches Weyr, exiled to Southern Weyr; dragon bronze Salth

T'ledon: watchdragon rider, at Fort Hold; dragon blue Serith

Tordril: fosterling, at Ruatha Hold, propsective Lord Holder at Igen

Torene: ancient Weyrwoman, at Benden Weyr

Toric: Lord Holder of Southern Hold

T'ran: rider, at Igen Weyr; dragon bronze Redreth

T'reb: rider, at Fort Weyr; dragon green Beth

T'ron: Oldtimer Weyrleader, at Fort Weyr; banished to Southern Weyr; dragon bronze Fidranth; also called T'ton

T'sel: dragonrider, at Benden Weyr; dragon green Trenth, fire-lizard bronze Rill

Vanira: see Varena

Varena (also called Vanira): rider, at Southern Weyr; dragon queen Ralenth

Viderian: fosterling (Seaholder's son), at Fort Hold

Wansor: Craftmaster glassmith, Smithcraft Hall, at Telgar Hold; also called Starsmith

Yanis: Craftmaster and Seaholder, at Half-Circle Sea Hold

Zurg: Masterweaver, at Southern Boll Hold